To Jane–
I ho
fills y
hours h
pleasure.

Suzanne Peran

A Room Without Toys

by

Suzanne Person

AuthorHouse™
1663 Liberty Drive, Suite 200
Bloomington, IN 47403
www.authorhouse.com
Phone: 1-800-839-8640

This book is a work of fiction. People, places, events, and situations are the product of the author's imagination. Any resemblance to actual persons, living or dead, or historical events, is purely coincidental.

First published by AuthorHouse 12/22/2008

ISBN: 978-1-4259-0979-6 (sc)
ISBN: 978-1-4259-0975-8 (e)

Library of Congress Control Number: 2005911336

Printed in the United States of America
Bloomington, Indiana

This book is printed on acid-free paper.

Dedicated to the memory of my mother and father
who filled my room with toys and my life with love.

Prologue
"Miss Victoria Windsor"

If it had been a month or so later, the guard thought afterwards, he might not have noticed her at all–the slim, blonde woman sitting on a bench across from the new little chapel recently dedicated by the Queen in memory of her late father, King George VI. By then the summer season would be at its height, St. George's Chapel–for that matter all the public buildings at Windsor–thronged with tourists and she might have gone unnoticed in the crowd. As it was, Simon couldn't be positive how long she'd been there. He first noticed her, however, only a short while before the building was due to close for the day. In fact, he was just making his last turn about the aisles.

She struck him as somehow familiar, but he soon forgot this point as coming closer, he observed she'd been crying. The tears had caused her make-up to run. Though why this one thought she needed make-up (he would describe her later to another guard as a "bloomin' beauty ") he couldn't imagine. Who was she, he wondered, her grief clearly a private thing and still fresh more than fifteen years after the King's death. He hated to intrude, but at last he walked up the three steps to the choir level and approached her, resting one hand lightly on her shoulder. At his touch she started visibly, her large green eyes widening briefly. "I'm.... I'm dreadful sorry, miss, but the chapel will be closing in a few minutes."

"Oh, is it that late? I'm sorry. I...ah...didn't realize I'd been here that long." Her voice was soft and yet clear, her accent quite evidently upper class. As she spoke, she glanced down at a pair of dark glasses he'd noticed in her lap and picking them up, she slipped them into place.

It's as if she needs to hide, Simon thought sadly. "Might I be of some 'elp, miss? Perhaps ring someone up to come and fetch you?"

"No." Strangely a look of annoyance passed across her face. "There's no one." She glanced back at the small memorial chapel. "Might I have just a moment more. I won't be long. I promise."

She listened as the guard's footsteps receded, echoing in the old stone chapel, and once more alone, she prepared to leave. Standing up, she smoothed her skirts and pulling her scarf up over her head again, she tied it firmly in place. For several seconds longer she continued to stand there staring at the tomb, but inevitably it was time. Touching her hand to her lips, she reached out to rest her fingertips lovingly on the side of the stone archway leading into the little chapel. "Good-bye, Uncle Bertie. I...I love you. I always will. Perhaps that's just it. Perhaps I can only admit to loving someone when that person is dead. I suppose it seems safe then. I...I wish you were still alive, though, to care for me. I need someone to...to... I need someone!" Only then did she turn away to walk slowly from the chapel without speaking again to the guard who stood at the exit waiting for her.

Crossing the lower ward of the castle and passing once more through the Henry VIII Gateway, she started back downhill toward the train station. As long as she remained in the chapel, warmed and comforted by memories of Uncle Bertie, her grief had been bearable. Now it tore through her, an actual physical anguish made more unendurable somehow by the glorious late spring afternoon. Even now–so many years later–it seemed as though England should still wear a gray drizzle of mourning for the dear, gentle man it had lost.

Dear God, she thought, loving hurts! It hurts and yet I keep falling into the same damned trap! Like a wounded animal, she instinctively sought relief from the pain and for her there was always one sure way. Quite near the station was a small pub.....

* * *

The telephone was ringing as Noel let himself into his flat after an evening of theatre with some friends. It would have seemed rather a "busman's holiday" for an actor to spend a night off attending a play, but he would be leaving for New York City the day after tomorrow and no one in his admittedly biased opinion could perform Shakespeare as brilliantly as his fellow Englishmen. Throwing the program on the desk, he slumped into the chair, loosened his tie and reached for the receiver. "Hello?"

"All right, St. John. Put the bitch on!"

Even blurred with liquor, the voice of Sean Patrick was unmistakable. Why in God's name did Victoria continually involve herself with men not worthy to lick her boots? In spite of himself Noel grinned. Where that lady was concerned, he seemed hopelessly addicted to cliches. "She's not here, Sean," he replied flatly.

"Like hell she isn't!"

"Look, you disreputable Irish bastard! <u>She's</u> <u>not</u> <u>here</u>! As far as I knew, she was having dinner with you, but apparently she had the good sense to stand you up!" He slammed down the receiver before the other man could say anything further. Almost immediately the telephone rang a second time. Angrily he snatched it up again. "God damn it!"

The caller sounded understandably startled. "Mr. St. John?"

"Sorry..ah..speaking."

"Constable in Windsor here, Mr. St. John. Seems a lady friend of yours got to feelin' a bit–shall we say–h'under the weather in one of our local pubs and the proprietor rang us up to collect her."

"Is she all right?" Noel was immediately alarmed. So that's where Victoria was, he thought. But why?

"Oh yes, sir. Nothing serious, sir. But I recognized Miss Windsor straight off and it didn't seem as 'ow a fine lady should be spendin' the night in my h'establishment. If you know what I mean, sir."

"That's most considerate of you."

"Not at all, sir. So I inquired of Miss Windsor as to who might come and fetch 'er and she asked that I ring you up."

"I'll be there as soon as possible."

During the approximately three-quarters of an hour it took Noel to drive from London to Windsor, he reflected on the five years he had known Victoria. They could be considered friends, he supposed, although she'd always been careful to keep a distance between them. There had been a few rare occasions when, quite by chance, he caught her with her guard down, but invariably when such moments had passed, she would retreat even further inside herself, often shutting him out of her life for a time as though to punish him. That horrible morning in Stratford shortly after they'd first met when he arrived at her flat to find her..... But even now that memory was too painful for Noel to dwell on for very long and besides, he told himself, tonight was different. Tonight she had asked him to come.

It was nearly one a.m. when he pulled his little red MG up in front of the Windsor police station and hurried inside. The constable stood up as he entered. A short, rather chubby man, he would have been quite unimpressive were it not for the luxuriant flowing white moustache which he had the habit of twirling between the thumb and forefinger of one hand as he talked.

"You don't have to tell me who you are, Mr. St. John. The missus and I, we enjoy the theatre and we seen you on the stage–two maybe three times–with Miss Windsor, too."

"Thank you very much," Noel replied distractedly. "Where is Miss Windsor?"

"My wife took her upstairs to our flat." The constable released the tip of his moustache long enough to jab at the air above his head indicating the upper floor. "I'll fetch 'er, sir. You just stay right 'ere."

Waiting anxiously, Noel glanced around at his dismal surroundings: unpainted wooden floors and institutional beige walls. How could she have come to this? He heard footsteps and the door through which the constable had vanished a few moments before opened again. Victoria appeared first, hidden still behind the dark glasses even though it was the middle of the night. " 'ere's the lady, Mr. St. John." Having held the door for her, the officer followed her into the room. "You can tike 'er along 'ome, sir." Victoria had simply stood there–silent and utterly passive–her hands plunged deep into the pockets of her trench coat, her head bowed and now at the words of dismissal she moved rapidly across the room and out the front door, not having so much as glanced in Noel's direction. "Go along now," the constable urged further. "There'll be no charges."

"Thank <u>you</u>, sir!" Noel seized the man's right hand in both of his. "You're very kind!" Outside he found her already in his car. Alone in the darkness she had taken off her glasses and now held them clasped tightly in her lap. He got into the driver's seat, started the motor and shifted into gear. Pulling out from the curb, the car sped off down the deserted street and soon they were on the motorway back to London. Several times he looked over at Victoria, but her eyes remained steadily downward and she said nothing.

They had been driving about twenty minutes when Noel first heard a small sound. For a moment he even thought he'd imagined it. Then he caught it again and this time he was sure she was crying. He wished she'd talk to him, tell him how she had come to be in Windsor, but she did not. Instead she merely continued to cry–more to herself than anything–and then even that dwindled away and she was quiet again. He knew better than to speak first, however, and only when he had brought the car to a stop in front of her Eaton Square townhouse, did Victoria finally break the silence. "Thank you, Noel," she whispered, reaching over to touch him briefly on the cheek. "Thank you for....for coming." She looked at him for a long moment. He could just make out her beautiful face in the glow from the dashboard. At last she simply shrugged and opening the door, she got out of the car, running lightly across the pavement and up the front steps to disappear inside the house.

* * *

All during the day Noel continued to wonder–why had Victoria been in Windsor; how would she seem when he saw her again that evening; whether, indeed, she would come to the party at all. On one point, at least, he should have known better. Victoria never missed a party–especially one being given in her honor. Actually it was in honor of the entire British rep company leaving on the following morning for the States, but Noel suspected that such a technicality would have escaped her notice. So of course she was there–in a low-cut, pale blue gown, every blonde hair sleekly in place. What did surprise him, however, was that she arrived with Sean Patrick. Their affair was rather an on-again, off-again thing, but after the other actor's irate phone call of the night before Noel had assumed <u>this</u> evening would be one of the "off's".

Victoria was, moreover, at her most delightful, floating about the room in a swirl of azure chiffon, hugging and kissing everyone, her pealing laugh clearly audible above the general hubbub of cocktail party conversation. Either she was too caught up in her well-perfected performance as the elegant, charming actress to notice him or she was deliberately ignoring him. It was late in the evening when Noel noticed she was missing from the party and going in search of her, found her alone in a small library– down the hall from the main foyer of the house and some distance away from the living room.

The door was ajar and for several seconds he stood there quietly, reveling as he always did in the chance to watch her unobserved. She was sitting on a low stool in front of the fireplace staring into the flames and the flickering light played across her exquisite features, here and there picking up the glimmer of blonde curls cascading down the back of her head. She had obviously gone in search of solitude and he'd about decided to go away, leaving her undisturbed, when she happened to turn her head and see him. "Noel, darling!" Victoria flashed a smile, extending one flawlessly manicured hand in his direction, her rings glittering in the firelight. "But why didn't you tell me you were here? Do come and sit with me, luv. I'm bored."

"You know you don't have to be that way with me, Victoria," he said, taking a step or two into the room. "Especially after last night. You...you asked me to come."

The lovely slim hand clenched into a fist, an expression of panic passing across her face. Helplessly he watched her fight to regain control of herself–the terrible effort it required. "Well, I had to have them ring someone up, after all. I didn't particularly care to spend the night in jail!"

"But...but what were you doing in Windsor in the first place? Please! You know you can trust me."

She hesitated and for a moment he thought she was about to answer him. Then all at once someone gave the library door a violent push sending it crashing back against the wall. "Last night not enough for you, St. John?"

Again, as over the telephone on the previous evening, the voice was instantly recognizable. Reluctantly Noel turned to face Sean Patrick. "Really, old chap, I told you that she......"

Victoria's mind was racing. So her current lover thought she'd spent the night with Noel. Well, better that than the truth which he would undoubtedly find extremely amusing. "We... we might as well admit it, luv," she interposed quickly. "Everyone's known about us for years anyway." Noel offered no further objection. If Victoria wished Sean not to know about the events of last evening, then let him think what he would. Besides it flattered his male ego to be considered as a serious rival.

"Of course I can't say I blame you." The Irish actor had continued on into the room–his swagger partly habitual, partly due to his state of inebriation. "She's bloody marvelous between the sheets! Though what such a magnificent wench sees in a pusillanimous toady like yourself is a mystery."

"You bastard!" Victoria sprang to her feet drawing her arm back to slap him–her anger, although she'd never have admitted it, far more on Noel's behalf than her own.

Sean grabbed her wrist. "The lady springs to your defense, St. John! How touching! But isn't it supposed to be the reverse? Well, somehow it seems appropriate!" Victoria struggled furiously to free herself, but he merely tightened his grip.

"Come off it, man," Noel objected at last, "you'll hurt her."

"My..my! Sir Galahad comes to the fair damsel's rescue after all. Oh, but wait a minute. Those damsels were supposed to be virgins, weren't they?"

"You Goddamned son-of-a-bitch!" Victoria drove her spike heel into Sean's foot.

With a yelp of pain he let her go. "Very well, madam. If you prefer to spend the night alone or with...." He waved one hand airily at Noel. "....it's fine with me."

Her face crumbled. "Please, Sean, don't. I...I'm sorry. You know I want to be with you."

"You should have thought of that sooner," he replied coolly. "Now if you'll excuse me, I'm sure I can find more pleasant company elsewhere." With a final unsteady bow in their general direction Sean turned to make his way uncertainly from the room.

Victoria sank back down on the stool, burying her head in her hands, and a terrible silence filled the room, broken only by the crackling of the flames on the hearth and the muted noises of the London traffic outside. Noel was still standing a few steps inside the door where he had remained throughout the whole miserable scene. He knew she'd probably rather be alone, but he couldn't bring himself to leave. "Victoria," he said at last–very softly.

"Oh, go away," she murmured not even lifting her head.

"That piece of Irish trash isn't worth it. Do you want another drink? I'll get it for you."

"Yes...I would. Thank you."

"Thank-you's" were rare from her and in those two simple words Noel glimpsed the depth of her despair. He went to the bar and returned quickly with Scotch for himself and Victoria's customary vodka. Handing her the glass with a slight flourish, he seated himself on the deep shag rag beside her. "I sit at your feet, m'lady," he said lightly, hoping to bring a smile to her lovely features. But instead she merely took a long drink. The liquor cut into her throat and she choked. "Are you all right?"

"Oh yes, I'm just fine. Can't you tell?" she observed mockingly, swallowing more of the vodka. "God, it takes more and more of this stuff to do any good!" There was another long silence which Victoria finally broke. "I...I do want to..to thank you, though."

Again–<u>thank</u> <u>you</u>! "For what...the drink?" He laughed a little. "You know us pusillanimous toadies. We live to be of service."

"Oh Noel–don't!" She lightly stroked his shaggy, brown hair. "And you know what I mean...for not giving me away about....about last night."

"Please, Victoria, tell me."

Again she hesitated, staring down into the clear depths of the liquor. "Yesterday was...was a mistake," she said at last, avoiding his gaze. "<u>This</u> is me." She raised the glass to take another long swallow. "This and begging some no-good, shanty Irish to go to bed with me because I don't like to sleep alone. Well, I suppose I should be out there," she said suddenly–just a little too brightly. She made a vague, sweeping gesture in the direction of the main room.

"There's no hurry," he replied quickly both because he wanted to keep her to himself as long as possible and because he feared what might happen.

"No, I...I should, I think." Victoria got to her feet only to sway and nearly fall. She sat down on the stool again. "It would seem I am just a little drunk, luv. Would you?"

Noel stood up and putting his right arm around her waist, he grasped her left hand in his and helped her to her feet. He felt her sway a second time, but he tightened his hold and she steadied herself. "You think I drink too much, don't you?" she asked as they moved together down the hall toward the foyer.

"No, Victoria."

"Dear liar," she sighed, touching his face with just the tip of her forefinger–an accustomed gesture, but one he nevertheless always cherished. At the living room door she shook off his support with a sudden show of impatience, momentarily gripping the door frame. "Open the door," she commanded.

"Are you sure you feel up to this, Vicki?" In his tender anxiety he inadvertently used the shortened form of her name–a mistake he hadn't made for some time.

"Oh God, Noel, you know perfectly well I abominate nicknames! Now open the damned door!" He submitted to her will without another word of protest. Allowing just enough time to pass for all eyes to turn in her direction, Victoria proceeded into the room, her walk betraying not so much as a hint of intoxication.

Noel knew better than to follow. Later he looked for her again. When he couldn't find her, he asked someone where she was. "Oh, you know Victoria," the other person replied with a knowing laugh. "She left with someone–one of the new RSC apprentices. But then it wouldn't make any difference to her who he was."

* * *

Victoria had indeed brought the fledgling Shakespearean home with her, but the fledgling had flown as soon as he'd gotten what he wanted, leaving her–ironically–once more alone and considering the amount of liquor she'd consumed, ridiculously wide awake. Long, empty hours lay ahead of her and at last she got out of bed to make her way over to the dressing table where, carefully concealed among the make-up, she kept a secret cache of sleeping pills. That damned snoop of a housekeeper had begun hiding her pills, but she hadn't found these yet. Victoria took two, washing them down with a little brandy from a decanter which was also on the dressing table and slipping back into bed, she waited for that marvelous sense of calm and well-being which was always the first sign that the sedative was working.

Martha doesn't have to hide the pills anyway, Victoria thought, curling up on her side. I know it's dangerous to take them on top of liquor. After all, I nearly killed myself that way once. Noel still doesn't know whether that was really an accident. Sometimes I'm not sure myself. Well, this time Martha's here, she reassured herself as the delicious drowsiness spread through her body and I <u>have</u> to get <u>some</u> rest or Noel will think...will think....that I....I...." Her drugged mind struggled to complete the thought, but consciousness was slipping away faster now and in her blissful euphoria it no longer seemed to matter what Noel would think.

She wasn't sure how much time had elapsed when the nightmare started. It was nighttime in her dream as well and she was walking along a narrow path in the woods. She was unable to discern exactly where she was because it was so dark. Then from some unseen point ahead of her she could hear her daughter calling to her. "Mummy, please! Help me, Mummy!"

"Olivia!" She began to grope her way toward the sound of the little girl's voice. "Where are you, darling? I can't find you!"

"Mummy! Mummy! I'm scared! Please, Mummy!"

Desperate to find her daughter, Victoria was running now. Mysterious hands or perhaps they were merely tree branches grabbed at her hair and clothing, but she pulled herself free. She had to reach Olivia–to take her in her arms and protect her. She felt as though she'd run forever when miraculously the child appeared a short distance ahead. "Olivia, it's all right now," she called out reassuringly. "You're safe, sweetheart. Mummy's here."

But to Victoria's horror the little girl's eyes only widened further in fear and she began backing away shaking her head. "Who are you? I don't know you!"

"Of course you know who I am. I'm your mother."

"You're not my mother!" Olivia screamed. "My mother <u>loves</u> me!"

"But I do.....I do......"

"You see–you can't even say it! That proves you're not my mother!"

"You don't mean that, darling." Crying herself now, Victoria reached out to her.

"I <u>do</u> mean it! You're <u>not</u> my mother! You're not!" Still screaming the hateful words, Olivia turned and fled, rapidly disappearing from sight again.

Horribly the nightmare recurred over and over again as held captive in the depths of a drugged slumber, Victoria remained its helpless prisoner. No sooner did the child run from her than she would once again hear her voice calling out of the darkness.

* * *

It always rains in London, but the weather that morning in early June belied the fact. The sky was a cloudless blue, the air warm and clear, and as she left the neighborhood market, Ruth Cornell was feeling particularly light-hearted. She'd been Victoria Windsor's personal maid for nearly a month now, but that would all be over as of today. The actress was leaving for the States. She had been fired, however, and wouldn't be accompanying her. Maybe that's why I feel so super, Ruth thought, and she giggled. As a favor to the housekeeper, she'd agreed to go out for a fresh loaf of bread and some oranges for Miss Windsor's breakfast, but it would be a while yet before the great lady was awake so she might as well take her time. Besides it was such fun to get Martha Kendall all worked up. Honestly the way that woman catered to Miss Windsor was positively silly.

Turning off Lower Belgrave Street into Eaton Square, Ruth slowed her steps even further. She gazed at the flower gardens just coming into bloom in the small private park; she stopped to exchange a few choice bits of gossip with another girl who worked in the neighborhood. Inevitably, however, she arrived at #14 and pushing open the iron gate, she walked up the steps and in the front door. She was supposed to use the service entrance, but that required descending a narrow, winding staircase, going through the basement and up another set of stairs to the kitchen which was a bloody nuisance. At any rate she'd been sacked already so she might as well use any damned door she chose and she rather enjoyed coming in this way. When no one was watching, she could pause for a moment in the front hall to stare up at the broad, curving staircase and the glittering crystal chandelier. She could dawdle as she passed through the empty dining room, gloating over the Queen Anne furniture, the highly polished silver and tall, graceful candlesticks. She could even forget for a minute that she'd had to polish all that silver. In short she could pretend she was the mistress of the house. God, she thought bitterly, as she pushed open the swinging door into the kitchen, what I couldn't do with all that money!

Miss Windsor's customary breakfast tray stood on a table in the center of the room already set with a juice glass, tea cup and saucer, pitcher of milk, sugar bowl, marmalade pot and assorted other dishes. As Ruth came in, Martha was measuring loose tea into the tea pot. "Did you use the front door again? Haven't I told you and told you.... Well, I suppose it doesn't much matter at this point."

"That's right. It doesn't." Ruth tossed the loaf of bread onto the counter.

Throwing her an exasperated glance, the housekeeper came over to open the bread and insert two slices in the toaster. "Well, can you at least help me get this tray ready? Miss Windsor's plane is leaving in three hours." Suddenly she realized the bread had been the only parcel. "Where are the oranges? I told you to get oranges! You know Miss Windsor prefers her juice freshly squeezed!"

"Sorry. The green grocer wasn't open yet." Unconcernedly Ruth removed the bottle of orange juice from the fridge, took a swig from it and filled the glass on the tray. "Did the lady have company last night by the way?"

"Miss Windsor is not to be an object of common gossip," Martha reprimanded her sternly. "Haven't I made that clear?"

The maid grabbed a slice of bread covering it with a thick layer of butter and marmalade. "Oh, yeah sure, Mrs. Kendall," she mumbled through a mouthful of sticky crumbs. "Only what I don't get," she went on a few seconds later after she had finally swallowed, "is why you always stand up for her. She treats you worse than anyone."

"She is my employer," Martha replied– a little stiffly. But even as she spoke, she automatically checked the egg timer and with about a minute to go she depressed the lever on the toaster. Preparing Miss Windsor's breakfast certainly required split-second timing, she thought, smiling ruefully to herself and then as usual she'll probably take one sip of tea and push the rest aside.

"That's right, Mrs. K. Keep an eye on that timer! Bad enough we're serving Her Royal Highness–God forbid–bottled juice!" She threw her hand against her forehead in a gesture of mock despair. "But a soft-boiled egg cooked a second less than the full six minutes! Whoever heard of a soft-boiled egg cooked for six minutes! It's ridiculous!"

"Perhaps that's why Miss Windsor discharged you." Martha's tone was as close to sarcasm as was possible for someone of her gentle disposition. "You never could be bothered to remember her taste in anything."

"Oh, come off it! How many maids have there been anyway?"

It was fortunate that at that moment the shrill whistle of the tea kettle saved Martha from having to answer the question. To be quite honest she'd long since lost count. "Pour the water into the tea pot, will you please?" The egg timer went off and removing the egg from the boiling water, the housekeeper rinsed it under the cold tap.

Ruth picked up the kettle and walked over to the table. "You know Tess, don't you? She works for the Huntingtons. Well, <u>she</u> told me that....."

"I am not in the least interested in another of your lurid tales about Miss Windsor." Martha's tone indicated plainly that the subject was closed. The toast came up and she quickly buttered it, her gaze meanwhile flicking instinctively over the tray one final time.. "Good. Everything's ready, but oh dear...." She looked at her watch. "...if she doesn't ring for her breakfast soon, I'll have to wake her. One last favor–I'd appreciate it if you'd take the tray up."

"Oh, no! I've been bounced, remember?"

Their discussion was interrupted just then, however, by the ringing of the telephone and at once Martha moved to pick up the receiver on the kitchen extension. "Miss Windsor's residence." The words by now were automatic.

There was a slight pause and then a small voice said, "Oh, I hoped my mother might answer herself."

"Who dares to call Madam at ten in the morning?" Ruth asked under her breath.

"Just a minute, please." Placing her hand over the mouthpiece, the housekeeper whispered, "Ssh–it's her daughter."

"That poor kid!"

"Be quiet! She'll hear you!" Martha raised the receiver to her ear again. "I'm sorry, dear. But I can't let your mother's breakfast burn, now can I?"

"May....may I please speak to my mother?" Olivia inquired eagerly. "I know she's leaving for the States today. My...my father won't let me see her, but I...I wanted to...to tell her good-bye."

"You see, honey, it's just that your mother's not awake yet. But I'll tell her you telephoned."

"Oh, that's all right. If she's late anyway, she probably won't have time to talk to me." The little girl was obviously close to tears.

"Now I'm sure she'll find the time."

"Thank you anyway," Olivia said politely. "Good-bye."

"What did you say that for?" Ruth muttered. "You know there's not a chance of her ringing up that kid!"

"Don't be so quick to judge her." As usual she came to Victoria's defense. "Neither of us really knows her."

"I don't want to know her any better than I already do. Now I <u>will</u> take that tray up for you. Then I'm getting the hell out of here!"

"Thank you." In spite of herself Martha smiled. "But please do try not to aggravate Miss Windsor this morning. She's probably not feeling very well."

"Not feeling well! Hung over is more like it!" Picking up the tray, the maid disappeared through the swinging door.

With a pleading glance heavenward or perhaps it was merely intended to reach only as far as the upper story of the house, Martha picked up the intercom phone and dialed her employer's bedroom.

* * *

It was several seconds before the telephone penetrated Victoria's consciousness and even then it seemed to be part of her dream. It was a while longer before the ringing roused her to some degree of wakefulness and she could identify the sound. At last she rolled over onto her back and reached for the receiver. Her lips were parched and she had to run her tongue over them in order to speak. "Yes, Martha, I'm awake."

"Good morning, Miss Windsor." The housekeeper breathed a sigh of relief. She always became uneasy when Victoria didn't immediately answer the intercom. She was careful, however, not to show her concern and her tone as she went on was matter-of-fact. "It's ten o'clock, ma'am. Your breakfast will be up directly." She waited for some reply although she didn't actually expect one and when the silence continued, she hung up.

Victoria, meanwhile, had merely let the receiver fall onto the bed. Even the motion of turning over to pick up the telephone had left her dizzy and she was shivering with cold. God, she thought, mornings are pure bloody hell. She swallowed back the bile threatening to rise in her throat and sitting up, she fumbled for the down comforter at the foot of the bed, huddling miserably under its satin folds. Ironically it seemed to symbolize her own life: luxurious, elegant and utterly useless for despite its warmth chills continued to wrack her body. It was a moment or so longer before she realized that her nightgown, even the sheets and pillowcases were soaked with perspiration and oddly that she was exhausted–so tired she might not have slept at all.

It was with some relief that she was prevented from further wonderings, at least for the time being, by the sound of footsteps approaching along the balcony followed by a light tapping on her bedroom door. "Good morning, Miss Windsor," a respectful voice murmured. "I've brought your breakfast, ma'am." Oh God–Ruth, Victoria thought. Of all people! Didn't I already sack her? Dammit, Martha, how could you? Having received no answer, the maid knocked more loudly. "Ah...Miss Windsor," she said again, still very politely, "your breakfast, ma'am."

Mealy-mouthed little snip, Victoria thought. I hope she doesn't think she's fooling me. "Yes," she finally said aloud, "you may come in."

Ruth entered. "It's a glorious morning, Miss Windsor." She came over to put the tray down on the bedside table, replacing the intercom receiver, and then she walked briskly over to the bay window and yanked on the cord operating the drapes. The curtains flew open with an audible swish and sunlight streamed into the room.

"What in hell do you think you're doing? You know I can't abide light first thing in the morning!"

"Aren't you feeling well, ma'am?" The girl closed the drapes again. "Perhaps a couple of aspirin?"

"And you can stop being so bloody obsequious! I know perfectly well you'll be as pleased to see the last of me as I will be to rid myself of you!"

"A reference is customary, ma'am," Ruth ventured from the doorway.

"Reference?!" The bedside clock which she flung at the maid's head crashed against the rapidly closing door and once more alone, Victoria lay back against the pillows. Her head was pounding and she wondered how she would ever get through the day ahead–the long flight, a strange hotel in a strange city... The bedside intercom buzzed again and she snatched up the receiver. "Yes?" she snapped.

"Your limousine will be here in an hour, Miss Windsor."

"I'm well aware of that fact, Martha!"

"Yes, ma'am and uh...your daughter's rung up to say good-bye. I told her you'd return the call."

Tears flooded Victoria's eyes at the mention of Olivia and for some odd reason she felt the same chilling fear she had experienced in her dream. "I...I can't, Martha..... not....not this morning. I...I don't feel well and I....I...."

"It would only take a few minutes, Miss Windsor. She sounded so anxious to talk to you."

"Please, Martha. You ring her up. Tell her....tell her....oh, I don't give a damn what you tell her! Tell her anything! And get up here! I need you!"

"Yes, ma'am." Walking through the dining room toward the front hall, Martha looked about much as Ruth had done earlier, but there was no envy in her gaze. Perhaps a complete change <u>would</u> help, she thought. This house could hold nothing but bad memories for Miss Windsor. But then from above her came the sound of Victoria's voice–"Martha, what in hell is taking you so long?"–and as she moved rapidly up the stairs and along the balcony toward the bedroom, she wondered unhappily if anything would really change. "Miss Windsor?" She tapped lightly on the closed door. Hearing no reply and thinking her employer might be in the bath, she opened the door calling her name again.

In the time she'd been in the actress' employ Martha thought she'd become accustomed to her moods and tempers, but nothing had prepared her for the scene which now met her eyes. Two of the valises she'd packed for the trip were open and most of the clothes flung about the room. Victoria was just opening the third suitcase and at the sound of the door she whirled about, both hands clutching articles of clothing. "Where in hell is that blue silk suit I was going to wear on the plane?"

"I told you yesterday, ma'am....."

But Martha got no further as with all her strength Victoria flung the clothes in her face. "God damn you! I am sick to death of your inefficiency! You can bloody well take your walking papers along with that sniveling little bitch downstairs!" With a frantic gesture she ran her hands through her tousled hair.

The housekeeper looked sadly at the lovely young face already showing the ravages of the life she led. In only three years the circles under her eyes had darkened, the lines on either side of the mouth become more deeply etched. Overwhelmed with love and pity, she slipped an arm around her employer's shoulders. "Please, Miss Windsor."

Was it only Martha's imagination or did the tense, defensive body relax? If in actuality it did, it was only for a second. Wrenching away, Victoria spun around to grab the other woman by the shoulders and shake her. "Don't you <u>ever</u> touch me like that again! How dare you so much as lay a hand on Victoria Windsor! Because that's who I am— <u>Victoria</u> <u>Windsor</u>! And no one touches me unless I allow it! Is that clear?" Just as unexpectedly she let her hands drop and moving away, she stood staring out the bay window of her bedroom. "Please go now, Martha." It was as if the violent emotion of the past few minutes had depleted her strength and she spoke very softly now.

"I'll be back in a moment, Miss Windsor. I had your suit in the kitchen pressing it." But the actress seemed intent on someone or something in the small park in the center of the square and made no reply. "Ma'am, did you hear me?"

As though her mind were returning from some great distance, Victoria turned slowly to face her. She shook her head as though to clear it, raising both hands to massage her temples. "Yes..all...all right. What...whatever you say. I...I'll be in the tub. I....I don't feel at all well this morning. Perhaps a...a warm bath...."

"Your car will be here in 45 minutes, Miss Windsor. I don't want to rush you, but..."

"Then why in hell don't you leave me alone?!"

"Yes, ma'am." Martha immediately left the room, closing the door behind her.

"Why do I do those things?" Victoria sighed wearily. "I....I don't....don't know. A..a drink... Maybe a drink will clear my head." She moved slowly to her dressing table and sinking down on the small stool, she reached for the brandy decanter and a small glass beside it. Her hands were shaking and it was all she could do to pour the dark red liquid. Some of it did indeed spill over onto the glass-topped vanity. Well, Miss Windsor, she thought to herself as she gulped down the burning liquid, you know what it means when you drink in the morning, but even as the words passed through her mind, she poured herself another.

Raising the glass to the reflection in the mirror to offer an ironic toast, she found herself looking at the same face which had moved Martha to pity a short while before. "God! Oh, my God, no!" In an attempt to blot out the image she dashed the brandy at the mirror, but the picture was still there–all the more horrible now dripping with brandy, dissolving like some sort of female Dorian Gray--and sobbing, she seized the decanter by the neck striking again and again at the mirror until it lay about her in pieces. "Very appropriate," she observed wryly to own image cracked now almost beyond recognition. "Shattered–just the way my Goddamned life is!" Glancing down, it was only then she became aware that her wrist was bleeding, gashed by the flying glass. It was at that precise moment Martha's knock sounded at the door again. Dear God, Victoria thought, when she sees the blood, her imagination will run wild!

"Miss Windsor, I have your suit," the housekeeper called. There was no reply. She raised her hand to knock a second time, but then the door opened–though only a bare few inches.

"I'll take it, Martha." Victoria extended her uninjured arm through the crack.

"If you'll let me come in, ma'am, I'll finish your packing."

"No...ah...that's all right."

"Miss Windsor, is something wrong? Please open the door."

"Just give me the suit and go away!"

Alarmed now, Martha gave the door such a push that she sent Victoria staggering backwards against the foot of the bed. "Damn you!" The actress laughed a little. "What are you trying to do to me?"

"Miss Windsor, you're bleeding! What happened?"

"Nothing 'happened' as you so dramatically put it. I accidentally broke my dressing table mirror."

"Let me bandage it for you, ma'am," Martha urged gently even as the unspeakable passed through her mind. Had it really been an accident?

"Didn't I tell you to keep your hands off me? I can take care of myself!"

"You can't bandage your own wrist, Miss Windsor. I think it may even require a few stitches."

"No...no stitches. All right–bandage it. Just hurry up!"

"I think there's some gauze in the medicine chest. And I'll draw your bath. I hate to be a nuisance, but you only have half an hour now before your limousine arrives."

"Well, you are a damned nuisance and besides, Noel will wait. He always does."

"Yes, ma'am." But I'm afraid the airline might not be so obliging, the housekeeper thought to herself as she poured Miss Windsor's special bath salts into the tub, expertly mixing the hot and cold taps to the perfect lukewarm temperature. Locating the gauze in the medicine chest as well as a tube of antiseptic ointment, she returned to the bedroom to find her employer once again seated at the dressing table staring at the cracked mirror. Martha moved quietly to her side and pushing back the sleeve of the dressing gown, she treated and bound the wound. Victoria submitted meekly to her ministrations–all fight apparently gone. "There, Miss Windsor," she said soothingly when she had finished, "your bath will be ready by now. That arm should be kept dry, you know."

"Yes—I'll be careful." Getting to her feet, Victoria moved obediently toward the bathroom. Martha watched her disappear inside and close the door. Absurdly now– touchingly–the actress' voice and manner reminded her more than anything of a small child. At last she began to collect, refold and repack the scattered garments.

Victoria, meanwhile, had turned off the water and removing her robe and nightgown, eased herself into the warm, sudsy water. With her head resting back against the contoured foam rubber pillow, she made a vain attempt to relax, to stop her head from throbbing and her mind from racing in its never-ending circles. Maybe another drink... "Martha, are you still there?"

"Yes, ma'am."

"My...my arm really hurts. Would you bring me a...a drink?"

Reluctantly Martha went to get the bottle of brandy from the linen closet where she kept it to refill the decanter and pouring some into the tumbler, she hurried to the bathroom door, knocked and entered. "Miss Windsor, you really shouldn't drink in the morning, you know." But even as she spoke, the housekeeper realized such an admonition was useless.

"Damn you! I did not hire you to be my mother! I had one of those and she was about as much use to me as you are!"

"Yes, Miss Windsor." Martha placed the glass on the stool beside the tub and silently withdrew.

With a trembling hand Victoria raised the brandy to her lips and lying motionless, she allowed it to trickle down her throat. Tears came involuntarily to her eyes as she thought once again of what her life had become and how disappointed Uncle Bertie would have been. Briefly waves of self-pity flooded over her, but then the discipline born of years of being alone took hold once more and she began to bathe herself as though the deliberate outward movements could calm her inner turmoil as well.

Martha, meanwhile, had finished straightening up the bedroom and repacking Victoria's suitcases and picking up two of them, she proceeded out the door and along the balcony. As she came down the last few steps, Ruth was just entering the front hall herself through a door just under and to the right of the staircase. She was also carrying two valises. "Well, all you have to do is look at that to see the difference between the great lady and me," the girl observed with a laugh as she put her two worn and faded suitcases down next to Victoria's lavender Italian suede ones. "But I guess I still wouldn't trade places with her."

"Then you do feel a little sorry for Miss Windsor." Martha searched the other woman's face for some sign of sympathy.

"I didn't say I felt sorry for her. I meant exactly what I said. I wouldn't be in her shoes if the rest of that gorgeous wardrobe were thrown in for good measure."

"All right, Ruth, all right." The front door chimes sounded just then and crossing the hall, Martha pulled open the massive oak door. It was, as she'd expected, Miss Windsor's driver.

The chauffeur touched his cap respectfully. "Good morning, Mrs. Kendall. Please inform Miss Windsor her car's here."

"Right away. You can take these two suitcases out now."

"Yes, ma'am." The driver entered and picked up Victoria's luggage.

"My, I wonder how he knew which ones were hers," Ruth mused.

"You're certainly in rare form today," Martha observed caustically. "But please leave now. No one needs another scene this morning."

"Don't tell me you're admitting she causes scenes!"

"And if <u>you</u> were honest, you'd admit that at least part of the time you have deliberately provoked her. Now you've simply got to get out of here!"

"Only too happy!" Ruth picked up her bags and started toward the door. Suddenly she dropped them and ran back to Martha. "Good luck!" She hugged the older woman and picking up her belongings one last time, she moved again toward the door. "You'll need it!" she tossed back over her shoulder as she disappeared from sight.

With Ruth at last safely out of the way Martha went back upstairs to get the rest of the luggage. Her knock was answered immediately this time and she entered to find Victoria partially dressed in the skirt to the suit and a pale blue blouse with full see-through sleeves and a huge bow at the throat. At the moment she was applying her base make-up, smoothing it painstakingly upward from her neck and blending it at the chin line. The large mirror having been broken, she was using her compact. It was at once apparent that the actress was again in control. Martha could only guess what this composure had cost her.

"I've come for the rest of your cases, ma'am."

"They're right there in front of you. Don't tell me you're blind."

"Yes, ma'am."

"You mean you <u>are</u> blind? Oh dear, what a pity!" Victoria cocked one perfectly shaped eyebrow.

"No, ma'am." Martha wished devoutly that Miss Windsor would not engage her in these battles of wits. She always ended up feeling foolish. "I meant yes, ma'am, I see the luggage. The car's here, ma'am."

"Well, they can bloody well wait!"

"Yes, ma'am." Martha took the other two valises down to the front door where the chauffeur was waiting and immediately returned upstairs, entering this time without knocking. "Is there anything else I can do for you, Miss Windsor?"

Victoria had finished with her base make-up and eye shadow and was concentrating on the application of eye liner. Nothing could absorb her attention as totally as her own face and at the unexpected sound of Martha's voice she jumped. The eye liner brush slid down one side of her nose leaving a long, black line behind it. "Damn you! Now see what you've made me do!"

"I'm sorry, Miss Windsor. I thought you heard me."

"It's obvious I didn't." Deftly she removed the error with cleansing lotion and went to work on the other eye. With that completed she put on her mascara, rouge and lipstick and at last she was ready. Getting to her feet, Victoria swayed slightly, but immediately caught her balance. "My jacket!" she commanded even though it lay over the foot of the bed easily within her reach. Martha helped her slip into the blue silk jacket and then reached for the broad-brimmed straw hat which she had previously placed on the bed next to the suit. "No, my scarf first."

"Which one, Miss Windsor?"

"The light blue one that matches my blouse. I already told you."

"No, ma'am. You didn't."

"I know perfectly well what I said. Are you insinuating I imagine things?" The actress' voice edged toward hysteria again, but with an effort she regained control of herself. "Very well then. Get it now, please!"

"Yes, ma'am." Martha went to the dressing table and pulled open the drawer which held the scarves. There was no pale blue one. "I'm sorry, Miss Windsor," she apologized. "I don't see it."

Victoria strode over and pushing the older woman aside, yanked the drawer all the way out, dumping its contents on the bed. "Where in hell is that scarf? What did you do? Steal it?"

"I have never stolen from you, Miss Windsor," Martha replied firmly.

"Oh, really!" She threw her a brief, contemptuous glance. "At any rate it appears this beige one will have to do." Victoria arranged the scarf over her head and deftly tied it in back, Martha waiting patiently to hand her the hat a second time. Finally she slipped into the matching cape and picked up her purse, gloves and a pair of sunglasses from the table. "Bring the cosmetic case and for God's sake, don't drop it!" And with that she was out the door.

Taking the make-up case, Martha started to follow her, but then almost at once she stopped retreating silently into the bedroom–just out of her employer's view. Miss Windsor had paused to study herself in the full length hall mirror. What an incredibly beautiful woman, Martha thought. No wonder she has all of London at her feet. But at the pace she's setting for herself, how long can it last? Finally Victoria nodded to her own reflection as though acknowledging the applause of an unseen audience and slipping the sunglasses into place, she turned in a whirl of royal blue silk, gliding swiftly along the balcony and down the stairs.

Martha followed to give the last case to the chauffeur. She watched from the doorway as Victoria moved down the steps, entering the car with a non-committal nod to her driver. Coming out onto the front stoop, the housekeeper continued to stare after the car until it vanished from sight around the corner and only then did she turn to go back into the house. Passing through the front hall, the telephone caught her eye reminding her of her promise to ring up Miss Windsor's daughter. With a sigh she lifted the receiver and began to dial.

* * *

It seemed to Noel as though he approached each meeting with Victoria with some degree of uncertainty and as the limousine turned into Eaton Square, he had instantly tensed. A moment or so later as they slowed and came to a stop, he found himself anxiously scanning the windows of #14. Ridiculous really–as if he could discern in their discreetly shuttered faces some sign of what to expect from the lady within. Shifting the transmission into neutral, the chauffeur turned to his passenger. "It will just be a minute, Mr. St. John."

"Now we both know Miss Windsor better than that," Noel observed with a chuckle. "Perhaps you should switch off the motor."

Grinning, the driver did as suggested and getting out of the car, he walked briskly across the pavement and up the steps and pressed the bell. Noel saw Martha Kendall open the door and the chauffeur entered, coming out again almost immediately with two pieces of Victoria's unmistakable luggage. The man was shaking his head and as he placed the cases in the boot, Noel distinctly heard him mutter. "Coo! And there are people starvin'!" Climbing the stairs again, he opened the door himself this time and emerged a moment or so later with yet two more valises. "Miss Windsor will be out shortly now, sir," he assured Noel.

But it was in actuality another ten minutes before Martha handed out Victoria's make-up case and the actress herself appeared. Holding onto the brim of her hat with one hand, she crossed the pavement to the waiting limousine, slipping into the back seat beside Noel with the same easy grace she displayed on stage. The chauffeur closed the door after her and went around to take his place behind the wheel, placing the make-up case next to him on the front seat. He turned on the motor, put the transmission in gear and the Silver Cloud Rolls Royce glided noiselessly along the square and out into the rapidly moving London traffic.

Victoria hadn't spoken when she got into the car and for quite some time they rode in silence. She appeared, each time Noel looked over at her, to be staring straight ahead through the car's windscreen and hidden as always behind scarf and hat and dark glasses, her face was much like the shuttered windows of her house. It gave no clue as to what was going on inside. One of her gloved hands lay on the seat between them and at last Noel covered it gently with his own bare one. "Good morning," he said softly. She made no reply. A few more minutes passed and he made another attempt. "There's just something about this city. I'll really miss it, won't you?"

For an instant he thought Victoria still wasn't going to answer, but finally she turned to face him. "I...I'm sorry, luv. I didn't hear you."

"I asked if you'll miss London."

"Oh...ah...yes, I suppose so. One place is pretty much the same as any other though, isn't it?" Even these few words seemed to require her last ounce of physical strength and mental concentration.

"Quite a hangover, hm?"

"No worse than usual.... Noel," she went on after a brief pause, " do you object dreadfully if we don't talk. I do feel wretched."

"Of course not," he immediately acquiesced. Grateful for the renewed silence, Victoria lay back and closed her eyes trying in vain, as she had a short while earlier in the tub, to stop the trembling inside. She brought up her hands to massage her temples, but the motion of raising her arms caused the sleeve of her jacket to slide back and glancing over once more, Noel saw her injured wrist, clearly visible now through the flimsy material of her blouse. Despite Martha's competent job of first aid the wound had bled some more staining the gauze. Involuntarily he gasped. "Victoria, what happened?"

"It was an accident. Not to worry, luv. If I ever decide to kill myself, I shall do a much more thorough job of it."

Horrified, Noel seized her by both shoulders, forcing her to face him. "Don't you <u>ever</u> say such a thing again, do you hear me? Don't even think it!"

"Damn you!" She laughed a little, trying to make light of it all. "Let me go!"

"Take off those dark glasses and look at me!"

"Please, no..." He ignored her and reaching up, he removed her glasses. In one motion Victoria pulled away, burying her head in her gloved hands. "No, please. I....I look so ugly this morning."

"You could never be ugly to me, my dear." Gently he took her hands down from her face.

She turned from him to stare out the window at the traffic. "Please–you know how I hate...."

"Hate what? Having people care about you? Well, whether you can admit it or not, you need that caring. You needed it two nights ago or you would have been the overnight guest of the Windsor constabulary."

Victoria whirled back to face him. "That's not fair!"

"Not fair? Not fair to remind you that you needed a friend and I was there?" She made no reply. "All right...all right....ah...." He cast about in his mind for a safe topic of conversation.

"So....ah.....tell me, Victoria, what do you think of our little theatre company?" Even to his own ear the words sounded stilted. He was an actor–trained in improvisation. Couldn't he have done any better than that?

Of course she knew Noel had deliberately changed the subject, but he'd offered her an avenue of escape from an uncomfortable situation and she gratefully accepted her cue. "Do you want my real opinion?" Her green eyes sparkled wickedly.

"Naturally that doesn't include me. It goes without saying that you fully appreciate my great talent, impish good looks and irresistible charm." He winked broadly.

"Oh, absolutely, luv!"

"Thank you, Victoria. I very much desire your good opinion of me as an actor." How stiff we both sound, he thought sadly. We've known each other for five years and we're reciting lines at each other as though it's just another scene in a play.

"The respect is mutual, believe me." Once again she willingly followed his lead. If she'd also noticed how unnatural they both sounded, she gave no indication. Still trying to appear casual, she glanced out the car window. "Not much further to the airport. Excuse me for a minute, will you, luv?"

She rummaged around in her large purse for her make-up and while Noel averted his eyes allowing her her privacy, she carefully inspected her face. "Do I look all right?" she asked at last almost shyly, facing him again for inspection.

How can such a beautiful woman need so much reassurance, he wondered, but aloud he simply said, "Perfect."

"We're in two plays together, aren't we? That will be jolly!"

"Looking forward to it!." Now it was Noel who took the cue from her and for the remainder of the ride they chatted easily about the company's stay in the States: rep is better than performing just one role–never gets boring; that actor– watch him–an absolute bugger at upstaging; this actress–limited in scope, but adequate for the roles in which she's been cast. With some relief her friend observed that Victoria was now entirely composed–her public face and personality in place–but then, too, such rigid self-control wasn't really healthy either and as the limousine moved off the motorway and under the sign for Heathrow Airport, he found himself once again dreading what lay ahead.

Seeing the sign herself, Victoria had removed her hat and scarf to check her hair–today pulled back in a chignon. Now she put the scarf on again, tying it more firmly in place–for all the world like a warrior girding for battle. Turning to Noel, she flashed her famous smile. "Well, here we are. Ready for the wolves to descend?"

"Then you are prepared to face the press, Victoria?" He attempted in vain to keep a note of apprehension out of his voice.

"I am never prepared for those bastards, Noel, but I am expecting them." The Rolls pulled up in front of the building for international departures and as they'd both anticipated, the car barely came to a stop before it was surrounded by reporters and photographers. Victoria replaced her hat and slipped the dark glasses into place once more. "Stay close, luv," she murmured under her breath.

His answer was a brief squeeze of her hand just before he opened the car door and stepped out, turning to assist her. They were greeted by an explosion of flashbulbs. There were cries of "Over here, Miss Windsor!"–"Miss Windsor, my readers want to know....."—"Miss Windsor, is it true that....."

Noel felt her grip on his hand tighten and as always he came to her aid. "If you'll be patient, I'm sure Miss Windsor will answer a few questions. You will have to understand, however, that we don't have much time."

"How about taking off the dark glasses," one photographer requested.

Victoria hesitated momentarily, but then she complied. This brought on a whole new barrage of flashes. She smiled graciously. "Now, ladies and gentlemen--- but please remember what Mr. St. John said. Our time is limited."

At first the questions were safe, pleasant ones.

"How long will you be in the States, Miss Windsor?"

"It depends on how the company is received," she replied. "It could be as brief a period as six weeks or as long as a year."

"Don't tell us you're admitting you could fail, Miss Windsor?" There was general laughter at that in which Victoria herself joined.

"What plays are included in the repertoire?" another reporter inquired.

"*Macbeth, Candida, The Devil's Disciple, The Importance of Being Earnest* and *Victoria Regina*."

"And which roles will you be performing?"

"Lady Macbeth, Candida, Gwendolyn in *Earnest* and Victoria Regina."

"Type-casting?" someone called out in reference to the last. Again there was laughter, but then the tone of the questioning began to change–subtly at first.

"Where's Sean Patrick this morning, Miss Windsor?"

"Sleeping it off, I should imagine." Noel caught the strain in her voice.

"Come off it, Miss Windsor, why do you try to pretend? That 'great romance' is over, isn't it?"

The wolves to which Victoria had referred earlier, only partly in jest, were closing in now for the kill and before Noel could intercede, the questioning continued. "Your daughter won't be accompanying you, Miss Windsor? What's her name, by the way?"

"Olivia," Victoria replied softly.

"How old is she?"

"Almost eight." Even more softly.

And now the leader of the pack went for the jugular. "She doesn't live with you, does she, Miss Windsor?"

That did it! In an instant Noel had an arm around Victoria. "Sorry, people. We have a plane to catch." Ignoring further questions, he literally pushed her past the reporters and through the door of the international building.

At once a slim young man in a BOAC uniform approached, gazing raptly at the actress. "Good morning, Miss Windsor. Ah...Mr. St. John..ah...good morning to you, too, sir." The latter was clearly an afterthought. Victoria acknowledged the greeting with a brief nod. Noel still had a hand at her waist and he could feel her trembling. "I'm sorry," the airline official continued, "but your flight is delayed about a half-hour. Of course our VIP lounge is at your disposal. If you would follow me, please. Your luggage will be attended to."

They moved through the terminal, apparently unnoticed, and yet Victoria became even more tense. "I hate public places," she whispered to Noel. "I always feel as though everyone is watching me." In only a few minutes, however, they were in a small, private lift. The door shut and they were moving upwards. "Olivia rang me up this morning by the way." Why in God's name am I telling him, she thought. Now he won't give me a moment's peace until I return the call. "To say good-bye, I suppose."

"Didn't you talk to her?"

"No, Martha did. I...I wasn't awake yet, you see, and I....."

The lift came to a stop just then and the door slid open again. The two men waited, allowing Victoria to exit first. "This way please, Miss Windsor." The attendant indicated the enclosed ramp to the right, sloping upward at a slight angle, and lined on both sides by windows looking out over the runways.

Invisible again, Noel thought good-naturedly. "You did ring her back though, didn't you?" He picked up their conversation again as they followed their escort up the ramp and along another hall.

"I...I told Martha to do it. She'll....well, you know she's staying a few days to close up the house and she....."

"That won't be a call from you," he insisted gently.

"I....I know, but I wouldn't be able to think of anything to say to her. I never can and I... I....."

"Just tell her you'll miss her and that you'll write to her. All she really wants is to hear your voice."

That was, of course, what Victoria had wanted–to be convinced. "Well, maybe I could. Now--while we're waiting for our flight. Then I wouldn't have to talk too long. I could....."

"Here we are, Miss Windsor–Mr. St. John." Their escort paused to open the door to the lounge, stepping aside to allow them to enter. "If you wish anything, just press the button you'll find at each of the chairs. An attendant will be with you immediately. Have a pleasant flight." Reluctantly he left them then with a last, lingering look at Victoria.

"Good morning, luv." A tall, thin man with dark blonde hair unfolded his arms and legs from one of the armchairs and came toward them grinning. "Do you feel as miserable as I do?" Dammit, Noel thought, why couldn't Sean have stayed away. "Get lost eh, St. John," the Irish actor suggested. "The lady and I need a moment alone."

Noel was relieved to hear that the other man's voice was at least pleasant this morning. "I'll do as you say, Victoria."

"Why don't you go find out about our flight?"

"As you wish then." He started to leave, but stopped at the door. "Don't forget about your phone call." He still remained, waiting for some answer from her.

For a second she hesitated, looking back and forth from Noel to Sean, obviously torn. "Why in hell do I try to fool myself?" She laughed harshly. "I'll never be a mother to that kid! Now go and do as I asked."

"Yes, Victoria." Obedient as always, Noel went to do as he'd been asked.

Inside the lounge Sean walked slowly toward Victoria. "Now that was a wise decision, my dear. You just aren't the maternal type. We both know what you are. Now come here!" He gathered her in his arms, forcing his mouth down over hers. Angrily Victoria pulled herself free to walk over and stare out at the runway, fighting to keep back the tears. But Sean had no intention of allowing her to escape so easily and he came to stand behind her. Slipping his arms around her waist, he attempted to kiss the back of her neck. "Damn that hat!" he muttered. "So then, how about a drink? I don't know about you, but I could use a little 'hair of the dog'!"

"God, no! Not this early!"

"Come off it, marvourneen! That wasn't toothpaste I smelled on your breath! I'd venture you've already had at least one today."

"That's none of your damned business!" She took another step or two away from him.

"Not so, luv. Not so. You know how concerned I am about your well-being."

Like hell you are, Victoria thought to herself. "But let's not spend our last few minutes together quarreling," she murmured and coming back to him, she slipped into his arms. "You're right, Sean, you're right! This <u>is</u> all I want and no one can give it to me the way you do. Come, luv, come." Putting her hand behind his head, she drew him down to her again and began to kiss him: soft little nibbles around the edge of his lips, the tip of her tongue flicking in and out, teasing him until Sean couldn't stop himself from responding.

His mouth opened to engulf hers and he brought his hands up to push her cape back off her shoulders, fumbling irritably with her suit jacket, the enormous bow at the throat of her blouse. "Dammit, woman!" he growled. "You wear too many bloody clothes!"

Just then, however, they were interrupted by the buzzing of the intercom phone on a near-by table and disengaging herself, Victoria went to answer it. "Yes?....Is Mr. St. John there?....Good." She replaced the receiver and turned back to Sean. "Sorry, luv. I have to board the plane." A smile played at the corners of her mouth.

"I swear to God you had that timed right down to the second." And in spite of himself he chuckled.

"You'll never know, will you?" She glanced at herself in a mirror on the wall to her left. "Heavens–look at me! Hot-blooded Celt!"

"Damn you, Victoria!" He moved to take her in his arms again, but she sidestepped him and began rearranging her clothing, leaning closer to the mirror to check her make-up.

The door opened. It was the same airline official. "The car is waiting to take you out to the plane, Miss Windsor. We thought you and Mr. St. John might like to board ahead of the other passengers." He eyed the actor enviously for a moment and then closed the door again.

Sean raised one shaggy, blonde eyebrow. "No public shuttle bus for you, I see."

Victoria gave one last glance at the mirror and walked to the door. "I won't ask you to see me out to the plane. Ta-ta, luv."

"Oh no, you don't!" He followed her from the room. "I'll come with you–at least to the car."

"Whatever you say, of course." So she had won–not only with him, but with the wolf pack who undoubtedly was still lurking about somewhere. Seeing Sean with her would shut those damned reporters up–at least for the time being. But oddly there was no sense of triumph–only a renewed weariness and a sudden terrible need to be alone. The cut on her wrist was throbbing and she smiled bitterly as she recalled that while Noel had inquired with great concern about her injury, her current lover had failed to so much as notice it. Following the attendant along the hall again and into the lift, she wondered why she even bothered when it all mattered so little. Yet a few moments later when the lift came to a stop and the door opened, she slipped her arm through Sean's and stepped out to meet the waiting press–flashing a dazzling smile.

"So you were here all along, Mr. Patrick," someone called out. "What were you trying to do, Miss Windsor–throw us off the trail?"

Victoria's smile grew even more radiant–that is, if you didn't look too closely at her eyes. "After all," she murmured coyly, "a lady is entitled to a little privacy."

"One picture, please," a photographer pleaded.

"Gladly." Sean pulled Victoria's hand all the way through his arm and covering it with his own, he favored them with his most irresistible grin. Flashbulbs filled the air once again.

Unobserved, Noel stood a short distance away watching and even as he hated every minute of it, he couldn't take his eyes off the scene. Finally to his relief the airline official was moving through the crowd of reporters. "I'm afraid it's time, Miss Windsor.

"Yes, of course." Sean and Victoria followed the attendant a short distance to a door opening onto the runway. Neither of them had noticed Noel leave the building ahead of them and go around the car to get in on the far side. "Good-bye, darling." Giving her lover a final brief kiss, Victoria slipped through the door and walked briskly out to the waiting limousine. Sean watched as the car began to move across the runway toward the BOAC jet. Almost in spite of himself he still stood there to see her climb the stairs to the plane and disappear inside, followed a short distance behind by Noel. What was there about this woman? Last night she had infuriated him and now more than anything he wanted to feel her in his arms again. "Bugger the bloody bitch!" he muttered before finally turning to stride away.

* * *

Victoria had been surprised to find Noel already in the car. On edge anyway, this was one of those times when for some reason she suddenly found his very presence intolerable. "Where in hell have you been?" she snapped.

He looked away from her out the car window. Apparently he was watching a plane taxi out onto the runway, but in actuality he was seeing Victoria as she had been a few minutes before–clinging to Sean and gazing up at him as if he were her entire world. Dammit, he was tired of being taken for granted–good old, faithful, uncomplaining Noel. He looked back at her. "I simply couldn't bring myself to intrude on your tender scene of farewell!" His normally gentle voice was noticeably harsh.

"What's the matter? Jealous?" Victoria was relieved to have the car pull up just then by the plane. Another airline official was waiting there to open the door for her and immediately she extended her hand to be assisted from the car.

"Good morning, Miss Windsor," the man said.

"Good morning," she replied coolly, hurrying past him and starting up the stairs toward the door of the plane.

"Mr. St. John, are you coming, sir?"

All at once Noel became aware that the airline official was still waiting, one hand on the open car door. "Oh–sorry, old man." He grinned sheepishly. "Rough night last night. You know how it is, what?" Getting quickly from the car, he gave the bewildered young man a hasty pat on the shoulder and followed after Victoria, taking the stairs two at a time.

There had been a great deal of interest and excitement among the various BOAC cabin attendants as to who would get this particular assignment and even though Victoria was reputed to be impossible to please, the steward and two stewardesses who had finally been given the first class section for this flight considered themselves fortunate. They had flipped a coin to determine which of them would greet her at the door. The girl who had won the toss stood now at the top of the stairs, her heart pounding, as Victoria and Noel climbed the last couple of steps. "Good morning, Miss Windsor. It's an honor to have you aboard," she managed to say with only a slight tremor in her usual crisp professional tones.

"I trust I will have complete privacy!" Victoria moved past the girl and on into the plane without so much as a glance.

The steward stepped forward to greet her next, bestowing on her his most winning manner. "Of course, Miss Windsor." He made the mistake of taking her arm to escort her to her seat.

"Don't touch me!" she hissed, wrenching her arm away. "And save all that charm for the empty-headed little ninnies you work with. It doesn't impress me in the least."

"Yes, Miss Windsor. This way please, ma'am." He turned to lead the way along the aisle, his male ego quite possibly damaged beyond repair. "As requested, we have curtained off this section for you and Mr. St. John. I presume you're traveling together."

"That is your second error of the day! I am not with Mr. St. John! I am alone and I wish a Bloody Mary immediately!"

"I'm sorry, Miss Windsor," he replied coolly as he held back the curtain for her. Who in hell did she think she was anyway? "We are not allowed to serve liquor until we're airborne." With a curt bow which he hoped salvaged at least some shred of his dignity, he went back to the rear of the plane to assist with the boarding of the tourist class passengers, anything to escape the scene of his humiliation.

"Bloody stupid rule!" Victoria entered the private area and pulled the curtain shut behind her almost in Noel's face.

The second stewardess approached hesitantly. "The entire first class section is reserved for the theatre company, sir. You may choose any seat."

"Thank you." He grinned ruefully. "For a minute there I was afraid I'd been relegated to one of the wings."

"Would Miss Windsor like her things hung up, do you think?"

"I'm fairly sure she'll want to keep them with her. But thank you anyway." Rewarding the girl with a warm smile, Noel took the aisle seat across from the curtained-off area. He listened carefully, but heard only muffled sounds of movement.

Victoria, meanwhile, had removed her cape, flinging it casually on the single seat facing the rear of the plane and dropping her hat and scarf on top of it, she sank gratefully onto the double seat which faced forward. With a trembling hand she removed her dark glasses and slipping out of her shoes, she put her feet up on the cape. "Noel," she called softly after a moment, "would you come in here, luv?"

Instantly he was on his feet moving to the partition. "Yes, Victoria." Entering the compartment, he closed the curtain again behind him and sat down beside her.

She was lying back in the seat, her eyes closed, but at last she opened them, reaching for his right hand with her left. "Forgive me, Noel."

"It is I who should apologize, Victoria. I....."

"No, luv." She placed one finger lightly against his lips to silence him. "You need never apologize. You put up with so much: my moods, my tempers..... How many times in the years we've known each other have I hurt you?" Helplessly Noel shrugged. There was no way he could answer that question. "Lost count, hm?" A smile touched her face briefly. "And yet you always forgive me, don't you? But...but I did want to explain to you that just now I....I really need to be alone. You do understand, don't you, luv?"

"Yes, of course. Call if you want me." Noel stood up and started to open the curtain.

"Except for Jon. As company manager maybe <u>he</u> can get me a drink!"

"Righto. See you later then, Victoria." Noel returned to his seat. Then he thought of the other members of the company who would shortly be boarding and he got up again and walked to the front of the plane. He was just in time. The regular shuttle bus, carrying the other first class passengers, was stopping at the foot of the stairs, the first one out being the company's artistic director, Sir Gregory Hayden. Dark hair graying at the temples, a neatly clipped moustache and blue eyes edged engagingly with laugh lines, he looked so much like everyone's mental picture of an English theatrical director, it had become rather a joke—definitely a case of typecasting, they would say. He was accompanied by his wife. Next out of the bus were Geoffrey Leicester and Cynthia Phillips, the former very much the matinee idol and the latter, the typical ingenue–small, dark and pretty. Noel met them halfway up the stairs, Sir Gregory being in the lead. "I must ask you not to disturb Victoria. She doesn't feel well and she's resting in her compartment."

Cynthia giggled. "I'll bet she doesn't feel well. I was at that party last night, too."

"I can't let you by until you promise not to disturb her," Noel insisted firmly, barring their path.

"Of course we won't," Greg assured him. "Though really, old chap," he continued, not unkindly, "you do rather make a fool of yourself over the lady."

He ignored the comment and finally stepped aside allowing them to pass. One by one they filed into the plane. Noel himself was just stepping through the door when another car screeched to a halt at the foot of the stairs and Jonathan Sinclair, the company's managing director, spilled out onto the runway. Disheveled, hair uncombed, flight bag in one hand and a briefcase in the other and a rumpled mac thrown over one shoulder, he came up the stairs at a run. "We're in trouble," Noel observed wryly, "if the company manager can't even make it to the airport on time!"

"I overslept." Jonathan replied with a grin. Following the rest of them into the plane, he took the empty seat next to Noel, but then all at once he looked around: the Haydens in the first seat, Geoff Leicester and Cindi Phillips directly behind them. "Where is she?" he asked. Noel silently indicated the drawn curtain across the aisle. Jonathan Sinclair had known Victoria even longer than Noel, dating back even to the years before she was an established actress. They had all first been together at Stratford where Jon had been the one to introduce the other two. Sometimes he wondered sadly if he had done Noel a disservice. "Oh, I see. Is she all right?"

"No, she isn't–not at all. She's...she's torn between what she really is and what she pretends to be and it's destroying her."

"I'm afraid I don't follow you, old man."

"No, I don't suppose you do." Noel smiled ruefully. "It seems no one does where that lady is concerned. She did want to see you for a moment, however. She...she would like a drink and of course they insist on adhering to the rules."

"And that's why they're called <u>rules</u>! However, I will say hello."

"Jon, please, she......"

But the other man ignored him, getting to his feet to move across the aisle. "Victoria?"

"Come in." He could tell by her tone that he was in for it, but he squared his shoulders and pulled aside the curtain. "Did Noel tell you what I wanted?"

"You know perfectly well, Victoria, that the airline has rules and it..."

"Bugger their bloody rules!"

Jon went on as if her interruption hadn't even occurred. "....would be unfair of me to ask a cabin attendant to break one of them. It could cost her her job."

"Speaking of which, I got <u>you</u> fired once, I seem to recall. I could very easily do it again!"

"Come off it! You know you don't mean that." Unlike Noel, Jon's patience had its limits. "Now stop being deliberately difficult!"

"Oh, is that what I'm being?" One perfectly shaped eyebrow arched expressively.

"Yes, and what's more–you're enjoying it!"

"Did you at least have my wine brought on board?"

"Of course. Will you be wanting it with your lunch?"

"Just the wine. I'm not very hungry."

"You really should eat something, Victoria."

"Oh, sod off! If you can't get me a drink, the least you can do is leave me alone."

"Yes, Victoria." With a distinctly mocking bow Jon pulled the curtain shut behind him and returning to his seat, he snatched up the briefcase from the floor in front of him, slamming it down on his lap.

Noel looked over at him once or twice, unsure as to whether he should speak. "Really, old chap," he said finally, "don't you suppose, if you requested it, they might make an exception."

Jon ignored him. He had removed several file folders from his briefcase and begun going through them: property and costume lists, cost estimates, performance schedules. Why, he wondered wryly, were things so much easier to deal with than people?

But the other man persisted. "You know Victoria can't help being the way she is. She....."

"Please! I have a considerable amount of paperwork to do and I would strongly suggest that for the sake of our long friendship we end, at least for the time being, any discussion of Victoria."

"But Jon...."

"Subject closed! I mean it!"

"All...all right. What...whatever you say, of course." With a sigh Noel subsided into silence. But as the hours of the flight wore on, he would glance often across the aisle at the closed curtain.

* * *

Alone once again, Victoria had curled up on the seat. God, she thought, I wish we'd take off. I need that drink! At last the lighted sign above her on the wall came on: "Fasten Seat Belts: No Smoking, Please." She put her feet back on the floor, slipping into her shoes. "Now who says I won't do what I'm told," she said to herself with a little laugh as she fastened her seat belt. A moment or so later the plane began to move and lying back in the seat again, she watched as they taxied out on the runway. Idly she ran the index finger of her right hand around and around the edge of the small window.

Then all at once for no apparent reason she started to cry–the tears welling up silent and unbidden. The runway blurred before her eyes and yet she continued to stare blindly out the window, unaware she was crying until suddenly she realized her face was wet. She fumbled in her purse for a handkerchief, but there was none. "Damn," she muttered under her breath, "I never have a hanky when I need one!... Oh, why did I have to think that," she whispered. "Why that of all things?" After all these years she could still hear his gentle voice so clearly. "Why is it a little girl never has a hanky when she needs one?" And superimposed over the runway there was a black, marble tomb in a small, white chapel: cold and so terribly final. "Oh, Uncle Bertie," she whispered aloud again, "if only...." The tears came faster now, welling up from a bottomless source over which she seemed to have no control. "I have got to stop this," she told herself sternly. "I am simply being weak and that is inexcusable!"

The plane gathered speed and feeling it leave the ground, Victoria leaned forward to look out the window again, continuing to watch as the cars and buildings dwindled away below. Soon she became absorbed in studying the green checkerboard design of the English countryside and the tears stopped as suddenly and inexplicably as they had begun. My goodness–airborne, she thought with a slightly hysterical giggle. Now I may drink legally! She pressed the call button by her seat. A stewardess appeared almost immediately. "Yes, Miss Windsor?"

"I would like a Bloody Mary."

"Yes, ma'am." The girl disappeared and returned a few minutes later with a tray on which there was a glass, a small bottle of vodka and a tin of Bloody Mary mix. Letting down the table from the wall, she placed the tray on it. She waited in vain for the actress to thank her and at last she left.

Victoria busied herself with mixing the drink. The seat belt sign went out and loosening hers, she curled up again taking a long, eager swallow, but liquor just didn't seem to do much good anymore. For a moment she almost called out to Noel or Jon to come and sit with her, but pride kept her silent. Only a short while before, after all, she had demanded solitude. She was almost relieved when a knock sounded on the wall of her compartment. "Your lunch, Miss

Windsor." The curtain slid back and she saw that both stewardesses were there, the girl in the lead carrying the tray and the other following with the bottle of wine in an ice bucket.

"I told Mr. Sinclair all I wanted was my wine!"

"Yes, ma'am. He said that, but Mr. St. John said to bring the food anyway in case you changed your mind."

"He had no right to do that," she replied crossly. No matter what she said or did, Noel stubbornly persisted in taking care of her. His concern touched her deeply, but she wasn't about to let anyone else know that. "Oh, all right, bring the tray in here although why people can't just leave me in peace is beyond me!" The first attendant entered and bent to remove the small tray with Victoria's drink still on it. "Don't touch that!"

"I have to put the lunch on the table, Miss Windsor, but the glass will fit on the tray, too." The other girl placed the wine bucket on the floor and they both withdrew as rapidly as possible.

Disinterestedly Victoria picked at the steak and potatoes. She did break the roll in half, butter it and take a few bites, but then she pushed the tray aside. She just never seemed to have much of an appetite. Finally she reached for the bottle of wine and pouring a glass, she lay back against the seat and closed her eyes. If only I could sleep for a while, she thought. But suddenly entirely without warning the tears started again, stinging and burning behind her eyelids. "What in hell is the matter with me?" she muttered angrily, blinking back the tears. "I'm not that bloody sentimental about dear old England!" But something was wrong with her today. She could never remember feeling so unsettled and twice now, just since she'd gotten on the plane, there'd been these ridiculous attacks of weeping.

This strange discontent had, in fact, begun two days earlier at St. George's Chapel–no, even earlier when she took the book and monogrammed handkerchief from their hiding place in her bureau drawer. Looking at them, it had been impossible not to wonder what Uncle Bertie would have thought of the woman she'd become and to realize sadly that he would have been bitterly disappointed. Why should that concern her now, however? Uncle Bertie had been such a fleeting part of her life–nearly 20 years ago–and what difference did it make whether he would have approved of her or not?

But it did matter terribly—why? Victoria found herself becoming oddly excited as though she were on the verge of some tremendous discovery. Because....because it didn't just start at Windsor, did it, she thought, or even that day I was able to look at the book again for the first time in so long? Somewhere deep inside I've known since....since I can't even remember when that something was wrong with my life. Going to Windsor–seeing myself through his eyes–only crystallized it all for me.

"I....I said to Noel last night at the party that Windsor was a mistake–that it wasn't the real me." Without even being aware of it she was whispering her thoughts aloud now. "But then why did I feel so contented there–more at peace with myself than I've been in years? Perhaps it wasn't a mistake! Perhaps it was the first right thing I've done in a long time. And....and what made it seem so right? Because....because I was remembering Uncle Bertie and how kind he'd been to me.....no, more than that. Because I....I was allowing myself to feel affection for someone and not just to feel it, but...but to express it out loud and.....and......"

Abruptly her elation faded and once again her eyes brimmed with helpless tears. It was just as she'd said that day at the tomb. She could admit to loving someone only when that person was dead, when....when it was safe. And what good was that? The memory of loving—of being loved–might comfort her briefly, but would do nothing to ease her loneliness, the terrible emptiness of her life. "Oh, I don't want to be like this," she whispered. "There...there has to have been a time in my life when I wasn't afraid to love and maybe if I can find my way back to that time, I can teach myself to love again. When...when was it–the last time I...I loved someone without fear or reservation? Besides...besides Uncle Bertie, I mean."

And all at once she knew. It had been the fall of 1945; she was unable to recall the exact date, but it was the day of her father's return from World War II. She'd looked forward to that day so eagerly and before it was over, her loneliness would have begun. Dear God, she had been only five years old............

Act One - "Vicki"

Chapter 1

Christened Victoria Olivia Windsor, she'd been born on her father's family estate in Westgate-on-Sea, Kent and for the first several years of her life its stone walls had constituted the boundaries of her world. Home was a rambling Tudor style manor house set in the midst of rolling green lawns. She had a large, sunny nursery filled with toys and a household of servants to look after her. Indeed it would have seemed the ideal place for a little girl to grow up.

From an early age, however, Vicki was aware something was amiss. Oh, the servants were all right although she did think Nanny rather mean sometimes, but more than anything she wanted a Mama and a Papa. Yet Vicki wasn't an orphan. She had parents. Malcolm Oliver Windsor, second son of Oliver Albert Windsor, the Earl of Carlisle, was her father and her mother's name was Catherine. She even called them Mama and Papa, but things still seemed wrong somehow.

Papa wasn't even a real person–just a framed photograph on the library mantel. The servants had explained to her that the funny clothes he had on were called a uniform and all those pretty pins and ribbons on the jacket were decorations. Her father, they told her, had gone far away to Australia when she was still only a baby to fly a plane for the King. Her Papa was a very brave man and she should be frightfully proud of him.

Secretly, however, Vicki wished her Papa were like Carleton, the family chauffeur. He had flat feet, everyone said in low tones as though that were something shameful, and so had been rejected for military service. All she knew was that Carleton hadn't had to go off to some place called Australia and she would often see him playing with his children: pushing them on the swing which hung from the big, old tree on the front lawn or sledding with them in the winter. Nanny always listened to her prayers, but every night after she'd left, Vicki would scramble out from under the covers to kneel again and say her own special prayer. "Dear God, please make my Papa have flat feet like Carleton so that he will come home and play with me. Amen." But she must be a wicked child indeed, as Nanny often told her she was, because she'd been saying that prayer for ever so long and nothing had happened.

Her mother was at least a real person who wore beautiful clothes and smelled good, but Mama found it "beastly dull" in Westgate-on-Sea and spent much of her time in a grand sounding place called London. Even when she did come to stay at the manor house for a few days, she had little time for her daughter. Often she would be accompanied by a man, always a different one, and never the man in the picture which confused Vicki even further. Lately there'd been one in particular whom she'd been told to call Uncle Henry.

Oh, but finally it seemed that God was answering her prayers! All that spring and summer she'd sensed the growing excitement. When she asked why everyone was so happy, the servants had told her that the war was almost over. She didn't know what a war was, but what she did understand was that once it was over, the King wouldn't need her Papa to fly his plane for him anymore and he would be coming home.

At the end of the summer there were parades and fireworks and she learned the war was indeed over! She waited and waited and then finally one night long after she was in bed, she heard her mother arrive. She tried to keep her eyes open, watching eagerly for the nursery door to open, but the next thing she knew Nanny was waking her to say that her mother was having breakfast in her room and wanted to see her. Happily Vicki jumped out of bed and donning her blue quilted robe and matching bunny slippers, she half-ran, half-skipped down the hall to knock on her mother's bedroom door. "Come in," Catherine Windsor's cool, refined voice responded.

Vicki pushed open the door and entered. "Good morning, Mama," she said, dropping a curtsey as her nanny had taught her.

"Come here, please," her mother said. "No, not on the bed," she added sternly as the little girl started to climb up beside her. Vicki stood obediently, hands clasped behind her back, looking up at her expectantly. "I suppose the servants have told you your father arrives home today."

"No, Mama, they didn't say it was today!" The child beamed delightedly. "Is he coming on the train? May I go to the station to meet him? May I, Mama, please?" In her excitement she jumped up and down clapping her hands.

"Stop that!" Her mother said sharply. "Really! I can't think what your nanny has been teaching you! A well-brought up young lady does not behave in such a fashion!"

"I'm sorry," Vicki said contritely, her spirits somewhat dampened. "But may I go to the station, please?"

"No, you may not. I'll wish to see your father alone."

In spite of herself she crept closer to the bed. "Mama, are you going to hug and kiss him the way Frances, the cook, does with her husband?"

"Really, Vicki! We are <u>not</u> servants! Now your nanny will give you your breakfast and dress you in your prettiest dress to greet your father."

"May I eat here with you, Mama, on the little table by the window?"

"I thought you took your meals in the nursery?"

"Yes, Mama," she replied in a small voice and with another curtsey she turned to walk from the room, closing the door carefully behind her. But today nothing could make her unhappy for long and by the time she'd eaten her breakfast and put on her best dress–light blue taffeta trimmed with lace–all her dejection was gone. It didn't even matter that Nanny was especially cross this morning, slapping her hand when she had trouble with the buttons on the dress and scraping her scalp with the hair brush.

At last she was ready. Her nursery looked out over the front lawn and the instant Miss Carpenter left her alone she ran to climb up on the window seat, remembering just in time to kick off her black patent leather shoes so as not to scratch the paint. Settling herself down cross-legged, she peered excitedly at the point where the gravel driveway emerged from the trees to circle the vast expanse of lawn, disappearing for a moment on the far side of the duck pond and passing eventually in front of the house directly beneath her. She wondered whether it would be the big blue Bentley in which Carleton drove her and her nanny to church on Sundays. After all, shouldn't it be the best for her Papa? She had only been there about twenty minutes when she saw a car slip noiselessly from the trees. It <u>was</u> the Bentley!

Vicki scrambled down from the window seat. She was halfway along the hall to the stairs before she realized she'd forgotten her shoes. Mama would be furious! She ran back to the nursery, but the shoes were nowhere to be seen. Throwing herself down flat on her stomach by the bed, she groped around under the pink and white polka-dotted spread and eventually found them. It took two tries before she had them on the correct feet and then there were those horrid buckles. Vicki could never decide which was more troublesome for her five year old fingers: buckles or laces and Nanny was so strict about her doing things for herself. At last she rushed out the door once more and down the hall, by now all but tripping over her own feet in her eagerness. Just as she reached the top of the wide front stairs, Jeffers, the footman, was coming up them carrying a large brown leather suitcase in one hand and a green canvas duffel bag in the other. "Oh, Jeffers!' she bubbled excitedly. "Where is my Papa?"

"In the library with your Mama, young miss," he replied.

"Thank you, Jeffers." Vicki ran on down the stairs and across the reception hall to the library, but before she could open the door, she heard a male voice inside. "....fine way to greet a man after all this time!" It must be my Papa talking, she thought happily, but her elation was short-lived.

"I'm sorry, Malcolm," her mother replied. "There's simply nothing left for us." She'd never known her Mama to sound quite so cold and a little lump of fear began to form in the pit of her stomach.

"You just couldn't be faithful to me, could you?" It was her Papa speaking again.

"Oh, come now! Did you really expect me to sit at home with a child for three years waiting patiently for you to return?"

"Yes, Catherine, actually I did, you see. Other men's wives remained true to their marriage vows. I had a right to at least hope mine would. Did you think I wanted to go off to the other side of the world and leave you alone with a two year old?"

"You could have requested to stay in England. A man in your social position– the son of an Earl–could have pulled a few strings."

"You knew I didn't believe in asking for special favors. You should have respected me for it."

"Respected you, ha! I thought you were selfish and spiteful!"

"Yes, well that is rather beside the point at the moment. I suppose you'll want a divorce so you can marry this Henry Montgomery. I won't stand in your way!"

"Most considerate of you, Malcolm. Now if you'll excuse me, I'll be packed and out of here tonight."

"May I at least see my daughter? She is mine, isn't she?"

Vicki heard the sharp crack of a hand across a face, followed by a few rapid footsteps and before she could move, her mother had flung open the door to find her standing there wide-eyed. "Oh God, Vicki! What in hell are you doing here?" Although the child tried desperately to answer, no words would come. She began to cry. "Answer me, you little brat! Eavesdropping, weren't you? I said–answer me!" But Vicki could only stand there, sobbing all the harder and shaking her head from side to side.

Suddenly she was aware that her father had knelt in front of her and was gently wiping away her tears with his handkerchief. "Hello, Vicki. I'm your Papa. Don't you think it's time we got reacquainted?" Malcolm Windsor picked his daughter up in his arms, carrying her back up the stairs and into her bedroom again to put her down on the window seat. It was the exact spot from which she'd so eagerly awaited his arrival a short while before, but of course he had no way of knowing that.

At last he seated himself beside her and for the first time he could really look at her. Her eyes were big and green like her mother's, but everything else from the blonde hair to the tiny pointed chin was a small, feminine copy of himself. Well, at least that settles the paternity question, he thought ironically. Vicki in her turn stared back. It was amazing to see a full-sized version of the picture on the mantel. Only now his clothes were like everyone else's. "Are you really my Papa?"

"Yes, Vicki. And what a pretty little girl you are."

"Thank you. But where's your uniform, Papa–like in the picture?"

"I've been discharged from the Royal Air Force, you see, so I don't wear one anymore."

"Oh." Vicki looked slowly around the room and after a moment she began to swing her feet, letting each fall in turn against the side of the window seat. It was a habit of hers whenever she felt bored or uneasy. Nanny had often scolded her for it. I don't know what's so special about a Papa anyway, she thought. He's just like all the men who come to visit with Mama; he even says the same stupid things! A small sigh escaped her.

A few minutes before when he saw his daughter again for the first time in so long, Malcolm had unthinkingly followed his natural impulse, picking her up to comfort her. But now an awkward silence filled the room, broken only by the unnerving banging of her heels against the wooden window seat, and that one sigh told him clearly she was just as uncomfortable as he was. He searched his mind for something they could talk about. "Do you have a nanny, Vicki?"

"Yes, Papa. Her name's Miss Carpenter." She inched closer to him. "Does.... does she have to stay now....now that you're home? I don't much care for her." Malcolm stared straight ahead drumming the fingers of one hand nervously on his knee. Vicki's eyes filled with tears and her lower lip began to tremble. Her father wasn't paying any attention to her. "Please, Papa." Kneeling up on the window seat, she placed one small hand on his arm.

"What, dear?" Finally he was forced to look at her.

"Papa, I asked if my nanny has to stay. I don't like her, Papa."

"Don't be silly, Vicki. Of course your nanny will stay. Your mother's leaving this evening and my work will keep me in London a good deal of the time. Someone has to look after you."

Now she was becoming frightened. "Where is my Mama going?"

"I think she should be the one to explain that to you. Now I have to get settled."

"May we have lunch together, Papa," she inquired hopefully.

"Do you usually eat with your mother?"

"I usually eat with Nanny," Vicki admitted reluctantly. "But I thought today might be special."

"I have a great deal to do, you see: phone calls, correspondence. You should probably continue in your regular routine." Malcolm Windsor had to get away from this child with her never-ending questions and her insistent hand on his arm and getting up from the window seat, he walked quickly to the door.

Vicki slid to the floor to follow him. "Please, Papa, I....I...." But she was incapable of putting her feelings into words: her longing to be loved and cherished–to be part of a real family. All she could do was stand there, eyes brimming with tears, looking pleadingly up at her father.

Malcolm's intentions toward his daughter were the best, but he had no idea how to deal with an unhappy five year old. She was, moreover, Catherine's daughter as well and a painful reminder of his wife's infidelity. All he wanted, at least for the present, was escape. "I'll see you later, Vicki." With a pat on her head he hurried away down the hall, trying unsuccessfully to ignore her heartbroken sobs.

* * *

A short time later Miss Carpenter entered the nursery to find it empty. The taffeta dress, frilly slip, patent leather shoes and white ankle socks were in a pile in the center of the floor, but Vicki herself was nowhere to be seen. Honestly that child was becoming more of a problem every day! With an exasperated sigh she turned on one heel and strode from the room again. She hadn't quite reached the stairs, however, when she encountered Catherine Windsor. "Where is Vicki?" her mother demanded. "I wish to speak to her."

"I'm sorry, Mrs. Windsor. I don't know. I was just on my way to look for her."

"Really, Miss Carpenter, you are exceedingly careless. If you don't fulfill your responsibilities more satisfactorily from now on, you will find yourself without a position and no references with which to seek a new one!"

"Yes, ma'am. I'll find her, ma'am." The nanny hurried down the stairs and across the entry hall, her heels pounding out an angry staccato on the polished tile. If she'd been annoyed with the little girl a short while before, she was furious now. "Vicki? Vicki, where are you..... dear?" There was no answer and quickening her pace, she moved out the front door and along the driveway, calling Vicki's name repeatedly, but even though she was careful to keep her tone even, there was no reply. By now she was growing alarmed. Cars traveled the narrow, winding road past the estate at terrifying rates of speed and on another side the land dropped off sharply to the rocky seacoast some distance below. Her career could be ruined! "Vicki, it's naughty of you to frighten Nanny. Now be a good girl and tell me where you are." Running now, she returned to the house, but then just as she started up the stairs, she remembered Vicki's secret place: an old, abandoned gazebo in the woods behind the house. The child could spend hours there with her dolls making believe–especially when she was due in the nursery for lessons. Angrily Miss Carpenter strode back down the steps and around the side of the house toward the woods.

The path toward the beach wound around and through a grove of towering elms through which one could just glimpse the blue of the ocean below and the gazebo itself was not even visible until you were almost on top of it. Even when she could see the summerhouse, there was still no sign of Vicki. Not until she'd come around to the side which faced out toward the water did she finally discover the child sitting on the single step, her chin in her hands, elbows on her knees. She was wearing a faded yellow pullover and red slacks with a gaping hole in one knee while on her feet were scuffed brown oxfords, as usual untied. Her blonde curls were hopelessly tangled and her face was streaked with dirt. "Vicki, didn't you hear me calling you?" At the sound of her nanny's voice the little girl jumped and when she looked up and saw the expression on the woman's face, she scrambled to her feet.

"Just look at you!" Miss Carpenter explained. "Your hair's a mess and your face is absolutely filthy! And wherever did you find those wretched clothes? I thought I threw them away!" Vicki wiped her nose on her sleeve and sniffed. "And will you <u>never</u> learn to use a hanky?" Dumbly the child stood there staring down at the ground and scuffing at the dirt with the toe of one oxford. "Answer me, young lady!"

Vicki swallowed once or twice. Fresh tears filled her eyes. "Nobody loves me," she said at last, but so softly the woman failed to understand her.

"Speak up! Haven't I told you not to mumble?" The little girl was sobbing now and although she repeated the words, this time they were completely garbled. "Well, never mind!' the nanny snapped. "If you insist on being naughty, we'll just put you in your room until you can learn to behave!" Seizing Vicki by the wrist, she started back along the path dragging her charge behind her. As they neared the house, however, the child's sobs grew in intensity until Miss Carpenter stopped so suddenly they collided. "Stop it! Do you hear me, stop it!" She knelt down in front of Vicki and shook her. "If I lose this position on account of you, you nasty brat, I'll see you pay! Do you hear me?"

Perhaps it was in these moments Victoria first discovered the rigid self-discipline which so characterized her in later years. In any case her crying ceased abruptly and with one last sniff, one last wipe of her nose and eyes with the sleeve of that disreputable jersey, she raised her head to look the woman steadily in the face. "Very well, Miss Carpenter. We may go in now."

With equal dignity they marched the rest of the way along the path to the front of the house, up the stairs and along the hall to the nursery. Inside the room Miss Carpenter pointed to the pile of clothing in the middle of the floor. "First, young lady, you will pick those up!"

The little girl obeyed, but then with everything gathered in her arms she hesitated. "What... what should I do with them now, please?"

"Honestly you are an idiot! You know where your clothes hamper is. All these things will have to be washed. You have made a mess of yourself as usual." Carrying the clothes into her bathroom, Vicki put them in the hamper and returned to stand dumbly in front of her nanny, awaiting her next instructions. "Now remove those horrid garments and this time I intend to see they are burned!" Without a word the child took off her pants and shirt and handed them to her. "Now then," Miss Carpenter concluded, "I will leave you alone so you can think about how thoroughly wicked you have been! That's why your parents are both leaving, you know. They can't bear to be here with you. I unfortunately have no choice. I'm stuck with you!"

All during this tirade Vicki had continued to stand there, staring blankly at some point beyond her accuser. "I'm.....I'm hungry," she whispered at last. "I...I didn't have any lunch."

"Well, perhaps <u>that</u> will teach you to behave." With these words the woman turned and strode from the room.

Vicki still stood for a few moments without moving. Finally, however, she went over to the window seat and lifting the right hand lid, she reached way in back where she'd hidden something under some building blocks. In order to do this it was necessary to hoist herself up onto the ledge of the seat and balance on her stomach, head down inside the cubbyhole. From behind all one could have seen were two chubby legs ending in the scuffed brown oxfords, still untied, and her small bottom in its white cotton underpants.

When the little girl emerged from her search, she was clutching a dirty, white object which could just be recognized as a toy lamb although most of its fleece, both ears and one eye had been missing for some time. "There you are, Snowball," she crooned, stroking it lovingly. "You must never be afraid, you know, because I'll never let anyone hurt you." At last she sat down on the floor in front of the window seat and cradling the lamb in both arms, she began to rock it back and forth.

* * *

For the next two years, then, Vicki's day-to-day existence would continue on much as it had been before her father's return. Busy with their new lives, both parents paid infrequent visits to the estate and in their customary absence Madeline Carpenter's rule in the nursery was absolute.

Though, in fairness to Malcolm Windsor, it must be said he at least felt a certain sense of responsibility for his daughter and in the beginning he came to see her somewhat more often. Invariably, however, these interviews were as awkward and uncomfortable as the day he'd arrived home and he allowed longer and longer to lapse between visits. One of the many RAF pilots rewarded with a knighthood following the war, Sir Malcolm was offered a BOAC vice-presidency–a prestigious position which took him all over the world–and his money and title as well as his aristocratic good looks provided him with no lack of female companionship. He knew he was derelict in his duty as a father. For the most part he managed to keep this realization buried in his subconscious, but the guilt was still there–like a nagging toothache–refusing to be ignored.

It was he who first noticed the change in Vicki. Once a warm, outgoing child, naturally obedient and eager to please, she'd grown increasingly hostile and withdrawn. He decided it was time for her to go away to school. His ex-wife refused to return his phone calls and so finally he made the selection himself. The Heathfield Abbey School for Girls was located just outside the village of Tetbury in Gloucestershire, about 100 miles west and slightly north of London in the picturesque section of England known as the Cotswolds. A Church of England convent school, it was noted for the quality of its education as well as the strict moral guidance of its students. Vicki would be eight years old on January 10th, just in time to enter for the winter term.

Malcolm himself had planned a New Year's skiing holiday in Switzerland so he left it to his solicitor, Nigel Bascombe, to make the actual arrangements. This included, by the way, breaking the news to his daughter–a task he did not relish. It happened to be on January 10th that Mr. Bascombe made his trip down to Kent. He had no way of knowing, of course, that the date had any special significance.

Jeffers, the footman, was sent to fetch the child. He found her in her room sitting at the small antique writing desk which had arrived the day before from her mother. "Someone to see you in the library, Miss Vicki."

At the sound of his voice she'd started guiltily although from where he was standing just inside the doorway he was unable to see what she'd been doing. "Excuse me, Jeffers. I didn't hear you."

"I said there's someone to see you in the library."

Perhaps it was because it was her birthday; perhaps it was because deep down inside she hadn't yet stopped hoping. She was sure the visitor was her father. "Thank you, Jeffers." There was just a trace in her manner of her former enthusiasm as jumping up, she hurried from the nursery and along the hall toward the stairs.

Curious what Vicki had been doing when he came into the room, Jeffers walked across to the new desk. He was shocked to discover several long, deep scratches in its highly polished surface. The scissors evidently used to inflict the damage were still there in plain sight. He wondered sadly why the child did such things, knowing full well she would be severely punished.

The door to the library stood open and the little girl ran happily into the room. Some man she'd never seen before was standing in front of the fireplace, legs slightly apart. He was smoking a small, thin cigar. "Stupid," she whispered to herself. "Stupid... stupid....stupid!"

"I beg your pardon, Vicki," he said. "Did you say something?"

"No, nothing."

"Well then, young lady," he went on with a nod, "I don't believe we've met. I'm Mr. Bascombe, your father's solicitor, and I've got something very exciting to tell you. In just a few days now you are going away to school–Heathfield Abbey in Gloucestershire. I'm sure you'll like it there."

Vicki simply stood there looking steadily up at the man as he talked. My father couldn't even come himself, she thought. But outwardly she accepted the news without comment. It didn't matter anyway. She couldn't possibly be any lonelier at school.

"Did you understand me, Vicki?" When the little girl did not respond in any way, the solicitor thought she might be puzzled about something.

"Yes, sir." Her face remained expressionless.

"No questions then?"

"Only one. What will happen to my nanny?"

"I also have instructions to dismiss her."

A half-smile flitted across the child's face. "I see," she murmured.

On the morning of her departure Vicki was out of bed and dressed long before a maid knocked on the door with her breakfast. A short time later, wearing her ermine trimmed cherry red coat and matching bonnet, she was sitting on the deacon's bench in the front entry hall waiting for Carleton to bring the car around. She'd only been there a few minutes when the slight, sandy-haired chauffeur appeared in the doorway. For a moment he studied her–the ladylike little face framed in fur, her feet in their patent leather shoes crossed primly at the ankles, her gloved hands clasping a book in her lap. The child had always seemed old for her age, he thought, but especially today. "All ready then, Miss Vicki?" he inquired kindly.

"Yes, Carleton, I am." She slipped down off the bench and walked past him through the doorway.

He followed at a respectful distance down the steps toward the car. "Are you looking forward to going to school?"

"Yes, I suppose so." Vicki knew it was the answer he expected. Sadly it had been some time now since she'd really looked forward to anything. "Have you put all my things in the boot?"

"Yes, Miss." He held open the rear door for her.

"Thank you, Carleton," Vicki said with all her eight year old dignity as she settled herself in the back seat.

The chauffeur closed the door after her and going around to the other side, he got into the driver's seat. He slipped the transmission into gear and the Bentley moved off around the circular driveway; as they were about to enter the woods, however, he slowed again. "Want to take one last look, Miss Vicki?"

"No, thank you. I want to go <u>now</u>, please."

"Yes, miss." The car moved on down the driveway and the house disappeared from sight. Glancing in his rearview mirror, he shook his head. The child was already absorbed in her book.

Chapter 2

Heathfield was an old school, established in the early 1800's, and its spacious grounds and redbrick buildings spoke eloquently of the tranquil permanence of class and privilege. On this first day of winter term, however, a steady stream of cars, busses and taxicabs passed in both directions through the main gate and the campus appeared very much in a state of barely controlled chaos–belonging quite definitely to the mid-20th century. Carleton stopped at the gate to ask directions to Burleigh Hall, the dormitory housing the younger girls, and as they passed under the stone archway, both he and Vicki looked about at the place which essentially would be her home for the next ten years. "Very pleasant, Miss Vicki," the chauffeur observed at one point. "I can see why Sir Malcolm chose it for you."

Vicki made no reply, knowing full well that her father hadn't even seen the school. As for herself, she hated Heathfield on sight. The buildings, all similar in design, looked like a prison and as they drove across campus, she saw girls everywhere–shrieking and hugging and kissing each other. She began to feel sick. A few minutes later, however, as they pulled up in front of Burleigh Hall, she was out of the car and halfway up the stairs before Carleton had a chance to come around and open the door for her. No one could accuse her of being a coward.

A nun, dressed in the dark blue habit of her Anglican order, sat at a table in the central hall. A sign read: *Registration: New Students*. "Yes, sir." She looked up inquiringly at Carleton who had followed Vicki into the building and now stood behind her.

"Yes, Sister," he replied removing his uniform cap. "I have a new student here for you–Miss Victoria Windsor."

"I'm Sister Elizabeth, Vicki dear. Welcome to Heathfield. I'm sure you'll be very happy with us."

"Say something, Miss Vicki," Carleton prompted her.

All this time she had been staring at the strange lady whose face was framed in starched white linen, her head covered with what appeared to be some sort of shawl. "Do you always dress in those funny clothes?"

"Miss Vicki, your nanny taught you better manners than that," the chauffeur remonstrated gently.

"That's all right." The nun smiled. "The younger ones are naturally curious about the habit. Yes, Vicki, I wear these clothes all the time."

The little girl's eyes widened. "Will I have to dress like that?"

"No, dear, although as a student, you will have a uniform. You may take your young charge's things on up to the second floor, sir," she said to Carleton. "Room 23. Turn right at the top of the stairs and it's the second room on the right. Now, Vicki," Sister Elizabeth went on, "your big sister will be ...ah...let me see..." She paused to consult a list on the table in front of her...."Sister Philippa. I'm sure you'll like her. Everyone does."

Vicki frowned. "What's a big sister?"

"Each new student has a postulant assigned to her to help her feel at home here at Heathfield."

"Thank you very much. I won't need anyone."

Sister Elizabeth was clearly startled. "Nonsense, Vicki, we all need someone." She was relieved to look up just then and see Philippa coming down the stairs with another of the new students and the child's parents. "Sister Philippa," she called, "I need you over here, please."

Hearing her name, the young nun excused herself and leaving the other family to say their good-byes in private, she came across the hall toward the registration desk.

Philippa was slightly older than the majority of postulants since she had received her University degree and begun a teaching career in a state-run school before joining the order a little less than a year before. She'd felt a lack of something in her life. As an Anglican sister, she knew she had found that something and she was always smiling, her soft, blue-gray eyes filled with joy. Philippa's natural sweetness drew all the students to her, but especially the younger ones, away from home for the first time and often homesick. "I have another of your new little sisters here," Elizabeth continued as the postulant approached. "Vicki Windsor. Vicki, this is Sister Philippa."

"I'm so happy to meet you, Vicki," Sister Philippa reached out to take the little girl's hand. "If you'll come with me, I'll bring you to the supply room to get your uniforms."

"Yes, ma'am." Looking steadily up at her, Vicki put both hands behind her back.

"Come along then, dear." Philippa made no further attempt to hold her hand, but instead simply turned to lead the way across the hall.

Vicki followed her–though with both hands still clasped firmly together behind her back. Carleton watched the small, proud figure move away from him, finally disappearing around a corner. "Is something wrong, sir?" Sister Elizabeth inquired after a moment as she became aware he was still standing there.

"I...ah....beg your pardon....uh, no, Sister. Take good care of her, will you? She's a very lonely child."

"She <u>has</u> both her parents, doesn't she?"

"Yes, but they....ah.... Well, I'll fetch Miss Vicki's things now." The driver left then before he could commit the unforgivable indiscretion of criticizing his employer.

* * *

"You call me Sister, you know, Vicki–not ma'am," Sister Philippa corrected her quietly as they walked along together.

"You're not my sister."

"I know I'm not. That simply means I'm a sister in this religious order."

"Oh......"

The two walked in silence the rest of the way to the supply room which was at the end of the corridor. The upper half of the door stood open, showing walls lined with shelves which held the various parts of the school uniform, arranged according to sizes. Several nuns were moving busily about the room, dispensing a neatly stacked pile of garments to each student: two navy blue wool skirts and navy blue wool pullovers, four long-sleeved white blouses, four pairs of navy blue knee socks and brown loafers. The girl directly ahead of them in the queue was also with her "big sister", but despite all the efforts of the young nun to comfort her she was clearly miserable, clinging to the postulant's hand and crying. She was a plain child with thin brown braids and pale, weak-looking eyes behind thick glasses.

"What's the matter with her?" Vicki asked–puzzled.

"She's probably a little homesick. That's natural for you new girls."

"Oh? Well, I'm not in the least homesick, thank you!"

Overhearing, the other girl turned around to stare at her. "You're not?" she whispered.

"Of course not! Only babies are homesick."

"Oh, Vicki, don't be cruel!" Sister Philippa was shocked. "She can't help missing her Mama and Papa, you know." What sort of family situation, she wondered, could possibly have produced such a strange, unfeeling child. But the other girl wasn't crying anymore and her eyes, as she stepped up to be given her school clothing, were wide with admiration.

Vicki was next at the window. "What do I do now?" she inquired of Sister Philippa once she had received her pile of garments. Her tone indicated clearly she wasn't really interested. She simply needed to know.

"I'll show you where your room is. Your driver was to bring your things up, I believe?" They returned to the front hall–mounting the broad front stairs together, around and up a second flight. As Carleton had been instructed, you turned right and went two doors down the hall, also on the right.

Vicki stood for a moment in the doorway. Fairly large, the room was rectangular in shape with three tall windows on the wall facing the door–quite superior to many public school dormitories, in fact. Four iron cots were arranged on each of the longer walls–the younger students being assigned eight to a room–and a small chest of drawers stood beside each bed. Each bureau held a small lamp, another unheard-of luxury in most schools. Two large wooden wardrobes stood at either end of the room–these to be shared, two girls to each. Five of the room's occupants were already there and of course the beds on the wall with the windows had been taken first. These four students were busy unpacking, chattering together as they worked. The door divided the other wall in half and the fifth girl was at the bed in the left hand corner. "Which bed do you want, dear?" Sister Philippa inquired.

Vicki thought of her room in the manor house–furnished with a canopy bed and decorated in pink and white with ruffled curtains both on the bed and at the windows. "I would have liked to be by a window." Her voice quivered and for just a moment she sounded like any other little girl away from home for the first time. "My own room has two windows and one has a window seat. I used to....used to...."

"There's nothing wrong with feeling a little lonesome at first, you know." Philippa put an arm around her shoulders, but at the touch she felt the child stiffen.

"I told you I'm <u>not</u> lonesome!" Impatiently Vicki pulled herself free. "I'll take the one in the other corner." And walking quickly to the end of the room, she sat down on the bed as if claiming possession.

"Would you like some help getting unpacked?"

"I can manage nicely, thank you."

"Very well, dear." Sister Philippa turned to leave, pausing at the door to address all the girls in general. "I'll be back at supper time to bring you all to the dining hall. Remember you are required to be dressed in the full Heathfield uniform."

Vicki had nothing to do until Carleton brought her things and after a while she found herself watching the four lucky girls who had arrived early enough to get the beds by the windows. Their natural youthful enthusiasm was so totally alien to her that it seemed as though she were watching a show of some kind, rather than other girls much like herself, and although she observed them with considerable interest, it never occurred to her to join them. She failed to notice the girl in the other rear corner of the room–the same one who'd been in front of her in the supply room queue.

Pamela was trying to put her things away, but with little success. Hopelessly confused, she did nothing but move from one side of the bed to the other and back again, picking up piles of clothing and putting them down again, all the time sniffing back the tears. Then all at once she happened to glance over at the bed in the other corner and she forgot everything else. The beautiful girl with the long, golden hair, like some fairy princess in one of her storybooks–this brave person who wasn't even homesick–was going to be in <u>her</u> room! "What are you staring at?" Vicki demanded crossly.

The princess had actually spoken to her! She approached hesitantly. "My... my name is Pamela Ashworth. What's yours?"

"Victoria Olivia Windsor!" she announced with a flourish. She'd always rather liked the sound of her own name.

At that moment Carleton appeared. With the assistance of the dormitory handyman he'd brought her trunk and two suitcases. He smiled at her kindly. "So here you are, Miss Vicki."

"Yes." At once she got to her feet. "You'll have to excuse me now, Pamela. I have to unpack."

"Is....is it all right if I take the bed next to yours?"

"It doesn't make any difference to me." She looked away, but the other girl, accepting her reply as an affirmative, went happily to move her belongings. "Please put the trunk there, Carleton." Vicki pointed to the foot of her bed. "And you may leave the small cases on the bed."

He did as she'd asked, but then he hesitated. "May I do anything else for you, Miss Vicki?"

"No, thank you."

"Well, I'll say good-bye then. The...ah...best of luck to you, young miss." She made no further reply and the chauffeur finally turned to go. All during the drive south and east back to Kent, however, he was unable to put the little girl from his thoughts. He knew boarding schools were an accustomed way of life for upper class children, but he couldn't shake off the feeling that somehow he personally had deserted her.

* * *

Despite living in a house full of servants Vicki had often been left to fend for herself and she'd easily donned the required clothing. Finished dressing in plenty of time, she was sitting on her bed brushing her hair, preparatory to fastening it back with a gold barrette.

Poor Pamela was once again having considerably more difficulty. She had finally managed the blouse and jumper, but the latter "felt funny". Actually she had it on backwards. Moreover, the action of pulling it on over her head had caused one of her braids to come partially undone as well as knocking one bow of her glasses off her ear. She hadn't even attempted the skirt. Looking over at the next bed, she observed Vicki just snapping the barrette into place. <u>She</u> was all ready and everything even looked the way it was supposed to. My goodness, but she was clever! Timidly Pamela came over to her. "I....I don't think I've got these on right. Would you help me, please?"

"I suppose someone always dressed you at home?"

"My nanny or my Mummy helped me." Pamela was a very honest child.

"Maybe Sister Philippa will help you. <u>She</u> <u>likes</u> babies!" The other girl walked slowly away, her eyes filling with tears. "Oh, come here!" Vicki snapped. "I suppose I'll <u>have</u> to help you! Take the jumper off." With the sweater removed it could be seen that the front of the shirt was buttoned wrong while the cuffs hadn't been done at all. Unbuttoning the shirt, she deftly redid it and then fastened the cuffs. "Where's your skirt?" Happily Pamela brought it from her own bed. "The zipper goes on the left," Vicki explained matter-of-factly. "Tuck the blouse in. Now the pullover. See the label. That goes in the back."

"What about my hair?"

"Do you have a brush?" Vicki removed the rubber band from the other braid.

"I...I think so." Pamela returned to rummage around in the top drawer of her little bureau.'

"Your hair's too thin to wear this way," Vicki went on as she brushed out the other girl's tousled hair and rebraided it. "You would look much better with it short. Now can you at least put on your own shoes and socks?"

Pamela was more and more impressed. Her new friend could <u>even</u> do <u>braids</u>! "Oh, yes—thank you so much!"

"Just don't think you can be bothering me all the time."

"Is everyone ready for supper?" Sister Philippa had appeared in the doorway. Out in the hall a moment later she signaled for quiet. "Now, girls, line up please by two's and take the hand of your partner."

"Don't!" Vicki folded her arms so that Pamela couldn't take her hand.

"But Sister Philippa said...."

"I don't care what she said. I don't want you holding on to me."

Neither of them had noticed the postulant approaching. "What's the matter, girls?"

They were both silent. Pamela was afraid she was going to be scolded; Vicki simply refused to answer.

"Is there a problem here, Sister Philippa?" Geraldine was the mistress of the junior school. "The girls should be on their way to the evening meal."

"Nothing I can't handle, Sister."

At that point the girl behind Vicki and Pamela in the line spoke up. "Sister Geraldine," she said sweetly, "Vicki wouldn't take Pamela's hand even though Sister Philippa told us to." With her pale blonde ringlets and enormous blue eyes Emily-Ellen Bowen was the sort of child adults think can do no wrong. Vicki's eyes narrowed. So this one was a tattle-tale. She'd remember that.

"Which one is Vicki?" Sister Geraldine asked.

"I am," she stated defiantly.

"<u>Did</u> you refuse to hold Pamela's hand?"

"Yes." The Windsor chin was held high.

"You may go ahead with the other girls, Sister Philippa. This young lady and I are going to have a little talk." Vicki stared down at the floor as the other girls filed past on their way to supper. "Is this your room, Vicki?"

"Yes." She followed the nun.

"Which is your bed?" Wordlessly the child turned to the right and walked back to her corner. "Sit down, young lady." Vicki obeyed. "<u>Now</u>–why did you refuse to hold your little friend's hand?"

"She's <u>not</u> my friend! I wouldn't have a stupid ninny like that for a friend!"

"You will <u>not</u> call other girls names. And that was <u>not</u> what I asked you. I want you to tell me <u>why</u> you refused to take her hand."

"Because I didn't want to."

"That is not a proper reason!"

"It's <u>my</u> reason."

"Very well, Vicki. I don't like to punish you on your first night at Heathfield, but you have to learn from the very beginning that when you are told to do something, you are expected to obey. Now I will give you one more chance to explain your behavior." The little girl looked steadily at Sister Geraldine, but said nothing. "All right, then. There will be no supper for you tonight."

For some time after the nun had left Vicki continued to sit on her bed until finally she became aware that the room was growing cold. Like most buildings in England at this time the Heathfield dormitories did not have central heating. Instead each room had two coal burning fireplaces, one at either end. Shivering, she moved around to the foot of her bed nearer the fire and drawing her knees up under her chin, she hugged them to herself. "I hate it here," Vicki whispered aloud to the big, empty room. Her eyes filled with tears and her insides seemed like one big hurt until she couldn't tell where the hunger pangs stopped and the pain of her loneliness began. At last she crawled under the blankets and in a while she felt warmer, but the ache refused to go away and the tears wouldn't stop falling.

After supper there was an informal gathering in the parlor of each dormitory with cocoa and cookies and when Vicki's seven roommates finally came upstairs, they found her asleep. The coal fire had gone out by now and the room was bitterly cold. "We had biscuits and cocoa after supper!" A large-boned tomboy type, Margaret Fitzwalter had immediately established herself as the leader in the room.

"And you didn't!" The latter was Emily-Ellen's contribution.

Awakened by their voices, Vicki sat up in bed. "Get away from me, you little tattle-tale! You'll be sorry! Wait and see!"

"Emily-Ellen's not the one who'll be sorry," Maggie retorted. "Everyone in this room is her friend and nobody likes you."

"I like you, Vicki," Pamela spoke up loyally.

"Well, I don't like you! Leave me alone! Everybody just leave me alone!"

Sister Philippa had come into the room just at the end of this, but she pretended not to have heard. "All right, now. Lights out is in half an hour. Everybody get soap, towel, toothbrush and paste." Obediently the girls scattered and a few minutes later they were all gathered at the door. "You know where the bathroom is," Philippa directed. "The first door on the left around the corner." Vicki was at the rear of the group. The last one to pass Sister Philippa, she kept her gaze averted. "Wait a minute, please, Vicki."

"Yes, sister." She stopped, but she continued to look straight ahead.

"What's wrong, dear?"

"Nothing. Why can't people just leave me alone?"

"Is that what you really want?"

"Yes!" She turned on the nun then, her eyes blazing defiance.

"All right, Vicki. You may go along to the loo."

At nine-fifteen the girls were at last settled, bedside lamps turned off. Sister Philippa did a final bed check and switched off the overhead lights. For a few minutes there was silence. "Vicki?" Pamela whispered.

"Go to sleep!"

"But, Vicki...here." The other girl thrust a packet at her. Something had leaked through the wrapping and the paper was soggy.

"Ick! What's that?" Vicki pulled her hand back and the parcel dropped on the floor between them.

"But I brought you some dinner. 'Cause it was my fault you got punished."

"Well, I don't want it!"

"All....all right, then." With a sigh Pamela subsided into silence.

Vicki lay quietly for a while, but when she was sure all the other girls were asleep, she slid out of bed, groping around on the floor. At last she found the package and sitting down on the floor, she unwrapped it to discover sliced roast lamb and boiled potatoes, coated in congealed gravy. Hungrily she devoured every bite. Nothing had ever tasted quite so good.

* * *

Each dorm had a private faculty parlor and having checked the other rooms on her floor, Philippa was finally free to join the others. The drapes were drawn against the winter darkness outside and the coal fire, more than adequate in this small room, warmed and welcomed her. The sisters were all busy–reading or writing letters or preparing for classes which would begin the next day–and the atmosphere was one of total peace. Sister Louisa was at a small desk in the corner of the room. At the sound of the door opening she'd glanced up and smiled. "Come visit." She patted the low hassock next to her chair. "What's been keeping you?" she continued as her friend came to sit beside her. "A problem with one of the new girls?"

Philippa nodded. "Vicki Windsor."

"Homesick?"

"Just the opposite. And...and she has a distinct aversion to....to being touched. A while ago when I went up to take the girls to the loo, she was screaming at the others to 'leave her alone'. I...I tried to talk to her, but she told me the same thing. She...."

"I couldn't help overhearing," Sister Geraldine spoke up from a sofa across the room. "That one's going to be trouble! You mark my words!"

"She's just terribly unhappy." Sister Philippa moved to sit beside the older nun.

"When you've had more experience, you'll stop excusing these girls for everything. A bad child is simply a bad child."

"Oh, I don't think we can say that, Sister," Elizabeth interposed mildly from an easy chair next to the sofa. "I was on the desk when Vicki arrived. She was one of the few girls brought here by a chauffeur. He was still standing there after you took Vicki to get her uniforms, Philippa, and when I asked him if he wanted anything, he asked us to look after her–that she's a very lonely child."

"Yes, she is, isn't she?" Sister Philippa replied thoughtfully as she returned to sit next to Sister Louisa.

"Hmph!" Geraldine muttered. "Molly-coddlers–the lot of you!"

"Really," Philippa remarked in a low voice to her friend, "a bad child is just a bad child."

"Sister Geraldine means well enough. She's just from another era."

"Means well enough! And withholding meals for punishment! It's like something out of *Oliver Twist*. I have to reach that girl! I have to!"

"If anyone can, you can," Louisa reassured her.

"I hope so." Moving over to a near-by rocking chair, Sister Philippa opened her Bible and settled down for her regular nightly study, but privately she worried whether she was, in fact, already too late.

Chapter 3

Vicki's early years had in no way prepared her for life at Heathfield. While her nanny could be excessively strict, there had also been many hours during which she was left entirely to own devices. Now all at once even Saturday and Sunday were neatly divided into blocks of time, each with its prescribed activity. Inevitably a moment would come when she rebelled.

It was on a day much as Robert Browning must have had in mind when he wrote–"Oh, to be in England now that April's there..." The sun was warm, the air fresh and clear and the tips of the tree branches were just beginning to turn yellowish-green with the buds of next summer's leaves. She was in reading class, the last one of the morning. In the front of the room Sister Eleanor was explaining consonant sounds. She had a low-pitched monotonous voice and Vicki found it difficult to concentrate. From her seat near the window she watched a gray squirrel scampering along the branches of a gnarled old tree just outside the building. How she envied him his freedom! Her eyes traveled beyond to the sky. Against a backdrop of brilliant blue, high white clouds were scudding past and after a while she found herself imagining what it would be like to ride on one of them. Sister Maria had told them in science class that clouds were actually cold and wet and gray like fog and that only the sunlight made them appear white, but Vicki couldn't believe that. She was sure they were soft and fluffy–just the way they looked–and she would snuggle down in one of them and sail endlessly across the sky. Suddenly she became aware that the teacher had called her name. "Yes, Sister?" She got quickly to her feet.

"I asked you to read, Vicki."

"Where....where are we, Sister?"

"Never mind, young lady. You may be seated. Please see me at the end of class."

Sister Eleanor lectured her severely, reminding her that God didn't like children who daydreamed, but Vicki heard little of it. She'd already learned with her nanny that by humming or counting or reciting the alphabet to herself she could shut out the sound of someone else's voice almost entirely.

A short time later, with Pamela in tow as usual, she was leaving the dining hall after the noon meal when all at once she knew she couldn't bear one more regimented minute. She came to an abrupt standstill in the middle of the sidewalk. "Pamela, do you want to go to stupid old Sister Maria's stupid science class this afternoon or do you want to have some fun?"

"Not go to science class?" The other girl's myopic blue eyes widened. "But we'd get into dreadful trouble!"

"No we wouldn't, silly! Sister Maria's practically blind! She won't even notice we're not there."

"What are we going to do, Vicki?" Pamela whispered.

"What are you whispering for? No one's around to listen. Now are you coming or not?"

She hesitated, torn between her natural tendency to obey the rules and her worship of her wonderful new friend. "We...we really shouldn't."

"All right. You just be a baby and go to class. I'll have all the fun by myself. Then you'll be sorry." Vicki started to walk away toward one of the gates which led off the school grounds.

Pamela couldn't stand it and ran after her. "Where are you going?" she asked breathlessly.

"I'm not telling you unless you come with me." Actually she had no idea at all at this point where she was going. "You'll tattle on me like Emily-Ellen. Sometimes I think she's your best friend, even though you say I am."

"Oh no, Vicki! You know you're my best friend! All....all right. I'll come with you."

"Well, hurry up, then!" Her pace quickened. "The longer we take to get to the gate, the more chance we have of being caught."

"V..V..Vicki," Pamela called after her, still hanging back. " wh...what will happen if we do get caught?"

"I already told you. We won't get caught because no one will miss us. The only way we might be caught is if you keep dawdling."

"I...I'm sorry," she apologized tearfully. "I wish I could be brave like you."

Vicki turned on her in a fury. "Pamela! Either you come with me now or you go back. But if you do come, you have to promise me you won't be blubbering all afternoon like some little ninny!"

The other child swallowed hard. "I...I do want to come. I really do. I...I promise."

"All right, then." Vicki began to move toward the gate again, half-running now.

Pamela tried to hurry, too, but she stumbled turning her ankle. "Please...please slow down a little," she called out. "I...I twisted my ankle." Apparently Vicki hadn't heard her, however, and so she did the best she could–hobbling gamely along on her sore ankle and periodically begging in vain for her friend to wait for her.

Ironically neither of them even noticed what a lovely place Heathfield was in the spring, its redbrick buildings set against the rolling green lawns, dotted now with crocuses and daffodils. Vicki's only thought was of the gateway which lay just ahead of her across the lawns and the freedom which was now within her grasp. Pamela, on the other hand, glanced continually behind her, certain that at any moment she'd feel a hand on her shoulder and turn to see a forbidding figure in its dark blue habit and starched wimple looking down at her in shocked disapproval. At last Vicki was through the gate and safe for the moment from discovery, she stopped to catch her breath and decide exactly what she was going to do. "Pam..." But her reluctant companion was nowhere in sight. A moment or so later the other girl came limping through the gate, her face flushed and one braid as usual partly undone. "What happened to you?" Vicki demanded. "And look at you–you're a mess!"

"I twisted my ankle. I called and called, but you wouldn't stop."

Vicki still hadn't heard her. Instead she was staring intently at the other girl's braids. Of course, she thought, her green eyes beginning to sparkle–the perfect adventure! "I don't suppose you have any money?" Triumphantly Pamela produced her change purse from the pocket of her Heathfield blazer. "Good–come on, then." She started to move along the road toward the village of Tetbury.

"What are we going to use the money for?" Pamela was thankful that at least her friend was walking now.

"If you don't stop asking questions, I swear I'll make you go back."

"All..all right." She subsided into silence and for a while Vicki could almost forget she was even there. It felt so good to be free, not to have Sister Somebody-or-other telling her it was time to do this or time to do that. The wind was cold, but the midday sun was warm on her face and for a few minutes she was actually happy. "Vicki, please tell me where we're going?" Pamela said at last as they neared the center of the town. "Vicki," she insisted finally in what was for her a rare burst of courage. "I...I have a right to know. After all, it's...it's my money!"

Vicki was busy studying the signs on both sides of the street. She'd first noticed the place when they passed it on one of Sister Hester's "health hikes" which were a regular and generally detested part of the Heathfield physical education program. Then she saw it. "Over there," she finally replied pointing a little further down the street to a small shop, the windows of which were edged in yellow, ruffled curtains. "You're going to have your hair cut."

"What?!" Pamela shrieked in alarm. "I can't!" Frantically she clutched one thin braid in each hand as if she could somehow protect them from mutilation. "My Mama would be awfully mad."

"When are you going to stop doing what your mama says? I've told you your hair looks positively dreadful like that. Now are you my friend or not?"

"I keep telling you I am."

"Well, if you really are, you'll do what I want you to do." Tired of listening to her objections, Vicki simply seized her by the hand dragging her across the narrow village street and into the shop.

"Yes?" One of the beauticians, a girl named Lila, came over as they entered.

Vicki pushed Pamela forward. "She wants to get hair cut."

Lila looked doubtful. "Does your mother know about this?" she asked Pamela.

Of course it was Vicki who answered. "We go to Heathfield. Her mother wrote one of the sisters and told her." Pamela simply gaped.

"Come on then," the operator directed. "Up in the chair." The little girl reluctantly climbed up and sat down, taking a firm grasp on the arms of the chair. Teeth clenched, her face contorted, she appeared to be awaiting execution rather than a mere haircut. "How short do you want it, dear?" As she talked, Lila was undoing the braids and brushing out her young customer's hair.

"Very short and sort of feathery around the face," Vicki directed briskly.

"Who's getting her hair cut, you or your friend?" the woman observed jokingly to Pamela. "She's doing all the talking."

"That's all right. She knows what to say, you see, and I...I don't." At the first snip of the scissors she gasped as if in pain.

"It only hurts for a while, honey." The beautician patted her reassuringly on the shoulder. Quickly she cut the hair off at the nape of the neck and then working with a razor, she layered and shaped it, brushing little wisps forward to frame the face. Thin as it was, Pamela's hair did have some natural curl and Lila was skillful with the razor. When she had finished, she gave the child a hand mirror. "There. Tell me what you think. Pretty good if I do say so myself."

Pamela held the mirror up in front of her face, but her eyes remained tightly shut. "Silly, look," Vicki said. "I knew I was right."

Slowly the other girl opened her eyes. She could hardly believe what she saw. Framed by the soft, wispy curls, her thin face had an almost pixie-like quality. Even her glasses appeared less noticeable. "Oh, my goodness! I....I'm almost pretty, aren't I, Vicki? Oh, not beautiful like you," she hastened to add, "but at least a little pretty."

"Much better, yes. Let's go. You have to pay her, remember. The sign says 'ten bob'."

"How....how much is a bob?"

"A shilling." Vicki sighed in exasperation. "Open your purse. There–see that paper one. Like a pound note, only smaller, and it says '10'. Give her that and a few pence extra. That's for the tip," she explained matter-of-factly. "Now come along."

Pamela followed her from the beauty shop, almost dancing in her excitement. "I like it, Vicki! I really like it!"

"I knew you would. Now–time for tea."

"Tea?!" At this latest thunderbolt Pamela instantly forgot her elation over her new hair-do. "Don't....don't you think we should go back now?"

"Honestly you <u>are</u> a bother! It's just a short way down that next side street," she explained as she led the way further along the main street and around the corner. "I noticed it the same day I saw the beauty shop. They had the most scrumptious tarts in the window. This is it," she said at last, glancing up at the sign. "Nina and Ida's," it read. "Tea and Homemade Pastries.". Vicki walked in with an air of easy confidence which gave the impression she went out to tea every day. Reluctantly the other girl followed her, looking so guilty you would have thought she was planning to rob the place. A small bell over the door tinkled to announce their entrance and Pamela jumped.

It was a tiny shop with room for only five tables along one wall, the other wall being taken up with glass enclosed shelves upon which were displayed an amazing assortment of tempting pastries. At this hour, with the noon rush over and tea time still nearly two hours away, an elderly couple were the only other customers. Nina and Ida, the proprietors, were unmarried sisters in their early fifties. Just then they were both busy in the kitchen. At the sound of the bell Ida snatched up an order pad from the counter and started to push open the swinging door into the dining room. Seeing the two girls in their dark blue skirts and school blazers, however, she stopped, withdrawing inside the kitchen once more. "Ring up Heathfield," she sighed.

"Not again!" her sister exclaimed throwing down the pastry cutter she'd been using to cut out the dough for a fresh batch of scones. "You'd think they could keep a closer eye on their students!"

"I suppose it's difficult with over six hundred of them."

Nina came to join her sister opening the door a crack to peer out herself. "I swear to God," she muttered, "they get younger every time."

"Ring up the school," Ida said again. "Meanwhile, I'll take their order. That way we can keep them here until someone comes to fetch them." Approaching the table, she forced her narrow lips into a smile. "I didn't realize Heathfield was on holiday, girls."

Vicki remained unruffled. "St. Swithin's Day," she lied blithely.

"Oh, I see." Well, we'll soon find out about that, Ida thought to herself. "May I take your order?"

"Tea with milk and a treacle tart, if you please.".

"I'll have the same," Pamela echoed weakly.

Nina, meanwhile, had gotten Heathfield on the line and been transferred to the junior school office. "Sister Geraldine speaking," a voice answered.

"Nina Wilkins, Sister. We have two of your girls here again. Quite young ones this time."

"Thank you, Miss Wilkins." Geraldine removed her wire-rimmed glasses and wearily rubbed her eyes. "One of our sisters has reported two girls missing from her class. That must be where they went. I'll send someone at once. I might have known," she added to herself and replacing the receiver, she pressed the button on the intercom which connected her with the outer office. "Please get me Sister Philippa," she directed briskly.

A few minutes later Philippa knocked and entered. "You wanted to see me, Sister?"

"Sister Maria sent a girl to report that Vicki Windsor and Pamela Ashworth were not in her class. Nina Wilkins just rang up. It seems they're in her tea room. Please go and collect them."

"Yes, Sister." Philippa knew without a doubt who the instigator of this little escapade was and a few minutes later as she walked toward the village, she couldn't help but worry whether the real trouble was still ahead.

It was Vicki's first taste of freedom in three months and this plus the dark, strong tea and treacle tart made for an intoxicating combination. She was enjoying herself immensely. Pamela, on the other hand, had barely touched her food. "What's the matter?" Vicki asked at one point through a mouthful of tart. "Aren't you hungry?"

"I guess not." The other girl pushed her plate away.

"May I have your tart then?"

"Sure, take it."

"I suppose you're still afraid we'll get caught, you silly goose! Don't you want your tea either?" Vicki managed to say all in one breath even as she reached for the pot.

It was just then that Sister Philippa entered the tea room. Pamela happened to be facing the door and glancing up at the sound of the bell, she gasped in horror, her worst fears realized. Vicki was already devouring the other tart, at the same time adding milk and sugar to her tea, and paid no attention. Philippa brought an extra chair over to the little table. "Having a good time, girls?" Then she noticed Pamela's appearance. "My goodness, you've had your hair cut, haven't you?" All the child could do was open and close her mouth. Then she started to cry.

"Don't be a ninny!" Vicki snapped. "This was all my idea: the haircut and the tea. She didn't even want to come."

""It's very commendable of you to take the blame, Vicki," Sister Philippa said, "but unfortunately you're both equally guilty of breaking the rules and you will both be punished accordingly."

"Well, that's just about as stupid as I would expect stupid old Heathfield to be?" she retorted scornfully.

"Vicki!" Pamela had suddenly found her voice. She didn't know whether to fear for her friend or to admire her for daring to sass a nun even if she was only a postulant.

Philippa, however, ignored the outburst. "Now, girls," she said quietly, getting to her feet, "if you're quite finished, Sister Geraldine is waiting for us in her office."

With admirable aplomb Vicki ate the last of the second tart and took one final swallow of her tea. Only then did she, too, stand up. "Come along, Pamela. As Sister says, we should be going." If Philippa hadn't been upset, she would have found the whole scene amusing.

The walk back to the school passed in silence, each of the three absorbed in her own thoughts. Pamela was so paralyzed with dread it was all she could do to put one foot in front of the other. Sister Philippa glanced back often at Vicki who was strolling along behind her and Pamela, apparently unconcerned. But what about Vicki herself? What was going through her mind----Of course, why didn't I think of this before! When you get in trouble, they telephone your parents. Now Mama and Papa will have to notice me!

The door to Sister Geraldine's office was open when they arrived. "Come in, young ladies. No, I won't be needing you, Sister," she added as Philippa started to follow them inside. "You may return to your regular duties."

No condemned prisoner hearing the institution gates clang shut behind him ever felt greater terror than poor Pamela at this moment. Vicki, on the other hand, sat down calmly in one of the chairs across from the desk and folding her hands in her lap, she stared resolutely back at the mistress of the junior school. Geraldine was not about to lose a war of nerves to an eight year old. Summoning her steeliest tone of voice, she began. "Pamela, what <u>happened</u> to your hair?"

"I...I had it cut," she stammered.

Briefly Sister Geraldine glanced upward as if imploring divine assistance. "Now girls, I'm sure you both realize you have committed a serious breach of our rules here at Heathfield."

"They're not 'our' rules," Vicki observed under her breath.

"What was that, young lady?" Actually Geraldine had heard the words. She just wanted to see whether the child would have the temerity to repeat them.

"Nothing." She spoke very distinctly now, looking at the nun as if to say–"You know perfectly well. Now what are you going to do about it?"

"Yes...ah...so then...". The nun cleared her throat as authoritatively as possible. "You will both forfeit your free time for the next three Sunday afternoons. Instead you will report to me here for additional religious studies. Is that clear, Pamela?"

"Yes, Sister Geraldine. Thank you, Sister Geraldine."

"Vicki?"

"Aren't you going to ring up our parents?"

"Is that what you want me to do?"

"No—I just wondered."

"That will be all for now, then. You may both report to class."

Outside in the hall Vicki turned on the other girl in a rage. "Just for that, I won't take you with me the next time!"

"Wh...what did I do now?" Her friend's anger hurt far worse than the sister's punishment.

"Thanking her for punishing us! You...you....you...."

Just then, however, Sister Philippa came out of the student records room across the hall. "Go along please, Pamela. I wish to speak to Vicki alone."

Pamela walked slowly away, her lower lip quivering. "I went with her and everything," she whispered to herself, "and she still doesn't like me."

"We've already been given our punishment," Vicki stated in an expressionless tone.

"I'm sure you have, but I wanted to know why you did it. Especially taking Pamela along and getting her into trouble as well?"

"I just felt like it, that's all, and no one made her come with me."

"But she adores you. She'd follow you anywhere."

Vicki's only reply was to say once again, "No one made her come with me."

"I want so much to be your friend, dear. Why won't you let me?"

"I don't need any friends. May I go now?"

"Yes–of course," Sister Philippa sighed. And so once again she had failed.

Leaving the dormitory, Vicki strode angrily away across the campus. All at once without warning Margaret Fitzwalter was standing in front of her on the sidewalk. In her unseeing fury she hadn't noticed her step from behind a tree and block her path. "So you got caught, didn't you?" Maggie jeered. "That will teach you!"

"Wh...what?" Momentarily she was thrown for a loss.

"I said you got caught! Serves you right! Nyah! Nyah! Serves you right! Nyah! Nyah!" Maggie capered around and around her, thumbs in her ears, fingers waggling in glee.

Suddenly Vicki understood. "You!" She pointed an accusing finger at the other girl. "You and Emily-Ellen are in that class, too. You...you tattled on us! Sister Maria would never have realized we weren't there if someone didn't tell her!"

"Nyah! Nyah!" Maggie continued her mocking dance. ""Nyah! Nyah!" Vicki made a grab for her tormentor, but the other girl escaped and still laughing, she ran away across the lawn.

"Never mind," she shrieked after the fleeing culprit. "I'll get even. You just wait and see!"

Long before the others were even finished in the bathroom that night, Vicki was curled up in bed pretending to be asleep. Peeking out from under the covers, she watched the little lamps go out as one by one the girls settled down. Only Margaret and Emily-Ellen were still up–standing over in one corner together whispering and giggling. Probably laughing at me, she thought bitterly. Sister Philippa appeared in the doorway. "Lights out, girls."

"Yes, Sister," they chorused sweetly and went obediently to their beds to turn out their lights. There was a brief silence and then an ear-splitting scream, followed seconds later by another. Sister Philippa was back in the room at once, flicking on the overhead lights. "What's the matter?"

"Our beds are all wet!" Emily-Ellen exclaimed. Coming over to inspect the damage, Philippa found that someone had indeed soaked the lower sheet of each bed, carefully replacing the blanket and spread to hide the evidence.

"I know!" Maggie cried out all at once. "Vicki did it!"

"Now, Margaret, can't you see Vicki is sound asleep? If she were going to play a prank on you both, wouldn't she want to be awake to see what happened?"

"She's faking! I know it was Vicki! I know it!" Maggie was shaking in childish rage.

"You must calm down, dear. You'll make yourself ill. Now if you'll come along with me to the linen closet, we'll get you both some dry sheets and pads. I don't think the water will have soaked through to the mattress. And I want the rest of you to get to sleep. We'll try not to make too much noise." Sister Philippa led the way from the room, switching off the lights again as she left. Both girls were still vehemently protesting that it was Vicki who had poured water on their beds.

"Vicki," Pamela whispered after a moment, "was it you?"

"You heard Sister Philippa. I'm asleep."

"It was you, wasn't it? My goodness, but you're clever!"

"Don't you dare tattle! Do you hear me?"

"I'd never tattle on you, Vicki. But you really are my friend though, aren't you?-- 'cause you tell me things."

"I won't be your friend anymore, Pamela, if you don't shut up!"

"Yes, Vicki."

All was quiet by the time Sister Philippa returned with Emily-Ellen and Margaret. Sister Louisa had come along to help and using just the small lamp on one of the bureaus for light, they quickly remade the two beds.

"Do you think it was Vicki?" Sister Louisa asked a short time later as they walked downstairs together to the sisters' lounge.

"Oh yes, probably," Philippa sighed. "I think they were the ones who told on Vicki and Pamela for skipping class. Actually, though, I'm almost relieved. Such pranks are quite normal behavior for an eight year old child."

For the few weeks remaining until spring holiday the war of harmless practical jokes continued and Sister Philippa watched with increasing hope as Vicki even made tentative overtures to the other student, bragging a little, perhaps, that she had two homes to go to on holiday. Ironically this was a special time for Vicki as well–sadly the best she was to know at Heathfield–and for much the same reason. For that short while she felt like all the other girls.

Then about a week before the holiday was to begin, her regular allowance check arrived from her father's solicitor. She was a little surprised because she'd half expected her father would wait and give it to her when he saw her. Opening the envelope, she discovered the amount was considerably more than usual and something else was out of the ordinary. Her father had enclosed a brief personal note.

Dear Vicki,

As it turns out, I will be on the continent on business at the time of your spring holiday so I'm afraid we will have to cancel our visit. I'm sending a little extra with this check and hope it will help to ease your disappointment. Buy yourself something special from your Papa. I'm sorry we can't see each other, but I know you'll have a good time with your mother and your new baby sister.

Love and kisses,

Papa

Vicki didn't know which hurt the most: that her father could dismiss her so casually or that he thought he could make it up to her with money. And why hadn't her mother told her about the baby? After all, it <u>was</u> <u>her</u> sister! Well, that didn't matter really. In just a little while now she'd be seeing her. She wrote her mother about the change in plans–that she'd be coming directly to Surrey and that she would be taking the train into London, arriving at Paddington Station at 16:30 hours. It seemed important somehow to explain it all clearly so there could be no possible misunderstanding.

The post was distributed each day at the noon meal and Vicki had soon learned to dread the moment. So many girls seemed to get at least one letter every day while she rarely received anything except her monthly allowance check. As a result she usually paid little attention as the nun at the head of the table called out the names. The day before holiday was to begin she didn't even hear Sister Philippa the first time. Ever since her father's note she had, in fact, prayed there would be no letter. Most certainly it would carry news she didn't care to receive.

"Vicki," Sister Philippa repeated, "I said you have a letter–from your mother, I believe."

Heart pounding, she stood up and walked to the head of the table. "Thank you, Sister. She slipped the letter into her skirt pocket before returning to her seat.

"Aren't you going to open it?" Margaret asked loudly enough for the whole table to hear.

"I'd rather wait until later." Vicki looked steadily down at her plate.

"Maybe your mother doesn't want you to come."

"Of course she does." Her head came up then as she hotly denied the accusation. For this was, of course, exactly what she feared. Why, after all, had she thought either of her parents <u>would</u> want her when they never had before. The meal seemed endless. When it was finally over, Vicki ran back to the dormitory to one of the few places at Heathfield allowing for any privacy–a stall in the lavatory. She locked the door and lowering the lid on the toilet, she sat down. Only then did she remove the envelope from her pocket and with trembling hands she opened it. Tears rushed into her eyes.

Dear Vicki,

How like your <u>dear</u> father to thrust all the responsibility for your spring holiday on me. However, I'm afraid it's impossible for us to have you as well. With a new baby in the house I simply cannot risk the germs you may have picked up at school. You are a sensible child and I'm sure you will realize this is the wisest course. Perhaps we can see each other over the summer.

Love,

Mama

Slowly Vicki lowered the letter to her lap. "She didn't even tell me the baby's name," she whispered. "She could have at least told me my sister's name." For sometime after that she continued to sit there, too numb with hurt to move. The tears in her eyes brimmed over, dropping one by one onto the letter which she still held in her lap. Large wet spots appeared on her mother's ivory parchment stationery. "Well, if she doesn't want me, she doesn't. That's all. I'll just stay here at school." Sniffing, Vicki wiped her eyes with the back of one hand. "But....but everybody else will be going home..." Fresh tears filled her eyes and drawing her legs up, she clutched them to her chest, burying her face in her knees and cried–huge, choking sobs so that after a while the back of her head began to throb.

All at once she heard someone else come into the bathroom and her sobs instantly ceased. Even then the rigid self-control was taking shape. The footsteps had stopped, too, however. There was a momentary pause. "Vicki?" It was Pamela. "Are you sick?"

"No, I am <u>not</u> sick! Go away!"

"You're always telling me that. I thought we were friends."

"No, you are <u>not</u> my friend. What you <u>are</u> is a silly goose! Now <u>go away</u> and <u>leave me alone</u>!"

"All...all right." With a sigh the other girl turned to leave.

Vicki wasn't sure how long she stayed there after that. Girls came in and out constantly, but she kept her feet pulled up and everyone assumed the stall was out of order. After a while it grew quiet and she knew afternoon classes must be about to begin. She listened carefully for another moment or so before tearing up her mother's letter and flushing it down the toilet. Coming out of the stall, she caught a glimpse of herself in the mirror over the washbasin. Her face was red and blotchy from crying and she splashed it with cold water before finally leaving the lavatory to go back to her room and get ready for class.

Stopping a minute to select the books she needed for the afternoon, she happened to glance over at Pamela's bureau which stood between their beds and there on the top was the framed photograph of her family: parents, two brothers and a sister. Vicki had often informed her with withering scorn that only babies had pictures like that. Now for some reason the picture infuriated her and throwing her books down on her bed, she yanked the photograph from its frame and tore it up. "Stupid picture!" she sobbed. "Stupid, <u>stupid</u> Pamela!" Grabbing up her books again, she ran from the room and along the hall, still crying. Sister Philippa just managed to get out of her way, but Vicki was too upset to notice.

Later that afternoon Philippa was in the living room of the dormitory, preparing to serve the students' tea, when Pamela came running up to her clutching the pieces of the picture in one hand. "Look what someone did to my picture! Who did it, Sister? Who?"

"I don't know, honey. I'm so very sorry." Philippa put her arm around the little girl's shoulders. "Come over here and sit down with me, will you?" Pamela allowed herself to be led over to a corner window seat where they settled themselves side by side. "Now, dear, please try to stop crying. After all you're going home tomorrow and you can get another photograph." It was true. Her parents would give her a new picture and her tears rapidly subsided. "Feeling better, then?" Sister Philippa inquired gently. She nodded. "Good. Now go along and have your tea." Philippa, however, remained there for some time–deep in thought. She had her suspicions, but she had to talk to Vicki.

* * *

The hours since she'd destroyed Pamela's picture were an aching, miserable blur in Vicki's mind. Now in evening study she sat hunched over a book open on her desk, her hands hiding her face. How could she bring herself to tell someone she would be staying at school for the holiday; how could she admit she had nowhere to go.

"Vicki—?" Sister Louisa touched her on the shoulder as she spoke.

She jumped. "Wh...what?" She brushed her hand across her eyes–carefully keeping her face averted.

"Sister Philippa is waiting in your room. She'd like to talk to you." Of course, Vicki thought bitterly, stupid baby Pamela's stupid picture! That's all anyone cares about!

"Now please, Vicki."

"Yes, Sister." Vicki closed her book and stood up. "I hate Sister Philippa!" she said over and over again as she walked upstairs and along the hall to her room, her hands clenched into tight little fists at her sides. "I hate her! I hate her!"

There simply has to be a way to reach her, Sister Philippa had thought as she sat on Vicki's bed waiting, but now as the little girl entered the room and she saw the expression on her face, she worried yet again that despite all her good intentions the child might already be beyond help. "Please, dear," she said with a smile and a quick pat on the bed beside her, "come and talk to me."

Obediently Vicki came over and sat down–not on her own bed beside the nun, however, but across from her on Pamela's bed–and she did not return the smile. Instead she simply sat there with her hands folded in her lap and looked steadily at Sister Philippa, waiting for her to begin. She won't let herself get too close to me, Philippa thought sadly, as she briefly studied her before speaking. "Vicki," she said finally, "do you know anything about what happened to Pamela's family picture?"

"You think I tore up that picture, don't you? Why do you think it was me? It could have been that horrid Maggie Fitzwalter!"

"I didn't say the picture had been torn up, you know," Sister Philippa observed quietly. "It could have been misplaced."

"So what if I tore it up! It was a stupid picture!"

Philippa reached across to lay one hand over Vicki's. "You can tell me. Did you tear up the picture because Pamela's going home on holiday and you're not?"

Pulling her hands away, Vicki glared at her accusingly. "How dare you! How dare you read my letter!"

"Oh, my dear—no! I would never do that. I simply guessed."

"I'm not your dear and I...I could go someplace if I wanted to. I just...I just decided to stay here." The performance might have been more believable, however, if her voice hadn't been shaking.

"Well, we sisters and the students who choose to stay here do have a lot of fun when everyone else is gone."

"Yes, that's...that's what I thought." Vicki felt her throat constrict. The tears were starting again and she couldn't let anyone see her cry. She looked down at her lap.

"Vicki, I want you to apologize to Pamela."

"You can't make me!"

"I don't suppose I can really, but I think deep down inside you like her and that you're sorry you tore up her picture and you want to tell her so. Now I'm going to leave you alone to think about it. Remember, dear, anytime you need to talk, you can come to me." With that Philippa stood up to go. She paused at the door waiting for the child to speak, but one glance at that stiff unrelenting little back told her it was hopeless.

Desperately Vicki fought to keep the tears back. Only when Sister Philippa's footsteps had receded down the corridor did she allow herself to cry and when she finally returned to study hall, she was once again dry-eyed. No one must discover her secret. But she was not to be so fortunate. Later as she was taking her pajamas out of her bureau drawer, Margaret came up behind her. "What was in your letter, Vicki?"

"None of your business!"

"You aren't going home on holiday, are you? Nobody wants you."

Vicki whirled on her. "That's not true. I am so going. Only I...I have to..to wait until Saturday for my mother to come and fetch me."

"Liar! Liar!" Maggie shrieked with glee. "Nobody wants Vicki! Nobody wants Vicki! Nobody wants Vicki!"

"Shut up! Shut up!" she screamed back, covering her ears with her hands.

Pamela had always been afraid of Margaret, but now all at once her loyalty to Vicki overcame that fear. "You're mean and horrid, Margaret Fitzwalter!"

"What's this?" Sister Philippa asked as she came into the room. She'd heard the two girls shouting at each other as she came down the hall, but she was surprised to find Pamela involved in the argument.

"N...nothing, Sister." Pamela was amazed at her own sudden courage.

"Why did she say that to you, Maggie?" Philippa felt the issue should be pursued.

"Oh, I don't know," Margaret replied with an exaggerated shrug. "Pamela's always saying silly things."

"No, I don't think she is. Do any of the rest of you know?" Philippa asked the others in the room. None of them dared defy Margaret and there was only silence. "Very well, girls. Now I realize you're excited about your holiday, but I want lights out on schedule and no talking. Understand?"

There was a chorus of "Yes, Sister...Yes, Sister."

"All right. I'll be back to check, remember. Now run along to the loo...all except Vicki, Pamela and Maggie, " she added as they all gathered up their things and started toward the door. Philippa waited for a moment, saying nothing further until everyone else had left. "Now I think we have a little more talking to do." Walking over to Pamela's bed, she sat down. "Come here, please." Pamela obeyed first, of course, sitting down beside the nun; Vicki followed to sit on her own bed and finally Margaret came to stand between the two beds at the foot. "Now," Sister Philippa continued, "is anyone going to tell me what happened?" She waited in vain. Pamela would say nothing and Vicki and Maggie simply glowered, each daring the other to speak. "All right. I can't make you talk to me, but I will accompany you to the bathroom so that I can be sure there are no more harsh words tonight."

Philippa did exactly that, waiting until all three had washed up and then walking them back to their room. When all the girls were in bed with their individual lamps out, she gave her final admonition about quiet and switched off the overhead lights. Alone outside she leaned back against the door and bowed her head, unshed tears stinging behind her eyelids. She felt utterly defeated. Why did the girls refuse to trust her?

* * *

Lights had been out about a half hour. Vicki was certain she must be the only one awake and in the blessed solitude afforded by the darkness she buried her head in the pillow and let the tears flow unchecked. But it takes more than a pillow to hide the sound of unhappiness from a friend. "Are you crying?" Pamela whispered. Desperately Vicki gritted her teeth together. Maybe if she were quiet for a while, the other girl might still think she was asleep. But neither can silence fool a friend. "Please don't cry, Vicki. You can come home with me."

New waves of humiliation swept over her. The last thing she wanted was to have anyone feel sorry for her, especially Pamela! "Will you shut up!" she hissed under her breath, fighting back the tears.

"But I really would like you to come home with me, honest. We'd have ever so much fun. Daddy would take us places and...." She got no further.

"Pamela! All you've done ever since we got here is hang around me. I'm sick to death of you so why would I want to go home with you?"

"Vicki!" Pamela was starting to cry herself now.

"And stop crying, you stupid baby! I'm glad I tore up your picture. So there!"

"Oh, Vicki," she gasped, horrified, "why did you do that?"

"Because I hate you! That's why!"

"You...you don't mean that! Please say you don't mean that!" Vicki turned on her side facing the wall and pulled her pillow up over her head to shut out the other girl's whispered pleas. "Never mind then," Pamela said finally. "I love <u>you</u> even if you don't love me back." After that neither of them spoke again although they both cried softly far into the night.

* * *

Classes ended at noon the next day and after dinner the dormitories were a flurry of activity as the girls hurried to finish packing in time for either the bus to the train station or the arrival of parents sometime during the afternoon. Vicki was nowhere to be seen. Pamela was still terribly upset about the previous night as well as her friend's apparent disappearance and Sister Philippa had some difficulty convincing her that under the circumstances the kindest thing she could do would be to leave without saying good-bye.

Vicki hadn't been far from Philippa's thoughts either that morning. But she had to be sure all her girls were safely on the way home and only when the last family car had disappeared through the main gate was she free to begin her search. She checked the child's room first and then the lavatory, but there was no sign of her and returning to the ground floor of the dormitory, she worked her way slowly and systematically upward, looking into every room and lav and calling Vicki's name repeatedly. Only as a last resort would she notify Sister Geraldine.

And just where was Vicki?

The day had been pure torment for her. Talk of home and family swirled all around her and only by keeping to herself at the back of the classrooms, eyes trained steadily downward, had she managed to hold back the tears. Scornfully she told herself over and over again that only babies went running home to their mamas, but by the time the last class let out, she knew she had to get away or everyone would see her cry.

The first one out into the hall, she hid under a stairwell for while before going back into the room to watch out a window until everyone had disappeared in the direction of the dining hall. Only when the campus appeared deserted did she finally leave herself, heading not for the dining hall, but back toward her dormitory. Keeping behind the buildings away from the sidewalks and lawns where someone might see her, it took a little longer, but at last sanctuary was in sight. She dashed up the steps and into the front hall.

Even here, though, there were wall-to-wall suitcases packed and ready, reminding Vicki all over again of all the girls who in just a little while now would be going home. She ran upstairs, but as she reached her floor, she heard footsteps below her somewhere on the stairs. She darted up a third flight and then a fourth, but the footsteps still followed her. Whoever it was had passed the floor below now and was coming up the last flight toward her.

She looked about frantically for an avenue of escape and after a moment a closed door caught her eye. Even a closet would afford a temporary hiding place. Vicki tried the knob. To her relief it turned and the door opened revealing a narrow, enclosed staircase. Just in time she was inside closing the door behind her and climbing the stairs, she opened another at the top to find herself in a tiny garret. It was dusty and except for a few wooden crates and broken chairs and tables, it was empty. Up under the roof the plastered walls slanted steeply and the one small, dormer-style window was so dirty she could barely see the beautiful April day outside.

At last she was alone and sinking to the littered floor, she folded her arms on the caned seat of an old chair, burying her head in them. Only then did she let the tears come. "Nobody wants Vicki—Nobody wants Vicki!" Over and over again she whispered aloud the same hateful words with which Maggie had taunted her the night before. She said them louder and louder sobbing until she choked, gagging on her own phlegm.

Exhausted, she must have dozed off for a while because all at once she caught the sound of excited voices below her. She crawled over to the window, rubbing one of the panes clean so that she could see outside. The busses must be about to leave for the station, she thought, and observing all the laughing, chattering girls as they trooped together across the lawn, Vicki tried to imagine what would be waiting for each of them at the other end of the journey. But since she possessed no personal memories upon which to base such imaginings, she soon gave up.

She was still sitting there when Pamela's parents arrived. Hungrily Vicki watched the other little girl fly down the steps into her mother's arms and then a moment later she saw Mr. Ashworth come around from his side of the car to pick his daughter up, swinging her high above the ground. She couldn't hear anything, but she could tell they were laughing together. Sister Philippa was there as well talking to Pamela's mother, it appeared. The whole scene seemed tiny and far away, reminding her of the time she'd looked through the wrong end of the groundskeeper's field glasses. It was as though her lonely, unloved existence was this uncared-for little garret and all she was ever to be allowed was a tantalizing glimpse of happiness through the one clean spot in a streaked and dirty window.

Vicki ached with a fierce and terrible longing and more than anything she wanted to call out, "Pamela, wait for me! Please wait for me! I do want to come with you!" She even raised her hand to turn the brass handle and push open the little window, but then her fearsome pride took over once more and the window remained closed. Instead she sat there motionless, staring unblinkingly down at the Ashworth family. She watched as first Pamela, then her mother and finally her father disappeared inside the car and shortly after that it began to move along the drive toward the front gate. Her friend was on the way home. Craning her neck, Vicki continued to gaze after the car until the last possible second and she found herself remembering another window and another driveway. Only that time, hopes high, she had waited eagerly for a car to appear. "Why doesn't anyone ever want me?" She whispered as new tears gathered, dripping down her cheeks and leaving little wet spots on the dusty window sill.

She wasn't sure how much time had gone by when she heard a voice calling her name from somewhere below. No one must be allowed to discover her hiding place. She got immediately to her feet only to find that the left one, which had been bent under her for so long, had gone to sleep. She shook it, stamping on the floor to get rid of the "pins and needles" as she'd once heard this condition described. Then she heard the voice again, sounding now as though it were coming from the bottom of the attic stairs. It was Sister Philippa! "Yes, Sister. I'm coming." Hurrying down the stairs, Vicki opened the door and stepped out into the hall. Her eyes were dry and her head held high.

"Oh, my dear! I've been so worried!" Philippa resisted the urge to take the little girl in her arms.

"Well, I just couldn't stand all that silliness," she stated flatly. "I thought I'd get out of the way for a while."

"You can bring your things over to the main house, dear. We're all going to have a jolly time. You just wait and see," the nun enthused--perhaps a bit too cheerily.

Vicki looked her full in the face for a moment as if to say, "You don't fool me and I know I don't fool you so let's forget the act, shall we?" Aloud she simply replied, "Thank you, Sister. It will only take me a few minutes." Philippa watched as with a touching dignity the child walked away from her along the hallway, disappearing down the stairs toward her own floor.

Chapter 4

All during the holiday Sister Philippa looked on helplessly as Vicki withdrew further inside herself. Even the other girls, arriving back at school for the start of a new term, sensed a change in her. Pamela was at first overjoyed. Vicki no longer called her names or told her to "leave me alone", but after a while she almost wished she would. It was like her friend was dead inside.

As the first summer holiday drew near, Vicki approached the dinner hour and the distribution of each day's post with renewed dread. Heathfield would be closed completely. Where would she go if no one wanted her this time? Her father's letter arrived about three weeks before the term was due to end in mid-July. It was only a brief note, but happy relief flooded over her as she read it.

Dear Vicki,

This is just to let you know I'll be picking you up myself on the last day of term. I have a luncheon meeting in London so I don't think I can get away before two. That should put me in Tetbury by six o'clock at the latest.

Love and kisses,

Papa

At least once a day Vicki reread that letter. Her Papa was actually coming to collect her! Maybe finally things were going to be different!

On the day the term ended Sister Philippa came down the front steps of the dormitory late in the afternoon to discover Vicki sitting at the bottom. All her belongings were collected around her on the ground and she was peering eagerly toward the main gate. Perhaps now might be the time to talk to her. In the happy anticipation of her holiday the child might let her guard down a little. "When do you expect your father, Vicki?" Sister Philippa smiled as she came to sit beside her.

"Six o'clock, Sister." Philippa couldn't resist a glance at her wrist watch. "Yes, I know it's early," Vicki said defensively. "It's...it's too nice to stay indoors."

"It's all right to be excited about seeing your father, dear. After all, it's been a while, hasn't it?" Immediately Sister Philippa realized her mistake. The little girl's green eyes blazed briefly with anger at this inference that her father had neglected her. Then her expression closed in on itself again and the nun inwardly cursed the thoughtless stupidity which had caused her to squander the moment.

"Is there anything else, Sister?"

"No...ah...Vicki."

"Well, good-bye then." Her eyes dropped to a book she held in her lap–a definite indication that she considered their conversation concluded.

"I'd like to make your father's acquaintance, dear. Do you mind if I wait with you?"

Vicki merely shrugged and continued her reading, but in truth she'd hoped Sister Philippa would be there when her father arrived. She had pictured the two of them chatting together as Philippa had done with Pamela's parents. She would see she was wrong, that...that everyone was wrong and that somebody did want her, after all. Now she awaited her father's coming even more anxiously, anticipating the moment when he would prove, once and for all, that she was indeed loved. When her father did actually arrive, however, Vicki didn't realize it was he until the car had stopped directly in front of her. It wasn't the chauffeur driven Bentley she'd been expecting, but a small, white convertible with her father himself behind the wheel. But that's even better, she thought happily. He's driven all the way here himself!

Sir Malcolm had passed the drive from London in a state of some consternation. He'd never felt comfortable with his daughter anyway and he was, in addition, suffering from a guilty conscience, partly because he hadn't seen Vicki since early the previous December when he made the decision to send her to Heathfield and partly because of the news he now had for her concerning her summer holiday. His discomfort increased as he observed the eagerness with which she jumped up and ran to meet him as he stepped out of the car.

"Papa!" With a smile which was already becoming rare for her Vicki reached up to hug her father, but his only response was a self-conscious peck on her cheek. For just an instant she could see Pamela's father enclosing his daughter in a bear hug and swinging her round and round, but she pushed the image from her mind.

Sir Malcolm had turned at once to Sister Philippa. "I can take the small valises and you may send the rest here," he directed briskly. Removing a memo pad from the breast pocket of his jacket, he jotted down an address.

"Yes, sir." Philippa accepted the slip of paper. Without saying another word Malcolm quickly stowed his daughter's cases in the boot, holding open the passenger door for her before going around to the other side to get in himself. Sister Philippa continued to look after them as the car moved toward the gate. To her joy Vicki even looked back to wave. It was only when they'd disappeared from view that she finally thought to glance down at the paper in her hand. "Oh no!" she gasped. "That poor child!"

Vicki, meanwhile, had settled herself happily in the passenger seat of the little car, her hair blowing behind her in the wind. At last she was actually on her way to her summer holiday with her Papa. She was somewhat disappointed that the friendly chat she'd envisioned between her father and Sister Philippa hadn't materialized. Still the nun had seen her father come to pick her up and that was what counted. "Where are we going, Papa?" she asked.

Sir Malcolm nervously cleared his throat. "To the house in Kent, of course."

A lengthy silence followed this brief exchange, a silence which grew more noticeable with every passing mile. "What are we going to do this summer, Papa?" Vicki finally inquired.

There was nothing to be gained, after all, by putting it off, Malcolm told himself, and it really was the most sensible arrangement for all concerned. He kept his eyes carefully on the road as he spoke, however, to avoid having to look at his daughter. "I've found a marvelous camp for you, Vicki," he announced cheerily. "It's in the Lake District. You'll have a super time there–I'm sure of it!"

A pain stabbed at the pit of her stomach. "I'm...I'm going to camp for the whole summer?" she whispered.

Malcolm Windsor hid his discomfort behind a matter-of-fact tone. "You'll have lots of sun and fresh air and there'll be other girls to play with. You'd find it frightfully dull in Kent, I'm afraid."

"But, Papa, I...I thought we'd be going somewhere together."

"I'm much too busy for a holiday, Vicki. I'll probably be in my flat in London most of the time."

Her lovely dream of a summer holiday with her father had shattered into a million pieces and once again she could hear the hateful words as clearly as if Margaret were right there in the car with them. "Nobody wants Vicki...Nobody wants Vicki." She stared down at her hands and finally, in spite of her determination to hide her disappointment, she began to sob.

"Vicki," her father scolded, "blubbering is not proper behavior for a young lady."

"Yes, Papa." She swallowed hard, choking back the tears. He will never see me cry again, she vowed.

Camp ended just two days before the fall term was to commence at school and this time it was Carleton who drove her from the camp in Lowness-on-Windermere to Kent and then back to Heathfield.

* * *

Although Vicki fortunately didn't realize it or perhaps simply refused to accept it, the pattern of her childhood was now established as terms at school came and went separated only by the holidays–holidays which better than anything typified that childhood.

Christmas, 1948: Spent at her mother's house in Surrey, just south of London. This was her first acquaintance with her half-sister, Rebecca, now nine months old. But Vicki wasn't allowed to hold the baby nor take her for rides in her pram nor do any of the other things she'd longed to do in her honored role as big sister. There were a great many seasonal house parties, moreover, and for much of the holiday Catherine and Henry Montgomery were absent. Rebecca's nanny was not pleased to have the added responsibility of another child and she made her feelings evident.

Spring, 1949: Another holiday spent at Heathfield, one of the "rejects" as Vicki had come to think of herself.

Summer, 1949: Back to camp.

Christmas, 1949: Malcolm Windsor had another of his sporadic attacks of conscience where his daughter was concerned and this time his letter to Vicki promised a nice Christmas in Kent for just the two of them. To give him due credit it must be admitted that his intentions were again the best and for the first few days father and daughter were together constantly. However, Sir Malcolm found the company of a child not quite ten years of age increasingly tiresome and by the end of the first week he discovered more and more excuses to be away. For the last few days of the holiday "business" kept him in London almost continually.

Spring, 1950: An organized bicycle tour of the Low Countries for girls, ages 10-14. The food made Vicki sick and two days after they began the trip in Holland, she developed blisters on both heels and had to ride in the van which carried their camping supplies.

* * *

Thus by her tenth summer Vicki had already lost one of the primary joys of childhood: anticipation. Why look forward to the holiday when she knew that once again her father's solicitor or Carleton or someone else who'd been paid to do so would collect her when the term closed and deliver her to camp, returning her to school once more in the fall. And she knew as well that for the six weeks in between she would be miserable. Most children didn't like Vicki and she found Camp Windermere even lonelier than Heathfield. Although she'd never have admitted it, she missed Pamela terribly.

The summer of 1950 was indeed much the same–until one particular day in crafts class. If there was one camp activity which Vicki disliked above all others, it was this. It wasn't the work with her hands; she rather enjoyed that. Most campers, however, made gifts for their mothers and fathers and she could just imagine how much either of her parents would appreciate a handmade wallet or key case. Then, too, the other girls seemed to gather naturally into groups, laughing and chattering together and leaving her entirely out of their camaraderie. Well, if the other girls didn't like her, that was fine; she didn't like them either and she stayed to herself. After Vicki's first two summers at camp the counselors, as well, had given up trying to get her to mix in. She was such an odd child. It was simply easier to allow her to do as she wished.

So on this day she'd been sitting alone on a rock outside the shed sewing together a leather pencil case for herself. Running out of gimp, she had no choice but to go inside to the supply closet and while she was searching through the drawer for her particular color, she couldn't help overhearing the conversation of the girls at the nearest table.

"Is he really coming?" one girl inquired eagerly.

"That's what my counselor, Cooky, said," someone else replied. "On Sunday, the regular visiting day."

Her curiosity was more than Vicki could stand. "Who's coming?" she asked.

The conversation stopped abruptly and the girls all turned to glare at her. Two of them had started attending camp the same year as she although, unlike Vicki, they only came for a fortnight, spending the remainder of the summer with their families. This, then, was the third summer they had been cabin mates. Usually Vicki didn't even speak to them and they hated to include her in their secret. At the same time they couldn't miss the opportunity to show off. "The King is coming, of course," the first girl announced importantly. "On Sunday."

Ever since Vicki could remember, someone had been reminding her of her illustrious ancestry. "You must remember who your great, great grandmother was," her mother or her nanny would say, "and always act like a little lady."

"Never forget, Victoria," her Grandfather Windsor would tell her–at least he was one person who'd never called her Vicki– "that my father was Prince Arthur, Duke of Connaught, and that you were named for his mother and your great, great grandmother, Queen Victoria."

Over and over again she'd heard it until she was tired of it. What difference did it make anyway? But these nasty girls thought they were so important and she wanted to show them up. "The King is my cousin," she stated proudly.

<u>That</u> stopped them! "What?!" one of the girls exclaimed–wide-eyed.

"The King is my cousin," Vicki repeated. "Queen Victoria was my great, great grandmother. I'm named after her."

"I don't believe you!" Another of the girls spoke up.

"It's the truth. You'll see. I'll prove it," Vicki maintained resolutely.

"Crafts class is nearly over, girls," the counselor called out just then. "Let's get your things put away." She was pleased to notice that at last the Windsor child was talking to some of the other girls.

Shelves along one wall of the shed held rows of cardboard boxes, one for each girl to keep her materials in and as they were all putting their projects away, Vicki could hear the others whispering. One girl even pointed at her. She dawdled over her box so that everyone else would leave ahead of her, but as the others walked out of the shed, she could still hear one of them exclaim, "Now Sunday's really going to be something!"

Vicki listened miserably until the last giggle had faded away in the distance. What <u>was</u> she going to do? Even if she did somehow find the courage to approach the King, he'd undoubtedly never heard of her and if she didn't at least try to speak to him, the others would be sure she was lying. Either way she'd be humiliated. Finally she decided that since she couldn't prove her kinship to the King, her safest course was to remain out of sight. Later she could make up a story for the benefit of the other girls.

Long before His Majesty, King George VI was due to arrive on the following Sunday, the campers were lined up on either side of the roadway–each clutching a tiny Union Jack. Many parents were there as well and when at last the Rolls-Royce came through the gate passing between them, everyone cheered mightily. The girls waved their little flags and from the back seat of the open car the King waved in return, smiling broadly.

By nature a rather shy man he found children easy company and visiting with his younger subjects was one of his favorite royal duties. Many years before when he was still the Duke of York, he had established a camp at which boys from the working classes and those from the aristocracy could meet and get acquainted and he'd greatly enjoyed the hours spent there. When his older brother's abdication had found him the unexpected and decidedly reluctant ruler of Great Britain, he nevertheless continued his interest in these "Duke of York" camps in particular as well as children in general. So although the King hadn't been in the best of health now for about a year, these visits to camps or schools were something he refused to give up.

Today he studied carefully the displays of arts and crafts painstakingly arranged for the royal perusal, asking the girls questions about their work and listening to their halting answers as attentively as ever he had any government minister. Later he was the most enthusiastic of all the spectators at the swimming events, foot races and tennis and volleyball games played for his benefit, heartily cheering the winners and gently consoling the losers.

As for Vicki, she had watched the King's arrival from an inconspicuous place and later as he walked among the exhibits, she followed along with the others, observing him longingly, but continuing to remain in the background. He appeared to be such a kind man that once for a moment she'd almost gone up to him to introduce herself, but then she lost her nerve and slipped away during the games.

In each of the various locations in which she spent her lonely childhood, Vicki managed to find a place of her own. Each was different yet in each she could hide herself away for a while from a hurtful world. In Kent it was the gazebo in the woods; at Heathfield the tiny attic at the top of her dormitory. Even here at camp she'd discovered the perfect spot: a flat rock partway up a hill by a small inlet in the lake. Not only was the inlet itself usually deserted, but on the rare chance that anyone did follow the path this far along the shore, she could easily disappear from view by simply lying down flat against the rock.

Today once again she had made her way to her private refuge and sitting down cross-legged, she stared out across the water. Normally she kept part of her attention on the path beneath so that at the slightest sound she could duck down out of sight, but this afternoon she was sure everyone would be watching the King so she hadn't even considered the possibility someone might discover her.

All at once she heard a man's voice say, "You're missing all the fun, young lady." She jumped. "I'm sorry, my dear," he apologized. "I didn't mean to frighten you." Looking down, Vicki thought her eyes must be playing tricks on her. The man standing on the path below the rock and smiling up at her looked just like the King. "What's the matter? Lose your tongue up there somewhere?" the man asked with a chuckle.

For a few seconds longer she continued to stare at him. My goodness, it was the King! Quickly she got to her feet. "Please...please excuse me, Your...Your Majesty," she stammered in confusion as she scrambled off the back of the rock and down the hill to stand in front of him and bob a hasty curtsey.

Now the King really laughed. "I certainly did startle you, didn't I?"

"No, sir...I mean yes, sir...well, that is people....people don't usually come along here, sir."

"Come here a great deal, do you?"

"Yes, sir."

"Is there a place where we could sit down...ah...what's your name, dear?"

"Vicki, sir."

"Could we sit down some place, Vicki? I'm supposed to be resting in the camp superintendent's cottage, but it's too fine a day to be inside, don't you think?"

The King himself was standing there on the path talking to her about the weather just as though he were like everyone else. She could hardly believe it! Only after several seconds did she finally recover her wits enough to reply, "Yes...yes, sir. There's...there's an old wharf down by the water. Would...would that be all right?"

"That will do just fine." Vicki noticed that even the short walk over the rather uneven ground at the edge of the lake caused the King's breathing to become labored. This frightened her a little, but once they were settled together on the edge of the wharf, feet dangling over the edge, she forgot her momentary anxiety. "Now then," the King said when he'd gotten his breath, "I presume Vicki is short for Victoria."

"Yes, sir."

"Victoria what?"

"Windsor, sir."

"Well now, that's certainly a name to be proud of, isn't it?"

"Yes, sir," she sighed. "That's what everyone keeps <u>telling</u> me!"

"Oh, they do, do they?" Again the King laughed. What a delightful child, he thought.

"Yes, sir. You see, sir, I'm....I'm...." She hesitated, uncertain how to continue.

"Go on, Vicki," he prompted gently. Here was the perfect opportunity to tell him about their relationship, but she couldn't think how to say it "Well, Vicki, I'm waiting." The King's eyes glowed with a suppressed smile. "We aren't by any chance related, are we?"

"Yes, only...only I didn't know how to say it," Vicki admitted in amazement. He seemed able to read her mind. "Queen Victoria was my great, great grandmother."

"Let's see now–she was my <u>great</u> grandmother so that would make us cousins, I think."

"I...I guess so. I tried to tell that to the other girls in my cabin, but they wouldn't believe me."

"They wouldn't, hm? Well, maybe they will when we arrive together for tea."

"Oh, thank you . But do you really want to?" Vicki positively beamed as she responded to this man's kindness with all the natural warmth and affection she'd learned to keep hidden.

"I certainly do," he affirmed with a smile, "but we still have some time for our own visit," he added consulting a watch in his waistcoat pocket. "Tell me some more about your family." As soon as he'd spoken the words, he regretted them. The glow died out in her eyes; her smile faded and she looked down at her hands clasped together in her lap. "But we don't have to talk about that if you don't want to. What would <u>you</u> like to talk about?"

"I don't care, sir." Vicki continued to gaze steadily downward, swinging her feet back and forth off the edge of the wharf.

"Do you like it at camp?"

"It's all right, sir." She shrugged. "I have to be some place so it might as well be here, I guess."

What a sad little girl, he thought. What can be wrong with a child who doesn't like to talk about her family and who looks upon summer camp as just some place to be. "If you could be anywhere, Vicki, where would it be?" At that question she finally raised her head and the King saw that her green eyes were brimming with tears. "I didn't mean to make you cry, Vicki. I could never stand to see <u>my</u> little girls cry."

"I'm...I'm not really crying, sir. It's just that usually...uh...well, usually..." But she could think of no way to explain her feelings and at last she gave up, ending it all with another elaborate shrug. The tears spilled over and rolled down her face–one teardrop perching precariously at the tip of her nose. Then all at once she realized what she was doing–crying like a baby in front of the King–and as usual she didn't have a handkerchief. She tried to sniff without doing it too loudly. "Oh dear, sir, I'm being dreadfully rude. I'm ever so sorry."

From the back pocket of his trousers the King produced a clean white linen handkerchief and handed it to Vicki. "There now," he said kindly. "Why is it little girls never have a hanky?"

"I don't know, sir." Carefully Vicki wiped her eyes and blew her nose. "My nanny always used to get cross with me about it." She looked doubtfully at the soiled hanky she still held in one hand. "What am I do with this, sir?"

"You keep it, why don't you, my dear. You never know when you might need it."

"Thank you, sir." She stuffed the hanky painstakingly into the pocket of her shorts.

"So then, Vicki, do you always come for this session of camp?"

"I'm here for the whole summer, sir," she replied with an air of resignation.

"And where do you live when you're not at camp?"

"Heathfield." Once more she was apparently resigned to her fate.

"Heathfield?"

"Heathfield Abbey School for Girls, sir. It's in Gloucestershire."

The King was beginning to think he'd made a serious blunder. "Are your parents living, Vicki?" he inquired as gently as possible.

"Oh yes, sir. It's just that....well, you see they're divorced and my mother's married again and she has another little girl to love and my father's frightfully busy with his job and all. I get in the way, I suppose. So I stay at school a lot and summers I come here." Once the words got started, Vicki couldn't seem to stop them. This man was much older than she and someone of whom she should be in awe, but for some reason she couldn't explain, he'd reached out and touched her in a way that all of Sister Philippa's kindness and concern had never been able to do.

When at last she stopped speaking, the King could think of nothing to say to console her, but fortunately he allowed the instincts of a father to take over and putting his arm around the child's shoulders, he drew her to him. That did it. Forgetting entirely the identity of her comforter, Vicki flung herself against his shoulder and sobbed as she hadn't permitted herself to do since that first spring holiday when she'd watched from the tiny attic window as all the other girls left for home. Only when the tears began to subside did she once again become aware of who this man was who had held her and let her cry. "Oh dear, sir, please excuse me." Quickly she sat up again, but then she noticed the large damp spot she'd left on his suit coat. "Oh my, look what I've done, sir," she gasped, horrified.

"You know, Vicki, I think that will dry. And it's been too long since a little girl has cried on my shoulder. I'm glad I was here when you needed me."

"Begging your pardon, sir, but why are you being so nice to me?"

"Why shouldn't I be, my dear?"

"It's just that no one much likes me and I....."

"Then there's something wrong with them because I like you very much. You know," he went on as an idea occurred to him, "I've just had a thought. Would it be all right with your parents if instead of staying here for the last fortnight of camp, you came to Balmoral with my family and me?"

Vicki didn't believe she could have heard properly. "I beg your pardon, sir?"

"I'm asking you to come up for a visit in Scotland. You do know where Scotland is, don't you?"

"I'm dreadfully bad at geography, sir. I know it's up north somewhere, though."

"Well, that's good enough." Once more the King threw back his head and laughed. "You know I haven't felt so good in a long time. You're just what the doctor ordered, Vicki. Will you come then? Will it be all right?"

"I'd like to ever so, sir, and my mother and father don't much care what I do."

"Oh, my dear! I can't believe that!"

"Whatever you say, sir." Immediately she acquiesced.

"Now if you're going to come for a visit, Vicki, I want you to think of me as just an old uncle who wants to enjoy the company of his pretty little niece for a while."

"Oh, I didn't agree because of who you are, sir. It's just easier to give in to grown-ups. You can't do anything about anything anyway."

The King was becoming increasingly disturbed by the little girl's attitude and he wondered whether he could really be of any help in only two weeks. Well, this would be only the first of many visits, he vowed. He slipped his arm around her shoulders again and smiled down at her. "And I don't want you to think of me as just another grown-up either, my dear, and so the first thing we have to change is this business of addressing me as 'sir'. Let me see." He paused for a moment, his eyes twinkling. "My nieces and nephews call me Uncle Bertie. Do you think you could manage that?"

Vicki's eyes got wider and wider. "Uncle Bertie," she whispered.

"Only for the benefit of your poor deaf old uncle, you will have to speak a little more loudly. Want to try it once more?"

She was starting to smile. "Uncle Bertie," she said again–this time quite clearly.

"Very good. Now we just have to arrange the date for you to come up and decide how you're going to get there."

Just then, however, the King's equerry appeared, walking rapidly along the path behind them. "Oh, Your Majesty!" Obviously he was much relieved at having found the King. "I became rather concerned, sir, when I went to the superintendent's cottage to wake you. You were supposed to rest, sir," he went on in a tone of respectful reproach as he came down the hill to stand beside the King on the wharf. "Her Majesty will be very annoyed with us both."

"Frightfully sorry to have worried you, Sir Kenneth. It was simply too lovely a day to nap and as you can see, I've made a new friend." The King took hold of the little girl's left hand with both of his. "And what's more I've discovered something extraordinary--this lovely young lady and I are cousins. Isn't that right, Vicki?"

"Yes, sir," she murmured self-consciously.

"Yes, who?" The King looked down at her with a slight smile.

"Yes, Uncle Bertie." And now Vicki's eyes positively shone.

"So then, my dear, shall we go have our tea?"

This time she simply nodded. A stab of fear went through her as she noticed that the King required his aide's help to get to his feet. Once again, however, her brief uneasiness was forgotten as the three of them walked back up the path toward the playing fields and the recreation hall beyond and Vicki experienced one of the few moments of genuine pleasure her childhood afforded her as she arrived for tea–hand in hand with the King.

During tea King George VI tried to divide his time and attention equally among all the children at his table, but just before he was scheduled to leave, he called her over to him. "When does this session of camp end, Vicki?"

"August 17th, Uncle Bertie." How good it felt just to say his name.

"I'll arrange everything with your parents and there'll be a car here to pick you up on the 17th. I'm very glad we've discovered each other, my dear."

His equerry appeared at the King's elbow as if out of nowhere. "Your car is ready, sir."

"Thank you, Sir Kenneth. Now don't forget, Vicki–the 17th."

"Oh, I won't forget. I promise! She hesitated for a moment and then beckoned to him. The King leaned over so that his face was only inches from hers. "May I give you a kiss, Uncle Bertie?" Vicki whispered.

"My dear, your old uncle would be honored." She carefully planted a kiss on his cheek and then on impulse threw her arms around his neck. The King responded with a hug and a kiss of his own.

Vicki stood on the porch of the recreation hall, watching and waving until the limousine disappeared from sight, and that night she lay awake staring up into the total darkness which enveloped the cabin and listening to the summer sounds of the woods. For once, however, it wasn't loneliness which kept her from sleep, but the most overwhelming happiness she could ever remember. And not once in all the hours before she finally fell asleep did she think she would be spending an entire fortnight with the Royal Family. Lying on her back hugging her arms to her chest, she whispered over and over, "Somebody really wants me. Somebody really wants me."

* * *

Two days after the King's visit to Vicki's camp the Royal Family left for its annual late summer sojourn at Balmoral, the Royal Residence near Braemar in the Grampian Mountains. The Princess Elizabeth and her husband, the Duke of Edinburgh, would not be going this year as she was momentarily expecting the birth of her second child and the royal party would, therefore, consist of King George and his wife, Queen Elizabeth, their younger daughter, Princess Margaret, and their 21 month old grandson, Prince Charles.

The Queen had been more than slightly distressed at the prospect of Vicki's visit. Increasingly concerned about her husband's health, she felt a ten year old houseguest would be an unnecessary additional strain, but she knew also of his kindness, his inability to ignore suffering or loneliness–especially in a child–and she'd realized it was futile to argue the point.

A bit of investigation on the part of Sir Kenneth had verified the little girl's heritage. Vicki was indeed a descendant of Victoria's through the Queen's seventh child, Prince Arthur; her grandfather was the Earl of Carlisle and her father, Malcolm Windsor, had been among those knighted for meritorious service during World War II. Her parents were divorced and her mother remarried as she'd said. Beyond that the King did not pry. Their reasons for treating their daughter as they did were not his affair. Vicki's parents, honored by the royal notice, had willingly given their permission for the visit. That the King was providing their daughter with the love and attention which should have come from them never entered their minds.

Vicki had learned it was better not to count on anything. Many times already in her short life she'd looked forward to something only to be bitterly disappointed so although she could hardly wait for the 17th of August to come, she dreaded it as well. She had no way of knowing, of course, that her Uncle Bertie was not a man to break his word, especially to a child, and the 17th did indeed bring the royal car, just as he'd promised, with the royal equerry himself to see her safely onto the train at Carlisle for the overnight ride to Perth and then on to Pitlochry. Sir Kenneth explained that a railway official there would help her change to the local train to Braemar where the King himself would meet her.

Now at last Vicki allowed herself to be excited. It was all really happening: her first journey by train, her first trip to Scotland and best of all, Uncle Bertie waiting for her at the other end. There was the added adventure of supper in the dining car and then going to bed in her own little room. What fun it was to sleep on a moving train, the motion of the railway car causing her bunk to rock gently back and forth. She felt very special the next morning being awakened by a porter with orange juice, tea and muffins for her on a tray and the man at the station treated her as if she really were a princess.

Even this was forgotten, however, as the little train bounced and rattled its way north out of Pitlochry, headed for Braemar, and Vicki glimpsed for the first time the majesty of the Scottish Highlands. Wild and desolate though the landscape was, she did not find it in the least frightening. On the contrary the towering mountains and plunging green glens seemed to welcome her, awakening in her a strange new emotion. She had never been here before and yet it was as though she were coming home.

When the train pulled into the Braemar station, Uncle Bertie was indeed waiting for her. It was not quite a fortnight since his visit to her camp and in that time he'd become simply that in Vicki's mind: her Uncle Bertie, the only person she could remember ever having loved and trusted. Now as she stepped down onto the platform and saw him standing there, however, he was suddenly once again the King of England and for a moment she hesitated unsure what to say or do.

"What–no hug and kiss, Vicki?" he said in a tone of mock reproach, opening his arms to her. In that instant he became Uncle Bertie again and her uncertainty vanished. She flew across the platform into his embrace, reaching up to kiss him on the cheek. "So you're here at last. We're going to have an awfully fine time, I can tell you that!" He turned to a uniformed servant who was standing respectfully in the background. "Bring Miss Windsor's things, will you, Fraser?"

"Yes, sir."

"Come along, my dear." The King offered her his hand to lead her over to where the chauffeur was waiting for them, one hand poised on the handle of the car door. "Nichols, this is my young cousin, Miss Victoria Windsor," he announced very formally.

"Miss Victoria, welcome." Bowing slightly, the driver opened the door for her.

"Thank you, Nichols," she replied politely, acutely conscious of her manners.

The King had stood back, allowing her to enter the car first, and now he seated himself beside her. The driver closed the door and moments later they'd left the village of Braemar behind them, climbing swiftly and smoothly into the hills toward Balmoral. "Well, Vicki, I have a new granddaughter since I saw you last," the King said proudly.

"Oh, that's nice." Uncle Bertie was obviously delighted at the event and she tried to sound pleased for his sake.

"Not too interested in babies, hm?" He smiled at her.

Vicki shrugged. "I don't actually know any babies personally. I have a little sister, but they don't let me play with her.....germs, you know," she went on to confide in such a matter-of-fact tone that the King's heart ached even harder for this lonely child.

"I'm afraid you won't be able to play with my granddaughter this summer either...."

"That's all right. I understand."

"No, no, my dear, you didn't let me finish," he said quickly, taking her right hand in both of his. "My granddaughter was born in London just three days ago and she won't be here this year. You'll have to wait until next summer to play with her. There <u>is</u> my grandson, however. He's nearly two and he probably won't give you a moment's peace." In spite of her determination to be dignified the little girl's eyes filled with tears. "Do you want to talk about it, Vicki?" As he spoke, the King removed his left hand from hers and put his arm around her shoulders. Slowly she shook her head. "All right, lovey. I won't push it," he said at once, accompanying the words with a brief hug.

For most of the rest of the ride, then, they did not speak, the King only occasionally breaking the silence to point out certain landmarks or a herd of shaggy, long-horned Highland cattle or the black faced sheep which appeared here and there along the roadside. He kept his comments light and jovial, trying his best to raise her spirits a little. For a long time nothing succeeded, but then all at once Vicki herself saw something which made her forget her tears. "Uncle Bertie!" she gasped, "The men have skirts on!"

He roared with laughter. "Don't let them hear you say that. They call them kilts and they're very proud of them."

"But why do they wear skir....I mean, kilts, Uncle Bertie?"

"It started hundreds of years ago, you see, because the shepherds found that their trousers got wet in the long grass. Scottish soldiers still wear them as part of their uniforms. I often wear one myself up here. It's actually very comfortable."

The car turned off the road then and traveling down a brief incline and through a grove of trees, they drove onto the grounds of Balmoral. Ahead of them across a wide meadow and sculptured green lawns Vicki could see the gray stone manor house. "Oh, it's beautiful, Uncle Bertie!" she exclaimed.

"Do you like it? You know it was the lady you're named after who first lived here. It was probably her favorite place."

"Maybe <u>that's</u> why I feel so happy here."

"Do you, lovey? I hoped you would."

A moment later the car came to a stop at the front door. As they entered the house, a woman descended the stairs to meet them. Vicki instantly recognized the Queen. "Well, here we are, my dear." The King slipped an affectionate arm around his wife's waist. "This is Vicki."

"How do you do, ma'am." Extending her right hand, the little girl dropped a curtsey. Nanny's constant reminders as to what constituted proper deportment for a well-brought up young Englishwoman had taught her well how to behave at such moments.

"Hello, Vicki," Queen Elizabeth replied accepting the offered hand. "It's lovely to have you visit with us."

"Thank you, ma'am. It's kind of you to have me." It wouldn't have been polite for her to show she'd noticed a certain lack of sincerity in the Queen's greeting. But then, too, perhaps she'd simply become accustomed to such treatment on the part of most adults.

"Lorna," the Queen spoke to a maid who had been standing unobtrusively off to one side during this conversation awaiting instructions, "if you would please see our young guest up to her room."

"Aye, ma'am." The maid came forward to pick up the luggage, turning to lead the way up the same stairs which the Queen had come down a few minutes before.

"This is a beautiful place," Vicki observed as she followed Lorna.

"Aye."

"Does that mean yes?"

"Aye."

"Is that all you ever say?"

"No."

It was Vicki's first contact with the dour Scot and after a while she gave up trying to make conversation. On the first floor Lorna indicated wordlessly that she intended to go left and still without speaking, she conducted Vicki along the hall to a corner room with windows which looked out over the mountains. As in the rest of the house both wallpaper and carpet were plaid. The woodwork glowed from frequent polishings and there was an enormous four poster bed. Somehow it looked more like home than any place she could ever remember. "Oh, I love this room!"

Vicki began to unpack, but not more than five minutes had passed when the face of a small boy appeared around the door frame. "Hello!" He lifted one hand to her, the gesture appearing to be part wave and part salute.

"You're Prince Charles, aren't you?" Along with all of Britain she'd seen countless pictures of the King's grandson.

Before the little boy could reply, however, a woman in uniform appeared behind him. "Therre ye be, wee laddie. I swearr by the blessed St. Andrrew himself, ye'll be drrivin' me fairr daft wi' yourr scamperrin's and scurryin's!"

With the more loquacious nanny Vicki had her first real chance to hear the rich sound of the Scottish brogue. The speech had a soothing burr to it, affecting her rather oddly– much in the same way as had her initial glimpse of the Highlands. Indeed she became so fascinated listening to the musical rise and fall of its cadence that she was unaware she'd been asked a question until the woman repeated it a second time. "I asked who ye'd be, lass?" the nanny said again, her eyes twinkling good-naturedly.

"I'm Vicki. I'm just visiting."

"Aye–the young cousin of His Majesty. Would that be it, the noo?"

"I beg your pardon," she inquired politely, discovering that in addition to its lovely sound the brogue was also at times quite unintelligible.

"Och, wee lassie, do ye no ken the brrogue? I'll be speakin' a wee bit morre slowly forr ye then. My name is Mrs. Lightbody and I take carre o' the wee Prrince herre."

Charles, meanwhile, had been studying Vicki and he decided now that he liked her. Marching over, he took her by the hand. "Take a walk," he announced.

"Is it all right?" Vicki inquired of the nanny.

"Aye, but ye'll no be mindin' if I coom along."

"Oh yes, please," she agreed.

The three of them set out together. Charles was eager to show his new friend about the grounds especially the pasture behind the house, one of his favorite spots. There were cows there ("Grampa England's cows," he explained proudly) as well as ducks in the pond and before they finally returned to the house for tea, he insisted on picking her a bunch of wildflowers.

Tea for the Royal Family was served in a small sitting room on the first floor. The nanny had left them to join the other members of the household staff for their tea so it was Vicki and Charles who entered together–hand in hand. "Well, I see you've already met my grandson." The King stood up coming over to pull a chair out for Vicki. "I might have known he wouldn't waste any time getting acquainted."

"Oh, we had a lovely walk!" she replied, settling herself happily in the chair. Uncle Bertie's gallant manner made her feel terribly grown-up.

"Vicki, I'd like you to meet my daughter, Margaret," the King continued, indicating the young woman seated on the other side of the Queen.

"How do you do, ma'am." Vicki got immediately to her feet again, going over to the Princess to shake her hand and drop yet another curtsey.

"How do you take your tea?" the Queen inquired as she poured another cup.

"Milk and sugar, please."

"Help yourself to sandwiches or biscuits, my dear," she went on handing the cup and saucer to Vicki. The Queen was relieved to observe that at least their young visitor was a sweet, well-behaved child. Perhaps having her here would not be as much of a problem as she'd anticipated. Then, too, Margaret, had agreed to be chiefly responsible for the little girl's amusement.

* * *

Vicki had never had so much fun: riding on a pony, hiking in the woods, swimming in the lake or riding on it in a motor launch. Margaret had secretly wondered how she would like spending an entire fortnight entertaining a ten year old, but she found Vicki to be mature for her age and a delightful companion. Charles was often with them as well, determined not to be left out of anything.

Only one mildly unpleasant incident marred her stay. She and Margaret and Charles had taken a pony cart off the grounds to have a picnic at another small lake near-by and then do a bit of exploring. Charles was supposed to nap after they ate. He was not particularly enthused with the idea, however, and while his aunt was trying unsuccessfully to convince him, Vicki decided to go off by herself for a short time. Just around the bend in the shoreline she discovered a large rock only a few feet from shore and removing her shoes and socks, she waded out to it, climbing up to seat herself cross-legged on the top.

She'd only been there a few minutes when she heard hoofbeats on the path behind her and looking over her shoulder, she saw a magnificent roan horse gallop through the clearing–a boy astride him bareback. Horse and rider were gone almost at once and Vicki turned to look out over the lake again, but then a moment later they were back. This time the rider reined in and jumped to the ground.

"Halloo, therre!" he called. Waving to Vicki, he splashed out to climb up beside her. He was a tall boy, apparently a few years older than she, with a tousled mop of auburn hair almost the color of his horse and large, dark eyes. He was dressed in a kilt and a short-sleeved jersey.

"Stop it, please!" Vicki protested. "You're getting me all wet!"

"Oh, am I noo?" the boy teased. Swinging around on the rock, he caught up a handful of water to toss at her.

"Get away from me!" she shrieked.

"Och, dinna be angrry wi' me! A bonny lassie like yourrself should always be smilin'." The boy grinned at her engagingly.

"And just exactly who do you think you are?" Vicki demanded in her most disdainful tone of voice.

"Ye'rre English, arre ye not?"

"Yes, I am," she replied proudly.

"Aye, that's what I thought. Everra Englisherr I've everr met has been stuck-up!"

"I am <u>not</u> stuck-up! You're a horrid boy. And you talk funny and you wear a skirt!"

"Och, why dinna ye stay doon in England wherre ye belong!" the boy yelled. Springing to his feet, he charged Vicki from behind pushing her off into the water. Then he jumped off the rock himself and splashed back to where his horse stood waiting, calmly nibbling at the lower branches of a tree. Holding onto the mane, the boy vaulted easily to its back. Vicki stood up in the waist-deep water. Her shorts and top were soaked and strands of her long hair dripped muddy water in her eyes. Watching her from his perch astride the horse, the boy roared with laughter. "That'll teach ye, English lassie!"

"I'll never forgive you! Never!" she screamed. Still laughing, he dug his bare heels into the horse's sides and they disappeared once more into the woods. Vicki was still sputtering when she returned to Charles and Margaret.

"Whatever happened to you?" Margaret inquired in amazement.

"I fell in the lake," was all she would say.

Afterwards she wondered why she'd hesitated to accuse her tormentor. What did she care if he got into trouble? But she never said anything further about the incident and soon she'd forgotten all about it. There were too many good times to think about to bother with one nasty boy.

* * *

Later in her life, however, it wasn't even the fun Vicki would remember, but the fact that for two magical weeks she knew what it felt like to be part of a family. Sometimes she even let herself pretend it was all real; that she was indeed a member of the family-- that Margaret was her big sister and Charles, her baby brother. And of course there was Uncle Bertie. If her dream could become reality, he would be her father. Oh, to have him for her Papa: gentle, loving Uncle Bertie. Well, at least she had him for now, she told herself, and during the time she was at Balmoral the hours spent with him were best of all.

King George VI was the sort of man who despite all his official duties never failed to find time for his family and this family now included Vicki. His health prohibited him from taking part in the more strenuous activities, but they all had meals and tea time together each day and she and Uncle Bertie enjoyed leisurely walks on the grounds of Balmoral with Charles often tagging along, of course. Sometimes the whole family would travel to interesting places in the area. For days before the trip to Loch Ness Uncle Bertie had teased her with lurid tales of the famous monster and Vicki was actually disappointed when they saw nothing. On the days they didn't go on major excursions the King would invariably take the two children down into the village of Braemar in the afternoon for ice cream or penny candy. When they returned, the Queen would pretend to scold her husband for spoiling the children's appetites; he would appear properly contrite and Vicki and Charles would giggle with delight at it all. The routine never varied, but they all enjoyed it immensely each time.

Most special of all the special moments, however, were the bedtimes. The first night of her visit Vicki was just about to turn out the light when there was a knock at the door. "Come in." She wondered nervously if she had done something wrong.

It was Uncle Bertie. "All set, lovey?"

"Yes," she replied doubtfully. "Is something the matter?"

"No, of course not." The King looked startled. "I've just come to say good-night."

"Oh." She appeared so puzzled that for a second he nearly inquired if she were unaccustomed to such bedtime visits. Just in time he stopped himself from asking the question. From the little he'd learned about her thus far, he already knew the answer.

"I'm afraid I'm indulging myself a bit here," he admitted. "I always enjoyed bedtime with my daughters, you see, and I rather miss it now they're grown."

"All right, then, if you wish." She still hesitated, however, uncertain exactly what was expected of her.

The King folded back the blankets and top sheet on the double bed. "Well, climb in then." Obediently Vicki did so and lying back against the enormous, overstuffed pillows, she looked up at him expectantly as if to say, 'What now?' He pulled up the covers again, gently tucking her in. Finally he drew a small, straight chair over by the bed and with a slightly embarrassed grin produced a book from behind his back. "I thought I'd read aloud to you for a while. Unless perhaps you think you're too old to be read to?"

Her eyes widened. "Oh, Uncle Bertie, I'd really like that. No one's ever read to me before."

"Very well." The King settled himself in the chair, holding up the book so she could see the title–*Little Women* by Louisa May Alcott. "This was always a favorite of my girls. Have you read it?" Vicki shook her head, wishing there were a way to hug this happiness to herself so that it could never escape. Opening the book, he began to read and thus was initiated one of the nightly rituals of her stay at Balmoral. They finished *Little Women* and had started in on *The Wind in the Willows* when it was time for her to leave. On the last night the King thought he heard a slight sound and glancing up from his reading, he saw the little girl was crying. "Vicki," he murmured, "oh, my dear." At once he moved over to sit beside her on the bed, putting his arm around her shoulders. "You don't want to leave, do you?"

"No, I don't," she sobbed. "I...I want to stay with you forever and ever."

He hugged her closer while with the other hand he drew a handkerchief from his jacket pocket and wiped her eyes. "You never do have a hanky, do you, Vicki?" he teased, hoping to make her laugh. But all she did was shake her head and cry even harder. "Vicki....Vicki, my dear, please. You'll make yourself sick."

The King knew, however, that words wouldn't really help and so for a while after that he simply sat there, holding her close and waiting patiently. Only when her sobs had abated somewhat, sounding touchingly now rather like hiccups, did he finally lay her back among the pillows, moving away a little and turning so that he could sit facing her. "Now, Vicki..." Putting one hand under her chin, he gently raised her face so that she was looking directly at him. "I want you to listen carefully and remember what I say. All right?" She nodded solemnly. "Yes, this visit may be almost over, but I promise you it's only the first of many. From now on we'll want you to spend part of every summer with us. Do you think you could abide our company for a whole month?"

"Oh, Uncle Bertie! Yes! Oh, Yes!" She started to cry all over again. "I've just had the most super time!"

"It's been just as wonderful for us, Vicki. I know little Charles will miss you terribly. Now let's finish this chapter and then I'm going to give you the book to take with you."

"All...all right." Bravely she swallowed back her tears and smiled up at him. "Uncle Bertie?" She beckoned to him to come closer so that she could kiss him on the cheek. "Oh, Uncle Bertie, I love you so much!"

The next day the King and the small prince came to see her off at the Braemar station. "Don't forget, lovey," the King whispered as he bent to hug and kiss her good-bye. "We'll see you next summer."

"I won't forget. I promise."

"Excuse me, Your Majesty." The conductor approached them just then and bowed respectfully. "I'm afraid the young lady will have to be boarding now."

Her eyes filling with tears, Vicki flung her arms around the King's neck for one final hug. "Good-bye, Uncle Bertie. Thank you for...for everything." The conductor was waiting, holding open the door for her, and as soon as she'd boarded, he closed it after her locking it securely. A whistle sounded and they began to move.

"Remember, Vicki," the King called after her as the train gathered speed. "Remember–next year."

Leaning out the window of her compartment, Vicki watched the man and the little boy standing together on the platform, both waving for as long as she could see them, but all too soon the train rounded a curve and they were lost from sight. For a moment she felt terribly lonesome, but then her ears caught the sound of the train wheels against the track beneath and their rhythmic clacking at once reassured her, reminding her as it seemed to do over and over again: "Next year......next year......next year...."

* * *

Philippa was just coming down the stairs into the entrance hall when Vicki arrived on the opening day of fall term. "Sister Philippa!" Running up to the nun, she threw her arms around her. "How are you? Did you have a good summer? Mine was super!"

"Yes, thank you, Vicki." With a thrill of joy she returned the hug. "At dinner tonight you'll have to tell me all about your holiday."

At once the girl moved away a little on the step, an odd expression passing across her face. "There's not much to tell really. I went to camp as usual. Has Pamela arrived?"

"Yes. She's already upstairs unpacking."

"Thank you, Sister."

Elizabeth looked up from her customary opening day post at the registration desk to watch Vicki run on up the stairs. She waited until the girl was safely out of hearing. "You haven't given up on her, have you, Sister? God bless you for your caring!"

"I tell you, Sister Elizabeth, there are times I wonder why I don't give up. Did you see how affectionately she greeted me a moment ago?"

"Yes, I did and I knew how much it would please you."

"More than you can imagine, but the minute I inquired about her holiday, she pulled back from me again."

"Perhaps this will answer your question, Sister, at least in part. Whatever you do, don't tell Mother Cecilia, but I keep something here to read during my spare moments and it's not the Bible. Drawing the current issue of *Illustrated London News* from under a pile of registration forms, Elizabeth skimmed through to a certain page and handed the magazine to Sister Philippa. The article was entitled "Royals on Annual Scottish Holiday". "Look at the top picture on the right hand page," she directed.

The picture she'd indicated showed the King and Queen, Princess Margaret and little Prince Charles in a motor launch on Loch Muick. Also in the picture was a young girl, sitting next to the King and holding Charles on her lap. "My goodness!" Philippa gasped. "That's Vicki!"

"Read the caption," Sister Elizabeth continued, "the last part."

"....and someone identified by a spokesman for the Royal Family as simply a 'young cousin of His Majesty's.' Vicki's related to the King?"

"She never told you?"

"She's never told me anything," Sister Philippa sighed.

"And don't expect her to say anything now." Elizabeth sounded thoughtful. "Look at the picture again and this time try to forget it's the Royal Family. What do you see?"

Philippa studied the picture intently. "It's really just a family, isn't it?"

"Exactly and knowing what we do about Vicki's situation, I'm sure that's what it meant to her. So don't be too upset, Sister, if she doesn't talk about her holiday. She doubtless considers it far too personal a thing to share with anyone."

"I....I think I understand."

"Oh and Sister, it wouldn't be wise either to expect too radical a change in her."

"I know, but at least she's turned the corner." And later that afternoon, passing Vicki and Pamela in the hallway, Philippa was further encouraged. Pamela had never looked so happy. She as well had apparently encountered a very different Vicki.

It soon became evident to everyone, in fact, just how much Vicki had changed. She was warmer and more open, not only with Sister Philippa and Pamela, but with other students and teachers as well. True, she remained a very private person, never answering questions about herself or sharing her thoughts with anyone. If someone happened to comment on her resemblance to the girl in the magazine picture, she would just smile and say "Really?" or "A lot of people have said that."

Meanwhile she hugged the memory of that magical fortnight to herself, feeding off it all during the fall months, the recollection warmed and strengthened by almost weekly letters from Uncle Bertie. They weren't long, but they were always personally written. This was also true of a letter which arrived early in December. Waiting as usual until she was locked securely in the lavatory stall before opening it, her eyes scanned hurriedly down the page, hungry as ever for his words. Her gaze came to rest at last on a paragraph near the end of the letter.

We had thought of asking you to join us for at least part of the Christmas holiday, but your parents tell us they want you with them. Of course we can understand that.

A wave of disappointment swept over her, but then almost at once it vanished and the dream which hadn't quite died in her sprang to life once again. After all, as wonderful as Uncle Bertie was, he couldn't take the place of her mother and father. In actuality, both parents had been rather annoyed by this second royal invitation, coming so soon on top of the first. Did the King think they didn't want their own daughter? Of course they did and if they divided the time between them, they'd each only have to have her for half the holiday.

* * *

The foundations of the wall had, in fact, been laid on the day her father returned home from the war–the day on which a little girl first knew she was not loved–and gradually since then, with each disappointment, each dashed hope, another stone had been added and another and still another. Many would approach over the years and finding her cold and hard, turn away. They saw only the wall. Others, drawn by her beauty, would love her or perhaps merely lust after her for a while. They, too, saw only the wall. Some, like Sister Philippa, glimpsing something of the lonely girl, the lonely woman all but hidden behind it, would attempt to breach the wall and a few to a limited extent would succeed. But for the most part she would remain a prisoner within her emotional stockade for some time to come. And as that Christmas approached, the wall would indeed require but a few additional stones.

She hadn't really felt well for more than a week, but years of being more or less on her own had taught her not to complain and this time for some reason she was particularly desperate to keep her illness a secret. Then, wouldn't you just know it, only about a few days before the holiday was to begin she passed out in class. Although she was conscious again almost immediately, that damned nun still insisted on taking her to the infirmary where the doctor soon diagnosed her with mononucleosis.

"You realize, of course," Sister Philippa observed sadly to Sister Elizabeth, "that now she will require care, there is a good chance neither of her parents will want her."

"Would you prefer I rang them up?"

"Please! I doubt I could even be civil!"

Mrs. Montgomery had meant to let them know earlier. They'd been invited to her husband's home for Christmas and a child from a previous marriage would be decidedly inconvenient. She was sure they'd understand.

Sir Malcolm was, after all, a man by himself with only a gentleman's gentleman to help him and it would be quite improper for them to tend to an indisposed young lady.

Vicki accepted the news with complete composure–probably because she had known it all along--and shortly after the term ended and most of the other girls had left for home, she uncomplainingly moved over to complete her convalescence in the convent where she'd spent so many other holidays. It was a profound relief when she was strong enough to leave her room and walk about the grounds and eventually down into the village. At last she could be alone–away from Sister Philippa's constant expressions of concern, away from the cloying sweetness of Sister Elizabeth.

* * *

The wall was nearly complete now. The very next spring she gave up on her father.

Suffering from his worst attack of parental guilt to date, Sir Malcolm had suggested a spring holiday together on the French Riviera and once again as at Christmas two years before he did indeed make a determined effort to "be a good father". I wonder why Papa has to try so hard to have fun, Vicki often wondered. I suppose it's my fault. Then one morning, still in bed, she overheard her father talking on the telephone in the next room. Apparently he was explaining to someone about his daughter. Then she heard, "All right! All right! I admit I'm bloody bored, but I promised her and this time by God I'm going to stick it out!" When he came in a few minutes later, she pretended she was still asleep and after he'd left, she packed her things and returned to England and Heathfield.

At this point, however, the wall still held an open doorway as all during the spring term and first weeks of her summer holiday, Vicki clung to the promise of Balmoral and Uncle Bertie. She even enjoyed a certain degree of popularity at the camp due to her celebrated departure via royal limousine the year before. Then the Queen's letter arrived. The King was ill and they would be unable to have her with them that summer. The door had begun to close.

As Christmas of 1951 approached, Catherine Montgomery for some reason conceived the notion of having her "two little girls" together for the holidays. "Wouldn't that be simply adorable?" she cooed to her husband. Henry Montgomery grunted an unintelligible reply. He secretly found even his own daughter a bloody nuisance and having two of the creatures around would be twice as intolerable, but he decided to let his wife have her fantasy. She'd tire of it soon enough.

Vicki had nearly refused the invitation and more than once on the drive from the train station she wished she had. Her mother's demeanor was decidedly cool and how odd the word "Mama" sounded to her own ears. Am I supposed to love her, Vicki wondered uneasily. Well, I guess I don't. I think I hate her. Does it make you an awful person if you hate your own mother? The Montgomerys' 18th century manor house was as unwelcoming as its mistress– highly polished floors and massive furnishings, tall gilt-edged mirrors serving merely to intensify the gloom. It just doesn't seem like a home, but then it isn't–at least not mine– Vicki thought, blinking back the tears.

It was the first time she'd seen 'Becca as the little girl called herself since her half-sister was a baby. This odd-appearing, yet somehow striking child with the soft, shoulder-length chestnut brown hair and enormous blue eyes made Vicki feel old and worldly-wise and full of pity. She spent as much time with her as Rebecca's nanny would allow: reading to her, coloring with her, playing at "make-believe"–doing everything she could to show the little girl she was loved. What she was trying to be, of course, perhaps without even realizing it, was Rebecca's Uncle Bertie.

For much of her stay, however, Vicki was alone. Catherine's surge of maternal feeling had indeed been short-lived and by the end of the first week the Montgomerys were again absent in London for days at a time. So now Vicki gave up on her mother as well. She was twelve years old, she told herself, and it was time to stop believing in childish illusions. The final bricks of the wall were laid that Christmas. It would take but one final tragic event to close the door and lock it.

* * *

When Vicki returned to Heathfield following the Christmas recess, her class passed from the junior school into the first form of the upper school. This meant additional privileges: more free time, unsupervised evening study and a smaller, cozier room shared by only four girls (Pamela and Vicki to be remaining together). An added advantage from Vicki's point of view was that Sister Philippa was no longer a daily part of her life. Although now a novice in the order, she still worked with the younger girls. But all of this meant very little to her or to anyone else for that matter. All anyone thought about or talked about was the King.

In January George VI had been too ill to carry out a planned tour of Australia and New Zealand, his daughter the Princess Elizabeth and her husband Prince Philip going in his place, and all month Vicki lived in dread, expecting news of Uncle Bertie's death to come at any minute. Then on the morning of February 8, 1952, she awoke to the tolling of the bell in the chapel tower. A sickening fear spread through her and she turned on her stomach, burying her head in the pillow in a vain attempt to block out the relentless bell. Yet the ringing continued until the room and even her bed seemed to echo its knell, the incessant sound proclaiming over and over again: next...year...next...year...next...year... next........year....as though deliberately mocking her with a promise of something which now would never be.

Gradually she became aware that many of the girls including the other three from her room had gathered outside in the hall, but she did not join them. Hers, after all, was a private grief. At last, however, Pamela returned, coming to kneel beside the bed. Her eyes brimmed with tears. "Vicki," she whispered, "the King is dead."

"I don't care. Leave me alone."

"All....all right." Clearly dismayed, Pamela got to her feet and walked away.

At that moment Sister Marion, one of the nuns in charge of the older girls, entered the room. Obviously she'd been crying as well. "Come along, girls." She paused a moment to wipe her eyes with a large, white handkerchief. "Chapel this morning will be a special memorial service for His Majesty." Vicki, however, had rolled over to lie with her back to the door, apparently ignoring her entirely. "Aren't you coming, dear?" Sister Marion inquired. She didn't really know her new students as yet.

"I don't feel well."

"But Vicki," Sister Marion remonstrated quietly, "The King......."

"I don't give a damn about the King!"

"What did you say?" The nun was positive she couldn't have heard correctly.

"I said I don't give a......"

"Very well, young lady!" Marion turned on her heel. "I will not stand here and argue with you. Mother Geraldine will deal with you later!"

Even after the room was finally quiet, Vicki continued to lie unmoving. "I didn't mean it, Uncle Bertie," she whispered at last. "You know I didn't. Only you weren't even a real person to them and how can they possibly feel so sad about someone they didn't even know." It was still some time after that before she could bring herself to get out of bed and dress. The dormitory was deserted by now and no one saw her move quickly along the hall, down the stairs and out the front door. Gradually she began to walk faster and then to run. Almost without knowing it, she was across the campus and out on the road, the crunching of her feet on the frozen ground the only sound in the still winter air.

The blast of a horn brought her abruptly to her senses and she discovered she was standing in the middle of the village's main street with no awareness whatsoever of either the distance traveled from the school or the amount of time elapsed. Cars were stopped in both directions. Bewildered, she just stood there. "Hey there, young lady," one of the drivers finally yelled, "get out of the road!"

"I'm....I'm sorry." She wasn't even sure in which direction she'd been going, but she moved out of the traffic and up onto the sidewalk. Why hadn't she sought out her accustomed spot in the attic of her old dormitory? Why had she come into town? Now she had to find some place to hide–some place where no one could find her. Turning the next corner, she found herself in one of the narrow streets common all over Britain. Brick row houses set directly on the edge of the pavement lined both sides, offering no possible hideaway. She'd about decided to go on when she saw a small stone church at the other end, forming a little cul-de-sac. If it were open, it would be the perfect refuge. With a quick glance back over her shoulder Vicki darted down the short street toward the minster and discovering to her relief that the side door was indeed unlocked, she slipped inside.

The interior of the chapel was dark and deserted, the only light coming in through narrow stained glass windows set high in the gray stone walls. Still searching for her hiding place, she walked slowly down the center aisle turning around and around. Finally as her eyes became accustomed to the gloom, she could make out a small gallery in the rear of the sanctuary–the perfect spot since it would probably be overlooked if they even searched the church at all, which in itself was unlikely. Returning to the vestibule, Vicki easily located the narrow, winding stairs which led up to the balcony and once there she settled herself in the far corner of the back pew where she couldn't be seen from below. At last she felt safe from discovery and pulling her feet up, she wrapped her arms around her knees. For a while then she simply sat there, idly studying a ray of light which filtered wanly through the dusty air from a window just behind and above her head.

In all the time since she'd gotten out of bed and begun to dress–even since conscious thought suddenly returned in the middle of the street a few minutes ago–she hadn't allowed herself to think about the death of her beloved Uncle Bertie, but now there was no more escaping its reality. The terrible loss was all around her there in the empty church–a palpable thing clutching her heart in its cruel fist. Gripping her legs more tightly, she pressed her face down against them, but the pain would not go away and she was certain she must die herself of the anguish.

In the first moments of numbed shock she hadn't cried, but now the tears flowed freely–great choking sobs that made her face burn and her chest ache. "Oh, Uncle Bertie," she whispered, "please don't be dead. You're the only person who's ever loved me. Please, Uncle Bertie, I need you dreadfully!" She knew even as she spoke the words how foolish they sounded, but in the extremity of her grief all she could think was how desperately she wanted him back. The sobs were coming harder now until she started to gag on them, her body heaving as if she would vomit, but since she'd eaten nothing that day, all that came up was bitter tasting bile.

"I have to stop," she muttered gritting her teeth together, but all she succeeded in doing was to change her sobs into hiccups. "Damn!" This was only the second time in her life she'd spoken that word, the first having been to Sister Marion just a short while before. It felt rather good so she said it again and yet again and all at once it struck her as funny. She began to laugh and then to cry again and then laugh and finally both at the same time until it made her sick all over again. Bending over the floor, she spat up more bile mixed with saliva–retching until her stomach ached. It was a long time before the heaving abated. Weak and exhausted, Vicki curled up on the church pew and after a while she fell asleep.

Awaking somewhat later, she sat up slowly, her body stiff and sore, and looked around her. She had no idea how long she'd slept, but the sanctuary was still deserted; no one had discovered her hiding place. "Of course they're not looking for me," Vicki said to herself. "No one cares what happens to me." As she spoke these words, the realization came over her once again that her Uncle Bertie was indeed gone and she was alone. She didn't begin to cry again, however; there were simply no more tears left.

Instead she continued to sit there huddled in a corner of the pew in the darkness, looking at nothing in particular. "What am I going to do?" she whispered at last. "There's no one left to love me and everyone I've ever tried to love has done nothing but hurt me. And it's....it's not just people like my mother and father who never loved me anyway. It's other people you think care about you–only they don't because if they really loved you, they wouldn't go away and leave you. So...so...I....I... guess that's the answer. I just won't let myself love anyone ever again." She had solved her problem rather neatly, it seemed, although for some odd reason there was no triumph in the revelation–merely an overwhelming sense of loss.

So the wall was now apparently complete, but Vicki was, in fact, much like the silly ostrich who when alarmed sticks its head in the sand and because it can't see anyone, assumes no one is there. Yet people were there: Sister Philippa and Pamela and later there would be others. She might refuse to love; she could not stop others from loving her.

Chapter 5

Sister Marion was mistress of the older girls and in the three years since Vicki had moved to the upper school, Philippa had undeniably made a nuisance of herself. Since early in December now she'd been toying with yet another idea–a particularly good one, she congratulated herself–and so on the first morning of Christmas holiday she was once again on her way to the lower level of the humanities building where Marion in her additional capacity as the school's drama coach had her office.

At the sound of the knock Marion glanced up from her desk. "Come in..oh, Philippa." She smiled. The identity of her visitor was no surprise. With each new term a group of girls moved up from the junior school and at some during the intersession they customarily conferred. "So what undiscovered gems are you sending me this time?" As she spoke, however, she noticed her colleague wasn't carrying any of the usual file folders. "Oh, good–just a visit! On the day after holiday begins I don't feel like working." She waved blithely at a chair. "You can push that pile of scripts off onto the floor." Creativity rather than neatness was her strong suit. Philippa accepted the offered chair although she moved the scripts carefully to a near-by table before sitting down. But then for a few moments she said nothing. "Oh, no!" Marion exclaimed. "Not Vicki again!"

"I know I've been a pest," the other nun admitted sheepishly, "but this time I really <u>do</u> have an idea. I don't know why I didn't think of it before."

Sister Marion hesitated briefly before replying. At Philippa's request she'd already made several attempts to establish some rapport with Vicki, only to be soundly rebuffed. Then, too, she remembered vividly the way the girl had acted on the morning of the King's death and she doubted whether anyone without actual psychiatric training could accomplish anything. She had come to fear, moreover, much as Sisters Elizabeth and Louisa, that Philippa's emotionally charged involvement with Vicki was unwise. But at the same time she found that now, as on each of the previous occasions, she couldn't refuse. Her colleague's concern was so touchingly sincere. "All right, Sister." She settled herself to listen patiently once again. "What is it?"

"It's so obvious! Can't you see it yourself?" Philippa's excitement bubbled irrepressibly to the surface as she talked.

"I'm afraid I lack your perception," Marion chuckled.

"Please don't joke about Vicki. What no one but me seems to realize is that unless someone can reach her and soon, it may be too late."

"All right, Sister. All right." Instantly she regretted her attempt at humor. "I certainly don't wish to make light of a serious situation–only to help you be less intense about it. I'm well aware Vicki is an unhappy girl. Now what do you think I can do for her?"

Looking down at her hands folded in her lap, Philippa took a deep breath. "You've talked so much," she said at last, "about how your work as a drama coach has helped the girls and..... well, I....I thought what a beautiful girl Vicki is and....and...." At this point, however, she happened to glance up and seeing the other woman's face, her words dwindled away.

"Oh, Philippa, my dear!" Marion shook her head. "The theatre is <u>not</u> a cure-all for every emotional problem. In fact it can be quite the opposite."

"I'm afraid I don't understand."

"You've often expressed concern about Vicki's inability to relate to other people. What better escape could she possibly find than pretending to be someone else? The theatre could actually prove quite <u>un</u>healthy for her."

Philippa looked dejected, but then she immediately brightened up again. "But don't you think she would be a good actress. She's so lovely and...."

"I don't want to destroy all your illusions, Sister, but that's no guarantee she has any talent."

"Couldn't she at least audition?" She was still loath to relinquish this, her latest hope.

"I'm willing to give any student a chance, but from what you've said and from what I've already observed myself, won't she immediately rebel against any such suggestion?"

"She's in your literature class. What if you asked her to help you during the Christmas recess?"

"She'll be here for the holiday then?"

"She hasn't gone home, if she'd ever had anything she could call home, in three years."

"Dear me–three years without going home!" Marion was genuinely shocked. "Well, I suppose I can at least ask her."

"Thank you, Sister. And who knows? You may be discovering a great actress!"

"Yes," the other nun laughed, "there's always a first time, isn't there?"

* * *

That evening all the people who would be remaining at school for the holiday were gathered as usual in the convent refectory for dinner. Sister Marion paused in the doorway to search for Vicki and after a brief perusal of the room located her at the far end of one of the long tables. Of course she was alone and as was often the case, apparently absorbed in a book. An old-fashioned gooseneck floor lamp stood behind her right shoulder at just such an angle that while her hair glowed in its light, her face, except for highlights on her cheekbone and forehead, remained in shadow. Clearly her isolation was deliberate. But I promised Philippa, Marion thought with a sigh, and I have to at least make the attempt. Walking quickly along the length of the tables, the nun sat down across from her . "May I speak to you for a moment, Vicki?"

The girl allowed just enough time to pass before raising her head to indicate that she resented the intrusion. "Yes, Sister?" Her tone managed somehow to sound simultaneously polite and disrespectful.

"I wondered if I might ask your help?"

"My help?" She lifted her eyebrows.

"Yes, since you're in my literature class and you always spend the holiday at school anyway, I thought perhaps....." Sister Marion realized at once that she'd made a serious blunder. "I... I'm sorry," she stammered. "I....I didn't mean that the way it sounded."

"It's all right," the girl replied flatly. More and more now she was learning to control the outward expression of her emotions.

"I....I only mentioned it, you see, because my drama club will be presenting Oliver Goldsmith's *She Stoops to Conquer* in the spring and it would be a great help to me if I could get a head start on the props and costumes."

"Do I have to?"

"No, of course not. Not if you don't choose to."

"Then I'd rather not, thank you."

"Very well." How Philippa could care so deeply for this girl, Marion couldn't imagine. She came close to walking away and afterwards she couldn't be sure exactly what prompted her to make one more attempt. Perhaps it was the prospect of having to report yet another failure to Sister Philippa. In later years, however, she liked to think and incidentally take every opportunity to relate that even then she'd sensed something special in a fifteen year old prep school student named Victoria Windsor. For whatever reason she turned back and to her own amazement heard herself saying, "How about at least trying out then?"

The girl raised her eyes from her book again–this time with an exaggerated sigh. "What, Sister?"

"You read aloud in class with such expression." That was actually true, Marion thought, again with some surprise. "Perhaps you might be interested in auditioning for a role." Inwardly Vicki had to admit the prospect tempted her. She was fully aware by now that she was attractive–that male heads turned when she entered a room– and she found the prospect of displaying herself on a stage appealing. Sister Marion could see that in spite of herself the girl was intrigued. "Auditions begin the second day of term if you decide you're interested," she tossed off casually before finally turning to leave.

"Go to hell!" the girl muttered at Marion's retreating back. When Vicki had informed Sister Marion three years before that she "didn't give a damn about the King", the nun's evident shock told her she'd happened on a marvelous way to upset the good Sisters of Heathfield. Since then she'd had her secondary level privileges suspended countless times for profanity. Her proudest moment had been the time she told her longstanding nemesis, now Mother Superior Geraldine, to "sod off, you bloody old bitch!". It had almost been worth the month's probation.

* * *

As Elizabeth had once reassured Philippa, the sisters did indeed do everything they could to make the holidays pleasant for the students remaining at school. This was especially true at Christmas, certainly the hardest time of all to be away from home. There was an enormous tree in the central hall of the convent and a sumptuous roast goose dinner. Names had been drawn ahead of time for the exchange of gifts, followed by a taffy-pull and caroling around the tree. Loneliness was difficult enough to bear by herself, but a thousand times worse surrounded by all that forced merriment. The girls were laughing and singing and wishing each other and the sisters a Happy Christmas and yet Vicki was positive they were as miserable as she was. During the caroling she slipped out to take a walk.

In the past several days since Marion spoke to her, she hadn't given the nun's suggestion much thought. The Heathfield Sisters were merely an unavoidable part of her day-to-day existence and Vicki paid them in general as little heed as possible. Today, however, she happened to pass the building which housed the school's drama program and for some strange reason–perhaps mere curiosity–she felt compelled to enter. Certainly no one would be there today and pushing open the heavy glass and metal door, she stepped inside.

The theatre was indeed empty, lit only by a few bare light bulbs hanging above the stage. Vicki moved down the aisle and up the stairs. Unerringly she found her way center stage and turning to face the audience, she stood for a long moment looking about her. All at once, still apparently with no conscious volition on her part, she reached out her arms toward the seemingly limitless space as though seeking to embrace an invisible someone or something out there in the darkness. It was precisely at this moment that Sister Marion entered the back of the auditorium. One thing's for certain, the nun mused with a silent chuckle, she's got the ego for it. Something kept her from confronting the girl, however, and she stayed carefully out of sight.

Vicki almost came to the first day's auditions, but then she changed her mind. Since that moment, standing alone on the empty stage, she had come to want a part in the play very much–not just any one of course, but that of Kate Hardcastle, the female lead–and she believed by now that whenever she really desired something, she was doomed to disappointment. Then, too, her pride made it difficult for her to admit to Sister Marion she was even interested.

Sister Philippa was waiting in the back as the last of the would-be actresses left the theatre. Plays were a popular activity since the men's roles were played by boys from the near-by Pritchard School and the convent-educated young ladies of Heathfield hungered for male companionship. Many of the girls spoke to Philippa as they passed, but as carefully as she watched, she didn't see Vicki among them. Not that she would have spoken to me anyway, she thought ruefully. Marion was still gathering her things together and Sister Philippa couldn't help noticing she appeared discouraged. "Didn't Vicki come?" Philippa inquired anxiously.

"Oh, heavens! I'd forgotten all about her. Auditions were a disaster!"

"If she doesn't come tomorrow, I'll speak to her."

"Philippa, my dear, when are you going to learn, she doesn't listen to you?"

The next afternoon's auditions were at first equally discouraging. There were a few new girls, but still no one who read very well. With a sigh Sister Marion finally turned to the young people who were assembled in the first two rows of the auditorium. "Now then, has everyone read who wished to do so?"

There was a moment's silence. "Sister Marion, I would like to read." Even at this comparatively young age, the voice was unmistakable.

"Yes, all right." Marion didn't know whether to be pleased or dismayed.

Everyone turned to watch as Vicki stood up from where she'd been sitting alone about half-way back in the hall and walked toward the stage. No one liked her. She clearly thought she was better than everyone else. Even now as she came to take a copy of the script, she glanced down at the other girls with undisguised disdain. "Where would you like me to read, Sister?"

"Which part were you interested in?"

"Kate." Simply–flatly–as if to say, "Who else?"

"Yes...ah....of course." The nun's mouth twitched. "Well then, Vicki, page 25 where Kate first meets Charles Marlowe. David," she went on to one of the Pritchard boys, "would you read Charles, please?" The young people took their places on stage, opening the playbooks, and Sister Marion settled back for yet another reading of the part of Kate Hardcastle. She'd listened to countless hopefuls butcher a role calling for a charm and sophistication which it was painfully evident none of them possessed. Yet, as she waited for the scene to commence, she felt herself once again tensing, hoping as always that this girl would prove the exception. Then Vicki began to read and suddenly the magic happened– that rare moment of joy in the career of an amateur theatrical director when he or she finds that one extraordinary talent worth all the hours of frustration and unrewarded drudgery. Slowly the script in which she'd intended to follow the scene was lowered to her lap and forgotten as Kate Hardcastle came to life before her eyes: the voice, the inflection–even the stance. It was really unnecessary, but for the sake of appearance she did have her do two more scenes.

"I think that will do, ladies and gentlemen. Thank you." Marion tried to sound matter-of-fact, but she was positive they could all hear the excitement in her voice. "The cast will be posted on the bulletin board outside my office tomorrow morning. Boys, Mr. Leonard will have the male cast members listed." Everyone trooped out–everyone, that is, except Vicki, who was still leafing through the script as she came down the steps leading from the stage. "Vicki, I'd like to speak to you if you have a minute."

"Is it important, Sister? I'd like to get some studying down before tea time."

"Yes, I think it is–rather." Anyone who thinks I cast a girl in my plays because I like her is much mistaken, she thought wryly.

"Very well." Vicki slipped into one of the front row seats, smoothing her blue woolen skirt under her and crossing her legs.

How does she manage to look so lovely in that outfit, the nun's thoughts continued irrelevantly, when it makes every other student appear dumpy and unattractive? "I've decided," she said aloud, quite graciously under the circumstances, "that I would like you to play the role of Kate." Most girls upon hearing they'd been given a part in one of her plays, would grin with delight, perhaps jump up and down; one or two of the less inhibited might even hug her. Many even remembered to thank her. Vicki's response was simply to tilt her head slightly to one side and arch her eyebrows. "Well, do you want the part or not?" Marion was understandably annoyed.

"Yes...all right," she said at last with a brief nod.

"Fine then. Rehearsals begin on Monday."

"I may keep this, I presume?" Vicki indicated the script.

"Yes, but....ah....I would prefer you not mention this to anyone until I post the full cast tomorrow."

"Why did you tell me now then?"

"I...I....just...ah...thought you might like to know."

"I could have waited." She shrugged. "But don't worry. There's no one I'd want to tell anyway." Without another word she stood up and started up the aisle.

"You could tell Sister Philippa," Marion called after her. "She'll be anxious to hear."

The girl paused–one hand on the swinging door leading from the auditorium. She muttered something which sounded suspiciously like "Bugger Sister Philippa!" and giving the heavy old door a shove, she strode on through and disappeared from sight. Sister Marion stared in fascination at the door which continued to swing back and forth as though in shock at such brutal treatment. She chuckled. She knew exactly how the door felt.

As Vicki walked quickly away across the campus, she couldn't help wondering why this moment, which should have been terribly exciting, seemed so empty. Putting her hand in her coat pocket where she'd shoved the script, she pulled out the thin, paper-covered book. Tears welled up in her eyes and with head down so no one who happened to pass her would notice, she half-ran toward her usual sanctuary. At this hour, however, almost everyone was in supervised study and much to her relief she encountered no one. Even the halls and stairways of her old dormitory were deserted. At last she hurried up the final short flight of stairs and pushed open the door to the by-now familiar little attic.

Sinking down on an old wooden packing crate to catch her breath, she looked about the tiny room. I don't think this place has changed since the first time I laid eyes on it, Vicki thought. And suddenly she could see herself as she'd been then–almost half her lifetime ago now–a lonely, unloved child who had sought a place in which to hide from the happiness of others and who had found it in a dusty garret as neglected and forgotten as she was. "And nothing else has changed either," she continued aloud. "I had no one then and I have no one now." She looked down at the script which she still held tightly in one fist. "Oh, dammit all anyway!" She hurled the book against the sloping wall of the attic and burying her head in her hands, she let the tears come.

Moments passed and at last she grew quiet. It was not a natural calm, however, but rather, as was to become increasingly so in the years ahead, an iron-willed self-control. She raised her head, gazing about again at the cramped, low-ceilinged room, and all at once she laughed–a brief, mirthless sound which would have been quite unnerving had anyone been there to hear it. "What in hell am I crying about? I'm going to be an actress and not just any actress but a great actress! Then everyone will want to know me and I can tell them all they can bloody well go to hell!" Vicki laughed again and with a toss of her head she got to her feet and walked over to where the book had landed. Picking it up with both hands, she held it out at arms' length. A half-smile played about her lips. "Well, Victoria Windsor, shall we begin?"

* * *

If Sister Philippa had anticipated that with Vicki's involvement in the school's drama program the girl would become less isolated from the rest of the Heathfield community, it was soon apparent that such hopes were in vain. From the first day of rehearsal she'd showed no interest in making friends with the other members of the cast, on the contrary indicating plainly that she intended to keep herself entirely apart from them. "Couldn't you ask them to include her then?" Philippa had pleaded at one point. "Vicki has never made friends easily, but....but..." she hurried on to add, ignoring Sister Marion's derisive snort, "but perhaps if someone else made the initial overtures......"

"No, I <u>can't</u> do that. <u>They</u> don't like her either," had been the other nun's acid reply. "Her superior attitude is insufferable. Whenever I ask her to repeat a scene for the benefit of another actor, she sighs or groans or mutters some choice bit of profanity just loud enough for me to hear it. I'll say one thing–working with Vicki has certainly enlarged my vocabulary!"

"I suppose it's because she's so much better than the others."

"Oh yes, she's good, probably the best <u>I'll</u> ever have, but that doesn't excuse her behavior. No professional director will put up with her, no matter how talented she is."

Philippa, of course, chose to hear only part of this. "Then you feel she's good enough to act professionally? My word! And just think–you'll be able to say you discovered her!"

"That I will," Sister Marion agreed with a chuckle. "Unless I kill her first!"

It was about two weeks before the dates of performance–just as rehearsal was concluding for the day–that matters came to a climax. "That will be all, everyone," Marion was saying, "except for Kate and Charles. I'd like to try that last scene just once more."

"Oh, God!" Vicki groaned.

"Young lady, I've asked you not to talk like that!"

"Excuse me, Sister Marion. I didn't know <u>He</u> was listening!"

"Vicki!—Never mind, David. I think perhaps I should speak to your co-star alone."

"All right, Sister. Good-bye, Sister." Hurriedly the boy gathered up his books and jacket, relieved to make his escape.

Vicki sat down in one of the armchairs already in place on the stage, making no attempt to hide her annoyance. With a sigh Sister Marion picked up another smaller chair and turned it to face her. She wondered wryly how Job and his proverbial patience would have fared if confronted with this young woman. "Well, now," she said at last, "I am waiting for an apology."

"Then you're going to have a long wait, Sister. I have done nothing for which I feel I should apologize."

"In that case, unfortunately, I will have no choice but to remove you from the cast."

For a second or two Vicki almost panicked. The play meant far more to her than anyone realized. Then immediately she saw how empty the threat was and it was all she could do not to laugh in the nun's face. "Now you know you don't want to do that." A mocking smile did play briefly across her lips. "I'm the only one in the cast with any real talent and you couldn't possibly replace me, now could you?" Without waiting for a reply she stood up to leave.

"I am not through with you!"

"Sod off!" Vicki turned on her heel and walked off the stage.

Sister Marion knew the girl should not be allowed to get away with such behavior; that she should be severely punished for her disrespect alone–not to mention the profanity. But at the same time she knew that unfortunately Vicki had spoken the truth and oh dear, how often did she find someone so gifted? It bothered Marion a little that by failing to report a student for disciplinary action, she was putting the play ahead of her responsibilities as a teacher. She spent a sleepless night thinking about it, but finally she said a prayer asking God to forgive her for the sin of pride and she decided to ignore the whole incident as if it had never happened.

Only one time in the weeks remaining before performance was she required to speak to Vicki directly and this was to check her name as it would appear in the cast list: "Kate Hardcastle.......Vicki Windsor." Years later Marion could still picture the girl as she studied the rough draft of the program. "Excuse me, Sister." It seemed as though the idea had just occurred to her. "I believe I prefer Victoria."

"Good heavens!" Sister Marion suddenly realized a few seconds later. "She was choosing her stage name!"

* * *

She Stoops to Conquer was performed three times: Friday and Saturday evenings and Sunday afternoon and after each of the first two performances all anyone talked about was Victoria Windsor. Vicki had dreamed what it would be like–being an actress– but she'd never imagined it would happen so soon. She had thought the adulation would begin only when she became famous, but here she had performed in just one amateur production and suddenly the nuns as well as her fellow students were showering her with praise. Most incredible of all, she also discovered–much to her relief–was that such worship did not require that she be pleasant in return. People were actually in awe of her, approaching deferentially to offer their congratulations and moving immediately away again. A mere regal nod of the head was sufficient acknowledgment on her part.

She only wished that the third and final performance was not being presented especially for the parents. Those silly people would only be interested in their own son or daughter while her talents would go unnoticed. What actually distressed her, of course, although she never would have admitted it even to herself, was that she would have no one there. She hadn't even told her parents about the play. It seemed pointless when she knew neither of them would come and afterwards at the special dinner in honor of the cast, their families and guests she would as usual be alone. "But what can I expect after all?" She laughed aloud at that–the same short, harsh laugh. "No one gives a damn about me. I should know that by now."

Vicki was wrong, however. There were at least two people who did indeed "give a damn". Suspecting that her friend would be alone after the Sunday matinee, Pamela had suggested a small private celebration: cake and ice cream, perhaps, and some gifts. Philippa, despite serious doubts as to how Vicki would receive such a gesture, agreed. They'd also decided to attend the performance together, feeling somehow that with them present Vicki would have family in the audience whether she was aware of it or not.

"Sister," Pamela whispered at one point, "did Vicki ask anyone to come?"

"I don't know that anymore than you do, dear." And the sadness in her tone was evident.

Closing at the end of the third act, the curtain reopened almost at once for the curtain calls. Cast members, entering one by one and bowing, were greeted with generous applause, but when Vicki came on stage, the applause became an ovation. Standing alone center stage, much as Sister Marion had first seen her two months before, she acknowledged the accolade with a low, sweeping curtsey. Philippa wondered sorrowfully at the girl's stunning self-assurance. At her young age it simply wasn't natural. The orgy of applause and curtsey, applause and curtsey continued on and on until she was certain she couldn't stand another minute of it. When at long last the curtain swished shut for the final time, the nun realized with a start that she'd been holding her breath.

"Are we going up on the stage, Sister?" Pamela inquired at once. "To see Vicki?"

"Yes, I suppose so." A good part of the audience had already begun to file down toward the front of the auditorium and somewhat reluctantly Philippa stood up, leading the way out into the aisle to follow them. By the time they'd finally made their way up onto the stage, however, it was thronged with people–every member of the cast and crew surrounded by family and friends–and there was no sign of Vicki. "I don't see her anywhere, Pamela." Secretly she was relieved. "Why don't we wait until the dinner and then we can......"

Just then she felt a sharp tug on the sleeve of her habit. "Oh, Sister, look!" Pamela whispered, nodding her head toward the rear of the stage.

Turning, Sister Philippa saw Vicki standing alone in a far corner of the set. A short while before the crowd had held her in the center of the stage with their applause, refusing to let her go; ironically now this same crowd had pushed her to one side. Indeed she was unaware anyone was paying her the slightest notice and as she stood there watching everyone else being hugged and kissed, her face openly betrayed her unhappiness. "Hello, dear," Philippa said quietly. At the sound of the gentle voice Vicki jumped.

"Oh, Vicki, you were super!" Impulsively Pamela threw her arms around her old friend.

"Please don't!" She pushed her away.

"We just wanted to tell you how proud we are of you, dear," Philippa continued as casually as she could, "and to ask you to have dinner with us."

Vicki turned slowly to look at Sister Philippa, a strained expression passing over her face, and for a few seconds she made no reply. She had, in fact, about decided not to attend the dinner even though it meant missing out on all the praise she would receive once everyone was through making such a fuss over those untalented dolts with whom she'd been forced to share the stage. Now here were two people wanting to be with her because they truly cared about her yet instead of being touched, or at the very least relieved, she felt only a choking panic. Her glance traveled from Sister Philippa to Pamela and back to Philippa again. "Well, I...I....all right...yes, I suppose so," she said finally.

"Do you want us to wait for you, Vicki?" Pamela asked.

"N....no." She shook her head and Philippa saw that same peculiar look–like a cornered animal, she thought suddenly–and this frightened her. "No," Vicki said again after a slight pause. "I....I have to change and...and take off my make-up. I'll...I'll meet you in the dining room." She somehow managed to slip by without having to touch either one of them and disappeared into the wings.

Philippa put an arm around Pamela's waist to draw her off the stage as well, back down the stairs leading into the auditorium and up the aisle toward the exit. "You know, dear, I wonder if perhaps this might not be the best time to give Vicki our presents. She's probably overtired and if we waited a few days...."

"No, Sister, I want to do it tonight–the way we planned." Pamela was as always polite, but there was a firmness in her tone Philippa couldn't help noticing. The girl had certainly changed in her years at Heathfield in more than merely physical appearance although the plain child had grown into a charmingly gamin-like young woman, contact lenses replacing the glasses.

"You're quite sure then, dear," the nun persisted gently, "no matter how Vicki responds?"

"No matter how–to...to let her know I'm still her friend."

Vicki was very late arriving at the dining hall. Everyone was in fact seated, the first course already being served, and she had yet to put in an appearance. Sister Marion was returning to her place after greeting the parents and other guests and as she passed their table, Philippa called her over. "Would you happen to know where Vicki is? We were to have dinner with her."

"Oh, she'll be here," Marion observed wryly. "I wouldn't worry about that. She's just waiting to make an entrance." Just then there was a burst of applause and the three of them looked up to discover Vicki standing in the doorway. "See what I mean! And now if you'll excuse me, I'm sure our star would not be pleased to find me here." Chuckling, she moved off around the edge of the room.

Vicki, meanwhile, was finally making her way through the crowd toward them, occasionally acknowledging the applause with a nod of her head. Without a word of explanation for her lateness she slipped into her chair and picking up her soup spoon, started to eat. The awkward silence continued all through the meal as she spoke only when absolutely necessary: to respond to someone who stopped at the table to compliment her on her performance or to reply to a direct question on the part of one of her dining companions. Even then she used the fewest words possible. When at last–mercifully–the meal was over, Pamela looked inquiringly at Sister Philippa.

The nun offered up a brief silent prayer. Aloud she said, "Vicki, we've planned a little party in your honor–nothing elaborate–just the three of us in my room."

"I'm really frightfully tired. If you don't mind, I'd rather not...ah...thank you."

"But, Vicki....." Her longtime friend's disappointment was evident.

"I think what she wants to say," Philippa interposed, "is that we have some simple remembrances for you and we were counting on your coming–at least for a bit." But the strain showed clearly on the girl's lovely face and watching her, Sister Philippa decided it might be wiser to cancel the celebration. Pamela would be disappointed, but the events of the "party" might hurt her far worse. "Of course, dear, we'll understand if you......."

"Well–all right," she suddenly heard Vicki say, "but I can't stay."

The walk across campus had never seemed so long to Philippa even though Vicki hurried on ahead as if she could somehow accelerate the whole process. Inside the room Pamela went at once to the small writing desk where the wrapped packages lay waiting. "You first, Sister," she said although she was obviously eager to give hers.

"Thank you, Pamela." Philippa picked up a prettily wrapped jewellery box.

During this brief exchange Vicki had stood in the middle of the room, nervously twisting a ring around and around on one of her fingers–looking everywhere but at them. Now she received Sister Philippa's gift with an all but inaudible "thank you". Tearing off the paper and ribbon, she dropped the wrappings on the floor, removing the cover just far enough to see the simple bangle bracelet inside. "Oh, that's very nice," she said, immediately replacing the lid and shoving it into her jacket pocket.

"Here." Pamela held the box out to her with both hands. "I...I hope you like it. I tried to find something special." Vicki accepted the package readily enough, but then for a moment she simply stared at it. At least the nun's present had been safe, but this was supposed to be "something special". Sister Philippa watched anxiously as the girl opened the second gift and fumbling with the white tissue paper, revealed a pale pink china figurine. "Take it out, please," Pamela directed quietly.

She removed the object as had been requested, but her hands were trembling and the nun could see tears in her eyes. She wants to care, Philippa thought--if only she could let herself. "What is it?" Vicki laughed nervously. "Two hands?"

"Turn it around," the other girl urged now. "Look at the front."

After a brief hesitation Vicki again did as she'd been asked, it now becoming evident that the figure, in actuality, depicted a handclasp. On its base was the one word: "Friends". "Oh no! Oh no! Why....why do you do this to me?" she exclaimed shaking her head, her voice choked with emotion. "I'm not your friend! I never was! Here.....here, take it....please....please!" She shoved the figurine at Pamela who--startled--failed to grasp it. It crashed to the floor between them. For just a moment Vicki still stood there. Then she turned and fled.

Briefly it was as though Pamela and Sister Philippa had themselves become statues. But at last Philippa went over to where the shattered gift lay on the floor and kneeling down, she began to gently pick up the pieces–one at a time. "You know, I really think this could be mended so that you won't even be able to tell it had been broken."

"No, Sister, I don't think it can be." Pamela smiled wistfully. "Thank you anyway. I'm going to leave now, too, if you don't mind."

"Please stay, dear. We'll.....we'll talk. Don't leave when you're so upset."

"Dear Sister Philippa," the girl whispered tearfully, coming to kneel beside her and rest one hand on her arm. "It's all right. Really it is. I've just finally learned my lesson, that's all. Good night, Sister." And with a quick hug she also left, closing the door behind her.

Alone, Philippa carried the broken pieces over to her desk and painstakingly glued them together again. Later when the cement was dry, she wrapped the figurine in the same tissue paper and placing it tenderly back in its box, she put it away on the shelf of her closet. She would leave it there, she thought, until the day came when Vicki might at last be able to accept it.

* * *

For Vicki, however, the incident of the figurine was all but forgotten in the nearly unbearable let-down she experienced in the days immediately following. More than she realized the play had filled, if only partly, the emptiness in her life. Each day there was a rehearsal to attend where for a few hours while she was pretending to be Kate Hardcastle, she could almost forget how lonely it was to be Victoria Windsor. Even at other moments when she would happen to see a group of girls gathered together–laughing about something and pointedly excluding her–she could tell herself she had lines to memorize and didn't have time for such adolescent foolishness. Most marvelous of all, of course, had been the actual performances–each culminating in the ovation she was sure was meant only for her. It seemed as though the applause would never cease, but inevitably it had, leaving only silence. And what was silence but a void and what was a void but emptiness and emptiness was once again nothing but loneliness–a loneliness far deeper and more profound that anything she had known before. And trapped as she was once again in the numbing Heathfield routine, her dream of one day becoming a celebrated actress seemed impossibly remote.

Then quite unexpectedly one day that dream was given new life. Sister Marion's class in English literature was to go to London to see Cartier's new production of Shakespeare's *The Tempest*. Even with what was at this point a limited acquaintance with the theatre, Vicki was aware of the name of Sir Terence Cartier. Sister Marion had shown them his classic films of *Hamlet, Richard III and Henry V* and she knew he was considered one of the world's foremost Shakespearean actors. Now she would actually see him perform in person. The excursion was on the whole a solitary experience for Vicki, sitting by herself on the train to London reading, eating her lunch in silence down at one end of the table, but on this particular afternoon it didn't matter. She was living only for the moment when the curtain would rise.

Something special and indefinable takes place in a theatre in that instant just prior to the start of a performance. As the house lights dim, the conversations die out and a hush falls over the audience–an all, but imperceptible pause during which members of that audience shift their individual minds from the everyday world of their separate existences to the world of make-believe. For that is what the theatre is, after all: a glorious place where people come to suspend willingly their disbelief, accepting whatever they see on the stage, however improbable it may be, as reality.

How Vicki despised the noise, the bustle, the meaningless chatter all about her. She was positive no other person in the audience truly comprehended or appreciated what was about to happen and she knew more surely than ever that it would never be enough for her to be sitting in the audience–that where she belonged was on the other side of the curtain, tensed and waiting for the moment she would feel the hot, blinding stage lights full on her face. At last the house lights did indeed dim and the curtain, barely visible now in the darkness, glided noiselessly upward and out of sight. "The theatre is where I belong," Vicki whispered to herself in that moment, "but where do I start? How do I start? I know so little and I'm damned if I'll ask Sister Marion. I bloody well wouldn't give her the satisfaction!"

As her attention became caught up in the performance, however, she stopped thinking, at least for a while, about her own theatrical career. True she'd seen films, even Sir Terence's own productions, of the works of Shakespeare. But nothing had prepared her for seeing living actors on a stage, for having them speak the lovely, musical words even as she was hearing them. Most of all the screen couldn't possibly do full justice to Cartier's genius and from his first entrance Vicki found herself gripped by his consummate skill as an actor.

The Tempest is believed to have been Shakespeare's final play and in one particular speech by the magical Prospero it seems as though the Bard is also saying good-bye.

Prospero: Our revels now are ended. These our actors,
As I foretold you, were all spirits and
Are melted into air, into thin air;
And, like the baseless fabric of this vision,
The cloud-capp'd towers, the gorgeous palaces,
The solemn temples, the great globe itself,
Yea, all which it inherit, shall dissolve
And, like this insubstantial pageant faded,
Leave not a rack behind. We are such stuff
As dreams are made on, and our little life
Is rounded with a sleep.
The Tempest, William Shakespeare, Act IV, Scene 1, Lines 148-158.

Sir Terence's voice seemed to caress the beautiful words and Vicki could hear throats being surreptitiously cleared, noses quietly blown, an audible sniff somewhere behind her. What must it be like to have the power to move an audience in that way? To do so she had to be more than merely another actress; she had to be the best–to one day deserve the privilege of standing side by side with Sir Terence on the stage, his equal in stature and reputation, but how?

The performance concluded and as the actors took their curtain calls, Vicki joined in the applause with a fervor which would have astounded anyone who knew her at all– applause which culminated in a standing ovation for Sir Terence. The let-down as the house lights came up, however, was just as agonizing from this side of the curtain. The play was once again over and all she had was her dream–stronger and brighter than ever perhaps-- but still only a dream. Before she or anyone else in her group could begin to leave, however, Sister Marion stood up at her seat. "Please stay where you are, girls. I have what I think will be a wonderful surprise for you."

A man came out on the apron of the stage. "Good afternoon," he said agreeably enough to the several students groups remaining in their seats. "My name is Pliny Nicholas and I am the assistant artistic director here at the Royal Shakespeare Company. Some of our cast have agreed to talk to you so get your questions ready. I must remind you, nevertheless, that this is a privilege and you should act accordingly."

"Aren't some people a royal pain?" Vicki heard someone behind her remark.

She turned on the unlucky girl. "Well, it is a privilege so shut up!"

Several people came out to sit informally along the edge of the stage, but Vicki's excitement really began to build as she saw that Sir Terence himself was among them. As the senior member of the company, it was he who opened the question and answer session. "Please feel free to ask any of us whatever you wish." He smiled warmly to put them at their ease. "And believe me, it is we who are privileged to talk to you so don't allow Mr. Nicholas to intimidate you."

"There you see!" the girl behind Vicki hooted.

"He's simply being gracious, you little twit!" But the first question was already being asked and she turned her attention back to the stage.

The questioning had gone on for nearly half an hour covering a wide range of topics from the characterization of various roles to the staging of a scene to the meaning and interpretation of a particular line. What better opportunity would she ever have to inquire about a career in the theatre, Vicki thought, and who could possibly be more qualified to answer her than Sir Terence Cartier? At last there was a lull and she raised her hand.

"Yes." Pliny Nicholas pointed to her. "The young lady on the aisle."

"Thank you." She stood up. She was the first to do so. "I'd like to ask Sir Terence a question, if I may." Neither had anyone had the temerity to address the revered actor directly and all eyes turned to her. A distinct murmuring could be heard among the Heathfield students. "Guess who?!....You might know!....."Who else would have the nerve?!"

"Yes?" Sir Terence smiled pleasantly.

"I was wondering what made you decide to become an actor?"

"Well, theatre was a great love of my parents even though they were not professionally involved in it themselves. I've been attending plays ever since I can remember."

Before anyone else could raise a hand, Vicki continued. "What is the best training for an actor? I mean–is a drama school a good idea or is it simply better to get as much practical experience as possible?"

It was obvious to Sir Terence by now that this young lady was no idle questioner and he thought for a minute before replying. "The theatre is like any profession," he said at last. "Some training in your craft is advisable–a good drama school where you will have the opportunity to learn movement, voice, etc."

"Is there a particular one you would recommend, sir?"

"The Royal Academy of Dramatic Art, perhaps, or the Central School is also excellent. Are you by any chance planning on being an actress?"

"Yes, sir, I am."

"Well, perhaps we'll be working together some day," Sir Terence observed charmingly.

"Maybe we will."

He chuckled a little. "I suppose you should tell me your name then so I'll remember you."

"Victoria Windsor, sir."

There was something in the way she said her name that made Sir Terence stop his pleasant banter and look at her intently. She was entirely in earnest

Chapter 6

Vicki was indeed in earnest. She <u>was</u> going to be an actress and she needed to plan accordingly. Her first move, she decided, must be to change to a school in or near London where she would be able to see a great deal of theatre and perhaps even begin acquiring the training Sir Terence Cartier had recommended. At Heathfield there would be nothing but the semi-annual plays–no classes in drama at all–and she was certain at any rate that Sister Marion had nothing further to teach her. Unfortunately changing schools would require the permission of one of her parents–bloody stupid rule, that!

Since she could apparently do nothing about the situation, however, she finally decided on her father–not that she cared any more for him; she had, in fact, barely given him a thought since the morning she fled the hotel in Nice over four years before. With a sigh of resignation she took a sheet of stationery out of her desk drawer. "Dear Papa...." But that was all she wrote. Dear Papa–to a man who'd made a mockery of both words. Crumbling up the first sheet, she threw it on the floor and took another one. After all, she thought, there's no need to make a total ass of myself.

Dear Father, (she wrote this second time)

I would like your permission to change schools. I have become interested in the theatre and I would prefer to be in or near London where I'd have the opportunity to see some plays and perhaps even take some acting classes. I would like to make the change for the fall term.

Thank you very much,
Victoria

Malcolm found the cold formality of the letter insulting and the mere idea of a daughter of his in the theatre appalling. His answer came from his solicitor.

Dear Vicki,

Your father has asked me to inform you that changing schools is out of the question. He does not, moreover, consider the theatre to be a suitable profession for a well-brought up young lady and he suggests you find an interest more in keeping with your station in life.

Sincerely yours,
Nigel Bascombe

"Damn!" Vicki wadded the letter into a ball and dropped it into her wastepaper basket. "Damn! <u>Damn</u>! <u>DAMN</u>! What bloody right does he have to tell me what to do? And why in God's name did I mention the theatre!" Briefly she considered trying her "dear" mother, but realized almost at once that ironically this was one subject on which they'd agree. Well, she would simply have to force them to give their consent. But how? There seemed to be no solution until one evening at dinner Vicki overheard a conversation between two girls at the next table; apparently they were discussing a friend of theirs.

"They're sending her to a different school?"

"Yes," the other girl replied. "Mother Geraldine's expelled her and her parents are going to transfer her to another school as far away from <u>him</u> as possible."

Vicki's mind raced. What could the girl have done? Staying out after hours only meant probation. Then she heard, "Well, you have to admire her–doing it right in the dormitory!" So that's it, Vicki thought exultantly a little later as she walked back to her dormitory! All I have to do is get caught with a boy in my room and Heathfield will expel me! Then my parents will have to send me to another school! And just think of the expression on Mother Geraldine's face!

Settling herself cross-legged in the middle of her bed, she opened a book. If anyone from whom she privately referred to as the "Holy Gestapo" checked on her, she would appear to be studying. "Operation Break-out" hit an immediate snag, however. She didn't <u>know</u> any boys. Her only regular contact with males except at play rehearsals were those horribly awkward tea dances with the Pritchard School. Now she needed a boy in her room and where was she going to find him?

Vicki took every opportunity to get off the school grounds and on Saturday afternoons she'd walk into the village to buy cigarettes or make-up, both of which were, of course, forbidden. In fact she had <u>started</u> to smoke expressly because it <u>was</u> forbidden. And so it happened that on the following Saturday she was strolling as usual along one of the main streets of Tetbury when suddenly she remembered Teddy. He was a local boy, an apprentice chemist apparently only a few years older than she and with an unfortunately prominent nose, but a fairly clear complexion. Easier to handle certainly than a more sophisticated Pritchard boy and she'd noticed him eyeing her in the shop although her Heathfield blazer had thus far kept him at bay.

Characteristically she put her plan into immediate action, going into the shop for a soda. Step #1 turned out to be ridiculously simple–a little casual conversation, one or two flutters of her illicitly mascaraed eyelashes and Teddy was spilling cherry syrup and dropping dishes–his bony Adam's apple leaping wildly. If this was all it required to fluster a male, Vicki thought, they must all be entirely stupid. He finally worked up the nerve to invite her to the cinema, but with an adorable pout she refused, blaming the strictness of the Sisters.

Step #2–Her suggestion that instead he come to the monthly Sunday afternoon tea dance being held at Heathfield the following week. He seemed just as flattered as she'd hoped he would be. Things were progressing nicely.

Vicki dressed for the dance with elaborate care–wondering how much make-up she could get away with. It was essential for her purposes that she appear worldly and sophisticated yet at the same time she couldn't risk having one of the sisters send her back to her room to "wash that filthy paint off your sweet, young face". I am definitely <u>not</u> sweet, she thought to herself, and I don't believe I was ever young.

A short time later, however, as she came downstairs to find Teddy waiting for her in the entrance hall grinning broadly, she came close to abandoning the whole idea. He was wearing a pink and purple plaid sports jacket, purple trousers, both of which were one or two sizes too short for him and the worst possible bow tie: iridescent pink polka dots against a purple background–- all color coordinated, you see, except for his brown shoes and white socks. She complimented him on his appearance and he blushed with pleasure. The outfit, it seemed, had been his older brother's, but "just like new and ever so swish," he thought. Well, after all, what did she care how foolish he looked. He was her ticket out of here. And as they entered the school gymnasium a short while later, she ignored the meaningful glances and openly derisive laughter of the other girls. The young apprentice chemist, meanwhile, stared about him goggle-eyed. Heathfield! Coo, weren't he the posh one though? Poor Teddy–he was only the first of the many males Victoria would use and discard.

Step #3 was the refreshment stand where the pink, watery punch they invariably served would provide her with the perfect cue and Vicki at once led the way there. Shyly she let it slip that she had something stronger in her room–genuine Scotch whiskey suitable for a "real man".

She had thought for a moment that Pamela was going to give her some trouble with Step #4–the dispatching of Sister Marion to their room at just the right moment. She supposed that was to be expected; they had barely spoken since the incident of the figurine. But the other girl finally agreed.

Once in the room, however, she nearly panicked. Teddy's sweaty hands were all over her, his open-mouthed, sucking kisses sounding unnaturally loud in the otherwise empty room. And what she had sold as "real Scotch" was in reality a mixture of two or three kinds of cough medicine with a few drops of rubbing alcohol for odor. Vicki held her breath as he raised the tumbler to his lips, but before he could take a drink, a knock came at the door. Years later she could still see Teddy's face at that moment– eyes almost popping out of his head, Adam's apple at last gone berserk and carrying the hideous bow tie along with it as though the two had somehow become miraculously joined.

The next morning as expected she was indeed summoned to Mother Geraldine's office. But from there on things did not go as planned. Her father, it seemed, had prevailed upon the school to give her six months' probation rather than expel her. "How much money did he give you, Mother Geraldine?" Vicki inquired bluntly.

"I have no idea what you mean, young woman!"

Vicki snorted. "No, of course you don't!"

Cruelest of all, perhaps, probation included a ban on all extra-curricular activities which would prohibit her from appearing in the fall production.

What could she do, Vicki asked herself, walking across campus from her interview with Mother Geraldine. What could she possibly do? It was late that sleepless night or rather early the next morning when the answer came to her. She sat up in bed. "Of course," she whispered excitedly, "how stupid of me! I've still been thinking like a child. I don't need any more schools–not like Heathfield anyway; what I <u>need</u> is to begin my training as an actress!" And so the solution was simple. When she was ready, she would just disappear. But when and how?

The first thing she had to decide was when. Then she could hide a calendar somewhere on which to mark off the days–to be able to say to herself only four months left or three weeks or two or one and finally to count the time in days. It took only a few minutes, in fact, for her to settle on one year, a nice even-sounding period of time–long enough to save a certain amount of money from her allowance and just short enough, perhaps, to be bearable.

<u>How</u> she would effect her escape turned out to be more of a problem. Running away from Heathfield where so many people knew and mistrusted her would be difficult. It would be easier to slip away unnoticed from her summer camp except for the fact that Camp Bureside, the Girl Guides sailing camp near Great Yarmouth which she'd attended now for the past two summers, was in the area traversed by the Norfolk Broads. The only direct route to and from the camp was by water and walking out to a main road carrying her luggage would allow them too much time to catch her up.

Then she remembered the day and a half spent traveling between school and camp when there was no one but Carleton to watch her. Furthermore, they customarily spent the night in Peterborough, surely a large enough town to have a railway station. On the way back to school that fall it was ridiculously easy to slip away after dinner to do a little reconnoitering. Proper British servant that he was, Carleton never sat with her at meals. She located the station without any problem–only two blocks from the hotel–and even picked up a train schedule. Returning to the hotel, she found him nervously pacing the lobby. She experienced a brief pang as she wondered what he'd do when she disappeared for real. But then it was her whole future at stake; she couldn't worry about the chauffeur. Back at Heathfield she carefully hid the train schedule and an extra copy of the school calendar under the clothes in her bottom drawer. Ten months to go and the time until then she would use to prepare.

Vicki could never be sure which had come first: her love of the theatre in general or the works of William Shakespeare in particular. She'd been one of the few students who genuinely enjoyed *As You Like It*, the first Shakespearean play they'd read in Sister Marion's lit class. That had been over a year before her acting debut in *She Stoops to Conquer*, but her deep and abiding passion for the Elizabethan playwright had only really been born with Cartier's performance in *The Tempest*. Whichever the order of her infatuation, it was after that she'd purchased a copy of the complete works of Shakespeare, beginning at once to read it through. The language was difficult at first, but she refused to give up. Now to the Shakespeare she added the playwrights available in the Heathfield library, quite a good selection actually.. With single-minded determination Vicki proceeded to read her way through the alphabet–from the American Albee to the Irishman, Yeats.

The one bright spot in the year was the school's spring production in which, her probation over, she was allowed to take part. Sister Marion knew it might be one of her few chances to attempt anything of this difficulty and she'd chosen *Romeo and Juliet*. Victoria's Juliet–her first Shakespearean role–would still be talked about years later.

* * *

She wondered afterwards why Carleton failed to find her behavior suspicious when he arrived to drive her to camp the following June. To hide her nervousness she chatted merrily away to him–quite unlike her customary stony silence. He did appear somewhat puzzled when she insisted on having all her luggage in her hotel room that night, but of course he would never have dreamed of questioning her.

The first train out of Peterborough for London was at 5:35 a.m.–plenty of time since Carleton never ate breakfast before seven. Still she held her breath. What if this one morning he got up early? The lobby was deserted, however, and by 5:20 she had bought her one-way ticket as well as a London newspaper and was waiting on the platform. It was not until many years later, not that she'd have cared at the time, that Vicki learned she had cost the chauffeur his job. For now at any rate all she could think was that at any moment she would see Carleton coming across the street after her and dammit, wouldn't you just know the bloody train would be late by nearly forty-five minutes.

Just as it seemed she could stand the suspense no longer, the train pulled in, she was on it and it was beginning to move. Vicki sat very still, gripping her handbag and the volume of Shakespeare in her lap. Feeling the train gather speed, she waited for the burst of elation she must certainly experience at finally being free. But nothing happened--- nothing–and vaguely she wondered what was wrong. At last she gave up and with a brisk shake of her head at her own silliness she turned her attention to more important matters. She still had part of Lady Macbeth's speech to memorize and she had no idea when the Royal Academy of Dramatic Art held its auditions. She also had the newspaper adverts to peruse in two particular categories: rooms to let and job openings: female.

* * *

As Vicki had not given a thought to Carleton, neither did it occur to her that for someone else her disappearance would be a far greater heartbreak.

"Tell me, dear Lord," Sister Philippa prayed fervently, "was I guilty of the sin of pride–to believe that I and I alone could reach her? Perhaps I was, but oh, I wanted so to help her. Now I finally have no choice.I must relinquish her in Your care and I take great comfort in the knowledge that although I may never see her again, she will never be out of Your sight.

"I accept that You in Your infinite wisdom understand far better than I what is best for Vicki. I do, however, have one prayer of intercession to offer on her behalf. It is a prayer I will continue to carry in my heart until somehow I learn it has been granted. Dear Father of us all, may she one day find the love she has never known; may someone else succeed where I have miserably failed."

* * *

No wonder the train had been late. It stopped at every village and the trip, which should only have taken two hours, required more than three. Thus it was nearly 9:30 a.m. when she stepped onto the platform at King's Cross Station, feeling vaguely there should have been some sort of welcoming ceremony. After all she was now an official resident of London! London.... London.....London! Chanting the magical word to herself over and over again, she made her way through the crowded, noisy station and out onto the street. After waiting and hoping for what had seemed like forever, she could hardly believe she was really here and for a few seconds she stood in the middle of the pavement staring at the people, the traffic, the buildings--even closing her eyes briefly to listen to the magnificent roaring clamor of it all.

Vicki was too sensible, however, to allow this euphoria to continue for long–the most pressing requirements being first a place to live and then a job. Her study of the adverts had not been encouraging. Flats were horribly expensive which left that peculiarly British institution: the bed-and-breakfast–no kitchen facilities or private bath, although apropos of its name she would receive her morning meal. Even worse the only jobs for which she was at all qualified were humiliatingly menial.

Well, the first absolute necessity, she thought now, was a roof over her head--at least for the night. For nearly two hours she trudged the streets around King's Cross, her shoulder bag hung around her neck and a suitcase in each hand, but every place she tried was either too expensive or they questioned her age. Her shoulder and neck muscles ached and she was getting a blister on one hand.

At last she approached a door with a rusty knocker in the shape of a man's face. At first it was funny; the man who answered the door looked just like the knocker: stringy shoulder length hair and his beard and moustache even looked rusty, streaked yellow as they were from chewing tobacco. Vicki's amusement was short-lived. The man wore a faded cotton bathrobe over a stained undershirt and all the time he talked to her he was continually reaching inside the robe to scratch his bony chest. Even his smile, more a smirk actually, struck her as obscene.

Suddenly London no longer seemed so thrilling and backing away from the door, she hurried away down the stairs. His high-pitched cackle followed her as she half-ran along the sidewalk, her suitcases banging against her legs and the shoulder strap of her purse threatening to strangle her. She didn't know why she was frightened. He hadn't actually said or done anything remotely suggestive. But she didn't stop until she'd turned the corner onto the main street again and then only to lean against a building and catch her breath. She noticed the street sign above her head–Euston Road. It was a while before she could move forward again, this time at a more normal pace. She wasn't sure exactly where she was heading; she was just walking, but after several minutes she became aware she was across from the train station again. So she had come full circle. What am I going to do, she thought. Briefly her courage deserted her and all she wanted to do was sit down on the curb and cry.

And perhaps she might have done exactly that if just then she hadn't happened to notice she was passing a pub and realized how hungry she was. It was no wonder. The last thing she'd had to eat was the stale bun washed down with weak, lukewarm tea in the Peterborough station. On this warm day in late June the double swinging doors of the pub stood open and Vicki caught a glimpse of bare floors and red painted tables and chairs. The cheerful, homelike atmosphere beckoned to her.

She had made a lucky choice. There was hardly anyone who lived or worked in the area or who even passed through on his way to or from King's Cross who didn't know "Danny's" or more particularly its warm-hearted proprietor. Dan Lester's father had been the first "Danny" and he himself had been born in the same flat upstairs where he and his wife now lived with their own two children. His only disappointment in life was that these two children were daughters and there would thus be no third generation "Danny" to carry on the family business. He didn't let even that bother him for long, however. Besides he openly and unabashedly adored his little girls.

A lifetime of enjoying first his mother's and now his wife's cooking plus an inordinate fondness for his own ale had long since cost Dan his youthful figure, but his ample girth only served to endear him all the more to his loyal clientele. If your wife or husband had left you, if you'd lost your job, if you were sick or even just lonely, you could count on Danny's sympathy. No matter what your problem, his eyes would grow moist, his double chin quiver with emotion; his pudgy hand would pat you on the arm and there would be a drink or a free meal or just a caring heart to cheer you.

It was still a little early for the regular lunch crowd and Dan was alone in the pub setting up glasses behind the bar when Victoria entered. At the sound of her footsteps he looked up and at once bustled over to take her suitcases and put them off to one side. "Just h'off the train, are you then, miss?" he inquired in a broad Cockney accent, his genial face wreathed in smiles. He even conducted her to a table and pulled out a chair for her. "Feelin' a bit peckish, I should h'imagine. Steak-and-kidney pie–specialty of me missus–comes 'ighly recommended."

Steak-and kidney pie–she hadn't had any for so long and she could almost feel herself salivating. But she knew anything that substantial would be well beyond her budget. Actually she should probably skip lunch altogether. "I'm sure it's delicious," she replied briskly, "but I have to watch my weight."

Poor little thing, Dan thought–h'aint got 'ardly a bob to 'er name, I wager. "Out in the world on your own then, ducks?"

"Why did you ask me that?" Instantly she was on her guard.

"Aaaooooow, don't tike it the wrong way, luv. You see, I got me a daughter only a bit younger than you and I........"

"How old is your daughter? I"m eighteen."

"You are? Coo, well as I was h'about to say, you don't look much older than my Betsey and she h'aint thirteen yet."

"Well, you're wrong. I'll.....I'll have a liverwurst sandwich and a lemon squash."

"Yes, miss. I'll fetch it right away, miss." All alone, Dan thought to himself shaking his head as he pushed open the swinging door into the kitchen and not very 'appy it h'appears to me.

"H'anything I can do, luv?" his wife inquired, glancing affectionately at him from where she stood at the enormous old black iron stove stirring a huge kettle of her homemade soup. Mrs. Lester's Scotch broth was as justifiably famous and equally in demand as her steak-and-kidney pie. In the rush of steam escaping from the kettle her thin, brown hair had formed a mass of damp curls against her red, shiny face and Dan thought fondly how beautiful she was.

"I tell you," he muttered, yanking open the door of the fridge. "I just don't know what this 'ere world is comin' to, I don't!" He took out the makings of the sandwich and the pitcher of lemon squash, carrying them over to the counter to work. Mrs. Lester was fully accustomed to her husband's peculiar habit of never giving a direct reply to a question and she smiled indulgently, knowing also he would eventually answer her. And indeed he did so just a few seconds later even as the thought crossed her mind. "No, luv," he tossed back over his shoulder as he made the sandwich, putting in an especially generous filling, his wife noted with a smile, as well as a few tomato slices. "Just the sandwich and a lemon squash. I can tike care of it m'self."

So used to him had she become, in fact, that now she responded to his earlier comment as though he'd just made it. "And what makes you despair of the world today, eh, Dan?"

He indicated the sandwich with a gesture as if to say, "That's why!"

"Liver sausage?" Bess chuckled.

"You know me better than that, me luv," Dan said with an embarrassed grin. "Not the sandwich. The young lady what's h'about to consume it." He placed the sandwich on a plate and poured the lemon squash. "Can't be a day h'over fifteen and all on her h'own in London. What 'er folks can be thinkin' of is beyond me!"

" 'Old on, Dan. There you go, h'off and runnin' again afore you know all the facts!"

"Claims to be h'eighteen," he muttered and picking up the plate and glass, he headed back out into the pub. "Coo, if she's h'eighteen, I'm....." But here he disappeared from sight and the rest of his words were lost to her.

Out in the pub Victoria had been able to hear the sound of their voices, punctuated frequently by laughter and even though she couldn't understand what they were saying, she experienced a by-now familiar stab of envy at their shared happiness. Tears of longing welled up in her eyes, but just then she saw Dan coming through the swinging door with her order and she quickly wiped her eyes with the back of her hand.

Dan wasn't fooled for a minute, however. Even if he'd failed to notice her pathetically defensive gesture, which he had not, the tears had left telltale gray streaks under each eye. He made no mention of it, of course. "There you are, miss." With a little flourish he put the plate and glass in front of her. "H'eat 'earty now."

All the time she was devouring the sandwich, Vicki was aware of him hovering solicitously somewhere in the background. Was this when she first thought of him as someone she could use? Sadly she failed to realize she didn't have to trick Danny into helping her. She would have only had to ask. But now with her lunch finished, she continued to dawdle, pretending to hunt for something in her purse, touching up her lipstick, powdering her nose.

Finally when it seemed she couldn't possibly postpone her departure any longer, he hesitantly approached the table again. "You know, miss, I don't want you should mish'appre'end my h'intentions. It 's just that I see a little girl like yourself and I think 'ow I'd feel if you were one of me h'own."

"I am <u>not</u> a little girl!" With some difficulty Vicki controlled her temper. "But it's true," she sighed. "I <u>am</u> rather on my own and so you see I have to be frightfully careful whom I talk to. Some men would take advantage of a girl," she confided shyly.

"Now I'd never do no such thing," he exclaimed horrified that anyone could want to harm her. "H'anyone'll tell you you're safe wiv h'old Dan 'ere!"

She smiled up at him, her eyes wide and innocent. "Yes, I knew that right away. Oh, please sit down," she added sweetly as he still lingered by the table.

Dan accepted her invitation, feeling absurdly pleased by her trust. Being totally without guile himself, he failed to realize that to Victoria trust meant simply that she'd found the perfect sucker. "Folks can't 'elp you?" he asked kindly.

Again Vicki's green eyes filled with tears, but this time they were part of her performance and she made no attempt to wipe them away. "My father was killed in the War." He might as well have been, she thought bitterly, for all the good he's ever done me! "And my mother's at home with little ones from a second marriage." Well, that was at least technically true.

"Where you from, luv?"

"You know that was simply the most super lemon squash I've ever had?" Vicki enthused, instantly changing the subject. "Could I have another?"

"H'absolutely, miss. On the 'ouse, you might say!"

"Thank you so much!" she murmured sweetly as he returned a few minutes later with the second drink. "Mmm, that's yummy!" she added appreciatively after the first sip. "So you see, I....I came to London to...to go to school in the fall. I...I want to be a secretary." Somehow that sounded like a more respectable profession. "But...but I.....I don't know where to begin to look for a job. I....I can't even find a room I can afford." Once more a little self-editing; it was better not to make any reference to her age. "There...there <u>was</u> one place, but the man...he.... he scared me and I.....I ran." All of this had come out in a rush leaving her a little breathless, but that merely made her appear all the more fragile.

Dan was leaning forward, looking at her intently. "This chap you spoke of–scruffy lookin' bloke? Yellowish moustache. Wearin' a plaid dressin' gown?"

Vicki nodded.

"Coo, ducks, you're better h'off not stayin' there. That un's a rum customer. Now I think I just might 'ave the h'answer to your problem." Getting to his feet, he patted her reassuringly on the shoulder. "You just wait right 'ere, Miss." He headed back to the kitchen. "You just wait right 'ere," he added a second time as he disappeared through the swinging door. Alone in the pub Vicki's immediate reaction was one of relief, but then strangely the relief gave way almost at once to a profound sadness. Impatiently she dismissed the sensation as more futile self-pity, failing tragically to comprehend that she found no true joy in tricking someone into helping her.

Meanwhile in the kitchen Dan had told his wife about the "poor little thing's" situation as well as his marvelous solution. "I don't know, luv." She shook her head doubtfully–as usual the more sensible of the two. "We could get a tidy sum if we let that room to someone."

"Come h'off it. We'd 'ave to fix it up a bit for that. Besides we could keep an eye on 'er, so to speak–'er bein' all alone in the world as it were. We'd want someone to do the same for one of h'our girls if they was out on their own, now wouldn't we? And you could use some 'elp in the kitchen."

Smiling fondly, Bess patted her tenderhearted husband on the cheek. "Dan, Dan– you don't even know if she's tellin' you the truth about 'erself."

"Coo, luv, wait 'till you see 'er. This un couldn't lie."

"I should know by now that when you get an h'idea in that 'ead o' yours, nothin' can get it out. Well, I suppose it can't do no 'arm now, can it?"

"Thank you, me luv!" Dan seized his wife by both shoulders, kissing her hard full on the mouth. "No wonder I'm such a 'appy man--married to the likes o' you!"

At the sound of her benefactor returning Vicki turned slightly in her chair, smiling up at him. He beamed at her in return. "I....I just 'ad to check wiv the missus. Now you'll 'ave to promise me ye'll stay out of this 'ere part of the h'establishment durin' hours. I mean, you say you're h'eighteen and all, but......"

"Don't you believe me?"

"Sure, miss, sure, but what wiv me 'avin' liquor on the premises, so to speak, I'd 'ave the local bobbies on me in no time. So 'ere's what I'm thinkin. You could 'elp the missus in the kitchen–wash dishes, 'elp us tidy up the place after closin'–mop the floor and such—the missus 'as got 'erself a bad back, you see–so a couple of hours durin' the noon rush and then six p.m. until midnight."

Vicki hesitated. Washing dishes, even mopping floors and this for a future luminary of the London stage! "What would you pay me?" If the wages were at least worth the unspeakable degradation, she might still consider it, however.

"Now I h'aint thought much h'about that. Let me see...ah...twelve and six an hour, I guess, so five pounds a day. Every day h'except Sunday–so thirty the week."

"Thirty the week," Vicki repeated after him, staring down at her hands clasped together in her lap. "I...I don't know, I...." Thirty pounds wouldn't be nearly enough and for such horrid, dirty work.......

"It's a fair wage, miss, believe me. H'old Dan—'e's not one to cheat you. I wish I could h'afford more, but I've h'only got me a small place 'ere and a wife and two daughters what depends on me for support, you might say—soooo...." This was his crowning touch and he couldn't stop himself from indulging in a slight dramatic pause...."we....we 'ave an h'extra room.. .not very large, but we'll h'include that and....and your meals. H'after all 'ow much can a little thing like you h'eat, 'ey?"

A roof over her head, all her meals and a job–all at once. Vicki could hardly believe her good fortune. "Yes, all right." She nodded briefly and stood up. "If you'd show me the room now."

Dan had eagerly anticipated the rush of tearful gratitude his announcements would occasion and he was more than a little disappointed at the girl's cool acceptance of his kindness. Characteristically, however, he did not dwell on his hurt for long. "Just follow me then, miss." Picking up her cases, he led the way through the second door in the rear of the pub, up an enclosed winding staircase and along a narrow hallway. "Right in 'ere, miss." He pushed the door open and stood gallantly to one side to allow her to enter ahead of him, following to put her cases down just inside the door.

The room was much as he'd said–quite small and with just one window. The only furnishings consisted of an old, iron bed, a low narrow chest of drawers and one straight chair. A badly discolored and cracked mirror hung above the tiny corner sink. "Well, it's certainly not much," Vicki observed haughtily. "No wonder you're giving it to me for nothing. You couldn't expect anyone to pay for it."

"The W.C. is just there." Dan indicated a closed door diagonally across the hall. "We 'ave to share. I 'ope you don't mind." In spite of himself he sounded apologetic.

"I suppose it will have to do then." She placed one of her suitcases on the bed and opened it. "Are you just going to stand there?" she demanded crossly when after a few seconds he still hadn't moved from the doorway.

"The missus could use your 'elp right now," he suggested hesitantly.

"I can't possibly start until tomorrow. I have to unpack and you certainly don't expect me to save anything for school on what you'll be paying me. I have to find a second job at least for the summer."

"Righty-o, miss. Tomorrow it is then. You know miss, you 'aven't even told me your name."

"Victoria Windsor!!" More and more now she spoke her name with a defiant pride. And each time she did so her determination grew to make that name mean something in the world.

"All right, Vicki, my girl!" Dan boomed out jovially.

"First of all, I said Victoria, not Vicki and second, I am not your girl!"

"Yes, miss, what-h'ever you say, miss." He left then, closing the door behind him. His wife often told him that people took advantage of his generous nature and perhaps she was right. For a minute walking back downstairs he was actually downhearted, but then he thought once more how alone the young lady was in the world and he felt better again just knowing she was safe under his roof where he could "look h'after 'er, so to speak." It didn't matter that she didn't seem grateful. For Dan acts of kindness constituted their own reward.

Alone in the room Vicki had some trouble forgetting the wounded expression she'd glimpsed briefly in Dan's mild, hazel eyes, but she reminded herself sternly that she couldn't allow herself to be so soft-hearted and soon she'd managed to put her benefactor's hurt feelings entirely from her mind. It took her less than a half hour to unpack and put her things away. A life spent primarily in public school does not provide for the accumulation of a vast amount of private property. And with that done she settled herself cross-legged on the creaky, iron-springed bed to reread the adverts. A second job for the morning hours would still leave her time in the afternoon to prepare her audition material. The most likely possibilities, however, sounded equally if not more degrading than washing floors and dirty dishes and in most cases paid even less–a chambermaid in a hotel, a waitress in a tea room or an attendant at a petrol station. Well, it seemed at this point she couldn't afford to be particular; she'd check out these three this afternoon.

Passing through the pub on her way out, she found the noon rush at its height. Quite in awe, she stood for a moment watching. Danny went by her at least three times-- once with plates balanced miraculously along the full length of each arm, another time with his fingers grasping the handles of an unbelievable number of beer mugs and yet again with a tray piled high with dirty dishes. At the sight of the latter Vicki nearly changed her mind about the whole thing. But she'd made her decision and she wasn't about to back down. After all one day when she was a famous actress, it would make for an amusing anecdote.

Back at King's Cross Station she bought a map of London and having located her various destinations, her next step was to consult the chart of underground fees. The hotel was closest at 6p; the petrol station next at a shilling. The tea room was on the outskirts of the city so that would only be as a last resort.

At the hotel, however, she barely got inside the door of the personnel office. The woman at the reception desk looked up as she entered. "I was interested in the job as a chambermaid," Vicki said in as grown-up a tone as she could manage.

"How old are you?"

"Eighteen." Damn, she thought, I have to say that more convincingly? I am an actress, after all.

"Are you really?" the woman observed ironically. "Why don't you come back in a few years when that's actually true."

"By then I won't need your grubby little job!" Vicki retorted and pivoting on one spiked heel, she walked out.

The filling station was nothing but two pumps and a run-down shack on a small, triangular shaped lot–an old warehouse being behind it and the two curbs meeting in a sharp point in the front. As Vicki crossed the street and approached, a tall, thin, nondescript figure came out of the shack. "Want something?" Even the gravelly voice provided no clue as to the age or even the sex of this odd individual.

At this point in her life 90% of Vicki's presence was pure bravado and she very nearly turned and ran. "I came about the part-time job."

The figure walked toward her, not stopping until their faces were just inches apart. "Wanted a boy."

"Why?" Vicki demanded more loudly as she tried not to wince. Whoever or whatever this person was, the breath emanating from its lips reeked of a combination of garlic and chewing tobacco. "The advert said the job was to pump petrol. Anyone can do that. Doesn't have to be a boy."

The figure paused long enough to turn its head and spit a long stream of tobacco juice. "Got a bit of moxie there, haven't you?" it remarked. The cultured accent didn't go with the shapeless brown pullover and rumpled corduroy trousers or the stringy gray hair, partially covered even on this warm day with a black, knitted tam, and only added further to the mystery of its owner .

"I think I can do the job if that's what you mean," she replied, now quite firmly. This amusing character--certainly the most unique she'd ever encountered--was, after all, more fascinating than frightening.

"Hours are 5-11 a.m.–Monday through Friday. Pay is 8 shillings, 6 pence an hour. Be here tomorrow morning."

Before she'd had a chance to answer or even to think whether the wages would be enough, the figure had turned back toward the shack. "Wait, please," Vicki called out. "You haven't told me your name. Mine's Victoria Windsor."

"Mine's Lou." And with this her new employer vanished from sight, leaving her none the wiser. Lou could just as easily have been Louis as Louise.. For a second or two she continued to stand there, but at last she simply shrugged. It didn't really matter anyway as long as she had the job.

Back in her room that evening after supper in the pub kitchen, Vicki could never remember being so tired, but at the same time she was proud of herself. Only her first day in London and she'd managed to find two jobs and a place to stay and with her room and board included with one of those jobs she could save almost all of what she'd be earning toward her expenses for the fall. Of course she wouldn't really know how she stood financially until she visited RADA for the first time tomorrow. She hadn't dared send for a catalogue for fear someone at Heathfield might become suspicious.

* * *

The next morning she dressed with particular care, wanting to appear older than her sixteen years. Along with personal possessions in general, her wardrobe was decidedly limited as well after the years spent in a school uniform, but she selected what she considered to be her most sophisticated outfit: a slim-skirted shirtwaist dress in a dark blue paisley material with white collar and cuffs, white high-heeled pumps and white gloves. Her make-up was heavier than she'd been able to get away with at school, but she applied it quite flawlessly, she thought, even with the terrible mirror in her room. Her hair was more of a problem. A chignon would make her look more mature, but at the same time her hair was one of her most stunning features and finally she simply gave it a thorough brushing and allowed it to hang free, held back from her face with a white band.

She was too nervous to eat breakfast. Instead she went out to find a kiosk and look up the Academy's address in a telephone book. 62-64 Gower Street, it told her, and upon asking directions of a bobby, she learned Gower Street was only a short distance along Euston Road. What sheer bloody luck!

Gower Street was indeed only a few blocks walk and turning left as the bobby had instructed, she began to watch eagerly for #62. Unconsciously her footsteps quickened. Most of the solid row of buildings on either side of the street appeared to be either small office buildings or private hotels, rather a mundane setting, she thought, in which to begin a whole new life. Even the building housing RADA itself was at first indistinguishable from those on either side of it and if it hadn't been for the numbers 62 and 64 on two low granite posts flanking the steps, she might actually have passed it by.

The year and a half since Sir Terence Cartier first suggested she attend RADA had seemed endless and now here it was; she had only to walk through the door. Why instead did she turn the other way and glancing briefly in both directions, cross the street to stand on the pavement and stare? Just possibly, although she'd never have admitted it, she was suffering from an attack of nerves. Afterwards, however, the moment was enduringly impressed on her memory and she would always be grateful for whatever impulse had prompted her.

Seen from this new vantage point, RADA no longer seemed so ordinary in appearance. True, the building was much like the others on the street: two lower floors of granite and four upper ones of red brick with a black, wrought-iron fence separating it from the pavement, but the entrance was distinctive, though understated and perhaps still not noticeable to anyone not looking for it. The words "Royal Academy of Dramatic Art" were carved into the granite above the door, but it was the two standing, bas-relief figures on either side which caught and held Vicki's attention: one male, one female, one with a serious expression on its face, the other smiling. The figures were facing the street, but at the same time they both wore theatrical masks which were turned sideways as though looking at each other. The odd thing was that the mask of tragedy was on the smiling face while the mask of comedy covered the sad face. It wasn't until much later Vicki would think about these figures and realize how perfectly they symbolized the unreality of the world of the theatre and more terribly how they had come to symbolize her own life. For now, however, she had put the moment off long enough. It was time to begin and recrossing the street, she entered the building.

Inside she found a small entry hall–very bare and once again quite ordinary in appearance with narrower hallways leading off to either side. To the right hand side of the door stood a small table with a sign on it stating, "Information". A pleasant looking girl sat behind it sticking stamps on large, manila envelopes. "Excuse me." Vicki's voice was suddenly lower and more musical–more like the voice which one day would be renowned. It was clear she'd done more in those few moments than merely step through a doorway.

"Yes?" The girl glanced up and smiled.

"I wish to apply for admission to the Academy." Vicki did not return the smile.

"In which field? Each department judges its own applicants."

"Acting, of course." Her tone indicated plainly that the girl was an idiot.

"Acting's at the end of the hall over there." She pointed across to the left.

Vicki merely nodded, whirling about to stride briskly down the indicated hallway. Upon first entering the acting department office, however, she found no one there. Photographs of recent RADA productions covered the walls and she began to walk slowly about the room, studying them with great interest. So absorbed did she become, in fact, that she wasn't even aware the department chairman had returned until he spoke.

One of Peter Harris' favorite stories in later years was of the day he'd come back from his mid-morning break to discover Victoria Windsor waiting in his office. Obviously, he remembered, she'd been entirely unconscious of the impression she made and although he never included this in the retelling, he'd taken advantage of her momentary preoccupation to study her fully. From this side view the dark tailored dress showed off to perfection her full breasts, slim waist and hips; her golden hair fell halfway down her back and her lips were moist and parted slightly. His pulse quickened in anticipation. "Might I possibly be of some assistance?" Peter's well-perfected charm held most of the female students entranced.

Victoria disliked being caught off-guard in this way and as she turned to face him, the mask fell instantly into place. "I wish to apply for admission to the Academy." She flashed him a smile. "I'm going to be an actress."

"Ah yes, of course." She probably has no talent, he thought; none of the really smashing ones ever do. "Please sit down, Miss....ah......?"

"Windsor"–the one word definitely aristocratic, in tone as well as lineage–and as she spoke it, Victoria slipped gracefully into a chair, smoothing her skirt under her and crossing her legs. She removed her gloves, placing both them and her purse on the corner of the desk. Outwardly she appeared all poise and self-confidence, but her heart pounded and she was sure her palms were perspiring. Suppose they required parental signatures or preparatory school records; suppose they discovered her real age.

But Peter Harris merely repeated the name after her as he himself sat down behind the desk. "And the first name, young lady?" He winked at her.

"Victoria."

"All right then, Vicki." He leaned down to open the drawer where the catalogues and admission applications were kept.

Act Two - "Victoria"

Chapter 1

"Excuse me–I said Victoria." Leaning back in the chair, she rested her hands lightly on its arms as though she were in fact her royal ancestor and the chair her throne.

Peter Harris had always been able to unnerve the young female applicants and her reply startled him. Clearly this girl was different, but that only made it more of a challenge. "I beg your pardon," he replied with a slight smile. "Victoria, then."

"Are you mocking me?" She gazed at him steadily.

"Now I would never do that, sweetheart."

"And I am not your sweetheart." Her green eyes blazed.

"Well, you have a few things to learn, Victoria," he stated precisely, "the first of which being that my name is Peter Harris and as chairman of the acting department I have a great deal to say about whether you will be accepted to RADA."

"And I presume," she replied with equal precision, "that my admission will depend solely on my talent."

By now it was Peter who was becoming rattled and it was with some relief he located the necessary forms and the catalogue, handing them to her across the desk. "Auditions will be held again the first week in August. Post the application and you will receive a specific appointment. You should have three selections prepared: five to ten minutes each."

"Thank you." She slipped on her gloves again and picked up her handbag.

"How about some lunch, Victoria?"

"No, I don't think so." Getting to her feet, she slipped easily around his desk and out the door.

Peter listened to the staccato of her high heels moving rapidly away down the hall. A wry smile played at the corners of his mouth. "Well, that young lady has pretty well cooked her goose," he observed aloud to the empty office.

Out on the street Victoria paused for a moment. She knew she'd made a poor impression, but she had become so accustomed to not caring what people thought of her, she'd forgotten there were going to be times when she would have to turn on the charm. Well, it was too late to worry about that now and she could only hope as she began to walk back along Gower Street that either her audition would be so spectacular that her behavior of today wouldn't matter or that her admission to RADA would depend on the opinions of others in addition to Peter Harris.

Back at the pub she hurried upstairs to her room and flinging herself down on the bed, she opened the RADA catalogue to the section for acting majors. Incredibly the course of study was everything she'd dreamed of: speech, theatre history, acting techniques, period dance and movement, pantomime–just from a cursory glance of the first year's curriculum. But she had unfortunately one other section to consider. It was entitled–"Fees". She located it all too easily and there–inexorably printed– was the bad news: "Tuition- four hundred pounds!"

She'd noticed a school calendar inside the front cover and flipping back there, she saw that opening day of term was August 26th. Quickly she counted the weeks–eight! Danny would be paying her thirty pounds a week at the pub and...wait a minute, what had he...or she... But she still hadn't the foggiest notion as to the gender of the station owner. Her irrepressible sense of humor bubbled to the surface. "Well, whatever," she said at last with a giggle. "Eight and six the hour, I think it was, five hours a day–five days a week so that makes twelve pounds, ten shillings the week."

Her total weekly wage thus amounted to 42 pounds and 10. Could she possibly live on the two and ten, thus enabling her to put aside the 40 toward her expenses for the fall? Luckily her job six nights a week would protect her from the temptation of spending money on the theatre in the evening although she just might be able to treat herself to an occasional matinee. Her escapade with Teddy had cost her ten pounds a week of her allowance, but during the past year she'd still managed to save nearly 100 pounds from which she'd really spent only the amount of her train fare. She even counted the change in her purse. Altogether it added up to 415 pounds, 12 shillings and 6 pence. Eight miserable weeks of dirty, degrading work and all she'd have to show for it would be barely one year's tuition at RADA. Well, that would have to do for now. It was nearly noon and she was due downstairs in the pub.

It wasn't until her second shift in the kitchen was over that for some reason it all seemed to overwhelm her. She came back upstairs to her room, but instead of going directly to bed, she sat down in the one chair and once there she didn't have the will to move. She found herself listening to the noise of the traffic below her on Euston Road, the same sound which had so thrilled her when she first arrived in London, but now only caused her barren little room to seem all the more silent in comparison. She'd almost have thought she was homesick–that is, if she'd <u>had</u> a home to miss. But of course she did not. Such feelings, therefore, were utter nonsense and at last she stirred herself to get to her feet and undress for bed. Washing up in the tiny sink, she crawled under the covers. To drown out the sounds of the traffic she recited Shakespeare to herself, but it was still after 2 a.m. before she fell asleep.

* * *

She was sure she'd set her alarm for four, but when she rolled over and looked at her little traveling clock, it was past 4:30. Had she forgotten to wind it? Had she turned off the alarm and gone back to sleep? Jumping out of bed, she hurriedly splashed water on her face and putting on navy blue slacks and a short-sleeved white blouse, she ran downstairs, out the back door of the pub and across Euston Road to the King's Cross tube stop. When she arrived at the filling station, the owner was already opening for the day. "You're late," was the muttered comment.

Victoria glanced at her watch. "Just five minutes."

"Five minutes is five minutes. From now on you'll be unlocking in the morning and I expect the station to be open on time. And you can't work dressed like that either; you'll be filthy in no time. There are coveralls and a shirt inside. I supply them and have them laundered. You can change in the loo. Door at the back of the office."

Not even attempting a reply, Victoria went on over to the shack and entered. The dark brown work clothes were indeed hanging on a hook behind the door and taking them down, she proceeded into the bathroom. The shirt, which she put on first, was enormous. The tail hung to her knees and her hands were totally lost in the sleeves, the shoulders coming nearer her elbows. Shrugging, she rolled up the sleeves and stepped into the overalls, pulling the braces up onto her shoulders and stuffing the voluminous shirt inside the trousers. For a moment she studied herself in the mirror. More than anything she resembled a baggy pants clown and opening the bathroom door, she came out into the office, walking with hugely exaggerated steps on the bottoms of the pants legs. In every actor, after all, there is of necessity a certain amount of pure ham.

The furniture in the "office" consisted of two basic pieces: one scarred and battered desk, one decidedly rickety chair and just at that moment the station owner was occupying both: feet propped up on the former, the latter balanced precariously on two legs. As Victoria made her comic entrance, the chair crashed down on all four legs. "I'll see if my supplier has a smaller size," Lou chuckled. "In the meantime....." Two large rusty safety pins were produced from the desk drawer. "Fasten over the waist and roll up the legs." For the first few customers her employer demonstrated the pumps, explaining the business of checking under the bonnet for oil and water, but very shortly she was on her own.

The station was conveniently located for commuters entering London and it was almost eight before there was a break in the steady stream of customers. Hot and tired, Victoria sat down on a bench in front of the shack to rest for a few minutes, stretching to ease her aching arms and shoulders. It was only then she noticed her hands–how filthy they were, the painstakingly manicured nails filled with grime. Gasping in horror, she jumped to her feet and ran back through the office to the bathroom. The dispenser there held a special type of abrasive soap powder, but a vigorous scrubbing only succeeded in lightening the color of her skin while leaving the nails virtually untouched. I can't keep this job, she thought in dismay. My hands will be ruined! How will I ever do films?

Outside at the pumps a horn sounded impatiently. Victoria hesitated. The horn blared again longer...a pause and then again. For a moment she continued to stand there, but then she remembered how much she needed the money. Well, I'll just have to buy some good strong soap and bottles and bottles of lotion, she thought, and she hurried out to wait on the customer. Eyeing the white Triumph convertible enviously, she failed to realize until it was too late who the driver was. "Fill it," the man demanded arrogantly. "And be damned quick about it!" Of all the bloody rotten luck—Peter Harris!

Without replying she moved at once to crank up the pump and removing the cap of the petrol tank, she bent to insert the nozzle. Maybe he wouldn't recognize her. After all, he'd only seen her once before and dressed very differently. With a sigh of relief she set the catch and straightened up to wait, only to find Peter regarding her with evident amusement in the car's wing mirror. Trying to ignore him, she finished filling the tank, replaced the cap and returned the nozzle to the pump. Finally she had no choice but to speak. "28 and 7, sir," she said with as much dignity as she could muster.

Peter, meanwhile, having gotten out of the car, stood with one foot crossed nonchalantly in front of the other grinning broadly. His hand still rested on the door handle and he made no move to pay her. So he's going to be difficult, she thought; I might have guessed. Remembering their prior meeting, however, she forced herself to smile and repeat the amount. At last he reached for his wallet, but then he paused with his hand only partway out of the breast pocket of his sports jacket. "Rather degrading job for a future luminary of the London stage–what?"

Mercifully another car pulled up at the pumps just then. "I have another customer, sir," Victoria murmured, continuing to smile.

"I beg your pardon?" He pretended not to have heard her.

"I <u>said</u> I <u>have</u> another customer." She swore she'd be gracious if she exploded.

Ever since Peter had stepped out of the car, he'd been studying her intently–the eyes which in the bright morning sunlight appeared even more startlingly green, the blonde hair now pulled back in a ponytail, the full breasts only partially concealed under the oversized shirt–and he was well aware how close she was to losing her temper. He could see the approaching storm clearly now, bubbling up through those incredible eyes like a turbulence begun in the farthest depths of a tropical pool and he wondered just how far he could push her before it burst through to the surface. "Well, are you going to pay me or not?" Victoria demanded finally when several seconds passed and he continued to stand there, his hand poised halfway from his jacket pocket–that damned infuriating smirk on his horsey face.

"Certainly....certainly." Chuckling, he withdrew his wallet the rest of the way and extracted the necessary amount.

"What is so damned funny?" She seized the money in such haste that it slipped through her fingers.

Gallantly Peter knelt to pick it up and handing it to her a second time, he thought it the perfect opportunity to expose her to a fresh dose of his redoubtable charm. "Do you know you're very beautiful?" he murmured as he stroked the inside of her wrist with his fingertips.

"Yes!" Snatching her hand away, Victoria turned abruptly to serve the next customer. Now I've really done it, she thought. How bloody stupid can I be? She needn't have worried. Peter Harris had not been in the least offended this time and he was still laughing as he got into the driver's seat and started the engine. Her anger was indeed like a tropical storm, he thought, and he hoped now she would be admitted to the Academy. He wanted to be the man to unleash all that passion.

Victoria found to her dismay that her hands were shaking and it was all she could do to fit the nozzle into the next car's petrol tank. She told herself it was merely anger at Peter Harris' insufferable rudeness, but what she couldn't admit even to herself was that she'd found even his mildly suggestive flirting upsetting. She fancied herself quite the sophisticate by now, but in truth she was still a convent-bred schoolgirl whose knowledge of sex was naively limited: composed half of the self-consciously scientific euphemisms of Sister Isobel's class in "health and feminine hygiene", which left a girl with the vague impression that as long as she stayed away from bees and flowers, nothing could possibly happen to her; the other half of the whispered rumors, half-truths and adolescent fantasies of other teen-age girls who were as badly informed on the subject as she was. Now suddenly Victoria found herself in the real world where she'd be expected to play by adult rules; where men would expect her to offer a great deal more than a mixture of cough syrup and rubbing alcohol and where no Sister Marion would knock on the closed door just in time to save her. A gush of petrol as the tank overflowed brought her back to the reality of the moment and she resolved for the rest of the morning not to allow her mind to wander. Almost before she knew it, she was on the underground again, heading back to her noontime shift at Danny's.

Her daily routine was thus established, varying only in minor detail for the rest of the summer. Up at four a.m. she pumped petrol from five to eleven. Returning to the pub, she snatched her own midday meal during the odd moments when there was a brief let-up in the seemingly endless procession of dirty dishes. Rarely did she finish before three. From six to midnight and often well beyond there were still more dishes and finally the inevitable floors to be mopped–both in the kitchen and in the pub itself. One thing and one thing only made the hard, menial work bearable. She'd posted her RADA application form and in return received a printed card informing her that her audition was scheduled for 4:30 p.m. on the eighth of August. The date was circled in red on a small calendar tacked up on the wall of her room and to fulfill her dream she could and would do anything, no matter how wretched and dirty.

Over the past year she had gradually compiled a list of possible audition pieces and now she made her final selections. Roles in her own age range she'd immediately rejected as not nearly impressive enough and after considerable thought she settled on a speech of Mary Tyrone's, the mother in Eugene O'Neill's *Long Day's Journey into Night*, a woman of at least 50–hands crippled with arthritis, drug addict; Shakespeare's Lady Macbeth, the famous sleepwalking speech, of course, but also the earlier scene where she plots her husband's ascension to the Scottish throne and for comedy–Lady Bracknell, the grand dame of Oscar Wilde's *The Importance of Being Earnest.*

Her next step was to purchase used paperback copies of the Wilde and O'Neill plays–*Macbeth,* of course, she already had–and rereading each work in its entirety, Victoria considered the motivation of each of the roles. What was the woman's mood, her innermost feelings at this point in the play? She believed it was vital she understand why the character was speaking these particular words in this particular scene. It didn't even occur to her that such insight into the art of acting was unusual in someone of her still limited experience. Finally she went over and over each speech, refusing to be satisfied until every tone, every inflection, every gesture was perfect.

Like the utterly open and honest man he was, Dan had accepted Victoria exactly as she'd first appeared and even after a full month he failed to understand she was acting a part. He would still try to include her as a member of his family only to find himself coldly rebuffed. One night in early August shortly after closing he came back into the kitchen where his wife was putting away the last of the clean dishes, wiping off the stovetops and counters. Victoria was as always mopping the floor. "Quite a crowd tonight, eh, ladies?" Dan rubbed his hands together in glee. Heavy business never failed to increase his already ebullient good humor.

"That it was, luv." Bess glanced up from her work to smile at him. Helping to run a family business wasn't the easiest life, but she knew women whose husbands drank too much or cheated on them or beat them and their children and she considered herself blessed. "Do you mind if I go on up? I'm a wee bit tired."

"Of course not, m'luv." Hugging her about the shoulders, he planted a noisy kiss on her cheek.

"Good night, Victoria." There was as usual no reply and after a moment Bess turned away, her slow, heavy footsteps on the stairs speaking eloquently of her weariness. She'd tried for her husband's sake to be kind to the girl, but really it was impossible to like her.

Dan couldn't help noticing that Victoria had made no effort to join in their camaraderie, but in his exuberance he couldn't stop himself from trying yet another time to include her. " 'ow h'about it, ducks?" he inquired grinning broadly. She glanced at him disdainfully, but still said nothing. Anyone more perceptive or perhaps less well meaning would have certainly stopped there, but he continued. "Quite a flourishin' little business you went and got yourself connected wiv, h'ain't it!"

Victoria gave one last swipe of the mop and replaced it in the corner closet. Only then did she turn to face him. "I wish you would try to understand something once and for all," she stated, her tone one of utter contempt. "I am <u>not</u> 'connected' as you say with your grubby little business and I never <u>will</u> be! Now am I through for the night?"

Nothing-- except, of course, his wife and daughters--took precedence in Dan's affections over his beloved pub and to hear it derided as a "grubby little business" hurt. Why then didn't he fire her on the spot? At the very least she'd been inexcusably rude. "Yes, Victoria," he replied quietly instead, "all through. Thanks for your 'elp." She gave him a look intended obviously as a silent comment on his unbelievable stupidity and disappeared rapidly up the stairs, her footsteps still light and quick after nearly seven hours of backbreaking work. Yet it was she and not his wife whom Dan pitied. "Poor little thing," he said to himself. And ironically in spite of all outward appearances he was right.

* * *

Shortly before 4:30 on the afternoon of August 8th Victoria stood again on the front steps of the Royal Academy of Dramatic Art, one hand poised to open the heavy, glass-paneled door. Her heart was pounding, though not from any apprehension of the approaching audition. Only those fearing failure had anything to dread. Well, time to get on with it, she thought and with a vigorous push of the door she went in. Directly ahead of her a crayoned sign with a red arrow indicated that auditions were to the left. At the bottom of a flight of stairs another arrow pointed upward and at the top Victoria found a small hallway. Two sets of swinging doors undoubtedly led to an auditorium. Several other applicants were also waiting their turn.

Two girls were perched on the stairs partway up to the next floor and another was sitting alone at the far end of a row of folding chairs set against one wall. A boy was stretched out on his back across the width of the hall arms folded under his head– he was actually asleep!-- while another paced the hall the long way. Amazingly the pacer always managed to step over the sleeper without so much as breaking stride. Victoria sat down at the other end of the line of chairs. To her distaste and displeasure, however, the other girl immediately moved over to sit next to her. "Isn't the waiting awful?" she confided shakily.

"Not particularly."

Clearly Victoria's manner was not meant to invite chumminess, but the other applicant was so desperate to talk to someone she didn't notice. "Which....which ones are you doing?"

"<u>What</u>?!"

"I....I just...just...ah...wondered what pieces you'd...ah...chosen. Mine are...."

"I don't give a damn what yours are!"

Before the poor girl could attempt any further reply, a man appeared at the swinging doors. "Miss Windsor?" he said consulting a clipboard he held in one hand.

"Yes." Victoria's voice and manner changed abruptly as with great dignity she rose to her feet and walked across the hall. Bestowing her most charming smile on the man, she slipped past him into the auditorium.

One of the girls from the stairs moved down now to sit on a chair. "Coo, 'ow did you like that un?" she inquired in a thick Cockney accent which would certainly go against her in the audition. "Bite your 'ead off one minute and all charm and sweetness the next! That's the sort they'll tike. Mark my words!"

But the girl who'd attempted to strike up a conversation with Victoria was still looking at the door through which she had just disappeared. "She wasn't even nervous!" Much like Pamela Ashworth years before at Heathfield she found such courage awe-inspiring.

For a second or two Victoria stood just inside the door and stared at the lighted stage. Starkly outlined by the darkness all around it, it seemed to beckon to her, symbolizing everything she'd ever wanted. All my life up to this point, she thought, has been as dark as this theatre and now all I have to do is walk down the aisle into the light and everything will change. Her musings were interrupted just then by the man who had called her name. "You may go on up and present your selections, Miss Windsor," he explained, coming up behind her. "Afterwards the committee may have a few questions."

She nodded and moving on down the aisle, climbed the short set of steps. Finally she took a few steps upstage, turning to face out toward the auditorium. The spotlights hit her full in the eyes all but blinding her, but that was just as well since she preferred not to know who was out there. One of them must certainly be Peter Harris. "Please begin, Miss Windsor," a somewhat raspy female voice requested from somewhere to her right. "Just tell us before each selection the play and the role you have chosen."

Just in time Victoria stopped herself from retorting, "What's the matter? Wouldn't you recognize them?" and instead merely announced that her first selection was a speech of Mary Tyrone's, the mother in O'Neill's *Long Day's Journey into Night* shortly after she's begun taking drugs again. From there she went on to the majesty of Lady Macbeth and finally the delightfully eccentric Lady Bracknell. Dead silence greeted the conclusion of this–her third and final selection–a silence which continued unbroken for several unnerving seconds.

Victoria wondered uneasily if she'd forgotten something. It was only three selections, wasn't it? Or perhaps she made some error in her choices. She was already too self-controlled, however, to allow any outward sign of her growing discomfiture and she simply stood center stage, hands clasped loosely in front of her, and waited. Observing her from his seat in the center rear of the auditorium, Peter Harris smiled in silent amusement. It will take more than a few seconds of silence to rattle this one, he thought to himself. At last, however, he decided she'd suffered long enough. "Are you finished, Miss?" He affected a bored tone. "I'm...ah.... sorry," he continued after a brief pause as though he were consulting with the other committee members, "what's the name on this one?"

"Damn," Victoria muttered under her breath, "Peter Harris!" Out loud she simply said, "Windsor!"

"Ah yes, Windsor." His chuckle was now maddeningly audible. "Well, are you finished, Miss....ah...Windsor?"

"Yes, I'm finished."

"I'd be interested why you picked out these particular speeches," a different male voice–a softer one–inquired from over to her left.

"I understood it was to be one serious modern play, one classical and one comedic from any era," Victoria replied.

"Then you're not aware you chose extremely demanding roles?" the woman asked. "Especially since I noticed on your application that your experience is limited to two roles in your preparatory school drama club?" Victoria didn't immediately respond although inwardly she cursed herself for being so damned truthful. "Miss Windsor, did you understand me?"

She tossed her head. "Of course I did. I was trying to decide how to answer such a silly question." Peter Harris tried unsuccessfully to smother the sound of his laughter with his handkerchief.

"What did you say?" It was evident that the woman had gotten up and moved nearer the stage–moreover that she was extremely irritated.

"Because talent has nothing to do with experience!" Victoria went on even as she realized she had once again jeopardized her chances by losing her temper.

"I have nothing further to say to this girl." The woman's tone was one of cold dismissal.

Tears rushed into Victoria's eyes as she started to leave the stage. Why had she been so stupid? "Wait, please, Miss Windsor," the milder male voice interposed just as she reached the stairs. "Do you perhaps have another selection more in your age range?"

A few minutes ago she would have explained scornfully that any actress can portray someone her own age, but now she realized she might still have a chance. "Yes–Juliet or Anne Frank." In spite of herself she sounded discouraged.

"Juliet is done so often. Could you possibly give us something from *The Diary of Anne Frank*?"

"I....I haven't prepared anything."

"We understand that–just one of the diary passages, perhaps."

Victoria couldn't remember the first time she had read Anne Frank's diary, but it was long before she even thought of being an actress and no matter how many times she'd reread it since then, the words of the little Jewish girl whose family had been driven into hiding by the Nazi occupation of Holland never failed to touch her profoundly. Perhaps she actually envied Anne. True–she suffered terribly, but she had also known the love of a caring parent–something Victoria couldn't even imagine. For whatever reason her voice as she spoke the words was filled with a sweet wistfulness. Her eyes still shone with the tears of her disappointment and her brief performance was totally winning.

"Thank you, Miss Windsor," Peter Harris said finally. "That will be all. Notices will be sent out in about a week."

Victoria walked as quickly as possible back up the aisle and out through the swinging door, ignoring the other applicants, and partway down the stairs she started to run. She didn't stop running, in fact, until she was out on Euston Road heading back toward King's Cross and then only because she'd stumbled and nearly fallen. Impatiently she wiped her tears away with the back of her hand and jamming her fists deep into the pockets of her beige linen skirt, she strode angrily along the pavement.

She had undoubtedly failed the audition and not because of any lack of talent. "Damn!" She realized almost at once she must have spoken the word aloud because a man who happened to be passing in the other direction appeared startled. What am I going to do, her thoughts continued, tinged now with desperation and inside the skirt pockets her hands clenched and unclenched, the nails digging into her palms. All I've dreamed about for over a year is RADA. I never bothered to consider what I'd do if they turned me down. And all because that woman, whoever the hell she is, is a bloody idiot!

It was actually a relief to once again be at work at Danny's–arms plunged up to the elbows in dirty dishwater. From now until well after midnight she would be too busy to think and then mercifully she would be so exhausted she'd be able to sleep.

* * *

Even as Victoria reported for this second shift, the admissions committee was meeting to discuss the day's auditions, acceptance requiring the approval of at least two of its three members. If she could have been there, she would have been able to see the other individuals attached to the disembodied voices she'd heard in the darkened auditorium–individuals who along with Peter Harris would determine her fate.

The woman was Claudine Arnold, instructor in acting and one of the directors of the three major productions presented each year by the Academy students. A short, dumpy woman, her body appeared compressed into a permanent "S" shape, her head protruding forward slightly while from there her figure (if you could call it that) swept down into a concave chest and a little, round pot belly. She wore her coarse white hair in a straight mannish Dutch cut.

Her wardrobe was limited, consisting exclusively of one dark blue suit and one light blue suit–both worn over a white nylon blouse with a limp bow at the neck. For some time now the waistband of both skirts had refused to go around Miss Arnold's misshapen middle, a problem she solved with a large safety pin. It remained impossible, however, to close the zipper and unfortunately she insisted on striding back and forth in front of her classes, hand on her left hip to hold back the suit jacket thus displaying the safety pin as well as the gaping opening.

The third person was "Tuck", instructor in theatre history as well as scenic and costume design and possessing a nature as gentle as his voice. A somewhat rotund little man, he tried in vain to ignore his overweight condition by wearing his belt below his belly; invariably his shirt protested the strain by popping a button or two at just this crucial spot. Tuck wore his hair combed down in all directions from a balding crown and his mild, near-sighted eyes peered out through rimless glasses–or rather over them since the glasses were forever sliding down his nose. As he lectured, he would habitually push them up again with the side of his forefinger–accompanying the gesture with a self-conscious clearing of his throat. His actual given name was Archibald Tucker, but most people had forgotten that fact if they'd even known it in the first place since no one called him anything but Tuck. This was less because it was a natural shortening of his last name than because he appeared the living reincarnation of the legendary Friar. A few students might begin by ridiculing Tuck; they all ended up adoring him.

For the first hour or so the committee's deliberations had proceeded smoothly, but now Peter Harris as chairman paused to study his list again. He'd put it off as long as he could. She was the last candidate to be considered. "Now----" He glanced at his female colleague—"Victoria Windsor."

"Absolutely not!" Claudine replied at once. Tuck could be distinctly heard to chuckle. "And what do you find so amusing, Archibald?" she demanded.

"Oh, nothing, nothing." He cleared his throat, pushing his glasses up on his nose again. "I just somehow had the...ah...feeling that would be your opinion."

"May I inquire as to why you are against Victoria's admission, Claudine?" Peter inquired soothingly even as he threw a pleading glance in the other's man direction as if to say, "Please don't get her going!"

"It's....it's obvious the girl has no talent on top of which she clearly lacks self-discipline!" The sound emanating from somewhere in Tuck's ample mid-section can only be interpreted in the written word–and that rather inadequately–as "Humph!" "<u>Will</u> you <u>please</u> <u>ask</u> <u>him</u> to <u>stop</u> that?!" Claudine was now employing one of her customary tactics with Tuck which was to talk around him rather than to him.

With a sigh of sorely tried patience Peter took on his customary role of peacemaker. "Well, Claudine," he replied at last, "since you have stated your opinion of Victoria, it <u>is</u> only fair, after all, to allow Tuck to give us his."

Removing his glasses, the other man began to search his pockets for a cloth to clean them, a very successful delaying ploy when he needed a few seconds to think or as in the present instance when he wished to be especially annoying. With the spectacles at last polished and replaced he looked deliberately past his longtime adversary at Peter and said very distinctly. "She has to be one of the most gifted and perceptive young actresses we've ever had apply to RADA."

"Not to mention beautiful," Claudine snorted.

"We are not taking Victoria's physical appearance into consideration," Peter interposed.

"Oh, we're not, are we?" she continued ironically. "Suppose you give us your opinion of her then."

"I'm afraid I'd have to agree with Tuck."

"Just as I thought," the woman sniffed. "And we know very well what your interest is in the girl!"

Tuck cleared his throat several times as once again he pushed his glasses back into their proper position. "There's no need to be nasty, Claudine."

"Thank you, but I can take care of myself," Peter Harris stated firmly. "It's clear," he continued to Claudine, "that you intend to vote against Victoria. It would seem, however, that the two of us outnumber you. Am I right, old man?"

Tuck barely resisted the urge to smirk. "Yes, Peter. I vote for acceptance."

"Very well. I think that concludes our business."

Claudine glared at them both and getting abruptly to her feet, strode from the room. "Whew!" Once more Tuck got out his handkerchief, but this time to mop his neck and forehead. "I knew this would happen when the young lady dared to defy her." He paused. "I say–are you...ah....in a frightful rush, old chap?"

"I have a dinner engagement." Peter stood up. "But we can walk to the tube stop together."

"Fine, fine." Tuck vaulted himself to his feet by means of the chair arms and gathered up his things. They left the auditorium together, moved down the stairs and out of the building, neither of them speaking until suddenly on the pavement in front of the Academy Tuck stopped, seizing Peter by the arm and turning his friend to face him. "She is good, isn't she?" he asked intently.

The other man merely nodded and after a quick glance in both directions he hurried diagonally across Gower Street toward the point at which it intersected with Chenies Street which in turn cut through to Tottenham Court Road and the Goodge Street Underground Station. But Tuck was not to be deterred and without bothering to check for approaching cars himself, he launched his body into the street. Brakes screeched; horns blared; drivers yelled obscenities, but he heard none of it, so intent was he on keeping up. Even under ordinary circumstances this represented quite a feat since it required two of his short, bouncing steps to every one of his companion's long strides and this evening for some reason his old friend seemed bent on escape. At last, however, Peter apparently took pity on him, stopping to wait at the corner of Chenies Street. Tuck came panting up to him. "How good?" he demanded.

Shaking his head indulgently, Peter smiled down from his height of nearly six feet at his friend's five feet, five inches. "Tuck, we go through this every time we hold auditions. You're always sure we've found the greatest actor or actress ever to set foot on the London stage and you know bloody well that nine out of ten of even our best never make it professionally."

"This time I'm sure," Tuck insisted refusing to be discouraged. "How good do you think she is?"

Peter started to walk away again, but at more deliberate pace. True–Victoria's defiance of Claudine had amused him, but that didn't mean he'd been unaware of the brilliance of her audition. There was a special excitement he experienced when he glimpsed that rare theatrical talent superior to the norm; a kind of prickling which ran up and down his backbone causing the gooseflesh to spread outward along his arms and legs. Claudine's accusations had shaken him, however, causing him to doubt his own judgment; after all Victoria was incredibly desirable. But now he could feel himself catching Tuck's fervor. He couldn't have been wrong if his colleague had seen it, too. It was at this point that his thoughts were interrupted once more by the sound of the other man's voice and with a start he realized they'd come out on Tottenham Court Road, a busy, crowded street, and he hadn't even been aware of it. "Damn it, Peter! How good?"

"Probably the best we'll ever see, Tuck." Peter paused for a moment on the curb before crossing over to the underground station. And he repeated it. "Probably the best we'll ever see."

"Then why didn't you defend her more vehemently?" Tuck demanded as they crossed together and entered the station. "You know Claudine always hates the pretty ones and this one had the spunk to talk back to her."

"Two reasons," Peter explained while they waited for the lift which at the older stations such as Goodge Street still served to carry passengers to and from the trains. "Claudine teaches elementary acting. Why antagonize her any further?"

The big, old-fashioned lift could be heard now creaking laboriously up from below and a moment or so later it slid into view, stopping at the street level. The attendant held back the heavy, metal door to allow the passengers to enter. The people who worked on these station lifts all looked the same, Tuck thought with his customary compassion– gray-faced, apathetic appearing individuals who obviously hated the tedium of their lives, but who also lacked the ambition to better themselves.

In the crowded lift cage–even walking through the low cement-lined tunnels leading to the train platforms–there was little opportunity to continue their discussion. Peter would be traveling just two stops south to Leicester Square where he was meeting his date at a pub while Tuck was going north all the way to Highgate where he shared a semi-detached with a widowed aunt and before they were to separate, they stopped again briefly to talk. "Peter," Tuck reminded him, "you said two reasons." Standing off to one side of the passageway out of the worst of the rush hour crush, the two men were still jostled as people hurried past them to turn left or right depending upon the direction in which they were heading.

"Oh yes, I did." Peter leaned one hand against the rough cement wall. At least, the other man reflected bitterly afterwards, he'd had the decency to look embarrassed. "The other...ah... is that Claudine's right. I do want to get her into bed." Clapping his friend on the shoulder, he turned to mingle with the crowd and the next instant he vanished from sight around the corner.

Tuck easily pushed his way through to the other side of the passageway and out onto the platform for the northbound trains. There were certain circumstances, he mused wryly, when his bulk was an advantage. Standing there waiting for the train, he kept seeing Victoria's lovely, young face and once he sighed profoundly, shaking his head. Claudine would be out to destroy her while Peter only wanted to use her for his own pleasure. He vowed he at least would be her friend and as he thought again of her potential as an actress, he nearly fell off the platform in his excitement.

* * *

Victoria spent the week following her audition in a state of abject misery. Certain now she would be turned down, all she wanted was for the waiting to be over. Perhaps when she'd actually seen the rejection in black and white, she could make other plans; until then she couldn't seem to do anything except haunt the postal box and suffer. One week to the day and there was still no word. Victoria was sure that in this case no news definitely did not mean good news and all through the long horrible day she'd had to fight to keep back the tears. The pub was closed for the night, in fact, and she was just finishing the floor, the job she despised the most, when Dan came hurrying into the kitchen. He was smiling uneasily and she saw at once he had a long, white envelope in his hand. "Now don't you go gettin' h'upset wiv me, young miss. But with the noon rush and then my h'account books to do in the p.m., h'it just sorta slipped my mind, you might say."

"Well, don't just stand there! Give it to me!" Snatching the envelope away from him, she saw at once the little masks of comedy and tragedy in the upper left-hand corner. A sharp pang went through her and her heart began to pound. Then the realization hit her. The suspense could have been over twelve hours ago if the letter hadn't "just slipped his mind". "How could you forget something like this?" she screamed at him.

Dan flinched. Gullibly he'd believed Victoria's story about being a secretarial student and so of course he had no idea of the envelope's significance. "B....b...beggin' your pardon, young miss. I didn't know h'it was that h'important."

"Important!" she shrieked. "You are without a doubt the most ridiculous, stupid little man on the face of this earth!" With her already well-developed sense of the dramatic Victoria picked up the pail of dirty, soapy water and dumped it all over the floor as Dan continued to stand there with his mouth open. "And you may wash your own floor!" With a toss of her head she turned to sweep grandly through the door and up the stairs.

Neither of them had noticed Bess who'd come from locking up for the night just in time to witness the brief scene. Without a word she took a dry mop from the closet and began to clean up the water. Finally Dan came to enough to comprehend what she was doing. "No, no, my dear." Gently he took the mop away from her. "Your back, you know."

His wife stood looking at him for a second or two. "Kindness don't do no good wiv some people, Dan. I'll tike care of it."

"I...I'd h'appreciate that, my girl." He was still shaking his head as he began to mop the wet floor.

Victoria, meanwhile, had arrived in her room and leaning against the closed door, she stared down at the letter as if miraculously she could discern its contents without opening the envelope. Then all at once she was tearing into it, all but demolishing it in her haste to remove the single sheet of stationery. Only one page–surely acceptance would have meant more forms to fill out, pages of instructions; one thin page undoubtedly signaled rejection. Hands shaking, she unfolded the paper and read:

> Dear Miss Windsor,
>
> Congratulations! It is my pleasure to inform you of your admission to RADA. It is my additional pleasure to notify you that the committee considers your potential as an actress worthy of a grant of 200 pounds to assist in the defrayal of your first year's tuition, fees and miscellaneous expenses.
>
> Please report to the Academy on Monday, August 26th at 9 a.m. for orientation and formal registration. Again my congratulations.
>
> Sincerely,
> *Peter Harris*
> Assistant Director
>
> Following the typed letter was a handwritten postscript. *—I trust we will be seeing a great deal of each other.—Peter.*

"I know what he's after," Victoria muttered to herself, but Peter's postscript was immediately forgotten as the full import of the letter's primary message swept over her–not only acceptance, but two hundred pounds of her tuition paid for! She had to tell someone! She could go back downstairs and tell Dan. He would..... But not even Victoria had the nerve to go to him with her news after their exchange of a few minutes ago. So there was no one to tell–no one with whom she could share the most exciting moment of her life.

She didn't know why, but all at once she thought of Sister Philippa. By now the Lesters would be upstairs in their flat and she hurried back down into the pub where there was a coin-operated telephone. She gave the operator the familiar number and when the pip-pip-pip sound came on the line indicating the connection had been made, she pushed in three one shilling pieces. It hadn't occurred to her that it was well past midnight and everyone at the school would have long since been in bed.

"Heathfield Abbey School for Girls," a cultured young female voice announced– undoubtedly one of the unfortunate first year postulants who were assigned to cover the switchboard during the night.

"Sister Philippa, please." Victoria's voice trembled a little.

There was a brief pause and then the well-remembered tones–"Sister Philippa here." She'd obviously been awakened from a sound sleep and it was only now that Victoria realized with a start how late it was. What am I doing anyway, she thought, and she quickly hung up. "Hello...hello....hello," Philippa said several more times, but the line had gone dead.

Victoria walked slowly upstairs and back in her room she began to pack. The next morning when Bess knocked at the door, there was no answer and entering, she found a note on the bed. "I thought I'd save you the trouble of sacking me!"

That evening found her settled temporarily in a bed-and-breakfast. During the last fortnight or so at Danny's she'd begun to think a small flat would allow her more privacy and accordingly she'd spent much of that day thinking and figuring–for what seemed like the hundredth time that summer covering endless pieces of paper with sums–to see whether she could afford it. She had indeed saved well over 400 pounds-- nearly the 415 she'd counted on. She would never, of course, have been able to save that much if she'd had to pay for rent and food. At the thought of Danny Victoria experienced a twinge of conscience, but quickly stifled it. With 200 of the 400 pound tuition taken care of, she had 200 plus to spare. Forty pounds a month for a flat perhaps and she could certainly eat on five or six pounds a week. In all that would be about 60 pounds a month times the nine months or so of the school year for a total of 540. By working nights she might just manage.

Two things became immediately apparent as Victoria began once again to study the adverts: the jobs hadn't grown any more appealing and the flats away from central London were as much as ten or even twenty pounds cheaper the month. Even considering the fare on the underground, it would be worth it to live further out. Several flats were advertised in the Hammersmith section on the west side of the city and the next morning she took the tube out of King's Cross..

The trip was a simple one, not even necessitating a change of trains since the Piccadilly Line ran diagonally northeast to southwest across the city. Traveling to RADA, if she did find a flat in this area, would be a bit more complicated as glancing up at the underground diagram in the Hammersmith station, she observed that Goodge Street, the closest stop to the Academy, was on the Northern Line. This would involve a change at Leicester Square, but even this was no problem at all to the well-seasoned cosmopolite she'd become in a mere two months. She felt absurdly pleased with herself.

Her euphoria was short-lived. The first flat was a disaster–on the top floor with only one narrow enclosed wooden staircase. The second wanted 60 pounds the month and at the third the woman once again questioned Victoria's age. By noon she was hot and discouraged and on top of everything else the pointed-toed, three inch spike heels she'd worn in an attempt to appear older pinched and rubbed everywhere.

Buying a cheese and tomato sandwich and a Coca-Cola in a delicatessen, she settled down on a bench in a small neighborhood park to eat her lunch and consider the remaining possibilities; there were only two. The first was on Netherwood Road which Victoria's map showed to be a side street off Shepherd's Bush Road. She'd only gone a short distance, however, when she passed a funny little triangular shaped building, its ground floor painted green with brown trim while the upper story was red brick. Between the floors a yellow stripe ran around the front two sides, black lettering proclaiming repeatedly that this establishment was indeed "Ollie's Alley". It was evidently a pub, but it was only as she was actually walking by that she noticed a sign in the window– "Waitress Wanted–Part Time". On an impulse she went in.

The bar was directly ahead as she entered and a man was sitting behind it on a stool. As she came in, he looked up, drying his hands on a towel. Then to her amazement he also stood up and up and still up and as he finally came around the corner of the bar and approached her, Victoria decided he had to be at least six feet, six inches and close to 20 stone. He was totally bald. Oddly at the same time the lower half of his face was all but lost in a luxuriant moustache and imposing patriarchal beard as if he were somehow trying to make up for the lack of hair on his head. She wondered later why she didn't find him in the least intimidating. Perhaps this awesome mountain of a man simply interested her; perhaps it was his eyes: the brightest blue she could ever remember seeing. "Unt vat can I do for you, kleine fraulein?" He had an extraordinary voice as well–hoarse and rasping–and she clearly detected a foreign accent. Then she realized he'd addressed her as fraulein and decided he must be German.

Here goes–mentally Victoria crossed her fingers. "I came about the job."

"Zat zo?" He peered down at her over tiny half-spectacles dwarfed even further by his massive features. "You are olt enough to vork in such a place, ja?"

Victoria began to relax. At least he hadn't said no. "I wouldn't apply otherwise." She flashed him a disarming smile.

"Vell, you look olt enough," he admitted, still doubtful. "But I have to be careful–ze polizei, verstehen-Sie? Excuse, bitte, the police–you undershtand?"

"I understand completely," she agreed seriously. "What do you pay, please, and what are the hours?" She couldn't help smiling. She was becoming an old hand at this.

"I need somevun–Monday to Saturday, seven to vun a.m., except Saturday ven ve must close at midnight–double behind ze bar. You can serve beer and ale from ze tap?"

Victoria found herself waiting for him to clear his throat. Whatever could have happened to his voice? "Yes, I can work those hours, but the wages?" Conveniently she'd overlooked the question about the tap. After all, how hard could it be?

"Businesslike," he observed with a wide grin and he added some other remark-- apparently in German. He was either praising her or teasing her; she couldn't be sure which. "Ja, of course. Abe pays gut; you vill see." He was still smiling broadly. "Ten shillings an hour– tips shplit between ze three of us–anuzzer pound or zo for each for ze night." She did some rapid mental arithmetic. That should mean at least 23 pounds, ten shillings a week–92 pounds a month. "Vell?" The man inquired after a moment. The word sounded like two pieces of sandpaper being rubbed together.

"I was just figuring out if that would be enough. I'm a student and I can only work evenings." Victoria managed to make her tone slightly condescending. "Do you know of any flats in the neighborhood?"

"Ja, I believe I do." He nodded so vigorously he almost lost his glasses. "My vife, a sister Esther she has vis flats. You go back to ze roundabout–you come zat vay, ja?–go around to ze ozzer side. At ze end of ze first block a little bakery zere is–light blue vis yellow trim and above–nice flats–gemutlich! You go see, ja? You tell Esther zat Abe sends you, ja?"

Already she was developing an ear for voices and dialects–storing them in her mind for possible future use. In fact she'd become so fascinated listening to this man that she neglected to pay attention to what he was saying. "Excuse me." She shrugged prettily. "Back to the roundabout and then where?"

"Zose kleine pink ears–I zink ze do not hear zo gut." He winked at her and obligingly repeated the directions.

Spinning about, Victoria walked rapidly from the pub. "Hold that job for a bit," she called back over her shoulder. "I'll be back."

For a minute Abe watched her go. "Himmel," he muttered to himself, "she didn't even say 'Danke'."

The bakery turned out to be only a few doors down from the delicatessen where she'd bought her lunch and Victoria found it easily. Specialty–what else but German breads and pastries? The woman behind the display case looked like the fairy godmother in every children's story ever written. She had a plump face and white hair curling all over her head like some sort of fluffy halo. The heat from her ovens had made her naturally rosy cheeks even redder. "Ja, kleine liebchen?" She beamed at Victoria.

"The man at Ollie's Alley told me you have flats to let."

The woman had apparently been standing on something because suddenly now she vanished from sight, reappearing almost at once around the corner of the counter to come and peer up at her. "A kleine madchen like yourself can do zis?"

"Excuse me, a what?"

"Kleine madchen–a little girl."

The woman was less than five feet tall and Victoria took full advantage of the height difference to stare down imperiously down at her. "I am <u>not</u> a little girl!" Was Abe's wife the same size as her sister, she wondered. If so, they must make an amazing couple.

"Vell, I don't know....."

"If Abe can hire me as a waitress, you can let me the flat." Immediately she was annoyed with herself. The last had sounded faintly desperate and that could only make her seem even younger.

"Ja, vell Abe, he ist freundlich...ah....kind-hearted. His vife, my sister Miriam, she alvays says zat......"

"May I see your flats?" The little lady still appeared doubtful, however, and Victoria gambled. "Well, really!" She tossed her head. "It looks as if I'll have to go elsewhere!"

"Now vait a minute." Quickly Esther reached out to take her by the hand and stop her from leaving. "I vill show you. Come vis me, bitte." Scowling, Victoria pulled her hand away. The woman noticed this, but made no mention of it. Instead she simply turned to lead the way outside. "At ze moment two I have to let." She opened the door next to the bakery and stepped into a narrow hallway. "I vill show zem boz and you can see, ja?"

The first was directly over the bakery and had a large living room, separate bedroom and kitchen. Victoria knew at once she could never afford it. "I don't need anything nearly so big," she said at once, trying not to sound disappointed.

"Ze ozzer vun ist smaller. Vat you call a bedsitter, ja? Come....come." Ist too kostspielig for ze kleine liebchen, she thought to herself. Vell ve vill make sure she can manage ze ozzer vun. Somevun has to look after her.

They climbed one more flight of stairs and walked toward the back of the building, the tiny landlady opening another door at the end of the hallway. The bedsitter or efficiency flat was a sunny, corner room almost as large as the living room of the flat below. A stove and a small fridge stood in an alcove to the left of the door while a sink in the far corner apparently served for housekeeping purposes as well as personal hygiene. A colorful braided rug covered the center of the floor and although it was quite evidently furnished in someone's cast-offs, the total effect was one of warmth and cozy homeliness. Victoria barely suppressed a forlorn little sigh; this flat, too, would certainly be well beyond her limited finances. "Oh no, it's much too shabby and run-down. I guess not." She was almost out the door when the woman's voice stopped her.

"Ja, I know. Ze furniture ist olt and ze water closet is off ze hall. Zat ist vhy I ask only...." Briefly Esther hesitated. The flat was actually 50 pounds a month, but it <u>was</u> poorly furnished and more than half an hour from central London on the tube. At the same time the rental price had to <u>sound</u> plausible. However badly the madchen needed a place, she was clearly too proud to accept anything resembling charity. "Zat is vhy I ask only zirty-five and ten ze monz. Zat ist fair, ja?"

Victoria spun about again so abruptly she nearly lost her balance. That was four pounds and ten below her limit! She came perilously close to throwing her arms around this dear tiny person. "In that case I suppose I can stand it. When may I move in?"

"At vunce, ja." Like many others in Victoria's life both before and since, she was puzzled, even hurt by her apparent lack of gratitude. "I am just two floors down, behind ze bakery. Just call for Esther if you need anyzing. Ze key ist zere on ze table," she added as she left the room closing the door behind her.

Victoria stood for a moment in the middle of the floor. It was all the hideaways she'd ever sought combined into one. It was the gazebo on her family's estate in Kent; the attic room in the Heathfield dormitory; the high flat rock at Camp Windermere and now there would be no one to intrude on her private world: no governess, no Sister Philippa and no...... But here her thoughts ground to a halt for the trespasser who'd dared to enter the last of these sanctuaries was Uncle Bertie. She strode to the table, snatching up the heavy, old-fashioned key. The door locked behind her, she hurried down the two flights of stairs, out the front door and along the street once again in the direction of the pub. But thoughts of Uncle Bertie would continue to come to her mind unbidden and at the most inopportune moments in the years ahead. The memory of that dear, gentle man refused to be so obliging as to simply go away.

When she entered the pub again a few minutes later, Abe was sweeping the floor.

"Well, I have a flat–poor, but adequate," she announced haughtily. "So I will be able to accept the job." Gott in Himmel, Abe thought, she sounds as zo she ist doing me ze favor. "I have to move today. I can start tomorrow." With that Victoria started to leave, but one point intrigued her. "You're not Ollie, are you?" she couldn't resist asking him in spite of her determination to sound suitably blase.

"Nein, nein, I am Abe–Abe Epshtein." Beaming now, he shook his head just as vigorously from side to side as a while before he had nodded in affirmation. "I begin to vork here vhen I come to England in 1946. Zen Sam Schultz, he own ze place. Perhaps he buy it from Ollie. I buy it vhen Sam–he gets too olt. Just last year. Verstehen-Sie–You undershtand?"

"Oh...ah...yes." She did not, of course, and as she finally left to walk back to the underground station, she was still laughing a little in amused bewilderment.

Arriving back at the flat a while later with her still meager belongings, she found a small brown paper sack outside the door. Inside were several warm, freshly baked rolls from the bakery downstairs. This custom would continue as long as Victoria lived in the flat and although the rolls, along with the inevitable pot of tea, were often, as was the case tonight, the only supper she'd have, somehow she could never bring herself to thank Esther for this kindness.

Now it was past midnight. The rolls had long since been devoured and yet she still sat motionless in the middle of the floor. Knees doubled up, she hugged her legs to her chest as unconsciously she continued to hunger for the simple human warmth she had never experienced. A pot of tea, long since grown cold, was on the floor in front of her and she hadn't even bothered to turn on a light. It was as though she were once more that forgotten small child defying anyone who might come to tell her it was time for bed.

The next evening Victoria reported for work at Ollie's Alley. Her shift began at seven, but the pub opened for the evening trade at 4:30 and she could hear the loud voices and raucous laughter when she was still a block away. Entering, she found the air thick with smoke and the place apparently already filled to capacity. The other waitress was in a state of perpetual motion about the room while Abe himself was behind the bar dispensing foaming steins of beer and ale. "Ah, you are here, kleine liebchen," he roared over the din. "Put your zings in ze back qvickly. Ve are very busy!"

Following his orders, Victoria left her cardigan and purse in the tiny kitchen and soon she was initiated into the routine. For the first week or so her arms and back ached from the heavy steins and trays of food and the hours spent on her feet left them bruised and blistered. She was young, however, and her body soon grew accustomed to the arduous life of a pub waitress.

Emotionally the toughening process took longer. At Danny's she hadn't come much into contact with the customers. Now she was right out among them and every time she stopped to take an order and to place foaming steins in a table, she could expect someone to slip an arm around her waist, gradually moving his hand up to her breast or perhaps try to run a finger up her leg. Victoria soon learned to use her elbows and high-heeled shoes to full advantage, warning an overly amorous customer to "Get your hands off me, you bloody bastard!" It was hard to believe she was only months away from an Anglican convent school!

Chapter 2

There came a day, however, just slightly more than three weeks later, when all of this ceased to have any significance–the morning on which she walked into RADA for the third time to commence in earnest her training as an actress. A sign was posted in the same spot as on the day of her audition, but this one was a directive for new students to report to the main auditorium. The hall also turned out to be the same one although today it was brightly lit and alive with the buzz of conversation. Sitting on stage with the other department chairmen, Peter Harris had seen Victoria almost at the moment of her arrival. Pausing in the doorway, she was unconscious of the stunning picture she created.

The director of the Academy, Bradford Carlisle, stepped up to the microphone tapping it briefly to be sure it was on. "Ladies and gentlemen, if you would please be seated. We are about to begin."

Small conversational groups immediately broke up as the students came forward to settle in the first several rows. Victoria waited until everyone else was seated and only then did she finally sit down herself–a few rows behind and removed from the rest. Highly amused, Peter watched her. Already the theatrical gesture, he thought smiling. It would, in fact, be some time before Victoria was so skilled in the theatrical gesture. But then Peter never really did understand her. Only long after it was too late would he discern at all her true nature and then but dimly.

Victoria only half-listened as first the director and then each department head welcomed them–making self-conscious little jokes and telling them how happy they were to have them at RADA. The one speaker to whom she paid any attention was Peter Harris and then just when he was outlining the first year course for acting majors. At last Peter was concluding. "As the final speaker it is also my job to inform you that class schedules will be distributed alphabetically. You'll notice four tables in front of the stage. Due to orientation, by the way, your first class this morning will be at 10:30."

Victoria made her way down the aisle to the furthest table to the right, vowing she wouldn't always come at the end. Damn it all! Wouldn't you know it would be Peter Harris! He'd patronized the filling station so frequently it had to have been purely for the purpose of tormenting her. And what the hell had he done with all that petrol?! Yes, Peter had indeed made certain he'd be at Table 4, but at the moment Victoria approached he happened to be looking down. "Name, please?" he tossed off carelessly.

"Victoria Windsor." The voice with its faint hint of arrogance already had an unmistakable ring to it.

Slowly Peter raised his head to find her regarding him coolly. "Well, Miss Windsor," he observed drily as he pretended to search through the stack of cards for her schedule although of course he knew exactly where it was, "are you sure this won't interfere with your duties at the pumps?" She glared at him, refusing to reply. "Ah, here it is." After what had seemed like forever, he finally removed her card from the pile, but then instead of immediately handing it to her he began to read through it himself as though to verify some particular point. "I see you have Claudine Arnold for beginning acting," he continued after a brief pause looking up again–a slow smile spreading across his decidedly equine features. "You may remember her from your audition. She certainly hasn't forgotten you."

"May I please have my schedule, Mr. Harris?"

"Certainly. Certainly." At last he handed her the card, watching with evident enjoyment as she strode away up the aisle. "Well worth taming, that one," he murmured under his breath to Tuck who was at the next table.

"Wh...wh...what?" the other man stammered in confusion although in actuality he'd heard all too well.

"Nothing, Tuck, nothing," Peter replied even as he wondered just how long the conquest would take.

"Son-of-a-bitch!" Victoria was so furious she failed to notice the girl in front of her had stopped to search for something in her purse until she walked into her. "Why in hell don't you watch where you're going?" she snapped.

"I...I'm sorry," the other girl apologized. "Oh....oh, wait a minute," she went on almost at once. "We met at the audition...remember?"

Already several steps further on, Victoria stopped and turned back. "Were you addressing me?"

"I...I was just saying that we'd met already–at the auditions. Looks like we both made it! My name's Melinda Cutler, by the way, but everyone calls me Mindy."

"I don't intend to call you anything!" Victoria continued on up the aisle and a moment later the incident was forgotten. After all, she wasn't at the Academy to make friends. Just down the hall from the auditorium she came across an empty classroom and welcoming the chance to be alone, she went in and sat down at one of the students' desks to look over her schedule. During their first semester RADA students received a general introduction to theatre in addition to beginning work in their major field and as a result Victoria's classes included theatre history, costume and scene design, modern dance, pantomime, period dance and movement, make-up and stage lighting as well as her introductory course in acting techniques and a workshop in improvisational theatre. Beside the course titles and hours were the names of the instructors. Quickly her eyes scanned the page and there, just as Peter Harris had informed her with evident glee, was the name of Claudine Arnold. "Damn!" She struck the desk with a clenched fist. "Of all the bloody rotten luck!"

Peter, meanwhile, had immediately turned the end of the alphabet over to someone else and hurried out of the auditorium himself, hoping to catch up with Victoria. He'd almost passed the classroom when he caught a glimpse of her out of the corner of his eye. He leaned against the door jamb and crossed his arms. "Well, well, so here you are." It was his bedroom voice and it rarely let him down.

A few seconds went by before Victoria raised her head to acknowledge his presence. "It would seem so." She lowered her gaze again as if her only interest were the listing of her courses. Actually she was sorry she had glanced up at all. He looked so silly posed like that she'd come close to laughing in his face.

Peter forced himself to continue smiling and coming on into the room, he leaned casually against the corner of the instructor's desk crossing his legs at the ankles. "So you want to be an actress?" His eyebrows shot upwards until they all but disappeared into his hairline. This particular feat of physiognomic gymnastics never failed to rattle the young female students, but it appeared to have been lost on Victoria whose ostensibly single-minded attention was once more on her schedule. He gritted his teeth–he would be charming if it killed him–and made a final attempt. "Do you have the talent to go with that beautiful face? You do know you're beautiful, don't you?"

"Surely you remember you tried that line on me once before." She was openly mocking him now. "And it didn't work then either."

Peter didn't enjoy being put down by a female, but then Victoria was clearly not the typical blonde featherbrain. Her seduction would require careful and perhaps lengthy strategy. Still the final result, he reminded himself, would be well worth it. He shifted tactics as easily and smoothly as his car's transmission changed gears: general category- boyish; sub-division-embarrassed, but sincere. He grinned at her disarmingly. "But what if it happens to be the truth?"

She favored him this time with a more lingering look, allowing herself to smile briefly in return. "In that case I suppose we'll have to allow it."

Involuntarily Peter clenched and unclenched his fists. God, he thought, how long will I be able to wait? Somehow he restrained himself and coming to sit in the desk next to hers, he once again switched his plan of action: general category - friendly; sub-division - conversational. "Frightfully sorry about Claudine by the way."

Victoria saw her chance. Peter was, after all, the chairman of the acting department. "Well, there was something I wanted to ask you," she admitted coyly.

"Anything...anything at all." He was at his most expansive.

"Couldn't I just skip the introductory acting course. After all I don't really need it."

"I don't know about the talent," Peter couldn't resist observing, "but you certainly have the ego."

"What do you mean–you don't know about my talent." She chose to ignore the second part of his remark. "You were at my audition."

"I should be totally honest with you, Miss Windsor. The vote on your admission was not unanimous and I could have...."

"Oh, come now, we both know who voted against me. What kind of bloody fool do you think I am anyway?"

There followed what was for Peter a long, disconcerting silence and one made no less uncomfortable by the fact that Victoria was sitting very close to him, a smile just tugging at the corners of her mouth. Trapped, unable to discern any dignified means of escape, his customary self-control snapped and jumping to his feet, he strode to the door. "You will follow your schedule exactly as you see it before you, Miss Windsor!" he shouted. "Perhaps that will teach you to treat your instructors with more respect in the future!" He had intended to punctuate these final words with a magnificent slam of the classroom door. Unfortunately it caught on his foot pulling his loafer half off and refusing to stop and adjust the shoe, he hobbled away down the hall followed relentlessly by peals of laughter from Victoria.

* * *

The classes were for Victoria a feast after years of famine and so for the first month or so she was content to remain in the background. Reveling in the chance to learn, she was willing to await her moment. When it did, in fact, come, it was due oddly enough to Claudine Arnold. Yet perhaps that wasn't so strange. If Victoria were eventually to be noticed as something more than the average RADA student, it would be in her acting class, no matter who the instructor.

They had received their first major assignment. A fairly routine one, it was called in theatrical parlance, a "stream-of-consciousness" exercise and consisted of voicing aloud the thoughts of some person or animal or even an inanimate object. Since theoretically the mind is never at rest, the actor is expected to speak continually. "Concentration is vital to an actor," Miss Arnold proclaimed striding up and down in front of the class, left arm as usual akimbo. Her voice was painful to listen to– high-pitched, nasal and with a pronounced Yorkshire accent. She would have benefitted immensely from the Academy's speech class. At the same time, however, as much as Victoria hated to admit it, her explanation as to the purpose of the exercise made good sense. "And if you allow anything to distract you," she was continuing, "your performance will suffer. Preparing and performing this assignment will help you to begin to develop this concentration." Specific instructions were to present an actual person out of history at some climactic moment in his or her life.

Victoria found the prospect of the exercise tremendously exciting. Choosing the right character to portray so preoccupied her, in fact, that she rode past her tube stop and later at the pub she forgot a stein under the tap until suddenly beer was pouring over the rim. "Here, here, liebchen, vat is it vis you tonight?" Abe inquired good-naturedly as he mopped up the mess, "You are all vet. Go home and shange. It is all right vis Abe–ja." He found it as difficult to be angry with Victoria as Danny had. At times her coldness puzzled him, but he also sensed the unhappiness hidden beneath and he was unfailingly kind.

"I'm all right," she snapped at him now. "Leave me alone!"

For the remainder of the evening, however, she kept her mind on what she was doing. Only when she was finally back at her flat settled in the middle of the floor– the inevitable pot of tea in front of her–did she allow herself to think of the assignment again. "I'll knock that ugly old bitch on her ass," she vowed and after much thought she decided to portray Joan of Arc alone in her cell moments before she is to be burned at the stake. The possibilities of such a scene were endless: Joan's memories of the outdoors, the colors, sounds and smells of her father's barnyard, her special pet–a mongrel dog, her faith in God, her first religious experience, a boy she'd once loved, a spider spinning a web in one corner of her cell, the rumblings of her stomach, the cold and dampness and climaxing, of course, with her dread of the fire.

It was all Victoria could do on the following Monday to concentrate on her morning classes. She was too excited to eat lunch, but she went to a small restaurant at the corner of Goodge Street and Tottenham Court Road just to have something to do until the acting class met at one-thirty. She was sitting alone at a corner table, sipping a cup of tea and nibbling disinterestedly on a scone when she happened to notice the girl who'd tried to strike up a conversation with her both at the audition and on the first day of classes. She was with a boy whom Victoria also recognized as an acting student although of course she had no idea who he was. They were holding hands, talking together in low voices and after a while she found herself watching them. How silly they were to have their minds filled only with each other! Yet she continued to stare at them, seemingly against her will. What would it be like, she found herself thinking, to have someone love me that much? I'm just as bad as they are, she reprimanded herself all at once. My mind's not on the exercise either! Disgusted with herself, Victoria tossed her check and the money on the counter by the cash register and hurried from the restaurant. At this hour the little theatre where the acting class met would be empty and she should be using the time to run through her presentation once more rather than wasting it in foolish wonderings.

Thus she was already there when the rest of the students began to come in–as usual in groups of two or three. Miss Arnold entered and with no advance pleasantries strode to the back of the room and sat down. "Would anyone care to begin?" Victoria's first impulse was to raise her hand, but she held back realizing that if other less impressive efforts were presented first, hers would seem all the more brilliant in comparison. And with one or possibly two slight exceptions these first performances were indeed much as she'd anticipated. Imagination, emotion, concentration–all the elements required to make such an exercise work–were almost totally lacking and yet Miss Arnold's comments were only mildly critical, proving once again the old bitch knew nothing about acting.

Finally everyone but Victoria had performed. What was the girl up to, Claudine wondered suspiciously. Could she have neglected to do the assignment? What a pleasure it would be to humiliate her in front of the rest of the class! But then she realized almost at once that Victoria would never give her the satisfaction of coming unprepared. Then what could it be? Of course, she thought at last, the nasty little baggage is waiting for me to call on her! For a second or two longer Claudine Arnold still delayed. What a blow it would be to Victoria if she overlooked her. Unfortunately she couldn't very well ignore the girl every time she gave an assignment so she might as well get it over with. "Miss Windsor?" she said finally as coolly as possible.

Only when all eyes had turned to her did Victoria rise to her feet and walk up on the low platform stage. "For my exercise I have chosen to portray Joan of Arc in the final moments prior to her execution for heresy." She pulled a stool forward–no one else had even thought to sit down–and settling herself, she stared at the floor for a moment willing all distraction from her mind. At last she lifted her head and began to speak and for the next five minutes or so Victoria's voice was the only sound in the room. There was envy, admiration–a few tears were even shed–but no matter what their individual reactions, they all listened and watched in rapt silence as the doomed Joan came to life before their eyes– a seventeen year old girl sentenced to die within the hour.

When she had finished, Victoria sat motionless, appearing almost to be in a trance. The silence was instantly shattered, however, by Miss Arnold's nasal tones. "Thank you, everyone. Next time we will be discussing the art of characterization within a play. Please read the material covering this in your text. Class dismissed." No one moved. Even those who disliked Victoria couldn't believe Miss Arnold would say nothing about a performance which even the most inexperienced neophyte among them had realized was exceptional. The only person who did not appear shocked or even surprised was Victoria herself. In fact she was halfway back to her seat when Claudine spoke again. "Is everyone deaf? I <u>said</u> 'Class dismissed'!" Finally one or two at a time people began to stand up, gathering their things to walk from the room still in silence. Victoria remained standing by her seat, carefully averting her eyes to discourage anyone who might be tempted to speak to her. Only when everyone else was gone did she pick up her purse, books and coat, preparing to leave herself.

Through all of this Claudine Arnold stayed in her seat. Even after the class had filed from the room, she continued to sit there watching this beautiful young woman collect her belongings with an exasperating calm. Finally, however, when Victoria was nearly at the door, she could no longer refrain from speaking. "Don't you wish to know what I thought of your 'little presentation', Miss Windsor?"

"Not really. You wouldn't recognize talent if it came up and poked you in that fat little belly of yours!" Victoria's exit was equally as dramatic as her performance of a short while before.

"Well, I never....I absolutely never......!" Claudine sputtered, snatching up her own purse and briefcase. Moments later, still fuming, she stormed into Peter Harris' office. "You see! I told you! But, oh no, you and Archibald wouldn't listen to me. Of course I don't see either of you helping me to deal with the wretched little snip!"

"Why, whomever could you be talking about?" The corners of Peter's mouth twitched.

"Damn you! You know bloody well who! I tried to tell you the girl had no talent, but you and Archibald insisted on admitting her. Well, she can't even handle the most basic acting exercise!"

Leaning back in his chair, Peter listened without comment to her ravings. "Yes, Claudine–perhaps you're right, after all," he replied at last. "I'll speak to the young lady."

She had fully expected him to argue the point and when instead he accepted her opinion without question, she was too stunned to doubt his sincerity as she might otherwise have done. "Yes...ah...well, I'm glad you...ah...finally see it my way. Th...thank you very much." Claudine beat a rattled retreat.

The talent of an actress like Victoria could not, however, remain for long on such a petty level. Sooner or later it could and would go far beyond the vengeance of a bitter old woman or the self-indulgence of an amateur Lothario. Since the beginning of the term Tuck had made it a habit to sit in on the introductory acting class–safely hidden away in the back of the theatre's tiny balcony–and today his patience had been amply rewarded. And thus Peter's lustful musings were broken into almost at once by the ringing of the telephone. "Harris here!" he barked into the receiver.

"Sorry, Peter. Did I catch you at a bad time?" the voice on the other end of the line replied. "It's Landon Ferris. Could you possibly pop down to the workshop for a bit?"

"Rather busy at the moment. Is it urgent?"

There was a brief pause. "I'm afraid it's me," Tuck puffed into the phone. "There's something I want you to see."

Peter shook his head, laughing a little in spite of himself. "What is it, Tuck?"

"First I'm afraid I have a confession to make. I....I've been sitting in on Victoria's acting class and I........"

"Oh God, Tuck, if Claudine ever saw you......."

"Not to worry, old chap, not to worry. Even someone of my size can be invisible when he chooses to be. Anyway Landon's going to ask Victoria to repeat her class exercise in his workshop. It really would be worth your coming down."

"As a matter of fact Claudine's just left my office and I should...ah...verify her report to me." Stopping briefly to inform his secretary where he could be reached, he made his way down one flight of stairs and along another corridor toward the theatre workshop. Female students and faculty members were taken aback not to receive one of the charming smiles or witty quips with which Peter customarily greeted them, but at that moment his thoughts were concentrated on one <u>particular</u> female. He was within minutes, he felt certain, of taking the initial step toward his objective. He'd hoped to slip unobtrusively into the room, but where his chubby friend was concerned, he should have known better.

"There you are, Peter!" Tuck bounded across the room to join him. "You won't be sorry, old chap. Believe me! Wait until you see her! What she does is....." Just then Victoria herself entered and although she passed directly by the two men, she appeared not to see them. As in the other class she sat alone–slightly behind and away from everyone else. "She always sits alone like that," he whispered. "For the life of me I can't understand how such a beautiful girl can be so lonely."

"Honestly, Tuck, you are bloody naive. It's purely for effect."

"No one wants to be alone, Peter."

At this point in their discussion, however, they were interrupted as Landon Ferris stood up in front of the group to begin the workshop. Fifty-ish with thick, shaggy gray hair and a drooping walrus-style moustache, he looked like someone you might have expected to find a hundred years ago in India stalwartly carrying the white man's burden. Even his manner belonged to another era–dignified, almost courtly. He began with a slight bow. "Before we begin our improvisational work today, ladies and gentlemen....."

Peter felt a sharp pain in his side as Tuck elbowed him in the ribs. "Will you please stop it!" he exclaimed in mock exasperation.

"....I would like to ask one particular young lady to repeat an exercise she has just presented in her acting class," Landon was continuing. "I've heard it was excellent."

"You see, Peter, you see!" Tuck chortled rubbing his hands together. "He heard she was excellent!"

"Oh, come off it! You're the one he heard it from! But watch now. She'll pretend she's surprised even though we both bloody well know she'll be expecting this."

"Why should she be expecting it? Why do you assume everyone's as cynical and calculating as you are?"

"Not everyone, old chap. Only certain people."

"And so," Landon was concluding his announcement, "we'd be pleased if you would honor us with your portrayal of Joan of Arc, Victoria."

At the sound of her name she started visibly and observing her closely, Peter and Tuck each saw in that reaction what he wanted to see, neither glimpsing the truth which oddly enough was that they were both right. Victoria did indeed believe too strongly in herself for such a request to have come as a surprise, but at that precise moment her mind had been on her recent confrontation with Claudine Arnold. "I...I beg your pardon. You....you were...ah... speaking to me?"

"I asked if you would repeat your Joan of Arc for us. I've heard some wonderful things about it."

"Oh, I...I...ah..." Victoria glanced about as if she were cornered. "Yes, ah....all right." After some further hesitation she at last stood up and moved between the chairs toward the front of the room.

"Have you seen her work, Peter?" Landon had come to sit in the row behind the other two men. "Can she possibly be as good as Tuck says she is?"

"To answer your first question–yes, I was at her audition. To reply to the second," he added with a grin, "no one can possibly be as good as Tuck says she is." His friend threw him a reproachful look and he felt vaguely disloyal, both to Tuck and even to Victoria herself, who was indeed just as good as Tuck said she was.

"Such a lovely, ethereal quality, hasn't she?" Landon remarked.

Peter uttered a snort. Lovely–certainly; talented–perhaps, but one thing Victoria definitely was <u>not</u> was ethereal.

Meanwhile, as in the previous class, Victoria had settled herself on a low stool, resting her head in her hands to prepare herself for the exercise. To her dismay, however, her thoughts raced in all different directions refusing to be brought under control and the concentration would not come. Who could have told Landon Ferris about her performance? Could this be an attempt on Claudine Arnold's part to humiliate her? No, she told herself firmly, she knows I'm good and the last thing she'd want is for someone else to see me. But who could it have been then? It certainly wasn't one of the other students. They were all jealous of her; she was positive of that.

At first the other students remained quiet, but gradually uneasy whispers began to spread through the group with here and there an occasional phrase able to be heard above the general murmuring. "Why doesn't she start?"..."What <u>is</u> she doing anyway?"......"I <u>told</u> you she was bonkers...." But just as the undertone was becoming generally audible, just as Tuck turned to defend Victoria against Peter's snort of derision, once again she looked up and began to speak. Some of the members of the workshop were also in Victoria's acting class, but others, seeing her performance for the first time, were actually awed. Even Peter Harris forgot for a while that his primary interest in Victoria was <u>not</u> professional. "Bang on target!" Landon whispered to Tuck. "She's magnificent." Tuck glowed with pride.

At the conclusion of her performance Victoria rose to her feet and all at once someone–no one knew who–began the applause. This was her first taste of anything anywhere near professional approval; the Heathfield faculty, parents were nothing, after all, but untutored "civilians" and it was a moment she would never forget. For others as well there would be an enduring memory of this day and in years to come they'd remember..."Oh yes, I saw Victoria Windsor when....." With a brief nod in acknowledgment of the applause she returned to her seat. For a second no one stirred and then Landon Ferris also stood up and walked to the front of the room again. The rest of the workshop would be a normal session–although the feeling that a special moment had occurred never completely disappeared.

Tuck seized his friend by the arm. "Get her out of Claudine's class! You have to get her out of Claudine's class! Here she was given her proper recognition. Claudine ridiculed her–she ridiculed her! Get her out of there! You have to get her out of there!"

"Certainly, old man, certainly." A smile tugged at Peter's mouth. "I'll see what I can do."

Horrified, Tuck saw his mistake. "You're going to take advantage of this, aren't you, to get what you want from her. Don't do it, Peter," he pleaded. "Don't use her!"

"Use her?" The other man's smile broadened. "Why Tuck, I haven't the foggiest what you're talking about."

* * *

Later that afternoon Frau Schneider was getting ready to close her pastry shop for the day when happening to glance up, she saw a slim, tweedy sort of man standing in the doorway. "Entschuldiken-Sie, bitte, mein Herr. I am just about to close," she apologized, "and already everyzing, it almost ist solt."

"Oh no, I only wished to inquire which flat is Victoria Windsor's," Peter explained, "but perhaps a biscuit or two. Do you have any ginger ones left? They're my favorite."

He bestowed his most irresistibly boyish grin on her.

Almost immediately, however, the smile vanished as to his shock this diminutive person straight out of Hans Christian Andersen snatched up a rolling pin and advanced on him furiously. "Nein, nein, she ist nicht here. Verstehen-Sie? She is nicht here!"

Unbelievably Peter found himself retreating. "I...I know this is her address." He prayed fervently the doorway was somewhere behind him. "All I needed was the flat number." The scene resembled nothing so much as a scuffle between a Yorkshire terrier and an Afghan hound with the Afghan definitely getting the worst of it.

"Raus! Raus!" the irate little woman fairly shrieked, beginning to beat him about the chest, shoulders and arms with the rolling pin. "She ist eine, gute kleine madchen! Raus! Raus!" As always in moments of extreme emotion Frau Schneider had lapsed almost totally into her native German and Peter had no idea what she was screaming at him. At any rate he was too busy trying to protect himself from the blows of the rolling pin even to attempt to understand her and finally he had no choice but to flee. Fortunately for his reputation as a London sophisticate, no one had been there to see him ignominiously routed by a tiny, German baker.

* * *

The next morning Peter was waiting in the hall outside the modern dance class when Victoria came out. Still dressed in her black leotard and dancing tights, she stopped for a moment in the doorway, apparently hunting for something in her enormous shoulder bag, and he took full advantage of her temporary distraction to look her over as he hadn't had the opportunity to do since that first day in his office. The action of turning her head and tipping it to one side to look in her purse had caused her long blonde hair to spill over one shoulder and through this silken golden curtain he could just glimpse her breasts rising and falling under the form fitting leotard. He allowed his eyes to travel downward, aware for the first time how tall she was–long-waisted and marvelously leggy. God! He wanted her more than he'd ever wanted a woman and he was getting bloody well nowhere.

At last she began to move forward again. Her attention was still on the frustrating search for her cigarettes and when she was a few feet away, Peter stepped in front of her blocking her path. They collided, her books and notebooks flying in all directions. "Dammit!" Victoria stooped to pick them up as she did so glancing up at him. "Oh, it's you! I might have known!"

"How nice to be loved," Peter observed wryly. He knelt to help her. "Mmm–you smell heavenly." He couldn't resist sliding a caressing hand over her shoulder and down along one arm.

Grabbing her belongings away from him, she stood up again. "As I believe I've already commented, you're not even original!"

Peter got to his feet as well. Grinning, he held up both hands in the traditional gesture of surrender. "All I wanted was to talk to you. I tried yesterday afternoon, but I couldn't get past your watchdog–small one, but extremely ferocious."

"What in God's name are you talking about?"

"Curly white hair. Comes armed with a rolling pin."

"Oh, Frau Schneider. Couldn't you simply have said Frau Schneider. And what in hell were you doing there anyway?"

"Believe me—I just happened to be in the neighborhood."

"Out where I live, <u>no one</u> just happens to be in the neighborhood!"

"Yes, you are rather a distance out, aren't you?" The sheepish duck of the head when added to the irresistible boyish grin usually proved unbeatable.

"Do you work on that routine in front of a mirror?" Maddeningly Victoria cocked an eyebrow at him. "Because it could use more practice."

"You are an insufferable bitch!" Peter's face was flushed with anger and there was no trace now of the charming smile. "And I would remind you once again that it might prove beneficial to your career here at RADA to be more pleasant to me!"

"That class was apparently omitted from my schedule. What is it called? Oh, yes-- 'The Care and Feeding of the Resident Rake'. Well, let's get one thing clear; you can bloody well stay away from me!" Pivoting about, she strode off down the corridor, the soft thudding of her ballet slippers on the linoleum seeming calculated to infuriate him.

Glancing around, Peter discovered to his chagrin that he hadn't been as fortunate as the day before at the bakery. Several students had witnessed the entire scene and not a man to suffer humiliation with equanimity, he vowed he would get his revenge. To begin with he left her in Claudine's class. Secretly Tuck was relieved. This jewel of a girl was better off not owing Peter anything in return for favors granted. Then in late October auditions were held for the first full production of the Academy season. The play was to be *The Barretts of Wimpole Street.* First year students did not customarily receive leading roles so they often didn't even bother to try out. Victoria thought that was ridiculous and she had auditioned to play the role of Elizabeth Barrett Browning.

Peter came up behind her as she stared in shocked disbelief at the bulletin board. "Cast list not what you expected, my dear?" he purred in her ear.

"YOU!!!" She spun about to face him. "This is because of you! How could you? You know I'm better than she is–a thousand times better! How could you?" She was so furious, so bitterly disappointed that for the only time Peter could remember, her eyes were filled with tears and for a few seconds he felt remorse. She <u>was</u> better, just as she'd said, a thousand times better and he had denied her the role purely out of spite. Then he also recalled the mortification he had suffered at her hands and any self-reproach was short-lived.

All RADA students were required to work in some capacity on each production. For *The Barretts* Victoria was assigned to the scenery crew and all the time she nailed and stapled and painted, she could hear Claudine Arnold below in the rehearsal hall screaming in frustration at Melinda Cutler, a particular favorite of hers, but a less than adequate Elizabeth. Well, the bitch had herself and Peter Harris to thank for casting the little twit in the first place.

Like a bad dream the scenario repeated itself with the second production in February: Shakespeare's *Othello.* Victoria had, of course, read for Desdemona, but was cast instead as merely one of the many nameless attendants who troop on and off the stage behind each of the Bard's nobly born characters. Actually having to watch someone else play a role she knew she could have done far better was extremely annoying and the sight of Claudine Arnold, gaping zipper, pot belly and all, mincing about the stage in an attempt to demonstrate how the character should be portrayed was all but intolerable.

And in the midst of this--"the winter of her discontent" –Victoria already had an admitted weakness for Shakespearean metaphors–came a greater torment.

London seemed–perversely–a city created for Christmas: the lighted streets, the crowds of happy, laughing people, the entire atmosphere remarkably Dickensian. Any second you must certainly turn a corner and encounter Scrooge or Bob Cratchit or Tiny Tim. Christmas Day itself she was determined to spend alone in her flat as though it were just another day and her plan might have succeeded had not Frau Schneider–dear cherry-cheeked, well-meaning Frau Schneider– come up to invite a lonely young girl for Christmas dinner. She was rewarded by having the door slammed in her face and from then on Victoria could no longer pretend she was unaware of what day it was. The bursts of laughter from the streets, the pealing of church bells in the distance, even the faint aroma of roast goose wafting up from Frau Schneider's flat below only served to remind her that it was Christmas and she was alone.

It was, moreover, during these weeks of the Christmas break that certain disturbing patterns began to emerge in Victoria's life–patterns which would hold her in their insidious grip for some time to come. First she discovered that several shot glasses of vodka–chosen after some experimentation as the least horrid tasting–snatched at odd moments during the evening when Abe wasn't looking were a great help in dulling the loneliness; that if indeed she'd had enough to drink, she might even be able to sleep that night. Secondly, to Abe's evident dismay, she apparently no longer found the attentions of the male customers so repugnant–though for the time being this went no further than casual flirting. After all, if she wasn't willing to sell herself to Peter Harris, she certainly wasn't about to give herself away.

* * *

The spring play was to be Enid Bagnold's *The Chalk Garden.* Although the least widely known of that year's principal female roles, Madrigal was perhaps the most intriguing–a young woman with a mysterious past who is hired to be the governess to Mrs. St. Maugham's granddaughter. Yet Victoria nearly decided not even to try out; it hardly seemed worth it when the outcome was inevitable until glancing disinterestedly at the bulletin announcing the auditions, she saw there was to be a guest director: Sir Terence Cartier. I've got a chance, she thought, joyous relief flooding through her. Finally I've got a chance.

Entering the auditorium on the day of try-outs, she immediately glimpsed Cartier sitting about halfway down the center aisle. She'd never forgotten his performance in *The Tempest* nor the fact that this revered actor had taken the time to pay serious attention to her questions. Her first impulse was to go up to him, to remind him of their previous meeting, but she stopped short of actually approaching him. If she spoke to him prior to the auditions, people would think she'd won the part because of personal influence.

"Good morning, Sir Terence," Peter murmured respectfully as he came to take the seat next to him.

"Good morning." Looking up from a copy of the script, Sir Terence smiled pleasantly. "Excuse me, I don't believe we've met."

"Peter Harris."

"Oh, yes." He acknowledged the introduction with a nod. "Chairman of the acting department." Peter couldn't help noticing, however, that the other man had first had to check the list of names fastened to his clipboard and his ego spiraled dizzily downward.

Tuck and Claudine came in just then–separately of course: Claudine sweeping between the rows to sit on the other side of Sir Terence while Tuck slipped as unobtrusively as possible into the row behind them. Amazing, Tuck found himself thinking drolly; from the back he looks just like everyone else. Peter introduced them both and then conducted Sir Terence to the front of the room, presenting him formally to the students who had come to audition. "The first role to be read for," he said in conclusion, "will be that of Madrigal."

Victoria was about the third or fourth actress to try out. It was all Peter could do to watch. If possible her talent had grown during the year and her fragile appearing blonde beauty made her the perfect Madrigal. But then she'd also been the perfect Desdemona, he reminded himself with a twinge of conscience. All at once Sir Terence was gripping him by the arm. "My God, she's brilliant! Why haven't I seen her in any other RADA productions?"

Strange, when Tuck grabbed him like that, he was annoyed; because it was Sir Terence Cartier, he felt absurdly flattered. "Well, she's...ah...only a first year student," Peter explained rather lamely.

"Yes, but *Chalk Garden's* your third production this year," Sir Terence persisted. "Where has she been until now?"

"Well...ah...ah...perhaps you simply didn't notice her."

"Oh, come now, old chap. Believe me, I would have remembered–for her beauty alone, not even to mention her talent."

Tuck wished he had the courage to speak up, but at least he was no longer on his own. And what more formidable ally could he possibly have hoped for?

It appeared at first, however, as though this meeting of the casting committee would have the same results. Claudine Arnold, who'd informed Peter in no uncertain terms beforehand that she for one did not intend to be railroaded, began the proceedings by proposing Melinda Cutler for the role of Madrigal and he had agreed. Plainly astounded, Sir Terence looked from one of them to the other for a moment. "And you, Mr. Tucker?' he inquired at last.

Tuck still hesitated. The distinguished actor might be there now to back him up, but he was well aware that a time would come when he would once again have to deal with Peter and Claudine on his own. ""Please, Sir Terence, I defer to <u>your</u> judgment." But his black, shoe-button eyes sparkled with suppressed excitement.

The other man studied him intently for a few seconds longer, a slow smile spreading across his face. "Ah yes, I see." The latter was spoken almost under his breath and only Tuck heard him. "Thank you. I appreciate that," he continued on more loudly. "Miss Windsor will be our Madrigal then. Is that agreeable to everyone?"

"Yes...ah...fine." Clearly under the circumstances Peter could only concede the issue as gracefully as possible. Perhaps he was secretly relieved that the matter had been taken out of his hands. "Now...ah...the granddaughter Laurel next?"

***

"Madrigal...........Victoria Windsor," the cast list read.

"Well, it looks like Peter Harris finally got his way"......"Did she have to sleep with the whole committee or just one of them?"....."Does that include Claudine Arnold?"......"I always wondered if the old sourpuss preferred girls".

Such overheard remarks caused Victoria considerable pain. More than she cared to admit– even to herself– she continued to yearn for the acceptance of others. However, she knew she'd gotten the part because she deserved it and when it came time for the performance, they would all know that, too. And what a joy it was to be acting again. Gliding about the stage, she felt gifted and beautiful, her loneliness all but forgotten. Plainly she had been born for the theatre; after all, look how everyone at Heathfield had admired her. She was soon to learn that her current director did not impress so easily.

For the first week or so Sir Terence allowed her her euphoria. Briefly he'd even found it amusing to watch her parade and posture about the stage, too overwhelmed by her own splendor to do any serious work. Then, too, since this was her first major role at RADA, perhaps she simply needed some time to get all of this out of her system. A day came, however, when he knew things had gone far enough. She was too talented an actress to be permitted to develop bad habits and it was better to pull her up short now before that talent was devoured by her ego. They were working on the scene in which Madrigal first meets Laurel, the child to be placed in her charge, and Victoria had just swept across the stage to pose with one hand resting on the mantelpiece. "And exactly what are you supposed to be doing, Miss Windsor?" Sir Terence asked suddenly, getting up from where he had been sitting to come and stand in front of the stage.

She glared down at him. "What do you mean....'What am I doing?' I'm acting!" How could he possibly have stopped her when she was being so bloody marvelous!?

"Ah, acting. Is that what you call it?" He smiled. "Thank you, everyone. That will be all for today—not you, Miss Windsor," he barked as she started to leave with the others.

With apparently single-minded concentration Sir Terence gathered up his things, seeming to forget Victoria entirely until everyone else had left and they were alone in the rehearsal hall. When finally he looked up at her again, she was perched on a table swinging her legs back and forth in an attempt to appear unconcerned. She failed to remember this as a habit from childhood. She was aware, however, that her nonchalance was pure sham. Now I've done it, she thought, as she watched him close his script and return his pen to the breast pocket of his jacket, finally bending to pick up his hat and coat. When it seemed to Victoria as if this unnerving silence must go on forever, he at last turned around, climbed the stairs leading onto the stage and walked toward her. "Sir Terence, I......"

"Miss Windsor, I am speaking to you! You are not speaking to me. Is that clear?"

Shut up, Victoria told herself, shut up! And in reply she simply nodded, bestowing on him her most helplessly feminine smile. "And save that for someone else. I know I'm too old for it and I'd like to think I'm too smart!" Instantly the smile vanished and he saw her green eyes widen. Good, he thought, she's still unsure enough of herself for me to reach her. "Well then," he continued aloud, "may I presume you're ready to listen?" She nodded again, but this time there was no smile. "I suppose like every would-be actor you think you're pretty good, am I right?"

"I............"

He raised his hand to silence her. "Reply not necessary. I'll assume the answer to be in the affirmative. Very well–I will give you that much satisfaction. Yes, you are good, probably one of the best–if not the best I've been privileged to see in some time."

To hear these words and from Sir Terence Cartier–to be told she was "the best he had seen in some time". "Oh, Sir Terence," she started to say, "I......"

"When I wish a response from you, Miss Windsor, I will ask for it. Now, as I was saying, you are good and it is precisely for that reason I will not allow you to get away with your little charade. And to reply to your earlier question–no, I do not call that acting. Acting is feeling, thinking, truly becoming the character you are portraying. Now tell me honestly, is that what you were doing just now?"

Victoria hesitated and lowering her gaze, she began to swing her legs back and forth as she'd done a few minutes ago. It was a while before she looked up again. "No, sir, it wasn't."

"Hallelujah!" Sir Terence threw back his head and roared with laughter. "There's hope for you yet!"

"May I go now?" she inquired meekly.

"Just one more thing. I want you to understand, Miss Windsor, that the next time you begin parading about the stage....." At this she suppressed a laugh herself. His estimate was devastatingly close to the truth. "...I will stop you again and the next time it happens and the time after that. Talent is a gift, but it is also an awesome responsibility and if you waste that gift as you've been doing here, you might as well not have it. Now you may go."

Without another word Victoria got down off the table and picked up her things and keeping her eyes averted, she walked slowly down off the stage and out of the auditorium. Over and over again she repeated to herself what Sir Terence had said and to her credit these were not so much his words of praise as the ones of admonition. That day Victoria had come to at least a partial comprehension of what it meant to be an actress and as rehearsals continued, all that was required on Sir Terence's part was an occasional reminder. "Miss Windsor, are you thinking?"....or.... "Miss Windsor, what is Madrigal feeling at this moment?"....or...a simple, but sharp "Concentrate, Miss Windsor!"

Sir Terence watched with tremendous pride and joy as over the concluding weeks of rehearsal Victoria's portrayal of Madrigal continually deepened both in color and dimension. At the same time he couldn't help observing that she took no part in the easy camaraderie which invariably develops among the members of a cast. Whether by choice or not she was always alone. Inevitably he found his mind drawn to thoughts of his own wife who, although beautiful and gifted, fought a constant desperate battle against the psychosis which threatened to engulf her. And there were so many others! Perhaps it was the price they were expected to pay for the gift, he thought, and he feared for Victoria.

With opening night now only a week away, her Madrigal was all he could have hoped for and Sir Terence thought it might be a good moment to approach Victoria on a more personal level. Flattered by his attention, she might accept an offer of friendship. He came up to her at the close of rehearsal as she was preparing to leave. "Madrigal really came to life today, Miss Windsor. I'm so pleased."

Oddly his voice appeared to startle her. "Excuse me, Sir Terence. I'm afraid my thoughts were elsewhere." Her tone was respectful, but cool.

"I was complimenting you on your work today."

"Is that wise? It might cause me to relax too much."

Sir Terence smiled to himself. He should have known better than to think her susceptible to flattery, but he tried again. "Are you hoping to work on the legitimate stage, Miss Windsor?"

"What?" Now she actually sounded annoyed.

"I was interested in your future plans. I thought perhaps if you had nothing more exciting to do, you might join an old gentleman for tea and we could chat."

For an instant Victoria hesitated. The kindness in his tone more than the fact that he was Sir Terence Cartier drew her to him just as Uncle Bertie had never seemed to her to be the King. But then somewhere inside herself she drew back from him. "As a matter of fact," she replied curtly, "I do have something much more exciting to do."

Friendship had been offered and she had turned it away yet ironically it was friendship she craved. With a longing she still couldn't entirely suppress, she'd watched once again as the other cast members became a close, happy unit from which she was pointedly excluded. It seemed sometimes as though she were forever destined to be on the outside–wishing desperately to be accepted and yet at the same time incapable of reaching out for that acceptance.

In addition the nights were getting worse. She was worried lest her lack of sleep eventually affect her work in class or at rehearsal. But already she possessed too much professional discipline to allow that to happen. And for the most part this would continue to be true. No matter what personal trials the woman Victoria Windsor might undergo, the work of Victoria Windsor, the actress, would never be permitted to suffer.

Opening night of *The Chalk Garden* finally arrived. Her Madrigal was masterful–mysterious, cool and strangely tragic--and as Victoria was to experience so many more times in the years to come, the audience rose to its feet as one to applaud her entrance for the curtain call. Acknowledging the ovation, she curtseyed in a manner which was to become her trademark, one hand to her throat and glancing downward as she sank gracefully to one knee. Once again, as at Heathfield, she found the applause profoundly moving. Borne toward her on waves of deafening sound, this outpouring of love carried her onward and upward to the heights of ecstasy yet marvelously this love required nothing of her in return but the performance she had already given. The relationship between herself and the audience, though intense, remained impersonal.

Too soon, however, the final curtain came down. Like an addict whose source of supply has been abruptly cut off, Victoria's euphoric state dissipated rapidly and by the time of the cast party only a short time later, her elation had vanished. Sitting by herself off to one side of the room, she smoked constantly, seeking release from her numbing depression in the vodka which by now she drank as easily as water. In between swallows she held the glass in one hand and staring down at it, she ran the tip of the forefinger of her other hand around and around the rim.

Peter Harris, meanwhile, prowled restlessly about the room and like a predator stalking his kill, he studied her. With her hair still drawn up in a bun as she'd worn it for the performance, she seemed to be more Madrigal than Victoria and wryly Peter wondered which of the two he actually desired at that moment. He noted also with considerable interest the amount of liquor she was consuming and not in tentative, ladylike sips either. She was evidently not a beginning drinker. Finally he decided the time had come and he walked across the room to draw up another chair and sit down next to her. "The evening of your great triumph, hm?" he murmured caressingly.

Victoria took another long swallow from the glass before she replied. "Yes, I suppose so." But her tone was flat.

If Peter had been thinking of anything except her seduction, he might have noticed her sadness–a sadness quite out of place for someone who had just been the recipient of such adulation. Victoria's feelings were the last thing to concern him just then, however, and all he saw was that her glass was nearly empty. "May I get our leading lady a refill?" His eyebrows shot upwards in the habitual mannerism.

Victoria shrugged and handed him her glass. I know what he wants, she thought as she watched him make his away across to the bar on the other side of the room.

So—what do I do? Sometimes I think I might as well get it over with, but God–I can't even bear to be touched. How can I............ But at this point her thoughts were interrupted as Peter returned with her fresh drink as well as one for himself. "Here you are, Victoria," he said as he handed her the glass, "but isn't straight vodka a little strong for a young lady like you?"

" You know your brand of charm would nauseate a sword swallower!"

"A sword swallower?" In spite of himself Peter laughed. "Come now, you can do better than that." He had intended to take it slowly, but she was so close to him, so arousing with her incredible sea-green eyes and her gleaming golden hair pulled severely back from her delicate English face. "My God, Victoria!" He reached out with both hands to grip her arms just below the shoulders. He was aware she'd flinched as he touched her, but he was unable to stop himself. "You are so damned beautiful! You know I desire you! I have–since the first moment I saw you. I thought I could buy you with what you wanted so badly, but I should have realized you were too proud for that. But come with me now–back to my flat. You don't belong here with all these people! You belong with me! Come now. Come, my beautiful Victoria, my beautiful, beautiful Victoria!" Dropping his hands and removing the glass from her unresisting fingers, he took her hand to lead her through the crowd toward the door.

With tears in his eyes Tuck watched them leave. "Oh, Peter," he whispered. "How could you?"

Without a word of protest Victoria allowed herself to be led from the room, through the darkened halls of the Academy and outside to Peter's car. Something deep inside seemed to have let go and it was just too much effort to resist. Perhaps she couldn't bear returning from her great triumph of the evening to her empty flat. Perhaps after so much loneliness she was reaching out for yet another kind of human contact which, like the adulation of an audience, required nothing from her in return. Perhaps she was merely too drunk to care. Her senses blurred with liquor, her conscious mind registered none of this, however. Much of the next hour or so was mercifully a total blank, pierced only once by the sharp pain as this man thrust himself into her.

When Victoria awoke early the next morning, Peter had already left and ironically she was once more alone. Her body was sore from his use of her, but she was unable to remember anything. Supposedly the crowning moment of a woman's life and she couldn't remember a damn thing–nothing except the fact that he'd hurt like hell.

* * *

The final irony in all of this was something which--providentially perhaps–Victoria was never aware. The events might, in fact, have been taking place even as she awakened alone in Peter Harris' bed.

Abe Epstein had been standing at the window of Frau Schneider's bake shop watching it grow light. "Wievel Uhr ist es?" Turning, he walked slowly back to where his wife and her sister were sitting together passing the hours with their knitting and their endless reminiscences about their young life in Germany before the rise of Hitler had torn their world apart.

"Es ist schon spat, Abe," his wife replied glancing at the tiny gold watch she wore on a chain around her neck. "Es is halb funf."

"Vell, she perhaps shtill comes, ja?" he said returning once again to the window to peer down the deserted street.

"I do not know vhy he vants to do zis ting, Esther. Such a shtrange vun she is. Not even nice to him and yet all he can tink–ve must have zis kleine party for her after her first performance."

"Ah, you do not know her." Esther Schneider shook her curly white head. "Behind zat cross outside she hides sad lonely inside."

"But all zis–balloons unt shtreamers–even zis kuchen you have baked and shtill she does not come."

"Nein, but she does not know about it zo it is not her fault, ja?"

"You are as bad as Abe." Getting up, Miriam went to join her husband at the window slipping a hand through his arm. "Abe, she does not come. Ve go home now."

"Ja," he finally admitted reluctantly. "You are right, liebchen. Ve go home. Guten nacht, Esther, danke." He bowed to her with typically Teutonic courtesy.

A small Viennese torte decorated with white icing and yellow roses and bearing the inscription, "Mazeltov, kleine liebchen," stood on a low table in the center of the shop. Alone now, Frau Schneider walked over to it. The candles had burned low, spilling wax onto the icing. With a sigh she blew them out.

Chapter 3

These would be the empty years: years which would have destroyed most people. But Victoria was not most people. She had been a courageous, determined child; she would grow into a courageous, determined woman and she would survive!

Her second year at RADA passed quickly, although in a professional sense certainly not uneventfully, as in that season's productions no other female student stood a chance. It was Victoria Windsor's Saint Joan, Victoria Windsor's Kate in Shakespeare's *The Taming of the Shrew* and in her culminating role at RADA Victoria Windsor's Blanche DuBois in Tennessee Williams' *A Streetcar Named Desire*. Each acting student was expected as well to take part in a senior project. Most worked with others in the preparation of a one-act play. Victoria, of course, had chosen to perform alone–no one else was worthy of standing on the same stage with her anyway–and after much thought she'd decided to present "An Evening of Shakespeare's Women", in particular Lady Macbeth, Juliet, Viola from *Twelfth Night*, Portia from *The Merchant of Venice*, Desdemona and Kate.

Her relationship with Peter Harris had continued. The forced intimacy of the situation more than the sex itself revolted her, but the alternative was to be alone. And at some point during that year, although neither of them noticed it happening, their roles had reversed. No longer was Victoria the one being used.

It all came down to an evening in late May–Victoria's farewell appearance on the Academy stage. Tuck was standing in the back of the auditorium watching with Peter when at some point during the performance he stole a sideways glance at him. At first Tuck thought it was simply a reflection from the stage lights, but then he realized with a start that the other man's eyes were filled with tears. All at once Peter turned abruptly away to stride from the theatre, across the vestibule and out the front door of the Academy. When Tuck caught up with him, he was sitting on the front steps smoking furiously. "How could you bring yourself to leave?" Tuck asked coming to settle beside him. "Victoria's last performance at RADA and all...I'd have thought..."

Peter laughed bitterly. "She doesn't need me in there! She's getting all the love she requires from that audience!" And before Tuck could even think of a reply, he had jumped to his feet again, pitching his half-smoked cigarette into the gutter. Storming across to the far side of the steps, he whirled about to point a finger–almost accusingly–at his old friend. "Do you know what she did to me last night?" he shouted so loudly that a girl who happened to be passing at that moment hurried away, glancing fearfully back at him over her shoulder. She'd always heard actors were crazy.

"How....about....uh...popping on over to the...ah... Pig 'n' Whistle then?" Tuck grunted breathlessly, struggling to his feet again.

"All right." Peter shrugged. "Believe me, I could use a drink."

The two men walked the block or so to the pub in silence. Even when they had purchased their mugs of ale and settled in a booth, neither spoke for several minutes. Peter, in particular, appeared lost in the contemplation of his glass. "There's something wrong with that girl, you know," he muttered at last. Misunderstanding his meaning, Tuck nodded thoughtfully in agreement, but that was as far as he got. "And I don't mean that line of crap you've been feeding me for two years! I means she's cold, totally inhuman. God, it's like making love to a zombie!"

"But that's what I mean." In his earnestness both of the little man's chins were quivering. "She doesn't want to be that way. She....."

Peter half-rose to his feet, the sudden motion jarring the table and causing their drinks to spill. "You start that again and I'm getting the hell out of here!"

"No, my friend, don't." Tuck reached up to touch him on the arm. "I won't say another word, I promise. Please–tell me what happened last night."

The other man hesitated, but finally he sat down again. "Well, actually the signs have been there for weeks now, but I...."

"Signs? Signs of what?"

"Signs that Her Royal Highness was finished with me, of course, but I was too stupid or perhaps too vain to accept them. Anyway two nights ago..."

"Peter, when did you realize you were in love with Victoria?"

"In love with her?" He spat out the words as if the taste of them turned his stomach. "Don't make me laugh!"

"Sure, old man, sure." Someone else might have thought that he was merely receiving his just deserts, but Tuck had never been a vindictive person.

"Where was I?" Peter rubbed one hand wearily over his eyes. "Oh yes, two nights ago at the opening night party, I asked if she was ready to leave and she said, 'No, but don't let that stop you'. How much plainer could she have made it? But last night there I was–like a bloody idiot–waiting for her in the wings."

Beginning to tell the story, he could visualize clearly Victoria as she stood alone center stage acknowledging the applause of the audience. Even after the ovation had subsided and the curtain came down, she continued to stand there–God, what an ego he could remember thinking–and only after several seconds did she finally turn and walk toward him. "Oh, I realize I should have known better." He shook his head ruefully at the memory of his own incredible stupidity. "But I still went up to her and put an arm around her–God, Tuck, I could actually feel her cringe when I touched her–and I whispered in her ear that she didn't need that audience...that she had me."

"Why didn't you just leave her alone, Peter?" Tuck put in at this point.

"Well, I fully realize that in your opinion I am an absolute ass," he observed drily, "but at any rate I walked back toward the women's dressing room with her and I said that if she was too tired, we could skip the party and go right back to my flat."

The present reality of Tuck and the noisy, smoky pub had faded entirely from his conscious mind now and he was actually reliving the painful scene of the previous night.

Victoria had stopped before the door of the dressing room. Once again with a terrible clarity Peter experienced the sensation of her–stiff, yet at the same time oddly unresisting within his embrace. "No, I don't think so." He could even hear her tone of cold dismissal. "I have to unwind after the performance and besides, I need a drink."

Why did I keep trying, he wondered to himself now, as he recounted the incident. Why did I allow her to humiliate me? "All right then, Victoria. I'll wait here for you."

"What in bloody hell do I have to say to make you understand? I do not want to see you tonight!"

For a few seconds he was silent, unable to ask the question for which, he supposed sadly, he already knew the answer. "It's not just tonight, is it, Victoria?" he said at last. "You're through with me, aren't you? You'll be leaving RADA and I'm simply no longer useful."

"What do you mean—'useful'?" Her green eyes narrowed into slits. "Are you insinuating that my success here has had anything whatsoever to do with you? Well, let me tell you something. In a few years everyone will know the name of Victoria Windsor while you will still be nothing but a teacher in a drama school!" And with this she entered the dressing room closing the door in his face.

With difficulty Peter brought himself back to the present moment, to the dimly lit pub and Tuck's fat, anxious face across the table from him. "So that's it, I guess." He attempted in vain to sound casual. "And believe me, I'm well rid of the bitch!"

"If it's any comfort, old man, she doesn't mean to be cruel. "She...."

"Oh, sod off!" Vaulting roughly from the booth, Peter hurried out of the pub into the darkness.

Alone, Tuck signaled the bartender for another ale, but when it was brought, he left it sitting untouched in front of him. Graduation was only a little more than a week away and then Victoria would be gone. "Whatever will become of her?" he worried aloud.

"Excuse me, sir?" the bartender inquired. "Did you say something?"

"Uh...no...no, I didn't." He downed half the fresh mug in one long swallow.

* * *

Victoria had given considerable thought to skipping the graduation ceremony. After all, it would only be another occasion at which everyone except her would be surrounded by loving friends and family. However, awards were always presented to the outstanding graduate in each of the major fields and so she decided to attend. She was indeed the recipient of the acting award, much as everyone including herself had anticipated, but when her name was announced, she showed no sign of excitement or even pleasure and somewhere between the ceremony and the luncheon following it, she disappeared. No one even remembered seeing her leave.

Victoria's own graduation celebration would consist of nothing but a pot of tea together with some of Frau Schneider's freshly baked bread and a little cheese, but in her relief at being by herself it seemed a feast. At last with her meal prepared she settled herself in her usual spot on the floor. The afternoon passed into the long, lovely spring twilight and still she sat there, her mind racing, as she considered a future which once more was uncertain. As long as she could remember, the Academy had been her dream. Then suddenly that dream had become a reality and now just as suddenly RADA was in the past and she was forced once again to make certain necessary decisions. Where would she live and how would she support herself until she could get her first acting role–for it was only her <u>immediate</u> future which was in doubt.

First she had to find a new job as well as a different place to live. It would have been simpler, of course, to stay exactly where she was, but for some time now she'd felt that both Abe and Frau Schneider, like Dan Lester before them, were becoming too involved in her life. And so changes were necessary. She had come in a way to enjoy the atmosphere of the pub: the impersonal social contact, the admiring glances of the men–even their lewd comments were somehow exciting–and so she would look for another waitressing job. All the other pub owners in the immediate vicinity were Abe's friends, however, and so it would have to be in a different neighborhood. She didn't want him checking up on her. Far older in appearance than her eighteen years, Victoria was certain the job hunting this time around would prove quite easy.

"The Golden Hind" was just a block off Leicester Square in the middle of the West End theatre district. A corner building, its ground floor was of highly polished wood, each wall having two bay windows with large heavy panes while above were two additional stories of brick, the upper windows being of the casement style opening to the outside. The pub was named, of course, after the ship of Sir Francis Drake and the decor was distinctly nautical: pictures of 16th century sailing ships, antique ships' wheels and navigational instruments, even a halfway decent painting of Sir Francis himself over the bar. "The Golden Hind" must certainly cater to a much more elegant clientele and between that and the West End location an actress could make some useful contacts.

The owner and proprietor of this establishment was a man with the unlikely name of Cassius O' Flaherty. Apparently his Irish father had suffered from classical delusions. Short and slightly built, Cassius had a particular fondness for small, thin cigars; in a bizarre way they suited him. He wore his dark, brown hair in an old-fashioned pompadour in the mistaken belief that it made him appear taller. His favorite moment of each day was the tallying of the previous night's receipts which he always did sitting at one of the tables, check stubs and money stacked up in front of him. He'd been warned this was a dangerous practice, but he couldn't deny himself the almost sensual pleasure of handling the coins, the pound notes, the five pound notes, the ten pound notes. At the staccato sound of high heels on the polished wooden floors he glanced up and his eyes widened, the money temporarily forgotten.

"You're staring." Victoria's laugh was low and enticing.

"And I'm sure you're accustomed to it." But inwardly Cassius cursed himself. With a woman he liked to be the one to take the offensive.

"Actually I am. Just as I'm sure you're more than accustomed to being rude. However, that's beside the point at the moment. I came about the position." It was only then he noticed she was holding the sign he'd placed in the window, "Waitress Wanted".

"So you need a job, do you?" he murmured allowing his eyes to travel over her well-proportioned figure, his gaze lingering briefly but perceptibly on her full breasts. "And what do you propose to do for me in return?"

"Subtle, aren't we?" It was starting again already then and with this repulsive little rodent of a man. The realization made her feel sick, but after all it might as well be with him, Victoria thought with a sigh, and easing herself into the chair facing him, she crossed her long, slim legs. The free leg swung lazily. "But there <u>are</u> other things to consider–hours, salary."

"Oh well, yes." Clearly, however, he considered such matters trivial. "Monday through Saturday–five to midnight. Wages are ten shillings an hour; you keep your own tips. And your name is?"

"Victoria Windsor."

"Victoria Windsor." He mimicked her haughty tone. "And who do you think you are, ducks—the Queen herself? Well around here yours truly, Cassius O'Flaherty, is the reigning monarch. Do I make myself clear?"

"Quite clear." He frightened her; he repulsed her, but dammit, she needed the bloody job! Tears of self-pity welled up in her eyes, but before he could notice she blinked them back, getting immediately to her feet.

Cassius stood as well, only to discover to his dismay that he was at least three inches shorter than she. He moved rapidly away behind the bar to minimize the height difference, but for the second time in a comparatively short period she'd managed to put him on the defensive. "A drink before you leave?"

"No, thank you. See you on Monday then." She was gone before he could say another word. And so within minutes of their meeting the tone of their relationship had been established–a constant battle of wits tinged with sexual overtones and seasoned with a growing mutual hatred.

Back out on the street Victoria consulted the newspaper again–this time for furnished bedsitters. These would once again have to be on the outskirts of the city; the prices in any good section remained prohibitive. There were a few possibilities in the area around Islington so returning to the Leicester Square tube stop, she caught the Northern Line heading south.

The first flat was already taken which was probably just as well since it was over an East Indian restaurant and the odor of curry and saffron was overpowering. Someone else was apparently as hard up as she was–undoubtedly another unemployed actor.

The second place was only a block and a half away from the first. In the basement of the building, it was dark and dirty–windows only at the front and back-- and she could hear highly suspicious scratching noises behind the walls. But hallelujah, it was only twenty-five pounds the month and the landlord was not likely to be in the least concerned about her welfare. And so on the following morning Victoria moved out of the warm, cozy flat over the German bakery and into the dismal, creature-infested basement bedsitter. To her relief she'd managed to sneak by Frau Schneider's ground floor flat without being seen–thus avoiding painful good-byes. Fortunately she wouldn't have to live like this for long, she thought, as she cleaned the new place, washing the walls and floors with disinfectant, sprinkling roach powder and setting mousetraps. It would only be a question of attending at most two or three auditions and she would be on her way to stardom, living in the luxury which ironically had been hers as a birthright.

Her RADA course in "Audition Techniques" had made two major recommendations: the first to try to join one of the major theatrical companies– "The advantages of being a member of an established company are obvious," they'd been told, "but in addition, being for the most part repertory in nature, they provide invaluable experience for an actor. The discipline of having to perform one role while rehearsing a second will provide the final and possibly the most rigorous part of your professional training." ; the second piece of advice–to hire a reputable agent. The former piece of advice Victoria deigned to accept; the latter she rejected out of hand. She could appreciate the importance of belonging to a company, but why should an actress of her talent have to have someone else find work for her?! So that evening, with her new home made as habitable as possible, she settled herself down–together with the inevitable pot of tea–for a study of the latest theatrical trade papers. Her customary spot on the floor was not particularly inviting, however, even after the thorough scrubbing she'd given it–not that the stained and lumpy sofa was much better.

It was all ridiculously simple, quite as she'd anticipated. The Royal Shakespeare Company, it seemed, would be conducting open auditions on the following Monday and Tuesday, the 18th and 19th of June. Victoria read no further. She would try out for the RSC and naturally they'd be thrilled to have her. The fact, moreover, that Sir Terence Cartier was the company's current artistic director would certainly do her no harm. She would prefer the company at the Aldwych Theatre in London, but she would condescend to accept the Stratford-upon-Avon company if they insisted. As a member of such a prestigious organization, she would soon acquire a reputation as an actress and the rest would happen of its own accord.

Auditions were being held in a rehearsal hall near the Aldwych and so on the morning of the 18th Victoria took the tube back into Leicester Square. On the seat across the aisle she noticed a newspaper. Having learned some time ago that a used paper served just as well as a new one, she reached over and picked it up, flipping by habit now to the theatre section. Large black print immediately drew her attention to the top of the left hand page. "Sir Terence Cartier was rushed to hospital last night after suffering a heart attack. The revered actor was stricken at his home and he......" Slowly Victoria lowered the paper to her lap. Then he wouldn't be at the auditions after all. She experienced an immediate, but brief sense of shame at her self-centeredness. But then Sir Terence didn't really mean anything to her anyway, she reminded herself, except that he might have been a help to her. Well, she had auditioned for strangers before and triumphed; she would again.

Coming up out of the Leicester Square underground station, she glanced distastefully in the direction of "The Golden Hind". Well that, she vowed, like her basement flat, was only temporary and as she made her way through to the Strand and thus along toward the Aldwych, even the street signs struck her as auspicious–Garrick, Kemble, Kean, each a revered actor out of the past; one day the name of Windsor must certainly join them. Inevitably she thought of Sir Terence again. Was his name already relegated to the dusty annals of theatrical history? He couldn't be more than 50–far too young to die--, but she couldn't allow herself to be so foolish and sentimental. All that mattered was the audition.

The rehearsal hall was on the second floor of an old office building. A large, rectangular room, drab and dusty, with bare unpolished floors, it was empty of furnishings at the moment except for a row of folding chairs set along one long wall and against the other, facing these, a table with two chairs behind it. To most, in fact, the room would have appeared entirely ordinary, but to those now entering, it represented the Royal Shakespeare Company and thus it held magic.

One of the chairs at the table was already occupied by an efficient appearing woman in blue-tinted glasses–her hair worn in a trim French twist. Occasionally she glanced up at the people who either were already seated along the wall facing her or who were just coming in through the double doors at one end of the hall. At last she made a few quick notes on a sheet of paper fastened to a clipboard and stood up, rapping sharply on the table for attention. "We will be requiring certain information from you," she announced crisply, "name, address, telephone number as well as any professional training and previous acting experience. The forms are here on the table. Undoubtedly you're already aware," she continued as people began to come up and pick up their forms and here her businesslike tone faltered noticeably, "that our much-loved director, Sir Terence Cartier, suffered a heart attack last night. You will be glad to learn, I'm sure, that as of the last bulletin we've received he is doing well, for which we are all, needless to say, most thankful. In his absence...ah...excuse me, please..." Embarrassed by her unwonted public display of emotion, she paused briefly to clear her throat before going on. --"In his absence," she repeated, "the associate director, Mr. Pliny Nicholas, will be conducting the auditions."

Victoria had been among the first to pick up one of the file cards and she only vaguely heard the latter part of the announcement. If she was aware of a rush of relief at the news of her one time mentor's probable recovery, she quickly suppressed it and sitting down again on one of the folding chairs, she went to work on the form, listing every role she'd played while conveniently omitting any mention of Heathfield and Sister Marion's drama club.

A single door opened at the far end of the hall and a slightly built, middle-aged man in gray slacks and a navy blue blazer entered, closing the door precisely behind him. A noticeable hush settled over the room as he strode across the floor and with a certain air of importance took the other seat at the table. Appearing to glance offhandedly about the room, he was in reality relishing the obvious effect of his entrance. People normally didn't pay him much notice. Pliny Nicholas was not the most prepossessing of men–sparse "pepper-and salt" hair, pasty complexion and long anachronistic sideburns. He remained convinced, however, that it was not his physical appearance which consigned him to relative oblivion, but the fact that fate had determined he should live and work in Cartier's shadow. His decisions, his opinions, mattered for nothing and the fact that Sir Terence or Terry, as he was "privileged" to address him, never failed to listen courteously to whatever he had to say only made the situation all the more intolerable.

Open auditions, of course, were a bloody nuisance–rarely yielding any significant talent–and Pliny was sure he could allow his mind to wander without fear of missing anything of importance. Then once this bit of twaddle was out of the way, he could really begin his work. Sir Terence would require at the least a lengthy convalescence and who knows–with any luck he might never be well enough to resume his duties.

Names were called at random and so for over an hour Victoria sat there listening to other people try out–people whose abilities ranged from quite good to mediocre to non-existent. At the same time, however, she observed Pliny Nicholas as anyone might have studied a potential adversary and it soon became apparent he was bored. At one point he actually stifled a yawn! Well, she thought, he bloody well better pay attention to me!

All at once she was aware that her name had been called. "Here." Rising easily to her feet, she walked to the center of the room. Everyone watched her. Even then–long before the mere sound of the name Victoria Windsor came to possess a magic of its own, they watched her–everyone, that is, except Pliny Nicholas, who was consulting his address book to select a pleasant companion for lunch. Well, Victoria thought with a slight smile, I will allow him a few moments' grace.

The advert for the audition had read as follows: "Each actor should prepare three monologues: two of which are required to be Shakespearean (one tragedy or history play and one comedy). The third may be the choice of the candidate." Victoria had immediately selected Lady Macbeth for the tragedy and Kate for the comedy. The third piece had been more difficult to decide on since the advert had given no indication as to whether it also had to be Shakespearean. This was the Royal Shakespeare Company, after all, but at the same time the company often did non-Shakespearean material. Finally she'd decided to play it safe by preparing one of each: Saint Joan, of course, and Juliet.

Lady Macbeth's two intensely introspective soliloquies with which she opened her audition required such complete concentration that for a while Victoria forgot everything else, but as she began Kate's tongue-in-cheek expressions of deference to her husband Petruchio, she turned to look at Pliny Nicholas, intending to play the speech off him for greater effect. She stopped in mid-sentence. He was cleaning his fingernails!! "What in bloody hell do you think you're doing?" she demanded.

Pliny's head came up. "Are you addressing me?"

"You're damned right I am, you pompous little sod!"

"What?!" Jumping to his feet, he slammed the flat of both hands down on the table. She had his undivided attention.

"Just who do you think you are anyway?"

"I think I'm the person who decides whether or not you will be invited to join the RSC," he replied, a strong hint of irony in his tone as coming around the table, he walked toward her. "And I must inform you frankly that right at the moment your chances do not look terribly good!"

Victoria stood unmoving, not in the least intimidated, and waited until he was directly in front of her. "This audition is probably more important to us than anything else in our entire lives," she said at last then in a voice shaking with anger, "and there you sit paring your Goddamned nails!"

A ripple of laughter passed through the room. Pliny heard it, of course, and he stiffened in renewed fury. "How dare you! I..."

"Well, let me tell you something! You can bloody well take the bloody Royal Shakespeare Company and shove it up your bloody ass!" With this Victoria spun about on one spiked heel and strode from the room.

In the stunned silence which followed Pliny Nicholas turned himself and walked slowly back to the table, fighting to regain his self-control. What would Cartier have done under these circumstances, he wondered. It never occurred to him that had the other man been there, the situation simply wouldn't have developed at all. Sir Terence would never have been so discourteous to his fellow actors in the first place.

* * *

Among the many others at this audition had been someone whose life was destined at several points to touch Victoria's. This would be the first.

Jonathan Sinclair was another recent graduate in theatre although he had attended the Central School. Central students considered the Royal Academy of Dramatic Art to be nothing more than a trade school with social status thrown in, but even if he'd known at this point that Victoria was a product of the rival institution, it wouldn't have mattered. He'd never seen anyone like her. Her portrayal of Lady Macbeth had thrilled him; her marvelous audacity in standing up to Pliny Nicholas had delighted him and she was so incredibly lovely. His own audition had been less than memorable and he'd been almost relieved when the director paid him scant attention. It was a nuisance anyway to have to begin his theatrical career by trying out as an actor when his primary interest lay in production management, but open auditions were often the only means of access to a major company.

Disappointed and humiliated, still raging at Pliny "Bloody" Nicholas, Victoria had already rounded the corner from Aldwych Circle into the Strand, heading back in the direction of Leicester Square, when suddenly she realized she'd left her purse with its few precious pounds and, far more irreplaceable, her beloved Shakespeare collection on the chair in the audition hall. Her steps slowed and involuntarily she looked back at the Aldwych Theatre and the rehearsal hall beyond it. She was standing there in the middle of the pavement debating whether to swallow her pride and return for her possessions or to keep her dignity, thus resigning herself to their loss, when Jonathan caught up with her. "I believe you left these," he gasped, his dash down two flights of stairs and along the Aldwych Circle having left him out of breath.

For a moment she stared at him. "Oh yes, I did," she said at last, accepting her belongings.

No "thank you" or "how nice of you"–but Jonathan was not to be so easily put off and he continued to follow her, rapidly getting out of breath again as he tried to strike up a conversation. "I say...but your audition was smashing!"

"Well, it would have been!"

Her unabashed ego made him smile, but then without ego, he thought, talent actually meant very little. "I'm Jonathan Sinclair, by the way," he volunteered helpfully, "but people usually call me Jon." Victoria merely glanced at him as if to say, "What does that have to do with me?" and quickened her pace a little. "I'm sorry." He grinned refusing to be daunted. "I'm afraid I wasn't paying much attention to the other names and I didn't catch yours."

She stopped so suddenly now that Jon had continued on a step or two before he was aware of it. "What in bloody hell do you want anyway?"

"Just....just to get to know you better." It was an admittedly hopeless cliche, but he was entirely sincere.

"I see," she said. "I thought so."

"At least tell me your name," he called after her as she began once more to walk away, "so when you're a famous actress, I can tell everyone I met you." He was sure the notion of fame would appeal to her and she did indeed hesitate. She even laughed, tossing her head. Her laugh had a harsh sound to it; Jon could hear no real mirth in it. At the same time, however, he saw the way wisps of her hair caught the sunlight and unfortunately the next words out of his mouth were, "Do you have any idea how beautiful you are?"

"Oh God, I might have known." By now they were only a few feet from the entrance to the Leicester Square tube station.

"At least your name," Jon pleaded. "How can it hurt to tell me your name?"

She whirled about to face him one final time, her hand on the railing of the stairs leading down into the underground. "Victoria Windsor," she announced with a flourish and with a brief nod–almost a bow, he thought–she disappeared down the steps.

"Victoria Windsor," Jon repeated to himself. "I'll remember that!"

Why can't people leave me alone, Victoria thought as she bought her ticket, stepping immediately onto the escalator which would take her down into the catacombs of the London underground. Well, in this case it doesn't matter; I'll never see <u>him</u> again. What I <u>should</u> be thinking about instead is the sodding mess I made of that audition! Not that I'm sorry it happened. I will allow no one to ignore me! He's the one who'll be sorry, she vowed a moment later, waiting for her train–just like Peter Harris. When I'm a famous actress, I swear I'll spit on the whole bloody lot of them! So lost, in fact, did she become in the prospect of her glorious revenge that if someone hadn't jostled her when the train arrived, she might still have been standing there when it pulled out. By the time she was coming up out of the station at Islington, however, she had begun to view her entire situation more realistically. She may have been grievously wronged, but she was still an out-of-work actress.

The main entrance to Victoria's building was only for those tenants affluent enough to live above ground. The door to <u>her</u> flat was actually <u>under</u> the front steps, reached by means of a narrow, semi-circular metal staircase. "I might as well be a bloody mole," she muttered and with a sigh of resignation at the uncivilized way in which she was temporarily forced to live, she inserted her key in the lock and turned the knob. What she did next would have appeared decidedly peculiar to anyone passing by on the street above her for prior to entering, she stamped loudly several times and then waited. Only when all the scratching noises had stopped and she was sure that the many and varied creatures with which she shared her home had retreated behind the walls, did she actually go in.

Putting the kettle on the hot plate, Victoria settled down immediately to a renewed study of the trade papers, making notes as to upcoming try-outs. Fortunately she had no way of knowing this was only the beginning, not that such foreknowledge would have stopped her. She soon learned that bored, indifferent directors like Pliny Nicholas were far from the exception; that very often, as had been the case at RADA, the people for whom she read were nothing more than disembodied voices in a darkened theatre. There were roles such as Laura, the daughter in Tennessee Williams' *The Glass Menagerie* for which she appeared too sophisticated; there were those such as Amanda in Noel Coward's *Private Lives*, enjoying yet another revival, for which she wasn't sophisticated enough; there were parts for which she was too young; parts for which she was too old. Attempts to outguess them by dressing to suit a particular role, perhaps altering her hair style, were in vain. There were so many unsuccessful auditions that after a while she lost track of where one ended and the next began and they all just seemed to blend together into one endless rejection.

More terrible, however, certainly far more telling in its lasting effect on her was the fact that for the first time in her life she was living an existence entirely devoid of human warmth and caring.

* * *

On her first evening at "The Golden Hind" Victoria reported for work in a skirt and blouse. It was what she and the other waitress had worn at "Ollie's Alley". Cassius was just coming out of his office as she entered. "Dressing room for you birds is in there." He jerked his head to the right. "Costume's got your name on it."

"Birds?" For just a second Victoria failed to understand. Then immediately she was furious with herself. After all she'd heard the word before. Even at Abe's she'd often been called a bird though never by him, of course.

"Yeah." His eyes were two amber slits. "A 'Vicki-bird', you might say."

"Ah yes, I see." There was no actual door, she noted wryly–only a curtain– and the dressing room was in reality the storeroom. The waitresses changed among the crates and kegs. But the costume was indeed there–her name pinned to it, written appropriately enough on the back of the label from a bottle of Guinness Stout. At first glance Victoria was delighted. Its full length red skirt, black velvet waistcoat and full-sleeved white peasant blouse were authentic to the period and more than appealed to her sense of the theatrical. Its one anachronistic feature was a slit in the skirt running all the way up to the top of the thigh and even this, she was certain, would have appealed to an Elizabethan gentleman. Tights were worn underneath and she slipped into these first–admiring her long legs outlined flatteringly in black mesh--, next the skirt and blouse and then the vest, turning at last to look at herself in the mirror.

She stopped and for several minutes she stood there staring at her reflection. The tops of her breasts were entirely exposed! Did she hesitate–perhaps even consider throwing over the job and walking out? If so, it was only for a moment and before she could change her mind, she walked quickly from the storeroom. Cassius was behind the bar filling a beer stein for an early customer. Like an actor in a bad comedy, he only became aware he was staring at her when the stein overflowed. "Will I do?" Plainly her laugh mocked him and her walk, as she moved toward him, was undeniably sensual.

"If you're not careful, bitch, I'll be only too glad to show you."

"I think I'm too much for you to handle, little man."

Before she had a chance to defend herself, Cassius had seized her by the wrist, bringing his face so close to hers she could smell his whiskey-scented breath. "Believe me, the only part of me that needs concern you is more than equal to the task."

"You disgusting bastard!" Then all at once Victoria became aware that despite an obvious effort on his part Cassius' eyes were continually drawn away from her face and down toward her low-cut bodice. "Come now," she murmured, "isn't there something you'd rather hold than my wrist?"

Cheeky broad deserves to be taught a lesson, he thought, but at the same time his gaze traveled involuntarily downward again to the neckline of her blouse and the swell of soft, pale flesh. "Yes, well, perhaps there is." He smiled slightly and although he still held onto her wrist, he brought his other hand up to trace the deliciously yielding line of her cleavage. His smile broadened until more than anything he resembled a human tom cat. Victoria felt her stomach turn over in revulsion. But unfortunately, she thought, I can't afford to be so bloody fastidious.

For the next two years, then, this was to be her existence: continual professional rejection, "The Golden Hind" and Cassius O'Flaherty. Yet oddly enough at the end of that time–just when the pattern seemed fixed–her life would take a major turn.

* * *

Andrew Roberts was a junior law clerk in a long-established and respected firm of solicitors located in Throgmorton Street in the old section of London--actually, of course, the original city. He was proud of the association and the Messrs. Granville, Granville and Carruthers were equally satisfied with Mr. Roberts. He was courteous, sincere and unfailingly dependable.

As long as he could remember, Andrew had been eager to be up and about in the morning. No matter what time he went to bed the night before he was invariably awake at five a.m. and up, showered and shaved by five-thirty. This allowed him a quiet hour or so for reading and studying and still gave him time to walk the dozen plus blocks to work where he and a fellow junior clerk, both bachelors, customarily cooked breakfast together in the staff lounge. Andrew, however, did most of the actual cooking since he usually arrived first and by then he was ravenously hungry. On this particular day he'd gotten there about eight and by the time the other clerk, Greg Allsworth, came in a half-hour later the coffee was perking, the eggs, sausage and tomatoes sizzling in the frying pan.

Greg tossed his rumpled mackintosh on one of the easy chairs, dropping his worn leather briefcase on top of it. He sat down at the small wooden table already set for their meal and sniffed the air appreciatively. "I swear to God, Drew, you'll make someone a bloody marvelous wife!"

His friend turned to smile good-naturedly over his shoulder. "That's not even original."

"But my remarks never anger you, do they? Does anything?"

Andrew thought for a moment while he served the breakfast. "No, I guess not." He shrugged. "Nothing ever strikes me as that important–certainly not enough to lose my temper over it. I suppose that's the main reason I chose this side of the law. I could never see myself as an irate barrister haranguing a jury." At last he sat down as well and for the first time that morning really looked at the other man. Greg was wearing what was for him a typical costume: rumpled corduroy jacket and an unironed shirt with the top button open. A stained tie, still bearing the evidence of other previous meals, hung untied around his neck. The mere thought of the condition of his trousers–mercifully hidden from view at the moment under the table– made Andrew shudder.

When he stopped to consider how different they were in their personal habits, it was amazing they'd been friends ever since their undergraduate days together at Cambridge. His own attire for the day was, as always, a dark-blue business suit (complete with waistcoat, of course), a spotless, starched white shirt and his maroon public school tie. That was rather beside the point just now, however. Greg had already been warned on several occasions about his appearance. "See here, old man." Andrew cleared his throat. "I have to...ah ...talk to you about...ah...something."

"Yes?" Greg had stopped eating to listen to him, hand poised halfway to his mouth, and all at once half the mouthful of eggs dropped off his fork. "Ooops! Sorry about that!" Grinning, he picked the eggs up with his free hand and popped them into his mouth, wiping his hand in his lap.

Andrew hoped fervently there was a napkin there although he seriously doubted it. "See here, old man," he said in his firm, but gentle voice. "Haven't they spoken to you about your ...ah...casual style of dress?"

"Oh, come off it, Drew. I like to be comfortable. That doesn't make me any less able a solicitor. I don't object to your looking like a mannequin in the window of an elite men's store."

"Nevertheless, my clothes are considered proper for our profession while yours are not."

"Well, never mind. I'm in far too good a mood to let anything bother me this morning." Whenever one topic of conversation made him uncomfortable, Greg would simply breeze casually on to another. "Tell me, have you ever been to The Golden Hind? It's a pub near Leicester Square."

"You're in serious danger of being discharged, you damned fool......"

The other man ignored him. "You see, the decor–everything in there–is Elizabethan and the waitresses wear these long red skirts slit up to here." He indicated the top of his thigh. "And these low-cut blouses that..... Well, you get the picture."

"Vividly!" Andrew chuckled.

"At any rate I popped in there last night after the theatre for a quick one and Drew, there's this one waitress." Greg leaned back in his chair hands clasped behind his head and stared intently at the ceiling as though envisioning what he was about to describe. "Tall, but not too tall, I'd say about 5'6" or 7"–about 9 stone...I mean, the kind of body that makes you ache to touch her and...." His voice dwindled away to a low, expressive whistle as if mere words were inadequate to the occasion. "So at any rate, I thought that once they've released us from our labors, we'd nip on over there and...."

It was just at this moment, however, that the interoffice phone in the lounge interrupted him with its insistent summons. Andrew picked up the receiver. "Roberts, here." He listened for a moment, his expression increasingly serious, and then hung up again turning back to the other man. "I'm afraid Granville, Senior, wants to see you in his office, my friend."

"Right-e-o." Greg took one last swallow of his coffee and rose slowly to his feet.

"Now for God's sake, be careful what you say!"

"Sure, Drew, sure." He tucked his briefcase under one arm–the handle having long since fallen off–and flung his mac over the other shoulder.

"Will you at least tie your tie?" Andrew called after him, but the door had already closed.

As the day went by without his once seeing Greg, he became increasingly concerned and about five o'clock, having cleared off his desk, he went to check up on him. There was no answer to his knock and when he opened the door, he found the room empty, stripped of all signs of occupancy. Andrew hurried back to his own office to grab his coat, umbrella and briefcase, intending to stop at the other man's flat on the way home, but as he came out of the building a few moments later and started along the street toward the underground, Greg emerged from a near-by doorway where he'd evidently sought shelter from the early October rain. "So it's off to The Golden Hind then, hm?" he exclaimed cheerily as he matched his steps to Andrew's. "Just the evening for it, I'd say!"

"You've been sacked, haven't you?"

"Look! I don't want to talk about it!" Grimly turning up his coat collar against the dampness, his friend strode faster along the rain and windswept pavement. "What I do want very much at the moment is a large whiskey----neat!"

They crossed Threadneedle Street together, catching the Central Line at the tube stop by the Bank of England. A short ride with a change to the Piccadilly at Holborn and another walk of a couple of blocks or so brought them to The Golden Hind. The gas candles were already lit, darkness on this dreary evening having come earlier than usual and the pub, as they entered, was cheerful and inviting. Three girls, all in the long skirts, peasant blouses and black velvet waistcoats, were moving busily about setting up for that evening's trade.

Andrew glanced about the room. "Well, which one's your goddess?" he inquired with a grin.

"Oh no, she's not any of these," Greg replied at once. "These are mere mortals. You'll know her when you see her, believe me!" It was precisely at this instant, almost as though she'd been waiting for her cue, that Victoria came out of the kitchen carrying a tray of clean glasses.

Long after she'd passed from his life, hurting him as cruelly as it is possible for a woman to hurt a man, the memory of Victoria as she looked to him in that first moment would remain an indelible picture in Andrew's mind: the delicate, fine-boned features, exquisitely framed in honey-blonde hair, the large luminous eyes, thickly lashed. Odd how positive he'd immediately been that they were green. He never saw the dark circles under those eyes which even her heavy make-up couldn't entirely hide; he failed to notice how tired and drawn she appeared. Perhaps it was the flattering glow of the gaslight, but more probably, even as he stood in the doorway watching her, he was already too much in love to believe she could be anything but beautiful.

With undisguised delight Greg observed the other man's reaction. "See what I mean?" he hooted as he delivered a resounding slap to his friend's back. "Venus lives!"

"Yes...yes, I do. I...I've never seen such a breathtakingly lovely face!"

"The face? Oh, never mind the face–that's already a little shopworn. Look at..."

"Shopworn?" Andrew was obviously puzzled. "I don't understand how you can say that."

"Ever the idealist! Ah well, old man, let's get ourselves a table before it gets crowded." He turned to lead the way across the room. "You can look at her face and I... well, I'll take care of the rest of her!"

"Is that all you see in a woman, Greg?" Andrew insisted as they seated themselves at one of the empty tables.

"What else <u>is</u> there?"

"Well, it's always seemed to me as though the basic equipment's the same."

"Agreed, but it's rather like the furniture in a room, you see. It's all in the way it's arranged. Now what can I get for you?"

"Please–let me."

"Absolutely not. Even temporarily without a situation I can still buy my friend a drink. Whiskey?" Before Andrew could offer any further objection, Greg stood up and walked over to the bar.

Although busy drying the glasses and placing them on the shelf behind the bar, Victoria had observed the two men who were evidently discussing her in some detail. One especially–the neat, well-dressed one–was obviously a professional man–dark-brown hair, expertly styled, and dark–rimmed glasses–certainly more attractive than the majority of men she'd been with over the past two years. The surest way to heighten his interest, of course, was to ignore him and so even as she began to move among the tables taking orders and bringing drinks, pausing to pay special attention to certain male customers, she gave no sign she'd so much as noticed him.

Andrew, meanwhile, continued to watch her with an intentness which was beginning to make Greg uneasy. "I say there, old man," he said at last. "It's all right to look. It's obviously even all right to touch. But she's completely wrong for you! Believe me!"

"You don't know that, Greg."

"Oh, but I do! That look on your face says marriage and children and take my word for it, this particular species <u>cannot</u> be domesticated.... Look, my friend," he went on insistently, "the girls in this pub are encouraged to carry their services beyond simply waiting on table."

"Oh, I can't believe that!"

"That's what I mean, Drew. You were born in the wrong century! Now let's get the hell of out here. Someday you'll thank me."

"You can trot along if you want. I'll see you tomorrow."

"See me tomorrow? Don't you remember? I....."

"Did you say something?" But even as he spoke, Andrew's eyes followed Victoria as she walked among the tables carrying a tray of brimming steins.

"No...ah...nothing, old chap. Nothing at all. Cheerio, then. I...I'll...ah...be in touch." The other man made no reply and at last Greg got to his feet to move reluctantly toward the door. Many times in the years to come he would remember tonight and blame himself for his friend's unhappiness.

Nearly two hours later Andrew was still there. For the most part he was content just to look at her, but occasionally as he watched her stop to speak to this man or that one, bestowing a kiss here, a caress there, he would find himself wishing she would pay him a little attention. At last the crowd began to thin out and he noticed her alone–at least for the moment–drawing beer from the tap. Heart pounding, he stood up and approached the other side of the bar. "Excuse me, miss."

Victoria knew at once who'd come up to her. She allowed a moment to pass, however, before turning around. She'd often used this delayed reaction to annoy; lately she found it equally effective to entice. "Yes?"

"Believe me," he smiled apologetically. "I don't usually do this sort of thing."

"Don't do what?" Victoria inquired with a slight laugh.

"Approach ladies in pubs. I..."

"Well, you should do it more often."

"Thank you." Rather naturally Andrew had taken her words to be a compliment.

She raised a mocking eyebrow–another well-rehearsed mannerism. "No, I mean you need a great deal of practice."

"I beg your pardon." He was growing more uncomfortable by the minute. "I....I don't wish to offend you, but I hoped I might buy you a drink now that the place has cleared out a bit."

Suddenly now Victoria looked at this man–really looked at him for the first time. Perhaps I was wrong, she thought, to view him merely as a companion for the night. He could–just possibly–turn out to be much, <u>much</u> more. "I should be able to join you in a few minutes," she said. Andrew had been so positive his invitation would be refused that when instead she'd accepted, he was too stunned to do anything but stare at her–open-mouthed."Well, are you going to stand there gaping at me? Buy me a glass of white wine and go sit down."

He managed somehow to rediscover the ability to walk and purchasing her drink as well as another one for himself, he returned obediently to his table. During the few minutes it took Victoria to deliver the mugs of beer, wipe off a couple of empty tables, finally picking up used glasses to bring them out to the kitchen, Andrew never took his eyes off her. He couldn't believe his own good fortune. She probably won't come at all, he told himself over and over again. She only said that to get rid of me. But then all at once there she was actually walking toward him–such a regal walk he noticed now–and he had to admit Greg was right about her figure. As she approached the table, he got quickly to his feet and came around to pull out the chair for her.

"I am utterly amazed." Slipping with an elaborate grace into the offered chair, she crossed her legs, allowing the slitted skirt to fall open revealing a slim, well-shaped thigh. "There's actually one gentleman left in the city of London."

"I...I didn't think you'd really come," he admitted as he walked around to the other side of the table and sat down again himself. "I....I've watched you all evening and I..."

"Yes, I saw you." She laughed merrily at his obvious bewilderment. "You didn't think I noticed, did you?"

"I...I couldn't help staring. You're....you're the most beautiful woman I've ever seen." Victoria acknowledged the compliment with a brief nod. The same old line, she thought, but I do believe he means it. It's just possible my plan may work! "Oh.....oh, please excuse me," he apologized. "Your....your wine." He reached across the table to place the glass in front of her, much as a peasant might have presented an offering to a queen. "Well, I.....I suppose I should introduce myself," he continued after a moment, clearing his throot. "I'm....I'm Andrew Roberts. I'm a law clerk with Granville, Granville and Carruthers. That's a...ah.... firm of solicitors in Throgmorton Street. May.....may I ask <u>your</u> name?"

Victoria took a sip of her wine before replying to his question, gazing at him intently over the glass. A wine goblet made such a marvelous prop anyway–seductive yet at the same time elegant. Even the particular drink she'd chosen was part of her plan; she would have preferred something a good deal stronger. Her expression betrayed none of this, of course, as replacing the glass on the table, she smiled at him. "Victoria Windsor," she said finally and with such an air of pride Andrew should have known at once she would never be contented to be simply a wife and mother. "And I," she went on with a toss of her head, "am an actress."

"I knew this was only temporary," he affirmed earnestly. "I knew you weren't just a barmaid."

"How kind of you to realize I don't belong here," she murmured, allowing her eyes to fill with tears. "I'm sorry. Do you have a handkerchief? I never seem to have one." She could hear Uncle Bertie's gentle voice as clearly as ever. "Why is it a little girl never seems to have a hanky when she needs one?" Oh God, she thought, why in hell did I have to say that? All at once she began aware Andrew was offering her his own handkerchief and with a grateful smile she accepted it, noting with some amusement that it was immaculate and freshly ironed.

"Do you have to support yourself?" he asked. "Don't you have a family?"

"No, I'm afraid I don't." Victoria hoped the little shrug which accompanied the words was sufficiently pathetic. The gesture would undoubtedly require more practice to become entirely effective.

Impulsively Andrew reached over to place his hand on hers where it rested between them on the table. "May I see you home? It's late for you to be out on the streets unescorted."

She smiled to herself. The pathetic shrug evidently needed no further rehearsal. "Oh, but it's such an imposition," she demurred. "I live way out past Islington."

"Please, it would be my pleasure."

"Well, all right, then," Victoria agreed as she stood up. "I just have to clean up behind the bar. You.....you will wait, won't you?" Was she truly afraid he might leave or was this just part of her performance? It didn't matter. Andrew looked into her eyes and was lost.

"Of course I'll wait," he reassured her. The next half-hour or so seemed the longest he'd ever known, but just when he felt he couldn't wait another minute, Victoria appeared from a back room, much as she'd done the first time he saw her; only now she was dressed in dark green slacks and a pullover and carrying a mackintosh over one arm and—incredibly–she was leaving with him. Standing up, he took the coat from her to help her on with it. How proud he felt following her to the door. It didn't even matter that as they walked from the pub to the tube station, she fell strangely silent. She was probably shy, he thought, and anyway it was enough for him just to be with her.

In reality Victoria was deep in thought. Should she invite him in? Suppose she continued to play the innocent and he never became smitten enough to propose? All during the ride out to Islington she was trying to decide and it wasn't until they were almost at her stop that she made up her mind. What the hell, she thought, I've carried it this far. "You.....you don't have to come any further with me," she said bravely as they came up out of the underground station. "You can cross over and catch the tube back. My flat's only three blocks from here."

"Absolutely not. I'll see you right to your door." Andrew felt very masculine and protective and as they started to walk again, he even summoned up the courage to offer her his arm.

"Oh, thank you," she murmured gratefully as she slipped her arm through his. "It's been a long night."

"That work's altogether too hard for you, Victoria." Oh, how fervently he wished it were up to him to take care of her, but as it was, he barely had the right to advise her. "Isn't there something less taxing you could do?"

Her only reply was the same little shrug which had worked so well back at the pub. She was immediately concerned because she'd employed that particular piece of business only a short while before. Even the most moving gesture if overdone can lose its effectiveness and apparently, since there was no instant expression of sympathy on his part, this one had already been used once too often.

She was wrong, of course. Andrew's heart had indeed been touched yet again, but he was too busy wondering how far they still had to walk and trying to work up enough nerve to ask her out on an actual date. "W...w...would you possibly be free Sunday afternoon?" he finally stammered. "I can borrow a chum's car and we could drive into the country for dinner."

"I'd like that." She glanced sideways at him with a quick, shy smile. It's working, she thought–even Sunday, the longest, loneliest day of the week! It was all she could do not to give a little skip of triumph.

"I'll pick you up at three o'clock then." He fairly beamed with pleasure, but then immediately his smile disappeared as Victoria stopped at what must be their destination. "Is this your flat?" he inquired anxiously, bending over slightly to peer at her door. "Have you a good, strong lock?"

"Oh, believe me, it's perfectly safe. The murderers and rapists are afraid of the rats."

"Oh, Victoria!" Andrew was more worried and upset than ever.

She laughed. "Though as a matter of fact I do have two locks plus a bolt."

"Well, I'll...I'll see you Sunday then." After a slight hesitation he leaned down to kiss her on the cheek and then he was gone, pausing once to wave before disappearing around the corner.

"Yes, I do believe I've solved my problem," Victoria said to herself as she turned to run lightly down the stairs to her flat.

Andrew arrived promptly on Sunday to take her on the promised outing. Soon after that he began to appear at The Golden Hind about a half hour before closing each evening to see her home. And just a little more than one month after they met and despite repeated warnings from Greg, he and Victoria went to a magistrate's office and were married.

Chapter 4

What a pleasure it was to quit her job at The Golden Hind–to tell Cassius O'Flaherty exactly what she thought of him. Most marvelous of all–for the first time since she'd arrived in London over four years before, she didn't have to worry about every penny. And no longer was she forced to endure the humiliation of offering herself to some man in the pub–any man so she wouldn't be alone. Andrew was there every night and his physical demands on her were no more annoying than anyone else's. It seemed, then, she could finally relax.

This blissful self-indulgence would be short-lived, however, for in one crucial area she allowed herself to relax a little too much. The morning of the wedding Victoria had reached by habit for her birth control pills. How vividly she remembered the distasteful little public health service doctor who'd grudgingly written her the prescription. Unfortunately it was a necessity. The last thing she wanted or needed was a baby. Now–suddenly–she stopped even as her hand grasped the container. The pills had given her headaches as well as causing her ankles to swell. And after all, she laughed to herself, if I get pregnant now, at least it won't be a bastard.

They had been married barely a month when she awoke one morning sick to her stomach and when she tried to sit up, the room spun about her. Weakly she sank down on the pillows again, fighting back the nausea. Andrew was standing in front of the dresser at the foot of the bed meticulously knotting his tie and he had observed her in the mirror. "What's the matter, darling?" He turned to look at her directly. "Are you feeling ill?"

God, Victoria thought, he is so bloody neat! "Don't be silly," she said out loud. "I'm perfectly fine. I....I didn't sleep very well last night–that's all. I...I think I'll stay in bed and perhaps I'll be able to nap a bit after you leave."

"Are you sure you're all right?" He came to sit beside her taking hold of her hand, but the motion of the bed only sent fresh waves of nausea sweeping over her.

Irritably she pulled away from him. "God, you are the damnedest old woman! Just get the hell out of here!"

"All right.....all right, sweetheart," he murmured placatingly as he stood up and backed away from the bed. "I'll....I'll ring you later to see how you're feeling."

"What you can do is to bloody well leave me alone!"

"Yes....yes, dear." Slipping on his waistcoat, Andrew picked up his suit jacket and left at once to avoid angering her any further. There had been moments in the weeks since they were married when he'd wondered if his new wife were really the sweet, gentle girl he'd taken her to be, but until now she'd never been openly nasty.

Alone, Victoria lay quietly for a while until finally it seemed she felt better. It might help, she decided, if she ate something–- a soft-boiled egg on toast perhaps and some tea. She managed to get up and make her way into the other room, but at the actual smell of food the nausea rose in her throat again and she just got to the bathroom in time. Every morning for the next two weeks or so she awoke feeling ill. Growing concerned, Andrew finally insisted she see a doctor, but quite inexplicably it seemed to him, this admonition–so lovingly intended–sent her into a rage. God, she thought, why in hell did I stop taking those pills? I might have known that with my bloody, rotten luck, I'd get caught! The day came, however, when she could no longer avoid facing the facts. Her monthly period was several days overdue and she'd always been so damned regular! She went to a lab for the necessary test–the following day to a doctor to learn the results.

"Mrs. Roberts, please." The receptionist's impersonal gaze flicked over the crowded waiting room. "Dr. Barrett will see you now."

"Yes." With her customary self-possession she rose to her feet and followed the other woman into the inner office.

The doctor was a slightly built man, balding and fifty-ish. "Please sit down, Mrs. Roberts. I'd like to talk to you first, if I may, and then my nurse will show you to the examining room and assist you to prepare." Victoria took the indicated straight chair on the other side of the desk and crossing her legs, she folded her gloved hands in her lap. Her face, as she waited for him to speak, was without expression. Dr. Barrett took a final look at the chart on his desk and closed the folder. "Well, yes, Mrs. Roberts.." He smiled....."the test was positive. I would say you're about one month pregnant."

She nodded. "That's what I thought. How do I arrange for an abortion?"

He blinked once or twice. "Then you and your husband do not want the child?"

"What in bloody hell does this have to do with him?" Her voice rose sharply both in pitch and volume. "I'm the one who's pregnant!"

The miracle of new life never failed to thrill Dr. Barrett and only his strict standards of professional behavior made it possible for him to answer this woman in an even tone of voice. "It's simply that under the law, Mrs. Roberts, your husband must consent to the abortion."

"Well then, I'll get his consent! I don't want this baby and by God, I'm not going to have it!" Before the doctor had a chance to say anything further, Victoria strode out of his office and through a waiting room full of women in all of the stages of pregnancy. From the shocked expressions on their faces they had evidently heard her outburst, but she didn't care.

"Damn!" She stabbed furiously at the lift button, beginning to pace impatiently as she waited. "Damn, it can't all be ruined so soon! Andrew will have to give his consent. After all, it's his fault I'm pregnant! Oh, where the hell is that bloody lift!" she exploded at last in exasperation. It was only then Victoria noticed the door marked "Stairs". Hurrying over, she yanked it open–in her overwrought state sending it crashing against the wall. She ran down the first flight, but turning the corner at the landing, she caught her heel and if she hadn't been holding on to the railing, she would have fallen. She laughed. "Well, maybe I'll have a miscarriage and save all of us the trouble." But she moved more carefully after that.

Returning to their flat each evening, Andrew could never be sure what he'd find. Sometimes the tiny living room would appear cozy and inviting–warmed by the coal fire, the lamps lit against the winter darkness and the table set for tea. Best of all, this meant Victoria was there herself, sweet and loving as only she could be when she was in one of her more benevolent moods. But then there were those other times when he was met by nothing except a dark, empty flat and he would spend several terrifying hours wondering where she was and worse–whether she was ever coming back. When she did at last return home, she was often drunk and he soon learned it only made matters worse to confront her. At such times now he'd usually pretend to be asleep. It might not be the bravest course of action, but it was the easiest.

Once again on this particular evening Andrew opened the door to discover only cold and darkness yet for some reason he sensed immediately he wasn't alone. "Victoria, are you here, sweetheart?" For a brief moment he actually found himself hoping there would be no answer, but then her voice came to him out of the darkness–so harsh as to be all but unrecognizable.

"Yes, I'm here." Unaccountably the room seemed to grow even colder. Andrew shivered. "No," she went on quickly as he started toward a table to snap the lamp on. "Don't turn any lights on! I can't stand to look at you!"

He was able to make her out now–sitting in an armchair near the window, the street light making her just barely visible. He went over to her. "What's the matter, Victoria?" he inquired as gently as possible.

"Matter?" She leaned forward, her hands gripping the arms of the chair. "Matter?" You bloody well know what's the matter!"

"I'm afraid I don't understand, dear, but if I've done something to hurt you, it wasn't intentional."

She came to her feet to face him then, her fists clenched at her sides. "You miserable bastard—I'm pregnant!"

"Are you sure?" Andrew was aware how foolish he sounded, but he could think of nothing else to say. Victoria let out one long piercing shriek and went for his face with her nails. He reacted instinctively, seizing her wrists in his own defense, but even as he struggled with her, Andrew was attempting to come to some sort of rational understanding of the situation. A woman was supposed to be happy, wasn't she, when she learned she was going to have a baby? Of course, he thought suddenly, it's just that the news had been unexpected. "Please, Victoria," he said at last, "if you'll try to calm yourself, we can talk about this. I realize we didn't plan on a baby so soon, but I'm sure once you're over the shock....."

"No, I don't want to calm myself and I don't want to talk about it!" With a sudden wrenching motion she managed to free her wrists, at once whirling about on him again. "What I want is an abortion!"

"But, Victoria, you can't really want to kill our baby!"

"Oh, don't be so bloody melodramatic! It's not a baby yet! It's just this thing inside of me. But the ridiculous part is–I need your consent! I don't know what Goddamned business it is of yours, but then laws are made by men!"

The calmness with which Andrew had faced every situation in his life threatened to desert him. "Well, I'm sorry, Victoria, but as the baby's father, I do have something to say about this."

"You still don't understand, do you?" He watched her beautiful face twist in scorn until it grew almost ugly. "I can't be saddled with a baby. I have more important things to do with my life!"

"What could possibly be more important than the creation of a new life? I'm sorry, Victoria," he said yet again. "But nothing you can say will change my mind."

At this her expression suddenly relaxed. She appeared almost placid. "All right then." Her voice as well was calm and yet somehow at the same time more threatening. "You leave me no other choice."

Fear stabbed at Andrew like a knife and the palms of his hands began to perspire. "No other choice?" he echoed weakly.

"No other choice," she repeated yet again and he realized with a start that she was smiling faintly. "There are people who will take care of this for me."

"Victoria, no! Those men are butchers! They could kill you!"

"As I said, you are leaving me no choice. I am telling you honestly that I don't want this baby. Therefore, if you force me to take matters into my own hands, you and you alone will be responsible." Her smile broadened; she knew she had won.

For a moment longer Andrew hesitated. He despised himself for his cowardice, but he couldn't risk losing Victoria and if he continued to refuse his permission, he would surely do so. Even if she survived the back-alley abortionist, she would never forgive him for opposing her. He sighed; he felt very tired "All right, Victoria, I won't fight you. Just tell me what I have to do." Suddenly the flat, which only a short while before had seemed cold, struck him as oppressively warm. "But right now, I need some fresh air–so if you'll excuse me." Andrew picked up his coat from the chair where he'd flung it and turning, fled back out into the night. He had just given his consent to the murder of his unborn child and it would take long hours of walking the darkened London streets before he could come to terms with that fact.

When he did finally return, it was well past midnight and Victoria was asleep. Sprawled on her stomach, she appeared almost childlike and for several moments he stood looking down at her. Perhaps, after all, he'd married her without really knowing her; perhaps she did not love him, had indeed <u>never</u> loved him, but he still loved her deeply and he would do anything to keep her. Just then she stirred in her sleep; it sounded almost as though she were calling out for someone. Hope rose anew in Andrew and he sat down on the bed, touching her gently. Her eyes opened, but seeing him, her face at once hardened. "Get away from me," she hissed. "You disgust me!" She turned away from him, burying her head in the pillow. He regretted profoundly having awakened her.

The next morning Andrew was up even earlier than usual. He'd been unable to sleep very much anyway and perhaps if he occupied his mind with the intricacies of the law, he could forget–at least for a while-- the pain of last night. He was relieved that as he slipped out of bed, Victoria did not move or say anything to him although it seemed impossible she could be asleep. He was just about to leave the flat when she appeared in the doorway of their bedroom. His back was turned and he didn't realize she was there until she spoke. "Be sure to ring up Dr. Barrett this morning, Andrew. I'd like to get this business taken care of as soon as possible."

He was glad she couldn't see the tears fill his eyes as she dismissed their unborn child as "this business". "I won't forget." But his voice still shook with emotion and as he hurried away down the stairs, he heard a heavy glass object shatter against the closed door. "I hate you! I hate you! I hate you!" she screamed over and over again. Only when he shut the downstairs door behind him did he finally escape the sound of her wrath.

Still shaking with anger, Victoria stood for a few seconds in the middle of the living room floor, but at last she walked slowly over to pick up the pieces of the vase she had thrown at the door. It had only been a wedding gift from Andrew's sister anyway and she'd always hated it. Well, I got what I wanted and that's all that counts, she thought as she worked. Yes—she <u>had</u> gotten what she wanted. Then why was there no feeling of triumph?

* * *

For the next several horrible days she and Andrew merely coexisted in the small flat, speaking only when necessary. As much as possible they avoided each other entirely.

The morning of her appointment, she awoke to find it raining steadily–a classic English day in early December–and it was easy to attribute her blue mood to the weather. Rain always depresses me, she thought, as she stepped into her slippers and putting on her robe, she went out into the other room. The coal fire–which as usual Andrew had tended before leaving for work–was burning cheerily in the grate and the combination kitchen-living room was warm and cozy. God, Victoria fumed, why does he always have to be so bloody considerate!

All at once a wave of nausea swept over her. She felt light-headed and for a moment she thought she was going to faint. Mercifully the sensation soon abated. Well, all that would be over with as of two o'clock this afternoon. Oddly–yet again–she experienced no sense of satisfaction at the thought, however, only a further deepening of her despair and at the same time an almost murderous rage at something... or..... someone. "Well, anyway," she said aloud to the empty room, "pregnant women are supposed to have moods, aren't they?" She laughed and laughed until ultimately tears mingled with the laughter, drowning it. Sobbing now, she sank into a chair at the kitchen table, burying her face in her folded arms.

She had no idea how long the telephone had been ringing. So many of her fruitless auditions ended with the almost classic cliche: "Don't ring us; we'll ring you" and perhaps this was actually one of those long-awaited calls. Halfway across the room, another dizzy spell hit her and she had to grab the back of the sofa to keep from falling. Dear God, she thought, don't let them hang up! Nausea rose in her anew, but she refused to let herself be sick and at last–miraculously–she reached the telephone. "Hello." Of course she sounded totally composed.

"Victoria?" It was a man's voice, unfamiliar to her.

"Yes, this is Victoria Windsor."

"I thought you might be interested. The actress playing Anya in that new production of Chekhov's *The Cherry Orchard* has hepatitis and they're auditioning for a replacement."

Victoria's mind raced. The production had received rave reviews and stepping into the role of Anya could be her big break. "Where?" She could barely contain her excitement. The voice supplied an address and a time: one to four that afternoon. "Yes, I've got it. Good-bye."

Jonathan Sinclair shook his head in amused exasperation as the wire went dead. She hadn't even bothered to inquire as to his identity–not that she'd have remembered him. It had been more than two years since their brief encounter on the pavement outside the RSC audition hall. But he had gone to a great deal of trouble to track her down and he'd anticipated some expression of gratitude on her behalf. Recalling now her behavior at that original meeting, Jon supposed he should have known better.

Victoria, meanwhile, hadn't given her caller a second thought. She located her Chekhov collection and spent the rest of the morning studying *The Cherry Orchard*–in particular the character of Anya–going over and over key scenes. The dismal weather was forgotten; her depression was forgotten; the scheduled abortion was forgotten.

She was one of the first to arrive at the audition hall. There were the usual index cards. By now she could have filled one of them out in her sleep. During the endless waiting for her name to be called she happened to glance down at her watch for some reason. It was nearly two-thirty. She had missed the appointment. "Well, never mind." She shrugged. "I can make another one." She felt much like a sentenced criminal at the moment of reprieve. Did she wonder or for that matter even note the sensation? Whether she did or not was unimportant; it, nevertheless, was there.

After the audition was over–she had ceased to judge her own work; she knew she was good and sooner or later someone else must realize it, too–Victoria returned home, inexplicably light-hearted, and when Andrew arrived some time later, he was surprised to discover her cooking dinner for him. She was even humming as she worked. How can she be happy, he wondered, and he felt sick to his stomach. How could he possibly eat anything? "Dinner should be ready soon, Andrew." She turned to smile at him. "I've made beef bourguignonne. I know that's one of your favorites and it's such a mean, nasty night and there's a salad and hot garlic bread...."

He couldn't keep quiet any longer. "How...how...can you, Victoria...after..... after..." But he couldn't bring himself to speak the words.

"After what?" At first she was puzzled, but then she understood what he meant. "Oh... that. I didn't go to the doctor." Joy flooded over him. She'd changed her mind; she did want the baby after all. But then she continued. "Something came up—an audition. I'll have to make a new appointment."

"Another audition?" Andrew inquired sadly. "Is that all you ever think about?"

"You should be glad! You're the one who wants me to have this thing."

"Thing! Our baby? God, I truly believe you're inhuman. Greg was right when he warned me not to marry you!"

"Oh, Greg warned you about me, did he?" Victoria arched one eyebrow. "Well, he wasn't above enjoying my company when you had to be in Bristol the week of our wedding."

If Andrew had been a different sort of man, he might have struck her. As it was, he simply strode from the room slamming the door behind him. When he came home, it was to find the flat empty, the cold food still on the table. His wife returned a couple of hours later, drunker even than usual. He didn't ask where she'd been.

Victoria did indeed make another appointment with the doctor, but that morning –by now it was early January–she awoke to discover it sleeting heavily, bits of ice pinging against the window panes and well, it seemed a pity to have to go out in such dreadful weather. She rang up to cancel. January passed and February and somehow she could never find time to have the abortion. She failed to realize that her excuses were increasingly flimsy–that once or twice she'd even caught herself looking at baby clothes. Finally, however, there came a morning in late March when she was no longer able to fasten her skirt. She made yet another appointment and this time she kept it.

How stupid they all look, Victoria thought as she sat among the other women in the waiting room–like a bunch of fat cows. Why then, in a vague way, did she envy them? Unwillingly her eyes filled with tears. "Mrs. Roberts, if you will come with me, please." Rising to lead the way into the inner office, the nurse eyed Victoria disapprovingly.

"Please sit down, Mrs. Roberts," the doctor said, accepting her file from the nurse. "I wish to talk to you prior to your examination."

"Talk to me!" Her self-control was near breaking. "Don't you remember....."

"Good pre-natal care is vital, Mrs. Roberts, both for you and your baby. Now I see from your records that your pregnancy was diagnosed in early December. Why have you neglected to keep even one of your appointments?"

Appropriate word–diagnosed, Victoria thought–diagnosed as in disease! "Pre-natal care? Those appointments were for my abortion!"

"Ah yes—of course, Mrs. Roberts." He nodded. "How could I have forgotten?"

"After all, a woman is more than a mere baby machine!"

"And you personally would find a baby inconvenient just at the moment?" He did not wait for her reply. "Then you should have found time to have the abortion."

"But I'm here to have it now."

"That's just it, you see. You're too late. Your pregnancy is into its second trimester and an abortion at this stage could endanger your own health–even your life."

Irritation, anger, blinding rage assaulted Victoria in rapid succession. But these more violent emotions soon ebbed before gentler, yet stronger ones: resignation first, then relief and finally an emotion more nearly resembling pure joy than anything she had yet to experience. She couldn't have the abortion! Her face betrayed none of this, however. If anything, her expression grew even more set.

"And I would strongly advise you, Mrs. Roberts," the doctor continued, "not to go anywhere else. Any reputable doctor will tell you the same thing."

"Yes, well, as you say, it appears I have no choice."

"Good. Now the examining room is right in there." He pointed. "Please undress completely and put one of the gowns on. I'll be with you shortly."

Without a word of protest Victoria obeyed, rising to proceed docilely through the indicated door. Removing her own clothing, she donned a hospital gown. It was extremely drafty and she felt ridiculous. Finally she climbed up on the table to wait. And through it all she kept telling herself--I don't want this baby. They can't force me to have this baby! Yet the happiness inside her refused to die.

The nurse came in first to prepare her for the examination and a moment later the doctor himself. The internal exam wasn't pleasant, but Dr. Barrett was extremely gentle in addition to being thorough. "Well, everything appears to be fine, Mrs. Roberts," he reassured her when he'd completed the exam and Victoria, dressed again, had returned to his office, seating herself across the desk from him as before. "I would estimate your due date to be early in August."

"You're positive I can't have the abortion, then?" she said again–flatly.

"The only reason I'd even consider abortion at this point, Mrs. Roberts, would be if your health were being adversely affected in any way. And despite the fact that you've probably done nothing to take care of yourself, you are in excellent physical condition. Now my nurse will give you your schedule of appointments. Please be sure that from now on you keep them. And don't hesitate to telephone me if you have any questions."

"Yes, doctor." Where was the infamous Windsor temper? Why didn't she tell him to "sod off"? She was still trying to understand why herself as she walked toward the door.

"Oh, yes," he added, "and Miss Newton will also give you a copy of the diet we recommend for expectant mothers. Please follow it as closely as possible. As well as a prescription for vitamins."

"Yes, doctor," she murmured meekly once again. Dr. Barrett's attention by now was on her file open on his desk and thus he only heard the door shut behind Victoria with a barely audible click. Quite a contrast, he thought wryly, to her last exit.

It was the heavenly kind of day peculiar to England in March–a slight nip in the air, but a cloudless sky and the sun warm on her face. Still Victoria hadn't made a conscious decision to take a walk and she had no idea where she was going– in fact as in the doctor's office she seemed to have no control over her own mind and body ––until all at once she turned a corner and found herself on Oxford Street, one of London's major shopping districts. About halfway along the first block she passed a shop specializing in children's clothing. Her steps slowed and she turned back to gaze at all the dear little things, in particular a white snowsuit embroidered with yellow ducks.

She had no idea how long she'd been standing there when something–she was never sure what–drew her attention away from the display and to her own reflection in the store window. There was a softness in her expression she'd never seen there before, a smile just touching her lips. Suddenly, as if with a snap of her fingers, Victoria's mind cleared and whirling about, she ran away down the street toward the Oxford Circus tube stop. For the remainder of the afternoon she had nothing to do but brood, twisting and turning the events of the past few hours until she'd wrung from them every last vestige of joy. Somewhere in this torturous process she managed as well to convince herself that her husband was entirely to blame–it was he who'd made her wait to have the abortion until it was too late–and when poor Andrew arrived home, she turned on him in retribution taking out all of her hatred and frustration–hatred and frustration which in reality, of course, were directed at herself.

But the worst of Victoria's anger had been vented–at least temporarily–and for the next few weeks an uneasy truce existed between them–at least until Andrew found the object concealed in the back of their bedroom closet. He strode out into the living room with it clenched in one fist. Victoria was, as usual, reading the theatrical trade papers and this only made him all the more furious. "And what is this for, may I ask?"

She looked up. Damn, she thought, I was sure I'd hidden it better than that. Now we'll have a great row. "What is what for?" she said aloud after a moment.

"You know damn well what I mean. This corset. You've been wearing it to auditions, haven't you–to disguise the fact you're pregnant?"

"What did you think I was using it for–a lampshade?"

"And another thing. They rang me up at my office today because you missed your last appointment with the obstetrician."

"Well, that damned doctor can just shove his instruments up his own ass because he's seen the last of mine! You knew I didn't want this baby and you still forced me to have it!"

"No one stopped you from having an abortion, Victoria," he replied quietly, "except yourself. Because deep down inside you really want this baby."

"Get out!" She clapped her hands over her ears to shut out Andrew's words-- words she could not accept. "Get out! Get out!"

"All right, all right. I'll be at my club if you want me."

"Want you? <u>Want</u> you? I never <u>wanted</u> you in the first place, you stupid sod, so why should I want you now? Didn't you hear me? I told you to get the hell out of here!" Victoria sprang to her feet, the newspapers falling to the floor forgotten and the sudden motion jostling the end table near her right hand and knocking over a small reading lamp. Automatically she caught the lamp, but then she appeared for the first time to notice it in her hand and yanking the plug from its wall socket, she struck out at him with it again and again. "Get out!" she sobbed. "Get out! Get out!"

"Yes, honey," Andrew murmured soothingly. He was far more afraid for her than for himself. "I'm going. I'm going." Even after he'd left, Victoria continued to swing the lamp blindly, sending empty vases, other lamps, even a small chair crashing to the floor. Finally she flung the lamp itself and running into their tiny bedroom, she threw herself sobbing on the bed.

Her rage so totally consumed her that initially she'd failed to notice the first faint stirrings of life inside her. But the baby kicked her again–more strongly this time– refusing to be ignored. Her sobs dwindled away as all her senses turned inward. Her breathing slowed and responding instinctively, she brought one hand up to stroke her abdomen which at five months was just beginning to swell noticeably with the new life she carried. "It's all right," she whispered. "It's all right. I didn't mean any of it. You know that, don't you? Hush, my little love, hush." She remained that way for a long time, caressing her stomach in slow, easy circles and crooning to her unborn child until at last she fell asleep.

By the next day, however, she'd pushed all memory of the moment from her mind and purchasing a new and stiffer corset, she continued her determined march from one audition to the next until one day she came the closest thus far to succeeding. A small, but reputable company was producing yet another revival of Oscar Wilde's *The Importance of Being Earnest* and Victoria had tried out for the part of Gwendolyn Fairfax, an elegant young woman, for which she considered herself eminently well-suited. She gave her usual flawless audition and then sat down with the others to wait for the results.

When the last hopeful had finished, the director rose to speak. He was holding the inevitable clipboard. I wonder, Victoria thought wryly, if they're born with those things already attached. "The following are requested to return," the man droned. He read a list of about fifteen names, but she heard only her own. For two days–until the call-back–her spirits were soaring. She was sweeter to Andrew than she'd ever been and once again his heart filled with hope. She <u>did</u> want the baby; he was sure now.

On the second day of readings she was asked to do the smashing argument scene between Gwendolyn and Cecily, one of her favorites–certainly another positive omen. They'd barely started, however, when the director stopped them. "Wait a minute there. The girl reading for Gwendolyn." He consulted his clipboard. "Victoria Windsor. You preggers, sweetie?"

Oh God, no, Victoria thought. "Of...of course not." she replied aloud.

"That's what I thought. Afraid we can't use you, ducks. Can't have Miss Fairfax in a family way, now can we, what?"

"Now just a minute. I....."

"Sorry, little mama. Next?"

Tears of discouragement stinging her eyes, Victoria walked off the stage and out the rear exit of the theatre. In the alley running along side the building there were the usual garbage cans and empty packing crates. She sank down on one of the crates burying her head in her hands. God, she thought, why didn't I have that abortion? "Excuse me, Miss Windsor." From somewhere behind her an unfamiliar male voice broke into her thoughts.

If there was anything Victoria hated, it was to be caught like this with her emotions so plainly revealed. "Yes?" Raising her head, she turned to look at the intruder, intending to intimidate him with a show of temperament. Instead she found herself studying him with considerable interest. With his longish brown hair worn parted in the middle, wire-rimmed spectacles and faded denim jeans and jacket he was actually quite ordinary in appearance–at least among the out-of-work theatrical types customarily seen at these auditions. Yet something about him intrigued her. Perhaps it was the fact that he had the liveliest blue eyes she'd ever seen; perhaps it was the way he stood there grinning at her, clearly delighted at having found her.

"Sorry if I startled you," he said. "I just wanted to tell you that I heard your audition in there."

"Then you didn't hear much." In spite of herself she laughed, forgetting entirely her discomfiture of a few moments before. "I couldn't have said more than a dozen words before he stopped me."

"Oh, well that." He grinned at her in such a genuine way that for some reason Victoria, who trusted very few people, sensed at once that he wasn't making fun of her. "I didn't mean that. I was referring to your original reading a couple of days ago. You're very good. Do you know that?" She saw no need to reply. There was no necessity to comment on the obvious. "You <u>do</u> know that, don't you?" His grin broadened. "That's part of what makes your performance what it is."

"What in hell are you talking about? Are you a producer?"

"This isn't the first time I've seen you either, is it? You read for the Chekhov play a few months ago, didn't you?"

"Congratulations! You have a magnificent memory! I repeat–what in hell are you talking about?"

"I'm getting to that. I'm getting to that. Since I saw you at the Chekhov auditions, I've done some checking around. You don't have an agent, do you?"

"Oh, so that's it. Not only are you not offering me a job–you're asking me for one! Well, I'm afraid I can't help you."

"I've made a frightful botch of this whole thing, haven't I? Wait....let me think." He paused to run both hands through his hair. "By George, I have it now." He grinned at her again. "See if you like this any better." He turned to walk away a few steps. With his back still turned to her he took something out of his jacket pocket and whirling about, he approached her a second time, bowed and with a flourish presented her with a business card. "Allow me to introduce myself, Miss Windsor. Leslie Matthews-- theatrical agent–at your service."

"Mr. Matthews." She nodded regally, entering into his game.

"Oh, the hell with it!" Flinging himself down on the next crate, he seized her by the shoulders.

She stiffened. "Don't touch me!"

"Sorry. Anything you say." He removed his hands, but nothing could dampen his enthusiasm. "Only you're absolutely smashing! You don't have an agent, do you?"

"I....I didn't consider one necessary." Was it only three years ago she'd been fresh out of the Academy–supremely confident that with but a single audition, her career would be launched? She still believed in herself, but after so many failures, maybe....

"Look—I can help you! I know I can!"

"My dear Mr. Matthews, if you were inside a few minutes ago, you also know that I'm pregnant."

"I'm not talking about now. When is your baby due?"

"This is incredible! I'm sitting in an alley discussing my pregnancy with a total stranger!"

"That's all right. You don't have to answer. Take my card and when you're ready to go back to work, give me a ring. Come on, take it," he urged as she hesitated.

At last Victoria accepted the card. She looked at him intently. "Yes, perhaps I will phone you."

"You won't be sorry," he promised fervently. He stood up then to leave, but he was still talking as he backed away from her down the alley. "Before I'm finished, the name of Victoria Windsor will light up the whole bloody West End!"

As he disappeared around the corner, Victoria was relieved to see he was finally facing forward. She looked down at the card in her hand. After all, anyone crazy enough to believe in her..... But she put the card in her purse.

Victoria was afraid to risk auditioning again and so with grim determination she settled down to wait out the four remaining months of her pregnancy. She would consider it as merely a term of bondage which must be served before her life could resume. She went back to reading plays; she restudied certain Shakespearean roles in greater depth and she watched herself grow more misshapen with every day. Oddly she no longer hated her husband for any of this. In fact she had no feeling toward him at all.

Watching her body swell with their child, Andrew wondered how she could possibly see herself as ugly. He knew, nevertheless, that she hated what was happening to her and now he found himself wishing she would blame him; scream at him, throw things at him. Even her rage would have been easier to take than her indifference. This was his child as well and he hungered to share the experience. Sometimes at night when she'd finally fallen asleep, he would rest one hand on her belly just to feel the child move inside her. He could never remember being so lonely.

Andrew was at work when her pains started and Victoria saw no reason to let him know. She walked to the corner newsstand to buy the latest theatrical trade papers and in the next few hours as her labor continued, she made a list of the upcoming auditions. The moment of her emancipation was at hand and as the contractions came closer and closer together, her elation grew. Finally when the pains were about fifteen minutes apart, she notified Dr. Barrett and telephoned for a taxi. Only when the admitting nurse insisted did she give her Andrew's office number.

* * *

The intercom in Andrew's office buzzed and he reached over to push the talk button. "Yes?"

"St. Mary's hospital rang, Mr. Roberts. Your wife is....."

She got no further as Andrew leaped to his feet and knocked his chair over. His jacket had been on the back of the chair, however, and when he went to put it on, he discovered it was pinned to the floor. He managed after several seconds of frantic effort to extricate the jacket, but then he tried to grasp the door handle with his hand still only halfway down the sleeve. By some miracle he finally made it into the lift and out onto the pavement to hail a taxi. "St. Mary's Hospital, Paddington," he directed the driver breathlessly. "And hurry! I'm about to become a father!"

"Well now, that's fine, sir," the driver replied with a grin. "I'll make sure you get there in time for the big event."

"Please, dear God," Andrew whispered fervently as they moved out into the traffic, "please let this be the beginning for us." He was still repeating the same prayer when the taxi pulled up in front of the hospital's main entrance. Even while he answered all the questions and signed the endless forms and especially when he was at last upstairs in the waiting room with the other expectant fathers, he continued to say it in his heart. He hadn't been there much more than an hour when a nurse entered and called his name. Eagerly he identified himself.

"Oh yes, Mr. Roberts." She smiled happily. "Congratulations! You have a beautiful baby daughter!"

"A...a little girl. And...and...ah, my wife?"

"Your wife is fine. You may see her in a little while."

"See my wife? I....." He hesitated.

"You <u>do</u> wish to see her, don't you, sir?"

"Oh...oh..yes,...of...of course, I do," Andrew replied just a trifle too quickly, the nurse thought.

When he pushed open the door to Victoria's room about a half-hour later, she was propped up in a sitting position studying her face in a hand mirror. Gazing at her, he let his imagination run wild. He would speak and his wife would look up and smile at him in their shared happiness. "Oh, darling, have you seen her?" she would say reaching up to embrace him.

"Not yet," he would reply holding her close, "but if she's half as lovely as her mother, she must be incredibly beautiful."

"Oh, Andrew, I love you so much....."

But just at that moment Victoria did indeed glance up. "Oh, it's you," she said flatly. "The admitting nurse said she was going to ring you. All the bloody stupid red tape just to have a baby. Well, anyway, thank God it's over with."

He misunderstood her or perhaps he wanted to misunderstand. "Was the pain terrible, sweetheart?" he inquired tenderly, coming to sit beside her on the bed.

"Don't jostle me, you idiot! In case you've forgotten, I just had <u>your</u> baby!"

Yet Andrew continued to try. "Did they tell you it's a girl? We...we...ah....never talked about names. Have you...ah...have you...ah..thought about it all?"

"I don't give a damn what you call her!"

"I'd.....I'd thought perhaps your names–only in reverse order."

She shrugged though inwardly this appealed to her vanity if nothing else. "Fine. Now if you don't mind, I'd like to get some sleep."

"Yes, Victoria. Yes, of course." he said at once, heading for the door. "I....I'll see you tomorrow." He left before she could tell him not to come, tears filling his eyes as he hurried away down the hall toward the lift. "Oh, Victoria," he whispered, "why?" Just then, however, he became aware that he was passing the nursery window. He stopped and began trying to read the tags on the bassinets.

One of the attending nurses noticed him and came to the door. "Sorry, sir. I'm afraid viewing time is over for this evening. You can see the baby tomorrow morning between ten and eleven o'clock." She started to lower the Venetian blinds.

"Please," he pleaded, "my daughter was only born an hour ago."

The look on his face touched her. "Well, perhaps just a peek then."

"Thank you." Andrew waited expectantly.

"Your...ah...name, please, sir?"

"Oh, sorry." He grinned sheepishly. "It's Roberts."

"Roberts," she repeated after him. "Just a minute, sir." Turning away, the nurse walked back among the rows of bassinets and a few moments later she came up to the window carrying a tiny bundle wrapped in a pink blanket. Like most newborn babies, Olivia Victoria Roberts was red and wrinkled and totally nondescript. Andrew was sure he had never seen anything so beautiful. After a while the nurse replaced the baby in her bassinet and returned to the door. "I noticed there's no name on the tag, Mr. Roberts. Have you and your wife selected one?"

"Yes." Or at least I have, he thought sadly. "Olivia Victoria."

"Oh, that's lovely—good. I'll put it on her records for you."

Thanking her again, Andrew finally turned to leave. On the ride home he tried to think about his new baby daughter and not the hurtful words of her mother.

* * *

The following morning Victoria was lying propped up in bed. It was a glorious summer day; the window stood open, a warm breeze just moving the thin curtains. They had awakened her at a ridiculously early hour to take her temperature and blood pressure, but by now she'd had breakfast and she was feeling lazy and contented. She smiled as she ran one hand over her marvelously flat stomach. She couldn't decide whether to give herself a manicure or to begin reading the biography of Dame Edith Evans she'd saved especially for this time. Dame Victoria Windsor, she mused; it had a nice ring to it.

All at once the door to her room opened slightly and a nurse's head appeared around it. "Roberts?" Victoria nodded–puzzled. "Just a minute." The head vanished from sight, but almost immediately the door opened all the way and the nurse entered carrying a small, pink bundle. "Visiting time," she burbled and before the usually quick-witted Victoria could say anything, the woman had placed the baby in her arms and left.

Oh God, no, she thought, I don't want to see her. Why didn't I tell them I <u>don't</u> <u>want</u> <u>to</u> <u>see</u> <u>her</u>! She opened her mouth to call after the nurse, but the bundle stirred emitting a soft cooing sound. Victoria's right hand, seemingly taking on a life of its own, came up to move the corner of the blanket aside and for the first time she looked down at her daughter. Olivia blinked once or twice in the sunlight, her head and two minute fists moving about in the jerky, uncontrolled motions peculiar to the newborn. Suddenly she sneezed. Tears welled up in Victoria's eyes. "Hello, my darling," she whispered and with one forefinger she gently caressed the baby's cheek. The tiny hands waved about once again and this time one inadvertently closed around her mother's finger.

The baby's grip was surprisingly strong. It felt like a vise. Somewhere in Victoria's mind a warning bell went off and at once she reached over to press the buzzer by her bed. Desperately she fought to keep from touching Olivia again, from even looking at her, and after what seemed like an eternity a different nurse appeared in the doorway. "Yes, Mrs. Roberts?"

"Take the baby" Victoria demanded, "and don't bring her back!" Shock had rendered the other woman incapable of movement and she still stood in the doorway. "What in bloody hell is the matter with you? Are you totally stupid? Here!" Victoria thrust the baby at her.

Startled by the sudden motion, Olivia began to whimper and it was all she could do not to hold her daughter close to comfort her. "Well, didn't you hear me? I said–Take her!"

"Y...yes, Mrs. Roberts, of course." The nurse moved forward quickly to take the infant and a few minutes later having returned Olivia to the nursery, she was relating the experience to a few incredulous colleagues. "You know I'm positive if I hadn't taken the baby, that woman would simply have dropped her on the floor!"

* * *

Andrew came every evening of Victoria's five day hospital stay. He was careful to coincide his visits with viewing hours in the nursery and after a brief stay with Victoria, who made it clear she didn't appreciate his company, he could don a surgical gown and mask and cuddle his baby daughter. But he refused to stop believing that once they were all together in the flat, everything would change. It was only while still in hospital that Victoria could ignore the fact of Olivia's existence. At home she'd have to care for the baby herself and he was sure no one could spend day after day with this dear little scrap of humanity without falling madly in love with her.

It was indeed impossible not to love Olivia, who was an incredibly good-natured baby. Most irresistible for Victoria was the fact that from the beginning her daughter seemed to recognize her. Every time she leaned over her–changing her, feeding her, bathing her, Olivia would grab hold of a strand of her mother's hair and tug at it, gurgling with happiness. One afternoon Andrew even came home to find her rocking Olivia and singing to her. What an exquisite picture they made–like an old Renaissance painting-- with Victoria's hair shining in the lamplight, her already beautiful face glowing with motherly love. He realized, however, that it was wiser to make no note of the moment.

With all her strength Victoria fought against the bonds of love which threatened to bind her to her child. She reminded herself repeatedly that she only planned to care for the baby personally until something else could be worked out, but then all at once Olivia was more than two months old and such arrangements were yet to be made. A day finally came in mid-October when she went out to do the marketing, as usual taking her daughter along. For some reason she felt particularly happy that day. A glorious sun shone down through the fall foliage bringing a touch of warmth to the chill autumn air and she found herself chattering to Olivia as she pushed the pram along–pointing out a squirrel or a pigeon or another small child. As though by fate, she arrived back at her building at the same time as another young woman who also had a baby in a pram as well as a toddler.

Cassie MacMichaels, as she introduced herself, attempted to strike up a conversation, understandably eager to talk to another adult. Overtures of friendship invariably made Victoria uncomfortable, but for some reason this person was especially irritating. Then all at once she understood why she disliked Cassie so intensely. Here was the perfect specimen of that species commonly called "wife-and-mother"– exactly what she herself was rapidly becoming unless she did something about it and bloody soon.

But if the other girl were indeed as she seemed, Victoria's thoughts continued, she might prove useful. Quickly before she had a chance to think about it, she made arrangements with Cassie to baby-sit on a regular basis and a short time later with Olivia settled in her crib for a nap, Victoria was deep in study of the too long neglected theatrical trade papers. God, how could she have let herself get so out-of-touch?! The memory of mother and child framed in a glowing circle of lamplight had never left Andrew. Now as he listened to Victoria's cool voice explaining the new arrangement, he seemed to watch the cherished image shatter.

What a marvelously clever scheme, Victoria congratulated herself. Any time there was a promising audition she had only to drop Olivia off downstairs. She was almost as free as before and she'd also contrived thereby to relegate her daughter safely to the background of her life. Then why did she feel so damned guilty? It didn't help her mood any that this new round of auditions was proving as fruitless as ever.

* * *

Victoria had, of course, been aware that a production of *Camelot*–already a hit on Broadway–would be opening in London after the first of the year and she was furious with herself for having all but missed the audition announcement. As it was, it was the final day of try-outs and she would have to go in cold, but then the hours of preparation she customarily put in hadn't done a damn bit of good either.

She hurried downstairs to the MacMichael's flat, but Cassie wasn't home. Several additional attempts were also in vain and by two o'clock she was frantic. Auditions only lasted until three. It wouldn't hurt to leave Olivia alone for a little while, she reasoned. She's fed and if I leave a bottle and a few of her toys, she'll be all right until I get back. With a last anxious glance in the crib–more motherly than she'd have cared to admit– she ran down the stairs once more and out the front door.

By the time she reached the theatre it was nearly two-thirty, but she noticed with relief that quite a few people were still waiting to read. The customary table stood off to one side of the stage. Waiting in the queue, Victoria thought the man taking down names looked familiar, but she'd attended so many auditions. Undoubtedly she'd seen him one time or another. When it was finally her turn, however, and he looked up to speak to her, an immediate grin of recognition spread across his face. "Victoria Windsor!" he exclaimed with evident pleasure as he added her name to the list. "You see– I promised you I wouldn't forget!"

"Is it too late?" she inquired a trifle breathlessly. "I've only just seen the advert and I......"

"You don't remember me, do you?" he replied in a tone of mock disappointment. "No, you're not too late. They're still auditioning Guineveres."

"How did you know I....."

"Would be trying out for the lead? I would expect nothing less," he teased her with the same friendly smile. "I'll slip your name in a little ahead in the list, O.K.?"

"Who in hell are you anyway?" she demanded finally. She found his attitude of easy familiarity distinctly annoying. What she failed to realize was that the greater part of her anger was directed at herself for having left her baby daughter alone.

"Jonathan Sinclair. The RSC auditions about three years ago."

"I'm sorry. I don't remember." She turned abruptly away to find an empty chair and wait for her name to be called.

Damn–the singing audition was first–although she had a fairly good voice, it had never been really trained–but as she finished and walked back to her seat, she felt she'd done quite well. At least she knew the words and hadn't used the sheet music as so many others had done. Moreover, her reading would more than compensate. Incredibly she had no more than sat down when she heard a voice from the darkened auditorium. "That last girl—ah, Windsor, I think. Have her read first, will you, Jon?" Jonathan Sinclair smiled appreciatively as he watched Victoria rise gracefully to her feet and move center stage, her manner betraying none of the excitement she must be feeling.

Her audition scenes were as always superbly done and as she started to leave the stage at the conclusion of the second one, unbelievably the all-powerful spoke again from out of the black void. "Wait, please, Miss Windsor. Sinclair, be sure you have her phone number."

"Well, no one else has impressed them like that," Jon smiled as he wrote the number by her name. "I'd say you all but have the part. I'll do what I can."

She walked away without a backward glance.

* * *

Andrew had decided to leave the office a little early that day, thinking that perhaps the girl downstairs wouldn't mind baby-sitting for a while that evening so that he could take his wife out to dinner. One floor below his flat he could already hear Olivia's screams. His insides turned over and fumbling in his trouser pocket for his keys, he took the last flight three stairs at a time. At last he got the door open and hurrying across the darkened living room to her crib, he bent to pick up the sobbing baby–wet, hungry and frightened, but thank God, unharmed. Where could Victoria be, he wondered, and anger over her neglect of their daughter mingled with the one worry which nagged at him constantly. Had his wife left him? Still holding Olivia up against him with one arm, he managed to put the jars of baby food and a bottle of milk on the stove to warm, all the while talking soothingly to the unhappy baby. Next he changed her wet nappy and he was just settling down to feed her when the door opened and in walked Victoria.

When she saw him sitting there, she stopped short. Andrew made such a sweet picture, Olivia nestled in one arm, a spoonful of food poised before her eager, little mouth. Unfortunately this only served to remind her of her own guilt. "Well, don't you look just precious!" she snapped, slamming the door shut behind her.

"Where in hell were you? I came home to find Olivia alone in the dark-- screaming!"

Remorse fed the flame of her anger. "I had to go out! And don't get hysterical! It didn't hurt her to cry for a while!"

"Didn't hurt her? She was terrified! Where were you? Another one of those damned auditions? When are you going to get that nonsense out of your head?"

"I am an actress! I never wanted to be a wife and mother! I hate that smelly little brat and I hate you!" Flinging off her coat, Victoria ran into the bedroom and once again the door slammed behind her. Andrew heard the key turn in the lock.

"That's not necessary, you know!" he yelled after her. "It's like sleeping with a block of ice."

The final irony would come about a week later. It appeared that Julie Andrews had agreed to repeat the role of Guinevere. So the whole affair had been for nothing and it had all but destroyed whatever relationship she'd ever had with Andrew. They continued to live together, but he slept on the couch and more and more she would leave Olivia downstairs early in the morning and be gone until late afternoon. He supposed she was still attending auditions, but she mentioned nothing about it and he didn't ask. This impasse continued through the winter and the change, when it came in early May, was by the merest chance.

Victoria had taken out her summer purse and upon opening it to put in her wallet, make-up, cigarettes, etc., she discovered a white oblong of cardboard clinging to its lining. She supposed that was why she'd missed it last fall. Turning it over, she read: Leslie Matthews: Theatrical Agent: 61-4486. Of course–the man she met in the alley after the *Earnest* audition. Cheeky bastard, she thought with a laugh. She started to throw the card away, but instead for some reason she found herself dialing the telephone. After only two rings she heard the click of a receiver being lifted. "Charlie's Fish and Chips," a cheery Cockney accent announced, " 'ot and toisty; h'eat 'em 'ere or tike 'em away."

"I beg your pardon." Victoria was thoroughly bewildered. "I must have reached a wrong number."

"Who'd you be wantin', then?"

"Leslie Matthews, but I......"

" 'old on." The receiver clunked down, but very shortly someone picked it up again.

"Leslie Matthews here."

"Mr. Matthews, this is Victoria Windsor. What in hell are you doing in a take-away shop? Don't you have an office?"

"Well, that's just it, you see. I don't!"

"Good God! Do you seriously expect me to......"

"I'm on Langley Street near Covent Garden. There's a pub just around the corner on Shelton called the Oxford Arms. I'll meet you there in about half an hour."

"Oh, all right—I suppose so, but....." However, he'd already hung up. Victoria nearly decided against it, but something seemed to tell her she should go and well before the appointed hour she was at the Oxford Arms, sipping a vodka and tonic and awaiting the arrival of Leslie Matthews, theatrical agent.

* * *

Victoria <u>was</u> an exceptionally gifted actress–he'd been convinced of that the first time he saw her audition-- but as the months went by and he hadn't heard from her, he had all but decided he never would. After all, he was no nearer establishing himself as an agent now than he'd been then and it seemed that nothing was ever going to go his way. Now suddenly after a full year she'd rung him up. This had to be the long-awaited sign that his luck was about to change. Entering the pub, however, at the end of the half-hour, he still held his breath until he saw her actually sitting at one of the tables.

She knew him at once: the same thick, tousled brown hair–even the same denim jeans and jacket. He waved at her cheerily and went up to the bar to buy himself a mug of ale. Looking at him more closely as he sat down across from her, she also remembered what she'd considered to be his most outstanding feature: those marvelous blue eyes. Matt, in his turn, had recalled that Victoria was a beautiful woman, but now he found himself staring. Leaning back in her chair, she ran the forefinger of one hand around the rim of her glass, rather enjoying his scrutiny. With all the angry words that had passed between her and Andrew he'd stopped praising her beauty. "Well," she said finally, "why should I sign with an agent who works out of a take-away shop?"

"I haven't exactly seen your name up in lights either," he observed wryly.

"Why, you son-of-a-bitch! You have one hell of a nerve....."

"Hold it, Miss Windsor!" He raised one hand, palm toward her. "Just because I find you an attractive woman, as well as considering you to be an exceptionally gifted actress, does not mean I am the least intimidated by you. And lovely and talented though you may be, you still haven't gotten any work. Am I right?"

She inclined her head briefly in reluctant assent. "Unfortunately, yes." She laughed. Actually Victoria <u>preferred</u> someone she couldn't intimidate. "And just how do two losers combine to find success?"

"Then I take it I'm hired."

"Not quite yet. First I'd like to hear exactly what you think I should do."

"Oh, no! No free advice! Suppose we agree on a six month trial. Within that time you are a working actress or we go our separate ways."

"And just what is your precise definition of a working actress?"

"At the very least–a solid supporting role." In spite of himself he smiled. "Or do you expect to start out with star billing?"

"I'm glad to see you can be as nasty as I can. You don't have to like me, you know. People usually don't." Yet for some reason it hurt her to say that.

"But I <u>do</u> like you. I admire nerve. In your profession it's mandatory. I do have one question though. Will you accept work outside London?"

Victoria hesitated. "How far outside?"

"Don't worry." He chuckled good-naturedly. "I won't bury you completely out of sight. But I also think our first objective must be for you to become a working actress. Then we can move on from there."

She never would have admitted it, but it felt good just to have someone say "we" and as she'd already thought several times since she came across his card, she had nothing to lose. Victoria extended her right hand across the table. "All right, Leslie. It appears I have an agent."

He did not immediately extend his hand in return, however. "One further condition–the only person I allow to call me Leslie is my mother. It's Matt."

A slight smile tugged at the corners of her mouth. "Matt–" She cocked her head at him. "And it's Victoria—never Vicki."

Now Matt offered his hand. "Agreed, Victoria." With his other hand he pulled a memo pad from the pocket of his jeans and handed it to her. "Address and phone number if you would." She complied and returned the pad. Pocketing it again, he stood up. "I'll be in touch," he called back over his shoulder as he strode jauntily from the pub.

Just one month later Matt kept his word. It happened to be a Saturday morning. Andrew had taken Olivia out in her pram–one of the few occasions these days when he was happy–and Victoria was just settling in for what she considered to be one of the world's great luxuries–a long soak in a hot, sudsy tub–when the telephone began to ring. "Damn!" Wrapping herself in a bath towel, she made her way across the living room to the phone. "This bloody well better be important!"

"I said six months, did I not? How about one month–almost to the day?"

"Matt!" she fairly shrieked, " a job? Where? When?"

"Well...ah...not exactly a job...an audition."

"Audition? God, I've had those sodding things for four years! If you can't do any better than that, you can go to hell!"

"Hold on just a minute. This is a private audition for which I've cashed in nearly every favor ever owed me so don't damn me to hell quite yet. Now it's ten o'clock Monday morning in my office."

"That damned take-away shop? That will make a smashing impression!"

"Not to worry! A friend's loaning us his office."

"A borrowed office? I might have known!" In spite of herself Victoria laughed. "Where is it?"

"Ten Broadwick Street in Soho–Room 320. Follow Beak Street in from Regent, then left on Lexington."

"All right, I'll be there. I don't expect anything to come of it, but I'll be there."

"Don't you even want to know about the job?"

"After four bloody years I don't give a damn! Can't you see, Matt? I want to act! It's....it's all I have..... I'll see you on Monday then." She hung up.

On his end of the line her agent hung up more slowly. What's wrong with her anyway, he wondered.

* * *

Matt had arrived early in order to remove all signs of his friend's business as a turf accountant from the borrowed office–scattering scripts, playbills, theatrical posters, etc. about the room. Lastly he stuck a cardboard sign up in the window of the door: "The Leslie Matthews Theatrical Agency". Damn, that looked good! Just perhaps today was the beginning, not only for Victoria, but for himself as well.

It was still a few minutes before ten as the taxi drew up in front of the building. The first to alight was Amanda Thatcher. Twenty years before, as Amanda Chase, she'd been one of the leading musical stars of the London stage when she left it all to become the wife of Philip Thatcher, owner of Thatcher Mills, one of England's major producers of linen. Friends bemoaned her choice: marrying a widower twenty years her senior, giving up fame in the London music halls to bury herself in the English Midlands, but Amanda had never regretted her decision. She'd been a faithful and loving wife to Philip and a caring stepmother to his three children and now after two years of widowhood, the two daughters married and only her stepson still at home, it was time to find some meaningful way of keeping herself occupied.

Standing on the pavement now waiting, she appeared more than equal to the task. At fifty years of age she was still a striking woman–heavier perhaps than when she'd been the toast of the West End–, but on her 5'10" frame the added stone or so only lent added majesty to her bearing. Her silver-gray hair was pulled sleekly back into a French twist and her make-up was artfully understated. She wore a rose-colored suit over a silvery chiffon blouse with matching wide-brimmed gray straw hat, gloves, purse and shoes–as always in the best of taste.

Amanda smiled at her companion as having paid the driver, he finally emerged from the taxi to join her. But for his thick Scots brogue, David Donald Douglas could have been one of Britain's leading Shakespearean actors. Since it wasn't possible to make a lifetime career out of playing Macbeth, he'd reluctantly made the move into university theatre and under his patient and devoted tutelage the University of Edinburgh drama department had grown steadily both in size and prestige. Sir Terence Cartier, a long-time friend from their early days together at the Old Vic, had tried many times to coax him back to the professional theatre, but David was too proud to accept any help.

Then six months ago he'd received Amanda's letter. She was planning, she said, to use some of the money from her late husband's estate to establish a professional repertory company in Stoke-on-Trent, a small industrial city in the English Midlands. Perhaps he'd heard of it since the Wedgwood China Factory was located there. At any rate might he be interested in accepting the position of artistic director? A new company with sufficient financial backing to ensure its survival! It wasn't easy to leave the University after so many years, but he couldn't refuse such an offer.

Many people found Amanda Thatcher intimidating, but from their first meeting David had refused to be cowed. To begin with he was big himself: 6'6" with a leonine head of white hair and on the increasingly rare occasions when she still attempted to dominate him, he'd simply rock back on his heels and roar at her. His brogue would grow thicker by the minute until ultimately he became incomprehensible and she would dissolve into helpless laughter.

Amanda did, in fact, respect him greatly, refusing as so many others did to call him "3-D", a nickname she considered demeaning. At the same time she rather hoped that eventually their relationship would be more than professional. For whichever reason she'd come today at his insistence. "I still think this morning rather a waste, I'm afraid, David," she admitted as they entered the building together. "If we decide definitely on that girl we saw yesterday, we'll have our full company."

"I rrealize that, Amanda, but I was asked to audition this gurrl as a perrsonal favorr, ye see." He pushed the call button and after a few seconds wait the lift arrived. It was an ancient one with no solid door–only a metal grating. Unfailingly courteous, David stood back to allow her to precede him inside. "It's Rroom 320, by the way."

"Any professional experience?"

"Oh, I doot that, Amanda. A verra orrdinarry office, I should imagine." He winked at her broadly.

"You know very well what I meant." She tried to look stern, but the corners of her mouth twitched. "The young lady we're going to see."

"The note didna say." He pressed Number 3 and with an alarming shudder the lift started upward. "But the audition won't take long and who knows, it might prrove worrth ourr trrouble."

Amanda smiled a little. "So then, is this finally to be our great discovery?" The company they had now all but finished assembling was something of a disappointment to them both. No established actor would agree to work in Stoke-on-Trent for so much as one season. Even the talented neophytes were reluctant to go so far from London. At last the lift creaked to a precarious stop at the third floor and exiting with some relief, they found themselves in a dusty, dimly lit hallway. There was a distinct odor of disinfectant. Amanda wrinkled up her nose. "I really don't know, David. No reputable agency would have an office in a building like this."

"Noo dinna go gettin' oopity and English on me, lass," he chuckled.

"Only if you'll refrain from becoming so Scottish that no one can comprehend a bloody word you're saying..... Oh, really, will you just look at that?" she went on pointing to Matt's painstakingly hand lettered sign.

By now even David was having his doubts and neither of them was particularly reassured by the outer office into which they first stepped: no secretary and only the barest of furnishings. "Hello, therrrre," he called out, the rolled "r" reverberating in the all but empty room.

"Yes. Come in, please." a voice answered from the inner office. This room was at least somewhat of an improvement. Theatrical posters covered the walls and on the desk was a battered portable typewriter as well as assorted scripts and programs. As they entered, a pleasant looking young man came to meet them cordially extending his right hand in greeting. "I'm Leslie Matthews." He shook hands with each of them. "I'm expecting Miss Windsor at any minute." Quickly he pulled a couple of wooden armchairs closer to the other side of the desk, surreptitiously dusting off the seats with the sleeve of his jacket.

"Yes, Mr. Matthews." Sitting down in one of the chairs, Amanda smoothly removed her gloves. "Perhaps in the meantime you might give us some information on the young lady. If you could wait a moment, please." From her purse she extracted a slim gold pen and a small leather notebook. Opening the notebook and uncapping the pen, she glanced up at Matt to indicate she was ready.

"Actually Miss Windsor is a recent graduate of RADA," he temporized, glancing uneasily at his watch. He'd hoped they would be so impressed with Victoria's audition that such questions could be avoided. "However, she did perform several major roles while at the Academy," he finished rather lamely.

"I see. No professional experience," Amanda stated flatly, writing rapidly in her notebook. She was well-acquainted with theatrical double talk. In the other chair next to hers she heard David chuckling.

"Miss Windsor is an extremely gifted young actress." Matt came quickly to his client's defense. "I agreed to represent her after I had seen her audition."

"Ah, then she <u>has</u> previously auditioned without success." Amanda continued to write busily.

The agent cursed himself for talking too much. Dammit, Victoria, he thought, where the hell are you?

"Ye apparrently believe strrongly in the lassie," David observed in his Scots accented voice.

"Indeed I do, Mr. Douglas," Matt replied as emphatically as possible, "and once you've heard her, I feel certain you will both agree with me."

It was nearly 10:30 before Victoria arrived, frantic at being so late. Desperate for this audition to be a success she'd redone her hair and make-up over and over again, changed her outfit so many times she'd lost count. At last she had decided on a paisley print shirtwaist in shades of pale green and gold, colors which complimented perfectly her hair and eyes. It was long sleeved, but the sleeves were full and feminine; the skirt flared just slightly. Strands of her honey blonde hair were pulled back on the sides and tied with a pale gold scarf, but most of her hair hung free, curling a little at the ends. Then naturally just because she was already late, she barely missed a train on the underground and had to wait ten minutes for another one. And of course that train stopped twice in the middle of nowhere for no apparent reason. Finally she couldn't seem to get the lift in the building and had to use the stairs. Half-running down the hall, she pushed open the door to the outer office.

Amanda Thatcher had been sitting for over half an hour in a hot, stuffy, dusty office waiting for an inexperienced actress who was apparently utterly lacking in self- discipline as well. Out of patience, she had put her pen and notebook away and drawn on her gloves again, preparatory to leaving. "I'm afraid there's very little point in our remaining any longer, Mr. Matthews. Our company is virtually complete anyway." Victoria couldn't know that even as she spoke, Amanda had already risen to her feet. All she heard was the stentorian voice pronouncing her doom.

The woman was understandably irritated at having been kept waiting and Victoria's first impulse was to burst into the room, reeling off her list of excuses and begging them to forgive her for being late, to listen to her, to give her a chance. And Amanda had taken but a few steps in the direction of the door when Victoria did indeed open it. "Matt, darling," she murmured, posing prettily with her hand on the knob, "I am frightfully late, I know. But the other audition ran longer than I expected. They just kept asking me to do more. I wouldn't have even come at all if I hadn't promised you."

At the sound of Victoria's voice David had also gotten to his feet and both he and Amanda studied her intently during this brief exchange. The run up three flights of stairs had ruffled her hair just slightly and brought a delicate pink to her naturally pale complexion. He thought she was exquisite. Amanda, on the other hand, admired how cool she was under pressure. Then she caught a glimpse of the girl's other hand-- clenched tightly into a fist at her side.

At last Victoria decided she'd ignored these two people long enough to indicate they were of no importance to her and she turned to face them. "I'm Victoria Windsor," she said as she advanced to meet them, her right hand extended to shake first Amanda's hand and then David's. The older woman couldn't help smiling. Clearly this young actress was informing them that if they didn't recognize the name, they were certainly the ones at fault.

Matt brought another chair forward, placing it almost at the side of the desk–giving her just the proper distance to create the best effect, Victoria noted gratefully. He cleared his throat. "Victoria, this is Amanda Thatcher and David Douglas. Mrs. Thatcher is...."

"Please, Mr. Matthews," Amanda interrupted him crisply, "I would like to do the talking. Miss Windsor, Mr. Douglas and I aren't acquainted with your work."

Matt came at once to her rescue. "As I believe I've already explained, Mrs. Thatcher, Miss Windsor has only recently...."

"And I would also prefer to have the young lady answer my questions herself so that we may get an impression of her voice and personality."

During this brief reprieve Victoria's mind was working frantically. She couldn't admit to four years of failure, but an outright lie would be too easy to check. Now as Mrs. Thatcher finally turned to her for a reply, she nodded briskly and taking a deep breath, she proceeded to list every role she had ever played.

"Imprressive, I'm surre, Miss Windsorr," David observed, "especially forr one sae verra young." It was the first time he'd spoken since Victoria entered the room. The Scots accent hit her with the force of a physical blow and all her self-possession vanished. "Can you no underrstand the brrogue, lassie?" David inquired kindly, misreading the reason for her blank stare. "Well, suppose you do the talkin'. What would ye like to do forr us?"

Tossing her head, Victoria favored David with a dazzling smile. "Why don't you tell me what you'd like to hear, Mr. Douglas?"

"But, Miss Windsor," Amanda interposed once again, "aren't you at all interested in what you're auditioning <u>for</u>? You haven't asked <u>us</u> anything: what company we represent, whether we're auditioning for specific roles, where our theatre is located—nothing."

Damn, Victoria thought, why don't I just get down on my knees and beg? Instead, however, she merely shifted her weight a little in the chair and crossed her legs. "You haven't given me a chance." She smiled again. "You've been asking all the questions." Matt couldn't help but admire her performance. He knew how much she wanted this job.

"You are evidently a very self-assured young woman, Miss Windsor," Amanda Thatcher was replying, "but it doesn't necessarily follow that you are an actress."

Victoria sat up a little straighter now. "And neither have I had the opportunity to show you that I am."

David liked the girl's spunk. Then, too, although he also suspected she'd had no professional experience, there was something about her– an air that excited him in a way no other prospective member of the company had succeeded in doing. He stepped in quickly again, wanting her to have a chance to show what she could do before she had entirely alienated his associate. "Well, Miss Windsorrrr....." Why in hell was his brogue having such an effect on her? Could it be just that fortnight at Balmoral? But that was so long ago now.... With a supreme effort Victoria forced herself to concentrate on what he was saying......"new theatrre in Stoke-on-Trent nearr Leeds in the Midlands. I grrant ye, 'tis a bit isolated, but we hope to establish an ootstandin' prrofessional reperrtorry coomp'ny....." But almost at once she found her mind wandering again. Stoke-on-Trent? Where in the bloody hell is Stoke-on-Trent? The name alone sounded dismal. But then she didn't actually give a damn where the place was; she'd go anywhere if they'd have her......."and now (only from David Douglas the word sounded more like a cross between now and new), Miss Windsorrr, we would enjoy hearrin' you do something. Some Shakespearre perrhaps, something moderrn and mix comedy and drrama–anything you'd like."

It had been harder than at any time before to pick out her material. It was inevitable, she supposed, that after four years of failure her self-confidence would have been shaken, but there seemed to be something wrong with every piece she considered. She shook herself mentally. What in hell was the matter with her? The turn-downs had had nothing whatsoever to do with either her talent <u>or</u> her material!

She would simply use what she knew to be her best–never mind that she'd done every one of them countless times before without success and finally Victoria had decided on Lady Macbeth's sleepwalking scene and Kate's final speech from *The Taming of the Shrew* for the Shakespearean material, the by-now dearly familiar Lady Bracknell from *The Importance of Being Earnest*– a sort of good luck piece since she'd performed it at her RADA audition–and concluding with Saint Joan. These four were undoubtedly her best. Now at David Douglas' invitation she stood up and pushing her chair back to give herself more room, she began.

A brilliant performance invariably reduced David to a state of emotional exhaustion, incapable of anything but helpless tears, and occasionally now as Victoria presented her selections, he simply shook his head from side to side, too drained even to reach for his handkerchief. Amanda's response was, perhaps, more intellectual, more restrained, but she, too, knew beyond a doubt that they were watching an incredibly gifted actress, the one shining light they had sought–seemingly in vain. At last Victoria turned to Matt as a sign she had finished. He was at once on his feet to return her chair to its original place and trembling, she sat down again to wait for Amanda and David's decision. At least once or twice during each of her selections she had stolen a glance in their direction, but neither seemed even to move. Now, however, she observed a long look pass between them; had she only imagined it or had David Douglas nodded?

She could never understand why it was at this particular moment that the magic happened. She'd certainly given just as impressive a performance countless times before. Perhaps it was the private audition; perhaps it was the extra edge which desperation lent to her work. Perhaps there was no explanation at all, but for whatever reason—or lack of it—unbelievably Amanda Thatcher turned to her and smiled. "Miss Windsor, Mr. Douglas and I appear to be in agreement. We would like to invite you to become a member of our company."

Victoria's initial impulse was to leap to her feet, screaming "YES! YES!" over and over again, but she would never have given Mrs. Thatcher the satisfaction. For a moment, indeed, she said nothing. "Well, naturally, I will have to consult with my agent," she murmured at last. "We hadn't really considered my joining a company so far outside London. Is there some place he can contact you?"

"We're stopping at the Dorchester, Miss Windsor," Amanda replied just as coolly, "but I'm afraid we can only allow you 24 hours. Come along, David," she concluded crisply, rising once more to her feet. "Miss Windsor..." And with a curt nod in Victoria's direction she sailed past her and out the door.

"It was a grreat pleasurre, Miss Windsorr, a grreat pleasurre." David bowed to her graciously. "I will be lookin' forwarrd wi' considerrable anticipation to dirrecting you."

"Oh, then you're directing." Victoria favored him with yet another smile. "Tell me, have you had much experience?"

"Well....ah...aye, as a matterr of fact, I....ah...have," he stammered, taken aback.

"Mr. Douglas, thank you for coming." Standing up as well, Matt came around the desk to offer his hand. "I'm certain that...."

"Are you coming, David?" Amanda demanded imperiously, returning to stand in the doorway.

"Aye, Amanda, aye....I'm coomin'....Miss....ah... Windsorr,." With yet another bow he followed his associate from the office.

The moment the outer door had closed Matt rounded on her slamming the flat of his hand down on the desk. "Victoria, are you insane? By tomorrow they could change their minds! And asking a man of Douglas' stature in the theatre if he's had much experience!"

"They won't change their minds. They want me." She paused to glance up at him coyly, a smile playing around the corners of her mouth. "And how do I know how much experience he's had. After all, he can't even talk properly."

"You do plan to accept, though, don't you?"

"I'm really not sure. If I bury myself in Stoke-on-Trent, I may never be seen again."

Reaching back to pull up the chair David had used, Matt sat down facing her. "I want you to listen to me, Victoria." With his hands clasped he leaned forward to rest his elbows on his knees, holding her gaze firmly in his. "Now you've had four years of fruitless auditions. I don't know why. There's no doubt you're a superb actress. But something clicked for you here today. And no matter how far outside London, it's a beginning."

Contrary to the way it might have appeared, Victoria was no longer hedging merely for effect. She couldn't help thinking that by joining a company way up in the English Midlands, she was somehow admitting defeat. Then, too, she found David Douglas' brogue so disturbing she seriously wondered if she could bear to listen to his voice through days and days of rehearsal. "I really don't know, Matt. I....."

"Victoria!–take this job or find yourself another agent!"

Her eyes dropped to avoid his steady regard. Her hands clasped and unclasped in her lap and it was several seconds before she looked up at him again. "All...all right. I...I guess so."

"Well, Hallelujah! I'll ring their hotel!"

"Oh God, let's not look too anxious. At least wait until this evening."

"All right, Victoria. I'll be in touch tomorrow with the details."

"Yes, Matt, fine." The situation for some reason had grown suddenly awkward and standing up, she walked toward the door. "I'll....I'll be waiting for your call then."

"You're entirely welcome, I'm sure," he observed with a wry grin, but of course she was already gone.

* * *

The damned lift was operating quite smoothly now–wouldn't you bloody well know it, though–but in her exhilaration Victoria chose to run down the three flights, arriving at the ground floor quite breathless and absurdly pleased with herself for having beaten the lift by several seconds. Pausing briefly to catch her breath, she continued on out of the building and along the street toward the underground station. She'd show the whole bloody lot of them now, she vowed–Peter Harris, Pliny Nicholas, Cassius O'Flaherty--even Andrew who'd never......

Her steps slowed and her elation faded somewhat—Andrew! What would he say? Well, he would simply have to understand, that's all! It was only temporary; she would eventually be returning to London. In the meantime they'd hire a nanny and he could bring Olivia up for visits on the week-ends. That way he would see her work, too, and he'd realize she was meant to be an actress. She had nearly reached her stop on the underground when she hit upon the ideal plan–a romantic dinner for two! Candlelight, champagne and soft music would certainly make Andrew more amenable-- and cheese fondue! The intimacy of the common pot made it the perfect dish! It would be fun–a bit of a lark actually–a game she fully intended to win.

She arranged to have Carrie keep Olivia through the dinner hour and by the time she heard her husband's key in the lock, she already had the table set, the champagne and salad chilling in the fridge. The candles were lit, Mantovani playing softly in the background, and she was just adding the last of the shredded mixture of Swiss and Gruyere cheeses to the bubbling wine in the fondue pot. She was still wearing the green and gold dress from the audition, but over it she'd added a yellow ruffled organdy apron.

Andrew had only taken a step or two into the room when he stopped short, unable to believe what he saw. Why would Victoria suddenly decide to cook him a special meal? He hated himself, but he couldn't help suspecting her motives. At the same time it seemed as though she had never looked more beautiful and he realized all over again why he'd fallen in love with her. Victoria glanced up from the stove. "The fondue's just about ready, Andrew, and Carrie's agreed to keep Olivia a little longer." She smiled at him. "Would you open the champagne, please, darling?"

Obediently he went over to the fridge and taking the bottle out, began to work to remove the cork. "What's the occasion?" he inquired lightly. Victoria, meanwhile, had brought the fondue, setting it over the alcohol flame and gone to the fridge herself for the salad. "You... you haven't answered my question," he prompted gently as he poured the champagne.

"Does it have to be a special occasion for me to cook dinner for my husband?" Victoria murmured sweetly. She reached across as she spoke to cover his left hand with her right and again she smiled. "But we really do have something to celebrate," she continued after a slight pause. "I...I finally....finally got a part today. Well, actually I was accepted as a member of a repertory company which is even better because I'll have the opportunity to play a variety of roles. It's marvelous training for an actor!" In her eagerness Victoria wasn't even aware that her words were coming faster and faster and she was surprised to discover when she stopped that she was actually a little light-headed.

"I'm very glad, Victoria. I know how much this means to you. You know it's not necessary for you to work, but of course, I wouldn't prevent it."

She experienced a flash of annoyance. What bloody right had he to decide what she could or could not do! "Thank you," she said.

If Andrew had caught the sarcasm in her tone, he made no mention of it. "What's the name of the company?"

"I don't know if it even has one yet. It's just being formed." But the game was spoiled for her now.

Then he asked the inevitable question. "Where is the theatre?"

"Stoke-on-Trent," she replied flatly.

"Where in the world is that?" Andrew's heart began to race. It had to be some distance. That would explain the dinner and he wondered sadly whether his wife ever said or did anything that wasn't coldly calculated in advance. Why, Victoria was wondering at the same time, had she ever concerned herself with his feelings? As she'd ended her affair with Peter Harris, it was now time to conclude her relationship with Andrew. It didn't make any difference that she'd actually married him, even borne him a child, because he'd never really touched her–only the outward facade of herself built up over the years. Absorbed in her own thoughts, Victoria was unaware quite a few minutes had passed since Andrew put his question to her. "I asked you where Stoke-on-Trent was?" he repeated, his uneasiness growing with every second of the long silence.

So she told him–just the bare geographical facts–no excuses, no pleading–just the location on the map. "The Midlands–a little south of Manchester."

"I see. And I presume this dinner was for the purpose of getting me to agree to your deserting your husband and child to indulge yourself in this foolishness!"

"I never loved you, you bloody fool! I only married you so I wouldn't have to work in that damned pub any longer. Besides I was tired of a different man every night and I wanted to try just one for a change."

He had known it for some time–known that she'd never really loved him. Then why did it hurt so much to hear her say it? "But what about our daughter?" His voice was shaking. "Even if I never meant anything to you, you must have wanted her. You could have had the abortion, but you didn't."

Oh God, Victoria thought, I did want her. I...I'll lose her if I leave... I'll..... "Of course I didn't want her!" she heard herself saying. "I just didn't get around to the abortion until it was too late." With a maddening calm she rose to her feet and walked toward their bedroom. "I'll be gone by the time you get home tomorrow."

* * *

For Andrew the following day was endless. He tried to believe Victoria wouldn't really leave him even though deep inside he knew she was already gone. Arriving home late in the afternoon, he ran up the stairs toward their flat, calling to her long before he reached the door, "Victoria," he called again as he fumbled to get his key in the lock and this time he could hear his voice breaking. The bedroom door stood ajar and when he spoke her name a third time, the word was a hoarse and hopeless whisper. The undeniable signs were all there: the unmade bed, the drawers pulled out, her half of the closet emptied. Before the inescapable reality could sink in, however, there was a knock at the door. Relief flooded over him. Of course..... of course! That was her now. She'd forgotten her key. "Victoria!" he called out once more and hurrying back across the living room, he flung open the door of the flat to find not his wife standing there, but Cassie MacMichaels with Olivia in her arms.

At once the baby reached out to Andrew, babbling her joy at seeing her father. He took her in his arms and as he held her warm, sweet little body close against him, he felt his eyes fill helplessly with tears.

"Is anything wrong?" Cassie inquired sympathetically.

"No, Mrs. MacMichaels, no. Thank you." Andrew started to close the door. He regretted appearing ungracious, but he was close to the breaking point.

"Wait a minute, please, Mr. Roberts." She stopped him from shutting the door by putting her hand up against it. "I just wanted to tell you that I'll be more than glad to keep Olivia all day while your wife's away."

"Away?" he repeated stupidly.

"When Mrs. Roberts left Olivia with me, she said she might be gone for a while so I thought perhaps......"

"Thank you again, Mrs. MacMichaels." Interrupting her quite rudely this time, he hurriedly shut the door, knowing that at any moment he must lose his self-control. For a few seconds Andrew continued to stand there holding his little girl close, too dazed even to think until at last a fat baby hand against his cheek brought him back to consciousness. "It's all right, sweetheart. It's all right." He brushed his lips against her downy hair. "I love you enough for two." Fresh tears welled up in his eyes. "Oh, Victoria," he whispered, "how could you?"

* * *

Leslie Matthews had arrived home at almost that same time to find his client sitting on the top step outside his flat waiting for him. "Oh, God," he exclaimed, "don't tell me you've changed your mind!"

"Is that all you can think of? Of course not, you bloody idiot! I...I need a place to stay for the night. Then I might as well....might as well go on up there....and no questions," she added quickly before he could say anything, "or I <u>will</u> change my mind.... and <u>you</u> will sleep on the couch."

In the morning Matt took Victoria to the train. He would never forget how she looked as she paused on the small step outside the railway car, turning to look back at him. "Well, Matt," she said, "this could be the beginning for both of us." He continued to watch as she disappeared from sight and even though he realized fully she was not the type to wave good-bye, he somehow felt he should stand there until the train pulled out.

Inside the car Victoria had been relieved to find a seat which at least for the present she would have to herself. She slipped her large valise into the storage space between the seats, lifting the smaller one and her make-up case onto the overhead rack. At last she settled down to begin rereading Anouilh's <u>Antigone</u>, the first of the plays she would be doing with the company.

As the train began to move, however, gradually gathering speed, she forgot the play for a while as inevitably her thoughts were drawn to everything that had happened to her in the six years since she'd arrived in London–to all the people whose lives had touched hers: to Danny.....Peter Harris.....Abe Epstein....Cassius O'Flaherty. It's funny, she thought; it seems either people use me or I use them. And still the names continued to come to mind... Andrew and....and...unavoidably....Olivia. Olivia–a life which had not merely touched hers, but a life she had brought into the world.

Ever since yesterday morning when she'd left her little girl with Cassie, Victoria had tried not to think of those last few moments. Now all at once she was remembering and with painful clarity. Olivia had laughed and gurgled all the way down the stairs, playing with her mother's hair and necklace and making it so hard to leave her. Victoria could even smell her sweet, baby fragrance; she experienced yet again the weight of the child in her arms just before she gave her to the other woman and hurried away, refusing to glance back.

Suddenly the passing landscape blurred. Odd, she thought, it hadn't looked like rain.

Chapter 5

Her long sought after dream was at last coming true. This had to be the happiest moment of her life. Why then, as the train slowed for her station, did she experience no excitement, not even a vague sense of anticipation? On the contrary she'd never felt more forlorn. Admittedly Stoke-on-Trent wasn't the most uplifting place imaginable. Looking down from the railroad embankment, Victoria saw the inevitable row upon row of identical brick houses–each set directly on the edge of the pavement so that the only yard any one house possessed was in the rear and this about the size of a Morris Mini-Rover. The nearest houses backed right up against the tracks yet incredibly almost every tiny yard boasted of a flower garden which managed to thrive despite the heat and fumes from the passing trains. But for some reason this only made the scene all the sadder.

The station itself was just as depressing–a squat, barren little building, also of brick, the platform dusty and litter-strewn. Well, that's exactly it, isn't it, Victoria thought to herself as she stood watching her train pull out. Why wouldn't I feel blue, coming to live in a place like this? It was a tremendous relief, somehow, to have her low mood so neatly accounted for and amazingly–almost at once–her spirits lifted. As Matt had said, she did have to begin somewhere and Stoke-on-Trent was definitely somewhere– albeit an ugly somewhere. Now she actually laughed. So many times in her life Victoria's sense of humor would be what saved her.

Oh, but God, I hope I won't be here too long, she thought a short while later as the taxi moved along what appeared to be the main street. Seen at close range, the town appeared if possible even more dismal, most of the buildings being constructed of the same faded brick as those she'd glimpsed from the train. She spotted one chemist, a green grocer, a newsstand and what at quick glance appeared to be a meat market. More than half of the businesses, however, were pubs–which actually was no wonder when she stopped to think about it. Anyone forced to live out his entire life in Stoke-on-Trent must certainly require an occasional drink! All at once the taxi swung sharply to the left into a narrow side street and stopped. "Theatre." The driver jerked his head to indicate the corner building to their right. "Ain't open yet though."

Victoria paid her fare and got out, reaching in again twice for her two suitcases and the cosmetic case. "I'm a member of the company." It was in vain she tried to sound matter-of-fact about it.

"Like the cinema better myself," he observed as he counted out her change.

"I'm sorry to hear that," she replied coolly and deliberately neglected to tip him. Jerking and backfiring–as though in contempt of either the actress or the non-tipper–the taxi moved away down the side street. Again as with the train Victoria stood for a moment looking after it. Did she possibly see each of these conveyances as a link to the life she had left behind her in London–to her baby daughter? If indeed she did, she was unaware of the fact and now finally she felt that excitement as with heart pounding, she once more picked up her luggage and entered the theatre.

The lobby was evidently still in the process of being decorated. The painting had been completed–the walls in a soft shade of gold with the woodwork done in a pale ivory. Chairs and sofas were only randomly placed about the room, however, with the gold brocade drapes, as yet to be hung, thrown across them and the floors remained bare. Rolls of new carpeting were stacked against the far wall. The building appeared deserted and glancing at her watch,

Victoria saw it was a quarter to one. Everyone must be at lunch which would give her the perfect opportunity to look around unobserved, in particular, of course, to see the stage. Ahead of her and to the right she noticed a broad staircase which in all likelihood led to the gallery. It would appear then that the three sets of double doors to her left, also covered in gold brocade, opened into the stalls. She left her belongings there and with a quick glance to make sure no one was watching, she walked over to the nearest door. It was unlocked.

The auditorium was in total darkness, the walls only barely visible, while the stage itself had apparently vanished altogether. Yet she did not find the blackness frightening. Rather it seemed somehow familiar, as though an old and trusted friend were waiting for her out there, and she walked without hesitation down the aisle. Gradually she was able to discern the dim outline of the stage. By the time she was standing directly in front of it, she could also make out the three or four steps leading up to it and climbing them, she crossed to center stage. In an unconscious reenactment of the moment at Heathfield she turned to face the audience, sweeping a low, graceful curtsey. She could almost hear the ovation.

All at once the sound of voices from the lobby brought her back to reality. The last thing she wanted was to be caught acting like a silly, stagestruck girl and she moved immediately out of sight into the wings. She was just in time as someone must have touched a switch in the rear of the auditorium bringing the house lights up. Though the stage itself was still in darkness, she was able to make out a door in the backstage wall and opening it, she found herself in the hall which ran alongside the auditorium. Back in the lobby once more, she picked up her purse and leaving the other cases where they were, she entered the theatre for a second time to discover that what had been empty and dark only a short while before was now full of light and action and noise.

Later, of course, the actors would become more blase, but at this point membership in the company was still new enough so that most came to watch rehearsals even when not actually involved in the scene. Today, as it happened, they were all present–the full complement of thespians–as a group creating for Victoria a different scene entitled perhaps, "Rehearsal". The focal point was a girl performing a relaxation exercise at center stage. First bowing her head, she next allowed her shoulders to slump and finally her whole body to droop forward from the waist, her arms dangling to the floor like a rag doll. Then almost at once she would uncurl to start the process all over again. Downstage and to her right a lone actor worked to develop his diaphragmatic muscles, his shouts of "Ha! Ha! Ha!" easily audible over the general chatter. Directly across from him another girl was standing on her head and back and forth across the upstage area two men fought an imaginary fencing duel. The remainder of the company provided the backdrop to the scene. Scattered about the stage, they drank coffee and smoked; a few were studying lines. Victoria experienced a renewed thrill. At last she was truly a part of it all.

Two people stood up from the front row and came towards her. Not quite halfway up the aisle, however, they stopped to look back at the stage evidently discussing something. The woman she recognized instantly as Amanda Thatcher. The man had reddish-blonde hair which hung well below his shoulders though the crown of his head was entirely bald. He was tall and so thin as to appear almost skeletal. His walk had been decidedly effeminate and now as he and Amanda stood talking, he held one hip thrust out to the side, his arms akimbo. In the six years since she entered the Academy Victoria had known several such men though few were as blatant about it. After a moment or so the couple turned to face her again, the man pointing to several spotlights fastened to the edge of the gallery and for the first time Amanda noticed her. "Ah, Victoria, there you are," she called out moving purposefully the rest of the way up the aisle to meet her. "Your agent rang up to say you were coming a bit early and we'd seen the luggage so I thought you must be about somewhere. Doing a little exploring, I suppose. So what do you think of our little theatre?"

"Yes, it is rather small, isn't it?" Victoria replied. "But I was looking for the loo actually."

That's right, Amanda thought, suppressing a smile. Don't admit you're at all excited. "Oh yes, Colin," she continued aloud as he came up to stand behind her, "Colin, this is Victoria Windsor, the final addition to our company. Victoria– my stepson, Colin Thatcher, also by our great good fortune a gifted scenic and lighting designer. Nothing like a little good, old-fashioned nepotism, I always say."

Colin acknowledged the introduction with a brief nod. Clearly she didn't interest him in the least and Victoria's original suspicions were confirmed. Amanda Thatcher's stepson was a nancy boy and the great lady remained blissfully unaware of the fact. Too far above the common horde, Victoria supposed. It never occurred to her that Amanda could know very well what Colin was and yet love him dearly. "I'm sorry, Mum," he was saying, his attention once more on the lights, "but we'll definitely need at least four more frenels. It may seem like an unnecessary expense at the moment, but in the long run it will be well worth it." His voice was high-pitched and faintly lisping, aptly completing the cliche.

"Well, if we're going to do this, we might as well do it right. Order whatever you need." Amanda patted Colin affectionately on the arm. "Come along then, Victoria, and I'll introduce you to the rest of the company." This one intrigues me, she thought, and as they walked down the aisle, she glanced over at the young actress. It will be interesting to see how she fits in with the rest of them. "May I have everyone together?" She waited until they had all gathered about her before continuing. "This is Victoria Windsor, the last of our actors to join us. Victoria, this is............and this is..........." She pointed out the individual connected with each name.

Victoria paid little attention to the introductions although two of the names <u>were</u> familiar to her. Allen Stewart and Melinda Cutler had been in her class at the Academy. Occasionally during the past four years she'd seen one of their names in a program and this had galled. Allen was at least a fairly capable, although unimaginative actor, but Mindy, who because of Peter Harris had cheated her out of two leading roles at RADA, possessed no talent to speak of–only a vacuous prettiness and the voice of a nervous chickadee. She'd heard somewhere that they were married–the bloody fools! Marriage could only ruin a career; after all, look what it had nearly done to hers.

All at once she became aware that Amanda was addressing her directly once again, "....And currently, of course, we are in rehearsal for our first production, *Candida* by George Bernard Shaw...."

"I know who wrote *Candida*, Mrs. Thatcher," Victoria interposed quietly.

Amanda looked over at her again–a slight smile tugging at the corners of her mouth, "Yes, I'm certain you do. Well, I'll give you your schedule and you can nip on over to the boarding house and get settled. Katie?"

A young girl with short curly brown hair–the rag doll of moments before–detached herself from the group and came over to them. She was dressed in faded jeans and a voluminous flannel shirt. "Yes, Mrs. Thatcher?" Katie's enormous brown eyes– in fact, her entire being– radiated friendliness.

"Could you show our new arrival where the boarding house is? You two are about the same age, I should think."

"Sure, Mrs. Thatcher. Hi, Victoria. I'm glad you could come early."

"How do you do," she replied coolly.

"Well, we'll let you people get to work," Amanda said. "Victoria, if you'll come with me."

The walk up the aisle of the theatre and down the hall to the company office passed in silence. Once inside Victoria immediately took one of the chairs facing the desk. Amanda, meanwhile, removed her cardigan, draping it over the back of her desk chair. As she was to notice on many occasions, her employer's taste in clothes was impeccable, the colors always perfectly coordinated. Today the cardigan was lemon yellow, exactly the shade of one of the many pastels in her floral print sheathe. A string of yellow beads and matching earrings completed the ensemble. Finally removing a folder from her cabinet, Mrs. Thatcher came to sit herself and opening the file in front of her on the desk, she folded her perfectly manicured hands on top of it. At last she looked up and prepared to speak. Instead she found herself studying this young actress once again–the way in which she simply sat there, her legs crossed, her hands folded in her lap, apparently–as at her audition–entirely self-possessed. "I believe you mentioned my schedule." Clearly Victoria resented the other woman's scrutiny.

"Yes, of course." So it was a facade, Amanda thought– a facade which evidently the girl was terribly afraid someone might penetrate–but outwardly she merely smiled. "Now, as I'm sure your agent has informed you, we plan at least for the present on a repertoire of four plays, the first of course being *Candida*..." She paused here to throw an amused glance in Victoria's direction..." by G. B. Shaw. The others will be *A Doll's House, The Merchant of Venice* and *Antigone* by Ibsen, William Shakespeare and Anouilh respectively, but then you're probably well aware of that as well." Amanda's hazel eyes twinkled maddeningly. "Just one other thing then and I'll let you get over to Miss Tuttle's and unpack."

"Yes?" Carefully Victoria kept her own face expressionless.

"Before we left London yesterday, I took the liberty of talking to some people at RADA about you. Your student performances were considered brilliant. Yet this is your first professional job. How do you explain that?"

"Never for one minute, Mrs. Thatcher, have I doubted I am a gifted actress. Unfortunately you and Mr. Douglas were the first to recognize the fact."

"Good!" Amanda nodded with evident satisfaction. "I didn't think you were the sort to indulge in false modesty. I'm glad to see I wasn't mistaken. You are a talented actress and that's why I'm starting you out with two excellent supporting roles: Ismene in *Antigone* and Jessica in *Merchant*. Rehearsals for *Antigone* will begin immediately after the opening of *Candida*. Now then-- any questions?"

"Just one actually. Who will be playing the female leads in these productions. I'm interested to know with whom I'll be working."

"So you can see if they're any better than you are?" Amanda's tone was half inquiry, half a statement of fact.

"No-- so I can see if they're anywhere near as good."

Amanda nodded again, partly to hide yet another smile. "As a matter of fact, Melinda Cutler will be playing both Antigone and Portia."

"Ah, yes." Victoria returned the nod. "She was in my class at RADA. I can replace her whenever you decide you've made a mistake. I'm a quick study. Will that be all?"

"Yes, thank you. You may go along now." Watching the girl leave, Amanda shook her head chuckling softly, but then almost at once she grew pensive. Was the ego as well merely part of the facade?

* * *

Coming out of Amanda's office, Victoria found Katie Webster sitting cross-legged on the floor waiting for her. A playbook lay open in front of her. The other girl glanced up and saw her. "Hi!" She jumped to her feet and dusted off her rear with one hand, leaning down to gather up her script with the other. "Need help carrying anything?"

"You can take one of those cases if you like." With a wave of one hand she indicated the two which still stood by the entrance to the auditorium.

"We turn right on the main street," Katie explained as she picked up one of the valises as well as the make-up case and headed outside, "and then it's only about two-and-a-half blocks. The place isn't half bad actually. The food's good and the rooms are clean. Of course the double rooms on the first floor are ever so much nicer. We could get a double together if you like."

The thought of sharing a room with another girl horrified Victoria. She'd had enough of that in school. "<u>No</u>...ah...thank you. I like my privacy." Much to her relief Katie didn't try to talk anymore after that.

The three story building which housed Tuttle's Boarding House appeared as though its owners had once been fairly prosperous. It was one of the few structures not joined to its neighbor on either side and even though the cement between the bricks had begun to crumble and the house needed painting, there was an air of genteel poverty about the place. The steps and walk were spotlessly clean and the windows behind which hung starched, white ruffled curtains sparkled in the afternoon sunshine. Due to the unseasonable warmth of the spring afternoon the heavy inside door stood ajar.

"Go ahead." Katie held open the screen door so that Victoria could enter ahead of her and then followed her inside, allowing the screen door to bang shut behind them. "Miss Tuttle," she called.

Almost at once a tall woman appeared at the other end of the hall. Once Lucy Tuttle had been an aristocrat, but those days were obviously in the past much as they were for her home. Her dress must at one time have been considered the height of fashion, but now it hung on her sparse frame and even her flat, Marcel-waved hair spoke of another era, an era when she had perhaps still hoped for a life beyond Stoke-on-Trent. Those hopes were long since dead now; she was the last of the once proud Tuttles and she was reduced to running a boarding house.

When Amanda Thatcher had first approached her concerning rooms for the theatre company, Lucy had been more than a little doubtful. In her aristocratic past actors were considered to be one step below convicted felons on the social scale and in addition they were notoriously bad credit risks. Amanda, however, had guaranteed the actors' room and board, to be deducted in advance from their wages, and Mrs. Thatcher herself was certainly quite respectable. So she'd finally agreed to admit Mrs. Thatcher's people, as she preferred to think of them, to the hallowed halls of Tuttle's.

The members of the repertory company had actually begun moving in about a month ago and in the time since then Lucy Tuttle's opinions had changed considerably. She discovered that actors were not all unprincipled reprobates and moral degenerates; that on the contrary they were for the most part hard-working people, dedicated to their chosen profession and willing to go anywhere to pursue it; moreover, that they were distinct individuals from many different backgrounds and–most amazing of all–that she actually liked many of them. Nevertheless, long held beliefs die hard and Miss Tuttle's initial reaction to Victoria was one of surprise. Everything about the girl spoke of class and breeding—not the sort she would have expected to be an actress. "Well then, girls, are you two going to take that nice double room Katie talked to me about?"

"I prefer a private room." Victoria was, of course, the one to answer the question.

"The double actually is a more pleasant room, Vicki," Miss Tuttle urged. Katie was a particular favorite of hers.

"In the first place I am called Victoria." Her tone grew icier. "And in the second place I believe I stated that I wished a room to myself."

"Well, not at a loss for words, are we?" Lucy observed crisply. Clearly she had committed the error of judging the young woman purely on appearance. The true aristocrat was unfailingly gracious–considerate of the feelings of others. But after all, she thought, what can I expect? She is an actress!

Victoria ignored the comment as though it had never been made. "And now I would very much appreciate being shown to my room."

"I...I'll take you up," Katie immediately volunteered, picking up the same two cases and starting up the stairs. Passing the first floor, she glanced wistfully at the large sunny double room before continuing on to the top floor. There she led the way to the back of the house and pushed open the door of the one remaining single. Secretly she still hoped that once the other girl saw the room, she would change her mind.

The furniture was decidedly sparse–just a single bed, dresser, small table and two straight chairs, but the walls were painted in a warm shade of rose and an only slightly worn Oriental rug covered the center of the floor. Poor Katie had no way of knowing what a vast improvement this was over Victoria's last flat before her marriage to Andrew–not that it would have mattered. Moving into the center of the room, Victoria put down the valise she'd been carrying, tossing her purse on the bed. "You can leave those anywhere." Her tone was clearly one of dismissal, but in the event she hadn't made her feelings evident, she returned to the door opening it wider.

"Your....your key's on the bureau." Katie set down the cases and walked quickly from the room.

The landlady was waiting in the front hall as the unhappy girl came down the stairs. "She's a strange one, isn't she? All the rest of you seem such a jolly sort. I'm surprised Mrs. Thatcher would have brought her here."

In spite of her disappointment Katie couldn't help smiling. "We weren't chosen on the basis of congeniality, Miss Tuttle."

* * *

Victoria next saw the other members of the company at tea. How she wished it were possible to avoid this enforced conviviality, but she couldn't afford to be so particular. Careful not to meet anyone's glance, she slipped into the first available seat. Perhaps if she made it clear from the beginning she wasn't interested in being chums, people would leave her alone.

Almost immediately, however, an older man sat down on her right. He was well above sixty, his flowing white hair and moustache making him appear a cross between Father Christmas and King Lear. "My dear young lady, we didn't actually meet this afternoon. My name is Karl Lindt." His speech still held traces of his Viennese origins. Victoria glanced at him briefly, but made no reply. "I beg your pardon, my dear," he murmured apologetically as he fumbled inside his jacket to turn up the volume on his hearing aid. "Did you say something?"

This time, however, her ear had also caught a distinctive clicking sound. "It must be very difficult," she replied finally.

He smiled at her. "Actually not–as long as the others on stage speak loudly enough......."

"No, I was referring to your false teeth. Have they ever fallen out on stage?"

Understanding at last, Karl subsided into a hurt silence. His ego was at best now a fragile thing and easily bruised. Through a long but less than distinguished acting career, he'd barely managed to earn a living and sometimes now even that seemed on the verge of slipping away from him. He was growing increasingly deaf and yes, although Victoria had no way of knowing it, there had been times when his dentures came perilously close to slipping on stage. Most terrifying of all, he'd begun to suffer from the one affliction an aging actor dreads above all else–loss of memory. He suspected he owed his membership in the company more to Amanda Thatcher's charity than anything, but pride was a luxury he could no longer afford. Oh, how dearly he loved to see the young ones like Victoria coming along and how he envied them. Yet at the same time how he pitied them for the inevitable heartbreak which lay ahead.

"It really isn't necessary to be unpleasant to him, Miss Windsor," a perfectly modulated voice gently rebuked her and turning to her left, Victoria at once recognized the actress who was portraying Candida. Cool and elegant, Althea Prentice was very much the lady. "Believe me, he will do anything for you and all he asks in return is a little simple kindness."

"I'm sorry. But I refuse to be bothered by a lot of meaningless drivel from some old fool."

Althea raised one eyebrow, a mannerism Victoria had once considered uniquely her own. Lately she was discovering to her distinct annoyance that <u>everyone</u> used it! "I only hope, Miss Windsor, that you never find yourself in his position: old and alone." I already know what it is to be alone, Victoria thought to herself. What in hell difference does it make if I'm old, too?

"She's as cruel and unfeeling as ever," Allen Stewart observed. Sitting diagonally across the table, he and his wife had been able to see and hear everything from the moment Karl sat down at the table.

"That's...that's why I know she'll do it to me all over again," Mindy whispered urgently, "--take my place, I mean. Unless maybe...maybe if we became friends......."

"Friends! Sweetheart, a barracuda doesn't have friends—only dinner!"

Melinda couldn't relinquish this last desperate hope, however, and a few minutes later she looked across the table to where her feared adversary was once more consuming her tea in solitary silence. "It's....it's nice to see you again, Victoria."

"I beg your pardon. Do I know you?"

"Ah..ah...yes, my husband and I were both in your class at RADA."

"Oh, come off it, Victoria," Allen interposed sharply. "You know us!"

Her gaze moved languidly from his wife to him. "Now <u>you</u> I do remember. You've put on a great deal of weight, haven't you?"

"It would appear," Althea commented drily to her neighbor on the left, "that the young lady is bent on alienating every other member of the company by the end of her first day here. She's certainly not the sort I'd have expected Amanda and David to select." Charlotte St. Onge was an immense, large-bosomed woman, heavily made up with a wealth of suspiciously jet black hair piled high on her head. Her immediate response to the other woman's remark was a deep, rumbling chuckle, barely audible but readily apparent, nevertheless, in the vibration of her ample body. "May I ask why you find that so amusing?"

"And precisely what sort are we all supposed to be? Besides I understand she's positively brilliant."

The so-called "male juvenile" of the company was Nathan Shepherd. Seated at some distance from Victoria, he had no chance to speak to her during the meal nor had he been able to hear what she was saying. He noticed only that she didn't eat very much and that she was the most beautiful girl he'd ever seen. When tea was over, Victoria was the first to leave the table, wondering how she could possibly endure three meals a day. Nate caught up to her in the front hall. "Hi! We didn't get a chance to chat during tea. I'm Nate Shepherd."

Last night at Leslie Matthews' flat had been the first in over a year and a half that she spent entirely alone. Even after they'd quarreled and Andrew slept on the couch, she knew she need only call and he would come in to her. Now all at once there was no one and by the end of that night Victoria had accepted the fact she would once again take a lover. But why a lover? Why not a chum like Katie? She by no means suffered from an inordinate need for sex. It was simply that sharing a room with another girl would entail actual intimacy while a lover would only expect the enjoyment of her body.

With this in mind she had noticed Nathan sitting near the other end of the table and staring at her with unabashed admiration. He was not unattractive–tall and slim-- sort of a "Hamlet" type. But then it seemed as though every young actor was a Hamlet type. He was certainly preferable to either the old one with the hearing aid or Allen Stewart, overweight and balding. She wanted Melinda's acting roles, not her husband. When Nate came up to her after tea, she hadn't as yet made her decision, but in the meantime it couldn't hurt to offer him a little encouragement. Slowly she raised her face to look up at him. "My goodness, how tall are you?" she exclaimed in coquettish amazement. It was quite a feat to play the flirt with her head cocked back at that angle, but Victoria was more than equal to the challenge.

"Six feet, seven inches actually," he responded with a laugh. She was as delightful as she looked. "But I won't seem so tall if we're sitting down. There's coffee in the front room."

"Yes, all right."

Nate turned to lead the way across the hall. "This way, madame." He pushed open half of the French doors and allowing Victoria to enter in front of him, he seated her with just a touch of gallantry on the window seat. "Black coffee or white?"

"White, please, with sugar."

Alistair Huntley–self-described leading man of the company with the graying temples and the pencil-thin moustache to prove it–had watched all of this with interest. Like Nate, he had ogled the newest addition to the company all during tea and as soon as she was left alone, he moved over to sit beside her. "I wouldn't have thought your taste ran to boys," he remarked leaning back against the window frame and crossing his legs. "I'm Alistair Huntley, by the way, although I'm sure you already know that," Victoria glanced up at him through coyly lowered lashes. Egotistical bastard, she thought, but in that instant she made up her mind. He slipped an arm around her shoulders, lightly caressing her bare arm. "I have whiskey in my room, by the way, if you prefer something stronger."

"How bloody marvelous!"

"Well, it didn't take her long," Charlotte St. Onge announced loudly as the couple disappeared together up the stairs. Poor Nate was just adding sugar and cream to Victoria's coffee. Amid the general amusement he looked over at the window seat. It was indeed empty.

"My, it pays to have influence," Victoria remarked a moment later with a laugh as they entered his room. "I am right, I presume, in my assumption that you don't have a roommate?"

Alistair had at once moved over to a low bookcase under the window where he kept the liquor. "I'm paying the difference. But please, my dear, make yourself comfortable." With a theatrical sweep of his left hand he offered her a choice of any seat in the room–including, of course, the bed. Victoria hated the oily way he had of calling her, "my dear". She chose the small sofa–no sense in making it too easy for him. "You know, my dear," he said as he settled himself beside her handing her one of the glasses, "when I learned that another young actress was joining our little troupe, I was terribly afraid she'd turn out to be another sweet, young thing like our Katie. I'm so glad I was wrong." Here he changed his own glass to his left hand leaving his right free to stroke first Victoria's arm, moving gradually downward and along her thigh. Wordlessly she submitted.

Finishing his own drink quickly, he put out his hand to take hers away from her, but she moved it out of his reach. "Uh...uh–drink first. That's the price you have to pay."

"Very well, my dear," he laughed. In actuality, of course, her meaning had entirely escaped him. "I'm sure it will be worth the wait."

Damn, Alistair thought, why was she taking so bloody long, but at last she had drained the glass and this time when he reached out to take it from her, she didn't prevent him. "Now come with me, my dear," he murmured with a low laugh. Alistair was proud of his chuckle. Women had told him it gave them the shivers. He brought her to her feet and leading her over to the bed, he lowered her onto it.

Victoria had long since learned to close off her mind from what was happening to her and if at all possible to enjoy it physically. Now as he caressed her, she could feel herself responding and instinctively she reached inside his light seersucker jacket and open-necked shirt to stroke him in return. But instead of the hirsute male flesh she had expected, her hand encountered a heavier, stiffer fabric and then something hard and unyielding–almost metallic. Oh my God, she thought, he's wearing a corset! She tried to hold back the giggles, but first one escaped her and then another.

"What is so Goddamned funny?" Alistair snapped. His preliminaries to lovemaking were not usually received in such a manner.

"N...n...nothing," Victoria managed to gasp.

"If I'm so bloody comical, you can get the hell out of here!"

Abruptly her laughter died away. "I'm sorry, please. It's just that......."

"Didn't you hear me? Get the bloody hell out of here!" Yanking her up off the bed, he pulled her across the room. With one hand he jerked the door open and with the other he pushed her outside. Before Victoria knew what was happening, the door slammed shut behind her. Well, at least the pubs were still open.

* * *

Watching the final two weeks of preparation for *Candida*, Victoria could see at once that David Douglas was indeed a gifted director. Then at last the production opened and it was her turn. Besides Melinda Cutler and Victoria the cast of *Antigone* included Alistair Huntley as Creon, the King; Charlotte St. Onge in the role of Eurydice, his wife; Nathan Shepherd as their son and Antigone's lover, Haemon and Karl Lindt who would be portraying Teresias, the blind prophet.

Antigone and Ismene's two brothers have both been killed in a civil war and Creon, their uncle, has decreed that only Eteocles will be given burial. The body of Polyneices, who led the rebellion, is to be left to rot on the battlefield. In the play's opening scene Antigone begs Ismene to help her bury their brother. The character of Ismene, a gentle, serene girl very different from herself, had been a challenge for Victoria and even on this first day of rehearsal her advance preparation was evident. Melinda's Antigone, by contrast, was timid and wooden, thus throwing the scene off balance by causing Ismene to seem the stronger of the two women. In the days that followed both Allen and David spent hours trying to help Mindy, but to no avail. She was out of her depth and what ability she did possess was all but obliterated by her paranoia that Victoria was only waiting to replace her–which, of course, she was. Ironically the moral dilemma of the play's title character and the artistic problems of her interpreter came to culmination on the same day.

King Creon has now ordained that anyone attempting to bury the corpse of the rebellious brother will suffer death by entombment and in the play's climactic scene he begs Antigone not to defy him. They had been working for most of the day on the scene and getting nowhere. The inevitable explosion came about three in the afternoon. David had just requested that

Melinda repeat a certain long speech for the fifth time and Alistair's patience gave out. "David!" he spat from between clenched teeth, "When you've finished giving acting lessons, I will be in the green room!" A stricken expression on her face, the girl watched him storm off the stage. Then almost immediately she burst into tears and fled in the opposite direction.

'Twas truly a great pity, David thought with a woeful chuckle, to muck up an exquisite piece of theatre with those ridiculous scraps of humanity called actors. "Well, ladies and gentlemen," he said at last, breaking the uncomfortable silence, "that would...ah....appearr to conclude the rehearrsal forr today." Victoria waited until the director was alone before getting up from where she'd been sitting out in the auditorium and coming up on stage. "Is therre somethin' ye'd be wantin' then?" David inquired.

"I told Mrs. Thatcher I would be willing to take over at any time. I just wanted to remind you of that."

The following day Melinda made the crucial mistake of refusing to attend rehearsal. "Well, it seems to me," Amanda sighed when David came up to her office to tell her, "that under the circumstances we have no choice. Ask Victoria to read for today so you can finish the blocking."

"But that's just what Mindy's afrraid of."

"I realize that, but rehearsals are on a tight schedule and we simply can't wait."

A short while later as the company began to assemble, David called Victoria and Alistair to one side. "I want to finish blocking the scene with Creon and Antigone today. Melinda's ill, Victoria, so if would you please read Antigone–temporarily." Unconsciously he stressed the final word.

"Of course," she replied mockingly. "Temporarily!"

So the rehearsal began with the same scene on which so many painful hours had been expended the day before. At least in terms of the script it was the same, but there all similarity ended. Today it blazed with all the heartrending agony of its two great antagonists. Amanda Thatcher had accompanied David to the auditorium to watch the scene and when the run-through was finished, he broke rehearsal for fifteen minutes to come and sit with her. For a few seconds neither of them spoke. "Well, after her audition," Amanda remarked at last, "I suppose we should have expected this." Absentmindedly he nodded. "And you know perfectly well that what you're thinking is out of the question," she continued in her brisk, no-nonsense voice. "Melinda's contract guarantees her two leading roles."

"Some people collect paintings or sculpturre, Amanda. I...I...collect performmances! Perrforrmances like that one! So many of the grreat ones arre gone now and I neverr thought I would..."

"Nevertheless, it's not worth a lawsuit. And don't look so glum, laddie. Melinda may well quit of her own accord. If she has any sense at all, she'll know she's frightfully outclassed."

Mindy did eventually return to rehearsals and a few weeks later *Antigone* opened to mediocre reviews. Individual actors were praised: in particular Alistair Huntley's Creon and Karl Lindt's Tiresias, but the production was generally considered to have suffered as a whole from the weak performance of Melinda Cutler as Antigone. "One could not help but wish," one reviewer concluded, "that the young actress, Victoria Windsor, who brings such depths to the supporting role of Ismene, could have been the one portraying the title role."

On the Monday following the opening of *Antigone* the company began work on the third play in the repertoire, Shakespeare's *The Merchant of Venice*. Portia is something of an enigma: dutiful and obedient yet at the same time strong and decisive and far more gifted actresses have found the role frustrating. Melinda's initial problem, however, was something far more fundamental. Bitterly regretting her decision not to take Shakespearean verse reading at

RADA, she stumbled over the strange, awkward sounding lines or worse, read them in a rhythmic, sing-song fashion. Victoria's experience with the Bard of Avon, on the other hand, went back far beyond RADA to the years when his beautiful words had been one of her few sources of comfort.

Inevitably *Merchant* opened to similar reviews and when she and Allen received Amanda Thatcher's summons, Melinda was actually relieved. Victoria was so much better than she could ever hope to be. She had accepted that–if only her husband could as well. But then they came out of the production office to find her rival sitting on one of the benches in the lobby. Of course she as well had been asked to come by Mrs. Thatcher, but to Allen, driven beyond the bounds of endurance, it was clear she had come purely to gloat. "You can't go on getting away with this, you know," he yelled, storming over to her. "Sooner or later it will all catch up with you!"

"Please forgive him, Victoria," Mindy apologized coming to stand next to her husband. "He really isn't a mean person, but when I'm hurt or disappointed, he's twice as upset as I am."

Reminding her yet again how alone she was, these words wounded her far more deeply than anything Allen had said. "How touching," she sneered. "Perhaps love can replace talent then. For <u>both</u> your sakes I can only hope so!"

Fortunately at that moment Amanda Thatcher also came out of her office. "Miss Windsor, would you come in now, please."

"Excuse me," Victoria murmured with elaborate courtesy. Standing up, she smoothed down the skirts of her dress and walked deliberately across the lobby into the office. "Then I presume you will wish me to take over the parts immediately?" It was not really a question.

Amanda smiled wryly. The girl could have least pretended to be surprised. "Well, there <u>is</u> the matter of memorizing lines...learning the blocking."

"As I believe I informed you when I arrived, I <u>expected</u> this would happen sooner or later. One run-though, however, might be helpful."

It was with some difficulty the older woman suppressed still another smile. "Are you sure you need even that much, Victoria?"

"Actually I don't, but <u>you</u> might find it reassuring!"

* * *

Thus with very little fanfare Victoria replaced Melinda in the roles of Antigone and Portia, simultaneously beginning rehearsals for Ibsen's *A Doll's House*, in which she had now also been cast. The idea of a woman who would allow herself to be so completely dominated was utterly foreign to Victoria and in some ways she found Nora even more difficult to empathize with than Ismene had been. Yet at the same time the character fascinated her. And what a consummate pleasure it was to work on a role from the outset without having to watch someone else destroy it first.

Having become instantly something of a local celebrity, certainly now Victoria was happy. Sadly she was not. She had succeeded in alienating every other member of the company and no matter how often she told herself she preferred to be alone, she was, in truth, profoundly lonely. The nights continued to be the worst. Lately the liquor didn't work as well and she would frequently spend the interminable hours prowling about her small room. Even the insomnia was to be preferred, however, to the nightmares, the worst of which was actually the simplest--the sound of a crying baby. Drowsily she would think Olivia needed her, but almost at once she would come fully awake and then nothing would ease the pain.

If only there were a man in her life again-- oh, not someone like Andrew who'd expected so bloody much in return-- just someone who would be there during the long, dark night. But in the nearly five months she had been in Stoke-on-Trent only Alistair Huntley had come close. Most of the regular pub clientele seemed to be common laborers–their skin coated with grime after a day's work in the factories. Finally it was mid-November and she'd met no one even faintly palatable.

Then just as it appeared that Victoria faced a long and lonely Midlands winter, it happened that a room became available at Tuttle's and that vacancy was taken by Michael Phillips, a teacher in the local grammar school–slim, slightly above middle height and most important of all, always freshly bathed. If it rained, Michael was waiting in the theatre vestibule with an umbrella; if it turned unexpectedly colder, he loaned her his coat; if she was hungry or thirsty, he took her to a pub. Her basic problem, however, remained the same since he never so much as set foot inside her room. In the weeks since he'd taken up residence at Tuttle's she'd all but openly propositioned him and yet he kept a respectful distance. At the same time he was always there–a protective, gentlemanly presence in her life-- giving her no chance to pick up anyone else. Damn, she thought, these upright, moral men were a bloody pain!

For Michael's part Victoria soon came to obsess him as no other woman ever had. Oh, how he wished he could take care of her forever! But from the first time he'd seen her on stage he knew this was a being he could never possess. Still he couldn't help being concerned about her. She always appeared tired, only coming completely alive on stage, and once or twice when he'd happened to see her in the morning-- normally she was still asleep when he left for school–she was noticeably hung over. This was especially troubling since with him she never had more than one or two drinks. Inevitably, of course, Victoria would have her way as finally one night, growing tired of waiting, she simply appeared at his door. As she came into his arms, Michael realized with a shock she had nothing on under her robe. Her cool indifference of the following day bewildered him still further. At breakfast she barely acknowledged him.. Yet that night she was back and now he knew he would never turn her away again.

It would have seemed, then, that her life was indeed complete. She was a working actress and she had a lover. What more could be required? But was that all there was to this person called Victoria Windsor? Many would think so, she herself being one of them. Fortunately there were to be others in her life as well–stubborn, caring people who refused to allow her to be contented with such an empty existence and on a cold Saturday in late February about two months into her relationship with Michael, she had a visitor who was one of those exasperating individuals.

It happened to be a day on which she was giving two performances: a matinee of *A Doll's House* and *The Merchant of Venice* in the evening. Such days were incredibly exhilarating, but also exhausting and as she hurried back to the boarding house in the late afternoon, all she wanted was a pot of tea and a long hot soak in the tub. She was halfway up the stairs toward her room when Miss Tuttle called to her from the downstairs hall. "Victoria, you have a guest in the front room."

For a second or two she stood unmoving. Who could possibly be coming to see her? But at last she turned to come back down the stairs, walking past the landlady without speaking and into the parlor. She stopped short. The last person she'd expected to see was her husband!

"Hello, Victoria. How have you been?"

Her annoyance increased. Only Andrew could greet her after nine months in as matter-of-fact a tone as if they had just said their good-byes that morning. "What in the hell do you want?" But looking at him, inevitably her next immediate thought was of her little girl. Olivia would be eighteen months old now–walking, probably talking a little. Olivia–all her anger melted away as the words were pulled from her seemingly against her will. "Andrew, how.....how....."

"How is our daughter?" It required every ounce of his emotional strength, however, to keep his voice level. He had vastly underestimated how it would affect him to see her again. "Olivia is fine," he managed to continue after a few seconds. "I found a very competent housekeeper."

"I.....I....see." Her eyes filled with tears and she turned away from him. "What are you doing here anyway?" she demanded crossly.

"You miss her, don't you?"

"What in bloody hell gave you an idiotic idea like that?"

"Come back to us, Victoria! Please! We'll....we'll start all over as though none of this ever happened." With a sinking heart he watched her back grow stiffer with each word he spoke and he knew already what her answer was. Desperately he seized on his last hope. "If not for me," he pleaded, "for our little girl. No hired housekeeper can take the place of her mother. If you could bring yourself to admit how much you love....."

How many times in the months since she'd left had she longed for Olivia–the sight and the sound, the smell and the feel of her and briefly she nearly weakened. Just in time she remembered–if she went back, she'd be giving up everything and for what? Eventually a child grew up and left, proving yet again what a mistake it was to love anyone. "No!"" She spun around again to face Andrew. "No... no... no...NO!!! N....O.....O....O!!!!" Her fists clenched and unclenched at her sides and her eyes brimmed with angry tears. "Now will you once and for all get the bloody hell out of my life!" She whirled about to run from the room. For a moment Andrew stood listening to the sound of her headlong flight up the stairs. Finally somewhere above him he heard a door slam and with a sigh he turned to leave.

It was perhaps a fortnight or so after this that Victoria received a thick, official looking envelope in the post, the return address being that of the solicitors' firm of which Andrew was a member. Opening it, she found the top page to be a letter informing her that divorce proceedings had been instituted against her on the legal grounds of desertion and that her husband intended to sue for full custody of Olivia. If she wished to contest either of these actions, a hearing had been scheduled; otherwise, she could simply sign the three copies of the enclosed document and return them.

So that was it then. She had only to sign her name and except for the formality of waiting a year she would be free to go on her way, relieved of the annoying encumbrances of marriage and motherhood. Impatiently she rummaged in her bureau drawer for a pen; after all, there was no sense in putting it off. But then with her hand poised over the document, she hesitated. It was one thing to end a loveless marriage, but quite another to relinquish all claim to her daughter.......... "Oh, the hell with it," she said finally, "I don't give a damn about her!"

"Yes, you do, Victoria. You love your little girl." It was the first time she'd heard the nagging inner voice, but it would not be the last. "You love her and if you give her up like this, someday you'll regret it."

"Shut up!" She was unaware she'd answered the voice aloud. "Shut up!" Quickly she signed each of the copies stuffing them with a frantic haste into the return envelope. Going to post it, unconsciously she started to run. "Leave me alone!" she sobbed, "Oh, please–just leave me alone!" But with whom was Victoria pleading?

* * *

It was inevitable that an actress of her caliber would attract attention beyond the narrow confines of Stoke-on-Trent, but when this did in fact occur, it was ironically due as much to yet another person's caring intervention in her life as it was to her talent. After the *Camelot* auditions Jonathan Sinclair had lost track of Victoria again and it was only by sheer good fortune that he came across a magazine article about the new Thatcher Memorial Theatre and noticed her name listed as a member of the company. He was delighted to have found her, but had she been forced to settle for this, he wondered–a struggling provincial rep company? Well, if he had anything to say about it, Jon thought with a grin, they'd soon have to manage without her.

And so a week or so later on an evening in late April he was waiting in the wings of the Shakespeare Theatre in Stratford-upon-Avon where he was now the assistant stage manager–waiting to remind Dylan Mallory, the famed Welsh actor, of a promise. He'd been a little surprised at his own temerity in asking a favor of someone of such theatrical preeminence, but now standing there watching the final scene of that night's performance, he knew he had gone beyond mere temerity to sheer bloody nerve!

The production was *Othello* and Dylan in the title role was at the height of his powers as a supreme Shakespearean tragedian in these, the play's closing moments. Visually as well he presented a magnificent picture, the long, flowing Moorish robes disguising the unfortunate fact that his physical type ran decidedly to overweight, a problem which in Dylan's particular case was made worse by a fondness for good food and well-aged Scotch. Equally impressive in this final scene was Sean Patrick in the role of the archvillain, Iago–his tall, slim figure brooding silently in the background in malevolent defeat. As pale-complected as Dylan was florid, Sean managed somehow to convey both an irresistible boyishness and an unspeakable evil. Offstage Dylan and Sean were close friends as well as drinking buddies. Unfortunately for Dylan, Sean's Irish constitution seemed to absorb the liquor like a sponge and except for the fact that his pale, blue eyes were habitually bloodshot, he showed no visible signs of their regular binges.

At last the scene concluded; the minor characters took their places on stage and the lights came up full for the curtain call. The principals entered in order of importance culminating, of course, in Percy Endicott, the actress portraying Desdemona; Sean and finally Dylan, the two men flanking Percy for the bows of the total ensemble. The moment the curtain touched down for the final time, Dylan and Sean draped their arms over each other's shoulders to walk offstage together in an exaggerated attitude of exhausted camaraderie. Both ignored Percy, considering her totally without significance as an actress. Each secretly thought, in fact, that she'd slept with the other in order to get into the company while the truth of the matter was that she had an uncle with substantial shares of stock. "Sean, my dear fellow," Dylan proclaimed with a theatrical wave of his free arm, "my system is in need of...nay, I should say <u>screaming</u> for sustenance of the alcoholic variety."

"Ah—so is mine! So is mine!" Here they stopped in the wings. "But alas, I have, as you know, trod these ancient and hallowed boards for the last time. Even as we speak, a limousine doth await to whisk me away to London and thus to Hollywood and fame and fortune on ye old silver screen!"

"Oh, come now." The other man chuckled. "I will grant these are ancient and hallowed boards; it might even be possible that a limousine 'doth await', but 'ye old silver screen'?" Suddenly Dylan dropped the easy, bantering tone which he and Sean customarily adopted with each other. "Seriously, old friend," he continued, "you were meant to be a stage actor. Films will only serve to corrupt an acting talent which I must admit with some reluctance is nearly as brilliant as my own!"

"Excuse me, Mr. Mallory," Jon interposed courteously, "but I spoke to Mr. Nicholas and you're not scheduled to perform tomorrow evening so...ah...you did rather promise, sir." He smiled a trifle uncertainly.

"Gambling debts again, eh, Dylan?" Sean winked broadly.

"God no, I've enough vices as it is. No, it....ah...seems our young friend here has an actress he wants me to see over at that new theatre in Stoke-on-Trent. So then, Jon, what time should we leave?"

"Thank you! Thank you, Mr. Mallory," Jon exclaimed fervently.

"I've told you countless times–it's Dylan-- and I'll only agree to go, if you'll bloody well stop drowning me in gratitude."

It took only a few moments on the following evening for the buzz of rumor to spread through the audience of the Thatcher Memorial Theatre and finally via the ushers to those backstage and as the house lights dimmed, anticipation was running high on both sides of the curtain. In the few seconds before the curtain rose Jon grasped the other man's forearm. "You'll see. Believe me, you won't be sorry you made the trip!"

Later Dylan would remember the occasion. In fact it became one of his favorite stories. "I've seen her perform so many times since then," he would say, "even worked with her, but I will never forget that night! She was playing Antigone. Of course my immediate reaction when she made her first entrance was that I had never seen such an exquisite woman–except, of course, for my wife of the moment," he would invariably add with a chuckle. "As she began to speak, however, I quite forgot her beauty or perhaps it became merely a part of the total effect she created on stage. As an actor one can easily become dismissive of another's talent. You see so much mediocrity that you almost come to accept it as the norm or perhaps your own conceit refuses to recognize the signs of brilliance in anyone else. But I tell you, my dear friends, sitting there in that small provincial theatre, I knew I was seeing an actress the likes of which are too few. I didn't applaud at the final curtain. I was physically drained, incapable of such exertion. I'm afraid that at first I rather disappointed Jon Sinclair, who'd been responsible for my coming. When he asked me what I thought, my only reply was 'Yes'."

"Is that all you can say?" Jon had exclaimed. "After that? My God, even I can't believe it. I'd only seen her audition, but now....I....I....." His voice dwindled away and he merely shrugged, helpless to continue.

"So I pointed out to him," Dylan would recall in continuing his story, "that my reaction was, after all, much like his–that a performance such as we had just witnessed did indeed render one speechless."

"Let's go backstage and talk to her!" Leaping to his feet, Jon started toward the aisle.

"Hold on, my young friend. Professional courtesy requires us to speak first to the owner of the company." Dylan consulted his program. "Ah...yes...Amanda Thatcher. I'm sure someone in the box office can direct us to her." At last then he stood up as well to follow Jon Sinclair out into the aisle. Their progress toward the lobby was slow, however, halted continually by people requesting autographs.

"You are unfailingly gracious," Jon observed as they finally approached the ticket window. "I find that amazing."

The other man shrugged off the compliment. "It's only a few minutes of my time, but it's much more than that to any one of them."

The clerk glanced up from her recording of that evening's receipts to find Dylan Mallory regarding her pleasantly through the grate. Her composure flew in fifty different directions. "Y....y....yes, sir? May...may I help you?"

"I wonder if we might see Mrs. Thatcher?" Somehow he managed to make even this simple statement sound faintly Shakespearean.

"Of....of course....ah....sir." The clerk fumbled with the switch on the intercom, spoke briefly into it and nodded. "If....if..you would come with me, Mr. Mallory." Emerging from the booth, the poor woman caught her heel and half-fell. Deftly Dylan caught her, almost appearing to escort her along the hallway, Jon observed with a grin.

Amanda stood in the doorway of her office waiting for them. Cordially she extended her hand in greeting. "Mr. Mallory–an honor to have you with us. Come in, won't you? And please, gentlemen, make yourselves comfortable." She indicated a sofa which stood against the right hand wall. Closing the door, she herself went around behind her desk pausing with her hand on the phone. "If it's all right with you, I'll ask my artistic director to join us."

"Of course, Mrs. Thatcher," Dylan agreed smoothly. "Many years ago when I was just starting to get work in London, I had the honor of playing Banquo to Mr. Douglas' Macbeth. It will be a pleasure to see him again."

"Yes," Amanda was saying into the receiver, "have Mr. Douglas paged to my office, will you? May I inquire, Mr. Mallory," she continued, coming over now to sit in an armchair facing the couch, "how you happened to pay our little theatre a visit?"

"Actually it was at Jon's request here." He indicated his companion. "Mr. Sinclair's on our production staff over at Stratford and he wanted me to see a young actress friend of his who's in your company."

"You're a <u>friend</u> of Victoria's?" Amanda turned to Jon, her eyebrows raised in an attitude of inquiry.

"So then, you're in fact already aware whom we came to see," Dylan observed before Jon had a chance to reply.

"Mr, Mallory, I may only be a retired music hall performer," she responded a trifle crisply, "but....."

At that moment, however, there was a brief knock at the office door and David strode into the room. "Dylan!" Beaming, he seized the visitor's right hand in both of his pumping it up and down. "I thought this might have somethin' to do wi' yourr bein' herre. 'Tis grrand to see you again, laddie!"

Dylan had immediately risen upon the older man's entrance and he returned the handshake with equal warmth. "Super to see you again as well. I'd heard of your fine work at Edinburgh of course, but it's good to have you back where you belong–in the professional theatre!"

"How verra kind of ye! Thank ye!" David looked pleased. "Noo–ye've coom aboot ourr lass, no doubt." Only as he said the word, it sounded more like "doot".

"Well, Jon, it seems our visit is a surprise to no one."

"They both know how good she is! That's why! I'm right, aren't I?" Jon's enthusiasm could be contained no longer.

"Yes, Mr. Sinclair," Amanda replied. "As I was about to say when David arrived, Victoria's brilliance is not lost on us."

"Aye, Dylan," her associate agreed, "we knew it was only a matterr of time. But tell me, laddie, is she trruly that good?"

"It's just as Mrs. Thatcher has said, David. I'm positive I can guarantee her a place in the Stratford company. She'd be interested, I presume?"

"<u>Interested</u>?" Amanda rolled her eyes. "That girl <u>lives</u> to act! Really, when I stop to think about it, it's all she <u>does</u> live for. Do you wish to speak to her now?"

"Not tonight, I think. I'm sure she's exhausted. And we've already booked rooms at a local hotel. Would it be possible for you to have Miss Windsor here in your office tomorrow morning–say about ten o'clock."

"Certainly, Mr. Mallory."

"Good–now, David, how about tipping a pint or two with Jon and myself. We've a lot of catching up to do, you and I."

"Aye, I'd like that." A few minutes later the three men were walking along together through a light spring mist heading for a pub near the theatre. "Ye know, Dylan," David remarked thoughtfully at one point, "Amanda's neverr rreally underrstood Victorria. Deep doon inside that lass somewherre, therre'a a frrightened wee bairrnie. Ye will have a bit of a carre overr herr, will ye not?"

* * *

Amanda and David weren't the only ones who realized at once why Dylan was there. Victoria herself had known as well, of course. And Dylan Mallory meant the Royal Shakespeare Company–ironically the first of her many fruitless auditions. Could that only have been five years ago? Sure that at last her time had come, she waited until long after everyone else had left the theatre, but no one sent for her.

It has to be me, Victoria sobbed aloud, as she paced the confines of her tiny room far into the night. No one else in the company's half as good, except maybe that Goddamned old lech, Huntley, and even he's a has-been who never was. So who else could it be? But then why didn't anyone say anything to me? And thus both her thoughts and her steps went on and on–circling endlessly until finally worn out, she curled up on the bed and fell asleep. In the half-light from the street lamp outside her figure bore a striking resemblance to that of a little girl who once many years before had determined she would stay up as late as she wanted to–because no one cared enough to tell her to go to bed.

The next morning when she came downstairs, as usual well after the breakfast hour, there was a message for her by the phone. "Victoria, Mrs. T. wants to see you in her office–ten a.m." It was Katie's handwriting. A glance at her watch showed it was nearly that time now. Such an important moment and no one had even bothered to wake her. Tears filled Victoria's eyes– tears that despite years of self-discipline were still close to the surface when she was alone and unguarded. Ashamed of her weakness, she blinked them back. "Of course," she said out loud, "everyone knows why she wants to see me and they're all jealous." And that, after all, was probably true.

It was a warm, spring morning and Victoria left immediately, not even stopping to go upstairs again for a cardigan. In fact she ran most of the way, slowing her pace only when she was within half a block of the theatre. Glancing about to be sure no one had observed such undignified haste, she walked more sedately the rest of the way all the while breathing slowly and deliberately and by the time she knocked on the office door she showed no sign of her mad dash from the boarding house. "Come in," she heard Mrs. Thatcher call out.

Pausing a second or two longer, she licked her lips and smoothed her hair and with one last deep breath opened the door. It was all she could do to control herself when she found that Dylan Mallory was indeed there along with David Douglas and another younger man who looked vaguely familiar. She paused in the doorway, one hand still on the knob. Dylan couldn't help smiling, appreciating as only someone could who had often utilized it himself, the carefully calculated theatrical gesture.

"Victoria, come in, please." Amanda indicated the armchair which faced the couch where Dylan and Jon were once again sitting. She herself was at her desk while David stood behind her leaning against the window frame.

After a moment Victoria came to enthrone herself in the chair crossing her legs. Her hands rested lightly on the arms, her right index finger tapping lightly on the fabric. This latter mannerism would in the years ahead become habitual, manifesting itself especially when she felt uneasy although outwardly it betrayed merely boredom or extreme irritation. Dylan studied her intently. She was, if possible, even more beautiful than she appeared from the stage. He sensed as well a certain air of strain though at the time he didn't find that disturbing.

Under the circumstances it was understandable. He saw no reason to prolong her uncertainty. He smiled. "Well, Miss Windsor, I had the distinct pleasure, I should say the honor of seeing your performance last evening. I cannot remember when I've been so moved. You are, as I'm sure you realize, an extraordinarily gifted actress!"

The response any one person would give to such a comment had always fascinated Dylan. Some would modestly deny it; others would accept the compliment, but with some degree of embarrassment. Victoria was the third type. "You are quite right, Mr. Mallory. I do realize I am, shall we say, gifted." Her words were accompanied by the elevation of one flawlessly shaped eyebrow, clearly mocking him or perhaps herself.

He could not resist testing her further. "In the light of such talent, Miss Windsor, how do you explain the fact that it was four years between your graduation from RADA and your first acting job here?" His own eyebrow shot expressively upward and now it was Victoria who couldn't tell just who was being mocked. "It was four years, wasn't it? I am right about that, I believe."

Her mind was racing. How in hell did Dylan Mallory know so much about her and just exactly what was he up to anyway? Was he seriously questioning her ability or was he simply testing her? When he stopped speaking, she said nothing for a few seconds, appearing instead to be fascinated by the motion of her right hand on the fabric covered arm of the chair. At last she raised her head and although the smile she bestowed on him was one of incredible feminine charm, her voice was coolly precise. "Unfortunately, Mr. Mallory, it took others somewhat longer to recognize my talent."

Dylan threw back his head and laughed. "But enough of this shilly-shallying, Miss Windsor. I'd like you to come to audition for the Royal Shakespeare Company."

Another audition? Nothing but another bloody audition?! The disappointment was an actual physical pain stabbing at her insides. "If I'm such a brilliant actress, Mr. Mallory, why in hell do I still have to audition?"

Amanda and David exchanged glances of exasperated amazement at Victoria's unbelievable nerve, but Dylan himself merely smiled. He remembered all too well what it was like: the years of failure, of wishing desperately that just one person would give you a chance and when that opportunity seemed finally within your grasp, the arrogant bluff because your ego as an actor wouldn't allow you to beg. "I'm afraid I have no real authority in the selection of the company, Miss Windsor. But believe me, you will have my wholehearted recommendation."

"Who is in charge of the actual selection, Mr. Mallory?" Amanda inquired.

"Our current artistic director, Pliny Nicholas." So–Pliny Nicholas again. She would be auditioning for the same man who five years before had had the bloody gall to ignore her. In spite of herself Victoria found she was also smiling. "Something amuses you, Miss Windsor?" Dylan asked.

"It's just I've auditioned for Mr. Nicholas once before, not that he'll recall the occasion."

"I don't see how he could have forgotten!" Ever since Victoria arrived, Jon had been waiting for her to turn to him suddenly in grateful recognition, realizing that of course it was he who had brought Dylan Mallory to Stoke-on-Trent. He should have known better, he thought ruefully.

"Ah yes," Dylan said. "Jon, forgive me,,, Miss Windsor, I'm sure you remember Jonathan Sinclair. He's the reason I'm here—actually."

At last, then, she looked at Jon and once again there was the expressively elevated eyebrow. "Really?" Somehow she managed to flirt with him while at the same time indicating clearly that she had no idea who he was.

"I've seen you audition–twice. The last time was for *Camelot.* The first was when you walked out on Pliny Nicholas." Oh God, Victoria thought. Why did he have to say that?

"She did what?" Dylan glanced quickly at Jon. "You never told me that!"

"He wasn't giving her audition the attention she felt it deserved." In spite of himself Jon laughed a little at the memory. "And she told him with anatomical precision what he could do with our beloved RSC."

Now it was Dylan's turn to chuckle. How often had he seen Pliny do just that, but this young woman was one of the few who had the courage to rebel at such treatment. Victoria breathed a sigh of relief. Evidently he wasn't going to hold that against her. Aloud she said, "I will allow no one to ignore me." Tossing her head, she focused her gaze with a terrible intensity on Dylan. "You of all people should understand that."

"I have the distinct feeling, Miss Windsor," he replied with a slight smile of his own, "that people are going to find you increasingly difficult to ignore. Now, Mrs. Thatcher tells me you would be free to come to Stratford on Thursday. I'm sure you have selections prepared."

"Yes, I do." Suddenly her green eyes came to life, sparkling with humor. It was a look he would come to know well. "Actually I could use the same ones. Mr. Nicholas won't remember them, I'm sure."

Again Dylan laughed, standing up to bring the meeting to a close. "We'll be expecting you, then—say, about one o'clock." Victoria extended her hand. He bowed slightly as he accepted it and compelled by an uncontrollable urge, he raised her hand to his lips. Again Amanda and David exchanged glances. Dylan Mallory was clearly paying homage to a newly crowned queen.

"I'll be seeing you then, Victoria," Jon interposed with a broad grin. She appeared not to have heard him. "Victoria," he repeated her name, "I said I'd see you."

With an evident reluctance she removed her gaze from Dylan. "Oh...ah...yes, Joe, wasn't it?" Was it deliberate, he wondered, or simply forgetful that she had addressed him by the wrong name?

A few moments later as the two men got into their car, Dylan glanced briefly at his companion. Had he been hurt by Victoria's callousness? "I don't mind if she doesn't remember me," Jon said in response to the other man's inquiring look. "Someday, when everyone knows her, I'll remember I was there at the beginning of it all."

Only her already thorough professionalism made it possible for Victoria to concentrate on her portrayal of Nora that evening. All she could think about was the coming Thursday when undoubtedly she would at last be invited to join the Royal Shakespeare Company.

Michael Phillips was as always waiting for her outside the theatre. During their walk back to Tuttle's Victoria was even more uncommunicative than usual, but he was accustomed to her moods by now and didn't think much about it. The next morning when Katie Webster told him the news over breakfast, he realized how naive he'd been. Sadly he knew as well that his relationship with Victoria was over. Once at Stratford she would have no further use of him.

* * *

Pliny Nicholas leaned back expansively in his canvas director's chair as pulling absent-mindedly at one of his graying sideburns, he listened with every appearance of genial accord to Dylan's glowing account of his visit to Stoke-on-Trent. Secretly, of course, he hated the man equally with Terence Cartier, but outwardly in the presence of such luminaries he became the perfect toady. "Yes, yes, she would appear to be an excellent addition to our company." He nodded vigorously, his mouth working into a fawning leer which in Pliny's case passed for a smile. "Of course you do understand we'll have to start her out with a few minor roles."

"Uh-uh...Plin...no. She's my Ophelia."

"Your Ophelia?" His already pasty complexion went several shades whiter. "An....ah.... an....ah...unknown actress play Ophelia to the great Mallory's Hamlet? No...ah... my dear boy, my dear, dear boy...ah...ah...." Helplessly Pliny stammered and stuttered and cleared his throat as he sought a way out of this situation without offending Dylan. "I...ah...ah...am afraid not. We....ah...have several....ah....established actresses in the company who deserve the role. They would be...ah....ah...offended and I...ah...must say justifiably so if the part were given to someone new to the company."

"You haven't seen her yet, man! God, an actress like this is a rare jewel! She is my Ophelia!—that is----" Here he paused, a glint of pure mischief in his eyes. He adored watching the insignificant little man grovel; he did it so beautifully. "That is, if you want me to do Hamlet for you this season."

His barb had evidently found its mark as the director gasped in obvious distress. "You... ah...wouldn't do that, Mallory old chap. I mean....I mean...you.....you wouldn't!"

"Ah, yes.... but you see, I would." Pliny harrumphed and muttered, his mouth working feebly. "But not to worry," Dylan went on after allowing the poor fish to squirm for a moment longer. "Once you've watched her work, you'll see there's no problem."

Thus on the following Thursday afternoon Victoria once again found herself looking at the streets of a strange town from the window of a taxicab–but how different it was from Stoke-on-Trent. Street after street of Tudor style buildings with their light stucco walls and dark brown beams proclaimed proudly their centuries old association with the Elizabethan age and in particular the name of William Shakespeare. As the taxi came to a stop at the famous red brick building which was her destination, she still had fifteen minutes before her audition so instead of going immediately inside, she walked through the small park in front of the playhouse toward the Avon River which flowed by on the other side–parallel to the street.

It was a glorious spring day, as if Stratford were putting on its most attractive face for her, and the gardens were a multi-pasteled riot of spring blooms with hyacinths, jonquils and tulips nodding in the light breeze. For several minutes Victoria stood looking down into the lazily drifting currents of the river. The water sparkled in the sunlight and set against the brilliant blue background were the famous Stratford swans-- hired, some wits maintained, by the theatre administration to provide additional atmosphere. Lost in the moment, she wasn't even aware someone had come up to stand behind her. "Worshiping at the shrine?" The voice of Dylan Mallory was unmistakable.

In an instant Victoria's expression altered and as she turned to face him, she betrayed no sense of wonder. She was, rather, the world-weary sophisticate who no longer found anything particularly exciting. "Well, it is all quite awe-inspiring, isn't it?" Such sentiments were, in fact, entirely sincere, but voicing them aloud, she managed to sound merely bored.

"Yes, but at the moment Mr. Nicholas is waiting for you inside and I know how eager you must be to see him again."

"Of course." Victoria laughed. "Dear, dear Pliny! Do you suppose he'll bother to listen to me this time?" She seemed cool and unruffled–supremely confident-- but as they walked back together toward the theatre, all at once she stopped and turning to Dylan, she touched him almost imploringly on the arm. "I....I brought a resume... pictures. Will.....will that be enough, do you think? Have....have you spoken to him about me? You....you promised." Once again, as on the occasion of their original meeting, he found himself studying Victoria. Was she actually as self-assured as she appeared on the surface or was the display of ego merely a facade as David Douglas had told him?

But if she were indeed putting on an act, why then did she seem totally lacking in awe of him–Dylan Mallory, a name customarily regarded with absolute respect? Because even now, he thought, with only one year of experience in a provincial rep company, she is my equal. She knows that and what's more, she knows I know it. "I'm sure whatever you brought will be more than sufficient," he nevertheless reassured her. "And yes, I spoke to him, in glowing terms, I might add. Oh, ah...and one more thing," he added as they began to walk again up the steps of the theatre and into the lobby. "I presume you're...ah...familiar with the role of Ophelia."

"You're doing Hamlet this season, aren't you?" Victoria stopped again and this time the hand which grasped his arm did not implore; rather it radiated an electric excitement, the sparks of which seemed mirrored in her luminous green eyes. "Aren't you?!"

"You're one of the ones who really love it, aren't you?

"It's everything that matters to me—everything!"

"A beautiful woman like yourself? I find that hard to believe."

Victoria ignored the compliment. "Do you want me for your Ophelia?" she insisted.

"Yes, but it will be much easier for both of us if Nicholas wants it as well."

Pliny Nicholas was waiting impatiently in the front row, the fingers of one hand pressed against the pain in his abdomen. Whenever he became upset, his ulcer flared up. He was convinced this girl was nothing but the latest of Dylan's mistresses, but rather than risk losing his Hamlet, he would condescend to audition the man's whore.

"Pliny, this is Victoria Windsor." Dylan made the introduction as just then he and Victoria arrived at the front of the theatre.

"Up on the stage," he growled, barely bothering to glance up. "Let's see what you can do." Victoria put down her purse and portfolio and as she started toward the stage, she could be faintly heard to make an observation. "Did she say something?" The director glared suspiciously at Dylan.

"No...ah...Pliny. I didn't hear anything." He turned away to hide his evident amusement as in actuality he'd heard Victoria quite distinctly.–"Charming as ever, the little bastard!"

This, however, was not an open audition and with Dylan only one seat away from him in an otherwise empty auditorium Pliny had no choice but to listen. "My God!" he exclaimed after a moment, "you were right! She's magnificent! Read the scene with her, man! Do it!"

As Victoria finished her speech from *Antigone*, Dylan joined her on stage, handing her a script. "The 'Get thee to a nunnery' scene."

`"Yes, all right." Although her tone was matter-of-fact, he could see the tension in every line of her exquisite face, in the slim, expressive hand which in the act of taking the script from him had trembled visibly.

So at long last Victoria shared a stage with an actor worthy of her and Pliny Nicholas would never forget he was there when it happened. "Victoria Windsor." Pliny spoke the name aloud, savoring the sound of it. And like so many before him he would feel he'd been the one to discover her. The scene ultimately concluded and Pliny was at once on his feet–no longer irritated, no longer blase, the pain of his ulcer all but forgotten-- not only on his feet, but halfway up the stairs to the stage. "My dear Miss Windsor," he burbled striding toward her, his hand extended in greeting. "Welcome to the Royal Shakespeare Company!"

With only a faint grimace of distaste Victoria submitted to his decidedly fishy handshake. After all, for the words he had just spoken, she would have shaken the flipper of Moby Dick himself.

Chapter 6

Victoria's agreement with the Thatcher Memorial Theatre ended on June 1, 1963 and on June 2nd she arrived in Stratford to sign her contract. I hope they don't think I'm overanxious, she remembered thinking with a laugh. She'd actually be earning considerably less, her wages no longer including room and board, but being a member of the Royal Shakespeare Company meant far more than mere money. Then, too, as she'd noted from the taxi on the day of her audition, the place had an undeniable atmosphere. The two rooms of her garret flat might be tiny, the ceiling slanting so sharply she could only stand upright in the center of the floor, but the building was authentic Tudor and from the leaded casement windows she could look over into the churchyard of Holy Trinity Church, Shakespeare's burial place. Even more important—after the enforced conviviality of the boarding house, she would have privacy.

* * *

The executive secretary of the Shakespeare Memorial Theatre had started in the ticket office nearly thirty years before and had taken over her present position in 1950. With her mousy hair, thick spectacles and a tailored wardrobe of blouses and skirts reaching to the mid-calf she did not appear the theatrical type, but Phoebe Shallett was the mainstay of the company. Managing directors and actors came and went, artistic endeavors being by nature shifting and uncertain; Phoebe remained and things ran smoothly. Hearing her office door open and close, she glanced up. "Yes?" This beautiful woman must be the expected new member of the company. She despised her on sight. Vain, foolish creature, she thought.

"I am Victoria Windsor," the vision announced. She'd always spoken her name with a ring of pride. Now she fairly trumpeted the two words and the gaze which flicked over the secretary was one of barely concealed contempt. Insignificant little wretch, Victoria thought.

"Mr. Nicholas will be back momentarily," Phoebe replied after a moment. "You may wait in his office." She rose to go and open the door. Oh, but how she hated to perform even such a simple task for this proud, disdainful woman.

"Bring me a cup of tea!" Entering the inner office, Victoria carefully held her skirt to one side as though to avoid any possible contamination. It is difficult to know what might have happened next had Pliny Nicholas not returned at precisely that instant.

"Miss Windsor," Phoebe muttered, "desires a cup of tea."

"Then get it, Miss Shallett," Pliny shut the door in his secretary's face. "Victoria, welcome, welcome, my dear!" Rubbing his hands together, he walked on tiptoe around to the back of his desk pulling out his chair to sit down. "Well, well, my dear," he continued as he reached over to open the upper left hand drawer and take out her contract, "we can't begin to tell you....."

"And where do you wish <u>me</u> to sit?" she inquired–just the hint of a bite in her tone.

"Please, Miss Windsor," he apologized, "forgive such a deplorable oversight." Coming rapidly around his desk again, he drew a leather upholstered armchair up to the other side. "If you would sit here, my dear."

A mere five years ago this odious little man had ignored her. Now he came willingly, even eagerly, to do her bidding. How bloody marvelous! The feeling of power was intoxicating and now that it no longer mattered what anyone thought of her, she need not concern herself whether people were offended by such cavalier treatment. If they didn't like it, they could leave her the hell alone! Ironically it was just as this thought crossed her mind that two men entered the room who, despite every indignity, every cruelty she could inflict, would remain her friends, refusing to "leave her the hell alone". One, of course, was Jonathan Sinclair.

The other was Noel St. John. "Victoria!" Jon exclaimed as they came in. "I'm so glad you're here."

"Oh, hello." She favored him with a brief glance before returning to her perusal of the contract. "Pliny, I see this is for two years. Is that the customary arrangement?"

"Ah...uh....yes. You weren't told that? With...ah...rare exceptions two years is the....ah.... rule."

"What exceptions?"

"Ah...established actors who agree to do one or perhaps two particular roles with the company." With a quick nod intended merely to show understanding, but which Pliny mistook for assent, Victoria once more lowered her eyes to the paper.

Watching her demolish Pliny Nicholas, Jon couldn't help smiling a little. "Victoria, I thought you might enjoy meeting a fellow RADA graduate–just a few years after you, I believe. This is Noel St. John. Noel–Victoria Windsor."

Noel was actually sorry when Jon made a second attempt to attract Victoria's attention. As long as she apparently remained unaware of their presence, he'd been free to study her unobserved. His friend's description of her as an "incredibly lovely woman" had in his opinion been vastly inadequate and he felt sure at that moment that he could have watched her silently and unseen for an eternity. Now all at once she was looking at him fully and his composure vanished. "Hi, Vicki." Noel was annoyed with himself for allowing his voice to crack like a nervous schoolboy and trying desperately to compensate for his lack of self-assurance, he smiled at her–an engaging grin revealing a set of uneven teeth. Unlike many actors he'd refused to have them capped. "Part of my charm," he would explain. At the use of the familiar nickname Jon had winced, knowing that for some reason she hated being called Vicki.

"The name is Victoria," she snapped and immediately turned her full attention back to the director. "I would prefer my agent see this as well before I sign it."

"Agent?" Pliny was understandably surprised. "You hadn't mentioned an agent so naturally I assumed........."

"Never assume anything where I am concerned. Of course I have an agent. I'll ring him and tell him to come up here." All three men noticed she'd said "tell him" and not "ask him".

"Please—use my telephone." Immediately he removed the receiver, handing it to Victoria.

For a few seconds she sat unmoving, the instrument poised in mid-air. "Well, may I have my privacy?"

"But of course. Gentlemen?" Pliny indicated the door.

"And find out where in hell that woman has gone with my tea!"

"Yes, Miss Windsor." Quickly he closed the door.

"God, she is incredible!" Noel murmured in an awed tone as he and Jon walked together down from the first floor where Pliny's office was located to the auditorium where *Hamlet* was already in rehearsal. "I've never seen such...."

"Sheer bloody cheek?" Jon interrupted him with a chuckle. "Well, you'll soon learn that is Victoria."

"Yes, Victoria–not Vicki. I won't make that mistake again. But I didn't mean her nerve actually–although I admit I admire that, too. I'm thrilled just to be here and there she is ordering Nicholas around as though he were her errand boy! No....I meant I've never seen such a beautiful woman. You didn't do her justice, old chap."

"Just don't ever let yourself forget. It will always be Victoria—never Vicki."

Noel stared at him blankly as they entered the auditorium together. "I already told you. I won't make that mistake again."

"You don't have the foggiest notion what I mean, do you? Look, Noel, Victoria is......" At that moment, however, the set designer called Jon away and he had no further chance, at least for the present, to explain to the other man just exactly what Victoria was.

* * *

Between the time that Leslie Matthews had put Victoria on the train for Stoke-on-Trent and the day when his telephone rang and she told him to come up to Stratford, communication between them had been limited. In the intervening months he had acquired a few additional clients, exchanged the kiosk in the fish-and-chips shop for an actual office and yet each time he attempted to advise her she ordered him to keep his "nose the bloody hell of my business!" Now, all of a sudden, she wanted him to check her contract. Victoria was nothing if not unpredictable. It would have served her right, he thought, if he refused to come, but the next day, of course, he drove up to Stratford.

It had been more than a year since he'd seen her and as he regarded her now from across the little table in the Rose and Crown pub, he observed a subtle, but disturbing change in her. As close as Matt could phrase it, she had withdrawn further inside herself. Yet oddly at the same time she was on the surface far more charming. It alarmed him, moreover, that she only picked at her lunch–although she consumed two vodka and tonics beforehand as well as an undetermined amount of wine with the little she did eat.

"So anyway, Matt," she was saying now gesturing broadly with her slim hands, one of which held her wine glass, "I can't abide a two year contract with one company. You'll have to do something about it!"

"Exactly what would you suggest?" He indicated the paper between them on the table. "This is a standard RSC contract."

"There are exceptions. Mr. Nicholas admitted that to me himself. For instance, Dylan's only doing one play although he is directing a second."

"Dylan?" Matt smiled at her immediately assumed familiarity with the distinguished actor.

"What else would I call him?"

"What else, indeed. Well, Dylan happens to be a major star while you, at least for the present, are not. You have no choice, I'm afraid. Take it or leave it."

"As an agent, you're no bloody use to me. I don't know why I bother with you!" Victoria stood up, but she lost her balance and sat down again.

Gallantly Matt ignored her clumsy attempt to leave. "Because whether you believe it or not," he replied quietly, "I do have your interests at heart." But he made the mistake as he spoke of placing his hand over one of hers where it lay on the table.

"Don't!" She pulled her hand away.

"I'll do what I can," he promised after a moment. "And if it comes to that, contracts can always be broken."

Victoria looked at him intently and now it was she who reached across to run her finger down the side of his face and along the edge of his chin. How was it that she, who couldn't bear to be touched, was becoming a compulsive toucher? Perhaps it was for effect or perhaps something continued to compel her to reach out for human contact. A strange smile played across her lips. "You know, Matt," she said. "Maybe you are worth something, after all."

* * *

It had been apparent from Victoria's first rehearsal that she was an extraordinary actress and other people in the company would find any excuse to watch her work. The attention was a marvelous tonic for her ego. She did not, however, view such recognition as an indication that she "had arrived" and therefore no longer needed to take her work seriously. She had, in fact, refused to indulge in such unprofessional behavior ever since Sir Terence had rebuked her for it while she was still at RADA. Now, watching Dylan Mallory, she knew she was only beginning to comprehend the demands of her craft and that furthermore it would require all her talent and self-discipline to create an Ophelia worthy of his Hamlet.

Noel would often think back on these, the first weeks of his acquaintance with Victoria. He had been assigned for the most part minor roles in *Hamlet*, the sole character of any consequence being Fortinbras, Prince of Norway, who only appears in the final scene. With Ophelia dead of drowning by the end of Act Four, he and Victoria had no rehearsal time together and thus for a while after her arrival in Stratford they saw each other merely in passing. On these occasions Noel would always speak and sometimes she would deign to answer him. But at this point their relationship remained impersonal and perhaps he could still have walked away.

Then late one morning Noel joined the many others who'd come to watch Victoria rehearse the play's famous mad scene.

"There's rosemary, that's for remembrance; pray, love,
Remember; and there is pansies, that's for thoughts...."

Ophelia's conscious mind has refused to accept either Hamlet's betrayal or the death of her father and now as she glides gracefully about giving away her flowers, she appears actually content. Clearly she has no idea where she is or who all these people are staring at her, but she does not find this at all alarming. She is safe in her private world and no one can hurt her. Other really quite competent actresses might feign insanity and do so convincingly. Watching Victoria, one felt a brief, yet genuine stab of fear that perhaps she has truly gone mad.

As the scene progressed, Noel found himself leaning forward gripping the back of the seat in front of him. After a while he became aware that his fingers were cramping yet he was unable to move. He was, in fact, so absorbed in Victoria's performance that he failed to realize Jonathan Sinclair had come to sit beside him until the rehearsal broke for lunch. Immediately excusing himself, he got to his feet to move rapidly down the aisle toward the stage.

"Where are you going in such a hurry?" Jon inquired.

"I...ah....wanted to talk to Victoria." Reluctantly Noel stopped. "I've been wanting to ever since you introduced us so I thought if I complimented her on her performance, it would give me the perfect opportunity. To...ah...tell you the truth I was also planning on asking her to lunch."

"I wouldn't, old chap," Jon called after him, but by then the other man was nearly at the bottom of the aisle and appeared not to have heard him.

Canvas chairs were scattered along the edge of the stage and with the scene finished Victoria had come to sit in one of them next to Pliny Nicholas, the play's director. As usual her legs were crossed and she was resting her elbows on the arm of the chair, the forefinger of one hand poised against her cheek. She was dressed in a sleeveless green turtleneck and pale, yellow slacks, the color of the latter seeming to intensify the gold of her hair. Consciously or unconsciously she presented an exquisite picture.

Noel took the unoccupied chair on her other side. "Hi, Victoria." The sound of his voice had startled her and she threw him a glance which would have discouraged anyone less determined. "You remember me, don't you?" he persisted. "We met the day you arrived, but we haven't really had a chance to get to know each other yet so I thought that......"

This time she looked at him directly and at some length. "I do not recall," she replied coolly, "indicating a desire to get to know you. In addition to which I am trying at this particular moment to listen to my director and you are being a bloody nuisance!"

Jon hurried up on stage to join them. "Rehearsal was magnificent, Victoria," he quickly put in.

"How perfectly charming of you to say so, luv," She extended her free hand to him. The other was still holding her script. "However, I am only beginning."

"You do remember Noel St. John, don't you?"

An expression of annoyance passed over Victoria's face. Why in hell did life have to be complicated by interpersonal relationships? With an exaggerated sigh she looked for yet a third time at Noel and now for the first time perhaps she really saw him– a round, slightly cherubic face topped by shaggy brown hair. But what caught and held her attention were his eyes–brown and alight with unquestioning devotion. In the future those who wished to be unkind would refer to Noel as her lap dog. It was true he'd follow her anywhere, doing her slightest bidding, reveling in her smallest kindness. Did Victoria at once sense this and decide to take advantage of it? Or did something hidden deep inside her, something all but lost, respond to his obvious adoration? For whatever reason she dropped her script into her lap and extended her other hand to him. "Of course," she murmured with her most beguiling smile. "Noel St. John. Of course I remember. How could I ever forget someone who so closely resembles a Pooh bear?"

Had Victoria intended the words to be affectionate or demeaning? It didn't matter to Noel. He saw only the smile, felt only the soft hand grasping his. He grinned at her in return. "Actually my full name is Noel Merrill Millington St. John." He ran the names together in a descending scale until the last sounded as though he'd all but swallowed it.

Victoria laughed delightedly. "You see, Jon, I told you he was adorable."

"May we escort you to lunch?" Jon asked before his friend could lose even this temporary advantage. "You like the Rose and Crown, don't you?"

"Why yes," she replied, "if I might have a minute to prepare myself for the company of two such charming gentlemen." Rising from the chair with her characteristically easy grace, Victoria moved away across the empty stage. Noel had immediately stood as well, of course, and the two men watched until she disappeared from sight.

"What I would like to know," Pliny muttered half to himself as he also got to his feet, gathering up his script, glasses, etc., "is how in hell I am supposed to direct her when every other male insists on treating her like the Queen of the May."

"Ignore him," Jon chuckled when the other man was out of hearing. "He's just annoyed because Victoria probably doesn't need a director at all."

"You're amusing today," Noel observed angrily. "And by the way thanks a whole bloody lot, chum. You knew I wanted to take her to lunch. What gave you the almighty cheek to include yourself?"

"Believe me, Noel. Alone–she would have refused you. Two of us are...well.....safe. And for God's sake keep it casual."

"I guess you're right," he agreed grudgingly. "She's not very happy, is she?"

"On two such brief meetings you can tell that?" But something about the tone of his friend's voice kept Jon from laughing.

"You mean you haven't noticed. When she smiles, it's only with her mouth. Her eyes are still so sad."

Victoria reappeared at that moment–hair brushed, make-up freshened, a gold cardigan which matched her slacks thrown over her shoulders. If she'd learned anything from Amanda Thatcher, it was how to dress even within her still limited budget. Smiling, she slipped an arm through each of theirs. "Now, gentlemen, are you ready to feed a poor, starving actress?"

Noel had learned something from Jon's remarks. "Ah, but my dear Victoria, we must suffer for the sake of our art!"

"Oh no, luv. Actors are only required to starve when they're unemployed. When we work, we eat!"

Noel laughed. One of Victoria's most endearing qualities, he was soon to learn, was her sense of humor. "The Rose and Crown it is, then?"

"Perfect!"

The Rose and Crown, a pub only about a block and a half from the theatre, was a favorite spot of the actors. Paneled in dark brown wood, its interior was divided into three sections: the bar, the buffet and the restaurant and as Jon already knew, Victoria preferred the latter. It was raised a few steps and thus more secluded; it was also the only section served by waitresses.

They settled themselves at a table and ordered drinks: a whiskey and soda for Noel, white wine for Jon and for Victoria a vodka and tomato juice, known more commonly in the States as a Bloody Mary. "Just don't tell Pliny that I'm allowing his actors liquor at lunch break," Jon pleaded rolling his eyes in pretended apprehension.

"Poor, dear luv!" Victoria reached across to cover his hand with hers. "We won't breathe a word, will we, Noel?" Her hand continued to rest on Jon's caressing it lightly and watching, Noel experienced a pang of jealousy. It was a sensation which was to become sadly familiar to him in the years ahead as circumstances forced him to observe her in the company of many different men.

On the whole, nevertheless, the luncheon was at first quite pleasant–the conversation light and sparkling with wit. Victoria had finished her drink in almost no time, however, and summoning the waitress with an imperious snap of her fingers, demanded another. When the woman returned a short while later for their lunch selections, Jon decided on a mixed grill and chips while Noel chose steak and kidney pie. Victoria, who'd claimed to be so hungry, ordered yet a third "Bloody Mary". The two men exchanged glances and Jon with the slightly longer acquaintance felt he had to speak up. "Don't you think you've had enough, Victoria?"

"Tell me, Noel," she fairly purred, "don't you find it dreadfully frustrating–a fine actor like yourself–stranded in roles like old bloody Fortinbras there." He felt ridiculously pleased at her praise even though at the same time he was fully aware she was merely using him to chastise their companion.

The waitress brought the drink Victoria had ordered, but Jon put up his hand to prevent her from placing the glass on the table. "I'm sorry. The lady has changed her mind."

"No, the lady has not changed her mind. Put the drink down, please!" There was the faintest hint of a hiss on the "s" in please. Clearly she was cautioning Jon to go no further.

But either he failed to hear the warning or he chose not to heed it. "Please, Victoria," he insisted, his own voice quiet but firm, "you won't be in any condition to rehearse this afternoon. If you have to drink, you must at least learn when to do it."

"You bastard!" She rose unsteadily to her feet, in the process knocking over her chair and coming dangerously close to falling herself.

Jon stood up to put a steadying arm around her shoulders. "Perhaps if you would just eat a little something."

Victoria wrenched herself free of him. "You'll regret this, you meddling son-of-a-bitch! I can promise you that right now!" She swayed slightly, but somehow managing to regain her balance, she hurried down the few steps past the buffet and out a side door into the street.

For a few seconds neither of the men spoke or moved, but at last Jon bent to set her chair upright and lowered himself slowly into it. "Well, old man," he sighed, "I trust you've learned something from this."

"Learned something? Surely she...ah...didn't mean that. She has you to thank for being here in the first place."

"But you see, that won't even occur to her and yes, I'm fairly sure she meant every word of it." Sadly Jon was right on both accounts. Victoria had long since forgotten, if indeed it had ever entered her mind in the first place, that anyone's kindness had played a part in her good fortune–she was in Stratford because she belonged there– and she did indeed mean every single word.

Arriving back at the theatre, she went at once to Pliny's office. Not stopping to knock, she flung open the door marked "private" and swept into the room. In a few years this entrance would be given its finishing touches with the addition of furs, jewels and designer clothes, but the entrance itself couldn't be improved upon. At the crash of the door hitting the wall Pliny had looked up–understandably startled. At once he rose to his feet–all solicitude. "Why, my dear, whatever could be the matter?" Damn, he thought, I am sick to death of temperamental actors!

Victoria sat down in the same leather armchair and crossed her legs, her free foot starting to swing–a characteristic mannerism. In time people would come to say that one could make a fair judgment as to "La Windsor's" mood at any given moment by the speed of this, her personal pendulum. Today the tempo was furious. "I find Jonathan Sinclair's behavior toward me insulting and I wish him dismissed!"

Automatically Pliny's fingers sought out his ulcer. "Well, perhaps if...ah...you could...ah... tell me exactly how he has.....ah...offended you?"

"It shouldn't be necessary for me to explain. And I might add that if you wish me to stay with the company, Mr. Sinclair will not remain!"

"Of course, my dear," Pliny capitulated at once, "whatever you wish." It stuck in his craw to bow and scrape to a neophyte actress less than half his age, but after all, how much did an assistant stage manager really matter? Even Dylan's attempt to intervene was half-hearted at best. She was the Ophelia of his dreams. He did, however, assuage his guilty conscience somewhat by quietly arranging for Jon's employment with the new, but already well-respected company in Ontario, Canada.

And so Jonathan Sinclair was gone; his crime?–he had dared to care about Victoria. Sobered, Noel wondered when it would be his turn.

But for everyone else, Victoria herself included, Jon's sudden departure was soon forgotten–at least temporarily–in the showering of praise which greeted the opening of *Hamlet*. Mallory's latest portrayal of the tragic Dane had been eagerly anticipated yet it was not Mallory's Hamlet which was on the lips of every Shakespeare devotee, but rather Windsor's Ophelia.

* * *

With *Hamlet* duly installed in the repertoire rehearsals began almost at once for *A Midsummer Night's Dream* in which Victoria was to be playing Titania, Queen of the Fairies, and Noel St. John the mischievous Puck, a role for which he was well and winsomely suited. They still had no actual dialogue together, but the two characters were often scheduled to rehearse on the same day and Noel soon became worried. Victoria didn't glow as he felt she should–an actress basking for the first time in the spotlight of theatrical renown. Rather she looked worn and pale, even sick. Then, too, he'd heard ugly rumors and although he tried to attribute such stories to professional jealousy, he couldn't help wondering whether–just possibly–they were true.

Dylan was equally concerned about the gossip, but he was finding it enough of a strain just being Victoria's director. He'd watched her clash with Pliny Nicholas over the interpretation of Ophelia, but as an actor himself he had been confident they could work together. He soon discovered he was mistaken. Perhaps it was because Victoria had considered Titania to be a simple character–certainly nowhere nearly as challenging as Ophelia or Antigone--and yet now the role seemed beyond her grasp. Frustrated and alarmed, she refused to admit she even had a problem. Instead she battled Dylan furiously over every movement, every line reading and rehearsals of her first scene with her husband, King Oberon, resounded with the head-on collision of two artistic temperaments.

Titania's other major scene is one of marvelously antic comedy. Oberon, with the assistance of his loyal minion, Puck, has put a spell on her while she is sleeping. She will fall in love with the first thing she sees upon waking which is, of course, a local laborer named "Bottom" upon whom they have also placed the head of an "ass". It was immediately apparent as they began the initial run-through that Victoria's difficulties with the role were yet to be resolved, but Dylan had given the matter some thought and he was almost sure he'd found the answer. "Stop, please." Leaving his seat at the director's table, he came up on stage.

"What in hell is wrong <u>this</u> time?" Victoria demanded crossly.

He saw the look on her face and he knew that if he didn't choose his words carefully, this one was going to be pip! "You know," he began quietly, "I believe I've figured out what's been troubling you about this role."

"Oh, really?" Her hands were clenched into fists at her sides. "I wasn't aware anything was!"

Just as I suspected, Dylan thought. She's terrified of failing. Aloud, however, he made no reference to her remark. "Is this the first time you've played a non-human?"

"I....I suppose it is, actually."

"I thought so and it occurred to me that might be the source of your problem. I encountered the same thing myself, you see–playing Caliban in *The Tempest*." At once he observed her relax. Just learning he'd met with a similar difficulty had helped. "...and I discovered," he went on quickly, "that I had to forget my normal human perception of the world. It's exactly the same with Titania. She's not a mortal woman and you can't play her that way. And as for our friend here, it might also help if instead of an ass' head, you pictured the face of an attractive man you've known."

"Well, that shouldn't be difficult! I've never known a man who wasn't an ass!...with the exception of you, of course, luv," she continued sweetly after a barely perceptible pause. All tension had vanished, however, and her eyes sparkled. "And you will <u>have</u> to admit it <u>is</u> rather a challenge to look lovingly at that thing!"

"Perhaps for a less gifted actress, Victoria, but not for you." She looked at him for a second or two, obviously trying to decide whether he was teasing her, reprimanding her or complimenting her, but she should have known better. He was, after all, the consummate actor himself and neither his face nor his voice gave her the slightest hint. "So start the scene again, please, and this time try it the way I suggested."

"Oh, but I always listen to my director."

"So that's what you've been doing. You certainly had me fooled." His eyes met Victoria's and their glances locked for a moment in silent and not entirely humorless combat. "May I continue my rehearsal now, madame?" he asked at last.

"But of course, sir."

"Thank you so much." Dylan was still chuckling as he left the stage. It appeared, after all, that Pliny's primary difficulty in dealing with Victoria had not been his failure to avoid such confrontations, but his inability to enjoy them. Returning to his seat, he noticed that having exited the scene a few minutes before, Noel had as usual stayed to watch. The other man would undoubtedly enjoy a recounting of what had just taken place on stage and pausing at the table to pick up his script, Dylan moved over to join him. "You know, Victoria really does have the most marvelous sense of humor. Just now she told me that......"

"Does she seem especially tired to you today?"

Dylan glanced at him quickly. Could he possibly not have heard the rumors? "Oh...ah... no more so than usual," he replied in an offhand manner. "She's been working very hard."

There was a long, awkward pause during which both men tried to pretend they were watching the scene just commencing again on stage. "It's true, then, isn't it?" Noel inquired at last in a choked voice, "...what I've heard?"

"Victoria's personal life is her own business. Until it begins to affect her work as an actress, I don't feel I have the right to interfere."

"But you're more than just her director, man! I hoped you were also her friend."

"You're already so much closer to her than I am, Noel. If anyone could speak to her, it would be you."

"Oh, but you see, I can't. Victoria sets very definite boundaries to any relationship and I learned from Jon Sinclair what happens to anyone who dares cross those boundaries."

"May I ask exactly what crime he committed?"

"He suggested one day at lunch that perhaps she'd had enough to drink–so you can imagine what would happen if I advised her not to....to....ah...well, I don't have to say it, do I?"

The other man merely shook his head and with some relief they both now turned their attention in earnest to the stage.

* * *

Well before the opening of *Hamlet* Victoria had indeed resumed her pub crawling. She'd awaken each morning sickened by the memory of the degradation to which she'd submitted herself the night before and yet darkness would find her once again in search of a companion. It had been some time, however, since she'd been forced to resort to such measures and she was out of practice. Twice she'd had to duck out a side door to avoid arrest for solicitation and finally came an evening slightly less than a fortnight into rehearsals for *A Midsummer Night's Dream* when it appeared her efforts were to be in vain. She'd been in three different pubs and now as she entered the fourth, it was dangerously near closing time. If she failed to find someone here, a long, lonely night stretched ahead of her.

Almost at once she saw him. He was also alone, leaning on the counter down at the end of the bar, and although in a dimly lit pub appearances can be deceiving, he appeared attractive enough: tall and slim with sandy hair. She sat down three stools away from him–it didn't pay to appear too anxious–and ordered straight vodka. Only when she was with someone did she dilute her liquor. She smiled at him–shyly. He took his cue and moved over, slipping onto the stool next to hers. "What are you drinking?" he asked.

"Vodka–neat." But the relief Victoria had felt when she first saw him was already tinged with uneasiness. Perhaps it was his eyes. In the semi-darkness of the pub they appeared bottomless sockets–devoid of expression. Or it could have been his hands as they gripped his beer stein–the skin stretched over ugly, protruding knuckles. They looked like the hands of a skeleton.

"Quite a strong drink, isn't it, for a lady?" Even his voice bothered her–hushed, obscenely insinuating.

"Believe me, I can handle it." If only there were time to find someone else.

"And such a beautiful woman to be here alone." And now the bony hand slipped over hers. Something told Victoria to back away before it was too late, but at that same exact instant the bartender called–"Time". "Straight vodka again?" the man asked.

"Still think it's too strong a drink for a lady?" she murmured.

"For a lady perhaps, but not for you." After that neither of them spoke again, both understanding this was not a social occasion, but merely the unavoidable preliminaries. "Closing–five minutes" came the inevitable announcement. "I have a bottle in my flat if you're still thirsty," he suggested.

"I am always thirsty," Victoria replied.

As they left the pub together, he gripped her forearm, his fingers digging into her flesh. It was as though he wanted to make sure she couldn't get away and he was walking so rapidly she could barely keep up with him. Once she stumbled, but he jerked her back to her feet. She was beginning to wonder whether there was still any possibility of escape when all at once he drew her into a dimly lit entryway and up a narrow, winding flight of stairs. He did let her go long enough to unlock the door and afterwards how desperately she wished she'd taken that chance to run. But before she could move, he had the door open and taking hold of her arm again, he half-pushed her into the room. Heart pounding, she noticed he not only locked the door again, but also drew a second bolt as well as a chain across the opening. Next he moved over to a small bedside table to turn on a lamp. She relaxed slightly as she saw him pick up a bottle and two water glasses. "Sorry, it's gin, not vodka."

"Well, it's the effect that matters." She made a weak attempt at a laugh; for some reason she didn't want him to know she was afraid. He filled the glasses and she reached eagerly for one of them, taking a long swallow and then another without even a breath in between. The liquor cut into her throat causing her to choke. Stupid, she thought, I might have known he'd have something cheap.

"What's the matter? My stuff not good enough for you?" Until then his voice had never risen above the hushed tones he'd used in the pub, but now all at once it had a definite edge to it. "Anything should do for your kind. Here----" Snatching the glass away from her, he refilled it. "—drink some more!"

At last Victoria had to admit to herself that she'd made a potentially fatal mistake. There could be far worse experiences, after all, than spending a night alone. "No, thank you. I don't think so. It's...ah...getting late. I should be leaving."

"Oh no, you don't!" He grabbed her again and pushed her down into the chair. "You cheap little sluts are all the same-- drink a man's booze and then you don't want to pay the price." His voice grew soft again, but now he no longer tried to hide the threat it contained. "Well, believe me, this time you <u>are</u> <u>going</u> <u>to</u> <u>pay</u>! Now drink!"

He shoved the glass in her face, but she pushed it away. "No, I don't want any more!"

"Oh yes, you do! For what I'm planning on doing to you, you need to be good and drunk!" He was gradually moving around behind her all the time he was speaking and suddenly now–before she was aware what was happening--his arm snaked around her neck pinning her head back against him while with the other hand he forced the glass into her mouth. Most of the gin spilled down the front of Victoria's dress, but enough went down her throat to start her choking again. Her stomach cramped in terror and a cold sweat broke out all over her body. She began to struggle in earnest.

"No, no, little whore. You see–God has chosen me as the instrument of His punishment!" Again and again he forced the liquor down her throat, but drunk as she was by now, her instinct for self-preservation remained. She managed to stand up, but she'd gotten only a few steps away from him when he grabbed her again and spinning her around, he slapped her full across the face with the back of his hand. The force of the blow sent her staggering across the room, half-falling against the edge of a table.

Desperately she tried to get to her feet, but in the next instant he seized her again, this time with both hands, and threw her toward the bed. She landed instead on the floor, striking the back of her head just hard enough to dull her senses, but–horribly–not enough to make her oblivious to what happened next as kneeling over her, he began to hit her. The blows fell indiscriminately on her face and body until mercifully she slipped toward unconsciousness, but not before he'd torn off her clothes and raped her.

When Victoria regained consciousness, it was just starting to grow light. Her first awareness was the sensation that she was resting on something extremely hard, something that no matter how far out she felt on either side of her apparently had no edge to it. It was a full minute before it came to her that she was lying on the floor and almost immediately afterwards that she was shivering with cold. Fumbling about herself, she discovered her clothing was in tatters and it was only then she fully recalled the hideous events of the previous night.

At once her heart contracted in renewed terror. Could the man still be there, waiting for her to wake up, waiting to begin all over again? Fearfully she raised her head. The effort sent a sharp pain shooting through her chest and back and up into her head, but it was a small room and she could see she was alone. With a sigh of relief she sank back down on the floor. Oh God, but this...this was his flat and sooner or later he would return. She had to get out of there–no matter how much it hurt and she forced herself first to sit up and then by holding onto a chair, to drag herself to her feet. There was the same stabbing pain in her chest each time she drew a breath, but she managed by clinging to the furniture and leaning against the walls to move toward the door.

In her relief at finding it unlocked it was only by the merest chance that she noticed a note, crudely printed in pencil, on a near-by table. "Soliciting is a crime, filthy whore. If you know what's good for you, you will tell no one. This is for services rendered." Beside the note was a half-crown engraved with the head of the late King George VI. Helplessly Victoria began to laugh. After all it really was too funny. She had been beaten and raped and in return she'd been a given a half-crown bearing the likeness of Uncle Bertie.

Dear God, what would he think of her, that good, kind man? Sobs mingled with laughter as grasping the bannister with both hands, she inched her way along the landing and down the stairs, one step at a time. "Oh, Uncle Bertie," she mumbled brokenly, "I'm.... I'm glad you didn't live to....to...." The sobs were great racking noises now and each one sent another pain shooting through her. She prayed she wouldn't pass out. In the doorway she stopped for a moment to gather her strength, but she didn't dare wait too long. Glancing up at the huge, old-fashioned clock hanging outside a tea room across the street, she saw it was not quite 5 a.m. Thank God, it was still early. There wouldn't be many people on the streets at this hour and she knew she must look hideous.

Afterwards she was unable to recall how she'd gotten back to her own flat, but she must have managed somehow because the next thing she knew she was coming to again, sprawled face down on her own bed–still dressed only in the remnants of her clothing. She didn't remember getting sick either, but the room stank of vomit. Waves of nausea rose up in her and she lay for a while unmoving–until all at once a horrible thought occurred to her. Would the beating leave her scarred? Was her beauty destroyed? Even the simple act of turning over onto her back was agony, but the possibility of permanent disfigurement was far more terrible. She probed gingerly with her fingertips and it was just as she'd feared; she couldn't find a spot which wasn't sore and swollen. I...I have to see myself, she thought desperately. Gritting her teeth against the pain in her chest, she pushed herself up to a sitting position. Her head was throbbing, but she held on to the headboard and pulled herself to her feet. She managed to cross to the sink and gripping the edge of it with both hands, she raised her head to look at herself in the mirror.

No! No! It wasn't possible! This ugly, distorted thing which looked back at her couldn't be Victoria Windsor, fabled already for her beauty. This was some hideous, perverted creature–so utterly repulsive indeed that for a moment she couldn't bear to look and she turned her head away. But Victoria hadn't reached this point in her life by being weak and willing all her courage, she turned back forcing herself to cold-bloodedly assess the damage. Her face appeared more than twice its normal size. Her left eye was almost closed and her lips stood out grotesquely–almost apelike–so puffed up that only the right hand corner of her mouth could open. Bruises mottled her usually pale skin and blood still oozed from a long, jagged gash which ran along the right side of her jaw from just below her ear nearly to her chin. "Oh, God," she mumbled, "how could I have been so stupid? I knew he was acting strange. It's...it's just that I'm so lonely and I....I...." Unable to decide what to do or where to go, Victoria sank to the floor, too miserable, too despairing to do anything but crouch there her arms wrapped around herself, whimpering.

* * *

Victoria had been due at rehearsal at ten o'clock. Punctuality wasn't one of her more noteworthy virtues, but by the time Noel reported at eleven Dylan was becoming concerned. "Victoria still doesn't have a telephone, does she?" he inquired at once.

"No, she hasn't." He laughed. "I mentioned it to her, but she said there wasn't anyone she particularly cared to talk to and if the Royal Shakespeare Company wanted her to have one, they could bloody well pay for it!" But there had been something in the other man's tone. "Is something wrong, Dylan?"

"I don't know, but she's not here yet. I could start with a different scene if you'll go on over and check on her."

"Yes, yes, of course, say no more." Noel was already halfway up the aisle of the theatre as he spoke. Yet when he actually stood outside her flat a short while later, it was difficult to bring himself to knock. What if she wasn't there? Worse–what if she <u>were</u> and...and.... But at last he rapped on the closed door. There was no answer and now he didn't hesitate, but knocked again more loudly, calling her name.

At the first sound outside her door Victoria's cries had instantly ceased. No one must be allowed to witness her humiliation. Then she heard Noel's voice. Oh, dear God, she thought, anyone but him. One look at those basset hound eyes and I'll fall apart. Then why did she cough a little, shifting her position on the floor if not to give herself away to him?

"I know you're there, Victoria. Now please let me in!"

Maybe, after all, it <u>would</u> be better to speak to him, she reasoned. Just to tell him I'm all right and convince him to go away. She knew very well, of course, that once he was sure she was inside, he would refuse to leave. "Noel, please go away. I'm.....I'm just not feeling well. I...I'll be all right, really I will."

"It's more than that! I know it is! And what's wrong with your voice?"

"My voice?" Could her garbled speech be due to more than just her swollen lips? Could her vocal cords actually have been damaged? Panic rose in her throat and she began to sob aloud. "Noel, please, <u>please</u> go away! Please!"

"I <u>will</u> <u>not</u>! Now either you open this door this instant or I...I...swear, I'm going to break it down!" Even in her extreme anguish the mental picture of chubby Noel ineffectually attempting to batter down her door was irresistible and now she was laughing and crying at the same time. "I mean it, Victoria! I will. I'll.....I'll....."

"Huff and puff and blow the door down?"

Briefly this stopped him. She couldn't possibly have said what he thought she said. And when he spoke again, his voice was once again quiet. "Please, Victoria. Let me in. You need help." He should have known better, he realized at once, than to use the word, "need".

"I don't <u>need</u> anyone!" she screamed. "Now get the bloody hell away from that door!"

"Very well, Victoria. I'll have no choice then, but to go downstairs and bring the landlady up here with her pass key. So which is it going to be?"

He waited silently for a few seconds longer and at last she gave in. "Don't, Noel, please. Wait a minute. I...I'm coming."

There was another slight pause and then finally he heard her moving slowly across the room. The door opened just wide enough to allow him to enter. She had stepped back behind the door as she opened it and it wasn't until she'd closed it again and turned around that Noel saw her face. His eyes widened in horrified disbelief. "Oh, my God, Victoria! What happened?"

"I might have known you'd come up with an original remark like that!" She looked abruptly away. She wasn't trying to hide her face from him; he'd already seen that. But she couldn't stand to see the pity on his. "Would you believe I was hit by a bus?"

"If that's what you want me to believe."

His voice was so gentle and now all her bravado was gone. "Oh, Noel!" She started to cry all over again, reaching out for him as a blind person might. For a moment he hesitated, unsure what to do, and in that same instant Victoria bent double in sudden agony and collapsed. Noel caught her just before she hit the floor and kneeling beside her, he supported her in his arms. "Oh, God," she moaned, "it hurts everywhere!....Oh God, Noel, he hit me...again and again! He wouldn't stop! And then he....then he.......... Oh God, he....he...." But she could go no further; she could only cling to her comforter and sob.

"Hush, Victoria, hush. It's all right now. It's all right," he whispered over and over again. He knew such words were meaningless, but the hideousness of it all so overwhelmed him that he could think of nothing else to say. Finally he gave up trying to talk at all and instead he simply held her as one would a hurt child. After what seemed like forever, but was really only a matter of fifteen minutes or so, her sobs abated and yet still Noel cradled her against him. He knew he should do something. Oh, but whenever again would he have the chance to hold her like this? "We....we have to get you some help," he said at last. "Do you want me to bring the police?"

"No, Noel...no police!" She sat up, pushing herself away from him.

"But you said someone attacked you!"

"Noel...Noel, dear, I.....I picked him up in a pub." She sounded terribly weary. "Now, please—I just want to be alone." Reaching over to grasp the edge of a near-by table, she attempted to pull herself to her feet, but the pain went through her like a knife and gasping, she sank to the floor again.

"At least let me get a doctor then."

"I don't want anyone, dammit! Now get the hell out of here!"

"But Victoria, I think some of your ribs are broken. You could puncture a lung. I'll....I'll get Dylan. He'll be able to keep it quiet. No one else need know. All right, Victoria?" For a while she made no reply and Noel's heart almost broke, watching her crouched there on the floor obviously in pain yet too proud to admit she needed help. "Victoria?"

"All....all right, Noel. All....right."

"Let me help you into a chair before I go. I don't want to leave you here on the floor." Again she hesitated for a moment, but at last she nodded reaching out wordlessly to accept his assistance. Gingerly he slipped one arm around her waist, helping her first to stand and then to walk the few steps to an armchair. More than once he felt her wince in pain, but she made no further outcry except for a sigh of relief as he lowered her into the chair. Next he went over to the bed to get a blanket, tucking it gently around her. "Will you be all right for a while now–while I go for Dylan?" Once more she merely nodded in silent assent and Noel left at once, afraid that if he waited any longer, she might change her mind and refuse to let him help her.

He had only gotten about halfway back to the theatre when he saw Dylan hurrying toward him. "God, where have you been?" The other man began shouting to him when they were still some distance apart. "I couldn't stand it any longer. Is she all right?" There was no possible way Noel could answer such questions when the two of them were still nearly half a block apart on a Stratford street filled on this summer morning with tourists. But as they drew closer, Dylan could see at once that the news wasn't good. "What is it, man?" he exploded when they were finally face to face. "Tell me!"

"You have to swear this will go no further."

"Of course! Don't be absurd!" In his anxiety he seized his friend by both shoulders and shook him. "Now tell me!" Noel took a deep breath and in as few words as possible filled him in on what had happened to Victoria–her unwillingness to involve the police–her need for a doctor."Yes, of course." Dylan wiped the back of his hand across his eyes. "There's a man whose discretion I know we can rely on. I'll fetch him."

The two men's glances locked briefly before they parted–both too preoccupied for formal leave-taking. Noel hurried back to Victoria's flat only to discover to his dismay that she'd relocked the door and no amount of pleading on his part could convince her to open it again. "Well...ah....I'll be going, then," he said finally. "Ah....take care of yourself," he added lamely as with a sigh he turned from her door to make his way down the stairs. He felt a profound sadness due to far more than merely the previous night's tragic event.

* * *

The doctor reassured Victoria there would be no noticeable scars. Even the jagged gash on her face, although it had required more than thirty stitches to close it, so closely followed the line of her jaw that it, too, would eventually be all but invisible. But studying her face for hours on end in the mirror, it seemed impossible she would ever look normal again. One thing above all about which she was certain. No one else must see her like this. Dylan and Noel told the others she'd been in a minor automobile accident– nothing serious, a few cracked ribs–but she was badly bruised and didn't wish to see anyone-- a useless admonition; no one cared to visit her. What the two men did not add was that the ban on callers included both of them as well.

And what was life like for Victoria–living in this self-imposed exile? To begin with there was only the blessed numbness, the body's natural anesthesia. Inevitably, however, the shock wore off and as her body came back to life, these days were succeeded by those of a physical agony worse even than she'd suffered in the immediate hours following the attack. At last, even as the numbness had receded, the pain abated as well, but at the same time Victoria made a terrible discovery. She had only begun to suffer. Her body might have started to mend; the healing of her mind and spirit would take considerably longer. Perhaps if she'd returned to work sooner, but instead she remained alone dwelling on her shame until at some point it came to extend beyond the actual beating and rape to the hours and days immediately following and to the people who had seen her like that–weak and humiliated–to the doctor, to Dylan, but oh, most especially to Noel. More and more the events of that terrible night became warped and distorted in her mind until finally he seemed more guilty of what had happened to her even than the man who had assaulted her.

* * *

On the morning Victoria was due to return to work, Dylan arrived at the theatre to find Noel already there filling the industrial sized percolator. It was jokingly remarked-- and indeed by many devoutly believed--that without coffee rehearsals might have proved impossible. "Doing your good deed, I see," Dylan observed lightly. The other man jumped and loose coffee spilled onto the table top and over the edge onto the floor. "Rather on edge, what?"

"Coffee?" Silently Noel cleaned up the mess and went back to his work.

Realizing of course that his observation had been deliberately passed over, Dylan said nothing further until the coffee was made and they were both seated in canvas chairs behind the director's table. Glancing over, he saw that Noel was hunched over his mug, holding it against himself as if to protect it from some unseen evil, and he thought he'd never seen anyone look so thoroughly miserable. "Just act natural," Dylan advised finally. "As if nothing's happened. Be casual."

"Casual, ha!" Noel exclaimed bitterly. "You didn't hear her voice the couple of times I tried to see her. She hates me! It's that simple!"

"Hates you? Oh, I can't believe that. You were so kind to her...when it happened."

"That's just it, you see. I...I was <u>with</u> her that morning. God, I'll never forget it!"

"But I went there, too, with the doctor. Does that mean she hates me as well?"

"Was she fairly in control by the time you got there?"

"I suppose so. But then I've never seen her when she wasn't."

"Well, I have. You remember what happened to Jon? Well, believe me, what I did was far, <u>far</u> worse."

"I'm afraid I don't follow you, old man. You didn't try to tell her what to do. You were simply there when she needed someone."

"Yes, and for that she'll never forgive me. I...I've lost her...whatever that means." He blinked back the tears. "I...I don't suppose I...I ever really had her, did I?"

Dylan placed a reassuring hand on his arm. "More important, my friend, if indeed that <u>were</u> the case, <u>she</u> would lose <u>you</u>." Noel impatiently shook off this attempt at comfort and leaving his untouched coffee on the table, he fled the auditorium to get control of himself before rehearsal began. He had made his exit just in time as shortly afterwards the cast began to gather. Gradually everyone had appeared with the exception of Victoria and Dylan decided to begin the day's work with Oberon and Puck. It would be better for Noel if he kept his mind occupied and perhaps by the time of her entrance, their Titania would be here.

It was strange, Victoria thought, as she walked the few blocks from her flat to the theatre. She'd longed for this moment of release yet now that the day was here, she was terribly nervous. Determined to allow no one to detect her uneasiness, she had selected her dress for that morning with particular care. The material was silk–draped in elaborate folds around a plunging neckline; the color was scarlet. It was the most flamboyant outfit she owned at the time and totally unsuitable for rehearsal, but it would create the desired effect of supreme self-assurance and that was what mattered. Her make-up as well was heavier than usual–not only the base necessary to cover up the scar along her jaw, but also the rouge, eye shadow and liner. Entering the auditorium from the rear, Victoria hesitated briefly before proceeding on down the aisle. The scene with Oberon and Puck was still in progress. It was the first time she'd seen Noel since that horrible morning and if she could have gotten to him at that moment, she would have gone for his face with her nails.

As the scene concluded, Dylan glanced around from his seat at the director's table and seeing her, rose at once to walk back and meet her. "Victoria, my dear, how...." He had nearly asked how she was, but just in time he remembered....... "how exquisite you look!" He raised her hand to his lips in a gesture of homage he knew she enjoyed. "And how terribly we've all missed you!" Her hand was ice cold, but he made no reference to the fact.

Victoria for her part had tensed as Dylan started to speak, dreading his expressions of concern. Instead his remarks had been quite charming and just then she very much needed to hear someone praise her beauty. "Aren't you the luv!" Her other hand came up to touch him on the cheek–an equally theatrical gesture.

"You're just in time," he went on smoothly as slipping the hand he was still holding through his arm, he turned to escort her up onto the stage. "We are ready for our Titania." With another rush of gratitude Victoria observed how he'd arranged for her to step directly into character, thus allowing no one the opportunity to talk to her. She'd spent many of the long hours of convalescence working on the role and her effort showed. Her Titania was at one and the same time charmingly fey and stunningly regal–everything one would expect of the Queen of the Fairies. Dylan and Noel watched the scene together and the instant it was over, Dylan was on his feet taking the steps up to the stage almost at one leap. "Bravo, Victoria!" he enthused and this time he raised both her hands to his lips. "Precisely what I wanted! I can see you haven't been idle!"

After a moment Noel came up on stage to join them. It was better, after all, to know the worst. "Beautiful performance, Victoria," he said as he came up to them.

She stared into his face for a beat and then turned her back on him. "Oh, come now, Dylan, you old flatterer, you must have something to say. We still have three weeks of rehearsal and I'm sure I can improve."

"Truthfully I don't see how, but I would like to do the scene with Bottom now."

"Yes, of course." Flashing him a smile, she moved off toward the center of the stage.

"Victoria, may I speak to you?" Noel inquired, but she did not so much as slow her pace. "Believe me," he persisted desperately, "I would much prefer you told me now how you feel rather than...."

Finally then she stopped, turning back to face him, and for a second he thought she was going to reply. Instead she looked directly over his left shoulder at Dylan. "May we get started now?" she asked sweetly. "I really feel this scene requires some work." And pivoting about on one spiked heel, she strode on across the stage to take her place.

Noel simply stood there watching her and after a moment Dylan came over to him, placing a sympathetic arm around his shoulder. "Just give her a little time."

"I don't know. Perhaps if I went away–worked somewhere else for a while."

"Give up your place in the company? Don't be a fool! Even Victoria's not worth such a sacrifice."

"I'm sorry. I just can't bear to have her look straight through me day after day as though I weren't even there."

Less than a week later, then, Victoria arrived at rehearsal to discover that a different actor had taken over the role of Puck. What could have happened to Noel, she wondered. Her initial impulse was to ask someone, perhaps Dylan, but at the moment he was one of the group around the coffee table. Besides if she inquired about Noel, people might think she actually cared enough to miss him. Her uncertainty must have been evident, however, because as soon as Dylan turned around and saw her standing there, he left the others and came over to her. "Looking for someone, Victoria?"

"And whom exactly would I be looking for, just as an example?"

"Well.....ah.....Noel, for instance."

The strangest look passed over Victoria's face. Invariably she was shocked when someone penetrated the facade she thought was perfect. "Oh....ah....isn't he here? I hadn't noticed."

How could she act so bloody innocent about the whole thing? For one of the few times in all the years they were to know each other Dylan was angry with her. "I don't see how you could help but notice since you're the one who drove him away!"

"And just what do you mean by that remark?"

"You know damn well what I mean. Noel had the almighty nerve to care about you and so you had to punish him!"

"You can go to hell, you bloody Welsh sod!" Turning, she started to walk away from him.

"That's right, Victoria. Keep trying to hide any real feelings you might have. Only it doesn't quite work." His tone was deceptively soft, but it's been said that Dylan Mallory can reach the last row of the top gallery with a whisper and although Victoria was over half the depth of the stage away from him, she heard every word.

* * *

When *A Midsummer Night's Dream* opened in late August, the critics were for the first time waiting for Victoria Windsor and as was rarely the case, they were in total accord, each trying to outdo the other in superlatives. They called her "ethereal," "charming," and "winsome". They spoke of her "awesome stage presence," her "command of the Shakespearean language," "her bell-like voice". At last, as she'd once vowed, her name did indeed mean something in the British theatre.

These reviews would prove to be much more than mere ego enhancers, however, of which at any rate she had no need. Because of them, two people out of the past would reenter her life, one for the moment at least only briefly and from the other side of the footlights; the other more closely and permanently, being as well the instrument which would move her once and for all into the spotlight of national attention.

Victoria had for some time now felt a growing fascination, almost an obsession, with her own face: the perfectly shaped eyebrows, the luminous green eyes themselves, the delicate bow-shaped lips–every feature often drew her into an intense study of herself bordering on the narcissistic. Moreover, there was now the added dimension of relief that the savage beating she'd received had indeed done no lasting damage. Pausing now in the application of her make-up for the Saturday matinee, she concentrated her attention on the scar running along her jawline. Already beginning to fade, it only gave her beauty an added air of tragic mystery. She was running the tip of a forefinger slowly back and forth along that scar–the effect was quite hypnotic–when a knock on her dressing room door brought her sharply back to reality. "Who is it?" she demanded. As always, she hid confusion with a show of anger.

"Pliny Nicholas, dear lady. I must apologize for disturbing you, but this can't wait, I'm afraid."

"Oh, very well. Come in!" But her tone indicated plainly that he'd better be brief.

"Ah, my dear Victoria–exquisite as always!" Gliding unctuously over to her dressing table, Pliny raised one of her hands to his lips.

His hand was inevitably warm and moist with perspiration and she found it revolting. "Don't be an ass!" she hissed, pulling her hand away. "What is it?"

Pliny hesitated, knowing only too well the probable result of his errand. He felt obligated, nevertheless, to go through the motions since the writer of the letter was an Anglican nun–a Sister Marion who said she'd been Victoria Windsor's first drama coach. Victoria Windsor–a pupil in a convent school! The thought boggled the mind! "A student group's here for the matinee," he said tersely. After all the sooner he got it over with, the sooner he could get out of there. "They'd like to speak with you for a few minutes–after the performance, of course."

"You know I see no one!"

"I thought that since they were students, you might….."

"That doesn't make a damned bit of difference."

"But these are……" Here Pliny paused again; undoubtedly it still wouldn't make a 'damned bit of difference' "….from your old school–Heathfield. I gather you were rather close to one of their chaperones: a Sister Philippa."

"I don't remember her!" What an odd mixture of emotions that name had prompted in Victoria. Affection fought with anger, both in turn drowning in a paralyzing panic. "But even if I did, I do not, as I've just reminded you, see anyone!" She turned abruptly back to the mirror, picking up a jar of creme rouge to continue applying her make-up.

"What should I tell them, Victoria?" Pliny inched toward the door. It was better when dealing with this particular lady to be near an exit.

"You can bloody well tell them whatever you bloody well please. Now get the hell out of here!" She hurled the rouge jar,

"Yes, Your Highness." Ducking the missile, he beat a hasty retreat. Very well, he thought bitterly, he would tell the good sisters the plain truth–in well-laundered language, of course–that Miss Windsor refused to see them. But why the hell should he bother? He'd send an usher to do the dirty work.

The poor young man–not far removed from prep school himself–felt he had to say something further to the sisters and he stammered on for a few painful sentences–about a previous commitment, how sorry Miss Windsor was not to be able to see them. Marion didn't believe him for a minute, but at the same time she found that in spite of herself she was disappointed. She'd half-hoped Victoria would see them if only to brag about her success. It would have been an unforgettable experience for the girls and then of course, there was Philippa–Philippa who at that precise moment was wistfully regarding the colored picture of Titania in the souvenir program. It's odd, Philippa was thinking, but I'd have recognized her anywhere--even after all these years. Maybe it's the eyes. How often, she recalled sadly, did I see those same eyes screaming defiance at me while all the time I knew how terribly she needed me.

Just then, however, the house lights blinked, signaling that the performance was about to begin and Marion and Philippa had no chance to talk until the first interval. Even then they had to wait until things had quieted down, the girls chattering together as they filed out of the auditorium, heading for the loo or the refreshment stand or the souvenir counter where, even though they couldn't meet Victoria Windsor in person, they could use a few precious shillings of their weekly allowance to purchase a picture of her or a poster of the company with her name in it. At last the auditorium was nearly two-thirds empty, the few remaining Heathfield girls absorbed in reading their programs. "Well," Sister Philippa remarked brightly, "what do you think of your protegee?"

"Yes, it would seem I'm quite a good judge of talent." Marion looked pleased with herself.

"I guess that was always the difference, Sister. You only saw the actress while I saw the girl. I hope she's happy."

"A member of the Royal Shakespeare Company? Don't be ridiculous!"

"I think it might require more than that," Philippa observed quietly.

"Why don't you go backstage by yourself after the performance?" Marion didn't know why she was even making the suggestion. "She might see you if you were alone."

"Oh, I rather doubt it." She shook her head. "I'm sure she wants no reminder of her days at Heathfield...or of me, either, I'm afraid. You know, when....when Vicki ran away–that....that was the one time I seriously questioned my calling. I felt I'd failed her."

"Oh now, Philippa, be sensible! No one could have done more......"

Neither of them had any way of knowing, of course, that all during this discussion they were being watched. As soon as the house lights came up for the interval, Victoria had hurried to a spot just behind the proscenium arch where she knew she could observe one complete side of the auditorium without being seen in return. Eagerly she pulled the teaser in front of the main curtain back to peer through the opening. The Heathfield girls were instantly identifiable--dressed in the exact same uniform she'd hated with a passion. Many of them were already heading up the aisle toward the lobby–she wondered how many were going outside to sneak a cigarette–and following the navy and white queue back to its point of origin, she easily located the two chaperones.

Sister Marion was there, of course, who'd been the first to recognize her potential as an actress, but her gaze passed rapidly over her former mentor coming to settle with a genuine hunger on Sister Philippa. I...I never thought I'd be so glad to see her again. "Dear, dear Sister Philippa, you were always so kind to me." Although she was unaware of it, she was speaking aloud now as if the person to whom her words were addressed might somehow be able to hear her. "No matter what I said or did, you never....you never..." All the gratitude and affection she'd refused to feel for the nun during her years at Heathfield flooded over her and tears welled up in her eyes. She looks so sad, Victoria's thoughts went on a moment later, again unspoken. I suppose it's because I wouldn't see her. Maybe I should--just for a few minutes. It's the least I can do.

She came within a breath of calling a stagehand over to take a message out to Sister Philippa when someone tapped her on the shoulder. Startled, she spun about to discover Pliny Nicholas standing there grinning in evident amusement. As Victoria turned to face him, however, it was Pliny's turn to be surprised–by the tenderness of her expression, by her eyes brimming with tears. "You could still send someone to tell them to come backstage, you know. It's not too late."

"Oh, but it is. Much too late!" She pushed her way past him and the moment was lost–perhaps forever.

* * *

Sir Terence Cartier had never forgotten the brilliant student actress he'd directed at RADA, but it had been a long and difficult convalescence following his near-fatal heart attack and it was over a year before he was able to return to work. By then Victoria had virtually disappeared and it wasn't until the fall of 1963 that he rediscovered her.

He'd just recently returned to London after a year of performing the title role in Anouilh's *Becket* on Broadway to find everyone talking about the new young actress playing Ophelia to Mallory's Hamlet. Then had come the opening of *A Midsummer Night's Dream* and reading the review, he thought immediately of his commitment to do *King Lear* as well as Shaw's *Caesar and Cleopatra* with the Royal Shakespeare's London company. Terry wondered why he hadn't thought of her at once and within moments he was on the phone to Stratford. "Pliny, old friend, do you suppose you might grant me a favor?"

"Anything for you, Terry, my dear, dear boy! You know that!" At the sound of the unmistakable voice he'd experienced the inevitable wave of resentment, softened little by the great man's brush with death. Others might marvel at his unfailing graciousness; to Pliny it always smelled faintly of noblesse oblige. On his end of the wire Terry suppressed a chuckle. He'd never taken his associate's fawning seriously. In fact he'd remarked to Dylan Mallory that undoubtedly Pliny had been secretly disappointed when he didn't die.

""Probably true, " Dylan had agreed. "I'm sure he'd have found a dead legend much easier to deal with."

"Actually, Pliny," Sir Terence continued now, managing to keep his voice businesslike, "I'd like to spring a young actress from your company to work with me here in London–Victoria Windsor to be exact."

"Say no more, Terry–she's yours! When do you want her?"

Something in the tone of his voice–even more servile than normally–struck Terry as odd. "You sound eager to be rid of her, Pliny. Her reviews were raves–though they only helped me to locate her. I remember her as a student at RADA. Even then she was brilliant."

"Granted, Terry, old chap," Pliny hedged. Leave it to Victoria to be a protegee of Sir Terence Cartier. I wonder how she managed that, he thought suspiciously. "Far be it from me to question the great Sir Terence as a judge of talent, but she is....ah...shall we say ...ah..... difficult to work with."

"Ah yes...even when I knew her, there was the ego. But....ah....not to worry, Pliny. I think I can handle her." To the other man's immense irritation Terry's amusement was now clearly audible. "Don't say anything to her. I'm going to be coming up there. There are some other people I'd like to see as well."

Sir Terence arrived a few days later, slipping unobtrusively into the rear of the auditorium after the performance of *Hamlet* had already commenced. He didn't want Victoria's portrayal affected one way or the other by the knowledge that he was in the audience. He was not to be disappointed. Obviously she had never forgotten his words: the responsibility inherent in her gift to give nothing less than her best. Sitting in the darkened auditorium, he smiled to himself; never had he been so proud!

When the final curtain had come down, he hurried backstage, oblivious to the excitement occasioned by his mere passage through the hallway, to knock at the door of her dressing room. "Whoever it is," she snapped, "get the bloody hell away from that door! I'm absolutely exhausted!"

He heard a harshness in her voice which hadn't been there six years before and it saddened him. "Victoria," he said after a brief pause, "it's Terence Cartier."

There were a few seconds of silence and then the door opened. Victoria posed prettily in the opening, her hand still on the knob. "Ah...obviously I didn't know who it was," she laughed, tossing her hair back from her face and managing to look embarrassed. "Won't you come in, Sir Terence." Backing up to open the door fully, she gestured gracefully for him to enter.

"I understand what it means, Victoria, to be tired after a performance, but I'd hoped we might go somewhere and talk."

"Please excuse me, Sir Terence," she murmured, "I'm never too tired for you." She smiled up at him, hoping that by employing all her charm she could make him forget her original rudeness. Little did she comprehend that he understood that rudeness and had already forgiven her. "If you don't mind waiting for a few minutes...please sit down." Victoria turned away back to her dressing table where she'd just begun to apply her street make-up when the knock came at the door.

Terry watched in silence as she painstakingly employed eye shadow and liner, mascara rouge and lipstick–sitting back after each stage in the procedure to study the results. "I seem to remember a cliche about 'gilding the lily'," he observed finally.

She glanced up at his reflection behind her in the mirror. "I'll only be a little while longer," she replied coolly and she made no reference to his charmingly phrased compliment.

"Ready at last," she announced a few moments later as she stood up from the dressing table. "My wrap is right there, thrown over the screen." Victoria indicated the shawl with a theatrical wave of one hand. She watched as he went to get it, standing unmoving as he draped it over her shoulders. "You're very patient with a lady." Turning her head just slightly, she glanced up at him, her eyes containing just a hint of flirtation.

"When an old gentleman is promised the company of a young lady as lovely as you, it's easy to be patient." Opening the door of the dressing room, he offered her his arm and they left the theatre together. Many of the cast, still lingering backstage, glanced at them curiously as they passed, but nothing better indicated the stature Victoria had already achieved than the fact that no one saw anything unusual in the person of her escort. A short time later they were settled in a booth in the bar of the Red Horse Hotel. "I thought perhaps a bottle of champagne to celebrate," Sir Terence suggested as he signaled a waiter over to the table and ordered.

Victoria was disappointed. Her usual choice was something a great deal stronger. In addition Sir Terence's presence meant she would have no chance to find a companion for the night. Sadly she'd known even in the days and weeks immediately following her brutal attack that once she recovered, her loneliness would drive her back to the pubs–despite the fact that there was nothing to prevent the same thing from happening all over again. Outwardly, of course, she gave no indication of any of this. "What are we celebrating?" she inquired instead as she removed a cigarette from her case and held it for Sir Terence to light for her, once more bestowing her most charming smile on him.

"Perhaps the reunion of old friends," he replied, picking up the matches from the table and returning her smile although his radiated genuine affection. Victoria acknowledged his observation with a nod of her head, but made no response. "Or perhaps your coming to work with me in the London company," he continued, his smile broadening.

She stared at him–at a loss for words. When he first appeared backstage, she'd assumed that his reason for coming <u>was</u> professional; so low an opinion did Victoria have of herself, in fact, that it would never have occurred to her that he simply wanted to see her again. But now when he announced his intentions so quickly and candidly-- when her long ago dreams were about to come true–for a few minutes she could think of nothing to say.

"Well," Sir Terence chuckled, "in future years I shall be delighted to tell everyone of the one time I saw Victoria Windsor speechless."

"Am I really that good, Terry? Am I?" She reached across the table to take his hand, grasping it with such fervor that her nails dug into him.

He looked back at her with an equal intensity, noting only in passing with a wry amusement how easily she'd slipped into the use of his familiar nickname while others waited breathlessly, hoping for his permission. "You don't really need an answer to that question, Victoria, I'm sure."

"Well, then!" Sitting back on the bench, she seemed to relax although Terry would soon learn she never relaxed entirely. "When am I to come to London and what are we doing together?" How good it felt to refer to Sir Terence Cartier and herself as "we".

Just then, however, they were interrupted by the arrival of the champagne and not until he'd approved the wine and the waiter had poured two glasses and withdrawn did Sir Terence continue. "Then I can presume you're interested?"

"Interested?!" Victoria tossed her head and drank deeply of her champagne. "And I presume you're joking!"

"You're right. I am." He smiled. "As soon as possible–to answer your first question–within the month at least–and to answer the second, I want you to do Shaw's *Caesar and Cleopatra* with me as well as Cordelia to my Lear."

"How bloody marvelous!"

"I'm glad you're pleased with the selections. Someday you will no doubt be able to choose your own roles, but for now I think you'll find these rewarding." Victoria said nothing, merely extending her glass to him for a refill.

"But tell me about yourself," he went on as he picked up the bottle to pour her some more champagne. "What's been happening to you since I saw you last?"

Holding the goblet in one hand, she ran the tip of the other forefinger slowly around and around the rim, studying the motion as though it required the utmost in concentration. When she finally looked up at him again, he wondered why he hadn't seen at once how tired she looked. He supposed he'd been so caught up in the excitement of finding her again, of discovering the thoroughly accomplished actress she'd become–fulfilling all his expectations of her–that he had simply failed to notice. "If you don't mind, Terry," she said finally, " I would prefer that our relationship remain purely a professional one."

Once he'd assumed that her rejection of his friendship had been because he was so much older, but now he saw her rebuff went much deeper. Well, I won't push it, he thought, at least for the present. "As you wish of course, Victoria," he replied aloud. "I'm sure our professional association will prove a most rewarding one indeed."

Chapter 7

People would remember, even years later, how Victoria Windsor's presence burst upon the world of the London theatre in a blaze rarely equaled, her debut all but eclipsing even the return of Sir Terence Cartier. It is a tribute to the magnanimity of the man that far from resenting her usurpation of the spotlight, he gloried in her triumph. It all began with the December 1963 opening of *Caesar and Cleopatra* as the audience simply refused to leave at the end of the performance.. Curtain call followed upon curtain call, first for the whole company and at last for Sir Terence and Victoria alone.

How charmingly she acknowledges the acclaim of an audience, Sir Terence thought as he held her hand, bowing in time with each of her sweeping curtseys. Yet he couldn't help noticing as well her odd demeanor each time the curtain descended, at once removing her hand from his as if she found even the intimacy of a handclasp disturbing. She appeared, moreover, to find no joy in her achievement. Instead she stood silent and unmoving, waiting for the curtain to rise once more–expecting it to rise–and then as it did, she would place her hand in his, turn on the radiant smile and prepare to bow again. Even when the curtain had come down for the last time, she remained there as if willing it to go up just once more."There'll be more applause the next time, Victoria," Terry observed in mild jest, taking hold of her arm just above the elbow as if to escort her offstage.

She pulled away from him. "Please don't!" As she came off into the wings, other cast members offered their congratulations, but her only response was a brief nod. She did not so much as pause in her flight until she had achieved the sanctuary of her dressing room. Almost immediately, however, a knock came at the door. "Who is it?" she demanded curtly.

"Clive Bannister."

During rehearsals Victoria had often noticed the tall, angularly handsome actor eyeing her in a speculative fashion–one obvious objective in mind. He was attractive enough–aquiline nose, pale hazel eyes and jet black hair–and it would be a relief to have a regular lover again especially now that a degree of fame was making her nightly pub crawls difficult. "Yes, of course, Clive." And now her voice was warm and inviting. "Come in, luv." As he entered, the telephone rang and giving him an adorable little pout of apology, she reached to answer it. "Yes?" She appeared annoyed, her perfectly manicured nails tapping a furious staccato on the glass top of the dressing table.

Damn, Clive thought. The last thing I need is to for someone to put her in a bad mood. "No!" Victoria was saying now into the receiver. "I have already told you that unless I specifically tell you otherwise, I will see no one!" It should have been evident that the matter was not open to discussion, but the person on the other end of the line had apparently made some reply because there was one final pause during which she still listened although the hand holding the receiver trembled visibly. "I don't give a damn who he says he is!" she retorted at last and slammed down the telephone.

* * *

The stage doorman winced and hanging up himself, he turned apologetically to the distinguished looking man waiting beside him. "I'm sorry, sir. Miss Windsor doesn't wish to see anyone."

"Thank you anyway," Sir Malcolm murmured courteously as he turned to walk away. "I....I appreciate your trying." Pushing open the heavy old stage door of the Aldwych, he followed the alley along the side of the building toward the street, intending to walk on down to the Strand and hail a taxi. As he came out in front of the theatre, however, he noticed the lobby was still lit, the doors standing open, and he couldn't resist the opportunity to spend a few more minutes looking at the photographs of the current production. Trying to appear nonchalant, Malcolm wandered from picture to picture until at last he stood before one showing Cleopatra ensconced on her throne in all her regal Egyptian splendor.

He'd been so relieved when he noticed his daughter's name in the list of the Aldwych Theatre company. It had been seven years since she ran away when she was only sixteen years old and despite countless sums spent on private detectives he was never able to learn her whereabouts. It had been even harder because he blamed himself. Granted–Victoria's mother also bore some of the responsibility, but he'd known Catherine was a cold-hearted bitch and he should have tried to make it up to the little girl. He remembered how happy Vicki had been the day he arrived home from the war. They could have had a wonderful relationship. Instead he'd wasted the precious years of her childhood nursing his wounded male ego and so he considered himself far the more culpable.

Now as he stood in the theatre lobby studying his daughter's face, the full awareness of what he had thrown away swept over him and the picture of Cleopatra blurred in a sheen of unshed tears. With a quick glance around him to see if anyone had noticed Malcolm pulled out a handkerchief and dried his eyes, but except for him and a man sweeping up cigarette butts at the other end of the room the lobby was deserted. "I don't blame you, sweetheart," he finally said out loud. "If I were you, I wouldn't want to see me either. But, oh God," he went on as once again his eyes filled helplessly with tears. "I was so proud of you tonight and I...."

"Excuse me, sir, were you speaking to me?"

"Wh...what?" Sir Malcolm spun about to discover that unnoticed by him the porter had been gradually moving toward his end of the lobby until now he stood directly behind him.

"I...ah...thought you said something, sir."

"Uh...no....I....uh...." Speechless with embarrassment, he fled the theatre to seek sanctuary in the bar of the Waldorf Hotel next door.

"May I help you, sir?" the bartender inquired.

"Yes—a double Scotch, please–<u>neat</u>"

In the years ahead Sir Malcolm would see every play in which Victoria appeared not once but several times although he never again attempted to speak to her. And finally this highly respected Knight of the British Empire, Order of St. George, stole a photograph of his daughter from the lobby of a theatre, framing it to keep on the desk in his den.

* * *

My Goddamned father, Victoria thought and as she turned away from the telephone, she was still shaking with anger. Does he really think he can step merrily back into my life and play the proud dad? Now–after I've gotten so far alone! Well, he can bloody well go to hell! Victoria willed herself to be calm and after a moment she glanced up at Clive who was still standing a few feet away from her. "If you tell me how beautiful I am when I'm angry, I will scratch your eyes out!" she warned him. Her tone was apparently one of stern admonition, but her eyes, even more startlingly green against the jet black Cleopatra wig, sparkled enticingly.

"Ah, but a superb actress <u>must</u> be capable of great passion." He congratulated himself for having used the situation to compliment her talent. He knew very well the actor's ego, being possessed of a sizeable one himself.

"How kind of you," she murmured raising one expressive eyebrow, "and I might add, how perceptive."

"And angry or not," he went on moving toward her, "you are a beautiful woman–an incredibly beautiful and desirable woman!" Watching him move toward her, Victoria studied his face–searching it intently as though she were trying to find there some deep feeling on his part; it was an expression she did not expect to see–an emotion she knew he did not feel. It did not matter, however; the effect was sensual and suggestive."Are you going to the cast party?" he inquired.

"Of course I am!" she snapped. "I've bloody well waited for this forever. Do you think I'd miss a single opportunity to revel in it?"

Clive didn't realize as yet how unexpectedly her mood could shift and he was afraid he'd offended her in some way. Casting about in his mind for some new way to ingratiate himself, he remembered how vain she was about her hair–always tossing it about in a way quite evidently intended to display it. "You are going to take off that black wig though, aren't you?" he pleaded disarmingly. "Rotten shame you have to wear it actually."

He is so damned obvious, Victoria thought wearily–all the standard techniques. "You haven't given me a chance, Clive," she teased. "You were so bloody eager, you got to my dressing room almost as soon as I did. But tell me, is this more to your liking?" Rising slowly to her feet and twirling about to face him, she removed the dark wig dropping it on the dressing table. Then one by one she pulled out the hairpins, letting each of them fall into his hand. Through it all her eyes never left his face. His, she noted wryly, had a tendency to wander to her cleavage. When the last pin was out, Victoria shook her head, allowing her hair to settle about her shoulders.

"Ah, much better," Clive whispered huskily as he brought up both hands to bury his fingers in its luxuriant golden depths. "Oh Victoria, I've wanted you ever since...."

"That can wait." With a little laugh she slipped away from him, moving behind the folding screen. "I have to change."

Maddeningly he could only catch an occasional glimpse of the top of her head as she removed her costume. "I suppose you'll be attending the party with 'Father Cartier'." His inflection suggested something between a statement and a question–both decidedly derogatory in tone.

How dare he show such a lack of respect, Victoria thought angrily; though why it should bother her, she couldn't imagine. Well, it definitely did not suit her present purposes to wax sentimental over Terry. She laughed. "Really, I don't know why they don't just make him a saint and get it over with. And what in hell would make you think I'd want to go with that old man?" A short time later she emerged from behind the screen. Her dress was yard upon yard of cherry red chiffon, accented just under the bustline and around the bottom of the long flowing skirt with a narrow gold brocade ribbon in the Greek key design.. It was high-waisted, the halter style top seemingly molded to her breasts and staring at her, Clive took one or two involuntary steps forward. He was prevented, however, from actually taking her in his arms by yet another knock at the door. "Would you get that on your way out?" Victoria requested.

"On my way out?" Clearly he was stunned. He'd considered matters between them all but settled.

"Oh, no, no, no, luv," Victoria laughed, touching his face. "I'm not sending you away, but a lady's lover should never watch her do her make-up–spoils the illusion, you know. Now be a good boy and wait outside."

Reluctantly Clive walked over to the door, getting there just as the knock was repeated. Opening it, he was relieved to see it was only Terence Cartier–no real competition. Terry found the younger man brash and irritating and he favored him with only the briefest of glances before looking past him to where Victoria was once again seated at her dressing table, a light cotton smock over her gown. "All ready, then?"

""Do I look ready?" She wrapped a towel turban-fashion around her head and reached for the jar of cold cream. "Anyway I'll be going with Clive so it won't be necessary for you to wait."

Terry knew that to remind her she'd already accepted his invitation would only cause a scene and accomplish nothing. "Of course, Victoria," he replied quietly, "I'll see you there, I should imagine." Without saying anything further he turned to leave.

Clive also stepped out into the hall, closing the door behind him, and alone inside the dressing room Victoria began to spread cold cream over the Cleopatra make-up. The intensity with which she invariably concentrated on her own reflection provided a welcome escape from her thoughts of the moment. She had treated Terry badly which, in turn, reminded her of Noel–whose kindness she'd repaid by driving him away. Then there was also the fact–of only minor concern–that she was commencing a new affair that night. All this she forced from her mind as she finished removing the stage make-up and applied her own.

Clive did not hear the door open and the first thing he knew Victoria had slipped an arm through his and looking down, he found her studying his face again in that peculiar way–at one and the same time profoundly disturbing and deeply arousing.

They made their entrance at the party about a half hour late, Victoria having deliberately postponed her arrival until she was certain most of the other guests would already be there. There was a burst of applause as people surged toward her and inclining her head in acknowledgment of the ovation, she began her progress through the room. Snatches of "Darling, this" and "luv, that" and "how terribly, terribly sweet" were distinctly audible. Only Terence Cartier and Dylan Mallory, who had come down from Stratford for the opening, stayed apart standing together off to one side and watching. "You seem to be the forgotten man here, Terry," Dylan observed drily.

He shrugged. "It's all new to her. Let her have the limelight."

"The question is–can she handle it?" They exchanged worried glances and although neither voiced his thoughts aloud, both were undoubtedly remembering Terry's former wife. "Who's that with her?" Dylan continued after a moment.

"Clive Bannister, another member of the company–not a very highly principled young man, I'm afraid."

The two men grew increasingly anxious as the evening wore on. Victoria was drinking steadily with Clive always at her elbow to hand her a fresh glass. Neither man wanted to make a scene by intervening and at last, unable to bear any longer watching her humiliate herself, they left. Victoria herself, however, stayed until the bitter end–in this case a distressingly apt cliche–the party finally breaking up shortly before 4 a.m.

In the back seat of the taxi she reached out at once for Clive. By then she wasn't even aware anymore who he was. "God, I want you!" she whispered throatily as slipping her hand under his jacket and shirt, she began to stroke his chest.

"I gather the bird's more than willing," the driver observed caustically, "but someone's got to give me an address."

"I'm afraid I have only a dingy bed-sitter," Clive replied apologetically, only slightly more sober himself. Victoria mumbled something, her head lolling against his shoulder.

"Look, mate!" At this hour the cabbie was in no mood to put up with any nonsense. "Sober up the little slut long enough to give me the address or you're both out on the street again!"

Vaguely Victoria had heard herself referred to as a slut. Slut, she thought, slut.... slut...... slut...... and she started to giggle. "Victoria," Clive prompted her.

"Oh, yes....ad....dress." Somehow she managed to whisper it in his ear, interspersing the words with soft, nibbling kisses.

"Seven Woods Mews–just off Park Lane," he repeated to the driver. "Oh God, Victoria, don't!" he gasped as he felt her stroking the inside of his thigh and drawing her to him, he covered her lips with his, slipping his tongue into her mouth. All during the ride they continued to kiss and caress with a steadily mounting passion, both finding the restriction of clothing increasingly frustrating. When the taxi finally came to a stop, Clive hurriedly paid the fare. By now he was too aroused to think of anything but relief. Inside the flat he looked frantically around for the bedroom. "Where? Dammit!"

She laughed, pointing to a narrow, winding staircase. Half-tripping in his eagerness, he followed her and once in her bedroom he began immediately to fumble with the back of her dress. "Anxious, aren't we?" she teased him as he finally managed to open the hook and move the zipper down. Working feverishly now, he undid her bra and Victoria stepped quickly out of the dress, shaking the bra down off her arms and letting it drop to the floor as well. Her breasts were much larger and fuller than they appeared under clothing and as she turned to face him, she watched his eyes widen in anticipation. With a groan he reached out for her, but she shook her head, backing away from him toward the bed, and tearing at his own clothes, he came after her. With no further preliminary he climbed on top of her.

Now was the moment Victoria always turned off her mind to what was happening to her, waiting only for the blessed release of sleep, but tonight she was not to be granted even these few hours of unconsciousness. Clive, on the other hand, did not so much as move when she got up. Coming downstairs himself several hours later, he found her in a bathrobe, curled up in a chair drinking tea and staring out the window into the narrow alley between the mews. "Any coffee around?" Only dimly aware someone had entered the room, she made no reply. "Victoria?"

She shook her head slightly as if to clear it. "Wh..what?"

"Ah...coffee...you know. Liquid–black–hot?"

"Oh, sorry...only instant. I drink mostly tea."

"What time did you get up anyway?" Clive asked as he put the kettle on to boil.

"Actually I....I....haven't slept. Usually when I've had that much to drink, it knocks me out, but not last night."

"Sex doesn't do it for you? World's cheapest sedative, you know."

"Well, not even that always works for me."

"I know a doctor who'll prescribe something–anything you need if you're willing to pay the price."

The thought of pills had always frightened her, but there'd been nights when she would have given anything to sleep. "Yes....ah...get me something, will you?"

That evening Clive knocked at the door of Victoria's dressing room and handed her a small bottle. "Everything's arranged, luv," he whispered with a quick kiss, "Any time you need more, just let me know."

The following week as rehearsal got underway for *King Lear*, Victoria found she'd quickly come to depend on the pills. Worse, she was building up a tolerance for them so that she continually required more. This was especially true when Clive had other plans. She knew there were other women–not that she cared, but her dread of being alone had reached nightmare proportions. A morning finally came when she arrived at rehearsal so badly hung over she could barely walk. She sank into a chair, not even removing her coat, and leaning back, she closed her eyes, willing her head to stop pounding. Suddenly someone was placing a mug of hot coffee in her hands. "Not feeling well this morning, Victoria?"

Damn, she thought, Terry. Sitting up and opening her eyes, she saw he had taken the chair next to hers. "I've always been a slow waker, luv." She smiled at him much too brightly.

"Have you had any breakfast, young lady?" he demanded sternly.

"God, no food, please. Even the thought of it makes me ill."

"I've something in my dressing room which I think might settle your stomach...."

"Dammit, Terry, stop clucking at me! You know how I hate it!"

"Yes, you can't bear to have anyone care about you, can you?"

"What?!" As always she was crossest when someone saw through her facade.

Sir Terence stood up to leave. "You heard me, Victoria. Very clearly, I'm sure." Before she could say anything further, he was gone.

"Hung over, I see," another voice whispered from behind her.

"Oh, Clive, luv, please!" She turned to look up at him, resting one hand pleadingly on his arm. "I need something stronger. I had to take four last night and this morning I feel bloody awful!"

"Try washing them down with liquor. That should do the trick."

"But isn't that dangerous?"

"Of course not," he reassured her smoothly. "But here..." Removing a bottle from his jacket pocket, he shook two pills into her hand. "These should take care of your problem. I was feeling a bit sluggish myself this morning. Thought I might be needing a pick-me-up."

"But can't you get trapped in a vicious circle–you know, uppers...downers.....?" She stopped. All that mattered, after all, was her work. Oh, what the hell, she thought, and she tossed the pills into her mouth, swallowing them with a little coffee.

When Terry next saw her, she was sparkling with life, vivacious and utterly charming. The conclusion was unavoidable and he felt terribly afraid. And by the time *King Lear* opened in February of 1964, a little over a month later, Victoria was indeed hooked. There were pills washed down with brandy to sleep at night and pills washed down with coffee or tea to wake up the next morning–the exact vicious circle she had feared. But Terry, who was hosting the party for the *King Lear* opening in his own home, vowed that at least on this one evening she would stay sober.

She soon grew suspicious, however. The waiter assigned to her table was clearly ignoring her and the couple of times she did manage to order a drink, it had obviously been diluted. When she demanded an explanation, the waiter mumbled something about "instructions". So Terry was rationing the liquor–how dare he! She slapped the poor, hapless waiter and stormed out!

Once again, then, the pattern of Victoria's life appeared fixed: her work, her current lover, the never-ending social whirl which was the inevitable result of fame–parties full of strangers who made a great fuss over her–and to ease her way through it all, the pills and liquor. That was her life. Neither could she change it nor did she wish to do so. Then why did she have the nagging feeling that something was missing.

Even that particular morning she was struggling to clear her head–drinking cup after cup of strong tea–when the envelope arrived in the post. At once she recognized the letterhead of Andrew's firm. Oh God, what now, she thought, but then she realized almost at once that it must be the final divorce degree. She carried the envelope back to the kitchen, but did not immediately open it. Instead she sat down at the table again, reaching for the teapot to refill her cup. Next she added milk and sugar, stirred the mixture thoroughly and took two or three long swallows. She would never have admitted, of course, that she was deliberately procrastinating and when she could find no further plausible excuse for delay, she slit the envelope and withdrew the bulky document. "Roberts v. Roberts," the lettering at the top of the first page proclaimed in black, uncompromising print, "Final Divorce Degree."

With every appearance of nonchalance Victoria flipped through the document skimming down each page. Whether or not she was consciously looking for a particular section, her rapid perusal came to an abrupt halt on the paragraph outlining the custody arrangements for one "minor female child: custody to be awarded to the father..." She stared at those words for several seconds, tears welling up in her eyes, and she felt again, as vividly as if it were yesterday, the warm, sweet sensation of Olivia in her arms in the final moments before she'd handed her to the woman downstairs and walked away.

"She'd be...ah...almost two-and-a-half now. She...she wouldn't even know me...she..... God, I'm getting maudlin over the whole bloody thing. I must really be hung over." Victoria shook her head impatiently and looked down again at the document...."with right of access awarded to the mother at the father's discretion."

"Right of access? Will he never give up?" Striding angrily across the room, she snatched the telephone receiver off the hook and dialed the number of the solicitors' firm.

"Granville, Granville, Carruthers and Roberts," the operator announced. That stopped Victoria for an instant. Puzzled by the silence at the other end of the line, the operator repeated the name of the firm, adding, "May I help you?"

"Yes, Mr. Roberts, please."

"May I tell Mr. Roberts who is calling?"

"None of your bloody business! It's a personal matter."

"I'm afraid I can't connect you, ma'am, without knowing your name."

"Oh, the hell with it!" She slammed down the receiver. "After all he can't make me see her!"

Victoria spent a great deal of time after that convincing herself that the motherly type she definitely was not and about a month later she was presented with the perfect opportunity to prove just exactly what sort of woman she was. The flowers were delivered to her dressing room about a half-hour before curtain, the card suggesting a late supper following the performance. The invitation intrigued her. Clive was becoming a bloody bore. All he ever wanted to do was go to bed with her probably because he couldn't afford to do anything else. This man sent long-stemmed yellow roses.

Her host turned out to be Nigel Fitzmaurice, eldest son of the Earl of Sheffield. He was a powerfully built, supremely elegant man in his early fifties, married although his wife preferred the South of France, an arrangement which suited them both. He promised he would spoil her shamelessly and he began at once to keep his word. That evening's meal–in his London townhouse–was long and leisurely, each course served with its own wine or champagne and Victoria discovered that good wine taken in sufficient quantity could have an even more pleasant effect than hard liquor. The following morning he sent her home wrapped in blue fox fur. And in between he had proved a practiced lover–all in all preferable to a poverty stricken actor who rutted like a barnyard animal.

Still Clive had his uses as well; for one thing he kept her supplied with pills. So all through that spring and summer she had not merely one regular lover, but two–Clive to take her to theatrical parties and the pubs and Nigel to take her cruising on his yacht and to his country estate–and both of them, of course, to take her to bed. Clive didn't find the arrangement as agreeable, however, and by early autumn he decided it was time to issue an ultimatum.

Invariably once the lovemaking was over, he would grow bored and restless and on one or two occasions he'd been about to leave. He was amazed at the instantaneous change in Victoria as she pleaded with him to stay. He'd never forgotten the incredible elation he experienced at seeing this proudly beautiful woman beg and after that he'd known that whenever he needed it, he had the power to make her crawl. On this particular night she was lying curled up on her side with her back toward him and although her posture was one of slumber, he could tell she was wide awake. He reached over to place his hand on her bare arm and at his unexpected touch she jumped. "Don't!" She pulled away from him. "Haven't you had enough for one night?"

"Hey, luv, we have to talk."

"Talk! I didn't know you were capable of anything requiring that much mental effort!"

"Look!" Grabbing her by the shoulder, Clive forced her over onto her back. She tried to turn her head away, but he held her down with one hand and with the other he grasped her chin, bringing his face to within inches of hers. "Now I want you to listen because if you don't, I can always leave and we both know you don't want me to do that!"

Her eyes filled with tears and she was thankful for the darkness. God, he can be so cruel, she thought, but after all it's only what I deserve. "What in hell can be so damned important?" she demanded, careful that her voice not betray her hurt.

"I want to know how long you plan to carry on with this Fitzmaurice."

"And I suppose you're completely faithful!"

"That's beside the point. I refuse to share you with that pompous ass of an Earl's son!"

"You do <u>not</u> own me! Do you understand that?" Victoria's voice rose sharply. "No one does. And I will do as I please!"

"Then you will do it without me, lady." Clive flung back the bedclothes and getting up, began to dress.

"Don't be ridiculous, luv," she murmured with a little laugh, trying in vain to keep her tone light. "It's the middle of the night." He appeared to be paying her no attention, however. "Please, Clive, don't leave!"

"Beg away, bitch! I am making my final exit!" Slinging his jacket over his shoulder, he plunged down the narrow circular staircase two at a time.

"Please, Clive—oh, please," she called after him, half-sobbing now. "Please! I'll... I'll do anything...anything...only please, I don't want to be alone." But below her the front door slammed and she knew he was gone. It was the middle of the night; there was no one she could call and finally she reached for the bottle of pills she kept by her bedside.

Her last conscious thought before drugged sleep overcame her was a vow of revenge and her first act the following morning before she was even half-awake was to ring up Terence Cartier, now managing director of the London company, and demand Clive's removal. Sir Terence complied without comment. He'd been suspicious for some time that Clive was supplying drugs to several in the company including Victoria. Moreover, he already had in mind the perfect actor to replace him.

Arriving for her next performance, Victoria saw the announcement on the message board– "Welcome back to England and to the Royal Shakespeare Company-- Noel St. John."

Noel himself, meanwhile, had come up behind her unobserved. He'd not really stopped to think about how or where he would first see her again after more than a year, but for some reason he'd assumed he would have some advance warning. Now instead he'd just happened on her–entirely unexpectedly–standing here alone in front of the bulletin board. Should he go up and speak to her, he wondered, as if nothing had changed or avoid her until he could ascertain how matters were between them, but just then she turned around and saw him. She looked so tired and drawn it was all he could do not to exclaim aloud in dismay. Somehow he remained silent, however, and then for a while he forgot all that as he waited for some reaction on her part. So much of their future relationship, it seemed, would depend on these next few moments.

Like Noel, Victoria had expected some chance to prepare herself for their first meeting–to decide exactly what she would do and say, how she would treat him. There had been none; she'd just learned of his return and there he was. Perhaps it was just as well. Caught so completely off-guard, her response was impulsive and utterly genuine. "Noel!" she exclaimed and he observed her expression soften slightly, but unmistakably. "I....I'm glad you're back." She appeared to be about to say more, but instead she turned away again and ran. It was far more, nevertheless, than he'd dared hope for.

* * *

So then, did Noel's return complete the puzzle? Victoria told herself it did–that of course a faithful, uncomplaining companion was all that had been missing–and if she wasn't especially happy with the finished picture, she accepted it. Someone else, however, remained unconvinced.

She'd just concluded a matinee performance of *Caesar and Cleopatra* to the usual tumultuous ovation. Yet how she continued to dread each final descent of the curtain and the eerie silence which followed as the applause died away. As always on this particular afternoon she hurried through the backstage to her dressing room, looking neither left nor right and speaking to no one. "Anna," she called out to her dresser as she entered, "get this damned costume off me. It weighs a ton!"

"How have you been, Victoria?" a still familiar male voice inquired quietly. He had been sitting in the back corner of the room and she hadn't seen him. Only when he spoke did he stand up and come forward.

"Andrew! What in God's name are you doing here? Haven't I made it perfectly clear..........."

"This isn't for me, Victoria. There's someone else I want you to see. I sent her out with your maid so that I could speak to you first."

"Someone else? Who? Oh no, Andrew....no..... I don't want to see her. Haven't I made that obvious, too? Now get out of here before they come back. Do you understand me?" But that's not true, she was thinking. I <u>do</u> want to see her. It hurts....I want to see her so much!

"Please, Victoria, just listen to me first."

"No, I don't want to listen! How many times do I have to tell you to stay the hell out of my life–you and that brat you tricked me into having...."

"Hold on a minute. No one stopped you from having that abortion except yourself.. Now listen, please, that's all–just listen."

"I have a dinner engagement."

"God dammit, Victoria, you listen! If you don't owe me that much–which I happen to think you do–you at least owe it to your daughter. Because whether you like it or not, she's a fact and not just a baby anymore, but an actual small person in her own right!"

"Very touching! How in hell did you get in here anyway? All right....all right. I'll listen, if only to get rid of you."

"I'm getting married again, Victoria."

"Congratulations!"

"The more you interrupt, the longer this will take me. I'm getting married again," he repeated, "and I can't help thinking it's important that Olivia know her own mother."

"Even if her mother's not interested."

"If you aren't interested, why did you sign the agreement?"

"What's that got to do with it?"

"The divorce agreement specifically gave you right of access."

"Oh. I....ah.....see. I...ah...didn't bother to read the damned thing."

"Never sign anything without reading it, Victoria. Didn't I at least teach you that much?" Andrew smiled a little. He wondered if she knew how transparent she was. "So at any rate," he continued quickly, "I decided to bring Olivia here. After that it will be up to you."

"But I told you....I don't want to...."

Before she could say anything further, however, the door opened and her maid entered, holding Olivia by the hand. The little girl was dressed in pale blue overalls and a pink pullover, her light brown hair held up in two pony tails, each tied with a matching pink ribbon. If only Victoria could have yielded to her first impulse which was to kneel down and enfold the child in her arms. Instead she stood frozen to the spot, unable to do anything but stare. Dear God, she thought, she's so sweet–so utterly adorable!

"Daddy!" Olivia exclaimed running across the room to him. "Where's the special lady you wanted me to meet?" Her voice was clear with no hint of baby talk–each word pronounced precisely.

It was Andrew who bent down and picked up their daughter. He studied Victoria's face intently. He could see how moved she was. If only he could find the right words. "Olivia, do you remember asking me why all your little friends had mothers and you didn't?"

"Yes, Daddy, but after you marry Em'ly, she'll be my mother, won't she, and then I'll be just like everybody else."

Oh God, Victoria thought, fighting back the tears. I don't want to feel like this. Yet more than anything she longed to reach out and take the little girl from Andrew-- perhaps sit down and hold her on her lap.

"Not quite, little love," Andrew was saying. "Emily will be your stepmother. This is your mother."

At last, then, Olivia turned her head and looked at Victoria and immediately her blue eyes widened in horror. It hadn't even occurred to Andrew how his former wife looked in her Cleopatra make-up; her eyes heavily edged in kohl and her own hair hidden under a long black wig, a crown in the shape of a serpent encircling her head. "No, Daddy, no!" the little girl screamed. "She's not my Mummy! She's a witch, Daddy! A witch! And she's got a snake on her head! Make her go away, Daddy! Make her go away!"

Victoria laughed harshly. "Well, Andrew, so much for the tender reunion. Now get out of here!"

"We'll wait until you get out of make-up. That's what frightened her. I should have thought of that."

"Look, Andrew, I....I...." She was trying very hard not to cry. "I don't bloody well give.... give a damn about her and it's apparent the feeling is mutual. Now get the hell out of here!'

Throughout this brief exchange Olivia continued to scream louder and louder until the noise had all but drowned them both out and Andrew finally had no choice, but to carry her from the room. "Any time you want to see her, Victoria, you only have to ask."

"GET OUT!!" she shrieked slamming the door after him. But then almost at once an expression of terrible grief passed over her face and walking over to her dressing table, she sank down on the little stool in front of it. "Oh, Olivia," she sobbed. "Olivia–my darling, my adorable little love. I'm so sorry. Oh, I'm so sorry, but I can't....I just can't......" She stared at her reflection in the mirror–the reflection which had frightened her own little girl, terrified her–sent her away screaming. Mechanically she picked up the cold cream, but her hand was shaking and she dropped the jar. "God," she murmured, "I need a drink." She reached for the flask she kept in a drawer of the dressing table, but to her dismay found it was all but empty.

Damn, she thought, the tears starting all over again. Damn! Damn! Damn! She'd lied about the dinner engagement. She didn't even have a performance that evening. There was nothing at all ahead of her, but a long, lonely night. Noel----she thought all at once. Of course—Noel's back. She picked up her telephone and asked to be connected to his dressing room.

Momentarily he answered. "St. John, here."

"Noel, it's....ah.... Victoria."

"Victoria? He wasn't sure he'd heard properly. Since his return a few weeks ago, she'd spoken pleasantly enough in passing, but until now she'd made no move to resume their old relationship.

"What in hell is wrong with you? Are you deaf? Hurry up! I need a drink!"

"Coming, Victoria," Noel replied although the phone had already gone dead. He grinned. It might not have been the most gracious invitation, but for now it was enough.

A short time later they were settled in a dark corner of a near-by pub. Noel was grateful for the late afternoon crowd; the crush of people made it possible for him to sit very close to Victoria, glorying in her perfumed nearness, while at the same time the noise gave him little opportunity to say the wrong thing. She removed a cigarette from a slim silver case and inserted it in a holder, a new affectation since he'd last seen her. He lit the cigarette for her and she inhaled deeply. "Is it still vodka, Victoria?"

"Yes, luv. How sweet of you to remember." She stroked his face with the tip of her forefinger.

It was the old well-rehearsed gesture, but Noel nevertheless relished the touch as with a smile he excused himself to go up to the bar. It took nearly ten minutes for him to get served and he was afraid Victoria might be annoyed. However, she only reached for the glass with a desperate eagerness which made him sad. His concern deepened as over the next hour or so she continually sent him to fetch her yet another drink. "Well, I don't know about you," Noel said finally–in as offhand a manner as possible, "but I'm starved. How about going somewhere and getting something to eat?"

Smiling slightly now, she once more caressed his cheek. "As subtle as ever, luv."

"What, Victoria?"

"You know I don't like to be told I'm drinking too much so instead you suggest getting something to eat."

"Good old transparent Noel, eh?" He grinned. "But I really <u>am</u> starving."

"Oh, very well, then. We'll go somewhere so you can eat. I'm really not very hungry."

Together they walked a few blocks to a small Greek restaurant near Leicester Square where Noel tucked into a plate of stuffed grape leaves while Victoria drank a great deal of wine and picked at a salad. His strategy hadn't succeeded, then, and despite some strong, black coffee by the time they left she was extremely drunk.

In the taxi Noel wondered what he should do next. He was apprehensive about leaving her alone yet at the same time he feared that any expression of concern on his part would drive her away again perhaps for good. After a while they pulled into the cul-de-sac between the mews and stopped at Victoria's door. She didn't move, however, and when Noel turned to look at her, he saw she was lying back against the seat with her eyes closed. "Victoria?" He touched her lightly on the arm.

"Hm? What?" Sitting up quickly, she looked about her–bewildered.

"We're here—your flat."

"Oh...ah...yes....ah....good night, Noel." She opened the taxi door herself and got out. He watched her move unsteadily to her door, fumble a moment with the key and then disappear inside.

"Lady 'ad a bit too much–what, mate?" the driver commented in a broad Cockney accent.

"That, my dear sir," Noel replied angrily, "is none of your damned business!"

Inside her flat Victoria stood motionless in the center of the living room–her mind so muddled that for a while she couldn't decide what to do. At last, however, she seemed to discover the stairs and although twice she stumbled and fell, she managed to make her way up them, leaving a trail of clothing behind her–her coat over the railing, her dress on one step and her half-slip on another.

Her bedroom was damp and cold–the coal fire in the grate having long since gone out. "For what I pay for this place," she mumbled, beginning to shiver, "you'd think it would have central heating." Instinctively she crawled under the covers of her unmade bed–like an animal seeking the comfort of its den–and in a while she felt warmer. But sleep eluded her–even drunk as she was–perhaps because every time she closed her eyes she saw a tiny girl in blue overalls and a pink jumper. "Dear God, Andrew, why?" she whispered in the darkness, her eyes filling with tears. "Why did you have to do it? I didn't want to see her. Now I'll keep seeing her and seeing her and seeing her."

She didn't know why she hadn't thought of the pills sooner. She wasn't sure how many of the tranquillizers she took; all she cared was that the anguish was receding and curling up on her side, she fell asleep.

* * *

Noel awakened very early the next morning–actually he hadn't slept much at all–and the first thing he did was to telephone Victoria. He only let it ring a few times, however, for fear of disturbing her so he wasn't really too concerned when she didn't answer. He walked to a restaurant for breakfast, stopping at a newspaper kiosk for the Sunday Times, and returning to his flat, he tried her number again letting it ring longer this time. There was still no answer and now he began to worry in earnest. He kept ringing her every fifteen minutes or so, then ten, then every five. At last he couldn't stand it any longer and throwing on his coat, he hurried outside to flag down a taxi. "Seven Wood's Mews," he instructed the driver—"off Park Lane and please hurry."

God damn me to everlasting hell, he reproached himself bitterly, if anything's happened to her. Why did I leave her alone last night? Clinging to the strap, he leaned forward in the seat to peer ahead as though by the simple force of his will he could speed the cab more rapidly toward its destination. Or why didn't I at least go over there first thing this morning? "Can't we go any faster?" he inquired urgently at one point. Traffic on a Sunday morning was comparatively light yet it seemed to him they were crawling. "It's rather an emergency, you see!"

At last a few blocks from the mews Noel paid off the taxi and ran the rest of the way. He rang the doorbell, but there was no response. He knocked loudly and still nothing. Horribly the situation reminded him of that morning in Stratford. "Victoria!" he called at first in a fairly normal tone, but when she still failed to come to the door, he began to pound on it calling her name repeatedly.

Someone touched him on the arm and he turned around to find a uniformed bobby standing there. "Is something wrong, sir?"

Knowing how Victoria would despise the notoriety, Noel's first instinct was to deny anything was the matter, but something told him he had to get into the flat. "My friend lives here," he replied. "She wasn't....ah....wasn't feeling well last night. I haven't been able to get an answer on the telephone and now she doesn't come to the door."

"Are you sufficiently concerned for me to ring for the rescue squad?"

He hesitated for only the briefest of seconds. "Yes, I am."

The man nodded. "There's a call box just around the corner on the main street. In the meantime you might continue trying to get a response here."

Noel did as requested but to no avail. Again it seemed like forever, but in actuality it was only a matter of ten minutes or so before the rescue squad's van pulled up in front of the house. After that it was only a few more moments until they'd forced the lock and were into the ground floor. It was immediately obvious there was no one in the tiny living room and kitchen and Noel started at once toward the stairs.

One of the squad stopped him with a touch on the arm. "Let us go up, sir," he suggested. "Sometimes these things aren't pretty."

His heart pounding with fear, Noel stood back and watched the others go up. Two of the three came back down almost immediately and going out to the van, returned a moment later, one carrying a rolled stretcher and the other a container of oxygen. "How is she?" he inquired anxiously.

"Can't talk now, sir," was all the reply he got as they hurried past him once more and up the stairs.

Seconds afterwards, however, the third man, who appeared to be in charge and who'd been the one to stop him from going upstairs, came down. "I'm sorry, sir. It appears your girl friend's overdosed."

The man sounded so matter-of-fact that Noel exploded in rage. "But you don't give a damn, do you? For you it's all in a day's work!"

"But that's just it, sir." And now as the man turned to look at him directly, Noel could see that his expression wasn't so much cold as it was profoundly sad. "I see too much of this sort of thing and it seems as though they're always young. If I let it get to me, I'd go bonkers for sure."

"Of course. I'm sorry. Is she....is she.......?"

"Right now she is still alive, yes. We'll be taking her to Middlesex Hospital if you want to follow us there. In the meantime I'll need some basic information: name, age, next of kin....."

Noel shook his head, trying to calm himself enough to give sensible answers to the man's questions. "Ah...her name is Victoria Windsor. She's...ah...." He hesitated. He wasn't really sure how old Victoria was.

At this point, however, the medical officer interrupted him. "The name sounds familiar."

"She's...ah...an actress with the Royal Shakespeare Company."

"Oh......how old did you say she is?"

"I'm not really sure. About 24 or 25, I think."

"Yes, as I said, they're always young. Family?"

"I don't know anything about her family. Sorry."

"You don't know much about your girl friend, do you?"

"She's not my girl friend," he replied sadly, "just my friend, but no, you're right. I know very little about her. She's....ah....a very private person."

The other two men came slowly down the stairs just then bearing the unconscious Victoria between them on the stretcher. The oxygen mask was in place and Noel could catch only a glimpse of her pale face and disheveled hair as they passed him.

"You could ride to hospital with us, if you like," the man with whom he'd been talking offered kindly.

"No, I'm sure she'd prefer I not see her like this. I....I would appreciate it, though, if you'd let me know how she is." Noel hurriedly scribbled his name and phone number on a scrap of paper.

"Be glad to, sir. And, believe me, if she gets through this, she has you to thank."

The ambulance was already starting up. What was there about the sound of a siren, Noel mused, moving to the door, which all by itself seemed to proclaim desperate tragedy? He watched as turning around, the vehicle stopped again just long enough for the third man to climb in the back, and then proceeded on through the gateway leading out into the main street.

He took a long look behind him at the empty living room before he finally closed the front door and walked away.

Chapter 8

It was late afternoon by the time Victoria finally awoke and a moment or so longer before she realized she was lying in a hospital bed. It had to be the worst hangover she'd ever had; she had never felt so weak and her head was pounding. For the first time someone–a doctor–spoke to her about her evident unhappiness, but she informed him it was none of his "bloody business". He also told her that if a friend hadn't been concerned about her and come to check up on her, she might very well have died. He wouldn't say who that person was, but he didn't have to. She rang up Noel, intending to tell him to sod off, yet when he actually answered–when she heard him say, "Hello," that one word in his gentle voice was enough in her present vulnerable state to bring on an attack of weeping. "Damn!" she muttered.

At this one brief expletive Noel chuckled to himself in amused relief. Just as the doctor had reassured him, Victoria seemed to be herself. "Hello," he repeated. He didn't admit to having heard her and almost at once she hung up.

It was three days before Noel saw her again–backstage prior to the performance of *King Lear*. He had been staring at the closed door of Victoria's dressing room for some time wondering whether to knock when all once it opened and she came out-- already in costume and make-up. She showed no sign of her recent ordeal, but at the same time the mere sight of her caused him to lose his nerve. He started to walk away, but it was too late. She'd seen him. "Noel," she called after him. It was her accustomed tone with him–somewhere between a command and a caress.

"Victoria," he replied, "lovely as ever."

"And why shouldn't I be? Are you insinuating I should look in any way different?"

Noel's mind raced. With her customary skill she was backing him into a corner. "Of course not...ah...Victoria. Why should you think that?"

The stammer had betrayed him, however, and taking a sudden step forward, she seized him by the wrist. "It <u>was</u> you, wasn't it?"

"I....I don't know what you mean." In vain he tried to free himself.

"You can't stop interfering in my life, can you?"

Noel gave up struggling against the slim, white hand which still held him in its iron grasp. They were about of a height and he found now that he was looking directly into her eyes. How large and green they are, he thought. Mentally he shook himself and from somewhere he rediscovered his courage. "Yes, it was I," he said aloud, pleased with the firmness of his tone. "And yes, I care about you and what's more, I intend to go on caring whether you like it or not."

For a long moment she looked back at him and in her face he could see with stunning clarity her aching need to be loved–all the more terrible because she was incapable of expressing it. "Noel St. John," she said at last–very softly. "You are a <u>damned</u> fool!"

The next few weeks were some of the worst Victoria had ever known. Ironically– shortly after Clive walked out on her–Nigel Fitzmaurice had succumbed to threats of disinheritance. So that "son of an Earl" was gone from her life as well and from two lovers she'd thus been abruptly reduced to none. Most of the time now when she wasn't on stage, she was alone–alone and more frightened than she could ever remember being: frightened of the night, frightened of the pills and liquor even as she craved them, and frightened, most of all, to go to sleep for fear she would never wake up. Curtly she refused Noel or Terry's invitations for lunch or dinner, the theatre or a Sunday drive, too proud to admit how lonely she was. Surely they were only making such offers out of pity. Neither of them could actually want to be with her.

* * *

No one paid Anthony Blake-Ashley any particular notice as he stood in the wings that evening watching the final moments of *King Lear*. Perhaps if they had, someone might have cautioned him that during Victoria's rapid progress from the stage to her dressing room no one spoke to her except possibly Noel St. John or Sir Terence and even they could never be sure of their reception.

Not that any manner of admonition could have stopped Tony at this point. Ever since he'd acquired the rights to produce and direct *The Divine Sarah*, a play based on the life of the immortal Bernhardt, he'd known whom he wanted for the title role. Now he'd bribed and cajoled his way past the guard at the Aldwych stage door and it was unlikely that a mere warning that Victoria never talked to anyone would have prevented him from approaching her as she came offstage after the curtain call. "Excuse me, Miss Windsor," he said politely. Of course she ignored him. "Miss Windsor," Tony persisted, "I wonder if I might have just a few minutes of your time."

At last then she stopped and turned to face him. Tipping her head back a little and sucking in her cheeks, she eyed him disdainfully. Like her royal ancestor and namesake, the lady clearly was not amused. "And just who are you?" she asked very precisely.

"I'm Tony Blake-Ashley, Miss Windsor and I...."

"That does not answer my question! What in bloody hell is a Tony Blake-Ashley?"

"Tony Blake-Ashley is a new theatrical producer and director, relatively untried but brilliant, I might add."

"Oh, I see." She laughed.

By pure luck he'd happened on the technique most likely to succeed with Victoria-- humor with just a dash of bravado–and he pressed on before he could lose even this slight advantage. "Yes, positively brilliant," he said again with a grin.

"I believe we've already established that fact," she replied, at once impatient again.

"Who also has the rights to this," he went on quickly, pushing the script into her hand. All the fruitless auditions, Victoria thought, and now someone just walks up to me and hands me a script!–even if that someone is only an unknown producer. After all Matt was once an unknown agent. She did not add, by the way–even privately–that until recently Victoria Windsor had been an unknown actress. "At least read it," Tony pleaded, misunderstanding the reason for her silence. "You're perfect for the title character–Sarah Bernhardt! Believe me!"

Now Victoria couldn't help but smile. They're even begging me, she thought. "I suppose I could read it," she finally replied, trying to sound off-hand about it. "Leave me your number and I'll ring you."

Tony was afraid to let her get away–afraid she would disappear inside her dressing room with his script and that would be that. "Or we could have a late supper," he suggested, "and I'll tell you about the play."

In the dimness of the backstage Victoria couldn't really see what he looked like except that he was fairly tall and broad-shouldered, his dark hair beginning to recede only slightly. "My, my," she said at last with what she knew was her most charmingly lilting laugh, "a script and a meal. Wait here while I change." She handed him back the script and moved away again toward her dressing room.

Just as Victoria closed the door, Noel appeared around the corner, intending as well to ask her out for supper. Seeing Tony, however, he stopped. "Are you waiting to see Miss Windsor?" he inquired although he didn't really care to hear the answer.

"You're Noel St. John, aren't you?" Tony smiled. "I've already seen Miss Windsor, thank you. I'm just waiting for her to get out of costume and make-up."

"Oh, I see." Noel turned away. Already, then, there was a new man. And he knew only too well this meant that temporarily at least he would move once again into the background of Victoria's life.

People who had only a superficial acquaintance with Victoria would have been astonished if they could have seen her in these moments as trembling with anxiety, she slipped out of her costume. She had so much to do if she were to appear at her most attractive. Yet at the same time she was terrified lest this man become impatient and leave and by the time she'd removed her stage make-up, applied her own and dressed again in a purple wool dress and matching cape, her poor maid had taken even more than the normal amount of verbal abuse.

She need not have worried. Tony would have waited forever. Even when Victoria at last emerged from her dressing room again and he was following her along the narrow hall leading to the backstage door, he still couldn't believe his good fortune. It was all he could do not to let out a whoop of triumph. He'd sent the stage doorman ahead to find a taxi–amazing how eager to please the fellow had suddenly become–and when they came outside, it was waiting for them. A few minutes later they were moving down the Strand. "It's only a short distance," he explained, "a little French place called *A La Maison*. I think you'll like it."

Victoria made no reply. In fact she'd said nothing since she came out of her dressing room and now she was staring straight ahead, apparently unmindful of him. One gloved hand was holding the collar of her cape up about her throat, the dark material accentuating her natural paleness, and a white chiffon scarf nestled softly over her blonde hair. Perhaps it was then he was first struck by her extraordinary beauty. How could he possibly have been so blind, Tony wondered, as all thought of the play vanished from his mind.

Though outwardly Victoria did indeed remain silent and immobile, inwardly her mind was racing. A starring role, she exulted, and inside her beige kid gloves her palms were perspiring. And a moment later–Sarah Bernhardt...a fascinating woman! And all the roles she played–didn't she even do Hamlet? And circling in, above and through such thoughts–God, I'm so tired of being alone! Can I possibly get him into my flat tonight? She glanced over at her companion in an attempt to guess his thoughts. He was studying her so intently it startled her. Tony smiled as their eyes met. "Do you want to know what I was thinking?" he asked.

"Please—" Victoria murmured. Turning to face him, she leaned back in the corner of the seat, fully aware that in the dark interior of the taxi, lit only briefly by passing street lights, she created an irresistible picture.

"I was thinking, I'm afraid, of the woman rather than the actress."

Victoria was overcome by a great weariness; to begin the game all over again was all but intolerable yet begin it again she must. "Well, after all, I am a woman, too, you know." And she allowed a smile to just touch her lips. By now every gesture, every facial mannerism, every tone and pitch of her voice were at her command to be utilized at will.

They drew up in front of the restaurant and Tony paid the driver and got out. As he came around to the other side, however, he discovered she was still sitting there, waiting with evident impatience for him to assist her from the taxi. Cursing his stupidity, he quickly did so, offering his hand to help her alight and walking ahead to hold open the door of the restaurant.

Victoria glanced about appreciatively as they entered. The room was decorated in pale blue and ivory tones; the carpet was ivory as well--thick and plush. *A La Maison* was evidently quite exclusive. Her interest in Tony Blake-Ashley increased considerably and as they followed the head waiter, she slipped her arm through his. In the center was an area for dancing and the short, flamboyantly mustachioed Frenchman escorted them to what he considered to be one of his best tables–on its very edge. Blue and orchid spotlights illumined not only the tiny dance floor, but this first row of tables as well. "Oh dear, Tony, this won't do at all," Victoria whispered snuggling closer. "Couldn't you find us something a little more....ah...intimate?" she inquired sweetly of the maitre d'.

"Naturellement, mademoiselle," he replied with an elaborate bow. At once he turned to show them to a booth two levels above the dance floor. "I understand perfectly. Only it is a pity, n'est-ce pas?" He gestured apologetically toward the candle in its smoked lavender globe. "In the darkness one cannot fully appreciate the face of a beautiful woman." He pulled out the table for them both to be seated and immediately withdrew.

Victoria smiled the same smile Tony had seen in the taxi. He was growing increasingly flustered. He couldn't remember when he'd been so drawn to a woman, so aroused by her mere presence. She took a cigarette from her case, inserted it in the holder and waited for him to light it. He failed to get the hint. "My cigarette, Tony." There was an instant edge to her voice. By now she was accustomed to having a man know what she wanted even before she knew herself and he'd already failed twice!

Tony hurriedly picked up the matches, but in his haste he also knocked over a glass of water. God, she thought, why are all men either total bastards or complete asses?! At last he managed to light her cigarette. "Would you like a drink, Victoria?"

Seeming not to hear him at first, she leaned her elbow on the side of the booth, the back of her hand resting against her forehead, her heavily mascaraed eyes closing in what appeared to be extreme fatigue. Eyes still shut, she brought the cigarette to her lips, drawing on it strongly, finally opening her eyes again to look at him steadily as she exhaled the smoke. Only then did she finally answer him. "Sorry, luv. I'm utterly exhausted. "Yes, I would.....vodka."

"On the rocks?" It was all he could do to speak.

"No....ah...neat...with a twist of lime." The waiter approached and Tony ordered. After that neither of them spoke again for some time as Victoria continued to use the cigarette to seduce her new lover. Tony's breath was coming more and more rapidly and his blood was pounding in his veins. He knew very well what was happening yet he couldn't tear his gaze away from those hypnotic green eyes, the rise and fall of her full breasts each time she drew on the cigarette. God, he wanted more than anything to touch her, to feel those moist, warm lips on his, to run his hands over..........

It was Victoria who first recalled the original purpose of his backstage visit. What in hell am I doing, she thought. Have I become so desperate that I'm putting the seduction of a lover, perhaps only for the one night, ahead of my career? The arrival at that moment of the waiter with their drinks served perfectly to break the mood and with a long, reviving swallow of her vodka she turned to the businesss at hand. "But tell me about the play, Tony," she said briskly. Her abrupt transformation from sensual seductress to coolly professional actress affected Tony exactly as if she'd thrown a pail of ice water in his face. He blinked. He's mine, Victoria thought triumphantly–whenever I want him. But first the play and then....later...... "Tony," she prompted him with a little laugh which she knew would only tantalize him further, "the play. You do remember the play, don't you?"

"The play?" he repeated after her as with considerable effort he forced himself to concentrate. "Yes, well as I told you backstage, it's based on the life of Sarah Bernhardt. A friend of mine wrote it. He's as untried as I am, but I think you'll agree he's created something memorable. The blending of Bernhardt's incredible personal life with the roles she played on stage is accomplished with remarkable skill and dexterity."

"You sound like an advert in one of the trade papers," Victoria observed teasingly.

Clearly she was laughing at him, but Tony didn't care. "The moment I saw you on stage," he went on, "I knew you'd be perfect for the part. You're an incredibly gifted actress, but I'm sure you're as aware of that as you are of your beauty." Victoria inclined her head in acknowledgment of both compliments. "Now how about a little supper while we discuss it?" he concluded.

Impatiently she waved the suggestion aside. A man didn't usually have to be told that her glass was empty–except perhaps Noel who was always trying with all the subtlety of a locomotive to stop her from drinking so much. "I'm not really hungry. But I would like another of these." More drinks were ordered. "Go on! Tell me more!" she commanded.

"The script will say it better than I can, I think. I should tell you as well that I'm not <u>entirely</u> lacking in theatrical experience–only it's been in rep–mostly in Scotland."

"God," she exclaimed laughing merrily. "I didn't even know they spoke English up there." She extended one slim, white hand to him–her rings glittering in the candlelight. "Let me see the script." Tony handed it to her, relishing even the fleeting sensation of her hand brushing against his. Victoria for her part became at once so absorbed in her reading that for the moment she was oblivious to her companion. The play was indeed a brilliant piece of work–and to portray Sarah Bernhardt! What a magnificent tour de force for an actress, she thought. This would doubtless be the role which would once and for all establish her on the London stage and not merely as a member of a company. She'd forgotten entirely there'd been a time–and not that long ago--when membership in that company was the one thing she desired above all else.

There <u>were</u> aspects of the "Divine Sarah's" life which Victoria found disturbingly similar to her own–a neglected child, a woman not above having another actor fired, a troublemaker who always wanted leading roles. But she pushed such coincidences from her mind. "Oh, Tony," she murmured fervently, at last reaching over to grasp his hand, "The part is an actress' dream! I want it!"

Glowing with excitement, Victoria was for one of the few times so far in her life entirely natural and thus she had never been more beautiful nor more arousing. Once again it required all of Tony's powers of concentration to bring his mind back to the play. "But....ah...what about your RSC contract?" he managed to inquire, clearing his throat and trying to sound professional.

"A minor problem. For this role I'll walk out if I have to."

"You're incredible, Victoria. Everything I've heard you were and more!"

"And what have you heard, Tony?" The hand which had continued to grip his began to move slightly, caressing him.

"Your beauty, your fire,,,,,"

"That I'll go to bed with anyone?" He swallowed, unable to think of an even halfway sensible reply. "Would you like to find out if it's true?" she asked when he still said nothing.

"Dammit, you know I want you, Victoria!"

She laughed and the very sound, soft and low in her throat, sent a shiver of renewed desire coursing through him. "Then let's get the hell out of here!"

Tony proved a gentle and considerate lover, one who from the first night they spent together loved her deeply. So low was Victoria's opinion of herself, however, that it never occurred to her someone might actually care for her and rather than being grateful for his tenderness, she would come to despise him as a fool.

* * *

Damn, Matt thought, watching the last few minutes or so of *Caesar and Cleopatra* from the wings, why couldn't he stay angry with her? He supposed it was all the memories–the long road out of oblivion they'd traveled together. But she was committing professional suicide and he had to stop her. True–she was a gifted actress, but it would be some time before she possessed the clout to take on the Royal Shakespeare Company. He just had to convince her to wait the six months until her contract expired. Already he was receiving offers for her and when the time came, she could have her choice: another play, television, films.

The final curtain came down and he slipped away to wait in her dressing room. Standing there in the wings, Victoria would feel she had to put on a show for the other members of the company; she was far more apt to be reasonable if they talked in private. It would further be to his advantage to catch her off guard and a moment later as the door started to open, he moved back against the far wall out of her immediate sight.

Thinking herself alone, Victoria couldn't resist striking a pose in front of the triple mirror. She nodded regally and tossing her head, she sent the black locks of her Cleopatra wig flying back over her shoulders. It was at that instant she saw Matt's reflection behind her, grinning in evident amusement. The great actress had been caught playacting like a little girl. Ordinarily she would have been furious at his intrusion, but she had an immediate suspicion as to the reason for his visit. With a little laugh she whirled about to face him and immediately she was into another performance--equally as entrancing as the one she had just given on stage–a bravura performance as the public Victoria Windsor. "Matt, darling, how absolutely marvelous to see you! We can chat while I'm changing, but I am expecting someone." Before he had a chance to reply, she spun away again to disappear behind the screen.

"Whom are you expecting, Victoria?"

"None of your bloody business, luv. Your only concern is my professional life! Now what did you want?" Her tone was clipped, impatient and many people would have been cowed by it.

Matt had known her too long, however. "Victoria?" There was no reply. "Victoria?" he repeated more insistently.

"What?!" No doubt now–she was annoyed.

Or more likely she was trying to sound annoyed. "Forget the act, Victoria," he said, unable to suppress a chuckle. "You don't frighten me in the least." Peeking around the side of the screen, she gave an amused look which clearly said, "Well now, you've got me." He realized with a start that–quite inadvertently–he'd caught her in a thoroughly genuine moment and he was so charmed by it that he nearly forgot why he'd come. After a moment Victoria came out from behind the screen wearing a robe and sitting down at the dressing table, she reached for the cold cream. "And just whom are you expecting?" he asked again.

Her head came up, their reflected gazes locking in the mirror. "Damn you, Matt..."

"Because as I'm sure you're already aware, I suspect the engagement may be professional rather than personal. And if this is the case, it definitely is 'my bloody business' as you so eloquently put it."

Victoria made no reply. Instead she deliberately unscrewed the jar's cover and apparently ignoring him entirely now, she began to smear cold cream over her stage make-up. Matt said nothing further. He simply opened the latest issue of *Time Out* to one particular page and placed the magazine on her dressing table. "Victoria Windsor–this season's theatrical sensation–to portray title role in new play," the article was entitled. She glanced down at it. "Oh.....I...ah...see."

Her ramrod straight back screamed defiance at him, but somehow she only succeeded in appearing absurdly like a rebellious small child all dressed up for Halloween, white mask and all. Watching her, Matt couldn't decide whether to laugh or cry. "The Royal Shakespeare Company will never let you out of your contract, Victoria," he said quietly. "They'll sue you for so much it simply won't be worth it. On top of that it's an unknown playwright, an untried director. Why did you ever commit yourself to something like this without consulting me?"

All the time he was talking, Victoria had been methodically wiping off the cold cream with one tissue after another, ripping each one in turn from the box. She had then picked up the pancake intending to apply her own base make-up, but now as he asked the question, she slammed the container down again on the dressing table. "Because you have no ambition for me!" she declared as spinning about on the stool, she rose to her feet to advance on him. "No drive, no guts! Can't you see this is what I've been working for–what I've given up everything to attain?" Damn, she'd wanted to sound gloriously furious, but for some ridiculous reason that same recurring picture of a little girl in blue overalls and a pink pullover had flashed across her mind as she was speaking and her voice choked with emotion.

Matt wondered anxiously just how close she was to cracking. She'd sworn the nearly fatal combination of pills and liquor had been accidental, but he couldn't be sure that was the truth. Possibly she didn't even know herself. "Believe me, Victoria," he stated calmly, but firmly, "I am thinking of precisely that–of all you've worked so hard to achieve– of all you'll be throwing away if you persist in this foolish idea. Your contract is due to expire in only six months. If you still wish to undertake this project, that will be time enough..."

"No!" she screamed at him. "I won't wait" Her eyes filled with tears. "Do you understand me? I've waited for ten years and I will not wait one Goddamned second longer! If you won't do it with me, then I'll do it alone! I've been alone ever since I can remember and I can bloody well do this alone, too!"

In those brief moments Matt glimpsed clearly her desperate loneliness and at once he wished he hadn't. But at the same time he also knew that from then on he would follow her unquestioningly through whatever course she set for herself. Someone had to be there who cared about her. Was there anyone else, he wondered. I know so little about her. But I suppose that's the way she wants it. "I still think it's a mistake, Victoria..." he started to say.

"Get out of here! Get the bloody hell...." Just then, however, a knock sounded at the dressing room door. Victoria's entire body went rigid and she bit down on the back of one hand with such force Matt was sure she must draw blood. "Yes?" she said finally and the voice which moments before had been shrill and hysterical was now low and musical.

"It's Tony, Victoria. About ready?"

"Just a bit longer, luv," she murmured coyly. "I'm such a beastly slowpoke." Had he heard her screaming at Matt, she wondered. He must have.

"Well worth waiting for, Victoria. And by the way I have the contract."

"It seems I was right then," her agent observed wryly. "It is professional although it appears it just might be personal as well."

"Did I or did I not tell you to get the bloody hell out of here?"

"You didn't allow me to finish. I still think it's a mistake..."

"You've established that fact!"

"Yes, but what you didn't give me the chance to add is that since apparently I can do nothing to stop you, I can at least try to keep the situation from becoming a total disaster. I'll talk to the RSC governing board, but I can't guarantee anything."

She had won! "Matt! You are a luv!" Running the few steps across the room, she threw her arms around his neck and hugged him. "Now smile at me like a good boy," she coaxed him prettily as with her hands still behind his head, she leaned back to look up at him. He knew he was being exposed to a heady dose of the Windsor charm; nevertheless, he couldn't keep from smiling at her. "There, that's much better," she approved, returning his smile with a dazzling one of her own, "and, oh Matt, it really is the most super play–based on the life of Sarah Bernhardt! Wait until you read it! You'll see I'm right!"

"Yes, I'm sure you are, Victoria." He grinned at her again. "But sometimes I can't help wondering just who is managing who!"

She laughed at that, the pealing laugh already associated with her, but Matt all at once realized with a pang of renewed fear that her laugh, much like the beautiful smile of moments before, was actually quite cold. "But right now I have to get dressed for a late supper with my new director." Removing her arms from around his neck, she returned to the dressing table to pick up the container of pancake once again and continue with her make-up. "His name's Tony Blake-Ashley, by the way. Introduce yourself on the way out, why don't you?"

So just like that I'm dismissed, Matt thought with a chuckle. He glanced down at Victoria, but she was already absorbed in the reflection of her own face and had apparently forgotten he was even there. Out in the hall he obediently presented himself as Victoria's agent and was relieved to discover upon some discreet questioning that the man was at least a legitimate director with considerable repertory experience. They both agreed that Victoria was a gifted actress as well as a beautiful woman, but any conversation after that was decidedly stilted. Like most of the men in Victoria's life, they had little to say to each other and after a few moments Matt went along.

Had he as well also slept with Victoria, Tony wondered. He was already jealous of every other man with whom she associated. About twenty minutes later, however, he forgot his anxieties, at least for the time being, as the door of her dressing room opened again and Victoria herself appeared. "Tony, luv." Coming up to him, she raised her face to be kissed.

"Oh God, Victoria," he breathed. "I never thought I'd fall in love with you–at least not so quickly!" In his ardor he failed to realize she made no reply.

* * *

Privately Terence Cartier agreed it was the right time for Victoria to move on–that as a member of a company she tended to get lost despite her brilliance. But even as managing director he was still only one vote out of the seven on the governing board and Victoria was indeed fined–thirty thousand pounds. It was not difficult, however, to convince Tony that half should be paid out of the ticket gross.

"What about the rest, Matt?" Dressed in a pale lavender silk robe, Victoria was stretched out on the couch in the living room of her flat. She had as yet to apply any make-up and the dark circles stood out against the pallor of her complexion with frightening clarity. She was taking long swallows of hot tea as they talked, the mug shaking slightly each time she raised it to her lips. Tony had taken her out last night to celebrate her last performance with the Royal Shakespeare Company and as usual she'd had a great deal to drink.

"I've settled on a two thousand pound a week salary for the new play and..."

"Pays to sleep with the director, what?" Victoria laughed so hard at her own joke that she choked, causing her hand to jerk violently. The hot, milky liquid sloshed over the edge of the mug and down the side of her robe. "Ouch!" she muttered, "God damn it!"

"You're being paid what you deserve as an actress! Don't be ridiculous! Now, as I was saying–five hundred of that will go toward paying off the rest of the fine. I'm in association with a business manager now so we'll let him take care of that."

"In association with a business manager," she repeated after him with an airy wave of her hand. "My, we've come a long way, haven't we?" Suddenly she became intensely serious. "But it's all worth it, isn't it? Isn't it?" Sitting up, she reached out to him, but the sudden motion spilled more of the tea and as a last resort Matt finally took the mug away from her.

"Yes, Victoria, it is worth it. Believe me, every bit of it!"

"Of course you're right, luv," she agreed, tossing her head. "Every damned bit of it!"

Shortly after that her agent left and Victoria lay back, wishing desperately that her headache would ease. A drink would have helped, but she couldn't seem to summon enough energy to get up off the couch and walk over to the bar to pour it. At some point she must have dozed off because the next thing she knew she was being awakened by the ringing of the telephone. Her head still ached and furious at whoever had disturbed her, she made a vicious swipe at the instrument which was on the end table near her head. She only succeeded, however, in knocking it to the floor. It was another several seconds before she managed to retrieve the receiver. "Victoria, are you all right?" an anxious voice was inquiring as she brought it to her ear. Of course it was Noel.

"I knocked the bloody phone on the floor. What in hell do you want?"

"I'm sorry if I disturbed you." Instantly he was apologetic. "But I didn't get the chance to say good-bye last night. You...ah...left with Tony and I....."

"Yes, I <u>left</u> <u>with</u> <u>Tony</u>! I wasn't aware that was any of your damned business!" Victoria lay back again, closing her eyes. She had, of course, observed Noel last night hovering in the background, but she had carefully avoided him. In fact she had <u>been</u> avoiding him ever since her decision to leave the RSC had become generally known, hoping to avoid a tender scene of farewell. Why couldn't Noel, or Terry for that matter, simply leave her alone? She had made it painfully evident she didn't want their friendship and yet they stubbornly persisted. All at once she realized Noel was speaking again. With great effort she brought her mind back to the sound of his voice only to have him stop talking. "Sorry, luv, I didn't catch that."

Her voice sounded softer now, though terribly tired. He was somewhat encouraged. "I...I only rang to see if you were free for lunch, but it seems I've picked a bad time."

"Lunch? Oh, Noel, I don't think so. I feel bloody this morning. I don't even plan to dress." Was Victoria at all aware that had she really wanted to drive Noel or Terry away, she could have easily done so? Instead she put them off with pathetically flimsy excuses which only made it all the more apparent how much she needed them.

"I've joined a private actors' club, Victoria–one little affectation to go with my modest success." A somewhat bantering tone was always more successful with her, he'd learned; she probably found it less threatening.

"Much more than modest, luv. Well, all right, but you must give me an hour at the very least. Where is the place? I'll meet you there."

"It's called "Garrick's', of course–on Garrick Street, a block off St. Martin's Lane. One hour. I'll be in the lounge. It's just inside the main entrance on your right. Very quiet. I'm sure m'lady will approve." She laughed. This was the first time he'd called her m'lady. It would become their special private joke.

He arrived at the club about fifteen minutes before Victoria was due–wanting time to arrange matters. Nothing must happen to disturb or annoy her in any way. "Good afternoon, Mr. St. John," the club steward murmured unctuously. "What a pleasure and honor it always is to have you with us, sir." Noel had to admit that such treatment was one of the main reasons he paid the club's ridiculously high membership dues. "Will you be lunching with us, sir?"

"Yes–in about a half-hour. And...ah....Mitchell, I'm expecting Miss Victoria Windsor to join me."

"Ah!" The man's face lit up with pleasure. "A most beautiful companion, if I may say so, sir."

"Miss Windsor and I are merely friends and...ah...please take care, although I'm certain any such reminders are unnecessary, that Miss Windsor is treated with the utmost deference."

"Say no more, sir. I will see to the lady personally."

Victoria arrived promptly–only half an hour late–escorted to the table, as promised, by the steward. She was dressed in an off-white wool suit and a purple velvet turban. She had begun now to wear dark glasses a great deal of the time. "Vodka and tomato juice," were the first words out of her mouth.

"It's customary to start with 'hello', I believe, Victoria."

"Very funny!"

The bartender had approached the table immediately he saw her come in and Noel gave him the order–a whiskey and soda for himself. "How can you see anything, Victoria? It's dark enough in here without those glasses."

"God, luv, all that beastly sunshine. This is London, dammit. Couldn't it at least have the decency to be cloudy?" She did remove the glasses, however, and even in the dimness of the lounge Noel could see she was heavily made up. "One of my affectations," she continued, waving them in the air before slipping them into her purse. With her sunglasses put away she took out her slim silver cigarette case and removing a cigarette, she inserted it in the by-now familiar holder leaning forward slightly so that he could light it for her.

The bartender returned with the order and they settled back to enjoy their drinks. Later on upstairs in the oak-paneled dining room Victoria even allowed herself to be persuaded to have a small quiche with a pot of tea. Perhaps it was on this day she came to accept Noel as a part of her life. It would be still some time before she called him a friend, but then she believed sincerely she had no friends.

For Noel as well the day was magic. It seemed as if Victoria were finally permitting him a degree of intimacy–more so, he hoped, even than she allowed the men who were her lovers. When they had finished eating, he sought about in his mind for some plausible excuse to prolong their time together, but it wasn't until they came out of the club and he noted once again the sparkling clear December weather that an idea came to him. "It's....it's such a beautiful day," he suggested. "Why don't we walk a bit?" To his happy surprise she agreed and they strolled together along St. Martin's Lane to Trafalgar Square and from there up the Strand, glancing in the shop windows as they passed.

At some point, however, he became aware that Victoria was no longer walking beside him. When Noel stopped to look around, he discovered her standing–of all unexpected places–in front of a toy store, apparently fascinated by the assortment of dolls, games and stuffed animals displayed in its front window. He waited, expecting that at any second she would turn away from the window, make some witty remark and they would move on. But she did not. Instead she continued to stand there while Noel hesitated uneasily a few steps behind her.

He had no way of knowing, of course, that in the last couple of months Victoria's footsteps had often slowed as she passed a shop selling children's clothing or toys. Today her eyes had been caught by a gigantic panda–nearly four feet in height–and even though for the first time she wasn't alone, she'd been drawn to pause. Oh, what a Christmas present that would be for Olivia, she thought, gazing helplessly at the window. She wouldn't scream when she saw that. She'd even taken a step or two toward the shop's entrance when she stopped. What in hell am I doing, she thought. It will start like this and then I'll be trapped! She spun around to leave so abruptly that she walked directly into Noel who'd had no chance to move. "Dammit! Get the hell out of my way!"

Victoria strode off down the Strand, a puzzled Noel following at some distance, but no matter how fast she walked, she couldn't get that panda out of her mind. I could have it delivered, her thoughts continued. I wouldn't even have to say who sent it, but I would know I'd given her something for Christmas. And to her companion's now thorough bewilderment, she suddenly whirled about yet again to pass him going in the opposite direction and disappear through the doorway of the store.

A slim, blue-haired saleslady bustled up to her. "May I help you, madam?" Order book and pen poised, she was ready for action,

Never in her life had Victoria felt so foolish. What in God's name was she doing in a toy store buying some ridiculous stuffed animal for a child in which she wasn't the least interested. "I....I've changed my mind." She hurried from the shop to find Noel waiting patiently on the sidewalk. For some reason she found the expression of total confusion on his kindly face absolutely infuriating.. "God, why in hell can't you just leave me alone?" Frustrated, feeling trapped, Victoria stood there looking from him to the store and back to him again and back one last time to the window. "Bugger," Noel distinctly heard her mutter as she reentered the toy store.

"Yes, madam." The saleswoman was once more all smiles. "I presume you've changed your mind yet again?"

"I wish to purchase the large panda in the window." Victoria's tone was crisp and businesslike. "Do you deliver?"

"We're too small an establishment to make our own deliveries. However, the service we employ is entirely reputable."

"Fine. Will you take a check?"

"Do you have some identification?"

"Identification?!" Her eyes blazed with anger. "I am Victoria Windsor!"

"Who?"

"Victoria Windsor! Oh, the hell with it!" She pulled out her wallet.

"Fine, Miss Windsor. Where do you wish the panda delivered?" Victoria stopped in the action of opening her checkbook. She had no idea of the address. All her communication with Andrew had been through his office. Of course, she thought, I'll send it there. Let him give it to her. She gave the address of the solicitors' firm, handed the woman the check and with great relief she turned to leave for the final time. "Do you wish to enclose a card, ma'am?"

"No, I....I...don't. Ah...yes...yes, I...I...do." The salesclerk handed her one of their gift cards edged with tiny circus clowns and taking out her pen again, Victoria rapidly wrote, "Merry Christmas, Olivia". She hesitated–staring at the card–unable to write more yet equally unable to put the pen away. The clerk reached out tentatively to take the card. "No!" she snapped. "I'm not finished!" Not allowing herself time to think, she added "Love from Your Mother," and thrusting the card at the startled woman, she ran from the shop.

Her friend made a valiant effort to keep up with her. "Victoria," he gasped at last, "haven't we walked enough? How about a taxi?"

"Wh...what?" She stopped in the middle of the sidewalk. "Oh, yes...ah...all right."

Relieved to be in charge of the expedition once more, Noel immediately stepped off the curb to flag down one of the large, old-fashioned black London cabs. He helped Victoria into the rear seat and gave the driver the Woods Mews address. But even then her erratic behavior continued. One minute she was in constant motion, apparently incapable of remaining still–often leaning forward to peer ahead through the traffic or grasping him convulsively by the hand–while the next she was sitting bolt upright on the seat, one clenched fist in its lavender suede glove pressed against her lips–not so much motionless as rigid.

What Noel was able to observe, of course, was merely the outward manifestation of Victoria's inner turmoil. Dear God, why did I do it, she would think one minute. Then almost on top of that would come quite a different thought–Oh, how I wish I could be there when she sees it for the first time as long as I...I could be invisible or something. God damn me for a bloody idiot, she accused herself bitterly at one point. I don't even want her to know I exist and then I buy her something like that.... Oh, dear God, please don't let her forget I'm her mother..... "Noel." She said his name aloud because all at once it seemed she must speak or lose her mind.

He was terribly relieved. Perhaps now she would explain it all to him. Instead she simply repeated his name and fell silent, beginning again the alternating periods of frantic activity and unnatural stillness. Well, this only proves I was right all along, Victoria told herself with a certain sense of ironic triumph. Loving's just not worth it. It hurts too much. And suddenly now the inner voice which she'd first heard on the day she signed the divorce papers was back. "So you're finally willing to admit you love her then?" "No." Again-unwittingly this time–she had spoken aloud.

"What, Victoria?"

"I didn't say anything."

"You said, 'No'. Just that, but I'm sure you said it."

"I should know if I spoke or not." Such as it was, that was the extent of their conversation. It wasn't until the taxi had pulled into the mews and stopped that she again broke the silence. "Noel....would...would you...ah...like to come in for a while?"

He didn't immediately answer her. He'd been in her flat only once with the rescue squad–never at her invitation. He hesitated only briefly, however. It would be foolish to question his good fortune and this was, in addition, another time when she shouldn't be left alone. "Thank you, Victoria," he murmured. While she unlocked her front door, Noel paid the driver and then followed her inside.

"Can I get you anything?" she asked as she removed her suit jacket tossing it over the back of a chair.

"No, thank you."

"Please, tea, at least." It was obvious she wanted something to do.

"All right," he agreed. "tea then."

She retreated to the tiny kitchen, relieved to be occupied. With a lover she knew how she was expected to behave, what she was expected to do; with this man she was uncertain and very much ill at ease. Sitting on the couch, Noel listened to the pleasant, homely sounds issuing from the next room. He was almost sure Victoria wanted to tell him about the toy store and if this were the case, their relationship was venturing into untried territory. Presently she came out into the living room carrying a tray which she placed on a low table in front of the couch and sitting next to him, she preceded to pour tea. She was still nervous; she spilled the tea and the milk and she refused to look at him–that is except for one pleading glance, imploring that he somehow understand. Noel watched all of this–wanting to help her, yet painfully aware one wrong word could shatter the moment. "Noel, I.... You see, I...."

"You know you don't <u>have</u> to tell me anything." She gave him a long look this time, mutely expressing gratitude for his patience, "Might I have some more tea, Victoria?" He handed her the cup, thus once more offering her a sanctuary in the familiar ritual of milk, tea and sugar.

She accepted–again with obvious although unspoken appreciation. I have to say something, she thought, as she finished the business of refilling his cup and returned it to him. If I don't, he could imagine almost anything. Of course...how simple. Just be casual... casual. "It's nothing actually, Noel," she said finally with a deliberate lightness. "The panda is for my...my.... ah...daughter, that's all. I'll...I'll bet you...you never thought of me as the motherly type."

"How old is she, Victoria?" Noel inquired, trying also to sound offhand about it and failing just as utterly in the attempt.

"Ah...a little over three...I think. I...ah...really don't keep very careful track."

"What's her name?"

"Olivia." That's my middle name. I guess you didn't know that either."

"Do you see her often?"

"Not unless you call once in three years often! Her father has custody–an arrangement which suits me perfectly. Oh, God," she put her cup down on the table so abruptly that the tea sloshed over into the saucer. "What in hell am I doing drinking tea anyway? I need something stronger!" Over at the liquor cabinet she filled a large tumbler with brandy and drank deeply of it.

"Victoria, I wish you wouldn't."

"Oh, Noel, get the hell out of here! You're a damned nuisance!"

"Whatever you wish. Be seeing you soon though, hm?" She made no reply, but simply took another long swallow of the brandy, apparently intending to ignore him. "Victoria, I said, 'See you soon'. " He couldn't bear to leave without at least a promise on her part as to some future meeting. "Ring me up sometime, will you?"

"I don't know. It depends on what mood I'm in."

"All right....all right." At last he acquiesced, knowing that to stay any longer would only anger her. "Good-bye, then." Noel left quickly and quietly.

Alone, Victoria finished her brandy and poured more. Perhaps if she could only get drunk enough, she could forget the whole, bloody stupid mess.

The brandy hadn't helped at all on that occasion, of course, and neither did it help a few weeks later as she sat alone in her darkened living room in the early hours of Christmas morning–utterly sleepless. But then ever since she could remember, she'd hated Christmas–perhaps because on this day more than on any other she was so conscious of being alone.

This particular year Tony had invited her to Surrey to meet his parents. Noel, terribly concerned about her being by herself for the holidays, had proposed they spend the day together. She'd told them both they could "bloody well go to hell!" Even Andrew when he called to thank her for the panda–that damned panda, what an asinine thing to have done–had suggested a holiday visit with Olivia and given her his home address. She'd recommended the same destination to him. She needed no one's pity!

She was terrified of the sleeping pills now, but by the time she went upstairs to bed, it had begun to grow light and in desperation she took two of them. When she awoke again, it was broad daylight and rolling over a little to look at the clock on her bedside table, she discovered it was nearly two in the afternoon. So she'd managed to sleep more than half the day away; now if she could just get through the rest of it. I won't even bother getting dressed, she thought, stretching luxuriously under the covers. With rehearsals for *Sarah* beginning right after the first of the year, I'll just enjoy being lazy.

It was another half hour before she finally got out of bed. She slipped into a robe and stopping in the bathroom to take a couple of aspirin, she went downstairs to fix herself a pot of tea. I suppose I should eat something, she thought vaguely, but she couldn't think of anything that appealed to her. As she carried the tea things out into the living room, she heard the sounds of children playing outside and putting down the tray, she walked across to the window, moving aside the curtain to look out. It was the same irresistible urge which had drawn her into the toy store.

Several boys were kicking a football about, but Victoria barely glanced at them. A little girl about Olivia's size and coloring was pushing a doll carriage along one side of the cul-de-sac, across and down the other and across again back to the starting point-- around and around. She had no idea how long she stood there watching, but after a while it seemed as though the tiny girl had indeed become Olivia. God, what am I doing, she thought suddenly. Shaking her head as if to clear it, she returned to the couch to pour her tea, but when she picked up the pot, she discovered it was cold. Why this should have seemed so tragic, she couldn't imagine, but she was desolate and burying her head on the arm of the sofa, she began to sob.

There never seemed to be one particular instant when Victoria arrived at a conscious decision. One minute she was crying on the couch and the next she was back upstairs in her bedroom applying make-up more lightly than was now her custom, returning as well to the simpler hair-do of a few years before with her hair drawn back and fastened at the nape of her neck with a matching scarf. After all, she reasoned to herself, it's Christmas–a special occasion. I certainly don't intend to make a habit of it.

"A special occasion? I thought it was just another day?!" It was the same taunting voice. "It's not just because it's Christmas though, is it? You want to see your daughter. You love her, don't you?"

"No, I don't!" Victoria spoke out loud now in an attempt to drown out her accuser. "I don't love her! I never have!"

"Then why didn't you kill her when you had the chance," the voice accused her, "before she was even born?"

"I...I...just didn't get around to it in time!"

"Don't you know what love is," the voice persisted mockingly, refusing to be silenced. "It's a trap! And you're a damned fool if you let yourself get caught in it!"

"I won't get caught!" Victoria maintained. " <u>None</u> of what you're saying is true! I...I will go just this one time–and only because it's Christmas!"

* * *

Andrew had placed Victoria's gift under their tree along with all of Olivia's others, many of which her new stepmother had purchased. The moment the little girl spied the panda, however, she made a mad dash across the room to throw her arms around it showering it with kisses and everything else was ignored. Knowing Emily would be hurt, Andrew kept trying to interest his daughter in her other presents, but to no avail. She would obediently open each of the packages as he handed it to her only to instantly push it to one side and return to the panda.

At last leaving Olivia happily sharing a picture book with her new friend, Andrew and Emily went together into the kitchen to prepare holiday high tea. "Really, darling," she observed almost as soon as the swinging door had closed behind them, "if I'd known you were planning on something so extravagant, I wouldn't have bought anything else." He started getting out plates, silverware, etc. hoping simply to let the remark pass. But his wife was not about to let that happen. "Didn't you hear me? I said I wish you'd told me."

"I...I...didn't buy it," he replied finally.

"Who did then? God, that thing must have cost more than a hundred pounds!"

"Her...ah...mother sent it."

"That woman!" Emily exploded in anger. "What does she think–that expensive gifts can take her place?"

"No, no, of course not. You don't understand Victoria. She....."

"Oh, I understand her all right. What I <u>don't</u> understand is why you married me when you're still in love with her."

"After the way she treated me? Don't be ridiculous! But I can't help but pity her, I suppose."

"Oh, Andrew, you're so sweet!" Emily came into his arms. "And I'm glad she didn't realize how lucky she was. Otherwise, I wouldn't be your wife now. I can manage in here. I'm sure Olivia would like to have you with her."

Tenderly he returned her embrace. "I love you, darling," he whispered. He wished, however, as he walked back through the dining room toward the front hall, that he could be sure. Then a moment later, standing in the archway into the living room, he forgot all of this at least for the time being. Olivia was trying to put the panda on the couch, but the toy was simply too tall for her. Each time she managed to lift it just so far before she'd drop it, trip over it and land on top of it, all the time laughing in pure glee. "What is going on here?" he chuckled.

"I'm trying to put Teddy on the couch so he can watch telly with me, Daddy/"

"Come on, I'll help you." Picking up the panda, Andrew placed it on the couch, sitting down beside it himself. "Now why don't you climb up over there on the other side? I'd like to have a little talk."

"All right, Daddy." Olivia scrambled up on the couch, presenting as she did so a beguiling view of pink ruffled slip and panties under her rose taffeta Christmas dress. At last she turned around to settle herself in a sitting position, two chubby legs ending in black patent leather shoes and white socks sticking straight out in front of her. Primly she smoothed down her skirt–very much the lady. There were times, he thought wistfully, when there was an air of dignity about his little girl strangely out of keeping with her years.

"Well, first of all, honey, it isn't a teddy. It's not even a bear actually. It's a panda. I think the real ones come from China–way over on the other side of the world."

"My goodness, I can't call him Teddy, then, can I?"

"No, we'll have to think of something else, won't we?"

"Yes, oh dear me, what?" Olivia drew up her legs and sitting cross-legged on the couch, she rested her elbows on her knees–her head in her hands. It was her customary position for serious thinking.

"Well, that can wait, sweetheart," Andrew said, taking Victoria's gift card from his jacket pocket. "I've something more important to show you."

"What's that, Daddy?"

"The card that came with the panda. It says–"Merry Christmas, Olivia. Love from your mother."

"But why didn't Em'ly tell me she gave it to me, Daddy?"

"No, not Emily. Your real mother sent it to you. You remember, don't you? We went to see her."

"Oh, the witch with the black hair. I didn't like her!"

"I explained to you, Olivia, that your mother is an actress. She doesn't actually look like that. Her hair's really blonde and she's very, very beautiful."

"But if she's my mother, why doesn't she ever come to see me?" Andrew searched for an answer to that question, but for the moment he could think of nothing to say. "Daddy," the little girl repeated insistently, "why doesn't my mother come to see me?"

"Well, sweetheart," he finally started to reply, "you see....." He was interrupted at this point, however, by the sound of the doorbell. "We'll talk more about this later, I promise, honey." Slightly relieved at the reprieve, Andrew rose to go to the door. He reached it just in time; as he opened it, their visitor was about to leave. "Victoria," he exclaimed, "I'm so glad!"

"Yes, well, I've changed my mind. I don't even know what I'm doing here actually."

"Please–now that you're here, come in."

"What will your wife think?"

"You have a perfect right to visit your daughter," he replied, choosing to ignore her sarcasm.

"No, Andrew. It was a mistake. This part of my life is over and done with." And this time she did indeed turn away and start down the front steps.

"Who is it, Daddy?" Tired of being left out, the little girl had followed her father to the door.

Victoria remained where she was–still poised for flight–yet somehow held there immobile. "You can still leave, you know." The jeering voice was back and now it almost seemed to be laughing at her as though uncannily it knew already what she would do. "You don't even have to look at her. Simply go on down the steps and walk away." But her tormentor was wrong. How much could it hurt just to look? The instant she turned back, however, she wished she hadn't. Her daughter was utterly irresistible.

"Oh!" Olivia exclaimed, "is she a princess, Daddy? She's so beautiful. She must be a princess!"

"Sweetheart–you already know who this is." Briefly he paused. The last time he'd spoken these words it had gone so badly. "This is your mother."

"Oh, my!" Olivia took a step or two backwards, overcome with wonder that this beautiful lady in the fuzzy coat could actually be her mother.

"Please, Victoria," Andrew said, "now that she's seen you, you have to come in."

"Very well." Reluctantly she stepped inside. "I can't stay but a moment, however."

"Leave whenever you wish," he assured her. "I won't stop you." He turned to lead the way into the living room and after a second or two's hesitation Victoria followed him. Olivia remained where she was, staring wide-eyed; normally a friendly, outgoing child, she was suddenly shy, rendered mysteriously mute. "Come on, lovey," Andrew encouraged her. "Your mother wants to see you." The little girl walked slowly into the room, her hands clasped behind her back. "May I take your coat, Victoria?"

Allowing him to help her out of her fur, she started to walk toward an armchair on the far side of the fireplace, a safe distance from Olivia. "No, please sit on the couch so she can sit next to you. You see–here's your gift. She was thrilled with it, weren't you, darling? I can't understand why she's so quiet. She usually chatters constantly. Olivia, say something to your mother."

"I'm a stranger to her, Andrew. Why should she say anything? This was a mistake. Please–I really should leave." But even as she spoke, she moved back across the room to the couch as he'd asked.

"Sit next to your mother, sweetheart. Tell her how much you love the panda."

Obediently the child climbed up on the sofa, revealing once again the little pink, ruffled bottom. Oh God, Victoria thought, she's so dear. Helplessly she felt the tears starting. Olivia still said nothing, however. She simply sat there perched on the edge of the seat, her two chubby legs swinging back and forth and her eyes fixed steadily downward on her hands which she held folded in her lap.

"Sweetheart," Andrew prompted her again, "thank your mother for your Christmas present."

The little girl had to swallow two or three times before the words would come out and even then they were so faint as to be all but inaudible. This was due at least in part, of course, to the fact that she continued to look down into her lap as she spoke them. "Thank you for the panda, Mummy."

It was the first time she'd heard herself called Mummy and Victoria felt a warm, sweet sensation bubbling up inside her. If only at that moment Emily hadn't come into the living room. "Andrew, I need your help in the kitchen." She stopped as she saw Victoria. "I'm sorry. I didn't realize we had a guest."

"This is Olivia's mother." Andrew tried his best to sound matter-of-fact.

"Oh, so you decided to come after all?" Emily turned pointedly to her husband. "Will she be staying for tea?"

"Certainly not!" Victoria stood up quickly. "Even I am not that civilized!" She strode across the room toward the archway, swooping up her coat from the armchair where Andrew'd left it as she passed.

Olivia didn't fully comprehend what was happening except that this glorious creature who was her mother had miraculously materialized out of nowhere and now she was going away again. Flinging herself down from the couch, she ran to hurl herself at Victoria, grasping her just about at the knees. "No, no, Olivia, please—let me go," she murmured, trying to disengage the small arms from around her legs. Andrew was convinced, however, that he'd heard a note of tenderness in her voice and a moment later he knew he was right. Victoria had, at last, succeeded in prying her daughter's arms away, but instead of leaving at once she knelt down and enfolded her in her arms.

"Mummy!" Olivia cried out in ecstasy, planting a wet, sticky kiss on her cheek. "Please don't go yet! I love the panda! I really do!"

"I'll...I'll come back, Olivia. I promise. I'll see you soon. All right?"

"All....all right, Mummy." But her lower lip had started to tremble.

Abruptly Victoria stood up. "Good-bye, Andrew." Before she could weaken, she hurried out the front door and down the walk and this time she did not look back. Why did I say that, she thought to herself. Why did I promise? I'm never going to see that child again!

Chapter 9

The past two months had been trying ones for Tony. He was Victoria's director; he was her lover. Yet she would accept neither direction nor love. He could deal with her artistic ego–her strength of will as an actress. He understood–in fact, respected that. Far worse were the many nights when awakened by the sound of her crying softly beside him, he knew he was not allowed to offer comfort–that to force his way into this world of her private sorrows would surely drive her away.

* * *

On the night of the opening--February 20th-- Victoria and Tony rode together to the theatre. She'd already informed him in tones which clearly did not invite contradiction that no one was allowed in her dressing room before a performance. So of course he merely left her at the door with a quick kiss and a whispered "Break a leg". She made no reply and Tony turned to go. Mentally he shook himself; even if his leading lady didn't need him just then, there were countless other last minute details requiring his attention. Oddly, except where Victoria was concerned, he was a strong, decisive person. The house lights were just beginning to dim an hour or so later as he slipped into the seat reserved for him a few rows from the back of the center section. He took a deep breath. His professional reputation would stand or fall on the basis of the next two and a half hours.

Why, he would wonder afterwards, had he worried? The play was, after all, basically a one-woman vehicle and thus that professional reputation had rested in the hands of Victoria Windsor. How could he not have known? Had he allowed their personal relationship to blur in some way his perception of her as an actress or had he simply been too close to the project to comprehend the full power of Victoria's performance as somehow she had managed to capture both the arresting, often bizarre, even tragic essence of the woman herself as well as her flamboyant, overstated method of acting–a style vastly different from her own. She was not merely portraying the "Divine Sarah"; she had become her.

It was a strange scene at the interval–the audience appearing to be in a state of suspended animation. He heard none of the customary light chatter. Even those who recognized Tony murmured but a few words in passing. After a while he noticed Noel St. John standing off to one side. How must he feel about me, he wondered. At last he approached the other man, hand extended in greeting. "Mr. St. John, I don't believe we've been formally introduced. I'm Tony Blake- Ashley."

"Yes, I know who you are."

"And you don't like me very well either, it seems. But then I can understand how you might resent me, knowing I am....I am...."

"That you are Victoria's lover?" Noel prompted him after a moment, not too gently. "I hope you don't think I'm jealous. My feelings for her are not of a physical nature." Why did that latter sound stilted even to his own ears? He meant it, didn't he? "But yes, it's true I don't much care for the men who take advantage of her loneliness-- not giving a damn whether she's hurt in the process!"

"Then you have no reason to hate me. Believe me! I....I love her. I would never knowingly hurt her."

"Then I don't hate you." His tone was kinder now. "I pity you."

"Oh, I know she'll never return my love. I've long since lost any illusions along that line." Just then, however, the lights in the lobby blinked off and on again several times signaling the end of the interval. "Are you coming to the party?" Tony inquired as they began moving back into the theatre.

"I haven't seen Victoria for the last few weeks," Noel admitted. "I'm not sure I'd be welcome."

"I am the host. Consider yourself invited."

"Thank you. I must say that's good of you."

"I'll see you later then." He stopped in the aisle, indicating his seat. "Director's relegated to the rear, as you can see." Was that man truly just a friend, Tony wondered bitterly as he watched him walk away. That remark about his feelings for Victoria not being physical was pure Jersey bull! Noel, meanwhile, had continued on down to his own seat a few rows from the front. Blake-Ashley seemed a decent enough chap. Then why did he dislike him so intensely? But the house lights came down then and as the second act commenced, both men forgot for a while their personal feelings for Victoria, gripped as they were once again by her performance.

One of Bernhardt's final stage appearances was in a one-act playlet entitled "Au Champs d'Honneur" ("On the Field of Honor"). Aged by then, an amputee hobbling about on a primitive wooden leg, the actress played a young French standard bearer willing to give his life rather than allow the battalion's flag to fall into enemy hands. Quite appropriately the climactic moment of "Au Champs d'Honneur" was also the closing scene of *The Divine Sarah*. Like Bernhardt before her, Victoria stood alone center stage–the French tri-color clasped in her arms. She had even insisted on the use of a stage prosthesis–her own leg bent double at the knee, her ankle strapped to her thigh. Tony had been afraid she might fall. A brilliantly gifted actress of the present era, she was portraying a brilliantly gifted actress of another era who in turn was portraying a World War One soldier, but somehow these three beings had become one– an heroic figure who, as the scene ends, sinks to the ground mortally wounded.

The curtain came down and for a moment there was silence. Then from somewhere a single voice called out, "Bravo!" That unleashed it. Applause rocked the auditorium. It seemed the ovation could not possibly become any louder and then Victoria made her entrance having, of course, shed the wooden leg. At the curtain call she must be all grace. She came from the back and as she moved downstage to take her place in the middle of the line, as if of one body the audience rose to its feet. Victoria appeared physically and emotionally drained, which was understandable after the performance she had just given, but what everyone failed to realize was that she was now merely giving yet another performance–that of a great actress physically and emotionally drained after the performance she has just given.

They simply wouldn't let her leave the stage. Whenever the curtain descended for what was apparently the final time, chants of "No! No! No!" would fill the air, building in volume and intensity until they had to bring it up again for Victoria to stand center stage–alone now– taking bow after bow. What in hell is wrong with me, she was thinking even as she inclined her head yet again in acknowledgment of the acclaim. Nearly ten years of trying and failing and now that I've finally made it, I feel nothing. When at last the curtain came down and stayed down, she turned and moved rapidly off the stage, wanting only the solitude of her dressing room.

As she entered, Maggie, her dresser, came to relieve her of the soldier's cap and jacket. "Oh, Miss Windsor, isn't it all super?" In her excitement the girl had forgotten that up until now Victoria had barely spoken to her. "I was watching from backstage!"

"I thought your job was in here–not gaping in the wings like some little twit!" Mercifully for her maid's sake Victoria was interrupted at that point by a knock on the door. "And get rid of whoever that is!" She sank onto the stool in front of her dressing table in an exaggerated posture of fatigue. "I'm utterly exhausted."

Hurrying to the door, Maggie opened it. "It's Mr. Blake-Ashley, ma'am."

In one graceful motion Victoria whirled about on the stool, extending her hand to him. "Tony, please come in!"

Moving to her, he bent to take her hand in both of his and kiss it. "Dear lady, words fail me!"

"Tony, luv–how sweet!" Victoria put her other hand to her throat, lowering her head in an affectation of modesty. She glanced up at him coyly. "You were satisfied, then?"

"Satisfied! Oh, Victoria, I....."

"But you will excuse me now, won't you?" she went on quickly. The last thing she needed at that moment was another of Tony's inarticulate expressions of devotion. "I have to get ready for the party." Clearly he'd been dismissed–at least for the present–and raising her hand to his lips yet another time, he obediently withdrew. The instant the door closed behind him, Maggie saw her mistress' expression alter. The smile vanished and in its place was an odd mixture of relief and contempt. Just then, however, Victoria reached for her jar of cold cream and as she did so, she caught a glimpse of her maid still standing behind her. "Didn't I make it clear that I desire privacy?"

"But I thought you would need my help taking off the rest of the costume. The boots always....."

"I'll do it myself!"

"Yes, ma'am." Maggie left without saying anything further, closing the door noiselessly behind her.

Automatically Victoria opened the jar of cold cream, but she'd applied only a single smear of it to one cheek when she stopped. Why don't I feel happy, she pleaded silently with her cold cream streaked reflection. But she allowed her thoughts to go no further, forcing herself to concentrate instead on her preparations for the party: first the removal of her stage make-up; next one of the luxuries that came with stardom-a hot shower in her private bath--and at last the painstaking application of her own face–far more important for now she would be portraying not merely Sarah Bernhardt, but Victoria Windsor. Finally at this point she allowed Maggie to return to do her hair, piling it high on her head in a gleaming chignon and then she slipped into her gown. And what care and thought she'd given to its selection! Her final choice had been jet black chiffon in the style of a Roman toga–one shoulder left bare. The color served perfectly to set off her hair and complexion and the flowing material, embedded with countless tiny rhinestones, streamed out behind her when she moved like the ripples of a lake sparkling in the moonlight.

It was about an hour later when Victoria and Tony arrived at the ballroom he'd hired for the occasion. The party had been a tremendous financial gamble–at the time he made the arrangements *The Divine Sarah* still being very much an unknown quantity. But personally he was hazarding far more. The party was for Victoria and he hoped she'd be grateful. In the entry hall he helped her out of the mink stole which had been his opening night gift to her (another considerable investment, needless to say) and the cloakroom attendant took it away. "Tony, it is simply too beautiful! You shouldn't have, luv," she murmured as she took his arm to walk into the ballroom. "Well, shall we?"

"Oh no, Victoria." Gently he removed her hand from his arm. "This is your night and your night alone. I'll be right behind you."

"Yes, that's true after all." A strange expression passed over her face. "I have done it alone, haven't I?" Two red-jacketed waiters opened the double doors leading into the ballroom and then came the final touch which Tony had considered truly inspired. As the doors swung open, the orchestra sounded a fanfare. Sadly it was all wasted on Victoria. All she could hear was that one word–alone–its bleak echo filling her head with the sound. Somehow she found the presence of mind to place one foot in front of the other and start down the stairs into the hall.

The head table stood on a low platform and from their vantage point at one end of it Dylan Mallory and Sir Terence once again watched her solitary promenade together, wondering even as they did so at the fact that though they were both well aware of her faults, they nevertheless continued to care deeply. And they knew as well they weren't the only ones; in the crowd here tonight were many others. Victoria made a great show of greeting Amanda Thatcher and David Douglas from Stoke-on-Trent– a highly theatrical peck on the cheek for each. It was as much Tony's triumph tonight and yet there he was, following along behind Victoria like an imitation Prince Philip. And of course there was always Noel St. John whose devotion bordered dangerously on the obsessive. They could just glimpse him hovering in the background.

"Well, her moment has finally come, eh, Dylan?" Terry remarked at one point.

"Yes, it certainly has," he replied. "I only wish she could enjoy it."

The older man's response to that observation could only be a rueful smile since just then Victoria was finally coming up the couple of steps leading to the head table. Tony immediately drew out her chair for her. "No, no, luv–not quite yet." Patting him on the hand, she moved along the rest of the table to bestow her attention on the fortunate few chosen to sit there, coming at last to Dylan and Terry. "Dylan, luv." She stroked his cheek with the tip of her forefinger extending her other hand to Terry. "Sir Terence."

Terry raised her hand to his lips. "You were magnificent tonight, my dear."

She acknowledged the compliment with a slight nod and only then did she allow Tony to lead her back to her place and pull out the chair for her. Dear God–I need a drink! It was the first conscious thought Victoria had allowed herself since she stepped through the doorway into the ballroom. It had been all she could do to hold the pose she knew everyone expected of her–the great actress in her moment of triumph. Actually she had no alternative; if she allowed it to slip even a little, the entire facade could shatter. "Tony, luv." Briefly she caressed his hand and her voice betrayed none of her inner turmoil. "Be a darling and get me a drink, will you?"

"Of course, Victoria." Tony signaled the waiter assigned to the head table and ordered.

A few minutes passed. Victoria's fingers drummed an impatient staccato on the table top. "What in hell is taking so long?"

"It's only been a short while....I was so proud of you tonight, my darling."

"I am not yours!" At last the drinks arrived. "Unless the service improves," Victoria snapped, "I intend to request a different waiter!"

"Excuse me, Miss Windsor," the man stammered. "The bar is very busy."

"Did you tell them it was for me?"

"No, ma'am, I...."

"The next time, do so!" She drank deeply of the vodka and as the warmth spread through her body, she experienced once again that miraculous sensation of release. Quickly she finished the drink and demanded that Tony order another and from then on, even as admirers came and went, she was never without a glass in her hand.

Tony was growing concerned. "Are you ready to leave yet?" he finally inquired. "It's nearly two-thirty in the morning. You must be exhausted."

"What you mean, luv, is that I'm jolly well getting blotto. You are correct and I intend to get more so."

As the crowd thinned out, Victoria's state of intoxication became increasingly noticeable to those remaining. Tony had begun going to the bar himself to avoid the knowing glances of the waiter. It was while returning from one of those errands that he happened to pass Noel. The other man seized his arm in an urgent grasp. "Can't you take her home?" he asked worriedly.

"If I suggest leaving one more time, St. John, it will be over between us."

"Noel, darling!" Victoria trumpeted merrily across the by now half-empty room. "Come here, luv!" Reluctantly he followed Tony up to the head table. Now was the wrong time for her to notice him. In her current condition she was capable of doing or saying anything. "Tony, what in bloody hell took you so long?" She snatched the drink out of his hand and in the process spilled some. "Naughty, naughty Victoria. You know that wasting vodka is a mortal sin!" She laughed loudly at her own drunken wit. Then all at once in the midst of one cascading peal of merriment her glance came to rest on Noel, who was still standing at the edge of the platform. Her laughter died away as she appeared to make a conscious effort to focus on him. Gradually a tipsily crooked smile of recognition spread across her face–a face that even in her advanced state of inebriation he found achingly lovely– and she waggled her forefinger at him in playful admonition. "Noel....Noel....Noel... Noel....Noel....Noel... you are very naughty, too. You haven't once come to say hello to me."

She started to get to her feet, intending to go over and give dear Noel a great big kiss, but the room spun around her in dizzying circles and abruptly she sat down again , upsetting the drink in the process. "Oh, dear." For a moment Victoria sat watching the wet stain spread across the blue linen tablecloth–a bemused expression on her face as though she were viewing some new phenomenon. Then she appeared to spot the empty glass and picking it up with an unsteady hand, she began to run a finger around and around the inside of the rim, raising it in turn to her lips to lick off the vodka.

Tony and Noel glanced anxiously toward Dylan who was still at his end of the table although Sir Terence had finally left about an hour ago. With a long sigh he stood up and came to join them. "Well, if neither of you stalwart gentlemen has the courage to cross the queen, I do." He sat down beside Victoria. "Time to go home, luv," he said quietly but firmly, taking the glass away from her and handing it to Tony.

Again it apparently took her a second or two to focus. "Hello, old Dilly..Dilly...Dilly." Draping her arm around his shoulders, she leaned against him to nibble on his ear. "Still faithful to the frumpy little wife of yours or are you ready for me?"

"Flattery will get you nowhere, beautiful lady. Time to leave."

"I...I don't want to go!" She sounded like a spoiled child.

"Victoria–listen to me!" His tone remained discreetly low, but he obviously did not intend to be ignored. "Tonight you have known theatrical triumph such as few of us have ever experienced. Do you want to end the evening by passing out in front of all these people or perhaps getting sick all over your expensive gown?"

Dylan knew very well how alarming Victoria would find the prospect of public humiliation. He was right. His words penetrated. "Very well." She nodded with that excessive solemnity peculiar to inebriates. "You may take me home."

"Tony, hold her other arm," Dylan suggested. "We can at least give her a reasonably decorous exit." Supported by her two escorts with Noel serving as rear guard, Victoria did indeed manage to cross the room and climb the stairs to the entry hall where they collected her stole. A moment later they were outside on the sidewalk. "Noel," Dylan directed briskly, continuing to take command of the situation, "see about finding a taxi, will you?"

"Righto!" He disappeared off around the corner at a trot.

"You'll be spending the night, I presume, Tony?"

"Yes, of course. Thanks, old chap. I know I should be firmer with her, but I...."

By now, however, the crisp night air had sobered Victoria up enough to make her aware of where she was. "What in hell am I doing out here?" she demanded angrily. She began to struggle to get away from the two men who were still standing one on either side of her holding her by the arms, but fortunately just then a taxi pulled up to the curb and Noel jumped out of the back seat. "Oh no," she exclaimed, renewing her efforts to free herself. "You can't make me go home!"

"That's what you think, Victoria," Dylan replied with a grin as the three men shoved her unceremoniously into the taxi, Tony following.

"How long can this go on?" Noel inquired worriedly a moment later as the two of them stood together watching the red rear lights of the cab dwindle away down the otherwise deserted city street.

"I've managed to combine acting and booze for years," the Welshman observed lightly. "I'm sure Victoria can do the same."

"How can you possibly joke about this?" Noel was genuinely shocked. "Can't you see she's destroying herself?"

"Believe me, I am more than aware how unhappy she is. But what else can we do for her? You better than anyone should know that."

"Well, yes, I suppose so," he admitted reluctantly. "Only I feel so damned helpless and I....."

"Victoria's very fortunate to have you for a friend. I hope you realize that."

"Yes," Noel sighed and his smile even under the dimness of the street light was noticeably bleak. "I just wish she knew it."

"Share a taxi, old man?"

"No...ah...thanks. I think I feel like walking."

The two men parted at the corner and now it was Dylan who continued to stand there alone, watching Noel move away with his hands clasped behind his back, his head bent in thought.

* * *

Victoria was at last an established London stage star and for someone of such lofty status, a mews flat–no matter how fashionable and costly–was simply no longer suitable. Accordingly she leased a townhouse in Eaton Square, engaged an interior decorator to furnish it and hired two full-time employees; a housekeeper and a personal maid. The latter need not be identified since she, like most of her successors, would not long remain. The housekeeper was Martha Kendall.

Being in a West End play rather than in a repertory company meant that she gave eight performances a week now–eight performances plus all the parties, interviews and television talk show appearances–and of course Tony and Noel, both more than willing to dance attendance upon her. And yet with all of this, there was still too much time–too many empty hours–when inevitably Victoria's thoughts would turn to her daughter. Not that Olivia was ever really out of her mind, but when people were there to distract her, she was able to push the longing deep into her subconscious where at least it was less painful.

She wished the terrible yearning would go away and leave her in peace, but a love which had survived nine months of an "unwanted" pregnancy and over two years of separation could not be so easily dispensed with. Then why not reach out to the little girl? Sadly such a prospect terrified her. So there she was, trapped between the forces of love and fear; one pulling her toward her daughter and the other keeping her away and neither would let her go. She did telephone Andrew to inquire about purchasing Olivia's Easter outfit, but when he suggested a mother-daughter shopping excursion, she hung up on him.

* * *

Was I wrong, Andrew asked himself yet again? Would it have been better to let the little girl grow up accepting Emily as her mother? But he didn't believe he was wrong! In spite of everything Victoria had said or done he was sure she loved their daughter. "They have the right to know each other," he whispered fervently. "They do!" And somehow he managed to hold on to that conviction even though following the Easter phone call there was once again no word from Victoria.

Gradually since Christmas the little girl's questions about her mother had come less and less often, ultimately ceasing altogether, but that wasn't surprising. She was not yet four years old, after all, and it was only natural that over a period of months she would forget. That in itself sorrowed him, but perhaps it was just as well. Time had such an endless quality for a small child and the waiting would be easier if she did not spend it in longing.

Afterwards Andrew wondered why he'd assumed that simply because Olivia had stopped <u>talking</u> about her mother, she had necessarily stopped <u>thinking</u> about her. Almost from her baby days his daughter had possessed the awareness of someone much older and he'd been in error to attribute to her the understanding of merely the average four year old. Then too, although outgoing in other ways, Olivia was already a very private person, often keeping her deepest feelings hidden. In that she was much like her mother. It was not until late July that Andrew discovered just how mistaken he'd been.

He arrived home early one Sunday afternoon from a rain shortened golf game to find Olivia sitting cross-legged on the floor of the living room. She was cutting something out of the newspaper and for a moment he remained silently in the archway watching her. Also like her mother she had the habit of sticking out her tongue, moving it furiously back and forth as she worked, as if by this peculiar feat of facial gymnastics she could somehow concentrate her efforts more fully. Looking at her, a wave of love swept over him "Cutting something out of the newspaper, hm?" Andrew inquired, finally coming on into the room to sit in a chair near her.

At the sound of his voice Olivia started guiltily and seizing the clipping in one small fist, she pushed it as far as she could under the rest of the newspaper which was scattered about on the floor. "I'm...I'm sorry, Daddy. I....I'll clean this up so Emily won't get mad." Hurriedly she began picking up the scraps of paper, a task made more difficult by the fact that she was attempting to accomplish it with only one hand while the other still held tightly to whatever she was trying to hide from her father.

"Princess, it's all right for you to cut something out of the paper. But why won't you show me what it is?" Olivia looked up at him–her eyes filling with tears–but at last she handed him the clipping.

Andrew was startled to see a picture of Victoria. She was clinging ostentatiously to the arm of an unidentified escort and flashing a dazzling smile for the benefit of the camera. You would never have guessed that passing the photographer a few seconds later, she had told him to "Sod off, you son-of-a-bitch!" The caption noted that fact, but luckily her daughter wasn't yet able to read. "So," he observed lightly, "a picture of your mother." Leaning down, he brought the little girl up to sit on his lap. "Sweetheart, why did you feel you had to hide it from me?"

"Be...because you don't like it when I ask about her." Vainly she tried to keep her lower lip from quivering. "So....so I thought you must hate her."

"Olivia, I don't hate your mother. She and I were wrong for each other, that's all. But she is still your mother and I want you to love her. Have you cut out other pictures?"

"Yes, Daddy." Fresh tears flooded her blue eyes.

"You know what I think? I think you should have a scrapbook to paste them in."

"Oh, could I? That would be super! And Daddy–would you please tell me what it says under the picture?"

"Ah...." Andrew hesitated briefly before returning the clipping to her. "Ah..just that she was seen leaving a restaurant."

For a second or two Olivia remained silent, staring down at the precious picture now once more clasped tightly in her hand. "Daddy," she said at last, "do...do you think maybe Mummy will come and see me next week for my birthday?"

"Do you want me to ring her up and ask her?"

The little girl thought about that for a moment. "No, I...I don't think so. It...it doesn't really count that way." She slid down off her father's lap. "I'm..I'm going to put this picture in my drawer with the others."

Coming out of the kitchen just then, Emily watched her climb the stairs.. "Have you been up to the nursery yet, Andrew, to see our son?" she demanded crossly. "No, of course you haven't. Olivia always comes first."

"Now you know that's not true. It's just that David's usually asleep at this time of day."

"Well, I do care about my son! I'm going to bring him down for his bath."

He sighed. So they were back to the same old argument.

* * *

Martha Kendall was a woman in her early 50's, slightly heavy, though she carried her weight well. She would have looked very much at home in the late 19th century when someone of her size might have been more graciously referred to as queenly. Her brown hair was lightly streaked with gray and she still wore it waved softly about her face in a style long out of fashion.

Martha had been Victoria's housekeeper for nearly six months now and in that time she'd often wondered why she stayed. After all at least four personal maids had come and gone in that same period of time. Why don't I quit, she asked herself again this particular morning as she carried Victoria's breakfast tray up the stairs and along the balcony to her bedroom. I suppose it's because I know she needs me. She shrugged and balancing the tray expertly on one arm, she raised the other hand to rap lightly on the closed door. "Breakfast, Miss Windsor. You said to wake you at ten."

"Yes," Victoria mumbled sleepily, "come in."

Entering, Martha moved at once across the room to put the tray down on the night stand. She started to help Victoria sit up in bed, but the actress pushed her away and the dear, motherly woman had to satisfy herself with plumping up the pillows. Sadly she observed that as usual her employer was hung over. Her eyes were bloodshot and her hands were shaking as she ran them through her tousled hair. "Where's Alice?" Victoria demanded. "I need her to help me dress."

"You fired Alice yesterday morning, Miss Windsor."

"Oh...ah...yes–so I did. Bring me my bed jacket, will you?"

"Yes, ma'am. She moved quickly to the closet. "Drink your juice and eat your breakfast while it's hot, Miss Windsor," Martha prompted gently as she took out the pale rose jacket, returning to the bed to hand it to Victoria.

"I'm not hungry."

The housekeeper expelled a sigh of sorely tried patience. "Will there be anything else, ma'am?"

"Yes–ring for my car for half-past twelve."

"Yes, Miss Windsor." She started toward the door.

"Oh...and you might contact the agency about another maid. Tell them to send someone halfway competent this time!"

"Yes, Miss Windsor." Martha left closing the door quietly behind her.

Alone, Victoria slipped into the bed jacket, picking up the glass of orange juice from the tray. She managed one or two sips of that–Martha even squeezed fresh juice for her–but the smell of the soft-boiled egg nauseated her. A drink, she thought, a drink will settle my stomach.

The phone was ringing as Martha came down the stairs and she hurried on into the kitchen to answer it. "Miss Windsor's residence."

"Good morning, Martha, my love."

She smiled, her natural good humor restored as the owner of that voice invariably seemed able to do. "Good morning, Mr. St. John?"

"Is the lady awake yet?"

"Yes, but...ah...she's...ah....not feeling terribly well."

There was a brief silence on the line. "I see," he said at last and from the tone of Noel's voice it was evident he understood the nature of Victoria's indisposition. "Well, she's expecting my call. We're lunching together."

"Just a minute, Mr. St. John. I'll buzz her bedroom."

Martha had to repeat the summons a second time before Victoria finally answered. "Yes, what is it?"

"Mr. St. John's on the line, ma'am."

"Oh...ah...yes. Ask him to wait, will you?" Dammit, Victoria thought. All Noel needs is to hear my voice and he'll know I'm hung over. She took two or three more swallows of the brandy, cleared her throat and wet her lips. Only then did she pick up the receiver again. "Noel, dear luv," she gushed. "Good morning."

"And how is m'lady this morning?"

"I'm fine! Why shouldn't I be?" Only Victoria could take a perfunctory inquiry as an invasion of privacy.

"No reason–no reason, of course." He hurried on before an argument could develop. "What type of shopping did you have in mind?"

"I've...ah...changed my mind about the shopping, luv. With a performance tonight I simply cannot exhaust myself."

Noel didn't immediately answer her. He'd been surprised when she'd telephoned him a few days before to suggest lunch. Such invitations were rare. Even more puzzling, however, had been this mysterious shopping trip for which she apparently required his assistance–a shopping trip about which she'd now just as inexplicably changed her mind. "Yes, well....all right," he agreed finally, knowing better than to question her. "Whatever you say. But we're still going to have lunch, aren't we?"

"Yes, of course. See you about one, luv."

* * *

The Cafe-Royal was one of Victoria's favorites. Just a few doors down from Piccadilly Circus on Regent's Street, it appeared from the outside to be merely another entryway in an area of London quite similar in character to New York's Time Square. Inside, however, were several small dining rooms, very intimate and very private, done in soft pastel shades, each with cream-colored woodwork and cut-crystal chandeliers. Most appealing of all to Victoria was a small army of French waiters who treated her like a queen.

Noel knew she preferred the blue room and it was here he settled himself to wait for her. He always liked to arrive first–not that that was difficult. Being there ahead of her gave him the chance to study her from a distance–unobserved– and then to watch her come toward him–noticing her effect on other men as she passed–and perhaps in that short space and time to imagine himself her lover. Looking about now, he thought what a fitting setting this indeed was for her and then just as Noel's glance fell on the entrance again, she appeared.

He watched as Victoria paused–or was it posed, he thought with a smile–in the archway. Ostensibly she was searching for him, but at the same time she was giving everyone in the room the opportunity to notice her. Even more amusing was the fact that the maitre d' seemed to sense just how long to allow her to stand there before approaching to bow with great ceremony over her extended hand and escort her to the booth. With a flourish he drew out the table so that she could slip in beside Noel and presenting her with a menu, with yet another bow he withdrew.

"Hello, luv," she murmured, leaning over to kiss him lightly on the cheek. Even at such a comparatively early hour her breath smelled of liquor, but of course Noel said nothing about it, merely resting his hand briefly on hers where it lay between them on the table. Victoria leaned back in the booth and with a sweeping gesture she removed her dark glasses, tossing her head. "Well, Noel, did you order me a drink? You know I simply cannot function until I've had a drink!"

"Of course," he replied with a smile even though he knew full well she'd already had at least one today, "don't I always? The waiter should be here momentarily."

And at that precise moment, once again as though on cue, the waiter arrived–drink in hand. "Mademoiselle Windsor," he murmured unctuously as with a low bow he placed the glass on the table in front of her.

"You know, Noel," she observed caustically when the man had left, "I am positive that with each one of those enchanting Gallic bows my tab goes up by at least ten shillings!"

"I'm afraid I can't agree. The French merely know how to appreciate a beautiful woman. We Englishmen could learn something from them."

"You mean you don't appreciate me." She pouted prettily.

Noel reddened. "Of course I do. You know I do. I...ah..." He cleared his throat. "I say... if you don't care to shop, I have my car with me. Perhaps a drive?"

Victoria laughed merrily. "No, thank you, luv! That little car of yours is a menace!" With this she turned her attention to the menu so that for a short while at least he wouldn't expect conversation. It was extremely difficult to be witty and charming when her thoughts were in turmoil and her present companion was so much harder to fool than most people.

"Have you decided, Victoria?" Noel inquired a few moments later.

"What?" Startled, she looked up at him and he saw clearly that her mind hadn't been on the menu."

"Have you decided what you want?"

"Ah....a cheese omelet and tea, I suppose."

Noel signaled the waiter and ordered, but before they could resume their conversation a woman approached their table. "Excuse me, but aren't you Victoria Windsor?'

"Yes, I am."

"I know I shouldn't bother you while you're having lunch..."

"Then why are you?"

"I...I beg your pardon?"

Victoria's voice became extremely clipped. "I was asking why, since you knew you shouldn't be bothering me, you were still doing it?"

"I'm...I'm very sorry, Miss Windsor," The poor lady beat a hasty retreat and although Noel tried not to show his disapproval, the expression on his face betrayed him.

"Oh, don't look at me like that!" she snapped. "The only thing I owe the public is a good performance." There was a long silence then during which Victoria had finished her drink and ordered another one. She drank more than half of that one, still saying nothing, looking everywhere in the room except at Noel. "Damn!" he suddenly heard her mutter–half under her breath.

"Damn what...or is it whom?" he inquired with his most engaging grin–hoping to improve Victoria's mood. The day had showed every sign of being a pleasant one before that foolish woman put in an appearance.

To Noel's delighted relief he could see he'd succeeded as in spite of herself she smiled. "Do you know you're a love? What would I ever do without you?"

Even such a comparatively casual expression of affection was rare for Victoria and if spoken words could only be captured, not on some cold impersonal recording device, but actually captured and held like a more tangible treasure, Noel would have done so with these. As it was, he could do nothing–not even put into words his own tender feelings for her. Instead he simply repeated his original question. "Well—damn what or whom?"

"Oh, damn everyone and everything in general, I suppose–with the possible exception of you, of course," she added and she allowed her hand to rest briefly on his.

Noel could hardly believe his good fortune. Not only had Victoria's mood improved once more; if possible she was in an even mellower frame of mind than when she'd first arrived at the restaurant. He could never remember having seen her so apparently at ease, both with him and within herself and he couldn't stop himself from taking advantage of such a happy circumstance. "Victoria?" He was interrupted, however, by the arrival of their lunch. For a while after that they were both occupied with pepper and salt, the pouring of milk and tea, the addition of sugar, etc. and by the time the invariable ritual was completed, Noel's courage had failed him. The moment had undoubtedly been lost and it was better to let it go.

"Noel?" Her melodious voice broke unexpectedly into his thoughts and he blinked at her foolishly. "Noel?" She repeated his name more insistently, but her green eyes were sparkling with good humor. He was relieved. He would far rather amuse her than anger her. "You were about to ask me something, I believe."

He swallowed hard. "Yes."

"Well?" Victoria raised one eyebrow. "What is it?"

"Ah....I...ah....how do you manage to raise one eyebrow like that?"

"That was your question?" She laughed. "Oh, come now!"

"Well, actually, I...ah....I...." He took a deep breath and made the plunge. "I....have been rather curious as to what sort of shopping could possibly benefit from my help."

"Oh–that." Abruptly Victoria's gaiety died and she gazed down at her plate, toying with her omelet.

"But if you'd rather not tell me," he put in quickly, "it's all right. You know that."

"No..ah...I don't mind. I...I... My...my daughter's birthday is...ah...Sunday. I had thought about getting her something, but as I told you on the phone, I've decided to forget about it." She still refused to look at him. Of course, Noel thought, her little girl. I should have known. "Well, say something," Victoria prompted angrily when he continued to remain silent. "I suppose you think it's bloody stupid!"

"I don't think it's 'bloody stupid' at all. Naturally you'd wish to remember your daughter on her birthday. Of course I don't know how much help I'll be, but why don't we give it a go?"

Victoria glanced up at him then and her answering smile was tremulous, but touchingly genuine. "All....all right, I....I guess. You won't be much good with the clothes, but...ah....toys are always fun to look at, don't you think?" Her eagerness was touching and Noel had to fight to keep the tears back. "Let's go then, shall we?" she suggested a short time later–pushing her plate away. "I'm not really very hungry."

"Whatever you say, Victoria." He started to reach for his wallet.

"No, no!" She slapped him playfully on the wrist. "I have an account here and it's the least I can do." They left together, beginning to stroll along Regent's Street. "There's a little girl's dress shop along here somewhere," Victoria explained, "and around the corner on Oxford there's a toy store." He couldn't help noting she knew the exact location of these places. "You don't mind, do you, Noel?" Unconsciously she'd started to walk faster, at the same time speaking more and more rapidly until at last she was half-running and her words had become an unintelligible jumble. Noel had actually gone a few steps past the dress shop before he realized she'd disappeared inside. At least this time he knew he could follow.

"Yes, ma'am," the clerk was saying as he entered.

"Yes....I wanted to look at some dresses and perhaps a play outfit for a four year old."

"Well, let's see.. Yes, that rack over there to your left–from the divider up to the yellow tag. Is the child average size for her age?" I don't know, Victoria thought helplessly. My own daughter and I can't answer a simple question like that. "If you're not sure," the clerk suggested kindly, "it's better to get a slightly larger size. She can always grow into it. Perhaps the next section to be sure."

Victoria still hadn't moved and at last Noel stepped up beside her to put his arm around her waist. She was trembling. "Come on then" he prompted gently, "Perhaps 'Uncle Noel" can be of use here after all." He began sliding hangers along so that she could look at the dresses and slowly he could feel her relax.

"Stop, Noel...oh look, how sweet! That one, I think, don't you?" The dress was yellow with countless tiny ruffles. Hanging from the post of the hanger was a small, matching parasol. "Keep going–one more anyway....well, maybe one more...." This went on for nearly fifteen minutes and by the time they were ready to leave, she'd selected three dresses and two sunsuits.

"Are these to be delivered, ma'am?" the clerk inquired.

"Yes." Victoria gave her Andrew's address. She paid for her purchases and they left continuing along Regent's Street in the direction of Oxford Circus. Oh God, she thought all at once, I want to see her again. I want to see her and hug her and.... "Noel, are you....ah.... busy on Sunday?"

"No, why?"

"I...ah...thought I'd take my...ah...daughter out somewhere to celebrate and it....it would be easier if you came along."

"Where did you think you'd like to take her?"

"I....I don't know actually."

"How about the Regent's Park Zoo then? We could have lunch in the outdoor café and children always enjoy animals."

"Yes....ah....all right."

If only others could see her at a time like this, Noel found himself thinking. They'd realize then, as he had known all along, that so much of what they accepted as Victoria Windsor was nothing but protective camouflage. By then they had reached Oxford Circus, the point at which Regent's and Oxford Street intersect, crossed Regent's and walked the short distance along Oxford to the toy store.

An incurable ham, Noel took full advantage of this treasure trove of available "props" to clown outrageously; waltzing with the walking dolls, "taming" the stuffed animals and at one point thoroughly unnerving the poor saleslady by setting an entire row of wind-up toys in motion at the same time. He didn't care how angry the woman became; he loved to make Victoria laugh. At last, however, they chose another stuffed animal: an enormous lion with mane and tail of yellow yarn as well as a baby doll complete with layette and cradle. Noticeably relieved, the clerk wrote up the purchase, but as Victoria started once again to give Andrew's address, Noel stopped her. "Let's take these with us on Sunday." he suggested.

"I...I haven't asked her father yet. He may already have made plans." Quickly she finished giving the clerk the address.

"Why don't we go somewhere right now and you can ring him up and check."

"Keeping me at it before I can lose my nerve, hm? Cheeky devil!"

"If you wish to place a call, Miss Windsor," the clerk proposed at once, "our phone is at your disposal."

"Thank you." Noel turned sharply to look at Victoria as she dialed the number of Andrew's law offices. Had she actually said, "Thank you."?

"Granville, Granville, Carruthers and Roberts," the receptionist answered the phone.

"Mr. Roberts, please."

"May I ask who's calling?"

"His ex-wife!" The forefinger of her left hand tapped in rapid staccato on the counter–a mannerism Noel had come to recognize as a sure sign of anger or nervousness .....or both.

"Victoria, good afternoon," Andrew said pleasantly enough. Several times in the last few weeks he'd almost telephoned her. Olivia wouldn't have to know. But now it was just as his daughter wanted. The call had come from her mother and the little girl was right; it was indeed better this way.

"Andrew, I....I was wondering...ah...about Olivia's birthday. Could....could I...see her? If it's....it's not inconvenient, of course. It would have to be Sunday. Does...does she like the zoo? I...I thought...perhaps I.....I....."

Andrew smiled as he listened to her halting words. "She loves the zoo," he replied, "and we'll be celebrating on Saturday. What time would you like to call for her?"

"Ah....about one, I guess...for....ah...lunch."

"Fine. She'll be thrilled, Victoria."

"Yes, well I don't know why she should be. At any rate I'll be there on Sunday."

Noel's telephone woke him at eight o'clock on Sunday morning. "Noel!" It was Victoria, highly agitated and–what was even more unusual for her at this relatively early hour–wide awake. "Noel." She repeated his name. "I....I've changed my mind about today. You can make other plans if you like."

"What's wrong?"

"Wrong?! What in hell do you think is wrong? It's eight o'clock in the morning and I'm wide awake and what's worse–I'm stone cold sober!"

Noel fought back the impulse to laugh. "Believe me, Victoria," he replied as matter-of-factly as possible, "it won't be that bad. I'll be with you and the animals will keep her occupied."

Victoria called for him at about quarter to one. With a start he realized she was on time! "She's in a dreadful state, sir," the chauffeur had warned in a whisper as he held open the door of the limousine.

Noel glanced over at her as he settled himself beside her in the rear seat. What was there about Victoria, he wondered, that created the strongest initial impression? Was it her incredible beauty which even a wide-brimmed hat and dark glasses couldn't entirely hide or was it the warm, lingering scent of her perfume? Or perhaps it was that certain, indefinable presence she seemed to exude so effortlessly. Then she whirled about on him. "So help me, Noel St. John," she muttered from between clenched teeth, "if this day turns out to be the disaster I bloody well know it bloody well will be, I will personally hang you from the top of Nelson's Column!"

* * *

"Daddy, my...my tummy doesn't feel good. I....I think I'm going to throw up." Olivia was standing in the bay window of the living room watching for her mother.

Her father sat nearby in an armchair, the Sunday Times spread out in front of him-- not that he was actually reading anything; he just couldn't bear to look at his little girl's face–the nervous excitement it held. "You couldn't possibly be sick, lovey," Andrew replied soothingly. "You ate hardly any breakfast."

Resolutely Olivia swallowed, looking once more up and down the street. "Do I look all right, Daddy? Maybe I should have worn one of the dresses Mummy sent instead of a sun suit?"

"We've been through all of that, princess." And now he couldn't help but smile. It had taken the child forever to make up her mind. "And you look lovely," her father reassured her for still another time. "Your Mummy will be so proud."

"Oh, I hope so, Daddy! I want so for her to.....Oh!" Suddenly Olivia stopped and dashed over to her father. "Oh, Daddy, she's here and she's in a great big car! Come and see!"

The limousine drew to a stop in front of the Roberts residence and the chauffeur got out, climbing the stairs to ring the bell. "Go get her yourself," Noel had urged.

"God, no!" Victoria exclaimed. "It's bad enough I have to think of something to say once she's in the car–not to mention the whole bloody rest of the afternoon!"

Andrew answered the door. "I'm Miss Windsor's driver, sir," the man explained.

Olivia appeared beside her father in the doorway. Her glow faded somewhat when she saw a tall, rather forbidding man in a gray uniform standing there. "Wh...where's my Mummy?"

"She's in the car, young miss," the driver explained. "We'll take good care of her, sir," he continued reassuringly and taking Olivia by the hand, he led her down the steps to the car.

Andrew's heart turned over as he watched the little girl in the aqua and white striped sun suit march bravely down the front stairs and across the pavement, her long, light brown pony tail with its matching aqua bow swinging behind her with jaunty determination. Olivia paused just before getting into the back seat of the limousine to look back and wave. "Have a good time, sweetheart," he called after her with an encouraging grin as he returned the wave. Please, Victoria, he thought as the child disappeared inside the car, please! She loves you so much.

As Olivia stepped into the limousine, it only half-registered in her mind that there was an additional passenger, a man who had drawn back his legs so that she could slip past him to sit in the middle of the seat. For on the far side of that seat was the glorious creature who was her mother, dressed in something which looked like orange sherbet. (Victoria's couturier would have been insulted. The material was georgette and the colour was called Tahitian melon!)

The chauffeur had gotten into the driver's seat by then and as they pulled away from the curb, the little girl sat staring straight ahead overcome with shyness. With those enormous dark glasses, Olivia thought, and that big hat held in place with more of the orange sherbet stuff it seemed as though her mother had no face. And so for some time she forced herself to be contented with little sidelong glances, but all she could see were Victoria's slim, flawlessly manicured hands folded gracefully in her lap. Guiltily she shoved her own stubby fingers with their bitten nails out of sight under her legs.

Noel waited, hoping Victoria would somehow ease the tension. She wouldn't even have to speak. All she'd have to do was slip an arm around those rigid little shoulders and hug the child. Go on, he thought, mentally urging her on. But Victoria continued to sit there silent and unmoving, although–ironically–what she longed to do was precisely what Noel was wishing she would do. Once she did actually start to stroke Olivia's hair, but her hand stopped just short of touching the child's head, hesitated briefly and withdrew. At last he couldn't bear another instant of this emotion-charged silence. "Well, Olivia," he announced with a significant clearing of his throat, "since <u>no one</u> is going to introduce me, I'll have to do it myself. I'm your Uncle Noel."

Olivia turned her head and actually saw Noel now for the first time–shaggy-haired with warm, brown eyes which reminded her of the spaniel puppies she'd eyed longingly in the neighborhood pet store. (Emily said a dog would bother the baby.) She liked him on sight. "I....I didn't know I had an uncle. Do...do..." And here she summoned up the courage to look directly at her mother. "Do I have an uncle, Mummy?"

There was that word again—"Mummy"–together with the same sweet pain it evoked. "It would seem you have," Victoria replied and she looked almost accusingly over her head at Noel----"self-appointed."

Her tone was so cold and detached and the hat and dark glasses hid so much of her face that Noel could only guess what she must be feeling. "Do you like animals, Olivia?" he inquired. Why can't <u>I</u> think of anything to say, Victoria thought frantically. And why in hell didn't I have at least one drink before I came out. This wouldn't be quite as horrible if I weren't so damned sober.

"Oh, yes," the little girl replied. "I love animals."

"Me, too. What's your favorite?"

"Oh, dear, let me see." She had to give such an important question serious consideration. "I think maybe the monkeys. They do such funny things. What's your favorite animal, Uncle Noel?"

"You know I believe I like giraffes. What about you, Victoria?"

At the sound of her own name she jumped. "What?"

"What's your favorite animal in the zoo?" Noel repeated.

"Oh...ah...." Victoria's mind was a total blank. "I...don't know...ah...really, I...."

Fortunately at that moment the limousine pulled up at the Prince Albert Road entrance to the park, the nearest one to the zoo, and the driver got out quickly to open the door. "What time do you wish me to return, Miss Windsor?" he inquired.

Victoria looked helplessly at Noel. "I...I would think about two hours," he replied.

"Yes, Mr. St. John." The driver got back into the car and the limousine moved back out into the traffic.

Two hours!!!–Victoria thought in a complete panic. Two hours! God, Noel St. John, I could kill you!

Regent's Park was at its most beautiful–flower gardens in bloom everywhere, fountains spouting water. Olivia ran ahead, chasing some pigeons. "Relax, Victoria," Noel murmured under his breath. She's a delightful little girl, but then I'd expect her to be. She's your daughter."

"I can't take any credit for that–any more than a cat who drops a litter somewhere and promptly deserts them."

"Here's the café," Noel called after Olivia. "How about some lunch first?" Locating a table off to one side, he gallantly ushered his two "dates" over to it. "My, but I'm lucky, aren't I?" he observed as he first pulled out Victoria's chair for her and then a second for the little girl, "to be out with two such beautiful ladies!"

Olivia giggled, her eyes opening wide with pleasure. "Am I really as beautiful as my mother, Uncle Noel?"

"Absolutely!"

"You are very pretty, Olivia." Victoria finally managed to speak directly to her daughter. And how much she wanted to add, "And I love you so much, my darling." But of course, she did not.

"Oh, thank you, Mummy! I think you're beautiful, too!" The child's smile was hesitant, but utterly adoring.

"What would you like to eat, Olivia?" Once again Victoria fought the impulse to touch the little girl.

"I'd like a cheese and tomato sandwich, please," Olivia said in her best grown-up voice, "and a glass of milk."

For the first time Noel relaxed a little. At least mother and daughter were talking to each other. "Victoria?" he asked.

"Nothing. I'm not hungry."

"At least a cup of tea, then?"

"All right."

"I'll be right back." Noel went up to the counter to place their order, but the instant he was gone the same deadly silence descended.

Ever since last Christmas Olivia had clung to the gradually fading memory of warm arms holding her close, but now it seemed almost impossible that such a memory could have anything to do with this mysterious lady with no face. She even sounded different. The lady who'd hugged her had a low, soft voice like the one she'd imagined the heroines of her favorite fairy tales might have, but this lady sounded cold and wicked like maybe the evil queen in *Snow White*. Maybe this wasn't her mother at all, but a witch who planned to kidnap her and turn her into a troll or something dreadful like that. Becoming more and more frightened, Olivia wished desperately she could get away and run home to her Daddy, but then almost at once she realized she didn't know where home was from here and her lower lip started to quiver.

Helplessly Victoria watched her daughter's blue eyes fill with tears and behind her dark glasses her own brimmed in anguished response. More than anything she wanted to do or say something to dry those tears and make Olivia smile and laugh as she'd done in the car with Noel or a few moments ago when she was chasing the pigeons. But there'd simply been too many years alone until now Victoria could only sit there–more frightened and miserable even than Olivia–a virtual prisoner behind her hat and dark glasses.

With Noel's help mother and daughter managed to get through the rest of the afternoon. Victoria walked uncomplainingly from one cage and animal house to the next, though hardly speaking more than a few words at any one time, and beside her marched Olivia, her hands clasped behind her back, her child's face set in dogged determination-- also saying very little. If it hadn't been so sad, Noel would have found the scene amusing. They were so much alike. It was only as they were about to leave the zoo that a moment almost happened. Near the exit was a souvenir stand and noticing it, Victoria's footsteps slowed. "Would you like something, Olivia?" she asked and for the first time that afternoon her voice grew soft with tenderness. At least she could show her love for her daughter by spending money on her.

The little girl gazed longingly at the rows and rows of dolls and stuffed animals, but after a few seconds she resolutely shook her head. "No, thank you," she said firmly. "Daddy said I shouldn't let you buy me anything. You already gave me so much for my birthday."

Instantly Victoria backed off. "Oh, I see." Disappointment was evident in her tone and for the third or fourth time that afternoon Noel was sure the dark glasses hid tear-filled green eyes.

"Well, come on, then!" he enthused with a grin, "everyone back to the car! My, but haven't we all had a super day!" Noel's attempt at cheeriness fell considerably short of success, however, and the ride back to Andrew's passed once more in dismal silence. Victoria stared fixedly out the side window of the limousine while Olivia huddled miserably in the center of the seat, looking down at her new white sandals.

After what seemed like forever, the car turned the corner from Portobello Road into Wheatstone and at the sight of her own front door the little girl brightened visibly. "Good-bye, Mummy. Good-bye, Uncle Noel. I had a very good time. Thank you very much,' she said politely, but in her scramble to get out of the car the words were all but lost. Victoria's heart contracted in actual physical pain as she watched Olivia run up the front steps to where Andrew stood holding open the door for her. Of course he'd been watching for them. Oh God, she thought, she's so happy to get away from me!

"Well, here we are, sweetheart," Andrew greeted his daughter as she ran toward him up the steps. "Did you have a good time?"

Dashing past without stopping, Olivia ran on through the hallway and up the stairs toward the second floor. "I....I had a wonderful time, Daddy." And a moment later he heard the door of her bedroom slam shut behind her. "Oh, Mummy," she whispered and now she finally allowed herself to cry. "I love you so much. Why can't you love me back?"

* * *

"How about dinner somewhere, Victoria?" Noel asked quietly after they had once again ridden in silence for several minutes.

"God, no! After this hideous afternoon all I want is to be alone!"

"That's just it. I don't think you should be. I..........."

But at this point Victoria interrupted him by leaning forward to slide open the partition separating them from the driver. "Mr. St. John will be going home first, Harrison."

"Yes, Miss Windsor."

"And close that bloody thing! I would like a little privacy!"

"Yes, ma'am." He quickly obeyed.

"Convenient, isn't it?" Noel observed drily. "Now that you can afford to <u>hire</u> whipping boys instead of having to depend on volunteers."

"And just exactly who are these volunteers? I suppose you're one of them?"

"Yes, I suppose I am. I...."

"Well, who in hell asked you to be?" And this time the partition flew open with a bang. "Stop this car! Mr. St. John is getting out.....<u>now</u>!" The car pulled over to the curb.

"Victoria, please...."

"Didn't you hear me? Get the bloody hell out of this car!"

Reluctantly acquiescing, Noel got out and shut the door after him. A couple walking by had stopped to watch the scene. "Girl friend a bit miffed, eh, mate?" the man remarked.

"Yes." Noel smiled ruefully. "You might say so."

Alone in the rear seat of the limousine Victoria removed her sun hat and lay back against the cushions, closing her eyes. Only by remaining utterly still could she possibly contain her emotions–emotions which no one, not even a hired driver, must be allowed to observe. And thus for the fifteen minutes or so remaining until the limousine turned into Eaton Square, she managed to appear merely weary. How it would have surprised her that her arrival home was so nearly identical to her daughter's. "Good night, Harrison." Accepting his hand, Victoria stepped out of the car and as she walked past him, her face was as expressionless as her tone.

Her housekeeper was waiting at the door. "Good afternoon, Miss Windsor."

She nodded curtly as she hurried through the doorway and across the entry hall. "Take the evening off. I won't be needing you."

"How about dinner, Miss Windsor?" Martha followed her as far as the foot of the stairs. "Would you like me to leave you something?"

By now Victoria had reached the top of the curving staircase and started along the balcony toward her bedroom. "I'm not hungry," she replied flatly. Her tone obviously did not invite discussion of the matter and she still hadn't so much as paused in her headlong flight toward the sanctuary of her room.

Standing helplessly in the downstairs hall, Martha watched the softly floating hem of her employer's skirt and finally the cream coloured patent leather pumps disappear from sight along the balcony. Wherever Victoria had been that afternoon, something must have gone terribly wrong, but she knew that to pursue the issue would only precipitate an ugly scene and after some thought she decided to go to the cinema. She remained apprehensive, however, and on her way to the theatre she stopped at a phone kiosk.

"Hello—St. John here."

"Good evening, sir. I trust I'm not disturbing you. This is Martha Kendall."

"Martha!" Upon learning the identity of his caller, he immediately became anxious. "What is it? Is Victoria all right?"

"I'm not at the house, Mr. St. John. Miss Windsor told me to take the evening off. But she was acting so strangely when she arrived home a short while ago and I..."

Noel exploded. "Then dammit, woman, why did you leave?"

"You know how useless it is to argue with her. But I'm still worried, sir, and I was wondering if perhaps you could just happen to pop in on her."

"I'm afraid that's not a terribly good idea, Martha. You see, she ordered me out of the car this afternoon."

"You were with her then, sir?"

"Oh, yes." He sighed. "I never miss any of the great disasters of Victoria's life. Otherwise who would she blame them on?"

"Mr. St. John, would I be asking you to betray a confidence if I inquired what happened today?"

There was a brief silence. "No, Martha, I don't think so," Noel replied at last. "We...ah.... took Miss Windsor's daughter out. Let's just say....that...ah....the occasion was not a smashing success."

"I....I didn't even know she had a daughter."

"No, I don't imagine too many people do."

"Should.....should I go back?"

"No, I don't think so. You won't be away too long and perhaps it is best to let her have some time alone."

"Yes, sir, and....ah...Mr. St. John, this conversation will remain between us. If she ever learned I'd rung you up....."

"It will be our secret, believe me and....ah....Martha, you might telephone me again a bit later on to let me know how she is."

"Oh, Mr. St. John–you're ever so kind, sir."

"Yes...well, I...ah...." He sounded actually embarrassed. "I'll be talking to you then."

The conversation ended there, but as the evening wore on, Victoria was to remain very much in the thoughts of them both.

* * *

For a moment–after shutting the door of her bedroom--Victoria had leaned back against it, once again closing her eyes. "Oh, sweetheart, I'm so sorry," she whispered, tears beginning to ooze out from under her lids. "I want...I want...so much to show you how much I....I love you. From the moment the nurse first placed you in my arms, I've loved you, but I....I...just don't seem to be able to...to....

How long she stood there, Victoria couldn't be sure. It was a while before she summoned up enough strength even to open her eyes; it was another moment or so until she walked away from the door. She dropped her hat and dark glasses on the bed and unzipping her dress, she stepped out of it, letting it fall. Sinking down at last on the stool in front of her dressing table, she reached automatically for the jar of cold cream. "Why do I do it?" she asked her reflection–once more aloud. "I know damn well I'm incapable of being a mother and yet twice now I've made the mistake of trying. I try and I fail and it hurts. Oh God, it hurts! And worse it....it hurts my little girl. Well, I've learned my lesson. I'm better off without her and God knows, she's better off without me."

With her make-up removed Victoria showered and putting on a nightgown and robe, she moved noiselessly along the balcony again and down the stairs, listening all the time to make sure Martha had actually left. She heard nothing; no one was there. Alone, she thought, as she reached the bottom of the stairs and walked on into the living room. God, sometimes it seems as though I've always been alone. Even today–-with Olivia– I was alone. Over at the liquor cabinet she eagerly grasped a fresh bottle of vodka and opening it, poured herself a glass.

It was perhaps two hours after this that Martha came hurrying along Lower Belgrave Street from the tube stop at Victoria Station. Turning the corner into Eaton Square, she was just in time to see Noel getting out of a taxi in front of #14. "Oh, Mr. St. John," she exclaimed as she came up to him, "I'm so glad you're here!"

Pausing only long enough to pay the taxi driver, Noel followed her up the stairs to the wrought iron front door. "Well, you see I got to thinking about another time when I stopped to worry if she'd be angry with me and it nearly cost Victoria her life."

Martha had been fumbling to get her key into the lock–her fingers grown suddenly clumsy–but at this last statement of Noel's she raised her head to stare at him–her eyes wide with horror. "Oh, Mr. St. John, you don't mean that she..." By then, however, they were in the front hall and she stopped short as they both saw Victoria lying on the couch–the now empty liquor bottle on the floor beside her.

"Martha, do you know where Victoria keeps her sleeping pills?" Noel's normally deep, resonant voice was high and tight with apprehension.

"Oh, dear God, do you think..I mean....she did once then, didn't she?...I mean that <u>was</u> what you meant when you said that....."

"Dammit, woman, will you stop yammering at me and go check the pills!"

"Y....yes, sir. I'm sorry, sir." Martha hurried from the room and Noel stood motionless, listening to the sound of her footsteps as they moved rapidly up the stairs and along the second floor balcony.

After a moment he bent to pick up the vodka bottle, returning it to the bar–as though at a time like this neatness somehow mattered. Actually, of course, he was trying to avoid looking at Victoria, but finally he couldn't help himself and staring down at her flushed face, her hair lying in a golden cloud about her head, he felt a stab of sadness. It was all such a waste. Then all at once Noel could feel his gaze being pulled downward–again almost against his will–to where her nightgown and robe had become disarranged revealing one breast and for a second or two his eyes were held there as he wondered hungrily what it would feel like to touch her. "Oh, God," he muttered under his breath, "St. John, you're disgusting!" Quickly he adjusted the front of her robe and turned away, profoundly ashamed of himself that at a time like this he could have.... but just then he heard Martha returning.

"Mr. St. John! Mr. St. John!" She was already calling to him before she was even halfway down the stairs. "Mr. St. John, they're all here! At least...at least I think they are!" By now she was back in the living room, quite out of breath, the bottle of pills clutched in one hand. "I just had the prescription refilled at the chemist's yesterday and the bottle looks as though it's still full."

Noel breathed a sigh of relief. "Well then, Martha, I think we should just go away. It's better if she never knows we saw her like this. Is anyone else working for her at the moment?"

"No, sir. She fired the last maid and she hasn't hired a new one yet."

"Good. Then we'll just close the French doors and leave her alone until she wakes up."

"Very well, Mr. St. John–whatever you say." The housekeeper's eyes filled with tears. "But....but could I at least fetch her a blanket?"

Chapter 10

The months following Olivia's birthday were not happy ones for those who cared about Victoria. The little girl herself kept trying to understand why her mother didn't love her while Noel was haunted by the picture of his friend as he'd last seen her. If only there had been more recent, more pleasant occasions to supplant that day in their memories, but neither of them had seen her since. Perhaps, however, they were the lucky ones.

It was Martha Kendall who was forced to watch her driving herself in an endlessly repeating cycle of theatre to party to bed–rarely alone, of course–theatre to party to bed and all, the housekeeper suspected, to keep from thinking about her daughter. And now there was the matter of this Christmas party–not even a cozy evening in the actress' own home, but in the Grand Ballroom of the Claridge Hotel. RSVP's were pouring in; that morning's post had brought yet another batch. How truly sad, Martha thought as she opened them, when she could be spending the holidays with her little girl. "More acceptances, Miss Windsor," she announced gaily as she came into the living room.

Victoria was stretched out on the chaise lounge reading one of the plays Matt had sent over for her consideration. Even though *The Divine Sarah* had another six months to run, countless producers, directors and playwrights were already trying to interest her in a particular work for her next production. She glanced up. "Leave them on the desk. I'll add them to my list later... I wish you'd tell me one thing though," she went on after a moment as with a slight laugh and a theatrical wave of one hand she indicated the scripts piled on the chaise beside her as well as additional ones scattered about her on the floor. "Where were all these people five or six years ago?"

"I'm sure I don't know, Miss Windsor."

"Can you believe that? Four bloody years and I couldn't get one damned job?"

"That seems impossible, ma'am." Again she gave the expected response.

"Martha, be a luv and bring me a pot of tea and ring up Mr. Matthews for me, will you?"

"Yes, Miss Windsor." The housekeeper withdrew to the kitchen, immediately putting on the kettle. Chloe, the current maid, was ironing some of their employer's personal laundry. "Careful of those shirts, dear," she warned the girl as she dialed Victoria's agent. "Miss Windsor likes razor sharp creases on the sleeves!"

"Coo–fussy one, h'aint she?" Chloe scorched the cuff and proceeded merrily on as though nothing had happened.

Chuckling to herself, Martha wondered how long this one would last. Leslie Matthews came on the line and she buzzed Victoria on the intercom. "I have your call, Miss Windsor."

"Victoria, how are you?"

"Bloody marvelous, darling–except for the fact that I've been reading scripts and I'm positively dizzy!"

"You can't fool me, Victoria. You object to all this about as much as I miss the fish and chips shop!"

"You've got me there!." Her musical laugh drifted over the wire. "Seriously though, I rang up to find out if you had any preferences."

"My God, don't tell me you're asking <u>my</u> advice?"

"Very funny, you bastard." But her tone was affectionate. "Are you free for lunch some day soon? I'd like to discuss it in person. How about...ah... Tuesday?"

"I have an appointment, but I'll change it. After all I owe all of this to you."

"Yes, you do, don't you? Why don't you come here–about one. I'll have Martha fix something. Bye, luv."

Matt sat looking at the receiver for a few seconds before replacing it–a bemused expression on his face. "Yes, I know, Victoria," he said to no one in particular, "and you owe me a great deal as well."

* * *

The following Tuesday morning Martha was interrupted midway in her luncheon preparations by the ringing of the telephone in the kitchen. All other extensions were, as always, turned off until her employer was awake. "Martha, it's Leslie Matthews. There'll be another person for lunch if it's not a problem for you."

"Miss Windsor...ah...doesn't like surprises, sir."

"Don't tell her then."

It was only ten minutes or so before her guest was due to arrive that Victoria finally came downstairs into the living room, easing herself down onto the chaise lounge. She was sure that in its current state her stomach would never agree to accept solid food. Thank God it's only Matt coming, she thought.

"Excuse me, Miss Windsor." Chloe wasn't aware that the actress' normal condition in the morning required hushed tones and since they were at opposite ends of a fairly long room, she spoke rather more loudly than usual.

"Where in hell do you think you are?" Victoria enunciated every word with icy precision, "the Roman bloody Coliseum?"

The maid, of course, had no idea what that meant. Perhaps Miss Windsor hadn't heard her. She raised her a voice a little more. "Excuse me, ma'am, I......"

"Where is Mrs. Kendall?!!" It had been a mistake to shout!

"In the kitchen, Miss Windsor. She...."

"Go get her!" Thoroughly bewildered by now, the girl didn't move. "Don't just stand there, you little twit! Go get Mrs. Kendall!"

Martha had been trying not to hear the discussion, audible even from the kitchen, but as the volume steadily increased, it became impossible to ignore. At last with a snort of exasperation she threw down the pot holder and went to take up her customary role as peacemaker. "I'm sorry, Miss Windsor. It's my fault." She motioned silently for the maid to leave the room. "I sent Chloe to see if you wished anything."

"Stop trying to protect the girl, Martha. She's an idiot!"

"Yes, Miss Windsor." She couldn't help smiling. Chloe was an idiot!

"And what in God's name are you doing out of the kitchen? Matt would never forgive us if his souffle fell!"

"Yes, ma'am. That was why I sent Chloe. I...." The housekeeper took a firm grip on her patience. "Never mind. Is there anything I can get for you?"

"Really–is it necessary for you to ask?"

"No, ma'am." Once when she'd first come to work for the actress, Martha had made the mistake of suggesting that perhaps it was a little too early in the day to drink. She hadn't committed the same error a second time. "May I send the girl in with it?"

"Oh, please!" Victoria held up one hand in a gesture of mute dramatic protest..."my head!"

"Complete silence...I promise."

"Very well, Martha. You may go back to the souffle."

"Yes, Miss Windsor." Martha withdrew and a few minutes later Chloe returned, walking in an exaggerated tiptoe and carrying a tumbler of orange juice on a small silver tray. Well, at least the colour was orange; the actual liquid content was 90% vodka. The maid's blatant lack of respect did not escape Victoria's notice, but the girl could have ridden in stark naked on a unicycle for all she cared. She merely took the glass and waved her from the room. Later, she thought, I can have Martha sack her.

This idea amused her and Victoria laughed a little as she raised the glass to her lips. Power could be as intoxicating as this vodka--oh, but not nearly as soothing, her thoughts continued as she took the first sip–and by the time the door chimes sounded a short while later, she felt that just possibly she could face lunch. She didn't move from the chaise yet, however. Her entrance would be more effective if she waited until Matt was seated in the dining room. Besides Victoria Windsor never answered her own door. She listened to the sound of her housekeeper's firm, steady footsteps moving across the front hall, followed by the click of the latch and the faint, groaning sound as the heavy wooden door was pulled open. "Good afternoon, Mr. Matthews," she heard Martha say.

"Good afternoon, Martha," Matt's always pleasant voice responded.

But before he could continue, a second male voice broke in. "My good woman," this other unfamiliar voice proclaimed in the tones of one accustomed to instant obedience, "if you have any mercy in your soul, a very large Scotch–neat and just a little sooner than immediately!" She had been about to be angry with Matt for bringing another guest without her permission. But someone whose sentiments at this time of day were so like her own? Victoria laughed; she decided she could be forgiving.

But now she supposed the time had come when she herself must put in an appearance. So gathering up all her strength and composure, Victoria got to her feet to move slowly back down the length of the room and into the front hall. Here she paused briefly, steadying herself by holding on to the newel post and watching Martha who was already serving the men their drinks. The predominant color of the dining room was gold and her housekeeper's arrangements for the luncheon complimented the decor perfectly: pale yellow linen tablecloth and a centerpiece of yellow rosebuds and white button chrysanthemums set on a mirrored mat. Victoria never stopped to think how expertly Martha entertained her guests. She had simply come to expect it. "Matt, darling!" She extended one hand and with a toss of her head–not nearly as theatrical as usual due to her shaky equilibrium–she proceeded on into the dining room.

The two men rose as she entered. Matt made the introductions. "Victoria, may I present Mr. Basil Fitzhugh who, I am sure you already know, is one of Britain's outstanding contemporary playwrights."

A tall, dignified man with a trimly clipped black mustache, Basil was impeccably dressed in a three-piece light gray flannel suit, rose and gray pinstriped shirt and rose silk tie. From his demeanor as he came to meet Victoria it was evident he was accustomed to fanfare trumpets accompanying his every movement. Clearly there had been an unforgivable oversight. "My dear Miss Windsor," he murmured, accepting her offered hand and raising it to his lips with a flourish. "Allow me," he added as he escorted her to her place at the head of the table. Indeed Victoria had heard of Basil Fitzhugh, but less as one of Britain's outstanding writers than as one of its outstanding rakes. Among his female "acquaintances", it was rumored, could be found several ladies of unimpeachable social background. Basil, someone had once quipped, was using *DeBrett's Peerage* as his personal little black book. As for his work as a playwright, he produced a popular type of trash-- West End sell-outs, but hardly works of great theatre.

"Would you like a drink as well, Miss Windsor?" Martha asked.

"Now what do you think, hm? I'll have another...ah....orange juice. We must have our Vitamin C, you know, gentlemen."

"Ah, yes," Basil agreed smoothly, "I, as well, am very much in favor of vitamins. And you may bring me a refill, my good woman." He waved his already empty glass.

Wordlessly Martha took it and returned to the kitchen. Why, she wondered, had Mr. Matthews brought this revolting individual into Miss Windsor's home?

"A bit of the hair of the dog, Mr. Fitzhugh?" Archly Victoria raised one eyebrow.

"My dear Miss Windsor, are you insinuating I'm hung over?"

"My dear Mr. Fitzhugh—I never insinuate. You, sir, are hung over!"

"And so, dear lady, are you!"

Matt winced. He'd anticipated sparks would fly when these two met, but not quite so immediately.

Victoria, meanwhile, merely threw back her head and laughed. "How very perceptive of you!"

Martha returned just then with their drinks and almost at once after that began to serve the lunch. She'd learned that speedy service cut down a little on her employer's drinking. Along with the cheese souffle there were a molded salad, hot rolls and a rose wine.

"My compliments, my good woman," Basil exclaimed at his first forkfull of the souffle, "but, Victoria, wouldn't a white wine have been more appropriate?"

"But you see, I prefer the rose."

"An excellent reason." He chuckled nodding in approval as he took another sip of the wine. "And I might add, a superior vintage. Again–my compliments."

"Victoria," Matt finally interposed, "haven't you wondered why I brought Basil with me today?"

"Oh dear," she murmured, "then it wasn't merely to amuse me?"

"Basil has a new play. He brought it to me specifically with you in mind."

An expression of distinct annoyance passed across Victoria's face. "Matt, I really don't feel Mr. Fitzhugh's material is....ah...suitable for me as an actress."

"Come now, Miss Windsor," Basil interposed. "I thought we realized at once that we both like to speak frankly."

"Well...ah...since you insist on total candor, Mr. Fitzhugh..." Although her one finger glided coquettishly around the edge of her wine glass, her large green eyes had narrowed into slits. "Ah...I must tell you quite openly that...ah....your reputation is more as a debaucher of woman than as a playwright and I would consider acting in one of your plays to be rather like romping about in a dustbin."

The Fitzhugh vanity was legend and although Basil himself freely admitted he wrote trash–very profitable trash, he would hasten to add–no one else was allowed to say so. Matt felt himself tensing, awaiting the inevitable outburst. Instead a smile spread across the other man's face. "On the subject of fornication, my dear Miss Windsor, you must, of course, be considered the expert." Basil toasted her with his wine glass. "However, what we're discussing here is a purely professional relationship, I believe."

Matt had often wondered if all the sordid rumors about Victoria could actually be true. Now he observed pain transfuse her eyes at the playwright's cruel jibe and he knew. He wished he did not, but he knew. He found himself studying her. At not quite twenty-six was her beauty already beginning to fade? Nonsense, he rebuked himself sternly a second or two later; she's as lovely as ever. Well, no matter what he couldn't allow anyone to insult Victoria in such a fashion. But certainly she herself would never accept such treatment. At any minute now she would rise to her feet in a magnificent rage and throw them both out and that would be the end of it.

Then incredulously he watched her begin to smile–at first only slightly and then more broadly-- her lips moist and parted, her full breasts rising and falling noticeably beneath the soft lavender jersey of her dress. It's as though she were actually seducing him, her agent thought, a sick feeling in the pit of his stomach. "Very well...ah... Basil," she replied at last, "as long as we understand each other. Let's discuss your play." For Matt should have remembered her indomitable pride. Now matter how the words had hurt her, she would never give either of them the satisfaction of knowing it.

"I say, old man..." Basil's smile was the smug one of a man who has once again proved his remarkable understanding of women, "I believe you brought a copy."

"My briefcase is in my car, Victoria." Matt was afraid that if he didn't get some fresh air, he would certainly insult Martha's excellent lunch quite inexcusably by vomiting it all over the pale gold carpet.

"Never mind, luv. Who better to tell me about the play, after all, than the playwright?" Her hand came to rest on Basil's. "I can read it later."

"Basically it's about a married couple, or perhaps I should say formerly married couple, who meet again at a seaside resort. Each is currently involved in an affair although neither has remarried. Right now, the title is *Once More–Forever.* But that may change."

"You <u>are</u> aware I won't be free to begin rehearsals until another fall?"

"Believe me, dear lady, you are worth waiting for." He sighed in exaggerated rapture. "Legitimate at last. Won't mother be pleased?"

"Once a bastard–always a bastard, Basil. And that remark sounds suspiciously like Noel Coward."

"There's one thing you must keep in mind, Victoria, if we are to work together. There is no such person as Noel Coward."

Matt could see now that what he had at first mistaken for an easy intimacy was in reality nothing more than an intellectual fencing match: thrust, parry and riposte; thrust, parry and riposte. He wondered sadly whether this was the life which lay ahead for Victoria. "Well, we'll be off then," he announced with a cheeriness which he in no way felt.

Victoria paid the two men the distinct compliment of seeing them to the door herself–extending her hand in turn to each one. Distracted, Matt merely shook it briskly; she raised one eyebrow in silent rebuke. Basil, on the other hand, once again raised the slim, white hand to his lips in courtly tribute. "Bye-bye, luvs," she murmured. "Oh, Matt," she called after them a moment later as they started down the walk, "bring Basil to my Christmas party. He'll enjoy the liquor–if nothing else."

"She's magnificent!" Basil roared, giving Matt such a vigorous slap on the back that the other man staggered slightly from the blow. "Will she do the play, do you think?"

"I never can tell what she'll do. Believe me–it's entirely up to her."

Back in the living room, Victoria settled down to read the script of *Once More–Forever.* She was surprised to find it delightful, the humor in excellent taste–not at all what she'd expected of a Fitzhugh play. Even more important, the lead role of the ex-wife was a marvelous one–the lines brittlely witty, the character charming. She had to credit Matt's professional judgment; it would indeed be the perfect change of pace from the high drama of *The Divine Sarah.* Later that afternoon she rang him up. "You were right, luv," she enthused. "It's bloody marvelous! I'm going to do it!"

"Look, Victoria, I...I've changed my mind. It's not right for you. Or perhaps I should say Basil's not right for you. I....I didn't like the way he treated you."

"Oh God, is that all? He was simply speaking the truth–a bit brutally, perhaps, but the truth."

"Please, Victoria. I wish you wouldn't say such things."

"Oh, Matt." His eyes filled with tears as he heard the terrible weariness in her voice. "Matt, I don't have to pretend with <u>you</u>, do I?" He could barely hear the click as she replaced the receiver.

* * *

Martha emerged from the kitchen just as the hairdresser came down the stairs. She'd been up in Victoria's bedroom for more than two and a half hours doing the actress' hair for her Christmas party. "All done, hm?" the housekeeper inquired as she escorted her to the door–more for the sake of conversation than anything else.

"Yes, finally." The other woman shook her head. "Nothing would please her today."

The party was due to begin at eight o'clock and at 7:30 the chauffeured limousine drew up in front of Victoria's townhouse, having already called for Tony Blake-Ashley a short while before. Tony had been aware for some time now that Victoria was tiring of him and he'd been surprised, therefore, to receive the invitation--most particularly because it had included a personal note asking him to be her escort. But then he supposed she accepted his attendance on her that evening for the same reason she continued to tolerate his presence in her life at all. No one better had come along. This was small comfort, however, and as he climbed the stairs to ring the doorbell, he tried in vain to shake off a sensation of impending doom.

"Good evening, sir," Martha said politely as she held the door open for him.

"Martha." Entering, Tony nodded to her. He removed his top hat, but declined her offer to take his evening cape.

"You may have a bit of a wait, sir," she suggested tactfully.

"Yes, well, that's true." Tony smiled as he spoke, but Martha could easily see it required an effort. "Perhaps I will remove it after all."

"Very well." She helped him off with it. "May I get you anything, sir?"

"No...ah....thank you." He sounded strangely vague as though his attention wasn't really on their conversation. "I...I'll just wait in here." Martha watched him walk into the living room. Poor Mr. Blake-Ashley, she thought. Miss Windsor doesn't treat him very well.

It was indeed three-quarters of an hour before Tony finally heard Victoria's footsteps above him on the upstairs balcony and getting to his feet, he hurried out into the hall. He thought that by now he'd become accustomed to her beauty, but as she came into view on the stairs, he stood transfixed–an enormous aching lump in his throat.

Victoria's dress was snow white chiffon with a plunging, v-shaped neckline. Chiffon was her favorite fabric; she liked the way it moved with her and with this particular gown its effect was heightened by an edging of white marabou, both on the deep cuffs of the handkerchief-style sleeves as well as around the bottom of the flowing skirt. Her hair was gathered up and off her face to tumble down the back of her neck in a cascade of shimmering Grecian curls and scattered in among the ringlets were a myriad of tiny jewels so that with each toss of her head she seemed to sparkle in her own miraculous light. "Victoria!" Tony finally managed to exclaim, "words fail me!"

She smiled, extending her hand for him to kiss it. "Hello, luv," she murmured and she raised her other hand to touch him lightly on the cheek, "how handsome you look."

He relished the feel of her fingers against his face and for the first time in weeks he almost believed their affair wasn't over. He should have remembered she was an actress.

Martha came up to them just then, handing her employer's full-length white mink cape to Tony. He placed it over her shoulders and then accepted his own cape and top hat from the housekeeper. "Come, luv!" Victoria commanded as in a swirl of white fur she preceded him across the hall. He hurried after her to hold open the door and she disappeared out into the night.

"Have a marvelous evening, Miss Windsor," Martha called after her.

"Thank you, Martha." It was Tony, of course, who had taken the time to reply before he followed Victoria outside closing the door behind them.

Victoria Windsor's Christmas party–its location, its list of illustrious guests–had been well-publicized. She'd made sure of that. And as a result people had begun to gather in front of the hotel at least two hours before the festivities were due to begin.

In the crowd, however, there was one particular young girl. Tall and slim, she was at first glance quite non-descript in appearance, her brown hair pulled back into a little rat tail. It would only have been if you took the time to study her that you might have found yourself intrigued and even then her face was striking rather than beautiful with high, prominent cheekbones and large eyes. But more than anything it was the expression in those eyes which would have held you. They were filled with a hungry yearning. And perhaps that was it; perhaps the girl was merely hungry. She certainly wasn't very well off–the thin, brown macintosh little protection against the frigid December night–and her face was reddened by the cold. But no--it was more than that.

It had been nearly fourteen years since Rebecca Montgomery had last seen her half-sister–Christmas of 1951 to be precise–when they were four and eleven years of age respectively. Since then, of course, Victoria had become the famous actress with her minks and her Rolls Royce limousine, but what of Rebecca? It hadn't been long before Catherine Windsor Montgomery became as bored in her second marriage as she'd been lonely in her first and when this occurred, she once again sought consolation in the company of other men. Henry Montgomery simply couldn't bear the shame. It was his young daughter who found him, the revolver with which he'd taken his own life still in his hand. In Rebecca's mind her mother had killed her father as surely as if Catherine herself had pulled the trigger and returning home from the funeral, she packed her few personal belongings and left.

It was just about that time the name of Victoria Windsor began to appear in the London papers and Rebecca read those accounts and gazed at the photographs with as desperate a longing as Olivia or Malcolm Windsor. For as Uncle Bertie had been the one spot of warmth and love in Victoria's childhood, Rebecca cherished the memory of that Christmas when her half-sister had shown her a little simple kindness. On two or three occasions she'd almost summoned up enough courage to go backstage, but at the last minute she would always lose her nerve. Then she had seen the story about the Christmas party in a newspaper and an idea came to her. She could go to the hotel and wait outside or perhaps, if she were lucky, in the lobby. Their eyes would meet and right there, even with all the other celebrities, her sister would take her in her arms and she would no longer be alone. After all, Victoria had probably tried to find her as well, but how would she have known where she was?

It hadn't even occurred to Rebecca that others would be there as well–others for whom the actress was nothing but an object of idle curiosity–and arriving at the hotel, she was dismayed to discover a large crowd already gathered in front of the main entrance. There was no chance of her getting inside. Along with the others, Rebecca watched eagerly as each limousine, each sleek sports car drew up under the hotel portico. There was a continuous chorus of ooh's and aah's–an occasional smattering of applause–as each newcomer passed through the crowd– among them Sir Terence and Lady Cartier, Dylan Mallory and his American film star wife and Noel St. John, all of them waving pleasantly to the throng–but with each arrival the excitement was building. It was obvious most had come for only one reason–to catch a glimpse of Victoria Windsor.

Then suddenly a Silver Cloud Rolls Royce turned the corner and pulled up before the entrance. "Yes!" someone near the curb called out, "it's her!"

"Who's with her?" someone else asked. "Is it still Blake-Ashley?"

"Who knows?" still another person remarked and a ripple of laughter passed through the crowd.

The chauffeur got out and moved back to open the rear door. Tony alighted first turning to help Victoria. Gasps of admiration followed by applause greeted her appearance and she paused to acknowledge the ovation–nodding regally in several directions–all the time flashing the famous Windsor smile. At last she slipped her hand through her escort's arm and together they moved quickly across the sidewalk to vanish inside the hotel.

Somehow Rebecca had managed to work her way through the crowd to the front. "Victoria!" she called out. But her sister never heard her.

* * *

The Grand Ballroom of the Claridge Hotel looked on this occasion very much as it might have at the height of its Edwardian elegance. Directly above the center of its elliptical shaped dance floor hung a single crystal chandelier, descending in tiers from the pale blue ceiling like an enormous sparkling wedding cake and in the radiance cast by its myriad of twinkling lights the gold silk brocaded walls glimmered as though in truth made of the precious metal. Additional pools of light spilled out from tiny electric candles placed at intervals in mirrored sconces along each side of the room. On the outside wall floor-to-ceiling windows were partially hidden behind pale cream-coloured velvet drapes held in place by golden ropes, the heavy tassels all but lost in the opulent folds of the material and only revealed by an occasional glint as the metal caught the light. Circular tables were arranged in a double row all around the edge of the dance floor–each table set with white linen tablecloths and napkins, the material of which was shot through with a golden thread, and each holding a single gold candlestick.

Against this sumptuous background men in the stark black and white of their formal attire mingled with women in every style and shade of gown imaginable and as the whirlpool of colour assaulted the eye, a cacophony of sound assaulted the ear. The orchestra had begun to tune up while at the same time from the swirling multitude of humanity rose a murmur of conversation as the guests, with the assistance of liveried attendants, searched for their gilt-edged place cards.

There were twenty-eight tables, each with chairs for three couples and when all had located their places, there would be few empty seats. But where had Victoria found so many to invite? Quite elementary actually–she'd gone through the most recent copy of *Who's Who in the British Theatre.* She was testing her drawing power and she'd not been disappointed. She was the newest star in the London firmament and the human ego being what it is, very few had questioned the invitation. "Excuse me, sir." One of the attendants approached Sir Terence. "You and Lady Cartier are at Miss Windsor's table." But then what was Terry doing at the party? Certainly an actor of his stature didn't require the further gratification of his ego; many doubted Terry even <u>had</u> an ego. Could it possibly be, whether Victoria claimed to be aware of the fact or not, that he considered himself her friend?

Spotting Terry at the preferred table, Dylan Mallory couldn't resist coming across the dance floor to speak to him. "What sort of class system is Her Highness observing this evening?" he inquired wryly. "Or is it simply that she disapproves of my recent divorce and remarriage? I adore Victoria, but she really has no right to condemn anyone else's actions."

"Oh, I doubt whether she's making any sort of moral judgment. It's more apt to be that your new wife is a bit too glamorous."

"Ah, yes." Dylan grinned. "That would do it, wouldn't it?"

Just then, however, Noel St. John came up to the table, like the Cartiers a short while before, escorted by a uniformed waiter. "Good evening, Noel." Terry immediately extended his hand. "Is Victoria coming with Tony?"

"Yes, I...ah...believe so."

"Gentlemen..gentlemen, good evening all." None of them had noticed the approach of Basil Fitzhugh until all at once he was standing in their midst bowing and smiling, offering his hand to each in turn. He knew they despised him and the fact that they were too polite to tell him so amused him. It was all he could do not to smirk in their faces as they graciously returned his greeting and handshake. How he wished he could have seen their expressions a moment or so later as he also took his seat–at Victoria's table.

"Well...ah...I should be getting back," Dylan said at last, breaking the awkward silence–awkward that is for everyone but Basil, who was enjoying himself immensely. "Terry... Noel..if either of you feels like joining the outcasts later, the leper colony is somewhere in that direction." Pointedly he had excluded one individual from the invitation. The insult was wasted. Basil was ordering a drink from one of the waiters and apparently hadn't heard him. Perhaps, after all, Dylan thought, striding away across the dance floor, he was one of the fortunate ones. At least he didn't have to spend the evening with Basil Fitzhugh. He was surprised, however, to find Leslie Matthews at his table chatting with his wife. "Matt!" He exclaimed, "you–among the lepers?"

The other man chuckled ruefully. "Temporarily at least. I tried to convince her not to do the Fitzhugh play."

"Please...please, Matt. Let me get you a drink. A man of your impeccable taste more than deserves it."

It was nearly nine and there was still no sign of Victoria, but of course, as everyone realized, she was waiting to make her entrance. No one, moreover, thought it coincidental that on a trilling run of the harp the doors opened and as the orchestra burst into a Viennese waltz, the couple of the evening appeared. All eyes were on them as they descended the steps leading down into the ballroom and began the walk across to their table. And indeed Victoria had spent a great deal of time deliberating every move she would make that night–every word, every gesture calculated to have the greatest possible effect. For this promenade across the dance floor, for instance, she still wore her mink cape. Later everyone would have ample opportunity to admire her gown; for now she'd spent far too much on the cape simply to hide it away in the cloakroom.

The choice of her table companions had required considerable thought as well: Tony–well, that was unavoidable–he was her escort and there was the matter of appearances; Basil because he was amusing; Noel because he was comfortable and finally Terry and his wife. Victoria regretted the necessity of having another woman at her table, but at least Lady Cartier wouldn't be any competition. It took comparatively little time to settle on a partner for the first dance. It would be Sir Terence–tall and elegant in stature and most important the leading figure of the British theatre.

Arriving at her table, Victoria extended her hand first to Terry, then Noel and finally Basil–murmuring each name in turn.

"Magnificent–as always." Terry bowed low over her hand.

"Victoria–so very beautiful," Noel said fervently.

"My God–the number of animals that meet their deaths simply to clothe one human female staggers the mind," observed Basil. Victoria laughed merrily. Yes, her choice of this man as a tablemate had been an excellent one.

For a few minutes she continued to stand by the table, thus giving everyone sufficient opportunity to admire her–also part of her plan. Finally she allowed Tony to help her out of the cape and pirouetting prettily about, she extended her hand again to Terry. "Lady Cartier, may I please borrow your charming husband to dance the opening waltz with me?"

"Of course." The other woman did not sound very gracious about it, however. Personally Genevieve Cartier found Victoria cold and calculating and she failed to understand how Terry could be so fond of her. He claimed his affection was purely fatherly, but she doubted that. After all she wasn't that much older than Victoria herself.

For a while everyone watched as Terry and Victoria whirled about the floor, but gradually other couples joined them and the evening had officially begun. Ever the gentleman, Tony had asked Lady Cartier for the first dance. As for Noel–he was content for the moment at least simply to watch Victoria, his eyes following her as she moved with an effortless grace about the floor. "Worshiping at the shrine, I see," Basil observed after a while. "Well, we know one thing for certain, eh, St. John? She's not one of the vestal virgins!"

The other man rose indignantly to his feet. "I find your comment about the lady extremely insulting! I ask you to withdraw it, sir."

But Basil merely looked up at him in evident amusement. "Come, come, old chap. The 'lady', as you call her, would be the first to agree with me. Now sit down and don't make an ass of yourself."

"If you will excuse me," Noel replied stiffly as with a certain sense of relief he retreated across the dance floor in search of the Mallory leper colony.

Tony, meanwhile, having turned Lady Cartier over to another partner, walked back around the edge of the floor hoping that Victoria would also have returned to the table by now. Instead he discovered to his dismay that at the moment Basil Fitzhugh was its only other occupant. Well, it was either resign himself to this revolting man's company or be forced to wander disconsolately about the dance floor like some absurd lost lamb in search of its shepherdess.

"Thank God!" Basil rolled his eyes eloquently heavenward.

"Oh, come now! You appreciate my company about as much as I do yours!"

"No, no, my good man. I was merely expressing gratitude that since I've driven away one of Victoria's champions, another has appeared to take his place."

"While you're communing with the Supreme Being," Tony responded evenly, "you might inquire as to why a woman as beautiful and brilliant as Victoria chooses to associate with such an utter boor as yourself."

"Bravo!" Basil applauded him. "At least you possess a modicum of wit which is more than I can say for the other fellow. But all this...ah...shall we say cerebral jousting on the field of honor has left me quite parched. I go in search of liquid refreshment."

Tony made no further reply, but simply watched as his table companion proceeded directly across the crowded floor in the direction of the bar, ignoring totally the annoyed looks of the dancers whom he jostled out of his path. Clearly they had no right to be there. I wish I dared go look for Victoria, Tony thought forlornly, staring down at the champagne goblet he held in both hands, twirling it aimlessly back and forth, but I suppose that would only make her angry.

"Mr. Blake-Ashley?"

"Yes?" To his surprise Tony glanced up to find Julian Christopher standing there. A veteran of nearly thirty years experience in both theatre and films, lately Julian had worked more on the Broadway stage than in London, his specialty being the suave middle-aged Englishman who was the accustomed staple of drawing-room comedy.

"I haven't had the opportunity to congratulate you yet, old chap," Julian smiled down at him–exuding that peculiarly British brand of charm which Tony personally found overrated. "I've been working on the other side of the pond, you know, and I only just saw *Sarah* a few evenings ago. It's magnificent and, I might add, she is magnificent! Where is she, by the way?"

"Dancing with someone, I should imagine," Tony somehow managed to reply. "I don't think she's been at the table since we arrived." He knew, of course, the real reason Julian had come over to the table. The man's reputation was fabled.

So she's tiring of him, Julian thought, unable to suppress a smirk and I don't wonder. It's rather like pairing Aphrodite with a plow horse. Out loud he merely asked, "May I?" He indicated one of the empty chairs and without waiting for a reply sat down, signaling the waiter. "Ah...martini...very dry. So your first London production, hm?"

"Ah...yes." Tony knew he should get rid of Julian before Victoria came back, but it just seemed too much of an effort. Perhaps he simply wanted to get it all over with– to suffer finally the agony of losing her so that he could begin to forget her.

* * *

Victoria had promised herself she wouldn't get drunk that evening. Later perhaps–in the early hours of tomorrow morning--if she found herself alone and sleepless; for now, however, she must remain in control. Every man there wanted to dance with her and after several sets without a break she laughingly begged her partner of the moment for a glass of champagne. A little champagne would only add an extra sparkle to her personality by removing some of her inhibitions and helping her to relax.

Her escort (She had no idea of his name and no interest whatsoever in learning it) gallantly ushered her into one of the small ante-rooms where a buffet had been set up for drinks and light refreshments. Supper was to be served at midnight. Handing her a goblet, he made some remark, but she was only half listening, her eyes everywhere but on him. She noted the elegant decor, the silver and crystal glistening in the candlelight, the waiters and waitresses in their stiffly starched black and white, but most particularly the faces of her guests, many far more famous than she.

Just six years ago, she thought, I was an unemployed actress sharing a basement flat with the rats and the roaches and now look! I don't know even half these people and yet they're all here because I am Victoria Windsor! She remembered the many times she'd pronounced that name with a desperate pride, well aware that to everyone else it meant nothing and she enjoyed a small private smile at the memory. The name of Victoria Windsor was definitely no longer meaningless!

I don't know even half these people; it was the same thought of but a few seconds before, but this time for some reason it struck her quite differently. And all at once she saw her glorious party for what it really was, after all--a room full of strangers. Fortunately at that moment she was rescued from her own thoughts by the realization that the gentleman with her had asked her a direct question and she had absolutely no idea what he'd said. "Don't you think so, Victoria?" he prompted her.

She flashed him a dazzling smile. "Oh, I couldn't agree more, luv!" Patting him lightly on the cheek, she slipped away before he could say anything further and made her way back into the main ballroom. As Victoria started back across the dance floor, she discovered that despite the fact that Tony was the only one of her selected tablemates still there–good, old, faithful Tony– that he wasn't alone. Her immediate reaction was one of annoyance; how dare anyone sit at her table uninvited? But there was something about this man! Perhaps it was his sleek, meticulously waved gray head; perhaps it was the fit of his evening jacket–obviously not a rental-- or perhaps it was the way that as she approached, he was expounding on some subject-- gesturing broadly, deliberately calling attention to himself. Who could he be?

Of course she gave this fascinating individual no outward indication that her interest had been piqued. Rather, as she slipped into the empty chair between the two men, she purposefully kept her back to him, all her attention apparently on her current lover. "Tony, luv, I've been neglecting you shamefully." She leaned across to kiss him on the lips. "The next dance is yours—I promise." It was a promise she was never to keep.

"Victoria..." Even the man's voice as he spoke her name held an invitation. She allowed a beat or two to pass–so much of dramatic technique, after all, lay in timing– before she turned to face him. "I'm Julian Christopher," he continued, enjoying her glance of obvious recognition. It was a special kind of ego trip to introduce yourself to someone when clearly no introduction was needed. She extended her hand to him and Julian raised it to his lips. Swiftly now–with an ease born of long practice–he commenced the opening moves in his plan of seduction. "I must admit your invitation rather puzzled me, however." Still holding her hand between both of his, he began to caress it. "After all–we've never met." But he never took his eyes from her face and a mocking smile played about his generous, though somewhat thin-lipped mouth. Clearly <u>he</u> felt he knew <u>why</u> he had been asked.

Always in the past Victoria had been the seducer and what an hypnotic sensation it was now to feel herself in the hands of a master. Involuntarily her breathing quickened; her heart started to pound. Dammit, even the palms of her hands were perspiring. It wasn't that Julian Christopher was particularly attractive. He was, in fact, faintly repellent. The debauchery of his lifestyle was evident in his pale, blue-veined face and there was something about his long, thin neck and heavy, drooping eyelids that gave him a distinctly reptilian appearance. Why then, did she find him so undeniably, so disturbingly sensual? Julian, meanwhile, had continued to study her from under hooded lids. She was evidently discomfited and that amused him. "Well, Victoria," he prompted her, laughing a little.

"Did she ever think," she managed to reply at last, "that it was all just a clever ruse on my part–so that I could meet you?"

At that he laughed again. "You are utterly exquisite, my dear," he murmured and now his hand slipped up under the full sleeve of her dress to stroke the inside of her arm.

Involuntarily she shivered. Dear God, she thought, what must he be like in bed? As though on cue, the lights dimmed and as the orchestra settled into a distinctly sensuous rhythm, a crystal globe suspended from the center of the chandelier began slowly to revolve, sending sparks of color flying along the walls and ceiling. Julian did not ask if she wanted to dance. Instead he simply stood up and drew her into his arms.

It was a strange dance–described by Basil Fitzhugh *sotto voce* to someone near him as the "mating dance of the horny–oh dear, you will excuse me–of course I meant the <u>horned</u> owl." Their feet never left the one spot on the floor. Even the swaying of their tall, slim bodies in time to the music was barely perceptible and only their hands could be seen to move, Julian's caressing the small of Victoria's back, hers teasing at the nape of his neck. They had both understood from the first moment of their meeting the nature of their relationship and already it was commencing.

Tony had dreaded this moment for so long and now that it had come, he was too numb with despair to speak a word of protest. It had been a relief when they got up to dance, even more so when they became lost in the crowd and he could no longer see them. So it was finally over. He waited for the blessed moment when his anguish would ease, but it did not come.

From the other side of the dance floor Noel had noted only that Tony was alone at the table and his initial reaction had simply been one of pleasure that Basil wasn't there. The less time he had to spend with that son-of-a-bitch, the better. It was only as he came closer that he was able to observe the expression on the other man's face–more thoroughly miserable that he could ever remember seeing him. Perhaps I'm fortunate, Noel thought, as he approached the table, never to have been her lover. The heartbreak when it's over must be unbearable. But aloud he merely asked, "Is she still dancing?" Deliberately he kept his tone light.

"Yes." Tony didn't even look up.

Noel searched the dance floor for Victoria and after a while he caught a glimpse of her–dancing very close to.... But he couldn't make out the man's identity. "Who with at the moment?"

"Julian Christopher." Tony half-choked on the name.

Filled with a profound sorrow, Noel could think of nothing to say. Once again his eyes swept the dance floor hoping, perhaps, to discover Victoria starting back toward the table. Maybe, after all, it had only been a matter of one dance although secretly he knew even then that wasn't the case. Indeed he located her just in time to watch her and Julian disappear through the double doors leading from the ballroom.

"What's wrong?" Anxiously Tony followed the direction of his gaze, but by then Victoria was gone from sight.

"I say, this thing's becoming a bloody bore. Why don't you and I hit a couple of pubs before closing time."

"Oh no, old chap, thanks anyway." Tony shook his head and his smile was noticeably bleak. "Victoria may totally ignore me, but she'll still expect me to see her home."

Noel placed a steadying hand on his shoulder. "You see–she's...ah...already left with...ah... Julian." He could actually feel the other man flinch.

It was several seconds before Tony could control his emotions enough to speak. "I...ah.... see." He drew a hand across his eyes. Was it to wipe away tears? Noel couldn't be sure. "Then perhaps I <u>will</u> take you up on your invitation after all. I seem to have this strange aversion to being publicly humiliated."

How often afterwards Noel wished he'd left Victoria's discarded lover to his own devices that night. After all, what in hell did he owe Tony Blake-Ashley? It wasn't the hours of following an increasingly maudlin companion from one pub to another that he resented. It wasn't even being thrown out of his private club where they'd gone when all the pubs were closed because by then Tony had degenerated to blubbering incoherency. It was being forced to listen as the other man revealed many of his most personal memories of Victoria– intimate details of their relationship which he never would have disclosed if he'd been sober and which Noel would have given anything never to have heard.

Victoria's party, by the way, continued on to its gala conclusion: the midnight supper. Most of the guests could not have cared less whether or not she was still there as long as the free food and liquor were available. There were some, however, for whom the gaiety of the occasion had exited along with their hostess. Leslie Matthews left soon after Noel and Tony. Both Dylan and Terry would have preferred to depart as well, but their wives refused to go just because Victoria had been ill-mannered enough to leave.

"What's she really like anyway?" Elena Mallory whispered in an aside to Lady Cartier. "I can't get a straight answer out of my husband. He can't see past those green eyes and that incredible pair of boobs."

"Actually I don't know her that well."

"You're hedging, Genie."

"True. My honest opinion of the lady—" A slight pause. "She's a calculating bitch with the morals of a common hooker."

"Yes, that's what I thought."

It was small wonder Victoria had no female friends.

* * *

But what of Victoria herself?

Upon first meeting Julian Christopher at the table and even more as they danced, she'd felt that special elation she invariably experienced at the start of an affair. And this time the identity of the man added an extra fillip of excitement. Julian Christopher was known as a connoisseur of beautiful women. As *Once More–Forever* would be the perfect move in her professional career, he was undoubtedly the perfect new lover. Then to walk out on her own party with him–someone would certainly have seen them leave together-- and by morning all of London would be talking about it.

Alone with him in the rear seat of his limousine, however, her exhilaration rapidly faded and for the first time since that horrible night in Stratford she was actually a little afraid of a man. Perhaps it was because Julian's manner had altered so abruptly. Gone were the overpowering charm, the slick compliments, the suggestive caresses. Instead, except for a brief conversation on the car phone--apparently instructions to a servant–he was unnervingly silent. Even more strangely he made no move to touch her. He remained, in fact, in the far corner of the seat and as he had done at the table, he appeared to study her. Like a hunter stalking its prey, Victoria thought. She wrapped her mink cape more snugly about her, but in spite of the warmth of the fur she felt cold.

You are magnificent, Julian was thinking, but you are too accustomed to having your way with a man. Well, my beauty, I will show you what it's like to be utterly in the power of a man and what's more, I will teach you to enjoy it. In only a short while the car had pulled up in front of one of the new buildings of luxury flats recently constructed along the Thames Embankment. Julian stepped out first. He did take Victoria's hand to help her alight, but almost at once he dropped it again as with a sweeping gesture he invited her to precede him inside.

His penthouse occupied the two top floors. It was a few minutes ride in the lift, but still Julian said nothing. An Oriental houseboy greeted them at the door, also in silence, and assisting her off with her cape, the impassive domestic ushered her across the marble-floored, mirrored foyer to push open the double doors leading into the living room, indicating with several rapid fire bows that she was to enter. Her host had mysteriously vanished.

The living room had apparently been envisioned by its original architect as starkly modern in mode. The walls were off-white and the floor covered in a wall-to-wall white shag carpet. Julian's personal decorator, however, had managed to create the effect of a Tudor manor house. Suspended from the cathedral style ceiling were dark hand-hewn beams. The furniture as well was heavy and oaken, elaborately carved and upholstered in dark velvets. The room was on three levels; to her right a semi-circular conversational well faced a massive stone fireplace which dominated that wall while at the far left end of the room a couple of stairs led to a raised dining area.

Victoria walked slowly across the room and up the stairs. The dining table was clearly an antique–from an actual manor house perhaps or possibly a monastery–and at its head stood a ponderous captain's chair capable of having supported Henry VIII at his most corpulent. She noted further with a certain amusement that the table was already set–some sort of covered dish on a hot plate-and a bottle of wine was chilling in a silver bucket. Julian's staff was evidently prepared to entertain with little advance notice. Floor-to-ceiling windows offered a breathtaking view of the Thames and for a while she stood watching the lights of the South

Bank on the opposite shore as well as the lanterns of passing boats and barges far below in the darkness.

Then suddenly for some reason she began to find the room oppressive: perhaps it was the excessive warmth, perhaps the cloying odor of an incense she perceived in the air; perhaps there was simply too much luxury, but for a brief moment Victoria longed to escape, to breathe the crisp December air outside. She did not move, of course, and all at once she heard his voice directly behind her. "Spectacular view, isn't it?" She jumped, whirling about to face him. He had changed into lounging pajamas and a dark green satin robe and once again he was studying her.

"Well, do you like what you see?" she inquired and her voice was unnaturally sharp.

Julian knew she was uneasy and he liked that. It meant that he was already in control of their relationship. "Shall we, my beauty?" Drawing back one of the chairs to allow her to seat herself, he remained for the moment, however, the epitome of charming propriety. "Since you lured me away from your party before supper was served," he continued smoothly as he moved around to his own side of the table to open the wine, "I took the liberty of having Lin Tiu prepare a little something." The cork came free of the bottle with a resounding pop and Julian poured two glasses of a very pale champagne. Quite naturally Victoria reached for one. She wanted the champagne–to let her fear dissolve in its bubbles. But instead of handing her the goblet, he pulled it back just out of her reach and laughed. "Anxious, aren't we, my beauty." It further amused him that her hand was trembling. "You're not afraid of me, are you, Victoria?"

"Of course not! Now may I please have my wine?" Dammit! She'd meant to sound disdainful. Instead she had seemed to be begging.

"Certainly, my beauty." Again he laughed. "Certainly." He leaned forward slightly to reach across the table and hand her one of the goblets, watching with evident appreciation as she raised it to her lips. "You are truly incredible, Victoria," he murmured, "born, as they say, for the pleasures of the flesh." He didn't appear to expect any reply to his remark. Instead he simply took her plate and removing the cover from the chafing dish, he helped her to what turned out to be a delicious Oriental dish consisting of pork, rice and vegetables in a richly seasoned gravy. Julian also served himself and then sat down across from her.

The meal appeared on the surface to be quite casual; they discussed the theatre, films, literature, even the state of the British economy, but through it all ran a definite sexual undercurrent. Constantly as they ate, their hands met–touching and caressing–and of course they drank a great deal of champagne–or at least Victoria did. The first bottle was replaced by another and still another and soon the wine had worked its wonders–blurring the edges of reality. Victoria felt warm and relaxed. "Julian, do we have to sit at the table?" Her speech was slightly slurred. "It would be so much more comfortable over in front of the fireplace." Regarding him over her goblet, she ran the tip of her tongue around and around the inside of its rim.

His answering smile was openly condescending. He, after all, was comparatively sober and he knew perfectly well it wasn't comfort she had in mind. "Well, yes, perhaps we can have our brandy there."

"Brandy–on top of all that champagne? Julian, are you trying to get me drunk?" For just a moment he was uneasy. Was she at all suspicious? But then she laughed, tossing her head. "Because if you are, you're doing a bloody rotten job of it! I'm still in an upright position!"

"That will be taken care of shortly, my beauty." Rising to his feet, Julian gestured toward the fireplace. "Well then, shall we?"

Victoria hesitated. Exactly what did he have in mind? But she couldn't allow him to see she was frightened and after a moment she inclined her head in what she hoped would pass for regal assent. "Very well, sir." But when she attempted to stand, she swayed and would have fallen if Julian hadn't moved quickly to catch her about the waist. His face had been close to hers as they danced. Why hadn't she noticed how old he looked–how dissipated–even evil. Uncontrollably Victoria shivered.

"There you are, my beauty," he murmured solicitously, "you've caught a chill here by the window. You'll be warmer by the fire."

Was she moving across the room under her own power or was Julian half-carrying her? Victoria couldn't be sure. It just seemed as though all at once he was easing her down on the sunken burgundy velvet couch facing the fireplace. Once again, then, there was the same unnerving silence as he paused to light the fire already laid and waiting, afterwards moving a few feet to the left to push a button just beneath the mantelpiece. The paneling slid noiselessly back to reveal a bar and filling the bottom of two large brandy snifters, he finally came to sit beside her handing her one of the snifters.

No games now as with the champagne–it was time. Yet he must still proceed carefully, each move being executed with such matchless subtlety that she would be unaware of what was happening until it was too late. Then, although she would want desperately to stop him, she would be incapable of doing so. He noticed she had finished her brandy and he poured some more for her.

During the next half-hour or so he watched her slip gradually downward until her head rested against the couch. Rather uncertainly now she held her empty snifter out to him and yet again he refilled it. At last he decided he could risk an experiment and this time as she drank he moved closer, beginning to stroke her neck and shoulders. She made no gesture of protest and he grew bolder, easing his hand down inside the front of her gown. Victoria sighed deeply, stirring in response to his touch, and again she offered no objection as he took the snifter away from her, drawing her into his arms. His lips were hard and insistent, at once forcing hers open. His tongue flicked about inside her mouth and she moaned softly, pressing herself against him. He laughed a little, low in his throat as slowly he moved down to bury his face between her breasts. "Julian," she murmured.

He could hear in that one word how aroused she was already–feel it in the way her breasts rose and fell against him. "You are a magnificent creature," he half-whispered, "but you have only begun to learn what a man can do to you." And releasing her slightly, he reached around behind her to unzip her gown, easing it down off her shoulders.

She couldn't be sure exactly when he'd started to caress her; she couldn't even remember lying back against the couch. It seemed as though one minute she was sitting there sipping her brandy quite decorously and the next she was lolling among the velvet cushions and he was stroking her, running practiced hands over her neck and shoulders. Before she knew it, his hand was inside her dress. Then his tongue was inside her mouth, her brandy snifter having inexplicably vanished. Erotic sensations were coming so fast now–one on top of the other–that she could no longer tell when one ended and the next began. She didn't even realize he'd unzipped her gown until she felt it slip down her arms, but the next instant even that was forgotten as he began to bite at the tops of her breasts where they spilled out over the top of her strapless brassiere. "Your breasts! Your splendid breasts!" he commanded hoarsely, "Free them for me, my beauty! Free them!"

By now Victoria needed no further prompting as she fumbled with the closure on the front of the bra, her fingers awkward and clumsy in her haste to let her breasts loose–to allow him to possess them. At last she unfastened the last of the hooks and experienced the glorious sensation of heavy breasts hanging free and unrestrained. Their mere weight was arousing to her, but then he began to fondle each in turn hefting it in his hand, flicking his tongue across the nipple. "Oh God–Julian!" she gasped. "Take me here--now!"

"Not yet, my beauty." Incredibly she heard him laugh. "You don't want it quite enough. Show me how much you want it. Undress for me–over there." He gestured toward a spot about midway between the couch and the fireplace.

"Julian—no!"

"You don't want me to send you away, do you? After all, where else could a whore go at this hour of the night?" Somehow she managed to get to her feet and swaying unsteadily, she let the gown fall to the floor, reaching at once for the elastic waistband of her full length half-slip. "No...no." He stopped her. "Much too quickly. Do you want to put it all back on and start over again?"

"Oh God, Julian, please!" She forced herself to undress slowly and enticingly, pushing down her slip, her tights and her underpants and kicking each garment away until at last she stood naked before him. Certainly now he would take her; certainly now he would grant relief from the terrible burning, throbbing ache which ran through her stomach and down between her legs.

"Good. Much better," he approved. "Now move a little. Shake those gorgeous tits for me!"

"Julian, I can't...can't bear it any longer!"

"You want it, don't you?"

"You....you know I do." Feverishly Victoria began to vibrate her shoulders, causing her breasts to sway back and forth. He looked almost bored and like a thing possessed, she moved faster and harder, faster and harder until it seemed as though her breasts must fly off. The sensation of her own breasts banging against her chest and against each other aroused her beyond the point of endurance. "Julian," she half-moaned.

"No!" Again he laughed, enjoying himself immensely. "No, I think I'll just look at you for a while."

"Oh, God!" She shuddered convulsively. "What do I have to do?"

"You haven't really shown me yet that you want it. Beg me."

"What?!"

So there was still a bit of pride left. He smiled. Well, even that would be gone in a moment. "You heard me. Beg!!"

"I will not. I.... Please. Oh, please, Julian!"

"That's not begging. Crawl! On your belly!"

He had won. Victoria did not so much as protest as dropping to her knees and then her stomach, she writhed toward him across the floor, no longer even human. "Please, Julian," she gasped. "Please!" Rolling over onto her back, she reached up to him imploringly. "Oh, God, I beg you! Please—I'm....I'm in agony!" Her hips were undulating now straining toward him and she was running her hands over her own body.

For a moment or so he still watched her, exulting in his triumph, but finally he knelt over her on the floor and pushing her legs up and apart, he took her–viciously, cruelly-- jabbing into her repeatedly. Groaning–sobbing–almost out of her mind with pain, Victoria arched her body against him, her nails raking his back. She could feel herself climaxing. She didn't want to–not with this insane, depraved man thrusting himself into her again and again, but waves of passion were flooding over her. Her body was moving with his. Higher and higher went the spirals of sensation until it seemed she could bear the ecstasy no longer.

Julian found the actual sexual act distasteful as well as somewhat tedious and he was relieved when he felt Victoria stiffen and go limp beneath him. After a brief wait he moved off her, straightened his clothing and rang for his houseboy. "Put her to bed for me, will you?" he ordered as he strode from the room.

It was nearly 10 a.m. when Victoria awoke the next morning. Briefly the unfamiliar surroundings confused her, but then she remembered almost at once where she was. She felt sick, but she managed to raise herself up to a sitting position and it was then she discovered her clothes laid neatly across a chair in one corner. Momentarily this bewildered her all over again. She didn't know when or where she'd removed them the night before, but she was almost sure it hadn't been in this room. She wouldn't let herself think about it, however. All she wanted–for now–was to go home.

Willing herself to her feet, Victoria walked into the bathroom, but at the sight of her face in the mirror she exclaimed aloud in horror. She looked so ugly–last night's make-up streaked, her eyes bloodshot and her hair like a bedraggled bird's nest. She washed her face, but a search of her clothes caused her to recall that she'd left her evening purse on the table in the ballroom. I've got to start carrying an overnight bag with me, she thought with a brief, harsh laugh. She dressed quickly. Why did her glorious gown now only depress her? Just as she finished, a knock came at the door–so polite as to be all but inaudible. No one must see her like this! "Yes?" she snapped.

The door opened and the little houseboy entered, bowing and smiling at her genially. "Mr. Clistopher ask me see you. You wish anything, missy?"

"Two things." Her words were icily precise. "My wrap and a taxi."

"No bleakfast, missy?" He looked disappointed. "Lin Tiu fix velly good bleakfast."

"No Goddamned bloody breakfast. My cape and a taxi. Is that too difficult to understand?"

"No, missy." Bowing again, he turned to scurry away. "Cape in flont hall. I go ling-ling taxi."

"That's right," Victoria said to herself. "Take it all out on a harmless little Oriental." And this for some reason struck her as terribly sad.

* * *

For the first morning in some time, then, Martha found that her employer's bed hadn't been slept in. It must be a different man, she mused sadly. Mr. Blake-Ashley always came here. The phone was ringing as she came down the stairs and she hurried into the kitchen to answer it. "Miss Windsor's residence. Good morning."

"Good morning, Martha. It's Noel St. John. I don't suppose Victoria's awake yet." There was a long silence–so long in fact that he thought the line had gone dead. "I say, Martha, are you there?"

"Yes, sir...ah...Miss Windsor's not here at the moment."

"Not there? Don't tell me she's gone out already?"

"No...ah...Mr. St. John–not exactly."

"Oh, I see, Martha–thank you. Ah...have her ring me, will you? It's about Christmas shopping for her daughter. I thought I might help again."

"I'll tell her, sir. Good-bye."

Noel hung up the phone. It was incredible how his mood had plummeted in a few short minutes. Victoria hadn't come home last night and that could only mean one thing... Julian Christopher.

It was perhaps an hour or so later that Martha looked out the front window just in time to see a taxi stop and her employer get out, as much as possible of her face and hair hidden by the collar of her fur cape. As she hurried up the stairs, Martha opened the door. "Pay him for me, will you?"

"Yes, Miss Windsor." Taking a small change purse out of her apron pocket, she went out to the waiting taxi.

"Coo," the driver observed, "these rich birds who stay out all night and don't even 'ave a quid for the fare,"

Martha gave him a withering look. "That remark just cost you your tip so I hope it was worth it." When she came back into the house, Victoria was more than halfway up the stairs to the second floor. The housekeeper remembered Noel's call. "Miss Windsor?"

Victoria stopped and turned slowly to look down. "Yes?"

Recalling the exquisitely groomed woman who'd left for the party the evening before, Martha was shocked by her employer's appearance. "Mr. St. John would like you to ring him up–about Christmas shopping for your daught...." The housekeeper stopped short. She'd remembered too late she wasn't supposed to be aware of Olivia's existence.

"My WHAT?!"

"N...nothing, ma'am. Just ring Mr. St. John." Martha moved away, hoping to escape into the kitchen. "Please excuse me now, Miss Windsor."

"Where in hell do you think you're going? Get back here!" Victoria pointed at the foot of the stairs.

"I...I'm sorry, Miss Windsor, I....."

"Shut up! It's not your fault that damned busybody can't keep his mouth shut!" In spite of herself Victoria's eyes filled with tears and Martha knew that as was so often the case her anger was not genuine.

"I'm certain Mr. St. John didn't mean to violate a confidence, ma'am. He....he must have assumed I already knew."

Reminded unexpectedly of her daughter, a sudden rush of emotion all but overwhelmed Victoria. And what a waste of effort her glorious display of outrage had been. She certainly hadn't deceived herself; she couldn't even fool Martha. Suddenly she noticed her housekeeper still standing there at the bottom of the stairs peering up at her–her expression one of evident concern. "And why in hell is a twenty-three year old bachelor so interested in shopping for a four year old anyway? Doesn't say much for his masculinity, does it? Ring him up for me, will you, and tell him to sod off!" Pivoting about again, she ran on up the stairs.

Martha also turned away and walked slowly toward the kitchen. What could she possibly say to poor Mr. St. John? She thought about it all the time she was tidying up downstairs and by late afternoon when she was preparing tea, she'd concluded it would be best to tell him the truth. He knew Miss Windsor too well to be fooled by......

Just then, however, the door into the kitchen swung open, crashing against the wall. At the unexpected noise Martha jumped, spilling loose tea all over the counter top, and she turned around to find Victoria standing in the doorway. "We mustn't deprive 'Uncle Noel' of the pleasure of shopping for his 'niece' now, must we? Take these...." Here she paused, taking a few steps into the room to throw several credit cards and a slip of paper on the table "....and go with him, will you, Martha? Pick out anything and charge the gifts to my accounts. Have the things sent. The address is on the paper." The housekeeper just stood there staring first at the cold, set expression on her employer's face and then at the articles on the table. "Well, what's the matter?" Victoria snapped. "Didn't I make myself clear?"

"Quite clear, Miss Windsor." Only then did Martha notice the actress was dressed to go out. "Then you won't be wanting tea, ma'am?"

"No. I'm not hungry. I'm leaving for the theatre early. I've already rung for my car." She disappeared back through the swinging door and a few seconds later Martha heard the front door shut behind her.

The limousine was parked at the curb waiting. Seeing Victoria come down the steps, the chauffeur hurried to get out to open the door for her. "To the theatre, Miss Windsor?"

"Yes." She got into the rear seat and immediately drawing the curtains which separated the passenger section from the driver's seat, she leaned wearily back against the leather cushions and closed her eyes. The motor started. She could tell from the motion of the car when they turned from Eaton Square into Lower Belgrave Street; another left turn and the noise of the traffic confirmed they were on Buckingham Palace Road, a major artery. She wasn't even aware she was crying until she felt a tear ooze out of the corner of one eye and trickle down her cheek.

When she'd first conceived the idea of dispatching Noel and Martha to select her daughter's Christmas gifts, she had experienced a profound relief. The problem was solved and so neatly, after all. But even before she stopped in the kitchen to leave her instructions with Martha, her elation had begun to fade. Olivia would receive many expensive gifts, but they would not be from her mother. And now–in the elegant solitude of a Rolls-Royce limousine--she found herself remembering with an agonizing intensity the previous Christmas when for one brief moment Olivia had clung to her. "I want my little girl," she whispered her voice breaking. "Dear God, I want her so much!"

This side of Victoria Windsor would still have some time to wait, however; would still have to struggle–at times against great odds–simply to survive. In the meantime there was Julian Christopher.

* * *

That first night they'd spent together turned out to be typical..although never again was the setting the living room. Julian had a place set aside for his peculiar pleasures. Reached by a small lift from the foyer, it was a curious sort of room: hexagonal in shape and windowless with the only furniture being an enormous bed set on a raised platform in the middle. Sheets and pillowcases were blood red satin. Walls and ceiling were mirrored so that one appeared surrounded by an endless procession of gigantic red beds marching off into infinity. Had the room not been such an utter cliche, it would have been obscene.

The exact nature of their erotic games, however, would vary from night to night. Were these planned in advance or merely a last minute whim? This she was never to learn. They could be autocratic sultan and frightened concubine one night–animals rutting in a barnyard the next. An adjoining room contained a sunken bathtub. He would undress her and bathe her before joining her in the water.

And there was one game she dreaded above all the others yet bizarrely each time they began she would find herself anticipating it. Its opening moves were much like any one of several others, but then he'd produce the ropes and she would know. Meekly she would allow him to bind her–all the while kissing and caressing her and arousing her still further. Then just as her need became unbearable, another woman would appear and Victoria would be forced to watch. Of course she could have closed her eyes, but she did not. She wanted to see it–all of it–and as the two bodies intermingled, grunting and sweating, her own would arch in response. It was undoubtedly the nadir of her life.

* * *

Their relationship was common knowledge, but it wasn't until a particular night in early March of 1966 –when along with the rest of London's theatrical elite Victoria and Julian were in attendance at the annual awards presentation–that anyone entirely comprehended its bizarre nature.

Victoria's nomination was her first. She was heavily favored to win and so she had given her costume considerable thought, finally choosing a low-cut Empire style gown of antique gold satin, the material studded with seed pearls. A pearl necklace, representing several weeks' salary, nestled seductively between her breasts and as was her custom for formal occasions, her hair was piled high on the back of her head.

It had been obvious from the moment he came to call for her that her escort was in a particularly foul mood even for him due primarily, no doubt, to the fact that he was not a nominee. Then as they entered the theatre lobby, they were approached by a man who, though considerably younger and somewhat shorter, bore Julian a striking resemblance; even the sardonic smile was the same. The other man's eyes moved over Victoria's face and figure in open admiration.

"What in hell are you doing here?" Julian muttered from between clenched teeth.

"Why not? I am an actor, after all."

"Well, just stay away from me. Little enough to ask, I should think."

"Yes. Yes, of course." Again there was the familiar mocking smile. "But I do wish you'd tell me one thing. How do you manage to attract such magnificent women? Frightfully annoying, actually. They're all nearer my age than yours!" For one terrible instant Victoria thought Julian was going to strike him, but the impertinent young man beat a timely retreat. "Cheerio, Dad!" With a jaunty salute he disappeared into the crowd.

"Dad?" Victoria couldn't resist taunting him. "Dad?" she repeated, raising one eyebrow.

"Shut up, bitch!" Julian hissed. He seized her upper arm with such force that she winced. Still holding her in the same relentless grip, he propelled her the rest of the way across the lobby and into the auditorium all the time bowing and giving the people they passed his most charming smile. But then so did Victoria even though for the entire walk to their seats his fingers bit into her flesh.

Once or twice after they were seated she glanced at him uneasily, but as the evening's program began, she all but forgot he was even there. Indeed she only half heard the presentations which preceded her category. This award would be the final proof she'd arrived as an actress. It seemed appropriate, somehow, and perhaps even a good omen that this year's master of ceremonies was Sir Terence Cartier. The moment finally came. Sir Terence stepped up to the microphone. "One of our final categories this evenings, ladies and gentlemen, is that of leading actress in a drama. The nominees are...." But Victoria heard only one name–her own–which came at the end since they were listed alphabetically. She felt as though it took Terry forever to open the envelope, but at last he withdrew the card and looked up smiling broadly. "I must say–I'm not at all surprised." He paused briefly and dramatically. "Victoria Windsor—*The Divine Sarah.*"

Any other young actress would have jumped to her feet and dashed up on the stage, squealing with delight–but not Victoria. Indeed for a second or two she didn't even move. Was she savoring the moment of triumph? Certainly! Was she waiting until all eyes had turned to her. Absolutely! "Milk it for all it's worth, won't you?" Julian muttered.

Even when Victoria at last rose to her feet and started to move toward the stage, it was not so much a walk as a royal progression. She didn't climb the steps leading up to the stage so much as she ascended them, holding her gown with one hand and giving the other to the usher for his assistance. This latter hand she then extended to Terry as she approached the podium.

He bent to kiss it in gallant tribute. "Victoria, my dear, I am so very pleased."

"Thank you, Terry," she replied, but she didn't return his smile. She simply accepted the award from him and turned to face the audience. Gracious as always, he stepped back to allow her the moment. And now she flashed a dazzling smile. "Ladies and gentlemen, as I'm sure you all realize, it is most gratifying when a performance which you yourself consider to be a personal triumph is so richly rewarded by your peers. Thank you for this great honor." With a final nod of her head in acknowledgment of the applause, she turned to accept Terry's arm and be escorted from the stage to the waiting reporters and photographers.

Noel had made up his mind that no matter what her reaction, he couldn't let the evening go by without telling Victoria how pleased he was for her and quite by chance, shortly after arriving at the party following the awards ceremony, he saw her coming out of the ladies' cloakroom. For a second, however, he very nearly turned away; she appeared desolate.

Actually Victoria had been in the ladies' room for several minutes–most of that time in one of the stalls. Still hiding in the loo, she mused bitterly, but she'd needed to be alone and at the moment that was the only place. Her exultation at receiving the award had soon dissipated–she didn't know why–and now she felt nothing. Then, too, Julian's mood had grown even <u>more</u> vile since she won the award–egotistical bastard! She'd gone to the ladies' room partly to escape him for a while and now she dreaded returning to the table. Always before he'd refrained from abusing her in public, but tonight he was capable of doing or saying anything. She shivered. Was there a draft coming from somewhere? Well, she couldn't spend the entire evening in the loo! She could just hear the conversation at their table.

"Where's Victoria?" someone would inquire.

"Where else would one find an alley cat," Julian would observe in an acid tone, "but in the sandbox."

She listened to make sure no one else was there and coming out, she sat down on one of the stools in front of the dressing table. She smoothed her hair along the temples, applied more blush, edged her lips a little more perfectly. At last, however, she gathered up her things as well as her composure–the public presence of Victoria Windsor–and reluctantly departed her refuge. She had only just stepped into the hall when the thought struck her. But it didn't matter, did it, how hideously Julian humiliated her tonight. She would still go with him–still allow him to do to her what he would. It was at this precise moment her old friend saw her.

Noel knew he would have no better chance to speak to her. As for the possibility she might be in a bad mood, he would have to risk it. It wouldn't be the first time he'd braved her anger and it undoubtedly wouldn't be the last. "Hello, Victoria." She started visibly. Oh no, he thought, I've startled her again. Where can her mind be at such moments?

"Oh...ah....hello, luv," she replied after a beat. Coming over to him, she reached out to touch his cheek with one hand, the other going to her throat in a gesture which managed at once to be ridiculously theatrical and profoundly moving. A brief smile passed across her features. "I didn't see you. It's been too long. How have you been?"

She's missed me, Noel thought, with an incredible joy. "Just fine, Victoria," he replied aloud. "I won't detain you," he added quickly before she could become annoyed. "I only wanted to tell you how thrilled I am for you and how richly you deserve the honor–but then, I'm sure you already know that."

"And just <u>what</u> exactly am I supposed to know?" Her green eyes glowed. "That you're thrilled for me or that I richly deserve it?"

He smiled. "Ah...from your acceptance speech, it would seem both."

Now she actually laughed out loud, her laugh for one of the few times he could remember possessing a genuine ring. "Noel, you really <u>are</u> a delight! Why don't I see more of you?"

As usual there was no explaining her moods. Just when he'd expected her to be impatient with him, she seemed in no hurry to leave. "You see as much of me as you let me, Victoria."

Her eyebrows rose and she laughed yet again. "That doesn't make sense, luv."

Noel looked at her steadily. "I think you understand me."

Suddenly she became very serious–then noticeably uneasy. "I....I have to get back to my table now." She started to back away from him.

"Victoria, are you all right?"

"Of course I am! On a night like this–achieving everything I've ever dreamed of. Why wouldn't I be?" Whirling about, she hurried on into the ballroom.

Even from where he stood, Noel could hear the applause beginning near the door where someone must have noticed Victoria's entrance and spreading outward in ripples as she moved through the room toward her table. He was unable to resist following as far as the doorway where unnoticed, he could observe her progress.

All at once a firm hand gripped him by the shoulder and Noel turned to find Jonathan Sinclair standing behind him grinning broadly. "Jon!" he exclaimed delightedly, seizing the other man's hand in both of his and pumping it up and down. Then, finding even this to be an inadequate expression of his feelings, he threw both arms around him. The two men hugged ferociously, pounding each other's backs in mutual affection. "Well, Jon, back from exile, I see," Noel managed to gasp when they had at last ceased this rather fierce form of greeting and he'd been able to take a breath or two. "Yours lasting a bit longer than mine, it would appear."

"But yours, my dear fellow, was voluntary. Mine, as I'm sure you recall, was not. Ah...how is the lady, by the way?" Noel shrugged. "You still feel the same about her, don't you?" the other man inquired as gently as he could.

"I...I suppose I always will. She grows more beautiful with every passing day and yet more.....more....." He waved one hand in the air–a mute expression of the helplessness he felt. "I...I really don't know how to express it, Jon. She's...she's drinking even more and there's always a man. Currently it's....it's Julian Christopher."

"Yes, I saw her with Christopher. Is he as bad as his reputation?"

"Much worse! Sometimes I think she deliberately chooses men she knows will abuse her.... but see here...." Noel shook his head as if to clear such depressing thoughts from his mind. ".....if you're not with anyone, there's room at my table. Ah....do you wish to speak to her?"

"No, I think perhaps for now I'll keep a low profile."

Table assignments had been by lottery to preclude any complaints about undue preference. Those who drew Victoria's table were thrilled by their incredible good fortune–not only to be at the table of one of that evening's winners, but also to be with the most talked about couple of the current London season. Later the majority of them would regret having been there.

At Victoria's approach the other three men immediately rose to their feet, one of them pulling out her chair for her. Not only did Julian refuse to stand, he actually slouched further down in his chair, extending his long legs out into the aisle so that several people nearly tripped over him. He was dragging deeply on a small, thin, foul-smelling cigarette, holding it up in front of his face between drags–his eyes squinted half-shut against the smoke.

"Thank you so much," Victoria said sweetly to the man who'd held out the chair for her. "It's so rare these days to meet a true gentleman." This latter, of course, had been purely for Julian's benefit.

He grunted some sort of unintelligible remark, but she paid him no attention, glancing instead around the room. What she was doing, though she was not immediately aware of the fact, was searching for Noel. How good it had been to see him, she found herself thinking now. Why do I continually drive him away? But I haven't driven him away, have I? He remains my friend despite everything I do. Just then she located him at his table halfway across the room. He was standing by it introducing another man who apparently was with him. Almost at once Victoria also recognized Jonathan Sinclair. Why was it I became so angry with him, she wondered to herself. Oh yes, I remember. He had the temerity to suggest I was drinking too much. She smiled. He should see me now!

"What is so bloody amusing?" Julian half-snarled under his breath.

How good it felt to discover she still had the capacity to irritate him. On the surface, however, she continued to ignore him as she removed a cigarette from her gold-leaf case and inserted it in her holder. Two lighters and a packet of matches appeared as if by magic. "My goodness," she murmured, "I don't know who to choose."

"Oh, sod off!" And this time Julian was fully audible.

The other men looked at him, obviously unable to believe their own ears. "Miss Windsor," one of them inquired pleasantly in what was quite evidently an attempt to make up for Julian's rudeness, "may I ask how long you've been an actress?"

Something had happened to Victoria in the time since she'd arrived back at the table, something which had first manifested itself in her remark about the current scarcity of gentlemen and something which now-- seemingly against her will–drove her to deliberately provoke Julian. She flashed a smile and tipping her head slightly to one side, she studied the man who had posed the question. She was the perfect picture of feminine enchantment and Julian glowered. " Do you mean," she finally said, "how long have I been acting or how long have I been a working actress? Those are two very different questions."

The three men laughed–delighted at having witnessed first hand the fabled Windsor wit. Their female companions were not quite so charmed. Perhaps sharing a table with Victoria Windsor was not the stroke of good fortune it had first appeared.

"But surely," another of the men remarked, "an actress of your incredible beauty and talent has never been out of work."

"That depends on what sort of work you have in mind," Julian observed drily.

Victoria experienced the first stirrings of excitement. It was beginning much more quickly that she'd anticipated. Purposively she turned her back on him, raising one hand to her throat–a gesture for which she was becoming famous. This would infuriate him even further; he knew it to be perfectly rehearsed and utterly phony. Then came the charmingly cocked eyebrow as the same hand reached across the table to rest lightly on top of the man's who had paid her this compliment. "How very kind of you," she murmured. "However, there was a period of time when there was not a producer or director in the London theatre who seemed to agree with you."

The third man, feeling left out, wanted to get his share of this beautiful woman's attention. "May I get you a drink, Miss Windsor?"

"Oh, luv, how terribly sweet of you!" With her other hand she now reached over to touch this man on the cheek. "I'm simply perishing for one! I was frightfully nervous, you know," she confided shyly, "about the award."

Julian snorted. "I feel it my duty, gentlemen, to remind you. You are in the presence of a gifted actress."

"Oh, but we quite agree," the first man replied. "And I might add, Miss Windsor, how privileged we are to share your table."

This time Julian did not give her a chance to respond. It was clear he had taken control. Her exhilaration increased, her heart pounding as though in anticipation of something. "You didn't give me a chance to finish, sir." And now he was actually smiling. "Or perhaps you simply failed to comprehend my meaning. You see–that's all it is–an act. The wit, the charm, and most especially the modesty–all nothing but an act. Now if any of you would like to try her out in bed–an experiment to which I and I'm sure she would willingly consent–there you would see the real Victoria Windsor. It's really rather a pity she chose to become an actress. She would have made such an incredible whore." All through this unbelievable oration no one else at the table attempted to speak. Even conversations at adjoining tables dwindled away until by the end an awkward silence prevailed among all those within hearing distance.

But what of Victoria herself? Anyone who ventured to look at her would have been shocked. Her lips were moist, parted slightly, and she was breathing deeply, her full breasts rising and falling under the lustrous satin. Her eyes glittered feverishly, eyes she never took from her lover's face. Every word Julian uttered struck her like a physical blow yet incredibly she had never been more aroused. She could almost feel his hands on her and she found herself fantasizing, imagining their copulating right there on the floor of the ballroom. Suddenly in the midst of all this she was aware of a different voice.

"Miss Windsor?"

Reluctantly she let go of her erotic daydream and bringing her mind back to reality, the first thing of which she was conscious was Julian's face. A smirk played across his lips as he drew on his cigarette inhaling deeply. He raised his eyebrows in an unspoken question.

"Miss Windsor?"

Victoria realized now that one of the other men at the table was addressing her and again with some effort she turned her attention to the person speaking. "Yes?"

"May I escort your home, Miss Windsor?" the man was saying. "Surely a lady will not allow herself to be treated in such an ungentlemanly fashion."

"But you see, sir," she heard herself replying, "Mr. Christopher is quite right. I <u>am</u> a whore–though with one important distinction; I am completely free of charge!" She rose gracefully to her feet. "Shall we go, Julian?"

"Of course." He stood up as well and chuckling low in his throat, he slid one arm about her waist to draw her to him. "As you can see, gentlemen, I am never wrong."

And indeed for much of that summer and into the early fall their relationship continued. Every evening after her performance his limousine could be seen waiting at the stage door and any party of note would find them there together. All this despite the fact that Julian now seemed to delight in publicly humiliating her. At times he would be openly physical, caressing Victoria's breast or thigh and watching the discomfort of those around them in evident amusement while at others he would turn on her, mocking and insulting her far more cruelly even than on the night of the awards presentation. The vast majority of those who had occasion to observe this immediately assumed Victoria was indeed exactly as Julian had characterized her. Only a few cared enough to feel a deep sadness and of those perhaps only Noel St. John understood that she simply believed she deserved nothing better.

Chapter 11

It was inevitable, nevertheless, that Julian and Victoria's affair would end, that sooner or later her pride would no longer allow her to accept his abuse. But when the break occurred–final except for a brief postscript a few months later–it came over what would have seemed in comparison to Julian's customary treatment of her merely an incident of minor rudeness.

The Divine Sarah had just closed after a twenty month run. It being a Saturday, there was no rehearsal for the upcoming Fitzhugh play and Julian, as always, had vanished with the dawn. Even Noel was away for the week-end. Until that evening's party at Basil's Victoria had nothing to do and with a long empty day stretching ahead of her she started drinking almost as soon as she awoke–first to ease her hangover and then because–frighteningly–for the first time she couldn't seem to stop. Even after she'd returned to her own home she continued to drink, eating almost nothing. Martha had the day off and the current maid hid in her room, too terrified to suggest her famous employer might be in need of solid food.

Somehow she managed to get ready for the party and finally flinging a fur stole over one shoulder, she started across her bedroom toward the door. Partway there, however, she lost her balance, landing against the wall, and for a few seconds she remained there laughing hysterically. Just as she finally opened the door, the bell sounded below. "Bastard!" she muttered, grasping the balcony railing to keep from falling. Evidently either Martha had returned by now or the new maid had ventured out of her room long enough to let him in because by the time she reached the top of the stairs Julian was waiting in the hall, tapping his gloves impatiently against the newel post. "Good evening!" she trumpeted. He glanced up, but from that distance he was unable to see that she was swaying slightly. Victoria began to make her way toward him, but partway down the stairs she lost her equilibrium a second time, almost toppling over the bannister. Once again she found her own clumsiness terribly amusing, but after a moment she regained her footing, managing the rest of the treacherous descent without mishap.

"What in hell is wrong with you?" he demanded. Even he'd never seen her this intoxicated at such a comparatively early hour.

"As if you didn't know, Julian darling, I....am...drunk. I've had nothing to do all day but drink and I am....very....very drunk!" She leaned one arm across his shoulders. "But that is all to your benefit..all...to....your....benefit. Well, shall we?" On the whole she navigated the trip down the front steps and across the pavement without serious difficulty and when at last they were settled in the rear seat of his limousine, she snuggled up to him, slipping her arms around his neck. "Want a sample?"

"Stay away from me, you drunken bitch!" He seized both her wrists, pushing her with such force that she landed hard against the far side of the car. "Your breath positively stinks!" After that a hostile silence descended between them, lasting until the limousine turned into Marlyebone Road just a block off Regent's Park. All at once Julian leaned forward to say something to his driver. The man immediately pulled the car over and leaving the motor running, came around to Victoria's side to open her door. "Get out!" Julian ordered her curtly.

She continued to sit there, staring at him stupidly. "What...what do you mean?"

"That would seem obvious–even to someone in your condition. I'm telling you to get out of my car!"

"But..the party....I...." Suddenly she understood. "You're....you're sending me in there alone, aren't you?"

"Ah, it would seem that the meaning of my words has at last penetrated your besotted brain. That is it precisely,"

"Oh no, Julian, please!" She knew that no amount of pleading would touch him, but in spite of this she found herself drawn to grasp his arm imploringly. "Even you can't be that cruel!"

"Really, my dear Victoria. You better than anyone should comprehend that I am capable of anything. As for tonight, I simply will not be humiliated by a drunken slut!"

Nothing he'd ever done to her–either publicly or privately–seemed quite as horrible as this, forcing her to arrive at a party unescorted–not even by the faithful Noel. "Oh, Julian, please no!" Her fingers tightened around his arm. "I won't drink any more tonight. I promise! And later–you...you can do anything to me! Anything! Only I can't go in there alone. I just can't!"

"Get the bloody hell out of this car!" His tone was now openly threatening. "Or I promise–you will regret it!"

Victoria hesitated for a second or two longer. Her heart was pounding and her hands were clenched into two small desperate fists in her lap, but her voice when she finally spoke was steady. "Very well, Julian. I will get out of this car, but...." Here she paused, turning to face him one last time. "But I promise.....I promise that if there is anyone who will regret tonight, it most definitely will not be I." At that moment she had no idea when her revenge would take place. She wasn't even sure what it would be. She was only very, <u>very</u> sure that she would have it.

For now she had no choice but to allow the chauffeur to assist her from the car and with considerable dignity under the circumstances she started up the short, circular driveway toward Basil's ridiculously ornate Regency mansion. Behind her, without actually being aware she was listening, she heard the car doors shut; a moment later and the sound of the motor had been swallowed up in the traffic. What was she going to do? So many people would be delighted to see her humiliated in this way. Indeed another car passed her just then, drawing up under the portico, and not waiting to learn the identity of the arriving guests, she slipped through the shrubbery and ducked down out of sight. Unfortunately the momentum started by the sudden downward motion pulled her over backwards and before she knew what was happening, she sat down.

The ground was cold and wet. She could imagine what the mud was doing to her pale blue gown, but it just didn't seem to matter and anyway people were arriving steadily now and she didn't dare move. She didn't know how long she sat there–the cars had long since stopped coming–but she was growing stiff and chilled. Vaguely she recalled leaving her fur wrap in Julian's car. Julian–that bastard! She wished there was someone to come and fetch her, but there was no one and anyway she had no money for a pay telephone. Well, she couldn't stay there; she was beginning to shiver. So finally with the help of one of the bushes she pulled herself to her feet and glancing in both directions to make sure the coast was clear, she stepped back out onto the pavement.

The cold had done much to sober her up, but her mind still wasn't too clear and her steps as she moved along the drive toward the street were stumbling and uncertain. Indeed for some time Victoria wandered aimlessly, unmindful of where she was or what she was doing. It wasn't until a car drove through a puddle in her path, splashing her with muddy water that she became fully aware she was walking the nighttime streets of London unescorted. It was about that same moment she noticed she was passing a neighborhood pub–its noise and light spilling invitingly out into the darkness–and pushing open one of the swinging doors with its amber-coloured bullet glass panes, she sought by instinct its promise of warmth and companionship.

In her dazed state she failed to grasp that she was no longer an unknown drama student and that furthermore she was wearing a floor-length formal gown with a distinctly muddy seat and in addition now a large wet stain spreading across the front of its satin skirt. Gradually she realized that as if by magic a path was opening in the smoky, crowded room as people moved backwards away from her; the place, moreover, looked oddly familiar. Have I been here before, she was thinking, when with startling clarity considering the din, she heard. "Isn't that Victoria Windsor?" At the sound of her name she instinctively turned her head in the direction of the speaker–a dead giveaway-- just as she heard someone else exclaim, "Coo, what's the likes of 'er doin' in Danny's?"

Of course–Danny's! The place hadn't changed in ten years: the same well-scrubbed wooden floor, the same red tables and chairs, even the bar with the gilt-edged mirror of which he'd been so proud. She became aware as well now that the noise level had dropped and glancing about, she discovered she was standing alone in the center of the room, surrounded at a distance of a few feet by a solid ring of humanity several layers deep. Coming out of the kitchen, Danny was at once conscious of the unnatural hush. "What's 'appnin?" he asked one of the waitresses who was behind the bar drying beer mugs.

"Look 'oo we've got 'ere!" she replied.

Now Danny was staring himself. It couldn't be, he thought. So glamorous and elegant now–she'd never come here. And yet there she was. Well, he supposed she'd just happened on the place. But something was wrong. Although she was trembling visibly, she made no move to escape. Walking quickly around the bar, he worked his way through the crowd. "I'm Danny, Miss Windsor," he said cordially. "The proprietor 'ere. Might I be of some 'elp?"

Even after so long the Cockney accented voice was familiar as well. Beyond that Victoria recalled the gentle owner of that voice and her immediate instinct was to reach out to him–perhaps to thank him for his unfailing kindness, but like so many of her tender impulses, this one would never be expressed. If anything, she became more aloof as if to deny such feelings even to herself. "Yes." She nodded imperiously in reply to his inquiry. "I seem to have...ah... become separated from my party. We were doing a bit of...." Here she paused, her glance sweeping the homely room..."slumming, you know, and I require the use of your telephone to ring for my driver."

She had risen so far above him. Why did she still feel a need to hurt him? But outwardly Danny merely smiled, bowing slightly. "Of course, Miss Windsor. My h'office is right in 'ere." His "h-office" as she remembered was in reality nothing more than a walk-in closet, but it did contain a chair, a desk and the needed telephone. He ushered her inside and closed the door, leaving her alone.

Victoria sank wearily into the straight, wooden chair, resting her elbows on the desk, her head in her hands. It seemed almost too much of an effort to pick up the receiver and dial and then when she did, there was no answer. Of course–she'd given her driver the night off. Frightened tears filled her eyes and as she continued to sit there trying to decide what to do, there was a knock on the door and Danny reappeared. "Were you h'able to get through, Miss Windsor?"

Why did he insist on calling her that? Obviously he had to remember her. "No," she snapped. "There's no answer."

"Per'aps a taxi?"

"I do <u>not</u> travel in taxis!"

"Of course, Miss Windsor, but since this is in the noiture of an h'emergency. I could 'ail one for you and 'ave 'im come round to the alley."

Victoria breathed a sigh of relief. Once again, it seemed, Danny was taking care of her. "Oh, very well then," she replied at last. "It will have to do, I suppose." But her tone displayed none of the gratitude she was feeling–merely a cool displeasure.

He nodded. "Wait 'ere, ma'am." Ma'am?! Worse even than Miss Windsor, but then it's the way I'm treating him, she thought. He would never presume unless I spoke first. I could....I could say something to show him I remember him...just a few words.....

After a moment or so Danny returned a second time, still refusing to come any nearer than the doorway. "The taxi will be around back in 'alf a mo', Miss Windsor. You'll have to walk through the kitchen, I'm afraid," he explained apologetically. "It's h'over 'ere." He indicated the rear of the pub.

The perfect cue, she thought. Just a brief smile and perhaps...."I remember where the kitchen is, Danny"----That would be enough. She said nothing, of course, hurrying past without so much as a glance in his direction. The kitchen hadn't changed any more than the rest of the pub. How many dishes had she washed in that sink? The taxi was indeed there, motor running. Victoria disappeared inside and as Danny stood watching, the vehicle backed out of the cul de sac and moved off down the street.

* * *

Noel and Victoria were working together again in *Once More–Forever*, giving him his first opportunity in a while to observe her on an almost daily basis. Her work was, of course, flawless–her portrayal of Marcia, the brittlely charming divorcee of the Fitzhugh play, a delight. Yet this part, which should have been far less taxing than Bernhardt, was apparently exacting a frightful toll. Then one day Noel came to understand what he thought afterwards should have been obvious all along.

At first as the cast began to gather that morning he didn't see Victoria. He experienced the inevitable flash of panic, but then after a moment he discovered her sitting in one of the folding canvas chairs off to one side of the stage. She had the privacy now which she claimed to crave as people willingly left her alone. She had as yet to remove her fur coat and her face was all but hidden by the customary dark glasses as well as a silk scarf pulled low over her forehead. But her moods no longer bothered Noel and pouring two mugs of coffee, he came to sit in the chair next to hers, handing her a mug. Such a luv, she thought, always so thoughtful. Gratefully she sipped the hot liquid. Only after some minutes did she speak and even then her voice was so low that the words were all but inaudible.

"Fine–thank you, Victoria." He did not inquire in return as to how she was feeling. That was painfully obvious.

"In answer to your unspoken question—I feel like hell, thank you."

"Rehearsal, ladies and gentlemen," the director announced. "Act One–Scene Two: Marcia and Nicky."

Victoria sighed and taking one last long swallow of the coffee, she returned the mug to Noel with a brief smile. He watched, profoundly concerned as she pulled herself to her feet, removed her scarf though not the dark glasses and began to unbutton her coat. Her friend stood up as well to help her off with the coat. Then all at once she just went limp. Quickly he slipped his arm around her waist and eased her back into the chair. "Why didn't you stay home today?" he demanded. "You could have missed one rehearsal."

"God, Noel," she murmured, "if I missed a rehearsal every time I was hung over, the play would never open."

"At least they can begin with another scene." He went to speak to the director.

"Why didn't she stay home then?" Somehow it sounded different when the other man said it.

"She's too much of a professional for that. Besides she's not making the request. I am."

"Ever the faithful watchdog eh, St. John?"

By now Noel was accustomed to snide comments about his relationship with Victoria. The canine theme remained a favorite. He'd learned to ignore them. "We'll be back in an hour." He returned to Victoria. She hadn't even moved. "Did you eat any breakfast?" he inquired with mock sternness. God, he thought, I sound like her father.

"I'm....I'm all right."

"That tea room you like so much is in the next block–at least tea and some toast."

"I might vomit it back in your face."

"I'll take my chances."

"I've dismissed my driver for the day."

"Don't tell me you can't walk one block."

"Oh, all right." She got slowly to her feet again.

Noel put an arm around her shoulders. "Do you mind?"

"Of course not." Helping her toward the stage door, he gloried in this rare chance to hold her yet at the same time he was fighting back the tears as every step seemed to take her last ounce of strength. As they stepped out into the narrow back street behind the theatre, he actually felt her shrink against him. "I...I don't know, Noel. I feel so weak."

"We'll take it easily, I promise, and the fresh air will help."

"Fresh air–in London?"

He could picture the perfectly shaped eyebrows behind the dark glasses–raised in amusement–and he smiled at her irrepressible sense of humor. It was one of the things that saved her, he supposed.

After that neither of them spoke. Noel wanted Victoria to save her energy although he also had to admit to himself wryly that he was afraid of breaking the spell. Victoria, on the other hand, was so moved by his tender concern she could think of nothing to say. Normally when the softer emotions were aroused in her, she would attempt to deny them with a show of temperament. This morning, however, she felt too sick even to do that and all she could do instead was to wish she could find some way of telling him how comforting his arm felt about her shoulders. The walk to the tea room required only ten minutes. The Rumanian owner greeted them, beaming with delight. "Ah, Miss Windsor, a pleasure and honor to serve you once more, dear lady. And Mr. St. John."

"One of the curtained-off booths please, Vladimir," Noel directed. "And please see to it we're not disturbed."

"I myself will wait on you, sir. I myself." The portly, bearded man conducted them smoothly to their table, presented the menus and immediately left, closing the curtains.

"So--tea and toast, will it be then?" Noel asked with a determined gaiety.

"Oh, please don't," she murmured, leaning back against the wall of the booth. "I'm in no mood for your cheerful elf routine."

In spite of himself he smiled. "Cheerful elf, hm?" But then almost at once he grew serious. "Is that all you see in me, Victoria–a cheerful elf?"

"Please, luv, I....." But her voice choked.

As promised, Vladimir returned himself to take their order. "Just tea and toast for both of us," Noel directed.

"We have some of those nice strawberry preserves you like so much, Miss Windsor," the owner suggested.

"That would be perfect. Thank you, Vladimir." It was still her escort who did the talking.

"Yes, sir. Very good, sir." And once again he withdrew.

Victoria hadn't really heard much of this, immersed as she was in the struggle with her own emotions. She despised weakness–most particularly in herself–and she was disgusted with the futile tears which she knew were even now reducing her eye make-up to a series of ugly gray streaks. She tried to tell herself that it was only because as usual she'd slept poorly the night before, but she knew it was more than that.

Since the day of that disastrous zoo excursion, she'd made no further attempt to see her daughter. After all–wasn't it obvious she was never meant to be a mother? Shopping for the little girl's fifth birthday she had once again delegated to Noel and Martha. Yet thoughts of Olivia continued to spring to her mind totally unbidden and at any inopportune moment they chose to do so.

She might be standing at the window either in her own home or that of her companion of the previous night, fighting off yet another hangover. She would be so dizzy and nauseous she could barely stay on her feet and then a small girl would go skipping by on the street below–long, light brown hair streaming out behind her. Tears would fill Victoria's eyes and she'd turn away from the window, but it would already be too late.

Another time she might be in a restaurant. Wine glass poised in one hand, she would be putting on what Noel teasingly called her "great lady of the theatre act" and utterly charming her companion when all at once she'd happen to notice a little girl's head just clearing the back of a near-by booth. Could it be? It was all she could do not to walk around to where she could see the child's face.

Or as in the case of last night when alone and wide awake she would go over and over her few precious memories of Olivia and when these were exhausted, fantasize others–quite simple things actually like reading to her or brushing her hair or walking together, hand in hand. It was so close to Christmas and...... Suddenly she became aware the proprietor had once again left them alone; moreover, Noel was studying her intently, his slightly pudgy face creased with earnest concern. "What are you staring at?" she snapped. "Anyway–get lost for a bit, will you? I have to fix my face."

"Certainly."

"And make sure they don't bring the order until I'm ready." She took a plastic pouch of cosmetics from her large handbag and propping the mirror up against the sugar bowl, reluctantly removed her dark glasses. If she'd been in a better frame of mind, her appearance might have struck her as amusing. Eyes rimmed in black, she resembled nothing so much as a raccoon. As it was, the sight was nowhere near laughable. Fresh tears welled up in her eyes.

"What in damnation is wrong with you?" she demanded of the apparition in the hand mirror. "Life has been a hell of a lot worse and <u>now</u> you decide to wallow in self-pity! Well, you can bloody well stop it this bloody minute!" Furiously she grabbed a handful of tissues to wipe off the streaked eye make-up and when Noel returned a while later carrying the tray of food himself, she was once again flawlessly made up and in control. He placed the dishes, tea pot, etc. on the table and leaving the tray outside, slid once more into his place across from her in the booth. "May I pour, luv?" Picking up the tea pot, Victoria gave him one of her prettiest smiles.

So the facade was once again in place. Noel sighed, almost preferring her despair of a few moments ago which at least had been genuine. He knew, however, he had to play the game by her rules. "Please, m'lady." He smiled in return. "I would be honored." She poured tea and milk for them both and adding sugar to her own, she took a long drink. "Toast, too."

Noel offered her the slotted silver holder with its triangular half-slices of cold toast–a British peculiarity. "That's part of the agreement, remember. With strawberry preserves."

Obediently she took one of the half-slices, even putting a little of the jam on it, but after one or two half-hearted nibbles she discarded it on her plate. "I don't know." She shrugged. "I just never seem to have any appetite."

"Eat at least that much, Victoria. Believe me, it will make you feel better."

"Don't smother me, Noel. You know damn well I can't abide it!" She half-rose to her feet as if to leave.

"All right," he agreed quickly. "Not another word, I promise. We don't have to talk at all if you prefer, but we might as well take the full hour."

Her move to go had, in fact, been pure bluff. She still felt far from strong enough to face rehearsal and at Noel's words she sank gratefully back into the seat. For a while neither of them spoke. Victoria drank several cups of tea and to his relief even ate not just the one half-slice of toast, but two more as well. Noel willingly accepted her need to be quiet. It was enough for him just to share such a private moment with her. It was enough for him to see her, if only for a brief while, at peace.

He was wrong this time, however. Victoria only <u>appeared</u> calm. In actuality her mind was racing. The thought had come to her first, of course, in the lonely darkness of last night and now in the gentle silence of the booth it was coming to the forefront of her mind once again, refusing to be ignored. Christmas is coming and I...I want to be with Olivia. She had to deny the thought–deny its very existence. "Well, you and Martha must have made some excellent selections." She tried to sound casual as though the remark were mere idle conversation.

"What?" But actually Noel knew very well what she meant.

"I <u>said</u>, 'You and Martha...."

"Never mind. You don't have to repeat it."

"Then why did you say 'what'?" Already there was an edge to her voice. She was being pushed into talking about it against her will now and of course that was Noel's fault.

"I...I didn't expect you to speak just then, that's all. But I'm glad you were pleased."

"Andrew said...she was very happy with the gifts. You...ah...might as well take care of it for Christmas, too. If you don't mind, of course."

"But you seemed to enjoy selecting the things yourself."

"Nonsense! I'm much too busy. Are you through? We should be getting back." This time she did stand up and pulling back the curtain, she walked rapidly toward the exit. Noel knew it was useless to argue and without a word he dropped some money on the table and followed her.

* * *

It was a little over a week later–a Saturday morning in mid-December–and since as usual they were between maids, Martha herself brought up Victoria's breakfast tray. To the housekeeper's surprise her knock on the bedroom door was answered immediately in a strong, clear voice and she entered to find the actress fully dressed and seated at her vanity, putting the finishing touches to her make-up. "Good morning, Miss Windsor."

"Good morning. You can put the tray on the table by the window. You know I do believe I'm even hungry this morning."

"It's good to hear that, Miss Windsor," she replied with an answering smile. Setting down the tray as Victoria had requested, she returned to the door. "Will you be wanting anything else, ma'am? If Mr. St. John's free, I thought we might do the shopping for Olivia this morning."

"Well, that's just it, actually. I..I've decided to go myself. I won't even bother with my driver. Ring up for a taxi, will you, in about a half-hour and...and you can plan an extra-special Christmas dinner. I...I thought I might have Olivia with me for the holiday." Martha stood there uncertainly, one hand on the doorknob. "What in hell is the matter with you?" Victoria inquired angrily. "Why shouldn't I buy her gifts? Why shouldn't I want her with me for Christmas? She is my daughter, after all."

"Yes, ma'am. I'm sure it will be a wonderful holiday for you both." Martha left quickly to avoid another outburst. "Mr. St. John's right," she said to herself as she made her way downstairs. "She really does love her little girl. But I suppose I should have realized that. I've always known the temper and the rudeness are only an act. But what must her own childhood have been like? Was there no one to love her–no one to teach her how to love?"

Victoria, meanwhile, had finished with her make-up, tucking her hair up under a turban-style hat, and finally now she went over to the breakfast tray. Sitting down at the little table, she spread the white linen napkin in her lap. There were freshly baked blueberry muffins and tea, but her ravenous appetite had vanished. She took a few sips of the tea and then for several minutes she sat there unmoving, looking idly out the bedroom window.

Eaton Square, like so many of the more elite London neighborhoods, had a small park in the center, private to residents. At some point she saw the gate on the far side open and a woman entered, holding a little girl by the hand. They moved out into the open area in the middle of the lawn and began tossing a ball back and forth. Was it only her imagination or could she actually hear the child's squeals of delight? The woman's not dressed like a nanny, Victoria thought; I suppose it's her mother.

Dear God, what must it be like, her thoughts continued as tears filled her eyes---to have a normal, natural relationship with your daughter–to watch her grow and develop? "Olivia," she whispered the name aloud, savoring its sound. It was an emotional indulgence she rarely allowed herself. "Oh, my darling, I love you so much!" Where had she even gotten the asinine idea of having Olivia with her for Christmas? It would never work! It would be another disaster-- worse even than the day at the zoo. Well, I <u>will</u> do the shopping, she decided at last, but I'll stop on the way out and tell Martha I've changed my mind about the holiday dinner.

The taxi let Victoria out at Oxford Circus and she began to walk along Oxford Street where most of London's department stores were located, heading in particular for Selfridge's, a favorite of hers. As was so often the case now, heads turned. Even the turban, the dark glasses, the collar of the fur coat held up about her throat could not quite disguise the unmistakable presence of Victoria Windsor. She ignored the glances, hoping no one would approach her. Today of all days she wanted to left alone.

The toy department at Selfridge's was every child's dream of Christmas come to life. On a table in the center of the floor the London of Dickens' *A Christmas Carol*-- Scrooge and Bob Cratchit and Tiny Tim–had been ingeniously recreated in miniature; there were people in old-fashioned costumes, gas street lights, even sleighs and horses which actually moved. A full-size carousel with six quite magnificent steeds stood to the left of the entrance while on a raised platform at the other end of the room, grandly ensconced on a bejewelled and gilt throne, was Father Christmas himself to welcome them all to his special domain. The room was thronged with happy, excited youngsters, most of whom were accompanied by at least one adult and Christmas elves in their colorful red and green costumes moved among the festive crowd serving punch and biscuits.

Victoria hesitated in the archway, overcome with doubt. I don't belong here, she thought, the panic starting. Dear God, why did I ever come? She knew she should leave, but something kept her there–a sweet and terrible longing to be part of it all. Then all at once she saw her, one of the children who were at that moment riding on the carousel. The little girl was laughing happily and slapping the reins on the horse's wooden neck. She was dressed in red overalls and a white pullover and her long light-brown hair was held back from her face with a red band. "Olivia," she breathed, absurdly pleased that even after more than a year she'd instantly recognized her daughter. More than a year? What better proof could there be she didn't belong here? The kindest thing I can do, Victoria's thoughts continued, is to break off the relationship now–completely. Let her forget me; after all, that's what I've wanted from the beginning. But Olivia forgetting her–forgetting who her mother was. The idea desolated her, rendering her immobile. She didn't notice that the carousel had stopped nor did she see Andrew help the little girl down from the horse and the two of them start across the room toward her....

"Mummy!" Olivia's piping little voice fairly bubbled with excitement. "How are you, Mummy?" Dazedly she looked down at her daughter, who was suddenly and unexpectedly standing in front of her and smiling up at her in obvious delight.

"Hello, Victoria." Andrew was also smiling. "I would have walked right by you, I think, but you can't fool your daughter." But Victoria just stood there saying nothing, doing nothing and the child's initial joy faded rapidly. "Have you had lunch? The restaurant on the top floor here is excellent and perhaps....."

"Oh no, I don't think so. I have several errands to do and I......"

"Mummy, <u>please</u>!" Olivia didn't know she had the courage to say even that much, but her mother was <u>really</u> there–her beautiful, adored mother–and she had to hold onto her if only for a little while.

The pleading in those two words tore into Victoria. My daughter loves me, she thought, and the knowledge awed her. "All...all right," she heard herself saying at last. "I suppose I can spare some time."

Olivia's smile of a few minutes ago returned. In fact she fairly glowed and hesitating for just an instant, she slipped her hand into her mother's. At the sensation of the small hand in her own Victoria's tears started again, but fortunately, she thought, the dark glasses will hide that. Indeed it would have been better had Olivia been able to see those tears. But at least she felt her mother's hand tighten around hers. "May we ride the moving stairs, Daddy?"

"Is it all right, Victoria? Perhaps you prefer the lift."

"No...the...escalator is fine."

So around and up they went–mother and daughter still hand in hand, Andrew noted following them–around and up until finally they arrived at the restaurant. It was only half-past eleven, early for lunch, and there were very few people eating. He was relieved. Somehow he imagined his former wife didn't care for crowds. The hostess escorted them to a corner booth where the windows afforded a view of Oxford Street far below. "Oh good, Daddy!" Olivia exclaimed, climbing up on her chair to kneel backwards and peer out. "This is one of my favorite tables because you can look down at all the funny little people on the street. Can you see, Mummy?"

Victoria rose to her feet again to go and stand beside her daughter and gaze down at the street. "Yes, I can see now. My, they seem so tiny, don't they?" That apparently satisfied Olivia and they both sat down again.

"What would you like to have, Victoria?" Andrew inquired.

"Oh...ah....an omelet, I think, and tea."

"What's an omelet, Mummy?" Somehow having her father here made talking easier.

"Actually it's scrambled eggs." How desperately she wanted to say darling or even luv, but the term of endearment wouldn't come out.

The little girl wrinkled up her nose. "Oh, poo, I thought it was something good. I hate eggs!" Andrew clearly saw the corners of Victoria's mouth turn up slightly. Why can't something happen between these two, he thought wistfully. Olivia leaned over just then to whisper something to her father. Victoria experienced a pang of envy as she watched her daughter's hand resting on Andrew's arm, her sweet, childish face near his ear. "Daddy, will Mummy take me to the loo?" He smiled.

"What does she want?" Unconsciously jealousy had sharpened her tone and Olivia at once lowered her head to stare miserably into her lap.

"She'd like you to take her to the ladies' room. Emily usually goes with her. We think she's still a little young to navigate it on her own."

"Of course I'll take her. After all I am her mother. She didn't have to whisper it to you like that."

"I...I'm sorry, Mummy." Olivia was still looking down, working busily now to reduce her paper napkin to shreds. "I didn't mean to make you mad at me."

"I....I'm not angry. Really I'm not. I....I....just....." Her voice dwindled away, but Andrew had heard the obvious emotion in those few stammered words.

"Of course Mummy will take you to the bathroom, sweetheart," he said quickly.

The two stood up then and walked across the restaurant together, but this time the child made no attempt to hold her mother's hand. Once they were inside the ladies' room, Olivia went directly into a stall. "I can do it myself, Mummy," she proclaimed proudly. "I just need help buttoning up in the back afterwards."

Victoria took advantage of these few moments to remove her dark glasses and check her make-up. Luckily nothing had smeared. She studied herself in the mirror. Do I look all right, she wondered. I want to look all right. Suddenly she became aware that the toilet had flushed and Olivia was standing behind her staring. Her immediate reaction was one of renewed panic. But then she observed the child's expression–so full of love–and all undeserved on her part. Quickly she covered her confusion by bending over to fasten the straps of Olivia's overalls, glorying in this rare opportunity to be close to her daughter. "What were you looking at?"

"Just you, Mummy. I...I see you in pictures all the time, but it's not the same as seeing you really and truly."

"It...it isn't, I suppose....Olivia. You're too young to understand, but....."

"Mummy, I don't mind if I don't see you very much. Honestly I don't, but I....."

Victoria said it all in a rush, not allowing herself time to think. "Would you like to spend Christmas with me? My play doesn't open until after the first of the year and I....."

"Oh yes, please. I'd like to ever so much. Let's go tell Daddy!" Olivia's hand slipped into her mother's again. How Andrew relished those few moments, watching them come toward him hand in hand. Things could have been so different, he thought sadly. The rest of the lunch passed pleasantly. Victoria would ring up about Christmas. As they rose to leave, however, the little girl's eyes filled with tears. The holidays seemed so far away. "May I please kiss you, Mummy?" she whispered.

"Olivia!" She knelt on the floor and put her arms around her daughter. "You don't have to ask."

All that afternoon as she shopped for Olivia–a special joy this time–even through the ride home in the taxi, Victoria was filled with a warm glow. She could still feel her daughter in her arms, the kiss on her cheek and Christmas for the first time held the promise of genuine happiness. "Martha!" she fairly sang out as she came in the front door laden with packages. There would be no having presents delivered this year. She would actually see her little girl open them on Christmas morning.

"Yes, Miss Windsor?" Martha emerged from the kitchen, wiping her hands on her apron. "I was baking scones for your tea."

"How thoughtful of you! Thank you!" She could never remember hearing her employer thank her for anything and the smile which accompanied the words had a new quality. The housekeeper could think of nothing to say. "Put these away somewhere, will you please?"

Please and thank you! But Martha did at last find her voice. "Yes, ma'am." She took the packages. "Would you like me to wrap them for you?"

"No, of course not." Now there was just the briefest flash of irritation. "I'll do it myself."

"Yes, Miss Windsor. I'll put these in the bedroom next to yours–if that's all right."

"Anywhere is fine." Victoria started up the stairs, but almost at once she stopped and turned back. "Oh...ah...and Martha, Olivia will be spending Christmas here after all." If she'd meant this statement to sound casual, she'd failed entirely. A few steps further up the stairs, she stopped yet another time. "Oh...and ring up Mr. St. John and see if he'll come for dinner. Could you manage on such short notice? Of course you can. You're bloody marvelous!" Pirouetting about again, she ran on up the stairs.

The housekeeper stood watching until Victoria had disappeared along the balcony toward her room and only then did she turn away herself to walk back into the kitchen. There was an extra bounce to her step and she couldn't stop smiling. In the kitchen she reached immediately for the telephone. It was Noel himself who answered. "Mr. St. John, it's Martha. Are you free for dinner?"

"I'm afraid not. I have a date."

There was a brief pause. "Could...could you possibly change your plans? I realize I'm overstepping the limits of my position, but I....."

"Martha, is something wrong?"

"No, sir–just the opposite. Miss Windsor went to do the shopping for Olivia herself and when she came back—well, I've just never seen her so happy. Mr. St. John...she asked me to ring you. Please you......you have to come! We simply can't let a moment like this go!"

"Of course we can't. And we...ah...won't mention that I broke a date to come. About eight as usual?"

"Yes, Mr. St. John. Thank you so much, sir."

Of course his date was furious–accusing him of breaking their engagement just because "the great lady had summoned him into her presence." Noel took very little notice. But why could Victoria possibly want to see him? Thinking that perhaps a tramp through the crisp December night would help him sort things out, he decided to walk the dozen or so blocks to Eaton Square. This plan of action, however, only succeeded in his wading ankle-deep into a puddle of ice water, getting himself hopelessly entangled in the lead of an indignant Yorkshire terrier and finally plowing at full speed into a rather portly bobby so lost was he in his own musings. He still had no idea, moreover, what lay ahead and as he turned the corner from King's Road into Eaton Square, Noel admitted to himself with a rueful chuckle that such frantic ponderings had been pointless. No matter what the mood of the evening, he would simply follow Victoria's lead, taking his cue from her as automatically as he did on stage.

He climbed the stairs to #14 and taking a deep breath, he rang the doorbell. Victoria herself answered the door and seeing her, Noel told himself with a sigh of relief that he'd been concerned over nothing. She was dressed in a full length gray wool hostess skirt and a pale pink cashmere pullover and her hair was tied back with a matching pink scarf. She wore only a minimum of make-up and most wonderful of all, she was totally sober. "Noel, dear luv!" Extending both hands, she drew him in through the door. "I hope I haven't interfered with any previous plans." The expression of his face gave him away. He wasn't a very accomplished liar. "Oh, dear, I did, didn't I? How naughty of me..but...but...." A strange expression passed across her face. "But you came anyway, didn't you? I mean...you put me ahead of your other plans?"

"Or perhaps I couldn't resist the prospect of one of Martha's delicious dinners." He was determined, if he possibly could, to keep the mood light.

"Oh, is that all?" Victoria pretended to pout as tossing his coat onto a chair in the hall, she linked her arm through his for the walk into the dining room. The table was covered with a pink linen cloth and in the center was an arrangement of pink rosebuds and baby's breath. Pale pink candles in silver candlesticks cast a shimmering light over platinum-rimmed china and iridescent rose-colored crystal goblets. Noel involuntarily drew in his breath. Victoria smiled. "I know. Isn't Martha a wonder? We must tell her how lovely it all is."

It seemed as though Victoria herself had never looked more beautiful. Perhaps it was merely that the subdued lighting was flattering. But there was more: an inner radiance which had nothing whatsoever to do with the candlelight. All during the meal they chatted easily, the conversation ranging over a variety of topics, Victoria laughing merrily at his flimsiest jokes, often reaching over to touch him on the arm as they talked. The dinner was like a dream Noel had often had as for the first time he saw beyond the shadow of a doubt the warm, sweet woman in whose existence he had always believed.

Then suddenly–shortly after Martha had served the dessert and coffee--the mood shifted. Victoria fell silent and at once Noel tensed. Perhaps, he thought, the real drama of the evening was yet to commence. "Shall we go into the living room for an after-dinner drink?" she suggested at last and even that rather routine hostess-type remark seemed fraught with undertones.

"Yes, I'd like that."

On the brief stroll across the front hall the easy intimacy seemed to return, however, and for a moment he once again relaxed. As before she took his arm, even resting her head briefly against his shoulder as they walked. "Would you, luv?" Victoria asked as she stretched out on the chaise lounge. "The fire is already laid and I would enjoy a brandy, I think."

More than anything Noel longed to tell her how lovely she was, how deeply he cared for her. But he knew better. Instead he simply did as she'd requested: lighting the fire with one of the long matches and then going over to the bar to pour two brandies. Here he added what he considered to be an inspired comic touch, whipping a bar towel over one arm and handing her one of the brandies with an absurdly exaggerated bow–the quintessential Neapolitan waiter. He was amply rewarded as Victoria laughed yet again at this bit of clowning. At last Noel returned to the bar for his own brandy and settled himself in a near-by easy chair, turning it first and placing it at an angle from which he could study her without actually appearing to do so.

Victoria did not immediately raise the brandy to her lips, however. Instead she cradled the snifter in one hand and with the tip of the index finger of the other traced an endless circular pattern around the rim. A mannerism she often employed in the process of seduction–he recognized it now as simply an attempt to hide her inner turmoil. It was several moments before she spoke. "Noel, I...I saw Olivia today."

"How...how is she?" Dear God, how inane that sounded!

But Victoria was too caught up in her own emotions to notice. "Fine....fine. I...I recognized her right away, you know, even though it's...it's been more than a year." He was becoming aware of a certain feverish excitement in her voice and his uneasiness returned. "It...it shouldn't have been so long, I know that. Only after....after that horrible time for her birthday, I....I've been afraid to try again. Anyway, she knew me, too, and I...I took her to the ladies' room–such a silly, little thing really, but I..... and she asked if she could kiss me and I....hugged her, Noel... I did and I...." The words were coming faster and faster now, almost tripping over each other. "I....I'm having her with me for Christmas Eve and Christmas Day. I mean....the play doesn't open until after the first of the year and I.... Tell me what you think, Noel, please. I'm crazy, aren't I? Crazy even to try?"

What could he possibly say? "Would you like me to be here? I could arrange it."

"No....no. I...I have to do this alone. I actually talked to her today. Of course Andrew, her father–you know—was there, too, but I can do it!"

"I believe you can, Victoria."

For a moment after that she was silent again, sipping her brandy. "Noel, I'm very tired. I really think I can sleep tonight and without the pills. Do you mind, luv?"

"Of course not." He stood up, placing his glass on a table next to his chair, and coming over, he bent to kiss her lightly on the top of the head. "Sleep well."

Later, however, alone in her bedroom, the lovely glow rapidly evaporated. "What's the matter with me?" Victoria whispered aloud in the darkness. "What in bloody hell makes me think I can be a mother?" But such insight brought no release–only a terrible grieving as though she'd lost something precious and irreplaceable.

The next morning she was more sure than ever that inviting Olivia for Christmas had been a mistake. The warm and easy feeling would vanish the instant they were alone together. If only she were a more communicative child, Victoria thought once. But then what can I expect? She laughed. She's my daughter, after all, isn't she? Obviously she had to cancel the invitation. As for Olivia–she'd be much happier spending the holiday with her father. "You know that isn't true," she whispered accusingly at her reflection in the dressing table mirror. "Olivia wants to come." Indeed there seemed no way out of her dilemma. Then late one afternoon about a week before Christmas she came out of the rehearsal to find a familiar limousine parked by the curb and quite unexpectedly the solution presented itself.

* * *

She recognized the car immediately, of course–the chauffeur standing at attention by the rear door–and for a few seconds she almost walked past, pausing just long enough to express one or two well-chosen obscenities. But she did not. Perhaps she never intended to. "Miss Windsor?" With a slight bow the driver opened the door for her and she saw that Julian himself was in the back seat, looking more than ever like a malevolent old snake.

At the sight of him Victoria felt her hands go ice-cold inside her fur-lined kid gloves. Dear God, she thought, what am I doing? But after only a momentary hesitation she stepped into the car. What the hell difference did it make anyway? "Victoria, my dear...." At once Julian slid one hand in under the full sleeve of her fox fur coat, caressing her lower arm. "How have you been?"

"Haven't you had the decency to slit your Goddamned throat yet?"

"Now you know you don't mean that." Without warning his hand closed over her wrist and he pulled her to him, bending her arm behind her. "Come here, you magnificent bitch!"

"Don't, Julian!" Victoria struggled to free herself. "That hurts!"

But he merely tightened his grip, deliberately twisting her flesh the wrong way. She gasped in pain and laughing, Julian brought his mouth down on hers forcing her back against the seat cushions, his tongue probing deep into her mouth. It was all she could do not to bite him. 'So tell me," he continued as he finally released her, "do you have any plans for the holiday? I've leased a villa in Cannes. Your play doesn't open until January 15th, I believe."

Going away for Christmas, she thought–the perfect excuse! "I have no plans I can't cancel. Christmas has always been rather meaningless to me anyway."

For the next few days Victoria still argued the issue with herself, but even as she struggled, she allowed herself to drift slowly but surely in the direction of her inevitable decision. Late that Sunday afternoon when Martha brought Victoria's tea up to her bedroom, she found her packing. "What....what are you doing, Miss Windsor?"

"What does it look like I'm doing? I'm packing. I'll be...ah...spending the holidays in the south of France with Mr. Christopher—not that it's any of your concern."

"Yes, ma'am." She knew it was useless for her to say anything further.

"Just leave the tray anywhere," Victoria rushed on nervously. For some reason the housekeeper's evident, though unspoken, disapproval bothered her. "Oh yes, and there are a few things there on the bed I will require you to press."

"Yes, ma'am." Placing the tray on the dressing table, she scooped up the clothes and silently withdrew.

The next morning Martha answered the front doorbell to find Julian's chauffeur standing outside. For one crazy moment she considered slamming the door in his face. "Miss Windsor's room is the last one on the right," she directed flatly.

"Yes, ma'am." He walked briskly past her and up the stairs, returning almost at once with the suitcases.

A few minutes later Martha watched from the dining room archway as Victoria herself came down, swathed in pale mink and wearing the inevitable scarf and dark glasses. "Oh, I almost forgot. Ring up Andrew and explain, will you? There's a luv." Without so much as a glance she disappeared through the front door, not stopping to shut it behind her.

So she <u>is</u> running away, Martha thought as with a sigh she followed to close the door. Well, there was no point in putting it off and going on into the living room, she sat down at the small writing desk in the front alcove to consult Victoria's address book. She found the number of Mr. Roberts' law office and reluctantly she picked up the receiver and dialed.

* * *

When Andrew arrived home that evening, his wife met him at the door. "You have got to speak to that child! She's packing as though it's for two weeks instead of two days and frankly I can't imagine that woman with a child around for even that long!"

"Neither can I," he muttered under his breath, continuing immediately on up the stairs. Ever since Mrs. Kendall's call he'd been dreading this moment and now he just wanted to get it over with. Entering his daughter's room, he found her trying to stuff yet another article of clothing into an already overloaded valise.

"Daddy," she fairly crowed, "I'm packing!"

"So I see." In spite of himself he smiled. "Sweetheart, can we move this suitcase off the bed for a few minutes so we can sit here together for a little talk."

"Sure, Daddy. Only I don't have much time. I've still lots and lots to do."

"Are you too grown-up to sit on Daddy's lap?" Happily Olivia shook her head and climbed on. I was wrong, Andrew thought; I should have told her her mother was dead. At last he somehow managed to say it–holding her close as he did so. "Olivia, your mother's plans have changed and she's had to cancel your visit."

There was a brief silence. "Oh, I see. All right." Her tone was cool and detached --so like her mother's, he thought. "I'd like to be alone now, please, Daddy."

"All right, lovey, but come down for your tea." Andrew went out, closing the door softly behind him. He stood in the hall listening as the child started to sob and for a moment he nearly went back in. No, he thought, she should be allowed her privacy. Olivia did come down for her tea, however, and once again he couldn't help but notice how like Victoria she really was. Except for a slight redness around the little girl's eyes he would never have known she'd been crying.

* * *

All during the flight to Cannes Victoria remained strangely uncommunicative and Julian grew increasingly irritated. "What in hell is wrong with you?" he growled as the plane came in for a landing.

At the moment he spoke her mind had been hundreds of miles away–specifically back in London with Olivia. "What?" she replied in a dazed tone.

"God damn you, bitch! You keep acting like this and I'll jolly well have you on the next plane back to England!"

Oh no, Victoria once again vowed to herself, this time I'll be the one to finish it. Her chance came when toward the end of the week Julian wanted to travel to Italy to attend a soccer game. "The hell with that," had been her reply. "Grown men kicking a ball around!" He'd made a remark about the type of balls she preferred and went off to see the game by himself or with another woman. Victoria didn't care. She gathered up her things to go down by the pool. The idea of even a day without Julian was bliss.

She'd been there only a little while, however, when a young man settled himself in another lounge chair just a short distance away. He appeared familiar, but it was several minutes before she could place him. Of course, she thought—Julian's son–and suddenly it came to her–the ultimate revenge. Once a scheme occurred to her Victoria was not one to delay and she stood up and walked over to him. Easing herself into a folding canvas chair facing him, she allowed her terrycloth beach robe to fall open revealing long, sleek legs. "Hello."

Ryan recognized her instantly, of course. "Victoria, don't tell me dear old Dad has left you unguarded!" The slow smile which spread across his face reminded her of Julian's, but there was a natural warmth to it lacking in the older man.

She laughed. "I <u>thought</u> you were Julian's son."

"Ah yes, there are very few who can point to one of the world's most notable dirty old men as their noble and immediate ancestor."

"You really hate him, don't you?"

"I've always considered patricide an honourable deed actually."

"I came with him on holiday for only one reason." Well, not <u>just</u> one, the same small voice reminded her. Damn, couldn't Olivia stay out of her thoughts even at a time like this? "For only <u>one</u> reason," she repeated, defying the voice to taunt her again. "To repay him for all his abuse and when I saw you sitting here, I came up with the perfect plan."

"Then I'm to be part of your plot? Bloody marvelous!" He rubbed his hands together in sadistic glee. The gesture looked like something out of a Victorian melodrama, she thought. But then this would indeed <u>be</u> a "Victorian" melodrama, wouldn't it? Her own wit delighted her. She'd have to tell that one to Basil. "What's your plan?" Ryan went on to inquire.

"My plan. Simply a mortal wound, luv, to his most vulnerable spot–his male ego."

He roared with laughter. "He may never recover. And I'm the weapon?"

"Precisely. What better revenge could there be than to walk out on him—with his <u>own son</u>?!"

"Bang on target! But how will he know you've gone with me?"

"Because we'll be sure to tell as many people as possible before we leave. It's no fun unless his humiliation is public. But just to be sure I'll also leave him a note."

"Dad's right about one thing. You <u>are</u> an incredible woman!" Taking her hand, he raised it to her lips, a mannerism he would have been dismayed to learn was a carbon copy of his father's. "And so very beautiful! Do you know how beautiful?"

Victoria sighed. Was there any man who was at all different? "I <u>should</u> know by now," she observed caustically, "I've been told so often enough!"

By the time Victoria and Ryan left to drive north to Paris, a dozen or so acquaintances knew they were going. Each lost no time in repeating the news and when Julian returned that evening, he didn't really require Victoria's note. But there it was–appropriately enough–on the bed. "Sorry, luv–I've decided I prefer the <u>younger</u> Christopher!"

Chapter 12

All her life Victoria had sought refuge from a lonely world. Childish hiding places were replaced with more adult modes of escape, but none of them worked for long. Even the world of the theatre–most magical of all–never lasted. Inexorably the curtain came down; the applause died away and reality returned. It was inevitable that one day her mind would seek a sanctuary of its own.

Ordinarily her euphoria lasted at least until the final curtain, but on the opening night of the Fitzhugh play the let-down had begun much earlier, the playwright having just joined the cast on stage. Curtain call followed upon curtain call and every time Victoria stepped forward from between Basil and Ian Hyde, her sophisticated graying co-star, to take a solitary bow, the acclamation grew louder. She should have been exultant, but instead–oddly–she was already experiencing a vague disappointment. True she'd been dreading the opening night party–the first such she'd be attending without an escort. Ryan Christopher might not have possessed his father's sadistic streak, but neither did he have his wit and she'd soon tired of him. But then everyone would have heard about her and Julian and they'd all assume she was alone by choice so that shouldn't have bothered her.

"Just be sure you make money, my dear," Basil observed to her drily under cover of the applause.

"Ah, yes, Fitzhugh–ever the aesthete!" She dropped yet another sweeping curtsey, at the same time raising one hand to her throat–her by-now famous mannerism of humble appreciation.

Noel had been next to Victoria until Basil unceremoniously pushed his way in between them and now from the other side of the imposing playwright he observed her anxiously. She barely smiled, seeming to accept the applause mechanically with no evidence of real enjoyment. Was she regretting Christmas, he wondered–not having spent it with her daughter? He suspected this was the case, although ever since she'd returned from France, she had managed outside of rehearsals to avoid him.

Victoria rose gracefully to a standing position once again, but this time as she glanced over her shoulder to step back into the line, she caught her old friend's eye on her. Damn him, she thought, and when the curtain came down for the final time, she hurried off stage, as usual speaking to no one. Abruptly dismissing her maid, she sank down on the stool in front of her dressing table, making no move to take off her costume or make-up. Indeed she was still sitting there some time later when a knock sounded at the door. With some effort she stirred herself to answer. "Who is it?"

"Noel. About ready to leave?"

"No...ah...I'm not."

She sounded peculiar. He became even more concerned. "If you need more time, I can wait."

"Go away! And stay the bloody hell away from me at the party, too. The last thing I need tonight is you following me around like a stray puppy."

"All....all right, then." This was the first time he could remember Victoria herself referring to him in this vein and as he walked away, he had to admit he was hurt. Later he would curse himself bitterly for not staying.

The sound of Noel's footsteps receding in the distance was the last thing of which Victoria was actually conscious. For a while she continued to sit there, but at some point something brought her to her feet, drawing her out the door and through the wings onto the stage. The set was the same one she'd seen through weeks of rehearsal and yet now Victoria looked about uncertainly at the various articles of furniture as though trying to understand where she was. All at once the elaborately carved sofa to the right of and slightly above center stage apparently caught her attention–or more precisely something on it. "Oh, my little lamb!" Her eyes shone with happy recognition and she hurried over to pick up one of the sofa cushions and hold it close. "It's all right, little lamb. It's all right," she crooned and curling up in one corner of the couch, she began to rock the pillow in her arms. "My nanny told me I had to throw you away because you're nasty and dirty, but I hid you where no one could find you and I will always keep you safe."

* * *

At the party Noel glanced at his watch for what must have easily been the hundredth time in the last hour. Where in God's name was Victoria? Then he noticed Sir Terence sitting on a window seat holding forth on some subject or other to the many admirers who were as usual clustered around him. "And so," Terry was saying as Noel moved over to stand at the edge of the group, "British theatre, and for that matter theatre in general, is not nearly in such dire straits as our detractors would have us believe. We have seen eloquent proof of that fact tonight."

"But tell me, Sir Terence," someone had the temerity to inquire, "did you feel Miss Windsor was at her best this evening?"

"Victoria is never anything <u>but</u> at her best." His voice dripped ice water and the gaze which flicked contemptuously over the poor soul who had dared utter such blasphemy was pure Richard III. "She is capable of nothing less."

"Terry," Noel interposed at this point, "I wonder if I might speak to you alone for a minute?" The people in the group glanced up at him, their reactions ranging from good- natured envy to open hostility. What must it be like to know Sir Terence so well?

Terry, of course, had understood at once why Noel broke into the conversation. "Of course. Ladies and gentlemen, if you would be kind enough to excuse me..... Noel?" He stood up putting an affectionate arm around the younger man's shoulders as they walked together out into the hall.

"She's not here yet!" Noel's voice was high and tight with anxiety. "At the curtain call she just wasn't herself. I'm going back to the theatre. Will you come with me?"

Without hesitation Terry nodded. "Let's go."

Fifteen minutes or so later a taxi let them out in front of the theatre, both pausing to glance briefly, but eloquently up at the marquee–now darkened. It was fortunate that the police didn't happen by as shortly afterwards two illustrious members of the British theatre worked feverishly to break off the lock on the stage door. "Victoria!" Noel called out anxiously the moment they were inside. There was no answer.

"Victoria!" This time it was Terry who called. Still nothing. They began an increasingly frantic search of the backstage area. Her dressing room door stood open. "Her fur's still here!" he exclaimed.

From there, for some reason, they went out onto the stage. Noel saw her first, curled up on the couch. "Oh, thank God!" He started toward her. "Victoria, where have you been? Why didn't you answer us when we called? We...."

Terry reached out to take his arm and stop him. "No...wait!"

"What?" At once Noel became annoyed, unable to comprehend the other man's hesitation.

"Look at her," Sir Terence insisted. "Can't you see she's still in costume? She never even got ready to come to the party! We must be very careful." He walked slowly across to sit beside her. He saw she was holding a sofa cushion, but for the moment he paid it no particular notice. "Victoria?" he said quietly.

"It's finally happened, hasn't it? I knew it!"

"Perhaps not. It's just possible if we talk to her calmly, we can bring her back before she slips too far away from us. You see, my friend, the dangerous thing about madness is that it can be so appealing."

"Appealing?" Noel felt a shiver run down his spine.

"Tell me, have you ever seen her so peaceful?"

"No, but....."

"Exactly. And why should she leave such a place and return to the real world where we both know she's unhappy?"

"But we have to make her want to come back. We can't lose her...not...not like this."

"Now you understand. Victoria?" he began once again, careful to keep his voice low and even. "Dearest girl, it's Noel and old Terry. You remember us, don't you?"

Finally now Victoria turned to look at him. "Uncle Bertie?" She smiled a sweet, childlike smile neither of them had ever seen before.....and who was Uncle Bertie? "Uncle Bertie," she said again, "this is my little lamb. Would you like to hold it for a while?" She placed the pillow gently in his arms, giving it one final pat. "But you must be very careful not to let Nanny get him. Nanny wants to kill him!" She grasped his arm imploringly. "We mustn't let her do that, Uncle Bertie! You have to promise me!"

"Oh God, I can't watch." Noel walked away across the stage, his fists clenching and unclenching in anguish.

"Then what do we do?" Terry demanded harshly. "Just allow her to slip away? After all, you did say she was happier this way."

"Damn you! You know I don't want that, but.....but....."

Ignoring him, the other man turned his attention back to Victoria. "I'm afraid it's not Uncle Bertie, Victoria, but it is Terry and Noel and we both love you, too, my darling." A tremor ran through her and she blinked once or twice, but she refused to look at him. "Please, dearest girl, I know how badly you want to run away, but we're here waiting for you. Please don't leave us. We would miss you dreadfully."

Again Victoria shivered. She didn't want to return, but the dear, familiar voice was calling to her, refusing to let her go. At last–reluctantly–her eyes met his. Relief flooded over him. Clearly now she knew who he was. "Terry?" Shakily she reached out to take his hand. She was ice cold.

"Victoria?" Noel came then to kneel in front of her.

"Noel?" She looked back and forth from one to the other, obviously confused. "I...I'm still at the theatre, aren't I?"

"Yes, Victoria." Terry was continuing to hold her hand and now he slipped his other arm around her shoulders. "Come, dear. We'll take you home now."

"I don't want to go home!" She pulled away from him and getting to her feet, moved downstage. "There's nothing for me there...no one." And still repeating those two terrible words–nothing...no one...nothing...no one... over and over again–she started to spin. Faster and faster she whirled, arms spread wide as though to seize hold of something, until the two men became afraid she'd fall off the edge of the stage. But then suddenly she stopped and looking at them, she at once saw their uneasiness, the concern on both their faces.

"Terry...Noel....I'm....I'm sorry. It's....it's just that ever since I can remember, this has been what I wanted and tonight it all seemed so meaningless." She returned slowly upstage to sink down on the couch again. "I...I don't know how long I've been sitting here. You.....you both came back, though, didn't you?" She looked from one to the other. "You.....you were worried and you....you..... Oh, Terry, please....please....." She made a pathetically imploring little gesture with her hands and understanding, he gathered her into his arms. "Oh, Terry... Terry...." Victoria began to sob.

"I know, dear. I know," he whispered tenderly. It seemed she would cry forever, but through it all he held her until at last she grew quiet. "Go and telephone my driver," he finally directed the other man. "I think we can take her home now and perhaps you should stay there tonight."

Noel nodded and went to do as he'd been asked. But, oh why couldn't she have come into <u>his</u> arms?

* * *

The next morning Noel was awake very early. In fact, he'd not really slept at all. He was feeling wretched, but as he came down the stairs, his nose caught the aroma of brewing coffee. Apparently Martha had gotten up even earlier. He pushed open the swinging door into the kitchen smiling his appreciation. "Exactly what I need! Bless you!"

"I couldn't sleep, Mr. St. John, after.....after you and Sir Terence brought Miss Windsor home. Is she still asleep?"

"I looked in on my way down. Yes, she is, thank God."

"What are you going to do, sir?"

"Terry said he'd come back this morning. Victoria seems to trust him."

"You mustn't feel, sir, that Miss Windsor only relies on Sir Terence. She depends on you more than you realize."

"You know, I was ashamed of myself last night–jealous because she went to Terry instead of me. What I'd do if she ever really fell in love with someone, I don't know." He paused for a moment, suddenly remembering something Victoria had said in her disturbed wanderings of the night before. "You know her about as well as anyone, don't you, Martha? Perhaps you'd know about her Uncle Bertie. Whether he's still alive. And if so, where we could get in touch with him?"

"Oh, she never talks about her family, sir. She....." Just then, however, the sound of the doorbell interrupted her.

"That will probably be Sir Terence. I'll let him in if you'll see to that coffee." Noel hurried through the formal dining room and across the hall to the front door. "Good morning, Terry. Victoria's not awake yet. Have you had breakfast?"

"No."

"Martha's making coffee. We're in the kitchen."

"Perfect! You know I have a particular fondness for kitchens and people never seem to feel I belong in them."

"It appears that neither of us have had breakfast," Noel said as he pushed open the swinging door once again. "Could we trouble you?"

As Sir Terence had predicted, the housekeeper looked properly startled to find the dean of the British theatre standing in her kitchen. "No trouble at all, but please, gentlemen, if you'll go into the dining room, I'll serve you there."

"No, no, Mrs. Kendall," Terry replied at once, "right here will be fine. Please don't put yourself out." How typical of him, Noel thought, to remember the name of Victoria's housekeeper. The two men settled themselves at the kitchen table. Martha poured two mugs of coffee and began to prepare breakfast.

"So," Noel inquired, raising his hands in a gesture of helplessness, "what happens now?"

"I...ah.....took the liberty of ringing up a psychiatrist this morning and I......"

"Last night she came to you of her own free will. Don't drive her away again by suggesting she see a psychiatrist!"

"And what have we accomplished by continually giving in to her? Absolutely nothing!"

"But if we cause her to turn away from us completely, what good will we be doing then?"

Martha had been trying very hard to ignore their discussion, but as their voices continued to rise in volume, she couldn't help frowning slightly. It was Noel who noticed her expression. "How do <u>you</u> feel about this, Martha?"

"Really, sir, it's not my place."

"I knew you'd say that." He smiled. "But I happen to think it very definitely <u>is</u> your place."

"I....ah....just feel," she finally replied, though still somewhat hesitantly, "that if you quarrel with each other, you'll be of little help to Miss Windsor."

"And do you have an opinion as to which of us is right, Mrs. Kendall?" Sir Terence inquired.

"I'm afraid I have to agree with Mr. St. John, sir. Even though Miss Windsor may indeed need professional help, the idea must come from her. In fact, it might be better if she didn't even realize you were both here this morning."

Terry shrugged his shoulders in reluctant surrender. "I won't argue the point any further. Mrs. Kendall, we will simply enjoy your excellent breakfast and quietly depart."

It would be several hours more before Victoria awoke, turning drowsily over so that she could see her bedside clock. Nearly eleven and yet she felt exhausted, her eyes burning with fatigue, her arms and legs heavy and aching. Of course, she thought, another hangover, but then she recalled that she'd had nothing to drink.

Noel.....Noel and Terry had brought her home from....from the theatre. She'd..... she'd just seemed to....to come to on...on the stage and....and they....they were <u>there</u> with her. But....but where....where had they come from? Suddenly–out of nowhere–another image flashed into her mind. It was as though she'd become the audience and she could see and hear herself sobbing in Terry's arms. "Weakness," she accused herself, "inexcusable weakness!"

But why hadn't she gone to the party? What was she doing on the stage? And why couldn't she remember? Oh God, she thought, I'm losing my mind! She broke out in a cold sweat and before the panic could take hold of her, she reached over to pick up the telephone receiver and buzz the kitchen on the intercom. "Yes, Miss Windsor," Martha replied immediately.

I swear she lives her life within arm's reach of that telephone, Victoria thought. "Brunch," she directed, "up here in about an hour."

Dear God, the housekeeper thought, tears welling up in her eyes, she's terrified, but she isn't going to admit it. "What would you like to have, Miss Windsor?"

"Tea, a soft-boiled egg–some toast...and ring the beautician. I'd like my nails done this afternoon —also a facial, I think."

"Yes, Miss Windsor."

"And my driver for about five o'clock. I'll be having dinner at the actors' club. Ring there and book an enclosed booth."

"Will anyone be joining you, Miss Windsor?"

"No, I'll be......<u>alone</u>!" The word was flat, harsh.......and <u>final</u>.

* * *

Andrew had made up his mind after the events of Christmas that Olivia would have nothing further to do with her mother. The little girl had accepted the decision too easily, he thought afterwards; he should have known she was stronger willed than that. Then a few days later his wife telephoned him at the office. Olivia had failed to come home from kindergarten.`

Somehow a little girl not quite five and a half had found her way to Oxford Circus on the tube and once there, a kind, grandmotherly woman helped her navigate the street crossings and brought her along Oxford Street as far as D.H. Evans, the first department store. For a few minutes Olivia stood just inside the main entrance. What could she possibly find for such a grand lady as her mother? At last she began to walk slowly around and around the counters which for her were just a little below eye level: jewellery, perfume—everything was so wonderful! Finally a salesclerk noticed her. "May I help you, dear?"

"I want to buy a birthday present for my mother, but she's a famous actress and she has everything!"

"Oh, I see." The woman smiled indulgently. "And how much do you have to spend on this famous mother?"

"One pound, six shillings," the child announced proudly. Patiently the clerk suggested several items within her small customer's price range. Nothing satisfied Olivia. She wanted so much to find something special–something which would make her mother love her–and then she saw it: a gold locket, hanging all by itself on a red velvet bust. "Oh—that, please!" she breathed fervently. "The locket!"

"I'm so sorry, but I'm afraid that costs almost twice as much as you have to spend."

"Oh." Tears filled the little girl's eyes.

Instantly the woman weakened. "But wait a minute. That may just be one of the items going on sale. She pretended to look at a list taped to one side of the cash register. "You happen to be in luck, young lady. The locket is on sale and for exactly what you have to spend."

"Oh, goody, goody!" Olivia jumped up and down, clapping her hands.

"I'll put it in a box and if you take it to the back of the store, they'll put paper and ribbon on it for you." She arranged the locket against the cotton and put on the cover, "I'm sure your mother will like it."

"I...I hope so. Thank you." Eyes shining, Olivia carefully handed over her one and six–all in coins of under a half-crown–and accepted the precious package. The clerk watched the little girl walk away, clutching her purchase. Only then did she go to the cash register to ring up the sale, reaching into a cabinet underneath for her own purse to make up the difference.

It was great fun seeing the lady put the pretty paper and ribbon on her package, but a few minutes later emerging once more onto the sidewalk, Olivia suddenly remembered that although she knew her mother's address, she had no idea how to get there.

"Lost, little miss?"

She looked up to see a bobby standing there smiling down at her. "No, sir. I know where I am. I just don't know how to get where I want to go."

His grin grew broader. "I see." He turned just in time to flag down a passing patrol car. "Well, you can tell them, luv, and they'll see you get there."

Martha was dusting the living room furniture and she happened to glance up just as a police car stopped in front of the house. A uniformed bobby got out and came up the stairs, holding a little girl by the hand. Puzzled, she went to open the door. "Yes?"

"Young lady says she belongs here, ma'am," the officer explained.

"I'm Olivia," the child trumpeted happily.

"Yes, it's all right—thank you." The housekeeper closed the door and stood looking down at the unexpected visitor–wishing vaguely she'd never seen her. Somehow it had been easier when Miss Windsor's daughter was only a name. "So you're Olivia," she said finally in as jolly a tone as she could muster. "I'm Martha. I work for your mother."

"Hello, Martha." She looked about eagerly as if expecting Victoria to appear at any minute. "Is my mother here?"

The housekeeper was tempted to lie. No, she thought, that wouldn't be fair to either one of them. "Yes, dear," she said finally, "but some friends are taking her out shortly to celebrate her birthday." Just then she heard the intercom buzz in the kitchen. "Wait there in the living room, will you?" Martha pointed out the direction. "I'll be right back." Olivia obeyed and Martha went quickly to pick up the telephone receiver.

"Where in the hell were you?" Victoria demanded crossly. "I thought you were pressing my dress."

"I finished that, ma'am. I was dusting the living room and......."

"I do not require a schedule of your duties, Martha–simply my dress."

"Right away, Miss Windsor." Perhaps it <u>would</u> be better to talk to Victoria face to face, but when she came out of the kitchen again carrying the pale aqua silk dress carefully on a hanger, Olivia was standing in the archway.

"Are you taking that up to my mother?" she inquired eagerly. "May I do it?" Before Martha could reply or do anything to prevent it, the little girl had grabbed the hanger and darted up the stairs. Arriving in the upper hall, however, she found a semi-circular balcony and leading off it five doors–all closed. Which one was her mother's bedroom? "Mummy?" she called out. Victoria was applying the finishing touches to her make-up and at the sound of the sweet, piping voice she jumped. Oh my God, she thought, what's she doing here? Perhaps if I don't answer her, she'll give up and go away. But Olivia wasn't to be deterred. "Mummy, I don't know which room it is!" Half the male population of London could tell you the exact location of my bedroom, the actress thought ironically, but my own daughter doesn't know. "Mummy!" By now the child was pleading.

Victoria sighed, closing her eyes with a great weariness or perhaps it was merely sadness, but at last she rose to her feet, walked to her bedroom door and opened it. "Here I am, Olivia."

The little girl ran along the balcony holding the dress high above her head. "I brought your dress up, Mummy," she announced proudly, "instead of Martha. I like Martha. Does she live here with you?" For a few minutes standing there alone in the strange house, she'd been frightened, but the fear had vanished the instant her mother appeared.

"Come in, dear." Her tone, however, was merely cordial. "Though I'm afraid you've come at a bad time. I'm just about to go out." Olivia followed her mother into the room, her joy already slightly dimmed, but still not forgetting to lay the dress carefully on the bed. Victoria seated herself again at her dressing table. It was her habit to study herself intently in a mirror, but now it provided the perfect excuse to ignore her daughter. She checked her eye make-up and edged her lips a bit more perfectly.

Suddenly she became aware that Olivia was standing behind her–also studying her mother's reflection as she'd done that day in the restaurant cloakroom. "Mummy, you're so beautiful," the child whispered. "Will I ever be as beautiful as you are?"

"Don't be silly. You're...you're very pretty now." How Victoria wished she could turn around and hug her. Why, then, did her voice sound so cold?

Olivia looked down at the precious gift-wrapped package which she still held clasped tightly in one hand. "Mummy, I....I came to...to bring you your birthday present."

If she'd been older, the little girl might have seen the strain in Victoria's face. As it was, she only heard her mother's voice saying quickly and coolly, "Well, thank you, luv. But I just don't have the time to open it right now. Leave it somewhere, would you?" Olivia edged forward to place the small box at the very corner of the dressing table, immediately backing away again to stand behind her mother. Victoria's eyes never left the mirror, her hands gripping the edge of the table as she gazed at the reflection of this dear, dejected little person who was scuffing at the rug with one foot and biting her lower lip to stop it from quivering. "Fine," she said at last, "now run along downstairs, will you, and ask Martha to ring up your father."

"Yes, Mummy." Swallowing hard, she walked quickly to the door. "Good-bye, Mummy."

"Bye-bye, luv. See you soon." Desperately Victoria kept her eyes on the mirrored image of her own face, refusing to look at her daughter who must by now be standing in the doorway.

As the little girl moved along the balcony and down the stairs again, the tears which she'd fought so hard to hold back in front of her mother began to fall freely. Reaching the downstairs hall, she found it empty. "I hate this house?" she sobbed with a vehemence unusual for her. "I can't find anyone and I...I just <u>hate</u> it!"

Martha pushed open the swinging door leading from the kitchen. "In here, lovey." Tears streaming down her face, Olivia half-ran to her. "Come on, then." The housekeeper led her gently over to one of the chairs at the kitchen table and from one of the enormous pockets of her apron she pulled out a handkerchief to wipe the little girl's eyes. "Now how about some biscuits and milk?"

"No.....thank you," Olivia added after a brief pause, remembering her manners. "My mother says you should ring up Daddy and tell him to come fetch me." Her voice, low to begin with, dwindled away until the last two or three words were all but inaudible.

"Do you know your phone number, dear?"

The little chin came up in a gesture of proud defiance and she recited the number distinctly. Martha at once picked up the receiver and dialed. "Hello," Andrew answered on the first ring. Obviously he'd been sitting right next to the phone.

Well, at least one of her parents loves her, Martha thought bitterly. "Mr. Roberts," she said aloud, "this is Martha Kendall. Your daughter's here and she's fine."

"Thank God. I'll be right there to collect her."

"No need to hurry, sir. We'll take good care of her."

"You <u>and</u> her mother?" Andrew's tone was noticeably sour.

"Yes, Mr. Roberts. Both of us." Martha hung up the telephone. "Your Daddy was so relieved, lovey. He was frightfully worried."

"Why.....why doesn't my mother love me?"

The housekeeper stopped to pull another chair out from the table and sit down next to the little girl. "You know, I think she does love you. It's just hard for her to express her feelings."

"I don't understand. If you love someone, why can't you show it?"

Victoria, meanwhile, had continued to sit staring into the mirror. It wasn't her own image she was seeing there, of course, but her daughter's face as it had been reflected there a few moments before–stricken and miserable. "Oh, Olivia, darling," she whispered, "I'm so very sorry. I....I love you so much, dearest; truly I do. But I see you looking at me that way and something happens inside me. I have to drive you away–destroy whatever feeling you still have for me." Just then her glance happened to fall on the gift-wrapped package on her dressing table. "Damn," Victoria muttered and snatching it up, she made as if to hurl the small box across the room. But of course she couldn't do that. For a breath or two she remained in that position, her hand seemingly frozen in the act of throwing. Then at last– trembling--she lowered it to her lap and began to unwrap it–carefully at first, then tearing at the paper and ribbon in her eagerness to get it open.

Jewellery was a special passion of Victoria's. It might be a piece she'd bought for herself or it might be a token from a male admirer, but it was always elegant and always expensive. Now she was sure she had never seen anything quite as lovely as this cheap, gold-plated locket. "Oh!" she breathed softly, "so beautiful. Oh–the sweet darling! Oh dear God, I....I can't let her leave like this!"

Jumping to her feet, she dashed out of her room and along the balcony toward the stairs before she had a chance to change her mind. "Olivia?!" What if her daughter had already left? But the little girl came running from the kitchen. They met at the bottom of the stairs, Victoria finding it entirely natural at that moment to sit on the steps. They were exactly at eye level. "Darling, I couldn't wait. I had to open it. It's just beautiful and....and it's perfect with the dress I'm going to wear today. Will you put it on for me?" The child ran up a few steps to stand behind Victoria and after several attempts managed to fasten the clasp. "Thank you, darling. Did....did you pick it out all by yourself?"

"Yes, Mummy, I did!" For the first time she wasn't tongue-tied in front of her mother. She had something exciting and important to tell her, but she'd barely begun when the doorbell sounded. Martha, who had remained discreetly out of view in the dining room, went to open the door. "Oh, Daddy." Olivia was clearly disappointed. "Mummy and I were having such a nice visit. Do I have to leave right away?"

"Victoria," Andrew replied, "that's up to you."

For a few seconds she hesitated. More than anything she longed for this closeness between herself and Olivia to continue, but the moment the possibility actually existed, she backed off. "I'm afraid I'm going out," she said briskly, getting to her feet. Frightfully undignified, after all, for a woman of her position to be sitting on the stairs. "You better go along with your father, luv. I'll....I'll ring up soon, I promise and....and we'll have lunch." She started to move away up the stairs.

"Mummy!" the little girl called after her.

Victoria stopped and turned back. She appeared impatient. What she actually was, of course, was terribly nervous. "Yes, darling?" Andrew looked up quickly. It was the first time he'd heard her use any term of endearment toward their daughter.

Olivia's lower lip was trembling just slightly. "I...I just.....I just wanted to kiss you good-bye."

"Of course, luv. I forgot." Victoria came back down to enfold her daughter in her arms, giving and accepting a kiss on the cheek. "Thank you for the locket. It's so pretty."

"You're welcome, Mummy. I'm....I'm glad you like it." Immediately the actress disengaged herself and this time she ran up the stairs without looking back. "Mummy, I....I love you." Olivia stood there watching until her mother had disappeared from sight along the balcony. Finally she gave a little sigh, inaudible to Martha and Andrew waiting below, and turned to come down. "All right, Daddy. I'm ready to go."

"Thank you, Mrs. Kendall," Andrew said.

Martha opened the door for them. "Mr. Roberts, you will let her come back?"

His answering smile held more than a trace of sadness. "That's not up to me."

The little girl was standing between them holding her father's hand and at the last words she looked up at him. "But....but Mummy asked me to—for lunch."

"Yes, dear. You know I'll let you come anytime."

"Oh, goody! Good-bye, Martha."

"Good-bye, dear." The housekeeper stood in the open door, watching them go down the front walk hand in hand. As she closed the door, however, another picture was far more vivid in her mind–that of Miss Windsor with her arms around her daughter.

"Why do I let these things happen?" Victoria demanded angrily of her reflection in the full-length mirror. "God, every time I see that child, I fall apart.....Oh, but why couldn't I have said that I love her, too?" Just then the doorbell sounded and forcing herself to stop thinking about her daughter, she removed her robe and reached for the dress, taking it off the hanger. For a second or two as she slipped the garment over her head, she could see Olivia again carrying it triumphantly along the balcony. She pushed the image from her mind, but she brought the locket out over the neckline–pretending to be casual about it as though it were simply too much bother to take it off.

Victoria ran lightly down the stairs. Jonathan and Noel were standing in the front hall, the latter holding a full-length sable coat. "My birthday gift to myself," she informed them gaily as he helped her slip into it. "Don't I have bloody marvelous taste?" Martha was there as well, waiting to hold the door open for them. Seeing Miss Windsor now, she might have wondered whether the whole incident with Olivia had been pure wishful thinking on her part, had she not also noticed that her employer was still wearing the locket.

At lunch Victoria chattered constantly, touching her companions' hands, their cheeks, frequently leaning over to kiss one or the other and in general being her most delightful. Both men knew that for some reason she was especially troubled that day. They wondered as well where the inexpensive locket had come from–gold-plated and oddly out of place with her silk dress and sable coat and made all the more evident by the tender way in which she continually touched it.

* * *

The next year or so was almost like the interval in a performance– a chance, perhaps, for everyone to draw breath before the next act--as on the surface at least nothing in Victoria's life changed. Martha, however, would never forget one night in particular.

The housekeeper was in her room off the kitchen about to retire for the night when she heard Victoria's voice in the front hall. Surprised, she glanced at her clock–only a little past midnight. Then she heard a second voice–male. She sighed. She should have known that if Miss Windsor came home this early, she wouldn't be alone. There were peals of drunken laughter. Apparently, however, they'd only stopped long enough to pick up a bottle because shortly afterwards she heard them go upstairs.

For a while after that the house was quiet. Then somewhere upstairs a door banged open. Martha could hear the voices again, raised now in anger, and a moment later she caught the unmistakable sounds of a struggle. Heart pounding with fear, she threw back the covers, but before she could get out of bed, she heard Victoria scream, then a series of thumps as though something–or someone had fallen down the stairs. Frantic running footsteps followed. Martha grabbed up her robe and just as she hurried out into the front hall, the door slammed behind someone making a hasty get-away. At once she saw her employer lying at the bottom of the stairs. "Oh, my God!" she exclaimed. "Miss Windsor!" She ran over to kneel beside her.

Incredibly–horribly–Victoria began to laugh. "Charming end to a charming evening–what?" She started to struggle to her feet.

"Please, ma'am. Don't try to move. I'll ring for the doctor."

"Hell no, Martha. A drunk never gets hurt, didn't you know that?" By now Victoria was indeed standing and holding onto the bannister, she managed to make her way up the stairs. Only when she'd reached the top step did she finally stop and let go of the railing, turning to look down at her anxious housekeeper. "Oh, come now! Aren't you even the tiniest bit curious?" She swayed slightly and grabbed the railing again to keep from falling. "Don't you want to know what caused my fall from grace?"

"I didn't think it any of my business, Miss Windsor."

Victoria laughed uproariously. "Hell, why not? You know everything about me. Goddamned bastard was impotent and he didn't much care for my admittedly indelicate observations on the fact." Still laughing, she moved along the balcony toward her room.

Early in the spring of that year she did finally keep her promise to invite Olivia for lunch, but the lovely closeness which existed between them briefly on her birthday had vanished. Once again mother and daughter could think of little to say to each other and the awkward silences grew longer and longer. A little more than halfway through the meal escape presented itself in the form of a telephone call from her agent. Would she possibly be free to talk over a couple of new scripts, he inquired.

"Yes, of course, Matt." Victoria hung up the telephone in the living room and ran upstairs to check her hair and make-up. Back downstairs she paused in her flight only long enough to grab a wrap from the closet before hurrying on across the hall toward the door. Through all of this she'd carefully avoided even so much as a glance in the direction of the dining room. It was bad enough that Olivia would be watching her, but by now Martha would undoubtedly have come to stand in the kitchen doorway as well. Why in hell could that woman always make her feel so bloody guilty? "Sorry, luv, I'd forgotten an appointment. See you soon." The door shut quickly behind her. She hadn't even waited for a reply.

Sometime during that winter a large yellow alley cat started hanging around the theatre. People fed it and so it adopted the place as its home. They named it Barrymore. One evening in mid-June Victoria arrived for a performance to find most of the cast and crew gathered center stage. "What's going on?" she asked.

The crowd immediately dispersed. "Nothing, Miss Windsor," someone murmured. "Good evening, Miss Windsor," said another. "Please excuse us."

Only Noel remained. "Now you know how the lepers must have felt," he observed with his crooked grin.

"Do you practice that smile in front of a mirror?" she retorted even as she experienced her usual rush of affection for this darling idiot.

"Everything about me is completely natural, Victoria. You know that!"

"Oh, you're impossible!" Then she discovered the reason for the gathering. In a large cardboard box left there last night Barrymore had given birth to four kittens.

"It seems Barrymore's first name is Ethel." Noel grinned at her again.

Victoria knelt down to look more closely at the kittens and he took full advantage of her preoccupation to study her. Her smile as she reached out to touch one of the babies gently with the tip of her index finger was soft and natural, lighting up her green eyes, and yet again he wondered why she found it so difficult to allow these tender feelings to show. She glanced up and he quickly looked away. "By the time of Olivia's birthday they'd be ready to leave their mother, wouldn't they? Little girls love kittens, don't they? Do you think her father would object?"

"I'm sure he wouldn't." Noel wondered if she were aware of the emotion in her voice.

"I'll wait until they're a little older–to choose one for her."

"Why not have Olivia come here and pick out the kitten herself?"

"No, I don't think so." Her good mood instantly evaporated. "I've already had my disaster as a mother for this year. But then I'm sure your friend Martha keeps you fully informed!"

"Maybe if you made more than one attempt in a year, they wouldn't <u>be</u> such disasters."

"God damn you, Noel St. John! Mind your own bloody business" She stormed past him into the wings, almost bumping into her co-star. A moment later the slamming of her dressing room door reverberated through the theatre.

Ian Hyde winced. "How can you bear it?" he inquired, coming to join the other man who was still standing center stage. "Her moods–that temper!"

Noel smiled a little. "I suppose I'm used to it. Once I was afraid she'd stay angry. Now I know better."

"Well, you might as well be the first to hear it, St. John. I've given my notice-- effective the end of the month."

"What a bloody shame, old chap. You're super in the role. Mind if I ask why?"

"Actually it was your little scene of a few minutes ago that made me think of it. It's 'La Windsor'! I can't stand working with her."

"You don't really know her," Noel remonstrated quietly. "But that's rather beside the point. Why walk out on a good role?"

"But this may be your big chance, St. John."

"Not the leading man type, I'm afraid. They'll bring in someone else."

Noel, as it turned out, was right on both counts. Victoria didn't stay angry with him although she did select the kitten and have her chauffeur deliver it. Olivia was thrilled, of course, although disappointed that her mother hadn't brought the gift herself. She named the cat "Victoria". Many would have considered that apt.

And the producer did indeed bring in another actor to play the male lead.

* * *

More important—-the end of the interval was in sight as two new men entered Victoria's life. One would soon pass from it again affecting her in no permanent way while the other would change her life forever. And yes, one of these was her new co-star.

Chapter 13

Sean Patrick and Victoria Windsor were, of course, not unknown to each other even though as of early 1968 they had as yet to be actually acquainted. Their paths had nearly crossed several years before–Sean departing the RSC only days before she became a member of the company–, but now he would be taking over the male lead in *Once More–Forever* and they were finally to meet. The evening before he was due to go into rehearsal Sean attended the performance with his friend, Dylan Mallory.

"Want to go backstage?" Dylan asked as they rose from their seats following the final curtain.

"No, I think I'll wait," the other man replied. "But God, what a magnificent woman! Tell me, as one chum to another, is she as bloody marvelous between the sheets as I've heard?"

"Well, as one chum to another, dear boy, you may find this as hard to believe as my wife does, but Victoria and I are far too good friends to be lovers."

"What a pity!" Sean adopted an expression of mock mourning possible only on his already lugubrious Irish countenance. "Then you can't tell me whether 'saints be praised!'-- that's all hers." He raised his hands to cup what were obviously two female breasts. To his amazement, however, Dylan didn't display his customary appreciation for the other man's bawdy sense of humor. "What's the matter, old chap? You look as if I were about to ravish your sister."

"I do feel protective of her, I suppose, but I also know perfectly well that won't stop you."

"Good. And now that's settled, me fine boyo, shall we hit a pub or two or three?"

Dylan laughed. It was impossible to remain annoyed with his old friend even though secretly he feared that Sean, like Victoria, would burn himself out before the age of forty.

The next morning Sean arrived for rehearsal prepared to turn on all his charm, only to learn he was to rehearse with Victoria's understudy. He was suffering from a monumental hangover as a result of last night's pub crawl with Dylan–lucky Welsh bastard was probably still sleeping it off–and to be treated so slightingly did nothing to improve his frame of mind. Who in the bloody hell did she think she was anyway?

* * *

Victoria did condescend to attend the final run-through on the Sunday before Sean was due to open in the role, but even then she was nearly three-quarters of an hour late. Noel was becoming uneasy as he did whenever she was noticeably overdue. Then, too, like so many others he'd been wondering what would happen when these two actually came face to face. Her new co-star was anticipating Victoria's arrival as well–not that he was about to let her know that. Positioning himself on stage where she couldn't help noticing him, he easily collected a group of adoring females and at the moment she walked in he was entertaining them with a long, elaborate ethnic story, his hands moving expressively as he talked.

As carefully as Noel was watching, he hadn't seen Victoria come in and when he first turned and observed her, she was staring at Sean, more totally absorbed in a man than he'd known her to be in some time. He sighed. He should have expected it, he supposed. After a moment he walked over to her. "Good afternoon, Victoria."

She glanced at him briefly. "Hello, luv." The words were accompanied by an absent-minded pat on the cheek, but her gaze returned at once to Sean and it was several seconds before she turned to look at him fully. "Am I sufficiently late, do you think?"

Noel shook his head. "Then this time it was deliberate?"

"Are you insinuating I am occasionally a bit tardy for my engagements?"

"Shame on me, Victoria!" He grinned. "However, if you mean is he thoroughly infuriated? Yes! But this wasn't really necessary–after making him work with your understudy!"

"I will not rehearse a role I can do in my sleep. God, long runs are a bloody bore!"

"Nevertheless–for an actor of his stature...."

"And what in hell does his height have to do with anything? Noel, shut up!" She winked at him before striding away across the stage.

Sean, of course, hadn't missed Victoria's arrival and now as she talked with Noel, he took full advantage of her brief distraction to study her in turn. Her blonde beauty was set off perfectly by the dark fur of her coat, but then he was sure she knew that. One of the woman standing near him followed the direction of his gaze. "Well, she's finally here! It would seem to me, Sean, you deserve more respect. I know I wouldn't have kept you waiting!"

A slow smile spread across his face. "Ah, but you see–Miss Windsor's worth waiting for." He bowed. "Ladies—excuse me."

They met–quite appropriately–at center stage.

Victoria extended her hand, glancing up at him coyly. "I haven't kept you waiting, have I?"

"Only about three and a half weeks," Sean replied very seriously, but he accepted her hand in his, raising it to his lips, and she'd seen the glint in his blue eyes.

"But if I'd been here right from the beginning, you wouldn't have appreciated me nearly as much."

He threw back his head and roared. "You egotistical English bitch!"

"You drunken Irish bastard!" Without skipping a beat Victoria picked up her cue, her pealing laugh blending perfectly with his bellow.

He slipped an arm around her waist and together they walked over to where the others were standing. "It seems Miss Windsor and I understand each other. We are ready to begin." And indeed they were!

When the run-through was finished, Noel headed for the prop table where he'd remembered seeing Victoria toss her coat just before her first entrance, but as he came across the stage, he saw Sean was there ahead of him. Slouched comfortably against the table–Victoria's coat slung up over one shoulder–the actor was skimming idly through his script, the ashes of his cigarette spilling onto the fur. Noel hesitated for a moment, unsure what to do. Then as he watched, Victoria came around the curtain and spotted Sean. Angrily she snatched the coat away from him. "You damned shanty trash! That happens to be Russian sable!"

The actor merely laughed, flicking his cigarette to the floor and stamping it out. "Never mind that, mavourneen." Smoothly he took the coat back draping it over her shoulders. "I'll keep you a lot warmer tonight that a lot of dead animals."

She turned to face him slipping her arms around his neck. "Is that a promise?"

His answer was to kiss her, his tongue thrusting into her mouth. He chuckled as he felt her respond. The rumors were evidently true. "But first," he said at last, "dinner and a few pubs." Arms around each other they walked toward the stage door. Neither of them had even noticed Noel. How many times has she just walked away, he thought sadly–not even giving me a thought.

It was nearly three o'clock the next morning when a taxi deposited two extremely intoxicated people on the sidewalk in front of Victoria's townhouse. With considerable difficulty Sean managed to extricate some money from his trouser pocket and pay the driver, vastly overtipping him. Climbing the front steps, however, he stumbled and fell pulling her down on top of him and for several minutes they sprawled there laughing. "God, you're bloody marvelous!" he gasped. "I've never known a woman who could match me drink for drink and still stand up." He took a second to look at their present position on the steps. "Well, perhaps I should rephrase that." At that they both went off into fresh gales of laughter.

"Do you suppose we could do this inside?" Victoria finally said. "I do have a reputation to maintain."

"I thought that's what we were doing."

Even in her present inebriated condition she understood him all too well. "God damn you, Sean Patrick!" Somehow she struggled to her feet and up onto the front stoop where she began the search through her purse for her door key.

He followed her and proceeded to make her task harder by nibbling at the back of her neck. "What're you so angry about, mavourneen?" he mumbled. "Mmmm, nothing smells nicer that perfume mixed with a bit of the strong stuff.... Faith and begorra, lass," he went on in a broad brogue, "and the way I'm feelin', ye'd better be findin' that key soon."

"Stop it, you damn fool!" Victoria was still hunting for her key, at the same time trying in vain to keep Sean away from her.

"Ring for a servant, why don't you? You do employ servants, I hope! Don't tell me I've fallen in with low company? At least a butler, two footmen, a cook and six maids, my girl, or I'll never darken your doorstep again!"

"Well, at the moment there's only a housekeeper who thinks she's my mother and I'd rather not disturb her."

"Hell, I don't mind!" Sean began to ring the bell with one hand, meanwhile pounding his other fist on the door. "Sainted mother–you did say she's your mother, didn't you–your wandering lass has come home and she's brought with her one fine broth of an Irish lad who happens to be horny as hell. Will ye be lettin' us in now?"

"Will you shut up?" she hissed. "And I can do without that ridiculous brogue!"

But just then Martha opened the door. "Finally!" He stumbled in over the threshold. "Where to?"

The housekeeper stared at them, saying nothing. "Go back to bed" Victoria ordered her. "I won't be wanting you tonight."

Sean, meanwhile, stood in the center of the hall swaying uncertainly. "No, right now what she wants is me, but what I need first, I'm afraid, is the WC."

"There's one up there." Victoria pointed to the top of the stairs. "And for God's sake stop acting like an ass!"

Sean staggered toward the stairs. "Hold on, little loo–I'm coming!" To her horror he was already unzipping his fly. Ignoring Martha's disapproving look, Victoria followed him. All at once she was completely sober. In her bedroom she automatically began to undress and after a moment Sean poked his head around the edge of the door. "Ah, there you are. All I could find were empty bedrooms. You planning on a large family?"

"God, you are disgusting! I should throw you out!"

"But you won't," he said, weaving his way toward her across the room. Victoria had just pulled her slip over her head and he bent to unhook her bra. "Did you know," he slurred, "that I hold the record in the UK, perhaps all of Europe, perhaps the entire world.... Aren't you going to ask me for what?"

It was just as well Sean couldn't see her face at that moment. Her expression was clearly not one of unbridled desire. She sighed. "For what?"

"Why for the man who can get the drunkest and still unfasten the lady's brassiere for her. The way I see it–it's the least I can do." At last he finished his task and sliding his hands around to the front, he hefted her breasts.

"What are you doing now? Weighing the meat?"

Her voice like her face was cold and set, but Sean failed to notice. He chuckled. "Merely finding out if my eyes could have deceived this poor benighted lad."

"And did they?"

"Mother of God and all the saints be praised–" Again the broad brogue–"they did not."

She laughed. Hadn't Julian taught her, after all, not to fight her true nature? And he'd taught her a great deal more as well. She laughed again. "But if you want more, you're going to have to catch me!" She backed away so suddenly that Sean tottered and half-fell. Victoria might have sobered up; he was still very drunk.

He made a grab for her, but she side-stepped him, the motion causing her full breasts to sway. "Ah, mavourneen," he pleaded. Again he reached out for her, but she slipped past him and around to the far side of the bed. He lurched after her, at the same time trying to pull off his jumper. In his drunken urgency, however, he'd entirely forgotten the buttons along one shoulder and blinded, he cracked both shins against the dressing table stool. He made one final lunge in her general direction. Managing at last to get the pullover off, he discovered she now lay naked on the bed. "Sure," he crooned, "and you're a magnificent sight!" He dropped his trousers, but when he attempted to step out of them, he tripped and went sprawling.

Peals of laughter drifted down to him from above, maddening him yet--bizarrely-- arousing him as never before. Groaning, he crawled up on the bed and with little further preliminary thrust himself into her. He heard her moan as she began to move under him. Dylan didn't know what he was missing. In the morning Victoria awoke to find Sean still asleep beside her. He looked much younger than when he was awake and bewitchingly Gaelic. It would be good to have a regular lover again.

* * *

It was perhaps a week or so after this that six off-duty members of the Scots Guards, Second Battalion, were gathered in one corner of a London pub. It would only have taken a few minutes of listening to their conversation to figure out that only two were actually Scots while the other four were English. The table in front of them was covered with empty mugs as well as six additional ones partially full at the moment, but rapidly being emptied as well. "So at any rate," one of the Englishmen was saying, "we weren't at the dance ten minutes when Gavin here had half the women in the room hanging on him." He indicated one of the other men with a jerk of his thumb.

The man who'd been thus singled out grinned broadly, ducking his auburn head in a show of modesty his companions knew only too well was feigned. "Och, Johnny, I canna help it. Poorr, starrved wee crreaturres see a fine brraw Highlanderr afterr all you puny, pasty-faced Englishmen. I feel sae sorrry forr them, ye see."

"Of courrse he does," the other Scot, a man named Ross, chuckled. "Just the way he pitied all the lasses back home in Glengowrrie. I must admit, laddie, I'll be glad when you finish yourr enlistment. Though I'll miss yourr coomp'ny, I willna miss the competition."

"Come off it, old chap," a second Englishman inquired, "do you mean to say you can get any woman you want?"

Gavin thought about that for a few seconds. "Aye, I believe I can." His brown eyes glowed with mischievous good humor. "Would any of ye carre to make a wee wagerr? Any lass ye'd carre to name. That waitrress overr therre perrhaps. She's a bonny one!"

"Och, no," Ross objected. "Too easy. We'll have to think of someone else."

"I know," still another of the Englishmen suggested all at once. "Victoria Windsor."

"Sounds like some sorrt of a monument!"

"The English actress," his friend explained. "There's a picture of her here in the newspaper. That's what made me think of her." He folded back the paper to a page in the theatre section and handed it to Gavin. The picture showed an elegantly gowned blonde woman leaving a restaurant on the arm of a slightly built man in a tuxedo.

"Who's that scrrawny gowk with herr?"

"Sean Patrick–an actor, too–Irish."

"Borrrrring!" He had a way of exaggerating his burr whenever he wished to place particular emphasis on something. "No contest, laddies, no contest. Still I'm not much for the actrress type. All painted oop like that–all those flounces and frrills."

"What's the matter? Afraid an elegant lady like that will throw you out?"

"Neverr happen!" Gavin waved his hand dismissively. "Lads–yourr bets!"

"Simple enough." It was Ross, his oldest friend in the group, who laid down the terms. "A date wi' Victorria Windsorr...ah....twenty pounds each and so m'laddie, failurre will cost you 100 pounds."

"I dinna intend to fail. I'd just like to ken a wee bit betterr the terrms of the wagerr. Is this just a date or....ah...." He rolled his eyes.

A brief consultation with the other four wagerers—"No, just a date. Besides, how could ye prrove the otherr?"

"Och, laddies!" Gavin shook his head in mock sadness. " 'Tis nae even a challenge!"

The next evening after the performance Victoria was as usual preparing to go out for a late night pub crawl with Sean. She was just putting the finishing touches to her make-up when her dressing room phone rang. "I'm sorry, Miss Windsor." It was the guard at the stage door. "He got by me before I realized what was happening."

"What are you talking about?"

"A man–sounds like a Scot."

"I don't give a damn about his nationality. How did he...." Just then someone knocked. "Mike, I swear I'll have your job for this!" She slammed down the receiver and striding across to the door, Victoria flung it open. The man was well over six feet and broad shouldered and he was leaning against the door jamb for all the world as though he had every right to be there. "Who in the hell are you?"

He roared with delighted laughter. "Aye, I like a gurrl wi' spirrit. But to answerr yourr question-- my name, lassie, is Gavin Hamilton." Before she, like the doorman, could be aware of what was happening, he was inside closing the door behind him and she got her first clear look at him.

He was indeed a tall man with a full head of auburn hair and dark eyes. He had a nose which in a less commanding face would have looked too big, but only gave his added power; a strong chin and a dimple in one cheek. She experienced the oddest sensation–as though she were falling forward–and his next immediate words were lost on her. "I'm afraid I didn't catch that," she finally managed to say. "I...I'm always tired after a performance and I......"

" 'Tis perrfectly all rright, lassie." Gavin grinned broadly. He was thoroughly accustomed to the effect he had on women and he was wondering already how he would spend the hundred pounds.

"And I suppose you think <u>all</u> women find you irresistible!"

"Och noo, lassie..."

"And why do you keep calling me lassie? What in hell do you think I am–a dog?"

"N...n...no....ah...lass. I...ah... I...ah...." For the first time he could remember a woman had Gavin stammering. " 'Tis...ah...only a way we have o' talkin' in Scotland. Did ye no ken I'm Scots?"

"I never would have guessed!"

"And I use it forr you because Victorria's too grrand forr a bonny wee gurrl like yourrself. It doesna suit ye at all."

"I don't recall giving you permission to call me anything! Listen to me!..." She suddenly interrupted herself...."carrying on a conversation with some half-mad Scot! What in hell are you doing here anyway?"

He was fairly sure by now it was a lost cause, but he had to carry it through. "Why–to offerr ye the pleasurre o' my coomp'ny tonight."

"What????!!! Get out before I call someone to throw you out!"

"Och, ye wouldna do that......"

Victoria grabbed up a container of cold cream from her dressing table. "If I ever did go out with someone who had the unbelievable nerve to come to my dressing room uninvited, it would not be with some egotistical son-of-a-bitch who sounds as though he's escaped from a tin of Walker's shortbread!"

He couldn't help but laugh at that. "Noo, lassie, arre ye surre ye dinna wish to rreconsiderr?"

"Reconsider??!!" She pulled her arm back to hurl the jar at him. "Get the bloody hell out of here!"

"I'm goin'. I'm goin'. Only ye dinna ken what ye'll be missin'!"

"O-O-U-U-TTTT!!!!!!!"

"Ye know, lass, ye'd look a considerrable bit betterr withoot all that paint on yourr face." Gavin quickly closed the door behind him, wincing as the cold cream jar thudded against the wood somewhere close to his ear, but as he walked away, he was still chuckling. The experience had been well worth the hundred pounds.

Inside the dressing room Victoria trembled with rage. How dare he? To treat her in such an offhand manner? There was another knock. "Get the bloody hell away from that door," she screamed.

"What's the matter? Did I miss a cue tonight?"

"Oh–come in, Sean."

He peeked his head around the door. "Are you sure it's safe?"

"Oh, shut up! Let's get the hell out of here. I'm very much in need of a drink—several, as a matter of fact."

"Just my plan, lass...just...."

"Don't call me that!"

"Don't call you what—lass? You never objected before."

"I know, but I've decided I don't like it!"

"All right. But what in hell is wrong with you?"

"I don't know...ah...nothing. Mind your own damned business!" Her mood remained terrible for the rest of the night–or at least until she began to get drunk. In fact even Sean couldn't remember seeing her quite that drunk. In the morning the events of the previous night were a confused blur in her mind; within a week she'd forgotten them.

* * *

Once More–Forever closed in late June and rehearsals for her next professional commitment, a revival of Cole Porter's *Kiss Me, Kate,* would not begin for a month. Victoria had been uncertain about attempting a musical, but Matt persuaded her it would be another excellent change of pace. She'd been further convinced by the fact that the play was based on Shakespeare's *Taming of the Shrew* and Will was, after all, an old friend. Finally Sean and Noel would be in the cast as well–both a lover and a chum in constant attendance: an eminently convenient arrangement. –And one unexpected bonus–the prospect of having to sing on stage eight times a week made her finally quit smoking. The habit, after all—like so much else about her—had been more for effect than anything.

At the closing night party Noel sensed a certain desperation in her. Undoubtedly she was dreading the hiatus. She and Sean had still been at the party when he left at two a.m. and so he waited until early afternoon before he drove over to her house, hoping she might accept a ride in the country. As he pulled his MG over to the curb, however, he recognized the Rolls-Royce parked there as belonging to Sean. Briefly he hesitated, but just at that moment the front door opened and the Irish actor stumbled out, disheveled and unshaven, still half-dressed in last night's evening clothes. He dove headfirst into the back seat of the limousine and it moved off into the traffic. Noel sighed, but after another moment he got out of his car and ran up the steps to ring the bell. Martha as usual answered the door.

"Mr. St. John!" She beamed in genuine pleasure. "I've a fresh batch of scones just out of the oven."

He grinned in return. "Do you know that I absolutely adore you!" As they walked through the dining room, they passed a maid heading upstairs with a pile of clean linen. "Victoria doesn't use this room very often, does she?"

"No, sir. What little entertaining Miss Windsor does are cocktail parties, that sort of thing. Very few sit-down dinners." In the kitchen she set a place for Noel with a cup and saucer and the plate of hot scones. "Tea, Mr. St, John?"

"Yes, thank you. What's that one's name, by the way?"

"Who? Oh, the maid. She's new...ah...Nora."

"Even you're not sure!"

"They don't stay very long."

"How long have you been with Victoria?" He gave the question more than its normal significance both by his tone of voice and a pointed elevation of both eyebrows.

"Three years or so, I suppose, sir. I haven't really kept track."

"Why do you stay when all the others don't?"

"Oh, Mr. St. John, you don't really need an answer to that question now, do you?"

They were interrupted at this point by the buzz of the intercom and the housekeeper went to answer it. "Yes, Miss Windsor."

"Martha–I'm bloody well starving up here. An enormous glass of orange juice, my very dear Martha, a fried egg, toast and our largest pot of tea–and was that Noel I just saw getting out of that ridiculous little car of his?"

"Yes, Miss Windsor."

"Smashing!–send him up with it when it's ready."

"I guess you could hear most of that, Mr. St. John," Martha said, hanging up the receiver. "It's....it's strange. She's usually, well, usually....."

"Hung over?" And now his smile was terribly sad. "That will come later, I'm afraid. Right now she is still very drunk."

It was about twenty minutes later when he carried the loaded tray up the stairs and knocked on the closed bedroom door. "Come in, you dear little luv!" He entered to find her still in bed, propped up among the pillows with the sheet held in front of her. It was immediately apparent she was naked. Grasping the sheet with only one hand now, she beckoned to him with the other. "Over here, luv."

He was horribly uncomfortable. "What....what...about the tray?"

"Oh, put that down anywhere for now. Really, Noel, haven't you ever wondered what it would be like? Haven't you ever wanted me?"

Yes, he'd wanted her, envied the men who possessed her yet now to have her offer herself to him in a way seemingly calculated to humiliate him. "Don't be absurd, Victoria! Put some clothes on and eat your breakfast!"

"Other men don't find me absurd. In fact, I'm considered rather good in bed. And to be perfectly honest, luv, I'm horny as hell! Sean was too drunk to be of much use last night and I....."

"How dare you! When you must know how I feel about you! To mortify me in this way, to....to....." He'd been standing there in the middle of the floor through all of this still holding the tray. Now he dropped it and fled.

The instant he was gone, remorse swept over her. "Noel!" she called after him and jumping out of bed, she snatched up a robe from a near-by chair and ran after him. "Noel, please wait! Please!" As Victoria came around the top of the stairs, he was almost at the bottom. He stopped when she spoke to him, but didn't turn around. "Noel, it was only a joke—a stupid joke. We...we didn't stop drinking all night and I...I....just felt like playing a joke on you." She came the rest of the way down the stairs to rest a hand on his shoulder. "I...I'm sorry. Please... don't be angry with me. What....what would I do without you, hm?"

At these words–words he'd never thought to hear from her–his anger dissipated at once. He reached up to cover her hand briefly with his. "We'll forget it...it ever happened then. I... I came because I thought you might enjoy a drive in the country." He tried to sound casual. All he wanted to do was put the whole appalling incident from his mind.

"I'll...I'll get dressed. Ask....ask Martha to fix us something. I'll....I'll be down in a little while."

"Shouldn't you get some sleep, Victoria?"

He felt her hand tense where it still lay on her shoulder. "No, I don't want to sleep. I couldn't anyway. Make me a Bloody Mary, will you; there's a luv." She turned and hurried back up the stairs.

Noel went on into the kitchen and delivered Victoria's message. "But what about the tray you just took upstairs?" the housekeeper asked shaking her head.

"I....I dropped it. Clumsy me! Perhaps..ah...the small table in front of the bay window in the living room. It's so much more cheerful in there." He left the kitchen again before Martha could ask any further questions.

It was nearly an hour before Victoria came back downstairs and into the living room. Noel looked up as she paused in the archway. She was wearing a coral colored, sleeveless dress with a full, pleated skirt and her hair was held back from her face with a matching scarf. But she had to have spent most of the time on her make-up. Every stroke was flawless. Oh God, he thought, she's....she's so beautiful and so...so sad. "Ah, there you are," he exclaimed, determinedly cheerful. "Your drink's in the fridge." He moved quickly behind the bar to get it for her.

Victoria noticed the small table in the alcove–set for two. "How perfect, luv. I've never really cared for that dining room."

"And Martha's busy with one of her souffles," Noel continued, bringing their drinks to the table. "So now, m'lady, have a seat and enjoy your Bloody Mary."

She obeyed, sipping her drink as she stared out the window. He searched his mind for a safe topic of conversation, but in a few minutes Martha came in to serve the brunch. When the housekeeper had finished and left them alone again, it was Victoria who spoke first. "Noel, what....what are you doing with your month's holiday?"

"No plans actually. I thought I'd stay in London for the most part–take in some theatre–I never get to do that when I'm working–visit with some friends in Brighton. Are you and Sean doing anything special?"

"Sean will be with his family in Connemara for some of the time. Then he's going salmon fishing in Scotland. He asked me to meet him in Scotland, but I said no. I hate Scotland!"

"I didn't know you'd ever been up there."

"Once–when I was a child."

It was obviously a topic she didn't care to pursue so Noel thought it best to change the subject. "What will you do then?"

"Maybe a month long binge. I've never tried that. Just shut myself up here and drink myself senseless!"

"I don't believe you, Victoria."

"It's stupid. I know it's stupid!"

He knew at once, then, that this must have something to do with her daughter. "I'm sure it isn't. Please-- tell me."

"I...I'd thought about taking Olivia somewhere for....for a fortnight," she said at last, "and it would help if you came, too."

"It's not stupid to love your little girl, Victoria."

"I....I don't love her. I feel responsible for her, that's all."

"Well, for whatever reason." He paused. "Only I can't or perhaps I should say I won't go with you. I will not be a crutch in your relationship with your daughter."

"Then I won't go either. I can't—not alone."

"If you really want to, you'll go with or without me." Noel stood up. "Now how about that drive?"

"No, you bastard. Get the hell out of here!"

He couldn't help smiling. "Yes, Victoria."

But Noel was a bastard! Hadn't he deserted her just when she needed him the most? Blaming her old friend wouldn't work this time, however, and the idea of a holiday with Olivia continued to nag at her. Well, perhaps Andrew would refuse. Certainly after last Christmas he'd have every reason. But he did, in fact, agree, albeit with a noticeable reluctance, and so now there was no way out for her. The travel agent offered a chalet in the Swiss Alps a few miles outside Lucerne, a house in southern Spain or a villa on the French Riviera. Victoria chose the latter. There would be the beach, of course, as well as a pool, and a staff was included. However, she also decided to take Martha along. Olivia had already met her housekeeper and that would help since Noel, the sod, had refused to come with her. The booking was for the last two weeks in July.

Andrew had never seen the little girl so excited as when he told her about her mother's invitation yet as the time drew nearer, he noticed she never mentioned the trip. Then one afternoon only a few days before she was supposed to leave he came home early to discover Olivia playing with a friend in their small back yard. "Daddy," she recited carefully, "this is my friend, Heather Lawrence." Sometimes he wished she weren't so polite. It seemed unnatural, somehow, in someone not quite seven. A short while later–settled nearby with his newspaper and a cold drink–he couldn't help overhearing their childish conversation. Heather, it seemed, would be spending a month in Scarborough. "That's nice," was Olivia's reply. "I'm not going any place special."

That evening at the little girl's bedtime Andrew climbed the stairs for his good night kiss, but coming into her room, he found she had as yet to get under the covers. Instead she sat cross-legged in the center of the bed, cutting out clothes for her paper dolls. He noted as well that her suitcases still remained off to one side, closed and upright.

"Hi, Daddy." Olivia smiled up at him--a little too brightly perhaps.

She really is so like her mother, he thought. "Hello, princess." He glanced again at the untouched valises. "You and Emily haven't started packing yet, I see."

"No, Daddy." She avoided looking at her father, appearing to concentrate on her work with the scissors. "There's plenty of time."

Andrew came to sit on the edge of the bed. "Olivia, why did you tell your little friend that you weren't going anywhere special? It seems to me that a holiday on the Riviera with your mother is very special." She shrugged, still refusing to look at him. "You're afraid she'll disappoint you again, aren't you?"

Tears filled the little girl's eyes and finally she nodded. "And if....if...I don't let myself count on it, then it won't hurt so much." She went on in a rush. "And I couldn't tell Heather, Daddy, 'cause then if I didn't go, all my friends at school would know."

"Would you feel better if I rang up your mother just to be sure?"

"Oh, would you, Daddy, please."

Of course he talked to Martha who hastened to reassure him. "Oh, we've already begun packing, sir, and I......"

"So then you'll be going along?"

"Well, you see I'm familiar with her needs and.... Mr. Roberts, may I speak frankly?"

"Please, I would appreciate it"

"Miss Windsor truly loves Olivia–she does. She's just...well...terribly unsure of herself as a mother."

The morning of departure, however, Andrew still couldn't help worrying. He was waiting with his daughter on the window seat in the living room. The little girl was dressed in a pale yellow sun dress and a white straw hat trimmed with daisies and yellow streamers and it seemed to him she'd never looked sweeter. He watched her peer up and down the street for the first sight of her mother's car, turning every so often to smile tremulously at him, and his heart ached for her. Had he made a mistake, he wondered, in giving his permission for this trip? Or perhaps his mistake had come years before in not simply letting Olivia forget her mother. Then suddenly they both saw the Silver Cloud Rolls Royce turn the corner, slowing to a stop in front of the house. "Oh, Daddy!" Olivia cried out jumping up and running to open the front door. "She's here! She's really here!"

"Yes, I see." Andrew followed to pick up the two suitcases which had been standing in the entry hall, surrendering them with some misgiving to Victoria's driver. He watched the man carry them down the steps and put them in the boot. Olivia was holding onto the doorknob and staring at the car. "Come along, princess," he encouraged her gently. "Your mother's waiting." When the little girl still didn't move, he squatted down next to her. "You don't have to go, you know, sweetheart, if you don't want to."

She looked at him steadily. "Of course I want to."

"Have a good time then, precious, and send us lots of postal cards."

"I will, Daddy, I promise." Olivia kissed him carefully on the cheek. "Bye, Daddy."

With tears in his eyes Andrew watched his daughter walk with a touching dignity across the front porch, down the steps and across the pavement. "Looking very smart today, young miss," the driver said with a slight bow as Olivia got into the car and he closed the door behind her.

"Good-bye, sweetheart," her father called after her. Apparently she hadn't heard him, but he remained on the front porch until the car disappeared from view.

Victoria had been unable to sleep at all the night before. Finally at four a.m. she took a couple of sleeping pills, washing them down with brandy. Each time she resorted to this ultimate remedy she remembered the time she'd nearly killed herself, but tonight she was desperate to sleep and if she didn't wake up in the morning, perhaps it was just as well. She had awakened, of course–nauseous and with a pounding headache. A glass of orange juice, liberally laced with vodka, had gotten her on her feet, dressed and into the car, but how in God's name was she going to manage an entire fortnight? Then to see Olivia frozen in the doorway, quite evidently terrified. Clearly Andrew had to talk her into coming.

"Such a pretty little girl," Martha remarked.

"What?" God, if only her headache would ease up. "Yes, she...ah...is, isn't she? Really–I wish you'd sit back here. That little seat must be frightfully uncomfortable."

"I'm just fine, ma'am, thank you." The housekeeper had deliberately taken the jump seat so as not to sit between mother and daughter. "Hello, dear," she went on as Olivia got into the car, patting the little girl on the hand. "Are you excited about our holiday? I know I am." She might as well have sat in the more comfortable rear seat, she thought, as the child carefully settled herself in the opposite corner from Victoria.

"Hello, Martha," Olivia responded politely. "Yes, I've been looking forward to it ever so much." But her eyes turned almost at once to her mother. Victoria was wearing a lavender silk suit and matching turban, her face once again all but hidden behind enormous dark glasses. "Hello, Mummy."

How she wished she could reach out to the little girl, sitting there so stiffly and as far away from her as possible. It would have been simple just to enfold her in her arms. They could chat about their holiday. One gloved hand did move tentatively in her daughter's direction. "Hello, Olivia." Cool and detached, Victoria's voice betrayed none of her inner turmoil, however, and her hands were once again clasped together in her lap.

The silence began then and continued, seemingly interminable, until Martha, much like Noel on the day of the visit to the zoo, was forced to say something for the sake of her own sanity. "Can you swim, Olivia?"

"Yes, ma'am. My Daddy taught me. Who taught you, Mummy?"

Victoria remembered her first swimming lesson vividly. A tall, muscular nun had begun the class by picking the girls up one at a time and throwing them into the deep end of the pool. "It....it was at school, I guess." She said nothing further and the silence resumed.

A short while later Martha made another attempt to initiate a conversation. "I know I'm looking forward to all that hot weather."

"I brought lots of sun suits and shorts and halters and stuff," the child replied eagerly. " 'Specially the ones you sent me, Mummy."

"I'm glad you liked them, Olivia, but it's Martha you should thank actually. She picked them out for you." Oh, Miss Windsor, Martha thought, that wasn't necessary. But Victoria herself had seen the hurt on her daughter's face. "I've....I've just been so busy," she added lamely, but the harm had been done and for the remainder of the ride to the airport no one said anything.

An obsequious airline official was waiting to escort them to the VIP lounge. Victoria walked briskly along beside him while Martha, taking Olivia by the hand, followed behind. The housekeeper was muttering furiously to herself. "What did you say?" The little girl was gazing longingly ahead at her mother, however.

"Nothing, sweetheart. Nothing at all."

In the lounge Victoria went directly to one of the large armchairs, swiveling it about so that she faced a picture window which looked out over the runways. She had not removed her glasses. "May I get you anything, ma'am?" the attendant inquired.

At once the public Victoria Windsor appeared. "Yes, luv." One gloved hand waved in the air. "A large Bloody Mary, please–on the rocks."

Unnoticed, Olivia had come forward to sit in the chair next to her mother. "Who....who's.... uh .... Bloody Mary, Mummy, and....and why is she on the rocks?"

In spite of everything a brief smile played across Victoria's face. "You wouldn't like it, dear. How about a lemon squash?" It would take so little, Martha thought, if they could only get past that certain point.

"Ma'am?" The attendant came over to where the housekeeper had remained, standing a little apart.

"Nothing for me, thank you. Olivia, why don't you and I take a walk around the terminal?"

"No, thank you," the child replied politely. "I'll wait here with Mummy for our drinks."

Victoria glanced at her daughter, but with the dark glasses Martha could only guess at her expression. "You can go if you like, luv," she said and her tone was softer than at any time since Olivia had gotten into the car.

"No, Mummy." And this time she shook her head emphatically from side to side. "I want to stay here with you."

"All right, then. I guess not, Martha."

The attendant returned with the drinks. Leaning back in her chair, Victoria took a long swallow of hers. The lovely warmth trickled down her throat, but she wished she'd ordered the vodka straight. How am I ever going to stand the next two weeks, she asked herself–especially sober? Mercifully someone came a few moments later to conduct them down to the airport limousine which was to drive them out to the plane. Olivia ran ahead up the stairs to the first class section, turning at the top to wait for her mother and Martha. "And I've never even flown before, Mummy," she exclaimed happily.

"Would you like to sit by the window, Olivia?" Victoria inquired as the stewardess led the way down the aisle and for those few seconds she sounded amazingly maternal. The little girl slid into her seat and looked up at her mother, obviously expecting her to sit beside her. Victoria hesitated briefly, but then she took the place next to her daughter. Martha sat across the aisle. All during the flight to Cannes the crew made a great fuss over Olivia, who was the only child in the first class section–even taking her up to the cockpit where the co-pilot held her on his lap for a while. Gratefully Victoria slipped into the background.

A car was waiting for them and in just a little over an hour from the time the plane set down they turned off the main highway into a narrow side road, traveling up and up the hill in a series of dizzying S curves. The pink stucco house stood high on a rocky promontory, surrounded on three sides by the turquoise blue of the Mediterranean. "What a magnificent view, Miss Windsor!" Martha exclaimed. "You certainly chose well!"

"It was entirely luck, believe me! I had no idea what the place looked like." Victoria walked rapidly across the lawn and up the steps.

A maid, dressed in the classic black and white uniform, starched apron and ruffled cap, was waiting to greet them, holding open the front door and smiling pleasantly. "Bienvenu, mademoiselle." The girl dropped a quick curtsey.

"This is my housekeeper, Mrs. Kendall." Victoria indicated Martha with a wave of one hand as she hurried past the girl and into the pale pink marble foyer. "She will explain how

I wish a household run. For now I would like to be shown my room so that I may rest before dinner."

"Oui, mademoiselle." But the genuine pleasure she'd felt at their arrival had drastically diminished. "Zis way, s'il vous plait." She led the way up a broad white staircase to the second floor. "We thought the front suite for you and your petite jeune fille. Zere is a small sitting room viz two bedrooms and a bath." In virtual terror Victoria contemplated an arrangement which would not even allow her the evenings away from her daughter. But what could she do with everything arranged so neatly. Instantly she despised the French girl. "Pour vous, madame," the maid continued to Martha, "zis room across ze hall. Claude will have your bags up toute de suite. You still have a good two hours of sun, but I must warn you zis 'ot Mediterranean sun is not good for zose lovely English complexions. Dinner will be at eight."

Olivia, meanwhile, was exploring–peeking into each of the bedrooms, even checking out the bath. She could hardly believe she would actually be sharing the suite with her mother and as she skipped happily from room to room, she was already imagining what it would be like–coming up here after tea each evening to read stories or color or cut out paper dolls or do any of the other jolly things all her friends did with their mothers. "Which bedroom do you want, Mummy?"

"I....I don't care." Victoria was staring out the window at the sea.

"I'll take this one then, please." Olivia was standing in the doorway of her chosen room. "The bed has a roof on it with yellow curtains. Mummy, what's that funny thing in the bathroom? It's shaped like a toilet, but it has taps–like the sink."

"That's a....ah.....never mind. You wouldn't understand."

The little girl merely shrugged–for the moment at least undismayed–and disappeared again into her room.

Since her unfortunate observation about the view, Martha hadn't dared say anything further and even now she remained silent, waiting uncertainly in the middle of the room and listening uneasily to this brief exchange. All at once Victoria strode over to her. The housekeeper blinked once or twice. "Please take her somewhere, anywhere! I have got to be alone for a while!"

"Oh, but Miss Windsor, you can't........"

"I have given you an order!" Her fingers dug into the other woman's fleshy upper arm. "Now get my daughter out of here before I scream the house down!"

"Olivia," Martha called, "shall we go down to the beach?"

The little girl came back out into the sitting room. "What about Mummy?"

"I...I have to rest, I'm afraid." Victoria edged toward her bedroom. "I'll....I'll see you at dinner." The door closed behind her.

"She's still tired, you know, dear," the housekeeper explained quickly. "She had a long run in the play."

Olivia was gazing at the door of her mother's room. "Do you really want to go down on the beach? I'll put on my bathing suit."

All during dinner Martha watched helplessly as the situation further deteriorated. To begin with Miss Windsor had obviously spent much of the time in her room drinking rather than sleeping. Then although she barely touched her food, she kept a decanter of wine next to her place and all during the meal she continually refilled her glass.

Olivia had returned from the beach, sunburned and full of enthusiasm. At first she chattered away about swimming in the ocean, hunting for shells, building a sand castle, but her mother said almost nothing in reply and gradually it seemed as though not only the child's enthusiasm, but even her sunburn faded. "Mummy," she asked at one point, "are you coming down to the beach with us tomorrow?"

"Oh, I don't think so, dear." Victoria poured some more wine and took a long swallow before continuing. "I burn very easily." Oh God, she thought, what in hell would I ever do on a beach? But the edges of the scene were blurring nicely now. What time was a seven year old supposed to go to bed anyway? All at once she became aware that Olivia had asked her another question. "Did you say something, luv?" she inquired and now Martha distinctly heard the slurring in her speech.

"I just asked if we could please drive into the village then and look in the shops. I'm going to buy presents for everybody!"

Again Victoria drank deeply of the wine before replying. "I...I don't like crowds, luv. But I'm sure Martha will take you."

"But Mummy......" Tears filled Olivia's eyes as all at once she felt terribly homesick.

"What?" She sounded annoyed, but inside she was hurting as badly as her daughter–worse perhaps because she was experiencing the little girl's pain as well.

"N...n....nothing. I'll....I'll go with Martha." Olivia stood up, her lower lip quivering, and moved slowly toward the doorway. "I'm....I'm really sleepy. I think I'll go to bed now."

"All right, luv." Victoria poured herself some more wine. "Do you need tucking in or anything?"

"No, Mummy. I'm a big girl now." She began to walk more quickly and by the time she reached the hallway she was running.

The two women sat in silence, not looking at each other, and listened to the little girl's footsteps recede rapidly away up the stairs. "Miss Windsor," the housekeeper finally started to say.....

"Shut up! Get the bloody hell out of here and leave me alone!"

The moment Martha opened the door into the suite, she could hear Olivia crying. She hesitated briefly, but she couldn't bear to listen to the little girl's heartbroken weeping and at last she crossed the floor to stand in the doorway of the bedroom. Still fully dressed, Olivia was sitting on the edge of her bed sobbing and wiping away the tears with the back of one hand. "Can I help you, honey?"

"I told Mummy. I'm a big girl now."

"Yes, dear, all right." So like her mother, Martha thought. "I'll see you in the morning."

It was several minutes before Olivia finally got up to change into her pajamas. Climbing into bed, she hardly noticed the lacy, yellow canopy which had so appealed to her earlier. Now it just wasn't her bed at home. But it had been a long day for a little girl. Exhausted–emotionally as well as physically–she was soon asleep.

She awoke the next morning to the sound of her mother's voice in the next room. Apparently she was on the telephone. "Oh, Nigel, darling! It's sounds super, but there's a slight problem."

Silence.....Nigel–whoever he was–must have been speaking and whatever he was saying must have been very funny because her mother laughed merrily. "I wish I could make her laugh like that," Olivia whispered fervently. "Then maybe she'd love me or at least like me a little." She got out of bed and started toward the door, but her mother was talking again.

"You see, my daughter's here with me...." Another pause followed by the same pealing laugh..."Yes, I know I don't seem like a mother and believe me, it's a bloody bore!"

Olivia backed away as though her mother had physically struck her. She stood there unmoving and only when she heard the phone being hung up did she finally go out into the other room. At the sound of the door opening Victoria turned and smiled–too brightly perhaps–but she did smile. She either failed or refused to notice that the whole scenario was bizarrely like the one played out by her and her father so many years before. "Oh, darling, there you are. You know--the more I think about it, the shopping would be fun. We'll go after lunch, all right, luv?"

"I don't want to go anywhere with you!" She fairly flung the words in her mother's face. "I just want to go home to my Daddy. <u>My Daddy</u> loves me!"

"Olivia....I....I....." But the words refused to come.

"See! You can't even pretend! Martha!" She ran from the room and down the stairs. "Martha, please take me home!"

The housekeeper met her in the downstairs hall. Gathering the sobbing little girl in her arms, she glanced questioningly up at Victoria, who stood at the top of the stairs looking down on them. "It appears the child wishes to leave. Take care of it, will you?" Pivoting on one heel, she strode back into the suite and slammed the door behind her.

Just a few hours later the arrangements had been made. Olivia was already outside in the car. Coming back into the house, Martha found her employer in the living room looking out the window–watching her daughter leave. "Miss Windsor?" Taken by surprise, Victoria whirled about to face her. She was crying. Martha had been about to ask coldly if there were any further instructions, but all that changed when she saw the tears. "Ask her to stay, Miss Windsor. She wants to, you know."

The actress tossed her head. "I don't have the slightest idea what you're talking about! Now don't you think you should be going along. We wouldn't want Olivia to miss her plane, would we?"

And thus her Riviera holiday with her daughter became instead an endless round of nightclubbing and gambling during which Victoria was never entirely sober and returning to London, her life went on–apparently unchanged. Yet at the same time she was experiencing a vague, but growing sense of unrest. And indeed the gentle, loving side of her nature–what was, in fact, her true nature–would not be much longer denied.

* * *

Kiss Me, Kate opened in early October, once again to rave reviews. The document was delivered a week or so after that. Victoria was out shopping and Martha had left the official appearing envelope on the table in the front hall along with the rest of the daily post. She was in the kitchen when her employer arrived home. She heard the front door close. There was a brief silence followed by the rapid staccato of Victoria's high heels on the polished hardwood floor of the dining room. The swinging door into the kitchen was flung open with a vengeance. "He's got no right, you know! No bloody right at all!"

"Excuse me, ma'am?"

"Andrew!? She waved a long, legal size sheet of paper in the air. "He's denied me all future visiting privileges. He can't do that! She's...she's my daughter, too, isn't she?"

Very well, Miss Windsor, Martha thought to herself–if you want to think for now that it's merely a case of proprietorship. Aloud she simply replied, "Of course he can't, Miss Windsor."

"Ring his office for me, will you? I'll be in the living room." Victoria strode back through the dining room and across the entry hall. How dare he, she thought. Well, she'd show him! No matter whether she cared anything about Olivia or not, she did have certain legal rights! The living room phone buzzed and all her angry bravado vanished in an instant. "Oh please, Andrew," she whispered. "Oh, please." The phone buzzed a second time before she walked over and picked up the receiver.

"Yes, Victoria?"

She had never heard him sound so cold. "I....I wanted to....to speak to you about... about seeing.....seeing Olivia."

Listening to her faltering words, Andrew steeled himself against the emotion she was still capable of arousing in him. "I understood the injunction had been served, Victoria."

"Yes, but....."

"Wasn't it clear to you?"

"Yes, but....."

Those pathetic, non-protesting "yes, but's" were tearing him apart, but he forced himself to go on. "I've given you ample opportunity to be at least something of a mother to our daughter–more than you deserve considering that you deserted her in the first place. And all you've done is hurt her–over and over again. Well, I'm sorry. It's done with. I intend to make sure you never see that child again!" When the silence continued for several seconds, Andrew thought she'd hung up on him. It wouldn't be the first time. "Victoria?"

"Yes, I'm still here."

He could hear the tears in her voice and despite all his resolution he weakened. "You don't really care anything about her and I just think...."

"That's....that's not true."

Andrew wasn't sure she'd spoken. "Did you say something, Victoria?"

"Yes! Go to hell!" And this time she did indeed slam down the receiver.

Sean arrived an hour or so later expecting to take her to their private actors' club for dinner, but finding her in the foulest mood he could ever remember, he went alone to a pub instead. During the performance he deliberately muffed his lines and confused the blocking and he never missed an opportunity to breathe in her face. Following the final curtain he allowed what he thought would be sufficient time for her to cool down and then he poked his head into Victoria's dressing room, not even bothering to knock. He grinned engagingly. "Ready to go, me fine beauty?"

She was sitting at the dressing table applying her own make-up. As was often the case, they were expected at a party. "Sod off! And you can jolly well sleep in your own bed tonight!"

"Ah, mavourneen," he murmured, coming up behind her to caress her arms and shoulders, "it doesn't matter in the least to me where we sleep."

Angrily she pulled away from him. "All that liquor has addled your already besotted brain! I didn't say anything about <u>us</u>!"

"Come off it, Victoria! You asked for it! <u>Now</u>–are you coming or not?"

"I don't know!"

"Very well then." He nodded curtly. "I <u>will</u> <u>be</u> at the party–if you deign to join us!" He strode from the room slamming the door behind him.

Victoria stared at herself for a long moment in the mirror. A wave of terrible desolation swept over her and she buried her face in her hands. "What's the matter with me?" she asked herself. "What's the matter with me?" Of course–<u>Sean</u> was to blame, upsetting her by going on stage drunk–how unprofessional. Well, she'd be damned if he was going to keep her away from the party!

She finished her make-up and dressing quickly, left the theatre. Seeing her come out, her chauffeur jumped from the car to open the rear door for her. "Will you be going directly home then, Miss Windsor?" He'd observed Sean Patrick leaving alone earlier.

"Of course not!" She gave him the address and arriving at her destination twenty minutes or so later, she ran lightly up the stairs to push the doorbell. "I'll ring if I need you," she called back over her shoulder to the driver. Once again she was the little girl who'd marched up the steps of the Heathfield dormitory–daring the world to call her coward. A liveried footman answered the door, took her coat and vanished. For a moment or so she stood in the foyer listening to the sounds of the gathering: an indistinguishable babble of voices, punctuated by frequent bursts of laughter and underlying it all, the inevitable background music. Dear God, she thought miserably, I'd rather be anywhere but here. But no one would have guessed that as seconds later she seized both handles of the French doors leading into the living room, pulling them open in a flourish of pale green chiffon. "Good evening, everyone!"

The woman who approached was a substantial personage, her chins cascading downward until the bottom one rested directly on her mountainous bosom, giving the impression of one unbroken mass of flesh. "Miss Windsor!" the good lady positively burbled, "we thought you weren't coming and we would have been so disappointed!"

Victoria supposed this imposing matron to be her hostess although she had absolutely no idea who the woman was. "Darling!" she gushed theatrically, "you must forgive me! I'm frightfully late, I know, but I simply had to rest after the performance. Acting is so exhausting..." At this point she happened to catch a glimpse of Sean who was standing off to one side leaning against the mantlepiece over the ornate marble fireplace. Their eyes met and he grinned, raising his glass in a mocking salute. She didn't miss a beat. "....especially when one's co-star is jolly well blotto!"

Sean walked slowly toward her, his smile growing broader. "Ah, but when one's co-star also happens to be one's mistress of the moment as well as a consummate pain in the ass, one must soothe one's poor bedeviled soul with a drop of whiskey."

"A drop, ha! It's a wonder your breath didn't rot the curtains!"

They began to circle each other now like two animals closing in for the kill. "Well, we all know what you are–the chairwoman of the Royal Temperance Society!"

"You Goddamned bastard!"

They were by now the center of attention and though Sean's anger was indeed genuine, he nevertheless was an actor. He was enjoying every minute of it! "Now, now, my dear. I've told you and told you–my mother and father's morals are not the issue."

"You never had parents! You crawled up out of the slime of an Irish bog!"

And still they circled. It seemed as if at any moment one of them must lash out physically at the other. "Since we're discussing the 'origin of the species'–so to speak–we all know where you came from—a kennel!"

"You should know! Your mother did!" At this last jab of Victoria's there was open laughter, but only a few of those listening and watching noticed its effect on her. She appeared startled as though until that moment she'd been unaware of their presence. Some even swore later she'd had tears in her eyes, but most instantly discounted the latter as ridiculous. Victoria Windsor didn't know how to cry. "I hate you, Sean Patrick!" she whispered her breath coming faster. "God, how I hate you!"

Sean watched the tops of her full breasts rising and falling with each respiration. He remembered vividly the sensation of touching them and absurdly in the midst of his rage he experienced a rush of desire which in turn only made him all the angrier. "Oh, you don't hate me, Victoria. You may think you do, but tonight or perhaps early tomorrow morning you'll feel differently."

She could think of nothing to say in retort and helplessly she felt the tears brim over, trickling down her cheeks. Frustrated and humiliated, she went at his face with her nails. "Bastard!"

"Bitch!" No tears for Sean. He merely smiled that same, damned mocking smile, even as he seized her by the wrists.

"Bastard!" Victoria shrieked again, struggling to reach his face.

"Bitch!"

"Bastard!"

Back and forth they went until finally she wrenched herself free and ran from the room. For a moment Sean stood there staring after her. It was unlike her to admit defeat - -to flee, as it were, from the field of combat. Then he had an idea. He grinned.

The final scene of this odd little drama would be enacted a few hours later. Coming home by taxi, Victoria had begun at once to drink, trying in vain to blot out the whole hideous day. Finally she lay down on the bed and she was just beginning to slip toward blissful oblivion when something roused her. She wasn't sure afterwards whether it had been the light or the sound of his voice, but pulling herself back from the edge of slumber, she managed to get up off the bed and make her way over to the window. It was Sean-- bugger his wretched Irish soul–marching up and down in front of the house, waving an electric torch and shouting at the top of his voice. "Now hear this! Now hear this! I couldn't find a red light so this will have to do!"

"Damn you, Sean Patrick!" She seized a figurine and threw it at the window, shattering the glass.

He roared with delight. This was more like it! "Yes, gentlemen, this is the place! London's most exclusive whorehouse!"

"Shut up!" Victoria screamed. "Shut up!" She grabbed her bedside lamp, flinging it blindly at the gaping hole in the window. She had to make him stop saying those things. The lamp fell harmlessly into the bushes, however, and Sean doubled over with laughter. "Yes, gentlemen–Victoria Windsor! She's here, she's available and she's free!"

"Go away! Go away and leave me alone! Please....oh, please..." Mindlessly now, like a trapped, tortured animal, she reeled away from the window, hands over her ears in a futile attempt to block out Sean's hateful words. Halfway back to her bed, she tripped over the rug, sprawling headlong. "Oh, God," she mumbled. "Oh, God! Oh, God!" It just seemed too much of an effort to get up again and she curled up there on the floor, sobbing her sad, little prayer over and over again until at some point she fell asleep.

"What in hell is wrong with that woman tonight?" Sean muttered to himself tossing the torch into a dustbin. He wondered where he could find a drink at this hour of the night..

For some time after that Victoria and Sean's relationship would be confined to the stage, the sparring of Kate and Petruchio–Fred Graham and Lilli Vanessi–given added zest by their personal animosity. Eventually their affair would resume, but it would never be the same.

"Balmoral Remembered"

Victoria was still in bed that Sunday morning in late March–as usual fighting a monstrous hangover. Idly she flipped through the pages of the *London Times* as she sipped a cup of tea and nibbled on a slice of cold toast. It was only by the merest chance she noticed the article.

> "Her Majesty to Dedicate Chapel at Windsor in Late Father's Memory," the headline stated and under it was a picture of the new little chapel.
>
> King George VI was a sovereign whose reign needs special commemoration–the article went on to state.– Called unexpectedly to kingship, he led his people through 15 years of war and peace. Before and throughout those years, his character and goodness endeared him not only to those who knew him but to a vast company in every land in the Commonwealth. His trust in God was simple and deep, his faith in Christ firm, his devotion to the Church of England sincere. He appreciated all in the Commonwealth who aspired to the true religion. St. George's Chapel was for him a place of regular worship and within its walls his faith was nourished and sustained. He reestablished the annual service of the Order of the Garter and the religious solemnity of the Installation of new Knights. He is remembered as a good, just and God-fearing King. It is for these reasons that this Chapel has been added to St. George's as both his memorial and his resting place. The remains of the late King have been recently moved to this, his final resting place, which will be dedicated on 31st March in the presence of his daughter, Queen Elizabeth II and his widow, the Queen Mother Elizabeth.

Long before Victoria reached the bottom of the column, however, the print was swimming in a sheen of unshed tears and she gave up trying to read any further, lying back instead against her pillows and closing her eyes.

Memories of the late King–of her beloved Uncle Bertie–flooded over her: the first time she'd seen him smiling up at her from the pathway below her private rock or a little while later as they sat together on the wharf by the lake, the King accepting with his easy equanimity her tears all over his suit jacket. He'd given her his handkerchief. It seemed she could even hear his voice—"Why is it that a little girl never has a hanky when she needs one?" Dear God–how many times had those words come back to haunt her? But most especially she remembered the precious days at Balmoral: his hand holding hers as they walked together, his arms enfolding her and once again the sound of his voice as he read aloud to her at bedtime. Oh–those bedtimes, two glorious weeks of bedtimes–- Uncle Bertie's face in the soft glow of her bedside lamp and..... The book! He'd given her the book to finish and although for a long time Victoria hadn't been able to look at it, she felt an overwhelming need now to see it again, to touch it– to make this dear man's memory come alive, warm and real once more.

Sitting up in bed, she swung her feet over the edge. Dizziness and nausea all but overcame her and with them a more recent memory: making love with Sean even though secretly she despised him. She sat there for a moment, the tears streaming down her face now and leaving little damp spots on her satin nightgown. "What would Uncle Bertie think of me?" she whispered. "Dear God, that good, kind man–what would he think of me?" By holding on to the foot of the bed Victoria was finally able to stand up and move the short distance to her dressing table. She sank to the floor, pulling open the bottom, left-hand drawer, and there under a pile of scarves was *The Wind in the Willows*. Hands trembling, she picked up the book and as she did so, a carefully folded white linen handkerchief fell from between the pages into her lap. There was no need to look, but she turned it over. Lovingly she traced the outline of the monogram in one corner— G VI R. "Uncle Bertie," she whispered. "Oh, Uncle Bertie. I.... I'm so very sorry." She didn't even hear the knock on the door. Only when her housekeeper spoke did she come back to reality. "Y....yes, Martha, what is it?"

Her employer's voice had sounded strange. "Are you all right, Miss Windsor?"

"Yes....thank you." The same tone, yet with an underlying gentleness and....thank you. How few times in the years she'd been with Victoria Windsor had she heard her say thank you?

"Can I get you anything, ma'am?"

"No....thank you." Amazingly <u>this</u> time she'd even laughed a little. "You know, I..I.." Suddenly for some reason she wanted to tell Martha she was aware of her unfailing kindness and that she appreciated it. But the words wouldn't come.

"Yes, Miss Windsor?"

"Nothing. Please....please, I'd like to be alone...if you don't mind."

She should go to Windsor–Victoria knew that–to St. George's. She owed him that much for the kindness he'd once shown a lonely little girl–not for the dedication ceremony with its crowds–but a more private pilgrimage later alone. Several times she went so far as to plan the excursion–an afternoon when she could slip away unnoticed by Noel or even Martha. But the thought of seeing his grave–of facing all over again the finality of his death–even worse of facing what she had since become–was too painful and always at the last minute she found some excuse not to go.

Then late that spring the Lincoln Center for the Performing Arts in New York City approached Sir Terence with an invitation for an RSC company to spend a season in residence. Victoria's sin of leaving the company earlier had long since been forgiven and she--as well as Noel--was asked to go. At first she'd been uncertain whether to accept. An American debut would be like starting all over, but she also felt a need to get away from London for a while and with Noel's and Terry's encouragement she agreed.

A six play repertory was selected in which Victoria and Noel were each to perform four roles. In two of the plays they would appear together: Algernon and Gwendolyn in Oscar Wilde's *The Importance of Being Earnest*, Banquo and Lady Macbeth. In addition she would be doing the title roles in both *Candida* and *Victoria Regina* while he was to portray Dick Dudgeon in *The Devil's Disciple* and Dromio, the identical twin servant brothers in *Comedy of Errors.*

They were to fly to New York on the first of June and finally with their departure only days away, Victoria knew she couldn't leave without first going to St. George's– to say good-bye. She picked an afternoon when Martha was out doing errands and with her identity carefully hidden by a plain beige mackintosh, scarf and dark glasses, she took a taxi to Waterloo Station where she boarded the train for Windsor. She need not have worried she'd be recognized. On this weekday morning before the start of the tourist season the cars traveling out from London were all but empty.

Arriving at Windsor by train, you can't avoid looking at the castle. It is simply there–from the moment you leave the depot–dominating the street below, brooding over it. For Victoria this was especially true, drawn there as she seemingly was by some force beyond her control, and as she walked slowly up the hill, she glanced continually at the wall and the old gray stone buildings towering above her to the left. In her present mood the tea rooms, the pubs, the souvenir shops which were to her right seemed wrong somehow as though placed there solely to show the late King a lack of the proper respect.

At the top of the hill the street curved around to the left and looking across at the castle again, Victoria saw a massive archway. "Henry VIII Gateway"– a discreet, black-lettered white sign informed her–"Public Entrance to Windsor Castle". "Well, this is it, I guess," she whispered. "I...I'm here. I might as well go in." She crossed the street, but as she passed under the arch, she felt a lump of apprehension settle in the pit of her stomach. St. George's Chapel was directly ahead of her now. She paid her half-crown admission fee at the little kiosk along the side of the building and directly beside it was a small doorway through which the public might enter. Immediately inside there was another sign with an arrow indicating the location of the "George VI Memorial Chapel". Her heart began to pound and her palms were damp with perspiration.

There weren't many in the chapel for which Victoria was grateful. One or two people glanced at her curiously as she moved across the chapel nave and turned right into the aisle beside the choir stalls. Did they recognize her or was it simply that there was an air about her? For whatever reason they left her alone and anyway nothing mattered except what now lay only a few steps ahead of her.

As she approached the memorial chapel, it appeared at first to be nothing more than another stone archway set in the outer wall of the aisle. In fact, Victoria nearly passed it by. Perhaps she half-hoped she wouldn't be able to find it. But then out of the corner of her eye she caught a glimpse of yet another sign– "George VI Memorial Chapel". She stopped, but even then for a few seconds she couldn't bring herself to look. How foolish, really, when she'd come this far–and at last she turned. How striking the new white marble was set against the background of the gray stone, darkened still further by the stain of centuries. Yet her gaze continued to avoid the tomb itself. She read the biographical information on a plaque to the right hand side of the entrance and the plaque to the left bearing the message which had been part of the King's Christmas broadcast in 1939, the first Christmas of World War II:

And I said to the man who stood at the Gate of the Year,
"Give me a light that I may tread safely into the unknown."
And he replied, "Go out into the darkness and put your hand into the Hand of God,
That shall be to you better than a light and safer than a known way."

The words seemed so typical of the King's gentle strength that it was as though she could hear his voice speaking them. Tears filled her eyes and Victoria knew she could no longer avoid the focal point of the chapel–the whole reason, after all, for her pilgrimage. Her glance traveled to the back of the small room to the altar and the candlesticks and finally, still with reluctance, to the white marble floor and once her eyes had come to rest on the tomb, she could not pull them away.

It was black marble, the gold lettering stating simply–George VI. The starkness of the black against the white spoke a soundless, but eloquent message of grief and standing there, Victoria did indeed grieve as she had not allowed herself to do on the morning the King died. Totally unmindful now of where she was or of the people walking by, she sank to her knees on the cold stone floor.

The words came pouring out seemingly of their own accord. "Oh, Uncle Bertie," she whispered, "why did you have to die? If you'd only lived, I might not be...the way I am. I suppose it sounds selfish to think of myself at a moment like this, but since you've been gone, no one else has cared what happened to me."

"That's....that's not true, Uncle Bertie. I...I can't lie to you. To others, perhaps, but not to you." She reached up to remove her dark glasses, revealing a face wet with tears, and slipped the scarf down around her throat. She who had concealed her true self for so long–concealed it behind dark glasses and heavy make-up; concealed it behind profanity and temperament–could not hide her face from him now anymore than she could speak anything, kneeling here before his memory, but the complete truth. "Other people have tried to be kind to me," she went on at last, "but I won't let them. It's as though I have to drive them away–even my own daughter. Oh, Uncle Bertie, she's so sweet and in spite of everything I've done she still loves me. And yet I can't seem to bring myself to love her back–or..or anyone else. I...I feel that love inside–I really do, but when it comes to showing it, I get frightened. But oh, dear God, I'm so lonely. Sometimes at night I wake up and I know I've been calling for someone. Maybe it's you. I don't know. I....."

Her voice trailed off, but she couldn't bring herself to leave. It was strange. She hadn't wanted to come and yet now she found being here profoundly comforting. It was as though the caring and kindness she'd received from this man when he was alive had somehow touched her again–even from beyond the grave. "Dear, dear Uncle Bertie," Victoria whispered tenderly. "I've never really lost you, have I?"

Chapter 14

For the first few hours of the flight Jon and Noel had maintained an uncomfortable silence, the former making a great show of shuffling papers, the latter pretending to study his lines. Even lunch was consumed without a word. It was a relief when the film began and it was only after that Jon finally spoke. "Noel....ah....sorry about earlier, old chap. But then you know I've just never had...ah...quite your patience with Victoria."

The other man grinned in return. "And I'm sure you know that where she's concerned, I'm not always entirely sensible."

They enjoyed a good laugh together over that and then for a while they chatted easily about other matters before at last resuming their individual tasks. Indeed the pilot had come on the intercom to announce their descent for Kennedy Airport before either spoke again. They'd been friends for years, however, and it felt good to have the tension gone. "Was anything in particular troubling her today?" Jon inquired as he worked to return the various forms and lists to his briefcase. "I heard about the party."

"It wasn't the party so much as it was...." Noel stopped.

"Was what? Oh, you mean the row with Sean. But I saw him getting into a taxi in front of the terminal just as I arrived. I assumed he'd come to see her off."

"Oh, yes." Noel shrugged. "But last night he was his usual boorish self. I should speak to her, I suppose," he went on after a slight pause as standing up, he slid past Jon into the aisle. The curtains had remained closed all during the flight, the cubicle silent, and he had no idea what he'd find. He rapped lightly on the wall. "Victoria?" There was no reply. "Victoria!" He repeated her name more loudly and rather more urgently. "Victoria, we'll be landing in New York in a bit."

At the first sound of Noel's voice Victoria had started and it was a moment before his words fully penetrated. She wasn't <u>at</u> Windsor. That had been two days ago. But he had said.. "landing". Could she possibly have spent the entire flight reliving all the lonely years which had brought her finally to Uncle Bertie's tomb? Why in God's name had she ever started on that long, tormenting journey anyway and what could she ever have hoped to accomplish?

Jon had forgotten entirely his earlier annoyance and equally concerned now, he also came out into the aisle "Victoria! Answer us at once!"

Not stopping to consult each other, both men reached up at almost the same instant to yank open the curtain separating Victoria's compartment from the rest of the first class section. The rod had only been a temporary measure, of course, attached by velcro fastenings to the luggage bin and before they knew what was happening, the curtains had come down engulfing them both. The next thing they heard was the marvelous sound of Victoria laughing. "Oh, dear," she gasped, "you have no idea how utterly ridiculous you both look!"

"So that's all we have to do to amuse her?" Jon observed under his breath when they'd finally managed to extricate themselves from the folds and were standing together in the middle of the aisle, breathless and feeling suitably foolish. "Make complete asses of ourselves?"

"Apparently so." But to hear Victoria laugh like that–with such total and natural abandon–Noel was more than willing to make an ass of himself at any time. Happily he noticed as well that the bottle of wine brought to her before take-off had hardly been touched. But what could possibly have kept her so occupied all the way from London, he wondered, that she'd even failed to hear the pilot's announcement?

One of the attendants came forward to relieve them of the curtains. "Gentleman, if you'll be seated. We will be landing now in less than fifteen minutes."

"Noel," Victoria said suddenly, patting the seat beside her, "why don't you sit here?"

"It would seem the lap dog's getting his daily ration of scraps," someone could be heard to remark.

Victoria saw clearly the hurt in her old friend's eyes and answering tears sprang to her own as she laid her hand over his. "People can be so cruel, can't they, luv? I.....I should know. No one has been quite as cruel to you quite as often as I have. I hope you can forgive me." It was only another of those impulses to be kind which she had sometimes known in the past, but this time she'd made no attempt to fight it. But....but it was more than just kindness, wasn't it, she thought, and the same odd excitement she'd experienced earlier began to stir inside her once again. I...I was feeling affection for someone–not only feeling it, but expressing it and <u>not</u> to someone who is dead, but to someone warm and alive who can return that caring. And....and if I can do it with Noel, I...I could....could... Inevitably Olivia came to mind, whose telephone call this morning she hadn't even bothered to return.

Noel couldn't resist the moment and raising his hand with hers still resting on it, he covered it with his other one. "What happened during the flight, Victoria? You seem.... ah.....different somehow."

Irritably she pulled her hand free. "You can never let well enough alone, can you?" But a moment later she continued, even resting her hand on his arm. "Please...I'm...I'm sorry." Incredibly he heard her voice grow softer and her eyes were luminous with unshed tears. "I... I don't know what's wrong with me today. I suppose I'm more nervous than I realized about New York." But just as reaching out to Noel had been more than an act of simple kindness, she knew that what she was experiencing now went far beyond a mere case of professional butterflies. Had her journey into the past indeed affected her in some way or was it, in fact, quite incidental to her feelings of the moment? Once again she thought about Windsor and she wondered if it <u>had</u> begun there–or much earlier.

Noel, as well, didn't buy her explanation. "It's more than that, Victoria. I really think that...." At that moment, however, the public address system interrupted him and shortly afterwards the plane touched down on the runway.

Jonathan Sinclair leaned forward from his seat across the aisle. "Wait, please, Victoria. There'll be a car here, too." She was fumbling through her purse and appeared not to have heard him. Actually the frantic physical activity was an attempt to mask her inner turmoil. Even sitting several inches away from her, Noel could feel her trembling. "Victoria?" Jon said again.

"What? Oh, yes, I....I heard you. I....I just wanted to check my make-up. I....I presume there'll be reporters here, too."

"I can easily arrange for there not to be."

"Oh, <u>would</u> you? You're an absolute darling!"

Her manner was, as usual, distinctly theatrical, but Jon, too, sensed a difference. The two men exchanged glances. But the curtain separating first class from tourist parted just then and a young girl of not more than eighteen stepped through. She had large, brown eyes and straight dark hair hanging free nearly to her waist. "Mr. Sinclair, I was just coming to ask if I might be of some help." Victoria was absorbed in the task of touching up her make-up, studying her face after each stroke, and the newcomer stared, positive no one that beautiful could live right on earth breathing ordinary air like any mere mortal!

"Yes, I believe you can," Jon replied. "Miss Windsor would undoubtedly prefer to drive directly into the city so perhaps you could take care of immigration for her..... Victoria?"

She looked up from her mirror. "Victoria...Noel, this is Millicent Smythe. She's going to be serving an apprenticeship with the company."

Millicent held her breath as the actress turned to look at her. "Oh, Miss Windsor, I can't believe I'm meeting you," she breathed "I've admired your work for simply years!"

Victoria glanced at Noel, raising that one expressive eyebrow as if to remark, "That long, hm?" But aloud she said, "How kind of you to say so. But I'm bloody awful at names or possibly Mr. Sinclair mumbles. Could you tell me yours again?"

"Millicent Smythe, Miss Windsor." Once more Jon and Noel exchanged glances. She'd probably only half-listened to the girl's name, but until now that had never concerned her. Also her little jest had obviously been intended to put Millicent more at ease and neither of them had ever seen her bother to do that before either.

"Victoria," Jon prompted, "Millicent will need your passport and luggage checks."

She looked bewildered. "I....I don't know where....."

"They're in your purse, Victoria," Noel at once reassured her. "I saw you put them in that little zippered pocket on the side."

"Oh...oh, yes, of... of course." Her hands were shaking slightly, but she managed to unzip the compartment, take out the passport and luggage checks and hand them to Millicent. "Thanks, luv."

"You're...you're more than welcome, Miss Windsor." Accepting the documents almost with an air of reverence, the young apprentice followed Jon back to the tourist section of the plane where the rest of the company had been seated..

"Which luv?" Noel inquired after a moment.

Victoria had returned to her make-up. "Hm?" She glanced up from her mirror again.

"You said, 'Thanks, luv,' and I was wondering whether you meant Millicent or me?"

"Well, Millicent is a luv." She tapped him on the tip of his nose and her eyes were sparkling. "You, on the other hand, are a bloody nuisance!" He grinned. "But I....I do overuse that word, don't I, Noel?" She grew suddenly thoughtful. "So that it loses all meaning. Love should be...should be...." She noticed all at once that he was looking at her oddly. "What in hell am I talking about anyway?" She laughed harshly, tossing her head as she reached across to pick up her scarf from the seat facing them. "I...I don't need this, do you think?" She stuffed it into her purse, not waiting for him to answer. She did, however, put on her hat, finally snatching up her gloves and dark glasses. "Where will you be staying in New York?"

"Jon and I are sharing a flat actually." Noel could still feel her trembling and she glanced continually out the window, watching the tourist class passengers walk toward the terminal. "Are you sure you're all right?"

"Of course I am. What a bloody stupid thing to ask me!"

" It's just that I'm....."

"Shut up, please! Just shut up!" He gave up then, remaining silent as the rear section of the plane gradually emptied.

"Well now, people, if you'd all listen for a moment." Jon Sinclair had returned to stand in the aisle. "Victoria, I thought Noel and I would keep you company. There'll be a mini-bus for the rest of you and a lorry for your luggage. You'll be going directly to Lincoln Center. For those of you who requested to live with an American family–your hosts will be meeting you there and the two hotels where I've leased bedsitters are within a block or two of the theatre."

About a half-hour later the limousine carrying Victoria, Noel and Jon had finally maneuvered its way through the tangled traffic of Kennedy Airport and out onto the Long Island Expressway heading into New York City. "Feels odd, doesn't it, driving on the right?"

Jon remarked at one point– not that he expected an answer. Neither of his companions had spoken since they got off the plane. "The hotel suite is only temporary of course, Victoria," he went on after a moment, "until Mrs. Kendall arrives next week."

"H...hotel suite?" she said vaguely.

"I told you about the Essex House, I'm sure. I booked you a suite there. It faces Central Park and the building where Noel and I will be living is only half a block away." She barely heard him. I'll be all alone, she was thinking. For this first week I won't even have Martha. "Victoria—" Jon's voice intruded gently on her thoughts once more.—"did you hear me?"

"It...it doesn't really matter," she replied at last– her tone expressionless. "One place is pretty much the same as another." She was sitting between them, her gloved hands clasped in her lap, and in the silence that followed both men looked at her often.

When the limousine pulled up in front of the Essex House, Jon stepped out onto the sidewalk, turning to help Victoria. Noel got out on the other side of the car. Unfortunately he'd looked the wrong way to check for traffic. Brakes squealed and horns blared. "Up yours, Yank!" he yelled.

Victoria smiled, but she still clung to Jon's hand. "Would you like us to see you to your suite?" he asked.

She'd heard him this time, but she couldn't seem to answer. She couldn't even make herself walk into the hotel. Instead she stood uncertainly in the middle of the pavement, looking from side to side and chewing on one corner of her lower lip– a habit neither of her companions had ever noticed before. By now Noel had come around the car to stand beside them. "I'm afraid it's me she doesn't want. I have a definite talent for saying the wrong thing, no matter how well-meaning my intentions."

"No, no, please." Victoria reached out her other hand to Noel. "Please come up–both of you. It's....it's just that it's been a difficult day and I...."

"Exactly," Jon interrupted her firmly, "and that's why we're going to get you settled and let you have some rest."

Why can't I suggest we have dinner together, Victoria thought as the three of them finally crossed the sidewalk and entered the hotel through its revolving door. Why can't I just say it? The lobby was richly decorated in shades of green and as they entered, a long corridor stretched ahead of them lit by enormous crystal chandeliers. The reception desk was to the left. "Yes, sir?" the clerk behind the counter inquired as they approached.

"Miss Windsor's suite, please," Jon replied.

"Ah, yes!" The man sprang instantly into action, bowing and smiling. "If you would be so kind as to sign our register, Miss Windsor. Your...ah...luggage?" he continued with an uncertain glance at the floor directly in front of the counter.

"Miss Windsor's things will be following separately," Jon explained as Victoria stepped forward to take the pen, grateful to be spared the necessity of speaking.

The clerk handed the bellboy the key. "Suite 1132, Miss Windsor. I trust the accommodations will meet with your approval. Please let us know if we may do anything to make your stay with us more pleasant."

Victoria merely responded with a nod and she, Jon and Noel followed the bellboy around the corner and along the long chandelier-lit lobby toward the lifts. "Oh, pardon me," Noel observed, glancing at a small brass sign on the wall. "Elevators–not lifts."

A few moments later they emerged on the eleventh floor walking to the right and then left to the end of the hall. The bellboy unlocked the door for them and Jon tipped him, accepting the key. "You'll see to Miss Windsor's luggage when it arrives?"

The boy looked down at the twenty dollar bill in his hand. "Yes, sir!" He walked away down the hall whistling.

"Now then, Victoria," Jon inquired kindly, "is there anything we can do for you before we leave?"

"Where.....where are you going?"

"To our flat, of course, or perhaps I should say apartment."

"That's right, Jon. If it's elevator, it must be apartment. Odd lot, these colonials, what?" Noel was still trying to lighten the mood.

Victoria smiled a little at that. The dear old thing was trying so hard to be droll, but that didn't change the fact that soon now she would be alone. "Suppose....suppose I ...I have to get in touch with you? What's....what's your address?"

"It's the Berkeley House. I don't know our phone number yet, but I'll ring you later and tell you."

"Wh...when?"

Noel observed the tension building again in her eyes–in every line of her body. No, it was more than tension; it was virtual terror and all at once he understood the reason, cursing himself for not grasping it sooner. My God, she's afraid of being alone, he thought, and yet at the same time she can't bring herself to ask us to stay. "Why don't we all have dinner together later?" he suggested aloud, hoping he sounded offhand enough, and as he watched the relief flood over her face, he knew he'd guessed correctly. "Perhaps room service here in the suite so you won't have to go out again. I'm sure there won't be any groceries in our flat and what good would two poor bachelors be even if there were."

"Are you sure you're not too tired, Victoria?" Jon asked.

"No, please come. I can rest beforehand, but please, please come." Her eagerness was touching.

"It will be our pleasure, m'lady," Noel assured her, taking in her right hand in both of his and leaning forward to kiss her on the cheek.

Victoria saw them to the door, kissing each of them again . She even stood in the doorway to wave to them as they turned the corner. Finally, however, she closed the door and for the moment she was indeed alone. At first she wandered aimlessly about the suite–through the enormous formal living room, pausing to glance down at the traffic on the street below and at Central Park on the other side; on through the entrance foyer where she opened a door to discover a small kitchenette and into the bedroom and bath, immediately turning around to retrace her steps back through the hall into the living room. "God," she said out loud, "I feel so strange. Maybe Noel's right; maybe something is wrong. I've....I've never felt like this before and I don't bloody well like it." A drink, she thought all at once. Of course–that's what I need!

A few minutes search turned up a small, well-stocked bar hidden behind a fake bookcase and pouring a glass more than half full of vodka, she curled up with it on one of the four sofas in the room. She took several sips, waiting for the liquor to produce its usual calming effect, but her agitation only grew. She raised the glass to her lips yet another time, but after hesitating briefly, she lowered it again without drinking. Then she abandoned it altogether on the coffee table and stood up to recommence her prowling. At last her restlessness was too much to contain and snatching up her purse, hat and dark glasses again, she headed for the door, remembering only at the last minute to take her key.

It was a perfect early summer day in New York, the air soft and warm, and Victoria walked and walked, losing all track of time and direction. Somewhere along the way she even shed the dark glasses, realizing that here her face was all but unknown. Such an awareness gave her a glorious sensation of freedom and by the time she hailed a taxi to take her back to the hotel, her disquieting thoughts of earlier had all but disappeared.

Not quite a week later Martha joined her–the very fact that she'd missed her housekeeper should have told her something, but it didn't–and by then Jon had located her a flat just two floors above the one he shared with Noel. It irritated her old friend somehow that the other man seemed to know Victoria's taste so well; the warm, autumn tones of the apartment's decor–its overstuffed, chintz-covered furniture–suited her perfectly.

And so as the summer passed, her life appeared to settle into its normal routine. Three of the plays in which she was appearing had already opened and she was in rehearsal for the fourth. New York actors– eager to be included among her intimates– were more than willing to suggest local bars and nightclubs and to join her in a bit of pub-crawling–American style. There was even a new lover–an actor in the company–Geoff Leicester. Sadly Noel resigned himself to the fact that Victoria hadn't changed at all. Then–perversely, it seemed–just as he was sure he had no further illusions, her actions confounded him once again. Rehearsal had just broken for the day and catching the scent of her perfume, he knew she was behind him even before she spoke. "Busy on Sunday, luv?"

"Ah....no." Self-consciously Noel cleared his throat, wondering yet again at the effect her voice, her very nearness, invariably had on him. "Nothing....ah...special."

"I thought I'd have a few people to dinner–well, actually just you and Jon and Millicent."

"I'd enjoy that. What's Martha planning to have?"

An expression of pure mischief played across her exquisite features. "Martha's planning on having the week-end off to visit some cousins in Boston. I'll be doing the cooking myself." She laughed delightedly at his expression of shocked disbelief. "Want to change your mind, luv ?"

"No, of course not. I just...ah...ah...never thought of you as...ah...as...ah..."

Again Victoria laughed, crinkling up her nose at him. "Perhaps the word you're searching for is domestic, hm? Well after all, you know, I did take domestic science at Heathfield."

"Heathfield?" She didn't reply. Why had she mentioned Heathfield? She hadn't thought of the place in years. Would...would Sister Philippa still be there? "Victoria?"

"Oh...ah...." As he'd only imagined the change in her, was he now imagining there were tears in her eyes? "A...ah...Church of England boarding school." The tears, if indeed they'd ever been there, were gone. "My goodness, Noel. Didn't you realize I was convent-bred?"

He blinked. "No....ah...I guess I didn't."

Dinner turned out to be a homesick Englishman's dream–roast beef and an amazingly light Yorkshire pudding--, but it was Victoria herself Noel would think about afterwards far into the night. She was dressed simply in a gold plaid hostess skirt and a gold cashmere pullover, her hair held back with a matching scarf. It was her face, however, which caught and held his attention. Perhaps it was simply that the heat from the stove had heightened her color, but he was sure it was more than that. She was, moreover, at her most charming. A little tense perhaps and she still drank too much wine, but there was a definite difference in her manner. Most significant of all was the kindness with which she continued to treat Millicent–amazing enough she'd even included the girl in the invitation in the first place.

Contriving to linger a while after the other two guests left, Noel begged a nightcap. It had begun to grow dark, the long lovely twilight of a fall afternoon and he took full advantage of the dimness of the room to observe Victoria. The lights from the city street below played across her face and he found himself thinking about another occasion not that long ago–the party on the eve of their departure from London. He'd watched her then, too, in the light from the fire. There is something different about her, he told himself. At some point, however, she turned and saw him looking at her. "What in hell are you staring at? Lately that's all you've done–stare at me– and believe me, I'm getting bloody sick of it!"

"A beautiful woman should be accustomed to being stared at."

"You're not admiring me; you're studying me. I suppose you're still insisting I've changed in some way–overnight!, as I recall–or perhaps the proper term in this case is 'overseas', since apparently this miraculous transformation occurred somewhere between London and here." In spite of himself Noel smiled. "And will you please tell me what is so damned funny?"

He continued to smile. "I'm afraid you are, Victoria. Even when you don't mean to be."

An answering smile tugged at the corners of her mouth, but then disappeared almost at once. "I....I really don't think I've changed, Noel," she murmured. "I still drink too much and what's more–I like drinking too much. I like being drunk and I still–shall we say–enjoy the company of men..." and here her tone turned deadly, "any man."

No matter how hard she tried, however, she couldn't convince herself. She felt different–filled with strange, indescribable longings yet oddly at the same time more at peace with herself than ever before. At times there was that same exhilaration she'd experienced on the plane as though she were on the verge of some tremendous discovery. But still she continued to tell herself that nothing had changed!. Perhaps she was simply afraid to believe; perhaps if she began to believe and it all turned out to mean nothing, she couldn't face the return of the emptiness.

* * *

Living in the same building, Jon and Noel customarily called for Victoria to take her to the theatre. It was a habit they'd just seemed to fall into, but one, Noel often thought gleefully to himself, which the Victoria of a few months ago would never have allowed. This particular evening they'd even had an early dinner together before going on to the theatre for the performance.

"Just a minute, please." Jon paused just inside the stage door to fish a typewritten notice out of the inevitable briefcase and tack it up on the call board. "I was telling you about this earlier, Noel."

"Oh—the NYU thing." The other man had come to stand next to him.

"Yes. I'd like to get someone of real stature in the company. It would make for some smashing PR!"

"Never directed, old chap. Not sure it's my thing really."

Unnoticed by either of them Victoria had moved over behind and between them to read the notice:

> Any member of the company interested in working with the NYU drama department as either director or guest artist, please let me know in the next few days. Thanks, Jon.

To pass my love of the theatre on to others, she thought. Well, admittedly the idea was exciting, but for her personally, of course, out of the question. She was so bloody awful with people and.... But this was yet another impulse which would not be denied. It was almost as though she stood off to one side watching and listening in disbelief as the words came out. "I don't know; it might be rather jolly."

Jon spun about to stare at her. It hadn't even occurred to him to consider Victoria. Noel also turned around, but more slowly--a grin spreading across his face. What better way to prove just how much she'd changed. "I don't hear you volunteering."

"Oh, is that so?" Well, if you'll act, I'll direct! Fair enough?"

Noel stuck out his hand. "Deal!"

For a second she hesitated, panic hovering at the edge of her mind. She pushed it back. "Deal," she replied shaking his hand.

The morning they were due at NYU for the first time Noel came upstairs to pick up Victoria. Martha opened the door at his knock. "She hasn't finished dressing yet, Mr. St. John. Have you had breakfast?"

"Yes, ma'am," he chuckled. "Believe it or not, I have. Jon and I can open cereal boxes now. Next we may even attempt toast."

Martha had always found the helpless male an object of great amusement. Now she simply looked at him before turning away to walk back toward the kitchen. "Perhaps just a cup of coffee then, sir?"

"Thank you. Has Victoria had breakfast?"

"She said she wasn't hungry." But even this simple statement sounded somehow accusing. The housekeeper went on into the kitchen returning a few moments later with Noel's coffee. She handed him the mug, but then continued to stand there.

"What is it, Martha?" Noel sat down on the couch, indicating for her to sit as well.

"Mr. St. John, you and I have known each other for some time now and..."

He smiled. "So long, in fact, that such preliminaries are no longer necessary."

"Yes, I suppose that's true." Finally she did sit next to him. She even managed a slight smile in return. "This thing at the University, sir–Miss Windsor told me <u>you</u> convinced her to do it."

"You should know by now that no one <u>convinces</u> Victoria to do anything. Actually it was more of a dare."

"Oh, but, sir, how <u>could</u> you? She was awake most of the night. I could hear her moving around out here."

"It's a new experience and she's understandably on edge, but.... Martha, you and I haven't had a chance to talk since we've been in New York and there's something I've been wanting to ask you." He put down his coffee cup and leaning forward with his elbows resting on his knees, his hands clasped together, he studied the housekeeper's face as he continued. "Have you noticed any change in Victoria?"

"Well, yes, I suppose I have. She's considerably more patient and there were these two girls in the lobby who asked for autographs. She was so kind to them. But....but at the same time she....she seems–I don't know–sad."

"She's fighting a lonely battle right now, Martha."

"I'm....I'm afraid I don't understand." Mr. St. John undoubtedly had Miss Windsor's best interests at heart, but sometimes she wondered about these theories of his.

Noel grinned. "I don't always make a great deal of sense, do I? Well, Victoria..... ah...... really wants to change, I think, and this decision to work at NYU is part of it. So no matter how hard it may be for her..." Just then, however, he observed the door of Victoria's bedroom opening and at once he stopped speaking, rising to his feet as she came out into the living room. "Good morning, m'lady."

She was wearing a cherry-red wool dress, a paisley print scarf in tones of red and royal blue fastened at her throat with a gold pin. Her hair was swept up into a bun on top of her head and as though in rebellion against this unusually severe style, tiny wispy gold curls had escaped, framing her face. Her make-up, as always, was flawless. "Noel, luv," She kissed him lightly on the cheek. "I'm frightfully sorry to have kept you waiting." With a vaguely apologetic wave of her hand she indicated her face, her dress, her hair. "I just couldn't get it right this morning. Martha, would you get my dark mink, please?"

The pleases and thank you's–that was another change, the housekeeper thought to herself as she went over to the hall closet to get the coat. Slipping the fur from its hanger, she returned to hand it to Noel. "You're always beautiful, Victoria," he whispered in her ear as he brought the fur up over her arms–allowing himself the luxury of letting his hands linger on her shoulders. "You never have anything to apologize for." She turned her head to smile gratefully at him and it was only then he glimpsed the pallor beneath her make-up, the dark circles under her eyes. "Ready to go, then?" he asked.

"Yes, of course. Martha, I should be back for lunch." She walked quickly across the room to open the front door of the flat, posing there briefly with one hand resting on the knob. "Well, Noel, are you coming or not?" In a swirl of fur she spun away from them again to step through the doorway, disappearing from sight along the hallway.

"Don't worry, Martha," Noel reassured her as he also turned to leave. "I'll take good care of her."

As they came outside, Victoria had as usual slipped on her dark glasses. Now she remained silent, hidden away behind them, as they waited together for the doorman to hail them a taxi. Oh God, she was thinking, why did I ever agree to this? Agree?! Hell, I bloody well volunteered! Now in just a little while all those people will be sitting there staring at me, waiting for me to say something! God, I'll feel as though I'm standing there stark naked! The doorman's shrill whistle sounded and she jumped, instinctively pulling her coat more snugly about her.

"Victoria?" Noel touched her on the arm. "The taxi."

"Oh....oh, yes–of course." She tried to smile at him.

"It's all right. Come along now." He put his hand at her waist to escort her across the sidewalk to where the doorman was waiting, holding open the door of the cab. Assisting Victoria into the back seat, Noel got in himself and gave the driver the address. The cab pulled away from the curb only to come to a stop again almost immediately. "I've got a riddle for you," he said after a moment. "What's the difference between a London traffic jam and one in New York City?"

She had been staring at a little girl walking hand in hand with her mother along the sidewalk. "Sorry, luv. I didn't hear you, I'm afraid."

He repeated the question. "Give up?....Ha! There is no difference. They're just on opposite sides of the street."

"That's the silliest thing I've ever heard!"

"Maybe so, but your mouth twitched. I saw it. Right there." He touched the corner of her lips with his forefinger.

"All right. I'll grant you a twitch. Are you satisfied?"

"Not entirely, but I suppose it will have to do for now."

"Noel, I'm sorry. Do you mind if we don't talk. I'm just not at my best first thing in the morning."

He resisted the urge to observe that for the average individual ten-thirty did not constitute the first thing in the morning. "Of course, Victoria."

Several times during the silence that followed he glanced over at her, but each time she appeared to be looking out the window again. He smiled shaking his head. She should have realized by now that she couldn't hide her feelings from him simply by hiding her face. Invariably she gave herself away and this time, as was so often the case, it was her hands. They moved constantly--playing with the fur at her cuff, smoothing her hair along her temples or just clenching and unclenching in her lap.

Then all at once, watching her and hurting for her, Noel had a thought. But maybe I no longer have to let her suffer in silence. Because if...if she truly is different, then I can be different, too. He looked at her hands again. At that moment they were clasped rigidly together in her lap. He reached over to cover them with one of his own. He felt her start at his touch, but incredibly she didn't pull away and after her initial reaction she relaxed. "Jon said they were thrilled you were coming," he said quietly.

Her gaze traveled from the window to rest on his hand where it still lay on top of her own. "Dear God, Noel, why did I ever say I would do this?"

"Perhaps because you wanted to do it."

She turned suddenly to face him and even more to his complete surprise, she whipped off her dark glasses. "Another deep and terribly significant bit of St. John philosophy, no doubt. And what in hell is it supposed to mean, may I ask?"

"No hidden meanings. Simply that. You wanted to do it or you wouldn't have volunteered. You did, may I remind you, volunteer, did you not?"

"Yes! God dammit!"

"Why?"

"How in hell do I know! You're supposed to tell me!"

"Do you really want my opinion because I've been offering it to you ever since we arrived in New York and you haven't been too interested."

"I haven't the foggiest idea what you're talking about!"

He looked at her face–all at once so alive–completely without subterfuge–and impossible as it was to imagine even more beautiful. "Victoria, whether you'll admit it or not, you have changed." She snorted in protest. "It's true," he insisted. "Tell me–even as recently as the day before we left London, would you have agreed to anything like this?" Once again she stared down at her lap for a long moment and finally she shook her head. "It will be all right," he reassured her. "Since you want to do, you can do it. And if nothing else, you're an actress. Give them the performance of your life!" The taxi drew up just then in front of the NYU theatre building. "And besides," he added as he opened the door and stepped out onto the sidewalk. "I'll be right there with you."

Before he could turn back to help her, she was out of the cab herself. "Bloody comfort that," she muttered under her breath as she strode past him and up the steps.

* * *

Jack Cabot looked down at his watch and then up at the revolving door which was the main entrance into the building. He'd repeated this ritual at least ten times in the last ten minutes, meanwhile circling the lobby and grumbling to himself.

The man waiting with him watched in evident amusement. "Calm down, Jack. How late is she anyway?"

"Over half an hour–half an hour!" Yet again he checked first his watch and then the door. "She's not coming, I tell you, Aaron. I knew it was too good to be true–getting Victoria Windsor."

"Only half an hour? Come on, man. How many years were you in the professional theatre? For an actress she's right on time! But then I've told you before you're in the wrong field. Actors can be damned aggravating. My light cables and flats obey without question–stay where I put them–never late–no temperament." Aaron Oblinsky did enjoy his work. Indeed he had known from the moment he took part with his fellow rabbinical students in a production of *Fiddler on the Roof* that he'd found his real love. He had never regretted the decision to forsake his religious studies although his parents never quite recovered. "But what do I tell my friends, Aaron?" his father was continually asking.

"I know....I know. But cables and flats are dead things. Actors are living, breathing creatures of talent and fire and brilliance!" Jack waved his arms in the air as he commenced yet another circuit of the lobby. How in hell did Aaron always manage to remain so damned unruffled anyway? "This whole thing was my idea, you know, and if she doesn't show, I'll look ridiculous!"

Just then, however, he saw the revolving doors begin to move. One–two sections passed by and Victoria Windsor appeared. She didn't simply come in, of course; she made an entrance–having given the door such a violent shove that Noel, who had been only a few steps behind her, stood watching helplessly as the sections flew past him.

Beaming, Jack moved forward to greet her, seizing her right hand in both of his. "Miss Windsor, this is indeed an honor! I'm Jack Cabot, chairman of the theatre department. I called Mr. Sinclair."

Jack was a big man, packing well over two hundred pounds into a frame somewhat under six feet and his size coupled with his recent anxiety as well as a blood pressure problem had left him flushed and sweating. He was precisely the sort of person she'd always found faintly repulsive. "Mr. Cabot–" Victoria flashed her most dazzling smile and although his hands were damp, she made no attempt to remove hers from his grasp. "How kind of you to invite me. And of course you know Mr. St. John," she went on to add as Noel, having finally maneuvered the revolving door, came up to join them. Gracious, charming–just as he'd suggested–she was giving a bravura performance as Victoria Windsor.

"Please, Miss Windsor, if you'll follow me, our students are waiting to meet you." At last mercifully Jack released her hands, turning to lead the way down the hall. "This, by the way, is Aaron Oblinsky. He'll be doing your sets and lighting."

Aaron hunched downward to acknowledge the introduction. With his thin sloping shoulders and dark-rimmed glasses, his hair painstakingly combed over his bald spot, a bony, prominent nose, he reminded Victoria more than anything of a vulture. What a perfect target for her stinging wit! Amazingly she liked him on sight. "How nice to meet you, Aaron." It was now she who extended her hand to take his, finding it as pleasantly cool and dry to the touch as Jack's had been warm and moist. "Can you manage, do you think, with this poor ignorant actress? You undoubtedly know so much more about all this than I do."

"Oh, I....I doubt that, Miss Windsor," he stammered.

Jack grinned as he watched his colleague come unglued. Calm and composed most of the time, perhaps, but apparently elegant English actresses had the capacity to unnerve him. "Just around the corner, Miss Windsor, and we're there." He placed a hand at her waist to direct her, a hand whose warmth she could feel even through the fur coat. Only Noel saw an expression of distaste pass briefly across her face. He couldn't believe she was even allowing this man to touch her.

Carrie Francks, the senior selected to stage manage the production, was waiting outside the auditorium for the private introduction Mr. Cabot had promised her. She'd loved the theatre ever since she saw *Peter Pan* when she was only six years old. Oh, how desperately she'd clapped for Tinkerbell to live! More than anything, she wanted to be an actress, but she just knew she was too plain and awkward so she stayed hidden away behind the scenes. Now as she saw Victoria come around the corner toward her, her heart began to pound. She took a step or two forward. "And Carrie Francks, one of our most competent student stage managers," Mr. Cabot was saying all at once. "I'm sure she'll be invaluable to you."

Victoria's smile had a special warmth to it as she not only took the girl's hand in hers, but covered it with her other one. "But you're so lovely. Why does Mr. Cabot keep you hidden away backstage?"

"Th...thank you." Carrie blushed. "I....I saw *Victoria Regina*, Miss Windsor. You... you were magnificent!"

"Magnificent! Did you hear that? I was magnificent!" She looked at Noel, laughing a little and arching her eyebrows, but all he noticed was that Victoria, who'd always shrunk from physical contact, was still holding the girl's hand between both of hers. "Now it seems it's my turn to thank you, luv. Well, Mr. Cabot, shall we?"

"Of course, Miss Windsor."

From behind the closed doors of the auditorium they could hear the hum of conversation. There was obviously a large group. Briefly Victoria glanced at Noel, her eyes widening in apprehension, and for the first time he realized exactly what this performance was costing her. "Steady, my girl," he just had time to whisper in her ear, accompanying the word with a pat on her back.

Jack Cabot held open the door, stepping back to allow Victoria and Noel to enter first, followed by himself, Aaron and Carrie. The conversation ceased instantly to be replaced by a speculative hum; heads turned as one and all strained to get their first glimpse of Victoria Windsor. The department chairman had taken the lead now and as they moved down the aisle, Noel could feel Victoria's gloved hand grasping his. "What in hell was that girl's name anyway?"

He squeezed her hand in return. "Carrie."

"God, I really <u>am</u> bloody awful at names, aren't I? I've got to do something about that." Noel enjoyed a private smile. Her kindness, her graciousness–it hadn't all been an act, had it?

Single file they climbed the narrow steps leading up to the stage. Several brown wooden armchairs had already been placed there and Aaron went over immediately to stand behind one of them, placing his hands on its back. "Miss Windsor?" She smiled at him again, moving across the stage to ease herself with her customary grace into the offered chair. With his assistance she slipped off her mink. She removed her gloves and crossing her legs, she at last turned slightly sideways in the seat–her hands resting lightly on the arms as though this were her throne.

Jack stepped up to the microphone. "Good morning. I fully realize you haven't come here this morning to see and hear me. I am not as celebrated and certainly not nearly as beautiful as our illustrious guest." There was laughter at that and even Victoria smiled a little. "So let me at once introduce our guest director for the fall production. Miss Victoria Windsor received her theatrical training at the Royal Academy of Dramatic Art in London. Among her many stage credits are included a season with the Royal Shakespeare Company during which she portrayed Ophelia to Dylan Mallory's Hamlet as well as Cordelia to Sir Terence Cartier's Lear. Following this there were several glittering seasons in the West End of London–most notably perhaps, her performance of the title role in *The Divine Sarah* for which she received the British equivalent of our 'Tony'. And this season, as you are all happily aware, Miss Windsor is honoring us with her presence on the New York stage, performing in repertory Lady Macbeth, Candida, Wilde's Gwendolyn Fairfax and Victoria Regina–quite an ambitious undertaking for an actress, but one to which, as I'm sure you will agree, our guest is more than equal. And now, Miss Windsor, if you'd please say a few words."

Noel had been watching Victoria closely all through this recital of her theatrical credentials. For all she showed any visible reaction Jack Cabot could have talking about a total stranger and he could only guess at her thoughts.

What <u>was</u> she thinking? Perhaps that she had every right to be proud–that in a comparatively short career she had indeed accomplished a great deal. But also, perhaps, that despite her success she had found no real happiness. Then suddenly Victoria became aware that the chairman was concluding his introduction. It was time once again for her to perform–because, as Noel had said, she could at least do that. She rose and walked slowly to the front of the stage–Victoria Windsor did not require a microphone–and for a moment she simply stood there, allowing the mere fact of her presence to have its effect. "Good morning, everyone." The clear, perfectly modulated and disciplined voice rang out in the small auditorium. "You know–I'm actually rather curious why you're all here–why in God's name you've chosen to pursue some branch or other of a profession which has an unemployment rate considerably above the average." She paused. "And right now you are all doubtless thinking–My goodness, she really <u>does</u> talk like that!"

A ripple of laughter ran through the group.

"And may I say–it is <u>not</u> true that if you wake an Englishman up in the middle of the night, he will talk just like everyone else." A louder laugh–Noel shook his head. She was charming them–slowly, but surely. "But you are also probably thinking," she went on after a moment, "that with the list of my stage credits as so generously provided for you by Mr. Cabot, I have no right to talk to you about the woes of an unemployed actor." It was somewhere right about here that something happened to Victoria and she was no longer performing. For what must have been the first time in her life she was standing in front of a group of people and being totally herself. Because there really <u>was</u> something she wanted to say to them. Perhaps it was this which in part at least had drawn her to the whole idea in the first place.

"Well, there was one point which Mr. Cabot graciously omitted in his story of my apparently meteoric rise to a position of some preeminence in the British theatre and for that I suppose I should thank him." Here she turned to smile at Jack. "Perhaps, however, it is one fact of which <u>you</u> should be aware. It was four years–did you all hear that?-- <u>four years</u>, forty-eight months and I have no idea how many weeks or days–I've always been bloody awful at mathematics–between the June I graduated from RADA and the day I got my first job as an actor and even that was with a new rep company in a grubby little industrial city in the English Midlands. I earned a living waitressing in pubs and even pumping petrol–oh, excuse me, gasoline, isn't it? And do you know that not once during all that time did I say–'I give up.'–'I'm sick of trying.'–'I don't want to act anymore.'—'I'll do something else instead.' Because the theatre truly does get into your blood and you have to be a part of it or you're not really living. So I'm going to presume <u>that's</u> the reason you're here and if it isn't, by God it <u>will be</u> before I'm through with you!" Again she paused. Her voice dropped and Noel could see individual members of the group lean forward, straining to catch every word. "Have you ever stood alone on a dimly lit stage in a deserted theatre and looked out over what would be the audience? Because I have–more than once– from the auditorium of a Church of England convent school to the Royal Shakespeare Company's Aldwych Theatre in London. It doesn't matter. The magic is still there, isn't it?"

"Well, I've decided on Noel Coward's *Blithe Spirit*." Suddenly she was all business. "It's a play I've never had a chance to work with and perhaps, since its essence is rather more essentially British than others, you may learn something from me in the process. Mr. Noel St. John will be portraying the major male role. All others will be open to audition. Books are available now in Mr. Cabot's office and try-outs will be next Monday, Tuesday and Thursday from one to three p.m." Another brief pause. "Yes, I know auditions are the most ingenious form of torture known to modern man, but unfortunately they are necessary. I survived them and so, believe it or not, will you." As she finally turned to go back to her seat, applause rocked the auditorium. Then one by one people rose to their feet. Victoria remained standing herself– smilingly accepting the ovation. My first, she thought–bemused-- just for being myself.

Later in the taxi on the way back to their building, Victoria was once again quiet. So many of our rides together, Noel thought, have passed in silence. He glanced sideways at his companion–but this time was different. She returned his glance and a smile tugged at the corners of her mouth–a smile beguilingly close to genuine. "Half-crown for your thoughts, luv."

He grinned with pleasure. "Only half a crown?"

"Well, let me hear them. I may consider raising the rate."

"Actually I was thinking that all your worry was for nothing." Not the complete truth, but not exactly a lie either.

Victoria's smile broadened. "I was bloody marvelous, wasn't I?"

"Bloody marvelous! May I ask exactly when you decided what to say?"

"Would you believe--just shortly after I began saying it?" Noel roared with laughter. "Will you come with me next week to the auditions? It might help them–to read with a professional."

"Glad to."

The remainder of the ride passed quickly and as had become the custom, Noel rode up to Victoria's floor with her. At the door of her apartment she started to look for her key, but then she paused, taking out her change purse instead. "Let me see." Once again there was that glorious twinkle in her eyes. "What is the current rate of exchange anyway?" She pushed about the change in the little tartan wool pouch, appearing to think for a moment, and finally extracted a quarter. "Here, luv." She pressed it into his hand, leaning forward as she did so to kiss him on the cheek. "I'm feeling generous." Grinning, he slipped the coin into his pocket. It would become his lucky piece. At last then, Victoria took out her key and inserted it in the lock. She turned to look back at him. "You know, Noel, maybe you were right after all." Unlocking the door, she disappeared quickly inside.

"About what?" he inquired plaintively of the closed door. There was no reply. "About what?" he called again more loudly.

Victoria still didn't answer him. Probably, in fact, she hadn't even heard him as inside the apartment she walked slowly through the living room into her bedroom. She closed the door behind her and sat down on the edge of the bed. "I have changed," she whispered as if to say it any louder might break the spell. "I have! Only a few months ago I could never have stood there and talked to those people. I could never have done it!"

Martha knocked at the bedroom door. "Miss Windsor, would you like your lunch now?"

"Yes....ah....thank you."

Smiling to herself, the housekeeper walked back toward the kitchen. Again---- thank you. Mr. St. John was right!

* * *

Ever since she could remember, it was her father who'd been there for her. Why then, Olivia would sometimes wonder now, did she continue to long for her mother? And what difference did it make that as the holidays approached, Victoria was thousands of miles away? She had only one vague Christmas memory of a warm, furry, sweetly scented embrace and what was that over the eight years of her life? But then one day at school the class began working on presents for their mothers–little floral sachets. Olivia knew it was hopeless–that even if her father agreed, her mother probably wouldn't want her–, but she knew she had to ask.

She waited until after tea that evening–until her stepmother had gone upstairs to put her half-brother and sister to bed. She and her father customarily spent this hour or so together anyway, he with the evening newspaper, she with her schoolwork. Andrew glanced up to smile at his daughter as she settled herself on the floor at his feet. "What is it you're studying tonight, then?"

"Just stuff." Olivia's heart was pounding and she pretended to be concentrating on the book which lay open on the rug in front of her.

"Just stuff, hm?" Chuckling, he leaned down to peer over her shoulder. "Oh, spelling, I see. Don't you want Daddy to help you with your arithmetic?"

She made a face. "Did you like arithmetic when you were at school, Daddy?"

"It wasn't my favorite subject either, but sometimes, you know, we all have to do things we don't like."

"Yes, Daddy." The child was silent for a moment. How could she bring up the subject of her mother? Then she had an idea. "Did Mummy like arithmetic?"

"I don't know." Andrew was unintentionally short with his daughter. But why after that hideous trip to France did she persist from time to time in bringing up Victoria? On the other hand if Olivia still had feelings for her mother, he was the one largely responsible. He gazed tenderly for a moment at the shining brown head–bent once again over the spelling book. "Sweetheart?" Olivia looked up and he saw with a pang of conscience that her blue eyes were full of tears. "I'm sorry I was cross with you. You're such a good little girl."

"Well, I am naughty sometimes," she admitted with a touching honesty, looking down again at her book. "Only....only you...you see there's something I want to ask you and now.... now I'm sure you're going to say no." Olivia took a deep breath. "Daddy, may...may I please write and ask Mummy if I may spend my holiday with her?"

For just a second Andrew thought he couldn't have heard correctly. "What?"

"I....I want to ask Mummy if I may come over for Christmas." Her lower lip began to quiver. "I....I promise not be disappointed if she says no."

"Oh, precious, after all the times she's hurt you, you still....."

"I...I know. But please may I at least write and ask her?"

"All right, Olivia." He sighed in resignation. "You know where the address is– in the leather book on my desk."

"Thank you, oh, thank you, Daddy!" Scrambling up beside him on the couch, she hugged him with all her strength. "I'm going to write my letter right now so that you can post it for me in the morning!" She jumped up and ran off happily in the direction of his study.

"Please, Victoria," Andrew breathed fervently. "Please just this once–surprise me."

After more than half a dozen tries, during which she'd ruined several sheets of her best stationery, this was what Olivia finally wrote.

Dear Mummy,

How do you like living in the States? It must be lots of fun to live in a different city. I am fine and working hard at school. Except I don't like arithmetic. Did you like arithmetic when you were at school? I asked Daddy, but he said he didn't know. I just joined the Girl Guides and I like it very much. I'm learning how to sew and how to cook.

It was at this point on each attempt that Olivia found herself stumped. It was as though once she put her request in writing, she would at once have her answer–an answer she wasn't sure she wanted to receive.

Mummy, (the letter at last continued) *I am writing to you especially to ask if I may please come to spend Christmas with you? I'm a big girl now and I can do everything for myself so I wouldn't be a bother to you or Martha so please, please, please, Mummy, write back real soon and say I may come.*

Love and kisses,

Olivia

Victoria's days were full now. All four plays in which she was appearing were in the repertoire and in addition a good part of Mondays, Tuesdays and Thursdays was being spent at NYU. First it had only been the rehearsals, but then a group of students had approached her about a master class in acting. She returned to her New York apartment that particular day in mid-December to find the table set as usual for dinner--the day's post to one side of her plate. Martha had heard her come in. "Would you like a drink, Miss Windsor?"

There was a brief pause. "No–just wine, I think. I have a performance tonight." She began to flip idly through the envelopes. Her daughter's plain, but still essentially childish handwriting was unmistakable.

"A letter from Olivia, I see," Martha remarked as she came in with the wine.

"Yes." When she said nothing further, however, the housekeeper finally put the goblet down and turned away. For several seconds Victoria continued to sit there staring at the unopened letter in her hand. Dear God, she thought, what does that child want now? Martha despised herself for snooping, but she stood just inside the kitchen holding the swinging door slightly ajar and watching as Miss Windsor tore open the envelope and read the letter. She clearly saw the distress on the beautiful woman's face as she threw the single sheet of stationery down on the table. "Dear God, no," Victoria whispered, resting her forehead in her hands. "Why do you keep trying, Olivia. You have to let me go."

"I roasted one of those little capons you like so much," Martha called out, wanting to give her employer time to compose herself.

"That...that would be nice–thank you."

And by the time the housekeeper came out of the kitchen again to serve the meal, Victoria was indeed in complete control. "How's Olivia?" It seemed a perfectly reasonable question since Miss Windsor already knew she'd seen the letter.

"Oh..ah...fine, she says." Her reply was carefully casual. "She's....ah....joined the Girl Guides. It....ah...doesn't seem possible she's old enough, does it?" Was that it, Martha wondered–she was saddened that her daughter was growing up so quickly? "Olivia wants to come for Christmas." And now Victoria simply sounded tired.

"That would be wonderful! You could......"

"Dammit, I will not be saddled with that child for the holidays!"

Why she chose this moment to defy her after so many years of accepting Victoria's every mood without question, Martha wasn't sure. Perhaps it was the softening both she and Noel had sensed in her, but it seemed as if Miss Windsor's life were ever going to change, it had to be now. "Oh, please, ma'am," she pleaded, "let her come!"

"<u>What</u>?"

"She loves you so much! All she asks is that you love her in return. And I think you do actually. No, I <u>know</u> you do. Oh, let her into your life. It will bring you more joy than you could possibly imagine."

"You miserable prying old bitch!" Victoria sprang to her feet, slamming the flat of both hands down on the table and upsetting the glass of wine. "How dare you interfere in my private life? And where in hell did you get the bloody idiotic notion that I love that child? I hate her!"

"Oh, Miss Windsor, that's not true. I don't......"

"Shut up, God damn you!" She gripped Martha by both shoulders and contorted with rage, her employer's face was mere inches away. "I wanted to kill her, you know, before she could even be born, but they wouldn't let me!"

"I'm sorry, ma'am. I don't believe you. You're just saying those things to shock me."

"Get the hell out of here and leave me alone!" Victoria pushed her away with such force that the older woman fell backwards against the couch. "And I don't mean just out of this room or even out of this flat! Get the bloody hell out of my life! You're fired–sacked! And don't expect any references! The only thing you'll bloody well get from me is your return fare to England!"

"I'll be out of here before you get home tonight, ma'am."

Martha stood up to walk slowly from the room as unbelievably the actress began to scream. Seizing anything she could lay her hands on–dishes, glasses, silverware–, she hurled them about the room and she screamed and screamed and screamed until the housekeeper thought she herself must go insane from the sound. Finally the bedroom door slammed and at least the screams were muffled. Coming back into the living room a few minutes later with a broom and dust pan, Martha listened while the screams turned gradually to sobs and at last–mercifully–there was silence. She swept up the shattered glass and china and when she'd finished, she tiptoed over to the bedroom door. When still she heard nothing, she carefully opened the door to discover with some relief that Miss Windsor had fallen asleep.

It was about two hours later when Noel arrived as usual to escort Victoria to the theatre. Martha answered his knock. "Come in, Mr. St. John. But if you'll excuse me, I have to finish packing."

"Packing?" He stepped inside and closed the door. "Where are you going?"

"Back to England, sir–on the nine o'clock flight."

"You can't. Not after all these years."

At last, then, she turned back to face him and he saw the tears in her eyes. "I have no choice, sir. Miss Windsor has discharged me."

"What....what happened?"

"I...I really don't want to talk about it and as I said, I do have to finish packing."

Noel didn't try to stop her. He wondered what he should do, but they did have to get to the theatre and after a moment he went over and knocked on the bedroom door. He had to knock a second time before Victoria finally opened it.

"Oh....ah....hello." She ran her hands through her hair. "I....I must have fallen asleep. I've been at University all day." For a few seconds she continued to stand there until at last some inner force seemed to propel her into action. As she moved across the bedroom to one of the closets, he could see she was weaving slightly. Was she drunk? He didn't think so and oddly he found himself almost wishing she were.

She stared dazedly for a moment at the open closet, but at last she selected a pair of slacks and a jumper. She went on into the bathroom and leaving the door open a crack, she began a stream of largely one-sided conversation. "What have you been doing all day, luv?" She gave him no opportunity to respond, however. "Have a drink, why don't you, luv?" He could hear the water running in the wash bowl; apparently she was washing her face yet she went on talking steadily as though she were afraid to stop. "That little Carrie is bloody marvelous, luv–so damned organized–and the girl playing Elvira is starting to come around, You know, I do believe she was afraid of me. Can you imagine anyone being afraid of me? I'm a pussycat, aren't I?" Stunned by the non-stop chatter, Noel could think of no answer. He'd never seen her like this. "Well, aren't I?" she demanded. "An absolute pussycat?"

"Yes....yes, of course you are," he finally managed to reply.

"I knew you'd agree. Anyway..." Her tone grew increasingly frenzied now. "Anyway–I've sacked Martha. No, don't say anything. It's important you listen. She interfered once too often. You know how she's been, Noel!"

"Yes, Victoria." There was nothing else he could say.

At last she emerged from the bathroom dressed and ready to go. Moving more purposefully now, she walked quickly through the bedroom and out into the living room. "Get me a coat, will you? I don't care which one." Grabbing up her purse and gloves from the desk, she came over to slip into the fox fur which he now held for her. "Marvelous taste, luv." She turned to pat him on the cheek. "As always." They left the apartment together, but then as they started along the hall toward the elevator, her non-stop flow of words resumed. "Olivia wrote and asked to come for Christmas. Of course you know that's out of the question. She's much better off with her father." For her at least that apparently settled the matter and finally now she fell silent.

So that's what happened with Martha, Noel thought. By now they were passing through the lobby of the building. Outside on the pavement they waited for the doorman to hail them a cab. "Victoria," he said quietly once they were settled in the taxi, "tell Olivia she may come."

"Dear God," she hissed under her breath, "not you, too." In spite of her emotional turmoil she was mindful that the driver could hear every word. A tense silence resumed and for the first time in a long time Noel watched her stride through the backstage area ignoring the greetings. The door to her dressing room slammed shut behind her.

More than a week went by. Victoria wrote her daughter a breezy note, explaining that she was terribly busy and a Christmas visit just wouldn't be practical. She was drinking heavily again and she'd returned to her old habit of picking up men at parties-- even in bars. It's as though she has to prove she hasn't changed at all, Noel thought sadly, and then he had an idea.

The following Sunday he and Victoria were driving together out to Westchester where a dinner in honor of the British rep company was being held in the home of the chairman of the New York State Theatre governing board. Well-hidden as usual behind scarf and dark glasses, she had barely spoken in the half hour or so since he'd called for her. Noel knew she'd given two performances the day before and partied half the night. She was undoubtedly tired as well as hung over. But he had a feeling it was more than that. He was right on both counts.

Drunk as she was, Victoria had indeed not fallen asleep until the early hours of that morning and then the nightmare about her daughter which she'd first had on the eve of her departure from London was back. But this time Martha and Noel were in the dream as well, pushing all sizes and kinds of stuffed animals in her face and chanting together--"Why don't you love her? She loves you! Why don't you love her? She loves you!" Suddenly the stuffed animals came to life and began chasing her. Bizarrely one of them turned into Sean Patrick wearing a leopard-skin loin cloth. All at once she became aware that Noel had spoken. "What?" she snapped.

"I said that it's probably just as well you told Olivia no. She probably didn't really want to come at all."

"You son-of-a-bitch! She wrote and asked me, didn't she?"

He knew immediately he'd touched a nerve; to what result he couldn't be sure. "It was more likely Andrew's idea. He's been trying to make a mother out of you for years, not even counting the original time."

"My God, but you're amusing this afternoon. For your information after that hideous trip to the south of France Andrew cancelled my visiting rights. Of course Christmas was her own idea."

Noel could hear the tears in her voice and he nearly relented. But no–he couldn't. He might be hurting her now, but it was worth it if she would only admit how deeply she loved her daughter. "Oh, come now, Victoria! Why would Olivia want to spend Christmas with you?"

"Because...because she loves me! That's....that's why!"

"<u>Loves</u> you!" He gave a snort of derision. "<u>Loves</u> you! Why in hell should she love you? What have you ever done in the eight years of her life to earn that love?"

"I never claimed to be a good mother. As a matter of fact I know I've been a damned, rotten mother!" She was sobbing audibly now. "But in spite of everything Olivia still loves me. She does!"

The trap was laid and baited. Noel paused briefly and then sprung it. "Prove it," he said softly. "Prove it."

"I don't have to prove my daughter's love to you. I know she loves me. That's what matters–not whether you believe it or not!"

He pushed the attack still further. "Afraid to find out?"

"I don't need to find out. God damn it–why are you doing this to me?"

"You can settle it very easily, you know. Ring up and ask Olivia to come. If she says yes, that would silence me once and for all, wouldn't it?"

"All right...all right! Damn you! I will....I will." The words came in short, agonizing gasps. "Tonight as soon as we get back."

"Oh, no! I don't trust you." At that moment they were passing a small shopping center and Noel swung the car in out of the traffic, pulling up beside a Dunkin' Donuts on the edge of the lot.

"What in hell are you doing?" Victoria demanded. "You've bloody well gone round the bloody bend!"

"Kiosk right there!" He indicated the telephone booth with a toss of his head.

Her green eyes blazed. "You expect me to make a private phone call in a car park?! Besides I don't have enough change."

"Bill it to the phone at your flat."

"All right! All right! I will gladly do anything to bloody well shut you up!" Victoria stormed out of the car and across the parking lot into the phone booth. But once inside she stood frozen one hand on the receiver, unable to bring herself to lift it off the instrument. Dear God, what if he's right, she thought. I've certainly given her reason enough to stop loving me.

"What's the matter? All the lines to England engaged?" Noel unexpectedly appeared behind her.

Why had he suddenly turned on her like this? "No, you bastard," she muttered. "I....I wasn't sure of the number."

"Oh–not sure of the number–of course."

She was trembling visibly as she finally took down the receiver, inserted a dime and dialed the operator. The preliminaries were ridiculously easy. The overseas operator came on the line and she gave her Andrew's number. Maybe it won't go through, she prayed fervently, and I can at least ring through later. But the line was ringing and almost at once her ex-husband answered. "Hello." Victoria was grasping the receiver so tightly that her fingers were cramping up and she couldn't seem to reply. "Hello," he said again.

"Andrew, it's Victoria," she managed to say at last.

"Oh." His voice turned instantly cold. "What can you possibly want? Your letter to Olivia made everything perfectly clear."

"She's....she's already received it then?"

"Yes. The postal service between the U.S. and the U.K. is quite efficient these days."

Dear God, he hated her! He'd never let Olivia come. "Andrew, is...is it too late to speak to Olivia?"

"Yes, Victoria. I'd say about eight years too late."

"I...I suppose it is." As she'd heard the anger in his voice, now he could hear the obvious emotion in hers. "But please....oh, please, just this one more chance."

The little girl, meanwhile, had come into the room just as he called Victoria by name. "Daddy? Is.....is that Mummy on the phone?"

Andrew turned to look down at her. Her eagerness was profoundly affecting. His gaze traveled to the receiver in his hand. "Sweetheart, your....your mother wants to speak to you."

Olivia walked slowly across the room to take the phone from her father. "Hello," she whispered.

It required all of Victoria's self-control not to break down completely. "Hello...darling. It's....it's Mummy."

"Let her hear how you feel," Noel urged her. "Don't fight it back!! Let her hear it!"

She glanced back at him—startled. She'd forgotten he was even there. "You know, Olivia, I've....I've been thinking. If....if you don't mind...I mean I'll...I'll be working most of the evenings, but...but...." Her voice faltered.

On the other end of the line Andrew watched his daughter's eyes fill with tears. "You.... you want me to come?"

"Yes....darling....very much!"

"Mummy, are...are you crying?"

"Yes, I.....I am. I....I..... But I'll wait to say it all when you get here. Tell...tell your father to cable me about your flight."

"My....my holiday is three weeks."

Three weeks when she'd never even been able to manage one day! "All....all right. If....if your father agrees."

"Oh, Mummy, I....I love you so much!"

"I....I love you, too, dearest. I'll see you soon then."

"See you soon, Mummy." The connection was broken and Olivia looked up at her father, her eyes shining. "Oh, Daddy, she said she loves me! She really said it!"

"Yes, sweetheart. I think she always has."

In New York Noel had already left the phone booth, slipping away unnoticed to allow Victoria to talk to her daughter in private. Now he watched as she walked toward him across the parking lot, crying unashamedly. There were no dark glasses to hide it. She got into the car and he started the motor pulling out into the traffic again. "So it would seem I was wrong," he observed lightly.

"Thank you, Noel." Her voice was still shaking. "Thank you for making me do it."

He removed one hand from the steering wheel to take hold of one of hers. "If you hadn't wanted to do it, you know, nothing I said could have persuaded you."

Her answering smile was tremulous, but touchingly genuine. "Yes, I suppose I have been known to be a little stubborn, haven't I?"

He laughed. "You—stubborn? Never!"

"Oh, Noel, she's coming! She's really coming!"
"Yes, dear lady, I know."

* * *

Olivia tried to tell herself this time was different–that this time her mother wouldn't cancel the visit, but still she jumped whenever the phone rang, whenever she heard the postman's whistle. For Victoria as well the week plus a day between her phone call and her daughter's scheduled arrival was a time of both anticipation and dread. Would she, despite all her good intentions, fail yet again? Then all of a sudden Olivia was coming tomorrow–the long-awaited tomorrow.

The day before would, of course, have to be–of all days– another Sunday. Noel and Jon decided to take Victoria out to brunch and perhaps the ballet, thinking it better she not be alone. "Oh, Noel, I....I couldn't possibly," she replied when he rang her up about noon to issue the invitation. "I...I have so much to do."

He could hear how tense she was. "Would you at least like some company for a while?"

"Oh, no, I just can't be with anyone! Wait, maybe–oh, never mind!" And she hung up. Five minutes later he was ringing her bell. She was at the door almost at once. "Noel...what in hell? Didn't I make myself clear on the phone?"

She was dressed in dark blue slacks and a red pullover, her hair held back from her face with a simple barrette, and Noel saw she was wearing no make-up. Dark smudges under her eyes told him at once how little sleep she'd gotten the night before. "Actually, Victoria, you made bloody little sense."

"Well, now that you're here, I suppose you might as well come in. But don't expect <u>me</u> to entertain you!" She turned away abruptly to walk back to the dining alcove where the table was strewn with newspaper clippings and brochures. Sitting down, she picked up a pamphlet and began making notes.

"What <u>are</u> you doing?" he asked.

"<u>That</u> should be obvious–even for a person of your limited mental capacity. I'm planning activities for Olivia's visit. If...If we have plenty to do together, I thought....I thought... maybe..." Suddenly she threw down the brochure. "Oh, Noel, I just know it's going to be another disaster and dear God, I do so want for it to be right this time."

He came to sit across the table from her, reaching over to cover her hand with his. "Then it will be—I promise you."

"You....you didn't mean it, did you–about her not loving me anymore?"

"No, Victoria, of course I didn't. But I had to make you admit how much you wanted and needed that love. You know," he went on after a moment, finally releasing her hand and picking up one of the brochures–one or two of the clippings. "These aren't the reason Olivia's coming. She's coming to be with her mother."

"Excuse me," she murmured. "I....I have to get a tissue." She stood up and moved toward her bedroom, but stopped in the doorway–one hand poised on the knob–and turned to look back at him. "You know, Noel, a wise and gentle man once told me I never have a hanky when I need one."

He watched her go on into the bedroom. Her last remark had totally mystified him, making him aware all over again how very little he knew about her. "Won't you reconsider, Victoria?" he asked when she returned. "At least a walk and perhaps lunch? It would do you good to get out for a while."

"Oh...all right, if you want to. Just let me put on my face."

Crossing the street in front of the building, they walked for over an hour in Central Park, enjoying the sunshine and the cold, crisp air. Victoria was grateful that Noel didn't push her to talk. Eventually they flagged down a taxi to take them to the Four Seasons for lunch and it was late afternoon when they finally got back to her apartment. As she inserted her key in the lock, Noel hesitated waiting for her invitation to come in, but she said nothing. "Well, I'll see you tomorrow then," he said at last, turning to leave.

Victoria watched her old friend walk away down the hall and the panic came surging back. "Noel," she called after him, "please...."

Her voice was so soft he wasn't even sure she'd spoken. He stopped to look back, discovering–somewhat to his surprise–that she was still standing in the doorway. "Did you say something?"

She started to shake her head–to deny she needed anyone–, but then she reached out to him. "Please– I...I can't be alone." He willingly returned, following her into the apartment and closing the door behind them. "Oh God, Noel," Victoria exclaimed seizing one of his hands in both of hers, "I want a drink! No–that's not exactly right. I...I want to get drunk–so drunk I can't think or feel..." Just as suddenly she let go of his hand, moving away to stand at the window and stare down at the darkening street–all the while drumming a feverish rhythm on the sill with her nails. "That's not true!" She whirled about again and came back to him–this time clutching the lapels of his overcoat. "I...I don't want to drink! Please—please don't let me! I can't be hung over tomorrow."

"Do you want me to stay here tonight, Victoria?" Noel asked gently as he slipped an arm around her shoulders.

He felt her slump gratefully against him and after a second she turned toward him a little touching his face. "Dear old thing. Thank you. I'll..I'll make sandwiches and tea and we can talk." The afternoon became evening; the evening night and still they sat side by side on the couch. They consumed pots of tea and they did indeed talk–or at least she did. Victoria, who once would never have admitted the details of her private life even to Noel, told him endless stories: about her pranks at Heathfield, about jobs she'd held before she could get work in the theatre, but nothing, he couldn't help but notice, about her family or the identity of the mysterious gentleman who had commented on her lack of a hanky. It was three a.m. before she fell asleep curled up at one end of the couch. How sweet, almost childlike, she is in her sleep, he thought. Dear God–let it work with her daughter this time! Oh, dear God–please let it work!"

Victoria had asked to borrow Noel's car for the drive out to the airport. It was important somehow that no one else be involved in this special day–no taxi driver, no hired chauffeur–not even Noel himself who had offered to go with her to help ease the tension. "What's the matter," she teased him. "Don't you trust me with your car?"

Chapter 15

There had never been an occasion for which Victoria dressed so carefully. Wanting to look her best for her daughter yet anxious not to appear too glamorous, she must have tried on and rejected at least a dozen outfits before at last deciding on a tweed pants suit and olive green turtleneck jumper. Her make-up was painstakingly understated and she chose the least ostentatious of her furs–the dark mink. The plane was due to land at 1:30 in the afternoon and being uncertain of the route to Kennedy Airport, she'd planned to leave about 11:30. This was one time she was not going to be late. Starting for the door, she reached automatically for a scarf and her dark glasses. "No," she said aloud to her reflection in the mirror, "I will not hide behind anything today and besides Olivia has always liked my hair."

The drive to Kennedy proved less complicated than she'd anticipated and by one o'clock she was pulling into a parking space at the International Terminal. Unfortunately when she went into the ladies' room for a final check of her appearance, she encountered a woman who raved on about *Macbeth* and asked for an autograph. Damn, Victoria thought, half-running now down the ramp leading to the arrival gates, life was a hell of a lot simpler when I could just be nasty! They were announcing the flight just as she got to the gate, but there would still be a delay while the passengers cleared customs. Victoria paced about the waiting room, at the same time trying to keep her eyes on the door leading out of the immigration area. She didn't want to miss the first glimpse of her daughter.

On the other side of that door, meanwhile, Olivia was waiting nervously for her luggage to come down the chute onto the carousel. "Do....do they ever lose things?" she inquired worriedly of Miss French, the flight attendant in whose charge she'd been placed at Heathrow.

"Not very often, believe me," the woman reassured her. "But it's a big plane, remember, and that means rather a lot of baggage."

Olivia nodded. "It's....it's just that I....I can hardly wait to see my mother." She glanced at the window through which people could be seen waiting to greet the arriving passengers, but the tinted glass made it difficult to make out faces. What if her mother wasn't there? Maybe she'd sent someone else–someone unfamiliar to her–or maybe no one would be there and she'd be all alone in a strange place. Her eyes filled with frightened tears.

"Don't worry, honey." The stewardess gave her a quick hug. "I'll wait with you if your mother isn't here yet."

"Thank you very much," Olivia replied politely even as she continued to search.

But a short while later they had located the two suitcases and each carrying one, they approached one of the customs officials. The little girl handed him her passport. "Well, well," the man said smiling broadly. "It appears the Redcoats have landed!"

"I beg your pardon, sir?" She looked puzzled. "My coat isn't red."

He chuckled. "Well, you look safe enough to me. Go along through." The stewardess picked up one of the valises again and started toward the door leading out into the main terminal. Doing the same, Olivia followed her–heart pounding.

Victoria had at last settled in one corner of the room away from the crowd and as the electric eye door swung open, she immediately spotted her daughter. Waves of love flooded over her and for a few seconds she hesitated–wanting to savor the moment. But then she saw the anxiety on Olivia's face. Dear God, Victoria thought, she's afraid I'm not here. "Darling!" she called out, moving rapidly through the throng of people, "over here!"

The child's face lit up in joyous relief. "Mummy!"

"Olivia!" Victoria knelt down and gathered her daughter in her arms–for once unmindful of the crowd around her. "Oh, dearest," she whispered, still holding her close. Finally then she released her, but only at arms' length so that she could look at her. "How are you, luv? Did you have a good flight?"

"Mummy, you're really here," Olivia whispered. "I mean–you came your...yourself!"

Victoria could think of nothing to say in reply; she wasn't even sure what she would say on the ride back to the city let alone for the next three weeks. But there was no panic–only a deep tenderness. Why have I always been so afraid, she wondered.

"Miss Windsor?" she heard a voice somewhere above her say.

"Yes?" Victoria stood up.

"You have a charming daughter. She's been a delight all the way from London."

"Thank you very much."

During this brief exchange Olivia never took her eyes off her mother's face. She was afraid to move, to breathe, even to blink for fear this would all turn out to be only another of the many dreams she'd had that one day her mother would want her. The stewardess had already handed Victoria the suitcase she'd been carrying. Olivia picked up the other one again and with good-byes exchanged, mother and daughter walked away together, up the ramp and across the main terminal toward the parking lot. "Where's your driver?" the little girl asked. "Waiting outside?"

Victoria experienced a flash of irritation which dissolved instantly into guilt. Of course her daughter had only seen her surrounded by the trappings of her success. "I'm afraid I'm the driver today....darling." How good it felt to use those terms of endearment which until now she'd always found so difficult to voice. "Do you think you can manage with your Mummy at the wheel?"

"Oh, yes. I just never thought of you driving a car yourself, I guess. I...I...." Olivia's voice trailed off and she stared down at her feet in their black patent leather shoes as they moved one in front of the other across the polished linoleum. It had always been so easy to anger her mother and she'd promised herself over and over again since the night of that wonderful phone call that she'd not do or say anything while she was here that would make her mother sorry she'd let her come.

How many times have I hurt her, Victoria thought meanwhile with a pang–so many times that she's actually afraid of me... "Well you see, darling, it just wouldn't pay for me to keep a car and chauffeur here." She was careful to keep her tone light. "Actually I borrowed your... your Uncle Noel's car today." She paused. Her natural sense of humor, always employed before to be clever–even to be cruel–could, after all, be used just as easily to help a little girl to relax. "So he's probably even more nervous than you are right now." Olivia glanced up and she winked broadly.

The child laughed happily. "Oh, Mummy, I can't believe I'm really here with you!"

"It does seem too good to be true, doesn't it, my darling." By then they were at the car. The two suitcases just fit into the back seat and moments later they were settled in the front. Victoria backed the car out of its parking space, paid the toll at the gate and soon they were on the road leading out of the airport. "Watch for signs that say 'Long Island Expressway', would you please, luv?" Why had it always been so hard to talk to her daughter when now she knew without the least bit of effort that something like this would make her feel important?

"All right, Mummy." Olivia leaned forward eagerly to watch the signs. "Oh, my goodness," she gasped the next moment, "the cars are on the wrong side of the road!"

Victoria laughed. "Only to you, luv. Here in the States, they're just where they should be, believe me." There was another pause, but this one was shorter. "My English mind, unfortunately, may not be." But to her horror Olivia's eyes suddenly brimmed with tears.. "No, no, I was only joking. It's all right. It's all right."

The little girl was crying in earnest now and Victoria became really concerned although for some reason it wasn't the old unreasoning panic. Pulling over into the breakdown lane, she stopped the car and turn to face the sobbing child. "What is it, darling? Please tell me." Olivia hesitated only briefly before flinging herself into her mother's arms. For a second Victoria was in turn startled, but then her arms tightened around her daughter. "It's all right, dearest. Please don't cry. Can't you tell me what's troubling you?" An awful thought occurred to her. "Didn't you want to come?"

"Oh yes, Mummy! She pulled back to look up into her mother's face. "More than anything else in the whole world!"

"Maybe those are happy tears, then, is that it?" Victoria asked tenderly, reaching up with one hand to brush the child's tousled hair away from her face.

Olivia smiled tremulously. "I guess that's it–happy tears. Oh, Mummy, I love you so much!"

"I...I love you, too." It was even more wonderful speaking those words directly to that dear face. "Oh, my darling. I have so much I want to tell you, but right now we'd both better dry our eyes and blow our noses so we can get this car back to the city before poor Uncle Noel dies of anxiety."

Olivia smiled and sniffed loudly. She opened her small purse and rummaged about inside. "I....I don't think I have a hanky."

Victoria shook her head, smiling in return. "You know I probably don't either. I never seem to have one when I need it."

"Me neither. Daddy says...." She stopped. "Is it all right if I talk about Daddy?"

"Of course it is."

"Well, I just wanted to be sure. 'Cause he gets awfully upset when I talk about you."

Luckily it wasn't the rush hour and with a quick glance over her shoulder Victoria had easily been able to slip the car out into the moving traffic once more. "Well, you know, darling, your father has every reason not to like me while I have no reason not to think well of him." Olivia looked bewildered. "But that's much too serious," Victoria continued quickly. "Tell me about school or the Girl Guides or whatever you'd like to talk about."

There was a brief silence while the child thought hard. "I....I like the Guides," she finally volunteered shyly.

"Is that all you have to say–'I like the Guides'?" Victoria was beginning to experience the same feelings of inadequacy she'd known many times in the past and unconsciously this lent a slight edge to her tone.

"I...I can't think of anything else, Mummy," Olivia confided tearfully. "I've never known what to say to you. Do...do I have to talk about anything?"

"No, luv. Of course you don't." And now her voice grew very tender. "Because you see, I....I understand. I've never known what to say to you either."

The little girl's blue eyes widened, "But how can someone as important as you not know what to say to people? And I'm your daughter."

"Don't you see, luv. That makes it especially hard. Because I want so much to say the right thing."

"Oh, dear!" Olivia exclaimed suddenly. "I forgot all about looking at the signs!"

"So did I," Victoria confessed. "Well, we'll just have to get off at the next exit and ask." When they did so, however, it was only to discover they'd been driving not toward the city, but further out onto Long Island. Mother and daughter looked at each other and began to laugh. There could have been no better icebreaker.

Noel had managed to wait until four o'clock before telephoning Victoria. There'd been no answer, of course, nor when he tried again ten minutes later or five minutes later and then every minute or so until finally he'd come upstairs to knock on her door–also to no avail. Since then he'd paced from her apartment to the elevator to the apartment to the elevator. By now it was after five and he was positive something terrible had happened. Suddenly he heard the elevator stop and with a wave of relief he recognized Victoria's voice. Incredibly he heard giggling; someone said, "Ssh–ssh!" and they appeared around the corner.

"Where in God's name have you been?" he sputtered. "Do you have any idea what time it is?"

"It....it wasn't Mummy's fault, Uncle Noel," Olivia said solemnly although the corners of her mouth twitched suspiciously.

"Ah—that's right," Victoria concurred. "The other driver was definitely at fault."

"Other driver!" he exploded. "What other driver? What's happened to my car?"

All at once they both burst into laughter and he realized he was being put on in grand fashion. "It seems we became rather lost," Victoria finally admitted.

"Oh, Uncle Noel," Olivia bubbled happily, "we went through the <u>same</u> toll booth <u>three</u> times, didn't we, Mummy?"

"We certainly did and finally the third time the man said–'Don't they teach you how to read in them limey schools?' " By now she had the door unlocked. "Coming in, Noel?"

"No, thank you. I just wanted to say hello to Olivia actually. I'll come down again with Jon before you go to the theatre."

Returning his car keys, Victoria gave him a quick hug and a kiss on the cheek. "Thank you for everything."

"You're welcome," Noel replied. "Both of you." He leaned down so that Olivia as well could give him a hug and a kiss and then hurried off down the hall, glancing back just as he turned the corner for one final wave.

"What did he mean, Mummy?" Olivia asked as they went on inside the apartment, Victoria closing the door behind them. "That we were <u>both</u> welcome?"

"Oh, I....ah...suppose he meant for the loan of the car."

"Oh." The little girl looked around the empty living room. "Where's Martha?"

"Martha doesn't work for me anymore, luv."

"Oh, Mummy, why? I was so looking forward to seeing her. I was looking forward most of all to seeing you, of course, but after that, Uncle Noel and Martha."

"We just couldn't get along, I guess." That was the truth, after all, or at least part of it.

"That's too bad. I liked her." But Olivia wasn't really that upset. What was a housekeeper, after all, when she had her mother.

"Well, believe it or not, I <u>can</u> cook." Victoria smiled–relieved that the little girl had accepted Martha's absence so readily. "And I've found someone to stay with you while I'm at the theatre. She's a student at the University where I'm doing some teaching. I'm sure you'll like her."

"Oh, Mummy, can't I come to the theatre with you?"

"I'm afraid you'd find most of the plays I'm doing frightfully dull. And I don't get home much before midnight. That's rather late for you, I should think. Now let's get you settled so we can have something to eat before I have to leave."

"All right." The child tried to smile. "Where's my room?"

Victoria had changed her mind about that at least once a day since she'd asked Olivia to come. Martha's room had seemed ideal, but then she got the idea of moving the other bed in next to hers so that she and her daughter could share a bedroom. Then she wondered whether she might need the nights to be alone and relax. But the housekeeper's room was off the kitchen at the other end of the apartment and after all the years already lost that seemed much too far away. It wasn't until today that she'd known what she wanted. However, she would let her daughter decide. "Well, that's up to you," she said now in answer to the question. "You can sleep in Martha's old room or we can move her bed into my room." Ever since Olivia could remember, she'd longed for her mother. Now they were even going to be roommates. It was all too wonderful to be true. "Well?" Victoria prompted gently.

"I'd....I'd like to share the room with you," Olivia whispered, "if it's all right."

"Oh, darling." Once more she reached out to draw her daughter close in her arms. "I was hoping that's what you'd say."

"Can we move the bed right now?"

"I thought Uncle Noel and Mr. Sinclair could do that for us. You haven't met Jon, have you? He's our managing director and he and Noel share a flat in this same building. But we can get you unpacked. In here." Victoria led the way into the bedroom. "I cleared out some bureau drawers and part of one closet just in case. That closet over there," she continued pointing, "and the drawers on the left in that chest."

"You really did want me to share your room, didn't you?" For the moment at least Olivia had entirely forgotten her disappointment at not being allowed to go to the theatre.

"Very much, yes, luv." Victoria swallowed hard. Together they unpacked the two valises and put away the clothing and toilet articles. "Well, I know one thing," she said decidedly at one point.

"What's that, Mummy?" She couldn't say that word often enough.

"You'll need a third suitcase to go home. After all, we are going to do some shopping while you're here, I should think."

"Could...could we get mother-daughter dresses? My friend, Heather, and her mother have them and we've never....we've never...."

"Come here, precious." Victoria sat down on the edge of her bed, motioning for Olivia to sit beside her. "Mother-daughter dresses, hm? I would be honored." She wanted to ask how Olivia could still love her that much, but she didn't have the courage. Instead all Victoria could do was to hold the little girl close as she'd so often dreamed of doing and it was several minutes before she happened to glance at the bedside clock. It was nearly six. "Oh, my goodness, luv, look at the time. You must be hungry. And I have some delicious lamb chops. I hope you like them. Tomorrow....tomorrow we'll go grocery shopping and you can pick out all your favorites." She stood up. "Want to help?"

"Oh yes, please."

Out in the kitchen Victoria turned on the oven for the frozen chips and prepared the chops for the broiler. Together they cut up vegetables for a salad and set the table. Conversation grew more casual now, aided by the fact that they had a job to do, and by the time they were settled in the dining alcove, any awkwardness between them had all but disappeared. When the doorbell rang at seven, Victoria couldn't believe how rapidly the time had passed.

"May I answer the door, Mummy?"

"Would you, luv. I'll start clearing the table."

Olivia ran to open the door, smiling happily up at the two men. "Hello, Uncle Noel."

"Hi, pussycat. This is Mr. Sinclair."

"I know. My Mummy told me."

"How long before I get to be Uncle Jon?"

She considered that weighty matter. "I shall have to think about that."

"Where is your Mummy?" Noel wondered if the spell still held.

But just then Victoria pushed open the swinging door from the kitchen. "We two poor helpless females need some masculine assistance." She smiled at them. "Jon, I presume you've met my daughter." Her voice fairly sang with pride.

Martha's bed was small and light and by tipping it on one side, the two men could easily move it from one room to the other. "Carrie hasn't come yet?" Noel asked when they were finished.

"No," Victoria replied, "and I'm already late, aren't I? Would one of you ring her up while I get ready? The number's by the phone." Olivia followed her mother into the bedroom. She hated to let her out of her sight. A few minutes later Noel knocked on the door. "Come in, luv."

He entered to find her seated at her dressing table brushing her hair, her daughter perched cross-legged on the bed watching. "Victoria, I'm afraid she's sick. She's been trying to find someone else. You know–I'm not performing tonight. How about Uncle Noel as a babysitter?"

"Mummy, may I please come with you?" Olivia pleaded. "I'm not in the least bit sleepy and it is my first night and I...."

Oh, honey, don't push her, Noel thought and somewhat apprehensively he waited for her answer. "Sweetheart, I..." Victoria paused. Much like the sanctuary of her bedroom, the hours at the theatre were to have been a welcome respite from her motherly duties. How long ago that all seemed now. "Oh, I suppose one evening won't hurt." She turned her head to smile at the little girl. "We can both sleep late tomorrow morning."

"Oh, Mummy!" Olivia jumped off the bed to run over and throw her arms around her mother's neck. "Oh, thank you! I'll be ever so good, I promise."

"Then after we get up, Uncle Noel will come with us grocery shopping to carry all those heavy bundles. Won't you, Uncle Noel?" Victoria threw him a glance which was pure mischief.

"My pleasure, ladies. My pleasure!"

At the theatre a short time later Victoria introduced everyone to Olivia, that same touching note of pride in her voice. "This is my daughter, Olivia...this is my daughter, Olivia"–over and over again.

"My," someone commented, "it must be exciting to have a famous mother."

The actress experienced another pang of guilt. Her little girl would have been far better off without a famous mother. "I don't know." Olivia was clearly puzzled. "She's just my mother."

When it came time for Victoria to prepare for the performance, Jon and Noel took her daughter out in front to watch the play from the audience. "You know, Mr. Sinclair," she confided happily, "I've never seen Mummy on the stage before." The play that evening was *Victoria Regina* and Olivia watched in astonishment as her mother aged from eighteen to eighty in the space of two and a half hours. "How does she do that?" she asked Noel at one point.

"Well, part of it is done with make-up," he explained in a whisper. "I'm sure she'll show you."

When the play came to an end, no one clapped harder than Olivia. Happening to glance down at her at one particular moment during the ovation, Noel saw her lips form two words: "My mother!" The curtain finally descended for the last time and the house lights came up. Here and there members of the audience stood and began to gather up their belongings, putting on coats, scarves and gloves against the winter night outside.

"Do we go backstage again now?" the little girl inquired eagerly. Several people in their immediate vicinity turned and stared. "What are they looking at, Uncle Noel?"

"You, I think, honey. You see..." He paused to bend down and whisper in her ear. "Not everyone gets to go backstage."

"Oh!" She giggled, clapping her hand to her mouth. "I forgot." She looked up at him and suddenly she grew thoughtful. "I guess everyone's not as lucky as I am."

He smiled and gave her a quick hug. "No, I guess they're not."

Backstage Jon left them to tend to some matters in his office and Noel took Olivia to Victoria's dressing room. The door was closed and he knocked. It was opened almost at once by her maid. The actress was still at her dressing table. She had removed the layers of latex used to form the famous jowls of the older Queen, but she had as yet to cream off her base. At the moment they came in she was talking on the telephone. Looking up and seeing who it was, she smiled and wiggled her fingers at them. "I'm sorry, Geoff," she was saying, "not tonight." The child immediately walked away, apparently to look at Victoria's costumes which were hanging on a rack against one wall. "Geoff, you know my daughter's here," Victoria went on, "and I want to spend every available minute with her." From the expression on her face Noel guessed the man had made some crude remark. Under different circumstances she would doubtless have responded in kind. As it was, she merely slammed down the receiver.

At the sound Olivia turned back to face her mother, swallowing hard to keep the tears back. "You...you can go out if you want to, Mummy."

"Come here, luv." She held out one arm to her daughter. Suddenly shy again, the child moved across the room to her mother. Victoria slipped the extended arm around her waist, drawing her close. "Noel, would you excuse us for a moment, please?"

"Of course." He and the maid left the room.

Once they were alone, Victoria turned to face the little girl, taking hold of both her hands. "Just now, darling, were you remembering that other phone call–in Cannes?"

She nodded. "Mummy–please, I don't want to be in the way so....."

"My dearest," she said emphatically even as tears threatened, "you are most definitely <u>not</u> in the way. But all this should probably wait until tomorrow. You must be tired, luv.... so for now we'll just say that the call in Cannes and this one have nothing to do with each other. All right?"

"Yes, Mummy." Olivia was a little confused, but somehow everything seemed all right. Just then she noticed the layers of latex which were sitting on various clay heads ready for the next performance. She wrinkled up her nose. "ICK! What's that?"

Victoria was relieved to have her daughter's attention at least temporarily diverted from the more serious subject. "That's how they make my wrinkles, luv. Some time I'll show you how I put them on. But for now let me get the rest of this stuff off so we can go home."

Noel returned a short time later with Jon. The watchman at the stage door had a taxi waiting and during the short ride back to the apartment building they were all quiet, each absorbed in his own thoughts. It wasn't until they were waiting for the lift that Victoria finally broke the silence. "Jon, dear luv..." She slipped her arm through his and rested her head briefly against his shoulder.

He looked understandably wary. "Yes?"

"I was...ah...wondering if I could...ah...have a couple of days off while my daughter's here?"

Instantly Olivia was wide awake. Noel saw the smile on the child's face, but could he possibly have heard correctly? Had Victoria actually requested to miss some performances–

Victoria who had told him repeatedly that the theatre was her life? The other man smiled, his thoughts much like Noel's. "I suppose your understudies could go on. When?"

The elevator arrived and they all got in, Victoria with her arm still through Jon's. She was very close to him; she was wearing no make-up and he thought she'd never looked more beautiful. "Well, actually..." She looked up at him coaxingly...."I was thinking of Christmas Eve and Christmas Day."

"Of course! Our biggest audiences! Do you know how many people will request a refund when they learn you're not appearing?" He tried to look stern, but unfortunately he couldn't stop smiling.

"I realize that." She laughed disarmingly, glancing over at Noel. "Nothing like humility, hm? Please, Jon, I....I wouldn't ask if it weren't frightfully important!" The elevator stopped at the men's floor and they stepped out. "Jon?" Victoria implored, catching the door to prevent it from closing.

"Oh, all right. Enjoy your holiday."

"Thank you." Her smile was radiant. "Perhaps we could all go to the Plaza for Christmas dinner–my treat." Victoria finally allowed the door to slide shut and the lift moved on upward. "Sleepy, luv?" she inquired.

"Only a little, Mummy." Olivia took hold of her hand.

"Only a little? Do you realize that back in England it's five o'clock in the morning?"

"It is? That means I've been awake almost a whole day then. And I didn't really sleep much the night before." How long ago that night seemed now–standing there with her hand clasped in her mother's–and how foolish all her fears.

The elevator came to a stop again at their floor and they walked down the hall to the apartment together–still hand in hand. Victoria hung up their coats. "Well, I'd say it's bedtime. How about you?"

The little girl hesitated. She hated to see this beautiful day come to an end. "I...I am a little hungry."

Victoria smiled. She couldn't remember another single day when she'd smiled so much. "Are you really or are you just trying to avoid going to bed?"

"Maybe some of both," Olivia admitted sheepishly.

"Oh, darling!" She leaned over to hug her daughter. "If your Daddy knew what I was doing....."

"I won't tell him. I promise."

Now Victoria laughed outright. "How about hot chocolate then and....and what?" Her midnight snacks had usually been more of the alcoholic variety.

"Cinnamon toast," Olivia proclaimed proudly. "We learned how to make it in Girl Guides."

"Cinnamon toast it is, then."

Together they prepared their snack in the kitchen, carrying it into the living room where Victoria lit the fire she'd laid earlier and settling cross-legged on the deep shag rug. "Is the toast all right?" Olivia inquired anxiously.

"Absolutely delicious," her mother assured her.

The atmosphere in the room, lit only by the flickering of the fire, was one of total peace and contentment. There could be no better time to talk and Victoria was afraid that if she let it go, the moment would be lost forever. "Darling?" Once again she was irresistibly drawn to reach out and stroke the child's shining hair. "Do....do you remember–in the car–I told you there was a lot I wanted to say to you?"

"Everything's all right, isn't it? I don't see how it could be any better."

"Yes, of course, but I wanted to....wanted to...." Desperately she hunted for the right words. Then all at once she knew. Before anything she needed an answer to one particular question–the question which earlier she'd been afraid to ask. "Olivia–dearest. Would...would you tell me something? Why...why over all these years..in spite of all the times I hurt you and disappointed you, did you never stop loving me?"

"You're my mother."

"But I'm afraid I didn't act like one."

"I...I didn't know how you were supposed to act. I've just always loved you."

Yes–even at her young age Olivia understood about loving, didn't she? Quite inadvertently, it seemed, she had stumbled on the right track. "Darling, did...did you ever think during all that time that I loved you just as much? That there were moments when I longed for you so terribly that it seemed more than I could bear? That I....I used to see other little girls with their mothers and wish so very much it could be us?" The child gazed down at the mug of hot chocolate now getting cold on the floor in front of her. "Please, sweetheart," Victoria continued gently, "just say exactly what you're thinking." Olivia's lower lip started to quiver. She was afraid that if she did say what was on her mind, her mother would be hurt and angry. "Won't you even look at me, luv?"

Slowly the little girl raised her head. "But....but, Mummy, if....if you loved me, why... why didn't you ever want to be with me? Like....like the Christmas I was supposed to come over or when...when we were in Cannes and you.....you....."

"Darling, did she ever think it....it could be possible to be afraid to love someone?"

"How can you be afraid to love someone?"

Victoria couldn't believe she was actually saying these things aloud to anyone– especially her daughter. "People....certain people hurt me very deeply when I wasn't even as old as you are...people I wanted to love and I.,...."

Olivia's eyes grew wider and filled with tears. "Who hurt you?"

"Well, mainly my...mother and father."

"Did...did they hit you?"

"No, luv. They....they just couldn't be bothered with me." She paused, struck suddenly by the horrible significance of her own words. "And what did I do but turn around and do the same thing to you, didn't I, my dearest? And it didn't make you afraid to love, did it, not even me?" Olivia looked dazed and Victoria could feel the old panic returning. What in hell made her think she could be a mother? She didn't even know how to talk to a child; she never had. "Never mind, luv." Hurriedly she picked up the dishes from the floor. "It's much too late and you should have been in bed a long time ago."

"No, Mummy, please!" Olivia began to cry in earnest. "I....I want to understand, really I do!'

Victoria immediately put the dishes down again and gathered her in her arms. "Don't, my dearest, don't! It's all right. It's all right." And before she knew what was happening she was crying herself, rocking the little girl in her arms. Even when at last they grew quiet, they remained cuddled together, arms around each other.

"Mummy?"

"Yes, my little luv?"

Olivia thought carefully about what she was going to say. "You don't ever have to be afraid to love me."

Tears threatened Victoria again. "I...I don't?" she managed to say.

"No, because....because I'll never, never, <u>never</u> hurt you and I'll always, <u>always</u> love you."

"You....you <u>do</u> understand, don't you? You are a very special little girl!" Olivia hugged tighter and Victoria leaned down to kiss her daughter on the top of her head.

They were silent once more then, the only sound in the room coming from the crackle and hiss of the flames while below on the street could be heard the muted noise of the traffic–quite light at this hour– the occasional blast of a horn, the high-pitched whine of a siren. After a while Victoria glanced idly down at her watch. Time seemed entirely irrelevant. "My goodness," she gasped, "do you have any idea how late it is?" There was no reply. Nestled against the mother for whom she'd longed for so many years, Olivia had fallen asleep. Tenderly she touched the child's face. "Darling, we better get you to bed."

"What, Mummy?" She stirred drowsily.

"Dearest, it's two in the morning. Let's go to bed." Victoria led the sleepy, little girl into the bedroom and helped her into her pajamas.

"I...I have to brush my teeth."

Victoria smiled. "I think that can wait until morning. Come on." She pulled back the sheet and blankets on Martha's bed. "Hop in."

"At least I have to say my prayers. Will you listen, please, Mummy?"

"All right." She sat down on the edge of the bed and Olivia knelt dutifully on the floor, folding her hands and closing her eyes. The sight of the child kneeling there beside her was almost more than Victoria's frayed emotions could withstand.

Olivia began with the customary, "Now I lay me down to sleep..." Then came what she called her "Please blesses". "Please bless my Daddy and Emily and David and Sara and...and my friend, Heather, and my teacher, Miss Cummings..but most of all, dear God, please bless my Mummy. I always did ask you to bless her, but now it's extra special because I'm with her. And thank you, dear God, because I kept praying that someday my mother would love me and now I know she always has...Amen."

When Olivia looked up at the close of her prayer, Victoria reached out again to touch her on the cheek. "What a beautiful prayer, luv. Thank you."

"It's all true," the child affirmed solemnly. " 'Cause you should never tell lies– especially to God."

"That's right," Victoria agreed with equal solemnity, "Now come on–into bed." Olivia slid obediently under the covers and she drew them up under her daughter's chin. The little girl held up her arms and her mother sat down again on the bed to hug and kiss her. "Good night, my darling."

"Good night, Mummy. I love you."

"I love you, too, dearest–so much. I'll be in in a few minutes. I just want to put the dishes in the sink." She stood up and started toward the door.

Olivia turned on her side and curled up. "It doesn't seem like I only got here today, does it, Mummy? It's like we've always been together."

That nearly destroyed Victoria entirely. "Yes, my luv, it <u>does</u> feel that way, doesn't it?"

She closed the door quietly. Tears were streaming down her cheeks as she picked up the dishes from their midnight snack and carried them into the kitchen. But how different these tears were from those she'd shed in the past. These were like some miraculous balm, cleansing and healing, washing away years of bitter loneliness. A short while later she was back in the bedroom, undressing quickly and noiselessly in the light from the city street below so as not to awaken Olivia. Before getting into bed herself, however, she stood for a moment looking down at the sleeping child and the night, which always before had seemed cold and empty, was full of love and warmth and belonging.

* * *

The next morning it was Olivia who stood watching her sleeping mother–just a little afraid to awaken her. Suppose yesterday was only a dream. No, it had been too real for that and besides she was hungry. She touched Victoria on one shoulder. "Mummy," she whispered, "wake up, please." Her mother stirred, mumbling something the child couldn't understand. She gave the same shoulder a little shake. "Mummy," Olivia said again–somewhat louder.

Finally Victoria rolled over from her side onto her back and opened her eyes. For just a few seconds she was startled to find her daughter standing by her bed. "Oh.... darling....what time is it?"

"Eleven o'clock."

"Eleven!" She glanced at her bedside clock. It can't be that late, she thought. I don't even remember lying down last night!

"Mummy—I'm starving!"

For as long as Victoria could remember waking up had been an unwilling return to painful reality. Today it was positively glorious. She smiled. "Absolutely starving, are you, luv?"

"I've been awake a whole hour and I....."

"Oh, darling!" Victoria flung back the covers, getting immediately to her feet. "Why didn't you wake me earlier?" The little girl shrugged. "Dearest–please come here a minute." She sat down on the bed again and drew her daughter over to stand in front of her. "You aren't still afraid of me, are you?"

"I...I didn't know if you liked having someone wake you up instead of waking up by yourself."

"I like having <u>you</u> wake me up."

Olivia smiled. Yesterday <u>had</u> been real. "Besides you looked like Sleeping Beauty. But then I got hungry."

Now Victoria laughed, hugging the little girl to her and kissing her on the cheek. "Well, let's get dressed and then we'll ring up your Uncle Noel and allow him to take us out for brunch."

"What's brunch?"

"Yes, I suppose that word might be new to you, luv. It's...let me see...the 'br' from breakfast and the 'unch' from lunch so it's kind of a special meal–half breakfast and half lunch."

"All right," Olivia replied, trying to sound very grown up, "we'll have Uncle Noel take us out for brunch."

Victoria smiled again, taking her daughter's face in both hands. "Do you know you are utterly adorable? I...I am so proud to be your mother."

"Oh, Mummy, are you really?" She threw her arms around her mother, but the force of the embrace sent the two of them tumbling backwards on the bed in gales of laughter. All too soon, however, the delicious moment was interrupted by the ringing of the telephone. "Damn," Victoria muttered under her breath, but they sat up and she reached for the receiver. "Hello."

"One moment, please, for an overseas call."

She put her hand over the mouthpiece. "I imagine it's your father, sweetheart."

"Oh, Mummy," Olivia gasped one hand flying up to her mouth. "I was supposed to ring him when I got here!"

She rolled her eyes. "Coo, luv, we're in trouble."

The little girl giggled.

"Victoria?" Andrew's voice was sharp with worry.

"Yes–I'm so sorry. Olivia forgot to ring you yesterday."

"It seems to me you might have seen to it!"

"I suppose so. But as I said, I'm sorry." Her tone was equally curt. Why after all these years did Andrew seem her enemy? "Would you like to speak to her? She's right here." Victoria handed the receiver to Olivia. "While you're chatting, I'll take my shower."

"Is he cross, Mummy?"

"Not with you, luv. But he was...ah...concerned, of course." Picking up her robe-- a deep purple velvet plush–from a near-by chair, she went on into the bathroom.

"Hi, Daddy," Olivia said into the mouthpiece. "It wasn't Mummy's fault. I didn't tell her I'd promised to ring you up."

Andrew shook his head. The child refused to stop defending her mother. "Well, never mind." He hesitated unsure how to say it. "Is your mother still there with you?"

"No, Daddy." She sounded puzzled. "She's in the bathroom."'

"Oh, I see....ah...Honey, is everything really all right? You can come home sooner, you know."

Olivia became alarmed. "I don't want to come home early! Oh, Daddy, everything is wonderful–just the way I've always dreamed!"

"I'm glad, darling. Write to me now and ring me in about a week."

"I will. I won't forget again. Bye, Daddy."

For a moment after he'd hung up the telephone Andrew continued to sit unmoving. It almost seemed as though Olivia were telling him the truth. Could the miracle have happened? Then why was he suddenly afraid?

Victoria, meanwhile, had finished her shower and was just slipping into her robe when she heard her daughter hang up the telephone. "It's all right, darling. You can come in."

When the little girl opened the door, her mother was tying her hair back from her face in preparation for putting on her make-up. "May I please watch you, Mummy?"

The application of her make-up had always been a private ritual. No one should witness the donning of her public mask. Suddenly now it was all different. "If you'd like, but would you do one thing for me first? Ring up your Uncle Noel and tell him to come fetch us in about an hour. The number's in the little book next to the telephone. Can you wait that long to eat, luv?"

"I think so."

Victoria laughed. "You sound doubtful. Fix yourself a snack then. There's toast and jam and milk."

Olivia went back to the telephone. "What's Uncle Noel's last name, Mummy?"

"Of course you wouldn't be apt to know that, would you? He's always been Uncle Noel to you. It's St. John."

The little girl looked up the number and dialed. Noel had been anticipating the call and was relaxing over coffee reading the newspaper while he waited. "Hello."

"Hello, Uncle Noel. It's Olivia."

"You know, I rather thought so since no one else calls me Uncle Noel."

She giggled. "Tell him to behave himself," Victoria called from the bathroom as she finished smoothing on her base and reached for the eyebrow pencil.

"Uncle Noel," Olivia relayed the message, "Mummy says to behave yourself." She laughed again. "He says he always does, Mummy. Uncle Noel, we've decided you may take us out for <u>brunch</u>." Unconsciously she stressed the new word she'd just learned.

"Oh, <u>brunch</u>, is it? My, won't we be elegant! But don't tell me you two lazy people weren't up in time for breakfast?"

"Uncle Noel, we didn't go to bed until two-thirty in the morning," she announced importantly.

"Shocking! Well, if I can eat a regular lunch, you have a deal."

"Oh, good. Mummy says in about an hour. Bye."

What could possibly have gone on until two-thirty in the morning, Noel wondered. But whatever it was, it must mean everything was all right.

Olivia skipped back into the bedroom and pulling over a small stool, she sat down to watch her mother. Victoria's head was tipped back, her eyelids half-closed and for a moment she'd forgotten everything but the fascination she invariably found in the study of her own face. "Why are you doing that?" the child asked wide-eyed. Victoria jumped. "Oh, Mummy, I'm sorry. I didn't mean to scare you."

But her mother smiled. "See that line along my eyelid. I tip my head back and close my eyes partway to give it a chance to dry."

"But why do you draw a line on your eye?"

The question annoyed her slightly, but privacy was only another word for loneliness, Victoria reminded herself, and she gave no outward sign of her passing irritation. "It makes your eyes look bigger and your lashes longer," she explained.

"But you have such beautiful eyes all by themselves. Why do you have to put all that stuff around them?"

"Believe me, luv, this is much less than I have used." The pressure was telling a little and she needed to ease her daughter away from her for a while. "But perhaps you should run along and start getting dressed, too. I'll be able to finish more quickly alone." No sooner had she uttered the words, however, than she regretted them as looking in the mirror she saw Olivia's face crumple in dismay. The little girl got up off the stool and moved away toward the bedroom. Damn, Victoria thought, haven't I already hurt her enough? "But then," she continued at once, "I suppose you're faster than I am since you don't have to put all this stuff on your face."

"I'm sorry I said that. I...I hurt your feelings, didn't I?"

Of course–that was it. The remark had hurt a little, just as <u>her</u> unthinking words had hurt her daughter. Loving <u>meant</u> letting yourself be vulnerable, but somehow that no longer frightened her. "I suppose so, sweetheart, but..."

"Mummy, please, I feel so bad." Olivia laid her hand on her mother's arm. "I said I'd never hurt you and now I already have."

Victoria turned around and sat down on the stool herself. "Oh, dearest.." She drew the child over and down on her lap. "I know you're probably much too big for this, but I've never had the chance to do it until now."

"That's all right." She put an arm around her mother's neck. "It feels nice. Mummy, I'm truly sorry. I....."

"Hush, luv, you don't have a thing to apologize for. It's only natural for you to wonder about things I do. I guess I just want to appear perfect in your eyes and I...."

"But you <u>are</u>, Mummy! I didn't mean anything wrong about the make-up. I....I just wondered, that's all and you really <u>do</u> have beautiful eyes."

"Thank you, luv." Victoria's arms tightened around the little girl's waist. "And then I suppose I've always realized myself that I wore too much make-up."

"Then why did you?"

"Well, just the right amount highlights your natural features–but why so much, hm?" The child nodded and again Victoria paused to think. "I suppose I was hiding behind it–just like the dark glasses and those silly scarves I always wore."

Olivia recalled their talk of the night before. "Because you were afraid?" she inquired solemnly.

"Oh, darling," Victoria whispered, "yes." She drew her daughter closer and they stayed that way for several minutes.

"Mummy, we're not going to be ready for Uncle Noel."

"You know you're right, but I don't care. I have a lot of hugging to make up for."

The little girl giggled happily way down in her throat and snuggled against her mother.

And so it was that when Noel arrived a half hour or so later, he at first got no answer to his knock. He could remember a time when this would have alarmed him. Now he merely knocked again more loudly. "St. John Escort Service reporting as requested. Let's look sharp here! Other clients to see to! What! What!"

At last the door opened a crack and Victoria peered out at him. He could see she was laughing. "Hmmmm." She appeared to be studying him. "Afraid you won't do—won't do at all. No..no...no...no." Shaking her head, she closed the door, but opened it almost at once again, smiling at him. "I'm frightfully sorry, Noel. We're running a little late."

Now that he was able to see her completely, he couldn't help himself and he stood in the doorway and stared. She had never looked so lovely. She glowed. She positively glowed. And her smile became broader as she saw the look on his face. "Well, are you coming in or are you just going to stand there?" She moved back toward the bedroom. "We won't be long."

"Victoria," he called after her, "am I allowed at least one 'I told you so'?" He grinned.

"Yes, I suppose you are." She ran back to throw her arms around his neck and kiss him on the cheek. "Oh, thank you. I never believed such happiness could exist, but...but we've got to hurry. My....my daughter is absolutely starving." She whirled about again and disappeared into the other room.

Anticipating a considerable wait, Noel settled himself in one of the comfortable armchairs. From inside the bedroom he heard constant chatter punctuated by frequent bursts of laughter. And this from a mother and daughter who could never find anything to say to each other! It was actually only about fifteen minutes before they came out ready to go. "Well, how often does a man have the opportunity to be the escort of two such lovely ladies?" he asked as he helped them on with their coats.

Olivia sighed wistfully. "Oh, Uncle Noel, I'll never be as beautiful as my mother."

"You know, I don't believe that for a minute. Shall we?" He held open the door and closing it again, he offered an arm to each of them. "I took the liberty of booking at 'The Top of the Sixes', Victoria," he continued as they walked together down the hall. "I know that's a favorite of yours and Olivia will be able to see the city."

With her free hand she reached up to pat him on the cheek. "Perfect, luv."

"Mummy," the little girl asked a few minutes later riding down in the lift, "are you and Uncle Noel going to get married someday?"

"Your Uncle Noel and I are much too clever to spoil a good friendship with marriage, aren't we, luv?"

"Your mother and I are just friends, Olivia."

"Oh...I see." She appeared satisfied, but secretly she still wondered.

* * *

It was only a short taxi ride to 'The Top of the Sixes'–so called because it is located at the very top of 666 6th Avenue. The maitre d' greeted them as they stepped off the elevator. Obviously he had been waiting for them. "Miss Windsor–good afternoon, madame." He bowed and kissed her hand. He saved his grandest manner for the famous and high-tipping and Victoria qualified on both counts. "Mr. St. John, sir." Another bow. "And who is this beautiful young lady?" He shook Olivia's hand with great ceremony.

"This is my daughter," Victoria explained. The same note of pride was evident in her voice and her old friend found it deeply touching.

The maitre d' escorted them to a window table drawing back the actress' chair for her while Noel did the same for Olivia and presenting each of them with a menu, he bowed once more and withdrew. "Goodness, Mummy," the little girl exclaimed, "he acts as if you really <u>are</u> a queen instead of just pretending to be one like you did in the play last night!" Victoria and Noel laughed. "I don't see why that's so funny," she protested.

"It isn't really, sweetheart." Noel was quite serious now. "Because your mother <u>is</u> a queen–actually."

"Oh, shut up!" Victoria slapped him playfully on the hand pretending to be embarrassed, but then she blew him a kiss. "Thank you, luv. That's sweet...but now let's see what we all want to eat."

She and Noel opened their menus, but Olivia ignored hers. Instead she stared open-mouthed at the city now spread out below them as far as she could see in any direction. "Is it bigger than London, Mummy?"

"Perhaps a little, luv. But not much. Now decide what you'd like to have and then you can look out the window as much as you like." Obediently Olivia turned her attention to the menu.

"Motherhood not as difficult as you thought, Victoria?" Noel raised an eyebrow in a facial mannerism she found ridiculously like her own. But she merely smiled in reply and shook her head.

At that point the waiter approached. "Cocktail, Miss Windsor?"

Noel saw her hesitate briefly. "Yes..a..ah..Bloody Mary, please," she replied at last.

"Mr. St. John?"

"Martini–very dry with a twist."

"And for the young lady?"

"Olivia?" Victoria reached over to touch the child lovingly on the arm. "Orange juice?"

"Yes, please. Mummy, what are strawberry c-r-e-p-e-s?" She spelled out the unfamiliar word.

"Crepes, luv. Very thin pancakes rolled up around strawberries and sprinkled with powdered sugar."

"Oh, that sounds yummy!" Olivia ran her tongue out over her lips. "I'll have that, and hot chocolate, please."

As the meal progressed, Noel couldn't help but notice the difference between the present occasion and their miserable day at the zoo. Then the little girl had barely spoken a dozen words to her mother. Now it was "Mummy, this" and "Mummy, that" and twice she even left her seat to come and sit in her mother's lap. But it was Victoria he enjoyed watching the most–brushing Olivia's hair back from her face, leaning over to put her arm around the child's shoulders and point out some spot of interest in the city below, even stealing a bit of her crepes and laughing all the time–a merry, pealing sound utterly unlike the harsh, mirthless laugh he'd actually come to dread. Unconcealed by either hat or dark glasses, her beauty sparkled irresistibly and he saw he wasn't the only one who noticed. Although at the moment she was unaware of the fact, Victoria was the center of male attention in the room.

When they had finished eating, they moved on to a large supermarket located on the ground floor of a near-by apartment building. Olivia pushed the shopping cart up and down the aisles while mother and daughter piled it high with every kind of food imaginable. And through it all Noel trailed uncomplainingly along behind them, not minding in the least that his presence seemed superfluous–that he was of no real use except when it came to loading the bags of groceries into a taxi and then helping to carry them up to the apartment. He knew that were it not for him all this might never have come to be and that was more than enough.

And thus it was that Olivia's visit began. The ten days between her arrival and Christmas Eve flew by and except for Radio City Music Hall and the Empire State Building they never did find time for any of Victoria's painstakingly planned activities. They did manage an elegant lunch each day at the Plaza or the Four Seasons or "21" and incidentally Olivia saw her mother's every performance; there was no further mention of a babysitter.

Perhaps, however, they both enjoyed the shopping most of all. After the years of having presents delivered, Victoria wanted the joy of watching her daughter select her gifts herself and together they bought dresses and jeans and sweaters and a powder blue winter coat trimmed with fox fur. The little girl would indeed require a third suitcase –if not a fourth.

And what would Christmas in New York be without a visit to the city's very own "mystical, merry toyland"–more commonly know as FAO Schwarz. Olivia chose a three and a half foot tall walking doll–one with no strings or batteries; she was emphatic about that. Of course her new doll, whom she named Victoria, had to have an extensive wardrobe. And one more thing–she wanted a doll's house.

With a pang Victoria gave the clerk the address in England. Naturally this larger item would have to be shipped. "It will get there almost as soon as you do," she tried to reassure her daughter, "and then it will be like having Christmas all over again."

"Not without you, it won't," the little girl whispered. She saw the pain on Victoria's face. "You...you wish I could stay, too, don't you?" All her mother could do was nod. Tears were too close to the surface. "Could we go home now, please, Mummy?"

"If you want to, luv—-of course,"

It was hard to think of anything to say after that; indeed they talked very little all during the block and a half walk back to their building. It was not, however, the uncomfortable silence of earlier years, but rather a mutual aching loss for words. Upstairs in the apartment they removed coats and hats and boots, still without talking, and Victoria lit the fire. "Tea, luv?" But as she gently brushed her daughter's hair, tousled now from her knitted cap, back from her face, she saw the blue eyes fill with tears. "Oh, sweetheart!" She reached out to hug her, but Olivia pulled away and ran into the other room.

Hurrying after her, Victoria found that she had flung herself face down on her bed. "Don't, dearest, please," she said, sitting down beside her to stroke the small anguished back. But the child only cried all the harder–great heartrending sobs which seemed more than her body could withstand. "Please, darling, sit up and look at me." Olivia shook her head, burrowing her face still deeper into the pillow. "Dearest, how can I put my arms around you if you won't sit up?" Somehow the little girl managed to scrunch herself up on all fours, turn around and throw herself into her mother's lap–all in one motion. "Well, that was quite a trick," Victoria observed lightly.

"Mummy, please, please, please don't send me back!"

"Oh, my darling, if you only knew how much I want you with me. But we're not being fair to your Daddy. He loves you, too, and he would miss you dreadfully."

"But he has Emily and Davey and Sara so I should stay here!" Olivia reasoned desperately, finally lifting a blotched and tear-stained face.

"Sweetheart–you don't know how it hurts me to have to say this, but when.... when I left you and your father, I...I really lost the right to have you with me."

"No, Mummy, no!" Dangerously close to hysteria by now, Olivia seized hold of her mother's shoulders, shaking them with all her childish strength. "You were afraid then so that doesn't count, don't you see?"

"All right, luv–hush, hush." Victoria began to kiss and caress and rock the distraught child. "You must stop, dearest. You'll make yourself ill."

"Mummy, please–please," she still begged although she was calmer now.

Dear God, I'm...I'm actually being given another chance, Victoria thought all at once, and if I don't at least try, I'll never forgive myself. "If you really want to come and live with me, dearest," she heard herself saying almost before she was aware that she was once again speaking out loud. "I'll do whatever is necessary."

Olivia sat up to look at her mother. "Oh, yes, Mummy. What do you have to do?"

"Hire a solicitor, I suppose. I'm sure Mr. Matthews, my agent, can suggest one."

"Then I can stay?"

Sadly Victoria shook her head. "No, I'm afraid not. Legal things like this can take months and in the meantime you'll still have to go back to England when the three weeks are up. If I kept you now, you see, I would be breaking the law and that would only hurt my chances in the long run."

"But....months," Olivia whispered forlornly.

"It....it will go by quickly and we...we can write and telephone and no matter what, I'll be home in May and then we'll see a lot of each other." The mood had to be changed, Victoria thought. Tomorrow was Christmas Eve and no gloom of impending parting could be allowed to dim that. She placed one hand on either side of her daughter's face and looked directly into her eyes. "We will be together finally, Olivia. That I promise you as fervently as I have ever promised anything! You do believe me, don't you, darling?"

The little girl's tears had vanished completely now. After all, her mother had promised. "Yes, Mummy, I believe you."

"Good. Besides we still have nearly a fortnight and we aren't going to let anything spoil that, are we?" Now since I don't have a performance this evening, how does this sound? Dinner at the Plaza where all those waiters spoil you so outrageously and then the cinema?"

Olivia shrugged. "Couldn't we just do stuff?"

"Stuff, hm? Well...ah...why don't we start out with a supper in front of the fire? Then we'll see what happens from there?" Supper was mugs of chicken noodle soup–a mutual favorite–followed by sausages cooked over the flames and finally chocolate ice cream. "You're right," Victoria agreed at one point. "This is much better than the Plaza,"

When they had finished eating and done the dishes, there were several hotly contested games of checkers, followed by the sharing of a coloring book and finally with her daughter in bed, Victoria excused herself. When she knew Olivia was coming, she'd purchased a copy of *Little Women*, the story Uncle Bertie had read to her at Balmoral. Now she took it out of the desk in the living room and returned to the bedroom, the book held behind her back. "Sweetheart, would...would you mind if I read to you for a while?"

"Oh, Mummy, please–would you?" Victoria must have read for over an hour until at last the child grew sleepy. "See, Mummy," Olivia murmured drowsily as she turned on her side, curling up in a ball under the covers. "Isn't stuff fun?"

It had been a perfect evening and not once had they allowed themselves to think of the pain of saying good-bye.

* * *

Christmas actually began for Victoria early on the morning of Christmas Eve when she was rudely awakened by an excited eight year old. "They're here with the tree, Mummy!" Olivia was kneeling on her bed and shaking her by the shoulder. "They're here with the tree!"

Victoria rolled over onto her back and opened her eyes. How many nights now had she known the luxury of falling asleep instantly without the help of pills or liquor– waking again the next morning refreshed and eager to begin another day?" She smiled up at her daughter. "Can you ask them to wait a minute, luv? I just want to splash some water on my face and run a brush through my hair." Was this the same woman who had customarily spent a minimum of one hour on her make-up?

"All right, Mummy." Olivia darted back into the living room. "My mother says–'Just a minute, please'," she announced proudly.

Victoria did indeed join them shortly. Her freshly brushed hair rippled in honeyed waves over her shoulders, its golden color even more startling against the deep purple of her robe, and her face glowed as much from happiness as its recent washing. The two men who were fastening the tree into its metal stand stopped their work to stare at her—open-mouthed. Victoria smiled a little. She was accustomed to male admiration, but what she failed to realize was that at the moment there was only her own natural beauty to occasion such a reaction. "Over there by the window, please." She indicated a spot which she and Olivia had already cleared of furniture and tipped them generously.

"Thank you, ma'am," they said appreciatively and touching the brims of their caps, they left.

"May we start decorating it now, please?" Olivia asked eagerly. Many of the Americans employed at the theatre had loaned them an ornament or two and others–- people they'd met in the lobby or the elevator, even the doorman and the lady at the local newsstand–had also contributed. They adored Olivia, of course, but Victoria would have been amazed how many of them liked her as well.

"Do you suppose we could at least have some breakfast first? Waffles, perhaps?" She'd learned this was a particular favorite of Olivia's.

The little girl grinned. "Well, I suppose I could wait for waffles."

"I rather thought so–then into the kitchen, m'lady!" Victoria made a sweeping bow in the direction of the swinging door.

"Oh, Mummy!" She giggled happily.

Ever since Olivia arrived, Noel had been torn: wanting to give Victoria and her daughter as much time as possible alone together yet hungry to witness their shared happiness. This morning it was especially difficult, knowing they would be decorating their tree, and about noon, unable to stay away any longer, he went upstairs. Briefly he stood in the hall outside the apartment, savoring the happy sounds he could hear even through the heavy metal door. The radio was playing Christmas music. At last he knocked.

At once there were running footsteps and Olivia flung the door open. "Oh, Uncle Noel, come in, but you're much too late! We're almost finished! We've been at it for ever so long, you know!"

"Have you?" he managed to reply for he'd barely heard a word she said. Victoria was standing a few steps back from the tree–an ornament in each hand–trying to decide where to place them and the expression on her face–rapt, open, utterly without affectation–drove everything else from his mind.

At last she turned to look at him. "Merry Christmas, luv. You know everyone was so generous with their ornaments, I do believe we've run out of room!"

"Mummy, may we please give Uncle Noel his present now?"

"Well, why not, hm? I think it's already under the tree."

Olivia plopped down flat on her stomach to rummage about under the lower branches and in only a moment or so she scrambled back to her feet, triumphantly grasping a large, flat package. "Merry Christmas, Uncle Noel!" she sang out happily, thrusting the gift into his hands. "From Mummy <u>and</u> me!" He sat down on one of the two couches and holding the package in his lip, began slowly to unwrap it. "Hurry up, Uncle Noel!" the little girl urged him.

"Let him take his time, luv," Victoria remonstrated gently, knowing somehow that her old friend would wish to hold onto the moment as long as possible.

At last Noel lifted the cover of the box and pushed aside the tissue paper. His vision blurred and had he been offered the greatest role of his career at that minute, he would still have been unable to utter a word. For inside the box lay a framed photograph of mother and daughter, dressed in identical long light blue dresses, ruffles at the wrist and throat, and seated side by side against a pale, ivory background. Hands joined loosely between them, they were smiling at each other so lovingly it hurt to look at them. He glanced up at Victoria and Olivia who were on the other couch facing him waiting expectantly for his reaction and as it happened, sitting in the identical pose. "I...I don't know what to say," he confessed. "I'll....I'll treasure it always, of course. I.....I...."

"Did you read what we wrote on it?" Olivia asked excitedly. "Well, <u>Mummy</u> wrote it, but I helped think it up and I signed my own name!"

Noel shook his head. In his overcome state at seeing the picture he hadn't noticed the inscription. Now he looked down again and read—"But for you, dearest Noel, this picture might never have been. Our love and gratitude always, Victoria and Olivia." There was no way he could stop himself. He was crying now and they came at once to comfort him, sitting one on either side–Olivia to rest her hand on his–Victoria to pillow her head against his shoulder. It was a moment he'd never expected to experience and for a while he simply reveled in it. "The afternoon is my treat, ladies," Noel said at last. "What is your pleasure?"

After some discussion they decided on a carriage ride in Central Park–their destination "The Tavern on the Green". After lunch they rented a toboggan and finally snow-covered, tired and happy, they flagged down a taxi to take them back to their building. Noel stopped in only long enough to collect his treasured gift. "After all," he teased Victoria, "some of us have a performance this evening!"

* * *

"Where are we going to church, Mummy?" Olivia asked later as they cleared away the last of the dinner dishes.

"Church?" Victoria replied rather stupidly. Her last attendance at any religious service had been Heathfield's compulsory chapel.

"Yes." Now it was the child who looked confused. "Christmas Eve."

"Oh...ah...I hadn't really decided." No, Victoria thought at once, I will not hedge. She put the dishes back on the table and sat down again in her chair. "To be perfectly honest with you, darling," she continued aloud, "I haven't been much in the habit of going to church. However, we can go tonight if you'd like."

"Oh yes, I would. I love the singing and the candles and everything!" Olivia had become extremely sensitive in a comparatively short time, however, to every nuance of emotion which touched her mother's face, no matter how briefly, and now she understood immediately that Victoria was troubled. "Mummy, are you all right?" the little girl inquired worriedly, also setting her dishes down and coming around the table to place one small concerned hand on her mother's arm.

"You've had a lovely life with your Daddy, haven't you, sweetheart?" Victoria's voice was choked with emotion.

"Yes, I guess I have." She was immediately apprehensive. "Why?"

"Perhaps you're better off with him, after all."

"Oh, no , Mummy! No!" Olivia's words tumbled out one on top of the other. "Is it because I asked about church? I don't have to go to church. I don't even like it that much, I......"

"Hush, luv, hush, you haven't done anything wrong...and you know, I think I'd <u>like</u> to go myself. There should be services listed in the newspaper. We'll just dump the dishes in the kitchen and then we'll have a look, shall we?" Victoria spoke quickly, trying to dispel the mood. Her remorse concerning the first eight years of Olivia's life was something with which she must deal herself. There was no reason to make her daughter feel guilty as well. A few minutes later they were settled side by side on the couch, studying the services listed in *The New York Times*.

"Let's go to one we can walk to, Mummy," Olivia suggested eagerly. "It'll be fun coming home afterwards. We can sing carols."

Victoria agreed although secretly she rather doubted the wisdom of walking in New York City after midnight. "I don't think this one's very far." She pointed to a particular listing. "Fifth Avenue Federated–just a block or two downtown from the Plaza."

They left for the church about ten-thirty. It was just beginning to snow–large, lacy flakes which glittered in the street lights as they walked hand in hand along Central Park South and up Fifth Avenue to the lovely old brownstone building. "Oh, Mummy," Olivia breathed fervently, "it really feels like Christmas Eve, doesn't it?"

Victoria had been deep in thought of other Christmases. And what miracle had brought her at last to this holiday–walking to church with her daughter through the crisp night air? "It's just perfect, my darling." She squeezed the little girl's hand even more tightly in hers. The church was already quite full when they entered. "Where do you like to sit, luv?"

"Down near the front so I can see everything. Oh, Mummy, look!" She led the way over to a small table where a carved wooden creche was displayed. With a cautious index finger she reached out to touch reverently the central figure of the baby Jesus.

Dear God, Victoria thought, thank you for not allowing me to miss all her childhood. "Ready to sit down, sweetheart," she asked aloud. Olivia nodded and they turned to follow an usher down the center aisle to the fourth row from the front.

The interior of the church was painted in a soft beige tone, the vaulting crisscrossed by dark brown beams. A single candle stood at the end of every other pew and along the sides and back of the chancel were multiple-branched candelabra. A bank of red poinsettias began on the floor, extending all the way up to the altar which itself was roped with holly. "Isn't it beautiful, Mummy?" Olivia whispered.

"Breathtaking, luv, but we mustn't talk now, you know."

"I keep forgetting. Daddy says the only person you should talk to in church is God and I guess, maybe Jesus, too."

"Your Daddy's absolutely right, dearest."

They didn't have long to wait, however, before the organ pealed forth the opening notes of the processional hymn, "Oh, Come All Ye Faithful". The children's choir appeared first in blue robes with white collars and huge black velvet bows under their chins, followed by the youth choir, the adults and finally the two ministers. The procession moved past them and up into the chancel to file into the pews. As the final words of the carol were sung, one of the two ministers approached the lectern to open the service. "It is with great joy that I welcome you here tonight," he said, "to celebrate the anniversary of the single most momentous event in the course of human history–the one which more than any other changed the world as it then existed. My heart is full as I speak to you tonight–full of the love of Christ, our Savior–by the Grace of God. Amen."

"What's his name, Mummy?" Olivia whispered, straining to see the order of worship in the dim light.

Victoria tipped her paper so that the candlelight fell across the correct spot. "It says–Senior Minister, darling." Let's see." She turned to the bottom of the last page. "The...ah... Reverend Jason Eliot."

"He looks nice, lots younger than Rev. Fletcher–the vicar at my church in London," she added by way of explanation.

Interesting, isn't it, Victoria thought, how a child will sense something in a person. The associate minister, Martin Davison, read the scripture and gave the pastoral prayer, but somewhat later in the service when the Reverend Eliot rose again and crossed the chancel to the pulpit to deliver his Christmas meditation, she found herself looking at him more closely. He wasn't the sort she'd have noticed in passing–just above average height, slightly built and he wore his brown hair closely cut–especially in a day when men's hairstyles were generally longer. What caught and held her attention, however, was the serenity of his expression. The effect was intensified as he began to speak–his tone soft, yet firm–and listening, Victoria felt oddly comforted as though he were talking directly to her.

"And so I command you," he was saying now in conclusion, "that ye shall love one another even as I have loved you. For God so loved the world that he gave his only begotten Son–that whosoever liveth and believeth in Him–shall never die, but shall know life eternal and everlasting in Christ Jesus–Amen." The carillon pealed from the steeple and rising again with the rest of the congregation to sing the recessional hymn, "Joy to the World", Victoria experienced an incredible exhilaration and all because this man had spoken to her.

As the two ministers followed the last of the choir down the center aisle from the chancel, Jason allowed his eyes to move over the congregation, smiling pleasantly in greeting whenever he saw a familiar face. All at once his gaze happened to fall on Victoria. Her blonde hair shone in the candlelight and her eyes were glistening–with unshed tears perhaps. Could his words have moved this beautiful woman so profoundly? Before he realized it, he had nearly walked up the heels of the last member of the choir recessing directly in front of him. Noticing the other man's reaction, Martin Davison smiled to himself. Perhaps the Reverend Eliot was human, after all.

Out in the narthex Jason listened as the final notes of the hymn were sung. Hurriedly he attempted to compose himself. "Quite a beautiful woman, hm?" his associate observed under his breath even as the first parishioners were approaching to greet them.

Jason stiffened. "Being a bachelor, you are perhaps somewhat more apt to notice such things."

"You know who she is, don't you? Victoria Windsor, the English actress."

"This isn't the time or the place, Rev. Davison," Jason remonstrated gently. "But I <u>am</u> familiar with the name." At that moment, however, Victoria and Olivia came out into the narthex and Martin watched as his boss' eyes were unavoidably drawn to her. He wasn't the only one. Heads turned as she walked the length of the hall toward the outside door, but only Martin dared approach her. He wanted to meet her himself, of course, but even more he wanted to see how Jason would react upon coming face to face with her.

"Miss Windsor, I'm Martin Davison, the assistant minister." He extended his hand in greeting. "It's an honor to have you worshiping with us this evening. I've already had the pleasure of seeing your Candida and I hope to attend other performances."

At such a moment it unsettled her to be recognized. "Thank you very much," she murmured a trifle breathlessly, but she smiled her most gracious public smile as she returned his handshake. "However, I really should be getting my daughter home to bed now."

"May I introduce you to someone first, Miss Windsor," he persisted. "It won't take but a minute."

"Very well," she agreed. But then almost at once she realized to whom he was referring and she became very nervous. Such a man seemed so far above her–not quite human somehow.

Martin placed a hand at her elbow to escort her across the narthex. "Jason, I knew you'd want to greet our distinguished visitor before she left." He observed the other man closely. "Miss Windsor, our senior minister, the Reverend Eliot."

A little hesitantly Victoria offered her hand. "Rev. Eliot, the service was terribly moving. Thank you."

Jason prided himself on his self-control and yet as he'd watched the actress walk toward him, he could feel his palms perspiring. Surreptitiously he wiped them on his robe before accepting her gloved hand. He felt it tremble slightly in his and for the first time he heard that bell-like English voice. "Miss Windsor," he managed to reply, "what a pleasure to have you with us." But he never took his eyes from her face and he held onto her hand considerably longer than was necessary.

It was Victoria, in fact, who finally removed her hand. "This is my daughter, Olivia," She turned to bring the little girl forward to join them.

"Rev. Eliot, I thought the whole thing was smashing!" Olivia enthused. "Lots nicer than church at home. The Vicar is ever so old and his teeth click when he talks."

Jason smiled indulgently. "And how old are you, young lady?"

"Eight."

"I have a son exactly the same age and a little girl not quite six. My wife and I would love you to meet them sometime."

The smile vanished from Olivia's face. "I'll only be here another week and a half. I...I live in London with my father."

"I'm sorry, Miss Windsor. Naturally I assumed....."

"That my daughter lived with me," Victoria replied shortly. "No, she doesn't. Come along, Olivia."

Jason watched her lead her daughter away and he wondered why he suddenly felt so lost.

* * *

Christmas Day itself was quiet and uneventful. Victoria and Olivia spent the first part of the day alone and then about two in the afternoon Noel and Jon came to escort them to dinner. How truly different she is, Noel thought happily as he watched Victoria laugh and joke with her daughter. But what will happen, he wondered further in sudden uneasiness, when the time comes for Olivia to return to England–a time drawing steadily nearer with each happy day mother and daughter spent together.

First, however, there was still New Year's Eve. A party was to be held on stage at the theatre after the performance, but as it happened, Victoria wasn't scheduled to appear that night. "Besides, Noel," she had remarked, laughing a little. "I'm not sure I want Olivia around a lot of drunken actors." She reached out to grasp his arm and now she was intensely serious. "Do you know I've been sober ever since she got here? I've....I've had a drink now and then, but I've been sober. Do...do you think I can still do it, after....after.." But she couldn't bring herself to finish the sentence.

It wasn't until the actual day of New Year's Eve that Victoria saw the advertisement in the newspaper. The same church they'd attended on Christmas Eve was holding a buffet supper and dance followed by a chapel service at midnight. "Would you like to go, luv?" she asked her daughter.

"Oh yes, Mummy, I would! Do you suppose that nice Rev. Eliot will be there?"

In spite of herself she reacted to the name. Did this man–so different from any other she'd ever known–have anything to do with her wishing to attend the party? Absolutely not, she told herself sternly. It's simply one of the few places in New York City to take a child on New Year's Eve! The advertisement gave a telephone number and requested that anyone wishing to attend make a reservation. Victoria went to the phone, picked up the receiver and dialed.

He should have known better, Jason supposed, as he let himself into the church that morning. His wife was already in a bad mood because of the New Year's Eve party of which she disapproved. They'd quarreled on and off about it for several days now. Then, too, during the nearly ten years they'd been married, she had doled out her sexual favors sparingly–never on the night before he was to preach, for example, when "his mind should be on higher things".

For the most part this didn't bother Jason. From childhood his father, also a minister, had lectured him severely on the necessity of curbing such base cravings. His wife, moreover, was not a woman apt to arouse a man to passion. Ruth was, charitably speaking, plain– her brown hair prematurely streaked with gray. There was nothing soft about her or warm or inviting. But that morning he'd come out of the bathroom to find her standing in front of the bureau brushing her hair. Normally she wore it bound up in a French twist, as tightly contained as her sensuality, but at the moment it still fell in chestnut waves down her back and the light was kind, making the gray appear as merely a glint against the brown. He came up behind her and pushing aside her hair, kissed her on the back of the neck. "Jason–don't!" She pulled away from him. "Lately that's all you think about! You're disgusting!"

So he'd left home early–aware that at this hour the church would be empty. Feeling vaguely ashamed, he was planning on spending the time in Bible study and prayer. He was thankful, at least, that their two children were spending the school vacation week with his parents near Chicago. They had already witnessed enough anger between their mother and father. He'd been there only an hour or so, however, when the ringing of the telephone disturbed his meditation. The office staff had the day off and with a sigh he moved to his desk to pick up the receiver. At the moment he didn't feel like dealing with anyone else's problems. "Fifth Avenue Federated Church–good morning." Of course his greeting betrayed none of his inner turmoil.

"Yes. I was ringing up about the New Year's Eve celebration. I'd like to book if I may."

The lilting English voice could belong to only one person. Jason was able to picture her with startling clarity despite the fact he'd only seen her once and he discovered to his dismay that the hand holding the telephone receiver was shaking. "Yes, Miss Windsor," he said in what he hoped was still a dignified, ministerial tone, "this is Reverend Eliot."

"I...I thought you sounded familiar." Her laugh pealed merrily. "And of course this damned accent of mine is a dead giveaway."

Jason felt a momentary displeasure. He found all profanity distasteful, but in a woman it was particularly upsetting. "Will it be just you and your daughter this evening?" he inquired and once again he was entirely successful in hiding his feelings.

"Yes. Will there be other young people present?"

"Certainly. Many families will be attending as a group. It's so difficult these days to be able to take a child anywhere and not encounter the consumption of alcohol." He actually sounded serious and now it was Victoria's turn to be annoyed. How could anyone be so prudish? "Will we see you later then?" Jason inquired.

"Yes, thank you. Good-bye."

Afterwards they both thought happily of the conversation–each for some reason forgetting the brief irritation he or she had at one point experienced.

When Jason returned home to change for the evening, it was to find that Ruth had a "headache" and wouldn't be attending the party. This concerned him somewhat because he knew there were already rumors about their marriage. At the same time he felt oddly relieved and for the first time since the New Year's Eve celebration had been planned, he discovered he was actually looking forward to the occasion.

Later, even as the guests were beginning to arrive and he moved from group to group, shaking hands and wishing people a Happy New Year–a blessed New Year–, he was aware of a certain distraction. His glance wandered continually toward the main door of the fellowship hall and more than once he failed to hear some remark addressed to him and was forced to ask the person to repeat. Then all at once Victoria appeared and he realized with a start that he'd been watching for her. She was wearing a full-length gown of a deep ruby velvet, the skirt slit on one side almost to the thigh. On Christmas Eve her hair had been hidden under a fur hat, but now it hung free, parted on one side, her face tantalizingly hidden from view by a golden cloud each time she turned her head. Jason immediately moved across the room to her. "Good evening, Miss Windsor. Welcome and Happy New Year to you and Olivia." It was typical that he would remember a little girl's name.

"Reverend Eliot." Smiling, Victoria extended her hand. He felt the blood rush to his face and as he turned to escort them to one of the tables along the edge of the dance floor, he felt as though his knees were about to give way. For a while he lingered there chatting–reluctant to leave her even briefly.

"Reverend Eliot!" a stentorian voice trumpeted from the other side of the room.

Jason sighed and excusing himself, he walked across to greet the woman who had thus summoned him. Esther Oglethorpe was an imposing matron who contributed generously to the church, but expected a great deal of bowing and scraping in return. "I'm so glad to see you, Mrs. Oglethorpe." He smiled as he shook hands with her. "The evening simply wouldn't be complete without you."

She smirked complacently at his compliment. Then she remembered why she'd wanted to talk to him. "Reverend Eliot, who is the woman with all that hair–the one in the red dress?"

"Oh...ah.... Victoria Windsor." Jason wondered why he felt guilty. "The English actress."

"Mercy! If my dear, departed husband–God rest his soul–knew that his church was letting in show folk, he would rise up in horror! The next thing we know it will be thieves and murderers!"

"Christ never judged those who came to him, Mrs. Oglethorpe, and neither should we." It was with some relief that he saw Ken and Kate MacAllister come in just then. "But now, if you'll excuse me for a moment, I must welcome some special friends."

Kenneth MacAllister and Jason Eliot had been students together at Andover-Newton Theological Seminary near Boston. Jason wasn't a person who made friends easily, but Ken, the son of Scottish immigrants, was a big, hearty man who had been willing to come more than halfway. He'd never regretted the effort. Recently appointed assistant professor of the New Testament at Union Theological Seminary in New York City, Ken and his wife had, of course, become members of the congregation. "Ken!" Jason seized his friend's hand warmly. "Bless you! You arrived just in time to rescue me!"

"Ah, yes!" The other man grinned. "Poor old Job might have had his problems, but you have Mrs. Oglethorpe."

"Where's Ruth?" Kate asked. She was nearly as tall as her husband and wore her short brown hair lightly frosted.

Jason's expression sobered. "Ruth is having one of her headaches. She won't be here tonight." His longtime friend looked at him steadily, but he merely shrugged in response.

"My goodness!" Kate exclaimed suddenly, "That's Victoria Windsor, isn't it? We saw one of her performances about two weeks ago. I didn't realize she attended this church."

"Christmas Eve was the first time. Would you like me to introduce you? Come along, then." He was exceptionally jovial–perhaps to conceal an uneasy conscience. "Miss Windsor, some friends of mine want very much to meet you. "Ken and Kate MacAllister--- Victoria Windsor."

"How do you do? This....this is my daughter, Olivia." She smiled pleasantly enough, but meeting new people was still difficult for her and she had no idea what to say next.

Luckily Kate was as friendly and outgoing as her husband. "Miss Windsor, we enjoyed your performance in *Victoria Regina* so much! Would you object to my husband and me joining you?"

"Of course not." But Victoria was beginning to wish she and Olivia were spending New Year's Eve alone together in the apartment. Fortunately just then the orchestra began to play and excusing themselves, the MacAllisters walked out onto the dance floor, settling into each other's arms with an ease born of years of practice.

"Would....would you care to dance, Miss Windsor?" Jason told himself he was being merely courteous. In truth he had wanted an excuse to touch her and as they moved about the floor, he was intensely aware of her nearness, the feel of her silken hair as it brushed against his cheek. "May...may I ask you a favor?" he managed to say after a moment.

"Yes?" She tipped her head back to look up at him and he wondered weakly what it would be like to kiss her.

"We...ah....we..." But the words just wouldn't come. Accustomed to the effect she had on men, Victoria smiled which only flustered him further. "The..ah....youth group is going to be presenting scenes from *Godspell.* Could you possibly watch a few rehearsals and give them some pointers? They meet on Sunday afternoons." Was this just so that he could see her again? If it was, he was honestly unaware of it.

"My...my daughter goes back to England next week. Perhaps after that."

Jason saw the expression on her face. "You'll miss her a great deal, won't you?" he asked gently.

Victoria's eyes filled with tears. "Yes."

Ken and Kate glanced often at the other couple "Ruth's driving him away, you know," she observed finally.

"I'd be more than willing to cut in on them." Ken winked at her.

"However, no one's driving you anywhere!" Kate administered a firm tug to one of his earlobes. "So fly right, fella!"

He chuckled. "Yes, ma'am."

The chapel service at midnight was simple, but moving. Jason was indeed an eloquent preacher and once again as on Christmas Eve Victoria felt profoundly comforted. When the festivities had concluded, he came over to where she and Olivia were putting on their coats and hats. "Are you walking?" he inquired.

"Yes." Victoria smiled at him again.

"May I accompany you? You and your daughter shouldn't be out on the streets unescorted at this hour."

"Thank you. We'd appreciate that."

They talked very little, but it was a pleasant, relaxed silence. How different he is from most of the men I've known, Victoria thought. He makes me feel safe. "Here we are," she said aloud as they approached the entrance to their building. "We'll be fine from here."

"Good night then." Jason was sorry the walk had been so short. "Call me up when you decide about *Godspell*."

"I'll do that. Good night."

"What an awfully nice man," Olivia observed as they rode up in the elevator. "But he's married, isn't he?"

"Yes, darling." Victoria laughed. "He is."

"Oh, dear," the little girl sighed. "That's too bad."

* * *

Inevitably the day came for Olivia to return to England. She was booked on a night flight leaving Kennedy at eight-thirty. Noel would be going with them to the airport.

"You wouldn't want me driving your car this time," Victoria had observed, trying to make light of it. "Please," she went on, "I don't know if I can stand watching her walk away from me through that gate. That's the real truth. I need someone there."

"Of course, Victoria," Noel had replied gently. "And I want to be there for you." But as he left his own apartment about six that evening, he rather wished he could miss the occasion entirely.

Victoria answered his knock almost at once and he was relieved that at least she appeared composed. "Noel–come in, please." Even her voice was fairly steady. "We're just about ready, I think."

Olivia came out of the bedroom as he entered. "Hello, Uncle Noel," she whispered. Her lower lip trembled suspiciously and she was clinging tightly to her new doll as though by doing so she could also hold onto her mother.

"The doorman let me park by the front entrance," Noel explained as he picked up the two suitcases waiting by the door. He felt ridiculous talking about commonplace things, but somehow he couldn't think of anything more significant to say. Then he saw that Olivia was also carrying a valise. "Seems to me you arrived with only two of these." He winked broadly at the little girl, but even this failed to get a smile out her.

"The rewards of an overindulgent mother," Victoria replied. "Well, I suppose we should be going."

The child backed away from them, shaking her head. "Not yet, please, Mummy."

"Noel, if you'd just go along down to the car? We'll be coming directly." He merely nodded and disappeared out the door. "Let's sit down together for a minute." Gently Victoria took the suitcase and put it down. Then she slipped an arm around her daughter's shoulders to lead her over to one of the couches. "Darling." She stroked her cheek and hair. "I love you so much."

"Don't!" Olivia said crossly, pulling away from the caress. "If you really loved me, you wouldn't send me back."

"Oh, dearest, you know that isn't true, don't you?" Stricken with guilt at her terrible words, the little girl made no immediate reply. Finally she nodded. "I'm glad because you know it's just as hard for me to <u>have</u> you leave. This apartment is going to seem very empty when I get back here from the airport." Victoria wished she hadn't said that because her throat caught on the last few words and she had made a firm vow not to cry until her daughter was on the plane. "But we'll be together very soon. Remember—I promised. I'll telephone my agent tomorrow about hiring a solicitor and I'll also get in touch with your father. That's only fair."

"Is Daddy going to feel awfully bad, do you think?"

"Maybe he won't mind too much. I think in a way he's always wanted us to be together." She glanced at her watch. It was nearly six-thirty. "But we do <u>have</u> to go now, I'm afraid, darling. We still have some time together, but we don't want to make your Daddy angry by having you miss your plane."

Olivia nodded solemnly. "All right. I...I'm ready." She tried to smile.

Victoria hugged her. "That's my good, brave girl."

Noel watched mother and daughter come out to the car, hand in hand as always. "I think we can all fit in the front." He smiled at them both.

Olivia sat in the middle. At first Noel tried to make conversation, but then he happened to glance at his two passengers and he fell silent. Victoria had her arm around the little girl who in turn was holding onto her mother's free hand with both of hers. Clearly they were communicating on a much deeper level. As they entered the airport grounds, however, each let go and they drew apart. It's as though they're preparing themselves to say good-bye, Noel thought, and he swallowed hard.

He made himself concentrate on finding a parking place and a moment or so later they were walking across the lot to the BOAC entrance. Once again Noel had the two suitcases. Victoria was carrying the other one while Olivia clung to her mother with one hand and the doll with the other. They checked in at the ticket counter and then there was nothing to do but wait and watch the second hand of the clock move slowly, but inexorably toward the boarding time of eight o'clock. Once again nobody spoke. About five minutes before, however, a stewardess approached. 'Miss Windsor?" Victoria jumped. "Excuse me, Miss Windsor. I'll be taking your daughter on board now."

So the moment had come as they'd both known it must. They embraced hard— clinging to each other with a desperate strength. "Go on now, luv," Victoria said at last. "You have to, you know."

"Yes, Mummy." Olivia stood up bravely. "I'm ready to go now," she said to the attendant.

"We'll take good care of her, Miss Windsor."

"Yes, I'm...I'm sure you will." Noel knew how close she was to falling apart, but somehow she controlled herself until Olivia had turned for one last wave and disappeared into the passageway leading out to the plane. "Oh. God!" Victoria exclaimed then. "Get me the hell out of here before I make a complete ass of myself!" Quickly they walked back through the terminal and out to the parking lot. Her eyes brimmed with tears, but she managed not to break down completely until she'd reached the privacy of the car.

Noel knew there was nothing he could do for her–at least for a while–except to let her cry. Actually she did talk to him from time to time, but for most of the ride back into the city her words were so mixed up with her sobs as to be all but unintelligible. He could make out Olivia's name, of course, as well as his own–the word "love" several times, but little else. Then suddenly, as they entered the city, he realized that for several minutes now Victoria had been silent and at almost the same instant he felt her hand on his arm. "You knew all along, didn't you, Noel? You knew how much I loved her?" He understood her quite clearly this time, but it didn't occur to him that she'd expected an answer. "Didn't you, Noel?" she insisted, a note of desperation creeping into her voice.

"Oh yes, Victoria," he said then, "I've always known."

Chapter 16

The first thing that struck Victoria as she entered her apartment a short while later was the silence. Noel had offered to keep her company, but she might as well get used to being alone again. She didn't bother to turn on any lights, but went at once to curl up in the corner of one of the couches, hugging her knees to herself–the old habit from childhood.

She didn't know how long she'd been sitting there when for some reason Jason Eliot came to mind–his gentle voice, his kind, blue eyes. She felt a compelling need to talk to him and moving over to her desk, she turned on a small reading lamp to look up his number in the telephone directory. There were two listings: one at the church and the other for his residence and without stopping to think she dialed his home number. After several rings a woman answered. She'd obviously been asleep and it was only then that Victoria looked at her watch, discovering to her dismay and embarrassment that it was nearly midnight. "I'm dreadfully sorry," she apologized. "I didn't realize it was so late. I....I wanted to speak to Reverend Eliot."

"Just a minute, please." Ruth made no attempt to hide her annoyance. More than once she'd suggested to her husband that he tactfully request his parishioners to confine their calls to reasonable hours. The calls continued to come, however, so either he hadn't heeded her suggestion or the members of the congregation refused to take a hint. She suspected strongly it was the former.

"Reverend Eliot speaking." Jason himself was apparently not in the least irritated by the lateness of the call.

"I've....I've already apologized to your wife," Victoria murmured. "I had no idea what time it was until after I'd rung up."

He didn't have to inquire as to the caller's identity. But for some reason he made an immediate, conscious decision not to use her name. "I place no restrictions on the hours of my calls," he said kindly. "How may I help you?"

I can't say I just wanted to talk to him, Victoria thought. After all, I barely know the man. Then she remembered the play. "I...I've been thinking about your youth group," she said finally. "I believe I could manage some time."

"I'd appreciate that, of course, but I don't think that's the real reason you called."

His intuitive grasp of her emotions startled yet at the same time reassured her. "My...my daughter left tonight to go back to her father in England," Victoria heard herself saying to her own amazement. What power did this man have over her?

"Would you like me to come over for a while?"

"Would....would you?" Victoria felt absurdly grateful. "Apartment Number 1016."

"I'm on my way," he said briefly and he hung up.

"Who was it this time?" Ruth inquired drowsily, turning over to go back to sleep.

"Just someone who needs me." Jason got out of bed and started to dress. In less than half an hour he was ringing Victoria's bell.

She came to the door almost at once. "You're so kind to come." She stepped back to allow him to enter. "I...I made coffee. I thought you might like some."

"Thank you, Miss Windsor. How thoughtful of you."

"Excuse me. I'll bring it in here." She disappeared through the swinging door into the kitchen and returned a few minutes later, carrying a tray with a carafe of coffee, cups and saucers, cream and sugar which she put down on the coffee table between the two sofas. She couldn't understand why, but she was terribly nervous. "White or black?"

"I beg your pardon?"

"I'm sorry." She laughed a little. "Do you take anything in your coffee?"

"Yes–a little cream, please, and one teaspoon of sugar." He watched as she poured the coffee, adding the cream and sugar. The dim light in the room only served to accentuate her beauty–her blonde hair, now held back from her face by a pale, cream-colored scarf, her lips—gleamingly moist and inviting. Worse still, he found his eyes traveling downward–lingering over her full breasts, slim waist and hips, her thighs outlined alluringly in black slacks. He knew he was only human and therefore weak, but to entertain such lustful thoughts when he'd come there in the role of spiritual counselor was an unforgivable transgression. "Tell me about Olivia," he said, keeping his voice carefully even. "Has she always lived with her father?" Victoria's eyes filled with tears and putting down his cup and saucer, Jason reached over to take one of her hands in both of his. It was cold and clammy and he rubbed it to warm her. Was it the man who did this or the minister? Very probably he didn't know himself. As for Victoria, it seemed natural for him to be holding her hand and she didn't question his action. "Perhaps you find it too painful to talk about your daughter?" he continued after a moment.

"No....no, I'd...I'd like to. I'm...I'm just not used to discussing my feelings."

"It's good to talk, you know." Finally–reluctantly–he let go of her hand. "God didn't mean for any of us to live in isolation. That's why he placed all of us here on this earth together. So that we might be a comfort and a solace to each other."

I...I can tell him anything, Victoria thought, and he will understand. "You see," she heard herself saying aloud, "I....I didn't really love Andrew–that's...that's Olivia's father. I....I only married him because...because I....."

"Because you were lonely perhaps," he interposed helpfully.

She'd married Andrew, of course, because she wanted someone to support her. But maybe she <u>had</u> indeed been lonely and to someone like Jason that would seem a more acceptable explanation. "Yes, I....I was terribly lonely," she agreed. "But then...then almost at once I became pregnant. I....I didn't want a baby. I...I...planned to have an abortion."

Jason was shocked! To him abortion was nothing short of murder. Then almost immediately he realized that of course she hadn't gone through with it. "But...but you didn't, did you?"

"No." She shook her head. "And...and then when she was born and they put her in my arms for the first time....."

"It must have been a moment of great joy. You must have been so thankful you didn't kill her after all."

She had thought the same thing many times herself, but somehow to hear him say it seemed like a condemnation and a new wave of guilt flooded over her. "Of...of course I was. But the whole thing–marriage, a baby,–felt like a prison to me and when I had the chance to join a repertory company outside London, I....I left."

This second admission dismayed Jason almost as much. What sort of woman would leave her baby to be an actress? He reminded himself sternly that he wasn't there to judge her. "How.....how old was Olivia then?"

"About....about nine months old–so sweet and bright and loving. I've...I've never forgotten that terrible moment when I gave her to the woman in the downstairs flat and... and walked away. I thought my heart would break." Tears filled her eyes again and this time it was she who reached out to him.

"Then you loved her even at the moment you left her," he remarked, tightening both his hands over the hand she had offered him.

"Oh yes–so much and...and yet at the time of the divorce when my husband offered me joint custody, I refused."

What must it be like, Jason wondered to himself, to have possessed this incredible woman only to lose her? But aloud he said, "What is there about loving, Miss Windsor, that you find frightening?"

How had he immediately discerned what her feelings had been then? Once again she was awed by the keenness of his perception. "Please–call me Victoria."

"That's not so unusual you know, Victoria." He savored the feel of her name on his lips. "Loving is....is a risking of self. It can be terrifying."

"I...I've never met anyone like you, Reverend Eliot."

"Jason...please."

"Jason then." She smiled—what a sweet smile, he thought. "But how is it possible for.... for you to understand so much?"

"I suppose that when I listen to someone, I hear not only the words actually spoken, but those unspoken as well."

Involuntarily she shivered. He would be someone from whom she could hide nothing. For some reason this realization made her distinctly uneasy, but then at once she dismissed such a notion as ridiculous. To possess such insight was, after all, a rare gift. "And....and you're not afraid to love, are you–to give of yourself to others?"

"It is part of my calling, I imagine." Neither of them was aware how smug he sounded. "But then neither are you any longer, are you, Victoria?"

"I...I am beginning to <u>learn</u> how to love...yes."

"And I would say you're succeeding. You and your daughter seemed very close. I'd like to hear how that came to be."

"Well. until...until this Christmas, every time I saw her was another bloody disaster."

Inwardly Jason recoiled once again at her use of the word, "bloody". "I'm sure it wasn't nearly as bad as you thought," he observed soothingly.

"You're very kind, but if anything, it was worse. I....I hurt her over and over again and yet she never stopped loving me. It's truly a miracle." Tears filled her eyes and trickled down her cheeks, but she began to talk as she'd never talked before: of all the awful times when she and Olivia seemed to have nothing to say to each other–even worse of the other instances when she'd canceled a visit at the last minute– and finally of her recent decision to seek custody. Suddenly she became aware it was growing light. "My goodness, I've kept you here all night!" She glanced down at her watch. "What will you wife think?" She laughed self-consciously. All night with a man, her thoughts continued silently, and all he's done is hold my hand.

"My wife is accustomed to these demands on my time," Jason was replying. "She knows that when someone needs me, I can't say no."

"If you'd really like me to watch your youth group rehearse, perhaps I could repay your kindness–even a little–in that way."

"Believe me, repayment isn't necessary, but we'd be grateful for your help. Next Sunday afternoon at two o'clock in the fellowship hall? That's where the New Year's Eve party was held."

"Yes, I'll be there."

Reluctantly Jason at last stood up to leave. Perhaps even at that moment he was already in love with her. "My office is directly inside the 54th Street entrance. Come there first and I'll bring you in and introduce you."

It seemed to Jason as though the following Sunday would never come. He'd half-hoped to see her at the morning service, but she wasn't there. Just shortly after two, however, a knock came at his study door and he hurried around his desk to open it. She was swathed in pale mink, the collar held up around her ears. The cold had brought color to her cheeks and her green eyes shone. He smiled. "Good afternoon, Victoria. You may leave your coat in here. I'll lock my office."

Her first impulse was to quip–"Don't tell me there are thieves in the Lord's House!" But she had a feeling Jason would not find such a remark amusing. Instead she merely thanked him and slipping out of its luxurious folds, handed him the fur. Underneath she was wearing a deep purple wool dress. Her hair was held back from her face with a lavender, paisley-printed scarf and her jewelry was an antique gold chain and matching earrings. She looked incredibly lovely and as he ushered her across the hall, he permitted himself the brief intimacy of placing a hand at her waist.`

The normal pre-rehearsal commotion died out instantly as they entered. A slightly older girl separated herself from the group and walked over to them. "Victoria," Jason said, "this is Lisa MacAllister, who's directing the production. You met her parents on New Year's Eve."

"I couldn't believe it when Reverend Eliot told me you were coming, Miss Windsor," Lisa exclaimed. "I'm pre-law at Columbia, but I'm taking a theatre history course and we've been to see both *Macbeth* and *Victoria Regina*! You are absolutely amazing!"

"Thank you so much," Victoria replied graciously although she was fighting her inevitable nervousness at having to talk to a stranger. "Why....why don't you have them go ahead? I'll know better what I want to say after I've seen them work."

"Okay, everyone." The young director moved into the center of the group. "Miss Windsor would like to see what you can do." The group gathered up on the small stage at one end of the hall and began to perform their abbreviated version of *Godspell*. Lisa couldn't believe it. The scenes had appeared fairly polished last Sunday, but this week, just when she hoped to impress Victoria Windsor, it looked as if they had never rehearsed at all. There were missed cues and forgotten lyrics and staging became hopelessly confused. More than once two people actually collided.

Victoria and Jason sat side by side watching the performance–that is, <u>she</u> was watching it. <u>He</u> was taking advantage of the fact that everyone else's attention was on the production to study her. The delicately featured English face viewed in profile was like an exquisite cameo. He observed her breasts, rising and falling with each breath, and her long, slender calves tapering into slim, graceful ankles. By leaning in just a little closer he could even catch the scent of her perfume, that same bewitching fragrance he had noticed the first time he met her. Looking over once in an attempt to gage the actress' reaction, Lisa couldn't help noticing that Reverend Eliot's attention was not directed at the stage and she was beginning to understand why her mother and father had exchanged interested glances when she told them that Victoria Windsor had agreed to help with the production.

Victoria made no comments, not even sidelong ones to Jason, until the performance was finished and the cast was sitting along the edge of the stage, waiting anxiously for her reaction. "Oh, Miss Windsor," Lisa exclaimed, coming over to sit on the other side of her. "I don't know what got into them!"

She smiled to put the girl at ease. "To begin with, if we're to be working together, I wish you'd call me Victoria. Miss Windsor makes me feel too bloody old!" Lisa knew Jason's feelings about even the mildest profanity and she glanced over at him. He frowned briefly, but said nothing. "Now why don't you all come down here and sit near me on the floor so we can talk more informally." Victoria accompanied the words with yet another smile, amazed that all at once she was entirely at ease. She waited until they'd all gathered around her before she continued. "First of all, I'd like to ask you something if I may." She paused again–ever the actress with an audience. "Do I make you nervous?"

Her question had caught them totally off-guard. It was the last thing they'd expected her to say and for a moment or so there was no reply. Then one or two of them began to smile–hesitantly at first–then to laugh and finally one of them, the boy who was portraying Christ, raised his hand. "We were awfully nervous, Miss Windsor, about performing for you. We've really done it much better."

"But why do I make you nervous?"

Another silence–'Why you're....you're Victoria Windsor," someone else said at last.

At that she laughed and Lisa looked at Jason again. There was a softness in his eyes she'd never noticed there before. She'd always thought of him as slightly stuffy. "So I'm Victoria Windsor," the actress was saying, "but do you know I started out just as many of you are starting here–in an amateur production–only mine was at school. It's the same thing, though, really, isn't it–people doing something because they enjoy it. Am I right? You are having a good time?" Several of them nodded. "Good, because if you're not, you're certainly putting in a lot of time being miserable." They all laughed at that, their nervousness gone. "So now that we have that settled," Victoria continued, "suppose I get out of your way and let you work. Then next week I'll come back and we'll begin all over again." She stood up to leave and Jason rose with her.

"Victoria, thank you," Lisa said. "I'll see you next Sunday then...actually before that. My class is coming to the matinee of *Candida* on Wednesday.

"Come backstage after the performance and say hello. Perhaps we could go somewhere for dinner and talk."

The girl beamed. "I'd like that."

"Good. I'll see you then. May I have my coat, Reverend Eliot?"

"Yes, of course." But he was disappointed she was leaving so soon. They left the hall together to go back across to his study and he took her coat from his closet, holding it for her to slip into. "May I walk with you?" Even as he spoke the words, Jason was amazed at himself.

"Please." Victoria turned her head to smile at him. She'd been dreading the rest of the long, lonely Sunday–the first since Olivia left. "Will you come up for tea– or perhaps you don't like tea."

"No–I like tea. Well then, shall we?"

They chatted easily together during the short walk back to her building, but once upstairs in the apartment an awkward silence fell. Victoria put her fur in the closet, taking his overcoat to hang up as well. "Please, make...make yourself comfortable," she murmured. "I'll put the kettle on and perhaps you might light the fire,"

A few minutes later she was back. The fire was already beginning to crackle cheerily on the hearth, making the room a cozy haven against the chill of the winter twilight outside. Jason had settled himself on a couch. "You know," he said as Victoria came to sit beside him, "this room suits you. It has a certain grace and elegance."

"Thank you." She smiled in response to his compliment. "But I'm afraid I can't take credit for the decor. I sublet the flat furnished."

He felt a strange desolation at the thought of her returning to England. Hurriedly he searched his mind for a topic of conversation. "Have you begun custody proceedings yet?" he inquired at last, sure she'd be eager to discuss her fight for her daughter. If she would only begin to talk, he could simply listen to that crisp British accent he found so enchanting.

"That reminds me. I'd like to ring Olivia up before it gets too late in London. You can listen for the kettle."

"Fine. Do they still 'hot the pot' in England?"

"Actually we do." She smiled at him again and he felt a warm glow. "How frightfully clever for a Yank." She disappeared into the bedroom and after a moment he heard her dial and speak to an operator,

* * *

It was nearly nine o'clock in London. Andrew was sitting alone in his study, rereading yet again the letter he'd received the day before from his ex-wife. He didn't know why it had been such a shock. The change in the little girl since the Christmas visit was unmistakable. He supposed, however, he'd simply been trying to ignore what was happening–until yesterday when this letter arrived and he was unavoidably confronted with the issue. Angrily he threw the sheet of lavender scented stationery down on his desk. "Dammit, Victoria," he muttered, "you have <u>no</u> right to do this after all these years–no right at all!" Just then he heard someone come downstairs and go into the living room. "Emily?" he called out.

But it was Olivia who appeared in the doorway–dressed in pajamas, robe and slippers. "I'm all ready for bed, but Mummy said she'd ring up on Sunday."

"Well, we both know your mother isn't exactly in the habit of keeping her promises, now don't we?"

Tears rushed into the child's eyes. "No, Daddy, you're wrong about Mummy and anyway–that was <u>before</u>."

"<u>Before</u> your wonderful visit, I suppose." Andrew hated himself for the open scorn in his tone–for the hurt he knew he was inflicting on his daughter–but he couldn't stop himself. He was so terribly afraid of losing her.

All at once Olivia noticed the letter on the desk–the handwriting now familiar to her. "Oh!" she said.

"'What do you mean–oh?" Andrew got up from his desk to come around and stand looking down at her. "You know about this letter?"

"Mummy said she was going to write to you."

"Then you know she's going to try to take you away from me?"

"I know my mother wants me!" Olivia spoke the words with such pride and joy that Andrew became furious.

"And just who loved you and took care of you until now? All the years your mother couldn't be bothered with you!"

"Mummy was afraid, that's all." Desperately the child defended Victoria.

"Afraid of what? Responsibility?"

"Afraid of loving someone."

"So that's the line she fed you! Get upstairs! It's past your bedtime! When your mother calls–<u>if</u> she calls–<u>I</u> will do the talking!"

Just then the phone began to ring and Olivia dashed for it. "Mummy!" she called breathlessly into the mouthpiece. "Mummy!" But it wasn't her mother's voice she heard, but that of the overseas operator–"One minute, please, for New York."

Before the connection could be completed, her father had snatched the receiver away from her. "What do you want, Victoria?"

"I'd like to speak to Olivia, if I may."

"No, you may not!"

She could hear the little girl in the background, however. "Mummy, he...he won't let me talk to you!"

"What in bloody hell is going on there?" Victoria demanded. Raised in anger, her voice was clearly audible in the next room. Jason wondered if he should speak to her about the fact that profanity bothered him. Then he reminded himself that he really had no right to tell her anything.

"There's no point in going on with this conversation," Andrew replied coldly. "Let me simply say for now that I intend to fight to keep my daughter!" He slammed down the receiver.

"I hate you, Daddy!" Olivia screamed at him with all the fury her eight year old body could contain. "I hate you! I hate you!" At last she whirled about to run sobbing up the stairs..

* * *

In New York Victoria came slowly out of the bedroom. Her face was ashen and she was shaking. "What is it?" Jason got at once to his feet moving toward her.

"Andrew...Andrew wouldn't even allow her to speak to me. Oh, Jason!" Her eyes filled with tears. "Jason, he'll never let me have her, never!"

He was standing right in front of her now and he looked so concerned. Neither one knew how it happened, but somehow she was in his arms. "Hush, Victoria, don't cry, please." He held her close stroking her back.

At last she raised a tear-stained face from his shoulder. "I've...I've never known anyone who was such a comfort," she whispered. Her face was close to his, her green eyes brimming with tears and her gracefully curved mouth trembling with emotion. All at once he was kissing her. "Jason," she murmured his name as their lips finally parted.

"Please forgive me, Victoria." He was horrified by what had just taken place. "That will never happen again. I can assure you." He grabbed his coat out of the closet and hurriedly left. In the days that followed Jason prayed almost continually, asking God to give him the strength to resist temptation, but his prayers were in vain. He could not stop seeing her lovely face so close to his or worse feeling again the sensation of her soft, moist lips yielding under his.

Victoria at the same time told herself sternly that a married minister was definitely off-limits even for a woman of her low moral standards. Yet despite her firm resolve she would find herself thinking of him at all hours of the day and night, of his tenderness and she would remember the safe feeling of being in his arms. Returning to the church the next Sunday, she was careful to go directly into the hall although a brief glance in the direction of Jason's office showed it to be dark and empty.

The production was indeed smoother than the previous week–too smooth, in fact. They were trying so hard, she supposed, they weren't having any fun. When the performance had concluded, they came at once this time to sit near her on the floor. Did they actually like her?! That thought made her smile and many of them smiled in return. She hesitated a moment before speaking– wanting to say the right thing–not wanting to discourage them. "Do many of you attend the theatre?" she asked finally. Quite a few of them nodded. "What makes the difference between enjoying and not enjoying a performance?"

"If it's well done," one girl suggested.

"True," Victoria agreed, "but sometimes a good performance still lacks something."

"I like anything with Victoria Windsor in it." It was the boy who was playing John the Baptist. He grinned.

Victoria laughed. "Flattery will get you nowhere–ah—what's your name?"

"Everybody calls me Shep."

"Shep–I'll remember that. Now what would you especially be looking for if you went to see a production of *Godspell*?"

"Several of us did go see a professional production of it," a voice volunteered from somewhere in the back.

"How was it?" she asked.

There were cries of "Fantastic!"–"Great!" A girl hesitantly raised her hand.

"Yes?" Victoria pointed to her. "You know it might help if you each identified yourself as you spoke. I confess to having a terrible memory for names, but it will at least be a beginning."

"It's....it's Cathy. They...they seemed so happy. It was contagious."

"Exactly–very good!"

Cathy glowed. Lisa marveled that this girl had even dared speak to Victoria. She had a clear, sweet singing voice, but until now she'd remained in the background. "So if the cast appears to be having a good time," the actress was continuing, "the audience can't help but enjoy themselves as well."

"That's what was wrong with <u>us</u>, wasn't it?" someone asked. "We...were just going through the motions."

"And we want the audience to have a true religious experience." It was Shep who spoke again.

Jason had left the church that morning as soon after the service as possible, but when it came time for the rehearsal, he couldn't stay away. He'd actually been standing in the doorway for quite a while listening to the discussion. He didn't wish to intrude nor even call attention to his presence. It was enough just to hear her voice–to watch her work her gentle charm on the young people–but now he was irresistibly drawn to contribute a word or two. "Yes, that was the reason the group chose this particular play," he said coming forward to join them. Victoria felt a rush of happiness at the sight of him.

"Even though some people object to our doing plays in the church," Lisa added.

"But it was the church that brought theatre back to life again after the Dark Ages," the actress observed, "with the passion plays." This time there was no mistaking the look on Jason's face and the MacAllister girl wondered if she should mention it to her parents. "But let's try a couple of the numbers again now," Victoria was saying at the moment, "keeping in mind our discussion. Lisa, would you object if I did some restaging. I'd like to move them off the stage; it's rather confining, I think, and too remote from the audience."

"Of course not–please."

"I'll be in my study," Jason said. "Vict..ah...Miss Windsor," he immediately corrected himself, "I'd like to speak to you before you leave."

"Certainly, Reverend Eliot. I'll stop by when we're finished." They had both made such an effort to appear casual that now not only Lisa but several of the young people noticed as well.

Rehearsal finally concluded about an hour later and heart pounding, Victoria walked across the hall to knock on his study door. "Come in," Jason called out. "Confirmation class for the seventh graders," he explained as she entered, indicating several books open on his desk, "although I must confess to having some difficulty concentrating."

"Would you prefer I not work with the young people?"

"No, of course not," he replied quickly. "That wouldn't be fair. You have such a wonderful way with them." He was still standing behind his desk and he paused now, looking down on his hands spread out on the blotter. "I'm not being truthful," he went on after a moment. "It's an excuse for me to see you. Otherwise, I....I... Do you find me boring company? You must know so many fascinating people."

Victoria thought of Sean Patrick, Julian Christopher. "The famous are not necessarily fascinating," she murmured. "Jason, the last thing I want to do is cause problems in your marriage."

"You're not causing the problems, believe me." He turned away to go over to the window and stand looking out at the traffic. "But you're so lovely, so tempting and I am, after all, only human."

"I'm sorry." She had no way of knowing at that moment how often in the coming months she would say those words. "I'm told there are only two more rehearsals and if you remember I'll be at the church during those hours, we can manage to avoid each other."

He turned from the window to look at her. Her hair seemed to have caught the glow of the sunlight and her pale, pink sweater was almost the color of her flesh. He found himself imagining her naked. "Thank you, Victoria." He half-choked on the words. "Thank you for helping me do the right thing."

"Good-bye, Jason. And thank <u>you</u> for all your kindness." Afterwards Victoria couldn't even remember the walk back to her building. She felt hurt and for some strange reason horribly guilty. As she let herself into the apartment, the telephone was ringing.

"Victoria, me darlin'. 'Tis Sean. I'm at the airport. I presume the bar is still well stocked."

She laughed–the old, hollow, theatrical laugh. "You know me better than that. Of course it is and I'm horny as hell!"

He roared delightedly in return. "You'll never change!"

Slowly Victoria replaced the receiver. She thought of the three weeks with Olivia, of her feelings for Jason and she laughed again. "Sean's right," she said aloud. "I'll never change." She went over to the bar and poured herself some vodka, toasting herself in the mirror. "Here's to the real Victoria Windsor! Why in hell have you been trying so hard to fool everybody, especially yourself?" She drank half the glass without stopping. Then she took the bottle with her to one of the sofas and in the hour it took Sean to get into the city she worked very hard for the first time in several weeks at getting drunk.

"Not fair at all," he muttered as she let him in. "You're way ahead of me. Come here, you magnificent bitch!" He pulled her to him and began exploring her face and neck with his eager, probing mouth.

It had been so long and in spite of herself she gasped with pleasure. Already she was becoming aroused. "Oh, Sean," she murmured throatily, "take me–now!"

Laughing, he swept her up in his arms and carried her into the other room, dumping her unceremoniously on her bed. "Just ' alf a mo, luv. Where's the bar?"

"The cabinet to the left of the fireplace and hurry, God damn your besotted Irish soul!" He disappeared into the living room again. He was only gone a few minutes and it would have been all right if in that brief interval she hadn't looked over at Olivia's bed which still stood beside hers. Somehow she hadn't been able to bring herself to have it moved back into the other room. For a moment she continued to gaze at it. She pictured her little girl curled up there asleep–so sweet and innocent–and turning over to bury her head in the pillow, she began to cry.

"Hey there, lady!" Rolling her over onto her back again, Sean ran a practiced hand over her breasts and stomach.

"Don't, please!"

"What in hell do you mean–'Don't please!' " He took a swig from the bottle and then threw it on the floor where it tipped over, spilling the whiskey out onto the rug. Kneeling over her on the bed, he grabbed her by both wrists.

"Sean, please!" Desperately she fought him, but he was so much stronger and in addition he was still sober. Finally she gave in–sobbing–and let him have his way. Dear God–he hurt! It had never hurt like that–even with Peter Harris the first time–and at some point she must have passed out.

It was dark when she came to. What time was it? Dazed and sick, she tried to turn her head to see the bedside clock. Waves of nausea flooded over her. She started toward the bathroom, but the sick feeling rose in her throat and she vomited on the floor. She barely made it back to bed before losing consciousness again and when she awoke this time, it was to the sound of the telephone. It had begun to grow light and her head was throbbing. "Hello?"

"Victoria–did I wake you?" It was Noel.

"As a matter of fact you did."

She sounded so weak that for one terrible moment he thought she seemed the way she used to after an all-night binge. At once he pushed the idea from his mind. "Are you all right?" he inquired anxiously.

"Of course I am! Mind your own bloody business!" She slammed down the receiver. It had been more than a month since she'd had a hangover and she'd forgotten just how miserable she could feel. Gradually she became aware that the room stank of whiskey and vomit. The smell made her gag again and forcing herself first to sit up and then to stand up, she moved out into the living room. I'll clean it up later when I feel better, she promised herself, wishing very much just then that she hadn't fired Martha.

Continuing on into the kitchen, she put water on to boil for tea and then she sank into a chair at the small dinette, resting her aching head in her hands. "Oh, Olivia, darling, you're so much better off with your father. Why did I ever think I could...." The doorbell sounded. "Damn you, Noel!" Victoria screamed. Giving her chair such a violent backwards shove that it fell over, she half-ran through the living room toward the front door. "Noel, why in bloody hell can't you...." She flung open the door. It wasn't Noel; it was Jason. "Oh, dear God!" Backing away, she covered her face with her hands, sick with humiliation.

Jason had heard all too clearly even through the closed door. Then on top of that she'd used the Lord's Name in vain. But he forgot his dismay almost instantly as he saw that she was not well. "Victoria, what happened?"

"Isn't that bloody obvious? Oh, go away, dammit!" She stumbled away across the room, but then she turned back to him running her hands through her hair. "Oh, Jason," she sobbed, "why did you have to see me like this?" Suddenly her knees gave way and she would have fallen had he not moved forward and caught her.

When she awoke for the third time, she was lying on one of the couches in the living room. Once again there was an odor, but now it was of freshly brewed coffee and as she pulled herself up to a sitting position, Jason appeared in the swinging door leading from the kitchen. This time he was the one carrying a tray with a carafe, two cups and saucers, creamer and sugar bowl. "I thought perhaps some coffee would taste good." He smiled his gentle smile. "Although perhaps you'd have preferred tea."

"C...coffee's fine." Weak tears trickled down her cheeks.

He appeared not to notice, however, as he came to sit beside her placing the tray on the coffee table. "I believe you also take cream and sugar, am I right?"

"Jason, I....I....."

"We'll talk when you're feeling better," he interrupted her quietly, but firmly. "Now drink your coffee." Meekly she obeyed. It felt good to have someone telling her what to do. It wasn't until Victoria had finished her cup and placed it on the tray, lying back against the cushions once more, that Jason spoke. "Now do you want to tell me what happened?"

"For God's sake haven't you ever seen a hangover before?"

"As a matter of fact I have."

"Although I don't imagine you've ever had one," she observed bitterly.

He hesitated. "I...I don't drink myself, but I....."

"Then where in hell do you get off commiserating with me? You don't know a damn thing about how I feel at this moment!"

"But I....I... do know pain when I see it and I...."

"Jason, I'm...I'm so sorry. It's just that I feel bloody awful!"

"Victoria, answer me a question honestly. You drank last night because of me... isn't that true?"

She thought of Sean. Had she begun drinking before or after his call? Events were fuzzy in her mind as they always were after a heavy binge and she couldn't remember. She did recall, however, with painful clarity what that Irish bastard had done to her!

"Oh, Jason!" Victoria wasn't even aware she was doing it, but she reached out to him with both hands and he took her in his arms. "I....I don't want to be like this. Help me –please, help me!" He held her close, forgetting her profanity, the stinking bedroom he'd cleaned while she slept–forgetting everything except the warm, lovely woman who clung to him and begged for his help. "Believe me," she went on, "all I want is your friendship. I'm sure you take your marriage vows very seriously."

At last he released her from his embrace and sat back away from her just a little so that he could look at her. "Oh, Victoria," he murmured, "you're so beautiful."

"I see." Her expression grew cold. "Why did I think you were any different?"

"No, wait, you don't understand."

"I understand that you want me. You do, don't you?"

Jason was horribly embarrassed at having her put it so bluntly. "If...if you'd just let me finish. You see, I....I did a great deal of thinking last night and this morning I told my wife I want a divorce. Victoria, I'm...I'm in love with you. Will you marry me?"

"Are you sure? It's....it's so sudden."

"Very sure. As I said, I've given it a lot of thought."

Despite everything he'd seen that morning this kind, decent man wanted to marry her! She wished she could think of a way to tell him how grateful she was. "Yes, Jason, I'll....I'll marry you."

"Victoria, my...my dear." He drew her into his arms again and she raised her face to be kissed. Willingly he lowered his lips to hers. Once again he was vaguely disturbed by the intensity of his physical response to her as almost at once he drew back. Victoria, on the other hand, found his kiss pleasant and she failed to notice its brevity.

The doorbell sounded, but before she could even move to answer it, someone began to pound on the door. "Victoria!" Of course it was Noel. "Victoria, open this door at once!"

She started to stand up and the room spun. "Jason, would you?"

"Of course." This lovely woman had consented to be his wife! He could hardly believe his good fortune. He went to the door and opened it.

For a second Noel was puzzled. Then he decided the man must be a doctor. "Is Victoria all right?" he inquired anxiously.

"Yes–still a little weak, but all right."

"Noel, luv," she called to him from the couch, "please come in." She smiled happily. Already Jason was taking care of her. She didn't even have to move. "Noel, this is Jason Eliot. Jason–a very old and dear friend–Noel St. John. Noel's in the theatre company with me." The two men shook hands cordially, but with no special warmth, each wondering about the place and importance of the other in Victoria's life. "Jason is the minister at the church where I've been helping with the youth group's production of *Godspell,*" she explained further to Noel. "It's the church Olivia and I went to on Christmas Eve and New Year's Eve. You knew we went, didn't you?" He nodded. "I'm glad you came, luv. Jason, would you bring another cup, please?"

Noel had seen the expression on the other man's face. Clearly he was in love with Victoria. It wasn't that which bothered him. He couldn't blame a man for loving her. It was the atmosphere, the mood of intimacy in the room which told him this was not merely another man in her life. Yet how long had she known him? How well did she know him?

There were so many questions he wanted to ask, but before he could say anything, Jason was back sitting beside her–his air distinctly proprietary. "Noel, how do you take your coffee?"

"Black, thank you." He accepted the cup and sat down on the other couch, facing them.

He didn't have to wonder for long. It was impossible for Victoria to contain her happiness and soon she put an end to his uncertainty–at least as far as her feelings for Jason were concerned. "Noel, I...I want you to be the first to know. We're...we're going to be married."

As she spoke, her eyes were on Jason and so she failed to see the dismay on her old friend's face before he got immediately to his feet, moving across to lean down and kiss her on the cheek and shake Jason's hand again. "I wish you every happiness, Victoria. Congratulations, Jason. You're a very lucky man." Neither of them knew just how fervently he meant those words.

* * *

Noel would never know how he made it through that evening's performance of *The Devil's Disciple.* Afterwards he turned down Jon's offer of companionship and for over two hours he sat in a bar going over it all in his mind. Was it simply that he was jealous? He really had no right to be. They'd never been more than friends. Victoria was a beautiful, desirable woman and very lonely. It had been inevitable she would remarry. But to a man she barely knew? Of course he wasn't jealous; he was merely concerned.

Even when he finally returned to his apartment, Noel was unable to sleep. Why had he taken such an instant dislike to Jason Eliot who certainly was preferable to the vast majority of Victoria's male companions and apparently devoted to her. But the man acted so damned smug as though he owned her. He simply had no right to step into her life and just take over that way–no right at all! So maybe he <u>was</u> jealous. But was he actually that selfish and self-centered that all his feelings were based solely on that one point?

Just how well <u>did</u> she know Jason Eliot anyway? As it began to grow light, Noel decided that at the very least he had to have an answer to that question. He owed their friendship that much–to caution her to be sure of her feelings–and once he was satisfied, he vowed he would wish her well. He knew Victoria would be at NYU most of the day and he planned on speaking to her that evening at the theatre. Tonight since they would be doing the less demanding *Earnest,* he hoped they could talk before the performance.

"Come in," she called out in answer to his knock–such a different greeting from her old, cross "Who is it?" As he came in, she glanced up in her dressing table mirror. "Ready so soon, Mr. Moncrieff? I'm nearly finished," she continued, returning to her work with an eyebrow pencil. "Olivia wanted to know why I put all this stuff on my face." She looked up at his reflection again and laughed happily at the memory.

"How <u>is</u> Olivia?" Noel wondered how he could ever steer the conversation around to Jason.

"Fine. At first after her father learned I was planning to sue for custody, he wouldn't allow me to talk to her. I'm not even sure he was giving her my letters. But things are better now. Andrew's a fair man, after all. I suppose he's afraid of losing her. I can't blame him for that."

"When will proceedings actually start?"

"Not before April or even May. You have to wait so bloody long to get on the court calendar." She paused, her mascara brush poised in one slender, expressive hand. "And yet even now it's so much better than it was. Do you know what I mean?" He said nothing. "You really came in to ask me about Jason, didn't you?" she teased him. "I suppose you realize I've only known him a short while."

"Well, I hadn't met him before so....."

"So naturally you assumed I couldn't have known him too long." Her green eyes sparkled wickedly. "Well, you're right actually," she admitted after a moment. "I only met him on Christmas Eve. But oh, he's so kind, so thoroughly decent. Do you know he was there with me the whole night after Olivia left and he never once touched me except to hold my hand?"

"I've done that, too, Victoria– on more than one occasion, if you remember."

"Of course I remember, dear, dear Noel."

Another knock sounded at the dressing room door. "Fifteen minutes to curtain, Miss Windsor."

"Thank you. Do you mind, luv? I do like a few minutes alone–even for Gwendolyn."

He still hesitated, however. He had not as yet said what he'd come to say and if he left now, he doubted he ever would. "Victoria, do you love him?"

A strange expression passed across her face. "Of course I love him! Would I be marrying him if I didn't love him?"

"I don't know," he replied quietly. "Would you?"

"Get the hell out of here, Noel St. John! What gives you the right to pry into my personal life?!"

He left without answering, closing the door noiselessly behind him. But rather than allaying his doubts, their conversation had only left him more concerned and uncertain than ever.

* * *

Jason was waiting in her dressing room when Victoria came offstage after the final curtain. "Darling," he whispered–a little self-consciously–for the term of endearment was new to him. Somehow he'd never been prompted to call Ruth "darling". He took her in his arms and she raised her face to be kissed. He complied briefly.

"Did you enjoy the play?" she asked, stepping behind the screen to change out of her costume.

"Ah...do...do...you want me to leave?" She laughed. "I don't understand why that's funny."

"It's not–just sweet. Of course you don't have to leave." She came out in a robe and sat down at the dressing table to remove her make-up. "You didn't answer me." It seemed important he approve of her work. "Did you enjoy the play?"

"Yes, it was very pleasant."

She felt a little let down, but then Gwendolyn was not her most challenging role. "You'll have to come and see the others–especially *Victoria Regina* or Lady Macbeth. Those are parts I can really sink my teeth into, as they say."

As they talked, she had finished creaming off the make-up and begun applying her own–a ritual that by now was automatic. "Do you work every night?" Jason asked after a while.

"The company gives eight performances a week, counting the matinees, and I usually do five of them. Why?"

"Being a minister's wife entails certain duties and responsibilities."

Perhaps it was at this moment that Victoria experienced her first stab of inadequacy. "But that's...that's only until June,"

"Can't you get out of the contract any sooner? I think you work much too hard."

"There–all done. I'm ready to go." She stood up and turned to him. "Oh, Jason!" She put her arms around his neck. "It's so good to have someone taking care of me."

They left the theatre together and started back toward Victoria's building. It was a glorious night–the air clear and cold with a few stars visible even above the lights of the city. "You know, " Jason said after a while, "we need to talk."

At once she panicked. "You've...you've changed your mind, haven't you, I mean about.... about wanting to marry me?"

"I...I love you. Why would I change my mind? But we do have to make plans."

By then they had reached her building. "Would you like to come up for a while?" she asked.

"You're not too tired?"

"I'm never tired after a performance. Actually I'm more exhilarated than at any other time."

"Then I'd like to. I can't see enough of you," he admitted as they walked through the lobby. "And when I'm <u>not</u> with you, I find myself daydreaming about you. The funny thing is–I've never been the type to daydream." There was another couple in the elevator so further talk had to wait. Walking along the hall toward her apartment, Jason once more took up their conversation of a few minutes ago. "Victoria, why would you ever think I would change my mind about marrying you?"

She covered her momentary confusion with the business of finding her key in her purse, unlocking and opening the door, hanging up her coat. Then with nothing else to do for the moment, she stood uncertainly in the middle of the room, nervously clasping and unclasping her hands. "Coffee or tea, Jason?"

"I really don't want anything. What I <u>do</u> want is to know what's upsetting you. Come sit on the couch and let's have a talk."

Victoria obeyed. He reminded her vaguely of the way she'd treated Olivia, but she only found that comforting. She reached out in what had become a compulsive manner to seize one of his hands in both of hers. "You're so good, so thoroughly decent and I..."

"And I can't believe anyone as beautiful as you can be anything but good and decent as well."

She laughed–a harsh sound which Noel would have instantly recognized. "You can still say that after yesterday?"

Jason's expression grew pained. He didn't like to think of Victoria as he'd seen her on the previous morning. "Anyone can drink too much once in a while."

"But you see–for me that isn't an unusual condition." Her tone had hardened, at the same time becoming more urgent.

"Please, Victoria." He took away the hand she had still been clutching and standing up, took several steps away from her. "You don't have to tell me any of this."

"Oh, but you see—I do. And you have to listen. Then if you still want to marry me..." She hesitated. Once she'd said it all she could lose him. "It's...it's not just the liquor, Jason. Sunday night there'd...there'd been a man here with me. I have no idea how many lovers I've had. Some of them were for long periods of time–others I picked up for the night at a party or in a pub. Maybe that's just the way I am. Maybe I'm incapable of being faithful to you."

All during Victoria's tortured confession Jason remained with his back to her–his fists clenched at his sides–his head bowed in anguish. He realized, of course, that theatrical people were less than moral, but to discover that his adored Victoria had sinned in this way, not merely once but over and over again, left him feeling sick. At last– mercifully–she stopped speaking, but even then he couldn't bring himself to look at her. Certainly she would seem different to him, aware as he now was of her impurity. "It's...it's all right," he heard her whisper after a moment. "Naturally you're disgusted by everything I've just told you. I understand."

He had to turn then to face her. She was slumped in one corner of the couch, her face buried in her hands, and looking at her–so penitent, so aware of her own iniquity— Jason experienced a wave of the purest Christian love. After all, his Savior had forgiven even such a one as Mary Magdalene; could he do any less? Quickly he was beside her kneeling on the floor in front of her, himself the penitent now. He raised her tear-stained face to kiss her and he saw with renewed joy that she appeared as beautiful as ever. "My dearest Victoria," he whispered fervently. "Don't you see none of that matters? I love you and I forgive you for everything you've done and been in the past."

She threw her arms around him. "Oh, thank you! Thank you! I....I need you so much. I...I love you." There you see, Noel, she thought triumphantly to herself. I <u>do</u> love him! I said it, didn't I?

After a few minutes Jason moved back to sit beside her. "Are you all right now, darling?" he asked patiently. Victoria merely nodded–too overcome with gratitude for his forgiveness to speak. "Then what I <u>wanted</u> to tell you was that I've decided to resign my pastorate."

"Resign? Oh, but why? You're a magnificent preacher!"

"I've discussed it with Ken MacAllister and the rest of the board. We all believe it's for the best."

"It's because of me, isn't it? Oh, Jason, I'm ruining your life!"

"Now how could you do that? I love you." Blindly she shook her head, waves of remorse flooding over her. "For some time now, Victoria," he went on quickly, "an organization called 'Prodigals' has been interested in engaging me as a counselor. Their work is primarily with teen-age runaways and after much thought and prayer I've decided that is my true calling."

She wanted him so desperately–wanted the safe haven he represented– and so she allowed him to convince her. "Really, Jason?" Her voice was shaking.

"Really, my darling." He gently touched her face. "And before I begin my duties, they'll allow me some time so that I may go to Reno and establish residency for a divorce." Actually he'd told "Prodigals" he was going to Nevada to attend a seminar on pastoral counseling. "Is six weeks sufficient notice to give them at the theatre?"

For a few brief moments she thought of the career she'd worked so hard to build, but then quickly the prospect of being loved, of no longer being alone, banished all regret. "Yes, I'm sure six weeks would be enough." Victoria's misgivings were gone and there was only a deep sense of peace as she surrendered her will to someone far wiser, far better than she. Jason left a few days later and Victoria informed Jonathan Sinclair that when he returned and they were married, she would be retiring as an actress. Both he and Noel tried to talk her out of it, but she was adamant. "I don't need all that anymore," he assured them with her most dazzling smile. "I'll be Jason's wife."

He came back toward the end of the first week in March and they were married the following Friday evening in Victoria's apartment–Ken MacAllister performing the ceremony. The guest list was necessarily limited and from the theatre company Victoria invited only

Noel and Jon. Jason had tried to dissuade her from inviting even them. He said they'd feel out of place. It almost seemed as though he were deliberately trying to cut her off from all her old associations, but such a thought was terribly disloyal to this fine, decent man. She told herself that of course she was wrong and as she stood beside him and repeated her marriage vows, she was sure she had never been happier. Jason, on the other hand, could think of only one thing–the wedding night. Had Victoria dressed that way, he wondered, just to tantalize him–the folds of her gold silk dress seemingly arranged in such a way as to accentuate the curves of her body.

At last they were alone heading out of the city on the Merritt Parkway, which at this hour was nearly empty of traffic. There would be just time for a week's honeymoon before Jason was to begin his new duties and they would be spending it on Cape Cod. He kept wanting to look at Victoria, sitting beside him in the car–this incredible woman who was now his wife–and he found it difficult to concentrate on his driving. "Cape Cod may seem a strange place to go in March"–he glanced over at her then and smiled–, "but believe me, darling, it's even lovelier in the winter–natural and unspoiled." Victoria merely smiled in reply. The joy she had felt during the ceremony had vanished and for some reason now she was filled with panic. But, oh why was she so terribly frightened? She should be experiencing nothing but utter contentment.

It was nearly two in the morning when they arrived at the White Hart Inn in Salisbury, Connecticut where they would be spending the night. It was a rambling old white clapboard building with a broad front porch. A light still burned over the front door in expectation of their late arrival and inside the dimly lit old-fashioned lobby a sleepy desk clerk was watching an old movie on a small portable television. As they came in, he was stifling a yawn. "Reverend Eliot?"

"Yes. Sorry to have kept you so late." As always Jason's tone was pleasant, but his handwriting as he registered was noticeably shaky. All he could think about was that in a very few minutes he would be alone in a bedroom with Victoria. Suddenly he became aware that the desk clerk was speaking to him again. "Excuse me, " he apologized. For the first time in his life could he be blushing?

"Room Eight, sir," the man repeated, a knowing smile beginning to creep across his face. "At the top of the stairs."

In the room Jason helped Victoria out of her coat, took off his own and methodically hung them up in the closet. Then for a moment or so they both stood there–trying not to look at each other. Jason cleared his throat. "Would...would you like to change first?" he asked finally.

Memories of other nights flitted through Victoria's mind. Never once had she been asked if she wanted to change first. Ordinarily she would have found this amusing, but now his words only proved all over again how thoroughly moral he was. Never could she possibly deserve him. "Thank you, Jason." She wondered if she sounded at all demure– wondered if Ruth were the only other woman with whom he'd ever had sex. She welcomed the privacy of the bathroom and as she slowly undressed, she realized she was trembling. "What in hell is wrong with me?" she muttered under her breath. "You might think I was a Goddamned virgin! But that's just it, isn't it?" She stared at her reflection in the medicine chest mirror. "The honor of <u>your</u> deflowering went to Peter Harris!"

When she came out, it was to find Jason sitting on the edge of the bed staring at the bathroom door. She smiled sweetly, pleading silently with him to come to her. She knew she looked beautiful–how could he help but want her–and once the first time was over, she would at least know what to expect during their intimate moments together.

Jason had imagined what it would be like, but nothing he'd envisioned had come close to the picture she made standing there before him–her breasts straining against the low-cut top of her nightgown–the outline of her body clearly visible through the filmy material. Desire flooded over him and getting quickly to his feet, he picked up his pajamas and robe from the bed beside him. "You...you look lovely." Somehow he managed to get past Victoria and through the bathroom door without touching her.

She stood without moving, listening as the door clicked shut behind him. A terrible thought occurred to her–of course, he's....he's thinking of all those other men and he finds me too repulsive even to touch. She pulled back the spread and slipped under the covers, burying her head in the pillow.

Jason had never known such physical sensations could exist as those which tore through him at that moment. He undressed as rapidly as possible, not even daring to glance down at his own body. By now he was so aroused that he knew he was no longer able to control himself. Would she notice? He was horribly embarrassed at the prospect, but when he came out of the bathroom, he saw with some relief that Victoria was already in bed, curled up on her side facing away from him and the room, moreover, was only dimly lit by a small bedside lamp. Turning off the light, he slipped into bed beside her. He reached out for her, but all he could bring himself to touch was her bare shoulder. "Victoria," he whispered hoarsely.

He....he did love her–in spite of everything–and willingly, happily she turned to give herself to him. The motion caused the strap of her nightgown to slide down off her shoulder, leaving one breast nearly exposed. His breath coming faster, Jason reached out to cup it in one hand. Incredibly he felt the nipple grow hard and now he was kneading the breast, reveling in the sensation of its firmness yielding beneath his fingers. But even this was no longer enough. So often he'd pictured her naked and now it was his right to see her that way. The material of her nightgown gave easily. For a moment he stared down at her, unaware he was drooling.

"Yes, my darling, yes," Victoria murmured. "Take me—take me now."

He tried to take off his own pajamas, but his fingers fumbled uselessly with the buttons and the string worked itself perversely into a knot. Groaning with frustration, Jason finally got them off and climbing on top of her, thrust himself into her. A great roaring noise filled the air and then somehow the sound was inside him as well like an enormous waterfall. His entire body went rigid in one final push and withdrawing from her at last, he fell back against the pillows, his flesh soaked with sweat. In almost no time he was asleep.

Victoria, however, lay awake for hours, happier than she could ever remember being. Sex couldn't be wrong if such a good, decent man could become so aroused. Curling up beside him, she pillowed her head against his chest and at last she also slept.

Chapter 17

The first physical sensation of which Jason was conscious the next morning was the pressure of something warm and soft against his arm. Coming after several seconds more to full wakefulness, he realized with a start that it was Victoria's bare breast. Lastly, and most humiliating of all, he realized that he himself was naked as well. He was filled with self-loathing.

Victoria rolled over onto her back just then and opened her eyes. She smiled, reaching up to him. Renewed desire swept over Jason and with it renewed shame. At once he drew away to sit up on the edge of the bed and slip into his robe. "I...I'd like to shower first if you don't mind." Standing up, he walked quickly toward the bathroom. "I...I'm so sorry about last night, Victoria. I....I can't imagine what came over me!" She lay quiet for a moment–too dazed and hurt to move. What had she done that she'd disgusted him so? Finally she forced herself to get up as well and put on her own robe. After that, however, she couldn't seem to decide what to do and she simply sat on the bed and waited. It was about a half hour before Jason came out again–showered and shaved. "Your...your turn, dear."

"Thank you." She gathered up her things and moved past him into the bathroom, avoiding looking at him. Clearly he was revolted by her and she couldn't bear to see that on his face. Only in the shower did Victoria allow herself to cry. It was too late for her to deserve life with someone good and decent and even though a few minutes later she did her make-up with special care, she felt ugly.

Jason smiled at her, however, as she came back out into the bedroom–the same gentle, loving smile– and she was somewhat reassured. "Hungry, darling?" he asked.

She smiled back tremulously, grateful once again for his forgiveness. "Not very, I'm afraid. I never eat much in the morning."

Over breakfast they discussed their plans for the coming days, the weather, the delicious scrambled eggs and hot corn muffins, everything except what was uppermost in both their minds–the previous night. During most of the remainder of the drive to the Cape Victoria read or watched the map for him. Once she slept for a while and by the time they arrived in Chatham where they would be staying, all tension seemed gone.

The rest of the honeymoon was pleasant enough: long walks on deserted beaches, candlelit dinners in small, intimate inns. Apparently, despite its unfortunate beginning, they had started to build a marriage. The situation was eased somewhat by the fact that after that first night Jason didn't make love to her again. This might have been because after long days in the out-of-doors they were both tired except that Victoria didn't sleep well at all. Lying awake for long hours in the darkness, she felt somehow cheated and worse, more alone than ever.

Then only a day or so after they returned to New York she had her first panic attack. She was lying beside her husband in bed, once again rigid with sleeplessness– the night stretching endlessly ahead of her--when with no warning the old unreasoning fear seized hold of her. She fought the feeling until she could bear it no longer. "Jason," she whispered, touching him on the shoulder. "Please, I'm so frightened."

"What, Victoria?" he murmured sleepily, turning to face her.

"Please, I can't stand it!" She clutched at him. "Please, I...I'm absolutely terrified."

"What are you afraid of, dearest?"

"I...I don't know." Helplessly she shook her head.

"When I'm afraid," he observed soothingly, "I find prayer a great solace."

"Oh, Jason, I can't pray!"

"Well then, I'll pray for you. Will that help?"

Briefly she felt a flash of irritation, but she pushed it from her mind. "Yes—please, would you?" So he prayed that God would send her peace of mind and an acceptance of her husband's love and a complete trust in him; that He would help them both to forget the past and work to build a new life together. Victoria found comfort in his words yet at the same time they reaffirmed what she already knew. She could never be worthy of him.

Jason, of course, soon became involved in his work, putting in long hours–hours which frequently extended far into the night–and since she'd resigned from the theatre company, she spent most evenings alone. Victoria told herself that although alone, she was no longer lonely, but often the time did seem long. Except for the MacAllisters, after all, everyone she knew in New York was in the theatre and also worked evenings. It was probably just as well anyway that she not see much of her fellow actors. Jason had made it evident these people no longer belonged in her life and she was so often guilty of displeasing him as it was.

She might be in the kitchen preparing dinner and a glass would slip from her hands or perhaps a knife nick her finger. "Dammit," she muttered under her breath.

"Please, Victoria," he would reprimand her gently, "you know I find profanity distressing."

Or they would go out to dinner–usually with the MacAllisters–and without thinking, she'd order a drink. Jason wouldn't say anything then, of course, waiting until they were home alone. "Victoria," he would inquire in an indulgent tone, "do you have to drink?"

"Well no, I suppose not."

"Then I'd rather you didn't–especially in public."

Her sense of humor prompted her to ask–""How do you feel about wine? Even Jesus drank that!" But she knew only too well what his reaction would be to such a remark.

Worst of all, however, were the nights when inevitably Jason would find himself aroused by her nearness and once more they would make love–although perhaps never again as passionately as on their wedding night. Each time Victoria enjoyed the lovemaking a little less–anticipating even as he kissed and caressed her–his certain, embarrassed "mea culpa" of the following morning. And with each stammered apology she felt a little dirtier, a little more sordid as she continued to crave what he clearly found shameful.

Then about two months after they were married the court set the date for Olivia's custody hearing–proceedings to begin the third week in May–and for a while everything else was forgotten.

* * *

Jason seemed unable to get away and so it was Noel, his commitment in New York concluded, who would be accompanying Victoria home to London. Her old friend had seen her only twice since the wedding. The first occasion was for dinner at the couple's apartment. Victoria appeared strangely ill-at-ease, glancing over continually at Jason as though for his approval. Then just a week or so ago they'd had lunch, just the two of them this time, but still she lacked her customary sparkle–a sparkle which until now had always been there–even in her worst moments.

During the early hours of the flight they chatted about Olivia, about their early days together in the theatre. After the film she apparently slept for a while and it wasn't until breakfast the next morning that Noel finally had the opportunity to bring up what was on his mind. "Victoria, are you really happy?"

"Am I happy? What a bloody stupid question!" Without being aware of it Victoria had indeed answered him and now he was more concerned than ever. Then a short while later stepping from the plane at Heathrow, they were greeted with the inevitable barrage of flashbulbs and he saw the famous Windsor smile turned on again for public consumption. For a moment it was almost as though the past year had never happened.

"Miss Windsor," someone called out, "I've been wondering why you weren't awarded custody of your daughter in the first place?"

"It's only been since my remarriage that I felt I could provide a proper home for her."

"I should think your new husband would want to be here with you," another reporter observed.

The smile dimmed slightly. "Unfortunately his work made it impossible for him to leave New York."

Damned rotten excuse–that, Noel thought bitterly, as he eased her through the crowd toward the waiting limousine. Once there they were quickly inside and the car moved off across the runway, around the terminal and out onto the road leading away from the airport, Matt, of course, as usual having already taken care of immigration formalities. Victoria leaned back against the cushions and closed her eyes– mannerisms which also reminded Noel painfully of the old days. But then after a moment she opened her eyes again and smiled at him–a more natural smile. "It will all be worth it, you know," he reassured her, "when you're back here at the airport and Olivia is with you."

"Oh, but Noel, suppose they decide I'm.. " She made an ironic face....." an unfit mother."

"They won't, Victoria. I'm sure of it."

"You're always there for me, aren't you? I haven't forgotten I have you to thank for this."

He smiled at her. "I've missed you, you know–both on stage and off."

"Thank you, luv. I've...I've missed you, too."

After that the conversation drifted easily through a variety of topics– all quite casual again–until the car came to a stop in front of the Waldorf where Matt had booked her a suite. He'd selected this hotel because it was next door to the Aldwych Theatre and he thought she'd find familiar territory a comfort. The hotel doorman was instantly at the curb–opening the limousine door for her. "Miss Windsor, allow me." He extended a hand to help her alight.

"Thank you." Accepting the offered hand, she stepped gracefully out onto the sidewalk. It felt rather good to be treated with such deference again.

Noel slid over to her side of the car. "I'll come back about seven and take you out for dinner," he promised.

"Oh, good! See you later then, luv." The limousine pulled away from the curb and she turned to walk across the pavement into the hotel.

Several passers-by, realizing who was getting out of the car, had stopped to stare, but then all at once a little girl pushed past them, arms outstretched. "Mummy!"

Instantly recognizing the sweet young voice, Victoria whirled about in the direction of the sound, bending down to receive Olivia into her embrace. "Darling, oh darling!"

A few of the more enterprising newsmen had followed the actress' car into London and now as mother and daughter hugged each other, flashbulbs popped again to record the moment. "Your name's Olivia, right?" someone asked.

"Don't answer any questions," Victoria said quickly before the child could reply. "Just come along inside."

A hotel official met them in the lobby. "Room 710, Miss Windsor. You may go right on up. Our housekeeper, Mrs. Simmons, is waiting there to let you in."

"My goodness, Mummy, I don't think I like being famous!" Olivia was slightly dazed by the whole episode.

Victoria laughed–totally happy again for the first time since her daughter had returned to London. "Oh, my darling!" She drew her close. "I've missed you so!"

"Have you truly? Even since you married that nice Reverend Eliot?"

"You know I have, dearest." The lift stopped at the seventh floor and they stepped out. "Only you should call him Jason now, you know."

"I'm so happy you're here, Mummy!" Olivia bubbled as she half-skipped along the hall hand in hand with her mother.

"So am I, luv." It seemed so natural for them to be together that for the moment Victoria hadn't stopped to think. It was only, in fact, when Mrs. Simmons, a large, cheery woman, had let them into the suite, given her the key and left them alone, that she remembered. "But I thought I wasn't allowed to see you before the hearing." The child stared guiltily at the floor. "Olivia–look at me." Reluctantly she obeyed. "I'm <u>not</u> supposed to see you before the hearing, am I?"

"Oh, but Mummy, it's been four whole months and I couldn't have you so close and not see you! I just couldn't!"

She tried not to think of what this could do to her case, but there was no need to alarm her daughter. The telephone rang and she went to answer it. "Hello?"

"Victoria! It's Matt. Welcome home!"

Home–Yes, London <u>was</u> home and yet she had committed herself to a life in the United States–because of Jason, of course–and how foolish she was to feel nostalgic about a place when she had this kind and decent man in her life. "It's good to hear your voice, luv," was all she said aloud.

"I can do better than that. I'm downstairs with your solicitor. May we come up?"

"Yes, of course. See you in a bit then."

She turned from the telephone to find her daughter standing there, her lower lip quivering. "Mummy, did I do something dreadfully bad by coming here?"

"Oh no, luv." Victoria touched her tenderly on the cheek. "How could anyone think it wrong for a little girl to want to see her mother?"

"It's...it's going to be all right, isn't it?" Olivia inquired tearfully. "I mean the judge will let me be with you, won't he?"

"I'm sure of it, darling." She hoped the doubt wasn't evident in her tone. "But tell me what you've been doing since your last letter," she went on as cheerfully as possible. "When's that Guides camping trip you wrote me about?"

"I....I haven't signed up for it yet. I...I thought I might living in New York by then so...."

"Oh, darling...." Victoria hugged her yet again. A knock came at the door. "Matt?" She didn't want to encounter any more reporters.

" 'Tis I, dear lady."

Victoria hurried over to open the door. "Matt, darling! Thank you so much for all you've done!"

He stepped over the threshold into her arms, kissing her on the cheek before turning to introduce the man who was still standing in the hall. "Victoria, this is Carl Michaels, the solicitor I've engaged on your behalf."

Carl Michaels was short and dark–very intense looking–with tortoise-shell rimmed glasses. He wore the obligatory three piece suit and derby, the latter of which he now carried in his left hand along with his briefcase and the inevitable rolled umbrella. "Miss Windsor." He graciously extended his hand. "An honor–I assure you."

"How kind of you, Mr. Michaels."

The solicitor moved over to a near-by chair to put down his things, but as he did so, he happened to notice Olivia. "Is this the child concerned in the litigation?" he inquired sharply.

"Yes, this is my daughter, Olivia." Victoria turned back to slip an affectionate arm around the little girl's shoulders and draw her forward to join the group. "Matt, you've never met her, have you? Olivia, darling, this is my agent, Leslie Matthews. You may call him Matt or Mr. Matthews or anything else you wish as long as it isn't Leslie."

"Hello, Olivia." Matt smiled at her kindly.

"Hi, Mr. Matthews. Mummy's told me all about you. How she met you in an alley before I was even born and everything."

"Has she now? Well, you know I've heard a great deal about you, too. The Girl Guides and your delicious cinnamon toast and....."

"This is all very touching, I'm sure," the solicitor interrupted curtly. "However, I thought you understood, Miss Windsor, that you were not to see your daughter prior to the hearing."

"And I thought that was absolutely asinine!" Victoria snapped. "I have every right to see her whenever I choose!"

"Mr. Matthews, you told me Miss Windsor would agree to anything I decided for the good of her petition."

Matt smiled ruefully. "I agreed, sir. But I'm afraid that's not quite the same thing."

"Please-- it was my fault." Olivia hurled herself bravely into the midst of the adult conversation. "I heard Daddy say what hotel my mother would be staying in and I just came here."

"Well, that was a very foolish thing to do, young lady!" Mr. Michaels said sternly. "Do you realize you may have seriously damaged your mother's chances of winning custody?"

The little girl burst into tears and Victoria turned on the unsuspecting solicitor in one of the most towering rages Matt had ever witnessed and he thought by now he'd seen them all. "And perhaps you can tell me,"she screamed at him, "just where you get the Goddamned bloody cheek to talk like that to an eight year old child? Get the hell out of here!"

"Victoria, please." Matt made what he knew in advance would be a vain attempt to calm her.

"Sod off, you son-of-a-bitch! You engaged the bloody bastard in the first place!" It was strange. Despite her genuine anger–despite her fear of losing Olivia forever–she felt exhilarated as for the first time in months she was able to let herself go in a glorious outburst of temper–liberally sprinkled with profanity.

"It is obvious, Mr. Matthews, that Miss Windsor should seek other legal counsel. So if you will excuse me!" Drawing himself up to his full height of five feet, four inches, the little man picked up his briefcase, his derby, his umbrella and his offended dignity and strode from the room.

"Please, sir." Matt followed him out into the corridor. "Let me bring her to your office tomorrow as planned. You did say the barrister would be there then, didn't you?"

"Well, really, if she throws one of those tantrums at the hearing, any chance she might have will be lost."

"I'll talk to her, I promise. Just wait until tomorrow before you decide definitely to drop the case."

"Very well," the solicitor finally agreed. "But get that child out of here!"

Just then the bellboys arrived with the luggage ending any further discussion between the two men. Carl Michaels began to walk away down the hall. "Tomorrow at eleven, right?" Matt called after him pleadingly. The other man merely responded with a wave of his derby before disappearing around the corner. "In here, please," the agent continued, indicating the proper door and knocking lightly before pushing it open. "Victoria, your luggage is here."

She was sitting beside Olivia on the couch, holding the little girl close and talking quietly to her. "Take care of it, Matt, will you please?"

He quickly showed the men where they could put the cases, tipped them and closed the door after them. Then he came over to sit on a chair facing them. "Olivia does have to leave, you know," he said, "before anyone knows she's here." He watched Victoria tenderly brush her daughter's hair away from her face. How truly different she is, he thought.

"I'm afraid it's a little late for that. There were photographers outside the hotel."

"Oh, I see. Well, then...."

"Please, Mr. Matthews," Olivia broke in anxiously, "did I ruin everything? I...I... just couldn't wait to see my mother."

"I don't blame you in the least." Matt reached over to pat her on the hand. "I couldn't wait to see her either. You want very much to live with your Mummy, don't you, dear?"

"Oh yes, please!" Olivia slipped both arms around her mother's waist, holding on with all her strength. "More than anything!"

Matt saw tears in Victoria's eyes and all at once he realized with a start how little make-up she was wearing. "Believe me, we'll do everything we can to make it come true." His words of reassurance were for both their benefits. "But for now I'm afraid you do have to go home."

"It won't be long, luv. I promise." Victoria hugged and kissed her daughter. "Matt, would you take her out one of the less conspicuous entrances and put her in a taxi?"

He nodded and stood up, taking his charge by the hand. "I'll be right back," he said to Victoria. "Then we can talk."

"Bye, Mummy." The little girl walked reluctantly toward the door, still looking back over her shoulder at her mother.

"Bye-bye, luv. See you soon."

When Matt returned a short time later, he found Victoria in the midst of unpacking. "Come in," she called out in answer to his knock. "I thought I should do something to help me keep my sanity," She had just taken a few cardigans out of a suitcase, but now she dropped them on the bed, spinning about to face him. "Matt, what are my chances? Please–be honest."

"Without legal counsel?"

"Oh yes, well..ah...what do I do about that?" She looked so adorably helpless, so unlike the Victoria he remembered that he couldn't help but smile. "I rather botched that one, what?" She smiled at him in return, but then he learned again that she hadn't changed entirely. "Well, you know, Matt, he had no bloody right to talk that way to Olivia. She's upset enough as it is."

"Yes, I know, Victoria, but Michaels is a highly competent solicitor and Joshua Epstein, a brilliant barrister. You couldn't have a better team working for you."

She made a face. "Then I have to be good. Is that what you're telling me?"

"We have an appointment with them at eleven tomorrow morning?"

"All right. Matt. I promise I'll keep my temper. Now then, with Michaels and Epstein safely in tow, what are my chances?"

"Well, you are Olivia's natural mother."

"Dammit, Matt!" Her eyes filled with tears. "Don't hedge! I know there isn't a chance in hell they'll give me my little girl." Her voice was shaking with emotion in spite of her effort to control it. "And oh God, Matt, I do want her so very much!"

"We won't give up hope yet, will we?" He put an arm around her shoulders. "Now suppose I order tea from room service and we can chat."

"Tea!" she exclaimed in mock ecstasy, blinking back the tears. "Real English tea! How bloody marvelous!"

* * *

His Lordship Sir Evelyn Hastings-Hargrove–-presiding judge in the case of Eliot v. Roberts concerning the custody of one minor child, Olivia Victoria Roberts—arrived in his chambers on the day of the hearing somewhat earlier than was his custom. He had already met with the two solicitors in the litigation and he'd spent hours studying the notes taken by his secretary during those meetings. The arguments on both sides were not out of the ordinary. The plaintiff was the natural mother with the strongest claim to the child while the counsel for the respondent had stated their intent to prove her unfit. He found custody suits to be invariably difficult, however, filled with more anger and bitterness than any other type of hearing over which he presided. Moreover, no matter how carefully he considered the evidence and no matter the decision at which he ultimately arrived, he knew someone would be hurt. A compassionate and sensitive man, Sir Evelyn needed the extra time, therefore, not to prepare himself mentally, but emotionally.

Andrew entered the courtroom first, accompanied by his barrister, Philip Cunningham, who with his solicitor–old friend and former associate, Greg Allsworth–had prepared his case. He'd tried more than once to persuade them to change their tactics. Why did Victoria's past have to be brought into this? "Phil," Andrew said yet again now, "are you positive that proving my former wife unfit is our only course of action? I've been a good father. Shouldn't that be enough?"

"Look here, old chap! I can still withdraw. Is that what you want? Because if I continue, I am going to present the strongest case possible and that's the one Greg and I have prepared for you." The barrister paused in the act of removing further papers from his briefcase. "Now do I go or stay?"

Andrew only hesitated briefly. "Stay, please." He wearily waved his hand. "I'll offer no further objections."

An uproar of clamoring reporters and photographers disturbed the hearing room for a moment as the doors opened again to admit Victoria and her barrister, Joshua Epstein.

A brilliant young man, Josh was olive-skinned with jet black hair and wide-set eyes so black in color as to appear almost opaque. He'd had some misgivings about accepting an actress as a client, but her charm, her wit, her genuine love of her daughter had entirely won him over. And she possessed the one quality he valued above all else in a client– unflinching honesty. During their preparatory conference he'd asked her what facts about her past could be used as evidence against her. "Almost everything," she'd replied. Her laugh held a bitter note, however, as she proceeded to tell him with painful candor about the style of her life up until the very recent past.

More than once now as they settled themselves at the table, Josh glanced over at her, greatly concerned. He could see how tense she was even though when she noticed him looking at her, she tried to smile. "It will be all right, Victoria," he reassured her yet again even as he doubted seriously the strength of their case. He'd tried to get her to give him the names of people he could call as character witnesses on her behalf, but she insisted there was no one. "I have almost no friends," was all she'd say.

Her barrister wasn't the only one watching Victoria. Andrew hadn't taken his eyes off her. She was even lovelier than he remembered–wearing very little make-up–and her green silk suit was the exact shade of her eyes. He supposed her hair was still long, but today it was hidden under a pill-box style hat. Her gloves were a soft beige kid.

A court stenographer entered from a back room and finally His Lordship, Judge Hastings-Hargrove. Due to Victoria's position as a public figure, it was to be a closed hearing with no others present. The opening remarks of each barrister did not differ in any significant detail from their written statements provided for Sir Evelyn in advance. Then as counsel for the plaintiff, Mr. Epstein presented his case first. He had only one witness: Victoria herself, stating simply but movingly how deeply she cared for her daughter. She also explained that she was now remarried to a fine man who would make Olivia a kind and loving stepfather.

Philip Cunningham rose to cross-examine. "Miss Windsor," he began smoothly, "may I first take this opportunity to tell you how much I've always admired your work as an actress."

Victoria had been horribly on edge–expecting the worst. She nodded briefly in response to this compliment. "Thank you very much."

"But never have you given a more impressive performance than the one we've all witnessed here today."

Her hands were clasped tightly in her lap. "I....I...don't understand what you mean."

"Oh, come now, Miss Windsor. Do you mean to say you weren't acting just now?" His tone was heavily ironic.

She looked at him steadily. "No, I was not. I love my daughter very much and I want to have her with me."

"How old was your daughter when you deserted her?"

Joshua Epstein was instantly on his feet. "Objection to the word, 'deserted', m'lord, as prejudicial to my client."

"Objection sustained," Sir Evelyn agreed. "You will rephrase your question, Mr. Cunningham."

"Gladly, m'lord. Miss Windsor, how old was Olivia when you left her?"

Briefly Victoria was back on that long ago morning when she'd handed her daughter to the woman in the ground floor flat and left. She could even smell that sweet baby odor that had seemed to cling to her long after she'd gotten on the train. "She...she...was...ah...nine months old."

"And this is the child you pretend to love?" Andrew looked down at the table in front of him. He couldn't bear to see Victoria's face. "Miss Windsor," Philip Cunningham prompted coldly, "would you kindly reply?"

"Objection, m'lord!" Josh was on his feet again. "There is no need to harass the witness."

But the judge ruled this time that this was acceptable cross-examination and requested that she answer. "I'm....I'm sorry." Victoria twisted her hands in her lap. "I...I didn't realize that was a question."

"Miss Windsor." Phil allowed himself a faint smile. She was already beaten and the most telling part of his case was yet to come. "Did you love your child at the time you left her?"

"Yes," Victoria whispered, "I....I did."

"Then why did you leave?"

"An...an acting job...in the Midlands. . I....I hadn't been able to get any work in London, you see, so I....I....."

"But you were married–why did you have to work?"

"I....I wanted to....to be an actress."

"And this was more important to you than your daughter?"

"No.....no!" Victoria vehemently shook her head. How could she possibly explain the forces that had driven her in those days when she didn't understand them herself.

"It isn't required that you continue, Miss Windsor. Tell me–how many lovers would you say you've had?"

"Objection, m'lord." Josh was now thoroughly indignant. "Counsel is being openly insulting to my client."

"As it is my intention, m'lord, to prove Miss Windsor an unfit mother," Phil Cunningham explained patiently, "it is necessary to establish the fact of her low moral character."

"You will answer the question, Miss Windsor," Sir Evelyn requested.

"How many?" she said blankly. How many lovers? Did that include the men she picked up in pubs? How about the man in Stratford who'd beaten and raped her? "How many?" she said yet again. She knew how important it was to say just the right thing and she couldn't seem to think clearly at all.

"May we understand, then, that you have lost count?" Victoria didn't answer. "Very well, madam. We will assume you have indeed replied." Phil's sarcasm was undisguised now. "It is also true, is it not, Miss Windsor, that you drink heavily...that, in addition, you have used various kinds of illicitly obtained drugs?"

Victoria fought as never before to regain control of herself and raising her head, she managed to say with a degree of dignity, "Not...not anymore...no, I don't."

"I see. Miss Windsor, at the time of your divorce I believe your husband offered you joint custody of your daughter and you refused. Why?"

She looked down at her hands still clasped together in her lap. She knew she'd lost and all she wanted was for this merciless questioning to end. Why had she even tried? All she'd done was raise Olivia's hopes and all for nothing. "I...I didn't have time for her. She was better off with her father." What the hell, it was all over anyway.

Philip Cunningham also knew he'd made his case. It was time to conclude his cross-examination and get on to his own witnesses. "And now you do?"

"Yes, I....I want her with me now." But her tone was flat, without emotion.

"Your present husband was married when you met him. Am I correct, Miss Windsor?" So that's it, she thought; I'm also a home wrecker. She actually laughed out loud. "You find that amusing?" Phil raised his eyebrows in shocked surprise–whether feigned or real, it was impossible to tell.

"About as amusing as an animal finds the trap it's caught in.... Yes, Jason was married when I met him. But it wasn't a happy marriage."

"Yes. Well, thank you, Miss Windsor. No further questions, m'lord." He turned away to walk back to his table.

Sir Evelyn banged his gavel. "Court is declared in recess until two p.m."

Victoria hadn't moved from the witness stand and after a moment Josh went up to her, touching her on the arm. "The judge has recessed the hearing," he said quietly. "Why don't we get some lunch?"

She looked about uncertainly. "Is...is he through with me, then?"

"Are...are you all right, Victoria?"

"Oh...oh, yes...thank you."

"Well, come on then. He took her by the arm and without a word she allowed him to lead her from the room.

"I...I never wanted to do this to her, Phil," Andrew said urgently. "This must go no further!"

"Tell me–do you wish to keep your daughter?"

"Yes, of course, but...."

"Then let me do my job."

* * *

Victoria ate very little–answering any question Josh put to her with the barest monosyllable. When he suggested, however, that she not return to court, she became agitated. "No, I have to be there! Don't you see? I have to hear what they say about me!" She was almost shouting and others in the restaurant turned to stare at her.

Josh wondered if he should call someone to come and be with her or for that matter whether there was anyone to call. Surely if there were, at least one person would have come forward to testify. Perhaps it was just as she'd said. Perhaps she truly had no friends. "Victoria," he asked her again as they left the restaurant together, "are you sure you feel well enough to go back in? It could get nasty this afternoon, I'm afraid." She didn't answer him and a moment later she alarmed him even more by almost walking into a man approaching from the opposite direction. Clearly she hadn't even seen him.

Back in the courtroom they had only a few minutes wait before Sir Evelyn returned, gaveled the hearing to order and asked if the plaintiff wished to present any further witnesses. "No, m'lord," Josh replied with a sigh. It wasn't a good feeling to know he was losing the case, especially when he was sure he could have done so much more. The respondent's witnesses were much as he'd anticipated. A former employer, Cassius O'Flaherty; two former lovers, Clive Bannister and Julian Christopher and two woman, one an actress, the other a stage manager had all been more than willing to testify as to Victoria's promiscuity or her drunkenness or her temper or any combination thereof. Josh did his best to discredit the testimony. It was, after all, only their word in each case and their motives were decidedly suspect: jealousy..revenge. Sadly he knew it was all in vain.

At first Victoria appeared to be listening intently, but as the afternoon session continued, she seemed to be having difficulty concentrating and finally it was clear she no longer heard a word of what was being said which was probably just as well. Perhaps the whole thing was, after all, worse for Andrew. He tried not to look at her, but again and again he would find his eyes drawn back to her face.

The stage manager had been the final witness. Both barristers offered their closing remarks and at last it was over. "Tomorrow morning I will be speaking with the child in question," Sir Evelyn announced in conclusion, "and at two o'clock all parties involved should be present in my chambers to hear my decision. Court is adjourned."

The sharp rap of the gavel brought Victoria back to some degree of awareness and she glanced about, a bemused expression on her face. Agonizing, her former husband stared at her, wishing–absurdly–that he could do something, but it was Josh who helped her to her feet and began to walk with her toward the exit. Unable to bear it any longer, Andrew hurried after them, catching her by the arm. "Please, Victoria, I'm sorry. I....I had no idea...." That was a lie, he thought miserably.

Dimly she heard a man speaking, but she was having trouble focusing on his face. She gave her head a little shake. "Oh, Andrew." She reached up to touch him on the cheek. "It's all right. Really it is. After all, it's all true, isn't it?" Her hand came to rest on his where it still lay on her arm and for a few seconds she appeared quite normal. "Oh, but you know, don't you," she whispered, her eyes filling with tears, "how much...how much I've...I've always loved her!"

Josh put his arm around her shoulders. "Let's go now, Victoria." Once again he started to lead her toward the door.

"Please, I....." Andrew attempted a second time to stop them.

Dropping his arm, the barrister rounded on him. "Haven't you done enough, you bastard?" And finally the unhappy man could only stand there, watching them leave. He'd won, hadn't he? Then why in hell did he feel so damned rotten?

Outside the courtroom Josh hesitated, wondering what he should do about his client, but almost at once a man appeared around the corner hurrying toward them. He recognized Noel St. John. "The lobby's full of reporters and photographers," the actor explained breathlessly. "We have a car out back in the alley and there's a lift for the freight."

They each took Victoria by an arm and unresisting, she let herself be led along the corridors in the same direction from which Noel had just come. "Who is we?" Josh inquired as the three of them got into the enormous old lift, the sides of which were padded for the carrying of crates and office furniture.

The other man's attention at that moment was more on the odd assortment of buttons and levers next to the door. "Oh...ah...sorry–Terence Cartier and I. He's waiting with his car and driver." The lift shuddered and at last they started to move.

"What I can't understand," Josh observed bitterly, "is why neither of you was willing to testify in her behalf. It's easy to be concerned now that the damage is done!"

"She said nothing about anyone testifying for her." Clearly Noel was dumbfounded.

"She told me she had almost no friends."

"Oh, dear God! That's not true and she knows it!"

Dazedly Victoria wondered why the floor was dropping away beneath her. Maybe these people with her could explain it, but their voices remained an incomprehensible babble–well, no matter..

At last they had her downstairs and out into the alley where the car was parked with the motor running. The rear door stood open and Terry was sitting on the edge of the seat, one foot out on the pavement, peering toward the building. The moment they appeared he slid over, reaching for Victoria. Easing her into the car, Noel turned back briefly to shake the barrister's hand. "Thank you. I'm sure you did your best."

Josh smiled ruefully. "Under the circumstances I'm afraid that wasn't much. We're to be in the judge's chambers at two tomorrow if she's up to it."

Noel nodded, at last getting into the car himself. "Ready now," he told the driver and they moved off down the alley and out into the traffic.

Terry had put an fatherly arm around Victoria and was holding her close against him. "Why is it always the beautiful ones?" he murmured more to himself than anyone.

"What I can't understand is why in hell that man she married let her go through all of this without him!"

"Why didn't he come with her?"

"Too busy praying, I should imagine," Noel muttered sourly. "Sometimes I think ministers talk a good game, but that's about it!!"

"A minister! Naturally I was aware Victoria had remarried–but a minister?"

"Well, I know one thing! He's going to haul his holy ass over here on the first plane!–unless he'd prefer to walk over, of course!"

"Noel," Terry said all at once, "do you realize she has no idea what we're saying?"

"I first noticed it on the way down in the lift. It's like the time we found her alone on the stage, isn't it?"

Terry nodded, gently stroking her arm. "Victoria, can you hear me, dear."

She made the same futile attempt to concentrate. Why did Andrew suddenly look and sound like her old friend?

Back in the hotel suite the two men took her at once into the bedroom and helped her under the covers. Meekly she submitted. Noel stayed with her for a few minutes and when finally he came out into the living room, he found Terry in the process of giving the hotel operator a phone number. He raised his eyebrows in an unspoken question.

"This time I refuse to listen to any arguments to the contrary." Sir Terence's tone clearly brooked no interference. "I am ringing up the psychiatrist."

"But it only looks like that night. She's much happier now. Once the trauma of the hearing's over, she'll be fine."

"Yes." Terry was speaking into the phone again. "Would you ask if Doctor Anthony has a few moments for Terence Cartier?" Irrelevantly despite the seriousness of the occasion, Noel thought–And who wouldn't have a few minutes for Sir Terence? "Thank you, yes. I'll be more than glad to wait," the other man was saying now. He put a hand over the mouthpiece. "I've seen this before, my friend, and believe me, I know; dear God, how well I know!" Rubbing his forehead distractedly, he did not continue, but Noel understood he was referring to his former wife's long ordeal with mental illness–an ordeal he'd no doubt shared. "Yes, Doctor Anthony," Terry said at last, "how kind of you to take the time. I needed to speak to you about a very good friend of mine."

But just at that moment Victoria let out a scream and Noel hurried back into the other room. She sat up in bed reaching out to him with both hands and he went at once to take her in his arms. She clung to him in terror. "Please, what am I doing back at the hotel? I don't remember getting here!"

"What's the last thing you do remember?" he inquired gently even as he wondered about the wisdom of asking the question.

"Andrew,,,,Andrew spoke to me. He said.....he said...something. I....I don't remember." Then all at once her mind seemed to clear. "Oh, Noel, they're never going to let me have my little girl! Oh, God!" She began to sob.

Coming to stand in the half-open door, Terry beckoned to the younger man. "Doctor Anthony has prescribed a sedative for tonight," he explained quietly. "I'm going to the chemist's to fetch it."

"No, I won't take anything!" Victoria had heard what he said and she got up off the bed and came over to them. "I'm afraid of pills. Really I'm all right now."

"Please, my dear," Terry said soothingly, "you need to sleep tonight. The doctor's assured me it's very mild. Now will you take it for me?"

"All....all right. Whatever you say." She gave in as if she were just too tired to fight him and returning to the bed, she curled up on her side.

"Do you want me to stay with you, Victoria?" Noel asked.

"No. I'm....I'm fine."

"Would you like me to ring Jason and ask him to come?"

"Oh please, you must promise you won't do that. He has so much on his mind with his work. I don't want to be a nuisance."

"All right," he agreed reluctantly. "I promise. You rest now. I'll be right in the next room if you need me."

She nodded and Noel quietly left the room. Terry had gone to pick up the prescription and he sat down to wait. Where and when would it all end for her, he wondered sadly.

* * *

At the sound of the knock Judge Hastings-Hargrove glanced up at the door of his chambers. "Come in," he called out.

His secretary entered, holding the hand of a little girl with long, light brown hair. "Here's a lovely young lady to see you, sir," she said kindly. "But I'm afraid she's rather nervous."

Sir Evelyn hadn't needed his secretary's urging to be gentle. "Olivia Roberts, then, is it?" he inquired. She nodded. "You know, my dear, I've been looking forward to our visit. Thank you, Miss Forman. That will be all." Olivia came slowly forward to sit in the chair across the desk from him. He smiled at her. "None of my information indicated you couldn't talk. You can talk, can't you?"

Again she nodded. Then she giggled. "I...I..mean–yes, sir. I can talk."

"Then suppose you begin by telling me just how much you understand of what's happening here."

"It's....it's...." Olivia looked steadily at the judge's blue eyes peering at her over his half-moon shaped spectacles. Nearly bald without his formal wig, he wasn't at all a frightening person. "It's to decide whether I'm going to live with my father or my mother."

"That's right. Up until now you've lived with your father. Am I correct?"

"Yes, sir."

"Why not your mother? It seems the usual thing for children, especially little girls, to live with their mothers."

Olivia couldn't think how to answer this question. In a way she comprehended why Victoria had been unable until now to be a real mother to her. But she wasn't sure how to make someone else understand. "I....I don't know," she said finally. "I...I've just always lived with my father."

The judge regretted the necessity of pushing this particular point a little further, but he considered the issue too crucial a one to evade. "Didn't your mother want you?" He hoped he wasn't being too blunt.

"My...my mother was....was busy."

"So busy that she didn't have time for you?"

"No.....<u>NO</u>!!" He saw the tears rush into her eyes. "My mother always wanted me and she's always, <u>always</u> loved me!"

Sir Evelyn smiled. The little girl's loyalty to her mother was profoundly touching. "And it's obvious that you love your mother very much as well."

"Yes....oh, yes!"

"Why?"

Olivia was becoming increasingly confused. She'd been determined to make the judge see how much she wanted to be with her mother, but there just seemed to be no place in this baffling maze of questions and answers to put the words. And why did she have to have a reason for loving her mother?

"Can't you tell me why, my dear?"

Helplessly she shook her head. "I....I just do, that's all." One tear spilled over, trickling down her cheek.

"But you love your Daddy, too, don't you?"

"Yes, sir."

"He's always been good to you, hasn't he?"

"You're...you're going to make me stay with Daddy, aren't you?"

"I haven't decided yet, Olivia."

"Please.....please! I want to be with my mother. <u>Please</u>!"

"Why?"

Again why! "Because....because my....my mother needs me."

"Well, you're a very special little girl," Sir Evelyn said. "I can well understand why both your parents want you so much. Thank you, dear. You may go now."

"Is....is that all?"

"Yes, dear. Thank you."

"But....but....."

The judge pressed the button on his intercom. "Miss Forman, you may come in and get Olivia now."

The secretary appeared at once. "Come along then, young lady."

Reluctantly the little girl stood up and walked to the door. Things hadn't worked out at all the way she'd planned.

* * *

Precisely at two in the afternoon the principals in the custody suit of Eliot v. Roberts together with their barristers were ushered into the judge's chambers. Olivia herself was now present as well. Noel had tried to convince Victoria not to attend–to allow her barrister to represent her, but she'd insisted she was all right. She did indeed appear cognizant of reality–pale and tense certainly–, but fully aware of everything that was taking place. Now she was sitting calmly beside Josh Epstein, but her eyes never left Olivia who was next to her father on the other side of the room.

Glancing down at the written statement on the desk in front of him, Sir Evelyn self-consciously cleared his throat. At best these were difficult moments. "Miss Windsor.... gentlemen." Again he cleared his throat. "In any custody suit the welfare of the child must, of course, be of prime importance and accordingly in the case now pending before me concerning one Olivia Victoria Roberts, I have given judgement that the child shall remain in the custody of her father."

Victoria's expression never changed. Perhaps this was partly because she'd already known what the decision would be, but also because even as he spoke, she was already drifting away in a lovely haze. She wasn't actually conscious that she was losing touch with reality. It was just so much more peaceful this way and this man who was doing the talking did sound too funny as though he were speaking from deep inside an echo chamber. She wanted to giggle, but it appeared to be such a solemn occasion.

Andrew's initial reaction was relief. He hugged Olivia to him. "No!" the child screamed and pulling away, she ran across the room to throw herself into Victoria's arms. "No! Oh, Mummy, please!"

The heartbroken sobs of her little girl pulled her mind back temporarily from the brink, maternal instinct bringing her arms up in an awkward, disjointed motion to draw her daughter close. "It's....it's all right, darling," she said, but her tone was oddly flat.

Olivia knew at once that something was wrong. She sat up so that she could see her mother's face. "What's the matter, Mummy?" She scrambled to her feet, turning on the judge in a childish rage. "I <u>told</u> you I wanted to be with my mother! I <u>told</u> you and you wouldn't listen!"

Andrew came over to take her by the hand. "Come along now, sweetheart. You'll....you'll be able to visit your mother often. I promise."

"No, <u>please</u>!" Desperately she tried to pull herself free of his grasp.

"Please come with me now, young lady. You're upset and you're upsetting everyone else."

"Yes, Daddy." At last, still sobbing, the little girl allowed herself to be led from the room.

With Olivia gone Victoria could finally let go of the painful reality. Oh, she was conscious there were other people in the room, but they were all apparently strangers. What am I doing here, she wondered, but she felt no panic, only a vague curiosity. Josh became suddenly aware as he closed his briefcase that for several minutes she had again said nothing. "Miss Windsor?"

She turned to face him. "Were you speaking to me?"

"<u>Victoria</u>?!" But she clearly had no idea who he was. "Will you get Noel St. John, please?" he asked the judge. "He's waiting outside."

Sir Evelyn became concerned. He'd witnessed tears, hysterics, even violent anger as the result of one of his decisions, but never anything like this. "What's wrong with her?"

"What's <u>wrong</u> with her? You've just taken her daughter away from her, dammit!"

My God, Josh thought, I've just sworn at him, but a possible citing for contempt was the least of his concerns at the moment. "Now get her friend in here, man!"

"Yes, yes, of course." Hurrying out into the hall, the judge found Noel on a bench diagonally across from the door. He was smoking, sitting hunched forward with his elbows resting on his knees. "Mr. St. John, I think we need you in here."

Jumping up, he threw away his cigarette and strode across the hall. The barrister met him just inside. "It's....it's much worse this time. She was denied custody and she....she....."

The other man silenced him with a gesture and going over to Victoria, touched her gently on the hand. "Hello, luv." She glanced up at him, as with Josh appearing mildly interested, but then almost immediately she looked away again. "May I use your phone, sir?" he asked the judge.

"Of course! Please!"

Noel picked up the receiver and dialed–praying Terry would be there. It was his wife who answered, but when he identified himself, it was only a moment before the dear man himself came on the line. "Is it Victoria?"

"She...she lost the suit. I can't get any response from her at all."

"I'll ring up Doctor Anthony. In the meantime don't startle her if you can possibly avoid doing so."

"Yes, Terry. Thank you! Thank you!" Noel hung up the phone, turning to look again at Victoria. She was sitting exactly as he'd left her–staring straight ahead, a strange half-smile on her face. He was filled with dread. Under the circumstances he considered himself freed from any promises he'd made and later that night he put a call through to New York.

Victoria's husband answered almost at once. He breathed a sigh of relief. "Jason, it's Noel St. John."

"Noel–oh, yes."

He ignored the condescension in the other man's voice. "I thought you should know. She was refused custody."

"I was afraid of that."

"Then why did you let her go through with it or why in hell didn't you at least come with her?"

"I've always considered profanity to be a rather weak mode of self-expression, St. John. As for my accompanying her, Victoria understands my calling to serve God. Did she <u>ask</u> you to telephone?"

"Of course not." Involuntarily his grip on the receiver tightened. How could Victoria possibly care for this damned, sermonizing prig? "In fact she made me promise <u>not</u> to. But that was before......" Quickly he recounted the events of the last few days.

"Where is she now? Is someone with her?" Gone now was the supercilious tone. The man was genuinely alarmed.

Well, at least that's to his credit, Noel thought bitterly. "A friend called a doctor. They took her in an ambulance directly to hospital."

"What does the doctor say?"

"That reality has simply become too painful for her so she denies its existence. He explains it as a defense mechanism."

"If I leave for the airport now, I should be able to get a night flight. What's the hospital?"

"It's Saint Elizabeth's–just off Wellington Road–near Regent's Park."

"Thank you," Jason murmured. "I do appreciate your calling."

* * *

Every time Noel closed his eyes that night all he could see was Victoria's face–devoid of expression except for that weird little smile. Consequently he slept very little and at 6:30 a.m. he gave up trying. Less than an hour later he was shaved, dressed and at the hospital. The receptionist at the front desk telephoned Dr. Anthony and then directed him to the psychiatrist's office. The door was closed. Noel knocked lightly and the doctor himself admitted him. Entering, he found Terry there as well. "I might have known you'd be here," the older man observed with a smile.

Noel smiled in return. "And I might have known you'd beat me to it. How is she, doctor?"

"Please sit down, gentlemen." Dr. Anthony's appearance and demeanor immediately reinforced the good impression Noel had received of the man the night before. Dark hair lightly sprinkled with gray, he was dressed neatly, but casually in a navy blue cardigan over a light blue open-necked shirt and khaki slacks. Leaning in a relaxed fashion against the corner of his desk, he nevertheless regarded them both intently from behind rimless glasses. Clearly, despite his deceptively informal manner, he was also judging them. "At the moment, Mr. St. John, as I've already explained to Sir Terence, Miss Windsor is still sedated."

"Noel," Terry interposed anxiously, "were you able to reach Victoria's husband?"

"Yes. He was going to get a night flight. He'll be coming directly here."

"I got the impression you don't think much of him."

"I....I don't know him that well," Noel hedged. "He's a kind person, I suppose. I think he genuinely loves Victoria."

Terry raised his eyebrows. "Now tell me, what's your real opinion?"

"He's a sanctimonious, overbearing, self-righteous son-of-a-bitch! That a direct enough answer for you, old chap?"

"Quite."

The doctor noted all of this with considerable interest although he made no attempt to enter into the discussion. "How long have you known her, Mr. St. John?" he asked finally.

Noel thought briefly. "Almost...ah...seven years now."

"And would you say she's basically a happy person?"

"Not really. Oh, she tried to hide it. No one could be more witty or charming."

"The public Victoria," Terry put in at this point. "Remember, Noel?"

He nodded. "Only too well. Then at other times she'd appear cold and unfeeling; she could be downright cruel. And she drank heavily. But those of us who cared about her knew differently–knew it was all a facade."

"And what about her life up to the point you met her?" Dr. Anthony inquired. "Her childhood in particular?"

"I've already said I know very little." Terry shrugged helplessly. "Except that her parents divorced when she was quite young. She's never talked much about her family."

"And I'm afraid I can't add much," Noel admitted regretfully. "I gather it was a lonely childhood though–boarding school, summer camps–no real home life to speak of."

"You've told me quite enough." The doctor shook his head. "Sadly it's all too common. A child deprived of love and security will often grow into an emotionally crippled adult. The facade you mentioned, Mr. St. John–that was also a defense mechanism–much like her withdrawals from reality. Sir Terence has informed me of the prior instance by the way."

Noel nodded. "I think I understand what you're saying, doctor. When are you planning to see her?"

"Anytime now actually." He consulted his watch. "But it might be better if you both waited here for the moment."

"Of course, Charles," Terry agreed. "You'll let us know?"

"Certainly. I have several other patients to see as well, but I'll get back to you as soon as I can."

Before Dr. Anthony could return, however, Jason arrived. Like Noel he was directed upstairs by the nurse at the front desk. Once again the office door was closed. He knocked and it was Noel who let him in, introducing him to Terry. If the American was impressed, he didn't show it, but then perhaps his mind was on Victoria. "How is she?" he asked at once.

"We were just waiting to hear as a matter of fact," Noel explained. "The doctor should be back any minute now."

As though on cue, the door opened. "Reverend Eliot?" The man offered his hand. "I'm Doctor Anthony. I'm glad you're here."

"How is my wife?" Jason inquired anxiously.

"She was beginning to come out of the sedative when I left her just now. We'll go up shortly, but first–if I might ask you a few questions?"

"Anything--of course."

"Mr. St. John and Sir Terence have been kind enough to give me some biographical information on your wife. What I would appreciate your telling me is whether during your marriage she has evinced any signs of emotional distress?"

Briefly Jason glanced at Noel and Terry. It had been all right for them to notify him, but now he would take over. "My wife is....is....subject to...shall we say...panic attacks–especially at night."

"She's always hated the nights." Noel wasn't even aware he'd spoken aloud. Jason had heard him, however, and he glared. Victoria was really none of this man's concern. Fortunately the actor would be remaining in London.

"Tell me, Reverend Eliot," the doctor continued, "has your wife seen a psychiatrist in New York?"

"I didn't consider it necessary. I prayed with her."

"Prayed with her?!" Dr. Anthony whipped off his glasses. "Reverend Eliot, your wife is emotionally ill. Prayer will help certainly, but she needs a trained therapist. Tell me—would you do nothing but pray if she'd broken her leg?"

"Well, of course not! I realize that..."

"Precisely! Well, gentlemen, shall we?" The doctor strode from the room. After a second or two Jason followed him and finally Noel and Terry. They got on the lift together and Dr. Anthony pressed the button for the third floor. "I'm sorry if I seemed abrupt just now, Reverend Eliot. I simply want what is best for your wife."

"Yes, of course. And I hope you know, doctor, that I never intended her harm."

"I'm sure you didn't." Privately, however, he'd begun to understand Noel St. John's feelings about the man. The lift came to a stop and filing out, the four of them started along the hall, Dr. Anthony and Jason walking together. "Now what I'm hoping," the doctor continued, "is that seeing you will bring your wife back to at least partial cognizance of reality."

"I pray I will be able to help her."

The other two men were once more trailing along behind. Noel at one point, indicating Jason, pantomimed a halo and praying hands. Despite the seriousness of the moment it was all Terry could do to keep a straight face.

Outside Victoria's door the doctor stopped. "Just her husband for now, please," he said to Noel and Terry. Inside the room he dismissed the nurse on duty. "I'll stand over here," he explained to Jason. "I want her to see you first. Just talk to her easily and naturally."

Until then he'd avoided looking at his wife. But she appeared exactly as she did when he awoke in the morning to find her asleep beside him and as he went to sit in a chair beside the bed, he experienced a great rush of tenderness. Victoria turned her head from side to side on the pillow. "No, please," she moaned softly. "I want....I want....." Jason looked uncertainly over his shoulder at the doctor.

"It's all right," he reassured him. "The fact that she's still attempting to communicate is actually a healthy sign. Let's find out what happens when she sees you."

All at once Victoria's eyes flicked open. A bewildered look passed over her face. "Oh, dear God, where am I? Please....where am I?" She began to scream. Out in the hall it was all Terry could do to restrain Noel from running into the room.

Jason took her hand in his. "Darling, it's all right. See—I'm here." She turned her head to look at him, but her screams only grew louder.

"She apparently doesn't recognize you, Reverend Eliot." Dr. Anthony came to stand beside him. "I'm sorry, but for the moment I'm going to have to sedate her again. Perhaps if you come back this evening."

Jason replaced her hand on the bed–gingerly as though he were afraid she might break–and getting to his feet, he left the room. Passing Noel and Terry without so much as a glance, he moved away down the long hospital corridor, hands clasped behind his back, head bowed–undoubtedly–in prayer.

* * *

Late in the afternoon Dr. Anthony came back alone to Victoria's room. "Miss Windsor?" he said quietly. She stirred and again she opened her eyes. But now there was no panic. Somewhere deep inside herself Victoria had found peace.

"Can you tell me your name?" he inquired. This was a customary first step in treating such a condition: to help the patient reestablish contact with his own identity and from there to move outward to the recognition of other realities. She looked at him blankly, however–uncomprehending. "I've enjoyed your work on stage so much," the doctor went on...Still no response. "But you are even more beautiful in person"... Nothing. "Your husband is a very fortunate man."...Still nothing. For nearly half an hour he continued to try, but there was not so much as the flicker of an eyelid to show him Victoria was even aware he was in the room.

In the days that followed he spent hours with his patient and when he couldn't be there, Jason was–talking soothingly to her, spending long periods in prayer. Noel and Terry were even allowed to try. It was all to no avail and Doctor Anthony was growing increasingly concerned. Unless someone reached her and soon, the withdrawal could become permanent. At last he decided he had no alternative but to take drastic action, but such measures as he was considering would require the permission of Victoria's husband. "Reverend Eliot, please come in," he called out in answer to the knock on his office door.

Jason entered. "Your message sounded encouraging, Doctor Anthony. Has Victoria begun to respond?" It was an accurate indication of the nature of the relationship between the two men, as well as their individual personalities, that after nearly a week of knowing each other under extremely trying circumstances, they continued to address each other by last name and professional title.

"I'm sorry if my message gave you false hope. It is quite the contrary, I'm afraid. The symptoms of withdrawal are becoming progressively pronounced. As I think I told you, the spells of panic were actually an encouraging sign–demonstrating at least some awareness of her external environment. For the last thirty-six hours now her retreat from reality has been so total it hasn't even been necessary to sedate her."

Jason sank into the chair in front of the doctor's desk. "Dear God, I feel so helpless!"

"I asked you to come, Reverend Eliot, because I need your permission to try something."

"Anything–please–anything!"

"Your wife's emotional collapse was undoubtedly caused by her failure to win the custody suit so what I am proposing is to bring Olivia here to hospital."

"Of course! Yes! That's the answer!" Jason exulted. "Praise God! But why haven't you done this before now?"

"Remember–this is the daughter she has just recently lost?... So, do we chance it?"

The other man's hesitation was brief. "I can't see we have a choice."

"Good! I hoped you would say that." A short time later the doctor walked determinedly up Andrew Roberts' front steps and rang the bell. Olivia's father would hopefully find him more difficult to refuse in person.

"Yes?" It was Andrew himself who answered the door.

"Mr. Roberts, may I speak to you for a few minutes. I'm your former wife's doctor and I....."

"Nothing about my former wife concerns me, sir." Andrew started to close the door in his face.

"Even though you are responsible for what's happened to her?"

"You're not one to mince words I see, doctor."

"When the welfare of my patient is involved—no, I'm not. Now–may we talk?"

"I suppose so, but I have only a few minutes to spare you." He stepped back, opening the door full and allowing the other man to enter. "In my den–over here." He indicated the room to the right of the front hall. Following him inside, Andrew pulled the sliding French doors shut behind them. "I don't wish my daughter to hear this," he explained. "Please sit down."

Dr. Anthony settled himself in an armchair to the right of the double doors and Andrew sat on the edge of the window seat, obviously ill at ease. The doctor could see no reason for not coming directly to the point. "Actually, Mr. Roberts, it's because of your daughter that I've come."

Ever since the hearing five days before, Olivia had only left her room for meals and to go to school. Much of the time she spent looking at the scrapbooks she'd kept of her mother as well as the snapshots she and Victoria had taken together at Christmas. The formal photograph like the one they'd given Noel stood on her bedside table. Over and over again she read her mother's inscription:"To my precious daughter–all my love always, Mummy." She was a normal eight year old, however, and now as she heard the doorbell, the sound of voices below and finally the closing of the sliding doors into her father's den, she thought it would be a good chance to go down to the kitchen for biscuits and milk. Passing through the front hall, she heard herself mentioned. The voice was unfamiliar and she couldn't resist stopping to listen.

"Olivia?" Her father sounded puzzled. "I don't understand what she has to do with all of this."

"When you let me in a few minutes ago, Mr. Roberts," the other voice went on accusingly–almost as though her father were guilty of something–"didn't you as much as admit that the custody hearing and perhaps your own part in it were directly responsible for Mrs. Eliot's emotional collapse." It was all Olivia could do not to rush into the room, but she knew if she went in, they would stop talking.

"May I ask what's wrong with Victoria?" she heard her father ask after a second or two of silence.

"Very simply–reality has become too painful for her and so she has withdrawn from it."

"And....and you feel the custody hearing brought this on?"

Dr, Anthony could see the depth of Andrew's own pain–the guilt he was feeling. He proceeded coldly and deliberately to use that guilt. "Then you do feel somewhat to blame?"

"Yes–dammit, I do!" The other man stood up and began to pace about the room. "I do feel responsible!" Suddenly he turned to face the doctor, running his hand through his thinning brown hair. "It's odd, you know. All I've wanted all these years is for Olivia and Victoria to know and love each other. Now it's happened and it's tearing me apart." All at once he became aware he was pouring out his innermost thoughts and feelings to a total stranger. "But I don't suppose that's much to the point now, is it? Where...where is she?"

"A small private hospital near Regent's Park–Saint Elizabeth's. Mr. Roberts, we've tried everything to reach her: friends, her husband. Nothing has succeeded. You must understand that the longer we wait, the more pronounced her withdrawal. That's why I thought perhaps your daughter,,,,,"

Now Andrew understood. "No! Absolutely not!"

"It was her love for her daughter that drove her over the edge. It's the one thing that could bring her back."

"I can't let her see her mother like that! It's out of the question."

The sliding doors flew open and Olivia burst into the room. "Please, Daddy, let me do it!"

"I'm sorry, sweetheart; it would be a horrible memory for you to carry with you for the rest of your life. I can't allow it!"

"You can't stop me! She's my mother and I'm going!" Olivia made a dash for the front door, but halfway across the hall her father caught up with her, seizing her by the wrist.

"Where you <u>are</u> going, young lady, is upstairs to your room until you can learn to do as you're told." Half-dragging her, Andrew strode up the stairs and along to her room where he finally let her go. "Inside, please." He pointed.

Sobbing, she obeyed and he closed the door and locked it. "Daddy! Oh, please! My mother needs me!"

Trying to ignore his daughter's pleading cries, Andrew hurried back down the stairs. He was surprised to find Dr. Anthony still waiting in the front hall. The doctor had been far from his thoughts. "I would ask you to leave now," he said coldly. "You can see the trouble you've caused."

"Did <u>I</u> cause it? I think we both know differently."

"Really, sir, you are....."

The doctor silenced him with a gesture. "Please, Mr. Roberts, there's no need to say anything further. I'm going. I sincerely hope you won't come to regret your decision." Turning abruptly away, he left before the other man could reply.

Alone Andrew walked into the living room, sinking down on the couch. "God," he whispered, "what a hideous mess I've made of it all!"

It had soon become apparent that her father wasn't going to respond to her entreaties and Olivia gave up, perching disconsolately on the edge of her bed. I have to get out, she thought, I have to! Her glance flew about the room searching for a means of escape. It stopped at the window. In the garden was an old gnarled oak tree. She'd often watched the birds and squirrels running along its branches, sometimes even imagining she was one of them. Now all she saw was a branch which grew close to the house. Quickly she changed into jeans–stuffing some coins for the underground into one pocket. Standing on a chair and holding onto the window frame with one hand, she reached for the tree limb with the other. Incredibly she could touch it! She grabbed hold of it bringing her free hand over and swinging from the branch, she worked her way along to the trunk. Once there it was an easy climb to the ground.

Her class had recently traveled by tube to the Regent's Park Zoo so she knew what line to take—what stop to get off. It had actually been easy, she thought proudly, as she ran up the stairs from the underground station and along the street toward the park. But she'd forgotten how large the park was and although she walked around the edge for over half an hour, she couldn't find the hospital. At last someone showed her where it was–about a block away from the park, it turned out, on a short cul-de-sac. Happily she walked up the stairs and into the small, white-painted lobby.

* * *

Andrew supposed he should go upstairs and talk to Olivia, but just at that moment he couldn't face such a discussion. For a while he tried to read thinking that might calm him, but he found it impossible to concentrate. When the telephone started to ring, he was tempted to ignore it, but the ringing persisted and finally with a sigh he got up from the couch to go out into the hall and answer it. Emily had taken their children to visit her parents in Devon and there was always the chance a client might require his services. Exasperated, he snatched up the receiver. "Andrew Roberts here."

"Oh, thank goodness," the female voice at the other end of the line exclaimed– obviously with some relief. "This is the reception desk at Saint Elizabeth's Hospital, Mr. Roberts. I believe we have your daughter, Olivia, here."

"What?!" He didn't think he could possibly have heard correctly.

"One of our staff caught her trying to sneak up the stairs. She says her mother is a patient here. Is that true?"

"Yes, it's true." Andrew felt terribly weary. "Please--keep her there. I'll come directly to collect her." A short time later he jumped out of a taxi in front of the hospital and carelessly tossing a ten pound note in the window at the driver, he ran up the stairs two at a time and into the lobby. At the reception desk he was directed to an office a short way along the hall to the left.

Inside with Olivia he found his recent visitor along with a tall, thin, white-haired man whom Dr. Anthony introduced as Lawrence Prescott, the hospital administrator. The doctor was sitting beside his daughter on a small, wooden bench against the left hand wall. He had an arm around her shoulders and was talking to her quietly. Lawrence Prescott had risen from behind his desk to acknowledge the introduction with a handshake. "You have a very determined little girl, sir. It seems she climbed out her bedroom window and down a tree into your garden."

"I see," Andrew replied shortly. "Well, come along then, young lady. We'll wait to discuss this when we get home."

To think that her mother was so close and she was still not to be allowed to see her. It seemed more than Olivia could bear. Tears filled her eyes, but she stood up obediently and walked over to look up at him. "I'm sorry, Daddy." She started to move past him toward the door.

Andrew sighed. "Doctor, I've changed my mind. Olivia may see her mother."

Whirling about, the little girl ran back to fling her arms around her father. "Oh, thank you, Daddy! Thank you!"

Taking her arms away from around his waist, he held her back away from him so that he could look down at her–the tears in her eyes answered now by those in his own. "But you must remember, darling, that your mother may not seem like herself."

Dr. Anthony came up to them and leaned down so that his face was nearly level with the child's. "Do you understand what's wrong with your mother?"

"Not....not really," she admitted.

The doctor smiled. "Well, I'm not surprised. I don't always comprehend it all myself, but come with me and I'll try to explain it to you on the way to her room. Mr. Roberts, you may go in with her if you wish."

"Thank you. I would feel better about all of this if I could be there," Andrew replied. "Believe me, doctor, I'm not a hard-hearted person. I'm only concerned that my daughter not be upset."

"Yes, I can see that. But as I said, my first concern must always be for my patient.....Now, Olivia," he went on as they arrived at the lift, "don't be alarmed if your mother doesn't seem to know you at first. It's....it's as though she's....she's far away from you and can't see or hear you very clearly." The lift came and they got in, the doctor pushing #3 on the board. "What I want you to do, you see, is just to talk to her about things you've done together. The one thing you must be careful not to do is to startle her in any way. Do you understand?"

"Yes, sir." The idea of her mother not knowing who she was scared her, but she was careful not to show it. If her father thought she was afraid, he might try even now to stop her.

The lift had come to a halt by then and the three of them walked quickly along the hall together. Outside Victoria's room the doctor stopped. "Here we are." He pushed open the door, coming in only long enough to open the blinds. Then he and the nurse withdrew. Victoria had blinked once or twice as the late afternoon sun flooded the room, but now she lay again, seemingly unseeing, locked away in her private world.

The little girl walked over to the bed. "Mummy," she whispered. "Mummy, it's... it's Olivia." Victoria appeared not to have heard her, however. She did not so much as turn her head in the direction of the voice. Olivia looked back at her father for reassurance.

"The doctor told you it might be this way," Andrew reminded her gently. "You have to keep talking to her. Don't give up so easily."

She turned back to the bed. "My....my dolly is just fine, Mummy. You....you know-- the one you gave me for Christmas that I named after you?" But Victoria continued to stare straight ahead. "Do....do you still like to sit on the floor, Mummy–the way we did– in...in front of the fire?" In spite of herself Olivia's voice was shaking. More than anything she wanted to run from the room, but she knew she couldn't. Swallowing hard, she went on. "Can....can you make the cinnamon toast all right yourself now? Do you remember the hot chocolate and cinnamon toast, Mummy, on the floor in front of the fire?"

When her mother still failed to respond, Olivia began to cry. Andrew came up behind her to put his arm around her shoulders. "Perhaps we better leave, sweetheart. We can come back tomorrow."

"No, Daddy!" She pulled away from him, climbing up on the bed. "Mummy, please!" she pleaded through her tears. "Mummy, I love you!" In her desperation she seized Victoria by the shoulder and shook her. "Please, Mummy, you're scaring me awfully!"

My little girl loves me....I'm scaring her. These frantic, emotionally charged words penetrated where calm, rational speech had failed and before Andrew could say anything –caution Olivia not to startle her mother–Victoria blinked, the vacant expression leaving her eyes. "No, darling, no. It's....it's all right." Her arms came up to draw her daughter to her and hold her close. "It's all right."

After several seconds Olivia finally sat up again so that she could look at her mother. "You acted as if you didn't know who I was, Mummy!"

"Now how could I ever forget you, my little love. You and your delicious cinnamon toast."

"You do remember! Did you ever learn to make it yourself?"

For the moment they'd both forgotten the hearing and all the unhappiness since then–everything but their shared memories of Olivia's Christmas visit. "You know, I just can't seem to get it right. Could you explain it to me just once more?"

"Well, I suppose so." Olivia settled herself more comfortably on the bed and began to explain yet again the procedure one must follow if one is to make really good cinnamon toast.

Tears all but blinding him, Andrew just managed to find his way to the door. It didn't matter anyway. Neither of them had noticed him leave.

"Well?" The doctor gripped him by the arm.

"They're talking about....about cinnamon toast," he said finally.

"What?"

"It's....it's all right. Olivia did exactly what you told her not to do. She shook Victoria and told her she was frightening her."

The doctor nodded his head and smiled. "The more I see, the less I know, I think, Mr. Roberts.... Well, we'll give them a little longer. This is only the beginning, of course. I have to decide what steps to take next."

It was not at that moment that Andrew made up his mind–not even as he'd watched mother and daughter together a few moments before. Perhaps in a way he had always known. "Well, I've already made my decision," he said firmly even as he experienced the most intense personal agony. He turned to go back into the room.

The doctor stopped him. "Please, Mr. Roberts, let them have this time together."

He smiled wistfully. "But you see, I intend to give them a great deal more than that."

At the sound of the door opening Victoria glanced up and when she saw who it was, her hand instinctively sought her daughter's. Olivia also moved closer to her mother. "Please–neither of you has anything to fear from me." Andrew's voice was choked with emotion.

Victoria looked up at him questioningly, her eyes brimming with hopeful tears. She had to know for sure. She had to hear him say it.

He nodded. "After all, it's all I've ever wanted–from the day she was born."

Olivia started to cry again herself. "Mummy, does he mean that....that...."

Now it was Victoria who nodded, opening her arms. The little girl threw herself into her mother's embrace. Over Olivia's head she sought Andrew's eyes with her own. Noiselessly her lips formed the words, "Thank you."

Chapter 18

So here she was once again, Victoria thought, flying westward across the Atlantic. Yet how different it was from a mere year ago–not only Olivia here with her, but a kind and gentle man to take care of them both. Could life possibly be more perfect? Oh, but why, then, had she found it so difficult to leave London–especially to say good-bye to Noel, who had, of course, come to see them off. It was probably just as well, however, that he would be thousands of miles away. Jason obviously didn't like the other man; she'd seen the expression on his face when she and her old friend embraced in farewell. They'd reached cruising altitude now and the flight attendants were coming around with drinks. Victoria watched the cocktails being served, at the same time wordlessly accepting her ginger ale and trying to settle herself more comfortably in the cramped tourist class seat which was all her husband had said they could afford.

After lunch the little girl quickly became engrossed in the film. Between Victoria's stay in the hospital and the legal formalities of assuming custody she and Jason had had very little time alone together and there was something she needed to ask him. "Darling?" She touched him lightly on the arm. "Please...may....may we talk?"

He had been in the act of opening his briefcase, but at her touch he hesitated smiling at her tenderly. "Of course–for a few minutes." He closed the briefcase again. "But if I can dispense with this paperwork during the flight, it will free up more of my time for actual counseling."

"I'm....I'm sorry I'm such a bother."

"You're never a bother, dearest. You know that."

"You're....you're so patient with me, Jason. I...I just wanted to be sure you thought I was doing the right thing–not staying for further therapy."

"Absolutely," he replied firmly. "It was only the strain of the hearing. After all, nothing like that's ever happened before, has it?"

She wondered if she should tell him about the time Noel and Terry had found her alone on the stage? No, she thought, that would only upset him and I've done that enough already. Besides her few sessions with the doctor had been terribly painful and she'd been relieved to avoid more of them. "You're right, Jason. Of course you are."

"I always am, my dear. You must learn to trust me." With an air of finality he opened his briefcase a second time and Victoria turned her attention to sharing the film with her daughter.

Oh, but she could never deserve this good, decent man. No sooner were they all settled together in New York than the same incidents which had marred the first months of their marriage began to recur. Of course these were her fault since she continually failed him. Most shameful of all–although, thank God, Jason remained unaware of this– she would lie awake for hours with him asleep beside her craving the caresses of a skillful, passionate lover. The conviction was born and grew; it was only a matter of time until she was unfaithful.

In a way, perhaps, she was already faith<u>less</u>. Why else would she miss the theatre so much and even more the people with whom she'd shared that world: Terry and Dylan Mallory, Jon Sinclair and Matt–occasionally even Basil and Sean–but oh, most especially Noel? How often some little incident would occur and she'd wish she could share it with him. Noel would enjoy hearing about that, she would think. They wrote regularly–oddly in some ways closer than ever– and yet words on a sheet of paper could never possibly take the place of a shared pot of tea.

Resolutely she turned away from it all. She stopped attending the theatre; she no longer read the theatre section of *The New York Times*; she ceased answering most mail coming from England. Finally she even began throwing letters away unopened. But it was not to be that simple. Victoria might swear she was through with the theatre. The theatre was not ready to let her go.

* * *

As part of its mission "Prodigals" ran a camp for emotionally troubled teenagers in Stratford, Connecticut, and that summer Jason was to serve as its director. The position included a rambling old house just off the grounds–perfect for Jason, Victoria and Olivia as well as Jason's own son and daughter, who would be visiting for the vacation. Victoria had been nervous about meeting Benjamin and Rachel, but her worries proved groundless. She found being a mother amazingly easy: hugging, kissing, clowning-- everything to which children responded--came as second nature to her and the two young Eliots, accustomed to their parents' more reserved personalities, adored her at once.

At first, then, the summer was happy, although uneventful. Jason was busy at the camp from early morning until quite late in the evening, but Victoria spent sun filled days on the beach with the three children and didn't really miss him. Actually she was discovering it was easier not to have to spend too much time with him. In addition the fatigue, resulting naturally from his long hours in the out-of-doors, provided the perfect excuse for his lack of passion as a lover.

Then about two weeks into their stay they had their first rainy day. Jason was involved with camp activities as usual, but the rest of them were forced to remain indoors. It was the weather, Victoria supposed, which had her feeling slightly depressed as she hurried to finish cleaning up after their lunch so that she could join the children. Coming out of the kitchen, she found Ben and Rachel busy at the heavy, old-fashioned table where they ate their meals: Ben, age eight, with a model airplane and Rachel, age five, with paper dolls. Olivia was flat on her stomach on the floor in front of the fireplace–as ever a favorite spot of hers–the newspaper spread out in front of her. Victoria stopped to check the little boy's work, playfully rumpling his thick, brown hair–so like Jason's. Then she helped Rachel with a particularly tricky outfit for one of the dolls before finally coming to settle on the floor near her daughter. "Rather a dreary day, what?" she commented to the children in general.

Olivia swung around up off her stomach. "Is something wrong, Mummy?"

"No, darling, of course not. I'm just feeling a bit dull today. I suspect it's the weather."

"Could we go to a play?" She reached down for the paper. "I was just reading about it."

Victoria smiled. "My, my–the theatre section already. I <u>am</u> starting you early on, aren't I?"

"I....I guess I got in the habit when I used to look for stuff about you before... before...."

She hugged the little girl close. "I understand, luv."

"Anyway–it says here there's a theatre right here in Stratford–just like Stratford at home in England."

"I'd heard there was a theatre here, but somehow it slipped my mind. I have more important things to think about now." But she still took the newspaper to read the advertisement for herself.

"Is that why you don't act anymore? I loved watching you in New York."

"Did you, sweetheart?" The American Shakespeare Theatre at Stratford, it seemed, would be presenting three plays by Shakespeare that summer: *King Lear, Much Ado About*

Nothing and The Tempest as well as Shaw's *Major Barbara.* She felt a pang of longing–quickly suppressed.

"How do you say that, Mummy?" Olivia pointed to the name of the theatre.

"Oh—that's Shakespeare, luv. William Shakespeare was a great playwright a long, long time ago," Victoria went on to explain. "You remember the play I did about the man who killed the king? Shakespeare wrote that."

"Why did the man kill the king, Victoria?" Ben had forsaken his airplane model to join them on the floor. He liked being close to his beautiful stepmother. She always smelled so good.

"Because he wanted to be king himself, Ben."

"Someday I'm going to marry a king and then I'll be queen." Rachel glanced up from her paper dolls just long enough to make this announcement.

"Are you, darling?" Victoria laughed happily. The theatre was an empty place indeed in comparison to this.

Olivia resented the intrusion of the other two children into what she'd considered to be a private conversation and at once she sought to regain her mother's undivided attention. "Mummy, do you know...." She stumbled over the name—"Sir..ah..Ter..Ter..."

"Terence Cartier. Yes, dear." She smiled. "But so do you. That's your Uncle Terry."

"Mummy, he's going to be at the theatre!"

"Where does it say that?" Victoria's attention was once more fully on the newspaper.

"There." Olivia pointed to an article. "Next to the advert."

"Of course. Why didn't I see that?" Eagerly she scanned the article.–"Renowned British actor to guest at Stratford," it began–going on to state that he would be performing King Lear as well as Prospero in *The Tempest.* "I did *Lear* with Terry in London." And once again, in spite of herself, she was the actress, proud of what she had accomplished.

"We'll go and see Uncle Terry, then, won't we, Mummy?" the little girl inquired excitedly.

Just to see Terry again! For some reason it seemed a long time although in fact it had only been about six weeks. "I don't think so, luv." Victoria shook her head. "He'll be much too busy."

"But he'd <u>want</u> to see you!"

"No, Olivia," she said sharply. "Now don't tease."

"Yes, Mummy." Her mother was rarely cross yet it always hurt a little when she was. "I'm sorry."

"So am I, luv." Victoria reached over to brush her daughter's hair back from her face–the old tender gesture. "It's just that part of my life is over and done with."

"I don't understand."

"No, I don't suppose you do." And she felt strangely sad.

Just then they heard the back door close. "Victoria?" Jason appeared in the doorway from the kitchen.

"Oh, darling!" She got up quickly and hurrying to him, she slipped her arms around his neck, raising her face to be kissed. She was so glad to see him–to be reminded of what was truly important in her life–that for a minute she'd forgotten he found such displays embarrassing.

"Victoria, dear." He kissed her lightly on the cheek. "We had the young people outdoors to work off some energy and I'm chilled through. Do you suppose I could have some coffee?"

"Of course." She went on into the kitchen, feeling a little disappointed as she always did whenever Jason failed to return a gesture of affection. But then she should learn not to expect that of him.

The telephone rang that evening just as they were finishing dinner. It was Ben who went to answer it. "It's for you, Victoria," he called out. "A man who talks just like you."

She laughed, pausing as she passed him on her way to the telephone to give the little boy a quick hug. "Hello."

"Victoria, dear. How are you?" It was Terry, but then she'd known it would be.

"I'm absolutely marvelous, thank you." she gushed. "And you?"

"Never overact, my love. I've told you that before, I believe."

"I haven't the slightest idea what you're talking about."

"Ah, yes–of course. Victoria, I have a tremendous favor to ask of you."

"Please–anything. I owe you so much in...in so many ways."

"I'm going to hold you to that because no other actress can equal your Cordelia. Will you do it with me again? You'll say yes, of course, and then I plan to persuade you to do Miranda as well."

"Wait–please. I'm here simply as a wife and mother."

"I know. The director didn't believe he could have Victoria Windsor only a few miles away and not even be aware of it."

"Terry, Jason....ah...prefers I not work and I....I....."

"You <u>do</u> miss it, though, don't you?"

Oh yes, she thought, so much! But aloud she replied, "Not really. You see, I don't need the theatre anymore."

"How fortunate for you, Victoria. But the theatre still needs you."

"No, Terry, I don't think so."

"Very well, my dear. I won't push. But rehearsals for *Lear* begin day after tomorrow if you change your mind."

"I...I won't change my mind, but I hope you'll come to dinner some evening."

"Just let me know when–<u>if</u> I don't see you at rehearsal."

As she hung up, turning away from the telephone, Jason was watching her–an affectionate smile lighting his face. "Who was it, darling?"

"Terence Cartier. He's at the theatre here in Stratford."

"Naturally he'd be concerned about you." He smiled again. "I hope you invited him to dinner."

"Yes, I...ah...did."

"Good. Well, I'm going over for the vesper service. Ben is coming with me."

"Jason...ah...Terry didn't call just to ask how I was. He'd...he'd like me to work with him this summer."

A displeased look passed over her husband's face. "I thought we'd agreed you were through with the theatre, Victoria."

She felt terribly disloyal. "I've...I've missed it, darling. I have to be honest with you. I love you and our life together, but...but part of me still wants to....needs to act, I guess." She shrugged.

"Well, it's your decision, of course. You know how I feel about it."

Ben came out of the kitchen just then. "Rachel and Olivia are coming, too, Dad."

"Fine....fine. Darling, shall we make it a family, then?"

"No....ah...Jason, not tonight I don't think." As soon as they'd left, Victoria hurried upstairs to their bedroom. Under her clothes in one of the bureau drawers was her beloved Shakespeare collection. Why do I feel the need to hide it, she asked herself. But then she opened the book to one of Cordelia's scenes in *King Lear* and soon forgot everything else. Her excitement building, she flipped over to *The Tempest*. Miranda would be new for me, she thought, and because she was less familiar with this play, she started to read it from the first act. She was about a third of the way through and so lost in another world that she wasn't even aware Jason and the children had returned until he spoke to her from the doorway.

"Victoria?" At his voice she started. "Victoria?" he repeated–puzzled. "I thought you'd stayed behind because the dishes weren't done from dinner."

"Oh, I...I forgot."

"What are you reading?"

"Nothing special."

"And yet it made you lose all track of time." He sounded annoyed.

"My....my Shakespeare. I...I was just reading it, that's all. I'll....I'll finish up downstairs." Jumping up, she put the book back in the drawer and hurried past him from the room. That night she had another panic attack–the first since her breakdown in London–and once more her gentle husband held her and prayed. In the morning she knew she must finally close that chapter in her life.

"Good, Victoria," he said quietly when she told him. "I knew you'd come to the right decision."

At the same time the least she owed Terry was the courtesy of informing him in person. Maybe this was only an excuse to see him–or to see the theatre– but for whatever reason she asked her daughter to go with her. Was that for moral support, she wondered with a laugh. Of course not–it was simply that the child would enjoy the visit.

Early in the afternoon they drove over to the older section of the town–the streets typically New England in appearance with white clapboard houses under leafy canopies. Walking up from the parking lot through a small birch grove, they could see the theatre set on a broad lawn–the sparkling expanse of the Housatonic River stretching away behind it toward the sea. "Oh, how pretty, Mummy!" Olivia exclaimed. "Does it look like the one in England?"

"Not really, luv." Inexplicably Victoria found conversation difficult at the moment. "Except....except that one's on a river, too, of course–the Avon. But...but the building's red brick. Actually this one looks more like it might have appeared in Shakespeare's day." She was relaxing a little now. It felt so good to talk about the theatre again–to share her love of it with her little girl. "See the weathered boards," she went on, "the octagonal shape–that's eight sides, luv–and the flag flying on the top. That's how they used to let people know there was going to be a play that day."

By then they had come up to the building. The doors stood open, but the place appeared deserted. "May we go in, Mummy?"

"I...I suppose so. Perhaps someone can tell us where to find Terry." They moved together through the wood-paneled lobby into the actual theatre–dark now except for the work lights. Victoria stopped in the back and just stood there. I....I shouldn't have come, she thought, but still she remained there staring at the stage.

"Mummy." Olivia touched her mother on the arm. "What is it?"

For a moment she appeared startled. "What?... Oh, darling." She reached down to caress the little girl's face. "Nothing. Let's go." She turned to leave, only to walk directly into Terry.

"Victoria!" he exclaimed–delighted. "I knew you'd change your mind. But you're a day early."

"Oh....ah... hello, luv. You know my daughter, of course."

"I certainly do. It's wonderful to see you again, Olivia."

"Hi, Uncle Terry."

"Terry, I...I haven't changed my mind." But even as Victoria spoke, her eyes strayed away from him and back to the stage.

"What is there about an empty theatre, hm?" he asked idly almost as though he were talking to himself. "It has the same effect on me. But come and see." He started to walk down the aisle. "The set is rather intriguing, I think. One basic framework..."

"No, I don't think so." Instead Victoria moved away toward the exit.

"Come on, Mummy," Olivia pleaded. "I want to see."

"Well then, young lady, I'll show you," Terry said smiling. He knew how Victoria must miss it all–knew it would only take a nudge. "And your mother will simply have to wait." He took Olivia's hand to escort her down the aisle. She didn't find it at all odd to be walking along hand in hand with perhaps the world's most revered actor. "Stay there," he instructed the little girl as they came up on the stage, "while I get the lights." In spite of herself Victoria was drawn down the aisle toward them. "Now let's test your mother's memory," he added under his breath. Smiling, Olivia backed away to sit on the floor and watch.

Lear: Now, our joy,
Although our last, not least; to whose young love
The vines of France and milk of Burgundy
Strive to be interess'd; what can you say to draw
A third more opulent than your sisters. Speak.
Cordelia: Nothing my lord. (By now Victoria had come up on stage beside Terry.)
Lear: Nothing?
Cor: Nothing.
Lear: Nothing will come of nothing; speak again.
Cor: Unhappy that I am, I cannot heave
My heart into my mouth; I love your majesty
According to my bond; nor more nor less.
Lear:How, how Cordelia! Mend your speech a little,
Lest you may mar your fortunes.
Cor:Good, my lord,
You have begot me, bred me, lov'd me: I
Return those duties back as are right fit,
Obey you, love you and most honour you.
Why have my sisters husbands, if they say
They love you all? Haply, when I shall wed,
That lord whose hand must take my plight shall carry
Half my love with him, half my care and duty,
Sure I shall never marry like my sisters,\
To love my father all. *
(**King Lear*, William Shakespeare, Act I, Scene 1, Lines 84-106.)

Unnoticed meanwhile by the three on stage, the artistic director had come to stand in the rear of the auditorium. "Terry! She's agreed then!" he called out, half-running down the aisle. "Fantastic! Miss Windsor, it's an honor to meet you!" By then he was up on the stage, extending his hand in greeting.

"Thank you!" Graciously she accepted his hand. "But I....I haven't agreed. We....we....."

"I'm afraid that's true," Terry observed regretfully. "We were merely reminiscing." Inwardly he was cursing the man's untimely arrival. A moment or so longer and he was certain she'd have given in. "Victoria, let me walk you and Olivia to your car. Right out here." He led the way through the wings and out a side door. "Quite a feeling, wasn't it?" he asked as they walked back together toward the parking lot. She didn't reply. "Weakening?" Now his eyes were twinkling.

"Damn you anyway," Victoria said quietly so that Olivia wouldn't overhear. "You bloody well know I am."

"You love the theatre." He had stopped just inside the trees, turning to look down at her intently. "Why should that change just because you're married? You do want to do this play, don't you?"

Victoria nodded, tears welling up in her eyes. "Very much."

"Well then?"

She hesitated only briefly. "Yes, all right."

"Hallelujah!" He threw his arms around her and hugged her.

"Come along, Olivia." Immediately pulling free of Terry's embrace, Victoria put an arm around her daughter's shoulders to lead her across the lot to their car. Quickly she unlocked the passenger door before going around to her side to do the same.

"Mummy," Olivia asked when they were both in the car, "is Jason going to be mad you told Uncle Terry you'd do the play?"

"Well, I don't know that, luv, but I'll find out, won't I?" Arriving home, Victoria went directly over to his office.

"Of course, dear." He accepted the news with equanimity. "If you feel you need it."

He made her feel terribly guilty, but for the present she refused to allow herself to think about it. Rehearsals were like coming home and she would return to the camp at the end of the day bubbling with excitement. Jason would listen politely, but somehow he never appeared very interested. He did, however, attend the opening performance of *King Lear*, along with Olivia as well as Ken and Kate MacAllister. Ben and Rachel had wanted to come as well, but Jason refused. He explained their mother wouldn't have approved, but Victoria knew the real reason. Their father didn't approve.

Victoria and Sir Terence entered together at the curtain call, a courtesy Terry extended to a friend and respected colleague since under ordinary circumstances Lear would take a solitary bow. The house rose as one to cheer them. Not content merely to clap, people stamped their feet as well. Shouts of "Bravo! Bravo!" filled the air. "She's simply unbelievable!" Kate exclaimed over the acclamation. "You must be so proud of her, Jason!"

"Yes, of course I am," he replied automatically.

Finally the ovation subsided, the curtain descending for the last time, and the house lights came on. "Are we going backstage, Jason?" Olivia inquired at once.

"There'll be too many people. We'll see your mother at home."

"Oh, Jason," Kate objected, "Victoria will be so disappointed."

"Well, why don't you take Olivia? Ken and I will go along."

"She'll want to see you, Jason," Ken put in at this point.

"I don't belong back there. Are you coming?"

The MacAllisters exchanged glances and Kate shrugged. "I'll go with Olivia, then," she said. "Leave me our car."

"What is it, old friend?" Ken asked a moment later as the two men left the theatre and walked toward the parking lot.

"Oh, nothing, nothing." He ran his hand through his hair.

"You were that much against Victoria working? Why?"

For several minutes the other man didn't answer. They got into the car and he started the engine, backing out of the parking space. Finally Ken repeated the question. "I....I just thought," Jason replied at last, "that once we were married, she wouldn't need this life anymore."

"It's been a long time since people in the theatre were considered beyond the social pale and particularly an actress of her caliber......"

"It's not that I disapprove, really. It...it just seems sometimes as though the theatre is...is a rival for her affections."

"Tell her that," Ken urged. "She'll be terribly hurt that you didn't come backstage."

"There's a cast party. She won't miss me."

"She'll want you at the party with her. Come on. Let's go back. We'll take Olivia with us and you and Victoria can go to the party."

"I'd be out of place. I'll be waiting at home when she's ready to come there."

"Will you at least talk to her then?"

"If I force the issue, she may feel pressured into making a choice."

"And you're afraid she'll choose the theatre? Jason, that woman loves you!"

"I wish I could be sure of that."

The other pair, meanwhile, had made their way behind the scenes, but they soon found it was quite another thing to get anywhere near Victoria. The hall leading to her dressing room was mobbed with well-wishers, luminaries of the New York stage who had come to see her and Sir Terence work together. Kate looked down to see Olivia's eyes full of tears. "What's the matter? Is it the crowd?"

"Maybe Jason was right," the little girl whispered.

"What, sweetheart?"

She shook her head. "Mummy's busy. Let's wait outside."

"Olivia, do you think all these people put together mean as much to your mother as you do?"

"I....I don't know."

"Oh, for heaven's sake!" Kate exclaimed. "Excuse me. Excuse me, please. This is Miss Windsor's daughter." Taking a firm grip on the child's hand, she began to push her way through the crowd, ignoring the dirty looks she received. Later when she told Ken the names of some of the people she'd unceremoniously shoved out of her way, he roared with laughter.

When they got to the door of the dressing room, however, the crush was just as thick. "Aunt Kate–never mind. Let's leave, please."

"Slip around there," Kate directed the little girl firmly, "near the wall. Go on. You can get close to your mother and get her attention."

Olivia looked up at her helplessly, but it was too noisy to argue. Heart pounding, she began to work her way around the edge of the room until finally she was almost next to her mother. She swallowed hard. "Mummy." The child's voice was so soft, however, that Victoria had no chance of catching it over the congratulations, the theatrical kissing and hugging. At first she'd kept watching, hoping Jason would at least bring Olivia backstage, but by now she'd given up. He's so angry he doesn't even want to see me, she thought sadly. "Mummy!" This time Olivia mustered up enough courage to speak more loudly and Victoria heard her.

"Oh, darling!" She leaned down to hug her. "How did you avoid getting trampled? Come up here. Excuse me, please, this is my daughter." She helped her stand up on the stool of the dressing table, slipping an arm around her waist.

Olivia put an arm around her mother's shoulders. "Mummy, I thought it was wonderful," she whispered in her ear. "But do you have to be dead at the end? I didn't like that much."

Victoria smiled and hugged her again. "It's only make-believe, luv. I'm fine."

"You've got the best spot there, young lady," someone called out. "Want to trade?"

Olivia shook her head vehemently, tightening her grip on her mother.

"He's only teasing you, luv," Victoria reassured her and gradually over the next half-hour or so the little girl began to enjoy herself. Everyone made a great fuss over her, but best of all she learned that no matter what else was going on, her mother was still her mother. At last everyone had left and Victoria could relax and remove her make-up. "A bit hectic, what?" She smiled at Olivia who was now standing beside her leaning on the dressing table.

"That was fun, Mummy. May I please come back?"

"If you'd like to, luv."

"Victoria," Kate finally had a chance to say, "you are not to be believed on that stage! How does it feel to be so incredibly gifted?"

"Oh, my! Well, thank you. I"m glad you and Ken could come."

Just then Terry stuck his head around the corner. "Ready to go the party?"

"I'm afraid not. I just got rid of everyone. Oh, Terry, this is my friend, Kate MacAllister."

"Mrs. MacAllister." He extended his hand, acknowledging the introduction.

Kate returned the handshake, dismally aware that her palm had gone cold and clammy. "Wonderful performance, Sir Terence," she managed to say.

"Thank you."

"Hi, Uncle Terry," Olivia piped up.

"Coming to the party, princess?"

She eyed her mother hopefully.

"No, Terry, she isn't."

"<u>Mummy</u>, I'm almost <u>nine</u> <u>years</u> <u>old</u>!"

"<u>No</u>, Terry, she isn't!"

He laughed. How good it was to see Victoria happy. "Well, perhaps some other time, then. Nice to meet you, Mrs. MacAllister."

Terry left and Kate let out her breath so loudly it sounded as though she'd been holding it all the time he'd been there. "He said it was nice to meet me," she gasped.

Victoria had begun applying her own make-up. She glanced up in her mirror and smiled. "And he meant it. That's the kind of person he is."

"But....but I didn't say anything in return. I just stood here gaping at him...like....like some stupid goldfish."

Now Victoria laughed. "Believe me, he's used to that."

"Mummy, may I please go out on the stage?" Olivia asked.

"Of course you may, darling." The little girl went out closing the door behind her.

"Why didn't Jason come backstage, Kate?"Victoria inquired when they were alone.

"He....he thought it would be too crowded. He said he'd see you at home."

"You've known him so much longer than I have. Do you think he's really angry with me for doing these plays with Terry?"

"I'm afraid that simply because I've known Jason longer doesn't mean I know him any better. Have you spoken to him about it?"

Victoria shook her head. "I...I can't talk to him. He makes me feel...I don't know.... inadequate."

"A woman of your beauty and talent? That's ridiculous! And I'm positive Jason wouldn't <u>want</u> you to feel that way. Do it when you get home."

"I'll....I'll try. I'll just put in an appearance at the party. You know, Kate," she continued after a brief silence, "Your friendship means everything to me. I've... I've never been at all close to another woman before."

Impulsively the other woman came over to lean down and hug her. "I find that hard to believe–someone so warm and outgoing." Victoria returned the hug, fighting back the tears. Kate could have no idea how much those words meant to her.

Arriving home not quite an hour later, she found Jason waiting for her sitting on the couch reading. He looked up as she came in. "Darling!" He got up quickly to take her in his arms. Such a display of affection was unusual for him and Victoria thrilled to it, raising her face to be kissed. During her brief stay at the party, however, she'd had one drink and when he smelled the liquor on her breath, he turned his head aside and hugged her instead.

Further guilt flooded over her and she couldn't bring herself to talk to him as Kate had urged. "I'm awfully tired, Jason," she said. "I think I'll go right to bed."

He said nothing about her returning to work either–not even some passing remark about her performance of that evening. Instead he merely replied, "I have a little more reading to finish. I'll be up in a while," So Victoria went on upstairs alone and later when her husband came to bed, she lay with her back to him pretending to be asleep.

The subject of her acting career never did come up although she continued to appear at the Stratford theatre for the rest of the summer season. When they returned to the city in the fall, there were several offers to do a play on Broadway, but she turned them down, compromising instead on a full-time position in the NYU drama department.

* * *

Victoria stepped out of the taxi in front of the university theatre building much as she'd done the previous fall, but halfway up the stairs she stopped. Had it only been a year ago she'd been terrified at the prospect of facing a roomful of strangers? "Good morning, Victoria," a familiar voice called out from below her on the sidewalk. "Forget something?"

She turned to find Aaron Oblinksy coming up the stone steps toward her two at a time. "Doing a bit of woolgathering, I'm afraid." She was a little embarrassed. "How was your holiday?" Aaron had spent the summer at the Dennis Playhouse on Cape Cod.

"Fantastic! I can't wait to tell you about it. Can we have coffee later?"

Victoria smiled. "Absolutely!"

"You know," he confessed as they walked together the rest of the way up the stairs and into the lobby of the building, "last year I was scared to death of you. That was before I got to know you and discovered how much I like you."

"Aaron!" Victoria stopped to reach up and pat his cheek, a gesture she now used only to show genuine affection, "Thank you, luv." A look of mischief crossed her lovely face. "Then of course you'll design the fall production I'm directing."

He held up his hands in mock surrender. "Trapped!" he grinned, "but seriously I was hoping you'd ask me."

"Miss Windsor!" Carrie Phillips came up to them beaming. She'd begun last year stage managing *Blithe Spirit*, but Victoria had coaxed her out on stage to play a small part in the spring musical, *Oliver*, and much encouraged, she was returning this fall as a graduate student.

Victoria turned to her. "Carrie, how <u>are</u> you?"

"About ten for coffee, Victoria?" Aaron put his hand on her arm. "Faculty lounge?" She nodded. "Good–see you then. Glad you're back, Carrie." He moved off down the hall to their right–heading for his design room.

"Me, too," Carrie replied. "Miss Windsor, I....I signed up for introduction to acting."

"Super, luv. I'd hoped you would."

"Well, I'm in <u>your</u> section first period. I hope you'll still feel that way once you've seen me work."

"I'm sure I will." Victoria glanced at her watch. "But now I think we're rather late. We're in the small theatre, I believe." They walked quickly along the corridor in the opposite direction from that Aaron had taken, turning one corner before at last entering the classroom assigned to Acting 101. At one time a lecture hall, it had recently been redesigned as an intimate theatre in the semi-round with a seating capacity of 250 on three sides of its low thrust stage. Carrie slipped into an empty seat near the door and Victoria continued on down to the front. The buzz of conversation subsided immediately as she put down her purse and holding a clipboard with a list of the twenty or so students enrolled in the class, she stepped up on the stage. All eyes were on her– some thrilled they'd been fortunate enough to get into her section, others terrified for the same reason.

"Good morning." Her glance traveled briefly over the group and she smiled warmly. "You are doubtless expecting me to begin by reading the roll. That, however, would be much too easy for you." There was an uneasy stirring, accompanied by an undercurrent of whispers, as everyone tried to guess what she was going to say next. "With very few exceptions," she went on noting their reaction with some amusement, "you'll be up here on your feet performing at least once a week. So–you might as well become accustomed to it. Starting from the front row here to my left, each of you will please come up here, introduce yourself and state any previous experience you've had including school productions, amateur theatre, anything–and why in God's name you <u>want</u> to be an actor!" They all laughed at the last, relaxing a little. Victoria took a seat in the back. "All right–please begin."

The procession, at first, was about as she'd expected. Some of the students were obviously nervous while others at least appeared self-assured; some were serious, even pompous, while others made an attempt at humor. As each student identified himself or herself, Victoria checked the names off against her list. But then one particular girl came to the front of the room. Tall and slender, she wore her short, light brown hair in a bouffant style, curled under at the ends. "Felicity MacDougall," she announced, "frrom Kinleygairr, Aberrdeenshirre, Scotland!" The latter part had been unnecessary. The brogue was unmistakable.

"So—a voice from home," Victoria couldn't resist observing.

"I'm no a bluidy Englisherr, Miss Windsorr," she replied, the "r's" burring softly.

It had been some time since anyone addressed her with such a total lack of respect. But the girl was so obviously without malice, Victoria couldn't possibly be angry ."Yes, well, that is evident," she replied laughing. "But actually, Miss MacDougall, I <u>am</u> aware of the existence of Scotland. I may be only a poor, benighted Englishwoman, but I do know that much." She was experiencing, moreover, her usual inexplicably strong reaction to the Scottish brogue. Was it gratitude toward David Donald Douglas or did it go back further to Balmoral and her beloved Uncle Bertie? No, she was almost certain it was something else–something dim and distant–perhaps a dream she'd once had. The whole thing was perfectly ridiculous!

Felicity, on the other hand, had been more than a little doubtful when she learned who'd be teaching her acting class. She'd only been in England once in her life– accompanying her father, Dr. Alexander MacDougall, when he attended a medical conference in London. She had found all "Englisherrs", as she persisted in calling them, to be stuck-up, snobbity folk and she bestowed what she darkly referred to as "the currse of the MacDougalls" on all who crossed her path. Once her father had gently reminded her that there was no such thing as a MacDougall curse. "Aye, Dad," she'd replied, "but the Englisherrs have such thick, wooden heads, they dinna ken that." Now the Scottish girl grinned at Victoria. "Aye, do ye noo? Then ye must be a wee bit brrighterr than most of yourr countrrymen."

"Might I ask why <u>are</u> you taking this course, Miss MacDougall?"

"I thought it would be a wee bit of a larrk. Ye know, Miss Windsorr, ye'rre nae half bad forr an Englisherr."

Victoria laughed again. "How extremely tolerant of you, Miss MacDougall. Next, please."

Following Felicity there were only a half dozen more students to introduce themselves. Finally Victoria herself returned to the front of the room to conclude the class with a few brief introductory remarks including the announcement of next week's auditions for the fall production, *The Diary of Anne Frank*. As the class began to stand, leaving the auditorium in chattering groups of two or three, Victoria also gathered up her things to meet Aaron for coffee. The school year had officially begun, but more was beginning for her–far more than she could ever possibly imagine.

* * *

Certain students in the introductory acting class immediately stood out. One, as Victoria had suspected would be the case, was Carrie Phillips. Much to the girl's delight, she would win the title role of Anne Frank as well.

Another outstanding young actress, and this was a surprise, was the feisty Scot, Felicity MacDougall. Her classwork showed a lively imagination: a Trafalgar Square pigeon, who having been hit on the head by a peanut, has forgotten how to fly; the trials and tribulations of a broken down washing machine. It was not as a student, however, but as a friend that Felicity would come to matter tremendously in her life. Their friendship began, suitably enough, in a unique fashion since theirs was to be a distinctly unique relationship.

The class assignment for one particular week was an idea she'd admittedly stolen from Claudine Arnold, her old nemesis at RADA---each student to present a character out of history at some crucial and dramatic moment in that person's life. Carrie had just given an extremely moving performance as Marie Antoinette on her way to the guillotine. The exercise was greeted with ringing applause and warm praise from Victoria. Carrie sat down again, cheeks red with embarrassment, but greatly pleased at her success.

"Next–let me see." Victoria consulted her class register, "ah, yes–Felicity MacDougall.

Felicity walked to the front of the class for the first time wearing her native dress: a kilt in the MacDougall tartan, a white blouse and velvet waistcoat. "I have chosen to speak to you today," she announced, her voice ringing with pride, "as Bonnie Prrince Charrlie on the occasion of the rraisin' of the standarrd at Glenfinnan at the beginnin' of the Forrty-Five!"

"Perhaps it might help," Victoria suggested, "if you could tell us first exactly what was the Forty-Five."

She glared. Clearly the actress had uttered blasphemy. "The Forrty-Five!" Felicity said it more loudly this time as if that should make it completely clear to everyone.

"No–you don't understand. It wasn't that we couldn't hear you."

The Scottish girl was the perfect picture of outraged incredulity. "Do ye mean to tell me,…." and amazingly her brogue grew thicker and more unintelligible in direct proportion to her indignation... "that ye dinna ken what is meant by the Forrrrrty-Five?" And this time she strung out the burr on the "r" in forty until it resembled nothing so much as the roll of a drum.

"I'm afraid not," Victoria admitted, making a vain attempt not to smile. The girl was so obviously in earnest.

"The Rrrrrrrebellion of Forrrty-Five!" And now she fairly trumpeted her defiance.

Laughter rippled through the class, laughter in which Victoria couldn't help but join. "Yes, I see." She was enjoying herself immensely, but then she did suffer from this foolish weakness for Scots. "Well, that tells us a little more, but I still have no idea what you're talking about and since I'm the only other person here from the U.K., I'm almost sure no one else does either."

"That's just the bluidy trrouble!" Felicity sputtered. "Ye'rre English! I've changed my mind. I will nae do the assignment!" Storming back to her seat, she proceeded to sulk magnificently for the remainder of the class.

Two more students were scheduled to present their exercises that day and when they'd finished, Victoria dismissed the class. "Oh....ah... Miss MacDougall, if I might speak to you for a moment before you leave."

"Aye, Miss Windsorr." She managed somehow to make even the actress' name sound vaguely insulting.

Victoria had never realized that one syllable could be so thoroughly maddening as that single, non-committal–"Aye". "I'm certainly willing to admit that my knowledge of Scotland is limited."

"Aye, Miss Windsorr."

"Is that all you're going to say?—'Aye, Miss Windsorr." She mimicked the dialect exactly.

"And ye will no make fun of the brrogue!"

"Well, at least I got you to say something else. Now will you please explain to me in words so simple that even a poor, ignorant Englishwoman can understand exactly what was the Forty-Five?"

Now Felicity couldn't help smiling. "Well, I dinna ken if I can make it that simple."

Victoria laughed. "You know, I don't believe I've ever met anyone quite like you!"

"Noo ye'rre makin' fun of me again!"

"No, Felicity, I am not!" She shook her head in amused exasperation. "Do you have such a low opinion of all Englishmen in general or just me in particular?"

"I don't actually know many Englisherrs perrsonally."

"Felicity." The idea seemed to come to Victoria out of nowhere. "Could we go some place–perhaps have tea and talk?"

The girl frowned doubtfully. "What do ye want to do that forr?"

"Let's just say that I like you and I want to get to know you better. Is that enough of a reason?"

"Aye, I suppose so."

"How about the cafeteria then? I have another class in an hour." Two unlikelier friends could not have been imagined and yet, as they walked together along the hall and down one flight of stairs to the basement where the cafeteria was located, their friendship had already begun.

"Have ye neverr been to Scotland then?" Felicity asked as they poured milk, added sugar and settled down to their beloved tea.

"Actually, you know, I would never make fun of the way you talk. I've always had a fondness for the Scotch brogue."

Felicity made a face. "If ye'rre rreally serrious aboot wantin' to learrn aboot Scotland, Miss Windsorr, the firrst thing ye must ken is that Scotch is what we drrink and nae what we arre."

"You are marvelous! You really are! But to...ah....answer your question, I've been to Scotland just once. I was...." Her voice faltered. "I was....only a child."

Her new friend's eyes grew soft in immediate response to her evident distress. " 'Twas nae a happy time forr ye then?"

She'd never mentioned Balmoral to anyone–not even Noel or Jason. Why, then, did she now feel like talking about it to an almost total stranger? "As a matter of fact," Victoria said softly, "it was a very happy time, perhaps one of the happiest I've ever known. Some....some... ah...distant relatives took me there on holiday. My parents were...were divorced when I was five, you see, and it was wonderful to spend time with a real family."

"Och, then ye have no family o' yourr own?" What would it be like to have no family? She couldn't imagine being so alone, she who had not only a mother and father who spoiled her outrageously, but also cousins and aunts and uncles and the whole village of Kinleygair for that matter and even the entire MacDougall clan.

"I'm sorry. I didn't mean to make you sad. And I do have a family now: a husband and a daughter."

"Well then, if ye have a laddie of ye verra own and a wee lass, ye must be verra happy indeed."

"Yes, I am, thank you." Victoria wondered why the words had a hollow ring to them. She searched her mind for a change of subject. "Where did you say you were from in Scotland, Felicity?"

"Kinleygairr in Aberrdeenshirre."

She shrugged helplessly. "Exactly where is that?"

"Ye'rre hopeless!" Felicity threw up her hands, upsetting her cup of tea all over the table, her lap and onto the floor. "Och, my mum's always told me I was a wee bit cloomsy."

Victoria went up to the counter for a handful of paper napkins and together they mopped up the mess. At last they were finished and the Scottish girl had a fresh cup of tea in front of her. "Felicity, at the risk of my china and glassware would you like to come to my home for dinner Friday evening?"

"Aye, I would." She was amazed she actually liked someone from England. "May I brring a wee bottle o' soomthin'?"

"No...ah...thank you. My...ah...husband doesn't drink."

"Och! The poorr laddie! Is he sick?"

"No, Felicity." Victoria tried not to laugh. "He's not sick. He's just....ah...." Fortunately the warning bell rang just then and she had to leave for her class. "I'll write down the address and give it to you in class on Friday," she promised, hurrying off with a quick wave. Only when she was halfway down the hall did she realize she'd learned nothing about the Rebellion of Forty-Five nor for that matter the exact location of Kinleygair. But she had definitely begun to know an extraordinary individual!

Felicity came to dinner that Friday as invited. Olivia liked her a great deal; Jason was pleasant although more serious. During the course of the evening Victoria managed to learn that Kinleygair was in the northeast corner of Scotland about halfway between Aberdeen and Inverness; that Felicity was in the States as nanny to the children of a colleague of her father's; that she was unofficially engaged to a distant cousin named Jamie and finally and most important of all that in 1745 Bonnie Prince Charlie had made a vain attempt to "rrecoverr the thrrone of Grreat Brritain from those bluidy, dastarrdly Hanoverrs and restorre it to the brrave and noble house of Stuarrt!"

"What did you think of her, darling?" Victoria asked later that night as they lay in bed, each with a book. She wondered sometimes if the reading were merely an excuse to avoid love-making, but she always pushed the thought from her mind.

"She's...ah...quite remarkable." But Jason's mind was not on their dinner guest. He glanced over at his beautiful wife so close to him in bed, so warm and desirable and in spite of himself he reached out for her, allowing himself the usually forbidden luxury of running his hands over her body, of kissing her breasts.

Awaking the next morning, Victoria forgot for a minute and nestled against him, more than willing to pick up where they'd left off the night before. Abruptly Jason pulled away, slipping out of bed. "I don't understand what comes over me sometimes," he mumbled. He disappeared–as always at these moments-- into the bathroom and pretending drowsiness, Victoria turned over on her side. Waves of sick guilt swept over her and she sobbed and sobbed, stifling the sound in the pillow. Finally she fell asleep again and secretly relieved, Jason left without waking her.

Then a few weeks after that, one evening in late October, Terence Cartier took Victoria and Jason out for dinner before he returned to England. She was feeling depressed because Terry was leaving and when he ordered her a drink before dinner, wine with the meal, she simply couldn't be bothered to object. Later home alone with the babysitter dismissed–they had the worst fight of their still brief marriage, culminating in his sleeping on the couch because he "couldn't stand the stink of her breath". That night she suffered another panic attack and there was no one there to comfort her.

The following day Felicity could tell even during class that Victoria appeared subdued. At the end of the period she came down to the front of the room, waiting for the other woman to gather up her belongings so that they could go together for what had quickly become their customary mid-morning break. "Miss Windsorr?"

"What, Felicity?" She still had the habit of massaging her forehead with one hand when she was upset or distracted.

"I...I was wonderrin' if ye werre botherred in yourr mind aboot soomthin'?"

"I...I do need to talk to someone. Can....can you keep a confidence?"

"To be honest with ye, Miss Windsorr, I do have a wee bit of a prroblem keepin' my mouth shut. My dad says it's incurrable. But I'll trry my verra best."

In spite of her preoccupation Victoria laughed. "Felicity, do you know I am becoming extremely fond of you!"

"Aye, Miss Windsorr, we Scots arre an endearrin' lot. Wait 'til ye meet my Jamie!"

"And what's your Jamie doing while you're larking about over here in the States?" Victoria inquired laughingly. Perhaps it was just as well to change the subject. How could she ever explain Jason to someone as uninhibited as Felicity?

"Oh, I suspect he's doin' a bit o' larrkin' aboot himself if I know my Jamie–he and that lot he goes aboot with. They'll all be coomin' overr herre with him as a matterr of fact."

Victoria raised her eyebrows in mock horror. "Don't tell me they're all coming to see you?"

Felicity looked at her quickly to see if she were serious. Then she grinned. "Och, Miss Windsorr, ye'rre havin' yourr wee joke again. No, they'rre coomin' to give some concerts at a coffee house."

By now they were in the line to get their tea and the conversation had to wait until they were settled at a table. "What sort of concerts?" Victoria asked.

"Folk music." Here Felicity paused in the act of stirring her tea to throw her friend a mischievous glance. "Scottish mostly."

"What a surprise!" Victoria's own eyes sparkled in return. "Do they all sing or play instruments?"

"Well, one of Jamie's chums has a rreally bonny voice–a braw laddie he is, too–overr six feet tall with auburn hairr and brrown eyes. Surre and the lassies always take a likin' to that one, forr fairr. Sooo, this one sings and plays the guitarr and Jamie and thrree otherrs have a quarrtet and they do a bit 'o dancin'. Have ye everr seen Highland dancin'?"

Victoria shook her head, smiling. "I'm afraid not, Felicity, but then what can you expect from an Englishwoman?"

"Aye, well, that's trrue, Miss Windsorr."

"That reminds me–I've been meaning to tell you. Outside of class I would really like to have you call me Victoria? After all, we <u>are</u> friends, aren't we?"

"Aye, but does no one everr call ye anythin' less forrmal?"

She shook her head. "I...I was called Vicki as a child, but... but I never liked it. So I'm afraid it's Victoria. Do you think you can manage it?"

"I'll do my verra best." Felicity smiled. Just then the bell rang. "Och!" she exclaimed, as always leaping to her feet at the sound. "We get to talkin' overr ourr tea and I'm always tarrdy to my next class. The prrofessorr thinks I'm a wee bit scatterrbrrained!" Somehow between the table and the exit the girl managed to bump into three people, drop her books and trip over nothing. When she finally reached the cafeteria door, she yanked it open with such force that a tray of clean dishes on a table against the wall went crashing to the floor. She went merrily on her way unperturbed. Victoria was still laughing as she also left for her next class. Felicity MacDougall– scatterbrained? How utterly absurd!

Perhaps Victoria and Jason's relationship would have deteriorated even more rapidly had they both not become increasingly involved in their own separate lives. They would go all day–sometimes several days in a row–without seeing each other except in passing. Her marriage could thus remain comfortably in the background of Victoria's life where for great parts of each day she could forget about it entirely. This was perhaps fortunate because deep down inside she knew things were very wrong and since Jason was perfect, she must certainly be the one at fault.

Then all at once Christmas was here and their life together, taking on the magic of the season, seemed for a while to be full of joy. Christmas Eve, with its special memory of their meeting one year ago, was spent at the Prodigals shelter where they could share their happiness, not only with each other and their children, but also the homeless young people. There was a religious service at midnight. Victoria remembered the first time she'd heard Jason preach; now he was her husband and she felt truly blessed.

Christmas morning was spent as a family and in the afternoon they drove out to Long Island for dinner at the MacAllisters. It was very late by the time they left to return to the city. Victoria sat close to Jason her hand through his arm, her head resting on his shoulder. Quiet moments of tenderness like this he could handle and occasionally he would turn to brush his lips against her forehead. Ben and Rachel were asleep in the back while Olivia was curled up on the front seat, her head in her mother's lap. With her free hand Victoria stroked her daughter's face and hair. She felt utterly contented. Any marriage, after all, required a period of adjustment. Perhaps now at long last their life together could really begin.

Then–just two weeks later–Jason received a phone call at his office. "Reverend Eliot, this is Colonel Herrick at the Pentagon." The brisk male voice spoke with obvious authority. "Your name has just come to the top of the list. Could you be ready to leave around the first of February?"

It was more than a year and a half since he'd volunteered to serve a three month chaplaincy in Vietnam and understandably he'd forgotten the commitment entirely. After all a great deal had happened to him in the meantime. At the time, Jason recalled now, he'd felt a need to make a contribution to the war effort and from a personal standpoint a three month separation from his wife seemed a good idea for them both. Three months away from Victoria was another thing altogether. The silence on his end of the line lengthened until it became noticeable.

"Reverend Eliot," Colonel Herrick went on finally, "I trust it hasn't become inconvenient to serve. You are very much needed."

"No—no, of course not, Colonel."

"Fine, then. Report to me here in Washington on February 3rd for a two week orientation prior to your tour of duty."

Jason went home that evening wondering how to break the news to Victoria. She had such a terror of being alone–especially at night. As he came into the apartment, the living room was softly lit, but deserted. Sounds of laughter could be heard coming from the kitchen and pushing open the swinging door, he saw her standing in front of the sink breaking up lettuce into a large salad bowl. Olivia was sitting at the table school books and papers spread about, but it was evident little homework was actually getting done. They enjoyed each other's company so much; sometimes he felt left out.

"Jason–hello, darling." Victoria smiled at him. "Dinner will be ready very soon."

She looked so beautiful and he would have liked to take her in his arms. Because Olivia was present, of course he did not. "I have a little writing to do," he replied. "I'll be in my study."

It was a quiet, pleasant evening, but when Olivia had gone to bed, Jason finally had no choice but to bring up the subject of his imminent departure. As he told her, he saw the expected reaction register on her lovely face. "Oh, Jason, no," she whispered. She had been sitting across from him in a chair, but now as she spoke, she moved to sit beside him on the couch. "Oh, darling, I'll miss you so!"

He took her in his arms gently caressing her back and shoulders. On those rare occasions when he could hold her like this–easily and naturally with no guilt or shame–he felt a special joy. "It will only be three and a half months, Victoria. The time will go quickly and you'll have Olivia for company."

Strangely it was all much easier than she'd anticipated. Like any "good wife" she helped Jason prepare to leave, washing his clothes and packing his suitcases, making careful note of all his instructions on insurance, the name and phone number of his attorney, everything of which she should be aware in his absence. Surprisingly none of this upset her in the least. She even drove him to the airport–together with Olivia walking him to his departure gate for the moment she'd expected would be the worst of all–the actual good-bye. It was over before she realized as with a final kiss and embrace, Jason hurried out through the rainswept darkness and climbed the stairs to the plane. At the top he paused turning back to wave. They both returned the wave and then he disappeared from sight.

"It's all right, Mummy." The little girl hugged her mother fiercely about the waist. "You've got me."

"Oh, sweetheart, thank you!" She returned the hug.

They walked back out to the car. It was a cold night, the rain beginning to freeze on the surface of the parking lot, as Victoria started the car and eased it out into the traffic. "Mummy, do you remember when I first came here and I thought all the cars were on the wrong side of the road?" Victoria didn't reply and the little girl leaned forward to look at her mother's face. "Are you all right, Mummy?"

"Yes, of course, darling. Now sit back and fasten your seat belt. The roads are getting slippery." What is wrong with me, Victoria thought. I feel.....I feel–she had to search for the word, but then suddenly it came to her. My God—I feel free!

Chapter 19

People were kind and well-meaning, often remarking comfortingly on Jason's absence. "How much you must miss him," they would say and she would invariably reply, "Oh, yes, I miss him terribly." Occasionally her wry sense of humor would prompt her to add–"This is a recording." But she resisted the temptation, scolding herself for even thinking it.

She and Olivia enjoyed long, cozy evenings together. Felicity MacDougall frequently joined them for the cinema, meals in all sorts of exotic restaurants, even a week-end at Mystic Seaport in Connecticut. The three of them spent the mid-semester break skiing in Vermont. The fact that they were all beginners only made it all the more fun. At the end of the day they were almost as sore from laughing as from falling down. For Victoria and her daughter especially it was the happiness of their first Christmas together all over again with no sadness of impending separation to mar it.

The MacAllisters, as well, were wonderful company. She often had them to dinner at the apartment; they went with her to the theatre, the opera and the ballet. At times she couldn't help wondering why Ken seemed so much more human than her own husband.

Then when Jason had been gone a little less than two months, Kate telephoned to invite them to spend the week-end. "Oh, thank you!" Victoria exclaimed. "You're sure we won't be a bloody nuisance?"

Her friend smiled. She found the Englishwoman's use of the word, "bloody" in so many and varied situations amusing and she couldn't understand why Jason was shocked by it. By today's standards it was really rather a mild oath. "You certainly will not be," she replied emphatically. "And for once Ken isn't preaching anywhere on Sunday so if it's warm enough, we can take the sailboat out on the Sound. Oh yes–and Lisa will keep Olivia entertained so you can just relax.'

"That's not necessary; I enjoy my daughter's company. But I know she likes Lisa."

"Good. Then come early Friday afternoon and plan on staying until late Monday morning. That way you'll avoid the commuting traffic."

* * *

"Welcome, you two!" Kate appeared at the kitchen door as their car came to a stop in front of the garage. "Need some help?"

Olivia was the first one out of the car. "No, thank you, Aunt Kate," she sang out. "We can do it."

"Hello, luv!" Victoria called as she got out herself, reaching in back for a suitcase. "Yes, we can manage although my daughter has definitely inherited my tendency to overpack. I told her we'll terrify the MacAllisters. They'll think we've come for a fortnight!" By now they were at the door.

"Absolutely not!" Kate assured her laughing as she hugged each of them. "We'd love to have you. Come on in." She turned to lead the way into the kitchen. "I'm afraid we <u>have</u> had a bit of a mix-up about this week-end, however," she added apologetically.

Olivia had put down her suitcase and headed straight for Muffin, the family cat, who was sunning herself on a window sill. Victoria rested her valise on a chair. "Mix-up?" She raised her eyebrows. What an expressive face she has, the other woman thought. I suppose it's because she's an actress, but it seems so natural. "Kate, if there's a problem, we could have come some other week-end."

"No, no, it's not a problem. It's just that we'll be having another guest as well."

Victoria's dismay showed clearly on her face. "Oh, I just knew that would bother you," Kate continued quickly. "I'm so sorry! But I hated to put you off and we really felt obligated to do this other thing. You're aware that Ken's father came from Scotland originally? But I can explain while we're getting you settled. Come along upstairs."

She nodded. "Come on, luv," she said to her daughter. Reluctantly the little girl left the cat and picking up her suitcase again, followed them up the stairs. What Victoria really wanted to do was to take Olivia and return to the city–to avoid what she was sure was going to be an uncomfortable situation. But this new person she had become couldn't bring herself to be rude.

"Right in here." Their hostess led the way into a lovely rose and white bedroom. "That closet to your left is empty and also the top two drawers in that chest over there." She pointed out the various spots as she spoke. "And this room does have its own bath."

They began to unpack, Victoria handing various items of clothing to Olivia and telling her where to put them. Often as they worked together, she would touch the child. "You are such an affectionate mother," Kate couldn't resist observing.

Victoria merely smiled in return. "So–who is this other guest?"

"Oh, yes–the...ah...son of a friend of Ken's father. He's coming over to give some folk concerts and Ken thought we should entertain him as a courtesy to his father."

"I wonder if he's one of this group I've heard about. There's a Scottish girl in one of my classes and she has some friends coming over the first of next week."

"It may be. I think this man's coming early to visit with us. Well, at least he's a countryman of yours. If you're finished unpacking, I thought we'd have tea and a snack. I'd like to wait dinner until Ken gets back from the airport."

"Then he's just arriving today?" Victoria remarked inquiringly as they went back downstairs. "You know though, Kate, the English and the Scots are actually quite different."

"In what way?" Their hostess put the kettle on to boil and they all settled around the kitchen table for their tea.

"It's rather like the difference between Handel's *Water Music* on the one hand and that bloody awful caterwauling that comes out of the bagpipes on the other."

Olivia laughed. "Mummy, Felicity keeps telling you that the pipes have a hauntingly beautiful sound."

Victoria laughed as well. "I know, luv, but I have yet to acquire a taste for them."

* * *

Hearing the flight from London announced, Ken stood up. Undoubtedly it would still take some time for people to clear customs, but since he only had a description of the man he was to meet, he wanted to have a good view of the arriving passengers.

He did indeed have a wait of another fifteen minutes or so before they began to come through the gate. For the most part they were typical tourists-clutching bags of souvenirs, looking bedraggled and extremely happy to be home. One particular group caught his attention, however: four girls clustered around a single man and all four talking at once. He had one girl hanging on each arm (a feat made more difficult by the fact that he was carrying a guitar case as well as his valise and a garment bag) while a third walked backwards in front of him and the fourth trailed along behind–woefully aware she had the least advantageous of the four positions. It was a few seconds before Ken realized with a start that this was probably the man he had come to meet: tall, auburn-haired and far more handsome–he thought ruefully–than any one man had a right to be. "Gavin Hamilton?" he asked, approaching the group.

"Aye–that I am," the man admitted with a grin. "Then ye must be Kenneth MacAllisterr." The brogue was a strong, lilting one and he had an engaging habit of ducking his head as he spoke.

"Oh, Gavin," one of the women sighed, "I can't remember when I've enjoyed a flight so much!" Ken noticed now that she and one of the other women were flight attendants. "The time went by so quickly."

"Thank ye, lass." He grinned again.

"You'll call me while you're here." Another of the girls reached out to touch him on the arm. "You promised."

"Aye, lass. I have the numberr rright herre." He patted one of the pockets of his belted trench coat which he wore open, the belt hanging loose.

"Oh, Gavin, I forgot to give you <u>my</u> number." The third girl searched frantically in her purse for a pen and a scrap of paper.'

"Just add it to this one," he suggested obligingly, digging the slip of paper out of his pocket. The original owner of the paper appeared properly deflated.

"I'll be in London again when you get back there," the fourth one–the other stewardess–put in eagerly. "I have a friend with a flat. I'll cook dinner for you."

"I'm verra sorrry, lass. I'll be goin' dirrectly oop to Scotland to help my dad wi' the sprring lambin'."

At last Ken had Gavin free of his entourage and they were walking out to the car. "Does that always happen to you?" he asked in amazement.

"I'm afrraid it does. I've always had a bit of a way wi' the lassies, ye see," The Scotsman made this rather conceited statement in such a matter-of-fact manner, however, that the other man couldn't help but laugh.

"How's your father?" Ken asked a few minutes later as he threaded his way out of the airport and onto the Expressway. "We've only a half-hour's drive incidentally. We live quite close to the airport."

"Dad's just fine, I'm glad to say. Worrkin' as harrd as everr on his sheep farrm. 'Twas a grreat disappointment to him that neitherr my brrother Rhuaridh (Gavin pronounced it, "Rurrry") norr I had any inclination to follow in his footsteps."

"What's your brother's name?"

"Rurry--R-H-U-A-R-I-D-H. 'Tis Gaelic forr Rroderrick," he went on to explain. "<u>My</u> name was originally spelled G-A-B-H-A-N. I've anglicized it much to my grranny's dismay."

"By the way I should tell you you're not our only guest this week-end. A friend of mine is on temporary duty in Vietnam as a chaplain and we also have his wife and daughter visiting with us."

"That's grrand! I always enjoy meetin' new people."

"You've probably heard of her–the English actress, Victoria Windsor?"

For more than one reason Gavin had never forgotten that night. "Aye, I've hearrd of herr," was all he said out loud.

Kate was in the kitchen preparing dinner. Lisa had taken Olivia up to her room to listen to music and thus Victoria was alone in the living room when she saw the headlights of Ken's car against the garage doors. The room, with its colonial furnishings in tones of orange and rust and forest green, was warm and homey and she was enjoying the peace of the moment, the crackling fire on the hearth and the Bloody Mary in which she was indulging herself in Jason's absence. All visitors to the MacAllister home were evidently brought in through the kitchen because almost at once she heard the men's voices–Ken's familiar to her by now and the other deeper and quite obviously Scottish.

"Go on into the living room and introduce yourself," Ken urged his guest. "I'll take your things upstairs and come right back down. Help yourself to a drink."

Gavin had the momentary advantage as passing through the darkened dining room, he had the chance to study Victoria briefly, unobserved in return. Dressed in royal blue slacks and a white turtleneck pullover, she was curled up at one end of the couch looking into the fire, her hands cradling a glass. Her blonde hair tied back from her face, her beauty was much as he remembered, but simpler somehow and fresher. He wondered what she'd say when she saw him. Would she recall their previous meeting?

At the sound of footsteps Victoria had glanced up at the archway leading from the dining room into the living room. She could see at once the man was too tall to be Ken and she steadied herself for the effort of having to make polite conversation until someone joined them At last he stepped into the light. He was indeed well over six feet and broad-shouldered–wearing brown corduroy trousers and a dark gold turtleneck jumper. He had a strong face–the bone structure pronounced–and thick, wavy auburn hair. Oddly he struck her as somehow familiar. "Good evenin', Miss Windsorr." There was the same soft burr on the "r" in her last name to which she'd become accustomed with Felicity and as he spoke, he smiled–a boyish grin which at once softened his features, revealing a dimple in his left cheek. "I seem to have been given the opporrtunity of intrroducin' m'self. My name is Gavin Hamilton." He identified himself with a bit of a flourish, his brogue broadening the "a" in his first name just slightly.

It wasn't until he spoke that Victoria realized with a jolt that she'd been staring. "Hello, Mr. Hamilton," she managed to reply.

"I was <u>also</u> instrructed to help m'self to a drrink and <u>that</u> is somethin' a Scotsman neverr rrefuses." He walked past her to the bar, carrying himself with the same unconscious pride with which he'd spoken his name. Quickly he poured himself a Scotch and came to sit at the other end of the couch, crossing his legs by resting the ankle of one on the knee of the other. He took a long swallow of his drink and sighed appreciatively. Victoria realized with some dismay that her heart was pounding. Gavin was watching her intently and he could tell she was bothered by something. Well, if she <u>does</u> remember the other time, he thought, I'll see that she soon forgets it. He smiled–the corners of his eyes crinkling and the dimple appearing again. "So..yourr husband's a frriend o' Ken's, I underrstand?"

God, I have never been so unnerved, she thought. What in hell is wrong with me? "Yes, she replied a little stiffly, "Ken and <u>my</u> <u>husband</u> were in seminary together."

Their eyes met. Hers reminded him of the North Sea in close to the shore where the reflection from the trees turns the water a greenish-blue while his, she could see now, were brown, so dark as to appear almost black yet glowing with a compelling warmth which seemed to radiate from somewhere deep inside him. He chuckled and the glow became a discernible twinkle. "My worrd! All this holiness may be just a wee bit too much forr me!"

Such utter irreverence was like a refreshing splash of cold water on her face. Victoria blinked and then she laughed, throwing back her head. "You are....you are...." She searched her mind for the word, but there was none.

"I am like no otherr laddie ye've everr met. Am I corrrect?" If possible the mirth in his eyes grew even stronger. He always enjoyed charming a beautiful woman, but for some reason this was particularly pleasant.

"You are......disgraceful!" She tried to sound annoyed, but the effect was spoiled by a twitch at one corner of her mouth.

"And <u>ye</u> have no doot been told a grreat many times that ye'rre a verra bonny lass?"

"Not exactly."

He frowned, momentarily at a loss. "Oh, ye mean ye've no been called a bonny lass beforre? Then ye've no known a Scotsman because he'd surrely have told ye that." He noticed suddenly that her drink was nearly gone. "Can I rrefill that forr ye, lass?" He smiled at her again.

That damned smile! If only he would stop smiling! "Yes, please." She handed him the glass. He stood up and walked toward the bar, carrying his own glass as well. "Do you know how to make a Bloody Mary?"

"A Bloody–Who?" Gavin whirled about to face her.

"I'm sorry." Again she laughed. How many times since he walked into the room had she found herself laughing. She supposed it was just as Felicity had warned her. The Scots were an endearing lot. "It's vodka, tomato juice, tabasco sauce and I like a slice of lime in it rather than lemon."

"What in God's name do ye want to do all that to good liquorrr forrrr?" he asked stringing out the burr on the last two words. "Ye'll have Scotch–neat. 'Tis much betterr."

"Mr. Hamilton," Victoria exclaimed in amused exasperation, "I don't like Scotch!"

"Therre's two things wrrong with that statement, lass." He poured two Scotches and returning to the couch, handed her the fresh glass. "Therre's no such thing as not likin' Scotch."

She looked down at the drink in her hand. "Mr. Hamilton, I said I......"

"Ye do ken what they say aboot Scotch, do ye not?"

"What?" Somehow she knew it was a mistake to ask.

"If God made anythin' betterr, He kept it forr himself." He winked.

"Oh really, Mr. Hamilton!"

"And that's the otherr thing."

"That's right. You did say two things, didn't you?"

"My fatherr is Misterr Hamilton." He appeared intensely serious now looking at her with those damned unnerving brown eyes and all at once she noticed for some ridiculous reason that the lashes framing them were auburn in tint matching his hair. "My name is Gavin."

"Gavin," she repeated after him, cursing herself for allowing her voice to shake.

"And you'rre?"

"Oh...ah... Victoria, of course."

"All that?"

"What do you mean...all that?" Bizarrely it seemed they'd even had the same conversation before, but that was clearly impossible. She could never have met such a man and not remembered him.

"It's too grrand and elegant. It doesna suit ye at all."

"I don't like Vicki."

He'd caught an odd note in her voice. Why did she so dislike being called Vicki? "No–not that. I'll have to think aboot it."

"You're going to decide what my name should be! You are impossible!"

His eyes began to glow again, the smile seeming to appear there first before it spread to his lips. "Aye." And once again they both laughed.

Ken had come back downstairs at some point to help Kate with dinner, but at each fresh burst of laughter he glanced worriedly in the direction of the living room. He was unable to hear the actual conversation, but this only made him all the more uneasy.

"What's the matter?" his wife asked finally. "Victoria was a little upset about our having another guest, but she seems to be enjoying herself."

"That's the trouble! That man is just too damned charming!" Ken's feelings about profanity weren't as strong as Jason's, but he only swore in extreme circumstances. "You should have seen it, Kate! Four women followed him off that plane!"

"Oh, darling, really! Victoria wouldn't....."

"Nevertheless, I think I'll join them." He put down the pan which contained the potatoes he'd been mashing and walked quickly into the living room. As he came through the archway, they were standing in front of a framed map of Scotland he had on one wall, Gavin pointing out a particular spot. It all appeared so innocent that Ken was a little ashamed of himself. "Dinner will be ready in a few minutes," he announced lamely, wondering if he sounded as awkward as he felt.

A short time later they were all seated around the dinner table enjoying a delicious meal of fried chicken. Gavin soon made himself the center of attention keeping them entertained with stories about his boyhood in the Scottish Highlands. Uneasily Kate observed Victoria's reaction. Maybe Ken was right. She'd never seen the other woman look quite like that– her lips slightly parted– and she never took her eyes off Gavin's face.

Then later that evening Lisa asked if their visitor were too tired to sing for them. "My grandfather plays the pipes and I think the traditional Scottish music is so beautiful."

Gavin grinned. "Ye have verra good taste, lass. You therre." He pointed a finger at Olivia. "The wee one with the bonny blue eyes. Will ye rrun oopstairrs and fetch my guitarr?"

"Yes, Mr. Hamilton." The little girl's high-pitched giggle had been clearly audible mixed in with the adult laughter at dinner and now she went eagerly to do his bidding, returning almost at once to hand him his guitar.

With an air of reverence he lifted the instrument from its case, deftly tuning a couple of strings. "Let me see noo–aye, of courrse. Nearrly everra-one knows this one, I think." And accompanying himself with a style of picking which conveyed magically a small boat rocking in the waves, he began to sing "The Skye Boat Song".

Speed, bonny boat, like a birrd on the wing,
"Onwarrd," the sailorrs crry.
Carrry the lad that's borrn to be King
Overr the sea to Skye.

His rich baritone voice filled the room caressing the words of the song and Victoria fought the sensation that she was floating–unable to do anything but allow the sound to sweep over and around her like a surge of wind.

They all went upstairs together calling their good nights as they went into the various bedrooms. Gavin's room was diagonally across from the one being shared by Victoria and Olivia. He paused, his hand on the doorknob, to look back at the two of them. "Good night, bonny wee one," he said to the little girl with a grin.

"Good night, Mr. Hamilton."

"Och, I told yet–'tis Gavin."

"Good night, Gavin." Suddenly she darted across the hall to give him a hug and a kiss on the cheek. "I like you!"

"Ye know–I like you, too. See ye in the morrnin' then, lass."

Olivia went on into the bedroom. "Do you call every female lass?" Victoria wondered why she found this habit of his irritating.

"Aye." His grin grew broader. "As forr you....." He pointed at her... "I'll gi'e the mattterr serrious considerration. Good night." He disappeared into his room, but for some reason

Victoria remained in the hall staring at his closed door. All at once it opened again and to her intense embarrassment he discovered her still standing there. "Did ye forrget somethin'?" he asked.

"No!" she snapped and stepping inside, she quickly shut her door. Unfortunately she could still hear him chuckling.

Undressing for bed a few minutes later, Gavin continued to smile. He realized now that on the occasion of their brief earlier meeting he hadn't even begun to appreciate this incredible woman. He stretched out under the covers, experiencing the inevitable flash of irritation as his feet came into contact with the footboard. No one, it seemed, made beds long enough for his 6 foot, 3 inch frame–especially at home in Scotland where most men except for his father were much shorter.

Victoria and Olivia, meanwhile, had also prepared for bed, the child slipping under the covers first and reaching up for a hug. "Oh, Mummy," she exclaimed, "isn't he the nicest man you've ever met?"

"I thought Jason was. And what about your Daddy?"

Olivia looked doubtful and a little guilty. "Well, they are, too, but...but...."

"Go to sleep now, sweetheart. It's very late." Victoria tried to keep her tone normal. There was no reason for her to be so upset. Hours later, however, she was still unable to sleep. She loved Jason. How could she possibly find another man so attractive?

* * *

Coming downstairs the next morning, Olivia found everyone else already in the kitchen, an informal breakfast in progress. "Good morrnin' to ye, wee one!" Gavin's voice boomed out. "And wherre's that bonny motherr o' yourrs?"

"Mummy's still asleep."

"How about a bicycle ride, Olivia?" Lisa asked. "I borrowed a smaller bike from the younger sister of a friend of mine. We'll be back before lunch."

"That sounds super, Lisa. Thanks awfully!"

"Well, I have some grocery shopping to do," Kate announced, "and someone should be here when Victoria wakes up."

"I have a bit o' worrk to do." Gavin poured himself some more tea. "I'll be herre."

"As a matter of fact," Ken put in quickly, "I was about to suggest some golf this morning."

"Verra frrankly–I'm terrrible at it and with the ceilidh this evenin', I rreally need to prractice. I feel as though I've left my vocal corrds back in Glengowrrie."

"Is that where you're from?" Kate inquired. "You know, perhaps one more cup of tea myself before I take on the supermarket." Ken was making a frantic assortment of odd facial and hand signals which any good wife would have understood to mean, "I want to talk to you". Whether deliberately or not she ignored him.

"Aye." Gavin slouched down in his chair and stretching out his long legs in their brown corduroy trousers and crossing them at the ankles, he sipped leisurely on his fresh mug of tea. " 'Tis a wee village in the foothills of the Grrampian Mountains aboot halfway between Aberrdeen and Inverrness. 'Tis a bonny spot, forr fairr."

"I'm surprised you could bring yourself to leave, " Ken remarked in a decidedly acid tone.

"If last night was any sample, Gavin," Lisa observed, "you don't need to practice."

"Lisa's right," Ken put in, genial once again. "And the exercise will do you good."

"Leave Gavin alone," Kate said. "He just got here yesterday and he's probably tired."

"I have a list of things I need, dear," her husband said pointedly. "<u>In</u> my den."

She barely glanced at him. "I'll get it before I leave."

"Kate! There's something on there I have to explain to you." He stood up. She looked around at the others and shrugged, but she got to her feet to follow him. Once inside the den Ken shut the door firmly behind them.

"This must be quite a confidential list," she observed with a grin.

"You are not to leave those two alone in this house! Do you understand me?"

"What—no list?"

"You know perfectly well there's no list! It's bad enough he has my wife and daughter eating out of his hand! What am I supposed to tell Jason when he gets back?"

"You're being positively silly! What do you expect Gavin to do anyway–run up to her room the minute they're alone and ravish her?"

"Oh, no. I'm sure he can wait until she comes downstairs!"

"Ken, you're impossible. Now I am going to the market! If you insist on playing watchdog, that's your business!" She strode from the den and snatching up her purse and jacket, she headed outside to the garage. Lisa and Olivia were already outside–the little girl trying out the strange bicycle in the driveway.

"What's the matter with Dad?" Lisa asked as Olivia rounded the other end of the driveway, temporarily out of hearing. "He was really rude. That's not like him."

"Oh, there's latent insanity in his family! Thank goodness you didn't inherit it!"

Lisa looked at her mother in astonishment, but before she could think of a reply, Kate had already pulled up the garage door and disappeared inside.

Back in his den, meanwhile, Ken had gotten out some books and a yellow legal pad. This would be a good chance to do some preparation for an upcoming lecture and he was determined not to leave their guest alone with Victoria. Very shortly, however, Gavin appeared in the doorway. "Ye've changed yourr mind then aboot the golf? Ye'rre no to concerrn yourrself wi' me."

Ken was finding the brogue increasingly irritating. He was becoming quite sure, in fact, that it was fake. "You're setting me such a good example." He forced a smile. "I'm going to do some work myself."

"I'll close this door then. I've no wish to disturrb ye."

"Oh, no–leave the door open. I'll enjoy the music."

" 'Twill not be verra bonny music I'll be makin', I'm afrraid. Och, how stupid of me. Will I be botherrin' the lassie oopstairrs?"

"I'm sure Mrs. Eliot won't object in the least. She certainly seemed to enjoy your singing last night." Ken turned his attention abruptly to his books.

Briefly Gavin remained there. He was unaccustomed to hostility. At last, however, he shrugged good-naturedly and returned to the living room. Ken heard the tuning of the guitar being checked and a short time later the Scotsman began to sing, going over and over certain passages. Perhaps he'd misjudged the man; perhaps, after all, he really did intend to work.

When Victoria finally awoke some time later, it was to the sound of Gavin's voice coming up from directly below her and for a few minutes she lay there listening. She found herself picturing the man that went with the voice and getting quickly out of bed, she went into the bathroom to take a shower. She was thankful the running water drowned out the music. It was nearly an hour before she finished with her shower, shampoo and make-up. Was she consciously dawdling–postponing going downstairs? Finally she had no choice; she had nothing else to do.

She could see Gavin from the hall–sitting on the couch. He appeared totally absorbed in the piece of music he was working on–playing a few chords and then stopping to make notations on the sheet music which lay in front of him on the coffee table. A second door led directly into the kitchen and she moved quickly and quietly past the living room relieved that apparently she'd been unobserved. There was a note for her on the table:

> *"Hi, Victoria. Mum's at the market and Olivia and I are going for a bike ride. There's juice in the fridge and rolls in the little oven. Make yourself a pot of tea. See you in a little while–Lisa.*

Victoria turned on the oven and put some water on to boil. Then she poured a glass of juice and set a place for herself at the table. She didn't know why she failed to realize that the music had stopped. She was pouring the water into the tea pot when he spoke. " 'Tis nae good to lie a-bed in the morrnin', ye know."

At the sound of his voice she jumped and boiling water splashed over onto her hand. "Ouch!" She dropped the kettle.

"Och, lass, I didna mean to starrtle ye." He moved forward to retrieve the kettle and put it back on the stove. "Did ye burrn ye bonny wee self?" He took hold of her right hand to inspect the damage.

"I'm all right, thank you!" Irritably she pulled away, going over to the oven to remove the rolls.

"My worrd, Gavin!" He shook his head. "No one seems to like ye verra much this morrnin'. Perrhaps ye should have stayed in Scotland." In spite of her determination to ignore him she glanced up and when he saw her looking at him, he winked.

"Oh, really!" she snapped, turning away to sit down to her breakfast. She drank her juice and then reached for the pot to pour a cup of tea. "Are you still standing there?"

"Well, if ye'd offerr me a cuppa, then I might sit doon to drrink it."

"For your information I intend to drink it all myself."

"This converrsation is not goin' the way I'd planned at all."

"Well perhaps, Mr. Hamilton, if you would stop trying to force yourself on people..."

"So we'rre back to Misterr Hamilton, then? Matterrs are definitely rregrressin'."

"You don't give up easily, do you?"

"No, I don't. Call it purre Scots stubborrness, if ye will....."

"That will do as well as anything. Now if I might be allowed to enjoy my breakfast in peace....."

"Aye, lass. aye. I willna botherr ye. If anyone inquirres as to my wherreaboots– which considerrin' my currrent popularrity–is dootful, I'm goin' forr a walk."

She heard him take the stairs to the second floor two at at time and come down again moments later. The front door slammed. Victoria finished her breakfast quickly, wondering vaguely why suddenly the day seemed a little bleak. She went on into the living room intending to find a book to read. Gavin's guitar was still there propped up against the couch–the sheet music spread out on the coffee table. How typically thoughtless of him–to leave his things about. She paced restlessly, glad a short while later to see Kate's car pull into the driveway,

"Victoria–hi!" her hostess called from the kitchen. "I just want to get the groceries put away."

"May I help?"

"No, it won't take long. Where's Gavin by the way?"

"He went out for a walk."

"You should have gone with him. It's too nice a day to be indoors."

"What are you trying to do? I'm a married woman!"

Kate paused in her work coming to stand in the archway. "That doesn't mean you can't be friends with a man for heaven's sake. No one would question my devotion to Ken and yet I find Gavin charming. And in your case he's almost a voice from home."

"My home is with Jason now!" Why did she feel so defensive? "You know," she went on hurriedly, "I've been thinking. Olivia and I should go back to the city. It's just too much for you to have all of us here at once."

Her friend came to sit beside her on the couch. "Is something troubling you, Victoria?"

"Why shouldn't I be upset? Jason's been gone for almost two months and I miss him very much."

"I'm sure you do. It's just that up until now you've been handling it so well."

"I appreciate your kindness, Kate, more than I can say, but I....I really do feel we should leave."

"Wait at least until tomorrow," she urged. "The parties at the Caledonian Club are such fun: Scottish reels and waltzes. And if Gavin bothers you, Lisa and Olivia and you and I could go out for lunch and perhaps do some shopping."

"Of course Gavin doesn't bother me," Kate wondered if the other woman was aware that her voice was shaking. "You....you hadn't mentioned a dance. I doubt we brought anything appropriate."

"That gives us the perfect excuse to go shopping. All you each need is a long dress–white or pastel--and I'm sure we have extra plaids."

"Plaids?"

"Yes, the woman don't wear kilts, just a plaid–that's a tartan scarf–pinned over one shoulder."

Later that afternoon the four women left the restaurant to begin their shopping. "What is the Caledonian Club anyway, Kate?" Victoria asked as they walked along together through one of Southampton's large shopping malls toward a certain dress shop.

"Americans of Scottish ancestry. The men have a pipe band and we all have weekly lessons in Scottish Country dancing and a party once a month."

"Their heritage means so much to the Scots, doesn't it?" she replied thoughtfully.

* * *

That evening Victoria was the first to be ready–unusual in itself. The simple white dress suited her, her fragile-appearing blonde beauty seeming to belong to another century. As she came downstairs, she was still carrying the tartan scarf–uncertain as to the correct way of wearing it. She was standing in front of the fireplace–from habit checking her appearance in the mirror there as she did before her first entrance in any performance–when Gavin's head and shoulders suddenly appeared behind her. She spun about to face him.

He was dressed in full Highland regalia: a kilt in the Hamilton tartan–three horizontal and three vertical bands of royal blue intersecting against a red background--, a royal blue velvet doublet and lace jabot. A plaid of the same tartan was drawn tightly across his chest, fastened on his left shoulder with a massive gold brooch, the voluminous folds cascading down behind him. My God, was Victoria's first thought, how could I ever have thought of a kilt as feminine?

He walked slowly toward her–the back of the kilt swaying slightly as he moved–his gaze on her intent. "I'm verra sorrry," he said, his deep voice burring softly over the "r's", "if I offended ye in some way this morrnin'. I do want verra much forr us to be frriends." She had no way of knowing that Gavin Hamilton had never before apologized to a woman. It was just as well. That powerful masculine body carrying itself with such pride in his native dress–those hypnotic brown eyes–were quite enough as it was.

As he came closer, Victoria realized that once again her heart was pounding. "That's...that's perfectly all right, I sure," she managed to reply. "It...it was just that you startled me and I did burn myself rather badly."

"Frriends, then?" He extended his right hand–a hand surprisingly slender in comparison to the rest of his frame. "Afterr all, Scotland and England have lived in peace noo forr overr two centurries. Shouldn't we be able to do the same?"

"I notice you put Scotland first," she observed, her eyes starting to sparkle.

"Aye," he replied, his own glowing in response.

"Well, far be it from me to disturb two hundred years of accord." She raised her hand to accept his, but as his fingers closed over hers, she felt herself trembling.

Normally when Gavin sensed that a woman was beginning to succumb to his charms, he would immediately press his advantage. Why then did he release Victoria's hand, moving back as though to study her in the dress? "I dinna ken how it happened," he remarked after a few seconds. " 'Tis an actual law that all lasses as bonny as yourrself must be borrn in Scotland." She laughed now. Kate was right, after all. Why shouldn't she find him likeable? Everybody else did. "May I fasten yourr plaid forr ye then?" he inquired, coming closer again. Forcing herself to remain still, she handed him the tartan scarf. "Och, I have to pity ye–knowin' ye'rre English."

"What is wrong now?" She felt the mirth bubble up inside her again. That's what was so unnerving–the intense masculine charm one minute and the boyishly mischievous sense of humor the next.

"And what do ye expect me to pin this on with? Do ye no have a brrooch of some kind?" Victoria shook her head. "I have anotherr one–smallerr." He hurried upstairs again, returning almost at once with a gold pin in the shape of a Celtic cross.

"Oh, Gavin–so beautiful! I can't wear that. Suppose I lost it? I'd never forgive myself."

"Ye willna lose it. 'Tis a good clasp. Herre–hold it so." He doubled over one end of the plaid and placed it on her left shoulder. She brought up her hand to hold it and he bent to fasten the pin. His head was very close to her face–the shining auburn hair brushing her cheek. He smelled of an aromatic mixture of a musk-like aftershave and pipe tobacco. "Therre," he said finally, stepping back to survey his work. "Noo–would ye be havin' a wee drram beforre we leave?"

"More Scotch?"

"Aye–of courrse."

"Thank you, I don't think so. What I could use is a crash course in Scottish Country Dancing so that I don't make a total fool of myself this evening."

He thought for a second. "Aye. There's one rreel simple enough forr even yourr cloomsy English feet."

"Oh–thank you!"

"Ye'rre verra welcoom, I'm surre—coom." He took her hand again and they began to walk through the dance, laughing together as at first she stumbled over the steps, but settling down to serious dancing as she soon caught on. "Verra good!" He applauded her. "Ye'rre learrnin' farr more quickly than most. Therre must be a recorrd herre. Shall we trry it to music?"

"Oh yes, I'd like to!"

"Grrand then!" Quickly he selected an album, putting it on the stereo, and by the time Ken and Kate came downstairs, Victoria and Gavin were moving smoothly through the dance steps. They made a striking couple–her blonde hair and fair complexion against his burnished auburn hair and sun-bronzed face.

Abruptly Ken turned away. "I'll get the car out." Kate still stood there watching them. They look as though they belong together, she thought uneasily. A moment or so later, however, Lisa and Olivia also came down and the rest of them went outside where Ken was waiting, the car parked in the driveway with the motor running.

It was one of the happiest evenings Victoria had ever known. She danced almost continually. But oh, when Gavin was her partner–his tall, handsome figure towering over her, one arm firmly about her waist, the pleats of his kilt flying out behind him. She seemed to float across the floor. It bothered her somewhat that Ken frequently cut in on them–almost as if he suspected something. There really was nothing wrong with their being friends.

Midway through the dancing Gavin gave a brief concert. While he was singing, Victoria glanced around at the people near her–faces of all ages rapt with attention– some of the older ones even crying as the music brought back memories of their homeland. "He really is a marvelous entertainer, isn't he?" Victoria observed under her breath to Kate as they joined in the applause after one of the songs.

It was all over much too soon. Almost before she knew it, they were back at the MacAllisters and she and Olivia were alone in their bedroom. "Didn't you just have the most super time, Mummy?" the little girl asked happily as she slid under the covers of her bed.

"Yes, I did, darling," Victoria replied, coming to sit beside her. Bedtime was still special for them both.

"Do you like Gavin?"

"Of course I do. Come on now, luv. Snuggle down and go to sleep."

Obediently Olivia turned on her side, curling up. "Good night, Mummy."

"Good night, sweetheart." Mother and daughter exchanged hugs and kisses. Victoria turned off the bedside lamp, going to undress in the bathroom. Once in bed, however, she continued to lie awake in the darkness reliving the evening. At some point she heard the door open across the hall. Footsteps moved past their room and down the stairs. She pictured Gavin in the kitchen, making himself an enormous sandwich no doubt and perhaps a pot of tea. Desperately she fought off the urge to join him and when at last she fell asleep, the same nightmare she'd had so many times before returned. She seemed to be searching for someone or something, but as always her quest was in vain and when she awoke, she discovered with a start that she'd been crying. She propped herself up on one elbow to look over at the other bed, but the little girl was sound asleep. At least she hadn't disturbed her daughter.

Finally she slept again herself and the next thing she knew Olivia was shaking her awake. "Mummy, breakfast is ready and Uncle Ken says we can take the sailboat out to an island in Long Island Sound for a picnic. Victoria opened her mouth to tell Olivia she'd planned to return to the city this morning, but she didn't have the heart to disappoint her–then maybe it was she herself who wanted to stay–and instead she dressed quickly, applied a minimum of make-up and followed her downstairs.

"You know what Gavin said to me, Mummy?" the child bubbled happily. "He said it's time we English lassies got some rroses in ourr cheeks." She rolled her "r's" in a perfect imitation of his brogue.

Victoria laughed. "That sounds like something he'd say."

"My goodness, Mummy. Isn't it too bad we're already married to Jason?"

Before she could reprimand her daughter for such disloyalty, the little girl had pushed open the swinging door into the kitchen. "Good morning, everyone!" Victoria said brightly, flashing her most dazzling smile.

Perhaps without realizing it, Gavin had been waiting for her to come down and now her actual entrance was a disappointment. There was a hard, brittle quality to her that reminded him of their original meeting in London. Even her smile was lacking something, leaving the green eyes strangely cold. She made no attempt to join in the breakfast chatter and she continued to remain silent on the drive to the marina. Finally he had her alone for a few minutes–Ken and Kate having gone to see the manager about launching the boat for the season; Lisa and Olivia walking out on the wharf to feed some crusts of bread to a flock of ducks that called the marina their home. Idly Gavin picked up a stone from the edge of the water hurling it far out into the Sound. "Arre ye angrry wi' me again then, lass?"

"Only a conceited ass such as yourrself would assume that my present mood has anything to do with you. As a matter of fact I didn't sleep well last night." She walked quickly away from him to meet Ken and Kate as they came out of the marina office. "I'm afraid Olivia and I are going to have to leave after all," she said. "I didn't sleep well last night and I'm feeling quite ill."

The MacAlllisters had discussed Victoria last night and now at her sudden indisposition they exchanged glances. "Suppose I take you back to our house and you can rest there," Kate suggested. "Olivia was so looking forward to the sail."

"I <u>want</u> to go home!" She was acutely aware she was sounding a great deal like the Victoria of a year or two ago, but she couldn't seem to stop herself. "And I'd rather my daughter not go out in a boat without my being present. She has to learn to accept disappointment! God knows I have!"

Ken, Lisa and Gavin remained at the marina and Kate drove Victoria and Olivia back to the house. As soon as the car stopped in the driveway, Olivia jumped out and ran inside sobbing. Kate followed Victoria into the kitchen. "It's Gavin, isn't it? You find him extremely attractive and that bothers you."

"I refuse to dignify that with a reply!" Victoria hurried from the room and up the stairs. Her daughter was already packing still crying softly. "Stop sniveling, Olivia. It's very annoying!"

"Mummy, why...why are you so mad at me?"

"Oh, darling, I'm not angry with you honestly. It's just as I said to Kate. I didn't sleep well and I'd like to go home and rest–that's all. Please try to understand."

"All right, Mummy." Nothing else really mattered, after all, as long as her mother still loved her.

A few minutes later they were back downstairs carrying their suitcases. Kate was still standing in the kitchen. "I'm so sorry, Victoria." She came over to hug her friend. "I...I shouldn't have said those things."

"It's all right. I'm....I'm sorry, too." She walked quickly to the door. All she wanted for the moment was escape. On the ride back into the city she forced herself to chatter to her daughter about inconsequential things and later that afternoon she suggested dinner out and a film.

Olivia was wide-eyed. "Jason doesn't approve of going to the cinema on Sundays!"

"Well, we just won't tell him," her mother replied flatly.

* * *

It was a relief to Victoria the following morning to be back at NYU where her mind was taken up with classes as well as rehearsals for the upcoming production of *My Fair Lady* which she was directing. As it turned out, however, she was not to be allowed to forget Gavin.

Felicity wasn't in class which was unusual and that evening the Scottish girl telephoned to apologize for her absence. "Ye see, Victorria," she bubbled, "Jamie and his chums arrrived today and it's been sae verra long since I've seen my Jamie!" As always when she became excited, her brogue was even thicker than usual and Victoria was having some difficulty understanding her. "Och, he's such a bonny lad, is my Jamie! He couldna believe I actually had an English frriend, but I told him ye werre everr sae nice in spite of such a terrrible handicap!" At last Felicity was forced to stop talking in order to catch her breath. "Arre ye still therre then?" she asked when a few seconds passed and Victoria hadn't said anything.

"To be perfectly honest, I wasn't sure you were finished."

"Arre ye all rright? Ye sound that queerr."

"Of course I'm all right. Don't be ridiculous!"

Felicity was somewhat taken aback. Sometimes she felt as if she didn't really know Victoria at all and continuing now, she sounded a little doubtful. "Well, I...I rang oop to ask ye to coom to theirr firrst concerrt." As she went along, she soon regained her momentum, however. "'Tis a wee coffee hoose rrun by the students at Columbia. Some of them hearrd Jamie and all o' them in Lundon last summerr so that's how it happened they'rre herre. So, will ye coom, then?"

"Ah...Felicity, this...ah...friend of Jamie's you mentioned. His name isn't Gavin Hamilton, by any chance?"

"Ye know him, then?"

"I met him this week-end. You....you knew he...he came a few days early to visit some friends?"

"Aye, Jamie said soomthin' aboot that. Well then, ye've got even morre rreason to coom, knowin' Gavin. What did I tell ye? Isn't he just aboot the most brraw laddy ye've everr seen? Och–when I was a wee lass o' twelve or thirrteen, I had the worrst crrush on him! But that was before I met my Jamie, of courrse!"

"Perhaps I shouldn't come. I....I might be in the way."

"In the way? Forr heaven's sake dinna go gettin' all daft and English on me noo, will ye, afterr my tellin' Jamie how grrand ye arre. Ye'll coom and I willna take no forr an answerr. 'Tis Wednesday at 7:30. We can go togetherr. See ye then. Bye!"

"No, wait, I...." But the line clicked and went dead. "Felicity, damn you!" she muttered, slamming her own receiver down. Well, I suppose at least I should go and meet Jamie, she thought after a moment. It's only a concert after all. I won't...ah... have to..ah...actually talk to him.

Felicity was waiting outside her last class on Wednesday afternoon. "So then, ye'rre coomin', arre ye?"

"It seems I'm not to be allowed to refuse," Victoria replied, smiling in spite of herself. "I've asked Olivia to come along. I hope that's all right."

"Aye, of courrse."

"She should be waiting in my office." They walked a couple of blocks to a restaurant which specialized in fish and chips and after dinner they traveled by subway to the Columbia campus. Victoria chuckled out loud as the train rattled its way uptown. "It's been quite a while since I rode the tube."

"Oh...and I suppose ye had a long black limousine with a chauffeurr and all."

"Well, yes, actually I did." Victoria's eyes sparkled. Teasing Felicity was such fun. Besides–for some reason–she felt particularly happy just then. "A Rolls-Royce–only it was gray–-a Silver Cloud." The Scottish girl blinked once or twice, but said nothing.

It was a cold, rainy night, but the basement room in the Student Union was already filled to capacity when they arrived. Jamie had saved them a front row table, however; a third chair was located somewhere for Olivia and they sat down, ordering two coffees and a hot chocolate. Jamie and three other men, forming a quartet called the Lochnagar Highlanders, opened the program followed by demonstrations of the Highland Fling and the stirring sword dance.

Finally Gavin was announced. A distinct murmur, noticeably female, ran through the room as he stepped up on the low stage carrying his guitar and settled himself on a stool. He was wearing the same clothes he'd had on the first time she saw him: brown corduroy trousers and a gold turtleneck pullover. "Good evenin' to ye all," he said with a nod. He smiled a special hello at Felicity. Then he noticed who was with her and he raised his eyebrows as if to ask–"What are you doing here?" Victoria looked away, appearing to concentrate on adding the correct amount of sugar and cream to a fresh cup of coffee.

He began to sing and now that she was no longer–for the time being at least–the focal point of his regard, she could relax a little. On and on he went from one song to the next, stopping in between only long enough to explain the historical context of the next selection. Then suddenly after one song he paused–idly strumming the guitar–a slight smile playing about his lips. "Ye know, I'm gettin' verra lonely oop herre," he said finally, "not that ye'rre nae verra fine coomp'ny for a laddy because ye arre. But I'd like someone right herre wi' me singin' along. Noo, as ye may be awarre, we'rre honorred tonight with the prresence of a celebrrated English actrress..." Oh no, she thought, he's <u>not</u> going to.... "...and I'm wonderrin'," Gavin went on the smile broadening, "if she wouldn't join me forr a wee bit. How aboot it, Victorria?"

There was a gasp and then thunderous applause. She glanced imploringly at Felicity as if to appeal for help from one mad Scot against another, but the girl merely shrugged and grinned as if to say, "What do you expect me to do about it?"

The applause continued unabated, several people near-by who had already recognized her watching to observe her reaction. Ever the professional, Victoria at last rose to her feet and walked the short distance to the edge of the platform where Gavin was waiting for her, smiling that damned charming smile and holding out one hand to help her up onto the stage. She accepted the hand, feeling its warmth close over hers as she had that evening at the MacAllisters and she was aware of his strength as he pulled her up to stand beside him. He continued to hold her hand as she smiled and bowed. "God damn you!" she hissed under her breath.

He roared with laughter. "Och noo, lassie, ye know ye dinna mean that."

"I don't know any such thing, you bastard!" But how good it felt to swear and have someone simply find it terribly funny.

Finally the applause died down. "A bonny lass, is she not?" Gavin asked everyone in general. " 'Tis a pity she's English."

"I'm afraid I'm not familiar with your type of music, Mr. Hamilton," Victoria murmured even as she continued to smile graciously.

"Noo, I'm surre we can find common grround somewherre, <u>Miss Windsorr</u>." He emphasized her name just slightly as if to say, "So we're back to formalities, are we?"

After a brief consultation they were indeed able to agree on two songs: "Try to Remember" from *The Fantastiks* and "My Cup Runneth Over" from *I Do, I Do*–both, since they were from musical comedy, being known to Victoria, but both also being folk music enough in style to be in Gavin's repertoire. The blend of her clear soprano with his baritone was glorious and the gathering greatly enjoyed the unexpected treat.

Victoria returned to her seat and the program concluded with a medley by the whole group. As soon as the last song had ended, even while the applause was still lingering on, Jamie was at their table. Felicity jumped up to hug him. "Oh, darrlin', I was that proud! Ye've gotten everr so much betterr since I hearrd ye last!"

"Well, it's Gavin they coom forr mostly, I think, but it means worrk for all of us."

"Jamie, this is Victoria Windsor and her daughter, Olivia."

"Hello, Jamie." Victoria smiled, extending her hand. But unconsciously she was looking past him. "I've heard so much about you. It's nice to meet you at last."

"Hello, Victorria." The young Scot's greeting was pleasant in a quiet way. He noticed the direction of her gaze. "Gavin'll be along in a bit. We'rre all headin' oot forr a wee drram and a sup–rright, lass?" This last was directed at Felicity.

"Aye–I've got a favorrite spot."

"We'll be going along then, I think." Victoria stood up. "It's late and tomorrow's an early day for both of us. Olivia?" But her daughter had disappeared.

"Oh, there she is," Felicity observed–pointing. "Overr therre." A crowd of girls had gathered around Gavin up on stage and he was signing autographs, his foot on the rung of the stool. Olivia was enthroned <u>on</u> the stool, one hand resting on his shoulder.

"I can't understand what's come over that child! I've never seen her so fascinated with anyone."

The Scottish girl grinned. "Gavin's appeal isn't limited to any parrticularr age group , ye see."

"Well, I'll soon put an end to that!" Victoria walked purposefully up on the stage.

"Hi, Mummy." Olivia smiled happily. "Isn't it nice to see Gavin again? He says we're all going to go get something to eat."

Gavin glanced up from the paper he was signing at the moment. "Ye arre coomin' with us, arren't ye?"

"It's a school day tomorrow, Olivia," Victoria protested weakly.

"It willna hurrt herr to miss one day." His eyes glowed with fun. "I've neverr found school of much use m'self."

"Mr. Hamilton!"

"Aye, I wanted to ask ye aboot that."

"About what?" Victoria was trying hard to be angry with him.

"I've irrritated ye again in some way, haven't I? That's why ye left in such a bluidy hurrry on Sunday."

"Why must you persist in the ridiculous notion that you have the power to affect me in any way whatsoever?"

"Don't be mad at Gavin, Mummy," Olivia pleaded. "He didn't do anything wrong."

"Thank ye, wee lass."

"Oh, I give up!" Victoria snapped. "But we can't stay late and you <u>will</u> go to school tomorrow!"

"Ye can always have a tummy ache, Olivia," Gavin said in a stage whisper, accompanying the words with an exaggerated wink. The little girl giggled.

"Mr. Ham.........."

"Ah...ah...ah." He wagged an admonishing index finger. "We'll have no morre o' that."

"If I call you Gavin, will you behave yourself?"

He grinned. "I'll trry my verra best. Coom, wee lass, and help me get my coat." He and Olivia disappeared backstage hand in hand.

Felicity came up to Victoria. "He's a difficult one to rrefuse, isn't he?"

"Oh yes, very much so." She shook her head.

Gavin and Olivia returned and soon afterwards they all left, trailing in a large, noisy group along the street and down into the subway. There were eleven of them in all and at the restaurant two tables had to be pushed together to accommodate them, Gavin at once settling himself at one end. Apparently it was a foregone conclusion this was his proper place. Felicity sat to his left with Jamie next to her, of course, while Victoria was on his right with Olivia beside her. The only two "Englishers" Victoria and Olivia soon found themselves lost in a swirl of Scots-accented chatter. There'd been a time when Victoria's ego would have demanded she be the center of attention. Yet now she was strangely content.

For Gavin's part although his attention seemed to be on the conversation, he was at all times acutely aware of the beautiful woman next to him. She was so close he could occasionally even catch a wisp of her fragrance and her left hand rested near his on the table. He wondered what she'd do if he covered that slim, white hand with his own.

When the waiter first approached their table, Victoria had ordered vodka and tonic for herself and coca cola for Olivia, but that was the last she thought of it. Each time the glasses were emptied, others miraculously took their places until she realized with a start that for the first time since she'd been married to Jason, she was becoming intoxicated. "No, Gavin, please." She stopped him as he started to call the waiter over again. "I've really had enough and Olivia and I should be leaving anyway."

"I'm afrraid I've no been verra good coomp'ny," he said apologetically. "We all get to talkin' aboot home, ye see." He appeared genuinely concerned that he might have hurt her feelings.

Briefly Victoria wondered what lay beneath the charming exterior, but the thought left no permanent impression on her mind. "No–really–we've enjoyed it."

"Well, the verra least I can do is to see ye safe into a taxi." Outside it was raining heavily. "We'll prrobably have betterr luck at the corrnerr," Gavin suggested, raising his large, black umbrella. "Underr herre noo--the both of ye."

They each took hold of an arm and the three of them walked quickly along the street. Through the sleeve of his trench coat Victoria could feel the firm muscles of his arm. It seemed no time before he'd flagged down a cab and tucked them both into it, but then he still stood there holding the door open. "Move overr," Gavin said suddenly. Startled, Victoria obeyed and he slid into the seat beside her. "It's too late for you two to be oot alone," he said by way of explanation. "I'll see ye home and take the tube back."

"You'll get lost," she suggested weakly.

"I'm a wee bit brrighterr than that, lass," he replied with a grin.

"Is someone going to give me the address?" the driver asked after a moment. He wished these damned foreigners would stay home where they belonged!

The three of them burst into laughter. "I'm so sorry," Victoria finally managed to give him the address. Once the laughter had subsided, however, an awkward silence filled the cab. Olivia soon fell asleep, her head against her mother's shoulder. Victoria looked steadily past the little girl out the window at the deserted, rainswept street, trying to ignore the sensation of Gavin's shoulder and thigh pressed against hers in the narrow back seat.

"Ye <u>do</u> have a dearr, wee lass therre," he observed at one point, glancing past her at the sleeping child, "Aye–a bonny one."

Victoria slipped an arm around her daughter and drew her closer. "Thank you. I think she's very special."

There was another silence after that lasting almost to their destination. Again it was Gavin who broke it. "Ye know, I did rratherr prromise the bairrn I'd see herr again–if ye'd no object."

"That's...that's very kind of you. She's....she's taken such a liking to you, but please don't let her make a nuisance of herself."

"She tells me therre's a fine zoo in Centrral Parrk. Ye'd be welcoom to coom along if it would make ye easierr in yourr mind."

"Yes...that...ah...might be better. Here we are," she added as the cab stopped in front of their building. She reached for her purse.

"No–lass, ye'll be insultin' me." He paid the taxi. "And dinna waken the wee one. I'll take her oop."

Victoria led the way holding open the door. Perhaps it was just as well, she thought with a slight smile, that the doorman went off duty at midnight. Carrying Olivia effortlessly, Gavin followed her through the lobby and into the elevator. Quickly they rose to the fifth floor and Victoria once again led the way unlocking the door of their apartment. "Her bedroom's the first door off the hall there," she directed. He disappeared with his sleeping burden, returning almost at once. "Thank you." She wanted very much to ask him to stay for coffee.

"I'm verra glad to do it." Had he ever turned and left such an appealing woman, he wondered. "Saturrday then. We'll make a day of it."

"Olivia will be so pleased!"

But still Gavin lingered. "Will ye be coomin' to the coffee hoose again, do ye think?" he inquired at last as the silence became noticeable.

"I suppose so–with Felicity."

"Coom Frriday then. That way it won't be a school night for the wee one." Brown eyes smiled down into green ones. "If ye coom earrly–say aboot six–I'll teach you a new song."

"I'd...I'd like that. Well....ah...it is late."

"Aye." He inched toward the door, but stopped again one hand on the knob. "Well, good night then."

"Good <u>night</u>, Gavin." Laughing softly, she made little shooing motions.

"Aye, lass, aye. I'm goin'. Good night then." At last he was out the door and there was an empty feeling in the pit of her stomach.

"Oh, Mummy!" Olivia came running out of her bedroom. "Did he leave?"

"Yes, darling, of course. But we're going to the coffee house again Friday night and to the park with him on Saturday."

"Oh, goody! He's so nice! You like him, too, don't you?"

"Yes, sweetheart, but it's very late now and we both have to get up early tomorrow morning."

"Do I <u>have</u> to go to school?'

"<u>Yes</u>! Olivia–go to bed!" But Victoria's attempt to sound stern had been such a total failure that they both laughed.

"Good night, Mummy." The little girl threw her arms around her mother and gave her a hug and a kiss.

"Good night, luv." Victoria returned the kiss. "See you in the morning." But she herself was a long way from sleep. Only after several cups of camomile tea and a lot of pacing could she bring herself to relax enough to go to bed. And when at last she fell asleep, some sound woke her again almost immediately. Weirdly it seemed as though it had been her own voice.

* * *

On Friday Felicity arrived late for class and slumping down in a seat in the back, she promptly fell asleep. When Victoria noticed her a little more than halfway through the period, she was furious. If she'd been honest with herself, she would have admitted that a great part of her annoyance stemmed from the fact that there had evidently been another party last night in which she wasn't included. When the class was over and the rest of the students had left, she snatched up her purse and briefcase and strode up the aisle to stand directly over the Scottish girl. "Wake up, damn you!"

"Oh...what?" Felicity opened one eye and looked woefully up at Victoria. "Och...my worrd–did I fall asleep? I'm sae verra sorrry." She scrambled to her feet. "I'm afrraid I got well flootherred last night and then Jamie and I...well, we..." She stopped, blushing bright red.

"Honestly–you are disgusting!" Victoria hurried on up the aisle.

"Victorria—!" Felicity ran after her, catching up just as she reached the door. "I ken I shouldna have fallen asleep, but is that why ye'rre sae angrry?"

"And I don't see why you damned Scots can't learn to talk properly. I swear to God if they ever cut one of you open, you'd be plaid inside."

"It's Gavin, isn it?"

"Why in hell must everyone insist on involving him in everything I say or do! I am a happily married woman!"

Victoria was walking rapidly along the corridor, but Felicity kept pace–refusing to be ignored. "Everraone was teasin' him, ye see, because he hadna coom back the night beforre and........"

"I suppose you think he spent the night!" Neither of them was aware that half-running down the hall as they were and talking rather loudly, they were attracting considerable attention.

"Well, he said he didn't," Felicity admitted, "but then Gavin has neverr found it necessarry to brrag aboot his conquests."

"No, I'm sure he hasn't!" Stopping at the elevator, Victoria jabbed at the call button.

"Arre ye no goin' to the cafeterria then?"

Victoria stared at her in amazement. "You really think we should just go and have our tea as usual, don't you?"

"Aye." The Scottish girl was the perfect picture of astonished innocence. "I told ye Gavin had a way wi' the lassies. Why should you be any differrent?"

The elevator arrived and Victoria stepped in, but she put up one hand to hold the door open. "You are absolutely impossible–you and every other damned Scot! You're insane–the whole bloody lot of you!" As she finally allowed the door to close, Felicity was still standing there with a puzzled look on her face.

Well, it was clear at any rate that they could see no more of Gavin and Victoria went home that afternoon determined to explain this to her daughter as gently but firmly as possible. And the next time she saw Felicity she'd make her understand as well. At the sound of her mother's key in the front door Olivia jumped up from the living room couch and turned off the television. "Mummy, we better go right away! 'Member Gavin said to come early so he could teach you another song!" She grabbed her coat from a chair and was pulling it on even as she came across the room.

"Yes, darling." Once again as at the MacAllisters, Victoria told herself it wasn't fair to disappoint the little girl. "Why don't we have supper in a restaurant? Just give me a few minutes to freshen up."

In a short while they were riding back downstairs in the elevator. "If we got those big sandwiches at the deli, Mummy, we could go right there without waiting to eat."

"Absolutely not. We will have a normal meal. Besides– we need to talk."

About a half-hour later they were settled in a small Italian restaurant close to the Columbia campus. They ordered their food and sat back to wait. "Mummy, are you going to tell me it's wrong for me to like Gavin so much?" Olivia inquired fearfully. "You said you like him, too."

"I'm...I'm married to Jason and I...I love him very much."

"I love Jason, too, but can't I still like Gavin? He's says such funny things and Jason is always so serious."

"Jason is a fine, decent man, Olivia, and he has serious matters on his mind...but the main reason I'm concerned is because you may become too fond of Gavin and he isn't the sort to form permanent attachments."

"I don't understand."

"It isn't necessary that you understand. We will simply enjoy Gavin's company while he's here and try not to miss him too much when he's gone."

"Both of us?" Just then the waitress brought their meal–spaghetti and meatballs for them both, coca-cola for Olivia and a half-carafe of wine for Victoria. "Both of us, Mummy?" the little girl asked again as they began to eat.

"Will you please just eat your dinner and stop asking silly questions!"

"I don't see why that's a silly question. You said that...."

"Olivia, be quiet!"

"Yes, Mummy." She'd lost all awe of her mother, but she also knew there was a certain point beyond which she could not push her. A short time later, however, she watched intently as Victoria poured herself a second glass of wine.

"What's the matter now?"

"Jason doesn't like you to drink, does he?" She was asking more for information than anything.

"So you're taking over the temperance duties while he's away, is that it?"

"No, Mummy. It's just that Wednesday night Gavin kept buying you another drink and I wondered if....."

"Young lady, you say one more word and we're going home! Do I make myself clear?"

"Yes, Mummy." Olivia ate the rest of her dinner in silence, but that didn't mean her mind was quiet as well. Grown-ups are funny, she thought. Gavin makes Mummy so happy and still she keeps saying she loves Jason.

Gavin was the only one of the group already there when they arrived although the students who ran the coffee house were busy setting up extra tables. Word was spreading about the folk group from Scotland–in particular its tall, handsome soloist–and they were expecting another large crowd.

"Gavin!" Olivia called out happily.

"Well, noo–'tis nearrly six-thirrty. I'd begun to think ye werre nae coomin'."

"We had dinner first," Victoria explained.

"Ah, I see then. Noo–I looked thrrough my music trryin' to find a piece simple enough for an Englishwoman to learrn quickly." He winked broadly at Olivia and she giggled. "You just sit doon therre, wee one," he said to her, "and tell us how we sound togetherr. Ye did say, the otherr evenin' at the MacAllisters, that you werre familiarr with the Skye Boat Song?"

"Yes, one of the few, I'm afraid." Damn, Victoria thought, why in hell am I so glad to see him?

"Herre's an extrra stool," he went on, "and I've got the words forr ye, as well." He handed her a typewritten sheet.

"I'm afraid I'm not dressed for climbing on a stool." She indicated the slim skirt of her gold suit.

"Och–that's no prroblem." Gavin leaned his guitar against one stool and putting a hand on either side of her waist, lifted her easily onto the other. Was it her imagination or did his hands linger at her waist somewhat longer than necessary? But then he sat down on the other stool and picked up his guitar. Beginning to strum softly, he sang the chorus through once. "Trry it with me noo–frrom the firrst verse."

Victoria listened a moment or so longer and then started to sing with him. At some point during the song Jamie and Felicity came in, stopping in the back to listen along with several of the waiters and waitresses. "Och, darrlin', I'll miss ye sae fierrcely," she whispered, "but I'll be glad when Gavin's gone."

"The laddy means no harrm. Ye ken that as well as I do." With a quick kiss Jamie went off backstage and Felicity came on down to sit with Olivia.

"Oh, dear," the little girl sighed, "they look so good together. I wish....I wish...."

Felicity was glad the music made a reply unnecessary. A moment or so later, however, the song came to an end and she watched Gavin lift Victoria down from the stool. Clearly his hands had lingered at her waist. Felicity knew it wasn't her imagination.

The actress smiled as she came over to join them. "I'm sorry about this morning, Felicity. Are only Scots entitled to "black and bloody moods" as you call them or are we English allowed an occasional one as well?"

Aye, you're with him noo, the girl thought to herself, so you forrget all your guilt and misgivings. Aloud she said simply, "'Tis all rright. I'm no a one to hold onto angerr."

"That's what makes all you Scots so totally beguiling, I guess. You have such warm, outgoing natures."

"Och!" Felicity muttered under her breath. "This morrnin' we werre insane; noo we'rre warrm and ootgoin'!" When the time came for Gavin to sing, she watched her friend closely. Victoria was obviously lost in the sound of his voice and when he asked her to join him, she went eagerly, doing not only the new song, but the two from the other night as well.

"Felicity," Olivia whispered at one point, "can you be in love with more than one person at the same time?"

"Of courrse, wee one. 'Tis possible to love many people." They all went out to eat again and Felicity grew increasingly uneasy as Gavin clearly gave Victoria much more of his attention than on the previous occasion–attention she evidently enjoyed. Once more, he left to see mother and daughter home and once more he did not return.

* * *

The next day Jamie awoke in the hotel room he was sharing with Gavin to find the other man already singing lustily in the shower. A short time later he heard the water stop running and getting out of bed, he went to open the bathroom door. His friend had wrapped a bath towel around his waist and was lathering his face in preparation for shaving. "Aye–good morrnin' to ye, laddie," Gavin said with a grin. "Did I wake ye wi' my caterrwaulin'? I'm verra sorry."

"Arre ye goin' oot?"

"Aye. I prromised the wee one I'd take herr to the parrk."

Jamie found himself remembering Felicity's concern of the night before. "I suppose herr motherr's coomin' along as well?"

"Aye. 'Twould be betterr since they dinna know me that well."

"Ye neverr needed an excuse beforre."

"What do ye mean–an excuse?" Gavin stopped in mid-stroke, half of his face still covered with lather.

"An excuse–to be wi' a lass."

"Aye, I take pleasurre in Victorria's coomp'ny. Ye must admit she's a beautiful woman. But I trrruly enjoy the bairrnie as well. 'Tis like the fun I used to have wi' my wee sisterr, Meghan, beforre she became too grrown-oop forr such sporrt."

"Ye enjoy childrren sae much. When arre ye goin' to settle doon and have some of yourr own?"

"I'm nae the marrryin' kind. Ye ken that verra well, Jamie."

"Is that why ye prreferr marrried women? No thrreat to yourr prrecious frreedom?"

Gavin had been taking their conversation quite lightly. Now he caught something in his friend's tone and he turned from the mirror to face him. "Ye needna frret yourrself, laddy. I'd do naethin' to hurrt Victorria. Noo–if ye'll excuse me, I'll get my clothes on. I'm takin' them to brreakfast. I'll see ye this evenin' at the coffee hoose." Dressing quickly but carefully in gray slacks and a dark red turtleneck pullover, he slipped on the inevitable trench coat and started toward the door.

"Ye trruly carre forr herr, don't ye, Gavin?"

He stopped one hand on the doorknob. "Och! Ye know me betterr than that!"

But later as Jamie recounted the incident to Felicity, he still wasn't convinced. "It was the look on his face morre than anythin'," he said, "when he told me he'd neverr hurrt herr."

It was the kind of golden day in mid-April when you forget New York is a big, noisy city. The air was clear; the sun warm and the Central Park Zoo glorious fun for all three of them. Victoria couldn't help remembering another day at another zoo. Then, of course, Noel had been their escort and through no fault of his the occasion had not been a happy one.

They had hamburgers, french fries and tall frosty milkshakes at an outdoor stand and then rented a boat for a row around the lake. Gavin continually insisted, however, that this was not Central Park at all, but Loch Ness and that "Nessie", as the Scots affectionately call their very own monster, would surface at any moment. Victoria laughed until her sides ached. She hated to have the day come to an end, but finally it was time to turn in the boat and start for home.

"Are we going to the coffee house again tonight, Mummy?" Olivia inquired eagerly as they walked toward one of the park exits.

"Don't you think Gavin's had enough of us for one day?"

"Neverr enough of the two bonniest lassies in New Yorrk City," he assured them.

"See, Mummy," the child exclaimed triumphantly. "We can get those big sandwiches and go right there and Gavin can teach you another song for tonight."

"It seems it's all decided forr us then." He grinned. "Noo–what arre these sandwiches?"

"Oh, my daughter has unfortunately discovered a delicatessen where they make these enormous and utterly indigestible sandwiches."

"Sounds perrfect!"

At the delicatessen Gavin insisted on the most inedible conglomeration of ingredients ever devoured by mortal man and Olivia, of course, would be satisfied with nothing less than the same. Victoria told them they would both have terrible indigestion and what's more, that they deserved it. She ordered sliced turkey with a little lettuce and tomato. "Och, wee lass, arre ye surre this one's yourr motherr?" He winked at the little girl. "She's got no courrage at all!"

Again there was the evening at the coffee house and again the late night supper and once again, of course, he took it upon himself to escort them home. "And what would ye like to do tomorrrow?" he asked at some point. It being a pleasant night, the taxi had left them at the corner and they were walking the rest of the way.

"Mummy, don't you think we should cook breakfast for Gavin tomorrow?" Olivia was much wider awake than any nine year old should be at two in the morning. Victoria's mind swam in confused circles. She was seeing altogether too much of this man. "After all he treated us today," the child continued insistently, "and it's only polite to return his hospitality." God, sometimes her daughter sounded like a little old lady!

"Perrhaps it's yourr motherr who's had enough of me, hm, wee lass?" Never had a woman made him feel so unsure of himself.

"No, no, of course not," Victoria said quickly. "Please...please come and...and bring Jamie and Felicity. But can we make it brunch–about noon?"

"That's half breakfast and half lunch, you see," Olivia explained importantly. "It's for when you sleep too late for just breakfast."

"Ah, I see, wee lass, thank ye," Gavin responded with due solemnity. "Won't we be grrand folk, though, havin' brrunch!"

As they neared the apartment building, their steps unconsciously slowed. "There's no need for you to come up," Victoria said before he had the chance to offer. "We'll be perfectly safe from here."

"Aye...well, good night then." He bent to receive Olivia's kiss. For a second he looked at Victoria, but then he turned and left.

"How long is Gavin going to stay in New York, Mummy?" the little girl asked as they walked into the lobby.

"I...I think Felicity said they'd be here about three weeks in all." Victoria pressed the elevator's call button.

Olivia sighed. "I'll miss him ever so much, won't you?" The elevator came; they got in and Victoria pushed the button for their floor. "<u>Won't</u> you, Mummy?"

"What <u>I'm</u> thinking is that Jason will be home soon." Her tone was noticeably sharp. "That's what matters to me."

"Oh yes, of course." The child looked a little guilty. "But Jason never makes you laugh. I've never heard you laugh as much as you did today."

They were at their apartment by then and Victoria took the key out of her purse to unlock the door. Her fingers seemed unusually clumsy. "It's late, sweetheart, and I want you to get right into bed."

"Whenever grown-ups can't think of what to say," Olivia observed, "they always tell you to go to bed."

"I have never known you to be so saucy! Now get to bed this instant!"

"All right." She moved reluctantly toward her bedroom. "But it's not fair."

"You say one more thing, young lady, and I'll cancel the brunch tomorrow. Do I make myself clear?"

"Yes, Mummy." Olivia went to bed without another word.

"Poor darling, you can't possibly understand," Victoria whispered as she went on into her own room and began to undress. A moment or so later, naked now, she walked over to her closet to take her nightgown down from its hook behind the door, but as she turned back, raising her arms to allow the garment to slide down over her head, she happened to glimpse herself in the mirror above her bureau. She dropped the nightgown on the bed and coming to stand in front of the mirror, she stared at the reflection of her own nude body. Her breasts, although full, were still firm, her waist slim, her stomach flat. What would Gavin be like as a lover, she wondered. Would he enjoy touching her– caressing her? Involuntarily her hands came up to cover her breasts, imagining instead that they were his hands–the same hands she'd felt strong and firm at her waist. All at once she stopped, shocked back to reality by the picture of herself fondling her own body. Sick with shame, she stumbled back to the bed to put on her nightgown and slip beneath the covers. It was a long time, however, before she slept.

Gavin, Jamie and Felicity arrived promptly at noon with their contribution to the brunch: a box of croissants. They had orange juice, scrambled eggs and bacon with coffee–hot chocolate for Olivia. Conversation was spirited and constant and Victoria was grateful it was unnecessary for her to take much part in it. After last night it was all she could do to be in the same room with Gavin. The few times she was forced to say something, she was certain everyone couldn't help but notice how her voice shook. As soon as the meal was finished, she stood up to clear the table, relieved to flee even temporarily to the sanctuary of the kitchen. Moments later, however, Gavin followed her, both hands loaded with plates. "I'm verra good at drryin', lass, if ye'd like some help."

"Somehow I was sure you'd be a male chauvinist," she replied lightly. "No, really. I noticed you and Jamie brought your guitars. Why don't you entertain us and Olivia and Felicity and I will be done in no time."

He shrugged good-naturedly although actually he'd been looking for a chance to spend a little time alone with her. She was dressed in a pale rose jersey dress, the top molded to her breasts, the skirt softly flared and moving with her as she walked. "You arre trruly the loveliest woman I've everr seen." He could no longer keep the words back. "How that husband of yourrs can leave ye like this is beyond me." He had come to put the dishes down beside the sink so that as he spoke the last words, he was directly at her elbow.

Angrily she whirled about to face him. "How dare you criticize my husband–a fine, Christian man who feels such a strong calling to serve God!" It had been a mistake to turn around. Gavin was standing very close, his brown eyes studying her with an obvious hunger. There was a beat and then he slowly lowered his head. Victoria could feel herself beginning to breathe more rapidly. Dimly she was conscious of tipping her head back– of reaching up and still up. His lips pressed against hers, probing gently as he caressed her back and shoulders, and she brought her hands up to bury her fingers in his hair.

"You forgot some things." Felicity pushed open the swinging door into the kitchen, but at the sight of Gavin and Victoria lost in an embrace, she quickly retreated. The worst part was that neither of them had even heard her.

Olivia laughed. "Felicity, you brought the dishes out again. I'll take them back."

"No, lassie, that's all right. I'll do it...I'm coomin' in!" she yelled and she gave the door a shove, sending it crashing against the wall. When she entered the kitchen a second time, they had separated. Victoria was standing with her back to the door, her hands gripping the edge of the sink, her head bowed.

"I...I think she wants ye to help herr." Gavin pushed past Felicity on his way from the room.

"Do ye want me to wash or drry, Victorria?"

She shook her head. "Felicity, please...please. I....I....."

"Dinna frret yourrself. It just happened."

At that Victoria finally turned to look at her, her face stricken with shame. "You.... you saw us?"

"Ye must put it frrom yourr mind."

"You....you don't realize. I...I haven't always led the best life. You....you know Jason. How could I.....could I...."

" 'Twas only a wee kiss. I tell ye–it meant naethin' to Gavin and ye shouldna let it botherr ye. Noo–we'll do the dishes and ye'll get yourrself settled doon and....."

"Oh no, Felicity, please...you all have to go. I...I can't see him again."

"Aye, if ye want us to."

Just then Jamie came out into the kitchen as well. "Felicity, Gavin and I arre leavin'. Arre ye coomin'?"

"Aye, I am."

"Good-bye, Jamie," Victoria whispered.

Olivia was horribly confused. First Felicity had acted so strange with the dishes and then her adored Gavin came out of the kitchen–not even noticing her–and after saying something to Jamie, left immediately. Now the other two were also gone– saying only hurried good-byes. For a few minutes the little girl continued to sit there, wondering what she should do, but finally Victoria came out into the living room. "Wh..what happened, Mummy? Is Gavin mad at me?"

She half-smiled at her daughter's innocent naivete. "No, luv, of course not." She took Olivia over to the couch and slipping an arm around her shoulders, hugged her close. This was as difficult a conversation as any they'd had since that Christmas that now seemed forever ago. "Darling, we...we won't be seeing Gavin any more."

"Oh, Mummy, why not? I like him so much."

"Olivia, dearest, I'm married to Jason and it's....it's not proper for me to see so much of another man."

"But I could still see him. I'm not married to anyone."

In spite of her inner turmoil Victoria laughed a little. "No, that's true—you're not. But I....I just don't know Gavin well enough to let you go without me."

"But he's my friend."

"Olivia, please don't beg. You're making this even more difficult for me."

"Did you tell him we couldn't see him anymore? Is that why he left?"

"I....I think he <u>understood</u> we wouldn't be seeing him again."

"Oh, Mummy! You hurt his feelings! He jokes a lot, but inside he's really lonely sometimes. I can tell."

The intuition of a child, Victoria thought. Was Olivia right? She made a visible effort to stir herself. "But....but that doesn't mean you and I can't still have fun together, now does it? How about a film and then supper at that little French restaurant with the thin pancakes you like so much?"

"All right, Mummy. Only the cinema again–on Sunday?"

"Well, luv, we might as well enjoy ourselves while we can." I can't believe I said that, Victoria thought in her bedroom as she quickly ran a brush through her hair.

"Ready, Mummy?" Olivia appeared in the doorway, but then she saw her mother's face–strained and white. "Mummy, do you feel all right? We don't have to go if you don't want to."

"Of course I want to, luv. It will be fun. Come along now." Grabbing up her coat, she hurried her daughter from the apartment, refusing to allow herself to think further.

* * *

All week long Victoria battled with herself. One minute she was sure she could enjoy Gavin's company on a purely friendly basis–the next she'd picture him clearly in her mind's eye or worse remember the sensation of his body pressed against hers and she knew she had to avoid seeing him again no matter how hurt and disappointed her daughter might be. When she's older, Victoria thought, I can explain.

The week was almost as hard on Felicity. Over and over again she kept seeing Victoria and Gavin in each other's arms. Then she would think about Jason Eliot–kind enough, perhaps–but rather a cold person. Was Victoria really happy with him? If you were <u>that</u> happy, did you have to keep saying so? And then there was Gavin. Ever since she could remember, she had adored this big handsome man. Yet she'd known so many women who had fallen in love with him only to find him growing bored and restless in a matter of weeks. Wasn't Victoria better off with her husband than Gavin, who for all his charm, wit and good looks would undoubtedly tire of her? But then she also kept seeing her old friend's face–visibly disturbed–as he strode past her out of the apartment. Could he finally have fallen in love?

Felicity even cut class on Monday and Wednesday because she didn't know what to say to Victoria. On Friday, however, she had to go. The class was doing one act plays at the moment and her group was scheduled to perform Synge's "Riders to the Sea". Their presentation finished, the cast waited expectantly for the customary evaluation. Instead Victoria abruptly dismissed the class, explaining she needed to clarify her notes and would speak to them on Monday. The group was visibly let down. Waiting until the rest of the students had left, Felicity came up to where Victoria had sat to watch the day's work. Any strangeness she'd once felt toward the Englishwoman had long since been replaced by a deep affection and now as she saw her friend's face, she forgot her own confusion in a rush of love and pity. "Could ye no have said a wee somethin'?" she asked.

Victoria was doodling on the pad of paper she held in her lap–small circles around and around and around. There were no notes on today's performance. At last the Scottish girl reached down to touch her on the arm. She jumped. "Oh, Felicity! Dear God, you startled me!"

"Ye no could say anythin' aboot the perrforrmance because ye didna hearr a worrd of it, did ye?"

For a few seconds Victoria made no reply. Then she shook her head and smiled ruefully. "No, I'm afraid not."

"If ye'd carre to talk, I can listen. Orr ye can tell me to mind my own bluidy business and I'll no be offended in the least."

She smiled again. "Thank you, luv, but this is something I have to work through on my own. You can't help."

That evening Olivia dawdled hopefully over her dinner. "Do you have homework?" her mother inquired sipping her coffee. The child nodded, stirring her spoon around and around in her ice cream until more than anything it resembled chocolate soup. "What are you doing?" Victoria's nerves were close to the breaking point.

The little girl's eyes filled with tears. "Please don't yell at me, Mummy!"

Lowering her cup to the saucer, she raised one hand to massage her forehead, a gesture Olivia knew very well after nearly a year with her mother as one of great weariness. "Oh, dearest, I'm so sorry."

"Gavin would make you laugh. He'd make you feel better."

Victoria's smile was distinctly ironic. Yes, Gavin would make her feel better. That was the whole problem.

Matters only got worse on Saturday when Olivia's response to every proposed activity was "I just want to go to the coffee house." Victoria had never known her daughter could be so stubborn! Inevitably they had their first real quarrel–a quarrel which ended with the little girl being sent to her room directly from the dinner table.

Only an early morning phone call from Felicity saved them from an even more miserable Sunday. It seemed the group was planning a boat ride up the Hudson River to Bear Mountain State Park for a picnic. "Oh dear, I don't know," Victoria temporized even as she contemplated the joy of spending another whole day with Gavin. "But....but I'm really not being fair to my daughter, am I?"

Verra well, Felicity thought, if that's what you want to tell yourself. Aloud, however, she simply agreed, " 'Tis trrue. The wee one would have a bonny time of it."

"All right. I suppose so."

"Grrand then." She gave her the time and place of departure. "See ye in a bit."

It was a beautiful day–unseasonably warm–and they found a lovely sunny spot at the back of the boat. Gavin spoke cordially on the pier, but once they had boarded, he took Olivia over to the railing to watch the process of untying from the wharf. Victoria sat on one of the benches. She closed her eyes, enjoying the warmth and the fresh air.

"I'm verra glad ye agrreed to coom." She didn't need to open her eyes to know who it was. But she did. "May I sit doon?" Gavin indicated the place next to her on the bench.

"Of course." Victoria steeled herself as he settled beside her, stretching out his long legs and crossing them at the ankles. "You must be looking forward to going home," she went on conversationally, watching the passing scenery. They were nearly clear of Manhattan now and the New York Palisades towered above them on the left. By gazing up at the cliffs she could avoid looking at him.

"Is it only my imagination," he asked quietly, "orr have ye been deliberrately avoidin' me?"

Felicity and Jamie had involved Olivia in a game of shuffleboard almost, it appeared, in a conscious plot to leave her alone with Gavin. "It....it seemed the wisest course under....under the circumstances."

"Please believe me. I didna intend forr it to happen, but ye werre so close to me and ye looked sae warrm and sweet...." Her eyes pleaded mutely with him to cease and he complied. "I'm sorrry. Frrom noo on I prromise I'll keep it casual."

"I....I love my husband." Her tone held a note of desperation.

"Of courrse ye do. But that doesna mean we canna have a pleasant day togetherr. Perrhaps I'll be forrtunate enough to see ye once orr twice morre at the coffee hoose and then this Scottish nuisance will be gone frrom yourr life."

"I....I never wanted you to feel that way," she said softly. "Olivia and I both enjoy your company. Of course we'll come to see you next week."

"Thank ye, lass. Noo shall we trry ourr hand at that shuffleboarrd?"

She nodded and they went over to join the others. For some reason Victoria felt more at ease after that. There was such happiness in just being with Gavin–such mindless, unthinking joy. Later, she knew, the guilt would assail her, but for now she didn't let herself think about it.

They hiked for miles along the trails of the park. His hand was always there to help her over rocks and other rough spots, but each time the path smoothed out again, he would immediately let go. At last, however, they came to a narrow rock ledge from which you could look down at the river far below. Felicity and Jamie went first with Olivia between them. "Arre ye game then, lass?" Gavin asked, holding out his hand and smiling down at her. All she could do was nod. "Well, then...." She took his hand and he led the way out onto the ledge. They inched forward until finally they came around a bend to find the others waiting for them in a spot where the path broadened out again. For a while they all stood there enjoying the breathtaking view. It was several minutes before Victoria realized they were still holding hands.

For dinner they grilled steaks over a charcoal fire. The group activity required almost no talking. Even while they were eating, there seemed to be little need for words and once they had finished, there was just time to clean up, douse their fire and get down to the dock to catch the return boat. The long day in the out-of-doors had made everyone sleepy and they were all still quiet even as the boat pulled away from the wharf and started back down the river. Once again Gavin sat next to her although carefully keeping his distance. "Tirred?" he asked.

"Yes. I'm....I'm not used to so much fresh air, I guess." The next thing she knew she awoke to find her head resting against Gavin's shoulder. At some point while she slept he must have slipped his jacket around her. It smelled strongly of his pipe tobacco, but then she realized he was also smoking at the moment–the fragrance filling the air around her. She hated to open her eyes because then she would have to sit up, but unconsciously, still drowsy, she moved against him.

"Couldna hold that bonny golden head oop any longerr, hm?" She couldn't resist opening her eyes then and Gavin leaned over to touch his lips briefly to hers. At once she pulled away from him and sat up. The loudspeaker announced they were docking and once again they were a group–walking off the boat and down into the subway. There was only the chance for hasty good-byes.

* * *

Can it be possible for time to drag on and yet still to have each day fly by before you're even aware it's come? That was the way it seemed to Victoria–all that last week before the folk group would be returning to Scotland. She wanted the time to pass quickly–to have the moment of Gavin's leaving over with–and yet she could hardly bear the thought that in less than a week now he would be gone. She did agree to go to the coffee house for the final performances on Friday and Saturday evenings. It meant so much to Olivia to see Gavin once or twice more. At the customary late night supper on Saturday, however, she found herself once again sitting next to him. As usual the small restaurant was crowded, but the noise, rather than making conversation unnecessary, only seemed to isolate them from everyone else, forcing them to talk to each other.

"Gavin, I....ah...." Dear God, what could she possibly say to him? What she needed at that moment was someone like Basil Fitzhugh to write her some clever, witty dialogue, but then Basil would undoubtedly have found the whole situation so ludicrous that for once he might just have been rendered speechless. Desperately she searched her mind for a safe topic of conversation. "Why...why don't you tell me about your family." Damn–could she possibly have sounded any more inane?

Gavin was very close to his family. They were terribly dear to him. They were also the last thing he felt like talking about at that moment, but he knew he had to reply– anything to ease the tension. "What would ye like to hearr, lass?" Carefully he kept his voice casual, but there was no trace of his customary easy smile. His gaze was, on the contrary, intensely serious and it unnerved her.

"Well...ah...are...are they all like you?"

"Not rreally." His eyes began to twinkle then. "Two of them arre gurrls." She laughed at that and they both relaxed a little. "Actually," he went on, "my brrotherr and I arre verra differrent. He marrried young forr one thing and he's the scholarrly type forr anotherr. I left the Univerrsity of Aberrdeen afterr my firrst yearr to enlist in the Scots Guarrds–as a piperr."

"Oh, I....I should have realized you'd play the bagpipes." I really know almost nothing about him, Victoria thought, and somehow she found that sad.

"Oh...aye, lass, I play the pipes. 'Tis in my genes, I suppose."

Again she laughed. "And you have two sisters?"

"Aye–Fiona is twenty-thrree and wee Meghan is seventeen."

"Do your parents still live in Scotland?"

An expression of intense pain passed over his handsome face. "My....my motherr died when Meghan was borrn."

His left hand lay on the table and impulsively Victoria reached over to place hers on top of it. "Oh, Gavin, I'm so sorry. You loved her very much, didn't you?"

Also without thinking he turned his hand over to grasp hers. "Aye, I did. Thank ye, lass."

"And your father has never remarried?....But I'm being too personal."

"No, ye'rre nae bein' too perrsonal. Ye'rre sae easy to talk to....Torri." It had come out then–quite inadvertently–his name for her. It wasn't a name he'd consciously chosen nor was he aware that as he spoke it aloud now for the first time, he caressed the word with the burr of his brogue far more tenderly than he had ever touched a woman with his hands.

At once Victoria tensed again. "So...so that's my name, is it?"

"I...I'm sorrry. It just slipped oot....Victorria."

"No–please. Tori is....is fine."

"Ye like it, then?"

"Yes...yes, I....I do. No one else has ever called me that."

"Aye...then 'tis suitable."

"Suitable?" Once again her heart was beginning to pound. "What...what do you mean?"

Just then, however, they were interrupted by the waiter bringing a fresh round of drinks. Victoria welcomed the distraction. It was happening all over again. They couldn't even carry on a casual conversation. Unfortunately at that moment she happened to glance down the table at Felicity who was watching them intently and she realized at precisely the same time that she and Gavin were still holding hands across the table. She snatched her hand away and got to her feet. "It's....it's dreadfully late. Olivia and I should be leaving."

"I've....I've offended ye again then by callin' ye that....that name." Somehow just then he couldn't say Tori.

"No, no, of course not," she replied hurriedly. "It's....it's just so late. Have a safe trip home, all of you. It's been wonderful. Come along, Olivia."

Gavin said nothing about seeing them home and only Jamie saw him down his Scotch in one gulp.

Outside Victoria and Olivia settled into a taxi. At once the child burst into tears. "Oh, Mummy, we'll never see Gavin again!"

"Jason will be home next week, darling," Victoria replied after a moment–fighting to keep her tone light and easy. "Gavin will always be a happy memory for us both, but he's not the sort to be a permanent part of anyone's life. Jason is. He's good and kind and dependable. You love Jason, don't you, sweetheart?"

"Yes, Mummy," the little girl replied dutifully–trying hard to believe it.

"Of course you do," Victoria said firmly, "and so do I."

* * *

Back in Scotland Gavin stepped off the plane at the Aberdeen Airport and into the welcoming arms of his family. "Well then," his father inquired, "did ye met my futurre daughterr-in-law in yourr trravels?" It was a version of the same teasing question he invariably asked whenever his son returned home for a visit.

He grinned good-naturedly, but then almost at once he grew serious. "Aye, but I'm afrraid she's alrready marrried."

"Laddy, arre ye serrious?"

Quickly Gavin laughed–tossing his head. "Of courrse not, Dad. Ye might as well accept the fact. I'm neverr goin' to settle doon."

Chapter 20

Victoria had been watching intently as each arriving passenger came through the airport gate. Even so for just a few seconds she failed to recognize him. He seemed shorter than she remembered–older–or perhaps he was merely tired. Then he saw her and he smiled–his pale blue eyes lighting up with genuine pleasure. "Oh, Jason!" She hurried toward him, holding out her arms.

He held her close, forgetting for a moment his aversion to public displays of affection, but then almost at once he stepped back away from her. "That can wait until later," he said quietly, but firmly.

"I love you so," she whispered–an unspoken plea in her voice.

"I know, dear. I love you, too." He'd permitted her to slip her hand through his arm as they walked together toward the luggage claim and now he gave her hand a pat. "How is Olivia?"

"Fine. We've....we've both missed you very much."

"It's good to be home."

"You look–tired."

"I kept irregular hours and the demands on me were never-ending."

"I'm sure, darling."

The flow of meaningless conversation continued–all the time they were waiting for his luggage, as they went out to the parking lot, even on the drive back into the city. Perhaps even they themselves weren't aware how stilted and unnatural they sounded. "Where is Olivia anyway?" Jason inquired as he maneuvered the car through the city traffic. By now they were just a few blocks from their apartment building.

"With Felicity MacDougall. You remember her, don't you–the Scottish girl who's taking one of my classes. She's been such good company while you were away."

"Yes, of course." Jason frowned thoughtfully. "You mentioned her often in your letters and I must admit that bothered me."

"Bothered you?" Annoyance colored her tone just a little. "You might think she was another man!"

"I would consider you incapable of infidelity, Victoria," he stated primly, but inside he cried out in anguish. He loved her, but he knew she was weak.

"I appreciate your trust, Jason," she murmured even as guilty memories of Gavin assailed her. Well, at least she hadn't technically been unfaithful. "But please–tell me what you don't like about Felicity."

"Later, Victoria, when we can really talk." By then they were in the parking garage under their building and his tone definitely closed the subject at least for then. Olivia came home shortly afterwards. Jason had brought gifts for them both: matching silk kimonos he'd purchased on a visit to Tokyo, jade earrings for Victoria and a doll in native Vietnamese dress for the little girl. His selections were those of a thoughtful, caring man and the three of them spent a happy evening together. Only when Olivia had gone to bed did Victoria begin to grow uneasy, dreading the moment when it would be time for them as well to retire. Later–alone briefly in their bedroom–she found herself wondering yet again what it would be like to have Gavin make love to her and it was just at that moment her husband appeared in the doorway. "About ready for bed, are you?"

She started guiltily as if he could guess her thoughts. "Yes, just a few more minutes." She puttered around at her dressing table much longer than was necessary: brushing her hair, applying various creams and lotions–postponing the inevitable as long as she could. Jason, meanwhile, had settled himself on his side of the bed and opened a book. He glanced up briefly and smiled as she lay down beside him. There was no one moment in which Victoria arrived at a conscious decision. It just suddenly seemed as if she couldn't bear to have him lying there beside her–all smug and self-contained and reading a book---*Baptist Missionaries in Nineteenth Century Japan* of all things!--and on his first night with her in more than three months. Reaching over, she stroked the side of his face with the tip of her index finger. "Did you miss me terribly, darling?"

"Of course I did, dear," he replied turning a page. "You know this is really fascinating. The juxtaposition of the Christian faith and the Asian culture......"

"Jason..." She slid her hand down along the side of his throat and inside the top of his pajamas. She felt him stiffen apprehensively and that made her all the more determined to prove to him once and for all that he was only human. "Jason," she whispered again and as she moved closer, she deliberately allowed her breast to graze his arm. She began to kiss his neck and ear-- little teasing kisses, flicking her tongue in and out. "You want me, Jason," she murmured soft and low in her throat. "You know you do. Admit you want me! Say it! Say–I want you, Victoria!"

He shuddered horribly. "Yes! Yes! I want you, Victoria!" Jason groaned. "God forgive me! I want you!" Night after night, thousands of miles away, he'd dreamed of her and now she had aroused him in a way he never believed possible. Even when he'd taken her once, he was still unsatisfied and only after a second even more frenzied session of lovemaking did he finally fall into an exhausted sleep. Victoria, however, lay awake for hours, reliving every moment. She felt whole, all thought of Gavin driven from her mind. Sadly she failed to realize that at the very height of his passion, her husband had pleaded with God to forgive him.

Awaking the next morning, she reached out for him, only to discover she was alone in the bed. "Jason," she called, "would you like me to fix you some breakfast?" There was no answer. She slipped on her robe and went down the hall toward the living room. Olivia's door was still closed. She knocked. "About ready, sweetheart?"

"Yes, Mummy–in a few minutes."

Victoria hurried along into the kitchen. Jason was sitting at the table drinking coffee–his back to her. "Good morning, luv." She came up behind him, leaning down to slip her arms around his neck.

"Don't!" he said harshly, pulling away from her and standing up. "Please don't!" Only then did she see his face–the expression of utter self-loathing it bore.

"Please, darling, I..." But she stopped as she realized she'd been about to apologize to him–apologize for wanting her own husband to make love to her.

"Yes, you were about to say something?" He sounded so beaten down with shame that she could only shake her head. "I'll be late tonight," he went on after a moment. "Perhaps you'd better not wait up for me."

She watched him walk from the room, making no attempt to stop him. Olivia came in soon afterwards chattering about her history project for school and Victoria pushed the entire incident from her mind. At least she thought she had. At the University she busied herself with classes and final rehearsals for *My Fair Lady* and that night she went to bed early. When her husband came home, she pretended to be asleep.

She didn't know how much later it was when the telephone began to ring. Jason often received calls at odd hours and so at first she paid little attention to the conversation, "What?!"

This time, however, he was clearly annoyed. "You're where? And you want me to do what?" There was a pause as evidently the person on the other end of the line responded. "Very well," he said after a moment. "I'll be there as soon as I can."

"What is it?" Victoria asked finally as he hung up the receiver and got out of bed.

"That 'friend' of yours–the Scottish girl." He bit off each word with an icy precision.

"What's the matter with Felicity?" Becoming alarmed, she started to get up herself. "Is she ill? Perhaps I should go."

"That will not be necessary." Jason picked up his clothes and walked toward the bathroom. No matter what, it seemed, he invariably dressed and undressed there. "She's been arrested for drunk and disorderly conduct and she needs someone to bail her out."

Victoria laughed delightedly. "Leave it to Felicity!"

"Well, I'm glad you find it amusing!" He still stood in the doorway to the bathroom holding his clothes and she went off into fresh gales of laughter–not at Felicity this time, but at Jason standing there in his pajamas and clutching his clothing to him–the perfect picture of outraged morality. "If you have no concern for yourself," he went on, "you might at least consider the example she is setting for your daughter." With that he went on into the bathroom emerging again in a few minutes dressed. "I'm very much afraid, Victoria, that I must ask you not to invite that girl into my home again." He left before she had a chance to reply.

"His home," Victoria whispered, staring at the bedroom door which he had closed behind him. "His home." Maybe this wasn't so funny after all.

By the time Jason returned Victoria and Olivia were in the kitchen having breakfast. Neither of them referred to the nature of his errand. In fact, they barely spoke to each other at all. Olivia couldn't help noticing. Things were so different when Gavin was here, the little girl thought with a sigh.

* * *

It didn't surprise Victoria when Felicity wasn't in class that morning. She couldn't be feeling very well and she was probably humiliated on top of it. Without her, however, the mid-morning tea break would be no fun and at the end of the period she returned to her office. She hadn't been there more than ten minutes, however, when her friend burst in without knocking. "I will no put oop with it!" Felicity sputtered. "Do ye ken what I'm sayin'? I will no put oop with it!"

Victoria laughed as much from relief as from amusement. The Scottish girl was obviously fine and not in the least embarrassed about last night's escapade. "Would you care to sit down?"

"I canna sit doon! I'm too oopset to sit doon!" She proceeded to pace back and forth in front of Victoria's desk muttering in Gaelic and shaking her fist at an invisible enemy.

"Felicity, please sit down. And please speak in English."

Stomping across the room one final time, the girl flung herself into a chair–legs sprawled out in front of her, arms folded, chin resting on her chest. "Och!" She shook her fist again. "The currse of the MacDougalls on the whole bluidy lot o' them! The currse of the MacDougalls, I say!"

"You know you admitted to me once that there's no such thing. Now will you please calm down enough to tell me what happened? Jason didn't say anything when he got back this morning."

"Aye, he's a cold one, that laddy o' yourrs–a cold one forr fairr. 'Tis no wonderr ye werre sae drrawn to Gavin. 'Twould be like a roarrin' firre afterr a blizzarrd in the Hielands!"

Victoria knew she should say something in defense of her husband, but the words wouldn't come. "Please, Felicity," she said instead, "I really do want to hear what happened–– from the beginning."

"Well–ye kent that everr since Jamie and the otherr lads left, I...I've been... been low in my mind...?"

"Yes, of....of course. That's...that's only natural." Victoria didn't like this conversation. It brought back memories of Gavin all too clearly.

"Finally last night it just seemed as if I couldna bearr it any longerr. Och, but I was in a black and bluidy mood! So I purrchased a wee drram and went forr a strroll."

"In the middle of the night? In New York City? Are you daft?"

Felicity ignored the comment. "I was doin' no harrm, I tell ye–just walkin' along the strreet, drrinkin' a bit noo and then and singin' to bolsterr my spirrits. I'd gone through 'Scotland, the Brrave' and was just starrtin' in on 'Scots, Wha Hae wi' Wallace Bled' when a patrol car pulled oop and they arrrested me forr doin' naethin–naethin' at all!"

"You were walking along a city street in the middle of the night, singing and drinking!"

The girl glared at her. "Och, ye'rre as bad as he is! The next thing I know ye'll be lecturrin' me aboot the evils of drrink, too!"

"Is...is that what Jason said to you?"

"Aye–that and the fact that I'm no longerr welcoom in yourr home."

"I....I know. I'm...I'm so sorry. I just don't see what I can do about it." Victoria shrugged.

"Aye, he's yourr laddy and ye canna go against him. 'Tis no matterr anyway. Afterr last night I ken I dinna belong herre. I'm goin' home."

"Oh, Felicity, no! I'd feel responsible somehow!"

" 'Tis no yourr fault. 'Twas havin' Jamie herre forr a while and Gavin and all. I'm sae verra lonely noo that they'rre gone." Even with her thoughts full of her own unhappiness she glanced at Victoria to see if there were any reaction to Gavin's name, but Felicity didn't know the years of experience her friend had had at hiding her emotions. Apparently there was no response at all. "Besides I won't be leavin' 'till classes arre overr. And therre's yourr play. I'd want to be herre forr that."

"I don't know what I'd ever do it without you–between stage managing and your art work on the set and programs-- you're irreplaceable."

"Och noo! Ye'll be turrnin' my head wi' yourr flatterry!" She stood up. "Well, I should be goin' along. I've got class."

Victoria got to her feet as well and came around to the other side of the desk. "You'll... you'll keep in touch, won't you? Write to me and tell me....tell me...."

Felicity knew very well what she wanted to say. "Aye, you know I will. Afterr all I've neverr had an English friend beforre."

"I'll....I'll miss you so much!" She could feel the tears starting.

"Och–dinna grreet. Dinna grreet." They embraced. "After all, it's not as though I'm leavin' rright away noo, is it?" They agreed to meet for tea before that afternoon's rehearsal and at last Felicity hurried away–as always late for her next class.

It seemed to Victoria as though she hadn't felt this lonely since the days before her daughter had come that Christmas nearly a year and a half ago now and taught her how to love. But that was just it, wasn't it? Olivia had taught her how to love and to allow others to love her in return and that didn't have to end simply because Felicity was leaving. She still had her little girl and....and Jason. She'd entirely forgotten for the moment all that had happened between them since he came home and on an impulse she reached for the telephone and dialed his office.

"Prodigals–Reverend Eliot speaking."

"Oh, Jason–darling. I'm glad you answered yourself. I...I wanted to talk to you."

"I have an appointment any minute now. Can it wait until I get home tonight?" He sounded preoccupied. "Victoria, I asked if it could wait?" He repeated his question.

"Yes." But now her tone was expressionless. "It can wait."

"I'll see you later then." No sooner had Jason hung up, however, than he regretted his abruptness and his last appointment completed, he hurried home to make it up to her. When he came in, she was curled up on the couch–reading. The floor lamp was behind and above her and her loveliness, set off by the pool of light around her, was like a Renaissance oil painting. Later he would often wonder what might have happened if he'd simply sat down beside her and taken her in his arms. He wanted to–certainly–with an aching desperation. "Victoria–darling." He smiled at her sweetly. "I'm sorry I'm so late. May we talk now?"

At the sound of his voice she glanced up and he was glad to see her answering smile. She wasn't that upset after all, it seemed. If it had been Noel or Terry or even someone who had known her for such a comparatively brief time as Gavin, he would have recognized this as merely her public smile–containing no genuine feeling at all–but to be fair to him, her face was in shadow. "Never mind, Jason. I've worked things out for myself."

"I'm glad, darling." Secretly he was relieved to avoid further discussion. "But you know I'm always here if you need me."

"Yes, of course–thank you." Quickly she lowered her head again–apparently to resume her reading, but in actuality to hide the tears in her eyes. After all, a man like Jason had so many more important things on his mind and since she could never be worthy of his love, the least she could do was not burden him with her silly, little problems. Probably it was just as well anyway. He certainly wouldn't regret Felicity's departure.

Classes at NYU concluded for the year and the Scottish girl left shortly afterwards. Victoria had been invited to return to Stratford, Connecticut for the summer, but she'd refused and now the weeks stretched ahead of her–seemingly endless. What was wrong with her? She should have been idyllically happy. The month of July they spent on Cape Cod. Benjamin and Rachel Eliot joined them once again and there were long pleasant hours spent in the out-of-doors: picnics, swimming, bike riding. Of course she was happy; she'd have been a fool to be otherwise.

The call from London came a day or so after their return to New York. "Matt!" Victoria cried out in delight at hearing her agent's voice. "Are you coming to the States?"

"Homesick?"

Maybe that was why she'd been feeling all at sixes and sevens. Maybe she was homesick. "A....a little, I....I guess."

"As it happens, I have the perfect cure. Come home."

"Matt, I...I can't. You know that."

"Oh, not permanently. Though you're missed–desperately. People just can't seem to believe you're not working. They all feel–as well as I, I might add–that it's a frightful waste."

"Thank you, luv. It's good to know I'm still wanted."

"But recently I've received one offer I had to tell you about. It would involve at most a month's location work here and the rest could be taped in New York."

"Jason doesn't like me to work. He...."

"Will you just listen, Victoria?"

"Yes, of course. See how I've changed, Matt." He pictured her green eyes sparkling as she teased him. "At least I'm willing to listen."

"The BBC is planning an extended mini-series on the three Queens: Elizabeth I, Anne and Victoria–probably eight to ten episodes each."

"Which one do they want me for?" In spite of herself she was getting excited.

"That's just it, you see. They want you to do all three roles! As I said, they would like to use the outdoor settings here: Hatfield House, Hampton Court, the Tower, Windsor Castle–while the weather is still good–but except for that...."

"Oh, Matt, it's....it's an actress' dream! Tell them...tell them yes ! I'll do it! I'll do it!"

"Smashing! They'll be delighted, needless to say, and I am absolutely thrilled. They'd like you here the first week in September. Can you manage?"

"Of course."

"Good! I'll find you a hotel suite. Victoria, will this cause problems with your husband? I wouldn't want to...."

"He'll have to understand." Her tone was decisive. "I've missed acting and oh, how I've missed London."

"What about Olivia?"

"I'll...I'll ask the MacAllisters if she can stay with them. She'll be less lonely that way. She's great chums with their daughter."

"The MacAllisters?"

"Friends of Jason's and...and...mine, too, I suppose. Matt, I'd like a housekeeper–- just someone to cook and do my laundry, etc. She wouldn't have to live in."

"I'll take care of everything, Victoria, including booking your flight. See you in September, then."

"Yes. Thank you, luv. Bye."

Victoria's elation carried her through the necessity of telling her family. Jason's look of obvious disapproval hurt, but not enough to cause her to change her mind. Her daughter, on the other hand, took the news very well–especially when she learned she would be living with the MacAllisters.

* * *

August seemed as though it would never end, but finally it was September 2nd and Victoria was boarding the BOAC jet for London. She was going home! It was a night flight, but she was too excited to sleep and the next morning as the huge jet circled low preparatory to landing, she leaned forward in her seat to look down at the lush green checkerboard of the countryside. Somehow England had never looked so beautiful. I suppose last time I was too nervous about the custody hearing to notice, she thought.

Matt was waiting with the car–customs and immigration formalities already taken care of for her as always. There were the inevitable reporters and photographers, but he found her amazingly patient–answering their questions and posing for their pictures. "Yes–my daughter's fine, thank you." Victoria flashed a smile–making her love for the little girl evident. "No, she won't be coming over. I'll only be here a month and she's in school.....Yes, I'm looking forward to the series–frightfully challenging!" Just then, however, happening to look past them, she saw a man striding through the waiting room in their direction and breaking away, she ran toward him. "Noel! Noel!" She flung herself into his arms. "How ever did you know when I'd be arriving, you clever old thing!"

"Not really very clever at all. I rang up Matt."

The reporters and photographers were all around them by now. "Your girl friend's married now, eh, St. John," a voice called out. "Rum go, old chap." Noel blushed–horribly embarrassed.

"Mr. St. John is an old and dear friend," Victoria said quickly, at once slipping an arm through his. "And if you'll excuse us, we have a lot of catching up to do."

Matt came around on her other side then and the three of them moved rapidly away across the terminal toward the car. "The suite's all arranged, Victoria," he said as they settled in the back of the limousine with her in the middle and it started toward the airport exit. "The Dorchester. I think you'll be pleased."

"I'm sure I will, luv. Thank you." For most of the ride they chatted casually, but as they came into the outskirts of the city, Victoria began to peer out the windows on both sides of the car–pointing excitedly first at one thing and then another. All at once she recognized one place in particular–Ollie's Alley. Could Abe Epstein possibly still be there? "Oh, stop, please!" she exclaimed. "Anywhere along here will be fine." The chauffeur willingly pulled over, bringing the limousine to a stop at the curb. He'd heard from some of the other drivers that Victoria Windsor was a real bitch to work for and he was finding it hard to believe this was the same woman. "You can wait or come with me, whichever you prefer," she invited her two companions as she slid past Noel and hopped out of the car.

"We'll wait, I think," he replied. "You can have your reunion in private,"

Victoria half-ran across the sidewalk toward the old pub. On the verge of entering, however, she hesitated–peering uncertainly through one of the dusty windows. But then she heard a raspy voice singing the opening waltz from Straus' *Die Fledermaus* and she knew she had to see him again. "Abe! Abe!" She rapped on the door.

She could hear him muttering to himself in German, his ponderous footsteps echoing across the wooden floor. There were some fumbling sounds with the lock and then he flung the door open–trying as she clearly recalled to appear forbidding–but his blue eyes still twinkled with good humor. Indeed, except for the fact that his beard and moustache were now snow white, he looked exactly the same. "Zo sorry, fraulein. Ve are not yet open, verstehen-Sie?" He even spoke in the same curious mixture of German and English."

"Abe, don't you recognize me?" she asked reproachfully.

He leaned down, peering over his gold-rimmed spectacles, and all at once his face burst into a million laugh lines. "Ach! It is ze kleine madchen, ja? For you I am alvays open!"

"You're...you're not busy, then? I wouldn't be disturbing you?"

"Ach! Dishturbing me! Vill you listen to her?" He clapped one hand against his formidable forehead. "Gott in Himmel! Dishturbing me! Come in! Come in!" He took a chair down off one of the tables, carefully dusting it for her with his apron and finally he brought another one for himself. It creaked alarmingly under his bulk, but amazingly it held together-- probably used to him, Victoria thought, smiling to herself. For a moment then he just sat there–his hands on his knees–beaming at her. "Ach! How shtupid is olt Abe! Zince you vorked here, you have become famous actress! Abe knows, you zee? Come! Look!" Seizing her by the hand, he led her across to one wall which she saw to her amazement was covered with pictures of her. In his excitement at seeing her again Abe had evidently forgotten that the Victoria he'd known would never have allowed him to treat her so casually. "I show zese to everyvun and I tell zem zee great actress, Victoria Vindsor vunce vork here. Zeh all zink I am meshugana, zat I am making it up, ja, but I tell zem, nein. She vas only eine kleine madchen zen, but it vas her!"

Her eyes filled with tears. "Oh, Abe, I wouldn't have thought you would <u>want</u> to remember me. I wasn't a very nice person in those days."

"Nein, nein. Inside you are zo lonely unt frightened, ve know." Victoria was actually crying now–so many people wanting to care about her and she had turned away from them all. "Ach, Abe! Now you make her sad! Dumkopf!" He put a big clumsy arm around her shoulders and hugged her. "I know–I have zum zauerkraut heating up in the kitchen. A big bowl of zat vill make you feel better–ja?"

"Oh, Abe–at this hour?" She laughed blinking back the tears.

"Ach, is gut to hear you laugh. You never laugh ven you are here. Esther alvays said zat....."

"How is Frau Schneider? Does she still have the bakery?"

"Oh, nein. She is....."

"She isn't....she isn't...." Victoria couldn't bear the thought of not seeing the dear little lady again.

'Ach, nein, nein. But she has ze art-ritis. Her daughter come to be vis her and run ze business."

"Tell her I'll come and visit her while I'm here." She looked at her watch. "I really do have to go now though." She paused. "Abe, do you suppose I could have some of that sauerkraut to take with me?'

"Ach, of courrse, kleine liebchen. Ist all right–Abe shtill calls you his kleine liebchen?"

"I'd be terribly hurt if you didn't."

"I vill get ze zauerkraut."

While he was gone, Victoria wandered around the pub reliving old memories. She was terribly glad she'd come. If only she could see others from the past as well... Abe was back almost at once–proudly carrying an enormous jar. "Danke." Smiling, she beckoned to him to lean over. He did so and she kissed him on the cheek. "Wait a minute," she said suddenly. "I'll be right back." Victoria ran lightly outside and across the pavement to the car. "Matt, do you have any photographs of me with you?"

"Just the last one you had taken before you left for New York. I'm dropping it off at the television studio for publicity."

"May I have it, please? You have others, don't you?" Matt nodded, taking it out of his briefcase and handing it to her. "And do you have a pen?"

"Is a good agent ever without one?"

He gave her the pen as well and she shoved the jar at Noel. "Hold this for me, will you, luv?" He looked at the container suspiciously, but finally accepted it from her. With the pen in one hand and the picture in the other Victoria walked rapidly back into the pub and leaning on the bar, she inscribed the photograph in her graceful, flamboyant script. "To my dear and good friend, Abe, with love from his kleine liebchen–Victoria." "There, now maybe they'll believe you," she said as she presented it to him.

"Danke! Danke! For zis I get zee frame! Danke!"

"You're very, very welcome. I'll see you soon then." Giving him one more quick kiss, she hurried out to the waiting car, once more slipping back into her place between the two men and with a final wave to Abe she at last retrieved the jar from a bemused Noel.

"What <u>is</u> that anyway?" he asked.

"Sauerkraut, you bloody idiot!"

He rolled his eyes. "You stop in the middle of Hammersmith, go running into some old pub and come out with sauerkraut?"

"You may think you know everything there is to know about me, Noel St. John, but you see you don't, after all."

A short time later they drew up in front of the Dorchester and instantly a doorman was there to open the rear door of the limousine. "Miss Windsor." He bowed.

Noel got out first, turning to help Victoria. Matt came around from the other side of the car and they hurried together across the sidewalk and into the lobby. "Miss Windsor!" The manager strode toward them, hand extended. "We are honored to have you staying with us."

"Thank you." She smiled warmly, accepting his hand. "I'm sure everything will be perfect." How charming she really is, Noel thought, but then I always knew she could be. The lift carried them swiftly upwards toward the twelfth floor. At the door of the suite Matt inserted the key he was carrying and pushed open the door, stepping back to allow Victoria to enter first.

The living room was small but attractive, the walls painted a pale blue. The furnishings were rose, pearl gray and off-white and the Oriental carpets combined many of the same restful tones. Something smelled delicious. "Your housekeeper is already at work, it seems," Matt observed as behind her back he and Noel exchanged conspiratorial glances.

"Oh, super! You found me someone!" Victoria whirled about to kiss him in thanks.

He indicated the kitchen doorway behind her with a jerk of his head. "Someone I think you know as a matter of fact."

She turned around again and there to her joy was Martha Kendall–her smile tentative, but affectionate. "Oh, you dear old thing!" Victoria ran to her and hugged her. "Oh, I'm so glad! You don't know how many times I've wished that....that....." Finally she merely shook her head, helpless to know how to continue.

Recovering from her momentary surprise, Martha had returned the embrace with equal warmth. "It's wonderful to see you again, Miss Windsor. But I should call you Mrs. Eliot now, shouldn't I?"

Victoria stepped back and the other woman, as always sensitive to her employer's moods, caught a strange expression on her face. "No, Miss Windsor will be fine."

"Well, Mr. Matthews suggested I have some lunch ready." Martha quickly changed the subject. "Mr. St. John, how are you, sir?"

"I was beginning to think you were ignoring me." Grinning, Noel stepped forward as well to embrace the by now thoroughly flustered Mrs. Kendall.

"Victoria," Matt put in, "let me show the rest of the suite. The bedroom and bath are in here." He led the way to the left across the living room and she followed him.

Noel, meanwhile, went with the housekeeper back into the small kitchenette. "Could I possibly smell blueberry muffins?" He sniffed hugely. "Do you know I've actually dreamed about your blueberry muffins."

She smiled as she checked the oven. "Yes, Mr. St. John. Blueberry muffins and a cheese souffle. I remembered Miss Windsor enjoyed my souffles–as much as she enjoyed anything in those days."

"May I help you?" He picked up the pile of plates and started back into the living room.

"Wait a minute, sir." Martha touched him on the arm. "What's her husband like–if you don't mind my asking? She seems happy and yet I....I...."

"That's it exactly, Martha. She <u>seems</u> happy and yet..... But to answer your question–he's a kind man, I think; he genuinely cares for Victoria, but at the same time he's rather....ah...you know, holier-than-thou. And I must admit it bothers me, too, that she's obviously thrilled to be back here even though it takes her away from him."

Just then Victoria appeared in the kitchen doorway. "Talking about me?" She cocked that one expressive eyebrow. Martha and Noel looked startled, then embarrassed and finally guilty.

The actress laughed. "Oh, come now! I know damn well you two have been discussing me in great detail for years. So-- what's the current consensus?"

They glanced at each other.

"Well, Victoria, I...." Noel searched for the right words.

"You see, Miss Windsor, we...." Martha attempted to help him.

Entirely serious now, Victoria came over to them and taking hold of one of each of their hands, she looked steadily from one to the other. "I'm only teasing," she said softly. "I've.... I've always known how much you both cared about me." Tears welled up in her eyes and her voice choked. "And even though I may not have shown it, I was and am deeply grateful."

"This isn't necessary, Victoria." Her old friend placed his other hand over hers.

"I know, luv, but I want to say it. Especially to you, Martha. I've already told Noel."

"As Mr. St. John said, Miss Windsor, you don't have to say anything." They hugged her between them. It was a very special moment. "Oh, gracious–my muffins!" Martha broke away to hurry over to the oven. "Mr. St. John will never forgive me!" They all laughed and the moment was gone, but the mood had been set for the entire luncheon. No one could ever remember seeing Victoria so at ease.

The men left soon after the meal, Noel promising to return to take her to dinner, Matt to pick her up in the morning for the drive to the BBC studios. A short time later having done the dishes, Martha came into Victoria's bedroom, intending to unpack for her. To her surprise her employer had almost completed the task herself. Two suitcases were already empty and the third nearly so. "Oh, let me do that, Miss Windsor," she objected. "That's what I'm here for."

"Actually I'm almost done," the actress replied. "You see, despite any previous impression I may have given you, I'm not helpless. How about making us a pot of tea and when I'm finished here, we can have a real visit."

"Yes, Miss Windsor. All right." What a pleasure it was now to be with Victoria and what a shame it would only be for one month. Later when they were settled on the couch, each holding a cup and saucer–the tea pot on the coffee table in front of them–the housekeeper asked whether she'd like her to return to the States with her.

"Oh no, I don't think so. It's not that Olivia and I wouldn't both love to have you. But Jason's salary won't allow us to hire any help and he's adamant about not using my money. "Oh, Martha, he's so good to us, so kind. It's little enough for him to ask."

"Of course, Miss Windsor. I understand. I'm glad you're happy." But privately Martha continued to wonder.

* * *

It was well into the evening, then, before Victoria was at last alone in the hotel suite. It had been some time since she'd been entirely by herself and she worked very hard at not being lonely. She read more than half of the "Elizabeth" script; she took a shower and washed her hair and yet it was still only ten o'clock when the telephone began to ring. She hurried to answer it. "Hello!" No one in London could possibly know already that she was here so it was probably Olivia or Jason calling from the States.

"Welcoom home, lassie!"

To her dismay the hand holding the receiver started to tremble. "How are you, Gavin," she managed to say. It was ridiculous that just hearing his voice again could do this to her. And how had he ever managed to learn her suite number?

"Och, so ye rrecognize m' bonny brrogue, do ye noo?"

She laughed. "Believe me, it's unmistakable!"

"Aye–so I've been told. And how have ye been..." He paused for just a breath.... "Torri?"

"Fine, thank you." She congratulated herself that she sounded completely unruffled.

"And what arre ye doin' at this verra minute?"

"Actually I was about to go to bed. I've a long day ahead of me– a read-through of the first several episodes and hours of costume fittings."

" 'Tis no matterr. A wee drram'll help ye sleep betterr."

She longed to see him again–to sit way back in the corner of some dingy little pub and drink and talk until closing. "No, Gavin, really," she replied quickly before she could weaken, "I'll be a wreck tomorrow if I don't get my sleep tonight."

"Surre and a bonny lass such as yourrself doesna rrequirre herr beauty sleep."

His voice had that beguiling tone already familiar to her and she knew if she were to see him again–over here without Olivia as a chaperone–it would be the worst possible mistake. "I'm sorry, but I simply can't."

"Och–Torrrri...."

"And don't call me that silly name. In fact–don't call me at all!" She hung up before he had a chance to say anything further.

* * *

The next morning, as promised, her agent picked Victoria up in the limousine. "Do I know any of the other people involved in the series, Matt?" she asked leaning back against the seat cushions.

"You look tired. Didn't you sleep well last night?"

"Actually I didn't." Victoria brushed off his question with a casual wave of one slim, graceful hand. "But I'm all right, luv. Really I am." She patted his arm.

"I suppose you miss Jason."

Guilt stabbed at her. "It would be strange if I didn't, wouldn't it?"

"Yes, Victoria." Matt knew he should answer her original question–warn her to expect certain"old friends". He couldn't seem to find his way back to the subject, however, through the maze of casual conversation. Then all at once the car was coming to a halt in front of the BBC studios and before either Matt or the driver could move, someone had opened Victoria's door, reaching in to help her alight. She accepted the hand without thinking and standing up, she found herself face to face with Anthony Blake-Ashley. Neither man had ever seen her blush before.

"Please, believe me." Tony still held her hand in his. "We are simply old friends."

Tears rushed into her eyes. "You're very sweet," she whispered, fighting to regain control of herself. "But then you always were. I can't imagine why I ever took you as a lover. Most of them were such bloody bastards!"

He laughed. He'd been doubtful about directing Victoria again. Noel St. John had assured him she was greatly changed, but it seemed impossible she could be that different. He had imagined how she would taunt him with their former intimacy. Seeing her now, however, he relaxed, realizing they could indeed enjoy a purely professional relationship. "Well, here we are." He indicated a studio they were just approaching, pausing to hold open the door and allow first her and then Matt to precede him inside.

As they entered, the cast and crew rose to applaud. Victoria might have the reputation of being difficult, but to work with an actress of her caliber was a rare privilege–not to mention the opportunity to bask in her reflected glory. The applause at last subsided and Victoria realized with a start that they were expecting her to say something. "Ladies and gentlemen, thank you.." She paused, smiling warmly, and only her two escorts were close enough to observe how nervous she was. "Your kind welcome has touched me more than I can possibly put into words."

Her statement was greeted with renewed applause. "Now then, could we all be seated for the read-through," Tony said at last. "I might add that I won't be stopping you today. I would prefer to let you be guided by your own instinctive reaction to the historical character you will be portraying. I will, however, be taking notes."

There were mixed laughter and groans at this as the cast members moved to take seats at the long table which had been set up in the middle of the floor for the read-through. Victoria reached to pull out a chair for herself, but before she could do so, someone came up behind her and drew it out for her. "Thank you so much." She glanced over her shoulder to learn the man's identity. She had no doubt, of course, that it would be a man. "Clive...ah....hello," she managed to say.

"Hello, Victoria." He pulled out the chair next to hers and sat down as well. "It seems I'm your Robert Dudley. Tell me, were Elizabeth and Dudley lovers, do you think?"

Speaking of "bloody bastards"! "And just what do you mean by that crack?"

"I was concerned with my character's motivation." He smirked at her. "If you, however, choose to construe my words differently...."

"You son-of-a-bitch! And I haven't forgotten what you tried to do to me at the custody hearing!"

Clive merely continued to smile. "But I was only thinking of the little girl's welfare."

"Like bloody hell you were!" Suddenly Victoria became aware that everybody else was seated as well, not only that–they were all staring at her. "Excuse me." She flashed a smile. "Just renewing old acquaintances."

For the period of the reading, however, she could even ignore the presence of this revolting individual at her elbow. To be working again was exhilarating! The reading broke for the morning shortly before noon. "May I take you to lunch, Victoria?" Clive asked as they all stood and stretched after three hours of sitting.

"No, thank you." She closed her script and picked up her purse. "It would ruin my appetite!"

"Perhaps later, then." He followed her as she started to walk from the studio. "The London nights are as long and lonely as ever, you know."

Victoria rounded on him with a vengeance. "You bloody sod! I could cheerfully scratch your eyes out!"

"But you won't. Oh—and by the way, the phone number's the same." With that Clive finally moved away whistling. Victoria just stood there, watching him.

"Are you all right?" She hadn't noticed Tony coming toward her from the other direction.

She forced her public smile back into place. "Of course, luv."

"How about some lunch? I thought we could....."

"Why will no one admit I've changed?" she hissed at the bewildered man. "Because I have, you know!" She turned and ran from the studio, failing even to see her agent standing off to one side waiting for her.

"Did I say something wrong?" Tony asked Matt worriedly. "Truly–all I want now is to be her friend."

"But other men out of the past aren't so kind, I'm afraid. I take it you never knew about Clive Bannister?"

"Of course not. I wouldn't have cast him in the role. And I can get rid of him."

"No–Victoria would see that as an admission of weakness."

"Nevertheless, I will speak to Clive about his behavior."

"I doubt that will stop him," Matt observed ruefully. "But thank you."

* * *

The telephone was ringing as Victoria let herself into the suite. Martha was busy in the kitchen so dropping her things on the couch, the actress hurried to answer it. "Well, I was beginnin' to think you werre trryin' to avoid me!" Damn, she thought, Gavin!

"Didn't I tell you not to ring me up again?"

He chuckled. "Aye, lass, but I decided ye didna mean it. Coom noo, ye ken verra well ye want to see me....."

That damned purring brogue and still more unnerving, the brown eyes she could picture so clearly glowing with mischievous good humor as he cajoled her. God, Clive was right! She hadn't changed at all. "I don't know any such thing!"

Victoria slammed down the receiver so hard that Gavin winced. "Anotherr one of those," he remarked to Jamie with whom he was once again sharing a flat, "and my hearrin' may be perrmanently damaged!"

The other man looked up from restringing his guitar. "Who was that you werre talkin' to anyway?"

"No one in parrticularr," he half-grunted. "I'm goin' to the pub. Do ye want to coom along?"

"I dinna think so. I should be wrritin' Felicity."

"Och, 'tis no good gettin' yourr mind and hearrt full to the brrim wi' one lassie. 'Tis actually unhealthy, I think." Grabbing his trench coat from a hook behind the door, Gavin strode from the flat. For a few seconds afterwards Jamie stared at the closed door, listening as his friend's footsteps receded rapidly down the stairwell. What could be bothering him?

* * *

Shooting on the Elizabeth sequence actually began the following morning at Hatfield House. It was here that the young princess had found refuge whenever–as was often the case during the reigns of her father, her half-brother and sister–she was out of favor at court. They were on lunch break when happening to glance up from Martha's delicious salad, Victoria saw Matt walking toward her. He was accompanied by a thin, somewhat horsey appearing man in a tweed jacket and gray flannel trousers. Dear God, they were coming out of the woodwork–these former lovers of hers! "Hello, Victoria," Peter Harris said extending his hand. "How are you?

"Peter—" She accepted his hand, but her tone was wary.

"He has an interesting proposition, I think, Victoria," her agent remarked by way of introducing the subject. She raised her eyebrows.

"May I speak to her alone, Matt?"

"That's up to the lady."

"Of course it's all right. Please, Peter, sit down." She indicated another folding canvas director's chair near her own.

He pulled the chair over closer before settling himself in it which allowed her several seconds both to collect herself and to study Peter. He had aged greatly since she last saw him. He could only be in his mid-forties and yet he looked ten years older. Or perhaps it was simply that he'd lost his air of easy confidence. "I'm sorry Matt put it that way." His voice had aged as well–husky and with a slight tremor.

"He doesn't know," Victoria replied lightly. "If all we did was discuss my former lovers, we'd have time for nothing else."

Peter did not so much as smile. "I came to ask if you could take over the class in advanced acting while you're here. Claudine has a bleeding ulcer."

"I'm not surprised."

"I realize you weren't fond of her."

"And I'm sure I would be the last person she'd want teaching her class. Really I don't think I should."

"Is it because of me....because I'm still there because believe me, I......"

"Oh no, Peter. That was so long ago. And I enjoy teaching. I've done some in the States, you know. Yes....all right, if you can arrange an hour that won't conflict with my shooting schedule."

"I'm...I'm grateful, Victoria. It would mean a great deal to the students to work with someone of your stature in the theatre. It's difficult sometimes to advise them properly when I've never....ah....never....." He shrugged, trying to appear casual, but she saw the sadness in his eyes and now she understood his defeated air.

She reached over to rest her hand on his. "You would surely have been successful in the theatre, luv, but you couldn't think of leaving RADA. You're needed there."

"Oh, God!" he exclaimed, pulling away and getting to his feet. "If you feel sorry for me, I must really be pitiful. After all, you yourself predicted this state of affairs years ago."

"What, Peter?" Clearly her puzzlement was genuine.

"It's not important," he replied after a moment, still refusing to look at her. "You told me that one day you'd be a great actress and I would still be nothing but a teacher at the Academy. It appears," he concluded with a weak laugh, "that you were right."

"Oh, I'm so sorry," Victoria gasped. "And I didn't mean it that way now! Please believe me!"

He finally turned back to her and now it was he who took her hand. "You know, Tuck used to tell me there was a very different girl–a warm, gentle person–hidden away inside you. It seems he was right."

"Thank you, Peter." She stood up to kiss him on the cheek. He embraced her, savoring briefly her soft, sweetly scented body. Then he released her and left without looking back.

Off to one side, unnoticed by either of them, Clive Bannister had watched the tender moment. "You see, old chap," he snorted to Tony, "she's already starting. You only have to wait–in the queue behind me, I might add."

Luckily Victoria didn't hear Clive's comment. Two of her former lovers had accepted her simply as a friend and she was feeling good about herself. She enjoyed a quiet dinner, but then just as she settled down to write a letter to Olivia, the telephone began to ring. "Hello."

"Ah and good evenin' to ye, lassie. I decided to gie ye one morre chance."

"You could have saved yourself the trouble," she retorted. "I've already told you twice I didn't want to see you. I should think that would be sufficient even for a stubborn, thick-headed Scot!"

"Well, I could say a worrd orr two m'self aboot cold, stand-offish English lassies!"

"If I'm so cold and stand-offish, why do you want to see me?"

"Why–to warrm ye oop a bit!"

Bang! Once again down came the receiver in Gavin's ear. Och, he thought, 'tis the last time I'll be rringin' herr oop!

* * *

That was on Friday and at more than one moment over the long, lonely week-end Victoria found herself wishing she hadn't hung up on Gavin that last time. He would have been such a pleasant companion.

No, she thought again, if I see him, I know what will happen. But how endless the hours seemed–even though Matt took her to dinner and the theatre on Saturday evening and dear Noel driving in the country on Sunday. There was an emptiness, a sense of a lack of purpose that left her strangely on edge. Sunday night was especially upsetting–full of decidedly erotic dreams about Gavin–and the next morning she was in no mood to face a new class of acting students.

Inevitably the casting board in the central hallway drew Victoria's attention–what memories it brought back–and so she failed to notice one particular student walk past. Nor of course did she see the startled look of recognition. So it's true, Rebecca thought, as she continued along the hall. Her famous half-sister was taking over the advanced acting class. But there was no joy at the realization— only a vague curiosity. For this was not the same Rebecca Montgomery who'd stood outside the hotel that December night in 1965 hoping Victoria would just smile at her.

The years since then had been difficult ones for the fragile-appearing girl with the doe-like hazel eyes. Her father dead–totally alienated from her mother-- she'd knocked about London alone. There were a few acting jobs–mostly low-budget little theatre in the far outskirts of the city–some modeling, but primarily hunger and bitter loneliness. This Rebecca was, indeed, much like her sister had been just a few years before and like her she took a seat in the classroom somewhat removed from the other students.

Outside in the hall, meanwhile, Victoria took a last deep breath and forcing herself to smile, she pushed open the door walking briskly to the front of the room. "Good morning." She saw them looking up at her expectantly, obviously nervous, and unconsciously her smile became more natural. They all smiled back–all except Rebecca, who remembered vividly the coldly beautiful woman who had swept past her unseeing on that long ago night. What a damned phony, she thought.

"As I'm sure you've already heard," the actress continued after a moment, "Miss Arnold is ill and for the next month or so I will be teaching this class." Her announcement was greeted by a burst of applause in which Rebecca once again did not join. Victoria responded with a slight nod--laughing a little as she went on. "Well, I hope you still feel that way a few weeks from now." At that they all laughed with her except, of course, her sister–whose expression, if anything, grew even more detached. Victoria paused briefly to glance down at her class list. "Now I customarily begin by asking my students to introduce themselves and I'd appreciate it if you'd do that for me now–beginning here in the front row, please." She sat down then to check off the names and one by one, the twelve students (seven girls and five boys) came up to tell her something about themselves. Victoria found it hard to concentrate, however; the moment recalled so strongly the previous fall in New York when she'd first met Felicity and through her had come to know Gavin.

She didn't see the tall, brown-haired girl step up to the front of the room–the last one in the class to do so since she'd been sitting the furthest back–until there was a perceptible silence and Victoria looked up to discover with a start that the girl was waiting to be noticed. "Yes, go ahead." With a private chuckle she remembered her original audition for Pliny Nicholas and the Royal Shakespeare Company. It appeared someone else had just as much nerve.

Her amusement was short-lived, however, as the girl cleared her throat and said in a clear voice, "My name is Rebecca Montgomery." Victoria leaned forward to look more closely at the slim, self-possessed young woman, but it could have been anyone. After all how old had Rebecca been the last time she saw her? "I've actually had considerable theatrical experience already," the girl went on, slightly rattled herself now by the evident reaction to her name. Somehow she hadn't thought her sister would even remember her. "With several major companies."

"Which ones?" Victoria couldn't resist asking–smiling a little. The listing of vague acting credits was a time-honored trick.

"I'm sure <u>you</u> wouldn't recognize them. They were somewhat removed from the West End."

Her smile broadened. "Yes, well my first acting job was in Stoke-on-Trent in the Midlands. You can't get much further from the West End than that."

The class laughed. Only Rebecca remained serious. "I know. I've followed your career closely, Miss Windsor."

How wonderful if this were actually her sister! They could each be the family the other had never had. "Miss Montgomery, would you object to my asking your age?"

Rebecca raised one eyebrow–a mannerism so like her own that it had to have been copied deliberately. "Of course not although I can't imagine why you'd want to know. I'm twenty-four."

That would be about right, Victoria calculated with a mounting excitement. My sister's not quite eight years younger than I. "Yes, well, thank you, Miss Montgomery. That will be all."

Later, however, when she'd dismissed the class, she saw Rebecca alone at the back of the room–the only one not leaving with someone else. Just like I always was, Victoria thought. I have to ask, even if I end up making a total ass of myself. But by the time she'd picked up her things the girl was already halfway to the exit. "Miss Montgomery, wait a minute, please." She hurried to catch up with her.

When she heard her name called, Rebecca stopped, but it was several seconds before she turned back with a sigh of long-suffering patience. Dear God, Victoria thought, it's like looking in a mirror. "Yes, Miss Windsor," the girl stated finally. "I am your half-sister." But she displayed no emotion at the fact.

"Oh, darling, I can't believe I've found you!" Victoria hugged her, but she felt the girl stiffen against the embrace, offering no response, and at once she released her. "You don't like being touched, do you? I'm sorry. I should have remembered."

"What...what do you mean?" Rebecca had never known anyone who seemingly comprehended her deepest feelings in this way. More than anything, she wanted to run.

"When one isn't accustomed to affection, it can be quite frightening." Her sister's voice remained maddeningly gentle. "But when you're ready, I'll be here."

"You....you don't have to bother with me."

"Oh, Rebecca!" In spite of her determination to be careful Victoria reached out a hand wanting to love, to comfort.

"Leave me alone!" the girl exclaimed, backing away. "Please–just leave me alone!" She turned and fled and Victoria made no further attempt to stop her.

* * *

Since her return to London Victoria had grown accustomed to finding Martha waiting for her with a good, hot meal and more important to sharing the day with her as she'd never been able to do in their earlier years together. I'll miss her when I go back to the States, she'd often think, and fresh guilt would assail her. In New York, after all, <u>Jason</u> would be waiting for her.

Tonight, however, there was no Martha–only a note explaining she'd had to leave early because her sister was ill. Stifling her disappointment, Victoria opened the door of the fridge and began bleakly to consider eating although she wasn't really hungry. "Why do I always end up alone?" she whispered forlornly–closing the door of the refrigerator again and wandering aimlessly out into the living room.

Just then the doorbell rang. "Oh, damn!" For some reason now she was actually annoyed at this unwarranted intrusion and striding over, she flung open the door to find Gavin standing there.

The Scotsman's eyes lit up with pleasure at the sight of her. How could he have forgotten how beautiful she was? "Good evenin' to ye, Torri." Victoria stared at him stupidly. She could feel herself beginning to breathe more rapidly, longing already to have him take her in his arms again, but once he did, she knew all vows of fidelity to her husband would be for naught. "Have ye lost yourr tongue then, lassie?"

"I....I told you on the telephone I didn't want to see you."

"Aye. That's why I didna rring ye oop this time." He looked so adorably mischievous.

"Oh...Gavin," she murmured.

He gestured into the room. "May I coom in then?" She nodded and stepped back, allowing him to enter.

Chapter 21

"As ye can see, lass, I didna coom empty-handed." Gavin held up a paper sack which obviously contained a bottle of liquor. He smiled, searching her face for a sign of her feelings. It seemed forever ago he'd left her in New York.

"If that's Scotch..." She tried to look serious, but inevitably an answering smile tugged at the corners of her own mouth.

"Och, Torri, I know betterr than that! 'Tis wine." He drew out the bottle with a flourish. Victoria had forgotten what a big man he was; the way his physical presence seemed to fill a room, the force of his personality radiating out in waves to engulf everyone within its radius. She was thrown entirely for a loss, unable to think what to say or do. Her uncertainty must have showed on her face because Gavin in his turn hesitated. "If ye rreally dinna want me herre, lass, ye only have to say so...." He took a step or two back in the direction of the door, pausing to glance at her questioningly.

All she had to do then was to ask him to go. She shook her head. "No, I don't want you to leave."

"Ah–good, then. Have ye had dinnerr, Torri?"

His burr lingered over her name and involuntarily she shivered. "As a matter of fact I...I was just rummaging through the fridge when you came. I...I think there are some steaks in there, if that's all right....maybe jacket potatoes and a salad?" Victoria moved quickly into the kitchen and began taking things out of the refrigerator. Suddenly she found to her amazement that she was actually hungry. Unconsciously she was even humming to herself as she washed the potatoes and put them in the oven and then started to break lettuce into a salad bowl.

Gavin came to stand in the doorway, watching her as she worked. "Ye enjoy cookin', then?" She hadn't realized he was so close. She jumped. "I do have a way of starrtlin' ye, don't I?" She looked at him–puzzled. "That morrnin' at the MacAllisterrs'."

"Oh....ah....yes. You're...you're so...so big, I guess, and yet you seem to materialize out of nowhere."

"Shall I carrry my pipes aboot wi' me. That'll gie ye ample warrnin'." His eyes glowed just as she'd remembered.

She laughed. "God, no! That would send me right through the roof."

Now he laughed as well. "Can I do anything?"

"How about mixing me a drink? A Bl....."

"I know. I know. One of those damned tomato-ey things."

Of course Gavin would remember what she drank. She busied herself with the salad, warmed and comforted more than she cared to admit by the simple knowledge that he was in the next room. In almost no time he was back carrying her Bloody Mary and of course, a Scotch for himself. "I'm glad to see ye at least <u>have</u> this stuff on hand." Putting her drink down on the counter, he waved his glass around. "Therre's hope forr ye yet, lass."

"I can't take credit for that, I'm afraid. The hotel stocks the bar."

"So–how long will ye be in Lundon?" he asked lounging against the counter near her.

It was so good to be with him–so good. With difficulty she concentrated on answering his question. "About....about a month, I guess, perhaps a little longer. You can never tell about the weather for outdoor shooting."

"Och—'tis a pity ye'rre nae filmin' in Scotland. It neverr rrains therre."

She looked up at him to see if he could possibly be serious. He winked at her. "Oh, you—honestly, you <u>are</u> impossible"

"Aye–so ye've alrready told me, I believe."

Again they laughed, but then their eyes met in that same endless way which had drawn them into their first embrace in New York. "Ah....what....what kind of dressing do you like on your salad?" Victoria asked, trying desperately to keep things casual.

"I'm not parrticularr." He moved away again toward the living room, realizing himself how difficult it was to be so close to Victoria without wanting to touch her. "Why don't I set the table? Wherre do ye keep things?"

"Glasses and dishes in the cupboard to your right–silverware in the drawer underneath."

So Gavin kept himself busy setting the table, laying a fire in the fireplace, finding a good radio station. Victoria finished the salad and put the steaks under the broiler. Finally they sat down to dinner. "So exactly what is this ye'rre worrkin' on at the moment?" he asked at one point.

"A mini-series on the three queens of England."

"<u>England</u>, is it noo?"

She smiled shaking her head. "Sorry–one English queen and two <u>British</u>. Is that better?"

"Aye."

Again their eyes met. With great effort Victoria pulled hers away. "What are <u>you</u> doing now?"

"Jamie and I are gettin' a job herre and therre, but....."

"I can't understand that! You're bloody marvelous! I could speak to some people. I'm sure if I......"

"No, lass," he replied firmly. "I will do it on my own."

"Don't be silly. People helped <u>me</u>–Terry and Dylan. Why without them, I....."

"Terry and Dylan?" Gavin raised his heavy reddish eyebrows, "That wouldn't be Dylan Mallorry and <u>Sirr</u> Terrence Cartier, would it by any chance? I keep forrgettin' the exalted coomp'ny I'm keepin'. Arre ye surre ye wish to associate with a merre morrtal such as m'self?"

"They're...they're just my friends–that's all. Please, I'm...I'm sorry." Impulsively Victoria reached over to touch his hand. "Ultimately you <u>will</u> make it on your own. I'm sure of it!"

Gavin looked down to where her hand lay over his and he couldn't stop himself from raising it to his lips. He glanced up to find her watching him. Her hand was trembling, but she made no move to pull away. "Thank ye, Torri," he whispered.

Now she finally did remove her hand. "Would...would you like some coffee?"

"Aye...thank ye."

It was with considerable relief that she fled into the kitchen. Why do I try to fool myself, Victoria thought, as she made the coffee, placing a small carafe together with two mugs, cream and sugar on a tray, but at last she had to go back out into the living room. She sat down to pour the coffee. "Gavin, I...I hope you don't think I was....ah....name-dropping a few minutes ago."

"Oh....that." He was slightly disappointed. He supposed he'd been hoping her words would touch on more intimate matters. "Dinna frret yourrself, lass. I ken ye meant well."

"And....and I don't want you to think of me in that way either."

Gavin leaned forward over the table resting on his elbows, holding the mug in both hands. Perhaps her statement did, in fact, have more significance to it that he'd first realized. "What do ye mean then, lass?"

Even though she refused to look at him, she could feel his gaze on her. "I....I don't want to be Victoria Windsor...not to you."

"Well then, ye dinna have to worrry. To me ye'rre simply a lovely woman whose coomp'ny I enjoy." She had to turn her head then to see the expression on his face and this time she could not look away. "But can ye pass the ultimate test?" he continued after a moment during which his eyes held hers steadily in their grasp–an unnerving twinkle just visible in their brown depths. "Do ye have any drrambuie in therre?" He went to look in the bar. "'Tis a Scotch based liqueurr, ye ken. The rrecipe was a gift to the Scots from Bonnie Prrince Charrlie himself!"

She couldn't tell for sure if he was serious; there was, at any rate, no drambuie in the mini-bar. "I'm...I'm sorry." But she wasn't exactly sure what she was apologizing for.

"Well, ye did say that the hotel stocks the barr and afterr all, 'tis an <u>English</u> establishment. What can I expect?" He smiled, his dimple appearing briefly. "Perrhaps a brrandy instead, then?"

"No--thank you." Somehow she felt that if she could possibly avoid the after-dinner drink, the course of the rest of the evening's events could be altered as well.

"Then at least brring ourr coffees overr to the couch. I've laid a firre."

"All....all right," she replied after a slight pause. The couch, the fire, the soft music from the radio–the whole scene was the classic one of seduction, but then she supposed she'd known from the moment she opened the door to him how the evening would end. Even as these thoughts passed through her mind, however, she went to join him. Putting the two mugs down on the coffee table, she finally settled herself in one corner of the sofa, resting her elbow on its low back, the tip of one index finger poised against her cheek.

He lit the fire and came to sit beside her. But then for a moment he studied her. "Why do ye pose like that?" he asked suddenly. "If ye dinna want me to think of ye as Victorria Windsorr, dinna act like herr."

She should have known by now that this man always said and did the unexpected, but once again she was taken by surprise and rattled, she took her hand away from her face. "I...I suppose I've gotten used to hiding behind her," she replied finally. "Maybe I can't be anyone else."

"Ah...but ye see...to me ye arre soomone else—Torri." Dimly she thought his burr was the way velvet would sound. "Can ye no see that?"

"That's true. I....I am a different person with you."

Stroking her face and hair, he moved slowly toward her. Over and over again he whispered her name–"Torri.....Torri......Torri."

And now she knew she was lost. "Gavin...oh, Gavin." She came easily into his arms, her mouth seeking his. When at last their lips parted, he raised his head for a moment to look at her, his gaze clearly asking whether it was all right to continue. Victoria nodded and lay back against the cushions. Her eyes closed, she felt his mouth travel down the side of her face to the hollow behind her ear and from there on down her neck, coming to rest in the warm, sweet curve at her shoulder. A slight pause and then he started up again–along the line of her chin. Briefly she tensed. Would Gavin wonder at the scar, but then his lips touched hers again and she forgot everything else.

They were never sure who made the move toward the bedroom–only that all at once they were walking in that direction, arms about each other's waist. Once there he immediately reached around behind her to unzip her dress and easing it down off her arms, he began to kiss her bare shoulders. Perhaps it was the months as Jason's wife, but for whatever reason Victoria could barely contain her desire. She unbuttoned Gavin's cardigan and then the shirt under it, running her hands through the mass of curly auburn hair on his chest. He slid the straps of her slip off her shoulders, letting both it and the dress fall to the floor. In her eagerness she immediately unhooked her own bra, but allowed him to remove it. Cupping a hand under each breast, he kissed them gently at first and then with an increasing urgency. Victoria moaned softly as she felt her knees buckle under her and Gavin picked her up to carry her to the bed.

She lay quiet while he stripped off her tights and underpants and then she watched him finish undressing himself. He had a magnificent male body as she'd always suspected–narrow waist, flat stomach, muscular thighs. She reached up to him and at last he lay down beside her, beginning again to kiss her–soft, teasing little nips, running the tip of his tongue out and over her breasts, the nipples now firm and pointed. His hands, meanwhile, explored on their own—her stomach, thighs–the warm moistness in between. And although before Victoria had always been more or less passive in the sexual act, merely submitting to her partner's needs, now her hands ran in turn over his body, wanting to learn it–the hardness, the male beauty of it as she'd never wished to do with another man. They spoke very little beyond urgent, repeated murmurings of each other's names.

Aroused as he was, when he finally took her, Gavin was incredibly gentle; in fact, although he couldn't have realized it at the moment, he'd never been so gentle with a woman. And for the first time Victoria knew what it meant to give herself totally to someone; to experience a feeling of release beyond mere physical climax. Even when he'd withdrawn from her, she continued to cling to him, wanting to prolong the moment. "Torri–ye'll be cold," he whispered, his voice husky with remembered passion. "Herre—wait a minute." He eased the top sheet and blankets from under her, covering her as tenderly as ever a father had tucked in a child and finally now he held out his arms to her. "Coom noo, lass." Dimly she was conscious of those same arms closing around her and the last thing of which she was conscious before falling asleep was the sure, steady sound of his heart beating just beneath her ear.

So many times after a night with a woman Gavin had found the following morning a terrible let-down, but this was <u>so</u> different! He awoke full of energy, feeling incredibly alive and aware of the joy of being a man. Stretching hugely, he raised himself up on one elbow to study Victoria, still asleep beside him. She was sprawled on her stomach, her face turned toward him framed in a tousled cloud of golden hair and the arm nearest him flung up over her head. Her beauty was profoundly affecting and he couldn't resist touching her–running the index finger of one hand gently along her cheek, down her throat and along the bare arm. At his touch Victoria stirred and turned over onto her back, the movement disrupting the covers and exposing a breast. He leaned down to kiss it. It was this which finally roused her. "Gavin?"

"Aye." He moved his mouth up gradually from her breast to her neck and cheek and finally her lips. Sleepily Victoria returned his kiss, but as she came fully awake, the guilt was there waiting for her in the recesses of her mind. Abruptly she pulled away from him, lying down again on her own side of the bed. "What's wrrong, lassie?" Propping himself up on his elbow again, he reached over to stroke her cheek.

"I've...I've never been unfaithful to my husband before."

"Then ye rregrret last night?" Gavin wondered why his voice turned suddenly harsh.

"No, that's...that's just it. I...I don't."

"Ah....good." He leaned down to kiss her yet again–a long, lingering kiss.

"We...we both know this won't last."

"Aye—I'm no a laddy forr any perrmanent attachment. Eventually I get rrestless."

But their eyes met just then, drawing them into yet another embrace. There was no move for the moment toward more lovemaking, but at the same time there was a hungry needing of each other that couldn't be satisfied. All at once Victoria happened to catch a glimpse of the bedside clock. "My God, it's nearly seven-thirty. The car will be here in an hour. If you'll let me shower first, I'll fix you some breakfast."

"Do ye have to get oop just yet?"

"I....I really do. I'll be late."

He still held her tightly, however, refusing to let her go. "Canna ye see, lass– ye'rre helpless in my grrasp!" He laughed, enjoying himself and her closeness immensely.

"You!" In spite of herself she laughed, too. And she began kissing and kissing him–lips, nose, cheeks, eyes–all the time laughing and experiencing the most incredible joy. Only the ringing of the telephone stopped her.

"Werre it not forr the fact that Alexanderr Grraham Bell was a Scot," Gavin muttered under his breath, "I would damn his soul to everrlastin' torrment!"

With difficulty she stifled her laughter, rolling over onto her stomach to reach for the phone which was on her side of the bed. "Hello."

"Good morning, Victoria." It was Matt. "Would you like me to ride out to the shooting site with you again today?"

Gavin, meanwhile, had slipped the covers down off her shoulders and now he was covering her back with soft, teasing little kisses. "Stop it!" Victoria whispered, one hand over the mouthpiece.

"What?" Her agent sounded puzzled.

"Nothing, luv–sorry. No, I won't need you today. The car's coming at eight-thirty, isn't it?"

"Did ye ken ye have the dearrest wee mole rright herre in the middle of yourr back?" Gavin kissed the spot before moving slowly on up to nuzzle the back of her neck.

"Will you please stop it!" Victoria hissed, trying with no success to be mad at him.

Suddenly Matt understood she wasn't alone. "I'll talk to you in a day or so then." He hung up quickly–embarrassed and just a little saddened. It seemed that in one respect at least she hadn't changed at all.

"Fine. Cheerio, luv." Victoria had failed to notice the abrupt change in her agent's tone. She didn't even realize that as she spoke these last few words he'd long since broken the connection. Replacing the receiver, she turned over onto her back to glare at Gavin in pretended fury. "I should be very annoyed with you!"

"Aye." He grinned at her. "But ye canna be angrry wi' a bonny Hieland laddy such as m'self, can ye noo?"

"No, dammit, and you bloody well know it!" Gavin roared with laughter. "But I'm afraid I do have to get up. There's a robe on the chair there. Will you hand it to me?" Reluctantly he did so, watching as she slipped it on and disappeared into the bathroom.

Quickly Victoria showered and applied a bare minimum of make-up, finding incredibly that she hated being even this far away from him. When she came out into the bedroom again, Gavin had put on his trousers although he was still naked above the waist. It required considerable self-control not to go to him. "I don't suppose ye have a rrazorr somewherre aboot, do ye?" He grinned rubbing his face. " 'Tis a wonderr I didna scrrape ye rraw!'

"I didn't mind, but I'm afraid you're right about the razor. What do you like for breakfast?"

"I don't suppose ye have any oatmeal eitherr?"

"Oatmeal....ick!" She made a face.

"No porridge! No rrazorr! What am I do wi' ye, lass?" He walked toward the bathroom waving his arms in mock irritation.

Victoria dressed in burgundy slacks and a white turtleneck pullover, running a brush through her hair and then tying it back from her face with a white and gold scarf. Gavin's baritone voice raised in song was clearly audible as he showered and smiling, she went to start breakfast. Oh God, I'm so happy, she thought over and over again–so happy!

A few minutes later he called to her from the living room. "The hotel must have a barrberr, Torri. I'll be rright back." She heard the outside door of the suite close behind him, but by the time breakfast was on the table he had returned, shaved and smelling marvelous.

"You didn't have to bother with that for me," she said.

"I couldna bearr m'self like that. I canna imagine everr grrowin' a bearrd. It itches! Hmmm!" He gave himself up then to the eggs and bacon, enjoying the food immensely. "Ye know, lass, ye'rre a verra good cook actually."

Victoria was eating very little herself, preferring to watch him. "And I suppose you're surprised?"

He glanced up quickly to see if she'd been angered by his remark, but her green eyes were sparkling. "But ye'rre nae eatin' yourrself. Arre ye no hungrry?"

"Actually this is quite a breakfast for me." She indicated her toast and coffee.

"Och! 'Tis nae enough to keep a wee birrdie alive–let alone a bonny lass like yourrself." He grinned, reaching across the table to take her hand. "Ah...Torri." Suddenly he was very serious. "Last night was....well...verra fine....forr me anyway."

"And for me." Victoria felt ridiculously young and shy. "Will....will I....I see you again while....while I'm here?"

"Is tonight too soon? I'll take you somewherre forr dinnerr."

"I'd...I'd love to see you again tonight, but I'd rather not go out if you don't mind."

"Aye, lass. Then I'll brring a few things."

"Oh, but you don't have to...."

"Includin' my rrazorr, if ye dinna mind."

She laughed. "Please–brring whateverr you need."

"Well then, I'll brring my soap on a rrope as well. I kept losin' that wee scrrap ye've got in therre."

"Gavin, I do have to be going."

"What time do you get thrrough?"

"I never know for sure, but usually by six."

"Well, I'll see ye aboot seven then."

"If I don't leave now, I have a feeling I never will." Victoria got up quickly, going to get a jacket from the closet. She picked up her purse and script, but at the door she paused.

"Torri." He had also put on his coat, the same old disreputable macintosh, and coming over to her, he took her in his arms one more time and bent to kiss her. Even when they at last parted, they still stood for a moment looking into each other's eyes and only then did they leave the suite, taking separate lifts down to the lobby. Gavin came out of the hotel just in time to see Victoria disappear into her limousine.

He continued to stand there until the car turned the corner. Suddenly the day ahead seemed very long to him, but he did have, in the meantime, certain practical matters to take care of. There was a pub which in the past had often hired him to play and sing during the lunch hour. He was in luck; at the moment they also needed a waiter. He could manage on that for a while and if Jamie wanted to continue working evenings-- admittedly it paid better in tips–the lad would have to go it alone temporarily. Of course he still planned on keeping the duo's upcoming week-end engagement in Edinburgh. That was an important break for them and besides, Gavin thought, he'd like the chance to show Victoria the Scottish capital. Felicity might be able to join them as well.

As for Victoria, it was soon apparent to everyone she was far from herself. Appearing distracted, she continually missed lines and cues. Twice she even giggled. No one could ever remember hearing her giggle. To Clive Bannister, however, it was obvious. "Who is he, Victoria?" he found a moment to whisper to her.

"What?"

"Your new lover. Who is he?"

Abruptly all her joy vanished. That's all Gavin was, after all, wasn't he–her latest lover–certainly not worth the ending of her marriage– and she made up her mind that that night she would send him away once and for all.

* * *

By six Gavin had been back to his flat to pack a few belongings, even shopped for dinner. He knew he was too early getting back to the hotel, but perhaps Victoria would have returned sooner than she'd expected as well. Pushing the buzzer at her suite, he waited impatiently for his first sight of her since that morning. It was not Victoria who opened the door, however, but Martha. "Yes?" The housekeeper eyed him suspiciously. Gavin's immediate and natural reaction was that, of course, he must have the wrong room. He leaned in a little to see the number on the door. "Twelve -oh-six," she informed him crisply.

"Aye–that's rright, then." He bestowed his most charming smile on her. "Is Miss Windsorr home yet?"

"Is she expecting you?"

"Aye, but I'm a wee bit earrly."

"Well, come in, I suppose," she said at last–doubtfully. It had been obvious to Martha when she arrived that morning that her employer had had company both at dinner and at breakfast. She'd hoped, however, that whoever it was hadn't also spent the night. She wanted so much for Victoria's wonderful new life to be permanent. She noticed now that this tall, handsome man was carrying a valise and her heart sank.

"I'm Gavin Hamilton." He grinned at her again and putting the suitcase down just inside the door–for all the world as though he'd every right to be there–he started toward the kitchen with the groceries.

"And just where do you think you're going?" Martha demanded.

"Only to put this doon, ma'am." He placed the bag on the counter, returning at once to the living room his hands raised in mock surrender.

"You're Scots, aren't you?" Her tone was approximately the same one she might have used to accuse him of being an axe-murderer.

"Aye, ma'am, I am." Gavin retreated to the couch. "If ye dinna mind, I'll just wait herre forr Miss Windsorr." For a big man he could appear terribly cowed and if Martha hadn't been so upset, she'd have found him amusing. Sitting there, he looked more than anything like a small boy summoned to the office of the headmaster.

Victoria let herself in with a key about a half hour later. Gavin stood up as she entered, but before either of them could speak, Martha came out of the kitchen. "Then you won't be needing me to start dinner before I leave, ma'am?"

The housekeeper's disapproval was evident and she felt her shame to be complete. "No, you may proceed as usual. Mr. Hamilton will not be staying."

"Torri–please."

Martha had never heard the actress called anything less formal than Victoria and she turned to stare at him.

"Please leave, Gavin." Victoria despised herself for being weak enough to need the other woman there, but the moment she'd seen him again, she knew that once they were alone, her resolve would falter.

"Ye'rre no bein' fairr, lass. At least let me talk to you firrst."

I can do it, she thought all at once–surely–proudly. I love Jason and I can do it! "Never mind, Martha. You may go."

"Yes, Miss Windsor." The housekeeper took her coat and purse from the closet and left quickly.

"I told you seven o'clock!" Victoria exclaimed angrily the moment the door had closed. "Why in hell did you have to come early?"

"I'm verra sorrry, but I couldna wait any longerr forr the sight o' ye."

"And please spare me the Celtic charm. Last night should never have happened!" She walked away from him.

"How can ye say that, Torri? Last night was glorrious. And I meant what I said. The day couldna pass quickly enough. I longed so to be with ye." Victoria had no way of knowing that Gavin Hamilton had never come so close to pleading with a woman. "Can ye honestly say," he went on moving toward her, "that ye havna thought of me at all today?"

She could tell by the sound of his voice that he was coming closer. She tensed–dreading and yet longing to feel his hands on her. "Now who's not being fair?" she managed to say.

"Ah–then this poorr Hieland laddy did crross yourr mind once orr possibly twice?"

He had to be standing within inches of her now. She would only have to turn and she would be in his arms. "Oh, Gavin," she whispered.

"Coom, lassie, coom." Now his hands did come up to caress her shoulders and she turned into his embrace.

"Dear God, Gavin–you touch me and I...I can't think straight."

"Aye, lass." He still held her against him, stroking her hair as he talked. "We arre drrawn to each otherr. We have been frrom the verra beginnin'. Ye ken that as well as I, do ye not?" All Victoria could do was nod. "Well then–I've brrought dinnerr–salmon in dill sauce. I think ye'll like it."

"You're going to cook?" She leaned back to look up at him–her uneasiness forgotten for the moment in her amusement.

"Aye. My grranny rrequirred everraone to learn–even the laddies."

"Then that means it's my turn to fix the drinks."

"Aye–ye can manage to pourr Scotch, I prresume."

"Well, I think even I can handle that."

"Brring the drrinks in herre and keep me coomp'ny."

Gavin went on into the kitchen and Victoria walked over to the bar. She poured his Scotch and mixed herself a vodka gimlet, twice spilling the liquor in her unconscious haste to be with him. At last carrying both drinks, she followed him into the kitchen. The fish was already arranged in a baking dish and at the moment he was mixing the sauce. Several small packets of herbs were scattered about on the counter. Putting down his glass, Victoria watched him for a moment. "My, but that looks impressive!"

"And just what have ye got therre?" Gavin eyed her glass suspiciously.

"You don't have to worry. You're not drinking it. But it's a vodka gimlet. It's made with lime juice."

"Och! Morre frruit! I don't know aboot ye, Torri." He winked at her. Victoria laughed, sipping her drink. "Ah...herre." He pulled the kitchen stool over near him. "Ye can obserrve the masterr chef in action." He lifted her onto the stool as easily as he'd done in the coffee house in New York, but now there was no need for pretense and he allowed his hands to linger at her waist before removing them. Deftly Gavin poured the sauce over the fish and slipped the dish into the oven. Then he made a salad as well as his own chips. And, of course, he'd brought wine again.

Over dinner he told her more about his childhood–his family. Victoria was content just to listen. "'Tis nae rright, Torri," Gavin said after a while. "I've done all the talkin'. 'Tis yourr turrn the noo." He had no way of knowing that he was treading on ground virtually untouched until then by anyone.

Victoria had been sipping her coffee, but now she abruptly put the mug down. "My parents were divorced when I was five," she said shortly.

He had observed the immediate change in her. "Och, Torri, I have aboot as much tact as one of my Dad's wee lambs. Ye dinna have to say any morre, if ye dinna want to."

She couldn't help laughing a little at that; the mental image of Gavin frolicking about like a newborn lamb was irresistible, but almost at once she grew sober again. "I...I want to tell you," she whispered after a moment. "I really do."

"Arre ye surre?" How could such a deep voice sound so gentle? She nodded. "Go on, then."

Speaking rapidly–hardly stopping for breath– Victoria told him about her early days on the estate in Kent with her father away at the war and her mother often absent in London leaving her in the care of a tyrannical nanny; of the years at Heathfield, her parents now divorced and plainly considering her an unnecessary encumbrance; of Sister Philippa who had tried so hard to love her. And for the first time she even spoke of Uncle Bertie and her sense of betrayal when the King died. Gavin said nothing all during this entire unhappy recitation– sensing somehow that had he interrupted her to comment in any way or even to express his sympathy, she might not have continued. He understood now why she'd been the person he first met backstage in her dressing room. But how could anyone have treated a little girl so uncaringly? At last, however, she fell silent and now she smiled at him self-consciously and shrugged. "You're... you're so easy to talk to, Gavin. I've...I've just told you things I've never told anyone else."

He smiled in return, reaching across the table to take her hand. "Then I'm glad I was herre to listen." He paused. "I have an idea. Why don't I find a good station on the rradio? We havna danced togetherr since the Caledonian Club in New Yorrk."

"Oh yes, I'd....I'd like that." How did he know without even asking that she didn't feel like talking anymore just then? A moment or so later Gavin had tuned in the radio, returning to take her by the hand and draw her to her feet. They danced for more than an hour before at last going to bed to make love again and finally to fall asleep, still in each other's arms.

* * *

The next day seemed even more endless, something to be endured until she could be with Gavin again, but Victoria was determined not to let herself be so obvious and using all her professional discipline, she somehow got through the day–rehearsals and taping in the morning, her class at RADA in the afternoon. She <u>had</u> hoped to have the opportunity to speak to her sister, but Rebecca took evident pains to avoid her. Once in the limousine on the way back to the hotel, however, the longing for Gavin--denied all during the day–flooded over her once again, sweeter and stronger than ever and driving everything else from her mind. Letting herself into the suite a short while later, she experienced a brief stab of disappointment as it was at once apparent he wasn't there yet. She was hanging up her jacket in the closet when

Martha came out of the kitchen. "Good evening, ma'am. I've started a roast beef for you. It should be ready in about an hour."

"There's nothing wrong, you know, with my having company in the evening," Victoria said defensively, "but if you'd rather not continue with me under the circumstances, I'll understand."

"Please don't feel you have to justify yourself to me, Miss Windsor. And of course I'll continue. I'll just plan on leaving earlier from now on to give you your privacy." The doorbell rang. "I'll get that." The housekeeper slipped on her coat and opened the door. It was, of course, Gavin.

"Good evenin' to ye, ma'am." Once again he smiled at her.

"Good evening," she replied curtly, brushing past him on her way out.

"She means well, Gavin. She worked for me for years before I went to New York."

"Aye, I see. Prrotectin' ye from the big, bad Hieland wolf then, is she?"

"I suppose so."

"Och, Torri, I've hungerred forr ye sae fierrcely all day!" He moved quickly across the room to take her in his arms. She felt his body stir against hers and very shortly they were in the bedroom. There were no long, leisurely preliminaries this time, but rather immediate lovemaking–almost savage in its intensity–and afterwards, both exhausted, they fell asleep. They couldn't be sure how much time had passed nor exactly what first awakened them: the incessant ringing of the doorbell or the fact that the suite was filled with smoke. Pulling on his trousers, Gavin hurried toward the kitchen. Victoria, meanwhile, had put on her robe and began opening windows. "Oh dear, is the roast ruined?" she asked, peering into the kitchen.

He presented a roasting pan in the middle of which was a small, charcoal-colored mound. "Aye, I would say so." He grinned.

By now the ringing of the doorbell had been replaced by a frenzied pounding. "Victoria, are you all right?" Noel could smell the smoke and he had never forgotten the time he found her unconscious.

"I'll finish gettin' drressed, lass." Gavin disappeared back into the bedroom.

"Noel–just a minute." Fastening her robe more securely about her, she went to answer the door.

"God in heaven, Victoria! What happened?"

"I fell asleep and Martha's roast burned. That's all. Ah...this really isn't a good time."

"I thought I might take you to dinner. Especially good idea with a burnt roast— what?"

Just then, however, Gavin came out into the living rom again. Noel wasn't at all fooled just because the other man was now fully clothed. "Noel, this is Gavin Hamilton," Victoria attempted to sound casual. "Gavin–Noel St. John, an old and dear friend."

The two men looked at each other, acknowledging the introduction with mere nods. "I guess you don't need company then, Victoria," Noel said quickly. "I'll be going along."

"Could...could we have lunch tomorrow—about one? We're shooting at Hatfield House at the moment."

"Fine, I'll see you then."

"Lunch with him, huh?" Gavin muttered when the other man had left.

Victoria came over to him, slipping her arms around his neck and looking up at him. "Why, Gavin Hamilton, are you jealous?"

"I've got no rright to be." He reached up to disengage her hands from the back of his neck.

"It's....it's just as I said. He's....he's an old and dear friend. There were so many times he kept me from falling apart."

He saw the remembered pain in her clear, green eyes and all the anger went out of him . "Aye, lass. aye. What shall we do aboot dinnerr, then?"

"Room service, I suppose. The menu's in the desk drawer."

* * *

The next day Noel arrived for lunch promptly at one. Victoria kissed him lightly on the cheek. "I'm afraid it will have to be just tea and a sandwich from the catering tent though, luv. I only have half an hour." In a matter of ten minutes or so he had bought their food and they were settled on a bench under the grape arbor where removed from the general crunch they could talk more easily. "Tell me absolutely everything, Noel," Victoria gushed, determined to keep the conversation away from herself. "How are things at dear old RSC these days? I hear your Malvolio is a sheer delight! I've been wanting to come see you, but at the end of a day of shooting I'm just too tired."

"Actually I <u>came</u> last night to say good-bye. I've been asked to go with a troupe to Australia and New Zealand. I won't be back until the end of January."

"But how unfair of you!" She pouted. "By the time you get back to London I'll be gone."

"You don't need me. You never <u>have</u> actually."

"What do you mean by that?" At once she was on the defensive. "I suppose you're referring to last night."

"As a matter of fact, I wasn't. Last night was none of my business."

"You're bloody right it was none of your business!" Abruptly her show of temperament dissipated and she reached over to touch him on the hand. "I know, Noel, I know. And I <u>love Jason</u>; truly I do. Only I....I can't help myself. I've never known anyone like Gavin."

"Then you're in love with him, Victoria?"

"Of course not. Didn't I just tell you I love Jason? But Gavin's so much fun to be with. He makes me laugh."

"I'm glad. There hasn't been much laughter in your life."

Finally she gave up and changed the subject. After all there really <u>was</u> no way of justifying her affair with Gavin. It was exactly as she'd said. She couldn't help herself.

* * *

Jason had been writing regularly–pleasant, carefully worded letters all about his work and how much he missed her. And she'd dutifully replied–pleasant, carefully worded letters all about her work and how much she missed him. Then the day of her lunch with Noel her husband telephoned. Martha had already left and Victoria was just unlocking the door when the call came. "Jason–hello." She'd rushed to answer thinking it might be Gavin and she sounded a little breathless.

"Are you all right, Victoria?" he inquired kindly.

"I....I could hear the telephone from outside in the hall and I hurried to answer it." That was truthful enough. "How are you, Jason?"

"I'm fine. But I got to feeling lonely, I guess. It must be lonely for you, too, dear. I wish I could manage to join you." No, she thought, I don't want you here. This is my time–away from you–back in England where I belong. "Victoria, did you hear what I said?"

"Ah...yes. You...ah...wish you could join me. It's...ah... all right. I understand it's impossible. And anyway," she went on, her tone sounding slightly petulant now, "I'm not really alone, you know. I do have friends."

"I...ah...realize that, Victoria, but I'm never sure how reliable those people are."

"Yes, well, I'm one of 'those people' as you call them."

"I'm aware of that fact. Otherwise you wouldn't be thousands of miles away."

"Please, you're....you're not being fair. I have a right to my career. It doesn't mean I don't love you."

"I suppose you and I simply have different ideas as to the duties and responsibilities of a good wife."

"There's really no point to this discussion, Jason. I'll....I'll be home as soon as I can–I promise. And I....I do love you."

"Of course you do, darling." His voice held its usual gentle tone now, but somehow, as was often the case, that gentleness tended ever so slightly toward condescension. "I love you, too, and I....ah....trust you."

"Th....thank you, Jason. Good-bye." She hung up quickly. If he truly trusted her, of, course, he never would have said so. Well, I suppose I can't blame him, after all, Victoria thought. He knows what I am.

Gavin let himself in just then, his arms full of bundles. "Ye'll neverr guess what I discoverred today, lass–a butcherr's shop rright herre in Lundon that sells sheep's stomachs and lungs and hearrts–everrathin'!"

"Wh...what?" Victoria had begun her terrible descent into self-loathing and here was Gavin–overjoyed at having located the insides of a sheep!

"A—Torri, ye havna lived until ye've had haggis!"

"Oh, Gavin!" She half-ran to him and tried to embrace him–packages and all.

"My worrd, lassie!" Laughing, he let the bags of groceries fall to the floor so that he could take her in his arms. Just maybe, he thought, the haggis could wait! "Have ye hungerred forr me all day, then, as I have forr you?"

"Yes, oh yes!" Taking Gavin by the hand, Victoria drew him into the bedroom–after all, if this was what Jason thought of her–and once there she started at once to undress. He watched–transfixed–as she moved seductively about the room, taking off a piece of clothing here–another there until at last she lay back on the bed–naked– her legs sprawled apart. "Come to me," she whispered throatily. "Take me now!'

"My God, Torri!" Almost unbearably aroused, Gavin required no further prompting. Hurriedly he stripped off his own clothing and lowering himself on top of her, he thrust into her.

Victoria groaned, arching herself to meet him, her nails raking his back. "Harder," she urged him, "harder! I want you to hurt me!" Their bodies began moving together– waves of the most intense passion either had ever experienced washing over them. Only when the ecstasy of it seemed almost unendurable did they finally climax and falling back away from each other bathed in sweat, they lay for several moments panting for breath. But something inside Victoria wouldn't allow her to rest. "Please, more," she gasped. "I can't get enough of you–never enough of you." Curling one leg over on top of him, she began using her entire body to caress him.

"Oh no, lass, 'tis my turrn the noo." Gavin pushed her away, intending to reassert his male domination of their lovemaking, but as he looked down at her lying there her eyes half-closed, her breasts and throat glistening with perspiration, a very different sensation came over him. He didn't understand why, but he was drawn to explore her body slowly and carefully and when at last they did make love again, it was softer and easier–lulling them both to sleep.

It was a moment or so before Victoria could be sure she was really awake and not still dreaming. But the terror–oh, that she knew at once and all too well. She was also suddenly and profoundly aware of how little she knew about the man who lay asleep beside her. Other men had walked out leaving her to fight the almost paralyzing panic with pills and liquor. I'm never afraid to waken Jason, she thought–dear, kind Jason—and look what I'm doing to him. But the fear wouldn't go away. "Gavin," she whispered, "please wake up." He merely mumbled in his sleep, however, and for a while Victoria continued to fight her battle alone. And still the terror was building until in spite of her efforts at self-control she was sobbing aloud. "Gavin, please, oh, please!"

"Torri?" At last he came dazedly awake. "What is it, lass?" Only a short while before she'd been a woman–stunning in her sensuality; suddenly now she was a terrified child. "Torri... lass, no, no. Coom....coom." Instinctively Gavin put his arms around her, drawing her close to him.

"Please....oh, please."

He was thrown completely for a loss. "Please what, lass? I dinna ken what ye want of me." But he continued to hold her rocking her a little as he'd sometimes done with his little sister, Meghan, when she had a bad dream.

"Gavin, please. I'm....I'm so frightened."

"Hush, lass, hush. It's all rright noo. What arre ye frrightened of ? Can ye tell me?"

"I....I don't know." Victoria still clung to him, but she was growing calmer now and the next thing she knew she was opening her eyes to discover it was morning and Gavin was gone. She was sure he'd been holding her when she fell asleep, but then–just as she'd feared–he must have left. Gavin Hamilton could have any woman he desired, after all. Why should he bother with some lunatic who was prone to screaming fits in the middle of the night.

But just then the bedroom door opened and Gavin stuck his head in. "Well, good morrnin' to ye, lass." He grinned at her. "Dinna move a muscle. I'll be rright back." And indeed he did return almost at once, carrying a breakfast tray which he set carefully over her, plumping up the pillows and helping her to sit up against them.

Victoria felt herself dangerously close to tears. "Please, you don't have to treat me like an invalid. I'm....I'm all right, really I am and I'm...I'm sorry about last night."

"Och noo, lass, everraone is entitled to a nightmarre once in a while." He came around to sit on his own side of the bed next to her. The events of the previous night had disturbed Gavin greatly and he just wanted to forget them. She'd been like someone in torment and he had hurt for her as he would for any helpless creature. Even the earlier erotic display of her body–although exciting to him at the time–seemed unnatural in retrospect. Had she been trying to prove something to him–or to herself? If it was her desirability as a woman, it wasn't necessary. "My dad used to rreferr to it as a case of the 'whilli-wumps'. It happens at night, ye see, because 'tis then the kelpies coom oot o' theirr dens and dance aboot, playing havoc wi' we poorr morrtals."

In spite of herself Victoria smiled. "Wh...what's a kelpie?" She picked up the glass of juice from the tray and he saw that her hand was shaking slightly.

"They'rre wee Scottish spirrits," Gavin explained as he poured tea for them both. "They live mostly nearr the rriverrs. They don't usually botherr wi' Englisherrs, but I suppose even they know a bonny lass when they see one."

She smiled again. "Th....thank you."

"I did naethin', lass." Now he was embarrassed. "Trry a scone while they'rre still warrm."

"You....you made scones?"

"Aye. You know, lass, I was thinkin' while I was gettin' brreakfast..."

"Cooking <u>and</u> thinking! My word!" Victoria raised her eyebrows.

Gavin glanced at her. He suspected her humor was forced, but he decided to let it go for now. Perhaps in time her good mood would be genuine. "Aye, lass, as rremarrkable as that may seem. Noo–I thought we should get oot o' the city this week-end. Can ye manage?"

"Yes...oh, yes. I...I'd like that."

"Good–we'll leave this afterrnoon as soon as ye'rre thrrough."

"Did you have a particular place in mind?"

"Aye—a frriend of mine from the Guarrds has a wee cottage doon in Devon. 'Tis a bonny spot—forr England." He winked at her.

"You know, Gavin, if you pick me up at Hatfield House, we can get an earlier start."

"Aye–but I thought that you...ah...."

"Wanted to be discreet?"

"Aye."

"I've decided that's silly," she replied flatly. "I should be able to leave by six."

* * *

More than ever that day, Victoria wanted the work to be done and she was at her most cooperative, accepting Tony's direction unquestioningly. They had spent the afternoon rehearsing the climactic moment when Elizabeth is told that her half-sister, Mary, is dead and she is now Queen of England. Only this scene to be taped, then, and the week-end could begin. She was submitting to the last minute ministrations of the wardrobe and make-up people when one of the production assistants hesitantly approached her . "Excuse me, Miss Windsor." Although one of the major changes in Victoria was her unfailing courtesy, people nevertheless continued to be somewhat in awe of her. "The guard at the gate wants to know if you're expecting a Gavin Hamilton?"

"Oh yes, thank you, luv." She smiled at the girl. "Yes, I am." He was really here then. As Victoria took her place for the scene, she felt ridiculously happy, but at the same time she was suddenly terribly nervous. He'd never seen her work before.

Gavin just managed to slip onto the set before it was closed for the taping and unobserved, he watched the scene. It was hard for him to believe that this incredible woman in the red wig and the green velvet riding habit could be the same frightened little girl who had clung to him in terror the night before. More than her appearance even was her manner. Perhaps it was because she'd told him about her distant kinship to the late King, but he swore he could actually see the strain of royal blood in her. Her carriage, her tone, every fiber of her being spoke unmistakably of rank and privilege as though-- miraculously-- Elizabeth Regina had been herself reincarnated to receive once again the mantle of royal rule. There was simply no trace of the person he knew as Tori. By the time the director called "cut", Gavin was wondering whether it might be best if he just left as quickly and unobtrusively as possible.

"Victoria!" Tony Blake-Ashley had rushed out from behind the cameras as soon as the scene concluded to grasp both of her hands in his. "Absolutely magnificent– beyond belief!"

Other actors in the scene also crowded around her, but Victoria barely heard them. She was looking for Gavin, but the bright lights made it difficult to make out anyone behind them. "Excuse me, excuse me, please." Managing finally to break free, she moved off the set where she could see more clearly. "Gavin!" She ran up to him eagerly. "It won't take me long to get out of all this. Do you want to come back to my trailer?"

"No, I....I'll wait herre."

"All I've done all day is think about the week-end," she confided–almost shyly--again a complete reversal of the queen he'd watched moments before.

"Have ye noo?" He found it hard to believe her thoughts had been on anything but the scene she had just completed.

Tony came up to them. "Can you work tomorrow, Victoria?"

"No, I can't," she replied quickly and firmly. "I've made plans." He looked questioningly at Gavin. "Tony, our director–Gavin Hamilton." She made a hasty introduction. "I'll be right back," she added and hurried away.

Tony studied the other man suspiciously. Was Clive right? Had Victoria indeed taken another lover–even though she was now married. "Have you known her long?" he asked after a moment.

"No."

"Just since she's been back in London then?"

"No."

"You're in the theatre?"

"No."

Finally despairing of getting anything out of the man beyond bare monosyllables, Tony excused himself. "Good to have met you," he lied.

"Aye." Neither was Gavin speaking the truth, of course. This was someone who belonged in Victoria's world while he, as he was now acutely aware, did not. Once again he considered leaving, but he couldn't tear himself away and less than twenty minutes later he observed her coming toward him again. She must have hurried, he thought, which pleased him. Moreover, dressed now in a pale rose and gray plaid pants suit and matching rose pullover with her own blonde hair tied back with a gray silk scarf, she looked like herself again. But still Gavin kept seeing her as she'd been a short while before: the great Queen--the consummate actress. Why in hell did she want to bother with a struggling folk singer? She smiled up at him, however, handing him her cosmetic case, and together they walked across to the car park. He stowed the case in the back of his tiny Morris Rover station wagon where he already had their suitcases and then he opened the passenger door for Victoria before at last getting in himself.

A few minutes later they were through the gate and off the grounds of Hatfield House. Victoria noticed that Gavin seemed unusually quiet, but the narrow winding country road doubtless required him to keep his attention on the driving. Even when they were on the motorway heading southwest toward Devon and he still had nothing to say, it didn't immediately bother her. It had been a long, tiring day and for a while it was enough to lean back in the passenger seat enjoying the coziness of the little car.

"Will my pipe botherr ye, lass?" he asked finally.

"No–I...I love the smell of your pipe." Once again there was silence. "Gavin, have you looked forward all day to the week-end as I have?"

"Aye."

'Really?"

"I said so, didn't I?"

"Yes, only I...I...." Her voice dwindled away. She'd never seen him like this. Gone were the easy charm and the boyish wit. Of course, she realized all at once, he's had all day to think about last night and he's decided he's had enough of me–only he's too kind to cancel our plans. Victoria felt tears of disappointment fill her eyes, but it was better to turn back now rather than burden him with her miserable company for an entire week-end. "Gavin," she said at last her voice trembling, "it's...it's because of last night, isn't it, that you don't really want to go?"

"Och, Torri, wherre in God's name did ye get a daft idea like that?"

"You're so quiet. But I don't blame you at all. Really I don't."

"Ye don't <u>blame</u> me?"

"Yes–after last night. If you've changed your mind about the week-end."

"Of courrse I want to go. Ye mustna mind me. I have my silent moments." His masculine ego wouldn't allow him to admit his sudden awe of her, but at the same time he wished to reassure her that he did indeed want to spend the week-end with her. There seemed no way out of his dilemma. It was fifteen minutes before he spoke again and even then he changed the subject completely. "Do ye mind drrivin' strraight thrrough? We'll stop at a wee inn forr dinnerr, but if we go on tonight, we'll have two full days therre."

"What...whatever you want to do is fine. I would like to have the two days there, though." She continued to sound somewhat forlorn, however.

"Arre ye still frrettin' yourrself, lass, overr this dourr Scot in whose coomp'ny ye find yourrself?"

"But....but you're...you're not usually like this so I can't help thinking that it's me.... the way I acted last night."

"Torri, ye mustna think aboot that any morre." Gavin's words came slowly. He was adept at charming a woman with pretty speeches; he was considerably less accomplished at expressing his real feelings. "Trruly I've....I've neverr known a lass sae easy to be with."

"Thank you."

He heard clearly the gratitude in those two simple words and he reached over to take her hand. How could such a beautiful and accomplished woman be so unsure of herself? "And I...I want this week-end to be verra special."

"What...what are we going to do?"

"Well, perrhaps I should begin by warrnin' ye 'tis nae a verra elegant place I'm takin' ye to. 'Tis only two rrooms with build-in bunks forr beds and a coal-burrnin' stove forr cookin'– although therre is indoorr plumbin', I hasten to add." She laughed and he was glad she was starting to relax. "And an enorrmous stone firreplace."

"It sounds charming!"

"I hope ye still think so by Sunday."

"I'm sure I'll love it, but you still haven't told me what we're going to do."

" 'Twill depend. Ye can neverr tell aboot English weatherr. I have inforrmed ye, have I not, that it neverr rrains in Scotland?"

"I....I just hope it pours the entire time we're in Edinburgh. That will shut you up."

"No, no, lass. 'Twill take morre than that." Now they both laughed and by the time they stopped for dinner all tension had vanished.

The proprietor of the inn welcomed them warmly. Gavin had informed him over the telephone that his lady companion would appreciate privacy so they were led not into the public dining room, but into a small parlor customarily used by the inn guests. Tonight, however, a sign on the door stated– "Sorry–private party in progress." The room was cozy and warm, the drapes drawn and the lights turned low. A small table already set for two stood in front of a cheerily crackling fire. "I hope this will do." If the proprietor had recognized Gavin's "lady companion", he gave no outward indication.

" 'Tis grrand."

"May I get you and the lady a drink?"

"Thank ye." Gavin ordered for them both and the man withdrew.

"This...this couldn't be more perfect." Victoria glanced about her. "Did you ask for a private room?"

"Aye."

"How thoughtful of you. Thank you." She came into his arms. How foolish he'd been, Gavin thought, pressing his lips to hers to confuse the real woman with merely a part she was playing.

The owner of the inn returned almost immediately with their drinks, knocking before entering. Reluctantly they stepped back from the embrace. "Coom in," Gavin called out, drawing back one of the chairs from the little table for her to sit down.

"Your drinks." The man set the glasses down on the table. "And the menus. I'll be taking care of you myself." Again he withdrew.

"Do you come here regularly?" Victoria asked, sipping her drink. "He seems to know you rather well."

"I sing herre quite often."

"Did you bring your guitar with you this week-end?"

"Aye, but I'm no herre tonight to enterrtain."

"Oh no, Gavin," she smiled, reaching across the table to touch his hand. "I hoped you would sing for me. I...I haven't heard you since New York."

"Aye—I'll sing forr ye. 'Twill be my pleasurre." He handed her a menu. "The steak-and-kidney pie is verra good–if ye like that."

"Bloody marvelous! Most Americans look ill at the mention of it!"

He laughed. "Aye, lass. I'll wait to see the exprression on <u>yourr</u> face when I make the haggis. So ye havna escaped it afterr all, ye see."

Victoria recalled clearly, of course, just what had prevented them from having the haggis the evening before and renewed shame flooded over her. She looked down at the table. The proprietor returned just then to take their order–his entrance once again prefaced by a knock. "What in hell does he think we're doing in here?" she snapped when he'd left again.

"Ye ken, do ye not," Gavin observed quietly, "that neitherr of us has done anythin' we should rregrret."

Even as she smiled at him in gratitude, he glimpsed the sheen of unshed tears in her eyes. "You're....you're right, of course. I won't think about it anymore."

Shortly after that their dinner was served and the meal passed in easy conversation, punctuated by mutual laughter and fleeting caresses. Back in the car Victoria settled into her place again. "That seat rreclines if ye wish to take a wee kip," Gavin suggested as he started the engine. "We should be therre by midnight."

"I'm wide awake," she assured him even as she stifled a yawn. The next thing she knew Gavin was touching her lightly on her arm. "Hm...what?"

"We'rre therre, lass." He smiled at her.

"Oh no, did I fall asleep? I'm sorry. I didn't mean to."

"Och, lass, 'tis no need to apologize and ye looked verra luvly lyin' therre. Coom noo. Let's get inside."

Each carrying a valise, Gavin with his guitar and Victoria her cosmetic case, they walked down a steep winding path from the road, around the cottage, across a narrow, screened-in porch and in the front door. The room was dark and cold. She stood in the middle of the floor–shivering. "Where's the light switch?"

"Ah—that's one thing I forrgot to mention–no electricity. Wait a minute." Gavin lit a match and by its flickering light located a kerosene lamp. Lifting the glass chimney, he touched the match to the wick and it leapt to life revealing a small bare room made cheerful and homey with braided rag rugs and paisley print curtains. The fireplace was directly ahead of the door; to the right were two built-in bunks and to the left a round table with four chairs. The tiny kitchen and bathroom were in a small ell extending to the back through a door to the left of the fireplace. They discovered a fire had been laid for them. Gavin quickly put another match to that. Victoria came to stand beside him and he slipped an arm around her, brushing his lips against her hair. "Sleepy?" he asked.

"No–dear God, how could I be? But you must be exhausted."

"Actually no. How aboot a snack?"

"Do you like hot chocolate?"

"Aye—Torri, would ye object to my puttin' the two mattrresses on the floorr in frront of the firre?"

"No, of course not."

"Good. Suppose I do that, then, while ye see aboot makin' us a wee sup."

Their lips met in a lingering kiss and at last reluctantly he released her. For a while after that neither of them spoke, Victoria busy in the tiny kitchen finding the makings of the hot chocolate, Gavin placing the two mattresses side by side on the floor, redoing the sheets and adding extra blankets. After a few minutes, however, she appeared in the doorway. "I'm afraid I need your help. I don't know how to use the stove."

"Aye. Of courrse." He came over quickly, kneeling in front of the cast-iron stove to lay a small coal fire inside and light it. From the angle where Victoria stood at the counter mixing the cocoa she was unable to see his face yet she found her eyes continually drawn to his back and strong shoulders, his head of thick auburn hair.

"What do you want to eat?" she inquired as Gavin finished and stood up again.

"I had an idea aboot that. Ye just wait and see." Whistling, he rummaged about in the cupboards and old ice box and taking out assorted ingredients, he began mixing them together in a large earthenware bowl. He's like a little boy sometimes, Victoria thought, although of course she didn't voice such an idea aloud. "I'll be rright back, lass," he said all at once and picking up an electric torch from the counter, he headed toward the door.

"Where are you going?"

Gavin made no reply, but simply disappeared outside–still whistling. She shook her head in silent amusement. He returned almost at once with two long, green sticks, stopping in the kitchen only long enough to wink at her and pick up his bowl again before going back out into the main room of the cottage.

"What <u>are</u> you doing?"

"Ye just get that hot chocolate rready and brring it in herre. Then ye'll find oot. Ye might also locate some jam orr jelly if ye could."

"<u>Gavin</u>!!"

"Neverr ye mind, Torri. I'll no say anotherr worrd so ye might as well not ask any morre questions."

"Honestly, you <u>are</u> impossible!"

"Aye, lass." Even from the other room she could hear him chuckling.

At last Victoria poured the hot chocolate into two heavy old stoneware mugs and placing them on a tray together with a jar of strawberry preserves, carried it all into the other room, beside herself by now with curiosity. She found Gavin kneeling in front of the hearth, holding the two sticks over the fire. Sitting down cross-legged beside him, she placed the tray between them on the floor. "Am I finally to be allowed to inquire as to the nature of your mysterious activity?"

He glanced at her and grinned. "In a minute, lass." Gavin reached down to pick up one of the mugs and took a noisily appreciative swallow. "Ah–that's verra good, Torri."

"Thank you." Victoria sat quietly for a moment watching the flames and sipping her own cocoa. "The dough's wrapped around the sticks?"

"Aye. 'Twas the only way ye could have hot brread in the mornnin' oop in the hills."

"Did you spend a lot of time there when you were a child?"

"Aye–weeks at a time in the summerr–tendin' the sheep."

"But you've never been interested in taking over the farm someday?"

"No. Much to my dad's rregrret. Ah–therre, that should do it." He removed the sticks from the fire and carefully drew one of them free of the dough. "Noo, lass, ye just fill the hole wi' jam." He held the bread for her as she dipped a spoon into the preserves, filling the hole as he'd directed. He took full advantage of her preoccupation to study her in the firelight. She seemed lovelier than ever somehow, her delicate face framed in her golden hair and he couldn't resist stroking her cheek with the tips of his fingers. At his touch she looked up and smiled. "Carreful noo, dinna burrn yourrself," he cautioned as he handed it to her.

Victoria took a bite of the hot bread full to the brim with strawberry jam. "Mmm, it's yummy, Gavin!" He roared with laughter. "What is so funny?"

"Ye've got crrumbs and jam all overr yourr bonny face. Ye look like a wee bairrnie." He leaned over to brush off the crumbs, kissing her lightly.

They talked very little after that–enjoying the shared quiet of the early morning hours. When they had finished their snack, he played his guitar and sang for her for a while and at last they curled up together under the blankets not even bothering to undress. Lying close in each other's arms, they were soon asleep. For the first time since the start of their affair they did not make love. But perhaps in another way that was exactly what they had done.

* * *

Gavin was awake nearly an hour before Victoria the next morning, but her head was pillowed against his chest and rather than disturb her, he lay quiet. Besides he found it pleasant just to lie there holding her close. At last, however, he felt her stir and then she raised her head. "Well, hello therre." He gave her a quick kiss. "Did ye have a good sleep?"

"Oh yes, thank you–marvelous!" Victoria snuggled closer against him.

"Naethin' like makin' a grrand lady sleep on the floorr–hm?"

"Oh, Gavin, please." She propped herself up again to look down at him. "I've told you I don't want you to think of me that way. I'm not....I'm...I'm...."

"Aye, lass, I know. I was only teasin' ye." He threw back the covers to get up.

"Oh, please–not yet," she pleaded.

"I'm just goin' to get the firre goin' so it'll be warrmer in herre. Lie snug noo and I'll only be a wee bit." Nestling down obediently under the blankets, she watched Gavin add paper and kindling to the glowing embers blowing gingerly until they burst into flame. Waiting a minute or so, he added a couple of larger logs and finally then he slid back under the covers, drawing her to him once more. "Hmmm." he murmured, "ye'rre nice and warrm." They kissed–lightly at first and then with more passion--, but for the moment it went no further.

"What are we going to do today, Gavin?" Victoria asked at one point.

"If the weatherr holds, I thought perrhaps a picnic on the beach. But firrst we could walk into the village. Therre are some bonny wee shops."

"Yes, I'd like that, I think–whatever you say. You know so much more about...about everything really than I do."

"I do, do I?" He smiled his slow, easy smile, pleased at her praise even in such a little thing. "Hungrry, lass?"

"Actually I am...and I'm not usually. What would you like?"

"We'll see what therre is, hm? But just forr the moment I dinna feel verra much like movin'."

It was nearly ten o'clock, then, before they finally got up to share a breakfast of fried eggs, coffee and more of the bread sticks cooked over the fire. A short while later after freshening up and changing their clothes, they started out for the village, strolling leisurely along the winding Devonshire road. It was a golden autumn day, the crisp air holding just a hint of approaching winter. Victoria felt incredibly at peace. Jason seemed a million miles away–someone with whom she simply had no connection. They spent the early afternoon exploring Clovilly, a picturesque little fishing village noted for its steep main street. Victoria enjoyed the shops, purchasing a skirt and jumper for her daughter in one place–a doll dressed in an old-fashioned costume in another. "I wish Olivia were here with us," she said as they left the last store, continuing on down the street toward the beach. "She'd really enjoy this and she likes you so much."

"Aye–she's a bonny wee one–forr fairr. I thought we'd walk back along the ocean. All rright?"

Victoria nodded and Gavin took her hand to help her climb over some rocks and down onto the beach. He still held it clasped firmly in his as they started out across the sand although the going soon became easier. And apparently she still felt the need of assistance because she made no attempt to take her hand away. They walked for several minutes in comfortable silence before Gavin finally spoke. "Torri?"

"Yes?" She raised her face into the sun and wind–reveling in the fresh air and the out-of-doors.

"I've....I've been meanin' to ask ye–do ye mind my callin' ye Torri? I've coom to rrealize no one else does."

"I....I told you that in New York–that...that no one else has ever called me that and....and you said that made it suitable."

"I did?" He smiled.

"And....and it is....suitable. When...when you call me that, I feel somehow it's who I am."

Chapter 22

Back at the cottage they packed the makings of a mixed-grill: chunks of beef, tomatoes, green peppers, onions and mushrooms and carrying the basket between them, they walked further on down the beach until they found a spot where a rocky cliff sheltered them from the wind. There under Gavin's direction they worked together to hollow out a place in the sand and lay a fire. At last they arranged the food on sticks, settling down cross-legged side by side to cook their dinner. "You love the out-of-doors so much," Victoria observed a short while later as they worked to push the food off onto plates. "How can you live in London? I should think you'd feel...confined."

"Aye, therre arre times I long forr the brraes o' my childhood. But I was seekin' a differrent way of life–parrtly purre youthful rrebellion, I'm surre, but also because I wanted my music to mean somethin' in the worrld." He shrugged–suddenly self-conscious. His ambitions had always been a private thing. He'd never spoken of them to anyone–not even to his father.

"Do you get home fairly often?"

"As often as I can. I....I hope I'll have the chance to show ye the Hielands soomtime--though perrhaps ye rrememberr how bonny it is therre."

"Remember?"

"Ye told me you'd been to Balmorral."

Involuntarily her eyes filled with tears. "Oh, yes, then it <u>is</u> beautiful."

"Och, lass. 'Tis a happy memorry. Ye mustna grreet."

"Greet?"

"Crry. Yourr bonny grreen eyes look like two wee lochs afterr the sprring rrains."

She smiled at that–though somewhat tremulously–and blinked back the tears. Was it thoughts of Uncle Bertie which had made her suddenly sad or the realization that in all probability she would never see the north of Scotland again–with Gavin? "Well anyway, I'll see Edinburgh with you next week."

"Aye, but 'tis only in the Hielands ye see the trrue Scotland." He paused. "Torri?"

"Yes?" She held out her glass for more of the sangria they were drinking with the mixed grill.

"Ye mentioned Edinburrgh."

"What's the matter?" She laughed, her brief sadness gone. "Did I say it wrong?"

"Actually–'tis Edinburra." He grinned in return. "But that's not what I was going to say. I was...ah....wonderrin' how ye'd feel aboot Felicity joinin' us."

"Oh, I'd love to see Felicity again. When she left New York, it wasn't under the happiest of circumstances."

"Aye." Gavin laughed. "She told us aboot her encounterr wi' the New Yorrk City constabularry. It could only happen to herr."

"Well, yes that and....and...." But somehow she couldn't bring herself to mention Jason's part in the episode.

"And what, lass?"

"Nothing." She shook her head. "Does....ah...she know about us?"

"Jamie does..so I suppose so....aye."

"Then I don't see why it should be awkward."

"Good–I'm glad." He pulled her closer to kiss her. "But we should be gettin' back noo–if we'rre goin' to have that haggis tonight."

Gavin put their fire out, burying the embers in the sand, while Victoria packed up the remnants of their meal. At last they started back along the beach, the basket once again swinging between them. "May I help?" she inquired when they were back at the cottage.

"I dinna think I should allow ye. Ye might rrefuse to eat it."

"Just exactly what are you planning to feed me?"

"Ye'll find oot soon enough, lass."

"Can't I at least watch you? I promise I'll eat it, no matter how disgusting it looks."

"Swearr—!"

"Oh, Gavin, really." But already she was beginning to giggle. "If I say I'll eat it, I will."

He ignored her laughing protest. "Rraise yourr rright hand, lass."

"What....what if I won't?"

"Ye dinna want to find oot!"

"Maybe I do." He made a grab for her, but she retreated. "Gavin, wh...what are you going to do to me?"

"Swearrrrr...."

"N...n...no." Slowly they circled the room, Victoria backing away from him–holding up her hands to protect herself, but laughing so hard by now she couldn't talk. The mattresses were still in the center of the floor, however, and all at once she fell backwards over them, sitting down hard.

"Torri—arre ye all rright?" Gavin knelt beside her, concerned suddenly he might have caused her to hurt herself.

"Yes, of course I am. I'm not that delicate!"

"Oh, is that so? Well, we'll see aboot that." He had entirely forgotten–at least for the moment–that only yesterday he'd been terribly in awe of this woman known to the world as Victoria Windsor. He started to tickle her.

"Oh no, please," she gasped. "I'm frightfully ticklish. All right! All right! I surrender."

Seizing her wrists, he pinned her to the mattress. "Swearr."

She shook her head still laughing, but then their eyes met and her merriment died away. Gavin released his grip on her and sat back on his heels, uncertain what she expected of him, but then Victoria reached up to him. Briefly he still studied her face almost as though searching for a sign of something. "Gavin, please," she whispered and he came the rest of the way down to her, pulling the quilt up over them both.

Afterwards they lay quiet in each other's arms. It was deliciously warm wrapped up together in the heavy old comforter and they felt thoroughly contented. Gavin stretched lazily in the drowsy stillness, his hand stroking her bare back and shoulders, and in response to his caress Victoria nestled closer, kissing him just below the ear. All at once he began to laugh, a marvelous silent chuckle deep in his chest from which she could feel the vibrations although he emitted no sound. "And just what is so funny?" she demanded, starting to laugh herself.

"Everra time I starrt to serrve ye haggis, we end oop in a horrizontal position. Arre ye that desperrate to avoid it?"

Still unaccustomed to his sense of humor, Victoria thought for a moment he could be serious. "It's not that. You know it isn't." She propped herself up to look at him and now she saw the twinkle in his eyes. "Oh, damn you anyway, Gavin Hamilton!"

He laughed even harder at that–hugging her closer. "What do ye want to do aboot dinnerr then, lass?"

"What about that inn we saw in the village?"

"Arre ye surre?" Even as he talked, he still caressed her lightly–enjoying the sensation of her skin under his hand. "I thought ye wanted to be by ourrselves?"

"I do, but we could just have dinner and come right back."

After a while, then, they got up and dressed and drove into town to the Tudor Rose Publick House, a lovely quaint old place with enormous bay windows looking out over the sea. They had fish and chips, wine and sherry trifle for dessert with coffee. As they were about to leave, however, they could hear musical instruments tuning up in another room. "What's that?" Gavin asked as he paid the check.

"We have a little band here on Saturday nights. You and your lady enjoy dancing?"

Smiling, Gavin took hold of Victoria's hand and they both nodded. "Right through those double doors there then. Enjoy yourselves."

They found a table–a small one tucked back in a corner of the hall and went immediately out onto the dance floor. Saturday night was the big night at the Tudor Rose and they were grateful that the crowded, dimly lit room afforded them so much privacy. "Happy, lass?" Gavin asked after a moment.

"Yes! Oh, yes!"

It was twenty minutes or so before they finally returned to their table. Gavin ordered drinks: Scotch for himself, of course, and a brandy alexander for Victoria. "What is that anyway?" he asked when the drinks arrived a few moments later. "Morre tamperrin' wi' good liquorr, I suppose."

She laughed. "I'm afraid so. It's made with brandy, creme de cocoa and milk or cream."

"Och, milk's forr wee bairrns. Arre ye surre ye dinna want a Scotch?" He started to raise his hand to signal the waiter.

"Yes–I am!" She caught his arm and pulled it down again.

"Well, ye've got sae many otherr fine qualities, I'll have to forrgive yourr rregrretable taste in spirrits." His other hand come over to cover hers, pulling her to him to kiss her lightly. "Would ye like to dance some morre?'

"Oh yes, I would."

It was one of the happiest evenings either of them could ever remember.

The next day–Sunday–Gavin leased a rowboat and they took another picnic lunch out to an island a short distance offshore. No one would have recognized Victoria Windsor in the sunburned woman who relaxed in the passenger seat of the boat, her hair blowing in the wind as they headed back toward shore at the end of the afternoon. It was time now, however, to lock up their little hideaway and return to London. Victoria especially was suddenly quiet as Gavin guided the little car off the winding Devonshire road and onto the motorway. "We'll coom back, lass," he reassured her–guessing correctly the reason for her silence.

"Of course," Victoria replied, attempting a smile, but she fully accepted the fact that reality and Jason would return all too soon. "You know, I've been thinking and I..ah...see no reason why...why you shouldn't just move in with me while I'm here. I mean it....it would be more convenient for you and I....I..." Her voice petered out as he made no attempt to reply. He was probably growing tired of her.

Gavin had never enjoyed anything in his life quite as much as these last few days, but he'd assumed that once the week-end was over, the old rules of their relationship would resume. Her invitation rendered him momentarily at a loss for words. " 'Tis nae necessarry, Torri," he said at last.

"Of course! How stupid of me to think you would want to."

"No, lass. "Tis not that. If ye trruly wish it, I'll move tomorrow." To his added surprise Gavin soon discovered their living arrangements wasn't the only thing that had changed. Victoria was more than willing now to go about London openly with him to restaurants, to supper clubs, to parties. It almost seemed as though she wanted their affair to become known.

* * *

"Talk to her, please," Noel had pleaded with Sir Terence. "She never listens to me. They're working at Hampton Court now. You could just happen to drop by to watch."

"Victoria's no fool, old chap. And besides what makes you think she listens to me– my gray hairs?" Terry agreed to try, however, and the following day he drove out to the shooting site. With a certain wry amusement he observed that Victoria was the only one who failed to notice his arrival. But then she was already in costume and make-up for the taping–standing off to one side since the farthingale, whalebone corset and stiff stomacher made sitting down all but impossible–and perhaps her mind was on the scene she was about to do. "Well," he said, going over to her, "back in England for more than fortnight and no time for an old, <u>old</u> friend."

She glanced up and now Terry saw the sparkle in those incredible eyes. "That old, hm? My, but you carry it well!"

"I don't have to ask how you are, Victoria. You look marvelous–the best I can remember."

"Thank you, luv!" She reached over to touch him briefly, but affectionately on the arm. "I suppose it's because I'm working again. It's like a tonic!"

"Miss Windsor, excuse me." The script girl came over to them. "We're ready for you."

"Fine. Wait, Terry, would you please?"

"Gladly. By any chance would you be free for dinner? My wife's in the country with the children and I'd enjoy the company."

"I'm....I'm sorry. I...I have plans."

The scene Terry would see was the one in which Robert Dudley comes back to court for the first time since Elizabeth has learned he is married. With a ferocious glee, prompted as much in this case by her personal feelings, Victoria/Elizabeth heaped abuse on poor, luckless Clive Bannister/Robert Dudley. In a moment of inspiration she seized a riding crop which happened to be lying on a near-by table and began beating him about the head and shoulders. "Cut!" Tony called out. "What do you think of our girl, hm, Terry?"

"I don't have to ask what you think, do I?"

"Am I through for the day?" Victoria asked eagerly as she joined them, blotting the perspiration from her face with a tissue.

"Absolutely!" The director grinned. "After that you deserve to leave a little early."

"May I at least give you a lift back into London then?" Terry inquired. "That will give us a chance to chat."

"Thank you. Just give me a few minutes."

Unconsciously Tony's eyes followed Victoria as she walked away. "Have...have you...ah.... met Gavin Hamilton?" he asked the other man.

"So that's his name. No, I haven't."

"I'm surprised she accepted your offer of a ride. Lately <u>he's</u> been picking her up."

"Actually that's why I came. I don't want Victoria to make a mistake."

"She won't listen to you," Tony advised shaking his head. "I've never seen her like this... so...ah....so...."

He didn't get to complete the statement as in an amazingly short space of time Victoria was back, shrugging into her fox fur coat as she came toward them. They both noted she was still in make-up--obviously in too much of hurry to bother to remove it. "All ready, luv," she said, slipping an arm through her old friend's. "May we go along? I'm.... I'm expected." A few minutes later as he maneuvered his Jaguar out of its parking space, Terry searched his mind for a way to open the conversation. Victoria, meanwhile, had settled herself in the passenger seat. "So, tell me, luv–was it dear meddlesome Noel who told you about Gavin or have you stooped to reading the gossip columns?"

He smiled. He was caught. Well, at least he wouldn't have to bring up the subject. "How did you know?"

"Well, you and he are two of the charter members of the 'Protect Victoria Windsor from Herself' Committee. That leaves only Dylan and he's in India shooting a film, I believe."

In spite of himself he laughed. "What about Mrs. Kendall? She is the fourth member of the quartet, after all."

She wrinkled up her nose at him–a new mannerism for the sophisticated Victoria. "Yes, well Martha has already given him her official frown of disapproval, but I doubt it was she. Code of British domestic service and all that."

"It was Noel," he finally admitted a trifle sheepishly.

"I thought so. I've kept expecting him to appear again himself. Or has he already left on the tour?"

"Tomorrow, but he....ah.....seemed to feel you wouldn't have time for him."

"Gavin is good for me. I wish you could both believe that."

"I'd like to meet him, Victoria. May I take you both somewhere for dinner? Your previous plans are with him, I presume?"

She didn't immediately reply. Gavin would undoubtedly resent the presence of a third person– especially Sir Terence Cartier. "Thank you, luv, but I don't think so."

"Very well. I won't push it. If you change your mind, you can always ring me."

"I don't expect you to understand, but this man is...is.... I don't know. I can't explain it. I've just never known anyone like him."

"But you see—I do understand," Terry said as he pulled the car over to the curb in front of her hotel. "Because I've had the same experience and believe me, just because you find yourself powerfully drawn to someone does not necessarily make it a good relationship."

"Believe me, I'm...I'm aware of that and I don't expect it to last." Victoria glanced down at her watch. "I....I should go up now. He'll...he'll be waiting for me." She leaned over to give her old friend a quick kiss on the cheek. "Thank you, luv. I'll be in touch, I promise. No, don't get out," she added quickly as he started to open his door.

"All right, dear girl. Take care then." Terry watched as she disappeared through the revolving door into the hotel. There was nothing more he could do.

* * *

Gavin had already arrived back at the suite an hour or so earlier, Martha looking up wordlessly from dusting the living room furniture as he came in. She'd made no comment when he moved in a few days ago, but as Victoria had observed wryly to Terry, she'd already bestowed on him her official frown of disapproval.

He didn't know why, but it bothered him that the housekeeper obviously didn't care for him. For now, however, he gave her a wide berth, settling himself in the bedroom. Spreading the partially filled sheet music out on the bed, Gavin continued work on a song he was composing. Sometimes he wondered why he kept trying. It seemed as though he were forever doomed to scratch out an existence working in one small, out-of-the-way pub or coffee house after another. The larger clubs all wanted rock or American country-western music and stubbornly he refused to compromise.

"I have to clean in here," Martha announced abruptly as she came into the room.

"Aye, that's perrfectly all rright."

"Good." She flicked the switch on the vacuum cleaner and it roared into life. With a good-natured shrug he moved into the living room, but Martha soon followed him--- seemingly in relentless pursuit. This time, however, Gavin moved around out of her sight and pulled the electric plug from the outlet. "What are you doing, sir?" she demanded angrily. "Unlike some people I have work to do. Now if you would please be so kind as to plug in the hoover."

He ignored her plea. "You don't like me, do you? Why? Does my bein' herre make too much worrk forr ye?"

"Begging your pardon, sir. It's not my place to have an opinion one way or the other as to who lives here."

"Coom noo, lass. Ye'rre morre than just Torri's housekeeperr. Ye'rre herr frriend as well, arre ye not?"

Martha looked at him –surprised he was so perceptive. No, she said to herself, I will not allow him to charm me. "That is precisely <u>why</u> I <u>don't</u> like you, Mr. Hamilton!"

"Have ye everr seen Torri sae happy?"

"And where did you ever get that name for her?" Now she sounded positively accusing.

"No one's everr called herr anythin' like that beforre, have they?"

"No," the housekeeper admitted reluctantly. "But that still doesn't make what you're doing right."

"Then ye'rre sayin' it's wrrong to be happy."

"It won't last, Mr. Hamilton. And when it's over–who will be hurt? I'm sure it won't be you."

At that he turned abruptly back to his music. He didn't care to think just then about it ending. Martha left shortly afterwards and when Victoria came in, it was to find a strangely subdued Gavin sitting on the couch staring into the fire. "Is something wrong?" she inquired, coming to curl up beside him and toy with the curls at the nape of his neck.

"Don't!" He pulled away from her.

"Have...have I done something to make you angry with me?"

She sounded so anxious that with considerable effort he pushed away his sober mood. He didn't really understand why he was so depressed anyway, "No, lass, of courrse not." He slipped his arm around her to draw her closer. "Forrgive a Scotsman and his daft moods."

So in spite of its beginning it was a happy evening and that night when they once again made love, she had never known Gavin to be so gentle.

* * *

Peter Harris was just coming out of his office when she arrived at RADA for her class. He knew it was foolish, but he found himself looking forward to seeing her each day. "Good morning, Victoria," he called out, hurrying to catch up with her. "I wonder if I might ask a favor? Would you assist in casting the fall production?"

"What's the play? Do I know it?"

"I would say you do. It's Enid Bagnold's *The Chalk Garden*."

"Ah, yes." She smiled. "It does sound familiar." Rebecca would be a perfect Madrigal, she thought: the large doe-like eyes, the thin, pale face with the high prominent cheekbones, the light brown hair pulled severely back in a chignon. Moreover, her classwork thus far had shown a poignancy which would suit the role ideally. "Who's the third member of the committee?"

"Someone new since you were here–Nigel Simmons."

"Peter, whatever happened to Tuck? I've often wondered about him."

"He got the chance to design professionally."

"How marvelous!" By now they had reached their respective classrooms which were directly across the hall from each other and she stopped. "But it's strange I never saw his name. I would have noticed it, I'm sure."

"He couldn't stand the pressure, I'm afraid. He began to drink heavily. The last I knew, he was in an alcoholic treatment center."

"Oh Peter, I'm so sorry!" Impulsively she reached out to touch him on the arm. "Do you know where he is? I'd like to help him if I could."

Briefly he studied her. "You really mean that, don't you?" he said after a moment. "I never knew you at all, I guess."

"Very few people did in those days. But what about Tuck?"

"Once he was discharged from the center, he dropped out of sight. No one really knows what happened to him."

By then the students were arriving for class. It was common gossip the two of them had been lovers when Victoria was a RADA student and many slowed their steps to stare at them. Unintentionally the scene had an air of intimacy to it with her hand still resting on his arm. "Auditions at eleven, Victoria, if you can manage," Peter said at last as he turned to go.

"Yes, fine. I'm not due on the set until one."

That particular day Victoria's class was doing poetry. Rebecca had chosen for her selection–"The Highwayman", the profoundly moving tale of a girl who fires off a shotgun to warn her lover of his impending capture even though she knows the shot will be fatal to her. The poem is noted for its haunting imagery and her sister's reading did it full justice. Before dismissing the group, Victoria asked her to remain. She would have done the same with any student whose presentation had been especially impressive. As the rest of the class filed out, however, Rebecca stood with her coat already on, her books in her arms–obviously impatient. "I won't keep you," Victoria said lightly. "I only wanted to compliment you on your work today."

"Blood will tell, after all, won't it, sister dear?" It was the same strange smile people had once noted in her–the corners of the mouth turning up only slightly while her eyes remained untouched.

"Yes, I suppose it will." Victoria smiled in return, but now her own eyes were lit with a reflected glow. "But then, too, I think a lonely childhood helps to create a gifted actor. Did you make believe all the time as I did?"

"I can't imagine what you're talking about. My childhood was ideal. My mother and I are still very close as a matter of fact."

"I'm sorry. It was foolish of me to assume our mother treated you as she did me. Of course your childhood was quite different."

"Yes, exactly–it was."

"Rebecca, could...could we go somewhere for...for coffee?" In her eagerness caution was forgotten. "I...I don't know about you, but I'm always hungry by this time in the morning."

"No....no, thank you." The girl turned and started to walk away.

"My treat." Victoria half-ran a few steps to catch up with her. "I remember only too well what it's like to be an impoverished drama student."

"It's...it's not that. I...I receive a very generous allowance."

"Well, my treat anyway." She couldn't see their mother bothering to send an allowance. "We are sisters, after all, and I want to get to know you. It's about time, don't you think, after so many years? How old were we when we last saw each other?"

"You wouldn't remember the last time."

"What?" Such an odd reply! Certainly she would never have forgotten seeing her own sister.

"Nothing. I've....I've got to go." Rebecca hurried away through the crowded corridor–her eyes filling with confused tears. "Who does she think she's fooling anyway," she whispered to herself, wiping the tears away with the back of one hand and smearing her mascara in the process. "She's never given a damn about me!" Then an hour later– make-up painstakingly repaired–she walked into the *Chalk Garden* auditions to discover that Victoria was a member of the casting committee. Well, now I'll find out just how much I can depend on her, she thought. Granted–she's only one of three, but she can certainly convince the others. She owes me that much!

Lacking as she was in any real belief in herself, Rebecca was unaware of just how impressive her audition was-- her reading of the role containing just the proper level of rigidly controlled emotion. Victoria could see that both men were profoundly affected. What Peter didn't realize, she thought sadly, was that much as she had done, her sister was merely playing herself. The next morning Rebecca smiled a tight little smile of triumph as she read her name on the cast list. "Congratulations! I'm so pleased." Unseen, her sister had come up behind her.

Slowly she turned to face Victoria. "Yes, well it certainly pays to be related to a member of the casting committee, doesn't it?"

"I'd never do that! Suppose you turned out to be bloody awful. Wouldn't I look the fool? But as a matter of fact, the decision was unanimous. You got the part because you deserved it." Nothing she could have said, however, would have convinced Rebecca.

* * *

Jamie had gone up to Scotland several days earlier to spend some time with his family. Of course Felicity inquired about Victoria almost as soon as he arrived. He'd managed to put her off, but now they were on the train from Aberdeen to Edinburgh and he knew he could no longer postpone telling her. "Well, Felicity..." Nervously Jamie cleared his throat; he was about to unleash the whirlwind. "I...ah...suppose ye've been wonderrin' why ye've no hearrd frrom yourr English frriend..."

"Ye suppose! Och! Ye ken verra well I've been worrried half to death aboot herr and to make matterrs worrse ye've been givin' me the grrand old rrun arroond. Ye needn't think ye've fooled me forr one minute, Jamie MacDougall, because ye have not!"

He smiled affectionately. No one could sputter quite like his lassie. "Believe me, darrlin', I was only trryin' to find a way to tell ye."

"Tell me what?" Were it not for the fact that they were on a moving train, she would undoubtedly have jumped to her feet and paced as was her habit whenever she was upset. As it was, she could only express her agitation by grabbing Jamie by the coat collar and shaking him.

"All rright...all rright, Felicity," he managed to get out, "I'll tell ye if ye'll just turrn me loose."

"Aye." Reluctantly she let him go and slumped back down in her seat. "But I swearr if ye dinna tell me this verra instant, I'll put the currse of the MacDougalls on ye, I will."

He shook his head. "Have ye forrgotten we'rre distant cousins? So the currse, if therre werre such thing in the firrst place, wouldna worrk on me. Now–if ye'll kindly be quiet forr one minute....."

"Aye, Jamie." Felicity clamped her mouth shut with such grim determination that he couldn't help but laugh. "Jamie!" She screamed so loudly this time that several people turned to look at them. "How is Victorria? Have ye seen herr?"

"No, I haven't." He sighed. "But...ah...someone else has been seeing a grreat deal o' herr."

"Someone else? Noo ye'rre talkin' in rriddles! I swearr I'll...." She stopped short. " 'Tis Gavin, isn't it? Och, why does he have to be that way?"

"Ye said yourrself that Victorria's husband's aboot as warrm as a winterr night in the Hielands. Can ye blame herr forr findin' ourr Gavin sae appealin'?"

" 'Tis him I blame! Him wi' his charrmin' ways!"

"I'm nae surre. It's differrent this time... But ye'll have a chance to judge forr yourrself. She's coomin' along this week-end."

"Oh dearr, Jamie! I'll be sae morrtally embarrrassed! Will they...ah...be sharrin' a rroom, do ye think?"

* * *

Victoria had requested a couple of days off so that she and Gavin could leave for Edinburgh early Thursday morning. She was grateful Tony didn't ask any questions, but then he'd probably guessed the reason. Her name was now being linked regularly with Gavin's in the tabloids. For some reason or other that fact merely amused her and thinking about it just then as they drove north along the motorway, she actually laughed out loud or perhaps she was simply laughing from pure happiness.

"What is it, lass?" Was it only his imagination, Gavin wondered, or did she look especially beautiful this morning? Dressed in a tweed pants suit and a dark brown turtleneck jumper, her hair was held back from her face with a gold barrette and she wore a bare minimum of make-up. It was becoming increasingly difficult for him to remember the Victoria who had lost him his bet just a few years before.

"It seems we've...ah...begun to make the gossip columns," she observed lightly, reaching over to touch him on the arm.

"And that trruly doesna botherr ye, lass?"

"There's just doesn't seem to be any point in being so secretive."

"Aye, Torri, I agree, but then 'tis easierr forr me. When we walk into a rrestaurrant orr a club, I ken 'tis not me the people arre starrin' at."

"Well, if they're female, it very well could be."

"Aye." He sighed in mock despair. "Can I help it–bein' such a brraw laddie?" She laughed. "Rready forr a bit o' brreakfast, then?"

"Yes--and I'm sure you are. I've never known anyone who could eat so much and so often."

"And ye, as I believe I've alrready noted, dinna eat enough to keep a mavis alive."

"A what?"

" 'Tis a wee birrd–aboot like a thrrush, I believe."

The next exit indicated food available. It was only one of those fast food cafeterias which had begun to appear in Britain, specializing– as such places all over the world– in runny eggs, cold, soggy toast, weak coffee and no atmosphere, but Victoria and Gavin noticed none of this. They had a marvelously silly meal laughing together over nothing and enjoying each other's company immensely.

Once they were on the road again, however, Gavin suddenly fell silent, wondering how best to bring up what could be an awkward subject. "Arre..arre ye lookin' forwarrd to seein' Felicity again?" he asked finally.

"Of course I am. She's one of my favorite people."

"Then ye..ah...willna find it embarrrassin'–herr knowin' that you and I...ah..arre...."

"I already told you I wouldn't." She paused, searching his face intently. "But I have a feeling you will."

"Dinna be daft," he denied vehemently. "Jamie and Felicity ken verra well the way I am wi' a lass."

"And that's all I am, after all, aren't I–just another lass!" She didn't know why it hurt her so much to say that. Gavin, on his part, could think of no reply. Victoria was like no other woman he'd ever known. Yet to dispute her accusation might give her cause to hope for a lasting relationship and as lonely as his life seemed at times, he had begun to accept the fact that he was incapable of any permanence. "That was unfair of me," she went on quickly when he continued to say nothing. "After all, we've both known from the beginning there would come a time when it would be over between us."

"Aye–but 'twill always be a warrm memorry forr me, Torri."

"For me, too." There was a long pause while they both tried desperately to think of something to fill it. "Is that all you wanted to say?" Victoria went on finally. "About Felicity?"

He cleared his throat. "Ah...no...therre was actually...ah...soomthin' else of a...ah... morre prractical naturre. Ye might say it...ah....concerrns the...ah...logistics of the week-end. Well.... ah....not the...ah...entirre week-end—only...ah..cerrtain parrts of it."

"What in bloody hell are you talking about? I realize you Scots are a muddle-headed lot, but if possible you're making even less sense than..." Suddenly she stopped, stared at him for a long minute and burst into laughter.

"What is so damned funny?"

"You weren't by any chance referring to the sleeping arrangements, were you?"

"Aye!" He stared straight ahead, refusing to look at her.

Victoria glanced over at him. A shade of red remarkably similar to the color of his hair was emerging from the collar of his shirt and creeping gradually up toward his ears. Could Gavin actually be blushing? For some reason, however, she sensed this wasn't the time to tease him. "If Felicity and Jamie know about us," she said quietly, "wouldn't it be ridiculous to pretend otherwise?"

"Aye." Still the monosyllabic response.

Victoria couldn't understand why he was upset. She had simply assumed they would share a room. "Gavin....I want to be with you,"

"Aye, lass...and I with you. I just didna want it to be uncomforrtable forr ye."

"Thank you for being so considerate." She wished she could sit closer to him, perhaps slip an arm through his and rest her head on his shoulder. "Damn these bucket seats!" she muttered. At that he laughed as well and they both relaxed.

* * *

The other couple had been waiting in the hotel lobby since shortly before eleven. It was now well past midnight and Felicity's mood was getting worse with every passing minute.. "Ye could have stopped him!" she sputtered at one point. "Ye ken that verra well."

"And just exactly how? Ye ken how Gavin is when he gets his mind set on a lass."

"That was differrent! The lass has neverr been a frriend of mine beforre!"

"Coom noo–ye've known a lot o' the gurrls he's rromanced."

"Victorria's English!" Felicity's tone indicated plainly that this should make the whole thing clear. Jamie looked at her blankly. "I swearr, Jamie MacDougall, ye'rre as thick between the earrs as a West Coast ha'ah! She's my firrst English chum! At first I thought she was everr sae grrand and elegant, but then I rrealized that was all a pose. Sometimes she's like a wee lost lamb and I...."

Just then Victoria came in alone through the front entrance of the hotel. "Felicity!" She ran across the lobby to hug her. "Oh, it's so good to see you! When you left New York, I didn't know when we'd see each other again and now here we are!"

Her friend returned the embrace with equal fervor, more determined now than ever to protect her. "Aye, herre we arre!" She hugged her a second time a little harder and then held her away at arm's length. ""So let's have a look at ye noo." The signs were unmistakable. Even after the long drive the other woman glowed. "Soo–wherre's Gavin?" But she sounded as though she had inquired as to the whereabouts of Jack the Ripper.

For a brief instant Victoria's smile dimmed. Was Felicity angry with Gavin for some reason? How could anyone be angry with Gavin? "He's...he's parking the car. Hello, Jamie."

"Hello, Victoria." He also looked at her intently. There was no doubt that she was incredibly lovely, but was that all his friend saw in her? He didn't know what to think.

Gavin followed Victoria into the lobby by just a few minutes, carrying their luggage. Coming up to the three of them, he put down the suitcases, feigning terrible fatigue. "I think the lass only brrought me with herr to tote herr barrge. What did ye pack, Torri?" he inquired, winking at her broadly, "brricks? How arre ye, Felicity? 'Tis grrand to see ye."

"Victorria, why don't we go on into the barr. We thought we should all have a wee deoch-'n'-dorris to welcoom ye to Edinburra." The Scots girl turned abruptly and walked away.

Victoria looked at Gavin as if to say–"What's wrong with her?" But then she shrugged and followed Felicity. A few minutes later the two women had settled themselves in the small, cozy pub connected with the hotel. Run as a private club for the guests, it managed to escape the strict British curfew laws. Victoria asked for brandy; Felicity, of course, ordered Scotch. "What is a wee deoch-and-doris anyway?" Victoria asked laughingly at last, hoping to lighten the mood.

"Oh...ah...'tis a last drrink beforre goin' to...ah. I mean beforre retirrin' forr the...ah...I mean....so..." She cleared her throat. "I've been...ah...wonderrin' aboot ye. I'd been expectin' to hearr frrom ye–knowin' ye werre back in the U.K. and all."

"I....I've been rather busy, you know." She had picked up a discarded swizzle stick and was making nervous patterns on the tablecloth as she talked.

"Aye, I suppose ye have." There was a long silence then lasting until the waitress brought their drinks. Unconsciously Victoria kept glancing toward the entrance. Having Gavin here would make things easier. Finally Felicity couldn't stand it any longer. "Can ye no stand to be away frrom him forr even five minutes?" she asked bitterly.

Victoria had actually been staring at the door at that precise moment and now she looked quickly away. "Sorry, I...I wasn't aware I was...." Hurt tears filled her eyes. "Please, I...I know what you must think of me, but I can't help myself. After all," she added weakly after a brief, pleading pause, "you yourself told me Gavin had a way with the lassies."

"Aye, but it seems ye no heeded the warrnin'."

"I...I've just never known anyone like him. But I've always realized it wouldn't last and when it's over, I'll go back to Jason, if....if he'll have me."

"So ye do still love your husband?"

"Of course I do, Felicity." Her voice was choked with emotion. "I...I realize he wasn't very kind to you that night, but he is a good man."

"Then how can ye do this to him?"

Unable to think of a reply, Victoria stared down at the snifter of brandy still untouched on the table in front of her. Where could Gavin possibly be for so long? Involuntarily she glanced toward the door again and just then the two men did indeed appear. "Did ye miss us?" Gavin asked jokingly as he and Jamie slid into the booth, each beside the expected female.

"One of us did anyway." Felicity noted with deepening despair the easy, familiar way with which he slipped an arm around Victoria's shoulders, drawing her closer to him.

He chuckled good-naturedly. "And I have a definite feelin' it wasn't you."

"Aye." She subsided into a ferocious silence.

The two men also ordered Scotch. "Why do I feel outnumbered?" Victoria made yet another weak attempt at humor.

Gavin was the only one to notice anything out of the ordinary about her tone. "Perrhaps ye tirred then, Torri?"

"I'm all right–really."

"No, I dinna think ye arre. Coom, lass." He stood up, moving back a little so that Victoria could walk in front of him and without another word she slid along the seat and got to her feet as well. "We'll see ye in the morrnin' then. I believe we'rre due to check oot the coffee hoose at ten."

For a few moments after they'd been left alone the other couple remained silent. "I tell ye–'tis differrent," Jamie insisted at last.

"I've seen him just as daft overr otherr lasses," Felicity stubbornly maintained. "He'll get overr herr soon enough."

* * *

Victoria and Gavin, meanwhile, had moved slowly across the deserted, dimly lit lobby, arms about each other's waists. The lift was standing there–empty, waiting. They stepped inside. Gavin pushed the button and the door slid shut. "Thank you," Victoria whispered turning to face him.

He slipped both arms around her waist and she leaned back to look up at him. "Forr what, lass?" He smiled down at her.

"For realizing I wanted to leave."

"And why couldn't ye simply have said, 'Gavin, I'd like to leave'? 'Twould have been verra simple actually." Before she could reply, however, the lift came to a stop at their floor and he took her hand to lead the way to their room.

They were both soon undressed. Gavin was the first one into bed and lying propped up against the pillows with his hands clasped behind his head, he was watching Victoria who was seated at the small dressing table. She'd already removed her make-up and at the moment she was brushing her hair. Happening to glance up all at once, she noticed his reflection behind her in the mirror, his dark brown eyes fixed on her with an unnerving intensity. "What in hell is so interesting?"

"Can I no look at ye then, lass?"

"I'd rather you didn't."

"What's trroublin ye, Torri?"

"Why does something have to be bothering me just because I object to being studied like some specimen in a laboratory?" Her voice rose sharply.

"Och, noo, lassie!" Gavin was determined to jolly her out of her bad mood. "Ye look farr too luvly sittin' therre to be some ugly squirrmy old thing in a bottle."

"Will you please just leave me alone? Why do you always have to try to be so bloody amusing?"

"Torri–lass–what is it? Can ye no tell me?" He got out of bed then to come and kneel in front of her. Tears rushed into Victoria's eyes. Mutely she shook her head. "Coom, lass," he said firmly, standing up and holding out a hand to her. She allowed him to lead her over to the bed, sitting down beside him. "Did Felicity say soomthin' to oopset ye? Is that it?" Victoria had been looking down to where Gavin still held her hand–now between both of his–, but at his question her eyes came up to meet his. Her lower lip began to tremble and the tears spilled over. "Och, ye look just like my sisterr Meghan when she was naethin' but a wee bairrnie." He reached over to the bedside and pulled two or three tissues from the box to dab under her eyes. "Will ye tell me noo what Felicity said to ye?"

"N...n...nothing I haven't already told myself," she whispered finally.

"And what's that?"

"That...that I'm foolish to throw away a good marriage for the sake of a brief, meaningless affair, that....."

Jumping to his feet, Gavin strode to the door. "God damn that meddlin' little blatherrskate! I'll teach herr a lesson she'll no be forrgettin' for soom time!" Victoria had never seen his frame of mind alter so abruptly.

"Please, she means well." She came over to where he stood with one hand on the doorknob, resting her hand imploringly on his arm. "Felicity's one of the first real friends I've ever had."

Gavin's anger dissipated as suddenly as it had appeared. Gently he caressed her cheek and then raised her face to kiss her. "Aye, lass." He still held her chin so that she had no choice but to continue to look up at him. "And havin' a frriend is verra imporrtant to ye, isn't it?" She nodded. "But I will speak to herr in the morrnin'," he insisted. "If we find joy in each otherr's coomp'ny, it canna be wrrong forr us to be togetherr even if it's only forr a wee bit and she should keep herr opinions to herrself." A few minutes later when they were both in bed, Gavin propped himself up on one elbow to look down at her lying beside him. "Therre's just one morre thing I want to say, Torri. When the time cooms and ye feel it's overr forr us–when ye feel 'tis time forr ye to rreturrn to yourr husband--ye need only tell me. I willna question yourr decision."

"Oh no, Gavin, don't say that," she pleaded. "I can't bear to think of it being over-- not yet."

"All rright, lass, all rright." He gathered her into his arms and held her close. "I willna mention it again."

It was nearly an hour before they finally slept and even then it wasn't over. Later that night Victoria had another of her panic attacks and as he held her and comforted her until she was once more asleep, Gavin would gladly have hurled Felicity MacDougall from the highest turret of Edinburgh Castle. Finally, however, he slept again as well and the rest of the night passed peacefully. In fact it was Jamie's knock which awakened them both the next morning. The two men were due at the coffee house, he reminded them, and Felicity had wanted him to tell Victoria she'd meet her downstairs for breakfast.

Gavin hurried to shower and shave, dressing in jeans and a black, turtleneck pullover. For the first time in their relationship they were oddly ill-at-ease with each other. They talked very little and of course neither mentioned the events of the previous night. "Afterr our meetin' Jamie and I will catch ye oop forr lunch and a bit o' sightseein'," he promised Victoria as finally he slipped on a suede jacket and headed for the door.

"Haven't you all seen Edinburgh many times?"

"Aye." He grinned. "But a Scot neverr tirres o' showin' off 'Auld Reekie'–especially to a Englisherr."

"Oh, I see. And I suppose it's vastly superior to London?"

"Aye, of courrse." Gavin still stood at the door. Victoria had put on her underwear and tights while he was in the shower and was heading for the bathroom now to do her make-up. "Torri?"

"Yes?" She stopped, turning to face him.

"Coom–lass." He held out his arms to her.

"Oh, Gavin!" She half-ran across the room to him, dropping her make-up kit on the bed as she passed. She came into his arms and they kissed–one long, lingering kiss followed by several short ones-- but even then he postponed leaving. It continued to amaze him that even after more than a month this woman still affected him so strongly.

* * *

Jamie and Felicity's argument concerning Gavin had continued into the early hours of the morning with neither able to convince the other of anything and now as they waited for their old friend to join them, each was determined to watch him closely, thus finally proving the other person wrong. They had only been in the hotel coffee shop about fifteen minutes when he came in. The hostess escorted him to their table and handed him a menu, but she did not immediately leave. Instead she hovered over him–checking the milk, the sugar, the pepper and salt, pouring coffee, even straightening his place mat and silverware–all in an obvious attempt to get his attention. Her efforts were wasted. Gavin was apparently studying the menu.

"Therre, do ye see what I mean?" Felicity observed under her breath. "Do ye see the way she's flirrtin' wi' him?"

"Aye," Jamie agreed–also in a whisper. "But do ye also ken he's payin' herr no mind?"

At last the woman gave up and withdrew. "Torri'll be doon in a bit," Gavin remarked a moment or so later still without looking up. "You lassies wi' yourr prrimpin' and fussin', I declarre I....." At this point, however, he glanced up to find them both staring at him and he fell silent. There was a long, awkward pause. "So," he continued finally, "it seems we arre simply pickin' it oop frrom wherre we left off last night."

"I willna say anotherr worrd," Felicity promised.

"No, but ye'll glarre at me the entirre week-end and ye'll no miss an opporrtunity to lecturre Torri aboot what a thorroughly dastarrdly lad I am."

"Please, both of ye," Jamie put in. "Canna we just forrget it and have a grrand time togetherr?"

"I'm sorrry, laddie. I will no have herr oopsettin' Torri wi' soomthin' that's none o' herr business."

"But ye see it <u>is</u> my business," Felicity insisted, "what wi' Victorria bein' my frriend. I'm only thinkin' of what's best forr herr."

"Oh, I see," Gavin snorted, "and so noo ye'rre the all-knowin' authorrity on what's best for everrabody."

"Do ye love herr?" she demanded.

"I've no prromised Torri anythin'," he replied. "But neitherr have I forrced m'self on herr." They both couldn't help observing that Gavin had ignored the question. This meant, Jamie was sure, that he really did love Victoria, but was embarrassed to admit it. Felicity, on the other hand, was equally positive that he didn't love her and was ashamed to admit it.

"And what aboot herr husband?" she asked.

"Please, Felicity." Jamie made one final attempt to restore peace. "He's rright, ye know. 'Tis none o' yourr business. And if we dinna orrderr brreakfast, we'll be late."

"I've lost my appetite!" Gavin growled. "So then, Jamie, arre we goin'?" He stood up to leave.

"No, please!" Felicity grabbed him by the arm. He looked down at her upturned, pleading face and his expression softened slightly. "Please, I canna bearr to have ye crross wi' me," she went on, still holding onto him even though she fully realized that had he really wanted to leave, she would have been incapable of stopping him. He hesitated for another moment, but then finally sat down again.

"We still have time to eat soomthin', Gavin," the other man suggested.

"Aye, all rright," he agreed grudgingly. "A coople o' frried eggs, perhaps...ah...toast and sausages."

"I'll find the waitress." Jamie got quickly to his feet and walked away.

Felicity glanced across the table, hoping to see something in Gavin's expression which would tell her he had indeed forgiven her. "Please tell me ye'rre no still angrry with me," she said at last.

"Och–noo. Dinna fash yourrself." He patted her on the hand. "I'm surre ye meant well."

"Thank you, Gavin." She smiled at him, but she wished she could shake the uneasy feeling that something was terribly wrong.

About a half hour later, the two men having left for their meeting, her friend joined her--fresher and younger-looking than she could ever remember seeing. But what would happen when the day came, as Felicity was sure it would, when Gavin was no longer a part of her life. "Good morning." Victoria smiled warmly although seeing the other girl made her uncomfortable all over again.

"Good morrnin'." She was determined the rest of their time together would be pleasant. "I'm afrraid I was sae hungrry that I ate wi' the lads, but I'll keep ye coomp'ny. Then I thought we could look in the shops."

"You know me. I'm never hungry in the morning. Just tea, please," Victoria told the waitress who approached the table just then, "and toast..and..ah...one fried egg, I guess."

"Yes, Miss Windsor."

"It must seem everr sae queerr," Felicity observed, " to have everraone know ye."

"I'm so used to it by now that I don't really think much about it." She laughed–a little self-consciously. "There are times, however, when it can be damned inconvenient."

"Ye...ye mean–goin' aboot wi' Gavin?"

She nodded.

"Victorria, I...I do want to say just one morre thing...."

"Yes?"

Felicity had heard her voice tremble slightly even on that one word and she felt a rush of pity for the lovely woman. "Ye'rre all confused, arren't ye?"

Victoria's eyes filled with tears. "You can't possibly imagine," she said softly, "the effect Gavin has on me. I..."

"Ye forrget he's been my frriend for morre than half my life. I ken verra well....."

"No, I....I don't mean the effect he has on women in general. I've never known anyone with whom I could relax so completely. I've never felt so happy or...or laughed so much or...or...." Finally she gave up trying to express her feelings and merely shrugged. There was a moment or two of uncomfortable silence before the waitress brought her breakfast and at once she busied herself with buttering the toast, putting pepper and salt on the egg, adding milk and sugar to her tea–glad to have something to do.

"I imagine you'd like to find soomthin' forr Olivia," Felicity suggested at last.

"Yes." Victoria glanced up as she stirred her tea–smiling gratefully for the change of subject. "I was thinking about a kilt actually. She'd love that. She liked...Gavin so...so much."

"He's always had a way with children. I've seen him with his niece and nephew–his brrotherr's childrren. Has he told ye aboot Rhuaridh?"

"A little. They're very different, aren't they?"

"Aye. Soomtimes it's harrd to believe they'rre even rrelated."

The tension further eased as Victoria ate her breakfast and they began to chat easily and naturally about Gavin. They enjoyed a pleasant couple of hours shopping and by the time they met the men for lunch, they had rediscovered the joy they'd always found in their friendship.

In the afternoon the four of them began their exploration of Edinburgh with a tour of the Castle. Others might have professional tour guides, but they had Gavin. A man who not only knew Scottish history, but cared profoundly about it, his commentary was nevertheless liberally sprinkled with humor, in particular remarks about the English. Before long they had gathered quite a crowd and the joy of the afternoon dimmed slightly for Victoria. Perhaps she was still uneasy about being seen in public with Gavin; perhaps she secretly resented his bestowing his easy charm on anyone except herself.

When they left the Castle, however, walking along High Street (Edinburgh's famed Royal Mile) on their trek back to the hotel, his attention was once again concentrated on her. An arm around her shoulders, he paused frequently to point something out to her.

" 'Tis grrand–sharrin' all this wi' ye, lass," he whispered in her ear at one point, tightening his grip around her shoulders as he spoke. She looked up at him and he leaned down to kiss her lightly. Fortunately neither noticed the other couple was watching them closely.

That evening Victoria and Felicity enjoyed the men's performance at the coffee house. All of Saturday was spent sightseeing and the evening again at the coffee house. By now they were having a marvelous time together and it seemed a shame to have it all come to an end on Sunday when the other three had to put Felicity on the train heading north and begin the drive back to London. Gavin promised, however, that he'd bring Victoria to the Highland Gathering being held at the end of October to celebrate Jamie and Felicity's betrothal.

* * *

After the long week-end with Victoria Gavin found the following morning strangely empty. The coffee house where he was still working was closed on Mondays and so he got the idea of surprising her at RADA. It happened that as he slipped into the back of the darkened auditorium, Rebecca and a male student were just concluding their presentation of the balcony scene from *Romeo and Juliet.* He had no way of knowing, of course, who the girl was. Although Victoria had mentioned her sister to him, there was no physical resemblance.

With the scene over the two actors sat on the edge of the stage to listen to the critique of their performance. Gavin soon discovered as the house lights came up that from his particular seat he was unable to see Victoria, but he thought it better not to attract attention to himself by moving. What she was saying meant little to him–he heard words like motivation, concentration–but after a while he became fascinated with the mere sound of her voice in the otherwise quiet auditorium. At last she dismissed the class and he stood up as well, intending once he was sure everyone had left, to sneak up behind her and kiss her on the back of the neck. As he started down the aisle, however, he saw the young actress who had just done the scene come over to speak to her and he stopped to wait until they'd finished their discussion.

Although Victoria was facing him, she was absorbed in the conversation and so for the first several seconds she failed to notice him. "You know perfectly well that isn't true," she was saying. "If I seem to judge your work more severely, it's only because I feel you're capable of more. It has nothing whatsoever to do with our personal relationship."

"I don't believe you," the girl replied. "You're afraid people will find out why I got the lead in the fall production so now you ridicule everything I do."

"And you know what I think? I think you're trying to prove you didn't deserve the role by deliberately giving poorly prepared performances in class."

By now Gavin realized he'd unintentionally become privy to what was meant to be a private conversation. He was trying to find some way of leaving unobserved–perhaps wait outside–when Victoria happened to glance past the other girl and see him. Her eyes widened in happy surprise and whatever she'd been about to say flew from her mind.

"Well?" Rebecca prompted impatiently.

"Yes...ah..." She tried to remember what she'd been talking about, but her mind was a blank. Gavin was enjoying the obviously unsettling effect he had on her and now he winked. The corners of her mouth twitched.

"What is so damned funny?" her sister demanded. "I suppose you think it's amusing when I feel you've made an unjust criticism of my work."

"No, it's not you. It's...ah..." Gavin executed a few steps of the Highland Fling and she collapsed helplessly into laughter. "Oh, will you behave yourself!" she gasped.

Finally Rebecca became aware someone was standing behind her and she whirled about to confront whoever had had the audacity to interrupt them. The handsomest man she'd ever seen smiled at her, his dark eyes crinkling disarmingly at the corners. "Good morrnin' to ye, lassie."

"What do you think I am?" she snapped. "A dog?"

Oddly the words struck Victoria as familiar. "Did I ever say that to you?" she asked Gavin with a slight laugh.

At the distance she was standing from him in the still dimly lit auditorium she was unable to see the expression which passed across his face. "Aye, but I didna think ye rrememberred."

Now Victoria was really puzzled. "Remembered what?"

"Rrememberred sayin' that to me."

Rebecca continued to stand there during all of this, looking back and forth from one of them to the other as though she were watching some strange new game for which she didn't understand the rules. All at once she realized that this impudent man, whoever he was, had to have been standing behind her for some time. "You...you knew he was there, didn't you?" she accused her sister. "And you let me go on talking!"

"No, luv, really. I....I only noticed him right at the end."

"I....I don't believe you."

Victoria's smile was now very sad. "I know you don't trust me, Rebecca, but then we weren't brought up to trust, were we? Gavin, perhaps you've heard enough by now to realize this is my half-sister, Rebecca Montgomery."

He nodded. "Torri has told me how happy she was to have found ye, lass, and I'm trruly sorrry if I intrruded. Ye see, I didna ken who ye werre at firrst."

Rebecca stared up at Gavin. She'd....she'd told him about her just as though she....she really mattered. Then suddenly a new awareness dawned on her; this had to be the man with whom her sister's name had been linked in the gossip columns. Well, she'd seen him here with her and now she knew it was all true. "You're Gavin Hamilton, aren't you?" she said. "Are you really her lover?"

He opened his mouth to protest, but Victoria silenced him with a gesture. "Yes, Rebecca, he is."

She had, of course, expected her sister to deny the accusation. "Well, I....I think that's disgusting!" Snatching up her things, the girl ran from the room.

When they were alone, Gavin took Victoria in his arms. "Torri, I'm sorrry. I only wanted to surrprrise ye, take ye forr soom lunch. I neverr expected to....."

"It's...it's not you." She looked up at him. "It's Rebecca. She....she won't let me close. No matter how hard I try....."

"Ye mustna frret yourrself, lass. Ye'll win herr overr eventually." He bent to kiss her lightly. "Noo how aboot that lunch?"

"Yes, all right." Victoria turned away to pick up her purse and briefcase. "But I actually said that to you once? When?" He didn't immediately reply. Instead he picked up her coat from where she'd thrown it on a chair and slipped it over her shoulders. If he told her now, she might assume all of this between them was nothing more than a renewed attempt to win his wager, but at the same time he felt the need to be completely honest with her. "Gavin, what is it?" She stopped and turned to look up at him again, searching his face.

He lightly caressed her cheek with the back of his hand. "Nothin' terrrible, lass---only soomthin' ye could misunderrstand if I didna explain it prroperrly."

"Can we go somewhere and talk then?"

"Actually I was thinkin' of pickin' oop a few things and havin' a picnic in the carr."

"You always have the most marvelous ideas!" she exclaimed, slipping her arm through his. "How do you ever manage it?"

"Ye'rre easy to please." He placed his other hand over hers where it lay on his arm. "The simplest things make ye happy."

"Just being with you makes me happy," she murmured looking up at him as they walked.

They said little more until they had stopped at a delicatessen where Gavin bought cold meats, bread, cheese and wine and they were parked near Hampton Court. With the car motor turned off they unpacked the food and he poured wine into paper cups while Victoria held them. Finally they were settled.

"When was it, Gavin?" she asked again, sipping her wine.

"When was what?" he replied, hoping to distract her. He still was unsure how she would react.

"You know perfectly well what I'm talking about. The first time you called me 'lassie', I said I wasn't a dog?"

"Aye."

"Are you sure? I don't remember."

"I know you don't."

"Gavin!"

"All rright. All rright. I'll begin by askin' ye a question. When and wherre did we meet forr the firrst time?'

"What a silly question! New York–last spring at the MacAllisters'–of course."

"Suppose I was to tell ye we met thrree yearrs beforre that–rright herre in Lundon?"

"Oh, that's impossible. I would have remembered."

""I'm that unforrgettable, hm?" His eyes twinkled.

"Gavin, really! But seriously–I...I could never have met you and forgotten it."

"Thank ye, lass, forr that." He smiled at her. "But the fact is, we did meet in the sprring of 1968."

"Where, Gavin? How?"

"Backstage in yourr drressin' rroom. Some...ah...frriends bet me twenty pounds apiece that I couldna get a date with ye. I...ah...lost the wagerr. Ye thrreatened to call a bobby and ye thrrew me oot."

" I...I do remember. That...that was you? You know...when...when you walked into the MacAllisters' living room, I had the strangest feeling I'd seen you somewhere before. But tell me, how much did I cost you in all?"

"One hundrred pounds!"

"Oh, Gavin, I'm so sorry!"

She sounded so sincere that he laughed. " 'Tis all rright, lassie." She turned to face him then and he could see tears in her eyes. "What is it, Torri? I've oopset ye, haven't I, wi' my foolish storry. I should neverr have told ye at all."

"Oh no, that's not it. I just wish that you'd won your bet, that we...well, that is..."

"Aye, lass." He touched her face. "But 'tis no matterr as long as we met at last."

"But you see–if we'd met then, I.... Oh, never mind. Can we go away again over the week-end?" she went on quickly, changing the subject.

"Aye, lass–of courrse." For some reason the conversation had begun to bother Gavin as well and he was more than willing to talk about something else. Apparently they were both indeed successful in putting the moment from their minds and yet their lovemaking of that night held a special and oddly bittersweet urgency.

It was about eight o'clock the next morning when the ringing of the telephone awakened Victoria. Reluctantly she stirred from her nest in Gavin's arms and reached for the receiver. She was instantly wide awake. "Jason...ah....hello," she managed to say. "What...what are you ringing up now for? It must be the middle of the night in New York. Is....is Olivia all right?"

"Everything's fine, Victoria." His quiet voice hadn't changed. "But I'm not in New York. I'm at Heathrow Airport." He couldn't have said what she thought he said. He couldn't possibly be in England. "Did you hear me, dear?" he went on when she did not respond. "I said I'm at Heathrow."

"Well, what in hell are doing there?"

"I am your husband, after all," he replied just as calmly. God–why was he always so damned in control? "And when you kept postponing your return home, I felt I should be with you. But we don't have to talk over the telephone. I'll see you in a little while, Victoria." Numb with shock, she again made no reply. "Victoria?"

"Yes...ah...Jason. I'll....I'll see you soon." For a moment or so after she hung up the receiver she continued to lie there in bed, one hand clutching the sheet to her as she'd done all through the conversation as if–miraculously–Jason were able to see her naked breasts over the telephone. "Gavin!" She leaned over and shook him. "Gavin! Wake up! You have to get out of here!"

"Hm—what, Torri? It canna be that late."

"Will you listen to me? Scrambling out of bed, she slipped into her robe. "My husband just rang up from Heathrow. He's on his way here. You have to collect your things and get out!"

"All....all rright," he murmured, turning over and burrowing deeper into the pillow. "Just a few minutes morre, lassie."

"Don't you dare go back to sleep!" Victoria hurried around to his side of the bed and seizing hold of his arm, began to pull at him. "Get up and get out now!"

"All...all rright, Torri." At last–thank God–Gavin was out of bed. "Just my showerr and shave and I'll be gone."

"You don't have time for that! Can't you get it through your thick skull? My husband's in England!" Her eyes filled with tears. "Please, Gavin, please! He can't find you here! Please!"

At last he was fully awake and now he understood. "Aye...aye, Torri. I'll leave as quickly as I can. Dinna frret yourrself, lass." All the time he was packing Victoria kept urging him on, begging him to hurry and in less than half an hour he was standing in the middle of the living room, holding his bags. "Well noo, 'tis been grrand."

"Yes...yes. Will you please get out of here!"

"Ye can always rring me oop, ye know, Torri, if ye have a frree evenin'."

"Gavin–neither of us ever expected this to last," she pleaded. "You said once that I only had to tell you when it was over. Well, I'm telling you now—it's over!"

Reluctantly he moved toward the door. "Aye, I ken that. At least forr the noo."

"No, not for now. Forever. Why can't you just accept that?"

"Aye, Torri, aye." He opened the door. "Ye'll take carre o' yourr bonny wee self, then."

"Will you stop all that Scottish drivel and get the hell out of here?!"

"Aye...aye, I'm goin'." Stepping outside, he shut the door behind himself and moved away down the hall without looking back.

With a sigh of relief Victoria turned to walk back into the bedroom to get dressed before Jason arrived, but partway across the living room her gaze happened to fall on Gavin's pipe, still resting in an ashtray on an end table. "Damn him! Damn him!" she shrieked and picking up the pipe, she hurled it into the fireplace where it shattered against the bricks. "Oh, no! Oh, no!" She began to cry and kneeling down on the hearth, she picked up the pieces, cradling them in her lap and sobbing as she hadn't sobbed since that night nearly two years ago when she'd put Olivia on the plane to send her back to her father.

Chapter 23

Jason gazed disinterestedly out the window of the taxi at the flat, brown autumn landscape, wondering vaguely why Victoria had always said England was so beautiful.

Victoria–his unexpected arrival had obviously not been a pleasant surprise and.... and that could mean only one thing. All the gossip he'd been reading in the newspapers– every filthy rumor his so-called friends had been more than willing to pass on to him– was all true. Well, after all, he had to remember the kind of life she'd led and once back in London under the unfortunate influence of her theatrical friends, he supposed it was inevitable. Had...had he been there just now even while she was talking to him, this....this Gavin Hamilton–lying next to her, touching her. Jason was afraid he was going to be sick.

* * *

At last Victoria had stood up again and still clutching the broken pipe in both hands, she walked through the bedroom into the bath where she dropped the pieces one at a time into a small wastebasket, noting with satisfaction how they sank out of sight among the soiled tissues. Well, that was that, then.

Somehow she washed herself and chose what to wear. A severely plain, dark blue wool dress with a single strand of pearls struck her as appropriate: demure and virginal. She sat down at her vanity to do her hair and make-up, but instead of beginning at once, she stared unmoving at her reflection. What would it be like, she wondered, being with him again after nearly six weeks? And how could she ever bring herself to tell him about.... For there was no doubt in her mind she would confess her infidelity–only when and how. With a long sigh she picked up her hairbrush, but she kept dropping it and finally she just grabbed a scarf from the drawer. She didn't even bother about the color. What in the hell difference did it make anyway? Doing her make-up was even more difficult. She couldn't stop her hands from shaking and her eyes continually brimmed with tears, causing the liner and mascara to run. She had to begin over again three times.

Her husband would certainly be here any minute now. How could she ever manage it all? Perhaps if she made a pot of coffee. That would give her something to do until he arrived and drinking it together would help to ease them through the first few minutes. She was plugging in the percolator when the doorbell sounded and she jumped, knocking the pot over. The cover came loose and coffee spilled out onto the counter, the water trickling over the edge onto the floor. The bell rang a second time–longer and more insistently. Somehow Victoria walked to the door and opened it.

"Hello, dear." Jason smiled at her as sweetly as ever.

"Ah... welcome to England. Please... come in." She returned his smile, hoping he didn't notice hers was forced, and stepping back, she held open the door for him. Coming into the flat and back into my life, Victoria thought. Involuntarily she shivered.

"Are you cold?" he inquired solicitously.

"A....a little, I guess. The...ah...bedroom's over there," she explained pointing. "I....I'm making coffee." She hurried back into the kitchen without waiting for him to reply. She cleaned up the mess, pausing often in her work to glance nervously toward the bedroom. I... I should have checked, she thought, to see if...if he....he left anything else. But what does it matter? I'm....I'm going to tell Jason anyway...eventually. She laughed out loud at that, but it wasn't a happy laugh. Finally she got the percolator started again and brought cups and saucers and milk and sugar out into the living room.

Jason came from the bedroom at almost the same moment. Victoria searched his face trying to learn whether he'd discovered anything to make her confession easier or at least cause it to come sooner, but his expression revealed nothing. "Very pleasant suite you have here, Victoria," he remarked evenly, sitting down at the table.

"I'm....I'm glad you like it. But...but why....why did you come?"

"I told you that on the telephone."

"You....you did?" She felt stupid, but then Jason always had a way of making her see herself as somehow inadequate.

"Yes, dear," he went on patiently. "Since you continued to postpone your return home....."

"That's....that's not true! The producers <u>requested</u> I remain in England somewhat longer than originally planned. The more actual locations we can use here, the fewer sets will have to be built in New York." Victoria experienced a wave of guilt even as she recited the oh-so reasonable explanation for her prolonged stay in London–the same one she'd used in her letters. How many times had Tony asked whether she objected to remaining?

"They should have considered that before they asked you to do the series." Was it her imagination or was there a slight edge to his voice. "As it is," he went on–no, the edge was definitely there–"they have caused you to neglect shamefully your duties as a wife and mother."

"Jason, you....you <u>know</u> how much I...I love you and Olivia."

"Do you? Sometimes I wonder."

"What a horrible thing to say!" Her temper flared. "You know I love you—both of you!" Victoria heard the percolator just then and got up to hurry into the kitchen–grateful for an excuse to leave the room. They couldn't quarrel–not after being apart for so long–not after she'd been telling everyone including herself that despite everything she loved him. When she returned with the percolator a few minutes later, Jason also appeared to have composed himself in the interval. She poured coffee for them both and sat down again.

"I..I don't want to argue, dear." His tone was once more even and he reached across to take hold of her hand. She fought the impulse to pull away. "It's just that I've missed you and... and perhaps I wouldn't object so much to your working if your career didn't bring you into contact with so many...ah...undesirable types."

Victoria put her cup down so suddenly that the coffee sloshed over into the saucer. "What do you mean by that?"

Jason also put his cup down, but with a careful precision and he also removed his other hand from Victoria's. Clasping his two hands together, he rested his elbows on the table. "I noticed on the telephone," he said slowly, "that you've fallen back into the habit of using some rather unfortunate language."

Frantically she searched her memory. What had she said to him over the telephone? She'd been so rattled it could have been almost anything. Then she remembered. "Oh, for God's sake! One Goddamned bloody hell!" But even as she spoke, she realized she'd managed to crowd four profanities into even this brief utterance. Jason merely bowed his head, wearily rubbing his forehead with the tips of his fingers. I....I can't handle this, Victoria thought all at once. Maybe tonight when I've had time to prepare myself, I can manage better, but now I... I've got to get out of here or....or I'll.....start screaming. "I...I'm sorry, Jason," she said aloud, rising abruptly to her feet, "but I'm due at RADA for my class and then I'll be taping all afternoon. I'll....I'll see you at dinner." She went over to the closet to get her coat. "What... what will you do with yourself all day?"

Jason also stood up. He wondered if she was going to him. He'd searched the bath and bedroom, but found nothing. "Actually there are some people interested in founding a Prodigals chapter here in London," he replied. "But I...I rather thought we'd spend my first day here together."

"Impossible....impossible." Victoria could hear herself chattering inanely on and on. "I'm much too busy to drop everything at a moment's notice. I'll see you tonight." She snatched up her purse and attache case from a small table in the entryway, turning again to fumble awkwardly with the lock on the outer door. "My housekeeper should be here any minute. She'll make you some breakfast." After what seemed like forever, she got the door open and she left quickly before he could say anything further, half-running down the hall toward the lift. At least there was no need to warn Martha. From past experience Victoria knew she could count on her discretion.

Left alone meanwhile, Jason poured himself another cup of coffee, taking it with him over to the window to look down at the street below. He prayed God would help him to forgive her.

* * *

The details of the drive across London that day would always be a little fuzzy in Gavin's mind. It was probably a miracle, in fact, that he hadn't killed anyone nor been killed himself in the process. The first he was actually aware of anything, however, he'd brought his car to a stop in the cul-de-sac behind his building and was getting out. His roommate was in the small kitchenette frying up some eggs when he let himself into the flat. Barely glancing at him, Gavin walked directly through to his bedroom to put down his valise and his guitar case, finally shrugging out of his coat and throwing it down on the bed.

Almost at once Jamie appeared in the doorway. "What happened? Did the lass thrrow ye oot?" The other man gave him a black look, but made no reply. Instead he simply opened his suitcase and began removing his things. "Coom, noo–ye've teased me often enough aboot a lass."

"Aye, I have, haven't I?" But through all of this what struck Jamie as the most bizarre was the way in which Gavin methodically–almost single-mindedly–continued to put away his clothes. He'd never been the neatest of roommates and now–all of a sudden–he seemed obsessed with folding his shirts, underwear and cardigans precisely, hanging his trousers and jackets correctly.

"Will ye stop that and talk to me?" Jamie exploded at last. "Ye'rre drrivin' me fairr daft!"

"Therre's nothin' to say. I told....." All at once he stopped speaking. His throat worked helplessly for a moment or so, but finally he swallowed and went on. "I..told.... Torri...that when it was overr, she'd only to tell me. I...I kept my worrd."

His tone was flat; the brown eyes which normally sparkled with good humor appeared lifeless and the question which had been in Jamie's mind for so long was answered. Impulsively he threw his arm around his friend's shoulders. "I'm verra sorrry, laddie. Trruly I am."

Impatiently Gavin shrugged off the comforting gesture and picking up the now empty valise, hurled it into the bottom of the closet. " 'Tis forr the best afterr all. Soonerr orr laterr I'd have gotten borred. I always do." Grabbing up his coat again, he headed for the door.

"Wherre arre ye goin'?" his friend called after him.

"Oot!" The door of the flat slammed shut behind him.

* * *

Victoria glanced at her watch as she stepped out of the car in front of the Academy. She was a little late, the perfect excuse to hurry along to her class without having to speak to anyone, but halfway along the corridor Peter Harris caught her up. How ironic it should be he. "I'm glad I happened to see you," he said as they walked along together. " I put a note in your box, but now you won't have to bother coming to my office."

"I'm rather late, Peter." She did not so much as slacken her pace.

"So am I. But this is my first year as Academy director and I'm finding that other commitments are causing me to lose rehearsal time on the fall production. Could you take over as director? Rehearsals are still in the evening."

At that she finally stopped, turning to face him. Her mind raced. Directing the play would mean additional time away from Jason–time, she told herself, she needed in order to readjust to her situation. "Yes, certainly," Victoria replied at last. "I'd enjoy it." She hurried on into her classroom before he could say anything further, striding briskly up to the front to put down her things and remove her coat. "Good morning, ladies and gentlemen." It was her customary greeting, but something in her tone made several people look up sharply. "We will continue with the scenes from full-length plays. Today, I believe, we are to see first Laura and Amanda from *The Glass Menagerie* and then Lady Bracknell and John Worthing from *The Importance of Being Earnest..*" It was a miracle she could even remember.

Victoria's critique following any classroom exercise was exacting. She'd been taught by Sir Terence never to give less than her best and as she'd told Rebecca, she expected the same from her students. Yet at the same time she always managed to find something worthy of praise. Today was quite different. Today she was in no mood to be charitable and her criticism of the first presentation was scathing. She ridiculed the two young actresses for attempting such difficult roles; she pointed out spot after spot where they'd failed to communicate their emotions to the audience and she concluded by inquiring as to "who in hell had admitted them to RADA in the first place". At last the girl who had portrayed Amanda worked up enough courage to raise her hand. "Yes, Miss Lawrence?" Clearly Victoria's tone dared the girl to protest.

"Miss Windsor, I...I don't consider your first point to be a valid criticism. You yourself played equally difficult roles when you were a student here."

"But you see—I had the talent for them." There were several audible gasps. None of them had ever known her to be cruel. "Now," she continued, ignoring or seeming to ignore their reaction, "may I see the second presentation? I can only hope it will be at least halfway decent."

There was an immediate buzz of conversation–normal between the longer class exercises. Until now Victoria had paid no attention to it, but today the chatter infuriated her–probably because she sensed it was about her. "And you will kindly show your fellow actors some consideration while they're preparing!" she rebuked them. "Perhaps if you'd concentrate on your classwork instead of your social lives, every damned exercise wouldn't be so bloody awful!" The talking stopped.

Rebecca glanced surreptitiously over at her sister. What was wrong with her? Then she remembered Gavin. Of course, she thought with some satisfaction, they've had a lovers' quarrel. Well, it serves her right!

The scene between Lady Bracknell and John Worthing was excellent. Sparkling performances did the clever Wilde dialogue full justice and when it was over, the class all turned expectantly toward Victoria. Certainly she couldn't help but praise this presentation no matter how bad a mood she was in. What they couldn't know, however, was that she'd heard almost nothing of the scene, most of her effort during it having gone into keeping her composure. What's wrong with me, she asked herself over and over again. Of course it had been a shock–Jason arriving so unexpectedly–, but I would have gone back to him eventually. He is my husband, after all, and I love him! I do!

"Excuse me, Miss Windsor," someone finally said quietly, "have you got anything to say to us? Class is over."

"Over?" How long had they been watching her, Victoria wondered. Could she possibly have spoken any of her thoughts aloud? If so, they must certainly think she'd lost her mind. "Of course I don't have anything to say," she snapped. "How could I even attempt to comment on that ridiculous piece of work! You're dismissed!" For a moment or so no one moved, but finally one or two of them stood up and gradually the room emptied. The silence was deafening.

Rebecca had no idea why she didn't leave with the rest of the class. It was mere coincidence they were sisters–she'd told herself that often enough–yet now for some reason she found herself waiting until the others were gone and then walking over to her. Victoria was slumped down in her chair one hand covering her eyes; clearly she was unaware anyone else remained in the room. For a moment Rebecca was relieved. It was still possible then for her to slip away unnoticed. She didn't go, of course. Instead, seemingly against her will, she knelt down placing her hand lightly on her sister's arm.

At the unexpected touch Victoria jumped. "Oh–luv, I...I'm sorry. Was...was there something you wished to talk to me about?"

"I....I just wanted to make sure you were all right."

Rebecca had never shown the slightest inclination toward intimacy. Why–suddenly now–was she so concerned? Am I acting that peculiar, Victoria wondered. "Yes, of course I'm all right." She smiled brightly. "I...I didn't sleep well last night."

"Oh, I see. Th...that's all it is, then." She couldn't think of anything else to say, but–strangely–she couldn't bring herself to leave.

"Really–I'm fine. Please don't let me keep you." Victoria sounded slightly frenzied now and it was with a visible effort that she got to her feet, turning to pick up her things. What was she supposed to do next? Was this one of the days she'd agreed to work independently with one or two of the advanced acting students or was this the morning she was also now teaching a class in the oral interpretation of Shakespeare?

"You....you asked me once if...if I'd like to have coffee. I could...could go this morning if you have time."

"No....no, I don't think so."

Rebecca had always shrunk from any physical contact. Now she was irresistibly drawn to slip an arm around her sister's waist. "All right then. I'll just walk with you to the faculty lounge. You'll feel better if you lie down for a while."

"I've already told you I'm fine." Pulling away, Victoria moved on up the aisle. But maybe the faculty lounge <u>was</u> a good idea. If she relaxed for a few minutes, her head might clear. Suddenly she stopped, however, turning back. "But....but thank you, Rebecca. Your kindness means a great deal to me especially....... especially today. In addition I'll be taking over the play from Mr. Harris and it will be easier for both of us if we're on better terms."

"Oh–you're going to direct?"

"I assure that at rehearsals I will continue to treat you like any other actress."

"That's...that's not it. I....I just thought Mr. Hamilton wouldn't like your taking so much time away....away from him."

Gavin!–From nowhere she could feel the tears starting and she swallowed hard, forcing them back–silly reaction anyway! "Fortunately, Rebecca, Mr. Hamilton's wishes no longer concern me. So I'll be seeing you at rehearsal then." Victoria spun around again and hurried from the auditorium. Had Gavin Hamilton walked out on her, Rebecca wondered. Could that be what was wrong? Then why didn't she feel triumphant?

* * *

The taping that day was another disaster. Victoria was completely unable to concentrate and at last she ran from the set in frustrated tears. It was only a little after five in the afternoon, then, as she got out of the car and walked slowly into the hotel. How could she ever bring herself to confess her infidelity to Jason? She hesitated before the entrance to one of the cocktail lounges, but that was all he'd need–to smell liquor on her breath–and she moved along.

When she let herself into the suite a few minutes later, she could smell dinner already cooking and in spite of her preoccupation she couldn't help smiling. No matter what else happened in her life, she could count on Martha and indeed the lady herself came out of the kitchen just then, wiping her hands on her apron. "Good evening, Miss Windsor. Reverend Eliot will be back shortly. He made a few phone calls and then he went out."

"Thank you, Martha." She put her things down on the usual table near the door, going to the closet to hang up her coat.

"Reverend Eliot seems very pleasant."

"Yes, he does, doesn't he." Victoria walked over to sit down on the couch. Happening to glance over at the cabinet behind the bar, she saw that it was empty. "Martha, where's the liquor?" She didn't know why she even bothered to ask when she already knew the answer.

"Reverend Eliot asked me to remove it. He said you wouldn't be needing it."

Victoria smiled, but it wasn't a natural smile and for the first time since the actress' return to London some weeks before, Martha was once again afraid for her. "I..I suppose you're wondering what happened." She tried in vain to sound casual. "Gavin's...gone. But then I never did expect it to last. I'm...I'm going to tell Jason about him."

"Oh, Miss Windsor, I....."

"Yes, Martha?" The pitch of Victoria's voice rose sharply. The whole thing was beginning to sound dangerously like one of the many scenes they'd had in the past.

"Nothing, ma'am." The housekeeper retreated into the kitchen to check the pots simmering on the stove, the roast in the oven. Coming out again, she took her coat from the closet, but did not immediately put it on. "I can stay, Miss Windsor, if you would like me to serve the dinner."

"Of course not!" More than anything she wanted her old friend to remain, but she couldn't bring herself to admit she dreaded being with her own husband. "I want to be alone with Jason! That's only natural, isn't it?"

"Yes, Miss Windsor." Martha knew it was useless to pursue the matter. "Of course you and Reverend Eliot would like your privacy. I'll see you in the morning then." She waited for a reply, but when there was none, she left.

Victoria hugged her arms to herself and leaning forward slightly to rest her elbows on her knees, she willed herself to stop trembling. I...I have to tell Jason tonight, she thought. I feel so guilty. That's probably why I'm on edge. At last she decided it might help to calm her if she kept busy. Martha had the dinner pretty well prepared, but Victoria managed to keep occupied–getting the dishes out, setting the table. She put two tall, pink candles into crystal glass candlesticks. Through it all, however, she felt as if she were holding her breath–waiting for something to happen as one waits during a summer storm for the next flash of lightening. At every noise from the hallway she tensed, pausing in her work to glance toward the door.

When Jason finally did arrive about a half-hour later, she was in the kitchen. "Victoria," he called out as he let himself in. "Where are you, dear?" At the sound of his voice her hands clenched briefly into fists, but then she moved immediately into the living room smiling in welcome. Jason took her in his arms, pleased she appeared so much more at ease. Perhaps, after all, it was only that his arrival had been unexpected. And Victoria was never at her best in the morning. Yes–he was sure now that all those newspaper accounts had been nothing but lies.

"Jason, I love you so much. I...I want you to know that."

"And I love you, too, Victoria." He kissed her tenderly.

"You can sit right down, darling." She slipped quickly out of his embrace which for some reason had immediately become intolerable to her.

Dinner was roast beef and potatoes with mixed vegetables. Inevitably Victoria's thoughts turned to another roast which had burnt to a crisp in the oven and it required an effort to bring her attention back to the present moment. "....but I told her your plans were too indefinite and that we'd have to wait and see what happened," Jason was saying.

She guessed he'd been talking about Olivia. Undoubtedly the little girl had wanted to come with him. "She's....she's all right with the MacAllisters though, isn't she?"

"Oh, yes." He nodded. "I don't feel they're strict enough, but then that's not my affair, is it?"

"Of course it is, Jason. But how do you feel they're not strict enough?"

"Nothing really major, I suppose–bedtimes, involving her in adult conversations–- that sort of thing-- but as I already said, it really isn't my affair."

Ridiculously Victoria thought to herself–I wish he'd stop using that word. "Please, Jason, I consider Olivia as much your daughter as mine."

"Nevertheless, you did prefer to have her stay with the MacAllisters."

"That was only because of your erratic schedule. I was worried she'd be alone too much."

"Yes, of course." Once again he'd apparently accepted her explanation and he went on to talk about the success of the Prodigals counseling program, his excitement over the founding of a new chapter in London. She was relieved to have him do most of the talking, but at the same time she couldn't help noticing he asked nothing about <u>her</u> work.

At last dinner was finished and they moved across to the other side of the room to have their coffee on the couch. God, Victoria was thinking, I need a drink! I wonder what Martha did with the liquor. But somehow she managed to pour the coffee although her hands were shaking and for one crazy minute she was unable to recall which of the two men drank his coffee black. Just in time she remembered and added cream and sugar. There was a long, uneasy silence during which Jason at least drank his coffee. Victoria's sat on the table in front of her untouched.

"Your coffee will be getting cold." Jason took one of her hands in both of his. "Almost as cold as your hands. What's wrong, dear?" He smiled–his same gentle smile although inside he felt sick. He was afraid he already knew what was troubling her.

"I'm sorry." She pulled her hand away. "But I'm....I'm frightfully tired and I could use a drink, if you don't mind. Where did Martha put it?" She stood up as though to go and get it.

"I really don't know. And anyway you don't actually <u>need</u> a drink. Alcohol is simply a crutch as I've explained to you many times."

"Yes, Jason." Victoria subsided meekly, sitting down again. So she wasn't to be allowed even that much help. For several long seconds she stared down at her hands clasped together in her lap. How could she ever find the words? "Jason, I....I....." Helplessly she shook her head, hot tears of guilt and humiliation filling her eyes.

"What can you possibly find so difficult to tell me, Victoria?" The horrible pain of betrayal gripped his chest and for one frightening moment he wondered if he were having a heart attack.

"Oh, my darling, I'm so very sorry, but....but I've....I've been unfaithful to you." At last the words were out–hideous, ugly ones that once spoken aloud seemed to hang in the air between them.

There was a brief, terrible silence. "It's...all right," Jason finally managed to say. "You..... you were lonely. I....understand, darling and...and I....I forgive you."

Perhaps it was the expression on his face; perhaps it was his voice, but suddenly it was all too clear to her. "You....you knew," she whispered, "didn't you?"

"I'd heard rumors, yes, but I....I chose not to believe them."

"Jason, I....I want to...to tell you about him."

"I....I would really rather not hear...."

"Please–it would help me if I told you."

"Very well. I always want to help you. You know that."

"Thank...thank you. Actually I....I met him at the MacAllisters while....while you were in Vietnam. He's...he's from Scotland. His father's a friend of Ken's father. We...we both just happened to be their house guests on the same week-end."

"So...it started then, did it?" His tone remained even.

"No...oh, no. Only when I...I came back to London."

"It isn't necessary to say anything further, Victoria. And now can we simply go on with our lives–forget it as though it never happened?"

"Oh, darling, can you really do that?" She blinked back her tears and for the first time she was able to look at him directly. "Can you forget it? Because....because I can. It didn't mean anything to me. But I feel so wretched about it."

"Yes–of course. I can forget it if you can."

"Th...thank you," she said again. But why had all his assurances of forgiveness only left her feeling all the more guilt-ridden and miserable?

"And now I think we should go to bed. This has been extremely trying for both of us."

"I....I should at least clear the table...."

"Let Martha do that in the morning." He gave her hand a solicitous pat. "That's what you pay her for, after all, and you did say you were especially tired."

She gave him no further argument, but stood up to lead the way into the bedroom where they both undressed in silence. Even after they lay together side by side under the covers– a measurable distance apart–neither of them spoke. Far more separated them, however, than merely a foot or so of unoccupied bed for all Jason's words of comfort and forgiveness had, of course, been nothing on his part but lies.

As for Victoria herself, she'd been relieved when at first her husband made no attempt to touch her, but as time passed and he still neither moved nor spoke, she came to understand the reason why she'd found so little solace in his words. There was no comfort in his forgiveness because he did not truly forgive. Then all at once she remembered one particular thing Jason had said and now she saw it in quite a different light. He said he had heard rumors, but chose not to believe them; not that he did <u>not</u> believe; he <u>chose</u> not to believe which meant, of course, that he'd believed them all along. Indeed that was very likely the whole reason for his trip–not because he missed her or was concerned about her–but because he wanted to check up on her. But why couldn't he have just come right out and asked her? Did he think she'd have lied to him or did he simply wish to find out whether she'd at least have the decency to confess?

The long, dark night dragged on–her loneliness ironically far more intense than when she had, in fact, been alone. Finally she could no longer bear to lie there motionless and making sure first that Jason was asleep, she got up, slipping into her robe. Dear God, if only she knew where the liquor was. She began to search for it, quietly at first, and then more carelessly as the need for a drink became intolerable. At last she found it in the back of a small cabinet over the refrigerator.

You didn't hide it very well, Martha, Victoria thought with a slightly hysterical giggle. In her desperation her fingers had grown clumsy and it was several terrible minutes before she could get the cover off the vodka. Not even bothering to get a glass, she took a long swallow directly from the bottle. She half-choked on the liquor, but the burning soon turned to a lovely warmth in the pit of her stomach and almost at once she began to relax.

"You're wrong, you know, Jason," she said aloud in the darkened kitchen. "Prayer is not the best way of easing tension."

She took another swallow and walking back into the living room, she curled up at one end of the couch to do something she'd hadn't felt the need to do in nearly two years–drink herself into oblivion. Jason found her there the following morning, the half- empty bottle on the floor beside her. Profoundly sad, he dressed himself and left without attempting to awaken her. Had he been wrong, he wondered, to fall in love with Victoria? By the time he'd met her, was she already so mired in sin that even his caring was not enough to save her?

* * *

For the first several days Gavin had forced himself to carry on with his normal routine. He continued working at the same coffee house during the lunch hour and even began singing evenings again in one or two other places. Then a week or so after he moved back into the flat, both men were invited to try out at a rather more elite supper club. Jamie was hired, but he found little pleasure in his own success. His friend's uncharacteristically lackluster audition had bothered him profoundly, but even more upsetting now was the proud man's easy acceptance of failure. "It doesna matterr anyway," Gavin shrugged. "Ye werre verra good, laddie–neverr betterr. Ye deserrved the job." By then they were at the entrance to their building and suddenly he thrust his guitar case into Jamie's hands. "Will ye take this oop forr me then? I feel like a bit of a walk."

"Would ye be wantin' coomp'ny?"

"No, laddie, but I apprreciate the thought." He clapped the other man affectionately on the shoulder and smiled at him. But it was merely the ghost of his usual engaging grin. Gavin turned up the collar of his suede, sheepskin-lined jacket and jamming his fists deep into his trouser pockets, he moved rapidly away until he could turn the corner and lose the concerned stare he could feel burning into his back. He lost track of where or how long he'd walked until all at once he found himself coming out along the Thames. His unhappiness would somehow have been easier to bear if the weather matched his mood, but instead–perversely–it denied every legend of London in November. The sky was a cloudless blue. Even the river itself sparkled in the sunlight. Strolling for a while along the Embankment, Gavin finally sat down on a bench, stretching out his legs and crossing them at the ankles. Two girls who were passing by stopped to stare at him, hoping no doubt that this handsome man would pay them a little attention. He appeared not to notice them, however, and reluctantly they moved on.

He had tried very hard in the days since he last saw her not to think about Victoria, but now sitting there alone, memories flooded over him: Tori walking by his side along a Devonshire beach; Tori–her delicate blonde beauty glowing in the firelight; Tori laughing merrily at his silly antics–laughing as he was sure she'd never laughed in her life; Tori clinging to him for comfort and reassurance; Tori lying warm and passionate and giving in his arms. Tori....

Tori....Tori...... "Torri." At last he whispered the sweet name aloud and sitting up, he leaned forward, elbows on his knees, to bury his face in his hands. Was it only then and there that the awareness came to him or had he, in fact, known for some time that he loved her? It didn't matter. The full cognizance tore through him now with a force more terrible that any emotion he'd experienced since the death of his mother when he was only sixteen. He had to tell her! He was aware there was little hope of Victoria returning his love, but he had never felt this way about a woman before and he wanted her to know. Perhaps, too, he simply needed to hear her voice.

Gavin jumped to his feet, his long legs taking the steps leading up from the Embankment two at a time. There were none of the familiar bright red telephone booths in sight, however, and at last half-running, he crossed the street to look further. It was several blocks before he came upon a kiosk and by then he was so anxious that when he tried to push the coin into the slot, it slipped from his hand. He hung up to dial a second time and after what seemed like forever, the hotel operator answered. He gave the number of the suite and waited impatiently, his fingers drumming a nervous rhythm on the side of the booth. It was a terrible let-down when Martha Kendall came on the line. He almost hung up, but even the housekeeper who had never liked him was a link to Victoria. "Hello, Marrtha," he said at last. " 'Tis Gavin Hamilton."

The Scottish brogue startled her. It was a voice she hadn't expected to hear again. Even more surprising was the rush of pleasure she experienced at the sound and she found herself picturing the man that went with the voice: the brown eyes with their maddening twinkle, the roguish grin which had never failed to unsettle her. Most of all she remembered how happy Miss Windsor had been with him. "Yes, Mr. Hamilton." Always the professional, however, she carefully kept her tone unexpressive of her feelings.

"Is...is it possible for me to speak to Torri?"

Martha heard the emotion in his voice and suddenly she pitied him. "I'm sorry, Mr. Hamilton. She's not here."

"That's all rright then. Neverr mind."

"Do you wish to leave a message, sir?" she asked quickly before he could hang up.

"Could ye ask herr to rring me back?" He couldn't believe she'd made the offer. "The numberr is 55-4610."

"I'll tell her, but....but I can't promise she'll return your call. She....she says it's over. She's.... she's trying so hard, Mr. Hamilton, but...but....."

"But..." he prompted.

"I've already said too much." Martha had immediately regretted her frankness. "I'll tell her you phoned, sir." That evening the housekeeper again suggested she stay and serve the dinner. Reverend Eliot was going out to an appointment and this would give her a chance to talk to Miss Windsor. She couldn't help noticing, moreover, how eagerly her employer accepted the offer this time.

Jason obviously didn't like her being there and during the meal Martha was careful to remain in the kitchen except when actually serving. From the other room she was unable to understand any of the actual conversation, but she could clearly hear Victoria's stilted, unnatural tone each time she spoke and her husband's quiet, soothing voice as he responded–a voice which was beginning to grate on her. Finally she brought out the coffee and dessert and a little while after that she knew the Reverend Eliot would be leaving. Martha listened for the outer door of the suite to close behind him and then she picked up a tray and went out into the living room. "May I clear now, Miss Windsor?"

Victoria was still sitting at the table, her hands gripping the edge of it as though she would certainly float out of the chair if she didn't hold onto something. "Oh yes–of course." She smiled a strange, tight little smile. "We're all finished."

Martha put the tray down and began to pick up the dessert dishes, the cups and saucers, coffee pot, sugar bowl and creamer. "Wouldn't you be more comfortable on the couch, ma'am?"

"I'm perfectly fine where I am, thank you. And never mind the dishes. You may leave now."

"I thought you might like some company."

"No, I wouldn't!"

"Yes, Miss Windsor," Martha acquiesced quietly, but after she carried the tray into the kitchen, she returned to stand by the table again. Victoria still hadn't moved. "You had a telephone call this afternoon, ma'am. Mr. Hamilton......."

"Did you tell him I'd phone him back?"

"I said I thought you wouldn't."

"You still haven't learned to mind your own business, have you?"

"If you wish me to resign my position with you again, you need only tell me"

"Oh no, please!" Victoria seized both of the other woman's hands in both of hers, looking up at her imploringly. "I'm sorry–please don't leave me!"

"Now you know very well I'll stay." Gently she freed one of her hands to put an arm around her employer's shoulders–grateful that at least now she could accept tenderness.

"Oh, Martha!" In response to the comforting touch Victoria turned to slip both arms around her old friend's waist, pressing her face against the dear, ample chest. "I...I don't know what's wrong with me! I...I wish Noel were here. I...I need someone to talk to."

"Miss Windsor, why don't you ring up Mr. Hamilton?"

"No! No, I.....I can't! If....if I see him, it will just start all over again and I can't let that happen. Jason would never forgive me. Sometimes I don't think he even....."

"Even what?"

"Nothing." Victoria's voice was flat now. She sounded defeated. "Please, I'm.....I'm really all right. You may go."

"Are you sure, Miss Windsor?"

"Of course I am! I should know how I feel!"

"Very well, ma'am." Martha agreed at once, going to the hall closet to get her coat. Nothing could be gained by upsetting Victoria further. "I'll see you tomorrow then." Later at her flat, however, she dialed the number Mr. Hamilton had left with her and asked the man who answered if she might speak to him.

Gavin came on the line almost at once. "Torri! Torri, I'm sae glad ye rrang me back, I......."

"Mr. Hamilton, it's...it's Martha Kendall."

"Oh."

"I'm....I'm sorry, sir. She says she won't telephone you and I thought I should tell you."

"Aye, Marrtha. Thank ye. Ye'rre verra kind–especially considerrin' the fact that ye neverr carred much forr me at all."

"That....that was only at first before....before I came to know you better and now when I realize...." She stopped. She had been about to step far beyond the self-imposed boundaries of her position which in her mind was unthinkable.

"When ye rrealized what, Marrtha?" She'd never known a man's voice could be so gentle.

"It's....it's not my place to say, sir."

" 'Tis the trrouble wi' you Englisherrs. Ye'rre too concerrned wi' prroprrieties! Ye have to rrun things from the hearrt, lass. Nae frrom a book o' mannerrs!"

Martha's eyes filled with tears. Here undoubtedly was the man Miss Windsor had always needed and apparently she was determined to turn her back on him. "Mr. Hamilton, there's nothing I can do to change her mind. She's very stubborn and self-willed and I...."

"Aye." But with that one word he managed to make stubbornness and self-will seem very endearing qualities indeed.

"Mr. Hamilton, you...you don't have to answer this if you don't want to."

"All rright."

"You....you love her, don't you, sir?"

"Aye, Marrtha...I do."

The silence went on for so long she almost thought Gavin had hung up. "Mr. Hamilton?"

"Aye, I'm still herre."

"I'll....I'll try to convince her to ring you, sir."

"No, Marrtha. Ye shouldna do that. At any rrate I'm thinkin' o' goin' home forr a bit. Lundon seems a verra cold and lonely place at the moment." And this time the line did indeed go dead.

Before he left, however, Gavin had to make one final attempt to communicate with Victoria in a letter. She could very well refuse to read it; Jason might even see the letter first and destroy it. But it was his one and only chance to tell her that he loved her.

* * *

It was a day or so later that Victoria let herself into the suite and walking slowly across the room, she slumped down on the couch, not even bothering to take off her coat. Her purse, script, gloves and umbrella fell unheeded to the floor.

Having heard her come in, Martha appeared in the doorway to the kitchen. "Good evening, Miss Windsor."

It was a long moment before Victoria turned to look at her. "Oh, it's....it's you. Is...is Jason here yet?"

"No, ma'am. He rang up to say he'd be late."

"Oh." She looked relieved, the housekeeper noted.

"So—I thought you might enjoy one of my omelets. You always liked those."

"What? I'm....I'm sorry." Wearily she massaged her forehead. "I'm so tired I can't even think straight."

"It's too much for you. Taping the series and teaching at the Academy and now directing the play there as well."

"You can't stop mothering me, can you, Martha?" But she didn't sound angry, only sad.

"How about a drink? It would help you to relax. Reverend Eliot doesn't have to know."

"No, I....I don't need a drink. Jason's right. It <u>is</u> only a crutch. Jason's always right—can't you see–always, <u>always</u> right."

"Yes, of course he is, Miss Windsor," Martha replied soothingly. "I'll get started on that omelet. Today's post is right there in front of you on the coffee table."

Victoria picked up the stack of envelopes, flipping through them without any real interest. A great many of them appeared to be simply more of the invitations which Jason discouraged her from accepting because she "needed her rest". The real reason, she knew only too well, was that he disapproved of her friends.

Then all at once she came upon a plain, beige envelope addressed to her in a strong, backslanting script. Although she'd only seen his handwriting a few times, she recognized it instantly and her hands were trembling as she tore open the envelope, unfolding the single sheet of stationery covered on both sides with the same, scrawling hand. As she began to read, she could almost hear the soft burr of his speech.

Torri–

I rrealize noo that I was wrrong to telephone ye and I'm verra sorrry. I willna botherr ye again and ye ken verra well I'm a lad o' my worrd. But I canna rest easy, lass, until I tell ye one thing–somethin' I'm as surre of in my verra hearrt as I'm surre that heatherr will bloom everra fall–and that is that I love ye.

Tears filled her eyes, blurring the page and she lowered the letter to her lap. He'd sworn all along as she had that their affair meant nothing and now he was writing to tell her he loved her. Well, he had no business loving her–no business at all. Almost against her will, however, she was drawn to read more.

Contrrarry to thought, I'm nae used to wrritin' love letters and perrhaps the whole thing doesna coom off all that eloquent–afterr all, I'm a singerr, not a poet. Though I did have a hand at verrse in my lessons as a lad, it's the firrst time I've wrrit such a thing to a lass.

Desperately Victoria fought back the tears. That damned charming Scotsman had no right still to affect her this way. She'd been so good–refusing to return his phone call and now this; he simply had no right–no right at all. Yet once again she raised the letter and read on.

I'll be rreturrnin' home to Glengowrrie in a few days. It seems that wheneverr I need strrength and consolation–that is wherre I go to find them. Jason turrns to the Lorrd; I turrn to the hills of Scotland. Well, therre's a fairr comparrison between us, do ye not think so? I'll no ask to see ye beforre I leave. I'll still love ye, but because I do, I'll rrespect yourr wishes.

So I'll returrn to Scotland and trry to put frrom my hearrt and mind this dearr English lass who has somehow found herr way in therre. Och, but it willna be easy. Ye do seem to have nestled in therre as warrm and sweet as once ye nestled in my arrms.

"Oh, Gavin!" Victoria was crying openly now. "You're not being fair. The way you have with words." But there was so little left of the letter now she might as well finish it.

Two nights ago I would gladly have choked the life oot of Jason forr makin' ye feel so beneath him, so much less than I know ye arre.

"No–Gavin–you're wrong," she whispered. "It's just that he expects more of me than I'm capable of being."

But that's passed–forr noo anyway. Life's a miserry forr surre, Torri, when ye canna have what ye want. I'll hope to hearr frrom ye, but if I don't, I'll be off to the Highlands.

Take carre of yourrself, dearr lass, and always ken that wherreverr ye arre and wherreverr I am, I'll always feel ye nearr me.

Forr aye–

Your Gavin

Victoria got to her feet and walked slowly toward the bedroom, intending to go on into the bathroom and throw the letter in the wastepaper basket among her discarded tissues and cleansing pads as she'd done with the broken pieces of Gavin's pipe on the morning he left. Halfway across the bedroom, however, she passed her bureau. Without stopping to think about it she opened the top drawer and thrust the letter in under her underwear–another place Jason would never look, she thought with a brief, mirthless laugh. It was so beautifully written, after all, it seemed a shame to throw it away. She'd keep it–simply as a memento. It wasn't that the writer of the letter meant anything to her. How could he when she loved Jason?

But would Jason ever truly forgive her? Victoria knew he was deliberately avoiding her, often not arriving home until well after she was in bed. Secretly she found it a relief. She'd hear him moving around in the other room and at once turn over on her side to feign sleep, even though she knew full well she'd still be awake hours later prowling the living room. Jason had to have discovered her more than once passed out on the couch and she wondered why he hadn't removed the liquor from the suite altogether. Perhaps he was testing her or perhaps he was merely resigned to the fact that she was weak.

What I should do, she thought at some point during one of those long nights, is to ask Doctor Anthony to prescribe a sedative–just to get me through all of this until Jason and I can work things out. The doctor gave her the prescription on the condition that she make an appointment to come in and talk to him. She agreed to the appointment--anything to get the pills; of course she had no intention of keeping it.

* * *

There'd been no answer to his letter–not that he'd expected one–and a few days later Gavin threw a valise into the back of his Morris Rover and turned the nose of the little car north. Had Victoria at least read the letter, he wondered; had she been at all touched by his words of love? His thoughts were so full of her that quite involuntarily he kept glancing over at the passenger seat as if by some miracle he would find her sitting beside him. But she was not there, of course. The seat was as empty as his heart felt; as empty as the years stretching ahead of him. In an ironic way he supposed the whole thing was almost funny. There'd been so many women in his life–women he casually discarded once he had tired of them. Wouldn't they all enjoy it if they could see him now. As was his custom, he would be traveling straight through and perhaps somewhere during the long drive he could come to terms with it all. It seemed foolish, in any case, to stop when he'd been having so much trouble sleeping.

The sun was just setting as Niall Hamilton closed the paddock gate behind him and started back toward the house. You would have known on sight he was Gavin's father. He had the same tall, strong build, the same thick, wavy hair–although at 55 Niall's was now silver gray--even the identical proud carriage. The most striking resemblance, however, was in the eyes–brown with the same irresistible twinkle–a twinkle which in the older man's case had been somewhat muted since the death of his beloved wife seventeen years before.

Niall had just reached the veranda which ran along the front of the old, gray stone farmhouse when he noticed an automobile moving along the road below, its headlights piercing the twilight of a Scottish November. He'd been expecting his eldest son for several days now, but he had learned some time ago that Gavin never ran his life by any definite timetable and his last letter, dated a little over a week ago, had been even less communicative than usual. Now he stopped, waiting as the car swung off the road and up the long, winding drive to come to a stop in front of the barn. The door opened, the light inside revealing that it was indeed Gavin. "Laddie!" He called out striding across the frost covered front lawn to greet him. They met about halfway, embracing affectionately. "We've been wonderrin' when ye'd be gettin' herre," Niall went on as the two men walked side by side toward the house. "Wi' Jamie and Felicity's gatherrin' only two days away noo."

Gavin paused on the front steps, turning back to look out over the horizon–the low hills surrounding the house still faintly visible silhouetted against the darkening sky. He had wanted so much to show all of this to Victoria. Now it seemed he never would. "It's good to be home, Dad," was all he said in reply as he continued on up the stairs to hold open the front door for his father.

Inside he was engulfed instantly in a wave of female affection: first his seventeen year old sister, Meghan, who had been curled up on the floor in front of the huge stone fireplace reading; then Fiona, twenty-four, a teacher at the local grammar school who had been correcting papers at the large family dining table to the left of the door and finally his Grandmother Hamilton from the kitchen. "Look at ye!" the little old lady scolded him fondly. "I suppose ye think that since ye'rre a grrand Lundon gentleman the noo, ye can trrack snow into my hoose. Did ye wipe yourr feet on the mat ootside the way I taught ye?"

"Aye, Grranny. Ye ken I've always been a well-behaved laddie." Despite his sadness Gavin winked at her.

"Och! I ken naethin' of the sorrt," she snorted, reaching up from her height of barely five feet to pat him on the cheek. "Ye've drriven me fairr daft everr since I can rrememberr." Wee Mary, as everyone outside the family called her, had come to care for her son's motherless children almost immediately after his wife's death and had ruled the family with a firm, but loving hand ever since. "Noo–take yourr case on oopstairrs," she ordered briskly, "and get rready forr yourr tea. And wash yourr hands! Ye ken verra well, I intend to check when ye coom doon!"

"Aye, Grranny." He bent to kiss her and picking up his suitcase, he obediently moved toward the stairs which started to the right of the fireplace and wound up around behind the chimney.

"Would ye be wantin' coomp'ny, Gavin?" Meghan inquired eagerly. Whenever her adored brother was home, she couldn't bear to have him out of her sight.

"No, lass." But he softened the refusal with his usual smile. "I willna be long, I prromise." He went on up the stairs disappearing around the corner.

Disappointed, she plopped down again cross-legged on the floor, her chin in her hands. "Noo, lass." Niall Hamilton came over to sit on the couch near her, lightly stroking her hair. "Ye ken yourr brrotherr is no himself." The girl nodded blinking back the tears.

Gavin indeed remained strangely silent all during tea and when the meal was over, he at once excused himself from the table. Niall noticed him a moment later staring into the fire and coming to stand next to him, he put an arm around his son's shoulders. "How aboot it, laddie? It's been too long since we've sharred a game of chess and a wee drram."

With an obvious effort he brought his attention back to what his father was saying. "Aye, Dad–fine."

"Unless ye'rre too wearry, of courrse. Did ye drrive strraight thrrough?"

Gavin ignored the question. "No–Dad–neverr too wearry forr a game of chess."

They arranged the small table and two chairs in their usual spot in front of the fireplace—the bottle of Scotch on the floor between then, but almost at once Gavin found he couldn't keep his mind on the game. It was odd. Victoria had never been here yet in his imagination he could see her– perhaps curled up on one of the couches–trying not to be impatient and yet wanting him beside her.

"Gavin– 'tis yourr go."

He blinked once or twice and looked up at his father. "My....my turrn?"

"Aye–the chess game."

"Oh–aye." He made a renewed effort to concentrate.

"Would ye rratherr talk, laddie? We all ken ye'rre trroubled aboot soomthin'."

Gavin gave a funny, little half-smile. Nothing could help–nothing but to feel Tori in his arms again and he knew that could never be. "No, Dad. 'Tis soomthin' I have to worrk oot forr m'self. The day afterr the gatherrin' I'll be goin' off into the hills forr a bit."

"It's always been that way wi' ye, hasn't it? This needin' to be alone wi' yourr thoughts."

"Aye, Dad."

" 'Tis such a lonely life, laddie. Will therre neverr be someone with whom ye can sharre those thoughts?" Niall had never seen such pain reflected on his son's face as there was at that moment and he realized that quite inadvertently he had come close to guessing the reason for Gavin's unhappiness. Perhaps Jamie would be able to tell him.

There is no form of festivity quite like a Highland gathering: athletic contests, dancing and piping competitions during the day and a gala ball in the evening with the men in full Scottish regalia and the women in their long dresses adorned with the plaid. "Do ye think Gavin will coom, Jamie?" Felicity inquired anxiously. They were standing in the reception line with their parents. "He didna coom forr the games and the pipin' and he neverr misses those."

"I canna believe he wouldna coom at all. He's no a lad to take frriendship lightly."

"But if he's trruly the way ye say he is, he'll no want to be dancin' and frrolickin'." A moment later, however, the Hamilton family arrived–including Gavin. He shook Jamie's hand with his customary warmth and bent to kiss Felicity on the cheek, but he moved on without speaking. "He didna brring a lass," Felicity observed under her breath even as the reception line continued. Jamie merely shook his head.

Soon the festivities were in full swing: reels, strathspeys, waltzes–all well lubricated with Scotch–but as the party went on, Felicity and Jamie kept seeing Gavin in the background pacing the outer perimeters of the hall. He wasn't talking to anyone; he wasn't dancing; he was not even drinking. At some point Gavin's father came over to them. "Jamie, I've been waitin' forr a chance to talk to ye. Do ye ken what it is wi' my laddie?"

"Aye, but I canna brreak a confidence."

"Well, I prromised naethin' to nobody," Felicity spoke up." 'Tis a lass, Mr. Hamilton."

"I thought that might be it." Niall nodded solemnly.

"He's coomin' overr," Jamie warned them.

"Felicity–Jamie," Gavin said quietly. "I hope ye willna be offended if I leave noo. I'm goin' off into the hills in the morrnin' and I'll want to be gettin' an earrly starrt."

There was such a terrible sadness in his eyes and Felicity knew there was no real comfort she could give him. "Aye, ye ken verra well 'tis all rright." The irony of it all, she couldn't help thinking as she embraced him, had been her concern that Victoria would be hurt.

"Can I walk oot wi' ye, laddie?" Jamie inquired.

"Aye, if ye want to." Gavin turned to leave with no further word and his friend followed him.

In the small vestibule Jamie waited silently as Gavin slipped into his tartan-lined greatcoat, but as the other man started across toward the outer door, he took him by the arm stopping him. He couldn't let him leave without at least saying something. "Will it help, do ye think then, to go oop into the hills?"

Gavin shrugged. "I just know I have to be alone. As ye could well see tonight, I'm no fit coomp'ny." He walked the rest of the way to the door, but with his hand on the knob he stopped to look back once more. "Be verra carreful, laddie. Ye have yourr darrlin'. Do naethin' to lose herr." And with that he was gone. Jamie hurried to catch the door before it could close again and he stood watching as Gavin strode along the path of light, finally disappearing into the darkness beyond.

* * *

No matter how hard she tried to avoid him, it seemed as though Jason was always there–like part of the air she breathed–unfailingly kind and considerate–why, Victoria wondered, when she knew he hated her–and with each day that passed she could feel the tension inside her building.

It was bizarre the way it happened–with no actual thought or prior planning– as though, just when her nerves had reached their breaking point, she was being shown the way out. She felt, in fact, amazingly at peace as easing herself out from under the covers so as not to disturb her husband, she went into the bathroom to get the bottle of sleeping pills from the medicine cabinet. Passing through the bedroom again, she paused to look down at him. "Good-bye, Jason," she whispered. "I'm sorry I've disappointed you." She wondered if she should kiss him, but after a moment she continued on into the living room. The whole scene had an unreal quality to it as though she were sitting in the audience watching herself in a play and mechanically without stopping to think of the consequences, she took all the pills left in the bottle–washing them down with vodka. At last she lay down on the couch to wait.

For just a moment as the drowsiness began to creep over her, she thought of Olivia and her eyes filled with tears, but then she decided that like Jason her daughter would be better off without her. I've been no good for anyone, she thought sleepily–Noel or Martha or Terry or Olivia or Jason–not even Gavin. Dear God–Gavin! I...I don't want to die! But her arms and legs–her whole body–were leaden now with approaching sleep and it was just too much of an effort to move.

Jason never knew what awakened him, but he noticed at once that Victoria wasn't in bed with him. Glancing toward the bathroom, he saw the door was open. He called her name, but there was no answer and at once he became annoyed. He got out of bed, stepping into his slippers. "Victoria?" he called again. She still didn't reply and pulling on his robe, he went out into the living room. It was there he discovered her on the couch. He assumed, of course, that once again she was merely passed out and kneeling beside her, he shook her speaking to her sharply. It was only then he saw the empty pill bottle near him on the floor. "Oh, Victoria–no! Why!" Desperately he felt for a pulse, relief flooding over him as he found one–thready and irregular–but at least she was still alive. But now he also noticed the vodka bottle on the coffee table.

"Dear God! Pills and liquor!" He hurried to the telephone and instinctively even as he searched through Victoria's address book for the name and number of the doctor who had prescribed the pills, he continued to pray. "Dear God! Just let her live! Dear God–forgive me for not being able to forgive her!..." Anthony–that was it–Dr. Charles Anthony–the same man she'd seen at the time of the custody hearing. He lifted the receiver and dialed.

"Doctor Anthony's office." The voice was professional, but impersonal.

"Thank God! May I please speak to the doctor!"

The woman sighed wearily. "This is his answering service. Doctor Anthony will be in his office at...."

"No...dammit!" He wasn't even aware he'd sworn. "This is an emergency–- attempted suicide."

Instantly the voice lost its detachment. "I'll ring you through, sir."

"Doctor Anthony." The man had obviously been awakened from a sound sleep.

Jason tried not to think of the precious moments that had been lost since he first discovered Victoria unconscious. "Doctor, this is the Reverend Eliot. My...my wife has taken an overdose."

"When?" At once the doctor was completely alert.

"I'm not sure. I just woke up and found her. Perhaps as long ago as two hours."

"Do you have any idea how many pills she took?"

"I presume it was the prescription you just gave her. The bottle is empty."

There was a momentary stunned silence. "Any pulse."

"Yes, but it's very weak."

"I'll dispatch the emergency squad and meet you at hospital."

Hanging up, Jason hurried back to Victoria. Gently he smoothed her hair away from her still, white face. "Please, darling, please–just hold on. Was this my fault, my darling? Was it?" His voice was choked with tears. "You've got to live so I can show you how deeply I love you–that I truly do forgive....forgive....."

It was all he could do to leave her long enough to put on his clothes, but by the time he was dressed, the emergency squad was at the door. Efficiently they lifted the unconscious woman onto the stretcher, slipping an oxygen mask over her head and into place on her nose and mouth. "You can ride in back with her if you wish, sir," one of the attendants told him.

"Yes–thank you." He grabbed up his overcoat and followed them into the hall. In a short while they were downstairs and out the side door of the hotel to an alley where the ambulance was waiting. The stretcher was lifted in and Jason got in afterwards.

"Right there, sir," the same attendant instructed, indicating a seat near Victoria. He checked her pulse. "Good." He glanced up reassuringly. "She's still with us." Picking up the short wave mike, he began to prepare the hospital's emergency room for their arrival.

As the ambulance pulled into the emergency bay, there was an instant flurry of activity around Victoria during which Jason only felt in the way. The stretcher was soon rolled into another room and moments later a man he recognized as Dr. Anthony hurried through the waiting room and disappeared through the same door. Once a nurse came out, but she could not or would not tell him anything. It was well over an hour before Dr. Anthony reappeared. He looked exhausted. "Reverend Eliot." He extended his hand. "Well, we got most of it out of her."

Fervently Jason grasped the offered hand. "Then she's going to be all right?"

"We can never be entirely sure, you see, until someone regains consciousness. A certain amount of the drug had already gotten into her bloodstream and there's nothing we can do about that."

"May I ask, doctor, what makes someone do something like this? There were so many incidents in my wife's past that could have driven her to....to...." He forced the words out..."to attempt suicide. She...she hasn't always led the best life and I....I..."

Dr. Anthony looked at him intently. It struck him as strange that the man was apparently making a moral judgment at a moment like this though now that he stopped to think about it there'd been something about Victoria's husband on the occasion of their previous encounter that made him distinctly uneasy. However, this was not the time to consider that either. "Any evaluation as to cause will have to wait, I'm afraid, until we're sure there are no physical effects from the attempt." In his effort not to let his personal feelings to show, however, his tone was rather cold.

"Well, I think I would prefer to have my wife's case handled by someone more genuinely concerned with her welfare." But in his anxiety Jason, in turn, had come off sounding merely pompous.

"I assure you, sir, I am profoundly concerned." By now the doctor was having some difficulty controlling his temper. "You may recall that at the time of her emotional collapse nearly a year and a half ago I tried to convince you both she needed counseling."

"And I'm still not sure that probing into her psyche is the answer to anything."

"Oh–?!" Dr. Anthony's eyebrows shot up in an amazed question mark. "And just what is–in your professional opinion?"

"It's true I'm not a psychiatrist, but as a minister I do a considerable amount of counseling myself and I find that a person of....shall we say...somewhat weaker moral fibre can easily be led into situations beyond that person's ability to...ah...cope."

"Yes, well, if you'll excuse me, Reverend Eliot, I wish to make sure your wife is comfortable." The doctor began to move away. He should have known better than to get involved in such a discussion at all.

But Jason followed him. "Yes, well as I've already stated, I intend to see that Victoria has a different doctor."

Dr. Anthony's only reply was a curt nod before he strode away down the corridor, taking his anger out on the swinging doors. A nurse met him on the other side–clipboard in hand–but she had to half-run to keep up with him. "Miss Windsor's in Room 320, sir."

"I'll be in my office for the rest of the night. I want vital signs taken every fifteen minutes. And she's to have no visitors–at least until I've talked to her in the morning." At that point, however, they entered Victoria's room and the conversation ceased as the doctor checked her heart and respiration, peering intently into her eyes with a tiny electric torch. At last he nodded, temporarily satisfied.

"Will she make it, do you think, doctor?"

"For this time, yes, I'm fairly sure she's going to pull through."

"But you're afraid this will happen again?"

"Miss Windsor has severe emotional problems–probably stemming from as far back as her childhood– and unless someone helps her get to the root of those problems, it will only be a matter of time before something like this occurs again."

* * *

Felicity walked dejectedly into her mother's kitchen and plopped down on one of the benches in the breakfast nook. Her relationship with Jamie had never been smooth, but since they'd formally announced their engagement, it seemed as though their arguments had only increased both in frequency and ferocity.

"What's the matterr, hinny," Nora MacDougall inquired gently as she put a mug of tea in front of her daughter. "Ye didna quarrrel wi' yourr jo again last night, did ye?"

"Aye!" The girl glowered at her tea as though it and it alone were the source of all her problems.

Nora shook her head in affectionate despair. She and her husband were placid, untroubled people and they were at a loss to explain Felicity. "What was it this time?"

"He wants blue currtains in the kitchen!"

"And that's what the arrgument was aboot?"

"Aye!" Felicity looked furious all over again.

Just then, however, Nora saw Jamie's jeep pulling into the yard. "Well, herre's yourr laddie noo."

"I dinna want to talk to him!" Picking up her mug, she started to get to her feet,

Her mother ignored her and opened the door to the knock. "I'll leave you two alone then," she said before the girl had a chance to go anywhere and immediately slipped out through the swinging door into the living room.

"What is it noo?" Felicity demanded. "Orrange polka dots on yourr blue currtains?" To her surprise Jamie didn't respond to her jab. Instead he asked her to sit down. "And ye dinna have to be so bluidy melodrramatic! Ye have no taste, Jamie MacDougall, and ye might as well admit it!"

All he did, however, was to sit down across from her and take hold of her hands. "Firrst of all," he began quietly, "ye should ken she came oot of it all rright."

"Noo ye'rre talkin' daft!" But something in his tone had alarmed her.

"Felicity–Victorria trried to commit suicide."

"Oh, dearr God–no! But ye said she was all rright."

"The news bulletin said she was conscious."

Felicity jumped to her feet–as always when upset unable to sit still. "Oh, dearr God–does Gavin ken what's happened?"

"He was the firrst perrson I thought of. I rang oop, but his Grranny said he hadna coom back frrom the hills. I left a message to telephone eitherr one of us. We should be the ones to tell him, I think."

"Aye." She nodded. "Och–poorr Victorria. What could have made herr want to do such a terrrible thing?"

It was three long days before Gavin returned. How could they ever tell him? How would he react? And to make matters worse their anxiety was unrelieved by any word of Victoria's condition other than what was given in the news media and these reports were liberally sprinkled with references to the actress' past. They had tried several times to talk to someone at the hospital, but of course no one would tell them anything.

Felicity was alone in the kitchen doing the supper dishes when Gavin came over the evening of the day he got back. Her father was working late at his clinic and her mother was helping him so it seemed she would have to be the one to tell him. To make it even more difficult it required only a glimpse of his face as he came up their back walk to know that the several days he'd spent alone in the Highland vastness hadn't helped at all. How could she ever tell him that Victoria had nearly died? She opened the door to his knock, standing back to allow him to enter. "Hello, Gavin."

He tried to smile at her. "How arre ye then, lass?" He bent to kiss her lightly on the cheek.

"Fine–therre's still coffee if ye'd be wantin' soom."

"No, thank you. I canna stay. Have you and Jamie set a date yet?" They'd come by then to sit facing each other in the breakfast nook–a favorite spot for everyone, it seemed, in the MacDougall kitchen.

"No and at this rate we neverr will. We arrgue aboot everrathin'." She couldn't imagine how they had come around to talking about her and Jamie, but then perhaps Gavin just needed to think about someone other than himself.

"Och, ye mustna do that, Felicity." He reached across the table to touch her arm in a gesture of great earnestness. She'd never seen him so serious. "Once ye've found someone ye can carre forr, ye must neverr let that perrson get away!" His fingers dug into her arm until involuntarily she winced. "I'm sorrry, lass." He quickly withdrew his hand. "Did ye want to see me forr some parrticularr rreason? Dad said you and Jamie have been rringin' me oop everra day while I've been gone. I trried to phone yourr jo, but therre was no answerr so I came herre."

"Jamie's worrkin' at the inn in Ballaterr, ye know."

"Aye, I'd forrgotten. My mind doesna seem to be worrkin' sae well these days."

"Gavin, I..I...." Desperately she hunted for the right words. "Torri...." Unconsciously she slipped into the use of his name for Victoria.

"Torri..what?" Again Gavin gripped her arm and this time he was completely unaware of her grimace of discomfort..

Felicity looked at him steadily as she spoke. "She....she trried to...to take...herr own life."

Helplessly she watched the pain on his handsome face. "But....but ye said–trried," he said after a few seconds. "Then....then she's all rright?" His grip intensified until in spite of herself she gasped. "Lass—I'm trruly sorrry," he apologized again. "I rreally am nae trryin' to severr yourr arrm in twa." In spite of his sadness he smiled–such a sweet smile that Felicity had to look away, her eyes filing with tears. How could she possibly have failed to notice until now this deeper side of Gavin's nature?

"Ye should go to herr," she whispered intently, placing her other hand over his.

He shook his head. "No, lassie. If anythin'–I'm the cause of all this. If she's all rright, that's all that matterrs."

"Gavin–if you'd just listen to me......"

"I'll be goin' along then, Felicity. Thank ye verra much forr yourr kindness." He got to his feet and hurried out, ignoring her pleas. But back at his father's house he immediately packed his things to return to London. He couldn't help himself; he had to be near her.

Chapter 24

Approaching Victoria's door that first morning, Dr. Anthony paused a moment before entering. The head nurse on the floor had already informed him she was fully awake and cognizant of her surroundings, but of all the various sessions he was called upon to have with a patient, this one–the first following a suicide attempt–was perhaps the most difficult. He supposed it was because he could never be sure what to expect. At last he took a final deep breath and pushed open the door. The room was in semi-darkness, the Venetian blinds still partly closed, but he could see that the hospital bed had been raised about halfway and that Victoria was lying there quietly, her arms at her sides. "Good morning, Miss Windsor," the doctor said in a pleasant, but non-committal tone. He preferred to allow the patient to set the mood of any session. "Would you object to a little more light in here?"

"It...it doesn't matter, but I'm afraid I don't look very attractive this morning."

Dr. Anthony walked around the bed to the window and with the blinds opened he turned back to look at her directly for the first time. Someone had brushed her hair and tied it back with a pink ribbon and despite her unnatural pallor and her complete lack of make-up she was as lovely as ever. "And I'm afraid I must disagree." He smiled at her as he pulled a chair over to sit beside her bed. "You are a remarkably beautiful woman, but I'm sure you're accustomed to hearing that."

"Yes." Victoria shrugged.

"So often, in fact, that you find it boring?"

"A woman is never bored by compliments." Here she paused. " I know you, don't I?"

"Yes–Doctor Anthony."

"Doctor Anthony." He noticed she still had the same habit of massaging her forehead. "Oh, yes—Olivia's custody hearing. Well, as I was saying, a woman is never bored by compliments."

"But basically they're meaningless. Is that what you're saying?"

"I suppose so." He watched her eyes fill with tears. "I...I've always known I was beautiful, but what does it matter when I've failed at everything else?"

"Is that why you attempted suicide?" Involuntarily Victoria gasped. "Does it disturb you," he inquired calmly, "to have someone come right out with it like that?" She made no reply. The tears were coming faster now and she possessed none of her customary self-control to stop them. "Because I don't say it to be cruel, Miss Windsor," the doctor went on after a moment, "but neither do I intend to evade the subject." He offered her a tissue from the box beside her bed. "<u>Was</u> that the reason?" he asked again when she had blown her nose and dried her eyes. For the second time since he'd walked into the room, Victoria shrugged and this time she said nothing. "Do you intend to talk to me?" Dr. Anthony said getting to his feet. "Because if you don't, I have better ways to spend my time."

"No, please don't leave." Victoria reached out to him.

He turned and came back to stand by the bed. "But are you willing to pay the price of my company?"

"In other words–if I want you to stay, I have to talk." There was just a slight glint of humor in her large green eyes.

The doctor smiled. "You have a marvelous resiliency, Miss Windsor. Very few people can joke so soon after a suicide attempt."

And now those same incredible eyes blazed with anger. "Do you make a point of bringing that up a certain number of times per minute and is it just a matter of sheer bloody luck?"

"We do have to begin at that point, you know. You have to comprehend fully what you tried to do to yourself and why–why you found life so intolerable that you felt compelled to seek escape from it."

Victoria looked down at her hands, now clasped loosely together over her slightly rounded abdomen, and shook her head. "I...I wasn't simply being evasive before. I...I really don't know why. I was lying in bed and all at once it....it just came to me–the way out. It..it all seemed so simple. It actually didn't even feel real."

"When I first came in here a few minutes ago, you said you considered yourself a failure." Tears filled her eyes again and this time she merely nodded. "Certainly not from a professional standpoint?"

"No! I'm....I'm very proud of my accomplishments as an actress!" The blonde head came up defiantly as if to say–You see, I have succeeded at something! "But at everything else, I've failed–as a mother, as a wife, even as a friend. While...while the pills were taking effect, I was just lying there in a..a kind of euphoria and I was thinking how much better off everyone would be without me."

"Does your husband make you feel as though you've failed him?"

"It's...it's nothing Jason has done. I <u>have</u> failed him. I...I've been unfaithful to him. He...he says he's forgiven me, but I know he really hasn't. How could he? Such a fine, decent man."

"And yet I thought the capacity to forgive was basic to the Christian faith. How can he be that fine–that decent if he is unable to forgive?"

"You can't expect a man to forgive that!" Immediately Victoria came to her husband's defense. "It's simply that I'm a worthless human being."

"So worthless, in fact, that you didn't deserve to live?"

"Is...is that what I thought? Is that why I...I..."

"Say it, Miss Windsor! Say it! You have to face the fact that you came very close to dying because once–just for a few minutes, perhaps–you wished to die."

"I...I can't understand it. There have been so many times when my...my life seemed intolerable and yet I never even considered..." She faltered again and raised her eyes to find Dr. Anthony studying her with a firm, yet kindly intensity. Swallowing hard, she went on...."suicide." He watched the full realization dawning on her face and all at once she sat bolt upright in the bed, reaching out to take hold of both his hands with both of hers. "Dear God," she whispered clinging to him. "I tried to kill myself! Why? I...I don't want to die. Oh, God–Olivia...Olivia! Will it have gotten into the newspapers in the States, do you think?"

"Would you like to ring her up? I'm limiting your use of the telephone, but I can make an exception."

"Not....not quite yet. I....I don't think I....I could." He saw the panic in her eyes.

"It's all right, Miss Windsor. In the meantime I can telephone the people she's staying with."

"Yes, of course." Immediately Victoria looked relieved. "The MacAllisters. They'll reassure her."

Dr. Anthony handed her his notebook so that she could write down the number and then he stood up to leave. "Well, I think we've talked enough for now. I've already put you through more than I intended for a first session."

"I...I'm really not tired. I...I feel like talking."

"Good! You do some thinking about all of this and I'll see you tomorrow."

Late that evening, however, Dr. Anthony was just leaving his office when the telephone rang. He had been awake since Jason's call at three a.m. and all he wanted right now was to go home. With a sigh of weary resignation he returned to his desk and picked up the receiver. It was one of the nurses. "Doctor, I'm afraid Miss Windsor is refusing to take her medication."

"I'll stop by on my way out." A few minutes later he was hurrying off the lift on Victoria's floor and along the hall toward her room. Pushing open the door, he found her backed into a corner, surrounded by two additional nurses and a male attendant as well as the woman who had telephoned him. "All right, people, you may all leave now," the doctor said briskly. "I don't think Miss Windsor is dangerous." Quickly and quietly they filed out of the room, a little ashamed at their overreaction.

"I...I won't take it," Victoria insisted vehemently–shaking her head. "I'll never take anything like that again—ever!"

"It's only to help you sleep. The first night can be pretty traumatic."

"I'm....I'm afraid to...to go to sleep."

"That's perfectly natural under the circumstances."

"I...I've always hated the nights anyway."

"Will you at least come back to bed and lie down?" he urged her gently. After a moment Victoria relaxed her tense vigilance against the wall and came over to the bed to slip under the covers again. "Why are the nights so terrible?" Dr. Anthony asked as he tucked the blankets in around her.

Once more Victoria shrugged. "I suppose because....because it's the worst time to be alone." Tears came into her eyes again.

"And yet–in all those years–you never once considered suicide?"

She shook her head. "I...I accidentally overdosed once, but I never even thought of...of trying to kill myself."

"Good. You can say it now." He patted her arm. "That means we can begin to deal with the reasons."

"It...it doesn't get any easier."

"Perhaps it never will."

"How thoughtless of me, Doctor Anthony," Victoria said all at once–reaching out to him with one slender, graceful hand. "You've probably been up since....Jason telephoned you this morning."

"How kind of you to think of me, Miss Windsor." He smiled as he took the offered hand in both of his. "Now will you allow me to give you a shot to help you sleep?"

He felt her tense slightly, but then almost at once she relaxed again. "All...all right," she said after a bit. "If....if you say so."

"I'll be right back." When the doctor returned a moment later with the hypodermic, she was still lying there unmoving. "Sure about this?" He indicated the needle. She nodded–looking up at him with an almost childlike trust which he found extremely touching. He gave her the injection in her upper arm and laid her hand gently down on the bed again.

"Will...will you stay with me until I fall asleep? I know I'm a terrible nuisance, but.... but it would help if I weren't alone."

"No one could ever consider you a nuisance, Miss Windsor." He sat down by her bed, once more taking hold of her hand, but a short while later he felt her tense up again. "You're fighting the drowsiness, aren't you? Now you know I would never do anything to harm you, don't you?"

She nodded, turning over on her side, and soon she was asleep. Dr. Anthony stayed a few minutes longer and then slipped noiselessly from the room.

When he returned the next morning, however, it was to find Victoria wide awake and highly indignant. "You've got one bloody hell of a nerve?" she exclaimed angrily.

"Good morning to you, too," he chuckled.

She hesitated. There were very few people whom she couldn't intimidate, but Dr. Anthony was apparently one of them. "You....you son-of-a-bitch!" She was attempting to maintain her mini-tantrum,, but the doctor saw the corners of her mouth twitch.

"Do you find profanity effective, Miss Windsor?"

Instantly her smile died away. "I...I shouldn't swear. Jason doesn't approve."

"Does your husband often criticize you?"

"Anyway I....I shouldn't swear in front of Olivia. I don't want her to acquire the habit."

"And how about you? How did you acquire the habit? Or did you simply find the use of profanity effective?"

"I suppose you agree with Jason then?"

Again Jason, Dr. Anthony thought. So many times the conversation came back to him. "Agree about what?" he asked aloud.

"That people in the theatre are a bad influence on me."

"Are they?"

"Do you always answer a question with a question?"

"Is that what I'm doing?"

"Oh, really!" Her eyebrows flew up in amused exasperation.

"You are a delight, Miss Windsor!" He smiled. "And I must tell you again, it is most unusual to be so upbeat only days after a suicide attempt."

"Is it?" She paused, appearing to think for a moment. "You know, it's strange. I feel marvelous! I haven't felt this good since...since..." She didn't complete the sentence, but in her mind she could see Gavin so clearly and suddenly she wanted more than anything to be with him just once more. "No...no!" she exclaimed. "Will I never learn?"

"Never learn what?"

"Nothing...nothing." Victoria shook her head and ran her hands through her hair which today fell free in golden waves about her shoulders. "Where was I?"

Dr. Anthony made no further reference to her strange outburst. This was clearly not the time to pursue the matter. "You know, Miss Windsor," he said instead, "a suicide attempt is often a cry for help."

She looked at him intently. "Is...is that what I was doing? Asking for help?"

"It's entirely possible. But for now I'd like to go back to when I came in. You were very upset with me. May I ask why?"

"This morning I asked the nurse why....why Jason hadn't been in to see me. I....I was afraid he was annoyed with me."

"Annoyed with you?"

"Well, I...I never seem to be able to please him. And I...I've tried so hard. I...I really have. Except....except....."

"When you were unfaithful to him?"

"Yes." Victoria reached for a tissue to dab at the corners of her eyes where tears were once again threatening to escape.

"Did the affair mean anything to you?"

"No...oh, no! It...it didn't. I told Jason that, but he still hasn't forgiven me. I already told you that, though, didn't I?"

"Yes...and I presume the nurse informed you that you were to have no visitors."

"But I shouldn't think that would include my husband."

"Especially your husband. I'm not convinced he has a healthy effect on you."

"My own husband? That's absolutely ridiculous! I...I want to see him."

"Do you?"

"Another Goddamned question! You're supposed to give me the answers–not ask one bloody question after another!"

"All right, Miss Windsor. I'll give you an answer since you've requested it, but you may not like it. No, I don't think you do want to see your husband. In fact, I think you're secretly relieved that I won't let you see him."

"You get the hell out of here! You're the one I don't want to see–you and your asinine ideas!"

"Because I further believe that he as much as anyone is responsible for your deep-seated feelings of unworthiness."

"How...how could Jason do that? Why would he do that? He...he loves me."

"Perhaps he does, but....."

"Perhaps? Of course he does!"

"Nevertheless, as long as I'm your doctor and you are a patient in this hospital, you will not see him." He stood up to leave.

"Wait–where are you going?"

"You told me–and I believe I'm quoting you correctly–'to get the hell out of here'."

"You're.....you're right about my swearing for effect." Clearly she wanted him to stay, but she couldn't come right out and say so.

"Am I?" He smiled. "Yes, I know–another question. And yet another–when did you start?"

"At Heathfield, I suppose. It's an Anglican Convent school."

"To shock the good sisters, I should imagine."

"Yes." The green eyes were sparkling again now. "My proudest moment was when I told the Mother Superior to 'sod off, you bloody old bitch!' I thought she was going to spit her teeth out." Dr. Anthony roared with laughter. Jason Eliot was a fool to want this charming woman to be any different. "But....but you're wrong," Victoria went on after a moment, "about it being Jason who makes me feel undeserving of love. I...I've never considered myself worth much. Even my own parents couldn't be bothered with me."

So a loveless childhood was again at the root of it all, the doctor thought. It seemed almost too pat an answer, but it was often the case. Out loud he replied, "So of course you couldn't be a worthwhile person if your own parents didn't care about you. Any child would think that. But surely there were others who loved you?"

Victoria hesitated–studying her graceful hands, resting quietly now in her lap. "Oh, there were people who tried to, but I wouldn't let them. I did everything I could to drive them away. Except one–an..uncle, but then he died and I felt betrayed all over again."

"And if I were to ask whom you love now, what would you say?"

"My husband, of course," she replied at once–defensively. "And my daughter. Oh, I do love Olivia. She's so sweet. But you've met her, haven't you?"

"Yes–a delightful little girl. Much the same as her mother. You know I do like you, Victoria. May I call you Victoria? I prefer to call my patients by their first names. It gives the relationship a tone of greater intimacy."

"Please." She smiled tremulously. "You really like me? Thank...thank you."

"It means a great deal to you to be liked, doesn't it?"

"Yes...oh, damn these tears!" Impatiently she reached for another tissue.

"And those are the only two people you love—your husband and your daughter?"

"A...ah...half-sister and...and a few close friends–Terry, Noel."

"No one else you'd care to mention?"

Suddenly there it was again–completely without warning–the longing to be with Gavin. He'd made her so happy. Guilt all but overwhelmed her. Of course she didn't love Gavin; she had only desired him. "No--no one." She was crying uncontrollably by now. "No one.... no one."

"All right then, Victoria. I'll be leaving now. We've accomplished a great deal, I think. I'll see you tomorrow."

She nodded–barely able to speak. "Thank...thank you, doctor."

Outside her room Dr. Anthony walked slowly away down the hall–deep in thought. First there'd been her reference to another time or place when she'd been happy and now her refusal to name another person she loved when obviously there was someone. With whom had she had the affair, he wondered.

Victoria, meanwhile, lay staring at the ceiling. Was it true–what Dr. Anthony had said? Was she relieved not to have to see Jason? So many times during their marriage he'd made her feel guilty or ashamed even when she sincerely believed she'd done nothing wrong. But of course I must be at fault, she told herself sternly. Jason is such a good man. He'd never criticize me if I didn't deserve it.

Yet she did feel more relaxed since...since.... Her mind stopped there, refusing to go any further, but Victoria had never been a coward and she wasn't about to become one now. "I....I tried to...to take my own life." She even whispered the words aloud to hear how they sounded. But why now? Why now? Why did I just get up out of bed and take all those pills? It was like a puzzle with one piece missing and no matter how hard she searched, that one piece still eluded her.

* * *

The following afternoon the doctor came again to continue their talk, beginning now to probe into her childhood. The session was extremely painful, but instinctively Victoria trusted him and with the aid of a continuous supply of tissues from the bedside box she talked about the emotional neglect of her parents, about the abuse of tyrannical nannies, and a great deal about Sister Philippa, who by the time she'd come into the young girl's life was already too late. These occasions were nearly as tiring for the doctor as they were for the patient and as he came out of Victoria's room after nearly two hours, the only things he wanted were a hot bath, a very dry martini and the tender ministrations of his understanding wife–in that order. To his dismay he found Miss Carter, the head nurse on the floor, waiting for him. "That was a long session, sir. You must be exhausted."

He nodded. "But I have the feeling I'm not going home yet. Why in God's name didn't I go into dentistry or better still–auto mechanics?"

The nurse smiled. "I'm afraid Reverend Eliot's waiting for you in the visitors' lounge. He's extremely annoyed that you haven't allowed him to see his wife. He says he wants you removed from her case."

"Yes, he's already told me that. I've been wondering why he hasn't done something about it. Well, no use in putting it off, what?"

When he entered the lounge a moment or so later, however, it was to find Jason sitting in one of the armchairs reading and making notes on a yellow legal pad. The other man glanced up and to Dr. Anthony's surprise his expression was completely composed. "Ah yes, thank you for coming," he said with an acknowledging nod. "I wished to ask why you continue to deny me the right to see my wife?"

The doctor did not immediately reply. He had just been informed that Jason Eliot was "extremely annoyed" and now this same Jason Eliot was calmly–almost rhetorically– inquiring why he was not being allowed to see his wife as though he merely required information. Was Jason simply a man of the best possible intentions who yet was ineffectual when the situation called for real action? But that wouldn't explain his constant moralizing and criticism of Victoria. Or was he someone (and this was what concerned the doctor) who was immediately intimidated when faced with a person of actual authority, but who enjoyed being that same authority figure when confronted by a somewhat less assertive person such as one of the nurses...or his wife. In either case nothing could be gained by antagonizing the man and when Dr. Anthony did finally speak, he was careful to keep his tone professional. "Unfortunately, Reverend Eliot, it is often those people closest to a patient who can do him or her the most harm...unintentionally, of course."

In the silence before the doctor finally answered him, Jason had closed his book, first meticulously marking his place, and put both it and his note pad down on the table next to him. "I'm afraid I fail to follow your reasoning," he replied precisely. "I care very deeply for my wife and I do not understand why seeing me would have an adverse effect on her."

"Simply <u>because</u> you do care for her, Reverend Eliot, as I know she does for you. At the moment the emotional strain would simply be too much for her."

Jason cleared his throat in a peremptory manner. "You know of course, do you not, that I possess the authority to remove my wife from your care."

Again the same threat, Dr. Anthony thought. Outwardly, however, he remained calm. "I don't think you want to do that. I have accomplished a great deal with your wife in a comparatively short time. I would think you'd wish that progress to continue."

The other man uncrossed his legs, immediately recrossing them the other way. Again he cleared his throat. "Exactly what type of progress?"

"Towards discovering the root cause of her emotional problems."

"For example?" Jason's tone was now openly scornful.

"She feels unworthy of being loved. It undoubtedly began when she was a small child. Her parents......"

"Ah, yes. The old story of the unhappy childhood. Isn't that theory somewhat overworked?"

It was with some difficulty now that Dr. Anthony kept his temper. "I assure you, sir, it is <u>not</u> merely a theory. There is a great deal of documented evidence that a lack of adequate love and caring during the formative years can result in emotional trauma– even outright psychosis– in later life."

"Nonsense, doctor! A mature adult is responsible for his own actions. Now I have to be leaving." Jason stood up. "Do what you will with my wife. Sooner or later you must release her from the hospital and then she will be where she belongs—with me. I can only hope and pray–" Here he paused to glance upward as though miraculously the roof would open allowing him to glimpse the heavens—"that you will not have done irreparable harm in the meantime." And with that he strode from the room.

Dr. Anthony followed as far as the door and stood watching as Reverend Eliot disappeared around the corner. There was no longer any question in his mind. Victoria's problems could most certainly be traced back to her childhood, but this man who swore such love and concern for her was the immediate cause. As long as she remained in hospital, he could keep her husband away from her, but–dear God–what would happen when she went home?

* * *

The doctor walked into her room the next day to find that for the first time she was sitting up in a chair, fully dressed and wearing make-up. Clearly it was only a matter of a day or so now before she would be ready to leave. He had no choice but to talk to her about Jason.

Victoria was wearing a rose-colored wool dress, her hair held back with a matching scarf. She was working at a small lap-desk. She glanced up as he came in and smiled at him. "A letter to my daughter," she explained. "I thought it would be easier to explain this way rather than over the telephone. I....I want you to read it though to...to see if you think it's all right."

"If you wish me to–of course." He accepted the sheet of paper and sat down in another chair facing her. "May I tell you how beautiful you look today?"

"Thank you." She smiled again and Dr. Anthony turned his attention to the letter.

My darling Olivia,

I know how terribly upset you must be by what has taken place in the last several days and for that, my dearest, I am so very sorry. I can only hope the MacAllisters have been able to reassure you. First, let me tell you, my love, that I am all right and I will continue to be all right. I can't really explain it all to you now, but when I see you again, I promise we will talk and talk until you're sure you understand.

You may tell the MacAllisters you will be coming to England in time for Christmas and that you'll be staying here until I'm finished. I miss you so much, my darling, and I want you with me.

No matter what else, Olivia, you must always remember how very much I love you and have always loved you.

Mummy

Dr. Anthony looked up when he had finished reading. Victoria was watching him, waiting anxiously for his opinion. "Oh yes, this will definitely relieve her mind. You were wise not to go into too much detail."

She glowed with his approval. "Thank you."

"Would you like me to post it for you?"

"Oh, would you? I'd appreciate that." The doctor watched as she rapidly addressed the envelope in her stylish, instantly recognizable handwriting. At last she handed it to him and folding her hands in her lap, she looked up at him expectantly, just the trace of a smile on her lips.

"As I'm sure you realize, Victoria," Dr. Anthony began as he slipped the letter into the breast pocket of his suit jacket, "you're about ready to go home–provided, of course, that we continue our sessions in my office. We still have a great deal of work to do." Had it been purely his imagination or had she tensed at the mention of going home? But that might have nothing to do with Jason. After an experience such as Victoria had just been through, the hospital often came to feel a safe place, a haven where the tensions of living in the real world could be avoided. "You do want to go home, don't you?" he went on– keeping his tone casual.

"Of...of course, I...I do. I'm...I'm very anxious to go home, to...to be with my husband."

"Because you see I'm not sure that's the best thing for you."

"That's..that's bloody idiotic! He...he loves me!" Does he love me, Victoria thought to herself. I used to think so, but I'm not sure anymore. No...no, he does love me. It's...it's my fault if I can't live up to his ideal of me–my fault, not his.

Her ears were so full of her own thoughts that she'd been totally unaware that Dr. Anthony was speaking and with some difficulty she forced herself to concentrate on what he was saying....."destructive love, not a healthy, healing love. Love should make you stronger. It should make you want to live, not want to die."

"Are you blaming my husband because I tried to commit suicide? How can you even think that? A kind, decent man like that....." Just then Jason walked in. "Oh—darling" Victoria ran to him. "Please take me home! I want to go home!"

He put his arms around her–looking accusingly over her shoulder as if to say, see what you've done to her? "I'll take my wife out of here now if you have no further objection." Dr. Anthony merely shrugged. "I'm sure you'll excuse us," Jason continued. "We would like a little privacy."

Slowly the doctor got to his feet and walked to the door. Opening it, he paused to look back at Victoria who still stood huddled against her husband. Turning willingly to the person who can destroy her, he thought. And unless she comes to me for help, I'm powerless to do a thing about it. "You will come to my office, though, won't you, Victoria?" he insisted gently.

"I believe I've asked you to leave, doctor." The other man's quiet voice now contained an undertone which was unmistakably threatening.

"Victoria—!" the doctor fairly pleaded. "You have to speak for yourself."

Finally she stirred in Jason's arms. "It's....it's all right, Dr. Anthony," she whispered. "Please leave."

He could see the tension in every line of her body and he was terribly afraid for her. "I am going nowhere, Victoria, until I hear you promise to come to my office."

"All right....anything...only please go."

"Yes, of course." At last then he reluctantly left the room.

When the doctor was gone, Victoria walked slowly away from Jason toward the window. She felt as though a heavy weight were pressing down on her chest making it difficult to breathe. "Shall I take you home now, dear?" he inquired in his most solicitous tone.

She hadn't even heard him. If only I could run away somewhere, she was thinking desperately–somewhere peaceful and quiet. When she'd failed to respond, Jason came up behind her, touching her gently on the arm. She jumped. "Wh...what?" She whirled about to face him.

"I'm sorry. I didn't mean to startle you. Shall we get you packed then?"

"Oh....packed...yes." But Victoria continued to glance about the room as if looking for something or someone.

"Is your valise here in the closet?" He indicated the door.

"Wh...what?" Fear–sickening, nauseating fear--was hammering against the inside of her head, all but drowning out his voice.

Just then one of the floor nurses entered the room. "May I help you get ready to leave, Miss Windsor?"

"You might pack her case for her," Jason replied. "It's in the closet." The nurse took the case out and laying it open on the bed, began to fill it from the drawers in the bureau.

Victoria remained silent. It was all she could do to hold onto herself and she mustn't let anyone see how frightened she was. If she did, they would undoubtedly insist she stay in hospital and her husband would be angry with her again. Jason, on the other hand, talked quite pleasantly to the woman as she worked. "It was the queerest thing," the nurse told one or two others somewhat later back at the duty station. "She didn't say a word the whole time I was in there; even when I asked her a direct question, it was Reverend Eliot who answered me, chatting away just as merrily as ever you please. You'd never think his wife had just attempted suicide."

* * *

"Well, here we are," Jason observed pleasantly as he unlocked the door of the hotel suite, standing back to allow her to enter first. "Doesn't it feel good to be out of the hospital, dear?"

"Yes...yes, of course," she managed to reply. The pounding inside her head was getting louder and it was hard to concentrate. She wished Noel or Martha or Terry were there, but at such disloyalty she felt guilty all over again. How could she want anyone else when she had her husband?

When Jason came out of the bedroom a moment later from putting the suitcase away, it was to find her still standing exactly where he'd left her. "May I take your coat for you, darling?"

"Oh...yes." Victoria looked down at herself, appearing bewildered. "My...my coat, yes." Numbly she allowed him to unbutton the garment and slip it down off her arms.

"Would you like to lie down for a while?" he inquired hanging up her coat and coming back to her.

"I...I don't know what I want to do." Mutely her eyes pleaded with him not to be angry with her.

"Well, Martha has left a fire laid. Suppose I light it and then I'll make us some tea and we can have a talk."

"All right...Jason. I....I'd like that. I really would." But her fists were clenched together so tightly at her sides that the nails were cutting into her palms.

"Come along then." He led her over and sat her down on the couch. Then he put a match to the fire. "I'll be right back, dear. If you want me, just call."

Victoria nodded and tried to smile. She hoped she was doing and saying the right things. She couldn't be sure and she wanted to please him. She didn't know what first drew her attention to the fire, but all at once she found herself staring at it. She wasn't even aware how much time had passed when Jason reappeared carrying a tray. "Here we are, Victoria." Settling himself beside her, he placed the tray on the coffee table. He looked over at her and smiled. Her hands were folded carefully in her lap and she was gazing into the flames. Her fascination with the fire unnerved him slightly. "Now then," he inquired as he poured the tea, adding milk and sugar to hers. "Isn't this better than being locked away in that hospital."

"I....I wasn't locked away."

"I didn't mean that exactly, dear. But you couldn't see me and that must have been enough to terrify you."

Victoria's mind went back to the days in hospital–days without pressure–days without Jason–and remembering the relief she'd felt at being free of him, renewed guilt all but overwhelmed her. "Of...of course, Jason. But...but Doctor Anthony felt that....."

"Doctor Anthony! Well, at least you're free of that man and his ridiculous theories! As if I'd do anything to hurt you!"

Jason didn't like Dr. Anthony. Was he going to prevent her from seeing him? "But...but I'm supposed to go to him for more therapy."

"That won't be necessary, Victoria." His tone indicated clearly that he considered the matter closed. "I prefer my own counseling methods and then, of course, nothing surpasses the therapeutic power of prayer."

He had never approved of her friends and now he evidently planned to shut her away from Dr. Anthony as well–shut her away from everyone indeed except himself. Involuntarily she shuddered and the cup and saucer dropped from her suddenly senseless fingers spilling tea onto the rug. "Oh my, I....I'm sorry." She looked like a little girl who knew very well she'd been naughty and deserved to be punished.

"It's all right," he at once reassured her, picking up the cup and saucer and replacing them on the tray. "I think perhaps it would be better if you did lie down for a while."

"Yes, Jason." Obediently she stood up to follow her husband into the bedroom. Not bothering to undress, she merely lay down on her back on top of the spread.

He covered her with a light blanket. "Try to sleep for a while, dear. Then later, we can talk. Would you prefer it a little darker in here?" Without waiting for her to reply, he moved over to the window to draw the drapes. "I'll just leave the door open a crack so that I can hear you if you need me."

He left her then, but even alone she couldn't relax. Rigid with tension, she continued to lie there on her back staring up at the ceiling. "Jason?" she called out after a few minutes.

He must have been very near the door because he appeared at once. "Yes, dear?"

"I'm...I'm so tense. Would...would you please bring me one of those tranquillizers Doctor Anthony prescribed?"

"Now I thought we'd agreed we were through with the doctor and his unfortunate methods. Let me pray with you instead. Believe me, you'll find it much more effective."

For the next few days, then, Jason was with her almost constantly. Only at night when he was asleep, did she have any solitude. He prayed with her; he read to her from the Bible. And whether consciously or not he used her weakened state of mind to work on her. "No, of course not, dear," he would say patiently when at first she still mentioned Dr. Anthony. "You don't need him. Now please listen and try to understand what I'm saying to you. When you're finished with the theatre and all the unfortunate elements associated with it...... When we're back in the States where we belong......

In the beginning Victoria tried feebly to hold on to her own ideas. She had to act; without her work she was only half-alive. She would never belong in the States. England was home..... England. Gradually, however, she gave up trying to fight him. Jason must know what was best for her. And anyway his will seemed much stronger than hers and she was so tired and it was easier not to struggle anymore.

* * *

Then a few days after Victoria's release from the hospital Jason returned to work. "Prodigals" was barely open in a store front a block or so off Piccadilly and already homeless young people were finding their way there. Word of mouth had it "not 'alf bad if you don't mind the Yank's sermons". Martha, of course, came back to look after Victoria. "Good morning, Mrs. Kendall." Jason's tone as he admitted her on that first morning was distinctly funereal. "Mrs. Eliot's still asleep. She is to have absolute quiet so no one is to be allowed to see her."

"Yes, sir. You know I'll take good care of her." She started to remove her hat and coat.

"I've left the number of my office there by the telephone," Jason explained pointing. "Please call me if you observe any problems developing. That fool of a doctor has done a great deal of damage and I still haven't been able to undo all of it."

"Reverend Eliot–please. I know it's not my place to ask, but...but how could this have happened?"

"It's quite simple," he replied firmly. "Victoria is a beautiful person, but she is weak and unfortunately she has come under the influence of some of the more depraved elements in our society."

"I'm....I'm afraid I don't understand, sir."

"I really can't take the time to go into detail now." Jason always managed somehow to make the person to whom he was speaking feel slightly below average in intelligence. "Also I'm concerned that if we continue to talk, we may awaken her."

He left then–almost at once. Martha had just started to clean up from his breakfast, however, when the bedroom door opened and Victoria came out into the living room. The housekeeper was shocked. Even on some of the worst mornings of her life Miss Windsor had never looked so haggard. Why, she's really ill, Martha thought. Can Dr. Anthony possibly have done that much harm? "Is...is he gone?" Leaning against the door jamb for support, Victoria peered nervously about the room.

"Yes, Miss Windsor. May I get you anything? At least tea and toast?"

"No, Martha, thank you. I…I just want to be left alone." Victoria walked across to the couch, curling up in one corner of it.

"I hope we didn't disturb you. Reverend Eliot said you were still asleep."

She smiled at that, but it was an unnatural smile. "Yes, I wanted him to think that."

The housekeeper came to sit beside her, taking hold of her hand. "Please, Miss Windsor, you're frightening me."

"Don't worry, Martha. You see, if it all becomes too much for me, I know a place where I can hide."

"Wh...where is that?"

"Ssh...it's a secret." Still smiling, the actress raised her forefinger to her lips. "And if I tell anyone, it will be spoiled. You understand, don't you?"

"Of course, Miss Windsor. I'll be in the kitchen if you need me."

For most of the day Victoria remained silent and unmoving although from time to time she would rock back and forth for a while, humming to herself. She did respond when Martha spoke to her directly, but the lunch with which the housekeeper tried to tempt her was left untouched on the coffee table. Suddenly, however, late in the afternoon she appeared to rouse herself. "What time is it?"

"Nearly four, Miss Windsor. Would you like tea? It's even the proper hour for it." Martha made a weak attempt at a joke.

Victoria's eyes widened in panic. "Oh....oh, no. I...I don't have time for tea." Getting to her feet, she swayed a little, but immediately steadied herself. "You see, I...I've got to get back to bed before....before...." Shaking her head, she hurried in the direction of the bedroom. "Tell him....tell him, I'm asleep."

Could Miss Windsor actually be afraid of her own husband, Martha thought. Dear God–then who's going to help her? She had Reverend Eliot's dinner ready for him when he arrived home, hoping that if he were prone to being harsh with Victoria, a good meal might soften him up a little. She'd chosen, unfortunately, to serve steak-and-kidney pie. Jason wondered how British food could possibly be so unappetizing, but of course he didn't complain, allowing himself a moment of pride at his extraordinary forbearance.

"Please sit down for a moment, Mrs. Kendall," he said when he'd finished eating, indicating the chair across from him at the small table. "I wanted to ask you how my wife is doing?" he went on as she settled herself. "You didn't telephone so I presume she had a restful day."

Martha could understand why Miss Windsor found this man intimidating. Even this quite natural question on his part made her uneasy. "I...I'm really concerned about her, sir. She just sat on the couch all day; she wouldn't eat and when I spoke to her, she barely answered me.

"I had instructed you not to disturb her!"

"I didn't, sir. She came out of the bedroom right after you left and she....."

"You say–she came out as soon as I was gone?" He looked at her sharply.

Immediately Martha realized her mistake. "I'm not exactly sure when it was, sir– just some time after you left."

"Yes, I see." Jason put down the coffee cup from which he'd been drinking all during their conversation and stood up. "Well, it seems Victoria and I still need to talk. We'll get nowhere if she deliberately avoids me." He walked briskly across to the bedroom door.

Martha hurried after him. "Please, Reverend Eliot–take her back to Doctor Anthony. She needs professional help."

"Nonsense. She needs me!" With this he went on into the bedroom and when the housekeeper left about an hour later, she could still hear his voice through the closed door. Miss Windsor had not said a word.

The next morning when Martha came to work, she was relieved to find that Victoria was, in fact, up and dressed, sitting at the table with Jason while he ate his breakfast. "Good morning," she exclaimed cheerily as she hung up her coat and hat. Maybe it would help if she, too, pretended everything was all right.

"Good morning, Mrs. Kendall." Jason's tone was at its most pleasant. "As you can see, Mrs. Eliot's feeling much better this morning." How desperately he wanted to believe this was true–that his talks with Victoria and his many heartfelt prayers were indeed what she needed. After all, she <u>had</u> gotten up this morning and even dressed herself, coming to join him at the breakfast table. It would simply require a great deal of time to undo Anthony's bungling.

"Yes, Reverend Eliot," Martha immediately responded, "she does seem more like herself today." Jason would never listen to her and it was better to let him think she agreed with him. But she observed Victoria just sitting there with her hands folded in her lap and she knew he was terribly wrong. She cleared away Jason's breakfast dishes, carrying them into the kitchen apparently to begin washing them. Everything must appear normal for once he was gone, she was determined to do something. Martha had long since forgotten her self-imposed rules of professional conduct. After all, hadn't Mr. Hamilton said she was not merely Miss Windsor's housekeeper, but her friend as well. Dear God, if only she knew where <u>he</u> was!

"I'm leaving now, Mrs. Kendall," Jason called out just then. "Mrs. Eliot will be fine, but you know where to reach me if you need me."

"Yes, sir." As soon as she heard the door of the suite close, Martha came back out into the living room. "Miss Windsor, why don't we go on over to the couch together and have a chat?" Without a word of protest Victoria stood up and walked over, curling up again in the same spot in which she'd spent most of yesterday. Tears rushed into the housekeeper's eyes as she followed to sit beside her. She would actually have preferred the demanding, imperious actress of earlier years. "You can't go on like this," she said as gently as possible. "You need to go back to Doctor Anthony."

"Jason knows what's best for me. He'll take care of me."

"Miss Windsor, please, I…." But here she was interrupted by the ringing of the telephone.

"I…I don't want to talk to anyone."

"Of course, ma'am. I'll take it in the kitchen." She hurried to answer the phone, hoping with all her heart the caller would turn out to be someone to whom she could turn for help. "Hello, Miss Windsor's residence." There was a brief pause on the other end of the line. Rebecca didn't even know <u>why</u> she was calling and when someone actually answered, she almost hung up. "Hello," Martha said again.

"I…I just rang up to see how…how Victoria was feeling after…after her accident."

"May I ask who's calling, please?"

Again Rebecca did not immediately reply. "Oh…ah…no one in particular. Just….just one of her students."

"How did you happen to have Miss Windsor's telephone number? Do you know her well?"

"I don't see what that has to do with anything."

"Because someone has to convince her to go back to the doctor."

"What do you mean?" The stab of worry she'd experienced at these words annoyed Rebecca a great deal. "Isn't she doing well?"

"No...no, she isn't–not at all--so I thought maybe you could....."

"I can't do anything," Rebecca interrupted her quickly. "There must be somebody else!" And the line immediately went dead.

It seemed then that it was going to be up to her and with a sigh–at once resigned and resolute–Martha replaced the receiver, turning to go back out into the living room. Well, if that were the case, she was indeed more than equal to the task. In the doorway, however, she paused for a moment to look at Victoria who was still exactly as she'd left her. But perhaps the answer lay at least partly in the woman herself. Surely someone who'd always been so vibrantly alive, so determinedly self-assertive could not possibly have submitted entirely to the will of another. "Miss Windsor?" Martha came over to the couch again now, leaning down to touch her employer lightly on the arm.

At the touch Victoria spun about to face her. Her eyes were no longer dead and impassive, but electric with terror. She clutched frantically at her old friend. "Dear God, Martha! I'm so frightened!'

"Can you tell me what it is you're afraid of?"

"That...that place I told you about. It's....it's calling to me."

"Miss Windsor, let me ring up the doctor."

"Jason feels Doctor Anthony is wrong for me."

"Do you think he's wrong for you?"

"No, but....."

"Is Doctor Anthony's number in your book?"

"Yes, but...but please don't telephone him. Jason will be angry and I want so much for him to...to..." All at once, however, a shuddering breath escaped her and she began to shiver, hugging herself about the waist with both arms. "Oh, no—please! Dear God--- please.... please!"

That decided it for Martha and hurrying over to the telephone table, she looked up the number and dialed. The doctor's service informed her he was at St. Elizabeth's Hospital that morning and gave her the new number. Quickly she dialed that, but then the hospital operator asked her to hold while she paged him. By now Victoria was lying on the couch in a fetal position, trembling uncontrollably, the sounds coming out of her barely human and with each new delay Martha became increasingly frantic. It seemed like forever before Dr. Anthony finally came on the line. "Oh, thank God," she murmured. "Doctor, I'm Mrs. Kendall, Miss Windsor's housekeeper."

"Yes, Mrs. Kendall?" He'd been expecting this call and now he was instantly on edge, dreading the worst. "What is it?"

"Miss....Miss Windsor's having a...a convulsion or...or something. She...."

"No need to say more. An ambulance will be there as soon as possible. In the meantime try to get one of those tranquillizers down her that I prescribed and...."

"I'm afraid her husband threw the pills out, sir. He said she didn't need them."

"Damn him! Well, just keep her warm then and as calm as you can."

Hanging up, Martha went quickly into the bedroom for one of the extra blankets and bringing it over to the couch, she tucked it around Victoria. Then all she could do was sit beside her and wait, stroking her hair and talking to her in a low voice.

When the ambulance crew arrived, one of the two attendants injected Victoria with a tranquillizer and when she grew quiet, they lifted her gently onto the stretcher. "Are you coming with us, ma'am?" the other man inquired respectfully of Martha. She nodded, grabbing her coat from the closet to follow them from the suite and down the hall to the lift.

A room was ready and waiting for Victoria when they got to the hospital. Deftly Dr. Anthony checked her vital signs and nodded, temporarily satisfied. Only then did he go back out into the hall where a worried Martha was waiting for news. "Mrs. Kendall?"

"Yes, doctor. How...how is she?'

"I won't really be able to tell you anything for several hours. I'd like to keep her sedated until I'm able to reach at least some tentative conclusions."

"I can't help feeling her husband is partly responsible."

"A very astute observation, Mrs. Kendall. In fact, after Miss Windsor's suicide attempt, I tried to convince her not to return to her husband, but he seems to have a great deal of influence over her."

"Oh yes–even today she begged me not to telephone you because Reverend Eliot would be angry."

"Then he's not aware she's back in hospital."

"No, he's not." Martha sighed. "I suppose I'll have to let him know."

"Don't worry. I'll take care of that. But first I'd appreciate your telling me how Miss Windsor has seemed to you."

"I wasn't there for the first few days, sir. Her husband stayed with her." The doctor rolled his eyes, but made no verbal comment. "And when I saw her for the first time yesterday morning," Martha went on, "I...I was shocked. I'd never seen her look quite so ill."

"Did she say or do anything in particular?"

"She hardly moved from the couch the entire day except sometimes she'd rock back and forth and hum to herself. I...I couldn't get her to eat anything. But...but what worried me the most, sir, was when she told me she knew a place where no one could bother her."

He nodded gravely. "And today?"

"About as I told you on the telephone except...except that now..now the place was calling to her. Doctor, could...could she be considering suicide again?"

"I rather think not. Often it is the mind and not the body which seeks escape. But I should telephone her husband now, I suppose." Martha gave him the number and he went immediately to his office. Nothing could be gained by postponing what he fully expected to be unpleasant.

"Good morning—Prodigals," the operator announced chirpily. "Remember–you can always go home again."

The doctor grimaced. He despised platitudes. "May I speak to Jason Eliot, please. Doctor Anthony calling."

"Reverend Eliot is just concluding a counseling session. Will you hold, please."

"Yes, of course." I wonder whose life the man's screwing up now, he thought bitterly.

A minute or so later Jason came on the line. "Yes, doctor?" Clearly he was annoyed. "What may I do for you? As I've already informed you, my wife is no longer any of your concern."

"But I'm afraid she is. Your wife became seriously disturbed again this morning. Your housekeeper notified me and we brought her back to hospital."

"Well, I shall see she is discharged at once."

"Reverend Eliot–I am prepared to get a court injunction in order to keep your wife under my care. Now are you at least willing to come down here and talk to me about it?"

There was a brief pause. "Yes–all right–about three?"

"Fine, Reverend. I'll be in my office." Dr. Anthony hung up the telephone with somewhat more force than necessary. If the man was so damned worried, what in hell was he going to be doing for the next four hours? In a few minutes, however, he'd calmed down enough to consider the entire matter more dispassionately. From their first meeting he'd handled Jason Eliot badly. It was extremely unprofessional of him to have sat in judgment on the man and worse–they'd both expended a great deal of energy being angry with each other, energy better put to use in helping Victoria.

"Reverend Eliot is here," his receptionist announced to him over the intercom– precisely at three o'clock.

The words had barely died away before Jason strode into the office without so much as a perfunctory knock. "Doctor–you will release my wife immediately!"

"Please sit down, Reverend Eliot. Believe me–your wife is in no condition to go anywhere."

"What have <u>you</u> done to her?"

It was fortunate that before Dr. Anthony had a chance to reply, he was interrupted once again by the intercom. "I'm sorry to bother you, sir, but Mrs. Kendall would like..."

"Tell her to come in," Jason demanded. "I wish to speak to <u>her</u> as well."

"Mrs. Kendall may join us," the doctor instructed. This time, of course, there was a knock. "Yes, come in."

"Please don't be angry, Reverend Eliot," Martha pleaded at once. "Miss Windsor was curled up on the couch, shaking all over and making these strange jabbering noises, and I didn't know what else to do!" Emboldened by her awareness of the doctor's support, she rushed on. "Please, sir. You're not helping her. I know you love her, but she's afraid of you."

Jason said nothing for several seconds, his gaze fixed steadily on the floor. "It's....it's true, you know," he whispered at last, his voice breaking. "I....I do love her."

"Mrs. Kendall," the doctor interposed gently, "perhaps I should talk to Reverend Eliot alone now."

"Yes, of course. You aren't angry with me, are you, sir?" She put her hand on Jason's arm. All he could do was shake his head. "It will be all right. You'll see."

"Now will you please sit down, Reverend Eliot?" Dr. Anthony asked again when Martha had left.

Jason slumped into a chair, his hands clasped between his legs, his head bowed in despair. "She...she <u>is</u> afraid of me, isn't she?" he said finally. "In the last few days I've tried to ignore it, but I'm not so blind I couldn't see it." Now that he was at last admitting all his fears and doubts to someone, he felt a profound relief and he couldn't stop talking. "Ever since I fell in love with her, I've been terrified of losing her. Now it's all coming true and the worst part is I'm making it happen. I'm driving her away."

Dr. Anthony came to sit facing him, reaching across to rest a comforting hand on his shoulder. "You can't blame yourself. But you must trust me. I'm going to do all I can to help her. You believe that, don't you?" Jason nodded. "Now there's very little you can do before morning. I suggest you go home and get some rest."

"May....may I see her tomorrow?"

"If she's calmer–yes–and if I may be present until we see how she reacts."

"And...and if she's...she's still afraid of me?"

The doctor tried to smile reassuringly. "Well now, we won't worry about that until it happens, will we?"

* * *

It hadn't helped Gavin at all to be back in London. It was, in fact, almost more than he could bear to be so near Victoria and not have the right to be with her. Always before a proud man, he seemed now to have stopped caring, supporting himself since his return to the city with various odd jobs. Often he'd just place his cap in front of him on the pavement, playing his guitar and singing until he collected enough to eat that night. Finally toward the end of the month he thought of the last coffee house where he'd worked with Jamie. True–he walked out on that job, but they'd always liked him so perhaps with the week-end coming up, they might be willing to use him. The owner did agree, somewhat reluctantly, to hire him–albeit only for that week-end and only in return for his supper and whatever he might receive in tips.

Once Gavin would have refused such an insulting offer, but now he accepted almost gratefully. As he ate his supper on that Friday evening, however, the bustle all around him in the club's kitchen only intensified his loneliness. Someone had left a newspaper on the table and he flipped idly through it as he ate. If he appeared occupied, people weren't so apt to talk to him and these days he found casual conversation difficult.

It was only a small item in the middle of the second page of the back section of the paper. Afterwards he wondered how he'd even happened to see it. "Actress Returned to Hospital" the article was headed and it went on to say that "Less than a week after her release from hospital following a suicide attempt, Victoria Windsor was readmitted to St. Elizabeth's Hospital yesterday morning. Her doctor was unavailable for comment." Gavin threw down the paper and grabbing up his coat, headed toward the rear exit. "Hey, where you going?" the owner called after him. "Show's about to start."

"I willna be able to perrforrm tonight."

"I've had it with you, Hamilton. Don't bother coming back!"

But Gavin was already gone, the door slamming shut behind him, and less than twenty minutes later he strode up to the main desk of St. Elizabeth's.

"Yes...ah...sir." Much like every other woman before and since, the receptionist reacted involuntarily to brown eyes, wavy auburn hair and that irresistible dimple.

"Would ye tell me, please, what rroom Victorria Windsorr's in?"

The girl blinked–surprised. "I'm sorry, sir. We aren't allowed to give out that information."

"Och, 'tis all rright, lass." He smiled at her. "I'm by way o' bein' a frriend of herrs."

"I'm afraid that makes no difference, sir. I have my orders."

"Aye–well, thank ye, then." Gavin turned away. For one of the few times he could remember, the Hamilton charm had failed him and just when he needed it most.

* * *

It was only under heavy sedation now that Victoria found peace. Each time the doctor allowed the medication to wear off hoping to be able to talk to her, her agitation would immediately return, forcing him to order her tranquillized once again. He hadn't even dared to consider allowing Jason in the room.

Only a nurse was there the first time it happened. Victoria lay in a drugged sleep, broken only by occasional disjointed mumblings, her condition of the past thirty-six hours apparently unchanged. Then all at once the woman was sure she'd heard a distinct word or perhaps even a name. Instantly she put down her knitting and came over to the bed. "Did you say something, Miss Windsor?" Roused from her slumber, Victoria moaned a little, reaching upwards with both arms although her eyes remained closed. "Is there something you want, dear?" The actress' arms fell back then to hug herself about the chest and she began to rock from side to side in the bed, whimpering softly.

Sadly the other woman turned away, but no sooner had she sat down again than Victoria spoke a second time. "Gavin....."

"Who, Miss Windsor? Did you call for someone?"

"Gavin....oh, please...Gavin." At long last the influence of the sedative had broken through her self-imposed inhibitions to lay bare her deep, unanswered need.

Hurrying out to the desk, the nurse sent someone else in to sit with Victoria. Then she telephoned Dr. Anthony in his office where he'd gone to rest for a while. "Doctor, Miss Windsor is calling for someone."

"At least that's some sort of response. Who? Her daughter?"

"No, sir...someone called Gavin."

"Gavin? I can't recall her ever mentioning that name. But perhaps if I come and talk to her, I can find out more." As he hurried down the hall a few minutes later, however, Dr. Anthony couldn't help wondering once again as to the identity of the man with whom Victoria had had the "meaningless" affair. Miss Carter was waiting for him at the nurses' station and together they walked the rest of the way to Victoria's room. Once again she was lying quietly although her arms were still clasped to her chest–something the doctor hadn't seen before. "Has she said anything else?" he inquired in a low voice of the other nurse.

"No, sir. Nothing I could understand."

"I'll stay with her for a while," Dr. Anthony told the two women and when they'd left, he came over to stand beside the bed. "Victoria–who is Gavin?' he asked quietly. Her eyes flooded with helpless tears and she began to turn her head from side to side on the pillow. "Do you want <u>Gavin</u>? Is that it, Victoria?" This time he'd strongly stressed the name.

"G..G...Gavin." Her tear-filled gaze came back now to the doctor's face and for the first time since her return to hospital on the previous morning, he felt she was actually seeing him. "Please....<u>please</u>!"

"If you'll just tell me who he is, my dear, I'll do my best to find him for you."

"Gavin." She rested one hand beseechingly on his arm. "Oh, please, I want Gavin."

Dr. Anthony tried for another ten minutes, but although Victoria continued to plead with him, he could learn nothing more of the man's identity. It seemed he had no choice but to ask Jason Eliot and after stopping at the desk to order another sedative for her, he took the lift down two flights to the visitors' lounge. He couldn't be sure how her husband would react if, as he surmised, this Gavin turned out to have been Victoria's lover, but as always the welfare of his patient came first.

Jason rose eagerly to his feet as the doctor entered. "She...she wants to see me?"

Dr. Anthony shook his head. He couldn't help feeling sorry for the man. "You can help, however. Your wife's asking for someone, but all we can get out of her is a first name– Gavin." Quite evidently stricken, Jason sank back into the chair, burying his face in his hands. The doctor waited before continuing to allow him time to collect himself. "Then you <u>are</u> familiar with the name?" he inquired as gently as possible. The other man did not raise his head, merely nodding in response. "His last name?"

"Hamilton," Jason replied at last, still without looking up.

"Do you know how we can get in touch with him?"

"No!" His voice was unnaturally harsh.

"Is he here in London?"

"I said I don't know." Standing up again, Jason moved away to stare out the window.

"Reverend Eliot–it appears you don't much care for this man." Dr. Anthony had decided it would be more effective to pretend ignorance. "But if you can tell me anything about him, you must not allow your personal feelings to interfere."

"In other words I shouldn't object to the fact that my wife is calling for her lover?"

"Very well, if you won't help me, I'm sure someone else will–perhaps Mrs. Kendall." Dr. Anthony turned abruptly to leave.

Pride and love waged a brief, but painful battle and it must be said to Jason's credit that his love for Victoria won. "No...wait. I...I do know someone I can call. What...what time would it be now in New York?"

The doctor glanced at his watch. "Five hours difference, isn't it? About ten o'clock, then. You may use the phone in my office."

Alone a few minutes later Jason went through the motions of placing a call to the States. He didn't know how he was going to explain to Ken MacAllister why he suddenly needed to get in touch with Gavin Hamilton, but he would think of something when the time came. For the moment, however, it seemed he was spared all that since Lisa answered the phone and told the operator her parents weren't at home. She took down the information, promising her father would return the call–no matter the hour. She tried to ask about Victoria, but the connection was broken before she could receive an answer.

To pass the time of waiting he decided to go down to the hospital coffee shop–not that he felt like eating; he just didn't want to be alone. At this hour the place was all but deserted. At one table a few nurses and residents were enjoying a brief respite in an otherwise exhausting night while at another a small family group was apparently keeping a vigil near a loved one much as he himself was. The only other person in the room was a man sitting alone at the counter and Jason slid onto the stool next to him, thinking that he, too, might appreciate company.

Gavin couldn't understand why he was still there. At least once an hour now for more than twenty-four hours he'd tried to see Victoria. The last time the nurse at the front desk had actually threatened him with expulsion and arrest. Yet he couldn't bring himself to leave and so he, too, had come to the coffee shop to pass the hours of waiting. Sitting there now–staring down into a half-empty mug of tea, long since grown cold–he was overwhelmed by a sense of his own impotence. He couldn't help thinking, moreover, how aptly the present situation summed up his whole, wasted life–all empty charm and good humor and serving no purpose whatsoever. He glanced up as another man sat down next to him. Now <u>there</u> was the typical solid citizen–three piece suit, dark, conservative tie and all—probably had never spent a useless hour in his entire life.

Jason ordered coffee, looking over as he did so at the man on the neighboring stool–a tall, strongly built individual, the overpoweringly masculine sort he'd always found vaguely distasteful. But the other man nodded and smiled and he felt he should say something–anything to drown out his own thoughts. "Time's certainly long, isn't it?" he said finally, "when all you can do is wait."

Hmm, Gavin observed to himself–American. But for the moment it was merely an idle thought. "Aye," he replied aloud, "although I was just thinkin' that ye appearred to be the sorrt o' laddie who could always be of use."

Jason was too struck by the irony of the remark to notice the man's brogue although not being British, he might not have found it instantly recognizable anyway. "Well, for the present at any rate that is not the case." He sighed heavily, taking a swallow of his coffee. "My wife... is...ah...emotionally ill and I can do nothing to help her. She wants.... she wants..." But here he broke off–shaking his head and waving his free hand as if to dismiss the entire subject.

The American accent–the disturbed wife. His companion could be none other than Jason Eliot–someone who could leave a woman like Tori and fly off to the other side of the world to do "his holy duty"–, but then almost at once Gavin forgot all that as he heard the man say that his wife didn't want him, that she wanted something or...or someone else. "Aye." And as he spoke, he watched the other man closely to observe the effect of his words. "But 'tis farr worrse when ye want to be wi' someone and ye dinna have the rright."

So this is Gavin Hamilton, Jason thought, just the sort who would use a woman merely for the satisfaction of his animal lust, but that was all Victoria seemed to want anyway. "You're Scotch, aren't you?" This was not a question on his part so much as a statement–a declaration of far more than simply the other man's nationality.

Inwardly Gavin winced at being called Scotch, but then what could he expect?" "Aye—I'm Scots."

For a few moments Jason was silent–looking down at the coffee cup now gripped tightly between his two hands. If he took this man to Victoria, he could very well lose her. But nothing mattered now but her recovery and certainly once she was herself again, she would realize what this man was. "And you're Gavin Hamilton, I suppose?"

"Aye, I am and I ken ye'rre Jason Eliot." As he pronounced the name, the "a" in Jason had an unusually grating sound, but perhaps that was only his brogue.

Jason hesitated briefly, then stood up off the stool. "Would you be so kind as to come with me, please?" Gavin's answering look was an unspoken question. "She's.... she's asking for you." He turned abruptly to stride from the coffee shop. In spite of everything Gavin felt a brief wave of pity for the man. Suppose their situations were reversed, but that wasn't the case, was it? He hurried after the other man, catching him up at the lift.

Neither spoke during the short ride up to Victoria's floor–each man occupied with his own thoughts. Jason was trying to resign himself to what was about to happen, at the same time feeling quite noble in his self-sacrifice. All Gavin could think was that in a matter of moments he would be with Tori again and oddly enough it was he who prayed–prayed that he could bring her back with his love. As they stepped off the lift, Dr. Anthony was just coming out of Victoria's room on his way to the nurses' station to order her another hypodermic. She was beginning to wake up again–calling repeatedly for Gavin–and she had to be kept calm until he could be located. He met the two men about halfway along the hall. It was odd, he would often think afterwards–this was the one and only time he saw them together.

"This is Gavin Hamilton," Jason stated flatly. "He's been here in the hospital all along."

"My good man!" The doctor shook Gavin's hand. "Please...come with me."

Jason remained where he was–watching them walk toward Victoria's room. Suppose he was wrong; suppose she never came back to him? But once again, it seemed, all he could do was wait.

"Mr. Hamilton–" Dr. Anthony stopped outside the door, placing his hand on the other man's arm. Gavin would have gone in at once–wanting only to hold Tori in his arms again, to tell her all the things he'd thought he would never have the chance to say. "Mr. Hamilton!" He repeated the name more insistently, gaining his attention at least temporarily. "She will not be as you remember her. She's deeply troubled and she....."

"But ye'rre wrrong therre, sirr. 'Twill not be the firrst time I've seen her trroubled." Impatiently he shook off the restraining hand and pushed open the door. Dr. Anthony started to follow him into the room. Gavin paused to look back at him. "And 'tis nae necessarry forr ye to coom in wi' me, sirr. I would do or say naethin' to harrm the lass."

As a psychiatrist he'd been privy to many emotionally charged situations in people's lives, but he had never known such tenderness could exist as he saw at that moment on this man's face. "Please, sir." The doctor stepped back gesturing into the room. "Please—I believe she's waiting for you."

Gavin merely nodded and turning back to open the door full, he went in. At the moment he entered Victoria was lying on her side facing away from the door, a small, bedside lamp illuminating only her head and shoulders. It was the sound she was making, however, which affected him most profoundly–a soft whimpering much like he'd heard when he happened upon an injured animal in the hills above his father's farm. What had that damned Eliot done to her?

The whimper was, in fact, her cry of submission, her final acceptance that no matter how deep her yearning, it remained futile. She could make no one understand how much she needed Gavin. And–oh, dear God–she did need him so. "Oh, Gavin," she whispered, "where are you?"

His eyes filled with tears and moving quietly across the room, he eased himself down on the bed so as not to startle her, taking hold of her hand. "I'm herre, Torri," he said softly.

Act Three - "Tori"

Chapter 1

She had longed for him so terribly, then, she'd even begun to imagine she heard his voice. Surprisingly, however, she did not find this frightening. It was on the contrary extraordinarily comforting and as long as she refused to look in the direction of the sound, she could almost believe he was really there. She supposed this meant she had finally lost her mind, but if it was only in madness she could have Gavin with her, she preferred it to a reality without him. But the voice called to her again. "Will ye no look at me then, lass?"

She could picture him so clearly. It was heartbreaking to think he was only there in her imagination. But at last she turned over onto her back and to her incredulous joy found that he was indeed sitting there on the edge of her bed smiling down at her and only then did she realize, holding her hand. "G...Gavin?"

Tenderly he smoothed her tousled hair. "Do ye mean to say ye dinna rrememberr my handsoom featurres that ye have to ask?"

"No...no, I just.... I mean, I...." Tears came into her eyes.

"Aye, lass. I ken it. Ye couldna believe I was rreally herre."

She nodded, her eyes fixed on his face. "Hold me...Oh, please hold me!" He willingly gathered her into his arms and immediately hers came up in response, clasping him about the neck. "Oh, Gavin...Gavin!" She pulled back a little then so that she could see his expression. There were tears in his eyes as well and she brought her hand up to touch his cheek. "No, no, don't cry. Don't."

"Coom lass, lie doon. Ye need to rrest."

"No!" She continued to cling to him with a surprising strength. "Please stay with me."

Gently he removed her arms to lay her back down on the bed. "Noo–did ye hearr me say I was goin' anywherre?" She shook her head. "So then." Once again he took her hand in both of his and now in spite of the solemnity of the moment his eyes twinkled. "I hearr ye've been askin' forr me."

"Only...only I...I had no idea you were still in London. You....you said in your letter you were going up to Scotland and I... Oh, Gavin—your beautiful letter. I....kept it. At the time I didn't know why, but I kept it."

"Did ye noo?"

"Did you....did you really mean what...what you said in it?"

He didn't need to ask to which part of the letter she was referring and she knew she didn't have to tell him. "Aye....aye, darrlin'. I...I love ye, Torri–verra, verra much."

"Oh, Gavin. I....I love you, too." And now she really began to cry.

"No...no. Hush noo, lass. Hush." He took her in his arms again, rocking her until she grew quiet. Only then did he place her back on the bed although he still leaned forward, his arms resting on either side of her. Their eyes met and he lowered his head to kiss her. Was this kiss any different than the many others they'd already shared? In a way perhaps it was because for the first time it spoke of their love far more eloquently even than their words of a few moments ago. Yet had not each kiss, each caress told of that love long before either of them had been enough aware of it to put it into words. When their lips at last parted, Gavin sat back up again although he still held her hand. She looked so beautiful lying there and all he wanted to do was savor the sweetness of her and vow with all his strength that he would never lose sight of her again.

There was a perfunctory knock on the door and Dr. Anthony entered. Moments before he'd stood helplessly by as Victoria fought the demons of her own private hell. Now she looked toward him as he came into the room and smiled. He was irresistibly drawn to smile in return. "Shall I prescribe this for all my patients? It seems to be a miracle drug."

"S..s...sorry." Her voice trembled slightly. "Pr..private stock."

"Well, I think we should let you get some rest now," the doctor suggested.

"Oh no, please." She tightened her grip on Gavin's hand. "Don't make him leave."

"Will you be quiet, Mr. Hamilton, so that she'll sleep?"

"I swearr on my solemn oath." He raised his free hand in affirmation.

"All right then. I'll see you in the morning, Victoria."

It was quite evident she hadn't even heard him. "Torri, darrlin'," Gavin prompted gently when she didn't answer.

"It's all right." The doctor smiled broadly. "She won't even notice I'm gone."

"Oh...Doctor Anthony!" Victoria laughed a little sheepishly. "I'm sorry. Good night. Th.. thank you for letting Gavin stay."

"Good night, Victoria. Sleep well." He strode off down the hall toward the nurses' station. Were it not for the fact that it was the middle of the night, he would actually have whistled. "Ladies," he announced with a bow, "I, thank the good Lord, am going home."

"How is Miss Windsor?" one of the nurses inquired.

"Miss Windsor's just fine, thank you. The gentleman who went in with me will spending the rest of the night with her."

"Oh, Doctor Anthony!" A young aide couldn't resist joining them. "The tall man with the auburn hair. Is he the one she's been asking for? I don't blame her. He's gorgeous!"

He laughed. "You know–I didn't notice."

As he was about to leave, however, the head nurse stopped him. "I hate to dampen your euphoria, sir, but Miss Windsor's husband is waiting for you in the lounge."

He grimaced. "Oh, damn!" he muttered under his breath, but he walked briskly across the hall to push the button for the lift. The man had the right, after all, to be told about his wife.

Jason was standing staring out the window at the darkened London street. He turned his head to glance at the doctor as he entered. "Everything's all right now, I presume." His soft voice was tinged with sarcasm. "I don't imagine Gavin Hamilton frightened her."

"Your wife is...ah...quiet now. Yes, Reverend Eliot."

"And am I to be allowed to see her?"

"I don't think that would accomplish anything."

"I see." Jason walked over and picked up his coat and hat from a chair where he'd thrown them. "Very well, sir, but I want you to know that I in no way consider this matter closed!" With a curt nod he strode from the room. A moment later as Dr. Anthony left the lounge himself to go down to his office and get his own coat, he did finally permit his lips to purse in a discreet whistle. Jason Eliot's threats had never amounted to anything and if by some chance this one turned out to be different, he somehow felt that a certain Scotsman was more than equal to the occasion.

When Victoria and Gavin were alone again, it was a while before either of them said anything although their hands expressed a tender message of awakening affection–each touching the face, hair, neck and arms of the other as if to be assured that the dear object of that love was truly there. Victoria was the first to speak. "You....you look tired, Gavin," she murmured, her forefinger tracing a hollow spot which ran along beneath his cheekbone. "I don't remember this being here before. You haven't been sleeping well, have you?"

"Och, Torri." Again he smoothed her hair. "Therre werre moments when I didna ken how I was goin' to bearr day afterr day wi' out ye. I thought that..." But here his voice choked and he was unable to go on.

"I'm so sorry for...for what you must have suffered. I don't know why I...that morning.. why I....."

"It doesna matterr, lass." He swallowed hard. "It doesna matterr. Neitherr will I everr underrstand how I could just leave wi'oot sae much as a worrd o' prrotest. But the doctor said ye should be gettin' a wee bit o' rrest. Noo I'll be rright overr herre." He stood up and started to move away, intending to sit in a chair in the corner of the room.

"Oh, not that far away–please!"

"Suppose I pull the chairr closerr to the bed then?"

"Still much too far. Please, darling, I've never forgotten what it was like to fall asleep with your arms around me."

He hesitated only briefly. After all he wanted more than anything to hold her again. "'Tis nae verra wide forr twa, I'm afrraid," Gavin observed with a grin as moving around to the far side of the bed, he slipped in beside her. "Especially when one of us weighs nearr fourrteen stone."

"Oh, I don't mind. I don't mind at all." Turning on her side, Victoria came into his embrace, resting her head against his chest. "Oh, Gavin," she murmured. "Oh, my love! It.. it feels so good!"

" 'Tis just as I rrememberred, lass. Ye fit into that spot as though 'twerre made forr ye."

He began to massage the small of her back in a slow, easy motion as he'd often done when they lay together and all remaining tension dissolved away. "Gavin, I...I don't want to fall asleep yet. Talk to me."

"If we dinna behave ourrselves, Torri, they'll be askin' me to leave. Ye wouldna want yourr laddie thrrown oot into the cold, would ye noo?"

"My...my laddie?" She raised her head so that she could see his face.

"Aye." He caressed her cheek. "Ye ken well that I am."

"My laddie," she murmured a second time as she cuddled back down against him. "It's... it's just that I'm afraid if I go to sleep, this will all turn out to have been a dream."

"Did I no say I was yourr laddie? Noo I'll be herre in the morrnin', I prromise."

Satisfied at least for the present, Victoria snuggled a little closer one arm across his chest, but the next instant her head came up again. "Gavin?"

"Aye, lassie." She observed the softness in his eyes, the tender smile she was sure no other woman had ever seen.

"Kiss me just once more."

"Do ye think ye have to ask?" One finger traced the line of her lips and then he brought his mouth to meet hers–gently moving and probing. He heard her soft murmur of contentment and he felt the awareness of her flow through him–not at all a physical desire, but an overwhelming flood of pure love such as he'd never thought himself capable of experiencing. He thought how easily he could have lost her and tears filled his eyes once more. "Torri....Torri.....Torri..." He whispered the dear name over and over again, interspersing it with quick kisses on her eyes, cheeks, nose and finally again her lips.

"Gavin...my dearest Gavin." She nestled close to him one last time and yet how hard it was to stay quiet–not to talk to him and hear the soft burr of his brogue in reply. But his arms held her close and she was feeling so deliciously sleepy. The next thing she knew a nurse was waking her with her breakfast. Victoria immediately sat up in bed. "Wh...where's Gavin?"

"Gavin?" The nurse had just come on with the morning shift.

"Yes... Gavin Hamilton."

Desperately she fought back the panic, but at that moment the door opened and Dr. Anthony appeared. "Good morning, Victoria."

"Gavin was here last night, wasn't he? I...I didn't imagine it?"

The doctor smiled. "No, he was here. I had one of the interns take him over to their residence to shower and shave."

"Oh!" She sighed in profound relief. "I...I woke up and he wasn't here and I...I.."

"It was all I could do to convince him to go, but I explained that I wanted a chance to talk to you alone and I would tell you where he was." He paused to pull a chair up beside the bed and sit down. "May we talk then?"

"Yes, of course."

"Go ahead with your breakfast."

"You know I am hungry." Smiling at him, Victoria reached for the dish of fruit.

"It's good to see the sparkle back in those green eyes," he observed. "Would you like to tell me about Gavin?" Her smile grew broader. "That smile says most of it, but is there anything you'd care to add?"

Victoria laughed, but then immediately she was serious as she considered where to begin. How could she possibly explain this incredible man who only yesterday had seemed gone from her life forever. "Well, I...I met him in New York actually–last spring and...and then when I came back to London, I saw him again and we...we...."

"Began that 'meaningless' affair you told me about?"

She nodded, a new smile tugging at the corners of her mouth. "I...I truly believed it was only a physical attraction. Gavin's so handsome. Don't you think so?"

Now it was the doctor's turn to smile. "I'm afraid I can't be considered an authority on that subject, but my nurses may never be the same."

"But...but when I think how happy I was just being with him, I can't understand why I didn't know that...well, that..." At last Victoria merely shrugged–laughing again a little self-consciously.

"You felt terribly guilty about the relationship, didn't you?"

"Yes. I...I'd always been afraid, you see, that eventually I would be unfaithful to..to Jason. Doctor, what...what about Jason? Does he know....does he know....."

"I had to ask him who Gavin was. All you'd tell me was his first name."

"So you....you asked Jason?"

"Yes...and..and the next thing I knew there they were, walking along the hall toward your room together. I still don't know where he found him. So... you were afraid you'd be unfaithful to Jason and therefore....?"

Victoria thought about it for a minute or so. "So...therefore I...I thought that was all Gavin was. I...I've always thought of myself as basically immoral, you see. There'd..... there'd been so many men..men who in most cases treated me horribly and yet I...I would still want someone there at...at night."

"You've never liked yourself much, have you?"

"Do you blame me? I've...I've treated people so badly–even my own daughter. No one's ever liked me. Why should I like myself?"

"Terry Cartier...Noel St. John...Mrs. Kendall...your daughter. They all seem to have found something in you to like–even to love."

"Well, I...I don't know what!"

"Did it ever occur to you, Victoria, that you acted the way you did to prove you were right about yourself? To prove you didn't <u>deserve</u> to be loved? But those who genuinely cared about you saw through all of that. But let's get back to Gavin...."

"Doctor," she said all at once, "may I leave hospital today?"

"In a couple of days perhaps, but....."

"May Gavin stay here with me then?"

"I stretched the rules to the breaking point last night, I'm afraid, so I....."

"Then I want to leave. I....I have to."

At once he observed her breathing rate beginning to accelerate. "Please, Victoria." He reached out to touch her.

"No...no!" She twisted away from him. "Where's Gavin? I want Gavin!"

"I'll see what's keeping him." The doctor hurried out of the room and down the hall toward the nurses' station, intending to ring the interns' residence. Just as he got there, however, the Scotsman stepped off the lift to stride toward him. Two student nurses trailed along behind him giggling and watching the scene, Charles Anthony experienced a brief stab of concern. Would such a man as this--who evidently could have any woman he wanted–be capable of giving endlessly and selflessly of himself to only one?

"Good morrnin', lassies." Gavin grinned at the two nurses behind the counter. They smiled back–one of them blushing with pleasure. Then he noticed the doctor. "How is she?" he inquired at once. "I hurrried as fast as I could."

Dr. Anthony searched the other man's face. He wished he knew him better. "Mr. Hamilton, she insists she's leaving hospital today. You have to convince her to stay at least a couple of more days. She's exhausted–both physically and emotionally."

"Aye, I'll talk to the lassie." Gavin hurried off down the hall toward Victoria's room, Dr. Anthony following him.

As the two men entered, they found she was already dressed. Her small valise lay open on the bed and she was throwing things into it. At the sound of their footsteps Victoria spun around, obviously frightened someone was going to try to prevent her from leaving. Relief flooded over her face as she saw Gavin. "Oh–darling!" She dropped what she was holding and ran to him. "They...they want to keep me here, but <u>you</u> tell them.... please..tell them!"

He slipped his arms around her and drew her close. "Tell them what, lassie?"

"Tell them I....I <u>have</u> to be with you!"

"It will only be for a couple of days," Dr. Anthony attempted to explain.

But Victoria refused to listen. "No...no! Please, <u>please</u> tell him. Tell him!" Her voice rose dangerously and she beat on Gavin's chest with her clenched fists.

"Perhaps if I talked to her alone," he said quietly.

Again Dr. Anthony studied him briefly. "All right, Mr. Hamilton," he said at last. "Perhaps that would be best." He left them then, allowing the door to swing shut behind him.

"Gavin–please!" Victoria began to pace the room in circles, her hands still balled into tight little fists. "Please don't make me stay here without you!"

He watched her despairingly. Nothing in his past had prepared him to love so deeply. "Torri, darrlin'," he said once and somewhat later, "Please, dearr wee lass" and "Coom noo, hinny," but she didn't appear to hear him and at last Gavin stepped in front of her, gripping her arms just below the shoulders. "Torri," he said firmly, "stop that and listen to me!" She half-collapsed against him, clinging to him with a physical strength which once again surprised him. "Ye have to ken, Torri, 'tis best forr ye to stay herre just a wee bit longerr. If anythin' happened to ye, it would fairr brreak my hearrt and forr surre there's nae much of it left the noo."

At the sound of his deep and yet tender voice Victoria instantly relaxed. He wasn't deserting her; he was only concerned for her welfare. "You can see it now, can't you, Gavin? All I need is your arms around me and everything's all right. Now will you please take me out of this damned hospital!"

"Doctor Anthony doesna think ye should, darrlin', and I...."

"Very well! With or without your help I am leaving!" Pulling away from him, she continued her packing with a vengeance.

Gavin didn't really know Victoria that well as yet and if he was unprepared for her physical strength, he was even more so for her determination of will. "Wherre will ye go then, hinny?" he inquired as gently as possible. " Ye canna go back to the hotel."

At that she hesitated briefly, but then she pulled on her coat, slammed the valise shut and fastened it. "I...I don't know exactly—somewhere. Terry will come and get me."

"Terry?"

"Yes–Terence Cartier!" She picked up the suitcase, fairly flinging the celebrated name in his face. "I do have friends, you know!"

Gavin sighed his surrender. If she was determined to leave, after all, it should be with him. "Coom then, lass." He put out his hand to take the valise from her. "But at least let me carrry that forr ye."

"Oh, you are a darling!" Victoria came up on tiptoe to kiss him on the cheek.

He tried to look disapproving, but after all what she wanted was to be with him and he slipped his free arm around her waist, grinning in return. "Aye, lass, but I swearr ye arre a morre mutton-headed daftie than Felicity at her worrst!"

She laughed. "I have the feeling I've just been insulted, but I don't even care."

Dr. Anthony was waiting outside in the hall. How good it was to hear her laugh, he thought. He wasn't surprised when a moment or so later the door opened and he saw that Victoria was wearing her coat and Gavin was carrying her suitcase. He'd suspected she would win the argument. "Well, you certainly are a determined young woman." He stepped forward to walk with them down the corridor. "At least you tried, Mr. Hamilton."

"Aye, I did but she's verra stubborrn. I dinna ken what I'm to do wi' the lass." He winked at her.

"Victoria," the doctor went on, "I will have to ask you to sign a statement that you're leaving of your own accord."

"Is that all I have to do?" she inquired eagerly. "Just show me where to sign."

They went on over to the counter and while the nurse on duty was getting out the proper forms, Dr. Anthony drew the other man off to one side. "Take good care of her," he urged, feeling slightly inane at the use of such an unprofessional cliche, but it was how he felt. "You can make all the difference, you know. If you can love her enough......"

"Aye, sirr." Gavin was indeed listening intently although his eyes were on Victoria who was standing a few feet away signing the forms. But then he turned to look at the doctor directly. "And I do love herr enough. Much morre than enough!"

"I believe that, Mr. Hamilton."

The legal formalities having been completed, Victoria joined them. "All ready." She slipped an arm through Gavin's. "May we go now, darling?"

"Aye, lass." He turned to push the button for the lift.

"Victoria—" The doctor touched her lightly on the hand. "I do want to see you in my office. Let's say the day after tomorrow–about eleven a.m.?"

"All...all right." But as she spoke, she moved a little closer to Gavin, tightening her grip on his arm.

"Both of you–actually."

"Aye–we'll be therre." The lift arrived then and Gavin reached in to hold the door open.

"Good-bye, Doctor Anthony." Smiling, Victoria offered him her hand. "Thank you so much for...for everything." Impulsively she leaned forward to kiss him on the cheek before going past Gavin into the lift. He followed her and the door slid shut behind them.

Dr. Anthony turned back toward the desk to prepare for his morning rounds. "Forget it, sir," the nurse teased him as she handed him his charts.

"Forget what?" He glanced up from the study of his first patient's records.

"All your tranquillizers and your psychoanalysis can never replace that." A toss of her head indicated the lift.

The doctor laughed. "Well, you know I don't think I would want them to," he replied, moving away to begin his morning's work. Not all of his patients were fortunate enough to have a Gavin Hamilton.

* * *

In the lift Victoria raised her face to be kissed. Smiling, Gavin willingly complied, but suddenly that wasn't enough. Putting down the valise, he took her in his arms and somewhere deep inside her a hard, cold lump which seemed to have been there ever since she could remember was beginning to melt away. "Where are we going?" she asked finally.

"To my flat, I suppose. Jamie's oop in Scotland again."

The lift stopped on the ground floor and they got out, hurrying across the lobby hand in hand toward the outside door. "Isn't that Victoria Windsor?" they heard someone observe. She laughed. "I didn't see her." Gavin's Morris Rover had been in the car park now for more than forty-eight hours and there were several tickets on the windscreen. "Oh, darling," Victoria gasped. "Those are because of me, aren't they?"

"Och, ye bonnie wee daftie, do ye no ken ye'rre worrth farr morre than a few parrkin' tickets? Well then," he continued as they got into the car and he started the motor, "we'll go to the flat, shall we, and get you settled. Then we'll see aboot gettin' in some grrocerries. I've not been much forr eatin' since I got back to London. All rright, Torri?"

"Anything..anything you say. I'm happy just being with you."

"Aye–well, 'tis mutual, darrlin'." A short time later he had parked in the small alley behind his building and getting out first himself, he came around to her side of the car to help her alight as well. In the light of the brilliant winter sunshine her beautiful face showed clearly everything she'd been through in the past few weeks and Gavin experienced a pang of worry. Should he have insisted she remain in hospital? What if tonight something went wrong? Then she smiled at him and his anxiety immediately lessened. Surely she was far better off with him than alone in a hospital room. He drew her into his arms and for a moment they simply stood like that. "Och, lass," he whispered burying his lips in her hair. "I could fairr burrst wi' happiness." At last he reluctantly released her and removing her valise from the car's boot, he took her hand to lead the way in the door and up the narrow, winding stairs to the second floor.

On the landing he put down the suitcase to hunt in his trouser pocket for the key and finally turning the knob, he pushed open the door. Victoria found herself in a large, sunny living room with windows along both outside walls which reminded her a great deal, in fact, of her first little flat over the German bakery. To her right she could see a small kitchen while a door on the left hand wall led apparently to a bedroom. Gavin followed her inside, closing the door behind them and putting her suitcase down. " 'Tis nae verra elegant, I'm afrraid, lassie, but I had no otherr place to brring ye."

Victoria took hold of his hand and looking around the room, discovered a couch against the far wall under the windows. She led him over to it and turning sideways, she reached for his other hand as well so that at last they were sitting facing each other. "Gavin, please. I've told you I'm not like that."

"What do ye mean, darrlin'?"

Frowning a little, she searched her mind for some way to make him see that she wasn't at all the glamorous woman with which he still apparently associated the name of Victoria Windsor. "You....you achieve a certain amount of success in a high-paying profession..."

"A <u>certain</u> amount?!"

"I....I truly do love the theatre, but part of the reason I became an actress was to satisfy an emotional need. I....I could receive affection from an audience, you see, and not really have to give anything in return. But no matter how people applauded me, the moment inevitably arrived when the curtain came down and I was left with nothing but my own empty life. So I...I bought a big elegant house and filled it with all the trappings of my success, but that didn't work either. Then I....I come to a place like this–peaceful and cozy-- and it feels like home to me especially because I'm with you. That's why you must never again apologize to me for something like this. Promise me you won't, my darling."

"Aye, I prromise, hinny."

"Oh, my love! I never knew I could feel like this. I never believed I'd see the look on a man's face that I see on yours at this moment."

Gavin had to ask her now. He'd half-planned the perfect romantic moment–perhaps that evening after dinner over a glass of wine–but now he knew he couldn't wait. He had to tell her that he wanted her to belong to him–that he, in turn, would belong to her forever. "Torri, I...I...." But what if she said no? What if she needed him for the moment, but didn't want to make a lasting commitment? Or perhaps, after all she'd been through, he should wait until she was stronger. "Torri, I....I..." He swallowed hard and the words when they finally did come out were more of a statement than a question– perhaps to save himself from the pain and humiliation of a direct refusal. "Torri, ye...ye do ken I want to marrry ye–that I want ye forr wife."

For a few seconds Victoria simply stared at him. "M...m...marry me?" Suddenly overcome with shyness, she looked down at their four hands still clasped together between them. "M... marry me? Are...are you sure?"

"Neverr surrer of anythin' in my life, lass."

"Even during those first weeks in London, I'd wonder sometimes what it would be like to spend my life with you, but I never thought...that....that...."

"Torri, will ye marrry me, darrlin'?" Victoria's eyes were fixed steadily now on his dear, strong face. Was she really going to be allowed to see that face the first thing every morning and the last thing every night? Was she never again to be alone or frightened? At last she nodded, hardly able to believe her own good fortune. "May I take that, then, as an affirrmative answerr?"

Again she nodded. "Yes, Gavin, I....I want very much to marry you, to...to be your wife."

"Torri." His burr as he whispered her name was the softest and most caressing she'd ever heard it. "I do love ye so, darrlin'." He held open his arms to her and she came eagerly into his embrace. "Well, we should be gettin' ye settled, I suppose," he continued at last and even as he spoke of everyday things, his voice shook with emotion. "Jamie's rroom's rright overr herre." He stood up, starting to lead the way toward the door she had noticed when they first came in.

"Where's...where's your bedroom, Gavin?"

He stopped, turning back to face her. "Off the kitchen, but I thought perrhaps ye'd rratherr..."

"Oh no, darling. I...I want to sleep with you unless...unless you....you don't want to."

He came back then to sit beside her again. "Och, hinny, I want to hold ye close everra night forr the rrest of my life, but...but that will be...be all I do want until ye'rre surre ye'rre rready. Do ye ken my meanin'?"

"Oh yes—yes, I do." This time it was she who made the move to come into his arms and he held her close for a moment. "You know–you are the dearest man in the entire world?"

"Aye–of courrse I am."

"Oh, you!" She slapped him playfully on the arm.

He chuckled. "But noo, hinny, as I said, let's get ye settled." He picked up Victoria's valise again and led the way through the kitchen into his bedroom. There was really only room in there for the double bed and a small chest of drawers. There was just one closet. Gavin swung the case up on the bed. Then he quickly emptied a couple of drawers in the bureau, also removing some of his clothes from the closet. "I'll just put these in Jamie's rroom and be rright back," he promised. With a quick kiss he disappeared with the armful of clothing. All Victoria really had to unpack were her things from the hospital. She'd need her clothes–not only from the hotel suite, but from the apartment in New York. She hoped Kate would pack up for her there. Gavin returned almost at once. "Hungrry, lass?"

"A...a little. Darling, I'll need my things from the hotel."

"Won't Marrtha get everrathin' togetherr forr ye?"

"Of course." She sighed with relief. "I...I don't want to see Jason again. He...he frightens me. I....I don't know why."

"He makes ye feel less than ye arre. He underrmines yourr faith in yourrself. He...he..." All at once Gavin broke off.

"He what, darling?" Victoria had finished putting her few things away and now she came to slip her arms around his neck.

"Naethin'. Let's have some lunch." He started to pull away from her.

"No, please!" She caught hold of his arm. "Have I done something to make you angry with me?"

"Of courrse not, Torri." At once Gavin took the step or two back to her and put his arms around her again. " 'Tis nae you I'm angrry with. 'Tis that...that..." (And here he first applied what was to become his customary epithet when referring to Jason)"....that bluidy damned prrreacherrrr!"

"Jason never did anything to you."

"Neverr did anythin'! He verra nearrly destrroyed the single most prrecious and irrreplaceable human bein' on the face of this earrth!"

"Dr. Anthony thinks that my feelings of inadequacy actually stem from my childhood. My parents....."

"Aye." He fairly glowered. "They'rre nae farr behind on my hate list!"

"You...you don't seem to be the kind of man to hate."

"Only people who have hurrt you. Well, noo..." Suddenly he was embarrassed---nonplussed at the depth of his own emotions. "What aboot ourr lunch? The larrder, as they say, is nearrly barre, but therre is a bit o' cheese and some brread. I can grrill some sandwiches. With tea?"

Reluctantly she slipped from his embrace. "Please–let me."

"No, no. Laterr on ye can do yourr wifely duty and wait hand and foot on yourr lorrd and masterr." He winked at her. "But forr the noo ye go sit wherre I can see ye while I get things togetherr."

Victoria returned willingly to the living room to curl up on the couch, hugging her knees to herself in the old habit. Happily she watched Gavin put on a pot of water for tea and then make the cheese sandwiches, placing them on the grill. Incredible–the contentment she felt at just being with him. And this was what she had so nearly turned her back on. "Gavin?" she said at one point. "Am I...am I really precious and irreplaceable?"

"Aye, Torri." He glanced at her tenderly, but then he noticed her position. "Och, hinny. Dinna waste yourr hugs on yourrself. Save them forr yourr laddie." She laughed. "Noo–sit doon to yourr lunch, darrlin'." He brought the things out to a small table which stood against the other outside wall between the windows. The room was warm and pleasant in the midday sun and Victoria could never remember anything tasting as good as that simple meal. Gavin watched with obvious pleasure as she ate the sandwich, drinking mug after mug of tea. Occasionally during the meal they spoke, but for that while it was enough just being together. "Tirred, Torri?" he asked gently when they had finished.

"A...a little. I...I didn't get much sleep last night, but at that I probably got more than you did."

"Aye, I could stand a wee kip. Shall we lie doon forr a bit? Then laterr we can fetch the grrocerries. All rright, darrlin'?"

She nodded and they stood up to walk together into the other room. For now they simply lay down on top of the spread, pulling a light quilt up over themselves. "As I believe I've noted on morre than one occasion," he whispered taking her in his arms, "ye fit into that spot as though 'twerre made forr ye."

Victoria nestled close to the warmth that was this dear man and the next thing she knew it was more than two hours later. Even then it was Gavin who kissed her awake. She stirred sleepily, instinctively seeking his lips with her own, and momentarily misunderstanding her intentions, he began to kiss her hungrily. Victoria felt the familiar desire come to life in her. Was she once again merely taking any man she could have just so she wouldn't be alone? "Please, I...I'm sorry," she murmured apologetically, turning her head away. "I...I can't. Not just yet."

"Aye, Torri. 'Tis all rright, darrlin'."

"I..I...still, well, want you in that way, Gavin, but..but...."

"'Tis all rright–have I nae told ye that? So then–shall we go get ourr grrocerries?"

"I...I don't think I feel like going out." She moved away, lying down again with her back to him.

"I willna let ye do this, hinny." He gripped her by the shoulders, turning her over so that she had to look at him. "Everrathin' is all rright. Noo–get oop and coom with me. We need soom things and I dinna want to leave ye herre alone."

"Gavin, pl...please." Weakly she shook her head, trying in vain to avoid his compelling brown eyes.

He slipped his arms all the way around her then, holding her close. "Ye <u>can</u> be strrong to get thrrough this, darrlin', and the strrength ye <u>dinna</u> have, I'll have <u>forr</u> ye."

What he said was true. She could feel his strength flowing into her and for a few minutes she continued to cling to him. "All right," she said at last. "We can go." They got up then and while he put their lunch dishes to soak, Victoria washed her face and brushed her hair.

"I...I'm sorry, darling," she apologized, coming out into the kitchen. "I...I don't even have my make-up."

"That bonny face doesna need any make-up." Kissing her once lightly, he helped her into her coat and they left the flat together, going downstairs hand in hand. " 'Tis only a shorrt way to the shops, darrlin'," he explained as they came out onto the sidewalk, "but would ye feel oop to a wee strroll firrst?"

"If you'd like. The fresh air would probably do me good."

"Frresh airr in Lundon?" Gavin wrinkled up his nose. "Not possible."

Victoria laughed. "Oh, you! I don't suppose there's any place on earth to equal your beloved Highlands."

"None at all," he avowed solemnly. "But ye'll see that forr yourrself verra soon noo." By now they had slipped their arms around each other's waists and were walking along quite briskly–each warmed against the chill November day by the nearness of the other.

"I... I will?"

"Of courrse. I want ye to meet my family, especially my Dad." Gavin threw back his head, laughing with a huge enjoyment. "Poorr man's aboot given oop hope of my everr marrryin'. I can harrdly wait to see the exprression on his face."

"When...when will we go?"

"As soon as Doctor Anthony thinks we can." But he'd caught the tremor in her voice. "Ye'll like my Dad, Torri. He's almost as adorrable as I am."

"Oh, Gavin!" She hugged him around the waist. "I...I'm sure I'll love him, but...but how will he feel about me? I mean...an actress and married twice before and...and English on top of it all."

He stopped and turned to face her, lightly touching her cheek. "He'll adorre ye, darrlin'– the minute he sees ye. Noo ye mustna frret aboot it."

"All right." They began to walk again then–once more hand in hand. "Gavin, where are you taking me?"

"You'll see. Actually you've prrobably alrready been therre many times."

"You're being very mysterious." She laughed a little out of pure happiness.

For a while after that they walked in silence. At last they came out along the river, but Gavin still led the way a little further until they arrived at one of the benches placed at intervals along the walkway and at last then he stopped, pulling her down beside him and putting an arm around her shoulders. "Therre," he announced, evidently satisfied.

Victoria looked around, trying to find some particular significance in the spot, but it was only the Thames Embankment. "There what?" she asked at last, her eyes coming back to his face–so strong...so sweet. A wave of emotion swept over her. "Oh, my darling, I....I love you so much," she whispered, coming into his arms. Without realizing it she'd made the moment perfect. But then almost at once she laughed, pulling away again just enough to look at him. "And exactly what are we doing–embracing on a public bench?"

"Well, ye see, lassie.." Gavin was irresistibly drawn to touch her hair. "It was herre on this verra spot that it finally came to me how I felt aboot ye."

"You are so dear! Who else would think of something like that?"

Briefly he hugged her to him again. "But it's cold and we've got ourr grocerries to buy." Together they stood up to move away from the Embankment toward the shops. Even the mundane task of grocery shopping was a joy. People continually turned to stare at them–even those who didn't recognize Victoria–drawn by the happy glow surrounding them and by the magnificent picture they made as a couple: the tall, auburn-haired man–the lovely, slim, golden-haired woman.

Back at the flat they made dinner and then snuggled close together before the grate. The lack of central heating in many of London's older buildings may often be an inconvenience, but at the same time nothing is cozier than a coal fire. They were no sooner settled, however, than there was a knock on the door. "Are you expecting someone?" Victoria found herself resenting any intrusion into their private world. He shook his head and got up to go and answer the door.

"Where have you been, you handsome devil?!" An attractive dark-haired girl darted past him into the room. "I just <u>happened</u> to be in the neighborhood and I thought I'd..." But then she saw that he wasn't alone. "Well, I might have known!" She moved closer to the couch to peer curiously at its occupant. "My God, you're Victoria Windsor, aren't you?"

Gavin had continued to hold the door open and now he acted immediately. "As ye've alrready noted, I'm not alone so...." He indicated the hallway.

"Well, my gracious!" the girl fumed. "We ordinary mortals don't stand a chance now."

She hurried out without looking back and he closed the door, coming back to sit beside Victoria again. "Sorrry aboot that, darrlin'."

"Oh, that's all right." But she looked away from him–evidently troubled.

"Torri, I dinna even ken who she was! That's probably how I firrst got into the habit of callin' everra gurrl 'lassie'. It saved me frrom havin' to rrememberr theirr names."

"Oh, it's...it's not that." She swallowed hard. "Gavin, would....would you still love me, if.... if I weren't who I am?"

"Dearrest wee soul, do ye no ken I've been waitin' forr ye all my life?! Noo, can ye coom to believe in my love? I'll neverr gie ye cause to rregrret it, darrlin'." The rest of the evening was peaceful and quiet and full of tenderness. It grew late and still they sat together on the couch, her head resting on his shoulder. "We should be goin' to bed, don't ye think, lass?" Gavin asked at last.

"Not....not quite yet. Today was so special, I hate for it to end."

" 'Tis only the beginnin' of a whole life togetherr, Torri–so will ye coom noo then?"

"All right." Victoria got up to follow him into the bedroom and a little while later she lay in his arms, savoring again the delicious warmth and security of his nearness.

And the first sensation of which she was aware the following morning was of those same arms still holding her close. Raising her head, she found he was already awake. "Well, good morrnin', sleepyhead," he said. "Do ye ken it's nearrly ten o'clock?"

"It is?" She nestled down against him again and he could feel her laughing.

"What is it, darrlin'?" He brushed his lips against her hair. "I ken I dinna look my best beforre I've shaved, but do I look that funny?"

"Of course not, luv. You look adorable, like a...like a rumbled teddy bear."

"Rrumbled teddy bearr?" Gavin pretended to be offended, but he couldn't help but grin at her.

"Rumbled, but absolutely adorable, I might add."

"Well, thank ye forr that much anyway, lassie. But then why werre ye laughin'?"

"When you told me it was almost ten, I couldn't help thinking how I used to suffer from insomnia. That's...that's how I got hooked on the pills and liquor, I suppose...as well as...as needing to have someone there with me."

"Torri, darrlin', the past is just that forr both of us–the past–and I've told ye..." The ringing of the telephone interrupted him just then, however, and Gavin reached over to answer it. "Aye, doctorr–just fine. She's rright herre."

Victoria took the receiver. "Good morning, Doctor Anthony."

He smiled–delighted by her clear, ringing voice. "It seems I don't have to ask how you are this morning."

"As a matter of fact, I feel marvelous!"

"Good–" There was a brief pause as he considered whether she was indeed strong enough to begin to deal with the realities of her situation. "Because I...I have some people trying to get in touch with you–Sir Terence for one."

"Oh." Victoria sounded relieved. "That's all right. I...I want Terry to meet Gavin. Who... who else?"

"Olivia's father. I'm sure he's only concerned about her under the circumstances. I assured him she's with some very reliable people."

"And...I suppose...Jason."

"Yes." Again Dr. Anthony hesitated briefly. "The Reverend Eliot."

"I...I don't want to see Jason."

"I certainly wasn't suggesting you see him. In fact I would strongly advise against it."

"Oh, good—but...but please tell Terry and Andrew where I am and that...that I'm all right."

"Well, I'll see you tomorrow then–at eleven."

"Yes, Doctor. I'll be there. Good-bye." Victoria handed the receiver back to Gavin who replaced it. "Oh, darling, Olivia's...Olivia's father.... What...what if he takes her away from me again?"

"I'm surre he wouldna do that, Torri."

"Will you come with me, please to...to see him. I...I can't face him by myself ."

"Do ye no ken yourr days of bein' alone arre overr? Noo–do ye think we could get oop and have a bit of brreakfast? I'm fairr perrishin' wi' hungerr."

"Of course, my darling. You go ahead. I know you like your shower in the morning."

"Och–I like that worrd."

"What word?"

"My!" He grinned and with a quick kiss he slid out of bed and headed for the bathroom. When he came out again about a half-hour later, dressed in gray flannel slacks and a navy blue turtleneck, he found Victoria busy in the kitchen. Smells of eggs, bacon and coffee filled the air. "Mmm, lass, it smells marrvelous!" He came up behind her to put his arms around her waist and kiss her on the back of the neck.

"Mmm–you smell marvelous yourself," she replied, turning around to slip her arms around his neck and raise her face to his. Gavin chuckled and bent to kiss her. "Oh, darling, things will burn if we don't eat and I...I do want to see Andrew this morning."

"Aye, lass, gladly. I'm starrved!" He went out into the living room to the table and Victoria followed with the coffee pot. It was a happy, companionable breakfast as more and more they were discovering how much they enjoyed simply being together.

* * *

Though ostensibly his attention was on the file which lay open before him on his desk, Andrew Roberts was in actuality lost in his own thoughts. If he were forced to take steps to regain custody of his daughter, it would destroy Victoria. But the little girl's welfare had to come first. He'd found his conversation with Dr. Anthony reassuring, but still.... The intercom buzzed and he jumped. He depressed the talk button on the instrument. "What is it, Miss Thompson?" He hoped he at least sounded professional.

"I'm sorry to disturb you, sir," his secretary said, "but Miss Windsor's here and I realize you've been wanting to get in touch with her."

"Thank God! Please ask her to come in." Feeling at once considerably relieved, Andrew rose to his feet. The secretary opened the door, ushering Victoria in, and he came around the desk to welcome her, but no words came out as he saw she wasn't alone.

"Andrew," she said at once, "this is Gavin Hamilton. He's...my....my... I mean we're.... Gavin, darling, this is Andrew Roberts, my...my...ah....Olivia's father. I....I....." Oh dear, how exactly did one introduce one's future third husband to one's first husband anyway? With her irrepressible sense of humor she could suddenly picture Jason there as well and in spite of the seriousness of the moment she giggled. This seemingly irrational behavior alarmed both men. "Oh no, I'm all right," Victoria continued quickly as she saw the expression on their faces. "It's just trying to introduce you to each other and thinking...thinking well, that.... that...." Then all at once she remembered that she could be about to lose custody of her daughter again and suddenly nothing seemed very funny. "Oh, Gavin, please..." She reached out her hand to him.

"'Tis all rright, Torri." He immediately slipped his arm around her shoulders, drawing her closer to him. "I'm surre he doesna want to take Olivia away frrom ye. Could...could we possibly sit doon, Misterr Rroberrts?"

"Yes, of course. How thoughtless of me." He pulled two chairs over to the desk and then went around behind it to sit down himself. "Perhaps, it might help, Mr. Hamilton, if you explained to me exactly what you have to do with all of this?" He hadn't intended to sound harsh, but he couldn't help recalling her response to any tender gestures on his part.

"Th....that's my fault, I'm afraid, " Victoria said softly. "Gavin and I are...are going to be married."

"Is that so, Mr. Hamilton?" Andrew inquired coolly.

He's jealous, Gavin thought, suppressing a smile, not that I can blame him. "Aye, Misterr Rroberrts," he said aloud and now he did smile warmly. "I...I would neverr I might add, sirr, trry to take yourr place in yourr daughterr's life, but I'll be therre when the wee lass needs me."

The other man looked at him steadily for several seconds. "Then Olivia likes Mr. Hamilton?" he asked Victoria, wondering fearfully even as he did so whether he would also eventually lose his little girl to this charming, yet gentle man. Ridiculous, really, to think that way when in reality he'd lost Victoria years before Gavin Hamilton came along–if he'd ever possessed her in the first place.

"Oh yes, even before I did," she replied eagerly, "or at least before I admitted I did. But.... but she'll...she'll always know who her father is and we'll....we'll be living here in London so you'll be able to see a lot of her."

"You and...and Mr. Hamilton are currently living together?" .

"Misterr Rroberrts," Gavin interposed, but then he interrupted himself. "Do ye no think that underr the cirrcumstances this business of Misterr Rroberrts and Misterr Hamilton is a wee bit rridiculous?"

Andrew smiled. In spite of his twinges of jealousy he couldn't help liking the man. "Yes... ah...Gavin, I suppose that's true."

"Good–Andrrew, then." His brogue made the name sound as though it began with a broad "a", the burr on the "r" stringing out the second syllable like the roll of a drum. He grinned in return. "Andrrew," he said again. Then once more he grew serious. "Torri needs me with herr and I considerr that morre imporrtant than any social prroprrieties."

"Believe me, I didn't mean to sound judgmental. I was merely thinking that temporarily it might be better for Olivia to stay with me. Wouldn't it take a little of the pressure off, Victoria, if you didn't have to concern yourself with her for a while?"

"You're...you're sure it <u>will</u> only be temporary? And how will we explain it to her? I don't want her to think I'm deserting her again."

"I'm sure that if...well, perhaps all three of us–were to talk to her together, she'd understand. As for the rest, you should know by now, Victoria, I would do nothing to betray you or <u>our</u> daughter."

It was Gavin's turn now to feel slightly put out by the other man's decidedly proprietary use of the word–"our". He stood up rather abruptly. "I think that's enough forr the noo, don't you, Torri?"

"Yes, I suppose so." She also got to her feet. "I'll let you know when Olivia will be arriving. In the meantime perhaps we could both ring her up to reassure her. I'll let you know the number."

"Yes, of course." Andrew rose and came around to the front of his desk again to see them out.

"Thank you." Victoria reached out her hand to him.

"I'm so happy for you both," Andrew assured them, shaking hands with Gavin as well. "I'll be in touch." He held open the door of his office, watching as they walked across the reception area together hand in hand. And so it seemed Victoria had at last found what she'd always needed–with someone else.

* * *

"So then, lass," Gavin observed a few minutes later as they came out onto the street, "ye werre worrried forr naethin', it seems."

Slipping her arm through his, Victoria smiled up at him. "I should have known. After all, he <u>gave</u> Olivia to me."

For a while they walked along the Strand in silence. The sun was beginning to break through the clouds. All at once Gavin stopped short in the middle of the pavement. "I think this calls for a celebrration. How aboot a picnic?"

"In November?" It would still take her some time to become accustomed to this man's rather unconventional inspirations.

"Why not?" St. James' Park's only a wee strroll and 'tis gettin' to be a bonny day–forr England," he added after the slightest pause.

"Oh–you!" She laughed.

"So how aboot that picnic, then?"

"All...all right."

"We can get sandwiches nearr Trrafalgarr. What would ye like, Torri?" he asked a short while later as they stood with the rest of the lunchtime crowd in front of one of those tiny, take-away counters found all over London.

"Ah..." Victoria studied the menu posted on the wall. "A cheese and tomato sandwich and tea, I think—please, darling."

"Aye." Gavin easily caught the attention of one of the girls behind the counter and gave their order. Several other patrons who'd been in the queue ahead of them glared. He paid for their food and they walked across Trafalgar Square together and under the Admiralty Arch into the park. They found a bench in the sun and spread out their lunch between them.

He'd said very little since they left the lunch counter and now Gavin sat hunched over his sandwich, elbows resting on his knees–once in a while tossing a crust of bread to the flock of pigeons who had immediately gathered at their feet. Victoria remembered their week-end trip to Devon when his silence had bothered her, but now she understood he was quiet only because something was troubling him. She'd noticed that once he paid for their lunch there were only a few pounds left in his wallet and now she wondered with a guilty start whether he might be worried about money. Because of her he probably hadn't worked regularly in over two months. Gavin was such a proud man. How could she possibly bring up the subject of his finances? But after some thought an idea occurred to her. She reached over to place her hand on his arm and bring him back to her. At her touch he turned to look at her, that special slow smile spreading across his face. "Aye, lass?" His burr was throaty with tenderness.

"So what will you do now, darling?" she inquired as casually as possible.

"What do ye mean, Torri?" He had indeed been worrying about money. Even the amount he'd reluctantly borrowed from his father during his last visit home was nearly gone and now he was at once on the defensive. Was she criticizing him for not working?

"I...I mean, you won't continue to travel, will you?"

"Well, of courrse not. The grreat actrress must live in Lundon. I wouldna be apt to forrget that noo, would I?"

Hurt tears sprang to Victoria's eyes. Quickly she blinked them back. "I'm...I'm sorry, darling. I...I...."

"It's gettin' cold," Gavin announced all at once, standing up. "We should be goin' back." He gathered up their trash, tossing it in a near-by barrel.

The next thing she knew he was almost to the Mall and she had to half-run to catch him up. "Wait, please," she begged at last.

At once he slowed, taking her hand in his. Before he met her, he'd about come to the conclusion that he would never find a woman who didn't bore him after a week and now his mind, his body, his very being was filled with her. How then could he have become annoyed over such an innocent question? "I'm the one who should apologize, dearr lass," he said, finally stopping altogether. "Ye werre only interrested in my plans and as my futurre wife, ye have everra right to ask."

"It's not that." She searched her mind for a way to say it without once again offending him. Then suddenly for some reason she remembered where they were. "Gavin, may I take <u>you</u> somewhere now? It's very near here."

He smiled down at her tenderly. "Of courrse. Wherre?"

"Please–just come." Taking his hand, she led the way across the Mall and along the pavement for a short distance on the other side. "Here," Victoria said at last, stopping at the bottom of a short flight of stone steps. "You see, I wanted to...wanted to..." But now she felt foolish. What could she possibly have had in mind? It would have been different if the man of whom the bust was a likeness were alive and she could bring them together, but Uncle Bertie was dead and she was being silly. "Oh...never mind. Forget it. It <u>is</u> getting cold."

Glancing up, Gavin of course recognized the late King George VI and immediately he understood why she'd felt compelled to bring him here. "No, darrlin', wait a minute. Excuse me, sirr," he said with a slight bow, "forr my imperrtinence, but we do have a bit in common. Ye carred forr the dearr lass herre when she was only a wee bairrnie and I love her verra deeply the noo. And lovin' herr, therre's no one I despise morre than anyone who's everr hurrt herr and at the same time no one I honorr above someone who cherished herr. I would hope, sirr, that ye would apprrove. I prromise I'll take good carre of herr. Coom noo, lass." He took her hand again, but she stood without moving, her eyes filling with tears. "Coom overr herre, hinny." He brought her over to sit with him on a low wall near the bottom of the stairs. "Ye dinna mind if he overrhearrs, I shouldn't think." He indicated the statue with a backward toss of his head.

Victoria shook her head–smiling now through her tears. "Thank you for understanding, Gavin."

"Aye, lass. I don't suppose ye have a handkerrchief?" Again she shook her head, his mention of a handkerchief bringing on fresh tears. "Noo what?" he exclaimed pretending exasperation, but his eyes gave him away.

"He...Uncle Bertie...used to tease me about never having a hanky. He...he gave me one of his. I....I want you to have it."

"No, lassie. He gave it to ye and ye should keep it. Noo–it rreally is gettin' cold. Shall we go?"

"Yes–all right." They both got up then to leave. Impulsively Victoria blew a kiss toward the statue. "You would have liked him, darling." Her voice was still shaking, but her eyes had begun to sparkle. "Even though he was English."

Gavin chuckled, slipping an arm around her waist as they walked away together heading back down the Mall toward Trafalgar again. "Aye, lass. Afterr all, he did have the good sense to take a Scotswoman to wife."

* * *

Later that day they had finished dinner and were cuddled up together once more before the cheerily burning coal in the grate. For a while they remained quiet, neither of them moving except for an occasional kiss or caress. "Torri," Gavin said at last, "aboot earrlierr today. I'm a verra prroud man, ye see, and I....."

"Oh, I know you are, darling. And I did try hard to be tactful, but I hurt your feelings anyway, I guess. I'm so sorry."

"Ye said naethin' wrrong, darrlin'. Only ye see, ye've made such a success of yourr life while I've wasted mine."

"If my being an actress bothers you, I'll quit–that's all."

"But when Jason made ye stop worrkin', ye werre verra unhappy."

"That...that was because he forced me to do it. This would be altogether different."

"Thank ye, Torri." He kissed her. "But I'm marrryin' ye knowin' how ye love the theatrre. I wouldna want ye to leave it on my account."

"Gavin, did I ever tell you it took me four years of auditions to get my first acting job? But I made it finally and so will you. It's only a matter of time."

"Is it?" He raised his eyebrows. "Soomtimes I think my rrefusal to settle doon to anythin' was just because secrretly I've always wonderred if I'm rreally any good at all."

Victoria looked at him for several seconds without speaking. Was his apparent self-confidence pure bravado? Could he actually doubt his own abilities? "Darling, how can you say that? You are incredibly gifted!"

Now he actually chuckled. "And I don't suppose ye'rre at all biased, of courrse."

"Gavin, don't be ridiculous. When I first heard you sing, I wasn't in love with you."

"Werren't ye?"

She smiled. "Well, maybe on the way to it, but...."

"So ye see,,,,,"

"No, I don't <u>see</u> anything. My opinion of your talent is entirely professional. It has nothing to do with the purely coincidental fact that I adore you."

"Thank ye, dearr wee lassie!" Gavin put one hand on either side of her face and leaned forward to kiss her "Yourr faith in me means a grreat deal. I willna let ye doon."

"But...but it wasn't really that anyway...." Victoria hesitated, but only briefly. She had blundered badly, after all, by trying to be careful. "This afternoon when I...I inquired about your plans, it wasn't because I have any doubts about your eventual success. When..when you paid for our lunch, I...I couldn't help seeing inside your wallet and...and...."

Instantly he was on the defensive again. "So that's it, is it? What arre ye afrraid of? I willna let ye starrve."

"Oh, darling!" She smiled at him tenderly. "I'm not in the least afraid of starving. But why should you worry alone? If we're truly to share our lives....." Just then, however, she was interrupted by a knock on the door. "Oh, no!" she exclaimed, her eyes dancing. "Not another old girl friend!"

"Ah, lass..therre werre too many to count....too many to count." As he went to answer the door, Gavin glanced over his shoulder and winked at her. He opened the door, however, not to an old girl friend, but to Sir Terence Cartier and for one of the few times in his life thus far he was rendered speechless.

"Excuse me," the actor said after a few seconds, "is this where I might find Victoria Windsor?"

"Terry!" she exclaimed, jumping up and running over to the door. "Oh, it's so good to see you! Doctor Anthony said you'd asked about me, but I never expected you to come here." She beamed at him.

"Ah...is someone going to ask me in?" He grinned good-naturedly.

"Oh, my goodness!" Victoria laughed. "Please excuse us. Do come in." They both stepped back to allow him to enter.

"May I take yourr things, sirr?" Gavin managed to say.

"Yes, thank you." Removing his hat and coat, Terry handed them to the other man who at once disappeared through the kitchen to leave the things in his bedroom.

"How sweet of you, luv!" She reached up to kiss her old friend on the cheek. "You're still looking after me, aren't you?"

"It's a difficult habit to break," he admitted, slipping an affectionate arm around her waist. "Although it appears someone else has accepted the job on a full-time basis."

People would soon learn they had only to mention a certain Scotsman to be rewarded with a radiant smile. "Yes, it would seem so." As Gavin rejoined them at that moment, however, Victoria realized she hadn't actually introduced them. If Gavin could never meet her beloved Uncle Bertie, he could come to know Terry. "Oh, I'm so sorry," she murmured. "Darling, this is Terry. Terry, this is Gavin." She made the presentation with some misgivings, worried Gavin would find it difficult, if not impossible, to see beyond the personage of Sir Terence Cartier to the warmhearted, caring man who had been so kind to her for so long. The two men shook hands, their visitor accompanying the handshake with a smile–Gavin for his part unusually serious, but with a slight nod to acknowledge the introduction. "Please, Terry, sit down," she urged, indicating a large, comfortable armchair to the left of and facing the sofa. She took Gavin's hand to lead him over to the couch where they sat close together, hands joined between them.

Briefly Sir Terence studied Victoria. Her face was perhaps a little thinner and there was just the slightest shadow under her eyes to show what she had been through in the past few weeks. But he'd never seen her looking so totally happy. "Are you positive you only left hospital yesterday? You look marvelous!"

"I <u>feel</u> marvelous! I....I want you to know, luv. The only other person I've told is Olivia's father." Here she paused to glance lovingly at Gavin. "We're going to be married." Somewhat surprised by the news, Terry looked searchingly at each of them in turn.. Victoria couldn't help noticing his reaction. "Please....please tell me you're glad for us. We..we love each other so much and....."

"It's...ah...quite evident there's a strong, mutual attraction," he temporized, "but have you known each other long enough to consider marriage?"

Of course, Gavin thought immediately, he doesn't think I'm good enough for her!

"Terry, please don't say anything to spoil this for me." Victoria's voice trembled slightly.

"I'm only wondering," he responded carefully, "whether perhaps you should be somewhat better acquainted before you...."

Gavin could keep silent no longer. "And just what exactly do you mean by that, sirrr?" As always when he was angered, his burr became thicker.

Terry had been wondering when he would say something. "Simply that, Mr. Hamilton. You haven't known each other very long and in addition....."

"And in addition the grreat Sirr Terrence doesna considerr me a worrthy husband forr the grreat Victorria Windsorr!" Gavin stood up, striding over to grab his coat out of the closet. "When yourr illustrrious guest has left, Torri, I'll be back. In the meantime I think I'd be morre comforrtable in the pub!"

"Darling–no, please!" Getting quickly to her feet, Victoria hurried over to place her hand on his arm. "Please don't leave. He didn't mean it that way at all!"

Terry saw the stricken expression on her face and at once he came to join them. "I assure you, young man, that you have completely misinterpreted my motives. I am most definitely <u>not</u> a snob and my only concern in this matter is the happiness of someone I couldn't care more about if she were my own daughter."

Gavin hesitated only briefly before throwing his coat down on a chair. "Aye, I'll stay." He returned to his place on the couch.

Victoria tried to smile. "Could...could I make tea?" Perhaps some refreshments would help and then, too, with her out of the room the two men would be forced to talk to each other.

"Thank you–yes." Terry replied at once.

"Gavin, all....all right?"

"Of courrse, lass." He smiled to reassure her. "If ye canna find soomthin', just let me know."

"Yes, thank you, darling." Victoria went out into the kitchen where she busied herself with filling the kettle and putting it on to boil. It will have to be Terry who speaks first, she thought as she worked.

And after a few seconds it was indeed her old friend's voice she heard. "So...you call her Tori?"

"Aye...aye, I do." At such a moment his natural inclination had always been to withdraw into a dour silence, but the man who was learning what it meant to love a woman knew how important it was to Victoria that he establish amicable relations with someone who up until recently had been nothing to him but a name on a marquee. But then, come to think of it, so had the name of Victoria Windsor and in spite of himself Gavin grinned.

Taking that as an encouraging sign, the other man went on. "Why that name, if I might ask?"

At once the smile disappeared. "Why not?"

Accustomed as Terry was to either the warm affection of close friends or the worshipful awe of most others, the Scot's attitude had him somewhat nonplused, but neither was he the sort to take offense at it. On the contrary he found it refreshing. "Believe me, Gavin, I am merely intrigued. I've never heard anyone use anything except her full name. When did you begin calling her that?"

"Shorrtly afterr....afterr we met. It...it just seemed to suit herr somehow."

It was then Terry began to lose his doubts. "<u>Tori</u>. Yes, you're right about that." He smiled. "It does suit her."

Gavin actually forgot for a moment that this was Sir Terence Cartier and instead he now found himself remembering something the actor had said earlier–that he cared for Victoria as though she were his own daughter. "Then ye do know herr verra well."

"As well as she'd let anyone know her in those days."

Victoria returned just then carrying a tray on which there were a tea pot, milk and sugar, mugs and a plate of biscuits. She set it on the small dining table near the windows. "Please..." She indicated the table and the two men joined her, Gavin bringing another chair for himself.

"Well," Terry observed as they all sat down. "I understand it's Tori now?"

At that she smiled. "I guess it is–at least to Gavin. He told me right away Victoria was much too elegant.." Here she paused to look at her future husband, her eyes sparkling..."and much too English." Their visitor laughed. "You can see though, can't you?" she went on pleadingly, "how good he is for me?"

"Believe me, Sirr Terrence–" Gavin covered Victoria's hand with his. "Ye can trrust me wi' the lass."

"First of all, young man, it's Terry."

"Aye," he nodded. "Terrrry."

When he came to know the Scotsman better, he would tell him he'd never realized until then how many "r's" there were in his name. For now, however, Terry decided it might be wiser not joke about his brogue. "And secondly if I'm not invited to the wedding, I shall be highly offended!"

All at once Victoria had an idea. "I've...I've really had nothing to do with my father for years. Will..will you give me away?"

"My dear girl, I would be honored!"

So all tension was gone and the rest of the evening passed quickly until Terry glanced at his watch. "Good heavens, it's nearly midnight. I must be going." He stood up. You will let me know as soon as you set a date." Victoria nodded, hugging him. How open and free she is, he thought, and he prayed it would last.

Gavin excused himself to get Terry's things. "You....you do like him, don't you?" Victoria whispered.

"Very much indeed. He is good for you just as you said."

"Jason wasn't, was he?"

"We all had our doubts about him," he admitted.

Gavin returned and Victoria instantly left Terry to stand next to him and link her arm through his. "Darling, Terry says you are good for me and....and Jason wasn't."

"Och! Anyone would be prreferrable to that bluidy damned prreacherr!"

The actor roared with delight. "Quite perceptive for an Englishman, hm, Gavin?" he inquired, extending his hand.

"Aye, Terrry, aye." Gavin laughed as well, grasping the other man's hand in both of his.

"Good night then, you two. I don't know when I've enjoyed an evening more." Gavin opened the door for him and walking briskly through, Terry started down the stairs. At the first landing, however, he paused to look back to where the couple stood together in the doorway, arms about each other's waists. Well, old chap, he thought, chuckling to himself as he continued on down the stairs, you arrived the doubting old cynic and you leave, the honorary father of the bride.

* * *

Alone again in the cozy little flat, Victoria and Gavin decided to leave the washing up for the morning and when he came out of the bathroom a short while later, she was already in bed. It seemed to him she had never appeared so sweet, so utterly desirable. Dear God, he wondered, how long can I lie beside her and not...not.... But he would allow his thoughts to go no further. She must be the one to give; he would not–he simply would not take. Slipping under the covers next to her, he propped himself up on one elbow. She had just taken a shower and the sweet, damp smell of her filled his nostrils, arousing him even though he had as yet to touch her. Once he did, he knew he would be unable to draw back.

Victoria had made up her mind, however, that tonight once again they would make love and now as he gazed down at her, she pushed the last of her fear and uncertainty away, raising her arms to bring him to her. "Are you surre, Torri?" he whispered.

She nodded. "Yes, my darling, very sure." At first he barely brushed his lips across hers, but when she still made no gesture of protest, he covered her mouth completely, probing gently at first and then harder and harder until her lips parted under his. Dimly she felt him begin to explore her body with his hands, caressing her as only he seemed to know how to do and as she arched her body upward to meet his touch, her very rational determination to give herself to him dissolved into a warm, throbbing yearning of her own. How could she ever have thought he was just another man?

Then all at once–despite her own mounting excitement–she became aware of his face. Strange she'd never noticed before that passion made his eyes deepen in color until the irises appeared almost black. More than his eyes, however, was his expression–one of infinite tenderness–and she knew with a beautiful certainty that for him as well this was far more than mere physical pleasure. At last then he took her and even these thoughts were lost as their bodies began to move together in waves of mounting passion. "Och, Torri----Torri!" Even as he finally withdrew from her, he still whispered her name and the last thing she remembered before falling asleep was his hand stroking her hair.

So many times she'd returned to consciousness in the morning vaguely aware she had allowed some man to use her body for his own selfish needs leaving her no less alone. Today, however, she awoke to the same tender touch of Gavin's hand on her hair. Sleepily she turned over on her back and opened her eyes. "Good morrnin', darrlin'." He had been so worried that he couldn't wait for her to wake up of her own accord. Had she really wanted him to make love to her last night? Suppose he had repulsed her? But then she smiled up at him and he breathed a sigh of relief. Apparently everything was all right. They lay quiet for a while in each other's arms and yet Gavin's mind refused to rest. He had to know for sure. "Torri?" he whispered and even at such a serious moment he savored the burr of her name on his tongue, "I need to know soomthin'." Victoria nodded, bringing her hand up to trace the firm line of his jaw. "Did....did ye trruly wish to make love last night orr did ye do it only because ye kent how fierrcely I wanted ye? Which I did, by the way," he couldn't resist adding with a grin.

She smiled in return. It was so easy to discuss the most intimate matters with him–so easy they could even joke a little. "Gavin, I....I truly wanted to...to give myself to you. I was only.... only afraid because I suppose I still wondered a little whether it was all only physical between us. But I....I learned something last night."

"Aye, darrlin?"

"That the most tender feelings can exist at the same moment as the strongest passion."

"Torri," he murmured, "I do love ye sae fierrcely, lass."

They moved into each other's arms again, lips searching for each other's now by instinct–hands moving over each other's bodies. The mood was shattered almost at once, however, by the strident tones of the bedside telephone. Muttering something nasty sounding in Gaelic, Gavin reached over to answer it. Victoria buried her head in her pillow, overcome by the worst fit of giggles she'd ever experienced.

* * *

Dr. Anthony became increasingly concerned as the time for Victoria's appointment had come and gone. Terence Cartier had rung up earlier that morning, but anything could have happened in the meantime and finally, unable to wait any longer, he gave his secretary Gavin Hamilton's phone number. The woman came in a moment or later red-faced and flustered. "She'll be here, sir," she announced, immediately turning on her heel to leave.

And Victoria did indeed arrive about a half-hour after that–breathless and apologetic. "I... I'm frightfully sorry. I...ah...completely forgot."

The doctor unabashedly stared at her. Could it have been only the cold air which had given her face such an incredible glow? "Who....ah...answered my secretary's call?" he inquired. "I've never seen her so rattled."

"Oh!" The corners of Victoria's mouth twitched. "That was Gavin. He...he put an ancient Celtic curse on her....ah....something about...ah....boils in her armpits and her fingers and toes dropping off, but...but he says he didn't mean it."

Dr. Anthony strove diligently not to laugh. "Where <u>is</u> Gavin? He did come with you, I imagine?"

"Oh, yes. Finding a place to park his car."

"May we begin then? I wanted to talk to you alone first anyway." He indicated that she should sit on the couch and he waited until she'd settled herself before going on. "How long have you known Gavin?"

"Why?" At once she was on the defensive.

"Sir Terence...ah....telephoned me this morning."

"Oh... Did Terry tell you how much he liked Gavin?"

"Yes, as a matter of fact, he did. But I still want <u>you</u> to tell me how long you've actually known him."

"All right...a...a couple of months, I guess. But....but we'll have to wait until my divorce from Jason is final so that will give us more time." Her eyes pleaded with the doctor to agree with her.

"Believe me, my dear young lady, when I saw you walk into this office a few moments ago–bubbling with happiness–all I could wish is that it would always be like that for you."

"But it's because of him–can't you see? I....I realize I have a lot to learn about him, but I already know the important things. He's so caring, so considerate. He didn't even make love to me until he was sure I wanted it."

"Then you and Gavin have had sex already since you left hospital?"

Victoria nodded, her green eyes sparkling again. "It...ah...would have been twice if your secretary hadn't rung up."

"So that was the reason for the curse?"

"Yes," she replied smiling, but then suddenly she was serious again. "I...I almost threw all of this away, didn't I, when I tried to kill myself? You're....you're right. It...it doesn't get any easier. Saying it, I mean. How could I ever have done that--<u>how</u>?"

"Well, that's one of the many things we'll be talking about."

"I....I had hoped I wouldn't need counseling—you know, now that I'm with Gavin."

"Your present happiness, Victoria, does nothing to change the fact that for years you've suppressed feelings of personal failure–a personal failure made all the more intolerable by your professional success. Until we get all those feelings out in the open, they will merely continue to fester."

"Gavin told me his father once said there was never a problem terrible enough to withstand the light of day."

"He sounds like a very wise man. Have you met him?"

"Not yet. We're....we're going up to Scotland as soon as you think it's all right."

"Don't tell me you're asking me?"

Victoria laughed, "My agent is always saying that, too. I must be a bloody terror!"

There was a brief knock and Gavin came in, smiling warmly. "What have you done to my nurse, old chap?" the doctor inquired as the two men shook hands. "You've positively unnerved the woman!"

The grin grew broader. "Och–Torri told ye then, did she? Dinna worrry. The toes and fingerrs'll grrow back."

Dr. Anthony cleared his throat once or twice. How did one maintain an even remotely professional atmosphere with these two? "We....ah....won't have time for a full session today, but I would like to speak to you alone for a few minutes as well."

Gavin had at once gone over to sit with Victoria, taking hold of her hand. "Therre's nae a thing ye can say to me that the lass canna hearr."

"It's all right, darling. I'll wait outside." Victoria got up and walked to the door. Dr. Anthony watched as the other man's eyes followed her from the room.

"I dinna ken why ye need to talk to me anyway."

"You don't really trust me, do you?"

"I just dinna ken what can be accomplished by pokin' and prroddin' aboot inside that bonnie golden head."

"Believe me, that lady has emotional scars which have been building up for years." Dr. Anthony hesitated briefly. "Are you aware she's only very recently made an attempt on her own life?"

"Aye." Gavin's face clearly betrayed his pain and for a moment the doctor regretted his rather cruel tactic. But then this man held Victoria's future well-being in his hands and he had to be sure of him.

"She doesn't like herself very much, does she?"

So many times he'd heard Victoria belittle herself and at last–reluctantly–he shook his head. "No–and I canna underrstand why. She's such a dearr, wee thing."

"You are very much in love with her, aren't you?"

Gavin looked at the doctor as though he were the one who needed help. "Arre ye daft—to be askin' such a question?"

"Well, there's no doubt you're good for her--for now at least."

"What in hell arre ye talkin' aboot? He stood up to stride angrily about the room. "Forr noo?! I intend to go on bein' good forr herr. She's sae damned good forr me. She...she makes me feel tallerr than Ben Nevis!! She....."

The longer Gavin talked the better the doctor felt about him, but now he was thrown for a loss. "I'm....I'm sorry, Gavin. Who is Ben Nevis?"

"Och!!" He threw up his hands in mock despair. "Englisherrs! 'Tis the highest mountain in the Brritish Isles. Naethin' like the puny wee hills ye have doon herre!"

Dr. Anthony looked suitably embarrassed. But he was glad he'd made the mistake. The man had obviously needed the emotional release. "You're not someone who expresses his deepest feelings easily, are you?" he observed carefully.

Returning to sit on the couch again, Gavin sighed. "No," he admitted, smiling ruefully, "I'm not."

"And yet in spite of your normal reticence," Dr. Anthony went on, "you spoke of your feelings to me. Why?"

" 'Tis imporrtant ye ken ye can trrust the lass in my carre."

"Yes, Gavin, I do trust you. But you also have to trust me. Because together we can help her."

"Aye, I do."

"Good then." The doctor stood up extending his hand. "I'll let you take her out of her now–as soon as we've set up a schedule of appointments."

Gavin rose as well and they shook hands again. "When may I brring herr home to meet my Dad? I've verra anxious forr them to know each otherr."

"Give me a week–two at the most–just to be sure she's really on the road back. Then you can go."

"Thank ye, sirr." Gavin opened the door and walked out into the reception area. At the sight of him Victoria jumped to her feet and came over to him. " 'Tis all rright, lass," he said at once, slipping his arm around her waist. "We just have to make some appointments forr ye and we can leave."

"What did you and Dr. Anthony talk about for so long?" Victoria asked a short time later as they came out onto the sidewalk. " I...I was becoming a little anxious."

"Aboot what, darrlin'?"

"Oh, I don't know...that he....he was warning you not to marry me or....or that he wanted to commit me somewhere....something like that."

Gavin stopped short. "No, Torri," he said very gently, "we wouldna do that to ye. The doctor just wanted to be surre I underrstood how imporrtant it was that ye coom to see him and I guess he wanted to be surre aboot me as well." Neither of them realized that from the window of his office Dr. Anthony was looking down on them–a smile on his face.

"Oh, I see," Victoria said, "and do you and is he?"

"Aye, hinny." He took her hand in his, leaning down to kiss her once lightly. "But noo yourr poorr laddie is fairr perrishin' wi hungerr. How aboot a wee bit o' lunch?"

Dr. Anthony continued to watch as they crossed the street together, still hand in hand, until they finally disappeared from his sight around the corner. Still smiling, he nodded in silent confirmation. Yes...he was content.

Chapter 2

At the first sound of her mother's voice on the telephone Olivia had cried from sheer relief, but almost at once she grew calmer and the news that her mother and Gavin were going to get married sent her into ecstasies. Grown-up were certainly peculiar, she thought. Uncle Ken had kept telling her everything was all right when it wasn't and now that everything was all right, he acted as though he were mad about something. Well, none of that mattered anyway. Her mother sounded just like herself and Gavin was going to be her Daddy and in less than a month now she would be going home.

Once settled in the flat with Gavin Victoria's first concern had, of course, been Olivia, but with the little girl reassured and happy–at least for the time being–she could concentrate on herself. There were practical matters to be taken care of such as having Martha and Kate MacAllister pack up her belongings. She discussed divorce proceedings with Carl Michaels, her solicitor. But most of Victoria's effort and energy during those first weeks out of hospital went into her work with Dr. Anthony.

Therapy continued to be no less painful as the doctor delved still deeper into her past–gently, but firmly exposing old emotional wounds to the healing light of reason. They talked in more detail now about her childhood, her first years in London– perhaps the loneliest of all--and of course the birth of Olivia and her subsequent desertion of her daughter which only proved yet again that she was a valueless human being. All this, however, she could also talk about with Gavin.

It came to be more difficult, however, as they discussed her relationships with men–how could she admit her shame–and she evaded his questions. When Gavin telephoned the doctor, he advised him to wait–that she'd let him know when she was ready. Gradually Victoria had come to comprehend that her apparent promiscuity stemmed only in part from her dread of being alone; that it was, in fact, due far more to her unconscious desire to debase and humiliate herself–to be treated as unfeelingly as she felt she deserved. But she still couldn't bring herself to reveal any of this to the man she adored. Then at last–inevitably-- she and Doctor Anthony began to deal with her relationship with Julian Christopher. Once again she refused to tell Gavin anything, saying only that it had been a particularly hard session, but then hours later in the middle of the night her screams awakened him. At once he reached over to bring her out of the nightmare. "Therre, therre, dearr wee one," he crooned, holding her close. "Will ye no talk to me? You'll feel betterr."

No, I won't, Victoria thought, because I will have lost you. "It...it was only a bad dream, darling. Therapy is terribly upsetting and I...."

"No, Torri, I willna accept that." He laid her back down on the bed then although one arm still cradled her. "Noo I want ye to tell me."

It hurt even more to hear the tenderness in his voice, to think of that same voice growing cold as its owner came to despise her. "It's too hideous. Don't make me! Please!"

"Tell me, Torri," his deep voice urged her in the semi-darkness. "Tell me."

"Only keep holding me–please."

"Aye, lass." He gathered her close again and waited. At last she began to talk and once she got started, she couldn't stop. The words came out in a torrent as sobbing, she told him everything, her words at times so garbled he could barely understand her: the pub crawling, the man who had beaten and raped her and paid her with a half-crown bearing the likeness of her Uncle Bertie and finally–Julian Christopher. Gavin felt the nausea rise up in him, but still he held her, stroking her hair, and let her talk it out. Even when she'd finished, he still cradled her in his arms until her sobs gradually ceased and she was quiet. "Torri," he finally said then, "I'm going to turn on the light."

"Oh, no–please!"

" 'Tis imporrtant. I want ye to see my face."

"All....all right then, but....."

He laid her down again then, reaching over to turn on the bedside lamp. Her face was flushed and tear-stained. "Let me get a cloth firrst though and wash yourr face."

"No...!" She grabbed hold of his arm. "No—tell me first. I...I have to know!" But then she saw his expression and she understood why he'd wanted the light. "Oh, Gavin...!" Fresh tears filled her eyes. "How can you still love me after...after everything I've just told you?"

"People used ye, Torri, when ye werre alone and lonely–used ye forr theirr own sick, perrverrted pleasurre. Why should that make me stop lovin' ye?? Noo the past is overr and done with and all that matterrs arre the yearrs ahead. Do ye believe me?" She nodded. "Then let me herre ye say it."

Her lower lip was quivering, but she managed to say it. "I believe you."

"And I know ye'll always love me."

"And...and I know you'll always love me. Oh, Gavin...thank you!"

"Forr lovin' ye? Dinna be daft!"

"For that and...and for...forgiving...."

"Torri, darrlin', when I think of people hurrtin' ye that way, takin' the dearr, sweet soul I ken ye to be and...and doin' those things to ye, I....I think I could actually kill them. They'rre the ones who should beg my forrgiveness...neverr you. Noo–I'm goin' to wash that bonny face and brrush yourr hairr and then I'll make ye a nice cup of tea. All rright?"

"All...all right." She sniffed and wiped her nose on the sleeve of her nightgown much as a little girl would have done.

"Och–and ye still dinna have a hanky, do ye? Firrst I'll get ye a tissue then." He went into the bathroom, returning a few minutes later to hand her a tissue, and then he did indeed wash her face with a warm cloth, gently brushing her hair and even braiding it and he made tea. Finally he lay back down beside her and holding her in his arms, he sang her an old Scottish lullaby.

"Gavin," she whispered as she nestled drowsily against him, "are you sure you want all of this? I'm a bloody nuisance."

"Torri, do ye no ken that I need to hold ye just as much as ye need to be held?"

This was a new thought to Victoria. Gavin seemed so sure and self-reliant. "You need me?" she whispered wonderingly and the next minute she was asleep.

She related all this to Dr. Anthony at their next session. "Good," he approved, "good. Then I think you're ready to make that trip to Scotland."

"I...I thought so myself. I....I know I still have a long way to go, but last night I....I learned something very special. I learned that I'll never again be alone."

* * *

And so a few days after that the little Morris Rover once again pulled out from the London access road onto the motorway–heading for the Scottish border. Gavin couldn't help remembering the last time he had traveled this same route–fleeing London in a vain attempt to forget Victoria. Now, impossible as he'd thought it then, she was sitting there beside him. Studying his face as he drove, Victoria thought she had never seen him look so happy. "Glad to be going home?" She touched him lightly on the arm.

Briefly he took his eyes off the road to glance over at her. "Glad to be takin' ye home, darrlin'?"

Secretly she'd been dreading this trip, been actually relieved when at first Dr. Anthony wouldn't allow it. She was sure Gavin's father would never approve of her. How could he–a woman of her reputation? "Gavin," she said now, "don't you think you should have warned your father that...that you were bringing me? That...that would at least have given him a chance to get used to the idea."

"Oh no, lass. Naethin' is goin' to deny me the chance to see his face when I tell him. Torri, ye'rre no still frrettin' aboot meetin' him, arre ye?"

"It's just that I've never wanted so much for someone to like me."

"And how aboot whetherr ye'll like <u>him</u>? Have ye thought aboot that?"

"I don't have to," she replied at once. "He's your father. How could he be anything but adorable?"

Gavin checked to make sure she was looking at him. "Aye, well I must admit that's trrue."

"Oh, you!" Victoria hit him playfully on the arm, but then at once she reached up to stroke his cheek with one fingertip. "I...I only want you to be proud of me, that's all and not regret...regret....."

"Oh, and exactly what am I supposed to be rregrrettin'?" he asked, still watching her out of the corner of his eye. "Lovin' ye, I suppose, and wantin' to spend the rrest o' my life wi' ye." Victoria knew by now when he wasn't serious and she laughed a little. "Well, good," he observed, "at least ye've got the sense to rrealize how rridiculous that sounds."

"I...I just want..." she started to say again, but her voice trailed off and she shrugged– a gesture he always found profoundly touching. "How...how long will it take us to get there, darling?" Victoria went on hurriedly, obviously wanting to change the subject.

"I'm nae entirrely surre. I usually drive strraight thrrough and I....."

"You see what a bother I am. Already I'm making you change your way of doing things."

"And suppose I want to do things differrently because of ye? Besides...'twill be fun to spend the nights togetherr in a wee inn."

"How...how far will we get today then, do you think?"

"Almost to the borrderr, I should imagine. We could prrobably make it the rrest of the way in anotherr day, but I want to arrrive in the daylight."

The long hours of driving gave them time to talk, to share memories, thoughts and feelings–both until then having been very private people. And as they talked, they watched the British countryside change gradually from the flat land and rolling hills of England and southern Scotland to the majestic mountains of the Highlands cleft by plunging valleys and glittering with numerous frozen lakes. "Does it appear at all familiarr to ye, darrlin'?" Gavin asked at one point. They were on the last lap of their journey now. By mid- afternoon they would be in Glengowrie.

Victoria was turning her head constantly to look at the glorious untamed beauty on all sides. She nodded smiling. "Except, of course, I saw it in the summer."

"We'll be herre then, too," he assured her, "if yourr schedule allows forr it."

"From now on my work takes second place." When he started to protest, she placed a hand on his arm to silence him. "Because <u>I</u> want it that way," she continued. "Did I ever tell you how I felt that morning–waking up on the train in Scotland?"

"I dinna think so, darrlin'."

"It was as...as though I...I were coming home. And...and it wasn't only that. Every.... every time I heard a Scottish brogue: the household staff at Balmoral; the first professional director to hire me was a Scotsman; even when I heard Felicity speak for the first time, there was something about the sound that warmed and comforted me."

"What arre ye trryin' to say, lassie?"

"I suppose that...well, somehow I sensed you were somewhere in my future. Is...is that totally impossible?"

"No, darrlin'. I think 'tis verra possible."

She smiled at him lovingly. "Gavin, speaking of Felicity. How is she? And Jamie?"

"To be perrfectly honest wi' ye, lass, the last time I was home I wasna much in the mood to concerrn myself wi' Felicity and Jamie." She reached over to caress him lightly on the cheek. "But soomthin' is verra wrrong between them," he went on after allowing himself a few seconds to savor the sensation of her touch. "They quarrrel overr everrathin'."

"But when I first met Felicity in New York, all she could talk about was her Jamie."

"Well, hopefully they'll be able to worrk things oot between them...."Oh, look," he suddenly interrupted himself pointing...."that hill overr therre in the distance...arroond and behind it and we'rre in Glengowrrie!"

After they had originally spoken about Victoria's first meeting with his father, they hadn't mentioned the subject again. Now all at once, it seemed, they were nearly there. "How.... how far is your home from the village?" She tried to sound casual, but Gavin had caught the tremor in her tone.

"Noo–did I no tell ye? Therre's naethin' to worrry aboot." In almost no time, then, they were through Glengowrie–the village being nothing more really than one or two shops, a tea room, a pub and a church. From there the road climbed sharply, winding in and through the snow-covered hills. At last they rounded one particular curve and Gavin pulled the car off to the side of the road and stopped. "Look just ahead therre, darrlin'," he said, his own voice shaking now with suppressed emotion. "Therre's a wee stone brridge turrnin' off to the left. Follow the rroad aboot halfway oop the hill and ye'rre therre."

Following his pointing finger, Victoria saw a large, rambling gray stone house with a white painted porch running all across the front. But her mind was more on the feeling evident in his tone as he described it to her. "It means so much to you, doesn't it, to bring me here?'

"Aye, dearr lass, aye." He leaned over to kiss her before releasing the brake. "Noo– herre we go." He put the little car in gear and they rapidly covered the last half-mile or so, at last turning off the road and over the little stone bridge. "Welcoom home, Torri." He grinned at her, his joy knowing no bounds. From there it was only a minute or so more before Gavin had drawn the car up in front of the barn and turned off the motor. Jumping out, he hurried around to open Victoria's door for her. "Coom, lass." With only the slightest of hesitations she took his hand, stepping out to stand next to him. How much better she looks already, he thought happily. "In the summerr," he explained aloud with a sweeping gesture, "therre's an enorrmous frront lawn."

They began to walk slowly together hand in hand toward where a path had been shoveled from the drive to the front steps of the house. "No, wait!" Suddenly he turned to climb up on a snowbank, reaching down to pull her up beside him. "Noo–look frrom herre all arroond ye!" He pointed slowly in an arc all along the horizon. Mile upon mile of rolling, snow-covered meadows surrounded them on all sides beyond which were the lower hills, dotted with pine trees and finally in the distance the mountains of the Grampian range rose in desolate white and purple splendor, silhouetted against the sky.

The notoriously capricious Scottish weather had cooperated most generously, it apparently having snowed just a day or so before and then rained, leaving a frozen crust on top. Today, however, the sky was a cloudless blue and all the world appeared a flawless, unbroken expanse of white, glittering in the brilliant sunshine. "Oh, darling," Victoria murmured, "it's unbelievable!"

"Aye....aye." Gavin nodded, satisfied that Scotland had put on her most spectacular show for his beloved Tori.

She looked up at his face glowing with pride. "You love it so, my dearest," she said at last. "How could you ever bring yourself to leave?"

"I don't know, Torri," he responded thoughtfully, putting an arm around her shoulders to draw her closer to him. "Soomthin' drrove me to seek soomthin' beyond this place just as soomthin' keeps brringin' me back. And afterr all if I'd stayed herre, I neverr would have found you."

Still standing high on the mounded snow, they turned to each other and kissed–a long, tender kiss, but their faces were getting cold and laughing, they moved back from the embrace. They were still laughing as they climbed back down off the snowbank and walked on toward the house, arms about each other's waists.

* * *

They'd been unaware, however, that from the moment of their arrival they were being closely watched from the house.

Whenever Gavin told his family to expect a visit, his sister Meghan kept a watchful eye on the spot where he always parked his car and very often, therefore, she was the first one out of the house to greet him–calling his name and running to throw her arms around him. It didn't matter that as on many occasions in the past, he'd said he was "bringing a lass". He often brought a woman with him, but when they actually got here, he would invariably ignore her, going off for hours with Meghan or their father.

This particular afternoon she had just come down the stairs which wound around from behind the huge stone fireplace and was on her way across the living room toward the kitchen. Of course she glanced toward the barn and as she observed the Morris Rover just coming to a stop, she let out a squeal of joy. But for some reason on this occasion she did not immediately run outside. Instead she stood looking as her brother got out of the car and walked around to the other side to open the door and help a woman out to stand beside him. From that distance Meghan couldn't see her face clearly or even the color of her hair since her head was covered by the hood of her coat, but she <u>could</u> see that her brother was holding her hand and at the same time pointing and talking with evident animation.

She was still watching, held there seemingly against her will, as the couple climbed up on a snowbank. Well, apparently he was just showing her the view, but he had his arm around her and then she saw him kiss her–a <u>long</u> kiss Meghan thought would never end. Tears welled up in her eyes and she turned and fled back up the stairs before they could come in. In the upstairs hall she encountered Fiona. "Meghan, what's wrong?" her sister asked.

"Gavin's home," she sobbed, running on past into her room and slamming the door behind her.

"Meghan—!" The older girl followed her to knock on the closed door.

"Leave me alone!"

"All rright—all rright, hinny." With a shrug Fiona gave up and went on downstairs. As she came into the living room, the couple was just climbing the front steps and she hurried to open the door. "As usual, Gavin, ye'rre just in time for tea," she teased him. "How do ye always manage to arrrive prrecisely at mealtime?"

He grinned. "Torri, this impudent lass, who is displayin' such a <u>disgrraceful</u> lack o' rrespect forr her elderr brrotherr, is my sisterr, Fiona."

The hood of Victoria's coat framed her face, soft curls escaping here and there to lie wispy and golden against the dark lining. The cold air had brought out the color in her cheeks and her green eyes shone. Fiona's eyes widened in admiration. Her brother invariably attracted beautiful women, but never quite like this one–and for some reason she looked familiar. "Welcoom..ah..Torri," she said at last. "Excuse me forr starrin'. Ye'rre sae luvly."

"Aye." Gavin smiled proudly and with what his sister couldn't help noticing was a distinctly proprietary air.

"Th...thank you," Victoria replied softly.

"Do I know you?" Fiona inquired. "I'm surre I've seen ye somewherre beforre. Is Torri a nickname?"

She looked helplessly at Gavin. "Aye," he said at once. "Torri is shorrt forr Victorria. Only ye willna call herr that. 'Twill be Torri to all of ye as it is to me."

"Oh, my goodness!" Fiona exclaimed suddenly. "Ye'rre Victorria Windsorr, arren't ye? I went doon to Lundon wi' my lit class frrom Univerrsity. We saw *The Divine Sarah*. Ye werre everr sae grrand! I've neverr forrgotten it!"

"It's kind of you to remember," Victoria murmured. So already a member of the family had recognized her. It would only be a matter of time now until his sister recalled everything about her and then they'd never accept her. "Gavin, would...would you please get my cases from the car?" Her voice sounded strained. "I'd like to unpack."

"Aye, I'll be rright back." Giving her a reassuring pat on the arm, he left them alone to hurry out to the car. This visit was so important and he realized that for Victoria at least it wasn't starting out well.

"I'm verra sorrry." Fiona could see it had upset their visitor to be recognized. "You must get sae tirred o' that, but I...."

"Not at all." But she could hear herself sounding a great deal like the Victoria of a few years ago–faintly imperious–and this was Gavin's sister. "I'm the one who should apologize," she went on her voice trembling. "It's just that it's been a long drive and I....I...."

"What's the matterr with me? I haven't even taken yourr coat. You must think all Scots arre half-mad, but then ye'rre used to my brrotherr, I suppose."

"Y....y...yes." Victoria slipped out of her coat. She'd chosen her most conservative appearing. The material was tan cashmere; the lining, however, was mink.

"Mmm–this is gorrgeous!" Fiona stroked the fur, but then she saw the same strained expression on the other woman's face. "Och, I've done it again, haven't I?"

"It's...it's all right."

"No, 'tis not. Ye'rre my brrotherr's guest and herre I am–blatherrin' away at ye."

Gavin came back in then with their suitcases. "Coom, Torri. I'll show ye to yourr rroom. Fiona, you'll let me know when Dad cooms in?"

"Aye."

"And tell Grranny I'll be doon to see herr as soon as I've gotten Torri settled."

"Aye." For a moment or so after Victoria and her brother had gone up the stairs together, Fiona continued to stand there looking after them. "Oh, my goodness," she whispered aloud to the empty room. "Do ye suppose?"

"Well, if therre's to be any tea this afterrnoon," she heard her grandmother sputter all at once, "someone's goin' to have to be givin' me a wee bit o' help!"

"Aye, Grranny, I'm coomin'." She hung up Victoria's coat and hurried on out into the kitchen.

"So–wherre is he?" As always Mary Hamilton was bustling about the room in what appeared to be a never-ending motion. "I did hearr the laddie, did I not?"

"Aye–'tis Gavin." Fiona took an apron down off the peg by the stove. "What would ye like me to do, Grranny?"

"The dough forr the scones is therre on the boarrd–rready to be cut oot. Och, 'tis glad I am I'm makin' scones–'tis one of the laddie's favorrites--and I think therre's a jarr o' that quince jam he's sae parrtial to."

"Ye know the rrest of us should be jealous--the way ye favorr Gavin. Ye always have."

"Och– 'tis all in yourr fancy! I've nae use forr him. He's a botherr and a nuisance. He'll have the place at sixes and sevens in no time!" But her tiny black eyes were dancing and her granddaughter didn't believe her for a minute.

"Gavin said to tell ye he'd be doon to see ye in a wee bit. He's showin' his guest to herr rroom firrst."

"Och!" Granny muttered, "he's got anotherr <u>English</u> lass wi' him, hasn't he?"

"Aye." Fiona busied herself with cutting out the scones. She hoped her grandmother would change the subject, but she should have known betterr. Once Granny got to carrying on about England, there was no quieting her until she'd said her piece.

"Well, I dinna ken what he sees in 'em."

"Grranny, the English havna been ourr enemies forr centurries noo and Gavin's guest seems verra pleasant."

"Och–that's just it–wi' theirr smooth ways and theirr nimity-pimity mannerrs. Ye canna trrust 'em. Ye marrk my worrds!"

"I know what it is," Fiona teased her. "He hasna coom to gie ye one o' his bearr hugs. As soon as I get these scones in the oven, I'll go tell him."

"Ye neednа botherr," the old woman replied with great dignity. "He's wi' his grrand English lady. And I should be gettin' oot the good china anyway. I'll no have herr thinkin' we'rre savages!'

"Neverr mind! Gavin'll soon coax ye oot o' yourr sulks."

" 'Tis nae sulks!" Granny insisted. " 'Tis havin' an Englisherr herre. Look what she's done alrready!"

"Torri hasna done a thing. 'Tis you–blatherrin' on aboot naethin'."

"Torri, is it noo? What sorrt o' name is that? And what do ye mean, she's done naethin'. Barrely in the hoose and she's turrned two of my grrandchildrren against me."

"<u>I</u> am going to get Gavin," Fiona announced finally, heading toward the enclosed back stairs which led directly up to the bedrooms from the kitchen. "He'll put an end to this nonsense."

As she left the room, she could hear her grandmother mutter, "Nonsense, humph!" just before she lapsed totally into Gaelic.

* * *

"Ye'll be rright in herre, darrlin'," Gavin had explained, leading Victoria along the upstairs hall into a large room at the rear. Two windows looked out on the hills behind the house while through another on the side wall she could see their car parked in front of the barn. Tears filled her eyes. "Oh, darling," she whispered, "Fiona already knows who I am."

He took her in his arms. "And I've <u>told</u> ye, lass, it doesna matterr."

Victoria slipped both arms around his waist, clinging to him with all her strength. "It's... it's just that I'm afraid that....that your family will think I'm wrong for you and then they'll convince you and I....."

"Och, hinny," Gavin said stroking her hair, "can ye trruly believe–even forr one minute– that anyone could everr change my feelings forr ye? And 'twill nae happen anyway. To them ye'll simply be Torri and they'll love ye as I do."

She drew back just far enough to see his face. "I'm sorry I'm being so silly. It's just that I'm finally learning what it feels like not to be alone and I....."She was prevented from going on, however, not by any further words on his part, but by the incredible tenderness in his eyes as he gazed down at her and all at once she knew beyond any doubt that whatever his family thought of her, he himself would go on loving her. And after all, wasn't that what mattered? At last Gavin bent to kiss her and she came eagerly into his arms again, tipping her head back and closing her eyes. Lost in the sensation of each other much as they had been when they first embraced in New York, they failed to hear the rapid footsteps coming along the hall.

"Gavin!" Fiona had run all the way up the stairs and it wasn't until she was standing directly in the open doorway that she realized she was intruding on a private moment. At the sound of her voice they moved apart, looking for all the world like two abashed teenagers. "Excuse me," she apologized at once. "I should have known. I guessed this wasna an orrdinarry visit."

"Oh, ye did–did ye?" Gavin grinned, ducking his head. It was an habitual mannerism whenever he was embarrassed although at the moment he didn't understand why he was feeling that way.

"Aye." She looked at Victoria. The other woman appeared so unhappy and uncomfortable that Fiona was drawn to come on into the room, placing a hand on her arm. "I'm trruly sorrry, Torri. Firrst I blatherr on at ye like soom starr-strruck bairrnie–then I brreak in on you and Gavin like that."

Seeing the genuine concern on the Scots girl's face, Victoria relaxed a little. "It's all right, really. I'm used to it for...for the most part. Only....only in this case, I...I...."

"You happen to be in love with my brrotherr. Am I rright?"

She simply nodded, but her smile would have been sufficient to answer the question.

" 'Tis a love that's rreturrned, Fiona," Gavin put in. "Do I darre trrust ye wi' a secrret? Because if ye brreathe a worrd beforre I can tell Dad, I swearr I'll thrrow ye in the deepest parrt o' the loch wherre ye'll have naethin' forr coomp'ny but the kelpies."

"Oh, I swearr!" she raised her right hand. "Torri kens how frrightened I am."

He grinned. "Well, then–" He slipped an arm around Victoria's waist, kissing her lightly on the hair– "This lass has agrreed to become my wife."

"I'm sae happy forr ye both." Was it her imagination, Victoria wondered, or had Fiona hesitated slightly? "Oh, but Gavin, I came oop to fetch ye," his sister went on–perhaps a little <u>too</u> quickly now. Grranny's miffed ye havna coom nearr herr and noo I've been gone a while and she'll be in a black-and-bluidy mood forr fairr."

"Go ahead, darling," Victoria urged him. "I'd...I'd like to shower before tea anyway. I want to be fresh when I meet your father."

"I'll show ye, hinny, beforre I go doon to Grranny. I can always jolly herr oot o' herr moods. I'm such a charrmin' laddie, ye know." He winked broadly at them both.

"I'll...I'll see you a little later then, Fiona," Victoria said as he took her hand to lead her from the room.

"Aye, Torri." The other girl smiled warmly.

"Is it the showerr ye'rre wantin', lass," Gavin asked a moment later as they walked down the hall, "or a wee bit o' time away frrom all these Hamiltons?"

"I...I just need to relax a little, darling–that's all–and...and you'll have a real chance to talk to Fiona."

"She likes ye verra much, I can tell. Herre we arre." He opened the bathroom door, reaching in to turn on the light.

Victoria touched him on the cheek. "Oh, dearest, what else could she say with me right there?"

"Och, Torri, when will ye coom to believe in yourrself?" He drew her close once again. "Noo I'll gie ye no morre than an hourr. Do ye hearr me?"

"Yes, darling–one hour."

Reluctantly Gavin released her then to return to Fiona. Victoria waited until she heard them leave before going back to the bedroom for her things. She discovered she was trembling and she did allow herself one of the tranquillizers Dr. Anthony had prescribed, "Dear God, let them love me," she prayed over and over as she walked down the hall again to the bathroom. "Please just let them love me."

* * *

Fiona was leading the way down the enclosed back stairs when she stopped, turning to face her brother in the darkness. "Gavin–I have to ask ye. Arre ye surre o' yourr feelin's?"

"Torri was rright then. She felt yourr good wishes werren't entirrely sincerre."

"Och–I've hurrt herr again, haven't I? I...I meant it when I congrratulated ye. Trruly I did. It's just that ye've waited sae long and noo to choose a lass from such a differrent way of life than yourrs."

"Ye mean–because she's Victorria Windsorrr." He exaggerated his pronunciation of the name even more than usual. "So ye can see noo why she was oopset to have ye rrecognize herr rright away. Please, Fiona, forr my sake, will ye just get to know my Torri."

"Aye, I will—I prromise. 'Twill not be harrd. She seems verra sweet."

"Thank ye, dearr sisterr." He bent to kiss her on the cheek.

"Ye know, Gavin, Dad's been worrried aboot ye–that ye'd just drrift thrrough life."

"To be honest I was a wee bit concerrned m'self."

Suddenly the crackle of Mary Hamilton's voice erupted from just below them on the other side of the door. "And what exactly arre ye two talkin' aboot oop therre? Ye should ken by noo that if ye canna say it in frront of me, ye shouldna say it at all!"

They still felt ridiculously as they had when they were much younger and their grandmother had caught them in a bit of mischief. Laughing together, they went on down into the kitchen. "Grranny!" Gavin's voice boomed out, "did I hearr that my favorrite lass is fairr perrishin' forr the sight o'me?"

"Humph!" She was trying hard to remember she was annoyed with him for having ignored her and worse for having brought another Englishwoman into her home, but her eyes were alight with her joy at seeing him again. "Humph!" she muttered a second time, "soomone has a verra good opinion of himself!"

"Och, ye love me, Grranny!" Effortlessly he picked up the tiny woman and swung her around. "Ye ken verra well ye do."

"Put me doon!" she sputtered. "Arre ye daft? I'm an old lady."

"Ye'll neverr be old. I willna allow it." But Gavin put her gently back on her feet, bending to kiss her on the cheek.

She peered up at him, still attempting to maintain a suitably stern expression, but that was all but impossible. She had adored him ever since he was a small boy and she found it extremely difficult to remain cross with him. In her eyes undoubtedly he was still the same small boy. "So," she said, "I'm gettin' oot the good china. I hope ye'rre satisfied."

"Aye, that's grrand, then. I...ah..." Gavin wondered how to tell her about Victoria.

"Carreful noo–ye ken how Grranny is." Fiona finished with the scones and put the sheet of triangular dough shapes into one of the ovens. "Everra time anotherr Englisherr sets foot in this house, 'tis the Duke of Cumberrland all overr again–marrchin' doon the glen!"

" 'Tis naethin' to joke aboot," Mary Hamilton insisted vehemently, punching and pulling at the dough she was kneading as though she actually had the Duke's head in her hands.

"They'rre dirrty forreignerrs and they should stay doon in the English bogs wherre they belong!"

"Well, ye betterr becoom accustomed to this parrticularr English lass," Gavin said at last, "because she's goin' to be my wife."

"Och, laddie! Ye canna do that!"

"Grranny, ye havna even met herr yet!"

"Aye, I've noticed that!" she sputtered on, still punching the bread dough as she talked. "Brring a hoity-toity English lady oop herre and suddenly ye'rre ashamed of yourr old Grranny!"

"Don't be rridiculous!" he exploded. "Ye know how prroud I am of ye. I just dinna ken verra well what I'm doin' today."

"Doesna matterr anyway," she affirmed solemnly as she finally shaped the poor battered dough into loaves. "Therre's nae an English lass alive can make a prroperr wife forr a brraw Scot such as yourrself."

"I...I love herr, Grranny." Gavin's tone was as soft and tender as a moment ago it had been loud and angry. "And so will you if ye'll only forrget she's English long enough to get to know herr."

"I don't want to get to know herr. Theirr ways arre differrent. 'Twill neverr change." She inserted the bread pans into the other oven and slammed the door shut. "Well, at least I can see she ne'err gets the Hamilton rring. 'Tis mine to gie noo wi' yourr dearr motherr in herr grrave. God rrest herr soul and prraise be she didna live to see this day!"

"I only wish she had!" he retorted. "She'd have loved Torri forr herrself. She wouldna have been some daft old woman still fightin' a warr that happened overr two hundrred yearrs ago!"

Involuntarily Fiona gasped. She had never heard her brother cruel to anyone, but most especially their grandmother. Gavin himself, seeing the hurt in the dear little lady's eyes, bitterly regretted the words as soon as he'd spoken then, but before he could say anything further, they heard the front door close.

"Hey therre, laddie," his father called out, "wherre arre ye?"

"In the kitchen, Dad. I'll be rright oot. Grranny, ye ken how dearrly I love ye and I wouldna hurrt ye forr anythin." He went over to put his arm around her shoulders. Suddenly she seemed particularly frail to him. "But I willna have ye speak that away aboot the lass I've chosen forr my wife."

Mary Hamilton ignored the apology. "Tell yourr dad–tea in aboot an hourr," she announced with even more than her customary matriarchal dignity.

Gavin knew better than to push the matter. Later he could talk to her again. "Will ye keep Torri coomp'ny forr a while, Fiona?" he asked instead. " 'Twill gie ye a chance to get betterr acquainted." He started toward the swinging door leading into the other room, but then he stopped, turning back again to his sister as a thought suddenly occurred to him. "Wherre's Meghan? Usually by this time she's attached herrself to me forr the entirre visit."

"In herr rroom. Ah...I'm afrraid she saw you and Torri drrive oop. She's not goin' to like the idea of yourr gettin' marrried, Gavin."

"Aye, I've thought of that," he admitted, "but she's goin' to have to accept the fact that I love Torri and she's goin' to be my wife." He glanced significantly at his grandmother before going on out into the living room.

Niall Hamilton was standing in front of the hearth, as was his custom about to light a taper from the fire with which in turn to light his pipe. "Laddie!" His father embraced him warmly. "How arre ye then? Feelin' a wee bit betterr aboot the worrld in generral?"

"Aye, Dad!" He got out his pipe as well and began to fill it. Two couches faced each other on either side of the fireplace and each man took his customary place on one of them. "So how is everrathin' herre?"

"Winterr's a quiet time–ye ken that." As he lit his son's pipe for him, Niall studied him carefully. Gavin's change of mood was remarkable. "I must admit I was verra concerrned the last time ye werre home. Perrhaps I shouldna mention it, but Felicity told me 'twas a lass had ye sae doon in spirrits."

"Aye, Dad." Even now his face sobered at the memory. He had so nearly lost her."But ye mustna let it rruin yourr life There'll be anotherr lass ye'll coom to carre forr."

"No, I dinna think so." He could feel a smile tugging at the corners of his mouth. This conversation was not going in the anticipated direction at all.

"But ye arre overr it, I see," Niall remarked wryly. "Suddenly it's verra amusin'." He leaned forward to regard him intently once more. "Do ye no ken, my boy, that ye canna drrift thrrough life neverr takin' anythin' or anyone serriously?" Now Gavin actually chuckled a little. " 'Tis naethin' to laugh aboot. Ye'rre nearr thirrty-fourr yearrs of age. Do ye no rrealize......"

"Dad," he finally exclaimed in amused exasperation. "everra time I've coom oop herre wi' a lass, ye've asked me the same question. Why in the blessed name of Saint Andrrrew, do ye choose this time to lecturre me aboot leadin' a morre meaningful life?"

"That question has becoom naethin' but a joke to us both."

"Dad, will ye no ask me?" So that was the reason for the change in him. All at once Niall understood and he, too, began to smile. "Dad, if ye dinna ask me this minute, I swearr I'll burrst!"

His father was grinning broadly now. "So then, is this a special lass ye've brrought home to meet me?"

Gavin had been anticipating this moment ever since he'd first known Victoria truly belonged to him. His father would make his inevitable inquiry and he would trumpet forth a triumphant, "Aye, Dad–I have indeed!" Now after considerable prompting, his father had finally asked the question and all he could think was that she was upstairs–so close–even as he had dreamed of her being. "Aye, Dad, I have indeed." But he spoke the words very softly and there was a tenderness in his eyes his father had begun to think he would never see there.

"Well, wherre is she?" Niall got to his feet. "All these yearrs ye parrade these lassies thrrough herre and noo ye finally brring home my futurre daughterr-in-law—she is my futurre daughterr-in-law, is she not...?" Gavin nodded, standing up as well. Once again now he was smiling. "....and ye hide her away somewherre."

"She's oopstairrs. I'll go get herr." He started toward the stairs.

"Wait, laddie. I canna help wonderrin'. 'Tis so soon–to feel sae deeply aboot a differrent lass."

Gavin paused, one foot on the bottom step and his smile grew broader. "Did I say she was a differrent one?"

"Well, no, you didn't," Niall admitted. "How mutton-headed can I be?"

"Dad–" He came back over to his father. "She's a bit nerrvous aboot meetin' ye."

"What have ye been tellin' herr aboot me?'

"Oh–soomthin' aboot shooting all Englisherrs ye find on the prroperrty."

"English–hm?"

"Aye, Dad. That doesna matterr to ye, does it? I've alrready told Grranny and she's verra oopset."

"Aye, I ken how my Mum is aboot the English." Niall Hamilton shook his head ruefully. "But I serrved beside too many brrave Englishmen in the warr and I ken 'tis time forr old prrejudices to be laid to rrest. Besides–all that trruly matterrs is that ye love herr. Noo– dinna keep the poorr lass waitin' any longerr. Orr me eitherr. Go on noo." His father listened smiling as his son's long legs took the stairs two at a time. More than anything, he'd wanted to see this lad of his married and now it seemed his wish was about to be granted.

Gavin had been somewhat concerned how he would find Victoria, but as he came along the upstairs hall, he could hear her chatting with his sister, their voices interspersed with the lilting sound of feminine laughter. Fiona was sitting facing the doorway and she looked up at him, her eyes full of mischief. "I was just tellin' Torri that the last time I saw ye blush like that was when I caught ye oot behind the barrn wi'...ah...what <u>was</u> herr name, Gavin? Anyway, Torri, I was nine so he was aboot sixteen, I guess, and he...."

"Please, Fiona." He laughingly held up both hands in a gesture of surrender. "Have merrcy!"

"I'll tell ye later, Torri," his sister promised with a nudge.

Victoria stood up and came toward him where he was standing in the door. "Gavin, did.... did you tell him?"

"Aye." He slipped an arm around her waist. "And he's verra pleased. I told ye he would be."

"You...you told him everything–I mean who I am–and it's all right?"

"Torri, I simply told him therre's a lass I'm in love with. The rrest's not imporrtant."

"Not important?!" She pulled away from him and walked over to look out at the snow-covered hills behind the house.

Brother and sister exchanged glances behind her back. It was Fiona who joined her at the window. "Gavin's rright, Torri," she said quietly. "It will nae matterr to Dad who ye arre. Alrready it doesna matterr to me and Dad is farr wiserr than I."

"But....but Fiona." Victoria turned to look at her. "You...you barely know me."

"Aye, that's trrue, but I do know my brrotherr. He wouldna choose lightly."

"Therre–ye see, darrlin'." He had come to stand on the other side of her. "Noo coom, lass. My Dad has been waitin' patiently forr this day."

At last Victoria nodded. "Let's go down." Her voice trembled only slightly.

"Aye." Gavin took her hand firmly in his and for a second time they walked along the hall together, this time going on down the stairs. At the corner of the fireplace he paused for a moment, however, bending to kiss her once lightly before they continued on into the living room.

Niall had heard them coming and he stood up again facing the stairs. What would she be like, he wondered–this one lass after so many. Then they came around the turn in the stairwell and he saw her for the first time–tall, slim, blonde and breathtakingly lovely. Of course, he thought wryly, for that son of mine she would have to be beautiful. He noticed as well that they were holding hands. They came toward him. "Dad, this...this is Torri." Even in those simple words Gavin's joy was evident.

Victoria looked up at what was amazingly an older version of the man she loved–the same brown eyes set in the same strong face–incredibly even the same smile warming and welcoming her even before he spoke. She extended her hand–her own smile shaky, but genuine. "Mr. Hamilton, I'm <u>so</u> very glad to meet you."

"Torri, is it?" Niall accepted her offered hand. "Och, lass, yourr hand's cold. Gavin said ye werre nerrvous aboot meetin' me. Noo, am I that frrightenin'?"

"Oh no, Mr. Hamilton." She denied it quickly and now Niall himself clearly glimpsed the anxiety in her large green eyes. "You...you shouldn't have told him that." She turned her head to glance reproachfully at Gavin who was standing beside her watching his father and waiting for his reaction.

"No, no, lassie. 'Tis all rright." Niall Hamilton reassured her. He was still holding her hand and now he patted it with his other one. "Noo– sit yourrselves doon." He indicated the couch facing his. "Overr therre so I can look at the two o' ye togetherr."

Gratefully she settled beside Gavin. With his arm around her shoulders, his free hand holding one of hers, it at once became easier. "Dad's rright, darrlin'," he said. "Yourr hand is cold. Arre ye warrm enough?"

"I'm...I'm fine–really." Victoria looked at him for a long minute this time and one fact about his son's chosen wife was immediately apparent to Niall. She was deeply in love with him.

"Well, Dad, what do ye think?" Gavin was smiling proudly.

At these words she made herself turn and look at Niall. Once again the older man found his gaze drawn to those magnificent eyes as plainly they pleaded for his acceptance. "Aye, laddie," he said after a moment, "ye've chosen well. She's bonny."

A smile of pure relief flooded across Victoria's face and those same eyes now reminded him startlingly of sunlight on the loch. "Oh, thank you so much, Mr. Hamilton!"

"Ye dinna have to thank me, lass. My son has chosen well; 'tis that simple."

"But...but you don't know anything about me. How can you be so sure?"

Niall glanced briefly at his son as if to ask–what's wrong with her. "Och, but ye see, lass, this is soomthin' I ken by instinct. Ye do feel it's rright yourrselves–both of ye, do ye not?" They looked at each other and for a few seconds they forgot everything but the wonder of each other's nearness. At almost the same instant they both realized neither of them had answered him. They began to smile, then to laugh and finally still laughing, they turned back to the elder Hamilton again. He joined in their merriment, enjoying it greatly. "I think ye've answerred my question. Have ye met the rrest of this family of ourrs yet, lass?:" he went on after a moment.

"Only Fiona. She's...she's been very kind."

"Have ye no explained to her," his father asked Gavin, "that we arre no just bein' kind?"

"Aye, Dad, I have," he murmured touching her cheek, " but I'm afrraid she still doesna ken it."

Niall leaned forward to rest his elbows on his knees, his pipe cupped in both hands. "Suppose ye find soomthin' to do wi' yourrself forr a bit, lad. Gie me soom time alone wi' this lass o' yourrs."

Gavin hesitated. "Torri?"

"Och, go on wi' ye noo." Dad Hamilton urged him. "She'll be perrfectly safe."

The moment had to come eventually, after all, Victoria reasoned with herself. "It's... it's all right, darling." She glanced over at Niall as though for verification and he smiled to reassure her.

"Aye—all rright, then." At last Gavin reluctantly removed his arm from around her shoulders and stood up. "I should go see Meghan anyway." Victoria's eyes followed him as he crossed the room and disappeared up the stairs.

"Ye've no met ourr Meghan, have ye?" Niall asked, still smiling. He wanted very much for her to feel at ease with him. "Wee Meghan adorres Gavin–but then I'm surre that's easy forr ye to underrstand."

"Oh, yes! I...I've never known anyone like him."

"Aye—I'm verra forrtunate in both my sons," he stated proudly. "But Gavin and I arre morre alike, I suppose."

"I...I can see that myself already. I...I...." Victoria wished she could think of something delightful to say to this warm, wonderful man who had so unquestioningly accepted her. But would that acceptance still be there, she wondered, when he realized who she was.

"So then--" Niall Hamilton settled back and began to clean his pipe in preparation for refilling and lighting it again. "Ye dinna mind this, I hope," he interrupted himself, gesturing with the pipe."

"Oh no, I...I love the smell of a pipe--especially now."

"Aye, I should imagine ye would. I fearr the laddie acquirred the bad habit frrom me. Well noo–as I starrted to say," he continued going back to work on his pipe, "just exactly wherre was my son forrtunate enough to meet ye?"

What a charming way of putting it, Victoria thought, as more and more she relaxed, sensing in him the same gentleness she had found in Gavin. "Oddly enough we met in New York–last spring...What?" she interrupted herself to ask, prompted by the thoughtful expression which had passed across Niall's face.

"Do ye ken that when Gavin rreturrned frrom the States, he told me he'd met a special lass therre, but that she was alrready marrried?"

At once she tensed again. He...he probably thinks I'm terrible, she thought–a married woman. "Yes, that was I," she said aloud after a moment. "But...but it was a very unhappy marriage and I...I..."

"No, lass–no." Here he got up from the couch where he'd still been sitting facing Victoria and came over beside her placing his hand over hers. " 'Twas only an obserrvation that the laddie has loved ye forr a long time noo."

Her smile was so sweet and at the same time touchingly shy. Niall found himself growing more and more sure that his son had indeed chosen well. "Yes," she said, "and...and I've loved him for just as long. Only we were both too blind or stupid to realize how we felt. Even when we...we met again in London in September, we...we still couldn't see it."

Good, he thought, she's beginning to open up to me now. "Is Torri a nickname?" He hadn't put the question in a manner to suggest he found it particularly significant, but at once two little anxiety lines appeared between her eyes and he worried he'd said something wrong. "What is it, lass?" How quickly she'd come to touch him profoundly.

"N...n...nothing. I....I...." But at last she simply shook her head, lowering her gaze to where her hands were clasped tightly together in her lap–the old gesture of mute despair.

"Tell me, Torri," he prompted her. Even his voice sounded like Gavin's and that made it hurt even worse. She had come so close–so close to having it all and now her next words must certainly ruin everything.

At last she looked up at him again–her green eyes glistening with unshed tears. "Mr. Hamilton, Tori is...is Gavin's name for me." Her tone was flat and defeated. "My full name is Victoria Windsor." Odd how once she had spoken that name with such a fierce pride and now she would have given anything to be able to deny her own identity.

"Well, Victorria Windsorr, is it noo?" Niall observed thoughtfully after a moment. "I've hearrd the name beforre, of courrse."

"Yes, I'm sure you have." And everything that goes with it no doubt, she added to herself with a barely suppressed sigh.

"Such a glamorrous prrofession and all. I would have thought Victorria Windsorr to be a verra differrent sorrt o' lass altogetherr. Ye dinna seem the type at all."

"I...I don't?" He wasn't reacting at all the way she'd feared. "What...what would you have expected Victoria Windsor to be like?" How peculiar it felt referring to herself in the third person as though Victoria Windsor were someone else–which...which she actually was, she supposed.

"Well. I...I would have expected....I don't know...." Now it was his turn to be slightly at a loss. After all he barely knew this girl. "Elegant clothes and jewellerry and all made oop–ye ken what I mean–that paint all overr yourr face and too hoity-toity to speak to us orrdinarry morrtals."

"Oh, Mr. Hamilton...." She was about to tell him there had been a time not that long ago when that was exactly what she was, but he didn't give her the chance.

"And herre ye arre," he went on immediately, " a sweet, shy lass–terrrified o' meetin' yourr futurre fatherr-in-law. Ye say Gavin was the one to gie ye the name of Torri. Noo that suits ye."

"I'm beginning to think it does, too, Mr. Hamilton."

"But this Misterr Hamilton business has to stop. Will ye call me Niall? No, no...not that." He paused briefly. "I dinna ken whetherr yourr own fatherr is livin' orr not?"

"I suppose he is. I haven't seen him for years. We're not at all close."

He'd observed the pain on her face at the mention of her father, but he realized he didn't know her well enough as yet to inquire further. "Well, then," he went on instead, "I'd like verra much to have ye call me Dad. Would ye do that?" All Victoria could do was nod, too overcome to speak. "Noo–while my son's oopstairrs," Niall continued in a conspiratorial tone, "suppose I brring ye into my den and show ye the family album. Would ye like that?"

"Oh yes!" She smiled delightedly. "I would!"

"Good." He stood up. "Let's do that, then, beforre he catches me at it." Laughing, Victoria got up as well to go with him. On impulse Niall held out his arms to her. "Well, daughterr—welcoom home."

She came happily into his embrace. Strange how even that felt like Gavin's. "Oh, Dad," she whispered, "thank you."

"Och, lass. 'Tis naethin' ye have to thank me forr. Noo how aboot those picturres?"

* * *

For some time after her heartbroken retreat Meghan lay face down on her bed sobbing, but after a while she heard her brother's voice in the hall and she sat up, quickly drying her eyes. Perhaps, after all, what she'd seen from the front window had meant nothing. Gavin would come to tell her he was home and everything would be the same as always. Almost at once, however, she became aware of another voice–unmistakably feminine, unmistakably English–and she flung herself down on the bed again to spend the next hour or so wallowing gloriously in self-pity. The room diagonally across from hers which had been Rhuaridh's was now the guest room and apparently <u>everyone</u> wanted to be with this woman who had no business even being here! She heard Fiona come up at least twice and her brother couldn't stay away, even calling this unwanted visitor darrlin' and dearrest! Peeking out once, she glimpsed a tall, slim woman going into the room, her head wrapped turban fashion in a towel.

After what seemed like forever, a knock finally came at her door and she heard her brother's voice again, this time speaking to her. "Meghan, whateverr arre ye doin'? I've been home overr an hourr. Arre ye angrry wi' me?"

"No...Gavin." She tried in vain to keep her voice from shaking.

"Well, may I coom in then?"

"Aye."

He opened the door, taking a step or two into the room to stand with one foot crossed in front of the other–his hand resting on the doorknob. He grinned at her. "Well, lass–have ye no got a hug forr yourr big brrotherr?"

"Oh, Gavin!" Jumping up off the bed, she ran to throw her arms around him.

"My worrd!" Chuckling a little, he took her arms down from around his neck and stepped back just enough so that he could see the tip of her nose. "Ye've no been grreetin', have ye?" Meghan looked up at him and her lower lip began to quiver, her eyes filling once again with tears. He was her very own Gavin and now someone was taking him away from her. "Och, lassie, I dinna like to see ye like this." He drew her over to the bed and sat down beside her. "Fiona said she thought ye saw us drrive oop. Did ye?"

Meghan nodded. "Aye, " she whispered so softly he could barely hear her.

He hesitated, wondering how to say it. When his little sister was first born, he'd almost hated her, blaming her for their mother's death. Later on, realizing how foolish this was, he had tried to make it up to her for his earlier bitterness. He supposed he'd spoiled her. "So then," he said finally, "I dinna have to tell ye that Torri is verra special to me. In fact she's goin' to be my wife."

"No, Gavin! Ye canna do that! 'Tis nae fairr. 'Twill spoil everrathin'!"

" 'Tis you who arre no bein' fairr, I think. I've been verra lonely. I've needed someone o' my verra own to carre for."

"But ye've got me and Dad and Fiona and Grranny and even Rhurrry–though he's nowherre nearr as grrand as ye arre of courrse."

" 'Tis nae the same, darrlin'...."

"No!" Jumping up off the bed, Meghan whirled about on him with her fists clenched, tears streaming down her face. "Ye canna call me that if ye call herr that! 'Tis one orr the otherr!"

"A man can love many perrsons in differrent ways, lass. Noo–will ye coom doonstairrs? I want Torri to meet ye."

"No, thank you!" She looked for all the world like the tragic heroine of every novel Sir Walter Scott had ever written and if it hadn't been for the seriousness of the moment, he would have laughed. "I'm no verra hungrry!"

"All rright." Gavin stood up and walked to the door. "But of all people I thought ye'd be happy forr me. I'm verra disappointed in ye, Meghan." With that he left, closing the door softly behind him. Victoria had so little confidence in herself. How could he ever convince her that his youngest sister's refusal to come down to tea was merely a case of adolescent jealousy?

As he came down into the living room, however, he found it empty. Hearing voices from his father's den, he went over to look in and at once he forgot Meghan entirely–at least for the time being. Victoria and his father were sitting side by side on a small settee, looking at something together and quite evidently enjoying both it and each other's company immensely. It was a moment he'd often envisioned and for a time he just stood there watching them. Then all at once he realized exactly what was giving them both so much pleasure. "Och, Dad!" he groaned. "Ye could have at least waited a day orr two!"

Victoria looked up and smiled. "Oh, Gavin! You were such an adorable little boy!"

He grinned. "Aye, I canna deny it."

"Och, Torri!" The older man threw up both hands in pretended exasperation. "Arre ye surre ye rreally want to marrry this lad? Do ye no ken he's impossible?"

Victoria's answering smile was as much due to her own boundless joy as to their wit. "Well yes, Dad, I do–but I seem to be in love with him so what can I do about it?"

Niall glanced up at his son. "Aye, the lass has done me the honorr of agrreein' to call me Dad. Afterr all, if she has to put oop wi' you, at least she's gettin' a grrand fatherr-in-law in the barrgain." Gavin threw back his head roaring with laughter. It was all he'd hoped for and more. "But I think that'll have to be all forr noo, Torri." Dad Hamilton closed the album, standing up and going over to place it on his old battered, roll-tip desk. " 'Tis time forr tea and as I'm surre ye ken, this lad o' mine rrequirres rregularr nourrishment!'

Gavin came over to take her by the hand and bring her to her feet as well. "Arre ye hungrry then, darrlin'?"

"Not very," Victoria murmured, suddenly self-conscious.

"What arre we goin' to do wi' the lass, Dad?" he inquired, pulling her hand through his arm and covering it with his other one. "She has the appetite of a wee mavis."

"Well, we'll just have to see she gets plenty of frresh airr and exerrcise." Niall came over to join them, slipping Victoria's other arm through one of his. "As well as a lot of love, I think." She looked back and forth from one of them to the other and her eyes filled with tears. Father and son exchanged glances across the top of her head and Niall cleared his throat. "Well, why don't I go see what's keepin' Mum and Fiona wi' ourr tea? Torri, ye wouldna object to my leavin' you two alone forr a wee bit? I ken verra well the laddie's nowherre nearr the charrmin' coomp'ny his Dad is."

Victoria smiled and like the morning mist in his beloved Highlands dissolving in the warmth of the sun, her tears vanished. "I think I can stand it," she replied, "if you're not gone too long."

"Ye hearr that, laddie?" the older man observed. "The lass shows verra good sense."

"Will ye get oot o' herre?" Gavin laughed. "Ye'rre worrse than I am if that's possible."

Niall finally left them then, still chuckling to himself as he walked across the living room toward the kitchen. "Wherre's ourr tea, Mum?" they heard him calling. "Gavin's lass'll be thinkin' we'rre plottin' to starrve herr to death!"

"How do you like that, darrlin'?" Gavin turned to face Victoria, slipping both arms around her waist to draw her closer. "Labeled forr life."

She tipped her head back to look up at him. "But I <u>am</u> Gavin's lass so why not call me that."

"And won't people wonderr who that is on the marrquee?" he teased her.

"Gavin–oh, Gavin!" Your father <u>knows</u>– he knows..who I am, I mean, and it's all right."

"So frrom noo on–" He brought up his hand to touch the tip of her nose with one finger....."will ye believe yourr laddie when he tells ye soomthin'?"

"I....I will. I promise. Darling, show me some more of the album."

"Och, Torri–ye <u>have</u> the man. What do ye carre aboot the bairrn?"

"Nothing fascinates a woman quite so much about the man she loves as the little boy he once was..or perhaps still is," she added after the slightest pause, her eyes sparkling.

"Aye," he agreed after a moment, his own eyes glowing in response. "I'll show ye the album. At least that way I can defend myself." Victoria curled up beside him on the same small sofa where she'd been sitting a short while before with his father, resting her arm across his shoulders and nestling as close to him as possible. "Soo, darrlin'–let me see." He flipped through several pages, glancing up at her briefly as he did so, perhaps partly to reassure himself that she was really there. "Oh, aye–that's one of me wi' Mum and Dad. He'd just coom home frrom the warr. He was a piperr. Led one of the firrst Brritish landin's at Norrmandy as a matterr of fact."

On they went through the album, the soft, yielding pressure of her breast against his arm reminding Gavin constantly of her nearness. At some point they came to a picture of him–seated on a horse. Merely referring to it in passing, he started to go on. "Wait a minute." Victoria stopped him from turning the page. "How old were you there?"

"I got that horrse forr my twelfth birrthday. Why?"

"I....I don't know. That picture looks familiar to me somehow."

"Well, perrhaps Dad alrready showed it to ye."

* * *

"Humph!" Mary Hamilton had muttered darkly at her son's description of Victoria as "Gavin's lass".

"What's the matterr, Mum?" Niall grinned affectionately at his diminutive, but iron-willed mother.

"Grranny' s a wee bit oot o' sorrts, Dad," Fiona replied as she picked up a tray with the tea things on it and went past him out through the swinging door to the living room at one end of which was the family dining table.

"That so, Mum? Gavin not paying ye any attention?"

"No—the laddie did coom to see me–when he could sparre the time frrom his grrand <u>English</u> lady, that is."

"Oh, that's it then, is it? Ye dinna apprrove o' Gavin's lass."

"She's <u>no</u> Gavin's lass. He's too canny a lad forr that!"

"But ye havna even met herr yet, have ye?"

"No–it seems Gavin's ashamed of his old Grranny."

"Dinna be daft! Ye ken verra well Gavin adorres ye. It's just that he's in love forr the firrst time in his life and his wits arre a wee bit addled. Can I carry soomthin' in forr ye?"

"No–ye go oot therre and keep an eye on herr!"

"I've told ye many times, Mum, that I serrved wi' the English in the warr and they..."

"Aye and ye've neverr been the same since! Noo leave me in peace orr ye'll neverr get yourr tea!"

Fiona looked up from setting the table as her father came out of the kitchen. "Grranny still goin' on, Dad?" she asked, stepping back a little to study the results of her work. The large round table was covered in a pale green linen cloth. The Hamilton china was creamy white with a narrow rim of lavender and she had complimented the color scheme perfectly with a centerpiece of dried heather flanked on either side by silver candlesticks.

"I'm afrraid so. ' Tis a bonny table, hinny," her father observed, putting an arm around her shoulders and giving her an appreciative hug.

"Thank ye, Dad. I wanted to make it especially prretty forr Torri."

"Ye like herr then?"

"Aye, I do. She's sae nerrvous aboot meetin' us all, Dad. If Grranny's not at least civil...."

"Well, ye know my Mum!"

"But why didn't Gavin take Torri rright oot to meet herr? Noo–on top of it all herr nose is oot o' joint."

"Prrobably for the verra rreasons we've just been discussin'."

"Which rreminds me, Dad," Fiona sighed. "Grranny's no the only one. Meghan hasna been oot o' herr rroom since Gavin and Torri arrrived."

"My motherr I canna handle, but <u>that</u> young lass will do as she's told." His tone indicated plainly he would brook no defiance.

Neither of them had noticed Meghan come downstairs just in time to hear the end of the conversation. "Ye willna have to do that, Dad. I'm herre."

"Well noo, that's morre like it, darrlin'." Niall went over to place a hand on each of his younger daughter's arms, bending down to kiss her on the cheek.

Up in her room she'd found it easy to put her brother's happiness ahead of her own feelings, but now she was once again having some difficulty controlling her lower lip. "Gavin said he... he was verra disappointed in me. I just couldna bearr it if he stopped lovin' me, Dad."

Hearing his sister's voice, meanwhile, Gavin had stood up, holding out his hand to Victoria. "Coom, lass. 'Tis time forr ye to meet the wee one o' the family."

She looked up at him searchingly. "She's....she's always been so important to you."

"Aye and noo–you arre," he replied firmly. They walked out together into the living room. "Meghan," he said quietly. At the sound of Gavin's voice she actually jumped. It meant she was about to meet this hateful person who planned to take her brother away from her. "Meghan," he repeated her name a little more forcefully. "Therre's someone I want ye to meet." She swallowed once hard and forcing a smile, she finally turned around. A tall, blonde woman was standing beside Gavin and holding possessively to one of his hands. How dare she, she thought indignantly. "Torri, this is my otherr sisterr, Meghan.

"Hello, Meghan.' Victoria stepped forward as she spoke. "You...you have a very special brother, but then I'm sure you already know that."

When Victoria moved forward, she'd come into stronger light and the Scottish girl observed with a sinking feeling that she was very beautiful. But then in the next instant that same realization brought new hope. Of course–<u>that</u> was why Gavin was attracted to her, but up here in <u>their</u> world he would soon see how entirely unsuited this elegant Englishwoman was to be his wife. "Aye," she replied coolly, "I ken it."

Granny came in from the kitchen just then carrying the teapot. "Ah, Grranny," Gavin said at once, "this is Torri–my futurre wife." Everyone had caught his barely perceptible stress on the last two words, but Mary all but ignored the introduction, not even pausing in her rapid progress toward the table.

"How do you do, Mrs. Hamilton," Victoria said. "I'm so happy to meet you."

"So!" The old woman drew herself up to her full and formidable five feet. "Ye think ye've got what it takes forr a Scotsman?"

"Noo, Granny." Gavin's voice was deceptively soft. " 'Tis no answerr to gie."

" 'Twill have to do!" she snapped. " 'Tis the only one I've got!"

"Well then, shall we all sit doon to ourr tea?" Niall Hamilton put in quickly, hoping that over the sociability of the meal the tension would ease. "Torri, if my son will agrree to sharre ye, I'd like ye to sit between us."

"Do I have a choice?" Gavin inquired.

"No," his father replied pulling out a chair for Victoria.

"I didna think so." Shaking his head, he took the seat on the other side of her.

"Oh, Mrs. Hamilton," Victoria exclaimed. "The table is simply lovely!"

" 'Twas nae me who did it." Mary picked up the teapot and began to pour. As the oldest female member of the family, this was her prerogative and she guarded it with a ferocious jealousy. " 'Twas Fiona."

"Oh, I....I see." She looked down in confusion.

"Thank ye, Torri," Fiona said at once. "I rreally trried to make it special forr yourr firrst tea with us." Victoria's head came up again to flash her a grateful smile which the other woman returned with equal warmth.

"So, Gavin," his father said, "have ye made any prrofessional plans?"

He grinned. "What arre ye trryin' to say, Dad? That noo I'm gettin' marrried, 'tis time I made soomthin' o' myself?"

"Have ye seen him worrk yet, Torri?" Fiona asked.

"Oh...oh, yes!" Instinctively she reached over to place her hand on Gavin's. "I think he's smashing!"

"And I keep tellin' herr she's a wee bit prrejudiced." Gavin gazed at her lovingly, covering her hand with his other one.

"And...and I keep telling him," Victoria insisted in return, "that my personal feelings have nothing to do with my professional judgement."

"He is good then, isn't he, Torri?" Fiona exclaimed excitedly. "Would ye like anotherr scone?" she added, passing the plate.

"Oh yes, please. They're so light! They're absolutely delicious!"

"Now those Grranny did make!"

"She....she did? They're...they're simply heavenly, Mrs. Hamilton!"

"Thank ye." Gavin's grandmother had been watching him intently all through the meal. But it was impossible for her to do this and not see Victoria, too–the way she had of touching him, the special smile she had for him, her obvious pride in him. I suppose she does feel soomthin' forr the laddie, Granny admitted to herself grudgingly.

Meghan, however, could not bring herself to be so charitable. All through the meal she had solemnly looked on as this interloper charmed everyone else at the table until at last she couldn't stand it any longer. "Excuse me, please!" She got abruptly to her feet. "I...I don't think I feel good." Pushing back her chair, she ran from the room and up the stairs.

"Oh, Gavin!" Again Victoria took hold of his hand.

"I think I'll just go have a talk with herr," Niall said also standing up. "It's time that lass grrew oop a bit."

"Oh, Mr. Hamilton, I....I mean, Dad," she corrected herself, "please don't be cross with her. I understand how she feels and believe me, it's all right."

"I hope ye ken it, Gavin. Ye've got yourrself a verra special lass herre." Niall bent to kiss her on the cheek before following his daughter up the stairs. Dazedly Victoria raised her hand to touch the spot he'd kissed.

"Well, Fiona," Mary Hamilton announced rather more loudly than necessary, "let's get cleaned oop!"

"May....may I help?" Victoria asked, getting to her feet and picking up a couple of the dishes.

"No...Torri," Fiona said firmly and she indicated the fireplace where her brother had gone to stir up the embers before adding another log. "Besides I think someone's expectin' coomp'ny."

Victoria smiled and putting the plate down again, she started to walk over to Gavin. But then she turned and came back to the Scots girl who had begun to clear the table.

"Th...thank you, Fiona. Thank you so much.....for everything."

"Oh, Torri." Fiona put the things she had in her hands back down on the table and reached out to embrace her. "Ye'rre welcoom. Dinna be daft!"

Victoria returned the hug before finally going over to Gavin. They stood side by side in front of the fire for a few minutes, arms about each other's waists. "Rrememberr the cottage in Devon, darrlin'," he asked tenderly after a moment, "the firrst night we got therre?"

"Gavin, how....how could we both have been so blind? We nearly lost each other."

"Aye, Torri. But fate wouldna allow it. Do ye no ken that?" She looked up at him then and he turned to take her in his arms.

"Humph!" Granny muttered, coming back out into the kitchen with the last of the dishes.

"What's wrrong noo?" Fiona asked, swishing her hands around in the hot, soapy water.

"Kissin'!"

"Oh." She laughed. "Well, what do you expect? They'rre in love. I like seein' my brrotherr in love. He's nae so afrraid o' lettin' his feelin's show. Coom noo, Granny. Ye canna help but like herr."

"She's still English!"

"Grranny! Ye'rre evadin' the issue........"

"And dinna use any o' yourr fancy univerrsity phrrases on me!"

"Grranny," Fiona laughed, "do ye like Gavin's lass?"

"Well, perrhaps a wee bit–just a wee bit, mind ye!"

Later on Granny was settled in her favorite armchair with her knitting; Fiona was correcting papers at the dining table while Gavin and his father had gotten out the inevitable chessboard. Only Meghan, adamantly refusing to come downstairs again, was missing, but nothing could spoil the evening for Victoria who alone was not occupied. It didn't even matter that the chess game was a mystery to her. Sitting close beside Gavin, she was content simply to watch the firelight play across his face, accentuating his cheekbones and turning his auburn hair the color of antique copper.

Gavin couldn't help remembering the last time he'd been home when Victoria had been present only in his longing imagination. Now she was actually there beside him, her fragrance filling the air around him. She said nothing and yet he was acutely aware of her. "Checkmate!" For the second time Niall Hamilton had taken his son's queen in under half a dozen moves. "Torri," he chuckled, "I dinna ken whetherr the lad's concentrration is worrse when ye'rre not herre or when ye arre."

Granny was the first to retire–as usual a bit earlier than the others–followed by Niall and then Fiona. Left alone at last, the lovers pulled one of the couches closer to the fire and settled down together–Gavin with his long legs stretched out toward the warmth of the hearth–Victoria curled up next to him with her head resting against his shoulder. "Gettin' sleepy, darrlin'?" he whispered.

At once he felt her tense slightly. "I....I don't want to go to bed quite yet. Can't we just stay here a little longer?"

"And suppose I was to tell ye that I'm plannin' to coom acrross the hall as soon as everrathin's quiet?"

"Oh Gavin, do you think we should?"

"I have no intention o' leavin' ye alone. Dad will underrstand. Noo shall we go on oopstairrs?"

* * *

The horizon was just growing light when Gavin awoke the next morning. There was something about being home that was better than an alarm clock. Victoria lay with her head pillowed on his chest, however, and when he tried to move, she snuggled closer against him. He smiled, wondering if he would ever grow accustomed to the wonder of waking up beside her. For a moment he considered asking her to go with him, but then he decided she needed her sleep. Finally he managed to slide his arm out from under her and ease out of bed. Moving noiselessly across the hall to his own room, he got his things and went on down the hall to the bath to shower and shave. At last he dressed and then before going downstairs to breakfast, he slipped back into Victoria's room to leave her a note. He failed to notice as he came back out into the hall a few minutes later that Meghan's door was open a few inches.

Granny was already up, of course, and the kitchen was warm and cozy from the coal fire in the grate. A pot of oatmeal bubbled away on the back of the stove and the tea kettle was just coming to a boil. By the time the rest of the family came down about an hour later Gavin had eaten his customary breakfast of oatmeal, fried eggs, fried potatoes and ham and gone out for an early morning ride.

"Dad!" Meghan caught up with her father just outside the kitchen. "I...I saw Gavin coomin' oot o' herr rroom this morrnin'!"

"Noo, lass," Niall remonstrated gently. " 'Tis none o' yourr business."

Before her father could say anything further, Meghan whirled about to run back up the stairs. "It's nae fairr," she sobbed. "Everrabody's on herr side!"

It was nearly ten o'clock and the bedroom was bright with sunlight when Victoria finally awoke to find Gavin's note pinned to the other pillow.

Darling–Forgive your laddie for running out on you your first morning here, but the sun was just coming up and the hills were calling to me. I'll tell Granny to make you some breakfast when you wake up and by the time you've eaten, I'll be back and we'll drive over to see Felicity.

It's so good to have you here with me, lass. I do love you so!

Gavin

For just a moment Victoria was a little hurt he hadn't waited for her, but then she remembered his joy at being home and she understood his impatience. Dressing quickly in rose and gray plaid slacks and a rose cashmere pullover, she brushed her hair and tied it back with a long gray silk scarf. Finally she applied a minimum of make-up and went on downstairs. It wasn't until she was standing in the doorway to the kitchen that she realized everyone else would be gone by now as well leaving her alone with Gavin's redoubtable grandmother. Just at that moment Mary Hamilton's back was turned. "Good...good morning," Victoria said hesitantly.

"Finally oop arre ye then?" In the three hours since the others had left Granny had enjoyed immensely grumbling aloud to herself about these hoity-toity English guests who expected breakfast in the middle of the day–lazy good-forr-nothin's, the whole lot o' them! Now she turned around to see Victoria standing there looking so apologetic and all her anger vanished.

"I'm...I'm sorry, Mrs. Hamilton. I didn't intend to sleep this late."

"Och, 'tis all rright, lass. Noo Gavin told me I should gie ye yourr brreakfast. What will ye be havin'?"

"Actually I...I eat very little in the morning. I just don't seem to be hungry."

"Aye, I can see that. Ye'rre farr too skinny. Noo–sit yourrself doon–a larrge bowl of oatmeal to starrt, I think." She began to bustle about the kitchen getting out plates, silverware, a mug for tea.

Meekly Victoria obeyed, sitting down at the kitchen table although she sensed the old woman's gruffness was not harshly intended. "I'm...I'm sorry, Mrs. Hamilton," she apologized again. "I...I don't much care for oatmeal." And renowned actress of the London stage though she might be, she felt herself somehow lacking.

"Ye dinna carre forr oatmeal?!" Granny stopped in the middle of the floor, turning to stare at her. "Och, but 'tis nae yourr fault, dearrie. 'Tis the way ye werre brrought oop, doon therre with all those Englisherrs and all."

With Victoria sitting down the two of them were just at eye level. She looked at the tiny old lady and began to laugh. "You mean–it's not my fault I'm English?"

Mary chuckled as well. "Oh dearr, dinna tell Gavin I said that. He's rratherr put oot wi' his old Grranny, I think."

"Now I can't believe that. He adores you. He's told me how much it meant to all of them to have you come here after his mother died."

"Well, my goodness!" Normally unflappable, such warm praise from an unexpected source had her quite flustered. "Herre I stand–blatherrin' on like a daftie when ye havna..ah..do ye ken 'blatherrin'?"

"Oh, yes!" Victoria smiled. No wonder Gavin loved this dear, little person. "My Scots vocabulary is growing by leaps and bounds!"

"Aye–well, as I was aboot to say, ye havna had yourr brreakfast. What can I get forr ye then, lass?"

"Is there more of that bread you baked for tea yesterday?"

"Aye." Granny beamed. "Would ye like soom, then?"

"Oh yes, please. It was absolutely delicious–and tea."

"That's all? Not even a nice frried egg?"

"All right—<u>one</u> egg."

" 'Twill be rready in a twinklin'." She put the kettle on to boil and broke an egg on the griddle. Then she cut off several slices of the bread.

Dear God, Victoria thought, how much does she expect me to eat? "Mrs. Hamilton?"

" 'Tis nae Missus Hamilton." Mary stopped working long enough to come over and pat her on the cheek. "If ye'rre to be Gavin's lass, 'twill be Grranny to ye, too, so ye might as well starrt gettin' used to it."

"Th...thank you." How many times since she'd arrived less than twenty-four hours ago had she found herself thanking someone for love and acceptance–things most people took for granted.

" 'Tis naethin' to thank me forr." Once again Granny was embarrassed. "Besides ye'll soon be Missus Hamilton yourrself, it seems, and we canna have two of us arroond noo, can we?"

"That's right." Victoria smiled. "I will be, won't I?"

"Ye like that idea, do ye? Well, the laddie's a dearr one–has been since he was a wee bairrn–but mind ye, he rrequirres a grreat deal o' patience."

She laughed. "Was Gavin really as much of a handful as he's told me?"

"Och–much worrse. He couldna sit still–rrunnin' hitherr and thitherr frrom sun-oop to sun-doon—hilty-skilty! Och, he wasna a bad one, though, trruly–just tentless. He'd drrive me farr daft wi' his prranks, but the next thing I knew, herre he'd coom' wi' a grrand bunch o' wildflowerrs and that beguilin' smile o' his and I'd forrgive him. Noo–herre's yourr brreakfast," she went on setting a plate with the egg and bread on it in front of Victoria as well as a steaming mug of tea. "And I intend to watch that ye eat everra bite o' it!"

Obediently she began to eat, discovering all at once she was hungrier than she'd thought. "Granny?"

"Aye–ye know I think I'll just get a mug o' tea m'self and join ye." And she did just that, settling herself across from Victoria at the kitchen table. "Noo, what did ye want to ask me?"

"Has...has Gavin always been so...so gentle?"

Mary Hamilton's black eyes glowed at that. "Aye. He was neverr one forr huntin' and trrappin' like his brrotherr. In fact he'd go rroond and sprring Rurrry's trraps. Och, they had soom grrand rrows aboot that!"

"They're nothing alike, are they?"

"No. Rurrry's canna help bein' a bit dourr and Gavin, as I'm surre ye've alrready kent, is just the opposite."

"Oh, yes!" Victoria stopped eating. "I've...I've never known anyone like him–so tender and loving–and yet so...so full of the joy of simply being alive."

"Aye—last night at tea–rright away I could tell how much ye loved him. Ye know—I...I want to tell ye how sorrry I am aboot the way I acted when ye firrst arrrived yesterrday. It was just yourr coomin' oot o' nowherre–so to speak–being sae differrent in oopbrringin' from the laddie and all, but I should still have welcoomed ye forr his sake."

Victoria reached over to take Mary's hand in hers. "Mrs. Ham....I mean, Granny–please, I...I understand. I...I am an outsider and Gavin's very special to all of you."

"Aye, but so will ye be and verra soon, I think."

Just then they heard the front door open. "Torri," Gavin called out, "arre ye oop, darrlin'?" Slam!! The door shut again with a resounding crash.

"Och!" Mary Hamilton muttered as she went to get another mug. "He's neverr learrned to close that doorr prroperrly!" Hearing his grandmother's voice, Gavin came out into the kitchen to find Victoria laughing merrily. He grinned. He'd been right to give them some time alone together. "And wherre did ye think she was anyway?" Granny asked with a wink at the younger woman, "that ye had to shout the hoose doon?"

He looked suspiciously from one of them to the other. "What has she been tellin' ye aboot me, Torri?"

"Oh, nothing, darling–absolutely nothing," Victoria avowed, but the corners of her mouth twitched.

"Well, sit yourrself doon and have yourr tea," his grandmother said, "and then I suppose ye'll be takin' the lass off soomwherre."

"Aye, Grranny. Overr to the MacDougall's."

* * *

A short time later having finished her breakfast, Victoria excused herself to go upstairs and get her purse. While she was gone, Mary disappeared into her own room behind the kitchen, returning almost at once with a small box. "Ye'll be wantin' to gie this to herr, I should imagine," she said tucking it into the pocket of Gavin's jacket.

"Aye, thank ye." He bent to kiss her. "Ye do like herr then?"

"Aye—aye, I do. Much too good forr the likes o' ye, as a matterr of fact."

"Och, Grranny!" He pretended to be crestfallen. "Ye dinna mean that."

"O' courrse I don't," she snorted reaching up to pat him on the cheek. "Aye, the Good Lorrd Himself intended forr ye to marrry, schemin' the way He did to brring ye togetherr."

"I love ye verra much," Gavin said tenderly. "Ye ken that."

"Get long wi' ye noo. Yourr lass'll be waitin' forr ye."

"Aye, Grranny." With another kiss he went out into the living room. Victoria was just coming downstairs again and hand-in-hand they went outside. A few minutes later they were settled in his car and he had turned it around, heading along the lane and back over the little stone bridge onto the main road. " 'Tis only a few miles to Kinleygairr," he told her.

"I can hardly wait to see Felicity's face when we tell her we're going to be married." She smiled happily.

"Ye like that idea, I see," he observed with a grin of his own.. "So do I, by the way..and speakin' o' gettin' marrried, we should be makin' it official." Gavin paused to study the road. "Aye, this will do nicely." He swung off into a small car park, coming to a stop in front of a low stone building. "This by the way..." He indicated the building with a toss of his head, "is wherre I went to grrammarr school–verra reluctantly, I might add." Victoria laughed, but then at once he was serious again, thinking how best to explain it to her. "Ye see, Torri," he said at last, "overr two hundrred yearrs ago the last o' the Stuarrts, the Bonnie Prrince Charrlie, made a trragically vain attempt to rregain the Brritish thrrone."

"Was that the Rebellion of Forty-Five Felicity told me about?"

"Ye've hearrd of it then?"

"Yes, although as I'm sure you can imagine, her explanation was more impassioned than enlightening."

"Aye." Gavin chuckled. "Well anyway, darrlin', an ancestorr o' mine fought forr the Bonnie Prrince. And just beforre the 'Rraisin' o' the Standarrd at Glenfinnan.."

"I'm sorry, darling, what?"

" 'Twas when the Prrince rraised his bannerr and the clans werre called to supporrt him. Glenfinnan is a bonny spot at the tip o' Loch Shiel nearr Forrt William. I'll show it to ye soom day. Anyway my ancestorr had chosen a lass forr himself. They were just betrrothed when he had to leave and so he gave herr a rring both as a pledge of his love and as a prromise he would rreturrn to herr. Everr since then the rring has been gi'en by the eldest son to his chosen wife." At last now Gavin took the little box from his jacket pocket where his grandmother had put it, opening it to reveal an antique gold ring set with three pearls. "I can underrstand, of courrse," he went on at once apologetically, "if ye'd rratherr have a diamond. It couldna be a larrge one, but I....."

"How can you even think that? This is exquisite and it....it means so much more to me... all the years of tradition and family heritage." Her eyes were luminous with unshed tears and he knew she was sincere. "Put it on me, please," she whispered.

"Aye....aye." His hands were trembling slightly, but he managed to pick up the ring and never taking his eyes off Victoria's face, he slipped it on the third finger of her left hand. For still another several seconds they looked at each other before Gavin took her face in his hands to kiss her. "Well then, shall we go on?" he said at last.

"You're not going to show me the school?"

"What would I want to do that forr? No—I just needed a place to stop and gie ye the rring. So, as I said—'tis noo official and ye canna get oot o' it."

"Oh Gavin, dearest–why would I want to do that?"

He smiled. "Well, I hope not." He started the car engine again and they drove back out onto the road.

"Did....did your family know you were giving me the ring today?"

"Well, Grranny did–aye. She went and got it forr me just beforre we left."

"She really does approve of me then, doesn't she?" she asked eagerly.

"Oh, aye." He chuckled. "Actually she told me ye werre too good forr me."

Victoria laughed. "She's so dear. We had the loveliest visit. Gavin...ah...." Her eyes sparkled. "She used two words though and I didn't know what they meant...one was tentless and the other was...ah....hilty-skilty, I think."

"Who was she talking about?" he inquired suspiciously.

"You as a matter of fact—as a child."

He chuckled again. "Well, 'tis a wee bit like tellin' tales on m'self. 'Tentless' means thoughtless or carreless and 'hilty-skilty- is...ah...scatterrbrrained."

"I rather imagined they were something like that."

"Oh ye did, did ye?" He pretended to be offended, but then he grinned at her and spoiled the effect entirely.

Shortly afterwards he turned off the main road again and soon they were driving through another tiny village–in appearance much like Glengowrie–coming to a stop just past the center in front of a white-washed house with a red-tiled roof. "Herre we arre," Gavin announced. "Parrt o' it is Alexanderr MacDougall's surrgerry. Ye ken that Felicity's fatherr is a doctorr?"

Victoria nodded, but just then she saw a tall, slim girl with brown hair come out onto the front porch and she jumped out of the car. "Felicity!" she called, waving excitedly. "Felicity!"

The Scottish girl was carrying an armful of braided rugs to beat for her mother. Hearing her name, she glanced up and letting out a shriek, she dropped everything, running to embrace her friend. "Torri!" Felicity exclaimed over and over again. "Torri! Torri! Torri! Whateverr arre ye doin' way oop herre in Kinlygairr? Forr surre ye'rre the last perrson I'd have expected to...." Then over Victoria's shoulder she saw Gavin still standing by the car, leaning on the door and grinning at them both. "Gavin! Ye'rre herre, too!" Felicity looked back and forth from one to the other. "Och!" She exploded all at once, running to hug and kiss him as well before finally leading him back to Victoria. "Ye came togetherr, didn't ye?" At that they both laughed. "Ye must think I'm daft! Of courrse ye came togetherr! We'rre just aboot to have lunch," she burbled on happily as they walked up the steps toward the front door, "so ye can join us." She stepped nonchalantly over the pile of rugs on the porch as though they weren't even there.

Exchanging amused glances, they followed her. "Oh dear, Felicity," Victoria groaned in mock distress. "I'm afraid I'm not very hungrry. Gavin's grandmother just made breakfast for me and I can't remember when I've eaten so much–even if I <u>don't</u> like oatmeal."

"Och, Gavin!" Felicity struck her forehead with the palm of one hand. "She doesna like oatmeal?"

"I'm afrraid not." Gavin shook his head as he held open the door for the two women. "Norr Scotch, but I seem to be in love with herr anyway so I have to overrlook such terrrible flaws in herr charracterr."

"I'll go tell Mum to set two extrra places forr lunch. We'rre just waitin' forr Dad. He's at hospital on rrounds." Hurrying away across the small, cozy parlor to the left of the entry hall, Felicity disappeared through a swinging door, but returned almost at once, continuing on without so much as an evident breath. "She'll be rright oot. So sit yourrselves doon and tell me everrathin'. Torri, arre ye....arre ye...well, all rright noo then? I mean....I mean...."

Victoria and Gavin had settled themselves hand in hand on a small love seat, Felicity pulling over a low, three-legged stool to sit in front of them. At this awkward, but touchingly sincere expression of concern Victoria reached over to place her other hand on her friend's. "Yes, Felicity, thank you. I'm...I'm fine now. You....you did know I was in hospital a second time?"

"Aye. That's one advantage o' havin' a famous frriend. Ye can learrn all aboot herr in the newspaperrs. Och, listen to me blatherrin' on as though it's all been a grrand larrk when ye've been thrrough sae much since the last time I saw ye....Wherre was it?" Victoria attempted to reply, but before she could say anything, Felicity answered her own question. "Oh, aye, that's rright—Edinburra. Well anyway, as I was sayin'–I was sae worrried, Torri, and...and I kept trryin' to rring oop, but no one would tell me anythin', but noo herre ye arre and ye'rre wi' Gavin so everrathin's all rright. Go on." She sat back, grinning happily at them. Victoria and Gavin exchanged glances again and burst into laughter. "Well, what is sae damned funny?" she inquired indignantly. "I swearr the one thing morre exasperratin' than eitherr of ye separrately is the two of ye togetherr... Och, I didna mean that. But stop yourr laughin', Torri, and go on wi' what ye werre tellin' me."

"I'm sorry," Victoria finally managed to gasp, "but I really haven't the foggiest <u>what</u> I was saying."

"The second time ye werre in hospital," Felicity prompted, somehow still managing to remember even after her own lengthy soliloquy.

"Well, I....I just woke up and...and Gavin was there. It was that simple."

"Aye, it usually is." The Scots girl's tone indicated plainly she had imparted a sage piece of wisdom.

"Gavin, how good it is to see you again!" Felicity's mother appeared through the same swinging door and came briskly across the room toward them. She was a short, slightly plump woman, totally unlike her tall, slim daughter both in physical stature and in her placid disposition. "And Felicity inforrms me 'tis underr happierr cirrcumstances than yourr last visit."

"Aye, Mrs. MacDougall." Gavin had stood up as she came in. "This is Victorria Windsorr. I'm surre ye've hearrd aboot herr frrom Felicity. Torri has done me the honorr of agrreein' to be my wife."

"Hello, dear." Flora MacDougall came over to take Victoria's hand, but got no further.

Felicity let out a whoop, far more startling to those present than the most ferocious Highland war cry. "Marrried?! Why didna ye tell me?" She threw herself at Gavin, hugging him with such force that had he been a smaller man, he would have been knocked off his feet. "When? Have ye set the date?"

"No, not yet," he managed to reply quite clearly for a man who was being choked.

"We...we have to wait until my divorce is final," Victoria explained, wondering why she felt faintly apologetic.

"Och, ye'rre well rrid o' that pious one!" Felicity snorted contemptuously. "And noo to wed such a brraw Hieland laddie !"

Flora gave her daughter a look of affectionate exasperation. "As I starrted to say, Torri... I may call ye Torri?"

"Oh yes, please."

"I'm sae verra happy forr ye both, Torri. Felicity has told us of yourr kindness to herr in the States and Gavin's always seemed like my own son so I feel ye'll be parrt o' ourr family as well."

"Mrs. MacDougall," Victoria replied, "I don't think I've ever known a people as warm and welcoming as the Scots."

"I'm home, Florra," Alexander MacDougall called from the kitchen. "Gavin's herre, I see." The doctor appeared at once through the swinging door.

"Torri and Gavin arre goin' to be marrried, Dad!" Felicity cried out. "Isn't that superr?"

"Gavin–I'm sae glad!" Alexander shook his hand. "And this is the lass, I take it."

"Hello, Dr. MacDougall." Smiling, Victoria offered him her hand as well. "Your daughter is one of the most delightful people I've ever known."

He grinned, returning her handshake warmly. "If ye think that, lass, ye'rre trruly a perrson o' rremarrkable forrebearrance!" At that they all laughed except, of course, Felicity who as usual couldn't see what was so funny. "Gavin," the doctor went on after a moment, "could we take a wee strroll aboot the yarrd while we'rre waitin' to sit doon to lunch?"

"Aye, of courrse." However, the invitation had obviously surprised him.

They went outside through the front door and Victoria followed Felicity and her mother into the kitchen. It was only about fifteen or twenty minutes before the meal was ready and Flora called out the back door to the men to come and eat. Gavin glanced significantly at Victoria as he entered, but everyone sat down at once at the table and they had no chance to talk. Lunch for the most part was festive, but Victoria kept wondering what he had to tell her. Something else was bothering her as well. Then all at once she realized what was wrong.

Jamie and Felicity had recently celebrated their engagement as well, but not a word was said about them.

When they had finished eating, Alexander MacDougall went on over to his surgery for his afternoon appointments. Flora refused to allow Victoria and Gavin to help with the washing up. "Felicity and I can manage. Noo you two go along," she urged affectionately, shooing them back into the living room.

"What's wrong, Gavin?" Victoria inquired anxiously as soon as they were alone.

"It seems Felicity and Jamie have brroken off theirr engagement."

"Oh, dear!" She put her hand on his arm. "I was afraid it was something like that!"

He put his arms around her. "Hinny, do ye ken how lucky we arre?" Victoria nodded, slipping her arms around his neck and looking up at him. "Would ye mind, lass, if I went overr to Jamie's forr a wee bit?"

"No, please, darling. That will give <u>me</u> a chance to talk to Felicity. Not that I've ever had any success before."

"I willna be long," he assured her and with a quick kiss he was gone.

It wasn't long after that before the Scottish girl came out of the kitchen. "Wherre's Gavin?" she asked at once.

Victoria hesitated. "Actually he's...ah...gone over to see Jamie."

"Oh, well! 'Tis a waste of time talkin' to that gowk! 'Twill do no good at all."

"What's a gowk, Felicity?"

"A...a...fool! A damned, stubborrn fool!" But she started to cry and Victoria hurried over to put her arms around her.

"What happened, luv? From the moment I met you all you could talk about was your Jamie. What could have gone so wrong?"

"Ye have nae a single doubt, do ye...I mean, aboot Gavin."

"Oh no, Felicity. All I want is to spent the rest of my life with him."

"That's just it, ye see. I dinna think I'm rready to settle doon. I've nae had my fill yet o' larrkin' aboot. Jamie willna listen to any o' that. He wants to get marrried rright away."

"Well, do you love him or not?"

"Oh, aye, I do. Ye ken that verra well. I've always loved him."

"And what if you make him wait too long and you lose him?"

"Och, Torri! He's my Jamie. I canna lose him!" For a second or two Felicity looked frightened, but then she tossed her head. "But if I do–well, that's that. Therre arre lots o' otherr laddies just as brraw!"

"But...but only one Jamie for you—just as there's only one Gavin for me. Felicity, sit down here for a minute on the couch and listen to me, please." The girl obeyed though clearly she was only humoring Victoria out of affection. "Felicity–" She took one of her friend's hands in both of hers. "I'm so afraid you're taking Jamie's love for granted, but then why shouldn't you? After all you've lived your entire life surrounded by people who love you. So why shouldn't you believe that no matter what Jamie will simply go on loving you. You're like a child, Felicity, who has grown up in...in a room full of toys so that when you're given merely one more, you can't possibly appreciate its worth. You can't even begin to imagine what Gavin's love means to me. For you see, I have always been that other child–the one for whom that one toy is infinitely precious–the one who has lived her life in a room without toys."

Chapter 3

Gavin, it seems, had been no more successful with Jamie, but nothing could really spoil their visit. They walked for miles along winding, snow-covered roads; they traveled by sleigh high into the hills for a winter picnic in one of Niall Hamilton's shielings; they spent an evening at a pub in near-by Ballater where Gavin had first sung in public. He sang that night. But Victoria found she could no longer look on him as merely another performer. He was the person she loved above anyone else on earth and she found herself observing things about him she was sure she'd never noticed before: the deepening of the laugh lines around his eyes when he smiled; his engaging habit of ducking his head and winking at someone as he sang or the way his hair fell in his eyes each time he bent over the guitar.

Most wonderful of all were the long, happy hours they spent with the rest of the Hamilton family although Meghan continued to refuse to enter into the fun and Rhuaridh never did appear. When, toward the end of their stay, Victoria asked Gavin why she hadn't met his brother, he replied simply that it could wait. But then Fiona had told her they weren't at all close so she didn't think any more about it.

All too soon, however, it was time for them to return to London. Fiona and Meghan had said their good-byes before leaving for the day. While Gavin took their suitcases out to the car, Victoria went into the kitchen with Granny who had insisted on packing them a lunch. Mary was sure her grandson never got enough to eat and someone had to see to fattening up this English lass. Niall followed them, putting a fatherly arm around Victoria. "Well lass, the next time ye coom, 'twill be forr a weddin'." She nodded smiling as she rested her head briefly against his shoulder.

"Rready to go, darrlin'!" The front door slammed shut with a bang.

"Torri!" Granny Hamilton rolled her eyes. "Will ye at least teach the laddie to close a doorr prroperrly!"

"I'll certainly try," she replied laughing. "But we both know he's incorrigible."

The two women embraced just as Gavin appeared in the doorway. Exchanging pleased glances with his father, he came over to the table to peek into the wicker picnic basket. "Och, Grranny," he exclaimed, " 'tis a good thing Torri doesna eat verra much. 'Tis barrely enough forr me."

They all walked out into the living room together, Niall going immediately along outside. It was a bitterly cold day with a strong hint of snow in the air so his mother would be saying her good-byes indoors and he knew she'd relish a private moment. "Ye take carre o' each otherr noo," the old woman muttered self-consciously, overcome with emotion.

"Aye, Grranny, we will," Gavin promised her.

She hugged and kissed them both, reaching up as well to pat each of them on the cheek. As usual her grandson picked her up several inches off the floor and she as always protested noisily, but not too convincingly at such treatment. Finally then the young couple turned to leave, Gavin holding open the door to allow Victoria to precede him outside. "Wait a minute," Mary Hamilton called out all at once, but when they looked back at her, she did not immediately continue. Instead she stared at them solemnly for a moment as if to imprint the picture on her mind. "Torri," she went on finally, "have ye gi'en much thought to yourr weddin' gown?"

"Well no, not really. I..I assumed that since I've been married before....."

"Doesna have to be white. I...I mentioned it because I'd like verra much to make it forr ye if ye'll let me."

"Oh, Granny, would you?" Putting down her purse and cosmetic case, Victoria hurried back to hug her yet again. "It would mean so much to me. I wouldn't even begin to know how to dress for a Highland wedding."

"I'll send ye soom picturres then and ye choose what ye like." Her dark eyes glowed with excitement. "Just let me know the measurrements and I can leave the finishin' 'till ye get oop herre."

"Torri," Gavin put in at last, "we have a long way to go today."

"Yes, darling." She glanced back at him. "Thank you so much, Granny," she said with one final hug. "We'll see you soon." Mary Hamilton stood at the window, watching them go down the snow-covered path together. She chuckled to herself as she remembered that less than a week ago she'd been determined not to accept "this grrand English lady" as Gavin's lass.

Niall Hamilton was waiting for them down by the barn. A large number of sheep and lambs had gathered at the fence when they saw him coming. They knew he never went near the pens without several carrots or cabbage and lettuce leaves in his pockets. He turned to smile at them both. "Yourr dearr motherr, Gavin, was always complainin' aboot my rrobbin' herr vegetable bins. Herre, Torri." He handed her a couple of carrots and some of the cabbage. "Ye might like to gie soom to the wee lambs."

His son looked up from stowing the last of their things in the car. "Between you and Grranny, Dad, I'll neverr get Torri oot o' herre."

"Well noo, laddie, ye canna blame us. We'rre just gettin' to know herr and we want to keep herr as long as we can."

Victoria had gone over to the fence with the treats and the sheep were all crowding close to be sure and get their share. At Niall's words she turned to give him an affectionate smile. "I feel the same way, Dad. Oh, Dad! Your sheep are just so cute!" The two men burst into laughter. "Well, why is that funny?" she asked, a little embarrassed. "So soft and woolly and those adorable black faces!"

"Darrlin' gurrl," Niall said, "I've hearrd my sheep descrribed in many ways, but neverr beforre has anyone called them cute."

"Coom, hinny." Gavin held open the car door for her. "Ye canna take any o' them with ye no matterr <u>how</u> cute they arre. They'll nae fit in my wee Rroverr."

"Oh, stop it!" She tried to look indignant, but this was one time that her acting ability failed her and she laughed merrily. "I don't suppose I'll ever live that down."

Gavin chuckled. "Prrobably not, darrlin'."

"Dad, good-bye." Victoria hugged and kissed him. "And thank you for everything. I can't begin to tell you how much this all means to me." At last then she stepped into the car, Gavin closing the door after her.

"Ye've got a dearr lass therre," Niall told his son. "Ye cherrish herr noo."

"Aye, Dad, I will." He also embraced his father before going around to the other side of the car and getting in himself. The elder Hamilton continued to stand there waving as long as he could still see the car and only when it had disappeared behind a snowbank did he turn to begin his morning chores.

* * *

Victoria was terribly nervous about returning to work and the night before she was still awake at three a.m. Gavin had apparently been asleep for some time, but it was a comfort just feeling him there beside her. If only I could stay like this, she thought, and never have to face the outside world again. But she knew that wasn't possible.

"Torri?"

The unexpected sound of his voice in the darkness startled her. "I...I thought you were asleep."

"Arre ye worrried aboot tomorrrow, darrlin? Is that it then?"

"It's...it's just seeing so many people for the first time since....since...."

"Aye, that's what I thought. And 'tis only naturral."

Victoria could feel the tears coming into her eyes. She wasn't being entirely honest. It wasn't people in general so much as someone like Clive Bannister who would doubtless take pleasure in tormenting her. "Oh, Gavin," she whispered reaching over to touch his face, "I.... I wish so you were the only man I'd ever....ever...."

"Oh, I see...that's it. Soomone oot o' the past."

"He's...he's acting in the Elizabeth sequence. He..he even testified against me at Olivia's custody hearing."

"Suppose I werre to coom wi' ye?"

She shook her head. "I...I don't know what he'd say to you."

"And do ye think I'd believe a worrd of it?"

"He's..he's not the only one. The director..... Oh, darling, I would give anything to have come to you pure and untouched....."

"And I, Torri...that I'd neverr known anotherr woman...."

"If...if only we'd met years before we did."

"Aye, lass, but ten yearrs ago–let's say–would eitherr of us have been able to apprreciate what we have togetherr?"

"No, I suppose not," she sighed, lying back down beside him. "Will you come with me today?"

"Aye, if ye'll coom wi' me in the evenin'. That coffee house wherre Jamie was worrkin' is givin' me an audition."

"Oh, I like that!" she exclaimed, hugging herself. "You do something for me and I do something for you!"

"Aye–'tis all a parrt o' lovin'. Torri, what did I tell ye aboot wastin' those hugs. Coom, lass." He raised one arm for her to slip underneath and then closed both arms around her.

She giggled, feeling a little bubble of happiness well up in her throat. Instinctively she began to move her hand around and around on his bare chest, feeling the thick, curling hair run through her fingers. "Gavin, why weren't you performing at the coffee house with Jamie? Don't you often work together?"

"Aye, lass."

Victoria could tell instantly by his tone that the mood had been spoiled. "What, darling? Did I say something wrong?"

"No, lass. 'Tis only my damned prride again. Actually, ye see, we did both audition therre, but they only hirred Jamie."

"What?!" She sat up in bed, holding the sheet up in front of her in an unconscious gesture of modesty which he found touching. "But that's ridiculous! He's not half as good as you! His voice—his stage presence–everything!"

Gavin completely forgot his discomfiture of a few minutes ago–enjoying immensely Victoria's indignation that anyone could prefer Jamie to him. "Actually, darrlin', 'twas rright afterr ye'd gone back to Jason. I wasna at my best."

"Then it was my fault!" She turned to throw herself against him, unaware the move now exposed both her breasts as they pressed against his chest. "Well, I'll be there tonight and that will make up for it at least a little, won't it?"

"Oh, Torri!" Rolling her over onto her back again, he began to kiss her face and neck, moving gradually down toward her breasts. "Everra minute I spend wi ye morre than makes oop for everrathin'." It was nearly four-thirty by the time they both finally slept and only three and a half hours after that the alarm went off. Groaning, Gavin reached over to silence it. "Torri?" There was no reply and when he rolled over on his side to look at her, he found she was still sound asleep. She looked terribly sweet lying there beside him sprawled on her stomach and he hated to wake her–hated it even more because beginning today he was going to have to share her. "Torri, darrlin'." He leaned down to kiss her lightly on the tip of her nose. " 'Tis time to wake oop, I'm afrraid, lass."

"Mmm." After a moment Victoria reluctantly opened her eyes to discover his were but inches away. "Good morning." The happiness she felt at just waking up to him made her smile.

"Good morrnin' yourrself, darrlin'." At once Gavin's hand slipped under the covers to glide lightly over her breast, down along her waist and over her stomach.

As always she found his caress profoundly affecting. "Oh, darling," she sighed after a moment. "I can't be late my first day back."

" 'Tis all rright, lass. 'Twill be plenty of otherr times. So then, if ye'll let me grrab a showerr and a shave, I'll cook us a bit o' brreakfast while ye put yourr face on–as ye say."

"Thank you, darling." Gavin gave her one more quick kiss before getting out of bed to slip into his robe and head for the bathroom. A few minutes later the telephone rang and sliding over to the other side of the bed, Victoria reached up to answer it. "Hello."

"Good morning." It was Leslie Matthews, her agent. "You're going back to work today, I believe. Would you like me to come with you?"

"Thank you, luv. You're very thoughtful as always, but Gavin...."

"It's still Gavin then?" He sounded a little sad.

"It will always be Gavin. We're going to be married as soon as I'm free." He said nothing. "Oh, Matt, please be glad for me and please stop by to meet him. I know you'll like him."

"All right then–probably sometime late this morning."

"Thanks–bye." Briefly she felt afraid again–perhaps talking to her agent had brought the real world too close–but the sound of whistling coming from the bathroom steadied her and by the time they left to drive to the studio, she was calm. Only when they actually stood in the hall outside the sound stage, did she hesitate.

" 'Twill be all rright, darrlin'." Once again Gavin put his arms around her. "I'll be rright therre everra minute." He bent to kiss her, first briefly and then more lingeringly and when at last he released her, she was ready to face the day.

* * *

The rehearsal hall, meanwhile, was alive with speculation. They all knew, of course, about Victoria's attempted suicide and her subsequent emotional collapse, but both Matt and Dr. Anthony had fiercely guarded her privacy and beyond the bare facts there was only hearsay, the rumors varying considerably in their proximity to the actual truth. 1) She had returned to the States with her husband; 2) She had been committed to a sanatarium due to a) a drug overdose or b) an alcoholic binge; 3) She'd taken off for a) the French Riviera, b) the Italian Riviera, c) the Greek Islands; d) Majorca or e) the Bahamas with–here insert the name of any living male or 4) She had entered an Anglican Convent.

Then the door to the sound stage swung open and Victoria entered–hand in hand with a tall, handsome, auburn-haired man whom many of them recognized. The couple was greeted with a cheer followed by resounding applause. Gavin couldn't help noticing how Victoria–ever the actress–waited until she had everyone's attention before she spoke. He smiled; it seemed he still had a lot to learn about his future wife, but he didn't mind. He was more than willing to devote a lifetime of study to the subject. "It's good to be back," Victoria said at last, smiling warmly. "I understand, however, that you've all carried on magnificently in my absence." At that there was a wave of laughter. "And for those of you who haven't met him already, this is Gavin Hamilton. We're..." She paused to glance up at him... "going to be married."

A few seconds of stunned silence met her announcement followed by renewed applause. It was at this point that Tony Blake-Ashley came into the studio. Wanting to make Victoria's return as easy as possible, he'd gone to Clive Bannister's dressing room to talk to him before rehearsal. He had failed miserably. To quote Clive exactly–"You may believe that crap about how much she's changed, but I don't! She'll be a Goddamned bloody bitch in heat for the rest of her Goddamned bloody life!"

"What is it?" Tony asked his script girl who happened to be near the door.

"She just announced she's marrying him," the girl replied. "You met him, didn't you, –the Scotsman who used to pick her up so often?"

He looked over to where Victoria and Gavin were standing, surrounded now by the cast and crew, and after a moment he made his way through the crowd to take her right hand in both of his. "Victoria, I'm so happy for you...." And now Tony extended his own right hand to the other man. "Gavin, we've met, I think."

"Aye." He returned the handshake although with no particular warmth and he offered no further response to the greeting.

"Do you need me in make-up, Tony?" Victoria asked.

"Not today, but the costume people would like to see you before we start."

"Do ye want me to coom, Torri?" Gavin inquired at once.

"No, darling, thank you. I won't be long." She touched him lightly on the cheek before walking away.

Tony had observed the expression on her face during this brief exchange and he couldn't help even now envying the man. What must it be like to have this woman look at you with so much love? Just then, however, he noticed Clive approaching and he tensed anticipating a scene. Well, at least Victoria wouldn't be there to hear it. "Well, my dear fellow, I understand congratulations are in order." The actor's smirk was decidedly unpleasant.

"Gavin, this is Clive Bannister," Tony said with a sigh. He saw a look of hatred pass across the Scotsman's face. He knows then, he thought, which probably means he knows about me as well. No wonder he's not very friendly.

"So, Hamilton," Clive continued, "welcome to the growing and, I might add, ever changing ranks."

Gavin looked down at this man who had dared to speak in such a fashion about Victoria. "I will thank ye verra kindly," he said, each word coming as a deadly rumble, " to rrememberr that Torri is to be my wife. And therreforre I dinna parrticularrly carre to hearr herr name sae much as mentioned by a rrepulsive, wee worrm of a man such as yourrself. In the futurre, if ye'rre forrced by unavoidable cirrcumstances to rreferr to herr, I would suggest ye keep in mind that a Highlanderr's dirrk is uniquely fashioned to fit prrecisely between an Englishman's rrribs!"

"Well...ah...yes...ah...excuse me," Clive stammered and backing away, he fled.

Tony had watched highly amused as the color gradually drained from the actor's face, but then Gavin turned to him. There was a brief pause during which he found himself thinking with some apprehension about the spaces between his own ribs and his palms started to perspire. "Well noo, Torri tells me ye werre kind to her," Gavin said finally. "I apprreciate that." But his brown eyes, which normally glowed with good humor, remained expressionless.

"It can't be easy for you," the other man murmured uneasily.

"I don't parrticularrly carre forr people who took advantage of herr loneliness..."

"See here, old chap, I......"

"Aye, as I already stated, ye werre kind to herr, but ye still used herr, didn't ye?'

"Yes, well if you'll excuse me, I have some last minute details to see to." Tony didn't know why he was so on edge. He knew he'd treated Victoria much better than most. Nevertheless, he was more than willing to join Clive in retreat.

A short while later Victoria returned from her costume fitting and the day's rehearsal was underway. With her work to take up her mind she soon forgot her nervousness and every time they stopped for a moment Gavin would appear at her elbow, bringing her tea or a drink of water or slipping a cardigan over her shoulders or simply putting his arm around her. How good it was to know he was there. Soon she found herself expecting him and each time no matter what else might be demanding her attention at the moment, she was careful to acknowledge his presence with a smile or a touch. The love between these two people was evident to everyone, but even if Gavin hadn't actually been there, they would have guessed Victoria's life had altered drastically during her absence. No one had ever seen her so content.

Matt stopped in as promised shortly before the lunch break. The scene on which they'd been working that morning was the one in which the elderly Elizabeth is being romanced by the Earl of Essex. Somehow Victoria was managing to portray not simply a faded and aging queen, but a faded and aging queen who is yet able to fascinate a man forty years her junior and almost at once he became engrossed in her performance. He didn't even notice that Tony had come to stand next to him until the other man spoke. "No matter what else happens," the director observed under his breath, " the gift is always there, isn't it?'

Matt nodded proudly. "She never fails to move me." He glanced about the stage. "Where is he? I offered to bring her this first day back, but it appears she was already taken care of."

"Very well taken care of, as a matter of fact–over there." With a nod of his head he indicated one of the folding chairs scattered at random around the periphery of the set. Gavin was leaning forward in his seat elbows on his knees, hands clasped together–- watching Victoria.

"What do you think of him?"

"You'll have to judge for yourself, I'm afraid. I'm so consumed with jealousy, I can't offer a rational opinion. Excuse me." Tony strode off—ostensibly to consult the script.

Shortly after that rehearsal broke for lunch. This time it was Victoria who came over to where Gavin was sitting. He stood up as she approached. Matt could not, of course, hear their conversation, but he understood at once what Tony had meant. This man was clearly her entire world. At one point he must have said something that amused her because she laughed. It was just at that moment that she happened to notice her agent. "There you are, you darling old thing!" She ran over to kiss him first on one cheek and then the other. For a moment he glimpsed the theatrical Victoria, but then she turned to extend one hand back to Gavin and the image vanished almost as soon as it had appeared. "Matt," she said–almost shyly now, "this....this is Gavin. Gavin–my agent and good friend, Leslie Matthews."

"Aye–'Tis grrand to meet ye." Smiling, Gavin slipped his left arm around Victoria's shoulders in a gesture at once affectionate and possessive, offering his right to shake hands with the other man. "Torri has told me sae much aboot ye."

"What have you done to her?" Matt asked. "She's radiant."

" 'Tisna verra complicated," he replied, hugging Victoria closer. "All I've done is love herr." At that she looked up at him again and smiled. "Can I get ye soom tea then, hinny?"

"Yes, darling, thank you. Matt?"

"Thank you, yes."

"I'll be rright back." Gavin bent to kiss her once lightly before walking away.

"You do like him, don't you?" Victoria asked at once.

"Would it matter?"

She laughed. "Not really–because I do! That's what's amazing! I'm so in love with him and yet I like him, too. Matt, how thoughtless of me. I haven't thanked you for guarding my privacy through all of this."

"That happens to be my job, Victoria." He found her gratitude actually embarrassing.

"Oh, no! You're not going to get away with that!" She shook her finger at him. "You happen to care about me, Leslie Matthews." But then all at once she became serious again and Matt could see the tears in her eyes as she reached across to lay a hand on his arm. "You always have. Not only you, but Terry and Noel and Martha–all of you. No matter how badly I treated you. I don't know why I used to do that–as if I wanted to drive you away– when I really needed all of you so terribly."

"None of us blamed you, Victoria," he assured her gently. "We all knew how unhappy you were."

Gavin returned then, carrying a tray with three mugs of tea as well as several sandwiches wrapped in wax paper. "Eat a sandwich, too, lass," he directed matter-of-factly. "That one's cheese and tomato. I ken ye like that."

"No, thank you, darling," she replied, reaching for a mug. "It's been an exhausting morning and I'm simply too tired to eat."

"Just exactly why ye <u>need</u> to eat," he stated firmly. "Noo ye'll have a sandwich orr I'll take ye overr my knee and think what it'll do forr the grreat Victorria Windsorr's image to be gi'en a spankin' in frront of the entirre cast." He winked broadly at Matt before turning back to her as if to say, "Well, what arre ye goin' to do?"

Meekly Victoria accepted a sandwich, glancing at her agent as she did so, and her eyes began to dance. "As you can see, luv, I am completely cowed–at last."

* * *

The "Harp and Lyre" was one of the few London supper clubs which refused to cater to current popular taste, seeking instead to preserve the rich cultural heritage of the British Isles and Ian Munro, its owner, was very selective in his hiring of performers. Gavin Hamilton's original audition had been a distinct disappointment and it was only to satisfy his daughter, Clara, that he'd agreed to give the Scotsman another chance. He didn't expect the result to be any different, however, and he'd deliberately settled on a Monday evening when the attendance was apt to be light. Then the man had the unbelievable audacity to arrive less than half an hour before show time. "You're late!" Ian growled at him. He paid no particular notice to the singer's female companion, thinking only how disappointed his daughter would be to discover Gavin Hamilton had brought a date.

"Aye." He and Victoria had lost track of time over dinner, but Gavin made no attempt to apologize for his tardiness. Instead he merely rested his guitar case on the stool in the center of the small stage and removing the instrument, he sat down on the edge of the platform to check the tuning. There had been a time when, if an audition didn't go well for one reason or another, he would merely shrug it off. Tonight, however, mattered terribly–too terribly for him to bother with minor matters such as courtesy. Feeling a light touch on his arm, he glanced up to find Victoria had sat down beside him and the look of love on her beautiful face only strengthened his determination.

The proprietor had already turned away in any case. It appeared that rudeness was another of this young man's unfortunate qualities. Just then, however, Clara Munro came out of the office carrying the completed seated chart and menus. Her eyes widened in surprise. "Dad, that's Victoria Windsor!"

"Where?" He glanced about excitedly. He'd always hoped the club would eventually attract a more notable clientele.

"There—with Gavin Hamilton."

"Oh, Miss Windsor!" he exclaimed. "You don't have to sit there!" Quickly he worked his way among the tables back to the stage. "Please–take your choice of any table–as my guest, of course."

Victoria bestowed her most enchanting smile on him. If Gavin wasn't particularly inclined to be gracious at the moment, she could be so for him. "I'm fine here for now, thank you. Later I would appreciate a table. However....." She hesitated, looking uncertainly about the room.

"Wherreverr ye want, darrlin'." Gavin had finished tuning the guitar, smiling to himself as he stood up to lean the instrument against the stool–ready for his performance. Even at such a moment he couldn't help reveling in the right he now had to call her darling in public and sitting down beside her again, he put his arm around her shoulders.

"I...I don't know. I'd prefer to be out of the light, but then I won't be able to see you as well."

"Perhaps a table at the front of the second level, Miss Windsor," Ian suggested.

"Oh, thank you! That would be perfect! How thoughtful of you!"

"I'll reserve it at once, Miss Windsor." He bowed slightly before withdrawing.

"Ye dinna have to be sae charrmin', Torri," Gavin muttered when the other man had left. But the way he felt just having her there with him made it impossible for him to sound too cross.

"Tonight's very important to you, isn't it, darling?"

"Aye, I....I want ye to be prroud of me."

"Silly," she murmured touching his cheek. "Don't you know I already am?"

The entertainment opened with the usual Highland dancing and a folk quartet and then Gavin was announced. An audible buzz could be heard as the audience got their first glimpse of the tall, handsome man dressed as always in corduroy trousers and a turtleneck jumper. "Good evenin'." He grinned at them as he picked up the guitar and settled himself on the stool. "And welcoom. Ye ken verra well, no doot, that I'm Scots." They laughed. "And so ye see I grrew oop lovin' the music I'm aboot to sharre wi' ye. This evening I trrust ye'll learrn to love it as well."

Deftly Gavin strummed a few chords for a last check of the instrument and then he began to sing. A hush fell over the audience as slowly but surely he wove his spell. One minute his song would tell of Highlanders driven off their land to make room for the English lord's sheep, his deep voice mourning their tragedy, and there wasn't a dry eye in the house. The next, his manner turning undeniably sensual, he'd sing a ballad. The women watched him, mouths open slightly, each of them wanting him more than she had ever wanted a man. Then just as all the males in the audience had begun to hate him, he'd launch into something like "Donald, Wherre's Yourr Trrooserrs?" and everyone laughed and relaxed, the tension broken. He stopped at various points during the set to visit with the audience–- accepting requests. It became rapidly apparent that his repertoire was extensive. Then toward the end of his performance he paused again, but this time Gavin merely stared at the floor, idly strumming the guitar. "What's the matter?" someone called out from the audience. "Forget the words?"

"Aye, maybe that's the prroblem." He grinned, ducking his head in apparent embarrassment. "Would someone be willin' to help me oot by joinin' me in a duet?"

Immediately several women raised their hands, more than willing to join him–in just about anything.

For a long moment Victoria looked down at the glass of wine she'd been nursing absentmindedly all the time Gavin was singing. This was obviously not a general invitation on his part, but one designed to ask her up on stage with him if she wanted to come, yet phrased in such a way that she could unobtrusively refuse if she chose not to do so. At last, however, she stood up and coming down the step or two to the main level, she made her way through the audience. She could hear the murmuring build as people recognized her. Finally applause broke out, but surprisingly none of this bothered her. All she saw or cared about was Gavin who had stood up as he saw her approaching to hold out his hand and help her up onto the stage.

"Thank ye, darrlin'," he whispered under cover of the applause as he slipped an arm around her waist and drew her to him. "I didna ken whetherr I should ask ye orr not, but I did want ye oop herre wi' me."

"I knew you did." She smiled up at him even as she graciously acknowledged the ovation. "And...and I wanted to be here."

"Is it all rright if I make an announcement?'

"Absolutely! It's time all these drooling females learned you're unavailable!"

He chuckled as he waited for the applause to subside. "It seems," he said when at last it was quiet, "that 'tisna necessarry forr me to intrroduce the lass." There was general laughter at that. "But what ye dinna ken is that we'rre to be marrried." Almost instantly the applause burst out again louder than before, accompanied by whistles and cheers and the stamping of feet.

"What have <u>you</u> got to say, Miss Windsor?" someone called out.

Victoria was still not at her best at such moments, but she knew that now the whole audience would be expecting her to respond in some way. "Th...thank you for coming," she said at last. "I'm sure you agree with me that we've heard an incredibly gifted performer this evening." Their applause showed they most definitely did agree. She smiled.

"It's not fair, Victoria," some woman called out. "He's gorgeous!"

She relaxed even more. "Yes, isn't he?"

Gavin looked suitably abashed. "Well noo, it seems that when I was in New Yorrk last sprring, I made the acquaintance of this English lass." There was more appreciative laughter as he proceeded to tell the story of how they'd met and he'd first asked her to sing with him. They began with the same two songs they'd done that night and then went on to others he'd taught her since then: "Loch Lomond," "The Skye Boat Song" and "These Are My Mountains". Finally she left the stage so that Gavin could conclude his program. All the way back to her seat people reached out to touch her and wish her happiness and Victoria, who at one time had found even such simple personal demands intolerable, responded easily and naturally to their good wishes.

When Gavin had finished singing and joined her, they were instantly surrounded. Everyone, it seemed, wanted an autograph or to take a picture. At one point Ian Munro appeared at the table as well. "While you're writing your name, young man, how about signing a contract? We'll start with three nights a week, but I have a feeling that's only the beginning."

"Oh darling, I'm so glad!" Victoria exclaimed. "I just knew it."

"What I can't understand though," Ian went on, "is how you could have been so unexciting the first time I heard you."

" 'Twas a time I thought I'd lost someone verra special." He glanced in Victoria's direction, making his meaning clear. "Therre's just one thing though. I'll need a wee bit o' time off arroond Chrristmas–forr ourr weddin'."

"Fine...fine!" The manager fairly beamed. "Please–have the reception here–as my guests, of course."

"Well, we may take ye oop on that laterr forr ourr frriends herre in Lundon, but the weddin' 'twill be at my Dad's–in Scotland."

* * *

All in all it had been a special day and Victoria was in no way prepared for the telephone call she received from her solicitor the following morning. It seemed that Jason was refusing to go ahead with the divorce unless she agreed to meet with him in person. The prospect of seeing this man again was unnerving, but Carl Michaels assured her it was far preferable to a long, difficult court fight and with Gavin's reassurance that he'd be there with her she finally agreed.

The meeting was set for the following afternoon–at Jason's office. "I...I feel as though I'm walking into a trap," she whispered, stopping on the pavement outside the storefront which housed the Prodigals headquarters.

"Just keep tellin' yourrself 'tis the last time ye'll everr have to see him." Gavin took her hand in his and together they continued on inside.

Jason happened to be coming out of his office just as they entered. Really– the unbelievable gall of the man-to show his face here! "I believe I said alone, Victoria," he observed sharply.

"I think Torri wants me with herr." Gavin's answering tone was even, but firm.

"And wherever did you get that ridiculous name for her? It doesn't suit her at all!"

"It happens to suit herr perrfectly! But then ye neverr did rreally ken herr, did ye?'

Victoria looked helplessly from one man to the other. "Please....please, both of you," she entreated. "Gavin, perhaps it would be better if I talked to him alone."

"No, Torri." He put a protective arm around her shoulders. "I told ye...."

"For God's sake, Hamilton, what do you think I'm going to do to her?"

"Och, Rreverrend!" Gavin's eyes rolled in exaggerated horror. "Ourr Lorrd's name in vain and frrom your sacrred lips!" For just a second Victoria forgot what an uncomfortable and unpleasant situation this was and the corners of her mouth twitched.

"You see what you've done to her!" Jason exclaimed. "For a while I thought there was hope."

"Hope? Forr what? To drrive herr perrmanently oot o' herr mind, ye Goddamned sanctimonious prrig!"

"Please, darling." Victoria put her hand on Gavin's arm. "This is only making it harder for me."

He looked down at her. Jason observed the gaze which seemed to leap across the space between them. Unfortunately it was such base drives which continued to govern Victoria. He felt terribly sad. What could he have hoped to accomplish? "Arre ye surre, Torri?" Gavin asked at last, covering her hand with his other one, and with a significant glance at Jason he bent to kiss her briefly on the lips. "I'll be rright herre if ye change yourr mind." .

"In here please, Victoria." Her soon-to-be ex-husband indicated the open doorway behind him.

Her eyes held Gavin's for one final moment. "Yes, all right," she murmured and walked past Jason into his office.

He closed the door behind them, appearing to ignore the other man entirely, but in actuality desperately aware of him, standing there like a large and very determined watchdog. Jason moved around to sit behind his desk, gesturing Victoria to a chair facing him. But oh, why did she have to look particularly lovely today? Her dress was a turquoise blue, the top of which was striped with narrow bands of white and gold, and the soft jersey seemed molded to her body. Was Gavin Hamilton able to satisfy the desires of that exquisite body as he'd never been able to do, he wondered. He watched the slow rise and fall of her breasts and for one crazy minute he thought she was trying to seduce him. He forced himself to look away. "So then, you're fully determined to go through with this?" he inquired at last.

Victoria had seated herself as he'd requested and while she waited for him to speak, she fought to remain calm. Her hands clenched and unclenched in her lap and the slow, even breathing which Jason found so arousing was in reality a relaxation technique Dr. Anthony had taught her. Only this, she kept telling herself over and over again–only this and it will all be over. And she thought about Gavin, of course, and Olivia and dear Noel and all the other people who found her good and lovable–not at all worthless and depraved as this man apparently had. She'd tried so hard to please him and to what point? So by the time Jason finally put his question to her she was fully prepared to answer him. "Do you mean the divorce?" Her tone was soft and low; again it struck him as sensual, but this was, in fact, her stage voice. It would have carried easily to the rear of London's largest theatre. "Of course I do. Is...is that why you had to see me–just to ask me that?"

Jason fumbled with various articles on his desk before replying. "I...I only wanted to...ah... hear you say it. To know it...it was your own idea."

Her green eyes blazed. "And just whose idea did you think it was?"

"This....Gavin Hamilton.." He half-choked over the name. "He has such a hold over you, I...I couldn't be sure."

"A hold over me? What in hell do you think he is? Some sort of bloody sorcerer?" He rubbed his forehead in despair. "Yes, Jason, yes. Occasionally I <u>do</u> <u>swear</u>!"

"But can't you see, Victoria–profanity only soils the lips of those who utter it."

She leaped to her feet. "Stop it! Just stop it! You will <u>not</u> do this to me again. I will not let you!"

"What am I doing to you? Only trying to help you–that's all I've ever done."

Outside Gavin had heard her raise her voice and unable to stand it any longer, he strode over to the office door, flinging it open. Instinctively Victoria went to him. "Arre ye finished then, Torri?" It was clearly not intended as a question.

"No, as a matter of fact, we are not." Jason stood up as well–irritatingly cool and condescending.

"Look, Rreverrend." And once again there was the exaggerated burr on the "r's". "I wasna talkin' to you."

"Well, perhaps you should, Hamilton, since it is <u>my</u> wife you have stolen!"

"Oh, no! Oh, no!" Advancing on the desk, Gavin slammed one fist down on it. Involuntarily the other man flinched. "Ye thrrew herr away! Noo-let herr go! Damn you!"

"Victoria, is this truly what you want?"

"<u>Please</u> yes, I....I do." She came to stand beside Gavin. Beside <u>him</u>—always beside <u>him</u>---, Jason thought despairingly "If I have to," Victoria went on after a moment, "I'll do it the hard way, but... but if you still have any feeling for me, don't make me wait. Don't put us all through so much unnecessary heartache."

All at once he had no more will to fight. He sighed. "I...I only wanted to be sure it was what you wanted. And it seems it is." In a bizarre way–even in this bitter moment of surrender–he found a certain humor in her pleading with <u>him</u> not to put them all through "unnecessary heartache".

"Gavin–" Victoria looked up at him. "Please wait outside–just for a few more minutes. I won't be long."

"Aye, lass." He turned to leave.

Suddenly Jason called after him. "Take..take good care of her....ah....please."

"Aye." The Scotsman walked out without looking back. "A hell of a lot betterr than ye everr did," he added under his breath.

"I just wanted to say thank you," Victoria murmured when Gavin was gone. "That's all, Jason–and good-bye. I suppose you'll be returning to the States."

"It seems there's no reason for me to stay here now."

"Yes–well, I...I should be going." She started toward the door herself now–anxious for it to be over.

"Victoria?"

"Yes?" One hand on the doorknob she turned to look back over her shoulder at him.

"Did...did you ever love me?"

"Jason–did <u>you</u> ever love me?"

"Of course I did. I still do."

"Did you? I wonder. Well, at least I <u>thought</u> I loved you."

Motionless, Jason watched his office door close behind her. Ridiculous, he thought. How could she ever have questioned his love for her? But what did it matter now? With the shutting of the door she was gone from his life and he felt an emptiness he doubted would ever entirely go away.

Just a few days later he did indeed return to the States, going on directly to Reno. The bitter irony of his destination did not escape him. Less than two years had passed since he'd gone there to divorce his first wife in order to marry Victoria. But in this current instance he at least had the satisfaction of knowing that he himself was entirely blameless.

* * *

The waiting period would have allowed the wedding to take place any time after December 27th. At first the symbolism of New Year's Eve was appealing, but then later they decided to move the ceremony back a day to allow for a long week-end before they would both be due back in London.

One thing only marred these weeks for Victoria. She had sent a letter to Sydney, asking her old friend to return for her wedding.

"Dearest Noel," she had written–

"I'm sure you already know everything that's happened in the past several weeks and I am sorry if you've had to hear it all first from someone else. But then, I have never treated you very well, have I? I can only hope you knew that despite the many times I hurt you, I was always deeply grateful for your unfailing friendship.

And so, <u>dear</u> friend, I want more than anything to have you there for my wedding to Gavin. I realize that the one time you met him was under very awkward circumstances. You thought, of course, that I was merely returning to old ways. But you see, I was not. Even then, although we were both too stupid to realize it, we were deeply in love. And now we are to be married at Gavin's family home in Glengowrie, Scotland and oh Noel, I do so want you to be there to share in my happiness. You who have been there for me through so much degradation and bitter loneliness–please come now to witness my total joy. You realized how wrong Jason was for me and yet you were at that wedding. Come now, please, to be at a wedding which is oh, so very right! I fully comprehend I am asking a lot of you–to fly thousands of miles–but I have asked far more of you in the past and you have never let me down.

Besides Terry is coming to be my surrogate father and give me away and Martha, who's been like a mother to me, will, of course, be there so that leaves only a brother and that, dearest Noel, is you.

I will be anxiously awaiting your reply.

My love to you always,

Victoria

The envelope was delivered to his dressing room less than an hour before the matinee performance of *Romeo and Juliet* in which he was currently appearing as Mercutio. Noel read the letter once through quickly and then a second time more slowly.

Both Terry and Martha had indeed written and called regularly. Just yesterday, in fact, there'd been another brief note from Terry telling him the date of the wedding. "I hope you can manage to come," he had said. "I know how much she wants you of all people to be there. She plans, I'm sure, to write and ask you herself." And so she had–beautiful words full of love–and all as she planned her marriage to someone else. It was almost humorous, Noel thought bitterly. It must be admitted that he failed to give his customary flawless performance that afternoon. He even confused the choreography in his fatal duel with Tybalt and after the performance the other actor waylayed him in the wings, yelled "Thanks a lot, old chap!" and punched him in the gut. It was fortunate he wasn't scheduled to appear in the evening production and after dinner served in his hotel suite he settled down with a bottle of whiskey to compose his reply.

"Dear Victoria," he'd begun and then for nearly half an hour he stared at those two words, meanwhile working with great diligence on the liquor. How ironic, he thought at one point, actually laughing out loud. She probably hasn't touched a drop in weeks and here I am trying to get drunk enough to tell her I'm not coming to her wedding. In the process he spilled whiskey on the paper and had to start all over again.

"Dear Victoria–" he penned again and finally after more staring and more drinking he continued on from there.

How very happy I am for you, my dear. Yes, I had learned of your approaching marriage from both Terry and Martha. But please try to understand why I cannot come and it isn't the distance which prevents me. I guess when it comes right down to it, I cannot bear to watch you pledge yourself to Gavin.

Yes, I was there for your wedding to Jason even though I believed you were making a mistake and I'm not very proud of myself when I realize that it was because I knew that marriage wouldn't last that I could bring myself to witness it–that eventually you would once again turn to me. But somewhere before that could happen, Gavin Hamilton came along and now as you say yourself and Terry and Martha have confirmed, you are at last deeply in love and I quote from them both, "happier than I have ever seen her". And this time when you pledge yourself, I'm sure it will be forever. No one wants you to be happy more than I, my very dear Victoria; no one wants more for you to know at last what it feels like to be safe and loved and yet I cannot bring myself to be there to see it.

I know how this will hurt you and for this I am deeply sorry, but at the same time I hope you will understand. My most heartfelt wishes to you both for every happiness. I hope Gavin fully appreciates how fortunate he is to claim you for his own.

My love always,

Noel

Arriving home first that afternoon, Gavin had noticed the letter among the day's post. The handwriting was unfamiliar to him, of course, but he saw the Australian stamp. He stirred up the coals in the grate and added more and with the room now growing warm and cozy, he opened a bottle of wine, placing it with two glasses on the coffee table. Whatever the news was, he would be there for her. He heard Victoria's footsteps on the stairs and moving quickly, he opened the door to the flat, gathering her in his arms as she reached the landing. "Therre's a letterr frrom Noel, I think, darrlin'---therre on the coffee table."

She hurried over to the couch to throw down her purse and script and shrugging out of her coat, she tore open the envelope. Gavin sat down beside her to pour each of them a glass of wine. From the expression on her face he knew at once what the answer was. "Oh, darling, he's...he's not coming," Victoria whispered, her eyes filling with tears. Mutely she handed him the letter to read for himself, watching as his gaze moved down the page. What a strong face he has, she found herself thinking even now. So many handsome men appear weak. At last Gavin finished reading and looked up at her again, his brown eyes soft with sympathy. "I'm verra sorrry, darrlin', but then ye must have kent Noel's always been in love with ye."

"No–oh, no! We...we...never...never......"

"I didna say that, lass. I said he was in love with ye."

"Gavin, I'm sure you're wrong. He never said....."

"Aye, I'm surre he hid his feelin's verra well."

"But why can't he come to our wedding just the same? Darling, would you write and ask him for me, please?"

"Can ye no see, hinny, the kindest thing we can do is to accept his decision."

"I suppose so," Victoria said slowly after a moment. "But Gavin, do you think after a while he'll be able to accept our marriage? I...I don't want to lose his friendship."

"We'll have to leave that oop to him, darrlin'." He handed her one of the wine glasses.

"I...I feel so terrible about Noel, but I just never cared for him–not in that way. I...I've never loved anyone like that, my darling, until you."

"So then, I am your firrst and only love and ye arre mine," he observed tenderly. They touched glasses and as Victoria sipped her wine, she realized with a stab of guilt that as long as she had Gavin not even her dear old friend's refusal to attend their wedding could hurt her very much or for very long.

Chapter 4

Thinking it better not to disrupt their daughter's routine, Victoria and Andrew had originally decided she should remain in the States until her school there broke for the holidays. But Kate MacAllister informed them that Olivia wasn't sleeping or eating properly and although the little girl's letters and telephone calls remained resolutely cheerful, it was evident she was becoming increasingly anxious. At last all concerned agreed she should return to England as soon as possible and a flight was booked for the first week in December.

The night before Olivia was due to arrive Victoria slept very little and now as they drove onto the grounds of Heathrow, Gavin glanced over to reassure her with a smile. "That wee lass adorres ye, hinny. Ye havna a thing to worrry aboot."

Andrew was already there, sitting near the gate for international arrivals. As he observed them coming toward him across the terminal, he noted with a renewed pang that they were once again hand in hand. "Are we late?" Victoria asked, sitting down beside him and slipping out of her fox fur coat. "The traffic on the motorway was bloody awful!" She was dressed in lavender slacks and a lavender and white striped cashmere jumper and she was so close he could catch the scent of her perfume.

"The plane's not due in for another twenty minutes." He actually managed to sound quite casual.

"Will you gentlemen excuse me then?" She smiled at them both. "I want to check my face."

They watched her walk away in the direction of the ladies' room. "Happiness agrees with her," Andrew remarked after a moment. "I've never seen her look....look lovelier."

Gavin glanced at him sharply. It was as he'd suspected; her former husband was still in love with her. Not that he blamed him or Noel or even that damned preacher for that matter. He allowed a moment of pity for each of the men who had loved Victoria and lost her–but only a moment. "Aye." It was his standard monosyllabic reply whenever he wished to discourage further conversation. He had another classic escape ploy. "Noo, I'm afrraid ye'll have to excuse me as well. I'm all oot o' pipe tobacco." He stood up and hurried away, returning just shortly before Victoria. Andrew noticed he'd brought her a cup of tea from the snack bar and he observed as well her look of loving thanks as she accepted it.

* * *

"Fasten your seat belt, sweetheart," the Pan Am attendant told Olivia. "We're going to be landing at Heathrow in about fifteen minutes."

"Yes, thank you." Obediently she buckled her seat belt, but she continued to lean forward, peering anxiously out the window.

"May I sit with you?"

"Of course," the little girl agreed politely. The whole cabin crew had been especially attentive, but then she supposed they knew who her mother was.

"Did you manage to sleep at all, dear?" the stewardess went on solicitously.

"Not very much, no." Olivia wished the woman would just leave her alone. Two years ago on almost this exact date she had been flying in the opposite direction to someone she barely knew and yet had loved for as long as she could remember. Since that time she had come to feel a part of her mother's life–safe and secure–, but it was three months now since Victoria had returned to England even though she was only supposed to be there for a month to work.

Secretly Olivia had hoped the rumors about Gavin Hamilton were true and that made her feel a little disloyal to Jason, who after all had been kind to her.

She would never forget the terrible day her mother had almost died. They'd called her to the school principal's office and Aunt Kate was there and...and told her. How could Mummy have wanted to leave her? All anyone would say was that everything was going to be all right, but she didn't believe them. Even Victoria's letter, although reassuring, did not entirely allay her fears. Then suddenly her mother had telephoned to tell her that she was marrying Gavin and soon the three of them would all be together. Only first she would be living with her father again for a while. Did Mummy and Gavin feel she'd be in the way?

These as well as many other thoughts had gone round and round in her head all during the short night of an eastbound trans-Atlantic flight and now as the plane circled to come in for a landing, she was still apprehensive and confused. Suddenly Olivia realized the woman had asked her another question. "Excuse me," she said, "I'm afraid I wasn't listening."

"I asked who would be meeting you?"

"Oh...ah...Mummy is...and my Daddy and...and...my...ah...Gavin."

"You mean the Scottish folk singer the newspapers say she's going to marry. Is that true?"

"That's...that's really none of your business." Olivia was rather surprised at her own temerity and she thought how her mother would appreciate the story.

"Well, excuse me!" Highly offended, the stewardess got up and moved to a seat beside another crew member. "Honestly," she whispered, "celebrities' kids are such brats!"

Olivia didn't even care she'd been rude and as the plane settled into its final descent, she crossed every possible combination of fingers and finally she even crossed her arms. If only everything would truly be all right.

* * *

Her mother and father were both there watching eagerly for her to come through the gate, but the only person she saw in that first instant was Gavin, the big, gentle man whom she'd adored from the moment she met him. Nothing could be very wrong as long as he was there and she ran toward him with her arms outstretched. "Welcoom home, bonnie wee lassie!" Grinning broadly, he knelt down opening his own arms to receive her.

She flew into his embrace. "Oh, Gavin! I didn't think I'd ever see you again!"

"It did seem that way, didn't it, darrlin? Lass," he prompted her gently after a minute, "yourr motherr." Torn, Victoria had remained off to one side watching the tender reunion. She couldn't help being a little jealous, but at the same time she was happy that these two special people in her life had accepted each other so readily.

"Oh, Mummy!" Instantly the little girl broke away to throw her arms around her mother. "I'm sorry, but I just saw Gavin and I...."

"It's all right, darling," she reassured her. "He has the same effect on me."

"You really love him, don't you?"

"Yes, sweetheart." Almost at once she'd gone back to her habit of stroking her daughter's hair. "Oh, my darling," she whispered. "I've missed you so."

"Are you all right, Mummy?" Olivia inquired anxiously. "I mean after...after..."

"I know, dearest." Victoria leaned down to kiss her. "I can only imagine what you've gone through. But we'll talk about it all, I promise."

"I...I only want to know one thing for right now, please. It doesn't make any difference, does it? I mean because of Gavin. You still want me with you, don't you?"

"Oh, Olivia!" She leaned down to enfold her daughter in that special world of soft, thick fur scented by her own special fragrance. "I will <u>always</u> want you with me! Nothing could ever change that!" Only then did Victoria remember that Andrew was still standing there waiting patiently–Andrew who over a year and a half ago now had selflessly given her the daughter she in no way deserved. "Sweetheart, your Daddy's here, too, you know."

"That's quite all right," he replied at once, bending to kiss the little girl. "It's a special pleasure for me watching the two of you together."

Victoria smiled at him. "Do you suppose that just possibly we could be friends?"

"I would like to think so, but now why don't we see about getting out of here? I presume you <u>did</u> leave New York with some luggage, princess?"

Finally then the four of them were walking toward the exit–Olivia holding her father's hand, Gavin and Victoria arm in arm. No, the child thought unhappily, this is all wrong. Tears blurred her vision and failing to see the moving walkway, she stumbled and fell. Andrew quickly helped her to her feet again, but then he saw at once that she was crying. "Did you hurt yourself, honey?" She shook her head.

"What is it, luv?" Victoria inquired tenderly.

Olivia looked up at her. She'd been worried her mother would appear different somehow, but she was as beautiful as ever. "Mummy, who...who am I going with now–you and Gavin or...or Daddy?"

"Oh, that's it, is it? Believe me, dearest, staying with your father again <u>is</u> only temporary. And as for right now, you're coming with Gavin and me." At that Olivia smiled, blinking back the tears. "I told you, didn't I," Victoria continued as they finally stepped onto the moving walkway, "that Gavin is on temporary duty with the Scots Guards again as a piping instructor?" The little girl nodded, holding onto her mother's hand now and gazing up at her intently. "Well, he has to work today, but I took the day off so we could spend it together."

They arrived at the exit then to find the sky cap waiting there with the luggage. Gavin went at once to get his car. Andrew bid his daughter an affectionate farewell and taking her suitcases, he as well headed off toward the car park. "Where am I sleeping tonight then, Mummy?" Olivia asked when they were alone.

"You'll be at your father's for about a fortnight, sweetheart. Then Gavin, Martha and you and I will heading up to Scotland for Christmas. The wedding is December 30th and after that Martha will bring you back to your father's until Gavin and I can find a place big enough for the three of us."

"Oh, I'm glad Martha's coming, too!"

"Yes, she's going to be working for us again. You'll like that."

"Who else will be at the wedding, Mummy? Uncle Terry and Uncle Noel?"

Victoria experienced a wave of sadness. "Your Uncle Terry, yes. In fact, he'll be giving me away. But not...not your Uncle Noel. He's on tour in Australia."

"Oh, that's too bad. I was looking forward to seeing him."

"Well, he'll be back eventually and then...then we'll see him." She wished she could be sure about that. "But Felicity and Jamie will be there and...and a whole new family for you to get to know: two aunts and an uncle and a wonderfully dear grandfather and even a great-grandmother."

For a moment Olivia solemnly contemplated all these new relatives, but then another thought occurred to her. "Then who will stand up with you, Mummy? I heard Lisa MacAllister call it that," she explained importantly. "She's standing up with a friend of hers who's getting married."

Victoria had planned to save this special news until later when the two of them would be alone in the flat for a while. But why not now? "Well, darling," she said after a moment, watching her daughter closely, "It's only going to be a small wedding so Gavin and I decided that....."

"Oh, Mummy!" She couldn't stop herself from breaking in. I do so like it when you say, 'Gavin and I'!"

Victoria smiled. "Anyway, luv, Gavin and I decided we'd each have just one special person so he's asked his father and I...I would like very much to have you."

"Me!!!!" she shrieked, jumping up and down. "Me! Out of everybody you want me?"

Just then Gavin pulled his car up to the curb. Olivia had kept her flight bag with her and he got out to put it in the back. "My worrd, wee one, is this all ye brrought? Yourr motherr needs an entirre baggage carr all to herrself!"

Olivia giggled. "Daddy took the rest. Gavin, I'm going to be in the wedding!"

"Aye, lass." He winked at Victoria. "I believe I hearrd soomthin' aboot that."

A short time later Gavin had dropped Victoria and Olivia off at the flat and they climbed the narrow winding stairs to the second floor hand in hand. "Do you and Gavin live here together?" the little girl asked in all innocence while she waited for her mother to find the key in her purse.

"Yes, darling, we do." Victoria unlocked the door and led the way inside. The very least Olivia deserved was honest answers to any questions she might have, while keeping in mind that she was, after all, still a child . "Are you hungry?" she added as they removed their hats and coats.

"No, Mummy. I...I just want to talk."

"All right, my love–come here." Victoria took her hand to bring her over to the couch and they settled down–arms about each other. "Oh, I can't believe you're really here with me. We'll be together from now on–I promise."

"Always and always, Mummy," Olivia affirmed solemnly, hugging her hard. It felt so good being close to her mother again especially after a separation filled with such worry and uncertainty. But there was one question she needed to have answered before any other and at once. She'd asked it of each of the MacAllisters, but only one person's response would truly satisfy her. She swallowed hard and once again her eyes filled with tears. "Mummy, why.... why did you want to....want to...die?" The last word was spoken so softly that Victoria could barely hear it.

She had known this would have to come up eventually. She'd hoped it could be postponed for at least a little while, but it was probably better to bring the difficult subject out on the open and get it over with. "My precious little girl," Victoria said very gently, stroking her daughter's hair. "I hope you didn't ever think it had anything to do with you."

Vainly Olivia tried to control the quivering of her lower lip. "Well, I...I did hear Uncle Ken say that...that you...you would never have done it if you cared about me at all."

"Damn him!" Victoria muttered angrily–more to herself than anyone .

"I...I knew I shouldn't eavesdrop, Mummy, but no one would tell me anything except... except that everything was going to be all right only...only I didn't believe them so I'd...I'd try to listen..."

Victoria took her in her arms again. "Ken was very wrong to say that, darling, but it's ironic really that you could have thought it was because I didn't love you. Because in...in a way it was because I do love you so much."

"Oh, Mummy," she gasped, "don't say that!"

"Just wait now, darling, please and listen carefully. Because I realize that once again I'm asking you to understand a great deal for a little girl....."

"Mummy!" Olivia was indignant. "I'm ten years old!"

"Oh yes, of course. Ten years old is practically ancient. The wisdom of the ages and all that..." In spite of the seriousness of the moment a smile tugged at the corners of the child's mouth. "There, luv." Victoria smiled herself. "That's better."

"But...but oh why....why would you ever do something like that because you love me?"

"I....I guess I felt a lot of people including you would...would be better off without me."

"Mummy, how could you think....."

"Believe me, Olivia, I...I have always been painfully aware of my failings as a mother."

"I....I won't let you say things like that about yourself. I won't! You're the best mother in the whole world!"

"You really love me that much, don't you?" Victoria's voice was choked with tears. "And then, darling, well, no matter how hard I tried, Jason always made me feel so unworthy."

"I knew it. I knew it was his fault more than anything. I never liked him, Mummy. I tried to for your sake, but I just couldn't."

"Whereas...Gavin?"

"Oh, Mummy—Gavin's...Gavin's super. He's....he's...."

"I know you like him, sweetheart–as a chum, but how about as a father?"

"Even better! Did...did he come to see you as soon as you got back to London?"

"Almost immediately, yes."

"It said in the newspapers you were having an affair. What does that mean?"

Victoria blinked once or twice. "Well, darling, you know how you asked me a few moments ago if Gavin and I were living together?"

"Oh, that's what that means, then." The little girl seemed satisfied at least for the moment. "Did....did you love Gavin even then, Mummy?"

"I think I was already in love with him in New York."

"But still you went back to Jason?"

Victoria nodded. "It wasn't until I woke up in hospital and Gavin was there that I realized how I felt about him."

"When did he know?"

"Very soon after I went back to Jason, I guess."

"My, my!" Olivia shook her head. "You were both stupid, weren't you?"

At that Victoria laughed, grateful that something had happened to lighten the mood. "You do feel better then, luv, now that we've talked?"

"Yes, Mummy, only...only you won't ever, ever do anything like that again, will you?"

"No, darling....never again, I promise. Every time I look at you and Gavin I'll be achingly aware of what I nearly threw away."

"Please, why can't I stay here with you? You said it was because it would be too crowded, but it looks to me as if there's plenty of room." Victoria laughed aloud at her daughter's sweet naivete. "What's so funny, Mummy?"

"As a matter of fact, precious, you are."

"I am?" Olivia looked indignant all over again. "Well, I don't see why! My goodness, but I'll be glad when I'm all grown up so I'll stop saying funny things when I don't mean to." But her sputtering little girl fury only made Victoria laugh harder. "Mummy!" At last, however, she began to giggle as well and mother and daughter hugged each other and laughed until they were both weak.

After that they were quiet for a while–their arms still around each other. It was Victoria who finally broke the silence. "You know, as anxious as you must have been about everything, I don't imagine you slept much during the flight."

Olivia sat up very straight. "Oh no, Mummy! Not a nap!"

"My, but we are good at mind reading, aren't we? You mean you're not in the least bit sleepy?"

"Well, maybe just a little, but...."

"That's what I thought. I'll get a pillow and a blanket and you can stretch out right here for a while."

"All right. I suppose so," she agreed reluctantly although when she stopped to think about it, she really was tired. Victoria returned almost at once and settled her daughter down on the couch. "Mummy, will you stay right here?"

"Of course, darling. This will give me a good chance to get some memorization done." She bent to kiss her, smoothing back her hair. "I love you, precious--so very much."

"Me, too," Olivia mumbled, already half-asleep.

Victoria didn't get many lines learned that morning. She kept putting her script down to look at Olivia. Finally she gave up trying to work and instead simply watched her daughter sleep. It was nearly noon by the time the little girl awoke and the rest of the day went by all too quickly. Victoria glanced at her watch as she placed their tea things in the sink. It was nearly four-thirty. She'd promised Andrew they'd be there by dinner time and there was one stop she wanted to make first. She looked down at Olivia who had followed her into the kitchen with the rest of the dishes. "We're going to have to be leaving fairly soon, I'm afraid, sweetheart."

"Oh, Mummy, do we have to?"

Victoria took the other dishes from her to add them to the pile, turning back at once to stroke her daughter's cheek. "I promised your Daddy, luv, and before that I want to take you to the Royal Academy of Dramatic Art where I went to school. There's someone special there I want you to meet–my sister, your Aunt Rebecca."

"I didn't know you had a sister, Mummy!" The child's eyes widened in happy surprise.

"There's a lot you don't know about me, I'm afraid, darling." Briefly Victoria hugged her close again. "But Rebecca's really only my half-sister, you see. She's eight years younger than I am and we didn't grow up together. Actually we'd lost touch until they asked me to come back to the Academy to teach and she turned out to be one of my students. We do have to be going though. I checked and her last class gets out at five."

A moment later then they had their hats and coats on again, going downstairs to hail a taxi. "Does Aunt Rebecca want to be an actress, too, Mummy?" Olivia asked at one point during the ride.

"I suppose she does, darling, since she's at the Academy, but we really haven't talked about it."

"But if she's your sister......."

"She's a lot like I once was, sweetheart, so it's hard to get close to her."

A short while later the taxi turned off Euston Road into Gower Street, coming to a stop in front of RADA. How strange it felt–coming here with her daughter. She took Olivia's hand to lead the way up the few steps into the building, across the small entry hall and through the labyrinth of corridors. "Did it look just like this when you were a student here, Mummy?" the little girl asked excitedly, craning her neck this way and that as they walked along together.

"It hasn't changed much, darling...Oh, here we are." Rebecca's class had indeed just finished– a workshop in audition techniques– and so of course Victoria knew many of the students. Immediately they clustered around her. She introduced Olivia to them all, but then she observed her sister trying to slip around the edge of the group, quite evidently hoping to leave unnoticed. "Oh, Rebecca, don't go–please." Reluctantly the girl stopped and waited while the rest of the class said their good-byes and went along. "I....I especially wanted you to meet your niece," Victoria continued. "This is my daughter, Olivia."

"It's super to meet you, Aunt Rebecca." the little girl said smiling. "I didn't even know I had an aunt until today."

Rebecca nodded coolly. "No, I don't imagine you did." She looked accusingly at Victoria as if to say— see, that shows how much I matter to you. "Is that all you wanted?"

"Well no, actually. I....I also wanted to ask you to come to my wedding. It's on December 30th–at Gavin's family home in Scotland."

"All the way up there–just for one day?"

"I'm sorry, luv. I should have said right off that of course you're invited for Christmas, too. You could drive up with us if you'd like. We'll be leaving on the 20th."

Rebecca hesitated. Her sister was obviously doing this for one reason only–because she felt sorry for her. Well, she didn't need anyone's pity. "I...I already have plans for the holidays."

"I see–well then, come up after that."

"Does he know you're inviting me?"

"If by he, you mean Gavin–naturally we talked over our guest list. Having the wedding in his home, we're limited for space."

"Oh, please come, Aunt Rebecca," Olivia put in.

Clearly Rebecca was feeling cornered again and Victoria knew if she didn't ease off a little now, her sister would certainly refuse the invitation. "Well, you can let me know in a day or so then. Check to see if you're free."

"Yes, I...I will. Th..thank you for asking me." She backed away, turned and fled and in a moment she had disappeared from sight around the corner.

Victoria sighed. "Well, darling, let's go." She put an arm around her daughter's shoulders. "Your father will be expecting you."

"Aunt Rebecca doesn't really have any place to go for Christmas, does she, Mummy?" Olivia asked as they walked slowly along the hallway themselves.

"What makes you think that?"

" 'Cause you said she's just like you used to be so she'd never admit she was lonesome."

Briefly Victoria hugged her closer, resting her cheek against the child's shining brown hair. "You're a very perceptive young lady?"

On the way out they met Peter Harris in the entry hall. "And this must be your daughter," he observed, smiling pleasantly.

"Yes, it is." Despite his friendly demeanor Victoria was immediately uncomfortable. Olivia could stand only so much truth about her mother.

"I'm Peter Harris." He shook hands quite formally with the little girl. "I was your mother's teacher when she was at the Academy."

"Did you know she would be a famous actress some day?"

"Oh, yes." He studied Victoria intently for a moment. "Even then I knew she was special."

"Darling, we have to be going," she said quickly and taking her daughter's hand firmly in hers, she turned away to continue on across the hall toward the front door.

"Glad to have met you, young lady," Peter said. "I hope you'll come again."

"Thank you—I hope so.." Olivia looked back to wave. "He's nice, Mummy," she added when they were outside. "I liked him."

"I'm glad, luv." She smiled to herself. Surprisingly enough, she had to admit that she liked Peter as well. At the corner of Euston Road she hailed another taxi and all too soon they drew up in front of Andrew's. Asking the driver to wait, Victoria followed Olivia up the stairs.

It was Emily who answered the door. "Oh, hello," she said coolly. "Andrew?" She called, turning at once to go back into the kitchen.

Almost immediately he appeared in the archway of the living room. "Thank you for being so prompt, Victoria."

"You're welcome." But she still had her arm around her daughter..

"It's all right." He came forward to place a hand on each of their shoulders. "You should both know by now that you can trust me."

"Yes, we can." On impulse Victoria kissed him lightly on the cheek. "May...may she spend the day with us on Sunday?"

"Of course."

"Thank you so much, Andrew–for everything. Olivia.." She leaned down to hug her. "I'll see you on Sunday then." She hurried away down the stairs before she started to cry. Oh, for a time to come when they wouldn't always have to be saying good-bye!

* * *

Gavin was especially sweet and loving that evening knowing how much Victoria must wish Olivia was there with them and the next morning since they were both free, he suggested an errand he thought would be a particularly pleasant one. "Ye know, lass," he said at breakfast, "we have to be thinkin' aboot pickin' ye oot a weddin' rring. Wouldn't this be a good day forr it?"

"Oh, yes." She smiled at him although something about the way he'd said it struck her as odd. It was a moment or so before she realized he'd said nothing about a ring for himself. "Did....did I understand you correctly just now? You don't wish to have a double ring ceremony?"

Gavin reached across the table now to cover her hand with his. "And what does my wearrin' a rring have to do wi' lovin' ye, darrlin' and wantin' ye forr my verra own?"

"You say you love me and yet you're embarrassed or...or ashamed to wear a ring. What exactly are you planning to do <u>after</u> we're married that you don't want to wear one?"

Immediately he withdrew his hand. "Torri, I've had all o' that. I <u>will</u> <u>be</u> a faithful husband. 'Tis nae necessarry to brrand me in that way."

"So that's what a wedding band is to you–a brand? And yet you expect me to wear one."

"A lass always wearrs a rring."

"And a laddie does not, I suppose. Tell me–I didn't notice when we were up there— does your father wear a wedding ring?"

"Well, aye, but...." Gavin knew he was being backed into a corner.

"Even though your mother's been dead all these years?"

"Aye."

"Then he didn't object to being branded?"

"Torri, if it means sae much to ye...."

"Oh, never mind!" Getting abruptly to her feet, she snatched up her coat and purse.

"Wherre arre ye goin'?" he demanded.

Where was she going? There <u>was</u> no place for her away from this man and she stood there motionless, her eyes filling with tears. "I.....I don't know," she whispered at last.

" 'Tis only a rring, lass," he said gently, "and rring orr no rring, I'll always be therre to love ye and carre forr ye so what arre ye frrettin' aboot ?"

Victoria looked at him–at the tenderness of his expression. "Well, you're right, I suppose, aren't you?" She smiled at him although somewhat tremulously. "So then we might as well go to the jewellery store this morning, don't you think?"

"Arre ye surre, darrlin'?" Gavin stood up as well taking her coat from her and holding it for her to slip into it.

"Yes, yes, I'm sure." She nodded decisively. "If...if you don't want to wear a ring, I shouldn't make you feel as though you have to. Now let's go." She walked quickly from the flat and ran ahead of him down the stairs. For just that moment she'd rather he couldn't see her face.

For a while as they drove across London neither of them spoke–for one of the few times thus far in their relationship ill-at-ease with each other. It was Gavin who finally broke the silence. "Did ye have soomthin' special in mind, darrlin'?" He hoped that he could somehow still make this a happy occasion.

"I thought something in antique gold." Victoria tried to smile at him, but on top of her disappointment she was starting to have misgivings about her choice of jewellers. It had been some time since she'd last been in the establishment of Cranford and Carnovsky, by Royal Appointment Jewellers to Her Majesty, Queen Elizabeth II–just before she left for New York in fact–and suddenly now she found herself remembering its understated elegance–the mahogany paneled walls–the lush carpeting–the discreetly recessed lighting. As they entered the store a short while later and she glimpsed the expression on her future husband's face, she was certain she had indeed made a serious mistake.

Gavin's father had sent him some money from an especially plentiful wool crop and he himself had pawned a second guitar he could do without for a while, but as he looked about at the display cases glittering with gold and gems, he was sure he could never afford a wedding ring worthy of his future wife. Then a small dapper man–the sort he loathed on sight–stood up from the reception desk and approached them. With his pencil thin moustache and wispy beard he reminded Gavin, in fact, of nothing so much as one of his father's goats. Certainly when the little man opened his mouth, rather than uttering sensible words, he would merely bleat.

He liked to be called Baron Carnovsky even though his family had lost the title at the time of the Communist Revolution and he habitually carried a rider's crop–supposedly from his father's days as a Cossack. He would slap it against his thigh as he walked and often he even used it to pick up a bracelet or necklace, extending it in turn to the customer. "Ah, Miss Windsor!" The Baron flourished the crop broadly now, bowing low. "We here at Cranford and Carnovsky were becoming concerned we had displeased you in some way. I assure you, madame, the sapphire and diamond pendant we sold you was of matchless quality!"

Sapphires and diamonds! Gavin very nearly walked out!

"Baron–!" Victoria smiled graciously and for the briefest of seconds she was once again the cosmopolitan lady instantly recognized in any of the smart London shops where she was a regular patron. Then almost at once she recalled the emptiness of those days and in the blink of an eye the moment was gone. "But this is a much more special occasion," she went on quickly. "This is Gavin Hamilton. We're going to be married and we wish to select a wedding ring."

Glancing up at Victoria's tall, virile companion, who must certainly outweigh him by four and a half stone, the Baron experienced a wave of revulsion. How could a woman so utterly exquisite submit to this hulking animal? Ah, but then you could never tell. He'd heard things about her. Perhaps she enjoyed such treatment. And business, after all, was business. He clasped one of the man's hands in both of his. "May I say, sir, you are getting a rare jewel which far outshines anything in my poor establishment." Gavin smiled at the flowery compliment. He agreed Victoria was a rare jewel, but he doubted the man's sincerity. Idly he contemplated the pleasure of picking up the "wee, timrous beastie" by the scruff of his neck and putting him through one of his own display cases. "But come..." The jeweller spun away to move around behind a case containing diamond engagement and wedding rings–drawing open the rear door with the tip of his riding crop.

"Oh no, Baron," Victoria said at once, "I want a simple gold band."

"Ah, but for a lady such as yourself, Miss Windsor," he protested, "it must be diamonds---never anything but diamonds!"

"If 'tis what ye want, Torri," Gavin said softly in her ear, one arm around her shoulders.

"I've already told you, darling," she said firmly, turning a little toward him. "I want an antique gold band."

He drew her away a few steps so that they could talk more privately. "Hinny, if 'tis because ye think I canna afforrd..."

Victoria let him go no further. "Gavin—" She put her hand on his arm, looking steadily up at him. "I.,..I <u>want</u> a gold band–to match the betrothal ring, but....but also because gold is solid and lasting–the way I hope our marriage will be. Do you see now?"

"Is that what a weddin' rring means to ye, lass?" He studied her with great tenderness, thinking she had never looked more beautiful. "Well, then," he continued after this brief, but loving pause, "let's look at the plain gold ones."

"As I was saying, Baron," Victoria finally turned back to him, "I would like something in gold--- more antique in color and design–to match this." She extended her left hand to him to display the Hamilton family ring. Gavin couldn't help noticing the pride in her gesture.

"Exquisite, Miss Windsor–utterly exquisite!" The Baron studied the ring for a moment. Privately he had to admit it was a piece of the richest craftsmanship. Perhaps this Scotsman wasn't quite so common as he'd first appeared. "How old is the ring, Mr. Hamilton?" It was only the second time he'd deigned to address Gavin directly.

"It dates back to the Rrebellion of Forrty-Five."

"I beg your pardon, sir?"

"Charrles Stuarrt's vain attempt to rregain the Brritish thrrone," Gavin explained with what was for him extraordinary patience. "That was in 1745 so the rring's been in my family forr overr two hundrred yearrs."

"I'm afraid my knowledge of British history is most inexcusably limited, but a ring of such fine workmanship–a most valuable piece–and you know I believe I have just the thing–just the thing!" The Baron rubbed his hands together, once again the genial and expansive salesman, and tapping the riding crop on his thigh, he led the way over to another display case. "You are correct as always, Miss Windsor. We must select a wedding ring which will do this beautiful old piece of jewellery full justice."

Gavin was still dubious about the man's sincerity, but he followed Victoria over to the other case, this one filled with gold rings in varying degrees of color and brilliance. The man removed one particular tray and placed it on top of the counter. "I think one of these will be exactly what you're looking for, Miss Windsor," the jeweller hissed, drawing his lips back over his teeth in what passed for him as a smile.

There were many styles ranging from perfectly plain bands to elaborately carved designs and in a variety of widths. What Gavin immediately noticed, however, with a pang of conscience was that all the rings were displayed in pairs: the woman's ring and directly below it in each instance, the man's. He saw again in his mind's eye the well-worn band on his father's left hand and he thought of the wedding ceremony itself–of Victoria placing the ring on his hand–of the significance of their two hands wearing matching rings. Suddenly he was aware she had asked him a question. "Sorrry, lass." Gavin grinned. "I'm afrraid I was lost in my own thoughts."

Victoria looked at him intently. Perhaps the whole business of wedding rings was distasteful to him. "I was asking," she said again, "if you saw something you especially liked?"

He brought his attention back to the tray of rings in front of them and for a minute or so after that they were both silent studying the rings–unaware that by now several of the other customers were regarding them with open interest. It was Gavin who actually first noticed the particular design: an apparent interweaving of two differently textured bands of gold, culminating in an elaborate knot at the top of the ring. "Look at that one, Torri." He pointed.

"Oh, yes," she breathed. She smiled up at the Baron. "May...may I see that one, please?"

"We call this design the Lover's Knot, Miss Windsor," he explained as he removed the ring from the tray. "May I?" he inquired.

"Yes....please." She had been gazing wistfully at the man's ring, but after a moment she slipped off the betrothal ring and giving it to Gavin to hold, she allowed Baron Carnovsky to slip the gold band onto the third finger of her left hand.

"A Loverr's Knot–hm?" Gavin took her hand away from the jeweller with a faintly possessive air as if to say–she belongs to me and this hand is part of the package. For several seconds he studied the ring with an unnerving absorption.

"Do you like it, darling?" Victoria asked at last.

He raised his eyes to look at her face then and he bent to give her a quick kiss. "Aye, lass, I do. The two bands arre like ourr lives, arren't they–meetin' and becoomin' one–joined forreverr by the loverr's knot." She had never known him to sound so thoughtful and it was a moment before his gaze left her and he turned back to the little jeweller. "Aye, we both like that one. Could I...ah....see the man's rring noo?"

Victoria drew in her breath. "Gavin, I...I thought you...you felt that....."

"Aye, lass. I ken what I said. I was wrrong."

The Baron couldn't imagine what was meant by all of this, but he took the man's ring out of the tray and slipped it in place. Gavin took only the briefest of glances at it. "Aye." He nodded, evidently satisfied. "Aye."

Victoria reached over to touch him on the arm. "Darling, are....are you sure?" Inadvertently she'd brought her left hand over so that it lay close to his. They looked at the matching rings and then they looked at each other.

"Aye, lass," he whispered. "Verra surre."

They left a deposit on the two rings. Hers needed to be sized and both were to be engraved with their initials and the date of the ceremony. They would be ready in about a week. At last they were outside again–walking along hand in hand. "Gavin," Victoria said after a while, "what...what changed your mind?"

He thought about it briefly before replying. "Torri, I...I was daft to say a man's weddin' rring is a brrand. "Tis a symbol of two people's commitment to each otherr—just as the woman's is."

"Do you know you are the most wonderful man in the entire world," she observed tenderly.

"In the entirre worrld, hm?" He cocked his head to look down at her out of the corner of one eye.

"And I suppose you wholeheartedly agree with that opinion?"

"Aye, lass, I do," he replied, but then he gave her a broad wink. They both began to laugh with such utter abandon that several people passing them on the street stopped to look back at them. <u>No</u> <u>one</u> could be <u>that</u> happy.

* * *

The remainder of the time until they were to leave for Scotland passed quickly. Only two incidents stood out in Victoria's mind–perhaps because each demonstrated just how much she'd changed. The first was profoundly moving; the other merely amusing.

She was alone in the faculty lounge at RADA when a knock came at the door. It was her sister. "Oh, how nice!" Victoria was pleased. This was the first time Rebecca had sought her out. "How about a cup of tea? I was just about to make one for myself. Gavin says I probably have tea in my veins instead of blood."

The girl didn't even smile. "No, thank you. I can't stay. I just came to tell you I won't be able to be at your wedding."

"Oh, 'Becca, why not?" Inadvertently she'd used her sister's childish nickname.

"Don't call me that! I hate that silly name!"

"I understand," Victoria said at once. "I've never liked being called Vicki either."

"And I wish you'd stop comparing us! I've already told you my childhood was very happy! Mother and I are <u>still</u> terribly close."

"I simply can't believe she could have changed that much."

"It was only you she didn't like. She....she told me I....I was her favorite."

"I'm glad—I really am–if that's true, but I suspect it isn't."

"You're just jealous!"

"Maybe that's it." Perhaps I can turn this around, Victoria thought–let her feel I need her. "I...I've never known what it was like, you see, to have a family. I...I've often wondered about you and now that we've found each other...."

"You're lying!" her sister blurted out. "I bet you don't even remember the last time we saw each other."

"Of course I do. I was twelve, I think, so you must have been about....."

"No– a long time after that. You see—you don't remember!"

"I'm afraid I don't then, Rebecca. Why....why don't we sit down together and you can tell me about it?"

"No....no, I don't want to sit down." Instead the girl began to pace about the small room, twisting the ring on her little finger around and around. Well, Victoria deserved to be told, after all, didn't she? "It...it was the big Christmas party you gave at the Claridge Hotel. I....I was in the crowd outside. You were all dressed in white fur like...like a queen or something."

Waves of guilt flooded over Victoria. That night had seen the beginning of her perverted relationship with Julian Christopher and all the time her own sister was alone outside in the cold and darkness needing her. "Oh, darling....darling, I am so very sorry." She came over to her sister taking both her hands in both of hers. "There...there were so many people and you were only a small child the last time I'd seen you. But...but we...we've found each other now and it's not too late for us."

Rebecca glanced down at her sister's hands still holding hers. "I want to...want to believe that," she whispered. "I...I always hoped I would see you again some day—that I could make you love me."

"But you see you don't have to <u>make</u> <u>me</u> love you. I already do. Dearest, I want so much for you to be at my wedding. Otherwise Olivia will by my only family there. Please come."

Their eyes met. It was the feature most alike in them although her sister's were more hazel in tint. Rebecca hesitated...wanting terribly to belong <u>somewhere</u>. "I....I'm sorry," she said after a moment. "I can't. I just can't."

"All right, luv." Victoria knew it could only do their relationship more harm if she pushed the matter further. Briefly she hugged her sister and then let her go. "We'll see you when we get back then. We'll be having a party at the coffee house where Gavin's working. Perhaps you could come to that."

Rebecca merely submitted to the embrace, making no move to return it. "All right," she murmured. She left the room without looking back.

* * *

Victoria wanted very much to see Margot Fonteyn and Rudolf Nureyev dance Prokofiev's *Romeo and Juliet* at the Royal Ballet. The company would be away on tour by the time they returned to London. Gavin had never been to a ballet and it took some coaxing on her part, but he finally agreed to accompany her. No sooner had the curtain gone up, however, than she knew she was in for a difficult time. Several male dancers made their initial appearance on stage and she heard the by now familiar burr close to her ear. "My worrd, Torri!" And only a moment or so later–"I dinna think I can let ye watch this, darrlin'. 'Tis indecent!"

"Gavin, ssh!" She attempted weakly to silence him.

But just a short while after that—"Aye, I see noo why Juliet wants the lad. She kens verra well what she'll be gettin'."

"Gavin, please," she hissed under her breath. As it was, they were the center of attention.

"Ye must admit it, lass. He might as well be as naked as a wee bairrn."

"He is most definitely <u>not</u> a wee bairn!"

The sophisticated London balletomanes glared at them. Some people had no respect for culture.

"Would ye like a drrink, Torri?" Gavin asked as they came out into the lobby at the interval.

"Yes, I would, I think. I've laughed so much, I'm parched. I thought *Romeo and Juliet* was supposed to be a tragedy."

He grinned. "So then, what would ye be havin'?"

"A...ah..champagne cocktail, I think, darling." He made a face at her selection, but then with a quick kiss he left her there to make his way across to the bar. She noted with amusement the many longing female glances he attracted as he moved through the crowd.

But then all at once an unmistakable voice boomed out from the other direction. "Victoria, my dear, <u>dear</u> girl!" She turned around to see Basil Fitzhugh coming toward her, the crowd opening before him much as God must have parted the Red Sea for the Israelites. In full evening dress, a pince-nez hanging around his neck on a gold chain, he held a goblet of champagne in one bejeweled hand. It was hard to imagine she could ever have belonged in his world. But that's just it, isn't it, she thought with a slight smile in the seconds just before Basil reached her. I didn't, did I? "Ah, my dear! He raised her hand to his lips. "But...to divorce the Pope in that way... sacrilege!"

"What?" For a moment Victoria was confused. "Oh–you mean Jason?" She laughed. "Different religion, I'm afraid."

"Doesn't matter," he affirmed solemnly. "Respect for the cloth and all that."

"Basil, it <u>is</u> good to see you again. How have you been?"

"Never better! But my dear, if I were you, I would take the advice of a friend and sack that agent of yours! I sent him a copy of my new play weeks ago and inconceivable as it may seem, he has entirely ignored me."

"I...I've been ill, you know. And then I'm currently doing the BBC series. Also I...I'm getting married again as soon as my divorce is final."

"I'd heard that! Really, Victoria, wasn't life less complicated when you simply took a new lover? All this beastly court business must be a bloody nuisance!" He waited beaming, anticipating some piece of her clever repartee. There was no one with whom he enjoyed a battle of wits more than this beautiful woman.

"It's....it's not like that."

"I beg your pardon?" For a moment he thought her humor was too subtle even for him.

"I love Gavin. I want to be his wife."

"But, my dear, how Victorian of you!"

In spite of herself the corners of her mouth twitched. "Basil–what would you ever do if my name were...ah....Francesca, for example?"

"But my dear, that's not even a challenge. I would simply have said how Franciscan of you."

"Come now, that doesn't even make sense."

"Brilliant humor doesn't have to make sense, my dear Victoria, and speaking of that..."

"Which—humor or not making sense?"

"Both—as a matter of fact–now that I think about it. Please tell me you're not actually marrying a Scotsman."

"Yes, Basil, I am–Gavin Hamilton. He'll be back from the bar any second. I want you to meet him."

"But you <u>can't</u> be serious! They're still living in caves up there– the whole bloody lot of them!"

"Now you know that's not true. And please don't make unkind remarks about someone I love very much."

"My God, Victoria–you've gone maudlin on me and worse you've lost your sense of humor!"

"Torri, hinny." Gavin had come up to them unnoticed. "I'm sorrry it took sae long."

"That's all right." She hesitated briefly. What would happen now? "Gavin–this is Basil Fitzhugh. He wrote that play I was in–*Once More–Forever.* Basil, this is Gavin Hamilton, my...my fiancé."

Basil wasn't accustomed to meeting people who had to be <u>told</u> who he was. It was all the proof he required that Victoria's future husband was indeed a savage. As for Gavin, he thought how much he'd enjoy taking this silly fop on a three day hike in the Highlands–not that he'd even last out the first day. He had a vivid mental picture of Basil Fitzhugh–still in full formal attire, of course–toiling up and down the mountains of northern Scotland.

"Are you enjoying the ballet...ah...what was your name again, my dear sir?" Basil placed the pince-nez on his nose tipping his head back to study the other man. The pince-nez incidentally had clear glass lenses; Basil carried it purely for effect.

"Gavin Hamilton." But as he himself spoke the name now, it had the ring of a battle cry.

"Most unusual first name, my good fellow."

" 'Tis Gaelic."

"Oh—<u>Gaelic</u>." Basil nodded as if in understanding. "One of the primitive tribes that lived up there somewhere, I believe." Off came the pince-nez again to be waved airily over his head indicating the general direction of north.

" 'Twas <u>nae a trrrribe</u>!" Victoria couldn't help smiling. You could always judge Gavin's mood by the thickness of his brogue. "But then I've neverr known an Englishman who wasna ignorrant."

Luckily at this point the lights blinked to signal the end of the interval and they started back toward their seats. The whole incident had been more amusing than upsetting, but Victoria was relieved to have the fencing match curtailed before either of the combatants had actually drawn blood. "Basil," she said quickly, "we'll be having a party here in London sometime in January for those people who aren't coming up to the wedding in Scotland. I hope you'll be able to be there."

"The wedding's in Scotland!" he exclaimed feigning horror. "What's he planning to do, my dear girl? Throw you over his saddle and carry you off?"

"No, sirr. We rreserrve that trreatment forr Englishmen–just beforre we rroast them on a spit forr ourr supperr." With that Gavin placed a firm hand at Victoria's waist to draw her away before the other man could get off a parting shot. When they were settled in their seats again, he glanced over at her and discovered she was laughing–her head down with her program hiding her face from the people around them. "What's sae funny?" It seemed terribly important to him somehow to learn whether it was he or Basil who was the object of her amusement.

She looked up at him then and smiled affectionately. "Oh, I was just picturing Basil roasting on a spit."

Chapter 5

It seemed to Victoria as though each of the phases of her life could best be typified by the Christmases. There had been the lonely ones of her childhood spent primarily at school; the early years in London when she'd tried to forget it even was Christmas; the elegant celebrations–that party at the Claridge Hotel where two-thirds of her guests were total strangers---and finally the holiday in New York with Olivia when her happiness had truly begun. But that first Christmas with the Hamilton family shone even above that–each moment like one of the shining ornaments hung on the enormous tree which dominated the warm, homey living room.

They arrived in Glengowrie three days before the holiday. Victoria couldn't help but smile remembering how nervous she'd been on her first visit just two months before. Now her feeling of homecoming was as strong as Gavin's and as they passed through the village, it was she who exclaimed over familiar landmarks pointing them out to her daughter and Martha.

As they finally came to a stop in the usual spot in front of the barn, Gavin's father was just shutting the gate at the bottom of the lane which led to the upper pastures where several large stone sheep cotes in the lee of the mountain sheltered the flocks from the winter gales. Immediately Victoria jumped out of the car, running to meet him. "Dearr lassie!" He embraced her and then held her back at arms' length to study her with great affection. " 'Tis the beginnin' of a verra happy time forr ye, I think."

"Oh yes, Dad." She came up on tiptoe to kiss him on the cheek. By then Gavin had come over to them. Father and son shared their customary bear hug.

Olivia, meanwhile, had scrambled excitedly out of the back seat, but now she stood off to one side, suddenly unsure where she fit into this new life of her mother's. Noticing her, Gavin immediately brought her over to join them. "So, Dad, ye can finally stop complainin' noo that I've neverr gi'en ye any grrandchildrren."

"Olivia, is it?" Niall inquired, bending down to look at her more closely.

"Yes, sir." At once the little girl felt reassured. No one who so closely resembled her adored Gavin could be anything but nice.

"Not sirr, wee lass." He held up an admonishing finger. "Grranddad, if ye would. And ye'rre as bonnie as yourr dearr motherr."

She smiled up at him. "Granddad, do you really have lots of animals?"

"That I do. And beforre ye go to bed tonight, I'll show ye soom o' them."

Victoria and Gavin watched fondly as the two became acquainted. "And this is Martha Kendall, Dad," she put in after a moment,–"an old and dear friend."

"Mrs. Kendall," Niall extended his hand to her, "welcoom."

Martha smiled in return. "Mr. Hamilton, you and your son have made Miss Windsor so happy. I'm very grateful."

" 'Tis easy to love the lassie," he replied slipping an arm around Victoria's shoulders.

"Oh, Dad!" She responded by putting her arm around his waist, nestling briefly against him.

"Well, coom along noo," Niall said at last. "And let's get ye all settled beforre tea." With his arm still around Victoria he turned to lead the way along the path to the house. Olivia followed hand in hand with Gavin and Martha. "We've put the wee one in a rroom wi' Fiona and Meghan," he explained as they walked. "We thought that would help herr get acquainted wi' herr new aunts. And wi' Fiona movin' into Meghan's rroom Mrs. Kendall can have herr rroom."

"We're certainly managing to disrupt things for you, aren't we?"

"Arre ye forrgettin'–'tis my son gettin' marrried...finally," he added after the briefest of pauses rolling his eyes. Victoria laughed merrily.

"What arre ye doin', Dad?" Gavin called out from behind them. "Tellin' morre atrrocious lies aboot me?"

"He doesn't have to tell me any lies, darling," Victoria flung back at him over her shoulder. "The truth is quite atrocious enough."

* * *

The very next morning an expedition set out from the Hamilton home: their vitally important mission the selection of the family Christmas tree, their means of transport one of the haywagons converted into a sleigh to make it easier to get about in the depths of a Highland winter. Victoria sat between Gavin and his father on the high front seat while Meghan, Fiona and Olivia nestled under the deep hay behind them. Meghan tried not to look at Victoria sitting so close to her brother her hand through his arm, but she found her eyes continually drawn there.

The air was cold–the sky leaden gray and heavy with more snow–and Victoria was very appreciative of Niall's advance Christmas present–a suede jacket with matching hat and mittens all lined with fleece from his own sheep. "I...I love my outfit, Dad," she said at one point. "Thank you. It...it was so thoughtful of you."

" 'Twas naethin, dearrie," he replied. "My Mum had your measurrements forr the weddin' drress, ye see."

"I know, but....."

Gavin put his hand over hers where it lay on his arm, stopping her. " 'Twill take the lass a bit morre time, Dad, to ken what it means to be loved."

"Aye." His father smiled warmly. "But then we Scots arre a verra patient people."

Finally they all got down from the sleigh and leaving the two Clydesdale horses with their noses contentedly immersed in bags of oats, they tramped further into the woods. Almost at once the group split up--Olivia going with Fiona; Meghan with her father and of course Gavin and Victoria. Everyone could hear snatches of the other conversations, but the snow-covered branches muffled the sound, making each couple feel they were, in fact, alone in the woods.

"Still nae verra happy, arre ye?" Niall inquired of his daughter as they trudged through the snow.

Meghan shook her head. "Oh, Dad! Wi' the weddin' only a week away, it...it even spoils Chrristmas! I knew Gavin would marrry eventually, but I always thought she'd be Scots."

"No wife he chose would have suited ye, darrlin'. Oh, he could dally wi' this gurrl orr that as long as he belonged to no one. But take carre, Meghan. If ye canna accept his lass, ye may lose Gavin altogetherr."

"But I've....I've rread aboot her, Dad. 'Tis bad enough she's been marrried twice beforre, but I don't know how many men......"

"Ye will say no morre, do ye hearr me? We will accept Torri as we find herr. Herr past is none of ourr concerrn."

"Well, I'm goin' to wait in the sleigh. This is all forr herr anyway!" Meghan whirled about to run back through the trees toward the road, half-falling twice in the heavy snow.

"It's so wonderful, Aunt Fiona," Olivia confided as they walked along together in search of that one special tree.

"What is, hinny?"

"Not only to get Gavin for a father, but two aunts and a grandfather and a great-grandmother. Besides–I....I've never seen Mummy this happy."

"Well, I'll tell you something. I've neverr seen my brrotherr sae happy eitherr."

"Oh, look! " the little girl whispered all at once.

Victoria and Gavin were standing only a short distance away through the trees. "Oh, darling," she was saying in a hushed voice, "it's...it's like another world–all clean and white. Snow always gets dirty so soon in London."

"Ye have to admit, lass, 'tis a dirrty city." He grinned down at her, but then almost immediately he grew serious. By now Victoria was accustomed to his lightning fast changes of mood. "But I don't rreally feel like jokin' rright noo, darrlin'. What I do want is just to hold ye forr a wee bit." She came willingly into his arms.

"If we sneak arroond this way, Olivia," Fiona whispered, "they'll neverr see us."

"What are we going to do?" The child's eyes were wide with excitement.

"Shake that brranch they'rre standin' underr, of courrse. Coom noo."

The next thing the couple knew a deluge of snow came down on them out of nowhere. "What?!" Gavin shouted, looking around for the culprit. Then he spotted his sister and Olivia, both of them shaking with laughter. "So then, Torri, are we goin' to stand forr such trreatment?"

"Certainly not!"

A free-for-all snowball fight erupted, accompanied by shrieks of merriment, and by the time Niall joined them they were covered with snow. When at last they arrived home with the tree, Granny pretended to grumble about "foolish bairrnies who neverr grrew oop" and " 'twould nae be herr fault if they all caught theirr deaths!" Only Meghan did not join in the fun.

* * *

The following day, Christmas Eve, was spent in final preparations for the holiday. The tree was set up in its traditional place in front of the double living room windows from where the lights could be seen for miles. When Gavin was a little boy, the decorations had all been homemade, but gradually much to his grandmother's disgust these were replaced by store-bought ornaments and electric lights. They all worked to string ropes of evergreen and holly about the room and Fiona used more of the greenery together with pine cones and red candles to make up the dining table centerpiece. The special Christmas cloth was Royal Stuart tartan shot through with gold thread and the table itself had been pulled out to its full length, the two leaves added in the middle converting its customary circle into the larger oval. Rhuaridh and his family would be coming making twelve in all for holiday high tea. Finally Gavin and his father carried in the yule log, placing it in the fireplace over the fragment of last year's log which would be used later to light it.

Victoria came downstairs about five-thirty dressed for the evening meal in a high-necked, ruffled white blouse and full-length red and green brocade skirt, her hair piled high on her head in a gleaming chignon. Except for the fire the tree lights were at the moment the only illumination in the room and at the bottom step she was drawn to stop and look at the scene. All at once the picture blurred as her eyes filled with tears. She wasn't even aware Gavin had come down the stairs behind her until she felt his hands on her shoulders. "Oh....darling." Momentarily startled, she glanced up at him.

He came around her to stand below her on the floor. "What noo! Grreetin', lass?"

"Oh, these are happy tears. Everything looks just the way a home should look on Christmas Eve. I...I've never seen anything so beautiful!"

"No, lass–this room has ne'err seen trrue beauty until tonight."

"Oh, Gavin." Victoria's tears were coming faster now and slipping her arms around his neck, she buried her head against his shoulder.

He put his arms around her waist and lifted her easily to the floor. "Oh, lassie, lassie," he crooned, "how did I everr live wi'oot ye, hm?" She raised a tear-stained face to him and he was just bending to kiss her when the doorbell rang.

"Please," she whispered, "let me go."

"Sick of me alrready?" he teased.

"Oh, darling, of course not, but that must be your brother and now I have to fix my face before....before...."

"Aye, lass–go on wi' ye noo. But don't take too long." He released her, but continued to stand there as she ran lightly up the stairs. Only in fact when the sound of her footsteps had faded away in the upstairs hall, did he finally turn and walk across the room. He knew only too well how his brother must feel about his marrying an Englishwoman. At last with a sigh he turned the knob and opened the door.

"Uncle Gavin!" His seven year old niece, Maurya, flew across the threshold into his arms. "Uncle Gavin!" David was not far behind his younger sister and was rewarded with a hug as well. Even Rhuaridh's children secretly preferred their uncle.

"Hello, Clairre." Gavin bent to kiss her sister-in-law on the cheek. A small, unassuming appearing woman, she wore her shoulder length chestnut hair in a simple pageboy style and her eyes were a washed-out shade of blue. Nothing better illustrated the difference between the brothers than the women they had chosen to marry.

Rhuaridh himself was the last to enter, the brothers shaking hands cordially enough. Although in fact only an inch or so shorter than Gavin, for some reason he usually impressed people as a much smaller man. Perhaps it was just that he seemed to blend into his surroundings–his eyes behind rimless glasses more hazel in tint, his brown hair only slightly tinged with auburn. It was rather like placing a wren next to a cardinal.

But this wasn't the main reason that ever since Rhuaridh could remember, he had resented his older brother. Although he'd never been able to understand why, people always liked him better. Even their teachers openly favored Gavin despite the fact that he'd been an irrepressible cut-up. Rhuaridh was a teacher himself now and whenever he spoke with one of his colleagues, they invariably inquired after his brother. And now Gavin was to take an English wife. Only his affection for the rest of his family brought him here tonight.

"Wherre is she, Uncle Gavin?" Maurya asked eagerly.

"Wherre's who, lassie?" he replied, bending down to tweak her button nose. "How did ye everr get a wee thing like that wi' a Hamilton forr a fatherr?" She giggled, bringing her hand up to feel her own nose. "Aye, 'tis still therre." He winked at her. "I've morre than enough o' my own."

"But wherre <u>is</u> she, Uncle Gavin? The grrand English lady ye'rre goin' to marrry?"

He straightened up then, eyeing his brother significantly. "She'll be doon in a bit, Maurrya. But in the meantime yourr grreat-grranny's in the kitchen and she's made those gingerr biscuits ye fancy." With the two children gone an uncomfortable silence filled the room broken only when Victoria came back downstairs. Gavin hurried to meet her, taking her hand to lead her into the room. "Torri, darrlin', this is my brrotherr, Rhuarridh, and his wife, Clairre."

The prospect of meeting this famous woman had terrified Claire. Now she noted the clamminess of the actress' hand, felt it tremble in hers and she observed that Victoria's smile as well, though genuine, was noticeably shaky. My goodness, Claire thought in amazement, she's as nervous as I am. As for Rhuaridh, he found himself staring. He'd heard she was beautiful; he hadn't realized how beautiful and this only served to anger him further. Of course his brother would be one to choose purely on the basis of physical attraction.

"Rrhuarridh..Clairre." Fiona came out of the kitchen just then to hug and kiss her brother and sister-in-law.

Following on her heels were Maurya and David. The little girl immediately ran up to Gavin and Victoria, her eyes shining with excitement, while her brother at the advanced and dignified age of nine stood back and watched. "Oh, Uncle Gavin," she breathed, "she looks like a prrincess!"

"Maurrya!" Rhuaridh said sharply, "behave yourrself!"

At once she stepped back, her eyes brimming with hurt tears.

" 'Tis all rright, wee one," Gavin assured her.

"I would ask that ye no interrferre in the rraisin' of my childrren," his brother stated coldly.

Luckily at that moment Niall Hamilton came in from his evening chores, accompanied by Olivia. Her soon-to-be grandfather was an incredible person in her eyes and as much as her mother would allow, she trailed after him. "Hello, laddie." Niall greeted his second son with a warm smile although Victoria couldn't help noticing they merely shook hands. But then probably Rhuaridh wasn't the demonstrative type. "Clairre...Maurrya...David." Niall did hug and kiss his daughter-in-law as well as his two grandchildren.

"Well, therre ye arre at last." Mary Hamilton bustled into the room. "The kettle's aboot to boil so ye can all sit yourrselves doon."

Christmas Eve in the Hamilton home, as was the Scottish custom, was even more festive than the day itself and the table was laden with all sorts of special delicacies: oatcakes, Dundee cake, Balmoral fruit cake, Inverness gingerbread in addition to the regular teatime fare. Niall presided over the seating arrangements. After himself, going counter-clockwise around the table, were Victoria, Gavin, Fiona, his mother, Claire, Maurya, David, Olivia, Meghan, Rhuaridh and Martha Kendall. For a while there was the business of passing food and then the table broke up into several separate conversations.

"What do ye think o' herr?" Rhuaridh inquired in a low voice of Meghan, aware that Victoria's friend was sitting on his other side.

At once his sister's eyes filled with tears. "I just hate herr. Look how she's got even Dad dotin' on herr."

Maurya, meanwhile, glanced surreptitiously across the table to make sure her father wasn't watching. "Mummy," she whispered, "why did Daddy get so angrry wi' me? She <u>does</u> look like a prrincess, don't ye think so?"

"Aye, hinny, I do," Claire replied,

Not a word spoken in Granny's immediate vicinity escaped her–no one could say the old lady was getting deaf–and she had, of course, overheard the exchange. "Will his feelin's everr change, do ye think, dearrie?" she asked.

Sighing, Claire turned to her husband's grandmother and shook her head. " 'Tis even worrse, I think, than when Gavin left to join the Guarrds in Lundon."

" 'Twill be differrent when he gets to know herr. Even <u>I</u> was wee bit dootful-- just at firrst, mind ye."

"A <u>wee</u> bit dootful?" Fiona put in laughingly from the other side of her grandmother. "Ye should have hearrd herr, Clairre. Torri was an ootlanderr and nae to be trrusted. Wasn't that what ye said, Grranny?"

"Be off wi' ye. I said no such thing!" Mary Hamilton hotly denied the accusation. "Torri's a dearr one and 'tis grrand to see Gavin in love that way. He's fairr daft aboot herr."

"What was that, Grranny?" Now it was Gavin who'd overheard. "Ye'rre not tellin' morre storries aboot me, arre ye?"

"Of courrse not. I've got betterr things to talk aboot than a fashious gowk such as yourrself."

"What did she call you?" Victoria rested her hand on his arm as she spoke.

" 'Tis naethin' ye'd carre to hearr, darrlin'," he assured her.

"I'll tell ye, Torri," Fiona offered gleefully. "She called him a...ah...'trroublesoom fool'. Would ye say that was accurrate, big brrotherr?"

"The trranslation is, aye," Gavin replied, grinning himself. "But cerrtainly not the descrription. Ye dinna think I'm a trroublesome fool, do ye, lass?" he said to Victoria. She pretended to think about it, her eyes sparkling with mischief, and everyone from Niall on Victoria's left all the way around the table to Claire burst into laughter. Gavin tried hard to look terribly aggrieved at such treatment, but finally even he had to join in the merriment.

Meghan and Rhuaridh only glared at Victoria with increased dislike. She had no right to be the center of attention like this. "We mustna frret ourrselves though, " her brother reassured her. "In the long rrun 'twill coom to naught, I'm surre."

"David," Olivia asked, "why does your father hate my mother so much?"

"Because she's English," he replied as though the answer should be obvious. "All Scots arre supposed to hate the English. They'rre ourr enemies."

"I'm English, too," she retorted. "Does that mean you hate me?"

"Aye, but then I don't like gurrls verra much anyway."

And so the conversation went around and around the table. And in spite of Rhuaridh's evident disapproval of Victoria the evening was a pleasant one.

Except for Grranny and Meghan, who volunteered to stay home to keep her grandmother company, they all left about eleven o'clock to travel by sleigh into the village for the midnight service. It was a still, cold night, the sky thick with stars as it can only be where there are no manmade lights to detract from their brilliance. The temperature was below zero, but all bundled up and buried under the hay, they were warm and cozy. Victoria was even warmer than most because Gavin had both arms around her. "Happy, darrlin'?" he asked at one point, nuzzling his cold nose against the sweet, warm spot behind her ear. She nodded, turning to look at him. Their eyes met and they kissed, a long, tender kiss–thinking that in the darkness no one would see them.

Rhuaridh did–"Disgusting!" he muttered to Claire who was sitting next to him. His wife made no reply. There were times she wished her husband were more like his brother.

* * *

Christmas Day itself was comparatively quiet and uneventful, but no less happy because of it. Gifts were exchanged, followed by a sleigh ride and several highly hilarious games of charades. A second and equally festive high tea concluded with the making of popcorn balls in front of the fire and finally a carol sing with Gavin accompanying them on his guitar. And Rhuaridh, Claire and their children were with her family.

The following day Fiona and Victoria went with Granny into her bedroom to begin to put the finishing touches to the wedding gown. Because of the holiday this was this first time Victoria would see it and she was perched expectantly on the edge of the bed, her face alight with anticipation. Mary glanced anxiously at her granddaughter as she went to take the dress from her wardrobe. More than once as they worked on it together, she'd asked if Tori would think it "grrand enough". "Ye have to close yourr eyes, ye know, lass," she directed now, "until I say ye can look."

Obediently she shut her eyes, "Only please hurry! I can hardly wait!" Fiona took advantage of the moment to study her future sister-in-law: the long, thick eyelashes, the finely molded face and graceful neck. She is so beautiful, she thought, her admiration untinged with jealousy. But the best part is that she seems unaware of it.

"All rright noo," Granny said after what had seemed like forever and Victoria opened her eyes. The ankle-length gown was of a pale, ivory crepe with ruffles edging the high neck as well as the bottom of the full-length sleeves and skirt. But it was the trim, a last minute inspiration on Granny's part, which was the crowning touch. Around the high neck, at the waist and just above each of the ruffles was woven a narrow blue satin ribbon.

"Oh...oh, it's perfect!" Victoria jumped up to hug the dear, little lady. "Exactly how I pictured it–only much, much more beautiful! Thank you! Thank you!" Mary Hamilton beamed. "And..and to think you...you both made it for me." Her eyes filled with tears.

"Ye mustna grreet, hinny," Granny admonished her. "A brride should be naethin' but happy. Noo drry those bonny grreen eyes orr ye'll be gettin' wee spots on the materrial."

A few minutes later with dry and shining eyes Victoria stood with her arms raised while Gavin's sister slipped the cloud of ivory crepe over her head. Putting her hands through the sleeves, finally she turned around to be zipped up the back. "We'll harrdly have to touch it!" Fiona exclaimed, "except perrhaps to take in the waist a bit and rraise the darrts herre at yourr brreasts. Oh, how I wish I had yourr figurre!"

"Och, she's too thin!" Just then a knock came at the door. "Aye?" It was Mary's no-nonsense tone of voice.

"Can I coom in, Grranny?" Of course it was Gavin.

" 'Tis that botherrsoom jo o' yourrs!" she observed to Victoria.

"Ah, Torri," he crooned, "tell them ye want me to see it, too."

"She'll do no such thing, Gavin Hamilton," Fiona stated firmly. " 'Tis bad luck forr ye to see herr in the drress beforre the weddin'."

"Sorry, darling." He could tell by Victoria's voice that she was smiling.

"Well, ye do ken we'rre goin' to the Rregistrry today?" After all, wasn't it his wedding as well?

The old lady nudged Victoria and winked. "And ye ken ye'll neverr get too big forr me to take my brroom to ye. Noo get along wi' ye."

"Aye, Grranny." Minding his grandmother was a difficult habit to break and he moved away from the door. Relentlessly the maddening sound of feminine laughter followed after him. "Daft lassies!" he muttered.

"Should I wear something on my head?" Victoria asked a short while later. She was standing on a low stool so that her future sister-in-law could pin up the skirt preparatory to hemming it.

"Well, I did have an idea?"

"Oh, what? Tell me!" Victoria whirled about to crouch down on the stool so that they were at eye level.

She laughed. "I canna believe I was everr afrraid ye'd be too grrand and elegant for all of us." Laughing, too, Victoria hugged her. "But if ye dinna stand still," Fiona went on returning the hug, "I'll stick ye wi' a pin and besides Gavin is waiting impatiently to take ye forr that license."

The other woman stood up again. "What was your idea?"

"Oh—aye–in the picturre wherre I found this dress, the gurrl had a small cap on the back of herr head."

"You mean like a Juliet cap?"

"Aye, well I thought it would look bonny with a bow of the blue ribbon in the back with long strreamerrs–especially wi' yourr hairr held back and hangin' loose."

"Oh, that would be perfect! I...I am going to have a drape of the tartan, though, aren't I... or....or isn't that allowed?" she added anxiously.

"Why wouldn't it be?"

"I....I thought perhaps since I'm...I'm not Scottish that...."

"Dinna be daft! Of courrse ye'll have a plaid, but Dad has that forr ye. And we've made surre the trrim on the drress matches the blue in the Hamilton tarrtan."

"It's called a plaid, isn't it? I must remember that."

"What arre ye doin' in therre?" Gavin yelled, pounding on the door now and from behind it there was another burst of laughter. "Och!" he exclaimed and they heard the outside door slam shut behind him.

* * *

Victoria came out of the house about a half-hour later to find him leaning on the fence near his car and looking out over the enclosure where part of his father's flock were frolicking in the snow. "Hello, darling," she murmured in his ear, slipping her hand through his arm and kissing him on the cheek. "I'm ready to go now."

Gavin glanced down at her. "Arre ye surre?" He had been determined to be put out with her. But her face was very close to his–framed in the fleece-lined hat his father had given her, wisps of golden hair escaping to curl against her pink cheeks. Her eyes were sparkling and she had never looked more beautiful. He gathered her in his arms, all his annoyance gone.

"Poor darling," she said at last. "But oh, wait until you see the dress!"

"I'm surre 'tis bonny, but 'twill be wasted on me, I'm afrraid. All I'll be lookin' at is my brride."

She smiled at him. "Can we go now?"

"Aye...aye. We'd betterr beforre Fiona gets ye in therre again wi' her damned pins!" He helped her into the car and a few minutes later they were across the little stone bridge, driving toward Ballater and the nearest Registry office. "If 'tis old Sandy MacGillivrray in the office today, darrlin', I should be warrnin' ye in advance he'll have a comment orr two to make. He's known me all my life, ye see. Rregisterred my birrth as a matterr o' fact."

"Oh, I'm so glad!"

"Aboot what?"

"That you were born." He grinned at her. "Gavin, there...there was something I've been wanting to ask you. I...I don't know when the idea came to me actually, but could... could we fit in one more person for the wedding? I wouldn't want her to stay at the Inn."

"Torri, Rrebecca's already told ye that....."

"No...not Rebecca. Sister....Sister Philippa from...from Heathfield."

He glanced over at her. "But I...I thought ye hated it therre, darrlin'."

"I...I did, but...but that wasn't her fault."

"And noo ye'd like herr to be at ourr weddin'. Would she object to sharrin' a rroom wi' Marrtha, do ye think?"

"I'm sure she wouldn't. They...they could compare notes as to which one of them I treated worse." Her laughter held a bitter note he'd never heard before. He decided he didn't like it.

"Dinna talk aboot yourrself that way, Torri," he remonstrated gently as he removed one hand from the wheel to take hold of hers.

"But...but it's true, Gavin, I......"

"And look how Marrtha loves ye–so she underrstood, ye see–and I'm surre the good sisterr did, too. Well, herre we arre," he went on as finally they drove along the narrow, busy main street of Ballater and around behind the Municipal Building to the car park. They entered through a rear door, climbing a narrow, dusty enclosed staircase to the first floor where Gavin led the way along a dimly lit corridor equally as dusty as the stairs. Stopping at the third door on the right, he knocked lightly on the opaque glass window.

"Aye–coom in," a high-pitched nasal voice invited them.

"They call him 'Piperr' MacGillivrray, Torri," Gavin whispered as he pushed open the door and stood back to allow her to enter first. "Ye'll ken why."

As they came in, a rotund little man, entirely bald except for a fringe of white hair, popped up from his desk and bustled around the counter which separated his office area from a sort of waiting room. "Tis sae good to see ye again, my dearr boy!" He seized hold of Gavin's hand, pumping it up and down. "And <u>this</u> must be the lassie. Och–yourr Dad's rright! She is a bonny one!"

Victoria smiled at the typically Scottish compliment. "Thank you, Mr. MacGillivray."

"Well, noo. Well, well, well." He hurried around behind the counter again to get out the necessary record books and forms. He had a habit of humming through his nose as he worked and the sound did indeed resemble bagpipes playing somewhere in the distance. Victoria exchanged amused glances with Gavin and he winked at her. "Well noo," the clerk said, finally facing them again across the counter. "I'll have to ask ye both some rroutine questions and then I'll just need yourr signaturres. Ye know, lass, I neverr thought this one would marrry a'tall." She smiled. In fact she couldn't seem to stop smiling throughout the entire process. "Och, Gavin," Piper observed at another point reaching across the counter to poke him in the chest with one chubby forefinger, "everra gurrl that cooms in herre smiles that way. She kens she's got the laddy firrmly in her grrasp!"

Only once did Victoria grow sober. The clerk was glancing over the completed forms before they signed them. "Oh yes, Miss Windsorr, I'll be needin' yourr divorrce degrree from... from ah..." He peered down at the sheet. "Misterr Eliot. I'll copy it and rreturrn it to ye, of courrse." Her hand was trembling as she removed the precious proof of her freedom from her purse and laid it on the counter. Gavin slipped an arm around her shoulders as if to say, "There–now it's all over."

At last they each signed the form and for a moment they stood there looking down at their two names. Glancing up at last, their eyes met and Gavin bent his head to give Victoria a brief kiss. As they stepped apart, however, they became aware that Mr. MacGillivray was leaning on his elbows on his side of the counter, peering up at them with an enormous grin on his cherubic face. They burst into laughter in which he wholeheartedly joined.

"Well, then," Gavin said as they turned to leave, "we'll be seein' ye at the weddin', I should imagine."

"Aye...aye, I wouldna miss it. And the missus, too. She was that pleased to be included." He was still beaming as the door closed behind them.

"Oh, darling, you were right," Victoria said as they walked hand in hand back along the hall and down the stairs. "He is adorable!"

"Aye, lass." He smiled down at her and squeezed her hand. "Noo then ye'll want to be rringin' oop Sisterr Philippa this evenin', I should imagine." She nodded, her eyes at once brimming with tears.

As soon as dinner was over, they went into Dad Hamilton's den where Gavin put the call through for her on the somewhat antiquated local phone system. " 'Tis rringin'," he said finally. "Would ye rrather I left ye alone then?"

"Stay–please," she replied at once, taking the receiver with one hand and reaching out to hold onto him with the other. He sat down beside her, holding her hand in both of his.

"Heathfield Abbey School for Girls." The voice on the other end of the line was young and cultured–one of the postulants, perhaps, or an older student. For just a second Victoria almost hung up. Why after so long would Sister Philippa want to hear from her? "Heathfield Abbey," the voice repeated when there was no answer the first time.

"Yes...ah...Sister...Sister Philippa, please."

"One moment, please."

Victoria tightened her grip on Gavin's hand. "Dear God, why am I doing this?!"

" 'Twill be all rright, lass," he reassured her. "Ye'll see."

* * *

As always on a mid-winter evening the convent parlor was cozy and inviting. Though most were occupied in some way: reading or writing letters or grading papers for the term which had just concluded, there was a constant hum of conversation and the teapot was kept full and hot. Sister Philippa, now mistress of the junior school, was engaged in the unavoidable task of bringing the class attendance records up to date. The postulant who was her current assistant was helping her. "Oh dear, Sister Emilia," she admitted with a sigh, taking a long swallow of her tea, "this is the part of my job I detest!"

Emilia grinned at her affectionately. Along with everyone else at Heathfield she adored her boss. The telephone on the small desk between them rang and she answered it. "Yes, may I ask who's calling, please?" There was a brief pause and Philippa saw her young associate's eyebrows rise sharply in surprise. "Sister, I didn't realize you knew Victoria Windsor." The nun's face went white and her hand shook so badly that the tea sloshed over, staining the page in the record book. "Are you all right, Sister?" the girl inquired anxiously,

"Oh, yes...yes, I'm fine and yes," she added as she took the receiver. "I...I knew Victoria Windsor when she was a student here." And irresistibly now she found herself drawn to use the name of the little girl. "Hello, Vicki."

"Sister Philippa, you....you took so long. I....I was beginning to think you...you didn't wish to speak to me."

The voice had matured and deepened since her days at Heathfield, but Philippa instantly recognized it. "You know me better than that, I hope."

"Yes, I....I do...only I....I wasn't sure."

"Oh, my dear. I...I've been so worried about you."

Victoria glanced at Gavin. "I....I don't know why. I....I treated you miserably and I...I....." Tears choked her and she pushed the phone at him, shaking her head. "I can't...I can't," she whispered, burying her head against his shoulder.

"Ah... Sisterr Philippa, this is....ah... Gavin Hamilton. I don't suppose ye ken who I am."

"I...I've seen your name, of course."

"Aye, well, Torri and I....."

"You call her Tori?"

"Aye..well, we'd like it verra much if....."

"No, Gavin, please." Victoria raised her head. "I...I want to be the one to ask her."

"Of courrse, darrlin'?" Philippa liked the sound of his voice. It was so gentle.

A moment later Victoria herself came back on the line. "Sister Philippa, I...I called to ask you to...to come up to Scotland for...for our wedding."

"You....you want me at your wedding? Oh, my dear, I...I would like that very much." She was close to crying herself now. So many times she'd reached out in vain to the little girl and now when she'd been certain the woman must have all but forgotten her, incredibly it was she who was making the overture.

"I'm so glad." Victoria smiled at Gavin. "The wedding's on December 30th, but it would be nice if you could come the day before."

"On the 29th, then. Certainly. Can I get there by train?"

"We're...we're not far from Aberdeen, Sister. Just let me know the time and we'll meet you."

"Well, I'll be seeing you then."

"Yes, Sister. See you soon. Good-bye." Slowly Victoria hung up the telephone, turning to Gavin. "Oh, darling, I can't believe it! She's really coming!"

* * *

Victoria and Gavin were standing together on the Aberdeen station platform when the overnight train from London pulled in a little after ten on the morning of the 29th. She was holding onto his arm with both hands. "I....I wonder if I'll even recognize her," she said nervously.

"Won't she be...ah....drressed in some parrticularr sorrt o' clothin'?" he asked. "Parrdon my Churrch o' Scotland oopbrringin'," he added grinning in that way he had which made him look about six years old.

"Oh–you!" She squeezed his arm, but at once she relaxed a little. He could always do that for her. Philippa's attire was, in fact, quite different than she remembered: a simple street length black coat and a short veil which covered only the back of her head, but she knew her instantly. "Oh, Gavin," she whispered, "I should have realized she'll never change. Sister.... Sister," she called out, waving and running across the platform to meet her.

Ever since the evening of the phone call Sister Philippa had worried how she would find Victoria. From the distance of the audience she'd seemed as lovely as ever, but up close might she appear faded and used up, destroying forever her memories of the child she had loved? To her joy, however, the girl stood before her now–smiling and not looking much older than the day she'd left Heathfield. "Oh, Sister Philippa!" Victoria threw her arms around her and hugged her.

The nun returned the embrace, tears filling her eyes yet again as she remembered all the times Vicki had rebuffed any gesture of affection. After a moment she held her back at arms' length to study her more intently. "Dear, you look absolutely marvelous!"

Gavin had allowed them a moment or so alone, but now he came forward. "Well noo, I think I'll just step in herre beforre the two o' ye flood ourr fine station with all those English tearrs." He picked up Philippa's valise.

"Oh, Sister," Victoria started to say, "this is...."

"Introductions aren't necessary, Vicki," she said at once. "You are undoubtedly Mr. Hamilton."

By now they were walking through the station toward the car park. "Just one thing though, Sisterr," he said. "Wheneverr anyone says Misterr Hamilton, I still think they'rre talkin' aboot my Dad. I'm Gavin."

Philippa laughed. "You know you look just the way I thought you would from hearing your voice on the telephone."

"I do? I hope that's good!" He grinned at them both. "Well, herre we arre. 'Tis only a wee carr, I'm afrraid."

"Why don't you sit in front, Sister," Victoria said quickly.

"Now don't be silly. I'm not that much older than you, Vicki, and you two should sit together." They were all soon settled to begin the drive along the winding roads back to

Glengowrie. "Oh, how beautiful–what magnificent country!" Sister Philippa exclaimed over and over again as they rode.

"I know," Victoria agreed at some point, "I...I feel so at home here."

"And when we get there," Gavin remarked with a wink, "Torri'll show ye all the cute sheep!"

"Don't listen to him, Sister," she defended herself although she couldn't keep a straight face. "You see the first time I came up here, I told Dad his sheep were cute. Now I'm never going to live it down."

When they arrived at the Hamilton home, Martha was waiting to take Sister Philippa up to the room they were to share and as Victoria had suspected, they would indeed talk about her. Her error had been in what they would say. They spoke of how they had grieved for her and they rejoiced mutually in her newfound happiness. But neither could or would speak a harsh word. For the moment, however, Philippa barely had time to unpack when there was a knock at the door. It was Victoria. "If you're not too tired, Sister," she said shyly, "I thought we could take a walk."

"I keep telling this girl," Sister Philippa said to Martha, "I'm not that much older than she is."

"I....I'm sorry. I...I didn't mean to...."

"I'm only teasing, Vicki," she immediately reassured her. "I always thought my teachers were ancient, too."

A short while later they were strolling together along one of the many roads which wound around and through the Hamilton pastures. In the brilliant light of the sunshine reflected on the snow Sister Philippa could see how incredibly well Victoria did indeed look–glowing with health and happiness. But she observed as well how nervous and uncertain she was. Several times the girl had glanced over as though she wanted to speak, but did not do so. "Well, I like Gavin," Philippa said at last to break the ice.

Her effort was amply rewarded as a dazzling smile flashed across Victoria's face. "Do you? I...I'm so glad."

"You know, I...I keep remembering the child and the young woman I once knew." She was conscious of moving very carefully now. Clearly there had been a great change in Victoria, but she wasn't sure just how honest she could actually be.

"And you still came?"

"Vicki..." But here Sister Philippa interrupted herself. "But perhaps you prefer Victoria now?"

"No, please, Sister. You...you always called me Vicki and I....I..."

'Vicki, then. Believe me, I knew how desperately unhappy you were and I..."

"Didn't fool you, hm?" she quipped, but Philippa could see the tears in her eyes,

"But perhaps you'd rather not go into any of that, dear. You've said it all anyway by asking me to your wedding."

"Oh, I hoped you'd see that, but I <u>want</u> to talk. I...I really do–to...to tell you even now when it's much too late, how sorry I am for all the times I hurt you..."

"Vicki, I've often blamed myself...." The nun's voice sounded incredibly kind. Why had she once found it so irritating?

"Blamed yourself? You did everything humanly possible!"

"But don't you see? I pushed too hard."

"You couldn't help that. You...you loved me or...or you tried to."

"No, Vicki—I <u>did</u> <u>love</u> you. All you could do was to stop me from showing it. May....may I ask you something?"

"Yes, please, anything."

"Was it Gavin who made the difference?"

"Actually it began the day I....I went to Windsor to see where...where Uncle Bertie is buried." Suddenly she could visualize the tomb as clearly as ever and inevitably the tears welled up.

"Somehow the late King succeeded where I failed, didn't he?"

"Yes, although I don't really know why, but then he...he died and I...I felt as though...as though I'd been betrayed all over again."

"That's a natural reaction to death–especially in a child."

"I suppose so, but it wasn't until I went to Windsor that day that I could admit how...how much I had loved him."

"Oh, but Vicki–love can be terribly frightening–the commitment it involves."

"How wise you are, Sister. Why didn't I realize that when I was a child? But the irony is that I very nearly did the same thing to my own daughter." Now it was Philippa who was fighting to keep the tears back. Could they really be walking together like this and talking so easily of the most intimate matters? "Did you know I lived in the States for a while?" Victoria continued after a moment.

"Of course I did."

"Stupid question?" The nun merely nodded. It was even more wonderful to observe the mood lightening a little. "Well, it may have started that day at Uncle Bertie's tomb, but the turning point really came the first Christmas I spent in New York. Olivia asked to visit me for the holiday and it...it just happened."

"Often the most beautiful things do happen quite simply."

"Sister, that....that boy in my room. I....I didn't really.... I mean, that...that was just a trick–- to get myself expelled."

Now Phillipa found herself actually laughing. "Oh, my dear, I <u>knew</u> that."

"Whatever happened to Mother Geraldine?"

"She died about two years ago....Vicki?" Suddenly the nun stopped, glancing about her in the Highland vastness as if someone might overhear. "Did...did you really call her.. 'a bloody old bitch'?"

Victoria nodded, her eyes sparkling. "Actually the full quote was 'Sod off, you bloody old bitch!' I thought she was going to have a stroke!"

Sister Philippa was enjoying herself more and more now. "You...you know no one at Heathfield refers to your running away anymore. About the time your first play opened in London you became a distinguished alumna."

Now it was Victoria's turn to laugh. "And what does Sister Marion have to say about that?"

"Oh, she takes full credit for having discovered you, of course."

"You know she <u>was</u> the first actually. Tell her I said that, will you? And..and tell her when I do another play to bring a group of students. They'd enjoy a visit backstage, don't you think?"

"Oh, Vicki, she'll be thrilled!"

"I'm glad, but I suppose we should be starting back. If we follow this road to the right, it should bring us around to the house again."

* * *

Gavin had gone riding with his father knowing Victoria would like some time alone with her old friend. He was just coming from rubbing down and stabling his horse when Terence Cartier drove up. "Terry, ye found us all rright then!" He strode up to the car, hand outstretched in welcome.

"My word—–a human voice." Grinning, the actor got out of the car to return the handshake. "I was beginning to think there were only sheep."

Just then Niall followed his son from the barn. "Terrry," Gavin said, "this is my fatherr, Niall Hamilton. Dad—Terrence Cartier."

"Sirr Terrence–an honorr to have ye with us."

"Uh-uh—it's Terry. And it is my honor to be father of the bride. How is she, Gavin?"

"Betterr everra day, thank God. I'll tell herr ye'rre herre." He bounded up the stairs and in the front door, as usual allowing it to slam shut behind him. "They've gone forr a wee strroll," he called as he came out of the house again. Bang went the door a second time. "Dad, is therre a jeep available?"

"Aye."

"Want to coom, Terrry?"

"Certainly."

"Grrand then. I'll be rright back." Gavin hurried away down behind the barn where the motorized farm equipment was garaged in the basement and a moment or so later the vehicle roared up the slope, stones and chunks of ice flying out from under its wheels, and screeched to a halt by the two men.

Sir Terence looked a little uncertain. "Is this how you finish off Englishmen these days, Gavin?"

"Aye—aye." He laughed heartily. "And even those who do rreturrn arre neverr the same."

"Well, I'll take my chances." Terry grinned as he climbed up into the jeep, but he gripped the dashboard firmly with one hand and the edge of the seat with the other.

Gavin gunned the motor and they sped off down the narrow, winding lane. "Neverr fearr," he said reassuringly. "I've been drrivin' these things since I was a wee laddie." At the moment, however, the acknowledged dean of the British theatre was virtually speechless. He merely nodded. "To answerr yourr question morre completely, Terrry..."

"Wh...wh....which question was that?" he managed to stammer.

"Aboot Torri. Do ye know she even asked a nun frrom herr public school to come up forr the weddin'?"

"Oh, that is a good sign!"

At the sound of the motor Victoria and Sister Philippa had stepped off to the side of the road to let the vehicle pass. Instead it skidded to a stop and Gavin jumped out.

"Darling!" Victoria put up her arms to be embraced.

"Hello, hinny." He held her close for a moment. "Sisterr, beforre this English lass o' mine gets ye hopelessly lost, I'll take ye back." He helped them both into the rear seat of the jeep.

"Oh, good!" Terry murmured fervently. "We may require religious assistance if we're going to get there in one piece!"

"Gavin," Victoria exclaimed, giving him a playful slap on the arm, "have you been scaring Terry?"

"Who? Me, Torri?" He grinned. " Ye know me betterr than that."

"That's just the trouble. Oh, Sister, I'm sorry. This is Terry Cartier. Terry, Sister Philippa from Heathfield. Perhaps Gavin's told you she was here."

"Yes, he did." Grimly the actor held on again as Gavin executed a rapid three-point turn and headed back down the road. "'l promise to greet you more properly, Sister," he shouted over the jolting and the roar of the engine, "when I am no longer in fear of life and limb."

Sister Philippa smiled. It was a moment before she fully realized who this man was. "Oh, my goodness!" she murmured.

Even in the midst of all this, however, both Philippa and Terry still noticed that Victoria's hand rested on Gavin's shoulder for the entire ride.

That evening after a brief informal rehearsal there was a dinner with Gavin's family, Olivia, Martha, Terry and Sister Philippa. Warmth, good food and a convivial atmosphere filled the cozy, firelit room.

But for Victoria and Gavin something extraordinary occurred in those last hours of December 29th as their sensations, their impressions of the world around them narrowed to merely each other. Conversation and laughter swirled around and about them, but they sat apart and silent on one of the couches near the fireplace, their hands intertwined. Although neither gave voice to the thought, they both wanted for the celebration–the excitement–to be over with, for there finally to be only the two of them.

* * *

It seemed to Victoria that Gavin kissed her awake the next morning with a special tenderness and when she opened her eyes, she found him looking down at her, his expression one of infinite love. "What time is it?" she whispered, touching his face.

"Seven o'clock." He grinned sheepishly. "I'm sorrry, lass, but I couldna wait any longerr to begin the day."

"You know, my love, a groom isn't supposed to see the bride until the wedding."

"And what am I supposed to do? Go arroond all day wi' my eyes closed?"

She smiled at him. "Want some breakfast?"

"What I <u>want</u> is my weddin' gift."

"You know there are moments when I can see the little boy in you so clearly."

He looked offended. "Is that anythin' to tell a lad on his weddin' day–in the full flowerr of his manhood–that he rreminds ye of a wee bairrn?"

"But I love the little boy in you, my darling. Of course I also love the man," she added, reaching up with both arms to draw him down to her. Before matters could proceed any further, however, there was a knock at the door.

"Torri?" It was Fiona. No one thought it at all inappropriate or embarrassing for Victoria and Gavin to be in the same bed even though their wedding was still hours away. They simply belonged together.

"Go away," Gavin muttered.

"Ye'll have herr all to yourrself soon enough, big brrotherr," she retorted laughingly. "And we still have some last minute worrk to do on the drress."

"I'll be there in a few minutes, Fiona," Victoria replied.

"Ah, Torri," he murmured reproachfully.

"I know....I know." She rolled over onto her side to nestle into his arms. "But it's only until this evening."

He held her close, savoring her nearness. "I'm nae surre I can wait that long to have ye forr my own wee wifie."

"Will it really seem that different, do you think, when we're married. I already feel that I belong to you."

"Aye, 'twill be differrent," he affirmed solemnly.

"Gavin, darling, I really do have to get up now. Fiona's waiting for me."

"Aye, lass." But he released her with great reluctance.

Victoria raised herself on one elbow to look down at him, "Will it make you feel any less abused if I give you your gift?"

He chuckled. "I suppose that would help a wee bit."

"You have to close your eyes though. It's not wrapped."

"Aye–all rright. What arre ye doin'?" he demanded impatiently after a moment as he heard her bare feet padding about the room.

"I had to put on my robe first."

Next he heard her open and close what sounded like the closet door. "So that's why it was locked."

"Yes," she replied laughing, "and I see I was right to do that."

He grinned. "I suppose ye got the key frrom Grranny."

She laughed again. "Yes. She doesn't trust you either. All right, you may look now."

When he opened his eyes, it was to see that Victoria was holding a clothes hanger on which was a complete new Highland regalia, the plaid held in its proper place, the lace on the shirt just showing at the cuffs and at the edge of the jabot. "Torri!" Gavin breathed. She came over then to lay the outfit on the bed for his closer inspection, watching much like a child would who has presented a gift and waits hopefully for approval. He stroked the pleats of the kilt–the wool of a much finer quality than anything he had ever owned. Almost reverently he touched one or two of the buttons on the velvet jacket. "Whateverr made ye think of such a gift, darrlin'?" he asked at last, loving her so deeply at that moment he could think of no adequate way of expressing it.

"I....I talked it over with Fiona and she ordered it for me from a tailor in Aberdeen."

"Torri, I dinna know what to say," Gavin admitted at last. " 'Tis a special thing ye've done forr me, lass."

"Then it...it was all right for me to do it? Fiona said you'd be pleased."

"All rright? 'Tis a farr sight betterr than all rright!"

Another knock came at the door just then. "Sorry, Fiona," Victoria called out. "I'm coming." She grabbed up her underwear from a chair and hurried toward the door. I"ll see you later, darling." She blew him a kiss and slipped out the door.

Gavin lay back in bed to enjoy a few moments of solitary contemplation on the wonder of the dear girl who almost unbelievably in only a matter of hours now would be his wife. Finally, however, he got up and went down the hall to the bathroom to shower. It was still impossible to contain his joy and he sang lustily as he soaped himself up and rinsed off. Even after the shower he was whistling as partially dressed, but still stripped to the waist, he prepared to lather up for shaving. Someone knocked on the door. "Aye, coom in," he called out.

It was Meghan and seeing her, he realized guiltily just how badly he had been neglecting her. "Hello, lass." He grinned at her affectionately, looking so much like the big brother she adored that tears filled her eyes again. "I'm afrraid we havna had much time togetherr this visit."

"It's...it's all rright. I...I prromised Dad I wouldna spoil things forr ye."

"Noo, Meghan, how could ye spoil anythin' forr me?" As he talked, he was working to apply lather to his beard.

"I'm....I'm sorrry, Gavin. I.....I havna been verra nice to Torri, have I?" He gave her a quick glance as he began to shave himself, but he made no reply. "Have I?" she insisted her voice trembling.

"I think ye ken the answerr to that yourrself," he observed at last in a quiet tone.

She nodded. She had never felt more miserable in her entire life. Ever since the day they went out for the Christmas tree, her father's words of warning had never left her–"Accept his lass orr ye may lose Gavin altogetherr." "Arre ye frrightfully angrry wi' me then?" she asked finally.

He looked over at her again as he finished shaving and rinsed off his razor. "Noo, I think ye know me betterr than that."

"Oh, Gavin–thank you!" Meghan threw her arms around him and hugged him, in the process getting her own face covered with the remains of his lather.

"Well, that saves me most o' the cleanin' oop, doesn't it?" he said with a grin as he rinsed a little anyway, dried off and splashed on after-shave.

She followed him eagerly as he left the bathroom to go back to his room and finish dressing. "May I...may I please do soomthin' to make oop forr it–a wee bit anyway?"

"Aye–ye could keep me coomp'ny."

"Wherre arre ye goin'?" Oh, the bliss of having her brother all to herself even if only for a little while.

"To Ballaterr. Misterr Davidson's made me oop soomthin' special–forr Torri's weddin' gift."

"Oh." At once a little of the joy went out of her face.

"Meghan–sit doon," he directed, indicating the bed with a toss of his head. She settled herself as directed and Gavin came to sit beside her. "Meghan, I...I love ye—I always will. Ye'rre verra special to me."

Her lower lip began to tremble and her throat ached with a terrible sense of loss. "But.... but it won't everr be the same again, will it?"

"I....I trruly wish I could tell ye it would be, darrlin', but I canna do that because.... because from this day on Torri will be the centrral perrson in my life."

The tears trickled slowly down Meghan's cheeks and she sniffed forlornly. He got up to go over to his bureau and get her a tissue. "Ye...ye love herr verra much, don't ye, Gavin?" She swallowed hard and blew her nose.

"Torri is... Torri is like soomthin' a man only drreams of. So will ye trry, lass--forr my sake?"

"I...I will, Gavin. I prromise."

"That's my lass." He put his arm around her shoulders and hugged her and kissed her on the cheek. "Soo then, arre ye coomin' to Ballaterr wi' me?"

She hesitated for a second. "No," she said at last decisively. "I'm...I'm goin' into Aberrdeen to that big flowerr shop. 'Twould not be a weddin' wi'oot white heatherr."

Gavin smiled at her gratefully. "Thank ye, darrlin'. Ye'rre a dearr one, for fairr."

Meghan threw her arms around him and jumped up to run from the room.

* * *

To be perfectly honest Gavin had preferred to make the trip into Ballater by himself anyway. It was an errand whose sweetness he wished to savor.

Although not well-known outside the exclusive circle of the Scottish clans, Davidson's Jewellers, Ltd. was an old and highly respected firm. It was, in fact, a Davidson who had designed and made the Hamilton betrothal ring. "Gavin–laddie!" Bruce Davidson looked up from his workbench at the sound of the bell. "Prreparred to give oop yourr frreedom, arre ye then?"

Gavin wondered why people always joked about weddings. How could they make light of such a meaningful occasion? But then he supposed he'd often been guilty of the same thing. "Aye....aye, all rready." His voice was tinged slightly with impatience. "But I'm eagerr to see the brrooch."

"In a bit of a hurrry, are ye? What's the matterr–afrraid the lass'll change herr mind. I wouldna worrry," he chattered on as he went into the back room where he had his safe. "I rrememberr when ye dated my Annie forr a bit. She'd have had ye in a thrrice and I'm surre she wasna the only one." Gavin endured the teasing in silence. Would he never live down his illustrious past? "Herre we arre, then." Bruce Davidson returned almost at once with a maroon velvet jeweller's box and opened it proudly for the other man's inspection of his work. He was a master craftsman and he knew it.

Done in antique gold, it was at first glance a traditional Luckinbooth brooch much like the one originally designed for the marriage of Mary, Queen of Scots–the initials "V" and "G" elaborately intertwined and at the point of union a dark, glowing topaz. Encircling this central design, however, was a quarter-inch wide rim on which were engraved the words, "Victoria and Gavin–For Aye and the date of the ceremony–30-12-71.

For a long moment Gavin studied it in silence. The brooch was exactly as he'd pictured it with the symbolic infinity of the circle and the two intertwined initials and its richness and elegance were perfectly suited to the woman who would wear it. At last he looked up, but if the jeweller had anticipated words of lavish praise, he was destined to be disappointed. "Aye." Gavin nodded solemnly in affirmation. "Aye."

Back home again, he bounded eagerly up the front steps. "Torri, wherre arre ye, darrlin'?"

"No, ye don't." Fiona greeted him at the door. "Go in thrrough the kitchen. We'rre decorratin' forr yourr weddin' and you and Torri are not allowed to see it until this evenin'."

"Well, would ye mind at least tellin' me wherre my brride is?"

Something in his expression made Fiona rise up on tiptoe to kiss him on the cheek. "Eitherr oopstairrs orr in the kitchen wi' Grranny."

"Oh, Fiona, I didna have a chance to tell ye." He grinned, "The kilt and all–they'rre bonny."

"I only ordered it." Seeing his obvious pleasure, she smiled in return. " 'Twas Torrri's idea. Noo–get on wi' ye." She shooed him off the porch and down the steps. "We've a lot to do beforre tonight."

"Aye.....aye, I'm goin'."

His soon-to-be wife and his grandmother were indeed sharing a cup of tea at the kitchen table–as well as a joke, it appeared. It was rare he had the opportunity to study Victoria unobserved and for a moment he stood on the small stoop peering in at her through the glass in the back door. She had apparently just washed her hair because her head was wrapped up turban fashion in a large bath towel. She was wearing no make-up and her face positively glowed. It was hard to believe this was the same woman he'd first met backstage nearly four years before or even the same woman he'd seen in a hospital bed only two months ago. Just then, however, Victoria glanced up and saw him standing there. She came over immediately to open the door. "Hello, my dearest. Fiona wouldn't let you in the living room either, I see."

"No." He smiled down at her. "Ye look sae beautiful, darrlin'," he murmured, bringing one hand up to touch her face.

"Like this?" She laughed happily.

He glanced past her at his grandmother who still sat at the kitchen table, beaming at them both. "Grranny, could I have a few minutes alone wi' Torri?"

"Aye...aye, of courrse." At once she got up to bring her cup and saucer over to the sink and still grinning broadly, she walked briskly across the kitchen, turning to wink at them both just before she disappeared through the swinging door into the living room.

"She's such a dear, Gavin," Victoria observed.

"Aye—will ye sit doon then, lass?"

"Would you like some tea?" she asked. "There's still some left in the pot, I think."

"No, I dinna want any tea." He chuckled a little. "What I <u>do</u> want is forr ye to sit doon."

"Yes, sir," she said with mock docility, doing as she'd been instructed.

He sat down across from her and placed the square velvet box on the table in front of her. " 'Tis nae sae grrand as yourrs, of courrse." For some reason he suddenly felt apologetic about his gift.

"Oh, Gavin, don't!" She placed her hand over his where it lay on the table near the box. "I bought the kilt for you to wear at our wedding. It wasn't to impress you. Besides your grandmother and sister made my dress and your father is giving me the plaid. May I open it now?"

"Aye, lass."

She lifted the cover then, disclosing the pin. "Oh, Gavin, it's...it's exquisite! It's a Luckinbooth design, isn't it, with our initials intertwined in the center? Isn't it?" she asked again when he didn't immediately answer her.

Gavin's mind had been on her face as she saw his present for the first time and he'd only half heard her. "Aye—darrlin'," he replied at last. "But take it oot o' the box and look morre closely."

She did as he'd told her and only then did she notice the inscription around the rim. He continued to study her, watching her lips move as she read the inscription. "Oh–Gavin!" She looked up at him and her eyes were filled with tears. "How did you ever think of such a perfect gift?"

She was caressing the pin between her thumb and forefinger and he put his hand over hers. "I waited a verra long time to marrry, hinny, because I couldna imagine spendin' the rrest o' my life wi' one lass. Noo I canna imagine life wi'oot ye. I wanted my gift to say that–that's all." He leaned across the table to cup her face in both hands and kiss her.

Chapter 6

Having left the upstairs to the ladies, father and son dressed for the wedding downstairs in Granny's bedroom. Their kilts, ruffled shirts and short velvet jackets were a proud statement of their Scottish manhood and all that remained were the plaids. This intricate maneuver, however, required more room and so they'd come out into the kitchen. "You firrst, laddie," Niall directly fondly. " 'Tis yourr weddin'."

Gavin merely nodded and held the plaid against the front of his left shoulder. Slowly he turned as his father wound the intricately pleated material across his chest, under his right arm and up again over his back.. At last, with the plaid now held in place by the massive Hamilton clan badge, Niall meticulously arranged the magnificent tartan folds which fell to below the hemline of the kilt. He glanced often at his son as he worked, but the younger man's face remained expressionless. "Well, laddie," he said finally, "ye'rre aboot rready, I would think."

"Hm–what?" Gavin blinked once or twice and shook his head. "Sorrry." His smile was endearing. "My...my thoughts werre elsewherre."

"Oopstairrs, perrhaps, in a cerrtain bedrroom?"

"Aye." The smile grew broader. "Hold this herre noo, Dad," he directed as he in turn set his father's plaid in place, "and turrn rroond so I can wind it."

Niall chuckled. "I was wearrin' the plaid when ye werre nae e'en a twinkle in yourr motherr's e'e. I dinna rrequirre instrructions."

"Ye know, I fastened Torri's plaid forr herr that firrst week-end in New York." Gavin's voice trembled with emotion and his fingers as he arranged the material were uncharacteristically clumsy. "I...I can still rrememberr how strrrange it made me feel–bein' sae close to herr and...."

"Gavin–darling." It was Victoria calling to him from the top of the back stairs.

"Aye—lass!" He started toward the door–hungry for the sight of her.

"Oh, no!" Niall Hamilton stepped in front of him. "Ye'rre both goin' to have to wait a few minutes longerr."

The two men heard her laugh floating down the closed staircase. "No, I...I only wanted to know if Jamie and Felicity have come. The last time I talked to her on the telephone, she wasn't sure."

"I'll go and see, Torri," Niall volunteered, "but you two have to prromise to behave yourrselves." Neither of them replied. "Gavin–" his father prompted.

"Aye–I suppose so." But he was obviously reluctant and Victoria turned to smile at Fiona who had followed her along the hall.

"I'll keep watch at this end, Dad," his daughter promised. "Noo, if ye want to get marrried, Torri, ye goin' to have to finish gettin' drressed." She took her by the arm to lead her back into the bedroom. Preparations were, in fact, almost complete with only the dress itself remaining. "Coom noo," Fiona urged, "beforre that brrother o' mind expirres from anxiety!" Victoria laughed and slipped out of her robe.

"Please, Mummy," Olivia said eagerly, "may I?"

"Of course, sweetheart."

"Careful of her hair, honey," Martha cautioned.

"I'll stand on something." The little girl dragged a chair over next to her mother and climbing up on it, she eased the ivory crepe over Victoria's head and upraised arms. Martha stepped forward to zip up the back and lastly Fiona settled the Juliet cap with its long blue streamers over her golden hair. Each wanted somehow to be even a small part of this day– to share in the happiness they saw shining in Victoria's eyes.

Just then a knock came at the door. "If that's Gavin," his sister remarked laughingly, "I'll kick him back doonstairrs wherre he belongs!"

" Tis Dad, Torri."

"Yes, Dad–come in."

It happened that at just this moment Victoria's back had been toward the door and so she was just turning to face it as Niall entered. "Och, Torri," he murmured, "ye'rre the loveliest thing I've seen since my Maurrya on ourr weddin' day."

"Oh, Dad– what a dear thing to say. Thank you. Are they here then–Jamie and Felicity?"

"Aye, darrlin'– but not togetherr, I'm afrraid."

"What's wrong with them?"

"Noo, lass–ye mustna let anythin' take away the joy of this day forr ye."

"Nothing could do that! How...how's Gavin?"

"Impatient! In fact I betterr get back doon therre orr he'll be charrgin' oop those stairrs at any minute."

"Before you go–fasten on my plaid for me." She picked up the tartan scarf from the bed and held it out to him. "Afterr all, it was yourr gift to me."

"Aye, lass, I'd be honorred." Niall cleared his throat and his eyes grew suspiciously moist.

"Herre's the pin." Fiona brought the wedding gift over from the dressing table.

"Have you seen the brooch, Dad?" Victoria inquired eagerly. "Did you know Gavin actually designed it for me himself?"

"Aye, lass, 'tis bonny." Painstakingly he pinned the plaid in place. In the simpler fashion correct for a woman it merely rested on the shoulder, coming down loosely across the back to be held by a loop at the waist of the dress. Smiling to herself, Victoria remembered her original puzzlement upon noticing the loop.

"Dad–" She still held him there with one hand on his arm. "Dad, I...I just wanted to say I'll....I'll try so hard to be the wife Gavin deserves. The way you....you've all accepted me..." Here she reached out her other hand to Fiona. They both hugged her and she felt the tears starting. "Oh, dear," she laughed, daubing under her eyes with the side of her index finger, "my eye make-up will be ruined."

"We'll go on doon and tell Terrry ye'rre rready," Niall said with one final hug. "Mrs. Kendall, Fiona...."

Martha hugged Victoria, too. "I'm so happy for you, my dear," she whispered.

"I...I know. Thank...thank you for everything–always." Her old friend patted her on the cheek before leaving. Fiona, the last to go, paused at the door to blow her a kiss.

Victoria turned to give herself one last check in the full length mirror. She pirouetted about so that the soft fabric of the dress swirled out around her and coming back to face the mirror once again, she raised one hand to touch the plaid. The simple, old-fashioned gown was the perfect setting for the Hamilton tartan. And lastly she brought her gaze to rest on the reflection of her own face. A thousand memories flooded over her. It seemed impossible she could ever have been the woman of those memories and oddly, despite everything, a young girl looked back at her out of the mirror–innocent and untouched– standing timorously on the threshold of marriage.

Olivia watched her go through her pantomime. "Mummy," she whispered at last, a little hesitant to break into her mother's private world.

For just a moment Victoria had forgotten anyone else was in the room. "Sorry, luv," she turned at once to smile at her daughter. "I guess I was daydreaming. Sweetheart, you look so beautiful."

The little girl's outfit–even to the Juliet cap–was identical to her mother's except that the material of her dress was red velvet and the trimming white ribbon and lace. "Not as beautiful as you, Mummy."

"Even more so, I think. Did you want to say something, precious?"

"Just how happy you look! And...and that I love Gavin, too, and I'm awfully glad you're marrying him!"

"Are you really?" She took Olivia's face in both hands and tilted her head up a little so that they were looking directly into each other's eyes. "And I want to tell you something, too–that tonight is the beginning of a wonderful new life–not only for Gavin and me, but for you as well."

"I know, Mummy.' Mother and daughter hugged each other.

"Ready, Victoria?" Terry asked from outside in the hall.

"Come in, luv."

He entered, coming at once to bend and kiss both her hands. "Victoria, my dear, words are truly inadequate!"

"Thank you, Terry." She kissed him on the cheek. "For everything. Oh, how I wish Noel could have been here tonight."

"You do understand why he couldn't be, don't you, darling?"

"I suppose so."

Terry drew her hand through his arm, covering it affectionately with his own. "Well then, I believe we're to wait at the top of the stairs for the music to begin." As they walked along the hall preceded by Olivia, he gave Victoria a last sideways glance. "Ready?" he whispered. She nodded, smiling radiantly. Another moment and they heard the unique and unmistakable sound of sheepskin bags filling with air. Terry felt her hand tighten momentarily on his arm. The pipes began to play "The Skye Boat Song"–an odd wedding march perhaps– , but it was the first song she'd heard Gavin sing and turning back to smile up at her mother, Olivia started down the stairs. When the little girl reached the corner of the fireplace, they followed.

Victoria wanted to remember everything and she had made up her mind to study every detail of the room. Now as she came down the stairs on Terry's arm, she noticed first that fresh greens and holly had been strung across the ceiling. They had practiced the procession, circling out as far as the front door before heading back toward the fireplace, but she saw now that an actual walkway had been formed by fastening additional ropes of holly to the chairs. The room was full of people, all standing at the moment, and thus it wasn't until they rounded the corner at the furthest point that she observed the two drapes of the Hamilton tartan, each wreathed in garlands of white heather, which framed the hearth. Finally her eyes came to rest on Gavin and from then on he was all she saw. Nothing suited him quite so well, she thought yet again, as his native dress: the blue jacket and white ruffled jabot setting off to perfection his ruddy complexion and auburn hair.

It was almost at this same precise instant Gavin had his first clear view of Victoria. Until then he'd just been able to catch an occasional fleeting glimpse of her over the heads of the crowd which merely served to madden him further with impatience. As she and Terry turned at the door, his fists clenched involuntarily in anticipation and then at long last he could see his bride. Dear God, he thought, there is no other woman quite as beautiful. "Torri," he breathed. He was unaware he'd spoken aloud, but his father heard him and smiled. Finally she was beside him. Unable to wait any longer, Gavin had actually taken a step or two forward to meet her, drawing her other arm through his. She felt the velvet of his sleeve under her hand and overwhelmed unexpectedly with shyness, she couldn't immediately bring herself to look up at him.

"Dearly beloved," the Reverend Wallace began, "we are gathered here in the sight of God and in the presence of this company to join together this man and this woman in holy matrimony...." It was hard for Victoria to believe that twice before she'd stood beside a man and listened to these words. Surely she was hearing them now for the first time. "Who giveth this woman to be married to this man?"

"I do," Terry's dear gentle voice responded, "on behalf of all those who have loved her for so long. We give her," he went on, "to someone whom we trust to cherish her for the rest of their lives."

She heard the word, "Aye" spoken somewhere near her ear and Gavin's hand came up to cover hers. At last then she was drawn to look up at him and once she did, the tenderness in his eyes held her there and she was helpless to look away. The minister inquired now as to whether Gavin would take her as his "lawfully wedded wife" and she was glad she was not only listening, but watching him as he replied, "I...do." He put just the slightest pause between the two words and his eyes never left her face.

It was her turn next to answer the same question–would she, Victoria, take him, Gavin to be her lawfully wedded husband. "I do." She was looking up at him steadily now and her voice carried easily to the furthest corner of the room.

"Join right hands," Reverend Wallace instructed them now, but Gavin added a special touch of his own by placing his left hand over hers as he repeated after the minister, "I, Gavin Atholl Hamilton, take thee, Victorria Olivia Windsorr, to be my lawfully wedded wife." His deep baritone voice recited the marriage vows with a steady sureness. Then the minister turned to her. "I, Victoria Olivia Windsor, take thee, Gavin Atholl Hamilton...." Her hand tightened convulsively over his as she repeated her vows and never on any stage had her voice conveyed such heartfelt emotion. Standing beside her mother, Olivia never once took her eyes off their faces during the entire recitation of their vows. Neither did Niall Hamilton next to his son.

When the time came for the exchange of rings, Gavin once again added his own touch as placing the ring on Victoria's finger, he raised her hand to his lips. At this profoundly moving gesture her eyes filled with tears and when she turned to take Gavin's ring from Olivia, she nearly dropped it. She managed to slip the ring on, however, looking up at him as she spoke the appropriate words. Inevitably they both remembered that originally he hadn't wanted to wear a ring and a brief smile of mutual understanding passed between them.

Finally, following a brief benediction, Reverend Wallace spoke the magical words, "I now pronounce you man and wife." They stood looking at each other–held by the emotional power of the moment–wanting to remember it as well as each other's face at this instant of union. "Ye may kiss the bride, Gavin," he prompted gently. Incredibly neither of them heard him and a ripple of laughter passed over the room. "Gavin," the minister said again, touching him on the arm.

"Hm—what?" With considerable effort he took his eyes from Victoria's face.

The laughter grew louder. "Would ye like to kiss your wife, laddie?"

"My...my wife." He turned back to look down at Victoria again. "Hello, wifie," he whispered.

"Hello, husband," she replied smiling up at him.

Martha had to look away at that point and her gaze found an answer in the tear-filled eyes of Sister Philippa.

At last Gavin bent to kiss her. Victoria came up on tiptoe, slipping her arms around his neck, and their lips met. They kissed and they kissed and they kissed. "Ah..hm..hm." Reverend Wallace cleared his throat.

There was no response. At last the pipes started up again and they stepped apart laughing. Arm in arm, they started to move out through the living room, but they had only gone a few steps when Gavin's joy overcame all decorum. With a resounding shout he seized Victoria around the waist and picking her up, he swung her around and around off the floor. Feeling dizzy, she laughingly begged him to stop and at once they were engulfed in loving arms, so many people reaching out to each of them: Niall, Olivia, Granny, Martha, Fiona, Sister Philippa, Terry–even Meghan and Rhuaridh.

The center of the floor, meanwhile, had been cleared for dancing and now the small orchestra swung into a lilting old waltz, "Cailin Mo Ruin-Sa," the Gaelic title translating as "The Maid I Adore". Gavin gazed down at her tenderly. "Well then, Mrs. Hamilton, may I have the honorr of the firrst dance?" Victoria merely nodded, coming into his arms and they began to circle the room in the graceful steps of the waltz.

"You...you were right," she said at last, smiling as she realized even as she spoke them that these were the first words she'd said to her new husband.

"Rright aboot what, darrlin'?"

"It...it does feel different, being...being your wife."

" 'Tis a good feelin', I hope." His voice was throaty with emotion.

"How...how long are we expected to stay, do you think?"

He chuckled and his brown eyes which a moment ago had been soft and tender were dancing with merriment. "So—my lass is anxious to be alone wi' me, hm?"

"I really am your lass now, aren't I?"

"Aye...aye." He bent to kiss her.

They were obviously lost in each other and for a while people left them alone. Finally, however, after half an hour or so, Niall Hamilton approached and tapped his son on the shoulder.. "Hello, Dad." Victoria smiled at him.

"No, no, Torri," Gavin protested. "If we ignorre him, he'll go away."

"I willna go away. I want to dance wi' my new daughterr." Niall clapped him affectionately on the back. "I'll take good carre o' herr, I prromise."

Standing alone in the middle of the dance floor, her brother appeared so utterly forlorn that after a moment Fiona came up to him. "Come on, laddie. I'll dance wi' ye."

"No offense." He grinned good-naturedly as he took her in his arms. "But 'tis nae exactly the same."

"Well, I wouldna think so." Just then Gavin caught Victoria's eye across the room. Raising her fingers from his father's shoulder, she wiggled them at him and smiled. Fiona looked up to follow the direction of his gaze. "Ye know," she said, "no one'll object if you two slip away fairrly soon."

"In a wee bit." He chuckled. "Tell me, did ye everr think ye'd see me sae totally daft overr one lass?"

"I knew it would eitherr be that way orr not at all. Love could neverr be anythin' half-hearrted orr casual forr ye. Ye've always felt everrathin' sae deeply."

"Well, daughterr," Niall was saying meanwhile, "I rrealize I'm no rreplacement forr m'laddie."

"Oh, Dad, I...I wanted to dance with you, too."

"Ye'rre verra dearr to say that, but I ken ye'd rratherr be wi' Gavin. Afterr all ye havna been marrried e'en an hourr. Seems that would classify ye as newlyweds."

Victoria smiled up at him and briefly she pressed her face against his. "But part of what makes all this so wonderful," she said, "is having you for a father-in-law."

"Thank ye, lass," he replied. "Ye'rre everrathin' I could have wanted forr my son–and speakin' of which–herre he cooms. I think ourr time togetherr is overr."

Just as Gavin got there, however, the dance came to an end. "All rright, Dad." He put a possessive arm around Victoria's waist to draw her to him. "I'll take my wife back noo if ye dinna mind."

The music started again almost at once, however, and this time it was Terry Cartier who cut in. "Father of the bride, you know, my good fellow," he observed, swinging Victoria away with an easy grace.

"Hmph!" Gavin turned to stride away across the floor.

* * *

The dance with Terry served as a sweet reminder of all the other people who–long before Gavin–had loved her and so when, just as the dance was ending, she spied Felicity, sitting alone and dejected, Victoria had to make one more attempt to talk to her. The Scottish girl humored her–even going with her into Dad Hamilton's den–but by the time Fiona came to tell her Gavin was about to sing, Victoria had to accept there was nothing she could do. Their future, after all, remained solely in the hands of Jamie and Felicity.

Back out in the living room Gavin was already standing on the low platform which had been set up at one end of the room for the pipers, one accordionist and two fiddlers which comprised the small orchestra. He had just slipped the strap of his guitar over his head, settling it on his shoulder, and at the moment Victoria came out of the den his head was bent over the instrument checking its tuning. He glanced up and grinned at her. "Therre ye arre, lass. I was beginnin' to think my new wife had deserrted me."

"I....I wouldn't do that, Gavin," she murmured, suddenly ill-at-ease.

"Torri, overr herre," Niall Hamilton called out, indicating the place next to him on the couch which he'd saved for her, and she hurried over to sink down gratefully beside him. Taking hold of her hand, he found it was cold. "Arre ye all rright, lass?" he whispered.

"Oh, yes. I'm just not good in situations like this. I...I wish I could be more like Gavin–casual and relaxed."

"But think how far you've come already?" She hadn't realized until then that Sister Philippa was on the other side of her.

"I....I have, haven't I?" All at once she was thoughtful. "It's just that I still have so far to go.....Sister, I've been meaning to ask you. Do you have Pamela Ashworth's address and phone number. I'd...I'd like to get in touch with her."

"She'd be thrilled, Vicki. And it's Pamela Stafford now, by the way. She's active in our alumnae association." Victoria smiled a little at that. Pamela <u>would</u> be just the one to be active in the alumnae association.

"As I'm surre ye ken," Gavin was saying now, "I'm nae herre tonight to enterrtain. Therre is one wee thing, howeverr, that I'd like to do forr ye. Well, actually 'tis forr my darrlin' lass herre, but we'll allow ye to overrhearr just this once." Everyone laughed including Victoria, her self-consciousness gone. "I've neverr been a man," he went on, "who could rreadily express his feelin's. I <u>have</u> found it a wee bit easierr when I could put those sentiments to music and that is what I am goin' to trry to do tonight. The tune is "The Skye Boat Song" for the same rreason 'twas ourr weddin' marrch this evenin'; 'tis one o' the few Scottish songs my poorr, deprrived English wife knows as yet. That will soon change." There was more laughter.

"That's the first song we heard him sing, do you remember?" Victoria whispered across to her daughter who was sitting on the other side of Niall Hamilton. Olivia nodded– her eyes shining.

"Noo–those of ye who have known me forr soom time are dootless amazed at what has taken place herre tonight," Gavin chuckled. "Ye all thought, I'm surre, that I'd neverr marrry. And to be honest I soomtimes wonderred myself. But then, ye see, I met Torri and I kent why I had waited. I was waitin' forr herr." His fingers began to move easily over the strings of the guitar in the same gently rolling accompaniment he always used with this melody. "But enough o' prreliminarries. Let me simply say that everra man cooms to his weddin' day wi' cerrtain thoughts, cerrtain emotions. These, my dearrest Torri, to the best of my poorr ability are mine." He sang the chorus first.

O'err plaid and o'err heatherr the candlelight gleams;
Sweetly the pipes do play.
Just as I've seen it in all of my drreams,
This is ourr weddin' day.

The song was indeed meant for Victoria alone and Gavin never took his eyes off her.

Lasses I'd known, yet still alone;
Emptiness filled my days.
Easy to do–to say 'I love you',
Tho' not but an empty phrrase.

Then therre was you and then I knew
Searrchin' was at an end.
The Scotsman was tame and ye became
My trreasurre, my love, my frriend.

As the pipes skirrl, my dearrest wee gurrl
Slowly cooms doon the stairr.
Tarrtan and white, my hearrt's delight,
In all the worrld most fairr.

Torri, my brride, stands by my side;
Each speaks the marrriage vow.
One lass I take; all otherrs forrsake,
Life has a meanin' now.

Now it is done; now we arre one
Purrest of joys unflaw'd.
Dearrest of wives, love joins our lives–
Unity blessed by God.

Niall soon became fascinated with watching his new daughter-in-law. Her right hand moved continually–to touch her wedding ring, Gavin's brooch, to stroke the plaid. Her lips were parted in a slight smile and her eyes shone with tears. At some point–he couldn't be sure when–one or two tears had escaped to trickle unheeded down her cheeks.

"Granddad," Olivia whispered, "Mummy's crying."

" 'Tis all rright, wee lass," he reassured her. "Those arre happy tearrs."

When the song ended, there was none of the hearty applause he customarily received–only a profound silence. People were too moved or perhaps even embarrassed at having been privy to such an intensely personal moment. Gavin was quiet himself for a few seconds, gazing down at the floor. When at last he did look up, it was to extend his hand to Victoria as if to say, "I'd like ye wi' me noo, darrlin'." At once she rose and came to join him, halfway there reaching out as if to shorten the time until they could be together. Their two hands met, clasping eagerly. He drew her up to stand beside him and then the applause came in celebration of the love shared by these two people–a love they had affirmed that evening by the taking of their marriage vows.

Gavin put his arm around Victoria's waist. "Will ye sing 'My Cup Rrunneth Overr' wi' me noo?" he whispered to her under cover of the applause. She nodded, smiling up at him and when the ovation had finally died down, he explained the significance of the song and that now, of course, the lyrics were doubly meaningful. "And, oh yes," he added, seemingly as an afterthought, "when we finish this, we hope ye'll excuse us."

Victoria sang the first verse. Her clear soprano was a surprise to most of the people there.

Sometimes in the morning when shadows are deep,
I lie here beside you just watching you sleep.
And sometimes I whisper what I'm dreaming of,
My cup runneth over with love.

And Gavin sang the second–his burr giving even this American musical comedy number a distinctly Scottish flavor.

Soomtimes in the evenin' when ye dinna see,
I study the small things ye do constantly.
I memorrize moments that I'm fondest of,
My cup rrunneth overr with love.

And finally they sang the last verse together although now it became a promise– not just to each other, but to everyone present–all the people with whom they'd shared this special night–that their love would endure, only growing stronger as the years went by.

In only a moment we both will be old.
We won't even notice the world turning cold.
And so in this moment with sunlight above
My cup runneth over with love....
With love....with love....with love....with love.

The song having concluded, Gavin gave his guitar to his nephew and taking Victoria's hand once more, he led her across the room and up the stairs.

Words had normally come easily between them and yet suddenly now, walking together along the upstairs hallway, they could think of nothing to say until at last, pausing in the doorway of Victoria's room, they turned to look at each other. Brown eyes met green eyes as they had so many times before in so many different places and situations. After a moment

Gavin bent to kiss her and only then did he speak. "Dinna be long, lass. We've got quite a drrive if we'rre goin' to get to Inverrness tonight." She nodded, but didn't move. His eyes began to crinkle at the edges. "Well, Torri, ye willna get rready to leave this way, I dinna think." Again she nodded–in complete agreement with these wise precepts being uttered by her new husband–, but she continued to stand there holding his hand. "What is it?" he asked after a moment..

"I...I hate to be away from you for even that long, I guess," Victoria replied at last. "I want you where I can see you and touch you. Otherwise, this might all turn out to be a dream."

" 'Tis nae a drream, darrlin'." He touched her new brooch lightly with the tip of his forefinger as if in affirmation of the words inscribed on it. "But do ye no ken, lass," he went on, his eyes beginning to glow again in fun, "that in orrderr forr ourr life togetherr to trruly begin, we firrst have to change ourr clothes."

"I don't see you moving either," she teased in return.

"Verra trrue, lass, verra trrue!" Chuckling, he went on down the hall to his own room. Suddenly he could see what Victoria meant and he'd never changed so rapidly in his entire life. But he cherished her gift too much to treat it casually and he carefully folded each item into his case before closing and latching it.

Fiona had come upstairs soon after the newlyweds to help her sister-in-law out of her dress and plaid and into the new heather tweed pants suit and turtleneck jumper she would be wearing on the drive. "Do you want this packed?" she inquired, holding up the dress.

"Yes. Gavin's taking his kilt and....and everything. We thought we might wear them again tomorrow night for New Year's Eve." Victoria went over to the dressing table, humming softly to herself as she leaned down to check her hair and make-up in the mirror.

"Ye'rre nae happy by any chance, arre ye?" Smiling, Fiona folded the dress and placed it in the suitcase.

"Now where would you get an idea like that?" Victoria laughed merrily.

"Do you want me to go see if my brother's rready?"

"No." She shook her head. "I'll go."

"Miss him alrready?"

"You know—I do. You could latch my cases for me though." Victoria hurried out of the room and along the hall to knock on Gavin's door.

He opened it almost at once–ready to go–dressed in corduroy trousers and a fisherman's knit pullover. "Hello there, lass" he grinned. "Is therre soomthin' I can do forr ye?"

She smiled back at him. "As a matter of fact, I was looking for someone to go on a honeymoon with me. Would you perhaps know of anyone?"

"Let me see herre." He looked behind him as though searching for someone. "Well, it seems therre's no one herre but me," he went on after a few seconds turning back to face her again, "so I'll have to do."

"Oh, dear!" Victoria pretended to be dismayed. "Well, I suppose, since I have no other choice...." Then all at once she didn't wanted to joke anymore. "Oh, Gavin!" She came into his arms. "I do love you so!"

"Aye, lass, aye." He held her close for a moment, reveling in the knowledge that at last she truly did belong to him. "So shall we go then?" he asked her at last.

She nodded. "Yes, I'm all ready."

"Yourr things in yourr rroom?" He picked up his valise.

"Yes–just take the large case. I can carry the other one."

"Otherr one?" He raised his eyebrows. "Ye do ken, do ye not, that we only have thrree days?"

"Oh, you!" She laughed and punched him in the arm.

"Ow!" he howled rubbing the wounded spot. "Och, Fiona," he complained as they came into the other room, "we've only been marrried two hourrs and she's alrready beatin' me oop!"

"Poorr laddie," his sister commiserated. "But I think you can take carre o' yourrself." Gavin took Victoria's valise in his free hand although he swore his injury made this extremely painful and laughing together, the three of them started along the hall. Suddenly Fiona stopped. "Stay herre a minute," she instructed them, "and let me go firrst. It...it should be just the two of ye." Leaving them there, she ran lightly down the stairs. "They'rre coomin'..... they'rre coomin'," she whispered excitedly. In the meantime Meghan had handed around small paper sacks of rice and now everyone formed into two lines leading from the foot of the stairs to the front door.

A moment later Gavin and Victoria came around the corner onto the landing and discovered what was in store for them. "Oh, no!" he exclaimed.

"Coom on then, laddie," his father urged, taking a large handful of rice.

"Come on, Mummy!" Olivia chimed in happily.

"Can soomone at least take ourr cases oot to the car," Gavin requested, "so we can rrun unencumberred?"

Two of the men willingly reached up to take them. "But wait forr us to coom back," one of them called over his shoulder as they disappeared outside.

In the few minutes of waiting Victoria's eyes came to rest on her daughter. Perhaps it was the long dress, but all at once she was painfully aware that Olivia wasn't really a child anymore and she thought with a rush of sadness of all the years she'd missed. "Darling," she said quietly, "come here, please."

"Yes, Mummy." She came over to stand at the foot of the stairs and look up at her mother.

Letting go of Gavin's hand, Victoria came to sit on the next to the bottom step. She wasn't even aware of all the people standing there. All she saw was her daughter's face–very close to hers now. "It will only be a little while, luv," she promised, "and then we'll have you with us."

"It's all right. I don't mind as long as I know we'll all be together soon."

By now Gavin had come down to sit beside Victoria. "And we will be, darrlin' wee one, ye ken that?"

Olivia smiled at him. "Are...are you really my Daddy now?"

"Well, ye alrready have a Daddy and I wouldna trry to take his place. But would ye mind havin' two Daddies?" She shook her head and they both leaned forward to embrace her. The other people in the room tried not to watch the little scene. As with Gavin's song they were being included purely by accident in a very private moment. But it was so touching and despite their honorable intentions their eyes were continually drawn back to it. "Do ye want to rrun wi' us, lass?" he went on to ask when they had finally released her, both sitting back to gaze at her lovingly.

"No." A grin tugged at the corners of the little girl's mouth. "I want to throw rice at you."

"Oh, you do, do you?" Victoria laughed.

Just then the men returned, having stowed the cases in the car's boot. "Coom along noo, Gavin," the other of the two yelled. "I've been waitin' a long time to thrrow rrice at yourr weddin'!" There was a roar of laughter from the crowd.

"Come on, Mummy." Olivia backed away. "Run!!"

"Aye, coom on, big brrotherr," Fiona called out.

They stood up again and Gavin held out his hand for Victoria to take hold of it. "Rready?" he asked her. She nodded and pelted with rice every inch of the way, they made a dash for the door. Even though it was starting to snow, the crowd followed them outside where Gavin first helped Victoria in on her side of the car and then hurried around to his own. The motor roared into life and they moved off quickly down the winding lane.

* * *

For the first hour or so they chatted casually, sharing their memories and impressions of the day, but gradually the conversation dwindled away and for a while they rode in silence. Actually for the most part it was Gavin who had stopped talking, but Victoria was not immediately concerned. The headlights reflected off the snow, dimly illumining the interior of the car as well, and making it seem their own private world– existing alone in an otherwise empty universe. She was happy just watching him. He shifted his left hand on the steering wheel and his new wedding ring caught the light, the antique gold gleaming dully in the semi-darkness. Irresistibly she found herself drawn to touch this symbol of their union. He glanced at her sharply and she thought she'd made a mistake. Gavin had once said he looked upon a wedding ring as a brand and now perhaps she had pointed it out to him as precisely that. "I...I'm sorry," Victoria said at once.

"'Tis naethin' ye've done, lass. I'm concerrned aboot the rroads. Perrhaps we should have stayed at Dad's tonight."

"Oh no, darling! I couldn't wait to be alone with you!"

He smiled a little at that, his dimple appearing in the dim light to be but a brief deepening of the shadow along his jawline. "Aye, lass." He took his left hand off the wheel for just a few seconds to reach over and give hers a quick squeeze. Replacing it, he himself glanced at the wedding ring. "Ye know," he said after a moment, "I'm verra glad I changed my mind aboot this. It means sae much to me, Torri, I....." But just then the car swerved so sharply that Victoria couldn't help but notice as well. "We've got to stop, darrlin'–the firrst place we coom to. 'Tis gettin' worrse!" He slowed down, but a few minutes later they skidded again, slamming sideways into a drift. Reducing the speed even further, Gavin peered anxiously ahead. The next village should be Tomintoul, but he wasn't sure how far that was. At least at this hour and in this weather they were unlikely to meet another car. Victoria couldn't help recalling his unequivocal statement that it never rained in Scotland, but tension was evident in every line of his face and body and she wisely decided this wasn't the time to tease him about the weather.

After what seemed like forever, they passed one or two houses and then a small chapel and with a rush of relief Gavin recognized the outskirts of Tomintoul. By now it was nearly eleven and at first everything appeared to be in darkness, but then they rounded a sharp bend in the road and in the central square of the village they discovered two lighted windows-- great splashes of welcome spilling out from them into an otherwise deserted street. The local pub was still open and Gavin brought the car to an uncertain stop in front of it. "Well, we can be grrateful," he observed, "that no matter what the weatherr a Scot must have his pint!" He tried to smile at her, but as he finally relaxed his grip on the steering wheel, Victoria could see that his hands were shaking.

"It's all right, darling," she whispered.

He reached over to take her in his arms. "Thank God!" he murmured fervently. "If soomthin' had happened–if ye'd been hurrt in some way–I would neverr have forrgiven myself."

"Now nothing did happen, did it?" She stroked the back of his head and neck to calm and reassure him.

He released her a little then and kissed her once lightly. "Do ye want to coom in wi' me, darrlin', orr wait herre?"

"I....I want to stay with you."

"Aye" was all he said in reply and after a moment they both got out of the car to fight their way hand in hand through the wind-driven mixture of snow and sleet to the door of the pub. Even on a stormy night in the Highlands the place was full and entering, they stepped in an instant from darkness and bitter cold into an atmosphere of warmth and smoke and noise. Gavin led the way through the crush of humanity still holding Victoria's hand. The people were three deep around the bar and it was several minutes before they could work their way up to the front. "Sorrry 'tis sae crrowded, darrlin'," he apologized.

"You're forgetting I used to work in places like this."

"Aye—laddie." The bartender finally addressed Gavin, "And what will you and your lass be havin' the noo?"

"Actually we'rre lookin' forr a rroom forr the night. We'd hoped to get to Inverrness, but the rroads are verra bad."

"Aye, laddie, aye. 'Tis no night to be oot and aboot." He moved away along the bar and raised a hand to shout something over the din.

"How can anyone hear him?" Victoria asked. She was forced to raise her voice even though Gavin was standing right next to her. He laughed and shook his head.

Evidently someone had, however, because a few seconds later another man joined them at the bar. Victoria was continually amazed at how Gavin and his father towered over so many of their fellow Scots. This man was barely as tall as she was. He wore a tartan cap even here indoors and his small blue eyes twinkled–though whether frrom his own good spirits or the liquid variety, she couldn't be sure. "Aye, Sandy?" he said.

"This is Gorrdie MacKinnon," the bartender informed them. "He and his wee wifie rrun a bed and brreakfast. These people arre in need of a rroom, Gorrdie."

"Aye....aye." He smiled warmly and Victoria decided that at least two-thirds of the twinkle was natural. "Katie and I would be that pleased to have ye. 'Tis nearrly last call and then we'll show ye the way. In the meantime coom back to ourr table and have a pint."

"Aye." Gavin replied at once and he slipped an arm around Victoria's waist to draw her through the crowd.

There was another couple in the booth as well as a plump, red-cheeked woman who was at the moment sitting by herself. Apparently this was "Gorrdie's wee wifie". Their host had managed to secure two chairs and was standing by the table beaming at them genially. "This is my Katie and these arre Davey and Lorrna Drrummond and ye arre...?"

"Gavin and Torri Hamilton." He experienced a ridiculous rush of pleasure at this, his first opportunity to introduce Victoria and himself as a couple.

"Wherre would ye be frrom, Gavin?" Davey Drummond asked.

"Glengowrrie–just this side of Ballaterr."

Victoria was sitting between Gavin and Katie MacKinnon. "Yourr laddie said yourr name is Torri?" Katie inquired at some point. " 'Tis an unusual name. Is it shorrt forr soomthin'?" She hesitated. "Did ye hearr me?" the Scotswoman went on when Victoria didn't immediately answer. "I'm nae surrprrised. The din in herre is soomthin' fearrful, isn't it?"

Victoria nodded. She had comprehended by now with some relief that she was being accepted simply as Gavin's wife. "Tori is short for Victoria," she replied at last.

"Oh, ye'rre English," Katie remarked, but it was obviously only an observation on her part. "Wherre did ye meet then?"

"In the States actually."

"Did ye hearr that, Katie?" Gordie interrupted at this point.

"Hearr what, lovey?"

"We have a pairr o' newlyweds herre. Gavin tells me they were just marrried this evenin'."

"My worrd!" she exclaimed. "And we'rre keepin' ye herre chatterrin'. Ye go on ahead, Gorrdie, and starrt oop a grrand firre in that big frront rroom wi' the prrivate bath. We'll bide a wee herre and then I'll brring them along."

"Aye, lassie, aye." Gordie got to his feet at once, shrugging into his coat. "Afterr all ye must be gettin' a bit tense aboot noo, hm?" He gave Gavin a conspiratorial nudge.

"Haud yourr wheesht!" his wife scolded him. "Get along wi' ye noo!"

"Aye, lass, aye," he chuckled, but he must have told everyone he passed on his way to the door because people began coming over to congratulate them and offer to buy them a drink. There were mildly off-color, but good-natured comments about getting the bride "well flutherred" or the danger of the groom's powers being blunted by drink and after a while Gavin became worried about the effect all this might be having on Victoria. It took only one glance at her to reassure him. Clearly she was enjoying herself.

About a half-hour later Katie said they could go and as they followed her to the door, they were roundly cheered. "I think we might as well walk," she suggested as they came outside. "'Tis only a wee bit doon the rroad and arroond the corrner and yourr carr will be fine wherre it is until morrnin'." They took the suitcases from the boot and each carrying one, they trudged through the snow to the MacKinnon house. The driving wind made conversation virtually impossible and Victoria was admittedly relieved that it was indeed only "a wee bit doon the rroad".

Gordie was waiting to hold the door open for them. " 'Twill be a while yet beforre yourr rroom's warrm, but the parrlorr is nice and cozy and I've put the kettle on." As he spoke, he turned to lead the way into the brightly lit living room where a coal fire was blazing away on the hearth.

Just then the tea kettle started to whistle. "I'll get that, lovey," Katie said at once, "and if ye'll gie me yourr things, I'll hang them oop in the kitchen to drry." She collected Gavin and Victoria's coats and hurried away with them.

"Sit doon....sit doon," Gordie urged them, indicating the couch and two armchairs drawn up around the fire. "We willna keep ye much longerr, but we dinna usually have guests in the winterr, ye see." This was his first clear look at Victoria. Her face glowed and her eyes sparkled. A slight smile played about her lips. He grinned. "Aye, ye can always tell a new brride. They've got that cerrtain look aboot them."

Victoria's smile broadened as she and Gavin settled down side by side on the couch– hands intertwined. "Well, we'rre verra glad we stopped herre," he observed. "Ye'rre verra kind."

" 'Tis ourr pleasurre, to be surre. Yourr lass doesna talk verra much, does she?"

"I'm...I'm very aware of being an outlander, I...I guess and...and anyway I'd rather let Gavin do the talking. He...he does it so much more easily than I do."

"Och," Gordie remarked, " 'tis a rrarre thing these days forr a wife to let her laddie do the talkin'."

Katie MacKinnon returned just then carrying a tray on which were four mugs of tea, a plate of scones, butter, jam, milk and sugar. "Oh, that looks marvelous!" Victoria exclaimed. There was such a natural sweetness in her manner and Gavin watched her with great pride.

"Well, I thought ye might be a wee bit hungrry. I rrememberr the day we got marrried. We werre both so excited we harrdly ate a bite and by this time at night we werre rright peckish. So...." she went on to her husband as she handed out the mugs of tea and passed the milk, sugar and scones...."Torri was tellin' me that she and Gavin met in the States."

"My worrd, what werre ye both doin' way overr therre?" Gordie took a hugely appreciative bite of one of his wife's scones.

Gavin and Victoria's eyes met briefly. She gave her head a barely perceptible shake and he understood that if the MacKinnons didn't recognize her of their own accord, she'd rather they not be told. "We werre both visitin' frriends," he said–a truthful enough reply.

"These scones are delicious, Mrs. MacKinnon," Victoria said. "Would you give me the recipe?"

"Thank ye–I'd be that pleased to."

Most of the rest of the midnight snack passed in similar casual conversation: Gavin's father's farm and its "cute sheep"; Katie's wondering questions about London which she'd never seen; Gordie's conviction that portions of the railroad from Inverness to Kyle of Lochalsh where they'd planned to take the ferry for the Isle of Skye would have been rendered impassable by the storm.. "Well, I think the rroom should be warrm and cozy by noo," Katie said at last and standing up, she took down the shallow covered pan with the long handle which was hanging on the wall next to the fireplace.

"I've been meaning to ask you about that." Victoria said as she and Gavin picked up their suitcases, following her up the narrow, winding stairs and into their room. "That's a bed warmer, isn't it?"

"Aye, I'm surrprrised ye kent what it is. Wherre did ye see one the noo?"

"In a museum, I suppose," Victoria replied in an off-hand manner. Actually one had been used as prop in the Elizabeth series.

"Ye see those tongs therre. When ye'rre rready forr bed, ye put a few hot coals inside." Katie demonstrated how the lid was raised. "Then ye just pass it back and forrth between the sheets. Ye can also wrrap the brricks Gorrdie's left by the firre in those pieces of flannel and put them doon at yourr feet. Well, I've kept ye long enough wi' my chatterr. Ye sleep as long as ye want in the morrnin' noo and just let me know when ye'll be wantin' yourr brreakfast." She paused at the door to look back at them, giggling a little at the happy prospect of a couple on their wedding night. "Good night, then."

"Good night...good night." By now Gavin was ready to push her from the room and when they were finally alone, he came at once to take Victoria in his arms. Sensing a certain lack of response on her part, however, he immediately drew back a little to look down at her. "What is it, lass?"

"It's nothing really." She made a move to pull away.

He tightened his hold on her. " 'Tis a grreat deal morre than naethin', I think. Noo tell me orr I swearr we'll spend the entirre night standin' in the middle o' the floorr and think how that'll disappoint the MacKinnons who at this verra minute arre dootless waitin' to hearr the crreakin' o' the bedsprrings."

Victoria was trying very hard at this point to remember what could possibly have been bothering her. "Oh you, honestly! What am I do with you?"

"Just love me, darrlin', that's all. Just love me." All tenderness now, Gavin cupped her chin and made her tip her head back and look up at him. For a moment he studied her face and then finally he bent to kiss her. Sighing deeply, she brought up both hands to bury them in his hair. Without a doubt the response was there now and he picked her up to carry her to the bed, their kisses increasing in intensity. He slipped a hand up under her pullover to caress her breast.

"Gavin–oh, Gavin! Let me! Let me!" She began trying to pull the jumper off over her head even though he was half on top of her.

"All rright! All rright!" He rolled over and sat up. "But hurrry!" Undressing rapidly, they slipped under the covers. In their ardor they had forgotten. The sheets were ice cold! "Yikes!" Gavin scrambled out of bed again–grabbing the quilt and wrapping it around himself. "Wherre's that damned thing she brrought oopstairrs wi us?"

Victoria was out of bed at almost the same instant–laughing so hard it was all she could do to open her suitcase and remove her robe. "Do...do you want your robe, too?"

"Aye...aye." He was laughing now, too. "Och—ye can talk all ye want aboot a cold showerr. A frreezin' bed is verra effective as well."

"Here, darling." She threw his robe to him, but she was shaking with mirth and her toss fell far short of the mark.

"Thank ye verra much," he observed wryly, but he grinned at her as he inched forward, holding the quilt around him with one hand and reaching for his robe with the other. "Why don't ye wrrap oop those brricks while I use that thing?" He nodded in the direction of the bed warmer.

"All right, darling." They were still laughing as they worked together to warm the bed. "Would you mind terribly, luv," she asked when they were finished, "if I put on my nightgown? It's flannel, I'm afraid, and not terribly alluring, but it's still not very warm in here."

"I dinna blame ye at all. I'm thinkin' verra fondly of my pajamas at the moment." At last they were settled. "Coom herre, lass." Gavin opened his arms to her. "Not exactly the way I planned it all," he chuckled, trying in vain to stifle a yawn. "I'm afrraid I'm aboot to commit the unparrdonable sin o' fallin' asleep on ourr weddin' night."

"There'll be plenty of other nights, darling," she assured him. "And it feels so good just lying close to you like this."

"Hm, hinny," he murmured sleepily, "werre it not forr the icy bed, things would have been verra...verra...differrent." His voice trailed off and the next second he was asleep. Victoria lay awake for a while, but the warmth of Gavin's nearness soon overcame her and in a short time she also fell asleep.

* * *

The next thing of which she was conscious was his voice speaking her name and opening her eyes, she discovered that at sometime during the night she had turned away from him onto her other side. Drowsily she rolled over, reaching out to him. He gathered her in his arms and they lay for a few minutes without speaking–Gavin rubbing the small of her back in a slow, easy motion. They kissed frequently, but somehow neither was in the mood just then for matters to go any further. It was he broke the silence at last. "Ye neverr did explain why ye werre a bit oopset last night. Will ye tell me noo?"

"It really was silly, I suppose, but it...it was all that talk about our wedding night. I...I got to wishing we'd...well...waited."

"And would ye have lost any of the nights we'd alrready sharred?"

"Oh no, darling! And then we....we had no way of knowing then, did we, that we'd eventually marry?"

"No, lass. We both werre a wee bit dense therre, werren't we?" He brushed his lips against her hair.

"What...what are we going to do today?"

"Well, 'tis prrobably trrue what Gorrdie MacKinnon said—that the rrailrroad will be blocked."

"Why can't we just stay here? Where are we, by the way?"

"Tomintoul."

"Where?!" Her head came up so that she could look at him.

"Neverr mind, lass," he chuckled. "Just lie back doon and behave yourrself!"

She obeyed although he could feel she was still shaking with laughter. "But I do like it here. The MacKinnons are so sweet and....."

"Of courrse they arre–they'rre Scots."

She ignored this and went on...."and there must be places around here to see."

"I did think we'd spend today herre. By tomorrrow the rroads should be open and we can drrive up to the coast and along to Inverrness. One night therre–and then back to Dad's. How does that sound to ye?"

"Fine. But if we're going to do all that in only three days," she teased him, "shouldn't we get started sometime this morning?"

"Aye, lass, I suppose we must and afterr all, as ye said, 'tis only the firrst o' many nights. But ye stay therre noo. I'll add morre coal to the firre and by the time I showerr and shave, the room will be warrmerr."

"You take such good care of me."

" 'Tis my pleasurre, hinny." With one last quick kiss he got out of bed to slip into his robe and tend to the fire. Finally he took his toiletries kit out of his suitcase and with a wink went on into the bathroom.

Victoria lay contentedly in the bed watching him move about the room. Even after he'd disappeared from sight, the sound of the shower running was a gentle reminder that he was only on the other side of the door. When the water had stopped, she waited a few minutes and then got up herself to go and knock.

"Who is it?" Gavin called out.

"Who is it?!" She flung the door open to find him bent over the washbasin– dissolved in laughter. A towel wrapped around his waist, he was just about to begin shaving and he looked so adorable that she flung herself into his arms–mindless of the lather on his face and hands. Continuing to chuckle, Gavin drew her to him. He tried to kiss her lightly, but he still got lather on her nose and chin. "May I duck in under you to put on my face?" she asked. "I can take my shower later."

"Aye." He cocked his head to one side to peer down at her. "I suppose that's one of the prrivileges of marrried life–sharrin' the mirrrorr?"

"Yes–aren't you fortunate?" She was back in a few minutes with her make-up, standing in front of him and leaning forward to apply base, eye liner, shadow and mascara, blush and lipstick. Somehow he managed to shave without cutting himself–quite an accomplishment when more than half his attention was on the dear blonde head just below his chin.

In about half an hour they were both ready. A door opened to the right of the stairs as they came down and Katie MacKinnon stuck her head into the hall to grin at them affably. "Well noo, I thought I'd hearrd ye oop and aboot. The tea's brrewin' and the oatmeal's hot. Coom on in and sit yourrselves doon." Gavin threw Victoria an amused glance. He knew just how much his new wife would appreciate the oatmeal.

"Just tea and toast for me, please," she said at once. "Or perhaps some of those scones from last night if there are any left."

"Yourr lass doesna eat verra much," Katie observed.

"No, but dinna worrry. I'll morre than make oop forr herr." He proceeded to put away a heaping bowl of oatmeal (thick and sticky, just the way he liked it), three eggs and sausage, toast and countless mugs of the strong, sweet tea. Victoria, on the other hand, had two mugs of tea and two scones. Katie continually beamed at them, enjoying watching what she innocently assumed was their first breakfast together. Not that they disappointed her–touching often during the meal. "Would we be inconveniencin' ye," Gavin asked at one point, "if we stayed herre again tonight?"

"Och, we'd be that pleased to have ye!" she assured him. "And therre are soom grrand sights herre aboot. The castle at Nethy Brridge is open in the winterr. A Black Watch rregiment drrills therre everra mornin."

"My Dad was wi' the Black Watch in the Warr."

"And tonight bein' Hogmanay," Katie continued, "therre'll be a dance in the village hall. Ye might enjoy that."

"Aye, we would–I think, hm, Torri?"

"It sounds lovely, yes."

"Good then–if ye'll gie us dirrections to the Castle, we'll go on overr therre."

"Gorrdie could prrobably do that betterr. He's the local postmasterr—doon just opposite the pub."

"Will ye be needin' anythin' frrom the rroom, darrlin'? I want my camerra." Gavin took a last swing of his tea as he stood up.

"Just my purse and my sunglasses."

"I'll be rright back." He leaned down to give her one more quick kiss before hurrying out the door and up the stairs.

"That laddie o' yourrs is in love forr fairr," Katie remarked. "And he's a brraw lookin' one, isn't he?"

Victoria smiled. "Oh yes, very braw."

"Ye've known him soom time then. Ye underrstand the Scots verra well."

"Between my husband and his family, yes, I'm learning quickly."

"Ye like the sound o' that worrd, 'husband', I think. Och, 'tis nae been that long since I wed my Gorrdie. I ken verra well how ye feel."

"Herre ye arre, lass." Gavin came back into the kitchen, putting her purse down on the table and handing her the dark glasses. The camera was around his neck. He took her coat down from a hook on the wall and held it for her to slip into.

Buttoning up the jacket, Victoria put on the matching fleece lined hat, pulled on her wellingtons and finally the mittens. "All ready, darling."

"Aye–well, let's go then." Shrugging into his own coat, he put out his hand for her to take it. He stood looking down at her for a moment and at last he turned to lead the way to the door.

"Tea's at five," Katie called after them.

"Aye....aye," Gavin called back, "we'll be herre in plenty o' time."

They walked back along the same route they'd traveled the night before. The storm had long since ended and the weather was perfect: crisp and clear. It being a week-day morning, however, the street remained deserted. Most people, like Gavin's father, were farmers of some sort, only coming into town on Sundays, market days or to the pub on an evening. Gordie MacKinnon greeted them with great enthusiasm, coming out into the street to point out the direction of the castle. "I took the liberrty," he went on, "of havin' some of the lads clearr the snow and ice off yourr carr."

"Aye–thank ye," Gavin replied. "We'll see ye this evenin' then. We'rre stayin' forr the dance."

"Aye–grrand....grrand! See ye then." He waited in the doorway of the post office while they got into the car and Gavin warmed up the motor. He was still standing there to wave good-bye as they finally moved off down the street.

"Where did the stereotype of the dour Scot ever come from?" Victoria wondered.

"Ye can ask that–havin' met my brrotherr?"

She laughed a little. "But as far as I can see, he's a minority of one. Everyone else is so warm and friendly."

"I think ye like my countrry, hinny."

"Oh, darling, of course I do." She reached over to touch him on the arm.

The old castle was set high on a hill, its ruins appearing even more dark and desolate somehow on such a glorious day. They left the car by the side of the road and began to climb hand in hand toward the main gateway. "Whatever could have happened to it?" Victoria wondered sadly.

"After the Forrty-Five a lot of homes werre destrroyed–as a punishment, I suppose."

"You mean the Duke of Cumberland's men did this?"

"Aye, lass."

She stopped suddenly in the center of the path, peering up at him with great earnestness. "Gavin, I'm so sorry!"

"What did ye do?"

"Oh, I don't mean me personally. The English–for such unnecessary cruelty. No wonder Rhuaridh feels the way he does."

"People like Rrhuarridh arre foolish, Torri. To go on holdin' hatrred forr soomthin' that happened overr two hundrred yearrs ago. And <u>ye'rre</u> cerrtainly nae rresponsible forr it anyway."

She smiled. "I guess I'm just seeing things from a different viewpoint. That's all."

Wanting to make sure, however, that Victoria didn't find their visit in any way a sad occasion, Gavin proceeded to indicate various "points of interest" to her: a red stain on the steps of the tower which he swore was blood, but looked suspiciously like catsup; a hole in the wall of what had once been the great hall which appeared exactly like all the other holes, but which Gavin demonstrated as having resulted from the swipe of a claymore held in the two hands of a mighty Highland warrior (not unlike himself, by the way) or a piece of paper which he solemnly affirmed to be part of the laird's last will and testament even though it was quite evidently the inside wrapper from a packet of crisps. By the end of the "tour" they had collected a crowd of wide-eyed English and American tourists who were evidently accepting his every word as unquestioned historical fact and Victoria was having to bite the insides of her mouth to keep a straight face. Away from the others finally, walking back down the hill to their car, she exploded with suppressed laughter. "Gavin, you are incorrigible! Those people will go home with the most dreadful misconceptions!"

He grinned. "Wasn't it fun though?"

"Yes, I must admit it was. But you really did it for me, didn't you?"

He put his arm around her waist and drew her closer. "Aye, hinny. To show ye that forr me the past is simply that—the past. Noo–has yourr historry lesson made ye hungrry? The man at the gate tells me therre's a grrand pub in Nethy Brridge."

"As a matter of fact, I...I am hungry."

"Good–let's go, then."

One of the pub's specialties, they discovered, was steak-and-kidney pie. Upon seeing the size of the portions, however, Victoria was properly dismayed. "Dear God," she gasped, "I'll never be able to eat all this!"

"I'll help ye oot, lass," Gavin assured her with a wink digging into his own meal with obvious relish.

They both enjoyed the homely coziness of the pub and for some time after they'd finished eating, they still lingered on drinking tea and talking. They were just beginning to think about leaving when a large, rather overdressed woman approached their table, the overbearing scent of her perfume having announced her impending arrival by at least half a dozen steps. She was wearing one of those fur pieces where the animal has apparently been caught in the peculiar process of devouring its own tail. "Frightfully sorry to bother you and all," she burbled, "but I simply had to ask. I told my friend you were Victoria Windsor, but she said what would Victoria Windsor be doing way up here." Victoria wasn't sure whether she was expected to reply since the woman's rather lengthy pronouncement hadn't actually ended in a question. "Well, are you?" the woman demanded after a moment.

"As a matter of fact I am." She hoped this would satisfy her.

"Why, I just knew it!" Before they realized what was happening, the woman had pulled over a chair from a near-by table and sat down between them. "Now I won't take much of your time, Miss Windsor, but I couldn't miss the opportunity to tell you how much I enjoy your work!"

Victoria glanced uneasily at Gavin–certain he would resent this intrusion even more than she did. She was right! "How very kind of you." She smiled pleasantly at the woman.

"You're quite welcome, Miss Windsor. You know what I think was my favorite–that witty little thing by Basil Fitzhugh. What was it called?"

"*Once More–Forever.*"

"Really? Are you sure?"

"Quite sure–yes."

"And that attractive man who appeared with you–Sean Patrick. How's he?"

"I...ah...wouldn't know. I...ah...haven't seen him for some time." The expression on Gavin's face was growing darker by the minute and at last Victoria understood fully what Felicity had meant by a black and bloody mood. "Perhaps an autograph?" she suggested —anything to get rid of the woman.

"Oh, thank you, Miss Windsor! I'll be right back." Bustling back to her own table, she began to rummage through her purse, all the time talking to her friend and gesturing excitedly in their direction.

"Gavin, darling, I'm sorry," Victoria said hurriedly during their few minutes alone.

"Aye." But his monosyllabic reply indicated the blackest fury.

"These things happen. You do understand, don't you?"

"Aye."

"Well, here we are, Miss Windsor." The woman returned now, dragging her reluctant friend behind her. "Mildred would just never forgive herself if she missed the chance to meet you, Miss Windsor."

"Hello, Mildred." Still trying to be gracious, Victoria accepted the pad of paper and the pen "And your name?" she went on to the first woman as she signed Mildred's autograph and handed it to her.

"My name is Eleanor–E-L-E-A-N-O-R." She spelled it out slowly as though the actress might be a little dense.

"Th...thank you, Miss Windsor," Mildred stammered, backing away as she might have from the presence of royalty.

Victoria rapidly signed the second autograph as well.

"Thank you very much, Miss Windsor."

"You're quite welcome, I'm sure." At last—mercifully–the woman left and without another word Gavin got to his feet, reaching inside his jacket for his wallet to pay the check. Victoria stood up as well. He helped her on with her coat, still without speaking, and turned to lead the way out of the pub. "Where....where to now, darling?" she asked once they were outside, hoping to lighten the mood.

"Back to the MacKinnons'. Ye'll be wantin' to do yourr prrimpin' and fussin' forr the dance tonight, I should imagine."

"That's...that's not fair," she replied breathlessly. Gavin's long legs were covering the distance back to the car in enormous strides and it was all she could do to keep up with him. "I only wear a little make-up now and that's just to look beautiful for...for you." Gavin heard the quaver in her voice and at once he slowed his step. "Darling, please." Victoria took hold of his arm. "Please tell me why you're so upset with me."

He'd stopped walking altogether now. Looking down at her, he saw the sea green eyes he adored brimming with tears and all his anger left him. " 'Tis naethin, lass," he assured her and taking a handkerchief from his trouser pocket, Gavin dabbed gently under her eyes where one or two tears were threatening to escape. "Tis naethin' at all. Wherre would ye like to go?"

"Somewhere we could talk, please." Now that he no longer seemed as remote, she immediately felt better and she blinked back the tears.

"Why not just a wee strroll then?" He put out his hand for her to take hold of it.

"I...I noticed some benches on the common. Couldn't we sit there for a while?"

"Ye willna be cold?"

"Gavin, I'm not so damned fragile as all that!"

He was relieved to see her spirit return. Dr. Anthony had cautioned him that Victoria would require a great deal of patience and understanding–especially at first. How could he possibly have gotten annoyed with her over nothing. "Aye, lass." He grinned. "I'll rrememberr that. Coom noo."

In silence they walked together along the street to the tiny village common. Even after they were both seated on one of the old wooden benches in the chill winter sunshine, neither of them spoke at first. Victoria stared down at her two mittened hands, clasped together in her lap while Gavin occupied himself, as was often the case when he was ill-at-ease, with the cleaning, refilling and lighting of his pipe. "Was it because that woman interrupted us?" she finally asked in a small voice. "I...I got rid of her as quickly as I could. I...I was so often rude to people in the past that now I suppose I....I try to make up for it by...by being kinder. I...I....." Gradually, however, as he made no attempt either to agree or disagree, she lost her courage and the words petered out.

"I alrready told ye, hinny—'twas naethin'," Gavin replied at last, reaching over to take one of her hands between both of his. " 'Twas only yourr daft laddie gettin' himself all oopset overr a trrifle."

She refused to allow him to drop the subject, however. "Please, my darling. I...I want to know so I can be sure it never happens again."

"Well, I rrealize noo how foolish I was. After all, ye havna been my wife forr a full day yet. I canna expect people to know."

"Oh!" Victoria laughed a little now–greatly relieved. "Then it was just because she intruded on our honeymoon?"

" 'Twasna even that. I told ye I'm daft. 'Twas all that Miss Windsorr business."

"You're going to have to expect it, darling. Many people will continue to call me that."

"But that's not yourr name anymorre!" He found himself becoming angry all over again, forgetting entirely his tender resolve of but a few minutes before.

Then all at once Victoria understood. "It wasn't because she called me Miss Windsor, was it?" He said nothing. "It was because I didn't correct her." He leaned forward to rest his elbows on his knees, puffing furiously on his pipe, and still he didn't reply. "I'm right, aren't I, Gavin?"

"Aye, Torri, aye. I...I want ye to be prroud o' bein' my wife."

"Oh, darling, I am."

"But if that's how ye feel, why don't ye show it?"

"Now that's just ridiculous!"

"Rridiculous, is it–to want my wife to be prroud o' me?"

"What in hell has my name got to do with being proud of you?"

"Well, if ye canna see it yourrself, I'm cerrtainly not goin' to explain it to ye. We should be goin' noo." He knocked his pipe against the bench several times to clean out the ashes and shoved it into his jacket pocket.

"Fine!" She stood up and began to move in the direction of the car. "As long as you insist on being so utterly idiotic!"

"Idiotic!" She heard him mutter as he strode past her. "Idiotic! Och!"

Gavin's rapid pace allowed him little chance to think, but he had more than ample opportunity for reflection once he reached the car as, unlike before, Victoria made no attempt to keep up with him. In fact she deliberately took her time, even stopping to look in the shop windows. All he could do was watch her and fume. Approaching, she saw at once he was furious and slowed her steps even further. "Get in!" he growled, yanking open the door.

With maddeningly exaggerated grace she slipped into the passenger side, drawing her legs in after her. Gavin slammed the car door after her and strode around to the other side to get into the driver's seat, slamming that door as well. He started the motor and jammed the transmission into first, the gears grinding in protest. The wheels spun as they pulled away from the curb, sending stones and bits of ice flying, and in a matter of minutes they were out of the village, speeding along the snow-covered country road. Victoria held on to the edge of her seat, bracing her feet against the floor, and even when the motion of the car began to make her nauseous, she refused to complain. At last, however, a moan of discomfort escaped her. Immediately concerned, Gavin glanced over at her. "Dinna ye feel well, Torri?"

"I'm fine!" she replied from between clenched teeth. At once he slowed down, pulling over to the side of the road. "I...I have to get some fresh air!" Victoria threw open the door and scrambled out to stand leaning against the car, breathing deeply of the clean, cold air.

Gavin got out of his own side and came around to stand beside her. "Arre ye surre ye want to go on wi' this whole thing?" he asked with a rueful grin.

"What...what whole thing?" she managed to reply between gulps of air.

"This marrriage. In less than twenty-fourr hourrs I've made ye crry and I've made ye sick."

"Oh, Gavin," she murmured, "of course I do."

"I love ye so, lass!" He took her in his arms. "I'm sorrry. I'm sorrry. I'm sorrry," he whispered over and over again.

"It's all right, darling," Victoria returned his embrace with equal fervor. "I...I feel much better now. We can go along."

"Arre ye surre, hinny?" He kissed her lightly on the hair. She nodded. "All rright, lass. I prromise I'll take it slowly." During the remainder of the drive back to the MacKinnons' they chatted about the weather, the castle, the dance that evening— anything and everything except what had caused their disagreement. Even when they went upstairs after tea to change, they avoided the subject. Perhaps they were afraid it would only start the argument all over again and they had discovered they definitely did not enjoy arguing. Perhaps it was simply that looking at each other–dressed as they had been at the moment they exchanged their marriage vows–made them both realize just how trivial the quarrel had been.

* * *

Nothing else quite compares with a Highland ball: garlands of heather, crossed claymores along the walls flanking proud family crests dating back hundreds of years and at the head of the hall, dominating all else, the banner of Saint Andrew and the Red Lion Rampant on a Field of Gold–the Royal Arms of Scotland. The festivities were already in progress when they arrived with the MacKinnons and against this background flashed the kilts of the men, the soft, pastel dresses and tartan plaids of the woman. Victoria gasped in admiration as they entered and Gavin grinned with pleasure. It was only the beginning of a glorious evening.

The polkas were the easiest, of course, but Victoria also managed the reels fairly well and even the strathspeys–slower, but more complicated. Oh, but most all she enjoyed the waltzes--Gavin's hand firmly at her waist, his plaid and the pleats of his kilt flying out behind him as they whirled across the floor. He's such a strong man, she thought, completely self-reliant and sure of himself. Yet this afternoon when I failed to correct that woman, he was deeply hurt. Why <u>didn't</u> I say something? Why would I want people to continue to call me Miss Windsor when I am so proud of being Mrs. Gavin Hamilton? Suddenly she became aware he'd said something. "What, darling? I'm sorry." She tipped her head back to look up at him.

" 'Tis a bad sign when a new brride's thoughts arre not on herr laddie."

She smiled. "But they <u>were</u> on you. What did you say?"

"Can we step ootside forr a bit afterr this dance? I'd enjoy a pipe, I think."

"Of course, darling. There's...ah...something I want to say to you anyway." They walked slowly up and down in front of the hall, Victoria wrapped snugly in a cape made of the Hamilton tartan–Fiona's Christmas gift–while Gavin only had on his velvet jacket. "Aren't you cold?" she asked, more in wonder at his hardiness than because she was actually concerned.

"No–lass." He grinned. "Only my hands a wee bit and I'll warrm them arroond the bowl o' my pipe."

Victoria pouted prettily. "You're supposed to say you've got your love to keep you warm."

"Oh well....ah...that'll be laterr," he replied with a wicked wink. "Only this time I'll make surre the <u>bed</u> is warrm firrst."

"Oh, darling, I do love you so," she whispered, managing in spite of the voluminous folds of the cape to slip an arm around his waist and snuggle against him.

"In spite of my actin' so daft this afterrnoon?" he inquired, immediately shifting his pipe to his other hand so that he could put his arm around her as well.

"You...you were right to be hurt this afternoon, Gavin."

"Oh–so ye think I was hurrt rratherr than angrry, do ye?" He drew deeply on his pipe to hide his discomfiture.

"I...I think you find it hard to admit that anyone, even I, can touch you so profoundly. So this afternoon you reacted in anger to hide the fact, maybe even from yourself, that you <u>were hurt</u>. And...and you tried to run away from me–just the way you did that day on the Mall." How well she knows me already, he thought, and oddly he did not find the realization in the least threatening. "You were hurt, weren't you?" she went on when he said nothing, "when I didn't correct that woman about my name? Weren't you, my darling?"

He cleared his throat. "Aye, lass, aye."

"And...and you had every right to be."

"But Windsorr is yourr prrofessional name and I have to underrstand....."

"I am Mrs. Gavin Hamilton," she said, every word precise and distinct although her voice trembled with emotion. "And nothing else has ever made me even half as proud."

"I...I dinna know what to say." Gavin's own voice was choked now with feeling.

Victoria stepped back to look up at him. "I don't believe it! The Silver Tongue of Scotland speechless! You've had me more than half-convinced there's a blarney stone up here somewhere as well."

He threw back his head and roared with laughter. "Och no, lass," he replied, throwing his arms around her in a bear hug. "That's forr those Irrish gowks. A Scotsman has the good sense to prreferr soomthin' a wee bit softerr and sweeterr smellin' than a rrrrrrrock." His deliberately exaggerated burr on the final word tickled her neck and she giggled. "Oh, ye like that, do ye?" he chuckled. "I'll have to rrememberr that and rroll all my 'rrr's' into that same spot."

"Oh...ah...excuse me," Gordie MacKinnon called to them from the porch of the hall.

"Aye....aye." Gavin strode across to him, pulling Victoria along behind.

"It seems my lass is nae as close-mouthed as yourrs. She's been talkin' a wee bit too much....."

"Oh, therre ye arre." Katie had followed her husband outside. "I'm afrraid I've told quite a few people aboot ye."

Oh no, Victoria thought, someone else has recognized me. "Have ye?" It was Gavin who replied.

"Aye—that we have a pairr o' newlyweds stayin wi' us and noo they'rre wantin' to toast ye. And ye'rre to lead the last rreel beforre midnight."

"Oh, that's lovely." Victoria was relieved and she smiled radiantly. "But do they realize half that pair is still stumbling through the Highland reels?"

" 'Twill nae matterr in the least." Katie beamed at them both. "Coom along noo–coom!" She took them each by a hand to lead them back inside right up to the front of the hall and onto the musicians' platform. "Herre...herre they arre, everraone!" A round of applause and resounding cheers greeted her announcement. "Gavin and Torri Hamilton," she went on when the ovation had at last subsided. "Pass the glasses noo--- pass the glasses!"

Tumblers already filled with Scotch were quickly handed about the room. It was Gordie MacKinnon who offered the toast. "May yourr love be as deep as a heatherred glen and as everrlastin' as Ben Lomond. May the Good Lorrd grrant ye a long healthy life togetherr and the joy o' many bairrns. Lang may yerr lum reek!" There was a resounding cheer and in one motion everyone tossed down the liquor.

"Lang may our what do what?" Victoria's eyes widened in puzzled merriment.

"Lum rreek," Gavin repeated for her, chuckling a little. "Long may our chimney smoke."

"Oh—well at least being toasted, I don't have to drink the stuff!"

"We'rre goin' to have to do soomthin' aboot that, lassie."

"Now really, darling, if I'm going to love something Scottish, wouldn't you rather it were you than your whiskey?"

"Aye, I suppose so." He grinned at her. "But coom noo," he went on as the fiddles tuned up to play again. "We have to lead that dance."

It was a wild, fast-moving reel, but no one seemed to mind that Victoria was a little uncertain of the steps. More important, Gavin never missed an opportunity to tell her how well she was doing and she thoroughly enjoyed herself. Immediately afterwards came the countdown to midnight and as the last chime died away, they all sang "Auld Lang Syne". Victoria was crying. So many other New Year's Eves as there had been Christmases and now to come to this one–the beginning of their new life together.

"What is it?" Gavin leaned down, drawing her closer.

"I'm all right, my darling," she managed to say, "–only terribly moved."

"Happy New Year, dearrest lassie," he whispered.

"Happy New Year, my only love," she replied raising her face to be kissed.

At last they were back in their room. Victoria went at once into the bathroom to shower and remove her make-up and when she came out a short time later, Gavin was in his robe, busily passing the bed warmer back and forth between the sheets. He grinned at her. "The brricks arre alrready in place, I might add."

"You are disgraceful, Mr. Hamilton!"

"Aye, lass, aye." He was chuckling as he finished with the bed warmer and replaced it by the fireplace. "That I will willingly admit." A moment later, however, as he turned and came back to her, his expression was intensely serious. Never taking his eyes off her face, he untied her robe and slipped it down off her shoulders. Her skin was warm and rosy from the hot shower, the tips of her breasts standing out hard and firm in the rush of cold air. "Torri," he whispered, "oh, Torri, darrlin'...darrlin'." He brought up his hands, touching her face first, before he allowed them to slide downwards over her neck and shoulders. At last he cupped her breasts, kissing each gently in turn as he had done on the first night they made love.

Victoria slipped her arms around his neck, pressing her body against his and reveling in the sensation of her, he stroked her bare back and shoulders. His eyes were dark with passion and he was breathing deeply. Turning to lead her over to the bed, he paused only long enough to remove his own robe before he slipped under the covers beside her. "Ah," he breathed, "warrm sheets!"

* * *

They slept late the next morning, getting up only in time to eat breakfast before going back to the castle to watch the muster of the Black Watch. They took their suitcases with them, intending to leave immediately afterwards. Bidding them a tearful good-bye, Katie MacKinnon made them promise to visit the next time they were up in Scotland.

The pipers and drummers of the Black Watch, First Battalion, created a magnificent spectacle of sight and sound as they marched on the esplanade of the ruined castle in the brilliant winter sunshine. The kilts flared out behind in a colorful flourish of pleats as the men turned their military corners and the sound of bagpipes and snare drums filled the air. Victoria and Gavin watched from a low hill slightly above the rest of the crowd, hoping to avoid another encounter with a member of her adoring public. "Oh, darling," she exclaimed at one point, "I've just never seen anything like it!"

"Aye, lass." He smiled, tightening his grip around her waist just briefly. Nothing pleased him more than his bride's newfound appreciation of Scottish culture.

At the end as they were turning to leave, however, they were stopped by a short, bristling bulldog of a man with a flowing gray handlebar moustache. He was dressed, Victoria noticed, in the uniform of the Black Watch although with more braid and metal and he was carrying a baton several inches taller than himself. "Ye have to be Niall Hamilton's laddie. Gavin, isn't it?"

"Aye, I am."

"Pipe Majorr Rross." He introduced himself with a brisk nod. "I had the honorr o' serrvin' wi' yourr fatherr in Frrance."

"Aye, sirr," Gavin immediately extended his hand in greeting. "I've often hearrd Dad mention ye."

"And who's this bonnie wee thing? Yourr fatherr's told me ye have quite a way wi' the lassies."

"Aye, sirr." He grinned, ducking his head. "But those days arre overr. This is my wife and we happen to be on ourr honeymoon."

"Do ye no have a name, lass, orr is yourr new husband just too mutton-headed to rrememberr it?"

"Victoria."

"Aye." He paused to study her more closely. "And yourr last name wouldn't be Windsorr by any chance?"

She wasn't about to make the same mistake twice. "It <u>was</u> Windsor, sir," she replied with a significant glance at Gavin. "<u>Now</u> it's <u>Hamilton</u>."

"Ye won't be keepin' this darrlin' gurrl off the stage, will ye, laddie? 'Twould be a grreat pity."

"I wouldna drream o' doin' that."

"Good—good. Could I prrevail on ye, then, to come home to lunch wi' me?"

"I'm afraid not, sirr," Gavin replied for them both. "We've only a couple of morre days and we want to drive along the coast to Inverrness beforre we head back to Dad's."

"Aye, I ken how it is wi' a young couple on theirr honeymoon." The already genial appearing man's laugh lines deepened even further. "Soom otherr time then and ye rrememberr me to yourr Dad noo."

"Aye, I cerrtainly will, sirr......Ye didna want to, did ye, darrlin'?" he asked when they were back in the car again.

"<u>No</u>—we...we have to share each other soon enough as it is."

"Aye–that's how I thought you'd feel."

The day was glorious, the view of the sea breathtaking and even with frequent stops they were in Inverness in time for dinner.

The next morning they shopped for gifts for Olivia and Martha as well as Gavin's family and then they rode out to see Culloden, site of the last futile battle in a futile war: the Rebellion of 1745. England and Scotland stood hand in hand looking out over the snow-covered, tree-edged meadow where once their countrymen had met in bloody conflict. "I'm glad 'tis noo instead of then, lassie," Gavin leaned down to whisper in her ear.

"Me, too," Victoria replied, kissing him on the cheek.

Finally in the afternoon they drove along Loch Ness. Gavin apologized for the frozen lake. "Nessie'll be sorrry to have missed ye, darrlin'."

"I <u>was</u> here once before, you know—in the summer. With Uncle Bertie."

"Does it make ye sad then–coomin' back?"

"Oh no, it's...it's a happy memory. Only I didn't see the monster then either. I'm beginning to think it doesn't exist."

"But no one except a Scotsman knows the trrick, ye see."

"And what's that?" Her green eyes sparkled.

"Why, ye soak pieces o' brread in Scotch, o' courrse, and thrrow them oot on the surrface o' the loch. Nessie'll coom oop everra time."

"Oh, you!" She burst into laughter.

"I'm verra serrious, lass." And he did, in fact, appear to be quite in earnest.

The long drive back to the Hamiltons' the next day didn't get them there until long after everyone else was asleep. "I'm really not sorry we didn't see anyone tonight," Victoria said as they undressed for bed. "It will be time soon enough to let other people back into our private world. And that's only the beginning."

And the next morning Fiona was indeed at their door before seven o'clock. "Aye," Gavin growled in response to her knock.

"Good morrnin' to ye, too, big brrotherr, but if we'rre goin' to get ye and Torri to the airrporrt in Aberrdeen, ye'll have to be gettin' that big lazy body o' yourrs oot o' bed."

"Verra funny," he grumbled, but Victoria saw he was smiling.

A short while later they were all at breakfast, but to Victoria's disappointment Martha had already taken Olivia back to London. "With the weddin' overr herr Dad seemed anxious forr herr," Niall explained. "Of courrse we told him we loved havin' the wee one wi' us, but he insisted."

"I understand." But the tears were audible in her voice.

"Neverr mind, darrlin'," Gavin quickly reassured her. " 'Twill be no time at all 'till we have herr with us forr aye." A long loving look was both given and received–a look Niall Hamilton immediately noted. It would seem the marriage had a firm beginning. "I hope it's not too much trrouble, Dad," he continued at last, "drrivin' my carr doon next week."

"Och, no–'tis the slow time o' the yearr forr me and it allowed you and Torri to have a honeymoon. Besides, 'twill gie me an excuse forr a visit."

At the airport there were hugs and kisses all around. "I....I was so nervous the first time I came up here," Victoria whispered as she embraced Gavin's father. "And now I'm a member of the family."

"Aye, lass," he replied, holding her close. He and Fiona waved as the newlyweds went out to the plane, continuing to stand there even as the plane taxied away down the runway and took off.

* * *

Back in London the true outside world was indeed waiting to intrude with a vengeance. Word had gotten out that Victoria Windsor and Husband Number Three would be returning on a certain flight out of Aberdeen and every major newspaper had sent a reporter and a photographer. Suspecting there might be a problem, Leslie Matthews had arranged for a car and driver. Later he decided to go along himself, but this turned out to have been a mistake. Several of the press recognized him and his presence was proof they were on the right track. Matt requested that the car be allowed to meet the Hamiltons at the plane. Then he himself started toward the gate through which the majority of the passengers would be deplaning, hoping to throw the bloodhounds off the scent.

One female reporter, however, trailed him doggedly every foot of the way along the corridor. "What's he like–this Scotsman she's married."

"Actually I don't know him that well as yet," he hedged.

"How long's this one going to last, do you think?" Moving at a fast trot, a man had come up on Matt's other side.

"I'm not a bloody prophet!" Why couldn't they leave Victoria alone even for a little while?

A uniformed official approached from the other direction. "Everything's arranged, Mr. Matthews. Miss Windsor's car will be allowed out on the runway."

"Not fair at all!" the woman reporter reproached him as she pulled an immediate U turn, heading toward one of the exits leading out onto the field.

"Most unsporting of you, old chap!" the other reporter accused him, following after the woman.

"Perhaps you'd...you'd like a ride out to the plane, sir?" the official suggested uneasily. "In case a situation develops?"

"A situation has <u>already</u> developed, you damned fool–but yes, I would."

* * *

The plane was too small to be divided into sections and Victoria and Gavin were the object of many curious glances as they sat together holding hands and talking quietly. For the most part, however, they were allowed their privacy.

At one point during the flight Victoria got up to use the lavatory in the front of the plane. In order to do so she had to pass the galley where the two attendants were preparing to serve coffee. Both bathrooms were occupied and while she stood outside waiting, they had a chance to observe her closely. If she noticed they were staring, she gave no sign of it. In a moment one of the lavatories became vacant and she disappeared inside. "Isn't she beautiful?" one of the girls whispered.

"Yes, I suppose so," the other agreed, "but I've got a chum who works the transatlantic run. Victoria Windsor was on her flight about two years ago and she says she's a real bitch!"

"I can't believe that. She looks so sweet." A few minutes later as the actress emerged from the lavatory again, the first girl approached her, heart pounding. "Ex...excuse me," she stammered, "I'd....I'd just like to wish you all the happiness in the world."

Victoria smiled in response. "Thank you. That's very kind of you."

Her graciousness emboldened the girl to go further. "M...Miss Windsor, I...I think he's smashing!"

"You know something," she laughed, " so do I! But, please, it's Mrs. Hamilton now. I'm sure you can understand how proud I am of that!"

"I certainly can!" Victoria went on back to her seat and the attendant turned back triumphantly to the other girl. "You see! Your friend is bonkers!" This same stewardess served their snack and later as the plane circled to come in for a landing, she came over to them yet again. By now she apparently considered them her private property. "Excuse me, Mr. and Mrs. Hamilton, the airport has just radioed us there'll be a car waiting for you. You will be allowed to leave ahead of the other passengers."

"Thank you very much," Victoria replied.

"It appearrs I'll have to becoom accustomed to the rred carrpet trreatment," Gavin muttered when the girl had left.

"It's Matt, that's all, darling. He...he always tries to make things as easy for me as possible."

"Aye, lass, 'tis all rright." He gave her a quick kiss on the cheek, but inwardly he vowed that as deeply as he loved her, he would not go through life known merely as the husband of Victoria Windsor.

Only a matter of ten minutes or so after that and they had landed, moving slowly along the maze of runways and finally coming to a stop at the gate. Victoria glanced idly out the window as the stairs were rolled into place. "Dammit!" she muttered under her breath. "Dammit!"

"What's the matterr?" Gavin leaned in a little so that he could see out himself. The car was indeed there as they'd been informed, but so was a considerable gathering of reporters and photographers. "Well, we'll rrun the gauntlet togetherr, hm, lass?"

"D...don't mind what they ask, please. They've absolutely no respect for anyone's privacy."

"I prromise, luv. Torri, look at me," he went on after a few seconds as he observed she was still troubled. With apparent reluctance Victoria turned to face him, but then she saw the tenderness in his eyes and immediately relaxed a little. "Ye ken, do ye not, that ye arre my verra own dearr lass and naethin' anyone else might say can change that." After a moment the attendant came over to tell them they could get off. Gavin stood up to pull their coats down from the overhead rack, helping Victoria into hers, and then slipping into his own.

With the stairs fastened in place the door of the plane was rolled back and they stepped out onto the platform to be greeted by the inevitable barrage of flashbulbs. There were cries of "Smile, Miss Windsor!"—"Over here, Miss Windsor!" Feeling Gavin stiffen in annoyance, she looked up at him anxiously. Quickly he smiled at her. "Neverr ye mind, lass," he whispered in her ear as they came down the steps together. "I'll strraighten them oot soon enough." Matt was standing by the car holding open the rear door and catching Victoria's eye, he shrugged ruefully.

"Why weren't we invited to the wedding, Miss Windsor?" someone called out.

"To begin with," Victoria replied smiling, "if you realize there's been a wedding, you must also be aware that it's Mrs. Hamilton now...or... Victoria, if you'd prefer," she found herself adding to her own amazement. With Gavin there even the press–her ancient adversary--didn't seem so threatening.

At her words a buzz ran through the crowd and miraculously Matt saw their temper change. "Introduce your husband to us, then," someone else requested.

"This....this is my husband, Gavin Hamilton." Love and pride were evident in Victoria's tone and the mood of the gathering altered still further. "But except for that," she continued after a few seconds' pause, "I'll let him speak for himself." Matt noted as well how she had at once stepped aside to allow Gavin to take over the spotlight. But then he'd also observed that from the moment they came to a stop at the bottom of the steps his arm was around her shoulders.

"What part of Scotland are you from, Mr. Hamilton?" still a third person asked.

"Glengowrrie–'tis a wee village aboot forrty miles inland frrom Aberrdeen. Ye do at least ken wherre Aberrdeen is. I rrealize Englishmen arre woefully ignorrant...aboot Scotland, I mean, o' courrse," he added after a perceptible pause.

A wave of laughter passed through the group.

"Does that include your wife?"

"Oop until rrecently–aye," Gavin replied, "but I'm in the prrocess o' educatin' the lassie." This time the laughter was louder.

"How do you like being called a lassie, Victoria?"

Her green eyes sparkled and for a moment she said nothing.

"You know," one reporter commented under his breath to the man standing next to him, "I don't think I realized until now just how beautiful she really is."

"Well, I did wonder at first," Victoria finally said, "if he were talking about his dog, but I'm getting used to it. Part of my...." Here she paused to glance lovingly at Gavin, "what did you call it, darling...my...ah...education."

"Aye, lass." He grinned down at her and in spite the people watching them, he was drawn to give her a quick kiss.

"Oh, Gavin," one of the photographers exclaimed reprovingly, "you could have warned us you were going to do that!"

"So noo I need perrmission to kiss my own wife?"

"Well, will you at least do it again?"

Only Victoria noticed the look of irritation which passed across Gavin's face. The expression vanished, however, almost as soon as it had appeared and as he turned to face her, his eyes clearly told her everything was all right. He had, in fact, decided to make it a moment of pure fun. He put his arms around her, but once in position he turned to the photographers. "Rready?"

Everyone laughed including Matt. Even the people still waiting on the stairs were enjoying themselves. Whereas people are usually impatient to get off a plane, they were in no hurry at all. But still Gavin toyed with the moment. He dropped his hands and turned his head away to clear his throat. Victoria looked out over the crowd, even to the people behind them, shrugging elaborately as if to say, "I don't know what to do with him, do you?"

At last, however, he took her in his arms again and with a last look at the photographers bent to kiss her: a long, tender kiss to which she involuntarily responded– putting her arms up around his neck–and briefly they were both oblivious to the watching crowd, even to the exploding flashbulbs. When they finally moved apart, Matt saw his opportunity and came quickly forward. "All right, ladies and gentlemen," he said pleasantly, but firmly, "I think you'll agree the Hamiltons have been more than generous. Now why don't we let them go?"

There was a general unspoken agreement and the group parted to allow them to walk to the car. With final waves Victoria and Gavin disappeared inside and closing the door after them, Matt got in front with the driver. No one knew who initiated it, but as the car moved away across the runway, there was a round of applause. "Gavin, it's good to see you again." The other man turned partway around to extend his hand over the back of his seat.

"Same herre, laddie," he replied. "And thank ye forr the rrescue. The blessed St. Andrrew himself couldna have guessed what they expected me to do next!"

"You're awful!" Victoria gave him a playful slap on the hand. "Matt, isn't he absolutely bloody awful?"

"Don't worry, old chap." The agent chuckled. "I don't think she means it."

"I'm nae concerrned in the least, believe me," Gavin assured him, slipping an arm around her shoulders to draw her just a little closer.

The car pulled around in front of the terminal and stopped to let Matt out. "I'll take care of your luggage and grab a taxi," he told them. "You two should have a little more time to yourselves. I'm afraid they want you at the studio tomorrow, Victoria."

Her smile faded a little at that. "Oh dear, so soon? I'd hoped for a few more days. But I can't blame them. They've been super through all of this. Will I see you soon?"

"Yes–we have several possible future projects to discuss." Getting out and shutting the door of the limousine again, Matt waved them smilingly away.

Victoria turned at once to Gavin. "Darling, I'm so sorry. I did want...want...."

"I know, dearr lass, but 'tis just as well. They'll be expectin' me at the Guarrds Barrracks firrst thing in the morrnin' as well."

"I guess what I really wanted," she admitted, "is to go on forever just being together, but that's not very practical, is it?"

"No, darrlin', I'm afrraid it isn't. But we will be togetherr frrom noo on and that's what matterrs."

* * *

How many times during their first weeks of marriage was Victoria to recall these words of Gavin's and think yet again how wise he was. Oh, not that being together every minute of every day wouldn't have been glorious. But they were together and that was indeed what mattered.

She didn't even object as the number of evenings they spent alone in the cozy little flat became fewer because it meant that Gavin was beginning to achieve the success he richly deserved. His original three nights at the supper club had grown to four and then five as he attracted larger and larger audiences. People might have come originally to get a look at Victoria Windsor's latest husband; they returned to listen to Gavin Hamilton.

Meanwhile, in a small street just off the Strand they'd discovered the perfect location for Gavin to open his own coffee house. An old building dating back to the latter half of the eighteenth century, it had been most recently operated as a discotheque with the improbable name of the "Cheshire Cat-a-Go-Go". Quite understandably the business had gone bankrupt.

The place might have even been a coffee house in the beginning. A massive stone hearth dominated the wall facing the door and two winding staircases led to a balcony extending all the way around the room where a second smaller fireplace stood directly above the large one below. At the moment, of course, this was all hidden under fluorescent paint and flashing strobe lights. Even the balcony had been divided into go-go cages. But Gavin could at once envision it divested of all its sleazy twentieth century trappings and restored to its former rich simplicity. Initial work turned out to be disappointing, however. There had been several previous remodelings and when all the subsequent layers were finally stripped away, the original oak paneling was found to be badly rotted. The interior would have to be gutted and entirely reconstructed and to be done properly down to the smallest detail would be an expensive undertaking.

The architect had just left their flat one evening after a particularly discouraging conference and Gavin was still sitting at the table staring at the sheets of paper covered with figures. He wanted this so much–to prove once and for all he could make something of himself–but the proposed cost was staggering. Feeling Victoria's touch on his hair, he looked up and tried to smile. "Perrhaps 'tis my Scottish blood, lass, but I canna abide goin' into debt."

She sat down opposite him at the table reaching across to rest her hand on his arm. If she didn't say this in just the right way, she knew he would refuse.. "Gavin, please let me......."

"No, Torri!" Abruptly he pulled away, standing up to walk over and look out the window. "I will do this myself orr not all. I willna accept yourr.....yourr charrity."

"Oh, believe me, this is not a donation," she responded lightly. "I'm making what I consider to be a wise investment."

He turned back then to look at her. " 'Tis a gamble, hinny. I ken that."

"I don't happen to think so."

"You believe in me that strrongly?"

"Oh, my darling!" She came over to him resting both hands against his chest. "You know I do–with all my heart! Haven't I told you that–over and over again? Now will you please let me help?"

"Aye–all rright," he finally agreed, though still reluctantly.

"Oh, thank you! Now I'll really feel a part of it all. I'll....."

"But only as my legal business partner. We'll have a solicitor drraw oop a contrract and I'll....I'll pay ye rregularr dividends."

"That means I may also offer an opinion once in a while...pick out drapes or something?"

"Aye," He chuckled a little now, his brown eyes glowing. "And think what fun we'll have at the stockholderrs' meetin's." Almost at once, however, he became serious again, drawing her into his arms. "Thank ye, darrlin', forr believin' in me. I prromise I willna let ye doon."

* * *

More and more Victoria would realize she was only beginning to know her new husband. Little episodes were continually taking place– silly and inconsequential perhaps–but each revealed to her all over again his dear, funny nature.

She'd decide to go shopping and he would turn down the invitation to accompany her. After all "a drress shop was no place forr a self-rrespectin' laddie," but he'd go along for the walk–"perrhaps brrowse aboot in a wee shop orr two in the neighborrhood". She'd be in the dressing room when inevitably there would come a tapping on the partition. Upon her reply Gavin's head would appear between the curtains, an engaging little boy grin on his face, and ignoring entirely her protestations that he wasn't allowed in there, he would join her. He looked absurd anyway–the little stool simply hadn't been designed to hold his tall, rangy frame–and his continuous comments about the clothes as well as the more intimate parts of her anatomy kept her in hysterics.

Impromptu lessons in Highland dancing would occur–often at midnight–Gavin crossing a broom and a mop in the middle of the floor and leading her patiently through the intricate steps of the sword dance.

On long winter afternoons Victoria would make biscuits and Gavin would try every tactic to steal a hot one off the baking sheet. She called him the "Scottish Scavenger". They both enjoyed old, sentimental films on the television. Invariably she'd cry. He called her "Weepin' Windsorr".

None of these were nearly so important to Victoria, however, as was the strength that just sharing her life with Gavin seemed to give her. She knew, at last, blessed release from fear and from loneliness. He loved her–without question, without reservation–and so gradually she was learning to love herself.

Perhaps a simple incident, occurring when they had been married about two months, summed it all up better than anything. It was a Sunday afternoon, one of the last they would spend alone together. They had located the perfect little house: living room, kitchen and one bedroom downstairs and three more smaller bedrooms upstairs. It had at one time been a carriage house and still possessed much of its original charm. They would be moving in around the first of March and Olivia would be joining them.

It had been snowing since early Saturday evening–a wet snow which stuck to the bare tree branches and iron grillwork–giving the city a graceful, lacy appearance. They'd had a late brunch and now Victoria was curled up at one end of the couch studying her lines for the next day's taping. By now they had begun work on the Queen Anne segment of the series. Gavin was sitting near her on the floor, composing a new piece on the guitar, but he was obviously in no mood to concentrate on his music. Every other minute he was shaking her script or knocking off her slipper to tickle her foot.

"Will you behave yourself!" Victoria reprimanded him although actually she was enjoying the attention. She herself was having some difficulty keeping her mind on the memorization with that dear, auburn head so close to her knee. Several times she found herself irresistibly drawn to reach down and toy with his hair.

"And ye'rre complainin' aboot <u>my</u> behaviorr?" He glanced up at her and grinned. A short time later he was up and prowling restlessly about the room and out into the small kitchen–glancing out the various windows and whistling "Scotland, the Brave". "Do ye want tea, darrlin'?"

"I don't think so–not right now, anyway."

"No tea!" he exclaimed, pretending great alarm. He came over to lie down on the couch, resting his hand in her lap and crushing the script in the process. "Arre ye surre ye nae ill, lassie?" He put his hand up to feel her head.

"I'm fine, thank you," she laughed. With one fingertip she drew a line from his forehead down over his nose to his chin. "And how do I explain the condition of this script tomorrow?"

"What scrript?" His brown eyes as he sat up to look at her were wide with innocence. Wordlessly Victoria held up the crumbled pages. "Oh, that script!" They both began to laugh and then all at once he grabbed her, pinning her down on the couch. "Och, lass– noo I've got ye at my merrcy! What will I do wi' ye, do ye suppose?"

"I hope you don't think I'm frightened?"

He gazed down at her for a moment–her hair spread out around her like a golden cloud and her lips slightly parted. He leaned down to kiss her–a long, lingering kiss. "I know," he exclaimed suddenly, " 'tis a perrfect day to make a snowman!"

"Wh...what?" Even after six months of knowing this incredible man and two of being his wife, she was still unprepared for some of the things he suggested. "Gavin, the weather is bloody awful: damp and cold. It's the perfect day for a fire and pots and pots of tea—not.... not making a snowman. Beside I....I don't think...I....I know how." Her eyes brimmed with tears and she looked away, suddenly ill-at-ease before his tender gaze.

Gavin took her by the chin and with great gentleness turned her back to face him. "Well then, 'tis time ye learrned, wouldn't ye say so?"

"I....I suppose it is," she whispered, trying to smile.

"So what arre we waitin' forr? Noo drress warrmly," he admonished with a shake of his finger, "includin' yourr Wellies."

"Yes....yes, darling. All right." Still reluctant and yet wanting to please him, Victoria got to her feet and walked back to their bedroom to get her things.

About a half-hour later they came up out of the underground at Trafalgar Square (Gavin insisting as always, of course, that the famous lions were, in fact, Scottish) and in just a few minutes they'd passed under the Admiralty Arch into St. James Park. Almost immediately he turned off the pavement, leading the way briskly across the fresh snow.

" 'Tis verra forrtunate that all those nambi-pambi Englisherrs arre hidden away indoorrs. Look at this!" He indicated the untouched snow with an expansive sweep of both arms and a toss of his magnificent head of auburn hair since as usual, no matter what the weather or temperature, he wore no hat.

"Oh, Gavin!" She laughed now. "Until a short while ago, I was one of those nambi-pambi Englishers."

"Aye, but ye have yourr Scots laddie noo to show ye the errrorr o' yourr ways."

"Yes, I....I do, don't I?"

"So then, since I am the teacherr herre," he said with mock sternness, "and ye arre the pupil, ye must listen verra carrefully."

"Yes, sir." Her eyes sparkled, partly from the cold, but mostly from pure happiness.

Under Gavin's direction they worked together to roll the huge balls of snow and pile them one on top of the other, finding sticks for the arms and dark pebbles for the eyes, nose, mouth and buttons. Passers-by occasionally stopped to watch, not that any of them recognized the woman bundled up against the cold as Victoria Windsor, but simply because the young couple were obviously having such a good time together.

Later on they were back in the tiny flat. Tea had been made and they settled on the floor in front of a glowing coal fire. "What is there about winter tea time that makes it so special, darling?" Victoria asked as she poured his tea and handed the mug to him.

"I suppose because 'tis cold and darrk ootside and it makes indoorrs seem even warrmer and cozierr."

For a while then they ate and drank in silence feeling so at peace that talk was not necessary. The storm had muffled even the customary sounds of the large city and the stillness was absolute. Afterwards they took their dishes into the kitchen and came back to sit together on the couch, Gavin's arms forming a snug nest for her. It was he who finally broke the silence. "I've got a prresent forr ye, darrlin'. Do ye want it noo orr laterr?"

Victoria's eyes had been closed as she savored the tranquillity around them as well as that within herself. Now she opened them to look at him. "For me?"

"No, forr Mrrs. MacPherrson doonstairrs, ye daftie. That's why I'm tellin' ye aboot it."

"What are you doing bringing presents to other women?"

He chuckled. "Well, do ye want it orr not?"

"Oh yes, please, Gavin." She sat up so that he could get to his feet and go over to the small coat closet. Taking a jewellery box from his jacket pocket, he came back to sit down beside her again and hand it to her. "What's the occasion?" Victoria asked even as she eagerly removed the ribbon and wrappings.

"No occasion, hinny," he replied one hand resting on hers to prevent her from opening the box until he'd finished what he wanted to say. " 'Tis only that I was thinkin' how we both feel aboot marrriage. That 'tis the joinin' with anotherr perrson to forrm a new entity."

"Yes, you....you said that in your song." She studied his face intently.

"Aye...and it made me rrememberr an old Gaelic prroverrb aboot marrriage. So I trranslated it as closely as I could into English. All rright." He removed his hand. "Ye may open it the noo."

Victoria lifted the cover and inside the box lay what appeared at first glance to be a round pewter disc on a chain. She started to remove it so that she could read the inscription, but to her surprise the disc broke apart along a jagged line and half of it still lay nestled in the cotton, each part having its own chain. "Gavin....what?" She was puzzled.

"Look, darrlin'." He picked up the other half, fitting the two pieces together once more. "Noo ye can rread it."

Victoria was beginning to understand now and her voice was trembling as she read the words aloud. "Alone—I am nothing; Together–we are one." She looked up at him again–her eyes brimming with tears. Helplessly she shook her head.

"Noo ye see," he said tenderly, slipping the more delicate of the two chains over her head–the heavier one over his own.

"Oh, Gavin," she whispered, "No one except you would have thought of this."

He smiled–that special smile she knew was for her alone. "Coom–lass–coom," he urged, opening his arms to her. He enclosed her in his embrace and at long last she knew she had come home.

About the Author

Suzanne Person is a graduate of Vassar College where her major field of study was drama. Since then she has had considerable experience in community and academic theatre as both an actress and a director. Playing Alice in Wonderland at the age of six, her love of the theatre did indeed begin even earlier in life than did her novel's main character.

She is an unabashed anglophile who has read and studied widely about the British Isles and has been known to bore hapless friends and relatives with royal genealogical trivia. She has traveled extensively in both England and Scotland, the last three visits having been for the specific purpose of acquiring background information for the novel. The first time I saw the Scottish Highlands, she says, it was as though I were coming home.

And thus *A Room Without Toys* is, in fact, the child born of her two great loves: the theatre and the British Isles.

After five years of living in the South, Suzanne has recently returned to her native New England—specifically Cape Cod— accompanied, of course, by four extremely spoiled cats and one seriously outnumbered dog, a lhasa apso mix named Casey. At least he should have the chance to see his name in print.

Breinigsville, PA USA
19 July 2010
242005BV00002B/7/P